LES MISÉRABLES

THE GOLDEN HERITAGE SERIES

LES MISÉRABLES

VICTOR HUGO

Galley Press

© This edition Galley Press 1987

Published in this edition by Galley Press, an imprint of
W. H. Smith and Son Limited, Registered No. 237811 England.
Trading as W. H. Smith Distributors, St John's House
East Street, Leicester, LE1 6NE.

ISBN 0 86136 654 9

Production services by
Book Production Consultants, Cambridge

Printed and bound in Yugoslavia by Mladinska Knjiga

CHAPTER I.

In 1815, M. Charles François-Bienvenu Myriel was Bishop of D——. He was an old man of about seventy-five, and had held the See of D—— since 1806.

Although this detail bears in no way upon the story we have to tell, perhaps it may not be without use, if only for the sake of exactness, to indicate here the noise and talk which went abroad concerning him from the moment when he arrived in the diocese. Whether true or false, what is said of men often holds as important a place in their lives, and above all in their fates, as what they do. M. Myriel was son of a member of the parliament of Aix; of parliamentary rank. It was said that his father, wishing him to be his heir, had married him very early, at eighteen or twenty, according to a custom sufficiently well recognised among parliamentary families. Charles Myriel had no objection to the marriage, had indeed, it was said, spoken frequently about it. He was well made in person, although his figure was small enough, elegant, graceful, and refined. All the early part of his life had been given to the world and to love affairs.

The Revolution came, and troubles happened with lightning rapidity. The parliamentary families, decimated, hunted, and tracked, were scattered abroad. M. Charles Myriel, at the beginning of the Revolution, emigrated to Italy. There his wife died from a chest trouble from which she had suffered a long time. They had no children. What next happened in the destiny of M. Myriel? The ruin of old French society, the fall of his own family, the tragic scenes of '93, still more fearful to the emigrants who viewed them from afar with frightful exaggeration—did these events raise in him the idea of vows and solitude? Was he, in the midst of one of these diversions and distractions which occupied his life, suddenly struck by one of those mysterious and terrible blows, which, by striking at his heart, sometimes overcome the man whom public disasters do not move, through hitting at his existence and his fortune? No one can say. All that is known is that, when he returned from Italy, he was a priest.

In 1804, M. Myriel was Curé of Brignolles. He was already old, and lived in profound retirement.

Towards the time of the coronation, a little business in

connection with his curacy, one does not know too well what it was, brought him to Paris. Among other powerful people, he visited Cardinal Fesch on behalf of his parishioners. One day, when the Emperor was paying a visit to his uncle, the worthy Curé, who was waiting in an antechamber, saw his Majesty pass. Napoleon seeing himself looked upon by this old man with a certain degree of curiosity, turned and said in an off-hand way.

"What honest man is he who looks thus on me?"

"Sire," said M. Myriel, "you look upon an honest man, and I upon a great one. Each of us may profit by it."

The same evening, the Emperor asked the Cardinal the name of this curé, and some time after, M. Myriel was quite surprised to learn that he had been made Bishop of D——.

For the rest, what truth was there in the tales told about the early life of M. Myriel? No one knew him. Few had known the Myriel family before the Revolution.

M. Myriel had to suffer the lot of all new-comers into a little town, where there are many chattering mouths and very few thinking heads. He had to suffer although he was bishop, and because he was bishop. But, after all, the stories with which they connected his name were only stories; noise, words, talk, even less than talk—*palabras*, as they say in the South.

Be that as it may, after nine years of the episcopate and of residence at D——, all these tales, subjects of conversation, which at the beginning had kept busy both petty towns and petty people, had fallen into utter oblivion. No one dared to speak of them; no one dared to remember them.

M. Myriel had arrived at D——, accompanied by an old lady, Mademoiselle Baptistine, his sister, who was ten years younger than he was.

Their domestic establishment consisted of a single maid-servant of the same age as Mademoiselle Baptistine, and called Madame Magloire. She, after having been servant to M. le Curé, now took the double title of Miss Baptistine's chamber-maid and housekeeper to Monseigneur.

Mademoiselle Baptistine was a lanky person, pale, thin, sweet; she was the living ideal of what is contained in the word "respectable"; for it appears necessary for a woman to be a mother in order to be venerable. She had never been pretty; her whole life, which had been simply a succession of good deeds, had finished by placing on her a kind of whiteness and transparency; and, in growing old, she had gained what might be called the beauty of kindliness. What there had been of transparency in her youth had become clearness in her maturity; and this transparency showed her as an angel. She was much more a spirit than a maid. Her person seemed formed of shadow; hardly body enough to say she had sex; a little substance containing a light; big eyes always lowered; a pretext for a soul to remain on earth.

Madame Magloire was a little, old woman, white, fat, busy, always breathless, at first because of her activity, and then because of asthma.

On his arrival M. Myriel was installed in his episcopal palace with the honours fixed by the imperial decrees, which rank the bishop immediately after the field-marshal. The Mayor and the President paid him the first visit, and he, on his part, made the first visit to the General and to the Prefect.

The installation being completed, the town was curious to see its bishop at work.

CHAPTER II.

THE episcopal palace of D—— adjoined the hospital. It was a vast and beautiful home, built of stone at the beginning of last century by Monseigneur Henri Puget, Doctor of Theology of the University of Paris, Abbé of Simore, who was Bishop of D—— in 1712. This palace was a veritable lord's residence. Everything there had a grand appearance, the bishop's apartments, the saloons, bed-rooms, the court of honour, very large with promenades under arcades, according to the ancient Florentine fashion, and the gardens planted with magnificent trees. In the dining-room, a long and superb gallery, which was on the ground floor and opened on the gardens, Monseigneur Henri Puget had given a ceremonial dinner on July 29, 1714, to my lords Charles Brûlart de Genlis, Bishop, Prince d'Embrun, Antoine de Mesgrigny, monk, Bishop of Grasse, Philippe de Vendôme, Grand Prior of France, Abbé de Saint-Honoré de Lérins, François de Berton de Grillon, Lord Bishop of Vence, Césarde Sabran de Forcalquier. Lord Bishop of Glandève, and Jean Soanen, Priest of the Oratory, preacher in ordinary to the King. The portraits of these seven reverend personages decorated the hall, and this memorable date, July 29, 1714, was engraved there in letters of gold upon a white marble table. The hospital was a house, narrow and low, a single storey high, with a little garden. Three days after his arrival the Bishop visited the hospital. The visit over, he begged the Director with right goodwill to go home with him.

"Monsieur the Director of the Hospital," said he to him, "how many sick folks have you at this moment?"

"Twenty-six, Monseigneur."

"That's what I counted," said the Bishop.

"The beds," replied the Director, "are well placed one against the other."

"Just what I noticed."

"The halls are but rooms, and it is difficult to keep the air fresh."

"So it seemed to me."

"And then, when there is sunshine, the garden is too small for the convalescents."

"Just what I was saying to myself."

"In epidemics, we have had typhus this year and military fever for two years, sometimes a hundred sick at a time, we do not know what to do."

"That's the thought that struck me."

"What would you have, Monseigneur?" said the Director.

This conversation had taken place in the dining-room on the ground floor. The Bishop kept silence for a moment, then he turned abruptly to the Director of the Hospital.

"Monsieur," said he, "suppose nothing but beds in this hall, how many do you think it would hold?"

"In my lord's dining-room?" cried the Director in stupefaction.

The Bishop looked round the room, and seemed to take measurements and make calculations with his eye.

"It would hold twenty beds," said he, as if speaking to himself; then raising his voice: "Now, Monsieur the Director of the Hospital, I am going to tell you something. There is a mistake here somewhere. There are twenty-six of you in five or six little rooms: there are only three of us, and we have room for sixty. There's some mistake, I tell you. You have my house, and I have yours. Give me my house. This is your home."

The next day the twenty-six poor sick people were installed in the Bishop's palace, and the Bishop was at the hospital.

M. Myriel had no possessions, his family having been ruined by the Revolution. His sister held an income of five hundred francs, which, at the presbytery, was enough for her personal wants. M. Myriel, as bishop, received from the State an allowance of fifteen thousand francs. The same day on which he went to live at the hospital, M. Myriel determined once for all to use this sum in the following way. We give here a note written in his own hand.

Note to rule the expenses of my house.

	Livres
For the little Seminary - - - - - -	1,500
Congregation of the Mission - - - - -	100
For the Lazars of Montdidier - - - - -	100
Seminary of Foreign Missions, Paris - - -	200
Congregation of the Holy Ghost - - - -	150
Religious establishments in the Holy Land - -	100
Committees of Maternal Charity - - - -	300
In trust for that of Arles - - - - - -	50
For the betterment of prisons - - - - -	400
For the comfort and deliverance of prisoners - -	500
For the liberation of fathers of families imprisoned for debt - - - - - - - -	1,000
Addition to the stipend of poor schoolmasters of the diocese - - - - - - - - -	2,000
Public Storehouse of Hautes Alpes - - - -	100
To the congregation of the ladies of D——, Manosque, and Sisteron, for the free education of poor girls - - - - - - - -	1,500
For the poor - - - - - - - -	6,000
Personal expenses - - - - - - -	1.000
Total - -	15,000

During all the time he held the See of D——, M. Myriel made no alteration in this arrangement. He intended this, as we see, *to regulate the expenses of his house.*

This arrangement was accepted with perfect submission by Mademoiselle Baptistine. For this holy maid, M. Myriel was at once her brother and her bishop, her friend according to nature, and her superior according to the Church. She loved and venerated him in all simplicity. When he spoke, she bowed ; when he did anything, she approved. Only the servant, Madame Magloire, grumbled a little. M. the Bishop, as has been seen, reserved to himself only a thousand pounds, which, added to Mademoiselle Baptistine's

annuity, made fifteen hundred francs per annum. With these
fifteen hundred francs, these two old women and this old
man contrived to live.

And when a village curé came to D——, M. the Bishop
still found means of aiding him, thanks to the strict
economy of Madame Magloire and the clever administration
of Mademoiselle Baptistine.

One day, when he had been about three months at D——,
the Bishop said :

"With all that I am pretty well short of cash !"

"Indeed !" cried Madame Magloire ; "Monseigneur is
the only one who has not claimed the income that the
department owes him for his carriage expenses in the town,
and his travelling expenses in the diocese."

"Ah! you are right, Madame Magloire," said the Bishop.
He made his claim.

Some time later, the Council-general taking this request
into consideration, voted him an annual sum of three thousand francs under this rubric : *Allocation to M. the Bishop for
carriage expenses, and travelling expenses for pastoral visits.*

This made the local people cry out, and on this occasion
a Senator of the Empire, an old member of the Five Hundred,
favourable to the 18th Brumaire, and provided with a magnificent senatorial residence close to D——, wrote to the Minister
of Religion, M. Bigot de Préameneu, an angry, confidential
note from which we extract these authentic lines :—

"Carriage expenses ! What is there to do in a town of
less than four thousand inhabitants ? Expenses for diocesan
visitations ! What good are these visits in any case ? And
again, why travel post in this mountainous country ? There
are no roads, and people travel only on horseback. The
very bridges of Durance at Château-Arnoux can hardly
bear the weight of an ox-wagon.

"These priests are all alike—greedy and avaricious. This
one played the good apostle when he came. Now he is
just like the rest. He must have carriage and post-chaise.
He must travel in luxury, like the old bishops. Oh, all
this priesthood ! M. le Comte, things are not going well
when the Emperor has given us up to these twopenny-half-
penny priests. Down with the Pope! (affairs were becoming
strained with Rome). As for me, I am for Cæsar alone,"
etc. etc.

This incident, on the contrary, rejoiced the heart of Madame
Magloire. "Good," said she to Mademoiselle Baptistine,

" Monseigneur began by others, but he has not quite failed to finish by himself. He has regulated all his charities. Here is three thousand francs for us. So there ! "

The same evening the Bishop wrote, and sent to his sister, a note in these terms :

Carriage and travelling expenses.

							LIVRES
Meat soup to the sick people in the hospital	-	-	1,500
For the Maternal Society of Charity at Aix	-	-	250
For the Maternal Society of Charity at Draguignan			250
For foundlings	-	-	-	-	-	-	500
For orphans	-	-	-	-	-	-	500

Such was M. Myriel's budget.

As to the episcopal perquisites, publication of banns, dispensations, private baptisms, sermons, the blessing of churches or chapels, marriages, etc., the Bishop seized upon these riches with no more eagerness than that with which he gave them to the poor.

At the end of a little time silver offerings increased. Those who had and those who had not, knocked at M. Myriel's door, some to seek alms, others to leave bequests. In less than a year the Bishop became the treasurer of all benefits, and the reliever of all cases of distress. Considerable sums passed through his hands, but nothing could make any change in his manner of life or add the least superfluity to his necessities.

More than that, as there is always more wretchedness among the lower classes than of fraternity among the higher, all was given, so to say, without being received ; it was like water on a thirsty land. He truly received money, but he never had any. Then he began to rob himself.

The custom being that bishops place their baptismal names at the head of their orders and pastoral letters, the poor people of the country had, with a kind of affectionate instinct, chosen, among the names of the Bishop, that one which had a meaning for them, and called him nothing but Monseigneur Bienvenu. We shall do as they did, and call him so when needful. For the rest, the name pleased him. " I love that name," he would say ; " Bienvenu counterbalances Monseigneur."

We do not pretend that the portrait we have given is absolutely correct ; we limit ourselves to saying that it is a likeness.

CHAPTER III.

M. THE BISHOP, though he turned his carriage dues into alms, did not on that account make fewer visitations. It is a trying diocese, that of D——. It has very few plains and many mountains, and, as a matter of course, almost no roads ; thirty-two curacies, forty-one vicarages, and two hundred and eighty-five sub-curacies. To visit all these is an undertaking, but the Bishop went from end to end of it. He travelled on foot when he was among his people, in a wagon when on the plains, and in a *cacolet* when in the mountains. The two old women went with him. When the journey was too sore on them he went alone.

One day, riding on an ass, he came to Senez, an old episcopal town. His purse, very bare at this time, allowed him no other means of conveyance. The Mayor of the town went to receive him at the gate of the Bishop's palace, and with scandalised eyes saw him get off his donkey. Some citizens laughed about it.

" Monsieur Mayor," said the Bishop, " I see you are scandalised. You think it is desperate pride in a poor priest to mount to a seat which was that used by Jesus Christ. I assure you I did it from necessity, not from vanity."

In these visitations he was gentle and indulgent, and preached less than he talked. He never used far-fetched reasonings and examples. To the people of one country he cited the example of a neighbouring country. In the cantons, where they are hard through necessity, he said :

" Look at the people of Briançon. They have given to the poor, to widows and orphans the right of mowing their meadows three days before all the others. Without payment they rebuild their houses when they are in a tumbledown condition, and it is a country blessed by God. For a hundred years there has not been a murder."

In villages where they were anxious for gain at harvest-time, he said :

" Behold the people of Embrun. If the father of a family, at the time of the harvest, has his sons serving in the army and his daughters in service in the town, and he himself, it may be, ill and greatly embarrassed, the Curé recommends him in the sermon ; and on Sunday, after mass, all the people of the village, men, women, and children, go to the poor man's field to make his hay, and carry his straw and grain to his granary."

To families divided by questions of money and inheritance he would say:

"Look at the mountaineers of Devolny, a country so savage that they do not hear the nightingale there once in fifty years. Well, when the father dies in a family, the boys go out to seek their fortune, leaving the goods to the girls, so that they may find husbands."

In cantons where they have a taste for law, and where the farmers ruin themselves with stamped paper, he would say:

"Look at the good peasants of the valley of Queyras. There are three thousand souls. Why, it is a little republic. There they know neither judge nor policeman. The Mayor does everything. He settles imposts, taxes each in conscience, judges quarrels gratuitously, divides patrimonies without charge, and gives judgment without fee. And he is obeyed because he is a just man among simple men."

In villages where no schoolmasters were to be found, he would cite again the people of Queyras.

"Do you know what they do?" he would say. "As a little place of twelve or fifteen hearths is not always able to maintain a schoolmaster, they have schoolmasters paid by the whole valley, who pass through the villages teaching as they go, spending eight days here and six days there. These teachers go to the fairs, where I have seen them. One knows them by the pens they carry in the band of their hats. Those who only teach reading have one pen; those who teach reading and arithmetic have two pens; those who teach reading, arithmetic, and Latin have three pens. Those fellows are fine scholars. But what a shame it is to remain ignorant! Act like the men of Queyras."

Thus he would speak, gravely and paternally; in default of examples he would invent parables, going right to the point with few phrases and fine figures of speech—the very eloquence of Jesus Christ, convincing and persuading.

CHAPTER IV.

IN conversation, the Bishop was affable and lively. He condescended to the level of the two old females who spent their life near him, and when he laughed it was a schoolboy's laugh. Madame Magloire was fond of calling him "Your Greatness." One day he rose from his easy-chair and went to fetch a book from his library : as it was on one of the top shelves, and as the Bishop was short, he could not reach it. "Madame Magloire," he said, "bring me a chair, for my greatness does not rise to that shelf."

One of his distant relatives, the Countess of Lô, rarely let an opportunity slip to enumerate in his presence what she called the "hopes" of her three sons. She had several very old relatives close to death's door, of whom her sons were the natural heirs. The youngest of the three would inherit from a great aunt 100,000 francs a year ; the second would succeed to his uncle's dukedom, the third to his grandfather's peerage. The Bishop generally listened in silence to this innocent and pardonable maternal display. Once, however, he seemed more dreamy than usual, while Madame de Lô was repeating all the details of their successions and "hopes." She broke off somewhat impatiently : "Good gracious, cousin," she said, "what are you thinking about ? " "I am thinking," said the Bishop, "of something singular, which, if my memory is right, is in St. Augustine : 'Place your hopes on Him to whom there is no succession ! '"

On another occasion, receiving a letter announcing the death of a country gentleman, in which, in addition to the dignities of the defunct, all the feudal and noble titles of all his relatives were recorded, "What an admirable burthen of titles death is made lightly to bear," he exclaimed, "and what sense men must possess thus to employ the tomb to minister to their vanity."

At times he displayed a gentle railery, which nearly always contained a serious meaning. During one Lent a young vicar came to D—— and preached at the cathedral. He was rather eloquent, and the subject of his sermon was charity. He invited the rich to give to the needy in order to escape hell, which he painted in the most frightful way he could, and reach paradise, which he made desirable and charming. There was among the congregation a rich, retired merchant, somewhat of an usurer, who had acquired £80,000 by manufacturing coarse cloths, serges, and caddis. In his whole lifetime M. Géborand had never given alms to a beggar, but after this sermon it was remarked that he gave every Sunday a penny to the old women begging at the cathedral gate. There were six of them to share it. One day the Bishop saw him bestowing his charity, and said to his sister, with a smile,

"Look at Monsieur Géborand buying a pennyworth of paradise."

When pleading on behalf of charity he would not let himself be rebuffed even by a refusal, and at such times made remarks which caused people to reflect. Once he was collecting for the poor in a drawing-room of the town. The Marquis de Champtercier was present, a rich, old, avaricious man, who contrived to be at once ultra-Royalist and ultra-Voltairian. This variety has existed. The Bishop on reaching him touched his arm, "Monsieur le Marquis, you must give me something." The Marquis turned and answered dryly: "I have my own poor, Monseigneur." "Give them to me," said the Bishop.

One day he delivered the following sermon at the cathedral :—

"My very dear brethren, my good friends, there are in France thirteen hundred and twenty thousand peasants' houses which have only three openings ; eighteen hundred and seventeen thousand which have only two openings, the door and the window; and, lastly, three hundred and forty-six thousand cabins which have only one opening, the door ; and that comes from a thing called the door and window tax. Just place poor families, aged women and little children, in these houses, and then see the fevers and maladies! Alas! God gives men fresh air, and the law sells it to them. I do not accuse the law, but I bless God. In the Isère, in the Var, in the two Alps, Upper and Lower, the peasants have not even trucks, but carry manure on their backs; they have no candles, and burn resinous logs and pieces of rope steeped in pitch. It is the same through all the high parts of Dauphiné. They make bread for six months, and bake it with dried cow-dung. In winter they break this bread with axes, and steep it in water for four-and-twenty hours before they can eat it. My brethren, be compassionate, behold how people suffer around you!"

Born a Provençal, he easily accustomed himself to all the dialects of the South. This greatly pleased the people, and had done no little in securing him admission to all minds. He was, as it were, at home in the hut and on the mountain. He could say the grandest things in the most vulgar idioms, and as he spoke all languages he entered all hearts. However, he was the same to people of fashion as to the lower classes.

He condemned nothing hastily, or without taking the circumstances into account. He would say, "Let us look at the road by which the fault has passed." Being, as he called himself with a smile, an ex-sinner, he had none of the intrenchments of rigorism, and professed boldly, and careless of the frowns of the severely virtuous, a doctrine which might be summed up nearly as follows :—

"Man is clothed with the flesh, which is at once his burden and his temptation. He carries it with him and yields to it. He must watch, restrain, and repress it, and only obey it in the last extremity. In this obedience there may still be a fault ; but the fault thus committed is venial. It is a fall, but a fall on the knees, which may end in prayer. To be a saint is the exception, to be a just man is the rule. Err, fail, sin, but be just. The least possible amount of sin is the law of man : no sin at all is the dream of angels. All that is earthly is subjected to sin. Sin is a gravitation."

When he heard many cry out and grow indignant, all of a sudden, he would say with a smile, "Oh ! oh, it seems as if this is a great crime which all the world is committing. Look at the startled hypocrites, hastening to protest and place themselves under cover."

He was indulgent towards women, and towards the poor on whom the weight of human society presses. He would say, "The faults of women, children, servants, the weak, the indigent, and the ignorant are the faults of husbands, fathers, masters, the strong, the rich, and the learned." He also said, "Teach the ignorant as much as you possibly can : society is culpable for not giving instruction gratis, and is responsible for the night it produces. This soul is full of darkness, and sin is committed, but the guilty person is not the man who commits the sin, but he who causes the darkness."

As we see, he had a strange and peculiar way of judging things. I suspect that he obtained it from the Gospels. He one day heard in a drawing-room the story of a trial which was shortly to take place. A wretched man, through love of a woman and a child he had by her, having exhausted his resources, coined false money, which at that period was an offence punished by death. The woman was arrested while issuing the first false piece manufactured by the man. She was detained, but there was no proof against her. She alone could charge her lover and ruin him by confessing.

She denied. They pressed her, but she adhered to her denial. Upon this, the Royal Procureur had an idea : he feigned infidelity on the lover's part, and contrived, by cleverly presenting the woman with fragments of letters, to persuade her that she had a rival, and that the man was deceiving her. Then, exasperated by jealousy, she denounced her lover, confessed everything, proved everything. The man was ruined, and would shortly be tried with his accomplice at Aix. The story was told, and everybody was delighted at the magistrate's cleverness. By bringing jealousy into play he brought out the truth through passion, and obtained justice through revenge. The Bishop listened to all this in silence, and when it was ended he asked : "Where are this man and woman to be tried ? " "At the assizes." Then he continued : "And where is the Royal Procureur to be tried ? "

A tragic event occurred at D——. A man was condemned to death for murder. He was a wretched fellow, not exactly educated, not exactly ignorant, who had been a mountebank at fairs and a public writer. The trial attracted the attention of the townspeople. On the eve of the day fixed for the execution, the prison chaplain was taken ill, and a priest was wanted to assist the sufferer in his last moments. The Curé was sent for, and it seems that he refused, saying, "It is no business of mine. I have nothing to do with the mountebank ; I am ill too ; and besides, that is not my place." This answer was carried to the Bishop, who said, "The Curé is right. It is not his place ; it is mine." He went straight to the prison, entered the mountebank's cell, called him by name, took his hand, and spoke to him. He spent the whole day with him, forgetting sleep and food while praying to God for the soul of the condemned man. He told him the best truths, which are the most simple. He was father, brother, friend—bishop only to bless. He taught him everything, while reassuring and consoling him. This man was about to die in desperation : death was to him like an abyss, and he shuddered as he stood on its gloomy brink. He was not ignorant enough to be completely indifferent, and his condemnation, which was a profound shock, had here and there broken through that partition which separates us from the mystery of things, and which we call life. He peered incessantly out of this world through these crevices, and only saw darkness ; but the Bishop showed him the light.

In the morning, when they came to fetch the condemned man, the Bishop was with him. He followed him, and showed himself to the mob in his purple hood, and with the episcopal cross round his neck, side by side with this rope-bound wretch. He entered the cart with him, he mounted the scaffold with him. The sufferer, so gloomy and crushed on the previous day, was radiant ; he felt that his soul was reconciled, and he hoped for heaven. The Bishop embraced him, and at the moment when the knife was about to fall, said, "The man whom his fellow-men kill, God resuscitates. He whom his brothers expel finds the Father again. Pray, believe, enter into life ! The Father is there !" When he descended from the scaffold there was something in his glance which made the people open a path for him ; it was impossible to say whether his pallor or his serenity were the more admirable. On returning to the humble abode, which he called smilingly his palace, he said to his sister, "I have been officiating pontifically."

As the most sublime things are often the least understood, there were persons in the town who said, in commenting on the Bishop's conduct, "It is affectation." This, how-ever, was only the talk of drawing-rooms ; the people, who do not regard holy actions maliciously, were affected, and admired him.

As for the Bishop, the sight of the guillotine was a shock to him, and it was long ere he recovered from it. The scaffold, in fact, when it stands erect before you, has some-thing about it that hallucinates. It is a species of monster, manufactured by the judge and the carpenter, a spectre that seems to live a sort of horrible life made up of all the death it has produced. Hence the impression was terrible and deep ; on the day after the execution, and for many days beyond, the Bishop appeared crushed. The almost violent serenity of the mournful moment had departed ; the phantom of social justice haunted him. He who usually returned from all his offices with such radiant satisfaction seemed to be reproaching himself. At times he soliloquised, and stammered unconnected sentences in a low voice. Here is one which his sister overheard and treasured up : "I did not believe that it was so monstrous. It is wrong to absorb oneself in the divine law so greatly as no longer to perceive the human law. Death belongs to God alone. By what right do men touch that unknown thing ?"

With the lapse of time these impressions gradually faded,

and perhaps were effaced. Still it was noticed that from this period the Bishop avoided passing by the place of execution.

M. Myriel could be called at any hour to the bedside of the sick and the dying. He was not ignorant that his greatest duty and greatest labour lay there. Widowed or orphaned families had no occasion to send for him, for he came of himself. He had the art of sitting down and holding his tongue for hours by the side of a man who had lost the wife he loved, or of a mother bereaved of her child. As he knew the time to be silent, he also knew the time to speak. What an admirable consoler he was! he did not try to efface grief by oblivion, but to aggrandise and dignify it by hope. He would say, "Take care of the way in which you turn to the dead. Do not think of that which perishes. Look fixedly, and you will perceive the living light of your beloved dead in heaven." He knew that belief is healthy, and he sought to counsel and calm the desperate man by pointing out to him the resigned man, and to transform the grief that gazes at a grave by showing it the grief that looks up to the stars.

CHAPTER V.

M. MYRIEL's private life was full of the same thoughts as his public life. To any one able of inspecting it closely, the voluntary poverty in which the Bishop lived would have been a solemn and charming spectacle. Like all old men, and like most thinkers, he slept little, but that short sleep was deep. In the morning he remained in contemplation for an hour, and then said mass either at the cathedral or in his house. Mass over, he breakfasted on rye bread dipped in the milk of his own cows. Then he set to work.

A bishop is a very busy man. He must daily receive the secretary to the bishopric, who is generally a canon, and nearly daily his grand vicars. He has congregations to control, permissions to grant, a whole ecclesiastical library to examine, in the shape of diocesan catechisms, books of hours, etc. ; mandates to write, sermons to authorise, curés and mayors to reconcile, a clerical correspondence, an administrative correspondence, on one side the State, on the other the Holy See ; in a word, a thousand tasks. The time which these thousand tasks, his offices, and his

breviary left him, he gave first to the needy, the sick, and
the afflicted ; the time which the afflicted, the sick, and the
needy left him he gave to work. Sometimes he hoed in his
garden, at others he read and wrote. He had only one
name for both sorts of labour ; he called them gardening.
" The mind is a garden," said he.

Towards noon, when the weather was fine, he went out
and walked in the country or the town, frequently entering
the cottages. He could be seen walking alone in deep
thought, looking down, leaning on his long cane, dressed
in his violet wadded and warm greatcoat, with his violet
stockings thrust into clumsy shoes, and wearing his flat
hat, through each corner of which were passed three golden
acorns as tassels. It was a festival wherever he appeared.
It seemed as if his passing had something warming and
luminous about it ; old men and children came to the door
to greet the Bishop as they did the sun. He blessed them
and they blessed him, and his house was pointed out to
anybody who was in want of anything. Now and then he
stopped, spoke to the little boys and girls, and smiled on
their mothers. He visited the poor so long as he had any
money ; when he had none he visited the rich. As he made
his cassocks last a long time, and he did not wish the fact
to be noticed, he never went into town save in his wadded
violet coat. In summer this was rather tiresome.

On his return he dined. The dinner resembled the
breakfast. At half-past eight in the evening he supped
with his sister, Madame Magloire standing behind them
and waiting on them. Nothing could be more frugal than
this meal ; but if the Bishop had a curé to supper, Madame
Magloire would take advantage of it to serve Monseigneur
with some excellent fish from the lake, or famous game
from the mountain. Every curé was the excuse for a good
meal, and the Bishop held his tongue. On other occasions
his repast only consisted of vegetables boiled in water and
soup made with oil. Hence it was said in the town,
" When the Bishop does not entertain a curé, he entertains
a Trappist."

After supper he would chat for half an hour with Mademoiselle Baptistine and Madame Magloire ; then he returned
to his room and began writing again, either on loose leaves
or on the margin of some folio. He was well read, and a bit
of a *savant*, and has left five or six curious MSS. on theologi-
cal subjects. In one of these dissertations he examines the

works of Hugo, Bishop of Ptolemais, great-grand-uncle of him who writes this book, and he proves that to this bishop must be attributed the various opuscules published in the last century under the pseudonym of Barleycourt. At times, in the midst of his reading, no matter the book he held in his hands, he would suddenly fall into a deep meditation, from which he only emerged to write a few lines on the pages of the book. These lines have frequently no connection with the book that contains them. Here is one.

"O you who are! Ecclesiastes calls you Omnipotence; the Maccabees call you Creator; the Epistle to the Ephesians calls you Liberty; Baruch calls you Immensity; the Psalms call you Wisdom and Truth; St. John calls you Light; the Book of Kings calls you Lord; Exodus calls you Providence; Leviticus, Holiness; Esdras, Justice; Creation calls you God; man calls you the Father; but Solomon calls you Mercy, and that is the fairest of all your names."

About nine o'clock the two females withdrew and went up to their bedrooms on the first floor, leaving him alone till morning on the lower floor. Here it is necessary that we should give an exact idea of the dwelling of the Bishop.

CHAPTER VI.

THE house which he occupied consisted, as we have said, of a ground floor and one above it; three rooms on the ground, three bedrooms on the first floor, and above them a storeroom. Behind the house was a quarter of an acre of garden. The two females occupied the first floor, and the Bishop lodged below. The first room, which opened on the street, served him as dining-room, the second as bedroom, the third as oratory. You could not get out of the oratory without passing through the bedroom, or out of the bedroom without passing through the sitting-room. At the end of the oratory was a closed alcove with a bed, for any one who stayed the night, and the Bishop offered this bed to country curés when business or the wants of their parish brought them to D——.

The surgery of the hospital, a small building added to the house and built on a part of the garden, had been transformed into kitchen and cellar. There was also in the garden a stable, which had been the old hospital kitchen, and in which the Bishop kept two cows. Whatever the quantity of milk they yielded, he invariably sent one hal every morning to the hospital patients. "I am paying my tithes," he would say.

His room was quite large, and very difficult to heat in the cold weather. As wood is excessively dear at D——, he hit on the idea of partitioning off with planks a portion of the cow-house. Here he spent his evenings during the great frosts, and called it his "winter drawing-room." In this room, as in the dining-room, there was no other furniture but a square deal table and four straw chairs. The dining-room was also adorned with an old buffet stained to imitate rosewood. The Bishop had made the altar which decorated his oratory out of a similar buffet, suitably covered with white cloths and imitation lace. His rich penitents and the religious ladies of D—— had often subscribed to pay for a handsome new altar for Monseigneur's oratory : each time he took the money and gave it to the poor. "The finest of all altars," he would say, "is the soul of an unhappy man who is comforted and thanks God."

In his oratory he had two straw prie-dieus, and an arm-chair, also of straw, in his bedroom. When he by chance received seven or eight persons at the same time, the Prefect, the General, the staff of the regiment quartered in the town, or some pupils of the Lower Seminary, it was necessary to fetch the chairs from the winter drawing-room, the prie-dieus from the oratory, and the easy-chair from the bedroom : in this way as many as eleven seats could be collected for the visitors. At each new visit a room was stripped. It happened at times that there would be twelve ; in such a case the Bishop concealed the embarrassing nature of the situation by standing before the chimney if it were winter, or walking up and down the room were it summer.

There was another chair in the alcove, but it was half robbed of the straw, and had only three legs to stand on, so that it could only be used when resting against a wall. Mademoiselle Baptistine also had in her bedroom a very large settee of wood, which had once been gilt and covered with flowered chintz, but it had been necessary to raise this settee to the first floor through the window, owing to the narrowness of the stairs : and hence it could not be reckoned on in any emergency. It had been Mademoiselle Baptistine's ambition to buy drawing-room furniture of mahogany and covered with yellow Utrecht velvet, but this would have cost at least 500 francs, and seeing that she had only succeeded in saving for this object 42 francs 5 sous in five years, she gave up the idea. But who ever attains his ideal?

Nothing more simple can be imagined than the Bishop's bedroom. A long window opening on the garden; opposite this the bed, an iron hospital bed, with a canopy of green serge; in the shadow of the bed, behind a curtain, toilet articles, still revealing the old elegant habits of the man of fashion; two doors, one near the chimney leading to the oratory, the other near the library leading to the dining-room. The library was a large glass case full of books; the chimney of wood, painted to imitate marble, was habitually fireless; in the chimney were a pair of iron andirons ornamented with two cases, displaying garlands and grooves which had once been silvered, which was a species of episcopal luxury; over the chimney a crucifix of unsilvered copper fastened to threadbare black velvet, in a frame which had lost its gilding; near the window was a large table with an inkstand, loaded with irregularly arranged papers and heavy tomes; before the table the straw arm-chair; in front of the bed a prie-dieu taken from the oratory.

Two portraits, in oval frames, hung on the wall on either side of the bed. Small gilded inscriptions on the neutral tinted ground of the canvas by the side of the figures indicated that the portraits represented, one the Abbé de Chaliot, Bishop of St. Claude; the other the Abbé Tourteau, Vicar-general of Agde, and Abbé of Grand Champs, belonging to the Cistercian order in the diocese of Chartres. The Bishop, on succeeding to the hospital infirmary, found the pictures there and left them. They were priests, probably donors, — two motives for him to respect them. All he knew of the two personages was that they had been nominated by the King, the one to his bishopric, the other to his benefice, on the same day, April 27, 1785. Madame Magloire having unhooked the portraits to remove the dust, the Bishop found this circumstance recorded in faded ink on a small square of paper which time had turned yellow, and fastened by four wafers at the back of the portrait of the Abbé of Grand Champs.

He had at his window an antique curtain of coarse woollen stuff, which had grown so old that Madame Magloire, in order to avoid the expense of a new one, was obliged to make a large seam in the very middle of it. The seam

formed a cross, and the Bishop often drew attention to it.
"How pleasant that is," he would say. All the rooms in
the house, ground floor and first floor, were whitewashed,
which is a barrack and hospital fashion. Still, some years
later, Madame Magloire discovered, as we shall see further
on, paintings under the whitewashed paper, in Mademoiselle
Baptistine's bedroom. The rooms were paved with red bricks
which were washed every week, and there were straw mats
in front of all the beds. This house, moreover, managed
by two females, was exquisitely clean from top to bottom :
this was the only luxury the Bishop allowed himself, for, as
he said, "It takes nothing from the poor." We must allow,
however, that of the old property there still remained six
silver spoons and forks and a soup ladle, which Madame
Magloire daily saw with delight shining splendidly on the
coarse table-cloth. And as we are here depicting the Bishop
of D—— as he was, we must add that he had said, more
than once, "I do not think I could give up eating with
silver." To this plate must be added two heavy candlesticks of massive silver, which the Bishop inherited from a
great-aunt. These branched candlesticks each held two
wax candles, and usually figured on the Bishop's chimney.
When he had any one to dinner, Madame Magloire lit the
candles and placed the two candlesticks on the table. There
was in the Bishop's bedroom, at the head of his bed, a small
cupboard in the wall, in which Madame Magloire each night
placed the plate and the large ladle. But the key was never
taken out.

The garden, which was spoiled to some extent by the
ugly buildings to which we have referred, was composed of
four walks, radiating round a drain-well ; another walk ran
all round the garden close to the surrounding white wall.
Between these walks were four box-bordered squares. In
three of them Madame Magloire grew vegetables ; in the
fourth the Bishop had placed flowers ; here and there were
a few fruit trees. Once Madame Magloire had said, with
a sort of gentle malice, "Monseigneur, although you turn
everything to use, here is an unemployed plot. It would
be better to have lettuces there than bouquets." "Madame
Magloire," the Bishop answered, "you are mistaken ; the
beautiful is as useful as the useful." He added, after a
moment's silence, "Perhaps more so."

This square, consisting of three or four borders, occupied
the Bishop almost as much as his books did. He liked to

spend an hour or two there, cutting, raking, and digging holes in which he placed seeds. He was not so hostile to insects as a gardener would have liked. However, he made no pretensions to botany ; he did not make the slightest attempt to decide between Tournefort and the natural method ; he was not a partisan either of Jussieu or Linnæus. He did not study plants, but he loved flowers. He greatly respected the professors, but he respected the ignorant even more, and without ever failing in this respect, he watered his borders every summer evening with a tin watering-pot painted green.

Not a single door in the house locked. The door of the dining-room, which, as we said, opened right on the cathedral square, had formerly been adorned with bolts and locks like a prison gate. The Bishop had all this iron removed, and the door was only hasped either night or day : the first passer-by, no matter the hour, had only to push it. At the outset the two females had been greatly alarmed by this never-closed door ; but the Bishop said to them, " Have bolts placed on the doors of your rooms if you like." In the end they shared his confidence, or at least affected to do so : Madame Magloire alone was from time to time alarmed. As regards the Bishop, his idea is explained, or at least indicated, by these three lines, which he wrote on the margin of a Bible : " This is the distinction : the physician's doors must never be closed, the priest's door must always be open." In another book, entitled *Philosophy of Medical Science*, he wrote this other note : "Am I not a physician like them ? I also have my patients : in the first place, I have theirs, whom they call the sick, and then I have my own, whom I call the unhappy." Elsewhere he also wrote : " Do not ask the name of the man who seeks a bed from you, for it is before all the man whom his name embarrasses that needs an asylum."

It came about that a worthy curé—I forget whether it were he of Couloubroux or he of Pompierry—thought proper to ask him one day, probably at the instigation of Madame Magloire, whether Monseigneur was quite certain that he was not acting to some extent imprudently by leaving his door open day and night for any who liked to enter, and if he did not fear lest some misfortune might happen in a house so poorly guarded. The Bishop tapped his shoulder with gentle gravity, and said to him, " Nisi Dominus custodierit domum, in vanum vigilant qui custodiunt eam."

Then he talked of something else. He was fond of saying too, "There is the Priest's bravery as well as that of the Colonel of Dragoons. Only ours should be quiet."

CHAPTER VII.

THIS is the proper place for an incident we must not omit, for it is one of those which will enable us to see what manner of man the Bishop of D—— was. After the destruction of the band of Gaspard Bès, which had infested the gorges of Ollioules, Cravatte, one of his lieutenants, took refuge in the mountains. He concealed himself for a while with his brigands, the remnant of Bès' band, in the county of Nice, then went to Piedmont, and suddenly reappeared in France, via Barcelonnette. He was seen first at Jauziers, and next at Tuiles; he concealed himself in the caverns of the Joug de l'Aigle, and descended thence on the hamlets and villages by the ravines of the Ubaye. He pushed on even as far as Embrun, entered the church one night and plundered the sacristy. His brigandage desolated the country, and the gendarmes were in vain placed on his track. He constantly escaped, and at times even offered resistance, for he was a bold scoundrel. In the midst of all this terror the Bishop arrived on his visitation, and the Mayor came to him and urged him to turn back. Cravatte held the mountain as far as Arche and beyond, and there was danger, even with an escort. It would be exposing three or four unhappy gendarmes to useless danger.

"And so," said the Bishop, "I intend to go without escort."

"Can you mean it, Monseigneur?" the Mayor exclaimed.

"I mean it so fully that I absolutely refuse gendarmes, and intend to start in an hour."

"Monseigneur, you will not do that!"

"There is in the mountain," the Bishop continued, "a humble little parish, which I have not visited for three years. They are good friends of mine, and quiet and honest shepherds. They are the owners of one goat out of every thirty they guard; they make very pretty woollen ropes of different colours, and they play mountain airs on small six-holed flutes. They want to hear about heaven every now and then, and what would they think of a bishop who was afraid? What would they say if I did not go?"

" But, Monseigneur, the brigands."

" Ah," said the Bishop, "you are right ; I may meet them. They too must want to hear about heaven."

" Monseigneur, they will plunder you."

" I have nothing."

" They will kill you."

"A poor old priest who passes by, muttering his mummery? Nonsense, what good would that do them ? "

" Oh, good gracious, if you were to meet them ! "

" I would ask them for alms for my poor."

" Monseigneur, do not go. In Heaven's name do not, for you expose your life."

" My good sir," said the Bishop, " is that all ? I am not in this world to save my life, but to save souls."

There was no help for it, and he set out only accompanied by a lad, who offered to act as his guide. His obstinacy created a sensation in the country, and caused considerable alarm. He would not take either his sister or Madame Magloire with him. He crossed the mountain on mule-back, met nobody, and reached his good friends the goat-herds safe and sound. He remained with them a fortnight, preaching, administering the sacraments, teaching, and moralising. When he was ready to start for home he resolved to sing a Te Deum pontifically, and spoke about it to the Curé. But what was to be done? there was no episcopal ornaments. All that could be placed at his dis-posal was a poor village sacristy, with a few old faded and pinchbeck covered chasubles.

" Nonsense," said the Bishop ; "announce the Te Deum in your sermon for all that. It will come right in the end."

Inquiries were made in the surrounding churches : but all the magnificence of these united humble parishes would not have been sufficient decently to equip a cathedral chorister. While they were in this embarrassment a large chest was brought and left at the curacy for the Bishop by two strange horsemen, who started again at once. The chest was opened and found to contain a cope of cloth of gold, a mitre adorned with diamonds, an archiepiscopal cross, a magnificent crozier, and all the pontifical robes stolen a month back from the treasury of our Lady of Embrun. In the chest was a paper on which were written these words : " Cravatte to Monseigneur Welcome."

" Did I not tell you that it would be all right ? " the Bishop said ; then he added, with a smile, " Heaven sends an archbishop's cope to a man who is contented with a curé's surplice."

" Monseigneur," the Curé muttered, with a gentle shake of his head, " Heaven or——"

The Bishop looked fixedly at the Curé and repeated authoritatively, "Heaven!"

When he returned to Chastelon, and all along the road, he was regarded curiously. He found at the presbytery of that town Mademoiselle Baptistine and Madame Magloire waiting for him, and he said to his sister, " Well, was I right? The poor priest went among these poor mountaineers with empty hands, and returns with his hands full. I started only taking with me my confidence in Heaven, and I bring back the treasures of a cathedral."

The same evening before retiring, he said too, " Never let us fear robbers or murderers. These are external and small dangers; let us fear ourselves; prejudices are the real robbers, vices the true murderers. The great dangers are within ourselves. Let us not trouble about what threatens our head or purse, and only think of what threatens our soul." Then, turning to his sister, he added, "Sister, a priest ought never to take precautions against his neighbour. What his neighbour does God permits, so let us confine ourselves to praying to God when we believe that a danger is impending over us. Let us pray, not for ourselves, but that our brother may not fall into wrong-doing on our account."

Events, however, were rare in his existence. We relate those we know, but ordinarily he spent his life in always doing the same things at the same moment. A month of his year resembled an hour of his day. As to what became of the treasure of Embrun Cathedral, we should be greatly embarrassed if questioned on that head. There were many fine things, very tempting and famous to steal on behalf of the poor. Stolen they were already, one moiety of the adventure was accomplished : the only thing left to do was to change the direction of the robbery, and make it turn slightly towards the poor. Still, we affirm nothing on the subject ; we merely mention that among the Bishop's papers a rather obscure note was found, which probably refers to this question, and was thus conceived : "The question is to know whether it ought to be returned to the cathedral or the hospital."

CHAPTER VIII.

THE Senator, heretofore referred to, was a skilful man, who
had made his way with a rectitude that paid no attention to
all those things which constitute obstacles, and are called
conscience, plighted word, right, and duty : he had gone
straight to his object without once swerving from the line
of his advancement and his interest. He was an ex-
procureur, softened by success, anything but a wicked man,
doing all the little services in his power for his sons, his
sons-in-law, his relatives, and even his friends : he had
selected the best opportunities, and the rest seemed to him
something absurd. He was witty, and just sufficiently
lettered to believe himself a disciple of Epicurus, while
probably only a product of Pigault Lebrun. He was fond
of laughing pleasantly at things infinite and eternal, and
at the crotchets " of our worthy Bishop." He even laughed
at them with amiable authority in M. Myriel's presence.
On some semi-official occasion the Count —— (this Senator)
and M. Myriel met at the Prefect's table. At the dessert
the Senator, who was merry but quite sober, said :
"Come, Bishop, let us have a chat. A senator and a
bishop can hardly meet without winking at each other,
for we are two augurs, and I am about to make a confession
to you. I have my system of philosophy."
"And you are right," the Bishop answered ; "as you
make your philosophy, so you must lie on it. You are on
the bed of purple."
The Senator, thus encouraged, continued :
"Let us be candid."
"Decidedly."
"I declare to you," the Senator went on, "that the
Marquis d'Argens, Phyrrho, Hobbes, and Naigeon are no
impostors. I have in my library all my philosophers with
gilt backs."
"Like yourself, Count," the Bishop interrupted him.
The Senator went on :
"I hate Diderot ; he is an ideologist, a declaimer, and
a revolutionist, believing in his heart in Deity, and more
bigoted than Voltaire. The latter ridiculed Needham, and
was wrong, for Needham's eels prove that God is unnecessary. A drop of vinegar in a spoonful of flour supplies
the *fiat lux* ; suppose the drop larger, and the spoonful

bigger, and you have the world. Man is the eel; then, of what use is the Eternal Father? My dear Bishop, the Jehovah hypothesis wearies me; it is only fitted to produce thin people who think hollow. Down with the great All which annoys me! Long live Zero, who leaves me at peace! Between ourselves, and in order to confess to my pastor, as is right and proper, I confess to you that I possess common sense. I am not wild about your Saviour, who continually preaches abnegation and sacrifice. It is advice offered by a miser to beggars. Abnegation—why? Sacrifice—for what object? I do not see that one wolf sacrifices itself to cause the happiness of another wolf. Let us, therefore, remain in nature. We are at the summit, so let us have the supreme philosophy. What is the use of being at the top, if you cannot see further than the end of other people's noses? Let us live gaily, for life is all in all. As for man having a future elsewhere, up there, down there, somewhere, I do not believe a syllable of it. Oh yes! recommend sacrifices and abnegation to me. I must take care of all I do. I must rack my brains about good and evil, justice and injustice, fas et nefas. Why so? because I shall have to give account for my actions. When? after my death. What a fine dream! after death! He will be a clever fellow who catches me. Just think of a lump of ashes seized by a shadowy hand. Let us speak the truth, we who are initiated and have raised the skirt of Isis; there is no good, no evil, but there is vegetation. Let us seek reality and go to the bottom; we must scent the truth, dig into the ground for it and seize it. Then it offers you exquisite delights; then you become strong and laugh. I am square at the base, my dear Bishop, and human immortality is a thing which anybody who likes may listen to. Oh, what a charming prospect! What a fine billet Adam has! You are a soul, you will be an angel, and have blue wings on your shoulder-blades. Come, help me, is it not Tertullian who says that the blessed will go from one planet to the other? Very good; they will be the grasshoppers of the planets. And then they will see God; tut, tut, tut. These paradises are all nonsense, and God is a monstrous fable. I would not say so in the *Moniteur*, of course, but I whisper it between friends. Sacrificing the earth for paradise is giving up the substance for the shadow. I am not such an ass as to be the dupe of the Infinite. I am nothing, my name is Count Nothing, Senator. Did I exist before my birth? no; shall I exist after my death? no. What am I? a little dust aggregated by an organism. What have I to do on this earth? I have the choice between suffering and enjoyment. To what will suffering lead me? to nothingness, but I shall have suffered. To what will enjoyment lead me? to nothingness, but I shall have enjoyed. My choice is made; a man must either eat or be eaten, and so I eat, for it is better to be the tooth than the grass. That is my wisdom; after which go on as I impel you; the grave-digger is there, the Pantheon for such as us, and all fall into the large hole. *Finis*, and total liquidation, that is the vanishing point. Death is dead, take my word for it; and I laugh at the idea of any one present affirming the contrary. It is an invention of nurses, old Boguey for children, Jehovah for men. No, our morrow is night; behind the tomb there is nothing but equal nothings. You may have been Sardanapalus, you may have been St. Vincent de Paule, but it all comes to the same thing. That is the truth, so live above all else; make use of your *me*, so long as you hold it. In truth, I tell you, my dear Bishop, I have my philosophy, and I have my philosophers, and I do not let myself be deluded by fables. After all, something must be offered persons who are down in the world,—the barefooted, the strugglers for existence, and the wretched: and so they are offered pure legends—chimeras—the soul—immortality—paradise—the stars—to swallow. They chew that, and put it on their dry bread. The man who has nothing has God, and that is something at any rate. I do not oppose it, but I keep M. Naigeon for myself; God is good for the plebs."

The Bishop clapped his hands.

"That is what I call speaking," he exclaimed. "Ah, what an excellent and truly wonderful thing this materialism is! it is not every man who wishes that can have it. Ah! when a man has reached that point, he is no longer a dupe; he does not let himself be stupidly exiled, like Cato; or stoned, like St. Stephen; or burnt, like Joan of Arc. Those who have succeeded in acquiring this materialism have the joy of feeling themselves irresponsible, and thinking that they can devour everything without anxiety, places, sinecures, power well or badly gained, dignities, lucrative tergiversations, useful treachery, folly, capitulations with their consciences, and that they will go down to the tomb after digesting it all properly. How agreeable this is! I

am not referring to you, my dear Senator, still I cannot
refrain from congratulating you. You great gentlemen
have, as you say, a philosophy of your own, and for yourselves, exquisite, refined, accessible to the rich alone, good
with any sauce, and admirably seasoning the joys of life.
This philosophy is drawn from the profundities, and dug up
by special searchers. But you are kind fellows, and think
it no harm that belief in God should be the philosophy of
the populace, much in the same way as a goose stuffed with
onions is the truffled turkey of the poor."

CHAPTER IX.

ANOTHER thing he did which the whole town declared to be
even more venturesome than his trip in the mountains among
the bandits. A man lived alone in the country near D——.
This man, let us out with the great word at once, had been a
member of the National Convention, of the name of G——.
People talked about him in the little world of D—— with a
species of horror. A Conventionalist, only think of that!
Those men existed at the time when people "thou-ed" one
another and were called citizens. This man was almost a
monster; he had not voted for the King's death, but had
done all but that, and was a quasi-regicide. How was it
that this man had not been tried by court-martial, on the
return of the legitimate princes? They need not have cut
his head off, for clemency is all right and proper, but banish-
ment for life would have been an example, and so on.
Moreover, he was an atheist, like all those men. It was
the babblings of geese round a vulture.

But was this G—— a vulture? Yes, if he might be
judged by his ferocious solitude. As he had not voted the
King's death, he was not comprised in the decree of exile,
and was enabled to remain in France. He lived about
three miles from the town, far from every village, every
road, in a nook of a very wild valley. He had there, so it
was said, a field, a hut, a den. He had no neighbours,
not even passers-by. Since he had lived in the valley the
path leading to it had become overgrown with grass.
People talked of the spot as of the hangman's house.
Yet the Bishop thought of it, and from time to time gazed
at a spot on the horizon where a clump of trees pointed
out the old Conventionalist's valley, and said, "There lives

a ‚soul alone," and he added to himself, "I owe him a visit."

But, let us confess it, this idea, which at the first blush was natural, seemed to him after a moment's reflection strange and impossible, almost repulsive. For, in his heart, he shared the general impression, and the Conventionalist inspired him, without his being able to account for it, with that feeling which is the border line of hatred, and which is so well expressed by the word estrangement.

And yet the shepherd ought not to keep aloof from a scabby sheep. But then what a sheep it was! The good Bishop was perplexed; at times he started in that direction, but turned back. One day a rumour spread in the town that a young boy who waited on G—— in his den had come to fetch a doctor : the old villain was dying, paralysis was overpowering him, and he could not live through the night.

The Bishop took his cane, put on his overcoat to hide his well-worn cassock, as well as to protect him against the night breeze which would soon rise, and set out. The sun had almost attained the horizon when the Bishop reached the excommunicated spot. He perceived with a certain heart-beating that he was close to the wild beast's den. He strode across a ditch, clambered over a hedge, entered a neglected garden, and suddenly perceived the cavern behind some shrubs. It was a low, poor-looking hut, small and clean, with a vine nailed over the front. In front of the door an old white-haired man, seated in a worn-out wheel chair, was smiling in the sun. By his side stood a boy, who handed him a bowl of milk. While the Bishop was looking at him the old man uplifted his voice. "Thanks," he said, "I want nothing further," and his smile was turned from the sun to rest on the boy.

The Bishop stepped forward, and at the noise of his footsteps the seated man turned his head, and his face expressed all the surprise it is possible to feel after a long life.

"Since I have lived here," he said, "you are the first person who has come to me. Who may you be, sir ? "

The Bishop answered, "My name is Bienvenu Myriel."

"I have heard that name uttered. Are you not he whom the peasants call Monseigneur Welcome ? "

"I am."

The old man continued, with a half smile, "In that case you are my bishop ? "

" Perhaps."

" Come in, sir."

The Conventionalist offered his hand to the Bishop, but the Bishop did not take it. He confined himself to saying : " I am pleased to see that I was deceived. You certainly do not look ill."

" I am about to be cured, sir," the old man said ; then after a pause he added, " I shall be dead in three hours. I am a bit of a physician, and know in what way the last hour comes. Yesterday only my feet were cold ; to-day the chill reached my knees ; now I can feel it ascending to my waist ; and when it reaches the heart I shall stop. The sun is glorious, is it not ? I had myself wheeled out in order to take a farewell glance at things. You can talk to me, for it does not weary me. You have done well to come and look at a dying man, for it is proper that there should be witnesses. People have their fancies, and I should have liked to go on till dawn. But I know that I can hardly last three hours. It will be night, but, after all, what matter ? Finishing is a simple affair, and daylight is not necessary for it. Be it so : I will die by starlight."

Then the old man turned to the lad :

" Go to bed. You sat up the other night, and must be tired."

The boy went into the cabin ; the old man looked after him, and added, as if speaking to himself :

" While he is sleeping I shall die : the two slumbers can keep each other company."

The Bishop was not so moved as we might imagine he would be. He did not think that he saw God in this way of dying : and—let us out with it, as the small contradictions of great hearts must also be indicated,—he, who at times laughed so heartily at " His Greatness," was somewhat annoyed at not being called Monseigneur, and was almost tempted to reply, Citizen. He felt an inclination for coarse familiarity, common enough with doctors and priests, but to which he was not accustomed. This man after all, this Conventionalist, this representative of the people, had been a mighty one of the earth : for the first time in his life, perhaps, the Bishop felt disposed to be severe.

The Republican, in the meanwhile, regarded him with modest cordiality, in which, perhaps, could be traced that humility which is so becoming in a man who is on the point of returning to the dust. The Bishop, on his side, though he generally guarded against curiosity, which according to him was akin to insult, could not refrain from examining the Conventionalist with an attention which, as it did not emanate from sympathy, would have pricked his conscience in the case of any other man. The Conventionalist produced the effect upon him of being beyond the pale of the law, even the law of charity.

G——, calm, almost upright, and possessing a sonorous voice, was one of those grand octogenarians who are the amazement of the physiologist. The Revolution possessed many such men, proportioned to the age. The thoroughly tried man could be seen in him, and, though so near his end, he had retained all the signs of health. There was something which would disconcert death in his bright glance, his firm accent, and the robust movement of his shoulders : Azrael, the Mohammedan angel of the tomb, would have turned back fancying that he had mistaken the door. G—— seemed to be dying because he wished to do so ; there was liberty in his agony, and his legs alone, by which the shadows clutched him, were motionless. While the feet were dead and cold, the head lived with all the power of life and appeared in full light. G—— at this awful moment resembled the king in the Oriental legend, flesh above and marble below. The Bishop sat down on a stone and began rather abruptly :

" I congratulate you," he said, in the tone people employ to reprimand ; " at least you did not vote the King's death."

The Republican did not seem to notice the covert bitterness of this remark, " at least " ; he replied, without a smile on his face :

" Do not congratulate me, sir : I voted the death of the tyrant." It was the accent of austerity opposed to that of sternness.

" What do you mean ? " the Bishop continued.

" I mean that man has a tyrant, Ignorance, and I voted for the end of that tyrant which engendered royalty, which is the false authority, while knowledge is the true authority. Man must only be governed by knowledge."

" And by his conscience," the Bishop added.

" That is the same thing. Conscience is the amount of innate knowledge we have in us."

Monseigneur Welcome listened in some surprise to this language, which was very novel to him. The Republican continued :

"As for Louis XVI. I said No. I do not believe that I have the right to kill a man, but I feel the duty of exterminating a tyrant, and I voted for the end of the tyrant. That is to say, for the end of prostitution for women ; the end of slavery for men ; and the end of night for children. In voting for the Republic I voted for all this : I voted for fraternity, concord, the Dawn ! I aided in the overthrow of errors and prejudices, and such an overthrow produces light ; we hurled down the old world, and that vase of wretchedness, by being poured over the human race, became an urn of joy."

"Mingled joy," said the Bishop.

"You might call it a troubled joy, and now, after that fatal return of the past which is called 1814, a departed joy. Alas ! the work was incomplete, I grant ; we demolished the ancient régime in facts, but were not able to suppress it completely in ideas. It is not sufficient to destroy abuses, but morals must also be modified. Though the mill no longer exists, the wind still blows."

"You demolished : it may be useful, but I distrust a demolition complicated with passion."

"Right has its passion, Sir Bishop, and that passion is an element of progress. No matter what may be said, the French Revolution is the most powerful step taken by the human race since the advent of Christ. It may be incomplete, but it was sublime. It softened minds, it calmed, appeased, and enlightened, and it spread civilisation over the world. The French Revolution was good, for it was the consecration of humanity."

The Bishop could not refrain from muttering :

"Yes ? '93 ! "

The Republican drew himself up with almost mournful solemnity, and shouted, as well as a dying man could shout :

"Ah ! there we have it ! I have been waiting for that. A cloud had been collecting for fifteen hundred years, and at the end of that period it burst : you are condemning the thunderclap."

The Bishop, without perhaps confessing it to himself, felt that the blow had gone home ; still he kept a good countenance, and answered :

"The judge speaks in the name of justice ; the priest speaks in that of pity, which is only a higher form of justice. A thunderclap must not deceive itself."

And he added, looking fixedly at the Conventionalist :
" Louis XVII. ? "

The Republican stretched forth his hand and seized the
Bishop's arm.

" Louis XVII. Let us consider. Whom do you weep for?
Is it the innocent child ? in that case I weep with you. Is
it the royal child ? in that case I must ask leave to reflect.
For me, the thought of the brother of Cartouche, an innocent
lad, hung up by a rope under the armpits in the Place
de Grève until death ensued, for the sole crime of being
Cartouche's brother, is not less painful than the grandson
of Louis XV., the innocent boy martyrised in the Temple
Tower for the sole crime of being the grandson of
Louis XV."

" I do not like such an association of names, sir," said
the Bishop.

" Louis XV. ? Cartouche ? On behalf of which do you
protest ? "

There was a moment's silence ; the Bishop almost
regretted having come, and yet felt himself vaguely and
strangely shaken. The Conventionalist continued :

" Ah ! sir priest, you do not like the crudities of truth,
but Christ loved them ; he took a scourge and swept the
temple. His lightning lash was a rough discourser of
truths. When he exclaimed, ' Suffer little children to
come unto me,' he made no distinction among them. He
made no difference between the dauphin of Barabbas and
the dauphin of Herod. Innocence is its own crown, and
does not require to be a Highness ; it is as august in rags
as when crowned with *fleurs de lis*."

" That is true," said the Bishop in a low voice.

" You have named Louis XVII.," the Conventionalist
continued ; " let us understand each other. Shall we weep
for all the innocents, martyrs, and children of the lowest
as of the highest rank? I am with you there, but, as I
said, in that case we must go back beyond '93, and begin
our tears before Louis XVII. I will weep over the children
of the kings with you, provided that you weep with me
over the children of the people."

" I weep for all," said the Bishop.

" Equally ! " G—— exclaimed ; " and if the balance must
be uneven, let it be on the side of the people, as they have
suffered the longest."

There was again a silence, which the Republican broke.

He rose on his elbow, held his chin with his thumb and forefinger, as a man does mechanically when he is interrogating and judging, and fixed on the Bishop a glance full of all the energy of approaching death. It was almost an explosion.

"Yes, sir; the people have suffered for a long time. But let me ask why you have come to question and speak to me about Louis XVII.? I do not know you. Ever since I have been in this country I have lived here alone, never setting my foot across the threshold, and seeing no one but the boy who attends to me. Your name, it is true, has vaguely reached me, and I am bound to say that it was pronounced affectionately, but that means nothing, for clever people have so many ways of making the worthy, simple folk believe in them. By the bye, I did not hear the sound of your coach; you doubtless left it down there behind that clump of trees at the cross-roads. I do not know you, I tell you; you have informed me that you are the Bishop, but that teaches me nothing as to your moral character. In a word—I repeat my question, Who are you? You are a bishop, that is to say, a prince of the Church, one of those gilded, escutcheoned annuitants who have fat prebends—the bishopric of D——, with 15,000 francs certain, 10,000 francs casualties, or a total of 25,000 francs,—who have kitchens, liveries, keep a good table, and eat water-fowl on a Friday; who go about, with lackeys before and behind, in a gilded coach, in the name of the Saviour who walked barefoot! You are a prelate; you have, like all the rest, income, palace, horses, valets, a good table, and like all the rest you enjoy them: that is all very well, but it says either too much or too little; it does not enlighten me as to your intrinsic and essential value when you come with the probable intention of bringing me wisdom. To whom am I speaking—who are you?"

The Bishop bowed his head, and answered, "I am a worm."

"A worm in a carriage!" the Republican growled.

It was his turn to be haughty, the Bishop's to be humble; the latter continued gently:

"Be it so, sir. But explain to me how my coach, which is a little way off behind the trees, my good table, and the water-fowl I eat on Friday, my palace, my income, and my footmen, prove that pity is not a virtue, that clemency is not a duty, and that '93 was not inexorable,"

The Republican passed his hand over his forehead, as if to remove a cloud.

"Before answering you," he said, "I must ask you to forgive me. I was in the wrong, sir, for you are in my house and my guest. You discuss my ideas, and I must restrict myself to combating your reasoning. Your wealth and enjoyments are advantages which I have over you in the debate, but courtesy bids me not employ them. I promise not to do so again."

"I thank you," said the Bishop.

G—— continued:

"Let us return to the explanation you asked of me. Where were we? What was it you said, that '93 was inexorable?"

"Yes, inexorable," the Bishop said; "what do you think of Marat clapping his hands at the guillotine?"

"What do you think of Bossuet singing a Te Deum over the Dragonnades?"

The response was harsh, but went to its mark with the rigidity of a Minié bullet. The Bishop started, and could not parry it, but he was hurt by this way of mentioning Bossuet. The best minds have their fetishes, and at times feel vaguely wounded by any want of respect on the part of logic. The Conventionalist was beginning to gasp; that asthma which is mingled with the last breath affected his voice; still he retained perfect lucidity in his eyes. He continued:

"Let us say a few words more on this head. Beyond the Revolution, which, taken in its entirety, is an immense human affirmation, '93, alas, is a reply. You consider it inexorable, but what was the whole monarchy? Carrier is a bandit, but what name do you give to Montrevel? Fouquier-Tainville is a scoundrel, but what is your opinion about Lamoignon-Bâville? Maillard is frightful, but what of Saulx-Tavannes, if you please? Father Duchêne is ferocious, but what epithet will you allow me for Père Letellier? Jourdan Coupe-Tête is a monster, but less so than the Marquis de Louvois. I pity Marie Antoinette, Arch-duchess and Queen, but I also pity the poor Huguenot woman, who, in 1685, while suckling her child, was fastened, naked to the waist, to a stake, while her infant was held at a distance. Her breast was swollen with milk, her heart with agony; the babe, hungry and pale, saw that breast and screamed for it, and the hangman said to the wife, mother, and nurse, 'Abjure!' giving her the choice

between the death of her infant and the death of her
conscience. What do you say of this punishment of
Tantalus adapted to a woman? Remember this carefully,
sir, the French Revolution had its reasons, and its wrath
will be absolved by the future. Its result is a better world ;
and a caress for the human race issues from its most terrible
blows. I must stop, for the game is all in my favour—
besides, I am dying."

And ceasing to regard the Bishop, the Republican finished
his thought with the following few calm words :—

" Yes, the brutalities of progress are called revolutions,
but when they are ended, this fact is recognised ; the
human race has been chastised, but it has moved onwards."

The Republican did not suspect that he had carried in
turn every one of the Bishop's internal intrenchments. One
still remained, however, and from this, the last resource of
Monseigneur's resistance, came this remark, in which all
the roughness of the commencement was perceptible.

" Progress must believe in God, and the good cannot
have impious servants. A man who is an atheist is a bad
guide for the human race."

The ex-representative of the people did not reply. He
trembled, looked up to the sky, and a tear slowly collected
in his eye. When the lid was full the tear ran down his
livid cheek, and he said in a low, shaking voice, as if
speaking to himself :

" O Thou ! O Ideal ! Thou alone existest ! "

The Bishop had a sort of inexpressible emotion ; after
a silence the old man raised a finger to heaven and
said :

" The infinite is. It is there. If the infinite had not a
me, the *I* would be its limit ; it would not be infinite ; in
other words, it would not be. But it is. Hence it has
a *me*. This *I* of the infinite is God."

The dying man uttered these words in a loud voice, and
with a shudder of ecstasy, as if he saw some one. When
he had spoken his eyes closed, for the effort had exhausted
him. It was evident that he had lived in one minute the
few hours left him. The supreme moment was at
hand. The Bishop understood it ; he had come here as
a priest, and had gradually passed from extreme coldness
to extreme emotion ; he looked at these closed eyes, he
took this wrinkled and icy hand and bent down over the
dying man.

" This hour is God's. Would you not consider it matter of regret if we had met in vain ? "

The Republican opened his eyes again ; a gravity which suggested the shadow of death was imprinted on his countenance.

" Sir Bishop," he said, with a slowness produced perhaps more by the dignity of the soul than by failing of his strength, " I have spent my life in meditation, contemplation, and study. I was sixty years of age when my country summoned me and ordered me to interfere in its affairs. I obeyed. There were abuses, and I combated them ; tyranny, and I destroyed it ; rights and principles, and I proclaimed and confessed them ; the territory was invaded, and I defended it ; France was menaced, and I offered her my chest ; I was not rich, and I am poor. I was one of the masters of the State ; the bank cellars were so filled with specie that it was necessary to shore the walls up, which were ready to burst through the weight of gold and silver, but I dined in the Rue de l'Arbre Sec., at two-and-twenty sous a head. I succoured the oppressed. I relieved the suffering. I tore up the altar cloth, it is true, but it was to staunch the wounds of the country. I ever supported the onward march of the human race towards light, and I at times resisted pitiless progress. When opportunity served, I protected my adversaries, men of your class. And there is at Peteghem in Flanders, on the same site where the Merovingian Kings had their summer palace, a monastery of Urbanists, the Abbey of St. Claire in Beaulieu, which I saved in 1793. I did my duty according to my strength, and what good I could. After which I was driven out, tracked, pursued, persecuted, maligned, mocked, spat upon, accursed, and proscribed. For many years I have felt that persons believed they had a right to despise me. My face has been held accursed by the poor ignorant mob, and, while hating no one, I accepted the isolation of hatred. Now, I am eighty-six years of age and on the point of death. What have you come to ask of me ? "

" Your benediction ! " said the Bishop, and knelt down. When the Bishop raised his head again, the Conventionalist's countenance had become august : he had just expired. The Bishop returned home absorbed in the strangest thoughts, and spent the whole night in prayer. On the morrow curious worthies tried to make him talk about G―― the Republican, but he only pointed to heaven From this moment he increased his tenderness and fraternity for the little ones and the suffering.

Any allusion to "that old villain G—— " made him fall into a singular reverie; no one could say that the passing of that mind before his, and the reflection that great conscience cast upon his, had not something to do with this approach to perfection. This "pastoral visit" nearly created a stir among the small local coteries.

"Was it a bishop's place to visit the deathbed of such a man? It was plain that he had no conversion to hope for, for all these Revolutionists are relapsed! Then why go? What had he to see there? He must have been very curious to see the fiend carry off a soul."

One day a dowager, of the impertinent breed which believes itself witty, asked him this question, "Monseigneur, people are asking when your Grandeur will have the red bonnet?" "Oh, oh!" the Bishop answered, "that is an ominous colour. Fortunately those who despise it in a bonnet venerate it in a hat."

CHAPTER X.

WE do not need to gauge the Bishop of D—— from an orthodox point of view. In the presence of such a soul we only feel inclined to respect. The conscience of the just man must be believed on its word; besides, certain natures granted, we admit the possibility of the development of all the beauties of human virtue in a creed differing from our own. What did he think of this dogma or that mystery? These heart-secrets are only known to the tomb which souls enter in a state of nudity. What we are certain of is, that he never solved difficulties of faith by hypocrisy. It is impossible for the diamond to rot. He believed as much as he possibly could, and would frequently exclaim, " I believe in the Father." He also derived from his good deeds that amount of satisfaction which suffices the conscience, and which says in a low voice, " Thou art with God."

We think it our duty to note that, beyond his faith, he had an excess of love. It was through this, *quia multum amavit*, that he was considered vulnerable by " serious men," " grave persons," and " reasonable people," those favourite phrases of our melancholy world in which selfishness is under the guidance of pedantry. What was this excess of love? It was a serene benevolence, spreading over men, as we have already indicated, and on occasion extending even to things. He loved without disdain, and was indulgent to God's creation. Every man, even the best, has in him an unreflecting harshness, which he reserves for animals, but the Bishop of D—— had not this harshness, which is, however, peculiar to many priests. He did not go so far as the Brahmin, but seemed to have meditated on the words of Ecclesiastes: "Who knoweth the spirit of the beast that goeth downward to the earth?" An ugly appearance, a deformity of instinct, did not trouble him or render him indignant; he was moved, almost softened, by them. It seemed as if he thoughtfully sought, beyond apparent life, for the cause, the explanation, or the excuse. He examined without anger, and with the eye of a linguist deciphering a palimpsest, the amount of chaos which still exists in nature. This reverie at times caused strange remarks to escape from him. One morning he was in his garden and fancied himself alone; but his sister was walking behind, though unseen by him. He stopped and looked at something on the ground. It was a large, black, hairy, horrible spider. His sister heard him mutter, "Poor brute, it is not thy fault." Why should we not repeat this almost divine childishness of goodness? It may be puerile, but of such were the puerilities of St. Francis d'Assisi and Marcus Aurelius. One day he sprained himself rather than crush an ant.

Such was the way in which this upright man lived: at times he fell asleep in his garden, and then nothing could be more venerable. Monseigneur Welcome had been formerly, if we may believe the stories about his youth and even his manhood, a passionate, perhaps violent man. His universal mansuetude was less a natural instinct than the result of a grand conviction, which had filtered through life into his heart, and slowly dropped into it thought by thought, for in a character, as in a rock, there may be water-holes. Such hollows, however, are ineffaceable, such formations indestructible. In 1815, as we think we have said, he reached his seventy-fifth year, but did not seem sixty. He was not tall, and had a tendency to stoutness, which he strove to combat by long walks; he stood firmly, and was but very slightly built. But these are details from which we will not attempt to draw any conclusion, for Gregory XVI, at the age of eighty was erect and smiling, which did not prevent him being a bad priest. Monseigneur Welcome had what people call "a fine head," which was so amiable that its beauty was forgotten. When he talked with that infantine gaiety which was one of his graces you felt at your ease by his side, and joy seemed to emanate from his whole person. His fresh, ruddy complexion, and his white teeth, all of which he had preserved, and which were shown when he laughed, gave him that open facile air which makes you say of an aged man, "He is a worthy person." That, it will be remembered, was the effect he produced on Napoleon. At the first glance, and when you saw him for the first time, he was in reality only a worthy man, but if you remained some hours in his company, and saw him in thought, he became gradually transfigured and assumed something imposing; his wide and serious brow, already august through the white hair, became also august through meditation; majesty was evolved from this goodness; though the latter did not cease to gleam, you felt the same sort of emotion as you would do if you saw a smiling angel slowly unfold his wings without ceasing to smile. An inexpressible respect gradually penetrated you and ascended to your head, and you felt that you had before you one of those powerful, well-bred, and indulgent souls where thought is so great that it cannot but be gentle.

As we have seen, prayer, celebration of the religious offices, almsgiving, consoling the afflicted, tilling a patch of ground, frugality, hospitality, self-denial, confidence, study, and labour, filled every day of his life. *Filled* is the exact word, and certainly the Bishop's day was full of good thoughts, good words, and good actions. Still, it was not complete. If cold or wet weather prevented him from spending an hour or two in the garden before going to bed after the two females had retired, it seemed as it were a species of rite of his to prepare himself for sleep by meditation, in the presence of the grand spectacle of the heavens by night. At times, even at an advanced hour of night, if the old maids were not asleep, they heard him slowly pacing the walks. He was then alone with himself, contemplative, peaceful, adoring, comparing the serenity of his heart with that of æther, affected in the darkness by the visible splendour of the constellations, and the invisible splendour of God, and opening his soul to thoughts which fall from the Unknown. At such moments, offering up his heart at the hour when the nocturnal flowers offer up their perfumes, he

could not have said himself, possibly, what was passing in
his mind ; but he felt something depart from him and something descend upon him.

He dreamed of the grandeur and presence of God ; of
future eternity, that strange mystery ; of past eternity, that
even stranger mystery ; of all the infinities which buried
themselves before his eyes in all directions ; and without
seeking to comprehend the incomprehensible, he gazed at
it. He did not study God ; he was dazzled by Him. He
considered this magnificent concourse of atoms which gives
visible forms to Nature, revealing forces in establishing
them, creating individualities in unity, proportions in
space, innumerability in the Infinite, and through light
producing beauty. Such a concourse incessantly takes place,
and is dissolved again, and hence come life and death.

He would sit upon a wooden bench, leaning against a
rickety trellis, and gaze at the stars through the stunted
sickly profiles of his fruit trees. This quarter of an acre,
so poorly planted, and so encumbered with sheds and out-
houses, was dear to him, and was sufficient for him. What
more was wanting to this aged man, who divided the leisure
of his life, which knew so little leisure, between gardening
by day and contemplation by night ? Was not this limited
enclosure with the sky for its roof sufficient for him to be
able to adore God by turns in His most delicious and most
sublime works ? Was not this everything, in fact, and
what could be desired beyond ? A small garden to walk
about in, and immensity to dream in ; at his feet, what can
be cultivated and gathered ; over his head, what can be
studied and meditated ; on the earth a few flowers, and all
the stars in the sky.

A final word. As these details might, particularly at the
present day, and to employ an expression which is now
fashionable, give the Bishop of D—— a certain "Pantheistic"
physiognomy, and cause it to be believed, either to his praise
or blame, that he had in him one of those personal philo-
sophies peculiar to our age, which germinate sometimes in
solitary minds, and grow until they take the place of
religion, we must lay stress on the fact that not one of the
persons who knew Monseigneur Welcome believed himself
authorised in thinking anything of the sort. What enlightened this man was his heart, and his wisdom was the
product of the light which emanates from it.

He had no systems ; but abundance of deeds. Abstruse

speculations are full of headaches, and nothing indicates that he ventured his mind amid the Apocalypses. The apostle may be bold, but the bishop must be timid. He probably refrained from going too deep into certain problems reserved to some extent for great and terrible minds. There is a sacred horror beneath the portals of the enigma ; the abyss is gaping before you, but something tells you that you must not enter : woe to the man who does so. Geniuses, in the profundities of abstraction and pure speculation, being situated, so to speak, above dogmas, propose their ideas to God ; their prayer audaciously offers a discussion, and their adoration interrogates. This is direct religion, full of anxiety and responsibility for the man who would scale its walls.

Human thought has no limits; at its own risk and peril it analyses and produces its own bedazzlement ; we might almost say that, through a species of splendid reaction, it dazzles nature with it. The mysterious world around us gives back what it receives, and it is probable that the contemplators are contemplated. However this may be, there are in the world men—are they men ?—who distinctly perceive on the horizon of dreamland the heights of the Absolute, and have the terrible vision of the mountain of the Infinite. Monseigneur Welcome was not one of these men, for he was not a genius. He would have feared these sublimities, on which even very great men, like Swedenborg and Pascal, fell in their insanity. Assuredly, such powerful reveries have their utility, and by these arduous routes ideal perfection is approached, but he took a short cut—the Gospel. He did not attempt to convert his chasuble into Elijah's cloak, he cast no beam of the future over the gloomy heaving of events ; there was nothing of the prophet or the magician about him. His humble soul loved ; that was all.

That he raised prayer into a superhuman aspiration is probable ; but a man can no more pray too much than he can love too much, and if it were a heresy to pray further than the text, St. Theresa and St. Jerome would be heretics. He bent down over all that groaned and all that expiated ; the universe appeared to him an immense malady ; he felt a fever everywhere ; he heard the panting of suffering all around him, and without trying to solve the enigma, he sought to heal the wound. The formidable spectacle of created things developed tenderness in him ; he was solely engaged in finding for himself and arousing in others the best way of pitying and relieving. Existence was to this good and rare priest a permanent subject of sadness seeking to be consoled.

Some men there are who toil to extract gold, but he laboured to extract pity; the universal wretchedness was his mine. Sorrow all around was only an opportunity for constant kindness. " Love one another " he declared to be complete ; he wished for nothing more, and that was his entire doctrine. One day the Senator, who believed himself a "philosopher," said to the Bishop : "Just look at the spectacle of the world; all are fighting, and the strongest man is the cleverest. Your ' love one another ' is nonsense." "Well," Monseigneur Welcome replied, without discussion. " if it be nonsense, the soul must shut itself up in it like the pearl in the oyster." He consequently shut himself up in it, lived in it, was absolutely satisfied with it, leaving on one side those prodigious questions which attract and terrify, the unfathomable perspectives of the abstract, the precipices of metaphysics, all those depths which for the apostle converge in God, for the atheist in nothingness : destiny, good, and evil, the war of being against being, human consciousness, the pensive somnambulism of the animal, transformation through death, the recapitulation of existences which the grave contains, the incomprehensible grafting of successive loves on the enduring *me*, essence, substance, the Nothing, and the Something, the soul, nature, liberty, necessity ; in a word, he avoided all the gloomy precipices over which the gigantic archangels of the human mind bend, the formidable abysses which Lucretius, Manou,St.Paul,and Dantecontemplate with that flashing eye which seems, in regarding Infinity, to enkindle the very stars.

Monseigneur Welcome was simply a man who accepted these mysterious questions without scrutinising them, without disturbing them, and without troubling his own mind with them ; and who had in his soul a deep respect for the mystery which enveloped them.

CHAPTER XI.

ABOUT an hour before sunset, on the evening of a day at the beginning of October, 1815, a man travelling on foot entered the little town of D——. The few inhabitants, who were at the moment at their windows or doors, regarded

this traveller with a species of anxiety. It would be difficult
to meet a wayfarer of more wretched appearance; he was
a man of middle height, muscular and robust, and in the
full vigour of life. He might be forty-six to forty-eight
years of age. A cap with a leather peak partly concealed
his sunburnt face, down which the perspiration streamed.
His shirt of coarse yellow calico, fastened at the neck by a
small silver anchor, allowed his hairy chest to be seen; he
had on a neck-cloth twisted like a rope, trousers of blue
ticking, worn and threadbare, white at one knee and torn at
the other; an old gray ragged blouse patched at one elbow
with a rag of green cloth; on his back a large new well-
filled knapsack, and a large knotty stick in his hand. His
stockingless feet were thrust into iron-shod shoes, his hair
was cut close, and his beard large. Perspiration, heat,
travelling on foot, and the dust, added something sordid to
his tattered appearance.

Nobody knew him; he was evidently passing through the
town. Where did he come from? The South perhaps, the
sea-board, for he made his entrance into D—— by the same
road Napoleon had driven along seven months previously
when going from Cannes to Paris. The man must have
been walking all day, for he seemed very tired. Some
women in the old suburb at the lower part of the town had
seen him halt under the trees on the Gassendi Boulevard,
and drink from the fountain at the end of the walk. He
must have been very thirsty, for the children that followed
him saw him stop and drink again at the fountain in the
market-place. On reaching the corner of the Rue Poiche-
vert, he turned to the left and proceeded to the Mayor's
office. He went in, and came out again a quarter of an hour
after. A gendarme was sitting on the stone bench near the
door, on which General Drouot had mounted on March 4th,
to read to the startled townsfolk of D—— the proclamation
of the Gulf of Juan. The man doffed his cap and bowed
humbly to the gendarme; the latter, without returning his
salute, looked at him attentively, and then entered the
office.

There was then at D—— a capital inn, with the sign of
the Cross of Colbas. This inn was kept by a certain Jacquin
Labarre, a man highly respected in the town for his relation-
ship to another Labarre, who kept the Three Dolphins at
Labarre, and had served in the Guides. When the Emperor
landed, many rumours were current in the country about

the Three Dolphins ; it was said that General Bertrand, in the disguise of a wagoner, had stopped there several times in the month of January, and distributed crosses of honour to the soldiers, and handfuls of Napoleons to the towns-people. The fact was that the Emperor on entering Grenoble refused to take up his quarters at the Prefecture ; he thanked the Mayor, and said, "I am going to a worthy man whom I know," and he went to the Three Dolphins. The glory of the Grenoble Labarre was reflected for a distance of five-and-twenty leagues on the Labarre of the Cross of Colbas. The townspeople said of him, "He is a cousin of the Grenoble man."

The traveller proceeded to this inn, which was the best in the town, and entered the kitchen, the door of which opened on the street. All the ovens were heated, and a large fire blazed cheerily in the chimney. The host, who was at the same time head cook, went from the hearth to the stew-pans, very busy in attending to a dinner intended ,or the carriers, who could be heard singing and talking noisily in an adjoining room. Any one who has travelled knows that no people feed so well as carriers. A fat marmot, flanked by white-legged partridges and grouse, was turning on a long spit before the fire ; while two large carp from Lake Lauzet and an Alloz trout were bubbling in the ovens. The landlord, on hearing the door open and a stranger enter, said, without raising his eyes from his stew-pans :

"What do you want, sir ? "

"Supper and a bed," the man replied.

"Nothing easier," said mine host. At this moment he looked up, took in the stranger's appearance at a glance, and added, "For payment."

The man drew a heavy leathern purse from the pocket of his blouse, and replied :

"I have money."

"In that case I am at your service," said the host.

The man returned the purse to his pocket, took off his knapsack, placed it on the ground near the door, kept his stick in his hand, and sat down on a low stool near the fire. D—— is in the mountains, and the evenings there are cold in October. While going backwards and forwards the landlord still inspected his guest.

"Will supper be ready soon ? " the man asked.

"Directly."

While the new-comer had his back turned to warm

himself, the worthy landlord took a pencil from his pocket, and then tore off the corner of an old newspaper which lay on a small table near the window. On the white margin he wrote a line or two, folded up the paper, and handed it to a lad who seemed to serve both as turnspit and page. The landlord whispered a word in the boy's ear, and he ran off in the direction of the Mayor's house. The traveller had seen nothing of all this, and he asked again whether supper would be ready soon. The boy came back with the paper in his hand, and the landlord eagerly unfolded it, like a man who is expecting an answer. He read it carefully, then shook his head, and remained thoughtful for a moment. At last he walked up to the traveller, who seemed plunged in anything but a pleasant reverie.

"I cannot make room for you, sir," he said.

The man half turned on his stool.

"What do you mean? Are you afraid I shall bilk you, or do you want me to pay you in advance? I have money, I tell you."

"It is not that."

"What is it, then?"

"You have money."

"Yes," said the man.

"But I have not a spare bedroom."

"Put me in the stables," the man continued quietly.

"I cannot."

"Why?"

"The horses take up all the room."

"Well," the man continued, "a corner in the loft and a truss of straw : we will see to that after supper."

"I cannot give you any supper."

This declaration, made in a measured but firm tone, seemed to the stranger serious. He rose.

"Nonsense, I am dying of hunger. I have been on my legs since sunrise, and have walked twelve leagues. I can pay, and I demand food."

"I have none," said the landlord.

The man burst into a laugh, and turned to the chimney and the oven.

"Nothing! why, what is all this?"

"All this is ordered."

"By whom?"

"By the carriers."

"How many are there of them?"

" Twelve."

" There is enough food here for twenty."

The man sat down again, and said, without raising his voice :

" I am at an inn, I am hungry, and so shall remain."

The landlord then stooped down, and whispered with an accent which made him start, " Be off with you."

The stranger at this moment was thrusting some logs into the fire with the ferule of his stick, but he turned quickly, and as he was opening his mouth to reply, the landlord continued in the same low voice : " Come, enough of this. Do you wish me to tell you your name? It is Jean Valjean. Now, do you wish me to tell you who you are? On seeing you come in I suspected something, so I sent to the police-office, and this is the answer I received. Can you read?"

While saying this, he handed the stranger the paper which had travelled from the inn to the office and back again. The man took a glance at it, and mine host continued after a moment's silence : " I am accustomed to be polite with everybody, so pray be off."

The man stooped, picked up his knapsack, and went off. He walked along the high street hap-hazard, keeping close to the houses like a sad and humiliated man. He did not look back once ; had he done so, he would have seen the landlord of the Cross of Colbas in his doorway surrounded by all his guests and the passers-by, talking eagerly and pointing to him ; and judging from the looks of suspicion and terror, he might have guessed that ere long his arrival would be the event of the whole town. He saw nothing of all this, for men who are oppressed do not look back, as they know only too well that an evil destiny is following them.

He walked on thus for a long time, turning down streets he did not know, and forgetting his fatigue, as happens in sorrow. All at once he was sharply assailed by hunger · night was approaching, and he looked round to see whether he could not discover a shelter. The best inn was closed against him, and he sought some very humble pot-house, some wretched den. At this moment a lamp was lit at the end of the street, and a fir branch hanging from an iron bar stood out on the white twilight sky. He went towards it : it was really a pot-house. The stranger stopped for a moment and looked through the window into the low taproom, which was lighted up by a small lamp on the table and a large fire on the hearth. Some men were drinking, and the landlord was warming himself; over the flames bubbled a cauldron hanging from an iron hook. This pot-house, which is also a sort of inn, has two entrances, one on the street, the other opening on a small yard full of manure. The traveller did not dare enter by the street door : he slipped into the yard, stopped once again, and then timidly raised the latch and entered the room.

" Who's there ? " the landlord asked.

" Some one who wants supper and a bed."

" Very good. They are to be had here."

He went in, and all the topers turned to look at him ; they examined him for some time while he was taking off his knapsack. Said the landlord to him, " Here is a fire ; supper is boiling in the pot : come and warm yourself, comrade."

He sat down in the ingle and stretched out his feet, which were swollen with fatigue. A pleasant smell issued from the cauldron. All that could be distinguished of his face under his cap-peak assumed a vague appearance of comfort blended with the other wretched appearance which the habit of suffering produces. It was, moreover, a firm, energetic, and sad profile ; the face was strangely composed, for it began by appearing humble and ended by becoming severe. His eyes gleamed under his brows, like a fire under a curfew. One of the men seated at the table was a fishmonger, who, before entering the pot-house, had gone to put up his horse in Labarre's stables. Accident willed it that on the same morning he had met this ill-looking stranger walking between Bras d'Asse and —— (I have forgotten the name, but I fancy it is Escoublon). Now, on meeting him, the man, who appeared very fatigued, had asked the fishmonger to give him a lift, which had only made him go the faster. This fishmonger had been half an hour previously one of the party surrounding Jacquin Labarre, and had told his unpleasant encounter in the morning to the people at the Cross of Colbas. He made an imperceptible sign to the landlord from his seat, and the latter went up to him, and they exchanged a few whispered words. The man had fallen back into his reverie.

The landlord went up to the chimney, laid his hand sharply on the man's shoulder, and said to him :

"You must be off from here."

The stranger turned and replied gently, "Ah! you know?"

"Yes."

"I was turned out of the other inn."

"And so you will be out of this."

"Where would you have me go?"

"Somewhere else."

The man took his knapsack and stick and went away. As he stepped out, some boys who had followed him from the Cross of Colbas, and seemed to have been waiting for him, threw stones at him. He turned savagely, and threatened them with his stick, and the boys dispersed like a flock of birds. He passed in front of the prison, and pulled the iron bell-handle; a wicket was opened.

"Mr. Gaoler," he said, as he humbly doffed his cap, "would you be kind enough to open the door and give me a night's lodging?"

A voice answered, "A prison is not an inn: get yourself arrested, and then I will open the door."

The man entered a small street, in which there are numerous gardens, some of them being merely enclosed with hedges, which enliven the street. Among these gardens and hedges he saw a single-storeyed house, whose window was illuminated, and he looked through the panes as he had done at the pot-house. It was a large white-washed room, with a bed with printed chintz curtains, and a cradle in a corner, a few chairs, and a double-barrelled gun hanging on the wall. A table was laid for supper in the middle of the room; a copper lamp lit up the coarse white cloth; the tin mug was glistening like silver and full of wine, and the brown soup-tureen was smoking. At this table was seated a man of about forty years of age, with a hearty, open face, who was riding a child on his knee. By his side a woman, still young, was suckling another child. The father was laughing, the children were laughing, and the mother was smiling. The stranger stood for a moment pensively before this gentle and calming spectacle. What was going on within him? It would be impossible to say, but it is probable that he thought that this joyous house would prove hospitable, and that where he saw so much happiness he might find a little pity. He tapped very slightly on a window-pane, but was not heard: he tapped a second time, and he heard the woman say "Husband, I fancy I can hear some one knocking."

"No," the husband answered.

He tapped a third time. The husband rose, took the lamp, and walked to the front door. He was a tall man, half peasant, half artisan; he wore a huge leathern apron, which came up to his left shoulder, and on which he carried a hammer, a red handkerchief, a powder-flask, and all sorts of things, which his belt held like a pocket. As he threw back his head, his turned-down shirt-collar displayed his full neck, white and bare. He had thick eyebrows, enormous black whiskers, eyes flush with his head, a bulldog lower jaw, and over all this that air of being at home, which is inexpressible.

"I beg your pardon, sir," the traveller said, "but would you, for payment, give me a plateful of soup and a corner to sleep in in your garden outhouse?"

"Who are you?" the owner of the cottage asked.

The man answered, "I have come from Puy Moisson; I have walked the whole day. Could you do it? for payment of course?"

"I would not refuse," the peasant answered, "to lodge any respectable person who paid. But why do you not go to the inn?"

"There is no room there."

"Nonsense! that is impossible; it is neither market nor fair day. Have you been to Labarre's?"

"Yes."

"Well?"

The traveller continued, with some hesitation, "I do not know why, but he refused to take me in."

"Have you been to what is his name, in the Rue de Chauffaut?"

The stranger's embarrassment increased; he stammered, "He would not take me in either."

The peasant's face assumed a suspicious look: he surveyed the new-comer from head to foot, and all at once exclaimed, with a sort of shudder, "Can you be the man?"

He took another look at the stranger, placed the lamp on the table, and took down his gun. On hearing the peasant say "Can you be the man?" his wife had risen, taken her two children in her arms, and hurriedly sought refuge behind her husband, and looked in horror at the stranger as she muttered, "The villain!" All this took place in less time than is needed to imagine it. After examining the man for some minutes as if he had been a viper, the peasant returned to the door and said, "Be off!"

"For mercy's sake," the man continued, "a glass of water."

"A charge of shot!" the peasant said.

Then he violently closed the door, and the stranger heard two bolts fastened. A moment after the window-shutters were closed, and the sound of the iron bar being put in reached his ear. Night was coming on apace : the cold wind of the Alps was blowing. By the light of the expiring day the stranger noticed in one of the gardens a sort of hut which seemed to him to be made of sods of turf. He boldly clambered over a railing and found himself in the garden; he approached the hut, which had as entrance a narrow, extremely low door, and resembled the tenements which road-menders construct by the side of the highway. He doubtless thought it was such : he was suffering from cold and hunger, and though he had made up his mind to starve, it was at any rate a shelter against the cold. As this sort of residence is not usually occupied at night, he lay down on his stomach and crawled into the hut : it was warm, and he found a rather good straw litter in it. He lay for a moment motionless on this bed as his fatigue was so great; but as his knapsack hurt his back, and was a ready-made pillow, he began unbuckling one of the thongs. At this moment a hoarse growl was audible : he raised his eyes, and the head of an enormous mastiff stood out in the shadow at the opening of the hut, which was its kennel. The dog itself was strong and formidable ; hence he raised his stick, employed his knapsack as a shield, and left the kennel as he best could, though not without enlarging the rents in his rags.

He also left the garden, but backwards, and compelled to twirl his stick in order to keep the dog at a respectful distance. When he, not without difficulty, had leapt the fence again, and found himself once more in the street, alone, without a bed, roof, or shelter, and expelled even from the bed of straw and the kennel, he fell rather than sat on a stone, and a passer-by heard him exclaim, "I am not even a dog." He soon rose and recommenced his walk. He left the town, hoping to find some tree or mill in the fields which would afford him shelter. He walked on thus for some time with hanging head ; when he found himself far from all human habitations, he raised his eyes and looked around him. He was in a field, and had in front of him one of those low hills with close-cut stubble, which resemble cropped heads. The horizon was perfectly black, but it was not solely the gloom of night, but low clouds, which seemed to be resting on the hill itself, rose and filled the whole sky. Still, as the moon was about to rise shortly, and a remnant of twilight still hovered in the zenith, these clouds formed a species of whitish vault whence a gleam of light was thrown on the earth.

The ground was therefore more illumined than the sky, which produces a peculiarly sinister effect, and the hill with its paltry outlines stood out vaguely and dully on the gloomy horizon. The whole scene was hideous, mean, mournful, and confined; there was nothing in the field or on the hill but a stunted tree, which writhed and trembled a few yards from the traveller. This man was evidently far from possessing those delicate habits of mind which render persons sensible of the mysterious aspects of things; still there was in the sky, this hill, this plain, and this tree, something so profoundly desolate, that after standing motionless and thoughtful for a while he suddenly turned back. There are instants in which nature seems to be hostile.

He went back and found the gates of the town closed. D——, which sustained sieges in the religious wars, was still begirt in 1815 by old walls flanked by square towers, which have since been demolished. He passed through a breach, and re-entered the town. It might be about eight o'clock in the evening, and as he did not know the streets, he wandered about without purpose. He thus reached the Prefecture and then the Seminary; on passing through the Cathedral square he shook his fist at the church. There is at the corner of this square a printing-office, where the proclamations of the Emperor and the Imperial Guard to the army, brought from Elba, and drawn up by Napoleon himself, were first printed. Worn out with fatigue, and hopeless, he sat down on the stone bench at the door of this printing-office. An old lady who was leaving the church at the moment saw the man stretched out in the darkness.

"What are you doing there, my friend?" she said.

He answered harshly and savagely, "You can see, my good woman, that I am going to sleep."

The good woman, who was really worthy of the name, was the Marchioness de R——.

" On that bench ? " she continued.

" I have had for nineteen years a wooden mattress," the man said, " and now I have a stone one."

" Have you been a soldier ? "

" Yes, my good woman."

" Why do you not go to the inn ? "

" Because I have no money."

"Alas !" said Madame de R——, " I have only twopence in my purse."

" You can give them to me all the same."

The man took the money, and Madame de R—— continued, "You cannot lodge at an inn for so small a sum, still you should make the attempt, for you cannot possibly spend the night here. Doubtless you are cold and hungry, and some one might take you in for charity."

"I have knocked at every door."

" Well ? "

" And was turned away at all."

The " good woman " touched the man's arm and pointed to a small house next to the Bishop's Palace.

" You have," she continued, " knocked at every door. Have you done so there ? "

" No."

" Knock there."

CHAPTER XII.

THAT evening, the Bishop of D——, after his walk in the town, had remained in his bedroom till a late hour. He was engaged on a heavy work on the " duties," which he unfortunately has left incomplete. He was still working at eight o'clock, writing rather uncomfortably on small squares of paper, with a large book open on his knees, when Madame Magloire came in as usual to fetch the plate from the wall-cupboard near the bed. A moment after, the Bishop, feeling that supper was ready, and that his sister might be waiting, closed his book, rose from the table, and walked into the dining-room. It was an oblong apartment, as we have said, with a door upon the street, and a window opening into the garden. Madame Magloire had laid the table, and while attending to her duties, was chatting with Mademoiselle Baptistine. A lamp was on the table, which was close to the chimney, in which a good fire was burning.

We can easily picture to ourselves the two females, who had both passed their sixtieth year : Madame Magloire, short, stout, and quick ; Mademoiselle Baptistine, gentle, thin, and frail, somewhat taller than her brother, dressed in a puce-coloured silk gown, the fashionable colour in 1806, which she had bought in Paris in that year, and still wore. Madame Magloire wore a white cap, on her neck a gold *jeannette*, the only piece of feminine jewellery in the house, a very white handkerchief emerging from a black stuff gown with wide and short sleeves, a calico red and puce checked apron, fastened round the waist with a green ribbon, with a stomacher of the same stuff fastened with two pins at the top corners, heavy shoes and yellow stockings, like the Marseilles women. Mademoiselle Baptistine's gown was cut after the fashion of 1806, short-waisted, with epaulettes on the sleeves, flaps and buttons, and she concealed her gray hair by a curling front called *à l'enfant*. Madame Magloire had an intelligent, quick, and kindly air, though the unevenly raised corners of her mouth and the upper lip, thicker than the lower, gave her a somewhat rough and imperious air. So long as Monseigneur was silent, she spoke to him boldly with a mingled respect and liberty, but so soon as he spoke she passively obeyed, like Mademoiselle, who no longer replied, but restricted herself to obeying and enduring. Even when she was young the latter was not pretty ; she had large blue eyes, flush with her head, and a long peaked nose ; but all her face, all her person, as we said at the outset, breathed ineffable kindness. She had always been predestined to gentleness, but faith, hope, and charity, those three virtues that softly warm the soul, had gradually elevated that gentleness to sanctity. Nature had only made her a lamb, and religion had made her an angel. Poor sainted woman ! a sweet reminiscence which has departed.

Mademoiselle Baptistine afterwards narrated so many times what took place at the Bishopric on this evening that several persons still living remember the slightest details. At the moment when the Bishop entered Madame Magloire was talking with some vivacity ; she was conversing with Mademoiselle on a subject that was familiar to her, and to which the Bishop was accustomed—it was the matter of the front-door latch. It appears that while going to purchase something for supper, Madame Magloire had heard things spoken of in certain quarters; people were talking of an ill-looking prowler, that a suspicious vagabond had arrived, who must be somewhere in the town, and that it would possibly be an unpleasant thing for any one out late to meet him. The police were very badly managed because the Prefect and the Mayor were not friendly, and tried to injure each other by allowing things to happen. Hence wise people would be their own police, and be careful to close their houses *and secure their doors thoroughly.*

Madame Magloire emphasised the last sentence, but the Bishop had come from his room where it was rather cold, and was warming himself at the fire while thinking of other matters ; in fact, he did not pick up the words which Madame Magloire had just let drop. She repeated them, and then Mademoiselle, who wished to satisfy Madame Magloire without displeasing her brother, ventured to say timidly :

"Brother, do you hear what Madame Magloire is saying ?"

"I vaguely heard something," the Bishop answered ; then he half turned his chair, placed his hand on his knees, and looked up at the old servant with his cordial and easily-pleased face, which the fire illumined from below : "Well, what is it ? what is it ? are we in any great danger ?"

Then Madame Magloire told her story over again, while exaggerating it slightly, though unsuspicious of the fact. It would seem that a gipsy, a barefooted fellow, a sort of dangerous beggar, was in the town at the moment. He had tried to get a lodging at Jacquin Labarre's, who had refused to take him in. He had been seen prowling about the streets at nightfall, and was evidently a gallows-bird, with his frightful face.

"Is he really ?" said the Bishop.

This cross-questioning encouraged Madame Magloire ; it seemed to indicate that the Bishop was beginning to grow alarmed, and hence she continued triumphantly :

"Yes, Monseigneur, it is so, and some misfortune will occur in the town this night : everybody says so, and then the police are so badly managed (useful repetition). Fancy living in a mountain town, and not even having lanthorns in the streets at nights ! You go out and find yourself in pitch darkness. I say, Monseigneur, and Mademoiselle says——"

"I," the sister interrupted, "say nothing ; whatever my brother does is right."

Madame Magloire continued, as if no protest had been made :

"We say that this house is not at all safe, and that if Monseigneur permits I will go to Paulin Musebois, the locksmith, and tell him to put the old bolts on the door again ; I have them by me, and it will not take a minute ; and I say, Monseigneur, that we ought to have bolts if it were only for this night, for I say that a door which can be opened from the outside by the first passer-by is most terrible : besides, Monseigneur is always accustomed to say Come in, and in the middle of the night, oh my gracious ! there is no occasion to ask for permission."

At this moment there was a rather loud rap at the front door.

"Come in," said the Bishop.

The door was thrown wide open, as if some one were pushing it energetically and resolutely. A man entered whom we already know ; it was the traveller whom we saw just now wandering about in search of a shelter. He entered and stopped, leaving the door open behind him. He had his knapsack on his shoulder, his stick in his hand, and a rough, bold, wearied, and violent expression in his eyes. The fire-light fell on him ; he was hideous ; it was a sinister apparition.

Madame Magloire had not even the strength to utter a cry ; she shivered and stood with wide-open mouth. Mademoiselle Baptistine turned, perceived the man who entered, and half started up in terror ; then, gradually turning her head to the chimney, she began looking at her brother, and her face became again calm and serene. The Bishop fixed a quiet eye on the man, as he opened his mouth, doubtless to ask the new-comer what he wanted. The man leant both his hands on his stick, looked in turn at the two aged females and the old man, and, not waiting for the Bishop to speak, said in a loud voice :

"My name is Jean Valjean. I am a galley-slave, and have spent nineteen years in the galleys. I was liberated four days ago, and started for Pontarlier, which is my destination. I have been walking for four days since I left Toulon, and to-day I have marched twelve leagues. This evening on coming into the town I went to the inn,

but was sent away in consequence of my yellow passport,
which I had shown at the police-office. I went to another
inn, and the landlord said to me, ' Be off.' It was the same
everywhere, and no one would have any dealings with me.
I went to the prison, but the gaoler would not take me in.
I got into a dog's kennel, but the dog bit me and drove me
off, as if it had been a man ; it seemed to know who I was.
I went into the fields to sleep in the starlight, but there
were no stars. I thought it would rain, and as there was
no God to prevent it from raining, I came back to the town
to sleep in a doorway. I was lying down on a stone in the
square, when a good woman pointed to your house, and
said, ' Go and knock there.' What sort of a house is this?
Do you keep an inn? I have money, 109 francs 15 sous,
which I earned at the galleys by my nineteen years' toil. I
will pay, for what do I care for that, as I have money ! I
am very tired and frightfully hungry. Will you let me stay
here ? "

"Madame Magloire," said the Bishop, " you will lay
another knife and fork."

The man advanced three paces, and approached the lamp
which was on the table. "Wait a minute," he continued,
as if he had not comprehended, "that will not do. Did you
not hear me say that I was a galley-slave, a convict, and
have just come from the galleys ? " He took from his pocket
a large yellow paper, which he unfolded. "Here is my
passport, yellow as you see, which turns me out wherever
I go. Will you read it ? I can read it, for I learned to do
so at the galleys, where there is a school for those who like
to attend it. This is what is written in my passport : ' Jean
Valjean, a liberated convict, native of '—but that does not
concern you—' has remained nineteen years at the galleys.
Five years for robbery with house-breaking, fourteen years
for having tried to escape four times. The man is very
dangerous.' All the world has turned me out, and are you
willing to receive me ? Is this an inn ? Will you give me
some food and a bed ? Have you a stable ? "

"Madame Magloire," said the Bishop, "you will put
clean sheets on the bed in the alcove."

We have already explained of what nature was the obedience of the two females. Madame Magloire left the room
to carry out the orders. The Bishop turned to the man.

"Sit down and warm yourself, sir. We shall sup directly
and your bed will be got ready while we are supping."

The man understood this at once. The expression of his face, which had hitherto been gloomy and harsh, was marked with stupefaction, joy, and doubt, and became extraordinary. He began stammering like a lunatic.

"Is it true? what? You will let me stay, you will not turn me out, a convict? You call me *Sir*, you do not 'thou' me. 'Get out, dog,' that is what is always said to me; I really believed that you would turn me out, and hence told you at once who I am! Oh, what a worthy woman she was who sent me here! I shall have supper, a bed with mattresses and sheets, like everybody else. For nineteen years I have not slept in a bed! You really mean that I am to stay. You are worthy people; besides, I have money, and will pay handsomely. By the way, what is your name, Mr. Landlord? I will pay anything you please, for you are a worthy man. You keep an inn, do you not?"

"I am," said the Bishop, "a priest living in this house."

"A priest!" the man continued. "Oh, what a worthy priest! I suppose you will not ask me for money. The Curé, I suppose, the Curé of that big church? Oh, yes, what an ass I am, I did not notice your cassock."

While speaking, he deposited his knapsack and stick in a corner, returned his passport to his pocket, and sat down. While Mademoiselle Baptistine regarded him gently, he went on:

"You are humane, sir, and do not feel contempt. A good priest is very good. Then you do not want me to pay?"

"No," said the Bishop, "keep your money. How long did you take in earning these 109 francs?"

"Nineteen years."

"Nineteen years!" The Bishop gave a deep sigh.

The man went on: "I have all my money still; in four days I have only spent 25 sous, which I earned by helping to unload carts at Grasse. As you are an abbé I will tell you: we had a chaplain at the galleys, and one day I saw a bishop, Monseigneur, as they call him. He is the curé over the curés; but pardon me, you know that, placed as we are, we (convicts) know and explain such things badly, and for me in particular it is so far away in the past. He said mass in the middle of the place on an altar, and had a pointed gold thing on his head, which glistened in the bright sunshine; we were drawn up on three sides of a square, with guns and lighted matches facing us. He spoke, but was too far off, and we did not hear him. That is what a bishop is."

While he was speaking, the Bishop had gone to close the door, which had been left open. Madame Magloire came in, bringing a silver spoon and fork, which she placed on the table.

"Madame Magloire," said the Bishop, "lay them as near as you can to the fire ; " and turning to his guest, he said, "The night breeze is sharp on the Alps, and you must be cold, sir."

Each time he said the word *Sir* with his gentle grave voice, the man's face was illumined. *Sir* to a convict is the glass of water to the shipwrecked sailor of the Medusa. Ignominy thirsts for respect.

"This lamp gives a very bad light," the Bishop continued. Madame Magloire understood, and fetched from the chimney of Monseigneur's bedroom the two silver candlesticks, which she placed on the table ready lighted.

"Monsieur le Curé," said the man, "you are good, and do not despise me. You receive me as a friend and light your wax candles for me, and yet I have not hidden from you whence I come, and that I am an unfortunate fellow."

The Bishop, who was seated by his side, gently touched his hand. "You need not have told me who you were ; this is not my house, but the house of Christ. This door does not ask a man who enters whether he has a name, but if he has a sorrow. You are suffering, you are hungry and thirsty, and so be welcome. And do not thank me, or say that I am receiving you in my house, for no one is at home here excepting the man who has need of an asylum. I tell you, who are a passer-by, that you are more at home here than I am myself, and all there is here is yours. Why do I want to know your name? Besides, before you told it to me, you had one which I knew."

The man opened his eyes in amazement.

"Is that true ? You knew my name ? "

"Yes," the Bishop answered, "you are my brother."

"Monsieur le Curé," the man exclaimed, "I was very hungry when I came in, but you are so kind that I do not know at present what I feel ; it has passed over."

The Bishop looked at him and said :

"You have suffered greatly ? "

"Oh ! the red jacket, the cannon-ball on your foot, a plank to sleep on, heat, cold, labour, the set of men, the blows, the double chain for a nothing, a dungeon for a word, even when you are ill in bed, and the chain-gang. The very dogs are happier. Nineteen years! and now I am forty-six; and at present, the yellow passport!"

"Yes," said the Bishop, "you have come from a place of sorrow. Listen to me; there will be more joy in heaven over the tearful face of a repentant sinner than over the white robes of one hundred just men. If you leave that mournful place with thoughts of hatred and anger against your fellow-men, you are worthy of pity; if you leave it with thoughts of kindliness, gentleness, and peace, you are worth more than any of us."

In the meanwhile Madame Magloire had served the soup: it was made of water, oil, bread, and salt, and a little bacon; and the rest of the supper consisted of a piece of mutton, figs, a fresh cheese, and a loaf of rye bread. She had herself added a bottle of old Mauves wine. The Bishop's face suddenly assumed the expression of gaiety peculiar to hospitable natures. "To table," he said eagerly, as he was wont to do when any stranger supped with him; and he bade the man sit down on his right hand, while Mademoiselle Baptistine, perfectly peaceful and natural, took her seat on his left. The Bishop said grace, and then served the soup himself, according to his wont. The man began eating greedily. All at once the Bishop said:

"It strikes me that there is something wanting on the table."

Madame Magloire, truth to tell, had only laid the absolutely necessary silver. Now it was the custom in this house, when the Bishop had any one to supper, to arrange the whole stock of plate on the table, as an innocent display. This graceful semblance of luxury was a species of childishness full of charm in this gentle and strict house, which elevated poverty to dignity. Madame Magloire took the hint, went out without a word, and a moment after the remaining spoons and forks glittered on the cloth, symmetrically arranged before each of the guests.

CHAPTER XIII.

AND now, in order to give an idea of what passed at table, we cannot do better than transcribe a passage of a letter written by Mademoiselle Baptistine to Madame Boischevron,

in which the conversation between the convict and the
Bishop is recorded with charming minuteness.

. . . .

"The man paid no attention to any one. He ate with
the voracity of a starving man. But after supper he said

"'Monsieur le Curé, all this is much too good for me,
but I am bound to say that the carriers who would not let
me sup with them have better cheer than you.'

"Between ourselves, this remark slightly offended me,
but my brother answered :

"'They are harder worked than I am.'

"'No,' the man continued, 'they have more money. You
are poor, as I can plainly see; perhaps you are not even
curé. Ah, if Heaven were just you ought to be a curé.'

"'Heaven is more than just,' said my brother. A
moment after he added :

"'Monsieur Jean Valjean, I think you said you were
going to Pontarlier?'

"'I am compelled to go there.' Then he continued, ' I
must be off by sunrise to-morrow morning ; it is a tough
journey, for if the nights are cold the days are hot.'

"'You are going to an excellent part of the country,' my
brother resumed. 'When the Revolution ruined my family
I sought shelter first in Franche Comté, and lived there for
some time by the labour of my arms. I had a good will,
and found plenty to do, as I need only choose. There are
paper-mills, tanneries, distilleries, oil-mills, wholesale manufactories of clocks, steel works, copper works, and at least
twenty iron foundries, of which the four at Lods, Chatillon,
Audincourt, and Beure are very large.'

"I am pretty sure I am not mistaken, and that these are
the names my brother mentioned ; then he broke off and
addressed me.

"'My dear sister, have we not some relatives in those
parts?'

"My answer was, 'We used to have some; among
others, Monsieur de Lucinet, who was Captain of the gates
at Pontarlier, under the old régime.'

"'Yes,' my brother continued, 'but in '93 people had
no relatives,—only their hands, and so I worked. In the
country to which you are going, Monsieur Valjean, there is
a truly patriarchal and pleasing trade. My dear sister, I
mean their cheese manufactories, which they call *fruitières*.'

"Then my brother, while pressing this man to eat,

explained in their fullest details the *fruitières* of Pontarlier,
which were divided into two classes—the large farms which
belong to the rich, where there are forty or fifty cows, and
which produce seven to eight thousand cheeses in the
summer, and the partnership *fruitières*, which belong to the
poor. The peasants of the central mountain district keep
their cows in common and divide the produce. They have
a cheese-maker, who is called the *grurin*; he receives the
milk from the partners thrice a day, and enters the quantities
in a book. The cheese-making begins about the middle
of April, and the dairy farmers lead their cows to the
mountains toward midsummer.

" The man grew animated while eating, and my brother
made him drink that excellent Mauves wine, which he does
not drink himself because he says that it is expensive. My
brother gave him all these details with that easy gaiety of
his which you know, mingling his remarks with graceful
appeals to myself. He dwelt a good deal on the comfortable position of the *grurin*, as if wishful that this man
should understand, without advising him directly and
harshly, that it would be a refuge for him. One thing
struck me : the man was as I have described him to you ;
well, my brother, during the whole of supper, and indeed of
the evening, did not utter a word which could remind this
man of what he was, or tell him who my brother was. It
was apparently a good opportunity to give him a little
sermon, and let the Bishop produce a permanent effect on
the galley-slave. It might have seemed to any one else that,
having this wretched man in hand, it would be right to feed
his mind at the same time as his body, and address to him
some reproaches seasoned with morality and advice, or at
any rate a little commiseration, with an exhortation to
behave better in future. My brother did not even ask him
where he came from, or his history; for his fault is contained in his history, and my brother appeared to avoid
everything which might call it to his mind. This was
carried to such a point that at a certain moment, when my
brother was talking about the mountaineers of Pontarlier,
' who had a pleasant task near heaven,' and who, he added,
' are happy because they are innocent,' he stopped short,
fearing lest there might be in the remark something which
might unpleasantly affect this man. After considerable reflection, I believe I can understand what was going on in
my brother's heart : he doubtless thought that this Jean

Valjean had his misery ever present to his mind, that the best thing was to distract his attention, and make him believe, were it only momentarily, that he was a man like the rest, by behaving to him as he would to others. Was not this really charity? Is there not, my dear lady, something truly evangelical in this delicacy, which abstains from all lecturing and allusions, and is it not the best pity, when a man has a sore point, not to touch it at all? It seemed to me that this might be my brother's innermost thought: in any case, what I can safely say is, that if he had all these ideas, he did not let any of them be visible, even to me; he was from beginning to end the same man he is every night, and he supped with Jean Valjean with the same air and in the same way as if he had been supping with M. Gedeon the Provost, or with the Curé of the parish.

"Towards the end, as we were at dessert, there was a knock at the door. It was Mother Gerbaud with her little baby in her arms. My brother kissed the child's forehead, and borrowed from me fifteen sous, which I happened to have about me, to give them to the mother. The man, while this was going on, did not seem to pay great attention: he said nothing, and seemed very tired. When poor old Mother Gerbaud left, my brother said grace, and then said to this man: 'You must need your bed.' Madame Magloire hastily removed the plate. I understood that we must retire in order to let this traveller sleep, and we both went upstairs. I, however, sent Madame Magloire to lay on the man's bed a roebuck's hide from the Black Forest, which was in my room, for the nights are very cold, and that keeps you warm. It is a pity that this skin is old and the hair is wearing off. My brother bought it when he was in Germany, at Tottlingen, near the source of the Danube, as well as the small ivory-handled knife which I use at table.

"Madame Magloire came back again almost immediately. We said our prayers in the room where the clothes are hung up to dry, and then retired to our bedrooms without saying a word."

After having said good-night to his sister, Monseigneur Welcome took up one of the silver candlesticks, handed the other to his guest, and said:

"I will show you to your room, sir."

The man followed him. The reader will remember, from our description, that the rooms were so arranged that in

order to reach the oratory where the alcove was it was necessary to pass through the Bishop's bedroom. At the moment
when he went through this room Madame Magloire was
putting away the plate in the cupboard over the bed-head :
it was the last thing she did every night before retiring.
The Bishop led his guest to the alcove, where a clean bed
was prepared for him ; the man placed the branched candlestick on a small table.

"I trust you will pass a good night," said the Bishop.
"To-morrow morning, before starting, you will drink a
glass of milk fresh from our cows."

"Thank you, Monsieur l'Abbé," the man said.

He had scarcely uttered these peaceful words when,
suddenly and without any transition, he had a strange
emotion, which would have frightened the two old females
to death had they witnessed it. Even at the present day it
is difficult to account for what urged him at the moment.
Did he wish to warn or to threaten ? Was he simply obeying a species of instinctive impulse which was obscure
to himself ? He suddenly turned to the old gentleman,
folded his arms, and, fixing on him a savage glance, he
exclaimed hoarsely :

"What! you really lodge me so close to you as that ?"
He broke off and added with a laugh, in which there was
something monstrous :

" Have you reflected fully ? Who tells you that I have not
committed a murder ? "

The Bishop answered : " God will take care of that."

Then with gravity, moving his lips like a man who is
praying and speaking to himself, he stretched out two
fingers of his right hand and blessed the man, who did
not bow his head, and returned to his bedroom, without
turning his head or looking behind him. When the alcove
was occupied, a large serge curtain drawn right across
the oratory concealed the altar. The Bishop knelt down
as he passed before this curtain, and offered up a short
prayer. A moment after he was in his garden, walking,
dreaming, contemplating, his soul and thoughts entirely
occupied by those grand mysteries which God displays at
night to eyes that can discern.

As for the man, he was so completely exhausted that he did
not even take advantage of the nice white sheets. He blew
out the candle with his nostrils, after the fashion of convicts,
and threw himself in his clothes upon the bed, where he

at once fell into a deep sleep. Midnight was striking as the Bishop returned from the garden to his room, and a few minutes later all in the house slept.

CHAPTER XIV.

TOWARDS the middle of the night Jean Valjean awoke.

He was born of a poor peasant family of Brie. In his childhood he had not been taught to read, and when he was of man's age he was a wood-cutter at Faverolles. His mother's name was Jeanne Mathieu, his father's Jean Valjean or Vlajean, probably a sobriquet and a contraction of *Voilà Jean.* Jean Valjean possessed a pensive but not melancholy character, which is peculiar to affectionate natures; but altogether he was a dull, insignificant fellow, at least apparently. He had lost father and mother when still very young : the latter died of a badly-managed milk-fever; the former, a pruner, like himself, was killed by a fall from a tree. All that was left Jean Valjean was a sister older than himself, a widow with seven children, boys and girls. This sister had brought Jean Valjean up, and so long as her husband was alive she supported her brother. When the husband died, the oldest of the seven children was eight years of age, the youngest, one, while Jean Valjean had just reached his twenty-fifth year; he took the place of the father, and in his turn supported the sister who had reared him. This was done simply as a duty, and even rather roughly by Jean Valjean; and his youth was thus expended in hard and ill-paid toil. He was never known to have had a sweetheart; he had no time for love-making.

In the evening he came home tired, and ate his soup without saying a word. His sister, mother Jeanne, while he was eating, often took out of his porringer the best part of his meal, the piece of meat, the slice of bacon, or the heart of the cabbage, to give it to one of her children ; he, still eating, bent over the table with his head almost in the soup, and his long hair falling round his porringer and hiding his eyes, pretended not to see it, and let her do as she pleased. There was at Faverolles, not far from the Valjeans' cottage, on the other side of the lane, a farmer's wife called Marie Claude. The young Valjeans, who were habitually starving, would go at times and borrow in their mother's name a pint of milk from Marie Claude, which they drank behind a hedge or in some corner, tearing the vessel from each other so eagerly that the little girls spilt the milk over their aprons. Their mother, had she been aware of this fraud, would have severely corrected the delinquents, but Jean Valjean, coarse and rough though he was, paid Marie Claude for the milk behind his sister's back, and so the children escaped punishment.

He earned in the pruning season eighteen sous a day, and besides hired himself out as reaper, labourer, neat-herd, and odd man. He did what he could; his sister worked too, but what could she do with seven children? It was a sad group, which wretchedness gradually enveloped and choked. One winter was hard, and Jean had no work to do, and the family had no bread. No bread, literally none, and seven children.

One Sunday evening, Maubert Isabeau, the baker in the church square at Faverolles, was just going to bed when he heard a violent blow dealt the grating in front of his shop.• He arrived in time to see an arm passed through a hole made by the blow of a fist on the glass. The arm seized a loaf, and carried it off. Isabeau ran out hastily; the thief ran away at his hardest, but the baker caught him up and stopped him. The thief had thrown away the loaf, but his arm was still bleeding. It was Jean Valjean.

All this happened in 1795. Jean Valjean was brought before the courts of the day, charged "with burglary committed with violence at night, in an inhabited house." He had a gun, was a splendid shot, and a bit of a poacher, and this injured him. There is a legitimate prejudice against poachers, for, like smugglers, they trench very closely on brigandage. Still we must remark that there is an abyss between these classes and the hideous assassins of our cities: the poacher lives in the forest; the smuggler in the mountains and on the sea. Cities produce ferocious men, because they produce corrupted men; the forest, the mountain, and the sea produce savage men, but while they develop their ferocious side, they do not always destroy their human part. Jean Valjean was found guilty, and the terms of the code were explicit. There are in our civilisation formidable hours; they are those moments in which penal justice pronounces a shipwreck. What a mournful minute is that in which society withdraws and consummates the irreparable abandonment of a thinking being! Jean Valjean was sentenced to five years in the galleys.

On April 22nd, 1796, men were crying in the streets of Paris the victory of Montenotte, gained by the General-in-chief of the army of Italy, whom the message of the Directory, to the Five Hundred, of 2nd Floreal, year IV., called Buonaparte; and on the same day a heavy gang was put in chains at Bicetre, and Jean Valjean formed part of the chain. An ex-gaoler of the prison, who is now nearly ninety years of age, perfectly remembers the wretched man, who was chained at the end of the fourth cordon, in the north angle of the courtyard. He was seated on the ground like the rest, and seemed not at all to understand his position, except that it was horrible. It is probable that he also saw something excessive through the vague ideas of an utterly ignorant man. While the bolt of his iron collar was being riveted with heavy hammer-blows behind his head, he wept, tears choked him, and prevented him from speaking, and he could only manage to say from time to time: "I was a wood-cutter at Faverolles." Then, while still continuing to sob, he raised his right hand, and lowered it gradually seven times, as if touching seven uneven heads in turn, and from this gesture it could be guessed that whatever the crime he had committed, he had done it to feed and clothe seven little children.

He was taken to Toulon, and arrived there after a journey of twenty-seven days in a cart, with the chain on his neck. At Toulon he was dressed in the red jacket. All that had hitherto been his life, even to his name, was effaced. He was no longer Jean Valjean, but No. 24,601. What became of his sister, what became of the seven children? Who troubles himself about that? What becomes of the spray of leaves when the stem of the young tree has been cut at the foot?

It is the old story. These poor living beings, these creatures of God, henceforth without support, guide, or shelter, went off hap-hazard, and gradually buried themselves in that cold fog in which solitary destinies are swallowed up, that mournful gloom in which so many unfortunates disappear during the sullen progress of the human race. They left their country; the church of what had once been their village forgot them; the stile of what had once been their field forgot them; and after a few years' stay in the galleys, Jean Valjean himself forgot them.

In that heart where there had once been a wound there was now a scar : that was all. He only heard about his sister once during the whole time he spent at Toulon ; it was, I believe, toward the end of the fourth year of his captivity, though I have forgotten in what way the information reached him. She was in Paris, living in the Rue du Geindre, a poor street, near Saint Sulpice, and had only one child with her, the youngest, a boy. Where were the other six ? perhaps she did not know herself. Every morning she went to a printing-office, No. 3 Rue du Sabot, where she was a folder and stitcher ; she had to be there at six in the morning, long before daylight in winter. In the same house as the printing-office there was a day-school, to which she took the little boy, who was seven years of age, but as she went to work at six and the school did not open till seven o'clock, the boy was compelled to wait in the yard for an hour—an hour of cold and darkness in the winter. The boy was not allowed to enter the printing-office, because it was said that he would be in the way. The workmen as they passed in the morning saw the poor little fellow seated on the pavement, and often sleeping in the darkness, with his head on his satchel. When it rained, an old woman, the portress, took pity on him ; she invited him into her den, where there were only a bed, a spinning-wheel, and two chairs, when the little fellow fell asleep in a corner, clinging to the cat to keep himself warm. This is what Jean Valjean was told ; it was a momentary flash, as it were a window suddenly opened in the destiny of the beings he had loved, and then all was closed again. ; he never heard about them more. Nothing reached him from them ; he never saw them again, never met them, and we shall not come across them in the course of this melancholy history.

Towards the end of this fourth year, Jean Valjean's turn to escape arrived, and his comrades aided him as they always do in this sorrowful place. He escaped, and wandered about the fields at liberty for two days : if it is liberty to be hunted down ; to turn one's head at every moment ; to start at the slightest sound ; to be afraid of everything, of a chimney that smokes, a man who passes, a barking dog, a galloping horse, the striking of the hour, of day because people see, of night because they do not see, of the highway, the path, the thicket, and even sleep. On the evening of the second day he was recaptured ; he had not eaten or slept for six-and-thirty hours. The maritime tribunal added three years to his sentence for his crime, which made it eight years. In the sixth year, it was again his turn to escape; he tried, but could not succeed. He was missing at roll-call, the gun was fired, and at night the watchman found him hidden under the keel of a ship that was building, and he resisted the *garde chiourme*, who seized him. Escape and rebellion: this fact, foreseen by the special code, was punished by an addition of five years, of which two would be spent in double chains. Thirteen years. In his tenth year his turn came again, and he took advantage of it, but succeeded no better: three years for this new attempt, or sixteen years in all. Finally, I think it was during his thirteenth year that he made a last attempt, and only succeeded so far as to be recaptured in four hours: three years for these four hours, and a total of nineteen years. In October, 1815, he was liberated; he had gone in in 1796 for breaking a window and stealing a loaf. Jean Valjean entered the galleys sobbing and shuddering: he left it stoically. He entered it in despair: he came out of it gloomy. What had taken place in this soul?

Let us endeavour to tell. Society must needs look at these things, because they are created by it. He was, as we have said, an ignorant man, but he was not weak-minded. The natural light was kindled within him, and misfortune, which also has its brightness, increased the little daylight there was in his mind. Under the stick and the chain in the dungeon, when at work, beneath the torrid sun of the galleys, or when lying on the convict's plank, he reflected. He constituted himself a court, and began by trying himself. He recognised that he was not an innocent man unjustly punished; he confessed to himself that he had committed an extreme and blamable action; that the loaf would probably not have been refused him had he asked for it; that in any case it would have been better to wait for it, either from pity or from labour, and that it was not a thoroughly unanswerable argument to say, "Can a man wait when he is hungry?" That, in the first place, it is very rare for a man to die literally of hunger; next, that, unhappily or happily, man is so made that he can suffer for a long time and severely, morally and physically, without dying; that hence he should have been patient; that it would have been better for the poor little children;

that it was an act of madness for him, a wretched, weak man, violently to collar society and to imagine that a man can escape from wretchedness by theft ; that in any case the door by which a man enters infamy is a bad one by which to escape from wretchedness ; and, in short, that he had done wrong.

Then he asked himself if he was the only person who had been in the wrong in his fatal history? whether, in the first place, it was not a serious thing that he, a workman, should want for work; that he, laborious as he was, should want for bread? whether, next, when the fault was committed and confessed, the punishment had not been ferocious and excessive, and whether there were not more abuse on the side of the law in the penalty than there was on the side of the culprit in the crime? whether there had not been an excessive weight in one of the scales, that one in which expiation lies? whether the excess of punishment were not the effacement of the crime, and led to the result of making a victim of the culprit, a creditor of the debtor, and definitely placing the right on the side of the man who had violated it? whether this penalty, complicated by excessive aggravations for attempted escapes, did not eventually become a sort of attack made by the stronger on the weaker, a crime of society committed on the individual, a crime which was renewed every day, and had lasted for nineteen years? He asked himself if human society could have the right to make its members equally undergo, on one side, its unreasonable improvidence, on the other its pitiless foresight, and to hold a man eternally between a want and an excess, want of work and excess of punishment? whether it were not exorbitant that society should treat thus its members who were worst endowed in that division of property which is made by chance, and consequently the most worthy of indulgence?

These questions asked and solved, he passed sentence on society and condemned it—to his hatred. He made it responsible for the fate he underwent, and said to himself that he would not hesitate to call it to account some day. He declared that there was no equilibrium between the damage he had caused and the damage caused him ; and he came to the conclusion that his punishment was not an injustice, but most assuredly an iniquity. Wrath may be wild and absurd ; a man may be wrongly irritated ; but he is only indignant when he has some show of reason somewhere. Jean Valjean felt indignant. And then, again, human society had never done him aught but harm ; he had only seen its wrathful face, which is called its justice, and shows to those whom it strikes. Men had only laid hands on him to injure him, and any contact with them had been a blow to him. Never, since his infancy, since his mother and his sister, had he heard a kind word or met a friendly look. From suffering after suffering, he gradually attained the conviction that life was war, and that in this war he was the vanquished. As he had no other weapon but his hatred, he resolved to sharpen it in the galleys and take it with him when he went out.

There was at Toulon a school for the prisoners, kept by some friars, who imparted elementary instruction to those wretches who were willing to learn. He was one of the number, and went to school at the age of forty, where he learned reading, writing, and arithmetic ; he felt that strengthening his mind was strengthening his hatred. In certain cases, instruction and education may serve as allies to evil. It is sad to say, that after trying society, which had caused his misfortunes, he tried Providence, who had made society, and condemned it also. Hence, during these nineteen years of torture and slavery, this soul ascended and descended at the same time ; light entered on one side and darkness on the other. As we have seen, Jean Valjean was not naturally bad, he was still good when he arrived at the galleys. He condemned society then, and felt that he was growing wicked ; he condemned Providence, and felt that he was growing impious.

Here it is difficult not to meditate for a moment. Is human nature thus utterly transformed? Can man, who is created good by God, be made bad by man? Can the soul be entirely remade by destiny, and become evil if the destiny be evil? Can the heart be deformed, and contract incurable ugliness and infirmity under the pressure of disproportionate misfortune, like the spine beneath too low a vault? Is there not in every human soul, was there not in that of Jean Valjean especially, a primary spark, a divine element, incorruptible in this world, and immortal for the other, which good can develop, illumine, and make resplendently radiant, and which evil can never entirely extinguish?

Grave and obscure questions these, the last of which every

physiologist would unhesitatingly have answered in the negative, had he seen at Toulon, in those hours of repose which were for Jean Valjean hours of reverie, this gloomy, stern, silent, and pensive galley-slave—the pariah of the law which regarded men passionately—the condemned of civilisation, who regarded Heaven with severity—seated with folded arms on a capstan bar, with the end of his chain thrust into his pocket to prevent it from dragging. We assuredly do not deny that the physiological observer would have seen there an irremediable misery; he would probably have pitied this patient of the law, but he would not have even attempted a cure; he would have turned away from the caverns he noticed in this soul, and, like Dante at the gates of the Inferno, he would have effaced from this existence that word which God has nevertheless written on the brow of every man : *Hope!*

Was that state of soul, which we have attempted to analyse, as perfectly clear to Jean Valjean as we have tried to render it to our readers? Did Jean Valjean see after their formation, and had he seen distinctly as they were formed, all the elements of which his moral wretchedness was composed? Had this rude and unlettered man clearly comprehended the succession of ideas by which he had step by step ascended and descended to the gloomy views which had for so many years been the inner horizon of his mind? Was he really conscious of all that had taken place in him and all that was stirring in him? This we should not like to assert, and, indeed, we are not inclined to believe it. There was too much ignorance in Jean Valjean for a considerable amount of vagueness not to remain, even after so much misfortune ; at times he did not even know exactly what he experienced. Jean Valjean was in darkness ; he suffered in darkness, and he hated in darkness. He lived habitually in this shadow, groping like a blind man and a dreamer ; at times he was attacked, both internally and externally, by a shock of passion, a surcharge of suffering, a pale and rapid flash which illumined his whole soul, and suddenly made him see all around, both before and behind him, in the glare of a frightful light, the hideous precipices and sombre perspectives of his destiny. The flash passed away ; the night fell, and where was he? He no longer knew.

The peculiarity of punishment of this kind, in which nought but what is pitiless, that is to say brutalising, prevails, is gradually, and by a species of stupid transfiguration, to transform a man into a wild beast, sometimes into a ferocious beast. Jean Valjean's attempted escapes, successive and obstinate, would be sufficient to prove the strange work carried on by the law upon a human soul ; he would have renewed these attempts, so utterly useless and mad, as many times as the opportunity offered itself, without dreaming for a moment of the result, or the experiments already made. He escaped impetuously like the wolf that finds its cage open. Instinct said to him, " Run away ; " reasoning would have said to him, " Remain ; " but in the presence of a temptation so violent, reason disappeared and instinct alone was left. The brute alone acted, and when he was recaptured the new severities inflicted on him only served to render him still more fierce.

We must not omit mentioning one fact, namely, that he possessed a physical strength with which no one in the galleys could compete. In turning a capstan, Jean Valjean was equal to four men ; he frequently raised and held on his back enormous weights, and took the place at times of that instrument which is called a jack. His comrades surnamed him Jean the Jack. Once when the balcony of the Town Hall at Toulon was being repaired, one of those admirable caryatides of Puget's, which support the balcony, became loose and almost fell. Jean Valjean, who was on the spot, supported the statue with his shoulder till the workmen came.

His suppleness even surpassed his vigour. Some convicts, who perpetually dream of escaping, eventually make a real science of combined skill and strength ; it is the science of the muscles. A full course of mysterious statics is daily practised by the prisoners, those eternal enviers of flies and birds. Swarming up a perpendicular, and finding a resting-place where a projection is scarcely visible, was child's play for Jean Valjean. Given a corner of a wall, with the tension of his back and hams, with his elbows and heels clinging to the rough stone, he would hoist himself as if by magic to a third storey, and at times would ascend to the very roof of the galleys. He spoke little and never laughed ; it needed some extreme emotion to draw from him, once or twice a year, that mournful convict laugh, which is, as it were, the echo of fiendish laughter. To look at him, he seemed engaged in continually gazing at something terrible. He was, in fact, absorbed. Through the sickly perceptions of an incomplete nature and a crushed intellect, he saw confusedly that a monstrous thing was hanging over him. In his obscure and dull gloom through which he crawled, wherever he turned his head and essayed to raise his eye, he saw, with a terror blended with rage, built up above him, with frightfully scarped sides, a kind of frightful accumulation of things, laws, prejudices, men, and facts, whose outline escaped him, whose mass terrified him, and which was nothing else but that prodigious pyramid which we call civilisation. He distinguished here and there in this heaving and shapeless conglomeration, at one moment close to him, at another on distant and inaccessible plateaux, some highly illumined group;—here the gaoler and his stick, there the gendarme and his sabre, down below the mitred archbishop, and on the summit, in a species of sun, the crowned and dazzling Emperor. It seemed to him as if this distant splendour, far from dissipating his night, only rendered it more gloomy and black. All these laws, prejudices, facts, men, and things, came and went above him, in accordance with the complicated and mysterious movement which God imprints on civilisation, marching over him, and crushing him with something painful in its cruelty and inexorable in its indifference. Souls which have fallen into the abyss of possible misfortune, hapless men lost in the depths of those limbos into which people no longer look, and the reprobates of the law, feel on their heads the whole weight of the human society, which is so formidable for those outside it, so terrible for those underneath it.

In such a situation Jean Valjean mused, and what could be the nature of his reverie? If the grain of corn had its thoughts, when ground by the millstone, it would doubtless think as did Jean Valjean. All these things, realities full of spectres, phantasmagoria full of reality, ended by creating for him a sort of internal condition which is almost inexpressible. At times, in the midst of his galley-slave toil, he stopped and began thinking; his reason, at once riper and more troubled than of yore, revolted. All that had happened appeared to him absurd; all that surrounded him seemed to him impossible. He said to himself that it was a dream; he looked at the overseer standing a few yards from him, and he appeared to him a phantom, until the phantom suddenly dealt him a blow with a stick. Visible nature scarce existed for him; we might almost say with truth, that for Jean Valjean there was no sun, no glorious summer days, no brilliant sky, no fresh April dawn. Some dim window light was all that shone in his soul.

To sum up, in conclusion, all that can be summed up in what we have indicated, we will confine ourselves to establishing the fact that in nineteen years, Jean Valjean, the inoffensive wood-cutter of Faverolles, and the formidable galley-slave of Toulon, had become, thanks to the manner in which the galleys had fashioned him, capable of two sorts of bad actions : first, a rapid, unreflecting bad deed, entirely instinctive, and a species of reprisal for the evil he had suffered ; and, secondly, of a grave, serious, evil deed, discussed conscientiously and meditated with the false ideas which such a misfortune can produce. His premeditations passed through the three successive phases which natures of a certain temperament can alone undergo, reasoning, will, and obstinacy. He had for his motives habitual indignation, bitterness of soul, the profound feeling of iniquities endured, and reaction even against the good, the innocent, and the just, if such exist. The starting-point, like the goal, of all his thoughts was hatred of human law ; that hatred, which, if it be not arrested in its development by some providential incident, becomes within a given time a hatred of society, then a hatred of the human race, next a hatred of creation, and which is expressed by a vague, incessant, and brutal desire to injure some one, no matter whom. As we see, it was not unfairly that the passport described Jean Valjean as a highly dangerous man. Year by year this soul had become more and more withered, slowly but fatally. With this withered heart, he had a dry eye. When he left the galleys, he had not shed a tear for nineteen years.

CHAPTER XV.

WHEN the time for quitting the galleys arrived, when Jean Valjean heard in his ear the unfamiliar words, "You are free," the moment seemed improbable and extraordinary, and a ray of bright light, of the light of the living, penetrated to him ; but it soon grew pale. Jean Valjean had been dazzled by the idea of liberty, and had believed in a new life. He soon saw what sort of liberty that is which has a yellow passport. And around this there was much bitterness ; he had calculated that his earnings, during his stay at the galleys, should have amounted to 171 francs. We are bound to add that he had omitted to take into his calculations the forced rest of Sundays and holidays, which, during nineteen years, entailed a diminution of about 24 francs. However this might be, the sum was reduced, through various local stoppages, to 109 francs, 15 sous, which was paid to him when he left the galleys. He did not understand it at all, and thought that he had been wronged, in fact robbed.

The day after his liberation, he saw at Grasse, in front of a distillery of orange-flower water, men unloading bales; he offered his services, and as the work was of a pressing nature, they were accepted. He set to work. He was intelligent, powerful, and skilful, and his master appeared satisfied. While he was at work a gendarme passed, noticed him, asked for his paper, and he was compelled to show his yellow pass. This done, Jean Valjean resumed his toil. A little while previously he had asked one of the workmen what he earned for his day's work, and the answer was 30 sous. At night, as he was compelled to start again the next morning, he went to the master of the distillery and asked for payment. The master did not say a word, but gave him 15 sous, and when he protested, the answer was, "That is enough for you." He became pressing. The master looked him in the face and said, "Mind you don't get into prison."

Here again he thought himself robbed. Society, the State, by diminishing his earnings, had robbed him wholesale. Now it was the turn of the individual to commit retail robbery. Liberation is not deliverance. A man may leave the galleys, but not condemnation. We have seen what happened to him at Grasse, and we know how he was received at D——.

As the cathedral clock pealed two, Jean Valjean awoke. What aroused him was that the bed was too comfortable. For close on twenty years he had not slept in a bed, and though he had not undressed, the sensation was too novel not to disturb his sleep. He had been asleep for more than four hours, and his weariness had worn off; and he was accustomed not to grant many hours to repose. He opened his eyes and looked into the surrounding darkness, and then he closed them again to go to sleep once more. When many diverse sensations have agitated a day, and when matters preoccupy the mind, a man may sleep, but he cannot go to sleep again. Sleep comes more easily than it returns, and this happened to Jean

Valjean. He could not go to sleep again, so he began thinking.

He was in one of those moods in which the ideas that occupy the mind are troubled. There was a species of obscure oscillation in his brain. His old recollections and immediate recollections crossed each other, and floated confusedly, losing their shape, growing enormously, and then disappearing suddenly, as if in troubled and muddy water. Many thoughts occurred to him, but there was one which constantly reverted and expelled all the rest. This thought we will at once describe. He had noticed the six silver forks and spoons and the great ladle which Madame Magloire put on the table. This plate overwhelmed him—it was there—a few yards from him. When he crossed the adjoining room to reach the one in which he now was, the old servant was putting it in a small cupboard at the bed-head. He had carefully noticed this cupboard—it was on the right as you came in from the dining-room. The plate was heavy and old, the big soup-ladle was worth at least 200 francs, or double what he had earned in nineteen years, though it was true that he would have earned more had not the Government robbed him.

His mind wavered for a good hour, in these fluctuations with which a struggle was most assuredly blended. When three o'clock struck he opened his eyes, suddenly sat up, stretched out his arms, and felt for his knapsack, which he had thrown into a corner of the alcove, then let his legs hang, and felt himself seated on the bedside almost without knowing how. He remained for awhile thoughtfully in this attitude, which would have had something sinister about it for any one who had seen him, the only wakeful person in the house. All at once he stooped, took off his shoes, then resumed his thoughtful posture, and remained motionless. In the midst of this hideous meditation, the ideas which we have indicated incessantly crossed his brain, entered, went out, returned, and weighed upon him; and then he thought, without knowing why, and with the mechanical obstinacy of reverie, of a convict he had known at the galleys, of the name of Brevet, whose trousers were only held up by a single knitted brace. The draughtboard design of that brace incessantly returned to his mind. He remained in this situation, and would have probably remained so till sunrise, had not the clock struck the quarter or the half-hour. It seemed as if this stroke said to him,

To work! He rose, hesitated for a moment and listened all was silent in the house, and he went on tiptoe to the window, through which he peered. The night was not very dark; there was a full moon, across which heavy clouds were chased by the wind. This produced alternations of light and shade, and a species of twilight in the room. This twilight, sufficient to guide him, but intermittent in consequence of the clouds, resembled that livid hue produced by the grating of a cellar over which people are continually passing. On reaching the window, Jean Valjean examined it. It was without bars, looked on the garden, and was only closed, according to the fashion of the country, by a small peg. He opened it, but as a cold sharp breeze suddenly entered the room, he closed it again directly. He gazed into the garden with that attentive glance which studies rather than looks, and found that it was enclosed by a whitewashed wall, easy to climb over. Beyond it he noticed the tops of trees standing at regular distances, which proved that this wall separated the garden from a public walk.

After taking this glance, he walked boldly to the alcove, opened his knapsack, took out something which he laid on the bed, put his shoes in one of the pouches, placed the knapsack on his shoulders, put on his cap, the peak of which he pulled over his eyes, groped for his stick, which he placed in the window-nook, and then returned to the bed, and took up the object he had laid on it. It resembled a short iron bar, sharpened at one of its ends. It would have been difficult to distinguish in the darkness for what purpose this piece of iron had been fashioned; perhaps it was a lever, perhaps it was a club: By daylight it could have been seen that it was nothing but a miner's drill. The convicts at that day were sometimes employed in extracting rock from the lofty hills that surround Toulon, and it was not infrequent for them to have mining tools at their disposal. The miners' drills are made of massive steel, and have a point at the lower end, by which they are dug into the rock. He took the bar in his right hand, and holding his breath and deadening his footsteps, he walked towards the door of the adjoining room, the Bishop's, as we know. On reaching this door, he found it ajar. The Bishop had not closed it.

Jean Valjean listened. There was not a sound. He pushed the door with the tip of his finger lightly, and with the stealthy and timorous carefulness of a cat that wants to get in. The door yielded to the pressure, and made an almost imperceptible and silent movement, which slightly widened the opening. He waited for a moment, and then pushed the door again more boldly. It continued to yield silently, and the opening was soon large enough for him to pass through. But there was near the door a small table which formed an awkward angle with it, and barred the entrance.

Jean Valjean saw the obstacle : the opening must be increased at all hazards. He made up his mind, and pushed the door a third time, more energetically still. This time there was a badly oiled hinge, which suddenly uttered a hoarse prolonged cry in the darkness. Jean Valjean started ; the sound of the hinge smote his ear startlingly and formidably, as if it had been the trumpet of the day of judgment. In the fantastic exaggerations of the first minute, he almost imagined that this hinge had become animated, and suddenly obtained a terrible vitality and barked like a dog to warn and awaken the sleepers. He stopped, shuddering and dismayed, and fell back from his tiptoes to his heels. He felt the arteries in his temples beat like two forge hammers, and it seemed to him that his breath issued from his lungs with the noise of the wind roaring out of a cavern. He fancied that the horrible clamour of this irritated hinge must have startled the whole house like the shock of an earthquake ; the door pushed by him had taken the alarm, and had called out ; the old man would rise, the two aged females would shriek, and assistance would arrive within a quarter of an hour, the town would be astir, and the gendarmerie turned out. For a moment he believed he was lost.

He stood still, petrified like the statue of salt, and not daring to make a movement. A few minutes passed, during which the door remained wide open. He ventured to look into the room, and found that nothing had stirred. He listened ; no one was moving in the house, the creaking of the rusty hinge had not awakened any one. The first danger had passed, but still there was fearful tumult within him. But he did not recoil ; he had not done so even when he thought himself lost; he only thought of finishing the job as speedily as possible, and entered the bedroom. The room was in a state of perfect calmness ; here and there might be distinguished confused and vague forms, which by day were papers scattered over the table, open folios, books piled on a sofa, an easy-chair covered with clothes, and a prie-dieu, all of which were at this moment only dark nooks and patches of white. Jean Valjean advanced cautiously and carefully, and avoided coming into collision with the furniture. He heard from the end of the room the calm and regular breathing of the sleeping Bishop. Suddenly he stopped, for he was close to the bed. He had reached it sooner than he expected.

Nature sometimes blends her effects and appearances with our actions with a species of gloomy and intelligent design, as if wishing to make us reflect. For nearly half an hour a heavy cloud had covered the sky, but at the moment when Jean Valjean stopped at the foot of the bed, this cloud was rent asunder as if expressly, and a moonbeam passing through the tall window suddenly illumined the Bishop's pale face. He was sleeping peacefully, and was wrapped up in a long garment of brown wool, which covered his arms down to the wrists. His head was thrown back on the pillow in the easy attitude of repose, and his hand, adorned with the pastoral ring, and which had done so many good deeds, hung out of bed. His entire face was lit up by a vague expression of satisfaction, hope, and beatitude—it was more than a smile and almost a radiance. He had on his forehead the inexpressible reflection of an invisible light, for the soul of a just man contemplates a mysterious heaven during sleep. A reflection of this heaven was cast over the Bishop. But it was at the same time a luminous transparency ; for the heaven was within him, and was conscience.

At the instant when the moonbeam was cast over this internal light, the sleeping Bishop seemed to be surrounded by a glory, which was veiled, however, by an ineffable twilight. The moon in the heavens, the slumbering landscape, the quiet house, the hour, the silence, the moment, added something solemn and indescribable to this man's venerable repose, and cast a majestic and serene halo round his white hair and closed eyes, his face in which all was hope and confidence, his aged head, and his infantine slumbers. There was almost a divinity in this unconsciously august man. Jean Valjean was standing in the shadow with his crow-bar in his hand, motionless and terrified by this luminous old man. He had never seen anything like this before, and such confidence horrified him. The moral world has no greater spectacle than this, a troubled, restless conscience, which is on the point of committing an evil deed, contemplating the sleep of a good man.

This sleep in such solitude, and with a neighbour like himself, possessed a species of sublimity which he felt vaguely, but imperiously. No one could have said what was going on within him, not even himself. In order to form any idea of it we must imagine what is the most violent in the presence of what is gentlest. Even in his face nothing could have been distinguished with certainty, for it displayed a sort of haggard astonishment. He looked at the Bishop, that was all, but what his thoughts were it would be impossible to divine ; what was evident was, that he was moved and shaken, but of what nature was this emotion? His eye was not once removed from the old man, and the only thing clearly revealed by his attitude and countenance was a strange indecision, It seemed as if he were hesitating between two abysses, the one that saves and the one that destroys ; he was ready to dash out the Bishop's brains or kiss his hand. At the expiration of a few minutes his left arm slowly rose to his cap, which he took off ; then his arm fell again with the same slowness, and Jean Valjean recommenced his contemplation, with his cap in his left hand, his crow-bar in his right, and his hair bristling on his head.

Beneath this terrific glance, the Bishop continued to sleep peacefully. A moonbeam rendered the crucifix over the mantelpiece dimly visible, which seemed to open its arms for both, with a blessing for one and a pardon for the other. All at once Jean Valjean put on his cap again, then passed rapidly along the bed, without looking at the Bishop, and went straight to the cupboard. He raised his crow-bar to force the lock, but as the key was in it, he opened it, and the first thing he saw was the plate basket, which he seized. He hurried across the room, not caring for the noise he made, re-entered the oratory, opened the window, seized his stick, put the silver in his pocket, threw away the basket, ran across the garden, leaped over the wall like a tiger, and fled.

Next morning at sunrise the Bishop was walking about the garden, when Madame Magloire came running toward him quite beside herself.

" Monseigneur, Monseigneur ! " she screamed, " does your Greatness know where the plate basket is ? "

" Yes," said the Bishop.

"God be praised," she continued; "I did not know what had become of it."

The Bishop had just picked up the basket in a flowerbed, and now handed it to Madame Magloire. "Here it is," he said.

"Well!" she said, "there is nothing in it; where is the silver?"

"Ah!" the Bishop replied, "it is the silver that troubles your mind. Well, I do not know where that is."

"Good heavens! it is stolen, and that man who came last night is the robber."

In a twinkling Madame Magloire had run to the oratory, entered the alcove, and returned to the Bishop. He was stooping down and looking sorrowfully at a cochlearia, whose stem the basket had broken. He raised himself on hearing Madame Magloire scream:

"Monseigneur, the man has gone! the plate is stolen!"

While she was uttering this exclamation her eyes fell on a corner of the garden, where there were signs of climbing; the coping of the wall had been thrown down.

"That is the way he went! he leaped into Cochefilet lane. Ah, what an abomination; he has stolen our plate!"

The Bishop remained silent for a moment, then raised his earnest eyes, and said gently to Madame Magloire:

"By the way, was that plate ours?"

Madame Magloire was speechless; there was another interval of silence, after which the Bishop continued:

"Madame Magloire, I had wrongfully held back this silver, which belonged to the poor. Who was this person? evidently a poor man."

"Good gracious!" Madame Magloire continued; "I do not care for it, nor does Mademoiselle, but we feel for Monseigneur. What is Monseigneur going to eat with now?"

The Bishop looked at her in amazement. "Why, are there not pewter forks to be had?"

Madame Magloire shrugged her shoulders. "Pewter smells!"

"Then iron!"

Madame Magloire made an expressive grimace. "Iron tastes."

"Well then," said the Bishop, "wood!"

A few minutes later he was breakfasting at the same table at which Jean Valjean sat on the previous evening.

While breakfasting, Monseigneur Welcome gaily remarked to his sister, who said nothing, and to Madame Magloire, who growled in a low voice, that spoon and fork, even of wood, are not required to dip a piece of bread in a cup of milk.

"What an idea!" Madame Magloire said, as she went backwards and forwards, " to receive a man like that, and lodge him by one's side. And what a blessing it is that he only stole! Oh, Lord! the mere thought makes a body shudder."

As the brother and sister were leaving the table there was a knock at the door.

"Come in," said the Bishop.

The door opened, and a strange and violent group appeared on the threshold. Three men were holding a fourth by the collar. The three men were gendarmes, the fourth was Jean Valjean. A corporal, who apparently commanded the party, came in and walked up to the Bishop with a military salute.

"Monseigneur," he said.

At this word Jean Valjean, who was gloomy and crushed, raised his head with a stupefied air.

"Monseigneur," he muttered, " then he is not the Curé."

"Silence!" said a gendarme. "This gentleman is Monseigneur the Bishop."

In the meanwhile Monseigneur Welcome had advanced as rapidly as his great age permitted.

"Ah! there you are," he said, looking at Jean Valjean. "I am glad to see you. Why, I gave you the candlesticks too, which are also silver, and will fetch you 200 francs. Why did you not take them away with the rest of the plate?"

Jean Valjean opened his eyes, and looked at the Bishop with an expression which no human language could describe

"Monseigneur," the corporal said, " what this man told us was true then? We met him, and as he looked as if he were running away, we arrested him. He had this plate——"

"And he told you," the Bishop interrupted, with a smile. " that it was given to him by an old priest at whose house he passed the night? I see it all. And you brought him back here? That is a mistake."

"In that case," the corporal continued, " we can let him go?"

" Of course," the Bishop answered.

The gendarmes loosed their hold of Jean Valjean, who tottered back.

"Is it true that I am at liberty?" he said, in an almost inarticulate voice, and if as speaking in his sleep.

"Yes, you are let go; don't you understand?" said a gendarme.

" My friend," the Bishop continued, "before you go take your candlesticks."

He went to the mantelpiece, fetched the two candlesticks, and handed them to Jean Valjean. The two females watched him do so without a word, without a sign, without a look that could disturb the Bishop. Jean Valjean was trembling in all his limbs; he took the candlesticks mechanically, and with wandering looks.

"Now," said the Bishop, "go in peace. By the bye, when you return, my friend, it is unnecessary to pass through the garden, for you can always enter, day and night, by the front door, which is only latched."

Then, turning to the gendarmes, he said :

" Gentlemen, you can retire."

They did so. Jean Valjean looked as if he were on the point of fainting; the Bishop walked up to him, and said in a low voice :

" Never forget that you have promised me to employ this money in becoming an honest man."

Jean Valjean, who had no recollection of having promised anything, stood silent. The Bishop, who had laid a stress on these words, continued solemnly :

" Jean Valjean, my brother, you no longer belong to evil, but to good. I have bought your soul of you. I withdraw it from dark thoughts and the spirit of perdition, and give it to God."

CHAPTER XVI.

JEAN VALJEAN left the town as if he were escaping. He made all haste to get into the open country, taking the roads and paths that offered themselves, without perceiving that he was going round and round. He wandered thus the entire morning, and though he had eaten nothing, he did not feel hungry. He was attacked by a multitude of novel sensations; he felt a sort of passion, but he did not know with whom. He could not have said whether he was affected or humiliated; at times a strange softening came over him, against which he strove, and to which he opposed the hardening of the last twenty years. This condition offended him, and he saw with alarm that the species of frightful calmness, which the injustice of his misfortune had produced, was shaken within him. He asked himself what would take its place; at times he would have preferred being in prison and with the gendarmes, and that things had not happened thus; for that would have agitated him less. Although the season was advanced, there were still here and there in the hedges a few laggard flowers, whose smell recalled childhood's memories as he passed them. These recollections were almost unendurable, for it was so long since they had occurred to him.

Unspeakable thoughts were thus congregated within him the whole day through. When the sun was setting, and lengthening on the ground the shadow of the smallest pebble, Jean Valjean was sitting behind a bush in a large tawny and utterly deserted plain. There were only the Alps on the horizon, there was not even the steeple of a distant village. Jean Valjean might be about three leagues from D——, and a path that crossed the plain ran a few paces from the bushes. In the midst of this meditation, which would have contributed not a little in rendering his rags formidable to any one who saw him, he heard a sound of mirth. He turned his head and saw a little Savoyard about ten years of age coming along the path, with his hurdy-gurdy at his side and his dormouse-box on his back. He was one of those gentle, merry lads who go about from country to country, displaying their knees through holes in their trousers.

Always singing, the lad stopped from time to time to play at pitch and toss with some coins he held in his hand, which were probably his entire fortune. Among these coins was a two-franc piece. The lad stopped by the side of the bushes without seeing Jean Valjean, and threw up the handful of sous, all of which he had hitherto always caught on the back of his hand. This time the two-franc piece fell, and rolled up to Jean Valjean, who placed his foot upon it. But the boy had looked after the coin, and had seen him do it; he did not seem surprised, but walked straight up to the man. It was an utterly deserted spot; as far as eye could extend there was no one on the plain or the path. Nothing was audible, save the faint cries of a swarm of birds of passage passing through the sky, at an immense height. The boy had his back turned to the sun, which wove golden threads in his hair, and suffused Jean Valjean's face with a lurid glow.

"Sir," the little Savoyard said, with that childish confidence which is composed of ignorance and innocence, "my coin?"

"What is your name?" Jean Valjean said.

"Little Gervais, sir."

"Be off," said Jean Valjean.

"Give me my coin, if you please, sir."

Jean Valjean hung his head, but said nothing.

The boy began again :

"My two-franc piece, sir."

Jean Valjean's eye remained fixed on the ground.

"My coin," the boy cried, "my silver piece."

It seemed as if Jean Valjean did not understand him, for the boy seized the collar of his blouse and shook him, and at the same time made an effort to remove the iron-shod shoe placed on his coin.

"I want my money! my forty-sous piece!"

The child began to cry, and Jean Valjean raised his head. He was still sitting on the ground, and his eyes were misty. He looked at the lad with a sort of amazement, then stretched forth his hand to his stick, and shouted in a terrible voice, "Who is there?"

"I, sir," the boy replied. "Little Gervais; give me back my two francs, if you please. Take away your foot, sir, if you please." Then he grew irritated, though so little, and almost threatening.

"Come, will you take away your foot, I say?"

"Ah, you are here yet!" said Jean Valjean, and springing up, with his foot still held on the coin, he added, "Will you be off or not?"

The boy looked at him in terror, then began trembling from head to foot, and after a few moments of stupor ran off at full speed, without daring to look back or utter a cry. Still, when he had got a certain distance, want of breath forced him to stop, and Jean Valjean could hear him sobbing. In a few minutes the boy had disappeared. The sun had set, and darkness collected around Jean Valjean. He had eaten nothing all day, and was probably in a fever. He had remained standing and had not changed his attitude since the boy ran off. His breath heaved his chest at long and unequal intervals, his eye, fixed ten or twelve yards ahead, seemed to be studying with profound attention the shape of an old fragment of blue earthenware which had fallen in the grass. Suddenly he started, for he felt the night chill ; he pulled his cap over his forehead, mechanically tried to button his blouse around him, stepped forward, and stooped to pick up his stick.

At that instant he perceived the two-franc piece, which his foot had half buried in the turf, and which glistened among the pebbles. It had the effect of a galvanic shock upon him. "What is this?" he muttered. He fell back three paces, then stopped, unable to take his eye from the spot his foot had trodden a moment before, as if the thing glistening there in the darkness had an open eye fixed upon him. In a few moments he dashed convulsively at the coin, picked it up, and began looking out into the plain, while shuddering like a straying wild beast which is seeking a place of refuge.

He saw nothing. Night was falling, the plain was cold and indistinct, and heavy violet mists rose in the twilight. He set out rapidly in a certain direction, the one in which the lad had gone. After going some thirty yards he stopped, looked and saw nothing ; then he shouted with all his strength, "Little Gervais, Little Gervais!" He was silent, and waited, but there was no response. The country was deserted and gloomy, and he was surrounded by space. There was nothing but a gloom in which his glance was lost, and a silence in which his voice was lost. An icy breeze was blowing, and imparted to things around a sort of mournful life. The bushes shook their little thin arms with incredible fury ; they seemed to be threatening and pursuing some one.

He began to walk again, and then quickened his pace to a run, but from time to time he stopped, and shouted in the solitude with a voice the most formidable and agonising that can be imagined : "Little Gervais, Little Gervais!" Assuredly, if the boy had heard him, he would have felt frightened, and not have shown himself ; but the lad was doubtless a long way off by this time. The convict met a priest on horseback, to whom he went up and said :

"Monsieur le Curé, have you seen a lad pass?"

"No," the Priest replied.

"A lad of the name of 'Little Gervais'?"

"I have seen nobody."

The convict took two five-franc pieces from his pouch and handed them to the Priest.

"Monsieur le Curé, this is for your poor. He was a boy of about ten years of age, with a dormouse, I think, and a hurdy-gurdy, a Savoyard, you know."

"I did not see him."

"Can you tell me if there is any one of the name of Little Gervais in the villages about here?"

"If it is as you say, my good fellow, the lad is a stranger. Many of them pass this way."

Jean Valjean violently took out two other five-franc pieces, which he gave the Priest.

"For your poor," he said; then added wildly, "Monsieur l'Abbé, have me arrested: I am a robber."

The Priest urged on his horse, and rode away in great alarm, while Jean Valjean set off running in the direction he had first taken. He went on for a long distance, looking, calling, and shouting, but he met no one else. Twice or thrice he ran across the plain to something that appeared to him to be a person lying or sitting down; but he only found heather, or rocks level with the ground. At last he stopped at a spot where three paths met; the moon had risen; he called out for the last time, "Little Gervais, Little Gervais, Little Gervais!" His shout died away in the mist, without even awakening an echo. He muttered again, "Little Gervais," in a weak and almost inarticulate voice, but it was his last effort. His knees suddenly gave way under him as if an invisible power were crushing him beneath the weight of a bad conscience. He fell exhausted on a large stone, with his hand tearing his hair, his face between his knees, and shrieked: "I am a scoundrel!" Then his heart melted, and he began to weep; it was the first time for nineteen years.

When Jean Valjean quitted the Bishop's house he was lifted out of his former thoughts, and could not account for what was going on within him. He stiffened himself against the angelic deeds and gentle words of the old man: "You have promised me to become an honest man. I purchase your soul; I withdraw it from the spirit of perverseness, and give it to God." This incessantly recurred to him, and he opposed to this celestial indulgence that pride which is within us as a fortress of evil. He felt indistinctly that this priest's forgiveness was the greatest and most formidable assault by which he had yet been shaken ; that his hardening would be permanent if he resisted this clemency ; that if he yielded he must renounce that hatred with which the actions of other men had filled his soul during so many years, and which pleased him ; that this time he must either conquer or be vanquished, and that the struggle, a colossal and final struggle, had begun between his own wickedness and the goodness of that man.

In the presence of all these gleams he walked on like a drunken man. While he went on thus with haggard eye, had he any distinct perception of what the result of his adventure at D—— might be ? Did he hear all that mysterious buzzing which warns or disturbs the mind at certain moments of life ? Did a voice whisper in his ear that he had just gone through the solemn hour of his destiny, that no middle way was now left him, and that if he were not henceforth the best of men he would be the worst ; that he must now ascend higher than the bishop, or sink lower than the galley-slave ; that if he wished to be good he must become an angel, and that if he wished to remain wicked he must become a monster ?

Here we must ask again the question we previously asked, Did he confusedly receive any shadow of all this into his mind ? Assuredly, as we said, misfortune educates the intellect, still it is doubtful whether Jean Valjean was in a state to draw the conclusions we have formed. If these ideas reached him, he had a glimpse of them rather than saw them, and they only succeeded in throwing him into an indescribable and almost painful trouble. On leaving that shapeless black thing which is called the galleys, the Bishop had hurt his soul, in the same way as a too brilliant light would have hurt his eyes on coming out of darkness. The future life, the possible life, which presented itself to him, all pure and radiant, filled him with tremor and anxiety, and he really no longer knew how matters were. Like an owl that suddenly witnessed a sunrise, the convict had been dazzled and blinded by virtue.

One thing was certain, nor did he himself doubt it, he was no longer the same man. All was changed in him, and it was no longer in his power to get rid of the fact that the Bishop had spoken to him and taken his hand. While in this mental condition he met Little Gervais, and robbed him of his two francs : why did he so ? assuredly he could not explain it. Was it a final, and as it were supreme,

effort of the evil thought he had brought from the galleys,
a remainder of impulse, a result of what is called in statics
"acquired force"?   It was so, and was perhaps also even
less than that.   Let us say it simply, it was not he who
robbed, it was not the man, but the brute beast that through
habit and instinct stupidly placed its foot on the coin, while
the intellect was struggling with such novel and extraordinary sensations.   When the intellect woke again and
saw this brutish action, Jean Valjean recoiled with agony
and uttered a cry of horror.   It was a curious phenomenon,
and one only possible in the situation he was in, that, in
robbing the boy of that money, he had done a thing of which
he was no longer capable.

However that may be, this last bad action had a decisive
effect upon him : it suddenly darted through the chaos
which filled his mind and dissipated it, placed on one side
the dark mists, on the other the light, and acted on his soul,
in its present condition, as certain chemical re-agents act
upon a troubled mixture, by precipitating one element and
clarifying another.   At first, before even examining himself
or reflecting, he wildly strove to find the boy again and
return him his money ; then, when he perceived that this
was useless and impossible, he stopped in despair.   At the
moment when he exclaimed, " I am a scoundrel ! " he had
seen himself as he really was, and was already so separated
from himself that he fancied himself merely a phantom, and
that he had there before him, in flesh and blood, his blouse
fastened round his hips, his knapsack full of stolen objects
on his back, with his resolute and gloomy face and his
mind full of frightful projects, the hideous galley-slave,
Jean Valjean.

Excessive misfortune, as we have remarked, had made
him to some extent a visionary, and this, therefore, was a
species of vision.   He really saw that Jean Valjean with
his sinister face before him, and almost asked himself who
this man who so horrified him was.   His brain was in
that violent and yet frightfully calm stage when the reverie
is so deep that it absorbs reality.   He contemplated himself,
so to speak, face to face, and at the same time he saw
through this hallucination a species of light which he at
first took for a torch.   On looking more attentively at this
light which appeared to his conscience, he perceived that
it had a human shape and was the Bishop.   His conscience
examined in turn the two men standing before him, the

Bishop and Jean Valjean. By one of those singular effects peculiar to an ecstasy of this nature, the more his reverie was prolonged, the taller and more brilliant the Bishop appeared, while Jean Valjean grew less and faded out of sight. At length he disappeared and the Bishop alone remained, who filled the whole soul of this wretched man with a magnificent radiance.

Jean Valjean wept long. He sobbed with more weakness than a woman, more terror than a child. While he wept the light grew brighter in his brain, an extraordinary light, at once ravishing and terrible. His past life, his first fault, his long expiation, his external brutalisation, his internal hardening, his liberation, accompanied by so many plans of vengeance, what had happened at the Bishop's, the last thing he had done, the robbery of the boy, a crime the more cowardly and monstrous because it took place after the Bishop's forgiveness—all this recurred to him, but in a light which he had never before seen. He looked at his life, and it appeared to him horrible ; at his soul, and it appeared to him frightful. Still a soft light was shed over both, and he fancied that he was looking upon Satan by the light of Paradise.

How long did he weep thus ? What did he do afterwards ? Whither did he go ? No one ever knew. It was stated, however, that on this very night the mail-carrier from Grenoble, who arrived at D—— at about 3 a.m., while passing through the street where the Bishop's Palace stood, saw a man kneeling on the pavement in the attitude of prayer in front of Monseigneur Welcome's door.

CHAPTER XVII.

THE year 1817 was that which Louis XVIII., with a certain royal assumption which was not deficient in pride, styled the twenty-second year of his reign. In that year four young Parisians played a capital joke.

These Parisians came, one from Toulouse, the second from Limoges, the third from Cahors, the fourth from Montauban, but they were students, and thus Parisians ; for studying in Paris is being born in Paris. These young men were insignificant, four everyday specimens, neither good nor bad, wise nor ignorant, geniuses nor idiots, and handsome with that charming April, which is called twenty years.

Their names were Felix Tholomyès, Listolier, Fameuil, and Blachevelle. Of course each had a mistress; Blachevelle loved Favorite, so called because she had been to England; Listolier adored Dahlia, who had taken the name of a flower for her *nom de guerre*; Fameuil idolised Zephine, an abridgment of Josephine; while Tholomyès had Fantine, called the Blonde, owing to her magnificent sun-coloured hair. Favorite, Dahlia, Zephine, and Fantine were four exquisitely pretty girls, still to some extent workwomen. They had not entirely laid down the needle, and though deranged by their amourettes, they still had in their faces a remnant of the serenity of toil, and in their souls that flower of honesty, which in a woman survives the first fall. One of the four was called the young one, because she was the youngest, and one called the old one, who was only three-and-twenty. To conceal nothing, the three first were more experienced, more reckless, and had flown further into the noise of life than Fantine the Blonde, who was still in her first illusion.

Dahlia, Zephine, and especially Favorite, could not have said the same. There was already more than one episode in their scarce-begun romance, and the lover who was called Adolphe in the first chapter, became Alphonse in the second, and Gustave in the third. Poverty and coquettishness are two fatal counsellors; one scolds, the other flatters, and the poor girls of the lower classes have them whispering in both ears. Badly guarded souls listen, and hence come the falls they make, and the stones that are cast at them. They are crushed with the splendour of all that is immaculate and inaccessible. Alas! if the Jungfrau were to be starving? Favorite, who had been to England, was admired by Zephine and Dahlia. She had a home of her own from an early age. Her father was an old brutal and boasting professor of mathematics, unmarried, and still giving lessons in spite of his age. This professor, when a young man, had one day seen a lady's-maid's gown caught in a fender; he fell in love through the accident, and Favorite was the result. She met her father from time to time, and he bowed to her. One morning an old woman with a hypocritical look came into her room, and said, " Do you not know me, miss?" " No." " I am your mother." Then the old woman opened the cupboard, ate and drank, sent for a mattress she had, and installed herself. This mother, who was grumbling and proud, never spoke to Favorite, sat for hours without saying a word, breakfasted, dined, and supped for half a dozen, and spent her evenings in the porter's lodge, where she abused her daughter. What drew Dahlia toward Listolier, towards others perhaps, towards idleness, was having too pretty pink finger-nails. How could she employ such nails in working? a girl who wishes to remain virtuous must not have pity on her hands. As for Zephine, she had conquered Fameuil by her little saucy and coaxing way of saying "Yes, sir." The young men were comrades, the girls were friends. Such amours are always accompanied by such friendships.

Wisdom and philosophy are two different things; and what proves it is that, after making all reservations for these little irregular households, Favorite, Zephine, and Dahlia were philosophic girls, and Fantine a prudent girl. Prudent, it will be said, and Tholomyès? Solomon would reply, that love forms part of wisdom. We confine ourselves to saying that Fantine's love was a first love, a single love, a faithful love. She was the only one of the four who was addressed familiarly by but one.

Fantine was one of those beings who spring up from the dregs of the people; issuing from the lowest depths of the social darkness, she had on her forehead the stamp of the anonymous and the unknown. She was born at M—— sur M—— ; of what parents? who could say? she had never known either father or mother. She called herself Fantine —and why Fantine? she was never known by any other name. At the period of her birth, the Directory was still in existence. She had no family name, as she had no family; and no Christian name, as the Church was abolished. She accepted the name given her by the first passer-by, who saw her running barefooted about the streets. She was called little Fantine, and no one knew any more. This human creature came into the world in that way. At the age of ten, Fantine left the town, and went into service with farmers in the neighbourhood. At the age of fifteen she went to Paris, "to seek her fortune." Fantine was pretty, and remained pure as long as she could. She was a charming blonde, with handsome teeth; she had gold and pearls for her dower, but the gold was on her head, and the pearls in her mouth.

She worked to live; and then she loved, still for the sake of living, for the heart is hungry too. She loved Tholomyès; it was a pastime for him, but a passion with her.

The streets of the Quartier Latin, which are thronged with students and grisettes, saw the beginning of this dream. Fantine, in the labyrinth of the Pantheon Hill, where so many adventures are fastened and unfastened, long shunned Tholomyès, but in such a way as to meet him constantly. There is a manner of avoiding which resembles a search. In a word, the eclogue was played.

Blachevelle, Listolier, and Fameuil formed a sort of group, of which Tholomyès was the head. He was the wit of the company.

Tholomyès was an antique old student of the old style. He was rich, for he had an income of 4000 francs a year— a splendid scandal on the Montagne St. Geneviève. Tholomyès was a man of the world, thirty years of age, and in a bad state of preservation. He was wrinkled, and had lost teeth, and he had an incipient baldness, of which he himself said without sorrow : "The skull at thirty, the knee at forty." He had but a poor digestion, and one of his eyes was permanently watery. But in proportion as his youth was extinguished, his gaiety became brighter ; he substituted jests for his teeth, joy for his hair, irony for his health, and his weeping eye laughed incessantly. He was battered, but still flowering. His youth had beaten an orderly retreat, and only the fire was visible. He had had a piece refused at the Vaudeville Theatre, and wrote occasional verses now and then. In addition, he doubted everything in a superior way, which is a great strength in the eyes of the weak. Hence, being ironical and bald, he was the leader.

One day Tholomyès took the other three aside, made an oracular gesture, and said :

"For nearly a year Fantine, Dahlia, Zephine, and Favorite have been asking us to give them a surprise, and we promised solemnly to do so. They are always talking about it, especially to me. In the same way as the old women of Naples cry to Saint Januarius, ' Yellow face, perform your miracle ! ' our beauties incessantly say to me, ' Tholomyès, when will you be delivered of your surprise ? ' At the same time our parents are writing to us, so let us kill two birds with one stone. The moment appears to me to have arrived. Let us talk it over."

Thereupon Tholomyès lowered his voice, and mysteriously uttered something so amusing that a mighty and enthusiastic laugh burst from four mouths simultaneously, and

Blachevelle exclaimed, "That is an idea!" An ale-house full of smoke presenting itself, they went in, and the remainder of their conference was lost in the tobacco clouds. The result of the gloom was a brilliant pleasure excursion, which took place on the following Sunday, the four young men inviting the four girls.

It is not easy to form an idea at the present day of what a pleasure party of students and grisettes was four-and-forty years ago. Paris has no longer the same environs; the face of what may be termed circum-Parisian life has completely changed during half a century; where there was the *coucou*, there is the railway carriage; where there was the fly-boat, there is now the steamer; people talk of Fécamp as people did in those days of St. Cloud. The Paris of 1862 is a city which has France for its suburbs.

The four couples scrupulously accomplished all the rustic follies possible at thaι day. It was a bright warm summer day; they rose at five o'clock; then they went to St. Cloud in the stage-coach, looked at the dry cascade, and exclaimed, "That must be grand when there is water!" breakfasted at the Tête Noire, where Castaing had not yet put up, ran at the ring in the quincunx of the great basin, ascended into the Diogenes lanthorn, gambled for macaroons at the roulette board by the Sèvres bridge, culled posies at Puteaux, bought reed-pipes at Neuilly, ate apple tarts everywhere, and were perfectly happy. The girls prattled and chattered like escaped linnets; they were quite wild, and every now and then gave the young men little taps. O youthful intoxication of life! adorable years! the wing of the dragon-fly rustles. Oh, whoever you may be, do you remember? have you ever walked in the woods, removing the branches for the sake of the pretty head that comes behind you? have you laughingly stepped on a damp slope, with a beloved woman who holds your hand, and cries, "Oh, my new boots; what a condition they are in!"

All four looked charmingly pretty. A good old classic poet, then renowned, M. le Chevalier de Labouisse, wandering that day under the chestnut trees of St. Cloud, saw them pass at about ten in the morning, and exclaimed, "There is one too many!" he was thinking of the Graces. Favorite, the girl who was three-and-twenty, and the old one, ran in front under the large green branches, leapt over ditches, strode madly across bushes, and presided over the gaiety with the spirit of a young fawn. Zephine and Dahlia,

whom accident had created as a couple necessary to enhance
each other's beauty by contrast, did not separate, though
more through a coquettish instinct than through friendship,
and leaning on one another, assumed English attitudes :
the first Keepsakes had just come. out, melancholy was
culminating for women, as Byronism did at a later date
for men, and the hair of the tender sex was beginning
to become dishevelled.   Zephine and Dahlia had their hair
in rolls.   Listolier and Fameuil, who were engaged in a
discussion about their professors, were explaining to Fantine
the difference there was between M.   Delvincourt and
M. Blondeau.   Blachevelle seemed to have been created
expressly to carry Favorite's dingy, shabby shawl on
Sundays.

Tholomyès came last ; he was very gay, but there was
something dictatorial in his joviality ; his principal ornament
was nankeen trousers, cut in the shape of an elephant's legs,
with leathern straps ; he had a mighty rattan worth 200
francs in his hand, and, as he was quite reckless, a strange
thing called a cigar in his mouth ; nothing being sacred to
him, he smoked.   "That Tholomyès is astounding," the
others were wont to say with veneration ; " what trousers !
what energy ! "

As to Fantine, she was joy itself.   Her splendid teeth had
evidently been made for laughter by nature.   She carried in
her hand, more willingly than on her head, her little straw
bonnet, with its long streamers.   Her thick light hair,
inclined to float, and which had to be done up continually,
seemed made for the flight of Galatea under the willows.
Her rosy lips prattled enchantingly ; the corners of her
mouth, voluptuously raised, as in the antique masks of
Erigone, seemed to encourage boldness ; but her long
eyelashes, full of shade, were discreetly lowered upon the
seductiveness of the lower part of the face, as if to command
respect.   Her whole toilet had something flaming about it ;
she had on a dress of mauve barege, little buskin slippers,
whose strings formed an X on her fine, open-worked
stockings, and a sort of muslin spencer, a Marseilles
invention, whose name of *canezou*, a corrupted pronunciation of *quinze août* at the Canebière, signifies fine weather
and heat.   The three others, who were less timid, as we
said, bravely wore low-necked dresses, which in summer
are very graceful and attractive, under bonnets covered
with flowers ; but by the side of this bold dress, Fantine's

canezou, with its transparency, indiscretion, and conceal-
ments, at once concealing and displaying, seemed a provo-
cative invention of decency ; and the famous court of Love,
presided over by the Vicomtesse de Cette with the sea-green
eyes, would have probably bestowed the prize for coquettishness on this *canezou,* which competed for that of chastity.
The simplest things are not infrequently the cleverest.

Brilliant from a front view, delicate from a side view,
with dark blue eyes, heavy eyelids, arched and small feet,
wrists and ankles admirably set on, the white skin displaying
here and there the azure arborescences of the veins, with
a childish fresh cheek, the robust neck of the Ægean
Juno, shoulders, apparently modelled by Couston, and
having in their centre a voluptuous dimple, visible through
the muslin ; a gaiety tempered by reverie ; a sculptural and
exquisite being—such was Fantine ; you could trace beneath
the ribbons and finery a statue, and inside the statue a
soul. Fantine was beautiful, without being exactly conscious
of it. Those rare dreamers, the mysterious priests of the
beautiful, who silently confront everything with perfection,
would have seen in this little work-girl the ancient sacred
euphony, through the transparency of Parisian grace !
This girl had blood in her, and had those two descriptions
of beauty which are the style and the rhythm. Style is the
force of the ideal ; rhythm is its movement.

We have said that Fantine was joy ; she was also
modesty. Any one who watched her closely would have
seen through all this intoxication of youth, of season, and
of love, an invincible expression of restraint and modesty.
She remained slightly astonished, and this chaste astonishment distinguishes Psyche from Venus. Fantine had the
long white delicate fingers of the Vestal, who stirs up the
sacred fire with a golden bodkin. Though she had refused
nothing, as we shall soon see, to Tholomyès, her face,
when in repose, was supremely virginal ; a species of stern
and almost austere dignity suddenly invaded it at certain
hours, and nothing was so singular and affecting as to
see gaiety so rapidly extinguished on it, and contemplation
succeed cheerfulness without any transition. This sudden
gravity, which was at times sternly marked, resembled the
disdain of a goddess. Her forehead, nose, and chin offered
that equilibrium of outline which is very distinct from the
equilibrium of proportion, and produces the harmony of the
face ; in the characteristic space between the base of the

nose and the upper lip, she had that imperceptible and
charming curve, that mysterious sign of chastity, which
made Barbarossa fall in love with a Diana found in the
ruins of Iconium.   Love is a fault ; be it so ; but Fantine
was innocence floating on the surface of the fault.

CHAPTER XVIII.

THE whole of this day seemed to be composed of dawn : all
nature seemed to be having a holiday, and laughing.   The
pastures of St. Cloud exhaled perfumes ; the breeze from
the Seine vaguely stirred the leaves ; the branches gesticulated in the wind ; the bees were plundering the jessamine ;
a madcap swarm of butterflies settled down on the ragwort,
the clover, and the wild oats ; there was in the august park
of the King of France a pack of vagabonds, the birds.   The
four happy couples enjoyed the sun, the fields, the flowers,
and the trees.   And in this community of Paradise, three
of the girls, while singing, talking, dancing, chasing butterflies, picking bindweed, wetting their stockings in the tall
grass, fresh, madcap, but not dissolute, received kisses
from all the gentlemen in turn.   Fantine alone was shut
up in her vague, dreamy resistance, and loved.   " You
always look strange," Favorite said to her.

After breakfast the four couples went to see, in what was
then called the King's Square, a plant newly arrived from
the Indies, whose name we have forgotten, but which at that
time attracted all Paris to St. Cloud ; it was a strange and
pretty shrub, whose numerous branches, fine as threads and
leafless, were covered with a million of small white flowers ;
there was always a crowd round it, admiring it.   After
inspecting the shrub, Tholomyès exclaimed, " I will pay
for donkeys ; " and after making a bargain with the donkey-
man, they returned by Vauvres and Issy.

On giving up the donkeys there was fresh pleasure ; the
Seine was crossed in a boat, and from Passy they walked
to the Barrière de l'Etoile.   They had been afoot since five
in the morning ; but no matter !   " There is no such thing
as weariness on Sunday," said Favorite ; " on Sundays
fatigue does not work."   At about three o'clock, the four
couples, wild with delight, turned into the Montagnes
Russes, a singular building, which at that time occupied
the heights of Beaujon, and whose winding line could be

seen over the trees of the Champs Elysées. From time to time Favorite exclaimed :

"Where's the surprise? I insist on the surprise."

" Have patience," Tholomyès answered.

The Russian mountains exhausted, they thought about dinner, and the radiant eight, at length somewhat weary, put into the Cabaret Bombarda, an off-shoot established in the Champs Elysées by that famous restaurateur Bombarda, whose sign could be seen at that time at the Rue de Rivoli, by the side of the Delorme passage.

A large but ugly room, with an alcove and a bed at the end (owing to the crowded state of the houses on Sundays they were compelled to put up with it) ; two windows from which the quay and river could be contemplated through the elm-trees ; a magnificent autumn sun illumining the windows ; two tables, on one of them a triumphal mountain of bottles, mixed up with hats and bonnets, at the other one four couples joyously seated round a mass of dishes, plates, bottles, and glasses, pitchers of beer mingled with wine bottles ; but little order on the table, and some amount of disorder under it. Such was the state of the pastoral which began at 5 a.m. ; at 4.30 p.m. the sun was declining and appetite was satisfied.

CHAPTER XIX.

LOVE talk and table talk are equally indescribable, for the first is a cloud, the second smoke. Fantine and Dahlia were humming a tune, Tholomyès was drinking, Zephine laughing, Fantine smiling, Listolier was blowing a penny trumpet bought at St. Cloud, Favorite was looking tenderly at Blachevelle, and saying :

"Blachevelle, I adore you."

This led to Blachevelle asking :

"What would you do, Favorite, if I ceased to love you ?"

"I?" Favorite exclaimed ; "oh, do not say that, even in fun ! if you ceased to love me I would run after you, claw you, throw water over you, and have you arrested."

Blachevelle smiled with the voluptuous fatuity of a man whose self-esteem is tickled. Dahlia, while still eating, whispered to Favorite through the noise :

"You seem to be very fond of your Blachevelle ?"

"I detest him," Favorite answered in the same key, as

she seized her fork again. "He is miserly, and I prefer the little fellow who lives opposite to me. He is a very good-looking young man ; do you know him ? It is easy to see that he wants to be an actor, and I am fond of actors. As soon as he comes in, his mother says : ' Oh, good heavens, my tranquillity is destroyed : he is going to begin to shout ; my dear boy, you give me a headache ; ' because he goes about the house, into the garrets as high as he can get, and sings and declaims, so that he can be heard from the streets ! He already earns twenty sous a day in a lawyer's office. Ah ! he adores me to such a pitch that one day when he saw me making batter for pancakes, he said to me, ' Mamselle, make fritters of your gloves, and I will eat them.' Only professional men are able to say things like that. Ah ! he is very good-looking, and I feel as if I am about to fall madly in love with the little fellow. No matter, I tell Blachevelle that I adore him : what a falsehood, eh, what a falsehood ! "

After a pause, Favorite continued :

" Dahlia, look you, I am sad. It has done nothing but rain all the summer : the wind annoys me, Blachevelle is excessively mean, there are hardly any green peas in the market, one does not know what to eat ; I have the spleen, as the English say, for butter is so dear ; and then it is horrifying that we are dining in a room with a bed in it, and that disgusts me with life."

At length, when all were singing noisily, or talking all together, Tholomyès interfered.

"Let us not talk hap-hazard or too quickly," he exclaimed ; "we must meditate if we desire to be striking. Too much improvisation stupidly empties the mind. Gentlemen, no haste ; let us mingle majesty with our gaiety. We must not hurry. Look at the Spring, if it goes ahead too fast it is floored, that is to say, nipped by frost. Excessive zeal ruins the peach and apricot trees ; excessive zeal kills the grace and joy of good dinners. No zeal, gentlemen ; Grimaud de la Reynière is of the same opinion as Talleyrand."

A dull rebellion broke out in the party.

"Tholomyès, leave us at peace," said Blachevelle.

"Down with the tyrant," said Fameuil.

"Sunday exists," Listolier added.

"We are sober," Fameuil remarked again.

"Gentlemen, be suspicious of women," Tholomyès

continued; "woe to the man who surrenders himself to
a woman's fickle heart; woman is perfidious and tortuous,
and detests the serpent through a professional jealousy."

"Tholomyès," Blachevelle shouted, "you are drunk."

"I hope so!"

"Then be jolly."

"I am agreeable," Tholomyès answered. And filling
his glass, he rose.

"Glory to wine! *nunc te, Bacche, canam*! Pardon,
ladies, that is Spanish, and the proof, Senoras, is this;
as the country is, so is the measure. The arroba of
Castille contains sixteen quarts, the cantaro of Alicante
twelve, the almuda of the Canary Isles twenty-five, the
cuartino of the Balearic Isles twenty-six, and Czar Peter's
boot thirty. Long live the Czar, who was great, and his
boot, which was greater still! Ladies, take a friend's
advice; deceive your neighbour, if you think proper. The
peculiarity of love is to wander, and it is not made to
crouch like an English servant girl who has stiff knees
from scrubbing. It is said that error is hnman, but I say,
error is amorous. Ladies, I idolise you all. O Zephine,
you with your seductive face, you would be charming were
you not all askew; your face looks for all the world as
if it had been sat upon by mistake. As for Favorite, O
ye Nymphs and Muses! one day when Blachevelle was
crossing the gutter in the Rue Guérin-Boisseau, he saw
a pretty girl with white, well-drawn-up stockings, who
displayed her legs. The prologue was pleasing, and
Blachevelle fell in love; the girl he loved was Favorite.
O Favorite, you have Ionian lips; there was a Greek
painter of the name of Euphorion, who was christened
the painter of lips, and this Greek alone would be worthy
to paint your mouth. Listen to me: before you, there was
not a creature deserving of the name; you are made to
receive the apple like Venus, or to eat it like Eve. Beauty
begins with you, and you deserve a patent for inventing
a pretty woman. You alluded to my name just now: it
affected me deeply, but we must be distrustful of names,
for they may be deceptive. My name is Felix, and yet
I am not happy. Miss Dahlia, in your place I would call
myself Rose, for a flower ought to smell agreeably, and
a woman have spirit. I say nothing of Fantine, for she
is a dreamer, pensive and sensitive; she is a phantom,
having the form of a nymph, and the modesty of a nun,

who has strayed into the life of a grisette, but takes shelter in illusions, and who sings, prays, and looks at the blue sky, without exactly knowing what she sees or what she does, and who, with her eyes fixed on heaven, wanders about a garden in which there are more birds than ever existed. O Fantine, be aware of this fact: I, Tholomyès, am an illusion—why, the fair girl of chimeras is not even listening to me! All about her is freshness, suavity, youth, and sweet morning brightness. O Fantine, girl worthy to be called Marguerite or Pearl, you are a woman worthy of the fairest East. Ladies, here is a second piece of advice: do not marry, for marriage is a risk, and you had better shun it. But nonsense! I am wasting my words! Girls are incurable about wedlock; and all that we sages may say will not prevent waistcoat-makers and shoe-binders from dreaming of husbands loaded with diamonds. Well, beauties, be it so: but bear this in mind, you eat too much sugar. You have only one fault, O women, and that is nibbling sugar. O rodent sex, your pretty little white teeth adore sugar. Now, listen to this, sugar is a salt, and salts are of a drying nature, and sugar is the most drying of all salts. It pumps out the fluidity of the blood through the veins; this produces first coagulation and then solidifying of the blood; from this come tubercles in the lungs, and thence death. Hence do not nibble sugar, and you will live. I now turn to my male hearers: Gentlemen, make conquests. Rob one another of your well-beloved ones remorselessly; change partners, for in love there are no friends. Whenever there is a pretty woman, hostilities are opened; there is no quarter, but war to the knife! A pretty woman is a *casus belli* and a flagrant offence. All the invasions of history were produced by petticoats; for woman is the lawful prey of man.

Here Tholomyès broke off.

"Take a breather, my boy," said Blachevelle.

At the same time the other three gentlemen struck up to a doleful air one of those studio-songs, which are composed extemporaneously, either in rhyme or prose, which spring up from the smoke of pipes, and fly away with it. The song was not adapted to calm Tholomyès' inspiration; hence he emptied his glass, filled it again, and began once more.

"Down with wisdom! forget all I have said to you. Be neither prudish, nor prudent, nor *prud'hommes*. I drink

the health of jollity ; so let us be jolly. Let us complete
our legal studies by folly and good food, for indigestion
should run in a curricle with digests. Let Justinian be
the male, and Merriment the female ! Live, O creation ;
the world is one large diamond ; I am happy, and the
birds are astounding. What a festival all around us ; the
nightingale is a gratis Elleviou. Summer, I salute thee.
O Luxembourg ! O ye Georgics of the Rue Madame and
the Allée de l'Observatoire ! O ye dreaming lobsters ! O
ye delicious nurses, who, while taking care of children,
fancy what your own will be like ! The pampas of America
would please me if I had not the arcades of the Odeon.
My soul is flying away to the virgin forests and the
savannahs. All is glorious ; the flies are buzzing in the
light ; the sun has sneezed forth the humming-bird. Kiss
me, Fantine ! "

Tholomyès, when started, would hardly have been
checked, had not a horse fallen in the street at this very
moment. Through the shock, cart and orator stopped
short. It was a Beauce mare, old and lean and worthy
of the knacker, dragging a very heavy cart. On getting
in front of Bombarda's, the beast, exhausted and worn out,
refused to go any farther, and this incident produced a
crowd. The carter, swearing and indignant, had scarce
time to utter with the suitable energy the sacramental
word, "Cur ! " backed up by a pitiless lash, ere the poor
beast fell, never to rise again.

"Poor horse ! " Fantine said, with a sigh ; and Dahlia
shouted :

"Why, here is Fantine beginning to feel pity for horses ;
how can she be such a fool ! "

At this moment, Favorite crossed her arms and threw
her head back ; she then looked boldly at Tholomyès,
and said :

"Well, how about the surprise ? "

"That is true, the hour has arrived," Tholomyès
answered. "Gentlemen, it is time to surprise the ladies.
Pray wait for us a moment."

"It begins with a kiss," said Blachevelle.

"On the forehead," Tholomyès added.

Each solemnly kissed the forehead of his mistress ; then
they proceeded to the door in Indian file, with a finger
on their lip. Favorite clapped her hands as they went out.

"It is amusing already," she said.

" Do not be long," Fantine murmured ; " we are waiting for you."

The girls, when left alone, leant out of the windows, two by two, talking, looking out, and wondering. They watched the young men leave the Bombarda cabaret arm-in-arm ; they turned round, made laughing signs, and disappeared in that dusty Sunday mob which once a week invaded the Champs Elysées.

" Do not be long," Fantine cried.

" What will they bring us ? " said Zephine.

" I am certain it will be pretty," said Dahlia.

" For my part," Favorite added, " I hope it will be set in gold."

They were soon distracted by the movement on the quay, which they could notice through the branches of the lofty trees, and which greatly amused them. It was the hour for the mail-carts and stages to start, and nearly all those bound for the south and west at that time passed through the Champs Elysées. Every moment some heavy vehicle, painted yellow and black, heavily loaded, and rendered shapeless by trunks and valises, dashed through the crowd with the sparks of a forge, the dust representing the smoke. This confusion amused the girls.

One of these vehicles, which could hardly be distinguished through the branches, stopped for a mement, and then started again at a gallop. This surprised Fantine.

" That is strange," she said ; " I fancied that the diligences never stopped."

Favorite shrugged her shoulders.

" This Fantine is really amazing, and is surprised at the simplest things. Let us suppose that I am a traveller and say to the guard of the stage-coach, ' I will walk on and you can pick me up on the quay as you pass.' The coach passes, sees me, stops and takes me in. That is done every day ; you are ignorant of life, my dear."

Some time elapsed ; all at once Favorite started as if waking from sleep.

" Well," she said, " where is the surprise ? "

" Oh yes," Dahlia continued, " the famous surprise.'

" They are a long time," said Fantine.

Just as Fantine had ended this sigh, the waiter who had served the dinner came in ; he held in his hand something that resembled a letter.

" What is that ? " Favorite asked.

The waiter answered :

"It is a paper which the gentlemen left for you, ladies."

"Why did you not bring it to us at once?"

"Because the gentlemen," the waiter went on, "ordered that it should not be delivered to you for an hour."

Favorite snatched the paper from the waiter's hands. It was really a letter.

"Stay," she said, "there is no address, but the following words are written on it: THIS IS THE SURPRISE." She quickly opened the letter and read (she could read):

"Well-beloved!

"Know that we have relatives: perhaps you are not perfectly cognisant what they are; it means fathers and mothers in the civil, puerile, and honest code. Well, these relatives are groaning; these old people claim us as their own; these worthy men and women call us prodigal sons. They desire our return home, and offer to kill the fatted calf. We obey them, as we are virtuous; at the hour when you read this, five impetuous steeds will be conveying us back to our papas and mammas. We are going, to quote the language of Bossuet; we are going, gone. We are flying away in the arms of Laffitte and on the wings of Caillard. The Toulouse coach is dragging us away from the abyss, and that abyss is yourselves, pretty dears. We are re-entering society, duty, and order at a sharp trot, and at the rate of nine miles an hour. It is important for our country that we should become, like everybody else, Prefects, fathers of a family, gamekeepers, and Councillors of State. Revere us, for we are sacrificing ourselves. Dry up your tears for us rapidly, and get a substitute speedily. If this letter lacerates your hearts, treat it in the same fashion. Good-bye. For nearly two years we rendered you happy, so do not owe us any grudge.

"(Signed)   Blachevelle.
Fameuil.
Listolier.
Felix Tholomyès.

"P.S.—The dinner is paid for."

The four girls looked at each other, and Favorite was the first to break the silence.

"I don't care," she said, "it is a capital joke."

"It is very funny," Zephine remarked.

"It must have been Blachevelle who had that idea," Favorite continued; "it makes me in love with him. As soon as he has left me I am beginning to grow fond of him ; the old story."

"No," said Dahlia, "that is an idea of Tholomyès. That can be easily seen."

"In that case," Favorite retorted; "down with Blachevelle and long live Tholomyès !"

And they burst into a laugh, in which Fantine joined ; an hour later, though, when she returned to her bedroom, she burst into tears : he was, as we have said, her first love ; she had yielded to Tholomyès as to a husband, and the poor girl had a child.

CHAPTER XX.

THERE was, in the first quarter of this century, a sort of pot-house at Montfermeil, near Paris, which no longer exists. It was kept by a couple of the name of Thénardier, and was situated in the Rue du Boulanger. Over the door a board was nailed to the wall, and on this board was painted something resembling a man carrying on his back another man, who wore large gilt general's epaulettes with silver stars ; red dabs represented blood, and the rest of the painting was smoke, probably representing a battle. At the bottom could be read the inscription : THE SERGEANT OF WATERLOO.

Though nothing is more common than a cart at a pot-house door, the vehicle, or rather fragment of a vehicle, which blocked up the street in front of the Sergeant of Waterloo, one spring evening in 1818, would have certainly attracted the attention of any painter who had passed that way. It was the fore part of one of those wains used in wood countries for dragging planks and trunks of trees ; it was composed of a massive iron axle-tree, in which a heavy pole was embedded and supported by two enormous wheels. The whole thing was sturdy, crushing, and ugly, and it might have passed for the carriage of a monster gun. The ruts had given the wheels, felloes, spokes, axle-tree, and pole, a coating of mud, a hideous yellow plaster, much like that with which cathedrals are so often adorned. The woodwork was hidden by mud and the iron by rust. Under the axle-tree was festooned a heavy chain, suited for a convict Goliath. This chain made you think, not of the wood it was intended to secure, but of the mastodons and mammoths for which it would have served as harness; it had the air of a cyclopean and superhuman galleys, and seemed removed from some monster. Homer would have bound Polyphemus with it, and Shakespeare, Caliban.

Why was this thing at this place in the street? First, to block it up; secondly, to finish the rusting process. There is in the old social order, a multitude of institutions which may be found in the same way in the open air, and which have no other reasons for being there. The centre of the chain hung rather close to the ground, and on the curve, as on the rope of a swing, two little girls were seated on this evening, in an exquisite embrace, one about two years and a half, the other eighteen months; the younger being in the arms of the elder. An artfully tied handkerchief prevented them from falling, for a mother had seen this frightful chain, and said, "What a famous plaything for my children!" The two children, who were prettily dressed and with some taste, were radiant; they looked like two roses among old iron; their eyes were a triumph, their healthy cheeks laughed; one was a rosy blonde, the other was a brunette; their innocent faces had a look of surprise; a flowering shrub a little distance off sent to passers-by a perfume which seemed to come from them; and the younger displayed her nudity with the chaste indecency of childhood. Above and around their two delicate heads, moulded in happiness and bathed in light, the gigantic wain, black with rust, almost terrible, and bristling with curves and savage angles, formed the porch of a cavern, as it were. A few yards off, and seated in the inn door, the mother, a woman of no very pleasing appearance, but touching at this moment, was swinging the children by the help of a long cord, and devouring them with her eyes, for fear of an accident, with that animal and heavenly expression peculiar to maternity. At each oscillation the hideous links produced a sharp sound, resembling a cry of anger. The little girls were delighted; the setting sun mingled with the joy, and nothing could be so charming as this caprice of accident which had made of a Titanic chain a cherub's swing. While playing with her little ones, the mother sang, terribly out of tune, a romance, very celebrated at that day:

" Il le faut, disait un guerrier."

Her song and contemplation of her daughters prevented

her hearing and seeing what took place in the street. Some one, however, had approached her, as she began the first couplet of the romance, and suddenly she heard a voice saying close to her ear :

" You have two pretty children, Madame."

" A la belle et tendre Imogène,"

the mother answered, continuing her song, and then turned her head. A woman was standing a few paces from her, who also had a child, which she was carrying in her arms. She also carried a heavy bag. This woman's child was one of the most divine creatures possible to behold ; she was a girl between two and three years of age, and could have vied with the two other little ones in the coquettishness of her dress. She had on a hood of fine linen, ribbons at her shoulders, and Valenciennes lace in her cap. Her raised petticoats displayed her white, dimpled, fine thigh ; it was admirably pink and healthy ; and her cheeks made one long to bite them. Nothing could be said of her eyes, except that they were very large, and that she had magnificent lashes, for she was asleep. She was sleeping with the absolute confidence peculiar to her age ; a mother's arms are made of tenderness, and children sleep soundly in them. As for the mother, she looked grave and sorrowful, and was dressed like a workgirl who was trying to become a countrywoman again. She was young ; was she pretty ? perhaps so ; but in this dress she did not appear so. Her hair, a light lock of which peeped out, seemed very thick, but was completely hidden beneath a nun's hood ; ugly, tight, and fastened under her chin. Laughter displays fine teeth, when a person happens to possess them ; but she did not laugh. Her eyes looked as if they had not been dry for a long time ; she had a fatigued and rather sickly air, and she looked at the child sleeping in her arms in the manner peculiar to a mother who has suckled her babe. A large blue handkerchief, like those served out to the invalids, folded like a shawl, clumsily hid her shape. Her hands were rough and covered with red spots, and her forefinger was hardened and torn by the needle. She had on a brown cloth cloak, a cotton gown, and heavy shoes. It was Fantine.

It was difficult to recognise her, but, after an attentive examination, she still possessed her beauty. As for her toilette—that airy toilette of muslin and ribbons which seemed made of gaiety, folly, and music, to be full of bells,

and perfumed with lilacs—it had faded away like the
dazzling hoar-frost which looks like diamonds in the sun ;
it melts, and leaves the branch quite black.

Ten months had elapsed since the "good joke." What
had taken place during these ten months? we can guess.
After desertion, want. Fantine at once lost sight of Favorite,
Zephine, and Dahlia, for this tie broken on the side of the
men separated the women. They would have been greatly
surprised a fortnight after had they been told that they
were friends, for there was no reason for it. Fantine remained alone when the father of her child had gone away
—alas ! such ruptures are irrevocable. She found herself
absolutely isolated ; she had lost her habit of working, and
had gained a taste for pleasure. Led away by her liaison
with Tholomyès to despise the little trade she knew, she
had neglected her connection, and it was lost. She had no
resource. Fantine could hardly read, and could not write ;
she had been merely taught in childhood to sign her name,
and she had sent a letter to Tholomyès, then a second, then
a third, through a public writer, but Tholomyès did not
answer one of them. One day Fantine heard the gossips
say, while looking at her daughter, "Children like that are
not regarded seriously ; people shrug their shoulders at
them." Then she thought of Tholomyès, who shrugged
his shoulders at her child, and did not regard the innocent
creature seriously, and her heart turned away from this
man. What was she to do now? She knew not where to
turn. She had committed a fault, but the foundation of
her nature, we must remember, was modesty and virtue.
She felt vaguely that she was on the eve of falling into
distress, and gliding into worse. She needed courage, and
she had it. The idea occurred to her of returning to her
native town M—— sur M——. There some one might
know her, and give her work ; but she must hide her fault.
And she vaguely glimpsed at the possible necessity of a
separation more painful still than the first ; her heart was
contracted, but she formed her resolution. Fantine, as we
shall see, possessed the stern bravery of life. She had
already valiantly given up dress ; she dressed in calico, and
had put all her silk ribbons and laces upon her daughter.
the only vanity left her, and it was a holy one. She sold
all she possessed, which brought her in 200 francs ; and
when she had paid her little debts, she had only about
80 francs left. At the age of two-and-twenty, on a fine

spring morning, she left Paris, carrying her child on her
back. Any one who had seen them pass would have felt
pity for them ; the woman had nothing in the world but her
child, and the child nothing but her mother in the world.
Fantine had suckled her child ; this had weakened her chest,
and she was coughing a little.

We shall have no further occasion to speak of M. Felix
Tholomyès. We will merely say that twenty years later,
in the reign of Louis Philippe, he was a stout country
lawyer, influential and rich, a sensible elector, and a very
strict juror, but always a man of pleasure.

About midday, after resting herself now and then by
travelling from time to time, at the rate of three or four
leagues an hour, in what were then called the "little
vehicles of the suburbs of Paris," Fantine found herself at
Montfermeil. As she passed the Sergeant of Waterloo, the
two little girls in their monster swing had dazzled her, and she
stopped before this vision of joy. There are charms in life,
and these two little girls were one for this mother. She
looked at them with great emotion, for the presence of angels
is an announcement of Paradise. These two little creatures
were evidently happy ! She looked then, and admired them
with such tenderness, that at the moment when the mother was
drawing breath between two verses of her song, she could not
refrain from saying to her what we have already recorded :

"You have two pretty children, Madame."

The most ferocious creatures are disarmed by a caress
given to their little ones. The mother raised her head,
thanked her, and made the stranger sit down on the door
bench. The two women began talking.

"My name is Madame Thénardier," the mother of the
little ones said ; "we keep this inn."

Then returning to her romance, she went on humming :

> "Il le faut, je suis chevalier,
> Et je pars pour la Palestine."

This Madame Thénardier was a red-headed, thin, angular
woman, the soldier's wife in all its ugliness, and, strange
to say, with a languishing air which she owed to reading
romances. She was a finikin woman, for old romances, by
working on the imaginations of landladies, produce that
effect. She was still young, scarcely thirty. If this
woman, now sitting, had been standing up, perhaps her
height and colossal proportions, fitting for a show, would

have at once startled the traveller, destroyed her confidence, and prevented what we have to record. A person sitting instead of standing up—destinies hang on this.

The woman told her story with some modification. She was a workgirl ; her husband was dead ; she could get no work in Paris, and was going to seek it elsewhere, in her native town. She had left Paris that very morning on foot ; as she felt tired from carrying her child, she had travelled by the stage-coach to Villemomble ; from that place she walked to Montfermeil. The little one had walked a little, but not much, for she was so young, and so she had been obliged to carry her, and the darling had gone to sleep—and as she said this she gave her daughter a passionate kiss, which awoke her. The babe opened her eyes, large blue eyes like her mother's, and gazed at what ? Nothing, everything, with that serious and at times stern air of infants, which is a mystery of their luminous innocence in the presence of our twilight virtues. We might say that they feel themselves to be angels, and know us to be men. Then the child began laughing, and, though its mother had to check it, slipped down to the ground with the undaunted energy of a little creature wishing to run. All at once she noticed the other two children in their swing, stopped short, and put out her tongue as a sign of admiration. Mother Thénardier unfastened her children, took them out of the swing, and said :

" Play about all three."

Such ages soon grow tame, and in a minute the little Thénardiers were playing with the new-comer at making holes in the ground, which was an immense pleasure. The stranger child was very merry ; the goodness of the mother is written in the gaiety of the baby. She had picked up a piece of wood which she used as a spade, and was energetically digging a grave large enough for a fly. The two went on talking.

" What's the name of your bantling ? "

" Cosette."

For Cosette read Euphrasie, for that was the child's real name, but the mother had converted Euphrasie into Cosette, through that gentle, graceful instinct peculiar to mothers and the people, which changes Josefa into Pepita, and Françoise into Sellette. It is a species of derivation which deranges and disconcerts the entire science of etymologists. We know a grandmother who contrived to make out of Theodore, Gnon,

"What is her age?"

"Going on for three."

"Just the same age as my eldest."

Meanwhile the children were grouped in a posture of profound anxiety and blessedness; an event had occurred. A large worm crept out of the ground, and they were frightened, and were in ecstasy; their radiant brows touched each other, and they looked like three heads in a halo.

"How soon children get to know one another," mother Thénardier exclaimed. "Why, one would take them for three sisters."

The word was probably the spark which the other mother had been waiting for. She seized the speaker's hand, looked at her fixedly, and said:

"Will you keep my child for me?"

Madame Thénardier gave one of those starts of surprise which are neither assent nor refusal. Cosette's mother continued:

"You see, I cannot take the child with me into the country, for when a woman has a baby, it is a hard matter for her to get a situation. People are so foolish in our part. It was Heaven who made me pass in front of your inn; when I saw your little ones so pretty, so clean, so happy, it gave me a turn. I said to myself, 'She is a kind mother.' It is so; they will be three sisters. Then I shall not be long before I come back. Will you take care of my child?"

"We will see," said mother Thénardier.

"I would give six francs a month."

Here a man's voice cried from the back of the tap-room:

"Not less than seven francs, and six months paid in advance."

"Six times seven are forty-two," said the landlady.

"I will give it," said the mother.

"And fifteen francs in addition for extra expenses," the man's voice added.

"Total fifty-seven francs," said Madame Thénardier.

"I will give it," the mother said; "I have eighty francs, and shall have enough left to get home on foot. I shall earn money there, and as soon as I have a little I will come and fetch my darling."

The man's voice continued:

"Has the little one a stock of clothing?"

"It is my husband," said mother Thénardier.

"Certainly she has clothes, poor little treasure. I saw it was your husband. And a fine stock of clothes too, a wonderful stock, a dozen of everything, and silk frocks like a lady. They are in my bag."

"They must be handed over," the man's voice put in.

"Of course they must," said the mother; "it would be funny if I left my child naked."

The master's face appeared.

"It is all right," he said.

The bargain was concluded. The mother passed the night at the inn, paid her money and left her child, fastened up her bag, which was now light, and started the next morning with the intention of returning soon. Such departures are arranged calmly, but they entail despair. A neighbour's wife saw the mother going away, and went home saying:

"I have just seen a woman crying in the street as if her heart would break."

When Cosette's mother had gone, the man said to his wife:

"That money will meet my bill for one hundred and ten francs, which falls due to-morrow, and I was fifty francs short. It would have been protested, and I should have had a bailiff put in. You set a famous mouse-trap with your brats."

"Without knowing it," said the woman.

CHAPTER XXI.

THE captured mouse was very puny, but the cat is pleased even with a thin mouse. Who were the Thénardiers? We will say one word about them for the present, and complete the sketch hereafter. These beings belonged to the bastard class, composed of coarse parvenus, and of degraded people of intellect, which stands between the classes called the middle and the lower, and combines some of the faults of the second with nearly all the vices of the first, though without possessing the generous impulse of the working man or the respectability of the tradesman.

They were of those dwarfish natures which easily become monstrous, when any gloomy fire accidentally warms them. There was in the woman the basis of a witch, in the man the stuff for a beggar. Both were in the highest degree susceptible to that sort of hideous progress which is made in the direction of evil. There are crab-like souls which constantly recoil toward darkness, retrograde in life rather than advance, employ experience to augment their deformity, incessantly grow worse, and grow more and more covered with an increasing blackness. This man and this woman had souls of this sort.

The man especially would have been peculiarly trouble-some to the physiognomist. There are some men whom you need only look at to distrust them, for they are restless behind and threatening in front. We can no more answer for what they have done than for what they will do. The shadow they have in their glance denounces them. Merely by hearing them say a word or seeing them make a gesture, we get a glimpse of dark secrets in their past, dark mysteries in their future. This Thénardier, could he be believed, had been a sold.er—sergeant, he said ; he had probably gone through the campaign of 1815, and had even behaved rather bravely, as it seems. We shall see presently how the matter really stood. The sign of his inn was an allusion to one of his exploits, and he had painted it himself, for he could do a little of everything—badly. It was the epoch when the old classical romance was inflaming the loving soul of the porters' wives in Paris, and even extended its ravages into the suburbs. Madame Thénardier was just intelligent enough to read books of this nature, and lived on them. She thus drowned any brains she possessed, and, so long as she remained young and a little beyond, it gave her a sort of pensive attitude by the side of her husband, who was a scamp of some depth, an almost grammatical ruffian, coarse and delicate at the same time, but who, in matters of sentimentalism, read Pigault Lebrun, and, "in all that concerned the sex," as he said in his jargon, was a correct and unmingled dolt. His wife was some twelve or fifteen years younger than he, and when her romantically flowing locks began to grow gray, she was only a stout, wicked woman, who had been pampered with foolish romances. As such absurdities cannot be read with impunity, the result was that her eldest daughter was christened Eponine ; as for the younger, the poor girl was all but named Gulnare, and owed to a fortunate diversion made by a romance of Ducray Duminil's, the mitigation of Azelma.

To be bad does not ensure prosperity ; and the pot-house was a failure. Thanks to the fifty-seven francs, Thénardier had been able to avoid a protest, and honour his signature ; but the next month they wanted money again, and his wife took to Paris and pledged Cosette's outfit for sixty francs. As soon as this sum was spent, the Thénardiers grew accustomed to see in the little girl a child they had taken in through charity, and treated her accordingly. As she had no clothes, she was dressed in the left-off chemises and petticoats of the little Thénardiers, that is to say, in rags. She was fed on the leavings of everybody, a little better than the dog, and a little worse than the cat. Dog and cat were her usual company at dinner: for Cosette ate with them under the table off a wooden dish like theirs.

Her mother, who had settled, as we shall see hereafter, at M—— sur M——, wrote, or, to speak more correctly, had letters written every month to inquire after her child. The Thénardiers invariably replied that Cosette was getting on famously. When the first six months had passed, the mother sent seven francs for the seventh month, and continued to send the money punctually month by month. The year was not ended before Thénardier said, "A fine thing that ! what does she expect us to do with seven francs ! " and he wrote to demand twelve. The mother, whom they persuaded that her child was happy and healthy, submitted, and sent the twelve francs.

There are certain natures that cannot love on one side without hating on the other. Mother Thénardier passionately loved her own two daughters, which made her detest the stranger. It is sad to think that a mother's love can look so ugly. Though Cosette occupied so little room, it seemed to her as if her children were robbed of it, and that the little one diminished the air her daughters breathed. This woman, like many women of her class, had a certain amount of caresses and another of blows and insults to expend daily. If she had not had Cosette, it is certain that her daughters, though they were idolised, would have received the entire amount, but the strange child did the service of diverting the blows on herself, while the daughters only received the caresses. Cosette did not make a movement that did not bring down on her head a hail-storm of violent and unmerited chastisement. The poor weak child, unnecessarily punished, scolded, cuffed, and beaten, saw by her side two little creatures like herself who lived in perfect happiness.

As their mother was unkind to Cosette, Eponine and

Azelma were the same ; for children, at that age, are good copyists.   A year passed, then another, and people said in the village :

"Those Thénardiers are worthy people.   They are not well off, and yet they bring up a poor child left on their hands."

Cosette was supposed to be deserted by her mother. Thénardier, however, having learnt in some obscure way that the child was probably illegitimate, and that the mother could not confess it, insisted on 15 francs a month, saying that the creature was growing and eating, and threatening to send her back.   "She must not play the fool with me," he shouted, "or I'll let her brat fall like a bomb-shell into her hiding-place.   I must have an increase."   The mother paid the 15 francs.   Year by year the child grew, and so did her wretchedness : so long as Cosette was little, she was the scapegoat of the two other children ; as soon as she began to be developed a little, that is to say, even before she was five years old, she became the servant of the house.   At five years, the reader will say, that is improbable, but, alas ! it is true.   Social suffering begins at any age.   Cosette was made to go messages, sweep the rooms, the yard, the street, wash the dishes, and even carry heavy bundles.   The Thénardiers considered themselves the more justified in acting thus, because the mother, who was still at M—— sur M——, was beginning to pay badly, and was several months in arrear.

Had the mother returned to Montfermeil at the end of three years, she would not have recognised her child. Cosette, so pretty and ruddy on her arrival in this house, was now thin and sickly.   She had a timid look about her.   "It's cunning !" said the Thénardiers.   Injustice had made her sulky, and wretchedness had made her ugly. Nothing was left her but her fine eyes, which were painful to look at, because, as they were so large, it seemed as if a greater amount of sadness was visible in them.   It was a heart-rending sight to see this poor child, scarce six years of age, shivering in winter under her calico rags, and sweeping the street before daybreak, with an enormous broom in her small red hands and tears in her large eyes.

The people of the place called her " the lark."   The lower classes, who are fond of metaphors, had given the name to the poor little creature, who was no larger than a bird,

trembling, frightened, and starting, who was always the
first awake in the house and the village, and ever in the
street or the fields by daybreak. Only this poor lark did
not sing.

CHAPTER XXII.

In the meanwhile, what had become of the mother, who,
according to the people of Montfermeil, appeared to have
deserted her child. Where was she? What was she doing?
After leaving her little Cosette with the Thénardiers, she
had continued her journey and arrivèd at M—— sur M——.
Fantine had been away from her province for ten years,
and while she had been slowly descending from misery to
misery, her native town had prospered. About two years
before, one of those industrial facts which are the events of
small towns had taken place. The details are important,
and we think it useful to emphasise them.

From time immemorial, the special occupation of the
inhabitants of M—— sur M—— had been the imitation of
English jet and German black beads. This trade had hitherto only vegetated, owing to the dearness of the material,
which reacted on the artisan. At the moment when Fantine
returned to M—— sur M—— an extraordinary transformation had taken place in the production of "black articles."
Toward the close of 1815, a man, a stranger, had settled in
the town, and had the idea of substituting in this trade gum
lac for resin, and, in bracelets particularly, scraps of bent plate
for welded plate. This slight change effected a revolution.
It prodigiously reduced the cost of the material, which, in
the first place, allowed the wages to be raised, a benefit for
the town; secondly, improved the manufacture, an advantage for the consumer; and, thirdly, allowed the goods
to be sold cheap, even while producing three times the
profit, an advantage for the manufacturer.

In less than three years the inventor of the process had
become rich, which is a good thing, and had made all rich
about him, which is better. He was a stranger in the
department; no one knew anything about his origin, and
but little about his start. It was said that he had entered
the town with but very little money, a few hundred francs
at the most; but with this small capital, placed at the
service of an ingenious idea, and fertilised by regularity and
thought, he made his own fortune and that of the town.

On his arrival at M—— surM—— he had the dress, manne rs, and language of a working man. It appears that on the very December night when he obscurely entered M—— sur M—— with his knapsack on his back, and a knotted stick in his hand, a great fire broke out in the Town Hall. This man rushed into the midst of the flames, and at the risk of his life saved two children who happened to belong to the captain of gendarmes ; hence no one dreamed of asking for his passport. On this occasion his name was learned ; he called himself Father Madeleine. He was a man of about fifty, with a preoccupied air, and he was good-hearted. That was all that could be said about him.

Thanks to the rapid progress of this manufacture which he had so admirably remodelled, M—— sur M—— had become a place of considerable trade. Spain, which consumes an immense amount of jet, gave large orders for it annually, and in this trade M—— sur M—— almost rivalled London and Berlin. Father Madeleine's profits were so great, that after the second year he was able to build a large factory, in which were two spacious workshops, one for men, the other for women. Any one who was hungry need only to come, and was sure to find there employment and bread. Father Madeleine expected from the men goodwill, from the women purity, and from all probity. He had divided the workshops in order to separate the sexes, and enable the women and girls to remain virtuous. On this point he was inflexible, and it was the only one in which he was at all intolerant. This sternness was the more justifiable because M—— sur M—— was a garrison town, and opportunities for corruption abounded. Altogether his arrival had been a benefit, and his presence was a providence. Before Father Madeleine came everything was languishing, and now all led the healthy life of work. A powerful circulation warmed and penetrated everything ; stagnation and wretchedness were unknown. There was not a pocket, however obscure, in which there was not a little money, nor a lodging so poor in which there was not a little joy.

As we have said, in the midst of this activity, of which he was the cause and the pivot, Father Madeleine made his fortune, but, singularly enough in a plain man of business, this did not appear to be his chief care ; he seemed to think a great deal of others and but little of himself. In 1820, he was known to have a sum of 630,000 francs in Laffitte's bank ; but before he put that amount on one side he had

spent more than a million for the town and the poor. The
hospital was badly endowed, and he added ten beds. M——
sur M—— is divided into an upper and a lower town; the
latter, in which he lived, had only one school, a poor
tenement falling in ruins, and he built two, one for boys
and one for girls. He paid the two teachers double the
amount of their poor official salary, and to some one who
expressed surprise, he said, "The two first functionaries of
the State are the nurse and the schoolmaster." He had
established at his own charge an hospice, a thing at that
time almost unknown in France, and a charitable fund for
old and infirm workmen. As his factory was a centre, a
new district, in which there was a large number of indigent
families, rapidly sprang up around it, and he opened there
a pharmacy that was free to all.

At first kind souls said, "He is a man who wants to
grow rich:" when it was seen that he enriched the town
before enriching himself, the same charitable souls said,
"He is ambitious." This seemed the more likely because
he was religious, and even practised to a certain extent a
line which was admired in those days. He went regularly
to hear Low Mass on Sundays, and the local deputy, who
scented rivalry everywhere, soon became alarmed about this
religion. This deputy, who had been a member of the
legislative council of the Empire, shared the religious ideas
of a Father of the Oratory, known by the name of Fouché,
Duc d'Otranto, whose creature and friend he had been.
But when he saw the rich manufacturer Madeleine go to
seven o'clock Low Mass, he scented a possible candidate,
and resolved to go beyond him; he chose a Jesuit confessor,
and went to High Mass and vespers. Ambition at that
time was, in the true sense of the term, a steeplechase.
The poor profited by the alarm of the honourable deputy.
for he also endowed two beds at the hospital, which made
twelve.

At length, in 1819, the report spread one morning through
the town that, on the recommendation of the Prefect, and
in consideration of services rendered the town, Father
Madeleine was about to be nominated by the King, Mayor of
M——. Those who had declared the new-comer an ambitious
man, eagerly seized this opportunity to exclaim: "Did we
not say so?" All M—— was in an uproar; for the rumour
was well founded. A few days after, the appointment
appeared in the *Moniteur*, and the next day Father Madeleine

declined the honour. In the same year, the new processes worked by him were shown at the Industrial Exhibition; and on the report of the jury, the King made the inventor a Chevalier of the Legion of Honour. There was a fresh commotion in the little town. "Well, it was the cross he wanted;" but Father Madeleine declined the cross. Decidedly the man was an enigma, but charitable souls got out of the difficulty by saying, "After all, he is a sort of adventurer."

As we have seen, the country owed him a great deal, and the poor owed him everything; he was so useful that he could not help being honoured, and so gentle that people could not help loving him; his work-people especially adored him, and he bore this adoration with a sort of melancholy gravity. When he was known to be rich, "people in society" bowed to him, and he was called in the town Monsieur Madeleine; but his workmen and the children continued to call him Father Madeleine, and this caused him his happiest smile. In proportion as he ascended, invitations showered upon him; and society claimed him as its own. The little formal drawing-rooms, which had of course been at first closed to the artisan, opened their doors wide to the millionaire. A thousand advances were made to him, but he refused. This time again charitable souls were at no loss. "He is an ignorant man, and of poor education. No one knows where he comes from. He could not pass muster in society, and it is doubtful whether he can read." When he was seen to be earning money, they said, "He is a tradesman;" when he scattered his money, they said, "He is ambitious;" when he rejected honour, they said, "He is an adventurer;" and when he repulsed the fashionable, they said, "He is a brute."

In 1820, five years after his arrival at M——, the services he had rendered the town were so brilliant, the will of the whole country was so unanimous, that the King again nominated him mayor of the town. He refused again, but the Prefect would not accept his refusal; all the notables came to beg, the people supplicated him in the open streets, and the pressure was so great, that he eventually assented. It was noticed that what appeared specially to determine him was the almost angry remark of an old woman, who cried to him from her door: "A good mayor is useful; a man should not recoil before the good he might do."

Father Madeleine remained as unaffected as he had been at the first. He had gray hair, a serious eye, the bronzed

face of a working man, and the thoughtful face of a philosopher.   He habitually wore a broad-brimmed hat, and a
long coat of coarse cloth, buttoned up to the chin.   He
performed his duties as Mayor, but beyond that lived solitary.
He spoke to few persons, liked to escape from compliments,
smiled to save himself from laughing, and gave to save
himself from smiling.   The women said of him, " What a
fine bear ! " and his great pleasure was to walk about the
fields.   He always took his meals with an open book before
him, and he had a well-selected library.   He was fond of
books, for they are cool and sure friends.   In proportion as
leisure came with fortune, he seemed to employ it in culti-
vating his mind : it was noticed that with each year he spent
in M—— his language became more polite, choice, and gentle.

In his walks, he would often take a gun with him, but
rarely fired ; when he did so by accident, he had an infallible
aim, which was almost terrific.   He never killed an inoffensive animal or a small bird.   Though he was no longer
young, he was said to possess prodigious strength : he lent
a hand to any one who needed it, raised a fallen horse, put
his shoulder to a wheel stuck in the mud, or stopped a run-
away bull by the horns.   His pockets were always full of
halfpence when he went out, and empty when he came
home ; whenever he passed through a village, the ragged
children ran merrily after him, and surrounded him like a
swarm of gnats.   It was supposed that he must have
formerly lived a rustic life, for he had all sorts of useful
secrets which he taught the peasants.   He showed them
how to destroy blight in wheat by sprinkling the granary
and pouring into the cracks of the boards a solution of
common salt, and to get rid of weevils by hanging up
everywhere, on the walls and roofs, flowering orviot.   He
had recipes to extirpate from arable land, tares and other
parasitic plants which injure wheat.

One day he saw some countrymen very busy in tearing
up nettles ; he looked at the pile of uprooted and already
withered plants and said, " They are dead, and yet they are
good if you know how to use them.   When nettles are
young, the tops are an excellent vegetable.   When they are
old, they have threads and fibre like hemp and flax.   When
chopped up, nettles are good for fowls ; when pounded,
excellent for horned cattle.   Nettle-seed mixed with the
food renders the coats of cattle shining, and the root mixed
with salt produces a fine yellow colour.   The nettle is also

excellent hay, which can be mown twice ; and what does it require ? A little earth, no care, and no cultivation. The only thing is that the seed falls as it ripens, and is difficult to garner. If a little care were taken, the nettle would be useful ; but, being neglected, it becomes injurious, and is then killed. Here men resemble nettles !" He added, after a moment's silence : "My friends, remember this,—there are no bad herbs and no bad men ; there are only bad cultivators."

The children loved him yet more, because he could make them pretty little toys of straw and cocoa-nut shells. When he saw a church door hung with black, he went in ; he went after a funeral as other persons do after a christening. The misfortunes of others attracted him, owing to his great gentleness ; he mingled with friends in mourning, and with the priests round a coffin. He seemed to be fond of hearing those mournful psalms which are full of the vision of another world. With his eye fixed on heaven, he listened, with a species of aspiration toward all the mysteries of Infinitude, to the sad voice singing on the brink of the obscure abyss of death. He did a number of good actions, he was careful to hide them as if they were bad. He would quietly at night enter houses, and furtively ascend the stairs. A poor fellow, on returning to his garret, would find that his door had been opened, at times forced, during his absence ; the man would cry that a robber had been there, but when he entered, the first thing he saw was a gold coin left on the table. The "thief" who had been there was Father Madeleine.

He was affable and sad. It was said, "There is a rich man who does not look proud ; a lucky man who does not look happy." Some persons asserted that he was a mysterious character, and declared that no one ever entered his bedroom, which was a real anchorite's cell, furnished with winged hour-glasses and embellished with cross-bones and death's-heads. This was so often repeated that some elegant and spiteful ladies of M—— came to him one day, and said, "Monsieur le Maire, *do* show us your bedroom, for people say that it is a grotto." He smiled and led them straightway to the "grotto"; they were terribly punished for their curiosity, as it was a bedroom, merely containing mahogany furniture as ugly as all furniture of that sort is, and hung with a paper at sixpence the piece. They could not notice anything but two double-branched candlesticks of an antiquated pattern, standing on the mantelpiece, and seemed to be silver. People did not the less continue to repeat, however, that no one ever entered this bedroom, and that it was a hermitage, a hole, a tomb. They also whispered that he had immense sums lodged with Laffitte, and with this peculiarity that things were always at his immediate disposal, "so that," they added, "M. Madeleine could go any morning to Laffitte's, sign a receipt, and carry off his two or three millions of francs in ten minutes." In reality, these "two or three millions" were reduced, as we have said, to six hundred and thirty or forty thousand francs.

Near the beginning of 1821, the papers announced the death of M. Myriel, Bishop of D——, "surnamed Monseigneur Welcome," and who died in the odour of sanctity at the age of eighty-two. The Bishop of D——, to add here a detail omitted by the oapers, had been blind for several years, and was content to be blind, his sister being with him.

The announcement of his death was copied by the local paper of M——, and on the next day Monsieur Madeleine appeared dressed in black, with crape on his hat. The mourning was noticed in the town, and people gossiped about it, for it seemed to throw a gleam over M. Madeleine's origin. It was concluded that he was somehow connected with the Bishop. "He is in mourning for the Bishop," was said in drawing-rooms; this added inches to M. Madeleine's stature, and suddenly gave him a certain consideration in the noble world of M——. The microscopic Faubourg St. Germain of the town thought about raising the quarantine of M. Madeleine, the probable relation of a bishop, and M. Madeleine remarked the promotion he had obtained in the increased love of the old ladies, and the greater amount of smiles from the young. One evening a lady belonging to this little great world, curious by right of seniority, ventured to say, "M. le Maire is doubtless a relation of the late Bishop of D——?"

He said, "No, Madame."

"But," the Dowager went on, "you wear mourning for him."

"In my youth I was a servant in his family," was the answer.

It was also remarked that when a young Savoyard passed through the town, looking for chimneys to sweep, the Mayor sent for him, asked his name, and gave him money. The Savoyard boys told each other of this, and a great many passed that way.

CHAPTER XXIII.

By degrees and with time all the opposition ceased. At first there had been calumnies against M. Madeleine— a species of law which all rising men undergo ; then it was only backbiting ; then it was only malice ; and eventually all this faded away. The respect felt for him was complete, unanimous, and cordial, and the moment arrived in 1821 when the name of the Mayor was uttered at M—— with nearly the same accent as "Monseigneur the Bishop" had been said at D—— in 1815. People came for ten leagues round to consult M. Madeleine ; he settled disputes, prevented lawsuits, and reconciled enemies. Everybody was willing to accept him as arbiter, and it seemed as if he had the book of natural law for his soul. It was a sort of contagious veneration, which in six or seven years spread all over the whole country.

One man alone in the town and neighbourhood resisted this contagion, and whatever M. Madeleine might do, remained rebellious to it, as if a sort of incorruptible and imperturbable instinct kept him on his guard. It would appear, in fact, as if there is in certain men a veritable bestial instinct, though pure and honest as all instincts are, which creates sympathies and antipathies ; which fatally separates one nature from another ; which never hesitates ; which is not troubled, is never silent, and never contradicts itself ; which is clear in its obscurity, infallible, imperious ; refractory to all the counsels of intelligence and all the solvents of the reason, and which, whatever the way in which destinies are made, surely warns the man-dog of the man-cat, and the man-fox of the presence of the man-lion. It often happened when M. Madeleine passed along a street, calmly, kindly, and greeted by the blessings of all, that a tall man, dressed in an iron-gray greatcoat, armed with a thick cane, and wearing a hat with turned-down brim, turned suddenly and looked after him till he disappeared ; folding his arms, shaking his head, and raising his upper lip with the lower as high as his nose, a sort of significant grimace which may be translated : "Who is that man ? I am sure that I have seen him somewhere. At any rate, I at least am not his dupe."

This personage, who was grave, with an almost menacing gravity, was one of those men who, though only noticed for a moment, preoccupy the observer. His name was Javert, and he belonged to the police, and performed at M—— the laborious but useful duties of an inspector. He had not seen Madeleine's beginning, for he was indebted for the post he occupied to the Secretary of Count Anglé, at that time Prefect of Police at Paris. When Javert arrived at M——, the great manufacturer's fortune was made, and Father Madeleine had become Monsieur Madeleine. Some police-officers have a peculiar face, which is complicated by an air of baseness, blended with an air of authority. Javert had this face, less the baseness. In our conviction, if souls were visible, we should distinctly see the strange fact that every individual of the human species corresponds to some one of the species of animal creation ; and we might easily recognise the truth which has as yet scarce occurred to the thinker, that, from the oyster to the eagle, from the hog to the tiger, all animals are in man, and that each of them is in a man ; at times several of them at once. Animals are nothing else than the figures of our virtues and our vices, wandering before our eyes, the visible phantoms of our souls. God shows these to us in order to make us reflect ; but, as animals are only shadows, God has not made them capable of education in the complete sense of the term, for of what use would it be ? On the other hand, our souls being realities and having an end of their own, God has endowed them with intelligence ; that is to say, possible education. Social education, carefully attended to, can always draw out of a soul, no matter its nature, the usefulness which it contains.

If it be admitted then that in every man there is one of the animal species of creation, it will be easy for us to say what Javert the policeman was. The Asturian peasants are convinced that in every litter of wolves there is a dog which is killed by the mother, for, otherwise, when it grew it would devour the other whelps. Give a human face to this dog-son of a she-wolf, and we shall have Javert. He was born in prison. His mother was a fortune-teller, whose husband was at the galleys. When he grew up he thought that he was beyond the pale of society, and despaired of ever entering it. He noticed that society inexorably keeps at bay two classes of men,—those who attack it, and those who guard it ; he had only a choice between these two classes, and at the same time felt within him a rigidness, regularity, and probity, combined with an inexpressible hatred of the race of Bohemians to which he belonged. He entered the police, got on, and at the age of forty was an inspector. In his youth he had been stationed in the galleys in the South.

Before proceeding, let us explain the words " human face " which we applied just now to Javert. His human face consisted of a snub nose, with two enormous nostrils, toward which enormous whiskers mounted on his cheeks. You felt uncomfortable the first time that you saw these two forests and these two caverns. When Javert laughed, which was rare and terrible, his thin lips parted, and displayed, not only his teeth, but his gums, and a savage flat curl formed round his nose, such as is seen on the muzzle of a wild beast. Javert when serious was a bulldog; when he laughed he was a tiger. To sum up, he had but little skull and plenty of jaw; his hair hid his forehead and fell over his brows; he had between his eyes a central and permanent frown, like a star of anger, an obscure glance, a pinched-up and formidable mouth, and an air of fierce command.

This man was a compound of two very simple and relatively excellent feelings, but which he almost rendered bad by exaggerating them,—respect for authority and hatred of rebellion; and in his eyes, robbery, murder, and every crime, were only forms of rebellion. He enveloped in a species of blind faith everybody in the service of the State, from the Prime Minister down to the gamekeeper. He covered with contempt, aversion, and disgust, every one who had once crossed the legal threshold of evil. He was absolute, and admitted of no exceptions; on one side he said: "A functionary cannot be mistaken, a magistrate can do no wrong;" on the other he said: "They are irremediably lost: no good can come of them." He fully shared the opinion of those extreme minds that attribute to the human law some power of making or verifying demons, and that place a Styx at the bottom of society. He was stoical, stern, and austere; a sad dreamer, and humble yet haughty, like all fanatics. His glance was a gimlet, for it was cold and piercing. His whole life was composed in the two words, watching and overlooking. He had introduced the straight line into what is the most tortuous thing in the world; he was conscious of his usefulness, had religious respect for his duties, and was a spy as well as another is a priest. Woe to the wretch who came into his clutches! He would have arrested his father if escaping from prison, and denounced his mother had she broken her ban. And he would have done it with that sort of inner satisfaction which virtue produces. With all this he spent a life of privation, isolation, self-denial, and chastity. It was implacable duty, comprehended in the police as the Spartans comprehended Sparta, a pitiless detective, a marble-hearted spy, a Brutus united with a Vidocq.

The whole person of Javert expressed the man who spies and hides himself. The mystic school of Joseph de Maistre, which at this epoch was seasoning with high cosmogony what were called the ultra journals, would not have failed to say that Javert was a symbol. His forehead could not be seen, for it was hidden by his hat; his eyes could not be seen, because they were lost under his eyebrows; his chin was plunged into his cravat, his hands were covered by his cuffs, and his cane was carried under his coat. But when the opportunity arrived, there could be seen suddenly emerging from all this shadow, as from an ambush, an angular, narrow forehead, a fatal glance, a menacing chin, enormous hands, and a monstrous rattan. In his leisure moments, which were few, he read, though he hated books, and this caused him not to be utterly ignorant, as could be noticed through a certain emphasis in his language. As we have said, he had no vice; when satisfied with himself, he indulged in a pinch of snuff, and that was his connecting link with humanity. Our readers will readily understand that Javert was the terror of all that class whom the yearly statistics of the minister of justice designate under the rubric —vagabonds. The name of Javert, if uttered, set them to flight; the face of Javert, if seen, petrified them. Such was this formidable man.

Javert was like an eye always fixed on M. Madeleine, an eye full of suspicion and conjectures. M. Madeleine noticed it in the end; but he considered it a matter of insignificance. He did not even ask Javert his motive, he neither sought nor shunned him, and endured his annoying glance without appearing to notice it. He treated Javert like every one else, easily and kindly. From some remarks that dropped from Javert, it was supposed that he had secretly sought, with that curiosity belonging to the breed, and in which there is as much instinct as will, all the previous traces which Father Madeleine might have left. He appeared to know, and sometimes said covertly, that some one had obtained certain information in a certain district about a certain family which had disappeared. Once he happened to say, speaking of himself, "I believe that I have got him ; " then he remained thoughtful for three days without saying a word. It seems that the thread which he fancied he held was broken. However, there cannot be any theory really infallible in a human creature, and it is the peculiarity of instinct that it can be troubled, thrown out, and routed. If not, it would be superior to intelligence, and the brute would have a better light than man. Javert was evidently somewhat disconcerted by M. Madeleine's complete naturalness and calmness. One day, however, his strange manner seemed to make an impression on M. Madeleine. The following was the occasion.

M. Madeleine was passing one morning through an un-paved lane in the town, when he heard a noise, and saw a group at some distance. He advanced to the spot. An old man, known as Father Fauchelevent, had fallen under his cart, and his horse was lying on the ground. This Fauchelevent was one of the few enemies M. Madeleine still had at this time. When Madeleine came to these parts, Fauchelevent, a toler-ably well-educated peasant, was doing badly in business ; and he saw the simple workman grow rich, while he, a master, was being ruined. This filled him with jealousy, and he had done all in his power, on every possible occasion, to injure Madeleine. Then bankruptcy came, and in his old days, having only a horse and cart left, and no family, he turned carter to earn a living.

The horse had his thighs broken, and could not stir. The old man was entangled between the wheels. The fall had been so unfortunate, that the whole weight of the cart was pressing on his chest, and it was heavily loaded. Fauchelevent uttered lamentable groans, and attempts had been made, though in vain, to draw him out ; and any irregular effort, any clumsy help or shock, might kill him. It was impossible to extricate him except by raising the cart from below, and Javert, who came up at the moment of the accident, had sent to fetch a jack. When M. Madeleine came up, the mob fell back respectfully.

" Help ! " cried old Fauchelevent, " is there no good soul who will save an old man ? "

M. Madeleine turned to the bystanders.

" Have you a jack ? "

" They have gone for one," a peasant answered.

" How soon will it be here ? "

" Well, the nearest is at Hatchet the blacksmith's, but it cannot be brought here under a good quarter of an hour."

"A quarter of an hour!" Madeleine exclaimed.

It had rained on the previous night, the ground was soft, the cart sank deeper into it every moment, and more and more pressed the old man's chest. It was evident that his ribs would be broken within five minutes.

"It is impossible to wait a quarter of an hour," said M. Madeleine to the peasants who were looking on.

"We must."

"But do you not see that the cart is sinking into the ground?"

"It cannot be helped."

"Listen to me," Madeleine continued; "there is still room enough for a man to crawl under the cart and raise it with his back. It will only take half a minute, and the poor man can be drawn out. Is there any one here who has strong loins? there are five louis to be earned."

No one stirred.

"Ten louis," Madeleine said.

His hearers looked down, and one of them muttered, "A man would have to be deucedly strong, and, besides, he would run a risk of being smashed."

"Come," Madeleine began again, "twenty louis."

The same silence.

"It is not the goodwill they are deficient in," a voice cried.

M. Madeleine turned and recognised Javert. He had noticed him when he came up. Javert continued:

"It is the strength. A man would have to be tremendously strong to lift a cart like that with his back."

Then, looking fixedly at M. Madeleine, he continued, laying a marked stress on every word he uttered:

"Monsieur Madeleine, I never knew but *one* man capable of doing what you ask."

Madeleine started, but Javert continued carelessly, though without taking his eyes off Madeleine:

"He was a galley-slave."

"Indeed!" said Madeleine.

"At the Toulon galleys."

Madeleine turned pale. All this while the cart was slowly settling down, and Father Fauchelevent was screaming:

"I am choking: it is breaking my ribs: a jack! something—oh!"

Madeleine looked around him.

"Is there no one here willing to earn twenty louis and save this poor old man's life?"

No one stirred, and Javert repeated :

"I never knew but one man capable of acting as a jack, and it was that convict."

"Oh, it is crushing me !" the old man yelled.

Madeleine raised his head, met Javert's falcon eye still fixed on him, gazed at the peasants, and sighed sorrowfully. Then, without saying a word, he fell on his knees, and, ere the crowd had time to utter a cry, was under the cart. There was a frightful moment of expectation and silence. Madeleine almost lying flat under the tremendous weight, twice tried in vain to bring his elbows up to his knees. The peasants shouted : "Father Madeleine, come out !" And old Fauchelevent himself said : "Monsieur Madeleine, go away ! I must die, so leave me ; you will be crushed too."

Madeleine made no reply. The bystanders gasped, the wheels had sunk deeper, and it was now almost impossible for him to get out from under the cart. All at once the enormous mass shook, the cart slowly rose, and the wheels half emerged from the rut. A stifled voice could be heard crying, "Make haste, help !" It was Madeleine, who had made a last effort. They rushed forward, for the devotion of one man had restored strength and courage to all. The cart was lifted by twenty arms, and old Fauchelevent was saved. Madeleine rose : he was livid, although dripping with perspiration : his clothes were torn and covered with mud. The old man kissed his knees and called him his saviour, while Madeleine had on his face a strange expression of happy and celestial suffering, and turned his placid eye on Javert, who was still watching him.

CHAPTER XXIV.

IN his fall Fauchelevent had put out his knee-cap, and Father Madeleine had him carried to an infirmary he had established for his workmen in his factory, and which was managed by two sisters of charity. The next morning the old man found a thousand franc note by his bedside, with a line in M. Madeleine's handwriting, "Payment for your cart and horse, which I have bought :" the cart was smashed and the horse dead. Fauchelevent recovered, but his leg remained stiff, and hence M. Madeleine, by the recommendation of the sisters and his curé, procured him a situation as gardener at a convent in the St. Antoine quarter of Paris.

Some time afterward, M. Madeleine was appointed Mayor. The first time Javert saw him wearing the scarf which gave him all authority in the town, he felt that sort of excitement a dog would feel that scented a wolf in its master's clothes. From this moment he avoided him as much as he could, and when duty imperiously compelled him, and he could not do otherwise than appear before the Mayor, he spoke to him with profound respect.

Such was the state of affairs when Fantine returned to her native town. No one remembered her, but luckily the door of M. Madeleine's factory was like a friendly face. She presented herself at it, and was admitted to the female shop. As the trade was quite new to Fantine, she was awkward at it and earned but small wages; but that was enough, for she had solved the problem,—she was earning her livelihood. When Fantine saw that she could live by it, she had a moment of joy. To live honestly by her own toil, what a favour of Heaven! A taste for work really came back to her. She bought a looking-glass, delighted in seeing in it her youth, her fine hair and fine teeth; forgot many things, only thought of Cosette, and her possible future, and was almost happy. She hired a small room and furnished it, on credit, to be paid for out of her future earnings,—this was a relic of her former ways.

She was very careful not to drop a word about her child, not being able to say that she was married. At the outset, as we have seen, she punctually paid the Thénardiers, and as she could only sign her name, she was compelled to write to them through the agency of a public writer. It was noticed that she wrote frequently. It was beginning to be whispered in the shop that Fantine "wrote letters," and "had airs."

It was noticed in the workroom that she often turned aside and wiped away a tear; it was when she was thinking of her child, perhaps of the man she had loved. It is a painful labour to break off all the gloomy connecting links with the past. It was a fact that she wrote, at least twice a month, and always to the same address, and paid the postage. They managed to obtain the address— "Monsieur Thénardier, Publican, Montfermeil." The public writer, who could not fill his stomach with wine without emptying his pocket of secrets, was made to talk at the wine-shop; and, in short, it was known that Fantine had a child. A gossip undertook a journey to Montfermeil, spoke to the Thénardiers, and on her return said, "I do not begrudge my five-and-thirty francs, for I have seen the child."

The gossip who did this was a Gorgon of the name of Madame Victurnien, guardian and porteress of everybody's virtue. She was fifty-six years of age, and covered the mask of ugliness with the mask of old age. Astounding to say, this old woman had once been young; in her youth, in '93, she had married a monk, who escaped from the cloisters in a red cap, and passed over from the Bernardines to the Jacobins. She was dry, crabbed, sharp, thorny, and almost venomous, while remembering the monk whose widow she was and who had considerably tamed her. At the Restoration she had turned bigot, and so energetically that the priests forgave her her monk. She had a small estate which she bequeathed to a religious community with great flourish, and she was very welcome at the Episcopal Palace of Arras. This Madame Victurnien then went to Montfermeil, and when she returned, said, "I have seen the child."

All this took time, and Fantine had been more than a year at the factory, when one morning the forewoman handed her 50 francs in the Mayor's name, and told her that she was no longer engaged, and had better leave the town, so the Mayor said. It was in this very month that the Thénardiers, after asking for 12 francs instead of 7, raised a claim for 15 instead of 12. Fantine was startled; she could not leave the town, for she was in debt for her rent and her furniture, and 50 francs would not pay those debts. She stammered a few words of entreaty, but the forewoman intimated to her that she must leave the shop at once; moreover, Fantine was but an indifferent workwoman. Crushed by shame more than disgrace, she left the factory, and returned to her room : her fault then was now known to all ! She did not feel the strength in her to say a word; she was advised to see the Mayor, but did not dare do so. The Mayor gave her 50 francs because he was kind, and discharged her because he was just; and she bowed her head to the sentence.

The monk's widow, then, was good for something. M. Madeleine, however, knew nothing of all this. These are combinations of events of which life is full. M. Madeleine made it a rule hardly ever to enter the female workroom; he had placed at its head an old maid, whom the curé had given him, and he had entire confidence in her. She was really a respectable, firm, equitable, and just person, full of that charity which consists in giving, but not possessing to the same extent the charity which comprehends and pardons. M. Madeleine trusted to her in everything, for the best men are often forced to delegate their authority, and it was with this full power, and in the conviction she was acting rightly, that the forewoman tried, condemned, and executed Fantine. As for the 50 francs, she had given them out of a sum M. Madeleine had given her for alms and helping the workwomen, and of which she rendered no account.

Fantine offered herself for a servant's place in the town, and went from house to house, but no one would have anything to do with her. She could not leave the town, for the broker to whom she was in debt for her furniture— what furniture !—said to her, " If you go away, I will have you arrested as a thief." The landlord to whom she owed her rent, said to her, "You are young and pretty, you can pay." She divided the 50 francs between the landlord and the broker, gave back to the latter three-fourths of the goods, only retaining what was absolutely necessary, and found herself without work, without a trade, with only a bed, and still owing about 100 francs. She set to work making coarse shirts for the troops, and earned at this sixpence a day, her daughter costing her fourpence. It was at this moment she began to fall in arrears with the Thénardiers. An old woman, however, who lit her candle for her when she came in at nights, taught her the art of living in wretchedness. Behind living on little, there is living on nothing. There are two chambers; the first is obscure, the second is quite dark.

Fantine learned how to do entirely without fire in winter, how she must get rid of a bird that cost her a halfpenny every two days, how she could make a petticoat of her blanket and a blanket of her petticoat, and how candle can be saved by taking your meals by the light of the window opposite. We do not know all that certain weak beings, who have grown old in want and honesty, can get out of a halfpenny, and in the end it becomes a talent. Fantine acquired this sublime talent, and regained a little courage. At this period she said to a neighbour, " Nonsense, I say

to myself; by only sleeping for five hours and working all
the others at my needle, I shall always manage to earn
bread, at any rate. And then, when you are sad, you eat
less. Well! suffering, anxiety, a little bread on one side
and sorrow on the other, all that will keep me alive."

In this distress, it would have been a strange happiness
to have had her daughter with her, and she thought of
sending for her. But what! make her share her privation? and then she owed money to the Thénardiers! how
was she to pay it and the travelling expenses? The old
woman who had given her lessons in what may be called
indigent life was a pious creature, poor, and charitable to
the poor and even to the rich, who could just write her
name, "Marguerite," and believed in God, which is knowledge. There are many such virtues down here, and one
day they will be up above, for this life has a morrow.

At first, Fantine had been so ashamed that she did not
dare go out. When she was in the streets, she perceived
that people turned round to look at her and pointed to her.
Every one stared at her, and no one bowed to her; the cold
bitter contempt of the passers-by passed through her flesh
and her mind like an east wind. In small towns an unhappy girl seems to be naked beneath the sarcasm and
curiosity of all. In Paris, at least, no one knows you, and
that obscurity is a garment. Oh! how glad she would
have been to be back in Paris. She must grow accustomed
to disrespect as she had done to poverty. Gradually she
made up her mind, and after two or three months shook
off her shame, and went as if nothing had occurred. "It
is no matter to me," she said. She came and went, with
head erect and with a bitter smile, and felt that she was
growing impudent. Madame Victurnien sometimes saw
her pass from her window; she noticed the distress of
"the creature whom she had made know her place," and
congratulated herself. The wicked have a black happiness.
Excessive labour fatigued Fantine, and the little dry cough
she had grew worse. She sometimes said to her neighbour,
"Marguerite, just feel how hot my hands are!" Still, in
the morning, when she passed an old broken comb through
her glorious hair, which flowed down in silky waves, she
had a moment of happiness.

She had been discharged toward the end of winter; the
next summer passed away, and winter returned. Short
days and less work; in winter there is no warmth, no

light, no midday, for the evening is joined to the morning ;
there is fog, twilight, the window is gray, and you cannot
see clearly. The sky is like a dark vault, and the sun has
the look of a poor man. It is a frightful season ; winter
changes into stone the water of heaven and the heart of
man. Her creditors pressed her, for Fantine was earning
too little, and her debts had increased. The Thénardiers,
being irregularly paid, constantly wrote her letters, whose
contents afflicted her, and postage ruined her. One day
they wrote her that little Cosette was quite naked, that
she wanted a flannel skirt, and that the mother must send
at least ten francs for the purpose. She crumpled the letter
in her hands all day, and at nightfall went to a barber's
at the corner of the street and removed her comb. Her
beautiful fair hair fell below her waist.

"What beautiful hair !" the barber exclaimed.

"What will you give me for it ?" she asked.

"Ten francs."

"Cut it off."

She bought a knit skirt and sent it to the Thénardiers.
It made them furious, for they wanted the money. They
gave it to Eponine, and the poor Lark continued to
shiver. Fantine thought, "My child is no longer cold, for I
have dressed her in my hair." She wore small round caps
which hid her shorn head, and she still looked pretty in them.

A gloomy work was going on in Fantine's heart. When
she found that she could no longer dress her hair, she
began to hate all around her. She had long shared the
universal veneration for Father Madeleine ; but, through
the constant iteration that he had discharged her, and that
he was the cause of her misfortune, she grew to hate him
too, and worse than the rest. When she passed the factory
she pretended to laugh and sing. An old workwoman who
once saw her doing so, said, "That's a girl who will come
to a bad end." She took a lover, the first who offered, a
man she did not love, through bravado, and with rage in
her heart. He was a scoundrel, a sort of mendicant
musician, an idle scamp, who beat her, and left her, as
she had chosen him, in disgust. She adored her child.
The lower she sank, the darker the gloom became around
her, the more did this sweet little angel gleam in her soul.
She said : "When I am rich, I shall have my Cosette with
me ;" and she laughed. She did not get rid of her cough,
and she had night sweats.

One day she received from the Thénardiers a letter in these words : "Cosette is ill with a miliary fever, as they call it, which is very prevalent. She must have expensive drugs, and that ruins us, and we cannot pay for them any longer. If you do not send us forty francs within a week, the little one will be dead."

She burst into a loud laugh, and said to her old neighbour, "Oh, what funny people ! they want forty francs ; where do they expect me to get them? What fools those peasants are !"

Still, she went to a staircase window and read the letter again ; then she went out into the street, still laughing and singing. Some one who met her said, "What has made you so merry?" and she answered, "It is piece of stupidity some country folk have written ; they want forty francs of me—the dolts."

As she passed through the market-place she saw a crowd surrounding a vehicle of a strange shape, on the box of which a man dressed in red was haranguing. He was a dentist going his rounds, who offered the public complete sets of teeth, opiates, powders, and elixirs. Fantine joined the crowd and began laughing like the rest at this harangue, in which there was slang for the mob, and scientific jargon for respectable persons. The extractor of teeth saw the pretty girl laughing, and suddenly called out :

"You have fine teeth, my laughing beauty. If you like to sell me your two top front teeth, I will give you a napoleon a piece for them."

"What a horrible idea !" Fantine exclaimed.

"Two napoleons !" an old toothless woman by her side grumbled, "there's a lucky girl."

Fantine turned quickly away and stopped her ears not to hear the hoarse voice of the man, who shouted : "Think it over, my dear : two napoleons may be useful ! If your heart says Yes, come to-night to the *Tillac d'Argent*, where you will find me."

Fantine, when she got home, was furious, and told her good neighbour Marguerite what had happened. "Can you understand it? is he not an abominable man? How can people like that be allowed to go about the country? Pull out my two front teeth ! why, I should look horrible ; hair grows again, but teeth ! oh, the monster ! I would sooner throw myself head first out of a fifth-floor window."

"And what did he offer you ?" Marguerite asked.

" Two napoleons."

" That is forty francs."

" Yes," said Fantine, " that forty francs."

She became thoughtful, and sat down to her work. At the end of a quarter of an hour, she left the room and read Thénardier's letter again on the staircase. When she returned, she said to Marguerite :

" Do you know what a miliary fever is ? "

" Yes," said the old woman, " it is an illness."

" Does it require much medicine ? "

" Oh, an awful lot."

" Does it attack children ? "

" More than anybody."

" Do they die of it ? "

" Very often," said Marguerite.

Fantine withdrew, and read the letter once again on the staircase. At night she went out, and could be seen proceeding in the direction of the Rue de Paris, where the inns are. The next morning, when Marguerite entered Fantine's room before daybreak, for they worked together, and they made one candle do for them both, she found her sitting on her bed, pale and chill. Her cap had fallen on her knees, and the candle had been burning all night, and was nearly consumed. Marguerite stopped in the doorway, horrified by this enormous extravagance, and exclaimed :

" Good Lord ! the candle nearly burnt out ! something must have happened."

Then she looked at Fantine, who turned her close-shaven head towards her, and seemed to have grown ten years older since the previous day.

" Gracious Heaven ! " said Marguerite, " what is the matter with you, Fantine ? "

" Nothing," the girl answered, " I am all right. My child will not die of that frightful disease for want of assistance, and I am satisfied."

As she said this, she pointed to two napoleons that glistened on the table.

" Oh, Lord ! " said Marguerite ; " why, 'tis a fortune ; where ever did you get them from ? "

" I got them," Fantine answered.

At the same time she smiled. The candle lit up her face, and it was a fearful smile. A reddish saliva stained the corner of her lips, and she had a black hole in her mouth—the two teeth were pulled out. She sent the forty francs to

Montfermeil. It had only been a trick of the Thénardiers to get money, for Cosette was not sick.

Fantine threw her looking-glass out of the window. Long before she had left her cell on the second floor for a garret under the roof,—one of those tenements in which the ceiling forms an angle with the floor, and you knock your head at every step. The poor man can only go to the end of his room, as to the end of his destiny, by stooping more and more. She had no bed left; she had only a rag she called a blanket, a mattress on the ground, and a bottomless chair; a little rose-tree she had had withered away, forgotten in a corner. In another corner she had a pail to hold water, which froze in winter, and in which the different levels of the water remained marked for a long time by rings of ice. She had lost her shame, and now lost her coquetry; the last sign was, that she went out with dirty caps. Either through want of time or careless-ness, she no longer washed her linen, and as the heels of her stockings wore out, she tucked them into her shoes. She mended her worn-out gown with rags of calico, which tore away at the slightest movement. The people to whom she owed money made "scenes," and allowed her no rest; she met them in the street, she met them again on her stairs. Her eyes were very bright, and she felt a settled pain at the top of her left shoulder-blade, while she coughed frequently. She deeply hated Father Madeleine, and sewed for seventeen hours a day; but a speculator hired all the female prisoners, and reduced the prices of the free work-men to nine sous a day. Seventeen hours' work for nine sous! Her creditors were more pitiless than ever, and the broker, who had got back nearly all her furniture, inces-santly said to her, "When are you going to pay me, you cheat?" What did they want of her, good heavens? She felt herself tracked, and something of the wild beast was aroused in her. About the same time Thénardier wrote to her that he had decidedly waited too patiently, and that unless he received one hundred francs at once, he would turn poor Cosette, who had scarce recovered, out of doors into the cold, and she must do what she could or rot. "One hundred francs," thought Fantine. "But where is the trade in which I can earn one hundred sous a day? Come! J will sell what is left!"

And the unfortunate creature became a woman of the town.

CHAPTER XXV.

THERE is in all small towns, and there was at M—— in particular, a class of young men who squander fifteen hundred francs a year in the provinces with the same air as their congeners in Paris devour two hundred thousand. They are beings of the great neutral species; geldings, parasites, nobodies, who possess a little land, a little folly, and a little wit, who would be rustics in a drawing-room, and believe themselves gentlemen in a pot-house. They talk about "my fields, my woods, my peasants," hiss the actresses to prove themselves men of taste, quarrel with the officers to prove themselves men of war, shoot, smoke, yawn, drink, smell of tobacco, play at billiards, watch the travellers get out of the stage-coach, live at the café, dine at the inn, have a dog that gnaws bones under the table, and a mistress who sets the dishes upon it, wrangle over a sou, exaggerate the fashions, admire tragedy, despise women, wear out their old boots, copy London through Pont-à-Mousson, grow stupidly old, do not work, are of no use, and do no great harm. Had M. Felix Tholomyès remained in his province and not seen Paris, he would have been one of them. If they were richer, people would say they are dandies; if poorer, they are idle scamps; but they are simply men without work. Among them there are some that are bores, some that are bored, some dreamers, and a few scamps.

In those days a dandy was composed of a tall collar, a large cravat, a watch and seals, three waistcoats over one another, blue and red inside, a short-waisted olive-coloured coat, with a swallow tail, and a double row of silver buttons, sewn on close together, and ascending to the shoulders, and trousers of a lighter olive, adorned on the seams with an undetermined but always uneven number of ribs, varying from one to eleven, a limit which was never exceeded. Add to this slipper-boots with swivel iron heels, a tall, narrow-brimmed hat, hair in a tuft, an enormous cane, and a conversation improved by Potier's puns; over and above all these were spurs and moustachios, for at that period moustachios indicated the civilian, and spurs the pedestrian. The provincial dandy wore longer spurs and more ferocious moustachios.

Eight or ten months after the events we have described in the previous chapter, toward the beginning of January, 1823, and on a night when snow had fallen, one of these dandies was amusing himself by annoying a creature, who was prowling about in a low-necked ball dress and with flowers in her hair, before the window of the officers' café. This dandy was smoking, as that was a decided mark of fashion. Each time this woman passed him, he made some remark to her, which he fancied witty and amusing, as : "How ugly you are !" "Why don't you go to kennel ? " "You have no teeth," etc. etc. This gentleman's name was Monsieur Bamatabois. The woman, a sad-dressed phantom walking backwards and forwards in the snow, made him no answer, did not even look at him, but still continued silently and with a gloomy regularity her walk, which every few minutes brought her under his sarcasms, like the condemned soldier running the gauntlet. The slight effect produced doubtless annoyed the idler, for taking advantage of her back being turned, he crept up behind her, stooped to pick up a handful of snow, and suddenly plunged it between her bare shoulders. The girl uttered a yell, turned, leapt like a panther on the man, and dug her nails into his face with the most frightful language that could fall from a guard-room into the gutter. These insults, vomited by a voice rendered hoarse by brandy, hideously issued from a mouth in which the two front teeth were missing. It was Fantine.

At the noise, the officers left the café in a throng, the passers-by stopped, and a laughing, yelling, applauding circle was made round these two beings, in whom it was difficult to recognise a man and a woman, the man struggling, his hat on the ground, the woman striking with feet and fists, bareheaded, yelling, without teeth or hair, livid with passion, and horrible. All at once a tall man quickly broke through the crowd, seized the woman's satin dress, which was covered with mud, and said : "Follow me." The woman raised her head, and her passionate voice suddenly died out. Her eyes were glassy, she grew pale instead of being livid, and trembled with fear—she had recognised Javert. The dandy profited by this to steal away.

Javert dispersed the onlookers, and began walking with long strides toward the police-office, which is at the other end of the market-place, dragging the wretched girl after him. She allowed him to do so mechanically, and neither he nor she said a word. The crowd of spectators, in a paroxysm of delight, followed them with coarse jokes, for supreme misery is an occasion for obscenities. On reaching the police-office, which was a low room, heated by a stove, and guarded by a sentry, and having a barred glass door opening on the street, Javert walked in with Fantine, and shut the door after him, to the great disappointment of the curious, who stood on tiptoe, and stretched out their necks in front of the dirty window in their endeavours to see.

On entering, Fantine crouched down motionless in a corner like a frightened dog. The sergeant on duty brought in a candle. Javert sat down at a table, took a sheet of stamped paper from his pocket, and began writing. Women of this class are by the French laws left entirely at the discretion of the police: they do what they like with them, punish them as they think proper, and confiscate the two sad things which they call their trade and their liberty. Javert was stoical: his grave face displayed no emotion, and yet he was seriously and deeply preoccupied. It was one of those moments in which he exercised without control, but with all the scruples of a strict conscience, his formidable discretionary power. At this instant he felt that his high stool was a tribunal, and himself the judge. He tried and he condemned: he summoned all the ideas he had in his mind round the great thing he was doing. The more he examined the girl's deed, the more outraged he felt: for it was evident that he had just seen a crime committed. He had seen in the street, society, represented by a householder and elector, insulted and attacked by a creature beyond the pale of everything. A prostitute had assaulted a citizen, and he, Javert, had witnessed it. He wrote on silently. When he had finished, he affixed his signature, folded up the paper, and said to the sergeant as he handed it to him: "Take three men and lead this girl to prison." Then he turned to Fantine, "You are in for six months."

The hapless girl shuddered.

"Six months! six months in prison!" she cried; "six months! and only earn seven sous a day! Why, what will become of Cosette, my child, my child! Why, I owe more than 100 francs to Thénardier, M. Inspector, do you know that?"

She dragged herself along the floor, dirtied by the

muddy boots of all these men, without rising, with clasped hands, and moving rapidly on her knees.

"Monsieur Javert," she said, "I plead for mercy. I assure you that I was not in the wrong. If you had seen the beginning, you would say so. I swear by our Saviour that I was not to blame. That gentleman, who was a stranger to me, put snow down my back; had he any right to do that when I was passing gently, and doing nobody any harm? It sent me wild, for you must know I am not very well, and besides he had been abusing me— 'You are ugly, you have no teeth.' I am well aware that I have lost my teeth. I did nothing, and said to myself, 'This gentleman is amusing himself.' I was civil to him, and said nothing, and it was at this moment he put the snow down my back. My good M. Javert, is there no one who saw it to tell you that this is the truth? I was, perhaps, wrong to get into a passion, but at the moment, as you are aware, people are not masters of themselves, and I am quick-tempered. And then, something so cold put down your back, at a moment when you are least expecting it! It was wrong to destroy the gentleman's hat, but why has he gone away? I would ask his pardon. Oh! I would willingly do so. Let me off this time. M. Javert, perhaps you do not know that in prison you can only earn seven sous a day—it is not the fault of Government, but you only earn seven sous; and just fancy! I have one hundred francs to pay, or my child will be turned into the street. Oh! I cannot have her with me, for my mode of life is so bad! O my Cosette, O my little angel, whatever will become of you, poor darling! I must tell you that the Thénardiers are innkeepers, peasants, and unreasonable; they insist on having their money. Oh, do not send me to prison. Look you, the little thing will be turned into the streets in the middle of winter to go where she likes, and you must take pity on that, my kind M. Javert. If she were older she could earn her living, but at her age it is impossible. I am not a bad woman at heart; it is not cowardice and gluttony that have made me what I am. If I drink brandy, it is through wretchedness; I do not like it, but it makes me reckless. In happier times you need only have looked into my chest of drawers, and you would have seen that I was not a disorderly woman, for I had linen, plenty of linen. Have pity on me, M. Javert."

She talked thus, crushed, shaken by sobs, blinded by
tears, wringing her hands, interrupted by a sharp dry cough,
and stammering feebly, with an agonised voice. Great
grief is a divine and terrible ray which transfigures the
wretched, and at this moment Fantine became lovely again.
From time to time she stopped, and tenderly kissed the
skirt of the policeman's coat. She would have melted a heart
of granite ; but a heart of wood cannot be moved.

" Well," said Javert, " I have listened to you. Have you
said all ? Be off now ; you have six months. The Eternal
Father in person could not alter it."

On hearing this solemn phrase, she understood that
sentence was passed ; she fell all of a heap, murmuring,
" Mercy ! " But Javert turned his back, and the soldiers
seized her arm. Some minutes previously a man had
entered unnoticed. He had closed the door, leant against it,
and heard Fantine's desperate entreaties. At the moment
when the soldiers laid hold of the unhappy girl, who would
not rise, he emerged from the gloom, and said :

" One moment, if you please."

Javert raised his eyes, and recognised M. Madeleine.
He took off his hat, and bowed with a sort of vexed
awkwardness.

" I beg your pardon, M. le Maire——"

The words " M. le Maire " produced a strange effect on
Fantine. She sprang to her feet like a spectre emerging
from the ground, thrust back the soldiers, walked straight
up to M. Madeleine before she could be prevented, and,
looking at him wildly, she exclaimed :

" So you are the Mayor ? "

Then she burst into a laugh, and spat in his face.
M. Madeleine wiped his face, and said :

" Inspector Javert, set this woman at liberty."

Javert felt for a moment as if he were losing his senses.
He experienced at this instant the most violent emotions
he had ever felt in his life, following each other in rapid
succession, and almost mingled. To see a girl of the town
spit in the Mayor's face was so monstrous a thing that he
would have regarded it as sacrilege even to believe it
possible. On the other side, he confusedly made a hideous
approximation in his mind between what this woman was
and what this Mayor might be, and then he saw with horror
something perfectly simple in this prodigious assault. But
when he saw this Mayor, this magistrate, calmly wipe his

face, and say, "Set this woman at liberty," he was stupefied with amazement; thought and speech alike failed him; the limit of possible astonishment had been overpassed. He remained speechless.

The Mayor's words had produced an equally strange effect on Fantine; she raised her bare arm, and clung to the damper of the stove like a tottering person. She looked around, and began to talk in a low voice, as if speaking to herself:

"At liberty! They let me go! I shall not be sent to prison for six months! Who said that? it is impossible that any one said it. I must have heard badly; it cannot be that monster of a Mayor. Was it you, my kind M. Javert, who said that I was to be set at liberty? Well, I will tell you all about it, and you will let me go. That monster of a Mayor, that old villain of a Mayor, is the cause of it all. Just imagine, M. Javert, he discharged me on account of a parcel of sluts gossiping in the shop. Was not that horrible! to discharge a poor girl who is doing her work fairly! After that I did not earn enough, and all this misfortune came. In the first place, there is an improvement which the police gentry ought to make, and that is to prevent persons in prison injuring poor people. I will explain this to you; you earn twelve sous for making a shirt, but it falls to seven, and then you can no longer live, and are obliged to do what you can. As I had my little Cosette I was forced to become a bad woman. You can now understand that it was that beggar of a Mayor who did all the mischief. My present offence is that I trampled on the gentleman's hat before the officers' café, but he had ruined my dress with snow; and our sort have only one silk dress for night. Indeed, M. Javert, I never did any harm purposely, and I see everywhere much worse women than myself who are much more fortunate. Oh, Monsieur Javert, you said that I was to be set at liberty, did you not? Make inquiries, speak to my landlord; I pay my rent now, and you will hear that I am honest. Oh, good gracious! I beg your pardon, but I have touched the stove without noticing it, and it smokes."

M. Madeleine listened to her with profound attention. While she was talking, he took out his purse, but as he found it empty on opening it, he returned it to his pocket. He now said to Fantine:

"How much did you say that you owed?"

Fantine, who was looking at Javert, turned towards him :

" Am I speaking to you ? "

Then she said to the soldiers :

" Tell me, men, did you see how I spat in his face ? Ah, you old villain of a Mayor, you have come here to frighten me, but I am not afraid of you. I am only afraid of M. Javert, my good M. Javert."

As she said this, she turned again to the Inspector :

" After all, people should be just. I can understand that you are a just man, M. Javert ; in fact, it is quite simple ; a man who played at putting snow down a woman's back, made the officers laugh ; they must have some amusement, and we girls are sent into the world for them to make fun of. And then you came up : you are compelled to restore order, you remove the woman who was in the wrong, but, on reflection, as you are kind-hearted, you order me to be set at liberty, for the sake of my little girl, for six months' imprisonment would prevent my supporting her. But don't come here again, faggot ! Oh, I will not come here again, M. Javert ; they can do what they like to me in future, and I will not stir. Still I cried out to-night because it hurt me ; I did not at all expect that gentleman's snow, and then besides, as I told you, I am not very well,—I cough, I have a ball in my stomach which burns, and the doctor says : ' Take care of yourself.' Here, feel, give me your hand ; do not be frightened."

She wept no more ; her voice was caressing ; she laid Javert's large coarse hand on her white, delicate throat, and looked up at him smilingly. All at once she hurriedly repaired the disorder in her clothes, let the folds of her dress fall, which had been almost dragged up to her knees, and walked towards the door, saying to the soldiers with a friendly nod of the head :

" Boys, M. Javert says I may go, so I will be off."

She laid her hand on the latch ; one step further, and she would be in the street. Up to this moment Javert had stood motionless, with his eyes fixed on the ground, appearing in the centre of this scene like a statue waiting to be put up in its proper place. The sound of the latch aroused him. He raised his head with an expression of sovereign authority—an expression the more frightful, the lower the man in power stands ; it is ferocity in the wild beast, atrocity in the nobody.

"Sergeant," he shouted, "do you not see that the wench is bolting? Who told you to let her go?"

"I," said Madeleine.

Fantine, at the sound of Javert's voice, trembled, and let go the latch, like a detected thief lets fall the stolen article. At Madeleine's voice she turned, and from that moment, without uttering a word, without even daring to breathe freely, her eye wandered from Madeleine to Javert, and from Javert to Madeleine, according as each spoke. It was evident that Javert must have been "thrown off his balance," as people say, when he ventured to address the sergeant as he had done, after the Mayor's request that Fantine should be set at liberty. Had he gone so far as to forget the Mayor's presence. Did he eventually declare to himself that it was impossible for "an authority" to have given such an order, and that the Mayor must certainly have said one thing for another without meaning it? Or was it that, in the presence of all the enormities he had witnessed during the last two hours, he said to himself that he must have recourse to a supreme resolution, that the little must become great, the detective be transformed into the magistrate, and that, in this prodigious extremity, order, law, morality, government, and society were personified in him, Javert? However this may be, when M. Madeleine said "I," the Inspector of Police could be seen to turn to the Mayor, pale, cold, with blue lips, with a desperate glance, and an imperceptible tremor all over him, and, extraordinary circumstance! to say to him, with downcast eye, but in a fierce voice:

"Monsieur le Maire, that cannot be done."

"Why?"

"This wretched creature has insulted a gentleman.

"Inspector Javert," M. Madeleine replied, with a conciliating and calm accent, "listen to me. You are an honest man, and I shall have no difficulty in coming to an explanation with you. The truth is as follows: I was crossing the market-place at the time you were leading this girl away; a crowd was still assembled; I inquired, and know all; the man was in the wrong, and, in common justice, ought to have been arrested instead of her."

Javert objected:

"This wretched creature has just insulted M. le Maire."

"That concerns myself," M. Madeleine said; "my insult is, perhaps, my own, and I can do what I like with it."

"I ask your pardon, sir; the insult does not belong to you, but to the Judicial Court."

"Inspector Javert," Madeleine replied, "conscience is the highest of all courts. I have heard the woman, and know what I am doing."

"And I, Monsieur le Maire, do not know what I am seeing."

"In that case, be content with obeying."

"I obey my duty; my duty orders that this woman should go to prison for six months."

M. Madeleine answered gently:

"Listen to this carefully; she will not go for a single day."

On hearing these decided words, Javert ventured to look fixedly at the Mayor, and said to him, though still with a respectful accent:

"I am very sorry at being compelled to resist you. Monsieur le Maire, it is the first time in my life, but you will deign to let me observe that I am within the limits of my authority. As you wish it, sir, I will confine myself to the affair with the gentleman. I was present. This girl attacked M. Bamatabois, who is an elector and owner of that fine three-storeyed house, built of hewn stone, which forms the corner of the Esplanade. Well, there are things in this world! However this may be, M. le Maire, this is a matter of the street police which concerns me, and I intend to punish the woman Fantine."

At this M. Madeleine folded his arms and said in a stern voice, which no one in the town had ever heard before:

"The affair to which you allude belongs to the borough police; and by the terms of articles nine, eleven, fifteen, and sixty-six of the Criminal Code, I try it. I order that this woman be set at liberty."

Javert made a final effort.

"But, Monsieur le Maire——"

"I call your attention to article eighty-one of the law of December 13th, 1799, upon arbitrary detention."

"Permit me, sir——"

"Not another word!"

"Still——"

"Retire!" said M. Madeleine.

Javert received the blow manfully, and with open breast like a Russian soldier; he bowed down to the ground to

the Mayor, and went out. Fantine stood up against the
door, and watched him pass by her in stupor. She too was
suffering from a strange perturbation: for she had seen
herself, so to speak, contended for by two opposite powers.
She had seen two men struggling in her presence, who held
in their hands her liberty, her life, her soul, her child. One
of these men dragged her towards the gloom, the other
restored her to the light. In this struggle, which she gazed
at through the exaggeration of terror, the two men seemed
to her giants,—one spoke like a demon, the other like her
good angel. The angel had vanquished the demon, and
the thing which made her shudder from head to foot was
that this angel, this liberator, was the very man whom she
abhorred, the Mayor whom she had so long regarded as the
cause of all her woes; and at the very moment when she
had insulted him in such a hideous way, he saved her.
Could she be mistaken? must she change her whole soul?
she did not know, but she trembled; she listened wildly,
she looked on with terror, and at every word that M.
Madeleine said, she felt the darkness of hatred fade away in
her heart, and something glowing and ineffable spring up
in its place, which was composed of joy, confidence, and
love. When Javert had left the room, M. Madeleine turned
to her, and said in a slow voice, like a serious man who is
making an effort to refrain from tears:

"I have heard you. I knew nothing about what you
have said; but I believe, I feel, that it is true. I was even
ignorant that you had left the factory, but why did you not
apply to me? This is what I will do for you; I will pay
your debts and send for your child, or you can go to it.
You can live here, in Paris, or wherever you please, and I
will provide for your child and yourself. I will give you all
the money you require, and you will become respectable
again in becoming happy, and I will say more than that:
if all be as you say, and I do not doubt it, you have never
ceased to be virtuous and holy in the sight of God! Poor
woman!"

This was more than poor Fantine could bear. To have
Cosette! to leave this infamous life! to live free, rich,
happy, and respectable with Cosette! to see all these
realities of Paradise suddenly burst into flower, in the midst
of her wretchedness! She looked as if stunned at the
person who was speaking, and could only sob two or three
times: "Oh, oh, oh!" Her legs gave way, she fell on

her knees before M. Madeleine, and before he could prevent it, he felt her seize his hand and carry it to her lips.

Then she fainted.

M. Madeleine had Fantine taken to the infirmary he had established in his own house, and intrusted her to the sisters, who put her to bed. A violent fever had broken out; she spent a part of the night in raving and talking aloud, but at length fell asleep. On the morrow, at about midday, Fantine woke, and hearing a breathing close to her bed, she drew the curtain aside, and noticed M. Madeleine gazing at something above her head. His glance was full of compassionate and supplicating agony. She followed its direction, and saw that it was fixed on a crucifix nailed to the wall. M. Madeleine was now transfigured in Fantine's eyes, and seemed to her surrounded by light. He was absorbed in a species of prayer, and she looked at him for some time without daring to interrupt him, but at last she said timidly:

"What are you doing?"

M. Madeleine had been standing at this spot for an hour, waiting till Fantine should wake. He took her hand, felt her pulse, and answered:

"How do you feel?"

"Very comfortable; I have slept, and fancy I am better. It will be nothing."

He continued answering the question she had asked him first, and as if he had only just heard it:

"I was praying to the Martyr up there;" and he mentally added, "for the Martyr down here."

M. Madeleine had spent the night and morning in making inquiries, and had learnt everything; he knew all the poignant details of Fantine's history. He continued:

"You have suffered greatly, poor mother. Oh! do not complain, for you have at present the dowry of the elect: it is in this way that human beings become angels. It is not their fault; they do not know what to do otherwise. The hell you have now left is the first step to heaven, and you were obliged to begin with that."

He breathed a deep sigh; but she smiled upon him with the sublime smile in which two teeth were lacking.

That same night, Javert wrote a letter, and next morning posted it himself. It was for Paris, and the address was: "Monsieur Chabouillet, Secretary to the Prefect of Police." As a rumour had spread about the affair in the police-office, the postmistress, and some other persons who saw the letter before it was sent off and recognised Javert's handwriting, supposed that he was sending in his resignation. M. Madeleine hastened to write to the Thénardiers. Fantine owed them over 120 francs, and he sent them 300, bidding them pay themselves out of the amount, and bring the child at once to M——, where a sick mother was awaiting it. This dazzled Thénardier. "Hang it all," he said to his wife, "we must not let the brat go, for the lark will become a milch cow for us. I see it all; some fellow has fallen in love with the mother." He replied by sending a bill for 500 and odd francs very well drawn up. In this bill two undeniable amounts figure, one from a physician, the othe. from an apothecary, who had attended Eponine and Azelina in a long illness. Cosette, as we have said, had not been ill, and hence it was merely a little substitution of names. At the bottom of the bill Thénardier gave credit for 300 francs received on account. M. Madeleine at once sent 300 francs more, and wrote, "Make haste to bring Cosette."

"Christi!" said Thénardier, "we won't let go the child."

Meanwhile Fantine did not recover, and still remained in the infirmary. The sisters had at first received and nursed "this girl" with some repugnance; any one who has seen the bas-relief at Rheims will remember the pouting lower lip of the wise virgins looking at the foolish virgins. This ancient contempt of Vestals for Ambubaïæ is one of the deepest instincts of the feminine dignity, and the sisters had experienced it, with the increased dislike which religion adds. But in a few days Fantine disarmed them; she had all sorts of humble and gentle words, and the mother within her was touching. One day the sisters heard her say in the paroxysm of fever, "I have been a sinner, but when I have my child by my side, that will show that God has forgiven me. While I was living badly, I should not have liked to have Cosette with me, for I could not have endured her sad and astonished eyes. And yet it was for her sake that I did wrong, and for that reason God pardons me. I shall feel the blessing of Heaven when Cosette is here; I shall look at her, and it will do me good to see the innocent creature. She knows nothing, as she is an angel. My sisters, at her age the wings have not yet fallen,"

M. Madeleine went to see her twice a day, and every time she asked him, "Shall I see my Cosette soon?"

He would answer :

"To-morrow, perhaps ; she may arrive at any moment, for I am expecting her."

And the mother's pale face would brighten.

"Oh !" she would say, "how happy I shall be !"

We have just said that she did not improve ; on the contrary, her condition seemed to grow worse week by week. The handful of snow placed between her naked shoulder-blades produced a sudden check of perspiration, which caused the illness that had smouldered in her for years suddenly to break out. Larmier's fine method for studying and healing diseases of the lungs was just beginning to be employed ; the physician placed the stethescope to Fantine's chest, and shook his head. M. Madeleine said to him :

"Well ?"

"Has she not a child that she is anxious to see ?" asked the doctor.

"Yes."

"Well, make haste to bring her."

Madeleine gave a start, and Fantine asked him :

"What did the doctor say to you ?"

M. Madeleine forced a smile.

"He told us that your child must come at once, for that would cure you."

"Oh," she replied, "he is right ; but what do those Thénardiers mean by keeping my Cosette ? Oh, she will come, and then I shall see happiness near me."

Thénardier, however, would not let the child go, and alleged a hundred poor excuses. Cosette was ailing, and it would be dangerous for her to travel in winter, and then there were some small debts still to pay, which he was collecting, etc.

"I will send some one to fetch Cosette," said Father Madeleine ; "if necessary, I will go myself."

He wrote to Fantine's dictation this letter, which she signed

"M. THÉNARDIER—

"You will deliver Cosette to the bearer, who will pay up all little matters.—Yours, FANTINE."

About this time, a great incident happened. However cleverly we may have carved the mysterious block of which our life is made, the black vein of destiny reappears continually.

CHAPTER XXVI.

ONE morning M. Madeleine was in his office, arranging some pressing mayoralty matters, in case he decided on the journey to Montfermeil, when he was told that Inspector Javert wished to speak with him. On hearing this name pronounced, M. Madeleine could not refrain from a disagreeable impression. Since the guard-room adventure Javert had avoided him more than ever, and M. Madeleine had not seen him since.

" Let him come in," he said.

Javert entered. M. Madeleine remained seated at his table near the fireplace with a pen in his hand and his eyes fixed on a charge book, whose leaves he was turning over and annotating. He did not put himself out of the way for Javert, for he could not refrain from thinking of poor Fantine. Javert bowed respectfully to the Mayor, who had his back turned to him; the Mayor did not look at him, but continued to make his notes. Javert walked a little way into the study, and then halted without a word. A physiognomist familiar with Javert's nature, and who had studied for any length of time this savage in the service of civilisation,—this strange composite of the Roman, the Spartan, the monk, and the corporal, this spy incapable of falsehood, this virgin detective,—a physiognomist aware of his secret and old aversion to M. Madeleine, and his conflict with him about Fantine, and who regarded Javert at this moment, would have asked himself, What has happened? It was evident to any one who knew this upright, clear, sincere, honest, austere, and ferocious conscience, that Javert had just emerged from some great internal struggle. Javert had nothing in his mind which he did not also have in his face, and, like all violent men, he was subject to sudden changes. Never had his face been stranger or more unexpected. On entering, he bowed to M. Madeleine with a look in which there was neither rancour, anger, nor suspicion ; he had halted a few yards behind the Mayor's chair, and was now standing there in an almost military attitude, with the simple, cold rudeness of a man who has never been gentle and has ever been patient. He was waiting, without saying a word, without making a movement, in a true humility and tranquil resignation, till the Mayor might think proper to turn round—calm, serious, hat in hand, and with an expression which was half-way between the private before his officer and the culprit before the judge. All the feelings as well as all the revolutions he might be supposed to possess had disappeared: there was nothing but a gloomy sadness on this face, which was impenetrable and simple as granite. His whole person displayed humiliation and firmness, and a sort of courageous despondency. By and by the Mayor laid down his pen and half turned towards him.

"Well, what is the matter, Javert?"

Javert remained silent for a moment, as if reflecting, and then raised his voice with a sad solemnity, which, however, did not exclude simplicity.

"A culpable deed has been committed, sir."

"What deed?"

"An inferior agent of authority has failed in his respect to a magistrate in the gravest matter. I have come, as is my duty, to bring the fact to your knowledge."

"Who is this agent?" M. Madeleine asked.

"Myself."

"And who is the magistrate who has cause to complain of the agent?"

"You, Monsieur le Maire."

M. Madeleine sat up, and Javert continued with a stern air and still looking down:

"Monsieur le Maire, I have come to request that you will procure my dismissal from the service."

M. Madeleine in his stupefaction opened his mouth, but Javert interrupted him:

"You will say that I could have sent in my resignation, but that is not enough. Such a course is honourable, but I have done wrong, and deserve punishment. I must be discharged."

And after a pause he added:

"Monsieur le Maire, you were severe to me the other day unjustly, be so to-day justly."

"What is the meaning of all this nonsense?" M. Madeleine exclaimed. "What is the culpable act you have committed? What have you done to me? You accuse yourself, you wish to be removed——"

"Discharged," said Javert.

"Very good, discharged. I do not understand it."

"You shall do so, sir."

Javert heaved a deep sigh, and continued still coldly and sadly:

"Six weeks ago, M. le Maire, after the scene about that girl, I was furious, and denounced you."

"Denounced me?"

"To the Prefect of Police at Paris."

M. Madeleine, who did not laugh much oftener than Javert, burst into a laugh.

"As a Mayor who had encroached on the police?"

"As an ex-galley slave."

The Mayor turned livid, but Javert, who had not raised his eyes, continued :

"I believed that it was so, and have had these notions for a long time. A resemblance, information you sought at Faverolles, the strength of your loins, the adventure with old Fauchelevent, your skill in firing, your leg which halts a little—and so on. It was very absurd, but I took you for a man of the name of Jean Valjean."

"What name did you say?"

"Jean Valjean. He is a convict I saw twenty years ago when I was assistant keeper at the Toulon galleys. On leaving the galleys, this Valjean, as it appears, robbed a bishop, and then committed a highway robbery on a little Savoyard. For eight years he has been out of the way and could not be found, and I imagined—in a word, I did as I said. Passion decided me, and I denounced you to the Prefect."

M. Madeleine, who had taken up the charge book again, said with a careless accent :

"And what was the answer you received?"

"That I was mad!"

"Well?"

"They were right."

"It is fortunate that you allow it."

"I must do so, for the real Jean Valjean has been found."

The book M. Madeleine was holding fell from his grasp ; he raised his head, looked searchingly at Javert, and said with an indescribable accent :

"Oh!"

Javert continued :

"I will tell you how it is, M. le Maire. It seems that there was over at Ailly le Haut Cloche, an old fellow who was called Father Champmathieu. He wasv ery wretched, and no attention was paid to him, for no one knows how such people live. This autumn Father Champmathieu was arres.ed for stealing cider apples : there was a robbery, a

wall climbed over, and branches broken. This Champmathieu was arrested with the branch still in his hand, and
was locked up. Up to this point it is only a matter for a
police court, but here Providence interposes. As the lock-up
was under repair, the magistrates ordered that Champmathieu should be taken to the departmental prison at
Arras. In this prison there is an ex-convict of the name of
Brevet, under imprisonment for some offence, and he has
been made turnkey for his good behaviour. Champmathieu no sooner arrived than Brevet cries out, 'Why I
know this man : he is an ex-convict. Look at me, old
fellow : you are Jean Valjean.' 'What do you mean?' says
Champmathieu, affecting surprise. 'Don't play the humbug with me,' says Brevet, 'you are Jean Valjean. You
were at the Toulon galleys twenty years ago, and I was
there too.' Champmathieu denied identity, and, as you
may suppose, the affair was thoroughly investigated, with
the following result. This Champmathieu about thirty
years ago was a journeymen wood-cutter at several places,
especially at Faverolles, where his trail is lost. A long
time after he is found again in Auvergne, and then in Paris,
where he says he was a blacksmith, and had a daughter a
washerwoman—though there is no evidence of this,—and
lastly, he turned up in these parts. Now, before being sent
to the galleys, what was Jean Valjean? a wood-cutter :
where? at Faverolles. And here is another fact. This
Valjean's Christian name was Jean, and his mother's family
name Mathieu. What is more natural to suppose than that
on leaving the galleys he assumed his mother's name as a
disguise, and called himself Jean Mathieu? He went to
Auvergne, where Jean is pronounced Chan, and thus he
was transformed into Champmathieu. You are following
me, I suppose? Inquiries have been made at Faverolles,
but Jean Valjean's family is no longer there, and no one
knows where it has gone. As you are aware, in those
places families frequently disappear in such a way ; these
people, if they are not mud, are dust. And then, again, as
the beginning of this story dates back thirty years, there is
no one in Faverolles who knew Jean Valjean : and beside
Brevet, there are only two convicts who remember him.
These two were brought from the galleys and confronted
with the pretended Champmathieu, and they did not hesitate
for a moment. The same age—fifty-four, the same height,
the same look, the same man, in short. It was at this very

moment that I sent my denunciation to Paris, and the
answer I received was that I had lost my senses, for Jean
Valjean was in the hands of justice at Arras. You can
conceive that this surprised me, as I fancied that I held my
Jean Valjean here. I wrote to the magistrates, who sent
for me, and brought Champmathieu before me."

" Well ? " M. Madeleine interrupted him.

Javert replied, with his incorruptible and sad face :

" Monsieur le Maire, truth is truth. I am sorry, but that
man is Jean Valjean : I recognised him too."

M. Madeleine said in a very low voice :

" Are you sure ? "

Javert burst into that sorrowful laugh which escapes from
a profound conviction.

" Oh ! certain."

He remained a moment in thought, mechanically taking
pinches of saw-dust out of the sprinkler in the inkstand,
and added :

" And now that I have seen the real Jean Valjean, I cannot
understand how I could have believed anything else. I beg
your pardon, M. le Maire."

While addressing these supplicating words to the person
who six weeks previously had humiliated him so deeply and
bidden him leave the room, this haughty man was unconsciously full of dignity and simplicity. M. Madeleine
merely answered his entreaty with the hurried question :

" And what does this man say ? "

" Well, Monsieur le Maire, it is an ugly business, for i.
he is Jean Valjean, he is an escaped convict. Scaling a
wall, breaking a branch, and stealing apples is a peccadillo
with a child, an offence in a man, but a crime in a convict.
It is no longer a matter for the police courts, but for the
assizes ; it is no longer imprisonment for a few days, but
the galleys for life. And there is the matter with the
Savoyard, which, I trust, will be brought up again. There
is enough to settle a man, is there not ? but Jean Valjean
is artful, and in that I recognise him too. Any other man
would find it warm ; he would struggle, cry out, refuse to
be Jean Valjean, and so on. He pretends though not to
understand, and says, ' I am Champmathieu, and I shall
stick to it.' He has a look of amazement, and plays the
brute-beast, which is better. Oh ! he is a clever scoundrel !
But no matter, the proofs are ready to hand ; he has been
recognised by four persons, and the old scoundrel will be

found guilty. He is to be tried at Arras Assizes, and I have been summoned as a witness."

M. Madeleine had turned round to his desk again, taken up his charge book, and was quietly turning over the leaves, and busily reading and writing in turn. He now said to the Inspector :

"Enough, Javert ; after all, these details interest me but very slightly ; we are losing our time, and have a deal of work before us. Javert, you will go at once to Mother Busaupied, who sells vegetables at the corner of the Rue Saint Saulve, and tell her to take out a summons against Pierre, the carter ; he is a brutal fellow, who almost drove over this woman and her child, and he must be punished. You will then go to M. Charcillay in the Rue Champigny ; he complains that there is a gutter next door which leaks, and is shaking the foundation of his house. But I am giving you a deal to do, and I think you said you were going away. Did you not state you were going to Arras on this matter in a week or ten days ? "

"Sooner than that, sir."

"On what day, then ? "

"I think I told you that the trial comes off to-morrow, and that I should start by to-night's coach."

"And how long will the trial last ? "

"A day at the most, and sentence will be passed to-morrow night at the latest. But I shall not wait for that, but return as soon as I have given my evidence."

"Very good," said M. Madeleine, and he dismissed Javert with a wave of his hand. But he did not go.

"I beg your pardon, M. le Maire," he said.

"What's the matter now ? " M. Madeleine asked.

"I have one thing to remind you of, sir."

"What is it ? "

"That I must be discharged."

M. Madeleine rose.

"Javert, you are a man of honour, and I esteem you ; you exaggerate your fault, and besides, it is another insult which concerns me. Javert, you are worthy of rising, not of sinking, and I insist on your keeping your situation."

Javert looked at M. Madeleine with his bright eyes, in which it seemed as if his unenlightened, but rigid and chaste conscience could be seen, and he said quietly :

"M. le Maire, I cannot allow it."

"I repeat," M. Madeleine replied, "that the affair concerns myself."

But Javert, only attending to his own thoughts, continued :

"As for exaggerating, I am not doing so, for this is how I reason. I suspected you unjustly ; that is nothing : it is the duty of men like myself to suspect, though there is an abuse in suspecting those above us. But, without proofs, in a moment of passion and for the purpose of revenge, I denounced you, a respectable man, a mayor and a magistrate ; this is serious, very serious ; I, an agent of the authority, insulted that authority in your person. Had any of my subordinates done what I have done, I should have declared him unworthy of the service and discharged him. Stay, Monsieur le Maire, one word more. I have often been severe in my life to others, for it was just, and I was doing my duty, and if I were not severe to myself now, all the justice I have done would become injustice. Ought I to spare myself more than others ? no. What ! I have been only good to punish others and not myself ? why, I should be a scoundrel, and the people who call me that rogue of a Javert, would be in the right ! M. le Maire, I do not wish you to treat me with kindness, for your kindness caused me sufficient ill-blood when dealt to others, and I want none for myself. The kindness that consists in defending the street-walker against the gentleman, the police agent against the mayor, the lower classes against the higher, is what I call bad kindness, and it is such kindness that disorganises society. Good Lord ! it is easy enough to be good, but the difficulty is to be just. Come ! if you had been what I believed you, I should not have been kind to you, as you would have seen. M. le Maire, I am bound to treat myself as I would treat another man ; when I repressed malefactors, when I was severe with scamps, I often said to myself, ' If you ever catch yourself tripping, look out.' I have tripped, I have committed a fault, and all the worse for me. I have strong arms and will turn labourer. M. le Maire, the good of the service requires an example. I simply demand the discharge of Inspector Javert."

All this was said with a humble, proud, despairing, and convinced accent, which gave a peculiar grandeur to this strangely honest man.

"We will see," said M. Madeleine, and he offered him his han d, but Javert fell back, and said sternly :

" Pardon me, sir, but that must not be ; a mayor ought not to give his hand to a spy."

He added between his teeth :

"Yes, a spy ; from the moment when I misused my authority, I have been only a spy."

Then he bowed deeply and walked to the door. When he reached it he turned round and said, with eyes still bent on the ground :

" M. le Maire, I will continue on duty till my place is filled up."

He went out. M. Madeleine thoughtfully listened to his firm, sure step as it died away along the corridor.

CHAPTER XXVII.

THE events which follow were only partially known at M——, but the few which were known left such a memory in that town, that it would be a serious gap in this book if we did not tell them in their smallest details. In these details the reader will notice two or three improbable circumstances, which we retain through respect for truth. In the afternoon that followed Javert's visit, M. Madeleine went to see Fantine as usual ; but before going to her, he asked for Sister Simplice. The two nuns who managed the infirmary, who were Lazarets, like all sisters of charity, were known by the names of Sisters Perpetua and Simplice. Sister Perpetua was an ordinary village girl, a clumsy sister of charity, who had entered the service of Heaven just as she would have taken a cook's place. This type is not rare, for the Monastic orders gladly accept this clumsy peasant clay, which can be easily fashioned into a Capuchin friar or an Ursuline nun ; and these rusticities are employed in the heavy work of devotion. The transition from a drover to a Carmelite is no hard task ; the common substratum of village and cloister ignorance is a ready-made preparation, and at once places the countryman on a level with the monk. Widen the blouse a little and you have a gown. Sister Perpetua was a strong nun belonging to Marnies near Pantoise, who talked with a country accent, sang psalms to match, sugared the *tisane* according to the bigotry or hypocrisy of the patient, was rough with the sick, and harsh with the dying, almost throwing God in their faces, and storming their last moments with angry prayer. She was bold, honest, and florid.

Sister Simplice was white with a waxen clearness. In comparison with Sister Perpetua, she was a sacramental taper by the side of a tallow candle. . Vincent de Paule has divinely described the sister of charity in those admirable words in which so much liberty is blended with slavery. "They will have no other convent but the hospital, no other cell but a hired room, no chapel but the parish church, no cloister beyond the streets or the hospital wards, no walls but obedience, no grating but the fear of God, and no veil but modesty." Sister Simplice was the living ideal of this : no one could have told her age, for she had never been young, and seemed as if she would never grow old. She was a gentle, austere, well-nurtured, cold person—we dare not say a woman—who had never told a falsehood ; she was so gentle that she appeared fragile, but she was more solid than granite. She touched the wretched with her delicate and pure fingers. There was, so to speak, silence in her language ; she only said what was necessary, and possessed an intonation of voice which would at once have edified a confessional and delighted a drawing-room. This delicacy harmonised with the rough gown, for it formed in this rough contact a continual reminder of heaven. Let us dwell on one detail ; never to have told a falsehood, never to have said, for any advantage or even indifferently, a thing which was not the truth, the sacred truth, was the characteristic feature of Sister Simplice. She was almost celebrated in the congregation for this imperturbable veracity, and the Abbé Suard alludes to Sister Simplice in a letter to the deaf, mute Massièeu. However sincere and pure we may be, we have all the brand of a little white lie on our candour, but she had not. Can there be such a thing as a white lie, an innocent lie ? Lying is the absolute of evil. Lying a little is not possible ; the man who lies tells the whole lie ; lying is the face of the fiend, and Satan has two names,—he is called Satan and Lying. That is what she thought, and she practised as she thought. The result was the whiteness to which we have alluded, a whiteness which even covered with its radiance her lips and eyes, for her smile was white, her glance was white. There was not a spider's web nor a grain of dust on the window of this conscience ; on entering the obedience of St. Vincent de Paule she took the name of Simplice through special choice. Simplice of Sicily, our readers will remember, is the saint who sooner let her bosom be plucked out than say she was a native of Segeste, as she was born at Syracuse, though the falsehood would have saved her. This patron saint was fitting for this soul.

Sister Simplice on entering the order had two faults, of which she had gradually corrected herself; she had a taste for dainties and was fond of receiving letters. Now she never read anything but a Prayer-book in large type and in Latin; though she did not understand the language, she understood the book. This pious woman felt an affection for Fantine, as she probably noticed the latent virtue in her, and nearly entirely devoted herself to nursing her. M. Madeleine took Sister Simplice on one side and recommended Fantine to her with a singular accent, which the sister remembered afterwards. On leaving the sister he went to Fantine. The patient daily awaited the appearance of M. Madeleine, as if he brought her warmth and light; she said to the sisters, "I only live when M. le Maire is here." This day she was very feverish. As soon as she saw M. Madeleine she asked him :

"Where is Cosette ? "

He replied with a smile, "She will be here soon."

M. Madeleine behaved to Fantine as usual, except that he remained with her an hour instead of half an hour, to her great delight. He pressed everybody not to allow the patient to want for anything, and it was noticed at one moment that his face became very dark, but this was explained when it was learnt that the physician had bent down to his ear and said, "She is rapidly sinking." Then he returned to the Mayor's office, and the office clerk saw him attentively examining a road-map of France which hung in his room. He then wrote a few figures in pencil on a piece of paper.

From the Mayor's office M. Madeleine proceeded to the end of the town to a Fleming called Master Scaufflaer, gallicised into Scaufflaire, who let out horses and gigs by the day. To reach his yard the nearest way was through an unfrequented street, in which stood the house of the parish priest. The Curé was said to be a worthy and respectable man, who gave good advice. At the moment when M. Madeleine came in front of his house there was only one person in the street, and he noticed the following circumstances: M. le Maire, after passing the house, stopped for a moment, then turned back and walked up to the Curé's door, which had an iron knocker. He quickly seized the knocker and lifted it; then he stopped again as if in deep thought, and, after a few seconds, instead of knocking, he softly let the knocker fall back in its place and went on with a spring of haste which he had not displayed previously. M. Madeleine found Master Scaufflaire at home, busy repairing a set of harness.

"Master Scaufflaire," he asked him, "have you a good horse?"

"M. le Maire," the Fleming replied, "all my horses are good. What do you mean by a good horse?"

"I mean a horse that can go twenty leagues in a day."

"Harnessed to a gig?"

"Yes."

"And how long will it rest after the journey?"

"It must be in a condition to start again the next morning if necessary."

"To go the same distance back?"

"Yes."

"Hang it all, and it is twenty leagues?"

M. Madeleine drew from his pocket the paper on which he had pencilled the figures; they were 5, 6, 8½.

"You see," he said, "total, nineteen and a half, or call them twenty leagues."

"M. le Maire," the Fleming continued, "I can suit you. My little white horse—you may have seen it pass sometimes —is an animal from the Bas Boulonnais, and full of fire. They tried at first to make a saddle-horse of it, but it reared and threw everybody that got on its back. It was supposed to be vicious, and they did not know what to do with it; I bought it and put it in a gig. That was just what it wanted; it is as gentle as a maid and goes like the wind. But you must not try to get on its back, for it has no notion of bieng a saddle-horse. Everybody has his ambition, and it appears as if the horse had said to itself: Draw, yes; carry, no."

"And it will go the distance?"

"At a trot, and under eight hours, but on certain conditions."

"What are they?"

"In the first place, you will let it blow for an hour halfway; it will feed, and you must be present while it is doing so, to prevent the ostler stealing the oats, for I have noticed that at inns oats are more frequently drunk by the stable-boys than eaten by the horses."

" I will be there."

" In the next place, is the gig for yourself, sir ? "

" Yes."

" Do you know how to drive ? "

" Yes."

" Well, you must travel alone and without luggage, in order not to overweight the horse."

" Agreed."

" I shall expect thirty francs a day, and the days of rest paid for as well. Not a farthing less. And you will pay for the horse's keep."

M. Madeleine took three napoleons from his purse and laid them on the table.

" There are two days in advance."

" In the fourth place, a cabriolet would be too heavy for such a journey and tire the horse. You must oblige me by travelling in a little tilbury I have."

" I consent."

" It is light, but it is open."

" I do not care."

" Have you thought, sir, that it is now winter ? "

M. Madeleine made no answer, and the Fleming continued :

" That it is very cold ? "

Monsieur Madeleine was still silent.

" That it may rain ? "

The Mayor raised his head and said :

" The tilbury and the horse will be before my door at half-past four to-morrow morning."

" Very good, sir," Scaufflaire answered, then scratching with his thumb-nail a stain in the wood of his table, he continued, with that careless air with which the Flemings so cleverly conceal their craft :

" Good gracious, I have not thought of asking where you are going ! Be kind enough to tell me, sir."

He had thought of nothing else since the beginning of the conversation, but somehow he had not dared to ask the question.

" Has your horse good legs ? " said M. Madeleine.

" Yes, M. le Maire ; you will hold it up a little in going down-hill. Are there many hills between here and the place you are going to ? "

" Do not forget to be at my door at half-past four exactly," M. Madeleine answered, and went away.

The Fleming stood " like a fool," as he said himself a little while after.

M. le Maire had been gone some two or three minutes when the door opened again; it was M. le Maire. He still wore the same impassive and preoccupied air.

" M. Scaufflaire," he said, " at how much do you value the tilbury and horse you are going to let me, one with the other ? "

" Do you wish to buy them of me, sir ? "

" No, but I should like to guarantee them against any accident, and when I come back you can return me the amount. What is the estimated value ? "

" Five hundred francs, M. le Maire."

" Here they are."

M. Madeleine laid a bank-note on the table, then went out, and this time did not come back. Master Scaufflaire regretted frightfully that he had not said a thousand francs, though tilbury and horse, at a fair valuation, were worth just three hundred. The Fleming called his wife, and told her what had occurred. " Where the deuce can the Mayor be going ? " They held a council. " He is going to Paris," said the wife. " I don't believe it," said the husband. M. Madeleine had left on the table the paper on which he had written the figures; the Fleming took it up and examined it. " Five, six, eight and a half; why, that must mean post stations." He turned to his wife : " I have found it out." " How ? " " It is five leagues from here to Hesdin, six from there to St. Pol, and eight and a half from St. Pol to Arras. He is going to Arras."

In the meanwhile the Mayor had returned home, and had taken the longest road, as if the gate of the priest's house were a temptation to him which he wished to avoid. He went up to his bedroom and locked himself in, which was not unusual, for he was fond of going to bed at an early hour. Still the factory porteress, who was at the same time M. Madeleine's only servant, remarked that his candle was extinguished at a quarter-past eight, and mentioned the fact to the cashier when he came in, adding :

" Can Monsieur the Mayor be sick ? I thought he looked very strange to-day."

The cashier occupied a room exactly under M. Madeleine's. He paid no attention to the remarks of the porteress, but went to bed and fell asleep. About midnight he woke with a start, for he heard in his sleep a noise above his head. He listened ; it was a footfall coming and going, as if some one were walking about the room above him. He listened more attentively, and recognised M. Madeleine's step ; and this seemed to him strange, for usually no sound could be heard from the Mayor's room till he rose. A moment later the cashier heard something like a wardrobe open and shut ; a piece of furniture was moved, there was a silence, and the walking began again. The cashier sat up in bed, broad awake, looked out, and through his window noticed on a wall opposite the red reflection of a lighted window ; from the direction of the rays it could only be the window of M. Madeleine's bedroom. The reflection flickered as if it came from a fire rather than a candle, while the shadow of the framework could not be traced, which proved that the window was wide open, and this was a curious fact, regard being had to the coldness. The cashier fell asleep, and woke again some two hours after ; the same slow and regular footfall was still audible above his head. The reflection was still cast on the wall, but was now pale and quiet, as if it came from a lamp or a candle. The window was still open. Let us see what was passing in M. Madeleine's bedroom.

CHAPTER XXVIII.

THE reader has doubtless divined that M. Madeleine is Jean Valjean. We have already looked into the depths of this conscience, and the moment has arrived to look into them again. We do not do this without emotion or tremor, for there is nothing more terrifying than this species of contemplation. The mental eye can nowhere find greater brilliancy or greater darkness than within man ; it cannot dwell on anything which is more formidable, complicated, mysterious, or infinite. There is a spectacle grander than the ocean, and that is the sky ; there is a spectacle grander than the sky, and it is the interior of the soul. To write the poem of the human conscience, were the subject only one man, and he the lowest of men, would be reducing all epic poems into one supreme and final epos. Conscience in the chaos of chimeras, envies, and attempts, the furnace of dreams, the lurking-place of ideas we are ashamed of ; it is the pandemonium of sophistry, the battlefield of the

passions. At certain hours look through the livid face of
a reflecting man, look into his soul, peer into the darkness.
Beneath the external silence, combats of giants are going
on there, such as we read of in Homer ; mêlées of dragons
and hydras and clouds of phantoms, such as we find in
Milton ; and visionary spirals, such as Dante introduces
us to. A glorious thing is the infinitude which every man
bears within him, and by which he desperately measures
the volitions of his brain and the actions of his life.
Alighieri one day came to a sinister gate, before which
he hesitated ; we have one before us, on the threshold of
which we also hesitate. Let us enter notwithstanding.

We have but little to add to what the reader already
knows concerning what happened to Jean Valjean, since
his adventure with Little Gervais. From this moment,
as we have seen, he became another man, and he made
himself what the Bishop wished to make him. It was
more than a transformation, it was a transfiguration.
He succeeded in disappearing, sold the Bishop's plate,
only keeping the candlesticks as a souvenir, passed through
France, reached M——, had the idea we have described,
accomplished what we have narrated, managed to make
himself unseizable and inaccessible, and henceforth settled
at M——, happy at feeling his conscience saddened by the
past, and the first half of his existence contradicted by
the last half ; he lived peacefully, reassured and trusting,
and having but two thoughts—to hide his name and
sanctify his life ; escape from men and return to God.
These two thoughts were so closely blended in his mind,
that they only formed one ; they were both equally absorbing and imperious, and governed his slightest actions.
Usually they agreed to regulate the conduct of his life ;
they turned him to the shadow ; they rendered him benefi-
cent and simple, and they counselled him to the same things.
At times, however, there was a conflict between them, and
in such cases the man whom the whole town of M——
called Monsieur Madeleine did not hesitate to sacrifice
the first to the second,—his security to his virtue. Hence,
despite all his caution and prudence, he had kept the
Bishop's candlesticks, wore mourning for him, questioned
all the little Savoyards who passed through the town,
inquired after the family at Faverolles, and saved the life
of old Fauchelevent, in spite of the alarming insinuations
of Javert. It seemed, as we have already remarked, that

he thought, after the example of all those who have been wise, holy, and just, that his highest duty was not towards himself.

It must be said, however, that nothing like the present had before occurred. Never had the two ideas which governed the unhappy man whose sufferings we are describing, entered upon so serious a struggle. He comprehended this confusedly, but deeply, from the first words which Javert uttered on entering his study. At the moment when the name which he had buried so deeply was so strangely pronounced, he was struck with stupor, and, as it were, intoxicated by the sinister peculiarity of his destiny. And through this stupor he felt that quivering which precedes great storms; he bowed like an oak at the approach of a storm, like a soldier before a coming assault. He felt the shadows full of thunder and lightning collecting over his head: while listening to Javert he had a thought of running off, denouncing himself, taking Champmathieu out of prison and taking his place. This was painful, like an incision in the flesh, but it passed away, and he said to himself, We will see! He repressed this first generous movement, and recoiled before such heroism.

Doubtless it would have been fine if, after the Bishop's holy remarks, after so many years of repentance and self-denial, in the midst of a penitence so admirably commenced, this man, even in the presence of such a terrible conjuncture, had not failed for a moment, but continued to march at the same pace toward this open abyss, at the bottom of which heaven was: this would have been grand, but it did not take place. We are bound to describe all the things that took place in this mind, and cannot say that this was one of them. What carried him away first was the instinct of self-preservation. He hastily collected his ideas, stifled his emotion, adjourned any resolution with the firmness of terror, deadened himself against what he had to do, and resumed his calmness as a gladiator puts up his buckler. For the remainder of the day he was in the same state—a hurricane within, a deep tranquillity outside,—and he only took what may be called "conservative measures." All was still confused and jumbled in his brain; the trouble in it was so great that he did not see distinctly the outline of any idea, and he could have said nothing about himself, save that he had received a heavy blow. He went as usual to Fantine's bed of pain, and prolonged his visit, with a kindly instinct, saying to himself that he must act thus, and recommend her to the sisters in the event of his being obliged to go away. He felt vaguely that he must perhaps go to Arras ; and, though not the least in the world decided about the journey, he said to himself that, safe from suspicion as he was, there would be no harm in being witness of what might take place, and he hired Scaufflaire's conveyance, that he might be ready for any emergency.

He dined with a good appetite, and, on returning to his bedroom, reflected. He examined his situation, and found it extraordinary,—so extraordinary that, in the midst of his reverie, through some almost inexplicable impulse of anxiety, he rose from his chair and bolted his door. He was afraid lest something might enter, and he barricaded himself against the possible. A moment after, he blew out his light, for it annoyed him, and he fancied that he might be overseen. By whom ? Alas, what he wanted to keep out had entered ; what he wished to blind was looking at him. It was his conscience, that is to say, God. Still, at the first moment, he deceived himself ; he had a feeling of security and solitude. When he put in the bolt, he thought himself impregnable ; when the candle was out, he felt himself invisible. He then regained his self-possession ; and he put his elbows on the table, leant his head on his hand, and began to ruminate in the darkness.

"Where am I ? Am I not in a dream ? What was I told ? Is it really true that I saw that Javert, and that he spoke to me so ? Who can this Champmathieu be ? It seems he resembles me. Is it possible ? When I think that I was so tranquil yesterday, and so far from suspecting anything ! What was I doing yesterday at this hour ? What will be the result of this event ? What am I to do ? "

Such was the trouble he was in that his brain had not the strength to retain ideas. They passed like waves, and he clutched his forehead with both hands to stop them. From this tumult which overthrew his wits and reason, and from which he sought to draw an evidence and a resolution, nothing issued but agony. His head was burning ; and he went to the window and threw it wide open. There were no stars in the heavens, and he went back to the table and sat down by it. The first hour

passed away thus, but gradually vague features began to
shape themselves, and become fixed in his thoughts, and
he could observe with the precision of reality some details
of the situation, if not its entirety. He began by noticing
that, however critical and extraordinary his situation might
be, he was utterly the master of it. His stupor only
became the deeper.

Independently of the stern and religious object he proposed to himself in his actions, all that he had done up to
this day was only a hole that he was digging in which to
bury his name. What he had always most feared, in his
hours of reflection as in his sleepless nights, was ever to hear
that name pronounced. He said to himself that this would
be to him the end of everything ; that on the day when that
name reappeared, it would cause his new life to fade
away, and possibly the new soul he had within him. He
shuddered at the mere thought that this could happen.
Assuredly if any one had told him at such moments that
the hour would arrive in which this name would echo in
his ear, when the hideous name of Jean Valjean would
suddenly emerge from the night and rise before him, when
this formidable light which dissipated the mystery with
which he surrounded himself would suddenly shine above
his head, and that the name would no longer menace him ;
that the light would produce only a denser gloom ; that
this rent veil would increase the mystery ; that the earthquake would consolidate his edifice ; that this prodigious
incident would have no other result, if he thought proper,
but to render his existence clearer and yet more impenetrable, and that from his confrontation with the
phantom of Jean Valjean, the good and worthy M.
Madeleine would come forth, more honoured, more peaceful, and more respected than ever,—if any one had told
him this, he would have shaken his head, and considered
such remarks insensate. And yet all this had really
happened, and this heap of impossibilities was a fact, and
Heaven had permitted all these wild things to become real.

His reverie continued to grow clearer, and each moment
he comprehended his position better. It seemed to him
that he had just awakened from a dream, and that he was
descending an incline in the middle of the night, shuddering and recoiling in vain from the brink of an abyss. He
distinctly saw in the shadows an unknown man, a stranger,
whom destiny took for him, and thrust into the gulf in his

place. In order that the gulf should close, either he or another must fall in. He had no necessity to do anything, the clearness became complete, and he confessed to himself—that his place was vacant at the galleys ; that, whatever he might do, it constantly expected him, that the robbery of Little Gervais led him back to it, that this vacant place would wait for him and attract him, until he filled it, and that this was inevitable and fatal. And then he said to himself—that at this moment he had a substitute, —that it seemed a man of the name of Champmathieu had this ill-luck : and that, in future, himself at the galleys in the person of this Champmathieu, and present in society under the name of M. Madeleine, would have nothing more to fear, provided that he did not prevent justice from laying over the head of this Champmathieu the stone of infamy which, like the tombstone, falls once and is never raised again.

All this was so violent and so strange, that he suddenly felt within him that species of indescribable movement which no man experiences more than twice or thrice in his life, a sort of convulsion of the conscience, which disturbs everything doubtful in the heart, which is composed of irony, joy, and despair, and what might be called an internal burst of laughter. He hastily relighted his candle.

"Well, what am I afraid of?" he said to himself; "what reason have I to have such thoughts ? I am saved, and all is settled. There was only one open door through which my past could burst in upon my life : and that door is now walled up for ever. This Javert, who has so long annoyed me, the formidable instinct which seemed to have scented me, and by heavens ! had scented me, the frightful dog ever making a point at me, is routed, engaged elsewhere, and absolutely thrown out ! He is henceforth satisfied, he will leave me at peace, for he has got his Jean Valjean ! It is possible that he may wish to leave the town too. And all this has taken place without my interference, and so, what is there so unlucky in it all ? On my word, any people who saw me would believe that a catastrophe had befallen me. After all, if some people are rendered unhappy, it is no fault of mine. Providence has done it all, and apparently decrees it. Have I the right to derange what He arranges? What is it that I am going to interfere in? it does not concern me. What ! I am not

satisfied? Why! what else can I want? I have attained
the object to which I have been aspiring for so many years,
the dream of my nights, the matter of my prayers—security.
It is Heaven that wills it, and I have done nothing contrary
to God's desire. And why has Heaven decreed it? that
I may continue what I have begun ; that I may do good ;
that I may one day be a grand and encouraging example ;
that it may be said that there is after all a little happiness
attaching to the penance I have undergone. I really cannot
understand why I was so afraid just now about visiting
that worthy Curé, telling all to him as to a confessor, and
asking his advice, for this is certainly what he would have
advised me. It is decided ; I will let matters alone, and
leave the decision to God."

Thus he spoke in the depths of his conscience, while
leaning over what might be called his own abyss. He got
up from his chair and walked about the room. "Come,"
he said, "I will think no more of it ; I have made up my
mind ; " but he felt no joy. It is no more possible to
prevent thought from reverting to an idea than the sea
from returning to the shore. With the sailor this is called
the tide, with the culprit it is called remorse ; God heaves
the soul like the ocean. After a few moments, he could do
no otherwise, he resumed the gloomy dialogue, in which it
was he who spoke and he who listened, saying what he
wished to be silent about, listening to what he did not
desire to hear, and yielding to that mysterious power which
said to him, "Think," as it said two thousand years ago to
another condemned man, "Go on."

Before going further, and in order to be fully understood,
let us dwell on a necessary observation. It is certain that
men talk to themselves ; and there is not a thinking being
who has not realised the fact. It is only in this sense that
the words frequently employed in this chapter, *he said, he
exclaimed*, must be understood ; men talk to themselves,
speak to themselves, cry out within themselves, but the
external silence is not interrupted. There is a grand
tumult ; everything speaks within us, excepting the mouth.
The realities of the soul, for all that they are not visible
and palpable, are not the less realities. He asked himself
then what he had arrived at, and cross-questioned himself
about the resolution he had formed. He confessed to himself that all he had arranged in his mind was monstrous,
and that leaving "God to act" was simply horrible. To

allow this mistake of destiny and of men to be accomplished, not to prevent it, to lend himself to it, do nothing, in short, was to do everything ; it was the last stage of hypocritical indignity ! it was a low, cowardly, cunning, abject, hideous crime. For the first time during eight years this hapless man had the taste of a bad thought and a bad action, and he spat it out with disgust.

He continued to question himself. He asked himself what he had meant by the words, "My object is attained." He allowed that his life had an object, but what was its nature ?—Conceal his name ! deceive the police. Was it for so paltry a thing that he had done all that he had effected ? Had he not another object which was the great and true one, to save not his person, but his soul—to become once again honest and good ? To be a just man ! was it not that he had solely craved after, and what the Bishop had ordered him ? Close the door on his past ? But, great Heaven, he opened it again by committing an infamous action. He was becoming a robber once more, and the most odious of robbers ! he was robbing another man of his existence, his livelihood, his peace, and his place in the sunshine. He was becoming an assassin, he was killing, morally killing, a wretched man ; he was inflicting on him the frightful living death, the open-air death, which is called the galleys. On the other hand, if he gave himself up, freed this man who was suffering from so grievous an error, resumed his name, became through duty the convict Jean Valjean, that would be really completing his resurrection, and eternally closing the inferno from which he was emerging ! Falling back into it apparently would be leaving it in reality ! He must do this : he would have done nothing unless he did this ; all his life would be useless ; all his reputation thrown away. He felt that the Bishop was here, that he was the more present because he was dead, that the Bishop was steadfastly looking at him, and that henceforth Madeleine the Mayor would be an abomination to him, and Jean Valjean, the convict, admirable and pure in his sight. Men saw his mask, but the Bishop saw his face ; men saw his life, but the Bishop saw his conscience. He must consequently go to Arras, deliver the false Jean Valjean, and denounce the true one. Alas ! this was the greatest of sacrifices, the most poignant of victories, the last step to take ; but he must take it. Frightful destiny his ! he could not obtain sanctity in the sight of Heaven unless he returned to infamy in the sight of man.

"Well," said he, "I will make up my mind to this. I will do my duty and save this man."

He uttered those words aloud without noticing he had raised his voice. He fetched his books, verified and put them in order. He threw into the fire a number of claims he had upon embarrassed tradesmen, and wrote a letter, which he addressed "To M. Laffitte, banker, Rue d'Artois, Paris." He then took from his desk a pocket-book, which contained a few bank-notes and the passport he had employed just previously to go to the elections. Any one who had seen him while he was accomplishing these various acts, with which such grave meditation was mingled, would not have suspected what was taking place in him. At moments his lips moved, at others he raised his head and looked at a part of the wall, as if there were something there which he desired to clear up or question.

The letter to M. Laffitte finished, he put it into his portfolio, and began his walk once more. His reverie had not deviated; he continued to see his duty clearly written in luminous letters which flashed before his eyes, and moved about with his glance, Name yourself, denounce yourself! He could also see the two ideas which had hitherto been the double rule of his life—to hide his name and sanctify his life—moving before him as it were in a tangible shape. For the first time they seemed to him absolutely distinct, and he saw the difference that separated them. He recognised that one of these ideas was necessarily good, while the other might become bad; that the former was devotion, the latter personality; that one said, "My neighbour," the other "Myself"; that one came from the light, and the other from darkness. They strove with each other, and he could see them doing so. While he was thinking, they had grown before his mental eye, and they had now colossal forms, and he fancied he could see a god and a giant wrestling within him, in the infinitude to which we just now alluded, and in the midst of obscurity and flashes of light. It was a horrible sight, but it seemed to him as if the good thought gained the victory. He felt that he was approaching the second decisive moment of his life; that the Bishop marked the first phase of his new life, and that this Champmathieu marked the second. After a great crisis, a great trial.

The fever, quieted for a moment, gradually returned, however. A thousand thoughts crossed his mind, but they continued to strengthen him in his resolution. At one moment he said to himself that he perhaps regarded the matter too seriously; that, after all, this Champmathieu was not interesting, and in any case was a thief. He answered himself—If this man has really stolen apples, he will have a month's imprisonment, but that is a long way from the galleys. And then, again, is it proved that he has committed a robbery? The name of Jean Valjean is crushing him, and seems to dispense with proofs. Do not public prosecutors habitually act in this way? A man is believed to be a thief because he is known to be a convict. At another moment the idea occurred to him that, when he had denounced himself, the heroism of his deed might perhaps be taken into consideration, as well as his life of honesty during the last seven years, and the good he had done the town, and that he would be pardoned. But this supposition soon vanished, and he smiled bitterly at the thought that the robbery of the 40 sous from Gervais rendered him a relapsed convict, that this affair would certainly be brought forward, and, by the precise terms of the law, sentence him to the galleys for life.

He turned away from all illusions, detached himself more and more from earth, and sought consolation and strength elsewhere. He said to himself that he must do his duty: that, perhaps, he would not be more wretched after doing it than he would have been had he eluded it: that, if he let matters take their course and remained at M——, his good name, good deeds, charity, wealth, popularity, and virtue would be tainted by a crime; and what flavour would all these sacred things have, when attached to this hideous thought; while, if he accomplished his sacrifice, he would mingle a heavenly idea with the galleys, the chain, the green cap, the unrelaxing toil, and the pitiless shame. At last he said to himself that it was a necessity, that his destiny was thus shaped, that he had no power to derange the arrangements of Heaven, and that in any case he must choose either external virtue and internal abomination, or holiness within and infamy outside him. His courage did not fail him in revolving so many mournful ideas, but his brain grew weary. He began thinking involuntarily of other and indifferent matters. His arteries beat violently in his temples, and he was still walking up

and down ; midnight struck, first from the parish church,
and then from the Town Hall. He counted the twelve
strokes of the two clocks, and compared the sound of the
two bells. They reminded him that, a few days before,
he had seen an old bell at a marine store, on which was
engraved the name Antoine Albier, Romainville.

As he felt cold, he lit a fire, but did not dream of closing
the window. Then he fell back into his stupor, obliged to
make a mighty effort to remember what he had been
thinking of before midnight struck. At last he succeeded.

" Ah, yes," he said to himself, " I had formed the resolution to denounce myself."

And then he suddenly began thinking of Fantine.

" Stay," he said, " and that poor woman ! "

Here a fresh crisis broke out. Fantine, suddenly appearing in the midst of his reverie, was like a ray of unexpected
light. He fancied that all changed around him, and
exclaimed :

"Wait a minute ! Hitherto, I have thought of myself
and consulted my own convenience. Whether it suits me
to be silent or denounce myself—hide my person or save
my soul—be a contemptible and respected magistrate, or an
infamous and venerable convict—it is always self, nought
but self. Good heavens ! all this is egotism under different
shapes, 'tis true, but still egotism. Suppose I were to
think a little about others ! It is the first duty of a
Christian to think of his neighbour. Well, let me examine :
when I am effaced and forgotten, what will become of all
this ? If I denounce myself, that Champmathieu will be
set at liberty. I shall be sent back to the galleys, and
what then ? What will occur here ? Here is a town,
factories, a trade, workpeople, men, women, old grandfathers, children, and poor people : I have created all this.
I keep it all alive : wherever there is a chimney smoking,
I placed the brand in the fire and the meat in the sauce-
pan : I have produced easy circumstances, circulation, and
credit. Before I came there was nothing of all this ; I
revived, animated, fertilised, stimulated, and enriched the
whole district. When I am gone the soul will be gone ;
if I withdraw all will die. And then, this woman, who
has suffered so greatly, who has so much merit in her
fall, and whose misfortune I unwittingly caused. And the
child which I intended to go and fetch, and restore to the
mother ! Do not I also owe something to this woman, in

reparation of the wrong which I have done her? If I disappear, what will happen? The mother dies, and the child will become what it can. This will happen if I denounce myself. If I do not denounce myself? Let me see."

After putting this question, he hesitated, and trembled slightly, but this emotion lasted but a short time, and he answered himself with calmness :

"Well, this man goes to the galleys, it is true, but, after all, he has stolen. Although I may say to myself that he has not stolen, he has done so·! I remain here and continue my operations : in ten years I shall have gained ten millions. I spread them over the country. I keep nothing for myself; but what do I care ? I am not doing this for myself. The prosperity of all is increased ; trades are revived, factories and forges are multiplied, and thousands of families are happy ; the district is populated ; villages spring up where there are only farms, and farms where there is nothing ; wretchedness disappears, and with it debauchery, prostitution, robbery, murder, all the vices, all the crimes—and this poor mother brings up her child. Why, I was mad, absurd, when I talked about denouncing myself, and I must guard against precipitation. What! because it pleases me to play the grand and the generous —it is pure melodrama after all—because I only thought of myself, and in order to save from a perhaps exaggerated though substantially just punishment a stranger, a thief, and an apparent scoundrel—a whole department must perish ! a poor woman die in the hospital, and a poor child starve in the streets, like dogs ! Why, it is abominable ! without the mother seeing her child again, or the child knowing her mother ! and all this on behalf of an old scamp of an apple stealer, who has assuredly deserved the galleys for something else, if not for that. These are fine scruples that save a culprit and sacrifice the innocent, that save an old vagabond who has not many years to live, and will not be more unhappy at the galleys than in his hovel, and destroy an entire population,—mothers, wives, and children. That poor little Cosette, who has only me in the world, and is doubtless at this moment shivering with cold in the den of those Thénardiers. There is another pair of wretches. And I would fail in my duties to all these poor creatures, and commit such a folly as to denounce myself! Let us put things at the worst. Suppose that I am committing a bad action in this, and that my conscience reproaches me with it some day ;—there will be devotion and virtue in accepting, for the good of my neighbour, these reproaches, which only weigh on me, and this bad action, which affects only my own soul."

He arose and resumed his walk. This time he seemed to be satisfied with himself. Diamonds are only found in the darkness of the earth ; truths are only found in the depths of the thought. It seemed to him that after descending into these depths, after groping for some time in the densest of this darkness, he had found one of these diamonds, one of these truths, which he held in his hand and which dazzled his eyes when he looked at it.

"Yes," he thought, " I am on the right track and hold the solution of the problem. A man must in the end hold on to something, and my mind is made up. I will let matters take their course, so no more vacillation or backsliding. It is for the interest of all, not of myself. I am Madeleine, and remain Madeleine, and woe to the man who is Jean Valjean. I am no longer he. I do not know that man, and if any one happen to be Jean Valjean at this moment, he must look out for himself, for it does not concern me. It is a fatal name that floats in the night, and if it stop and settle upon any man, all the worse for that man."

He looked into the small looking-glass over the mantelpiece, and said to himself :

"How greatly has forming a resolution relieved me ! I am quite a different man at present."

He walked a little way and then stopped short. "Come," he said, " I must not hesitate before any of the consequences of the resolution I have formed. There are threads which still attach me to Jean Valjean which must be broken. There are in this very room objects which would accuse me, —dumb things which would serve as witnesses, and they must all disappear."

He drew his purse from his pocket, and took a small key out of it. He put this key in a lock, the hole of which could scarcely be seen, for it was hidden in the darkest part of the design on the paper that covered the walls. A sort of false cupboard made between the corner of the wall and the mantelpiece was visible. In this hiding-place there were only a few rags—a blue blouse, worn trousers, an old knapsack, and a large thorn-stick, shod with iron at both ends.

Any one who saw Jean Valjean pass through D—— in October, 1815, would easily have recognised all these wretched articles. He had preserved them, as he had done the candlesticks, that they might constantly remind him of his starting-point ; still he hid what came from the galleys, and displayed the candlesticks which came from the Bishop. He took a furtive glance at the door, as if afraid that it might open in spite of the bolt ; and then with a rapid movement he made but one armful of the things he had so religiously and perilously kept for so many years, and threw them all—rags, stick, and knapsack—into the fire. He closed the cupboard, and, redoubling his precautions, which were now useless since it was empty, dragged a heavy piece of furniture in front of it. In a few seconds, the room and opposite wall were lit up with a large red and flickering glow ; all was burning, and the thorn-stick crackled and threw out sparks into the middle of the room. From the knapsack, as it burned with all the rags it contained, fell something that glistened in the ashes. On stooping it could be easily recognised as a coin ; it was doubtless the little Savoyard's two-franc piece. He did not look at the fire, and continued his walk backwards and forwards. All at once his eye fell on the two candlesticks which the fire-light caused to shine vaguely on the mantelpiece.

"Stop," he thought, "all Jean Valjean is in them. They also must be destroyed."

He seized the candlesticks—there was a fire large enough to destroy their shape, and convert them into unrecognisable ingots. He leant over the hearth and warmed his hands for a moment ; it was a great comfort to him.

He stirred up the ashes with one of the candlesticks, and in a moment they were both in the fire. All at once he fancied he heard a voice cry within him, "Jean Valjean ! Jean Valjean !" His hair stood on end, and he became like a man who is listening to a terrible thing.

"Yes, that is right ; finish !" the voice said, "complete what you are about ; destroy those candlesticks, annihilate that reminiscence ! forget the Bishop ! forget everything ! ruin that Champmathieu ; that is right. Applaud yourself ; come, all is settled and resolved on. This old man, who does not know what they want with him, who is perhaps innocent, whose whole misfortune your name causes, on whom your name weighs like a crime, is going to be taken for you, sentenced, and will end his days in abjectness and horror. That is excellent ! Be an honest man yourself ; remain Mayor, honourable and honoured, enrich the town, assist the indigent, bring up orphans, live happy, virtuous, and applauded ; and during this time, while you are here in joy and light, there will be somebody who wears your red jacket, bears your name in ignominy, and drags along your chain at the galleys. Yes, that is an excellent arrangement ! Oh ! you wretch ! "

The perspiration rolled off his forehead, and he fixed his haggard eye upon the candlesticks. The voice within him, however, had not ended yet. It continued :

" Jean Valjean ! there will be around you many voices making a great noise, speaking very loud and blessing you, and one which no one will hear, and which will curse you in the darkness. Well, listen, infamous man ! all these blessings will fall back on the ground before reaching Heaven, and the curse alone will ascend to God ! "

This voice, at first very faint, and which spoke from the obscurest nook of his conscience, had gradually become sonorous and formidable, and he now heard it in his ear. He fancied that it was not his own voice, and he seemed to hear the last words so distinctly that he looked round the room with a species of terror.

" Is there any one here ? " he asked, in a loud voice and wildly.

Then he continued with a laugh, which seemed almost idiotic :

" What a fool I am ! there can be nobody."

There was somebody ; but He was not of those whom the human eye can see. He placed the candlesticks on the mantelpiece, and then resumed that melancholy, mournful walk, which aroused the sleeper underneath him. This walking relieved him, and at the same time intoxicated him. It appears sometimes as if on supreme occasions people move about to ask advice of everything they pass. At the end of a few moments he no longer knew what result to arrive at. He now recoiled with equal horror from the two resolutions he had formed in turn ; the two ideas that counselled him seemed each as desperate as the other. What a fatality that this Champmathieu should be taken for him ! He was hurled down precisely by the means which Providence at first seemed to have employed to strengthen his position.

There was a moment during which he regarded his future :

—denounce himself ! great heavens ! give himself up ! He thought with immense despair of all that he must give up, of all that he must resume. He would be forced to bid adieu to this good, pure, radiant life,—to the respect of all classes,—to honour, to liberty ! He would no longer walk about the fields, he would no longer hear the birds sing in May, or give alms to the little children ! He would no longer feel the sweetness of glances of gratitude and love fixed upon him ! He would leave this little house, which he had built, and his little bedroom. All appeared charming to him at this moment. He would no longer read those books or write at the little deal table ; his old servant would no longer bring up his coffee in the morning. Great God ! instead of all this, there would be the gang, the red jacket, the chain on his foot, fatigue, the dungeon, the camp-bed, and all the horrors he knew ! At his age, after all he had borne ! It would be different were he still young. But to be old, coarsely addressed by anybody, searched by the gaoler, and receive blows from the keeper's stick ! to thrust his naked feet into iron-shod shoes ! to offer his leg morning and night to the man who examines the fetters ! to endure the curiosity of strangers who would be told, "That is the famous Jean Valjean, who was Mayor of M——." At night, when pouring with perspiration, and crushed by fatigue, with a green cap on his head, to go up two by two, under the sergeant's whip, the side ladder of the hulks ! Oh, what wretchedness ! Can destiny then be malignant like an intelligent being, and become monstrous like the human heart ?

And do what he might, he ever fell back into this crush-ing dilemma, which was the basis of his reverie. Remain in paradise, and become a demon there ; or re-enter hell, and become an angel ? What should he do, great God ! what should he do ? The trouble, from which he had escaped with such difficulty, was again let loose on him, and his thoughts became composed once more. They assumed something stupefied and mechanical, which is peculiar to despair. The name of Romainville incessantly returned to his mind, with two lines of a song which he had formerly heard. He remembered that Romainville is a little wood, near Paris, where lovers go to pick lilac in April. He tottered both externally and internally ; he walked like a little child allowed to go alone. At certain moments, he struggled against his lassitude. and tried to recapture his intelligence ; he tried to set himself, for the last time, the problem over which he had fallen in a state of exhaustion,—must he denounce himself, or must he be silent ? He could not succeed in seeing anything distinct. The vague outlines of all the reasonings sketched in by his reverie were dissipated in turn like smoke. Still, he felt that, however he resolved, and without any possibility of escape, something belonging to him was about to die ; that he entered a sepulchre, whether on his right hand or his left, and that either his happiness or his virtue would be borne to the grave.

Alas ! all his irresolution had seized him again, and he was no further advanced than at the beginning. So struggled beneath its anguish this unhappy soul.

CHAPTER XXIX

THE clock struck three. He had been walking about in this way for five hours without a break, when he fell into his chair. He fell asleep, and had a dream. This dream, like most dreams, was only connected with his situation by something poignant and mournful, but it made an impression on him. This nightmare struck him so much that he wrote it down at a later date, and we think we are bound to transcribe it verbatim, for whatever the history of this man may be, it would be incomplete if we omitted it. It is the gloomy adventure of a sick soul. It is as follows : Upon the envelope we find this line written : "The dream I had on that night."

"I was in a field, a great, sad field, on which no grass grew. It did not seem to me to be day, but it was not night. I was walking with my brother, the brother of my boyish years, of whom I am bound to say I never think, and whom I scarce remember. We were talking, and met travellers. We spoke about a woman, formerly a neighbour of ours, who always worked with her window open, as she occupied a front room. While talking, we felt cold on account of this open window. There were no trees on the plain. We saw a man pass close by us ; he was a perfectly naked man, of the colour of ashes, mounted on a horse of an earthen colour. The man had no hair, and I could see his skull, and the veins on his skull. He held in his hand a wand, which was supple as a vine-twig and heavy as lead. This horse-man passed and said nothing to us.

"My brother said to me: 'Let us turn into the hollow way.'

"It was a hollow way in which not a bramble or even a patch of moss could be seen; all was earth-coloured, even the sky. After going a few yards, I received no answer when I spoke, and I noticed that my brother was no longer with me. I entered a village that I saw, and I fancied that it must be Romainville. The first street I entered was deserted; I entered a second street, and behind the angle formed by the two streets a man was standing against the wall. I asked this man, 'What is this place? where am I?' but he gave me no answer. I saw the door of a house open, and walked in.

"The first room was deserted, and I entered a second. Behind the door of this room there was a man leaning against the wall. I asked him, 'To whom does this house belong? where am I?' but the man gave me no answer. I went out into the garden of the house, and it was deserted. Behind the first tree I found a man standing. I said to the man, 'Whose is this garden? where am I?' but he made me no answer.

"I wandered about this village and fancied that it was a town. All the streets were deserted, all the doors open. Not a living soul passed along the street, moved in the rooms, or walked in the gardens. But there was behind every corner, every door, and every tree, a man standing silently. I never saw more than one at a time, and these men looked at me as I passed.

"I left the village and began walking about the fields. At the end of some time I turned back and saw a great crowd coming after me. I recognised all the men whom I had seen in the town, and they had strange heads. They did not appear to be in a hurry, and yet they walked faster than I, and made no noise in walking. In an instant this crowd joined me and surrounded me. The faces of these men were earth-coloured. Then the man I had seen first and questioned when I entered the town, said to me, 'Where are you going? Do you not know that you have been dead for a long time?' I opened my mouth to answer, and I perceived that there was no one near me."

He awoke. He was chilled to the bone. A wind, cold

as the morning breeze, was shaking the open window.
The fire had died away, the candle was nearly burned out,
and it was still black night. He rose and went to the
window ; there were still no stars in the sky. From his
window he could see the yard and the street, and a dry
sharp sound on the ground below him induced him to look
out. He saw two red stars, whose rays lengthened and
shortened curiously in the gloom. As his mind was half
submerged in the mist of dreams, he thought, " There are
no stars in the sky : they are on the earth now." A second
sound like the first completely woke him, and he perceived
that those two stars were carriage lamps, and by the light
which they projected he could distinguish the shape of the
vehicle—it was a tilbury, in which a small white horse was
harnessed. The sound he had heard was the pawing of the
horse's hoof on the ground.

"What's the meaning of this conveyance?" he said to
himself; "who can have come at so early an hour?"

At this moment there was a gentle tap at his bedroom
door. He shuddered from head to foot, and shouted in a
terrible voice, "Who's there?"

Some one replied, "I, sir;" and he recognised his old
servant's voice.

"Well," he continued, "what is it?"

"It is getting on for four o'clock, sir."

"What has that to do with me?"

"The tilbury has come, sir."

"What tilbury?"

"Did you not order one?"

"No," he said.

"The ostler says that he has come to fetch M. le Maire."

"What ostler?"

"M. Scaufflaire's."

This name made him start as if a flash of lightning had
passed before his eyes.

"Ah, yes," he repeated, "M. Scaufflaire."

Could the old woman have seen him at this moment she
would have been horrified. There was a lengthened silence,
during which he stupidly examined the candle flame, and
rolled up some of the wax in his fingers. The old woman,
who was waiting, at length mustered up courage to raise her
voice again.

"M. le Maire, what answer am I to give?"

"Say it is quite right, and I am coming down."

CHAPTER XXX.

THE postal service from Arras to M—— was still performed in small mail-carts, dating from the Empire. They were two-wheeled vehicles, lined with tawny leather, hung on springs, and having only two seats, one for the driver, and another for a passenger. The wheels were armed with those long offensive axle-trees, which kept other carriages at a distance, and may still be seen on German roads. The compartment for the bags was an immense oblong box at the back; it was painted black, and the front part was yellow. These vehicles, like which we have nothing at the present day, had something ugly and humpbacked about them, and when you saw them pass at a distance or creeping up a hill on the horizon, they resembled those insects called, we think, termites, and which with a small body drag a heavy lumber after them. They went very fast, however, and the mail which left Arras at one in the morning, after the Paris mail had arrived, reached M—— a little before five a.m.

On this morning, the mail-cart, just as it entered M——, and while turning a corner, ran into a tilbury drawn by a white horse, coming in the opposite direction, and in which there was only one sitter, a man wrapped in a cloak. The wheel of the tilbury received a rather heavy blow, and though the driver of the mail-cart shouted to the man to stop, he did not listen, but went on at a smart trot.

"There is a man in a deuce of a hurry," said the courier.

The man who was in such a hurry was he whom we have just seen struggling in convulsions, assuredly deserving of pity. Where was he going? He could not have told. Why was he hurrying? He did not know. He was going on unthinkingly. Where to? Doubtless to Arras; but he might also be going elsewhere. He buried himself in the darkness as in a gulf. Something urged him on; something attracted him. What was going on in him no one could tell, but all will understand it,—for what man has not entered, at least once in his life, this obscure cavern of the unknown? However, he had settled, decided, and done nothing; not one of the acts of his conscience had been definitive, and he was still as unsettled as at the first.

Why was he going to Arras? He repeated what he had already said on hiring the gig of Scaufflaire, that, whatever

the result might be, there would be no harm in seeing with
his own eyes, and judging matters for himself ; that it was
even prudent ; that he was bound to know what was going
on ; that he could not decide anything till he had observed
and examined ; that, at a distance, a man made mountains
of molehills ; that after all, when he had seen this Champmathieu, his conscience would probably be quietly relieved,
and he could let the scoundrel go to the galleys in his place :
that Javert would be there and the three convicts who had
known him,—but, nonsense ! they would not recognise
him, for all conjectures and suppositions were fixed on this
Champmathieu, and there is nothing so obstinate as conjectures and suppositions, and that hence he incurred no
danger.   It was doubtless a black moment, but he would
emerge from it.   After all, he held his destiny, however
adverse it might try to be, in his own hands, and was
master of it.   To this latter thought he clung wildly.

In reality, to tell the truth, he would have preferred not
to go to Arras.   Yet he went.   While reflecting, he lashed
the horse, which was going at that regular and certain trot
which covers two leagues and a half in an hour ; and as the
gig advanced, he felt something within him recoil.   At daybreak he was in the open country, and the town of M——
was far behind him.   He watched the horizon grow white ;
he looked, without seeing them, at all the cold figures of a
winter dawn.   Morning has its spectres like night.   He did
not see them ; but unconsciously, and through a sort of
almost physical penetration, these black outlines of trees
and hills added something gloomy and sinister to the violent
state of his soul.   Each time that he passed one of those
isolated houses which skirt high-roads, he said to himself :
"And yet there are people asleep in them."   The trot of the
horse, the bells on the harness, the wheels on the stones,
produced a gentle and monotonous sound, which is delightful when you are merry, and mournful when you are sad.

It was broad daylight when he arrived at Hesdin, and he
stopped at the inn to let the horse breathe and give it a feed.
This horse, as Scaufflaire had said, belonged to that small
Boulonnais breed, which has too large a head, too much
stomach, and too small a chest, but which also has a wide
croup, dry, fine legs, and a solid hoof : it is an ugly but
strong and healthy breed.   The capital little beast had done
five leagues in two hours, and had not turned a hair.

He did not get out of the tilbury.   The ostler who brought the oats suddenly stooped down and examined the left wheel.

" Are you going far in this state ? " the man said.

He answered almost without emerging from his reverie :

" Why do you ask ? "

" Have you come any distance ? " the ostler continued.

" Five leagues."

" Ah ! "

" Why do you say, ah ? "

The ostler bent down again, remained silent for a moment, with his eye fixed on the wheel, and then said as he drew himself up :

" Because this wheel, which may have gone five leagues, cannot possibly go another mile."

He jumped out of the tilbury.

" What are you saying, my friend ? "

" I say that it is a miracle you and your horse did not roll into a ditch by the roadside. Just look."

The wheel was, in fact, badly damaged. The blow dealt it by the mail-cart had broken two spokes, and almost carried away the axle-tree.

" My good fellow," he said to the ostler, " is there a wheelwright here ? "

" Oh, yes, sir."

" Be good enough to go and fetch him."

" There he is, close by. Hallo, Master Bourgaillard."

Master Bourgaillard was standing in his doorway : he examined the wheel, and made a face like a surgeon regarding a broken leg.

" Can you mend this wheel ? "

" Yes, sir."

" When can I start again ? "

" To-morrow ; there is a good day's work. Are you in a hurry, sir ? "

" In a great hurry ; I must set out again in an hour at the latest."

" It is impossible, sir."

" I will pay anything you ask."

" Impossible."

" Well, in two hours ? "

" It is impossible for to-day ; you will not be able to go on till to-morrow."

" My business cannot wait till to-morrow. Suppose, instead of mending this wheel, you were to put another on ? "

" How so ? "

" You are a wheelwright, and have probably a wheel you can sell me, and then I could set out again directly."

" I have no ready-made wheel to suit your gig, for wheels are sold in pairs, and it is not easy to match one."

" In that case, sell me a pair of wheels."

" All wheels, sir, do not fit all axle-trees."

" At any rate try."

" It is useless, sir ; I have only cart-wheels for sale, for ours is a small place."

" Have you a gig I can hire ? "

The wheelwright at the first glance had seen that the tilbury was a hired vehicle ; he shrugged his shoulders.

" You take such good care of the gigs you hire, that if I had one I would not let it to you."

" Well, one to sell me ? "

" I have not one."

" What, not a tax-cart ? I am not particular, as you see."

" This is a small place. I have certainly," the wheel-wright added, " an old caléche in my stable, which belongs to a person in the town, and who uses it on the thirty-sixth of every month. I could certainly let it out to you, for it is no concern of mine, but the owner must not see it pass ; and besides, it is a caléche, and will want two horses."

" I will hire post-horses."

" Where are you going to, sir ? "

" To Arras."

" And you wish to arrive to-day ? "

" Certainly."

" By taking post-horses ? "

" Why not ? "

" Does it make any difference to you if you reach Arras at four o'clock to-morrow morning ? "

" Of course it does."

" There is one thing to be said about hiring post-horses— have you your passport, sir ? "

" Yes."

" Well, if you take post-horses, you will not reach Arras before to-morrow. We are on a cross-country road. The relays are badly served, and the horses are out at work. This is the ploughing season, and as strong teams are re-quired, horses are taken from anywhere, from the post-houses like the rest. You will have to wait three or four hours, sir, at each station, and only go at a foot-pace, for there are many hills to ascend."

"Well, I will ride. Take the horse out—I suppose I can purchase a saddle here ? "

"Of course, but will this horse carry a saddle ? "

"No, I remember now that it will not."

"In that case——"

"But surely I can hire a saddle-horse in the village ? "

"What, to go to Arras without a break ? "

"Yes."

"You would want a horse such as is not to be found in these parts. In the first place, you would have to buy it, as you are a stranger, but you would not find one to buy or hire for 500 francs,—nor for a thousand."

"What is to be done ? "

"The best thing is to let me mend the wheel and put off your journey till to-morrow."

"To-morrow will be too late."

"Hang it."

"Is there not the Arras mail-cart ? When does that pass ? "

"Not till to-night."

"What ! you will take a whole day in mending that wheel ? "

"An honest day."

"Suppose you employed two workmen ? "

"Ay, if I had ten."

"Suppose the spokes were tied with cords ? "

"What is to be done with the axle ? Besides, the felloe is in a bad state."

"Is there any one who lets out vehicles in the town ? "

"No."

"Is there another wheelwright ? "

The ostler and the wheelwright replied simultaneously : "No."

He felt an immense joy, for it was evident that Providence was interfering. It was Providence who had broken the tilbury wheel and stopped his journey. He had not yielded to this species of first summons ; he had made every possible effort to continue his journey ; he had loyally and scrupulously exhausted all resources ; he had not recoiled before the season, fatigue, or expense ; and he had nothing to reproach himself with. If he did not go further, it did not concern him ; it was not his fault, it was not the doing of his conscience, but of Providence. He breathed freely and fully for the first time since Javert's visit. He felt as if the iron hand which had been squeezing his heart for twenty hours had relaxed its grasp ; God now appeared to be on his side, and declared Himself openly. He said to himself that he had done all in his power, and that now he had only to retrace his steps tranquilly.

If his conversation with the wheelwright had taken place in an inn-room, it would probably have not been heard by any one,—matters would have remained in this state, and we should probably not have had to record any of the following events, but the conversation took place in the street. Any colloquy in the street inevitably produces a crowd, for there are always people who only ask to be spectators. While he was questioning the wheelwright, some passers-by stopped around, and a lad to whom no one paid any attention, after listening for some moments, ran off. At the instant when the traveller made up his mind to turn back, this boy returned. He was accompanied by an old woman.

" Sir," the woman said, " my boy tells me that you wish to hire a conveyance ? "

This simple speech, made by an old woman led by a child, made the perspiration pour down his back. He fancied he saw the hand which had let him loose reappear in the shadow behind him, ready to clutch him again. He replied :

" Yes, my good woman, I want to hire a gig."

And he hastily added, " But there is not one in the town."

" Yes, there is," said the old woman.

" Where ? " the wheelwright remarked.

" At my house," the old crone answered.

He shuddered. The fatal hand had seized him again. The poor woman really had a sort of wicker-cart under a shed. The wheelwright and the ostler, sorry to see the traveller escape them, interfered :

" It was a frightful rattle-trap, and had no springs,—it is true that the inside seats were hung with leathern straps —the rain got into it—the wheels were rusty, and ready to fall to pieces—it would not go much further than the tilbury —the gentleman had better not get into it,"—and so on.

This was all true, but the rattle-trap, whatever it might be, rolled on two wheels, and could go to Arras. He paid

what was asked, left the tilbury to be repaired against
his return, had the horse put into the cart, got in, and
went his way.   At the moment when the cart moved ahead,
he confessed to himself that a moment previously he had
felt a sort of joy at the thought that he could not go where
he was going.   He examined this joy with a sort of passion,
and found it absurd.   Why did he feel joy at turning back?
After all, he was making this journey of his free will, and
no one forced him to do so.   And assuredly nothing could
happen, except what he liked.   As he was leaving Hesdin,
he heard a voice shouting to him, "Stop, stop!"   He
stopped the cart with a hurried movement in which there
was something feverish and convulsive that resembled joy.
It was the dame's little boy.

"Sir," he said, "it was I who got you the cart."

"Well?"

"You have given me nothing."

He who gave to all, and so easily, considered this demand
exorbitant, and almost odious.

"Oh, it's you, you beggar," he said; "well, you will
not have anything."

He whipped up the horse, which started again at a smart
trot.   He had lost much time at Hesdin, and would have
liked to recover it.   The little horse was courageous, and
worked for two; but it was February, it had been raining,
and the roads were bad.   The cart too ran much more
heavily than the tilbury, and there were numerous ascents.
He took nearly four hours in going from Hesdin to St. Pol:
four hours for five leagues!   At St. Pol he pulled up at the
first inn he came to, and had the horse put in a stable.   As
he had promised Scaufflaire, he stood near the crib while it
was eating, and had troubled and confused thoughts.   The
innkeeper's wife entered the stable.

"Do you not wish to breakfast, sir?"

"I did not think of it," he said, "but I am very hungry."

He followed the woman, who had a healthy, ruddy face.
She led him to a ground-floor room, in which were tables
covered with oilcloth.

"Make haste," he remarked, "for I am in a great
hurry."

A plump Flemish servant-girl hastened to lay the cloth,
and he looked at her with a feeling of comfort.

"That is what I wanted," he thought, "I had not
breakfasted."

He leaped upon the bread, bit a mouthful, and then slowly laid it back on the table, and did not touch it again. A teamster was sitting at another table, and he said to him :

"Why is their bread so bitter ? "

The teamster was a German, and did not understand him ; he returned to his horse. An hour later he had left St. Pol, and was proceeding towards Tinques, which is only five leagues from Arras. What did he do during the drive ? what was he thinking of ? As in the morning, he looked at the trees, the roofs, the ploughed fields, and the diversities of a landscape which every turn in the road changes, as he passed them. To see a thousand different objects for the first and last time is most melancholy ! travelling is birth and death at every moment. Perhaps, in the vaguest region of his mind he made a comparison between the changing horizon and human existence, for everything in this life is continually flying before us. Shadow and light are blended ; after a flash comes an eclipse ; every event is a turn in the road, and all at once you are old. You feel something like a shock, all is black, you distinguish an obscure door, and the gloomy horse of life which dragged you, stops, and you see a veiled, un- known form unharnessing it. Twilight was setting in at the moment when the schoolboys, leaving school, saw this traveller enter Tinques. He did not halt there, but as he left the village, a road-mender, who was laying stones, raised his head, and said to him :

"Your horse is very tired."

The poor brute, in fact, could not get beyond a walk.

"Are you going to Arras ? " the road-mender continued.

"Yes."

"If you go at that pace, you will not reach it very soon."

He stopped his horse, and asked the road-mender :

"How far is it from here to Arras ? "

"Nearly seven long leagues."

"How so ? the post-book says only five and a quarter leagues."

"Ah," the road-mender continued, "you do not know that the road is under repair ; you will find it cut up about a mile further on, and it is impossible to pass."

"Indeed ? "

"You must take the road on the left that runs to

Carency, and cross the river ; when you reach Camblin
you will turn to the right, for it is the Mont Saint Eloy
road that runs to Arras."

" But I shall lose my way in the dark."

" You are not of these parts ? "

" No."

" And it is a cross-road ; stay, sir," the road-mender continued, " will you let me give you a piece of advice ?   Your
horse is tired, so return to Tinques, where there is a good
inn ; sleep there, and go to Arras to-morrow."

" I must be there to-night."

" That is another thing. In that case go back to the
inn all the same, and hire a second horse. The stable boy
will act as your guide across the country."

He took the road-mender's advice, turned back, and half
an hour after passed the same spot at a sharp trot with a
strong second horse. A stable lad, who called himself a
postilion, was sitting on the shafts of the cart. Still he
felt that he had lost time, for it was now dark. They
entered the cross-road, and it soon became frightful ; the
cart fell out of one rut into another, but he said to the
postilion :

" Keep up a trot, and double drink-money."

In one of the jolts the trace-bar broke.

" The bar is broken, sir," said the postilion, " and I do
not know how to fasten my horse, and the road is very
bad by night. If you will go back and sleep at Tinques,
we can get to Arras at an early hour to-morrow."

He answered, " Have you a piece of rope and a knife ? "

" Yes, sir."

He cut a branch and made a trace-bar ; it was a further
loss of twenty minutes, but they started again at a gallop.
The plain was dark, and a low, black fog was creeping
over the hills. A heavy wind, which came from the sea,
made in all the corners of the horizon a noise like that of
furniture being moved. All that he could see had an
attitude of terror, for how many things shudder beneath
the mighty breath of night ! The cold pierced him, for he
had eaten nothing since the previous morning. He vaguely
recalled his other night-excursion, on the great plain of
D—— eight years before, and it seemed to him to be
yesterday. A clock struck from a distant steeple, and he
asked the lad :

" What o'clock is that ? "

"Seven, sir, and we shall be at Arras by eight, for we have only three leagues to go."

At this moment he made for the first time this reflection —and considered it strange that it had not occurred to him before—that all the trouble he was taking was perhaps thrown away; he did not even know the hour for the trial, and he might at least have asked about that; it was extravagant to go on thus, without knowing if it would be of any service. Then he made some mental calculations: usually the sittings of assize courts began at nine o'clock, this matter would not occupy much time, the theft of the apples would be easily proved, and then there would be merely the identification, four or five witnesses to hear, and little for counsel to say. He would arrive when it was all over.

The postilion whipped up the horses. They had crossed the river and left Mont Saint Eloy behind them. The night grew darker and darker.

CHAPTER XXXI.

MEANWHILE, at that very moment, Fantine was very happy. She had passed a very bad night, she had coughed fearfully, and her fever had become worse. In the morning, when the physician paid his visit, she was raving; he felt alarmed, and begged to be sent for as soon as M. Madeleine arrived. All the morning she was gloomy, said little, and made folds in her sheet, while murmuring in a low voice, and calculating what seemed to be distances. Her eyes were hollow and fixed, they seemed almost extinct, and then, at moments, they were relit, and flashed like stars. It seems as if, on the approach of a certain dark hour, the brightness of heaven fills those whom the brightness of earth is quitting. Each time that Sister Simplice asked her how she was, she invariably answered, "Well. I should like to see M. Madeleine."

A few months earlier, at the time when Fantine lost her last modesty, her last shame, and her last joy, she was the shadow of herself; now she was the ghost. Physical suffering had completed the work of moral suffering. This creature of five-and-twenty years of age had a wrinkled forehead, sunken cheeks, a pinched nose, a leaden complexion, a bony neck, projecting shoulder-blades, thin

limbs, an earthy skin, and white hairs were mixed with
the auburn. Alas ! how illness improvises old age ! At
midday, the physician returned, wrote a prescription,
inquired whether M. Madeleine had been to the infirmary,
and shook his head. M. Madeleine usually came at three
o'clock, and as punctuality was kindness, he was punctual.
At about half-past two Fantine began to grow agitated,
and in the next twenty minutes asked the nun more than
ten times, " My Sister, what time is it ? "

The clock struck three. At the third stroke Fantine,
who usually could scarce move in her bed, sat up ; she
clasped her thin yellow hands in a sort of convulsive grasp,
and the nun heard one of those deep sighs, which seem
to remove a crushing weight, burst from her chest. Then
Fantine turned and looked at the door ; but no one entered,
and the door was not opened, She remained thus for a
quarter of an hour, with her eyes fixed on the door, motionless, and holding her breath. The nun did not dare speak
to her, and as the clock struck the quarter, Fantine fell
back on her pillow. She said nothing, and began again
making folds in her sheet. The half-hour passed, then the
hour, and no one came. Each time the clock struck Fantine
sat up, looked at the door, and then fell back again. Her
thoughts could be clearly read, but she did not say a word,
complain, or make any accusation : she merely coughed in
a sad way. It seemed as if something dark was settling
down on her, for she was livid and her lips were blue. She
smiled every now and then.

When five o'clock struck, the nun heard her say very
softly and sweetly, " As I am going away to-morrow, it
was wrong of him not to come to-day." Sister Simplice
herself was surprised at M. Madeleine's delay. In the meanwhile Fantine looked up at the top of her bed, and seemed
to be trying to remember something : all at once she began
singing in a voice faint as a sigh. It was an old cradle-song
with which she had in former times lulled her little Cosette
to sleep, and which had not once recurred to her during the
five years she had been parted from her child. She sang
with so sad a voice and to so soft an air, that it was enough
to make any one weep, even a nun. The Sister, who was
accustomed to austere things, felt a tear in her eye. The
clock struck, and Fantine did not seem to hear it : she
appeared not to pay any attention to things around her.
Sister Simplice sent a servant-girl to inquire of the porteress

of the factory whether M. Madeleine had returned and
would be at the infirmary soon : the girl came back in
a few minutes. Fantine was still motionless and apparently
engaged with her own thoughts. The servant told Sister
Simplice in a very low voice that the Mayor had set off
before six o'clock that morning in a small tilbury ; that he
had gone alone, without a driver ; that no one knew what
direction he had taken, for while some said they had seen
him going along the Arras road, others declared they had
met him on the Paris road. He was, as usual, very gentle,
and he had merely told his servant she need not expect him
that night.

While the two women were whispering with their backs
turned to Fantine, the Sister questioning, and the servant
conjecturing, Fantine, with the feverish vivacity of certain
organic maladies which blend the free movements of health
with the frightful weakness of death, had knelt up in bed,
with her two clenched hands supported by the pillow, and
listened with her head thrust between the curtains. All at
once she cried :

" You are talking about M. Madeleine : why do you
whisper ? what is he doing, and why does he not come ? "

Her voice was so loud and hoarse that the two women
fancied it a man's voice, and they turned round in alarm.

" Answer ! " Fantine cried.

The servant stammered :

" The porteress told me that he could not come to-day."

" My child," the Sister said, " be calm and lie down
again."

Fantine, without changing her attitude, went on in a
loud voice and with an accent at once imperious and heart-
rending :

" He cannot come : why not ? you know the reason.
You were whispering it to one another, and I insist on
knowing."

The servant hastily whispered in the nun's ear, " Tell
her that he is engaged at the Municipal Council."

Sister Simplice blushed slightly, for it was a falsehood
that the servant proposed to her. On the other hand it
seemed to her that telling the patient the truth would
doubtless deal her a terrible blow, and this was serious
in Fantine's present condition. The blush lasted but a
little while : the Sister fixed her calm sad eye on Fantine,
and said :

"The Mayor is gone on a journey."

Fantine rose and sat up on her heels, her eyes sparkled, and an ineffable joy shone on her sad face.

"He has gone to fetch Cosette," she exclaimed.

Then she raised her hands to heaven, and her lips moved : she was praying. When she had finished she said, "My Sister, I am willing to lie down again and do everything you wish : I was naughty just now. I ask your pardon for having spoken so loud, for I know that is wrong, good Sister ; but, look you, I am so happy. God is good, and M. Madeleine is good : only think, he has gone to Montfermeil to fetch my little Cosette."

She lay down again, helped the nun to smooth her pillow, and kissed a little silver cross she wore on her neck, and which Sister Simplice had given her.

"My child," the Sister said, "try to go to sleep now, and do not speak any more."

"He started this morning for Paris, and indeed had no occasion to go there ; for Montfermeil is a little to the left before you get there. You remember how he said to me yesterday when I asked him about Cosette, 'Soon, soon' ? He wishes to offer me a surprise, for, do you know, he made me sign a letter to get her back from the Thénardiers. They cannot refuse to give up Cosette, can they ? for they are paid ; the authorities would not allow a child to be kept, for now there is nothing owing. Sister, do not make me signs that I must not speak, for I am extremely happy : I am going on very well, I feel no pain at all ; I am going to see Cosette again, and I even feel very hungry. It is nearly five years since I saw her : you cannot imagine how a mother clings to her child,—and then she must be so pretty. She has such pretty pink fingers, and she will have beautiful hands. She must be a great girl now, for she is going on for seven. I call her Cosette, but her real name is Euphrasie. This morning I was looking at the dust on the mantelpiece, and I had a notion that I should soon see Cosette again. Good Lord ! how wrong it is for a mother to be so many years without seeing her child ! she ought to reflect that life is not eternal. Oh ! how kind it is of the Mayor to go ! Is it true that it is so cold ? I hope he took his cloak. He will be here again to-morrow, will he not ? and we will make a holiday of it. To-morrow morning, Sister, you will remind me to put on my little cap with the lace border.

Montfermeil is a great distance, and I came from there to this town on foot, and it took me a long time ; but the stage-coaches travel so quickly ! He will be here to-morrow with Cosette. How far is it to Montfermeil ? "

The Sister, who had no notion of distances, answered, " Oh, I believe he can be here to-morrow."

" To-morrow ! to-morrow ! " said Fantine ; " I shall see Cosette to-morrow ! my good Sister. I am not ill now ; I feel wild, and would dance if you permitted me."

Any one who had seen her a quarter of an hour before would not have understood it ; she was now quite flushed, she spoke with an eager natural voice, and her whole face was a smile. At times she laughed while speaking to herself in a low voice. A mother's joy is almost a childish joy.

" Well ! " the nun said, " you are now happy. So obey me and do not speak any more."

Fantine laid her head on the pillow, and said in a low voice, " Yes, lie down, behave yourself, as you are going to have your child. Sister Simplice is right : all in this place are right."

And then, without stirring, without moving her head, she began looking around with widely opened eyes and a joyous air, and said nothing more. The Sister closed the curtains, hoping she would fall off to sleep. The physician arrived between seven and eight o'clock. Hearing no sound, he fancied Fantine asleep. He entered softly and walked up to the bed on tiptoe. He opened the curtains, and by the light of the lamp saw Fantine's large calm eyes fixed on him. She said to him :

" Oh, sir, my child will be allowed to sleep in a little cot by my bedside ? "

The physician fancied she was delirious. She added :

" Only look ; there is exactly room."

The physician took Sister Simplice on one side, who explained the matter to him : that M. Madeleine was absent for a day or two, and being in doubt they had not thought it right to undeceive the patient, who fancied that he had gone to Montfermeil, and she might possibly be in the right. The physician approved, and returned to Fantine's bed, who said to him :

" In the morning, when the little cat wakes up, I will say good-day to her, and at night I, who do not sleep, will listen to her sleeping. Her gentle little breathing will do me good."

"Give me your hand," said the physician.

"Oh yes, you do not know that I am cured. Cosette arrives to-morrow."

The physician was surprised to find her better : the oppression was slighter, her pulse had regained strength, and a sort of recovered life was animating the poor exhausted girl.

'Doctor," she continued, "has the Sister told you that M. Madeleine has gone to fetch my darling ? "

The physician recommended silence, and that any painful emotion should be avoided : he prescribed a dose of quinine, and if the fever returned in the night, a sedative ; and as he went away, he said to the Sister, "She is better. If the Mayor were to arrive with the child to-morrow, I do not know what would happen : there are such astounding crises, great joy has been known to check diseases, and though hers is an organic malady, and in an advanced stage, it is all a mystery. We might perhaps save her."

CHAPTER XXXII.

It was nearly eight o'clock in the evening when the cart we left on the road drove into the yard of the post-house at Arras. The man whom we have followed up to this moment got out, discharged the second horse, and himself led the white pony to the stables ; then he pushed open the door of a billiard-room on the ground-floor, sat down, and rested his elbows on the table. He had taken fourteen hours in a journey for which he had allowed himself six. He did himself the justice that it was no fault of his, but in his heart he was not sorry at it. The landlady came in.

"Will you sleep here, sir ? "

He nodded in the negative.

"The ostler says that your horse is extremely tired."

"Will it not be able to start again to-morrow morning ? "

"Oh ! dear no, sir ; it requires at least two days' rest."

"Is not the bureau of the post in this house ? "

"Yes, sir."

The landlady led him to the office, where he showed his passport, and inquired whether he could return to M——

the same night by the mail cart. Only one seat was vacant, and he took it and paid for it. "Do not fail, sir," said the clerk, "to be here at one o'clock precisely."

This done, he left the hotel, and began walking about the streets. He was not acquainted with Arras, the streets were dark, and he walked about haphazard, but he seemed obstinately determined not to ask his way of passers-by. He crossed the little river Crinchon, and found himself in a labyrinth of narrow lanes, in which he lost his way. A citizen came toward him with a lanthorn, whom, after some hesitation, he resolved to address, though not till he had looked before and behind him, as if afraid lest anybody should overhear the question he was about to ask.

"Will you be kind enough to tell me the way to the courts of justice, sir?" he said.

"You are not a resident of the town, sir?" replied the man, who was rather old; "well, follow me. I am going in the direction of the courts, that is to say of the Prefecture, for the courts are under repair at present, and the sittings take place temporarily at the Prefecture."

"Are the assizes held there?" he asked.

"Certainly, sir: you must know that what is now the Prefecture was the Bishop's palace before the Revolution. Monsieur de Conzié, who was Bishop in '92, had a large hall built there, and the trials take place in this hall."

On the road, the citizen said to him:

"If you wish to witness a trial you are rather late, for the court usually closes at six o'clock."

However, when they arrived in the great square the citizen showed him four lofty lighted windows in a vast gloomy building.

"On my word, sir," he said, "you have arrived in time, and are in luck's way. Do you see those four windows? they belong to the assize courts. As there are lights, it is not closed yet: there must have been a long trial, and they are having an evening session. Are you interested in the trial? Is it a criminal offence, or are you a witness?"

He answered:

"I have not come for any trial: I only wish to speak to a solicitor."

"That is different. That is the door, sir, where the sentry is standing, and you have only to go up the large staircase."

He followed the citizen's instructions, and a few minutes later was in a large hall, in which there were a good many

people, and groups of robed barristers were gossiping together. It is always a thing that contracts the heart, to
see these assemblies of men dressed in black, conversing in
a low voice on the threshold of a court of justice. It is
rare for charity and pity to be noticed in their remarks, for
they generally express condemnations settled before trial.
All such groups appear to the thoughtful observer so many
gloomy hives, in which buzzing minds build in community
all sorts of dark edifices. This hall, which was large and
only lighted by one lamp, served as a waiting-room : and
folding doors, at this moment closed, separated it from the
grand chamber in which the assizes were being held. The
obscurity was so great, that he was not afraid of addressing
the first barrister he came across.

"How are they getting along, sir?" he said.

"It is finished."

"Finished!" This word was repeated with such an
accent, that the barrister turned round.

"I beg your pardon, sir, but perhaps you are a relative?"

"No, I know no one here. Was a verdict of guilty
brought in?"

"Of course ; it could not possibly be otherwise."

"The galleys?"

"For life."

He continued in a voice so faint that it was scarce
audible :

"Then, the identity was proved?"

"What identity?" the barrister retorted. "Nothing of
the sort was required ; the affair was simple,—the woman
had killed her child, the infanticide was proved, the jury
recommended her to mercy, and she was sentenced to
imprisonment for life."

"You are alluding to a woman, then?"

"Why, of course ; a girl of the name of Limosin. To
whom were you referring, pray?"

"To nobody ; but as the trial is over, how is it that the
court is still lighted?"

"It is for the other trial which began about two hours
back."

"What other trial?"

"Oh, it is clear too ; he is a sort of beggar, a relapsed
galley slave, who has been robbing. I forget his name,
but he has a regular bandit face, on the strength of which
I would send him to the galleys if for nothing else."

" Is there any way of entering the court, sir ? " he asked.

"I do not think so, for it is very full. However, they are taking a recess, and some persons have gone out. When the court resumes, you can try."

" Which is the way in ? "

" Through that large door."

The lawyer left him. In a few minutes he had experienced almost simultaneously, and confusedly blended, every emotion possible. The words of this indifferent person had by turns pierced his heart like needles of ice, and like red-hot sword-blades. When he found that the trial was not over, he breathed again ; but he could not have said whether what he felt were satisfaction or pain. He walked up to several groups and listened to what they were saying ; as the trial list was very heavy, the President had selected for this day two simple and short affairs. They had begun with the infanticide, and were now engaged with the relapsed convict, the " return horse." This man had stolen apples, but it was proved that he had already been at the Toulon galleys. It was this that made his affair bad. His examination and the deposition of the witnesses were over ; but there were still the speech for the defence and the summing up, and hence it would not be over till midnight. The man would probably be condemned, for the public prosecutor was sharp, and did not " miss " his person ; he was a witty fellow who wrote verses. An usher was standing near the door communicating with the court, and he asked him :

" Will this door be opened soon ? "

" It will not be opened," said the usher.

"Will it not be opened when the court resumes its sitting ? "

" It has resumed," the usher replied, " but the door will not be opened."

" Why not ? "

" Because the hall is full."

" What ! is there no room ? "

" Not for a soul more. The door is closed, and no one can go in."

The usher added after a pause : " There are certainly two or three seats behind the President, but he only admits public functionaries to them."

So saying, the usher turned his back on him. He withdrew with hanging head, crossed the waiting-room, and slowly went down the stairs, hesitating at every step. He was probably holding counsel with himself; the violent combat which had been going on in him since the previous day was not finished, and every moment he entered some new phase. On reaching the landing he leant against the banisters and folded his arms; but all at once he took his pocket-book, tore a leaf from it, wrote in pencil upon it, "M. Madeleine, Mayor of M—— sur M——;" then he hurried up the stairs, cleft the crowd, walked up to the usher, handed him the paper, and said to him with an air of authority: "Hand this to the President." The usher took the paper, cast his eye upon it, and obeyed.

Without himself suspecting it, the Mayor of M—— enjoyed a species of celebrity. During the seven years that his reputation for virtue had filled the whole of the Bas Boulonnais, it had gradually crossed the border line into two or three adjoining departments. In addition to the considerable service he had done the chief town, by restoring the glass-bead trade, there was not one of the one hundred and forty parishes in the bailiwick of M—— which was not indebted to him for some kindness. He had ever assisted and promoted, when necessary, the trades of other departments; thus he had supported with his credit and funds, the tulle factory at Boulogne; the flax-spinning machine at Nivers, and the hydraulic manufacture of canvas at Bourbus sur Cauche. The name of M. Madeleine was everywhere pronounced with veneration, and Arras and Douai envied the fortunate little town of M—— its Mayor. The Councillor of the Royal Court of Douai, who presided at the present Arras assizes, like every one else, was acquainted with this deeply and universally honoured name. When the usher discreetly opened the door of the judges' robing-room, leant over the President's chair, and handed him the paper, adding, "This gentleman wishes to hear the trial," the President made a deferential movement, took up a pen, wrote a few words at the foot of the paper, and returned it to the usher, saying: "Show him in."

The unhappy man whose history we are relating had remained near the door of the court at the same spot and in the same attitude as when the usher left him. He heard through his reverie some one say to him, "Will you do me the honour of following me, sir?" It was the same usher who had turned his back on him just before, and was now bowing to the ground. At the same time the usher handed him the paper ; he unfolded it, and as he happened to be near the lamps he was able to read, "The President of the Assize Court presents his respects to M. Madeleine." He crumpled the paper in his hands, as if the words had a strange and bitter after-taste for him. He followed the usher, and a few minutes later found himself alone in a stern-looking room, lighted by two wax candles standing on a green baize covered table. He still had in his ears the last words of the usher, who had just left him : "You are in the Board's withdrawing room ; you have only to turn the handle of that door, and you will find yourself in court behind the President's chair." These words were mingled in his thoughts with a confused recollection of narrow passages and black staircases, which he had just passed through. The usher had left him alone—the supreme moment had arrived. He tried to collect himself, but could not succeed ; for it is especially in the hours when men have the most need of thought that all the threads are broken in the brain. He was at the actual spot where the judges deliberate and pass sentence. He gazed with stupid tranquillity at this peaceful and yet formidable room, in which so many existences had been broken, where his name would be echoed ere long, and which his destiny was traversing at this moment. He looked at the walls and then at himself, astonished that it was this room and that it was he. He had not eaten for more than twenty-four hours, he was fagged by the shaking of the cart, but he did not feel it ; it seemed to him that he did not feel anything. He walked up to a black frame hanging on the wall, and which contained under glass an autograph letter of Jean Nicolas Pache, Mayor of Paris, and Minister, dated, doubtless in error, Juin 9 an II., and in which Pache sent to the commune a list of the ministers and deputies under arrest at their own houses. Any who saw him at this moment would doubtless have imagined that this letter appeared to him very curious, for he did not remove his eyes from it, and read it two or three times. But he read it without paying attention. He was thinking of Fantine and Cosette.

Even while musing, he turned, and his eyes met the brass handle of the door that separated him from the assize court. He had almost forgotten this door, but his eye, at first calm, rested on it, then became wild and fixed, and was gradually filled with terror. Drops of perspiration stood out between his hair and poured down his temples. At one moment he made with a species of authority blended with rebellion. that indescribable gesture which means and says so well: "By Heaven, who forces me?" Then he turned hurriedly, saw before him the door by which he had come in, walked up, opened it, and went out. He was no longer in that room, but in a passage, a long narrow passage, cut up by steps and wickets, making all sorts of turns, lit up here and there by lamps resembling sick persons' night-lights—the passage by which he had come. He breathed, he listened, not a sound behind him, not a sound before him, and he began to fly as if he were pursued. When he had passed several turnings, he listened again,—there were still the same silence and gloom around him. He panted, tottered, and leant against the wall; the stone was cold, the perspiration was frozen on his forehead, and he drew himself up with a shudder. Then standing there alone, trembling from cold, and perhaps from something else, he thought. He had thought all night, he had thought all day; he now heard but one voice within him, which said, "Alas!"

A quarter of an hour passed away thus. At length he inclined his head, sighed with agony, let his arms fall, and turned back. He walked slowly and as if stunned; it looked as if he had been caught up in his flight, and was being brought back. He entered the Board's room, and the first thing he saw was the handle of the door. This handle, which was round and made of polished brass, shone for him like a terrific star; he looked at it as a sheep would look at the eye of a tiger. His eyes would not leave it, and from time to time he took a step which brought him nearer to the door. Had he listened he would have heard, like a species of confused murmur, the noise in the adjoining court, but he did not listen and did not hear. All at once, and without knowing how, he found himself close to the door; he convulsively seized the handle, and the door opened. He was in the court-room.

CHAPTER XXXIII.

HE advanced a step, closed the door mechanically after him, and gazed at the scene before him. It was a dimly lighted large hall, at one moment full of sounds, and at another of silence, in which all the machinery of a criminal trial was displayed, with its paltry and lugubrious gravity, in the midst of a crowd. At one of the ends of the hall, the one where he was, judges with a vacant look, in shabby gowns, biting their nails or shutting their eyelids ; barristers in all sorts of attitudes ; soldiers with honest harsh faces ; old stained wainscoting, a dirty ceiling ; tables covered with baize, which was rather yellow than green ; doors blackened by hands ; pot-house sconces that produced more smoke than light, hanging from nails driven into the wall ; upon the tables brass candlesticks,—all was obscurity, ugliness, and sadness. But all this yet produced an austere and august impression, for in it could be felt the grand human thing called law, and the great divine thing called justice.

No one in this crowd paid any attention to him. All eyes converged on a single point, a wooden bench placed against a little door, along the wall on the left of the President. On this bench, which was illumined by several candles, sat a man between two gendarmes. This man was the man ; he did not seek him, he saw him ; his eyes went there naturally, as if they had known beforehand where that face was. He fancied he saw himself, aged, not absolutely alike in face, but exactly similar in attitude and appearance, with his bristling hair, with his savage restless eyeballs, and the blouse, just as he was on the day when he entered D——, full of hatred, and concealing in his mind that hideous treasure of frightful thoughts which he had spent nineteen years in collecting on the floor of the galleys. He said to himself with a shudder, "Great God, shall I become again like that ? " This being appeared to be at least sixty years of age ; he had something about him rough, stupid, and startled. On hearing the sound of the door, persons had made way for the new-comer, the President had turned his head, and guessing that the gentleman who had just entered was the Mayor of M——, he bowed to him. The public prosecutor, who had seen M. Madeleine at M——, whither his duties had more than once called him, recognised him and also bowed. He scarce noticed it, for he was under a species of hallucination ; he was looking at a judge, a clerk, gendarmes, a number of cruelly curious faces,—he had seen all this once, formerly, seven-and-twenty years ago. These mournful things he found again,—they were there, stirring, existing ; it was no longer an effort of his memory, a mirage of his mind ; they were real gendarmes, real judges, a real crowd, and real men in flesh and bone. He saw all the monstrous aspects of his past reappear, and live again around him, with all the terror that reality possesses. All this was yawning before him ; he felt terrified, closed his eyes, and exclaimed in the depths of his mind, Never ! And by a tragic sport of fate which made all his ideas terrible and rendered him nearly mad, it was another himself who was there. This man who was being tried everybody called Jean Valjean. He had before him an unheard-of vision, a species of representation of the most horrible moment of his life played by this phantom. All was there,—it was the same machinery, the same hour of the night, almost the same faces of judges, soldiers, and spectators. The only difference was that there was a crucifix over the President's head, which had been removed from the courts at the time of his condemnation. When he was tried God was absent. There was a chair behind him, into which he fell, terrified by the idea that people could see him. When he was seated he took advantage of a pile of pasteboard cases on the judge's desk, to hide his face from the spectators. He could now see without being seen : he fully regained the feeling of the real, and gradually recovered. He attained that phase of calmness in which a man can listen. Monsieur Bamatabois was serving on the jury. He looked for Javert, but could not see him, for the witnesses' bench was hidden by the clerk's table, and then, as we have said, the court was very dimly lighted.

At the moment of his entrance, the counsel for the defence was ending his speech. The attention of all was excited to the highest pitch ; for three hours they had seen a man, a stranger, a species of miserable being, deeply stupid, or deeply clever, being gradually crushed by the weight of a terrible resemblance. This man, as we know already, was a vagabond who was found in a field, carrying a branch covered with ripe apples, which had been broken off a tree in a neighbouring orchard. Who was this man ? Inquiries had been made, and witnesses heard ; they were unanimous, and light had issued from every incident of the trial. The prosecutor said : " We have got hold not only of a fruit-stealer, a marauder, but we hold under our hand a bandit, a man who has broken his ban, an ex-convict, a most dangerous villain, a malefactor of the name of Jean Valjean, whom justice has been seeking for a long time, and who, eight years ago, on leaving Toulon, committed a highway robbery with violence on a Savoyard lad, called Little

Gervais, a crime provided for by Article 383 of the Penal
Code, for which we intend to prosecute him hereafter, when
the identity has been judicially proved. He has just committed a fresh robbery, and that is a case of relapse. Find
him guilty of the new offence, and he will be tried hereafter
for the old one." Before this accusation, before the unanimity of the witnesses, the principal emotion evinced by
the accused was astonishment. He made gestures and
signs, intended to deny, or else looked at the ceiling. He
spoke with difficulty, answered with embarrassment, but
from head to foot his whole person denied. He was like an
idiot in the presence of all these intellects ranged in battle-
array round him, and like a stranger in the midst of this
society which seized him. Still, a most menacing future
was hanging over him; the probability of his being Jean
Valjean increased with each moment, and the entire crowd
regarded with greater anxiety than himself the sentence
full of calamity which was gradually settling down on him.
An eventuality even offered a glimpse of a death-penalty,
should the identity be proved, and he was hereafter found
guilty of the attack on Little Gervais. Who was this man?
of what nature was his apathy? Was it imbecility or
cunning? Did he understand too much, or did he understand nothing at all? These questions divided the crowd,
and the jury seemed to share their opinion. There was in
this trial something terrific and something puzzling. The
drama was not only gloomy; it was obscure.

The counsel for the defence had made a very good plea.
He had begun by explaining away the robbery of the apples.
The barrister had established the fact that the apple robbery
was not materially proved—his client, whom, in his quality
as defender, he persistently called Champmathieu, had not
been seen by any one scaling a wall or breaking the branch;
he had been arrested with the branch in his possession, but
he declared that he found it on the ground and picked it up.
Where was the proof of the contrary? This branch had
been broken off and then thrown away by the frightened
robber, for doubtless there was one. But where was the
evidence that this Champmathieu was a robber? Only one
thing, his being an ex-convict. The counsel did not deny
that this fact seemed unluckily proved. The prisoner had
lived at Faverolles; he had been a wood-cutter; the name
of Champmathieu might possibly be derived from Jean
Mathieu; lastly, four witnesses unhesitatingly recognised

Champmathieu as the galley-slave, Jean Valjean. To these
indications, to this testimony, the counsel could only oppose
his client's denial, which was certainly interested : but, even
supposing that he was the convict Jean Mathieu, did that
prove he was the apple-stealer ? it was a presumption at
the most, but not a proof. The accused, it was true, had
adopted a bad system of defence ; he insisted in denying
everything,—not merely the robbery, but his quality as
convict. A confession on the latter point would have doubtless been better, and gained him the indulgence of his
judges; the counsel had advised him to do so, but the
prisoner had obstinately refused, probably in the belief that
he would save everything by confessing nothing. This was
wrong, but should not his scanty intellect be taken into
consideration ? This man was visibly stupid : a long misery
at the galleys, a long wretchedness out of them, had
brutalised him, etc. etc. ; his defence was bad, but was that
a reason to find him guilty ? As for the offence on Little
Gervais, the counsel need not argue that, as it was not
included in the indictment. The counsel wound up by imploring the jury and the court, if the identity of Jean Valjean
appeared to them proved, to punish him as a criminal who
had broken his ban, and not apply the fearful punishment
decreed to the convict found guilty of a second offence.

The public prosecutor then replied. He was violent and
flowery, as public prosecutors usually are. He congratulated
the counsel for the defence on his "fairness," and cleverly
took advantage of it ; he attacked the prisoner with all the
concessions which his counsel had made. He appeared to
allow that the prisoner was Jean Valjean, and he therefore
was so. This was so much gained for the prosecution, and
could not be contested ; and here, reverting cleverly to the
sources and causes of criminality, the public prosecutor
thundered against the immorality of the romantic school,
at that time in its dawn under the name of the "Satanic
School," which the critics of the *Quotidienne* and the *Ori-
flamme* had given it ; and he attributed, not without some
show of reason, the crime of Champmathieu, or to speak
more correctly, of Jean Valjean, to this perverse literature.
These reflections exhausted, he passed to Jean Valjean himself. Who was this Jean Valjean? Here came a description of Jean Valjean, a monster in human form, etc. The
model of this sort of description will be found in the recita-
tion of Theraméne, which is not only useful to tragedy but

daily renders great services to judicial eloquence. The audience and the jury "quivered," and when the description was ended, the public prosecutor went on, with an oratorical outburst intended to excite to the highest pitch the enthusiasm of the country papers which would appear the next morning. "And it is such a man, etc. etc. etc., a vagabond, a beggar, having no means of existence, etc. etc. etc., accustomed through his past life to culpable actions, and but little corrected by confinement in the galleys, as is proved by the crime committed on Little Gervais, etc. etc. etc.,—it is such a man who, found on the high-road with the proof of robbery in his hand, and a few paces from the wall he had climbed over, denies the fact, the robbery, denies everything, even to his name and his identity. In addition to a hundred proofs to which we will not revert, four witnesses recognise him, Javert, the upright Inspector of Police, and three of his old comrades in ignominy, the convicts Brevet, Chenildieu, and Cochepaille. And what does he oppose to this crushing unanimity? he denies. What hardness of heart! But you will do justice, gentlemen of the jury, etc. etc. etc."

While the public prosecutor was speaking, the prisoner listened with open mouth, and with a sort of amazement in which there was certainly some admiration. He was evidently surprised that a man could speak like this. From time to time, at the most energetic apostrophes, when eloquence, unable to restrain itself, overflows in a flux of branding epithets, and envelopes the prisoner in a tempest, he slowly moved his head from right to left, and from left to right, in a sort of dumb and melancholy protest, with which he had contented himself ever since the beginning of the trial. Twice or thrice the spectators standing nearest to him heard him say in a low voice : " All this comes from not asking Monsieur Baloup." The public prosecutor drew the attention of the jury to this dull attitude, which was evidently calculated, and which denoted, not imbecility, but skill, cunning, and the habit of deceiving justice, and which brought out in full light the "profound perverseness" of this man. He concluded by reserving the affair of Little Gervais, and by demanding a severe sentence. The counsel for the defence rose, began by complimenting the public prosecutor on his "admirable speech," and then replied as well as he could, but feebly ; it was plain that the ground was giving way under him.

CHAPTER XXXIV.

THE time for closing the case had arrived. The President ordered the prisoner to stand up, and asked him the usual question : " Have you anything to add to your defence ? " The man, who was rolling in his hands the hideous cap he had, made no reply, and the President repeated his question. This time the man heard, and seemed to understand ; he moved like a person who is waking up, looked around him, at the public, the gendarmes, his counsel, the jury, and the court, laid his monstrous fist on the woodwork in front of his bench, and, suddenly fixing his eyes on the public prosecutor, began to speak. It was an eruption ; from the way in which the words escaped from his lips, incoherent, impetuous, and pell-mell, it seemed as if they were all striving to get out before each other. He said :

" I have this to say. That I was a wheelwright in Paris, and worked for Master Baloup. It is a hard trade is a wheelwright's ; you always work in the open air, in yards, under sheds when you have a good master, but never in a room, because you want space, look you. In winter you are so cold that you swing your arms to warm you, but the masters don't like that, for they say it wastes time. Handling iron when there is ice between the stones is rough work ; it soon uses a man up. You are old when quite young in that trade. At forty a man is finished. I was fifty-three, and had hard lines of it. And then the workmen are so unkind. When a man is not so young as he was, they call him an old canary, an old brute ! I only earned thirty sous a day, for the masters took advantage of my age, and paid me as little as they could. With that I had my daughter, who was a washerwoman in the river. She earned a little for her part, and the pair of us managed to live. She was bothered too. All day in a tub up to your waist, in the snow and rain, and with the wind that cuts your face. When it freezes, it is all the same, for you must wash ; there are persons who have not much linen, and expect it home ; if a woman did not wash, she would lose her customers. The planks are badly joined, and drops of water fall on you everywhere. Her petticoats were wet through, over and under. That penetrates. She also worked at the wash-house of the Enfants Rouges, where the water is got from taps. You are no longer in the tub ; you

wash at the tap before you, and rinse in the basin behind
you.   As it is shut up, you don't feel so cold.   But there is
a stream of hot water which ruins your sight.   She came
home at seven in the evening, and went to bed directly, for
she was so tired.   Her husband used to beat her.   He is
dead.   We were not very happy.   She was a good girl,
who did not go to balls, and was very quiet.   I remember one
Shrove Tuesday, on which she went to bed at eight o'clock.
I am telling the truth.   You need only inquire.   Oh yes, inquire ! what an ass I am.   Paris is a gulf.   Who is there that
knows Father Champmathieu ? and yet, I tell you, Monsieur
Baloup.   Ask him.   What more do you want of me."

The man ceased speaking, but did not sit down.   He had
said all this in a loud, quick, hoarse, hard voice, with a sort
of wretched and savage energy.   Once he broke off to bow
to somebody in the crowd.   The affirmations which he
seemed to throw out hap-hazard came from him in gasps,
and he accompanied each by the gesture of a man who is
chopping wood.   When he had finished, his hearers burst
into a laugh; he looked at the public, seeing they were
laughing, and understanding nothing, he began to laugh
himself.   That did him mischief.   The President, a grave
and kind man, began speaking.   He reminded the " gentlemen of the jury " that " Monsieur Baloup, formerly a wheelwright in whose service the accused declared that he had
been, was a bankrupt, and had not been found when an
attempt was made to serve him with a subpœna."   Then,
turning to the prisoner, he requested him to listen to what
he was about to say, and added : " You are in a situation
which should cause you to reflect.   The heaviest presumptions are weighing upon you, and may entail capital punishment.   Prisoner, I ask you for the last time to explain
yourself clearly on the two following facts : In the first
place, did you, yes or no, climb over the wall, break a
branch, and steal apples, that is to say, commit a robbery
with escalade ? secondly, yes or no, are you the liberated
convict, Jean Valjean ? "

The prisoner shook his head with a confident air, like a
man who understands and knows what answer he is going
to make.   He opened his mouth, turned to the President,
and said :

" In the first place——"

Then he looked at his cap, looked at the ceiling, and held
his tongue.

"Prisoner," the public prosecutor said in a stern voice, "pay attention. You make no answer to the questions that are asked you, and your confusion condemns you. It is evident that your name is not Champmathieu, but Jean Valjean, at first concealed under the name of Jean Mathieu, your mother's name ; that you went to Auvergne ; that your birthplace is Faverolles, and that you are a wood-cutter. It is evident that you stole ripe apples by clambering over a wall, and the gentlemen of the jury will appreciate the fact."

The prisoner had sat down again, but he hurriedly rose when the public prosecutor had finished, and exclaimed :

"You are a very bad man—you, I mean. This is what I wanted to say, but I could not think of it at first. I have stolen nothing, for I am a man who do not eat every day. I was coming from Ailly, and walking after a flood, which had made the whole country yellow ; the very ponds had overflowed, and nothing grew in the sand except a few little blades of grass by the roadside. I found a branch with apples lying on the ground, and picked it up, little thinking that it would bring me into trouble. I have been in prison and bullied for three months, and after that people talk against me, I don't know why, and say to me, Answer. The gendarme, who is a good-hearted fellow, nudges me with his elbow, and says, Why don't you answer ? I cannot explain myself, for I am no scholar, but only a poor man, and you are wrong not to see it. I have not stolen ; I only picked up things lying on the ground. You talk about Jean Valjean and Jean Mathieu. I do not know these persons ; they must be villagers. I used to work for Monsieur Baloup, Boulevard de l'Hôpital, and my name is Champmathieu. You are a very clever fellow to tell me where I was born, for I don't know. It is not everybody who has a house to come into the world in. That would be too comfortable. I believe that my father and mother were persons who went about the roads, but I do not know it after all. When I was a boy I was called little, and now I am called old. Those are my Christian names, and you can take them as you please. I have been in Auvergne. I have been at Faverolles. Well, bless me, may not a man have been at those two places without having been to the galleys ? I tell you that I have not stolen, and that my name is Champmathieu. I worked for M. Baloup, and lived in his house. You will vex

in the end with your nonsense. What is everybody after me
for, like a mad dog ? "

The public prosecutor, who was still standing, here
addressed the judge.

" In the presence of these confused but very clear denials
on the part of the prisoner, who would like to pass for an
idiot, but will not succeed, we warn him,—we request that
it may please you, sir, and the court to recall the prisoners
Brevet, Cochepaille, and Chenildieu, and Police-inspector
Javert, and examine them again as to the identity of the
prisoner with Jean Valjean."

" I must remark," said the President, "that Inspector
Javert, having been recalled to his duties at a neighbouring
town, left the hall and the town immediately after giving
his evidence ; we authorised him to do so with the consent
of the public prosecutor and the counsel for the defence."

" Perfectly correct, sir," the public prosecutor continued.
" In the absence of Inspector Javert, I believe it my duty to
remind the gentlemen of the jury of the statement he made
here a few hours ago. Javert is a worthy man, who
honours by his rigorous and strict probity inferior but
important functions. His evidence is as follows : ' I do not
require moral presumptions and material proof to contradict
the prisoner's assertions, for I recognise him perfectly.
This man's name is not Champmathieu ; he is Jean Valjean,
an ex-convict of a very violent and formidable character.
It was with great reluctance that he was liberated when he
completed his time. He had nineteen years' hard labour
for qualified robbery, and made five or six attempts to
escape. In addition to the Little Gervais robbery and the
larceny of the apples, I also suspect him of a robbery
committed in the house of his Grandeur the late Bishop of
D——. I frequently saw him when I was assistant gaoler
at Toulon, and I repeat that I recognise him perfectly.' "

Such a precise declaration seemed to produce a lively
effect on the audience and the jury, and the public
prosecutor wound up by requesting that the other three
witnesses should be brought in and re-examined. The
President gave an order to an usher, and a moment after
the door of the witness-room opened. The usher, accompanied by a gendarme, brought in the prisoner Brevet.
The audience were all in suspense, and their chests heaved
as if they had but one soul among them. The ex-convict
Brevet wore the black and gray jacket of the central

prisons; he was a man of about sixty years of age, who had the face of a business man and the look of a rogue— these are sometimes seen together. He had become a sort of gaoler in the prison to which new offences had brought him, and was a man of whom the officials said, "He tries to make himself useful." The chaplains bore good testimony to his religious habits, and it must not be forgotten that this trial took place under the Restoration.

"Brevet," said the President, "as you have undergone a degrading punishment, you cannot be sworn."

Brevet looked down humbly.

"Still," the President continued, "there may remain, by the permission of Heaven, a feeling of honour and equity even in the man whom the law has degraded, and it is to that feeling I appeal in this decisive hour. If it still exist in you, as I hope, reflect before answering me ; consider, on the one hand, this man whom a word from you may ruin, on the other, the justice which a word from you may enlighten. The moment is a solemn one, and there is still time for you to retract, if you believe that you are mistaken. Prisoner, stand up. Brevet, look at the prisoner. Think over your past recollections, and tell us on your soul and conscience whether you still persist in recognising this man as your old mate at the galleys, Jean Valjean."

Brevet looked at the prisoner, and then turned to the court.

"Yes, sir, I was the first who recognised him, and I adhere to it. This man is Jean Valjean, who came to Toulon in 1796 and left in 1815. I came out a year later. He looks like a brute now, but in that case age has brutalised him, for he was cunning at the hulks. I recognise him positively."

"Go and sit down," said the President. "Prisoner, remain standing."

Chenildieu was next brought in, a convict for life, as was shown by his red jacket and green cap. He was serving his time at Toulon, whence he had been brought for this trial. He was a little man of about fifty years of age, quick, wrinkled, thin, yellow, bold, and feverish, who had in all his limbs and his whole person a sort of sickly weakness, and immense strength in his look. His mates at the galleys had surnamed him Je-nie-Dieu. The President addressed him much as he had done Brevet. At the moment when he reminded him that his degradation robbed him of the right of taking an oath, Chenildieu raised his head and looked boldly at the crowd. The President begged him to reflect, and asked him if he still persisted in recognising the prisoner. Chenildieu burst into a laugh :

"I should think I do! why, we were fastened to the same chain for five years. So you are sulky, old fellow ? "

" Go and sit down," said the President.

The usher brought in Cochepaille. This second convict for life, who had been brought from the galleys and was dressed in red like Chenildieu, was a peasant of Lourdes and a semi-bear of the Pyrenees. He had guarded sheep in the mountains, and had gradually glided into brigandage. Cochepaille was no less savage, and appeared even more stupid, than the prisoner ; he was one of those wretched men whom nature has sketched as wild beasts and whom society finishes as galley-slaves. The President tried to move him by a few grave and pathetic words, and asked him, like the two others, whether he still persisted, without any hesitation or trouble, in recognising the man standing before him.

"It is Jean Valjean," said Cochepaille. "He was nick-named Jean the Jack, because he was so strong."

Each of the affirmations of these three men, evidently sincere and made in good faith, had aroused in the audience a murmur of evil omen for the prisoner—a murmur which grew louder and more prolonged each time that a new declaration was added to the preceding one. The prisoner himself listened to them with that amazed face which, according to the indictment, was his principal means of defence. At the first the gendarmes heard him grind between his teeth, " Well, there's one." After the second he said rather louder, and with an air of satisfaction, " Good ! " At the third he exclaimed, " Famous ! " The President addressed him :

" You have heard the evidence, prisoner ; have you any answer to make ? "

He answered :

" I say—famous ! "

A laugh broke out in the audience and almost affected the jury. It was plain that the man was lost.

"Ushers," said the President, " procure silence in the court. I am about to sum up."

At this moment there was a movement by the President's side ; and a voice could be heard exclaiming :

"Brevet, Chenildieu, and Cochepaille, look this way."
All those who heard the voice felt chilled to the heart, for
it was so lamentable and terrible. All eyes were turned in
the direction whence it came; a man seated among the
privileged audience behind the court had risen, pushed
open the gate that separated the judges' bench from the
public court, and stepped down. The President, the public
prosecutor, M. Bamatabois, twenty persons recognised him,
and exclaimed simultaneously, "Monsieur Madeleine!"

CHAPTER XXXV.

IT was indeed he; the clerk's lamp lit up his face; he held
his hat in his hand, there was no disorder in his attire, and
his coat was carefully buttoned. He was very pale and
trembled slightly; and his hair, which had been gray, when
he arrived at Arras, was now perfectly white—it had turned
so during the hour he had passed in the court. Every head
was raised, the sensation was indescribable, and there was
a momentary hesitation among the spectators. The voice
had been so poignant, the man standing there seemed so
calm, that at first they did not understand, and asked each
other who it was that had spoken. They could not believe
that this tranquil man could have uttered that terrific cry.
This indecision lasted but a few moments. Before the
President and the public prosecutor could say a word, before
the gendarmes and ushers could make a move, the man, whom
all still called at this moment M. Madeleine, had walked
up to the witnesses, Brevet, Chenildieu, and Cochepaille.

"Do you not recognise me?" he asked them.

All three stood amazed, and indicated by a shake of the
head that they did not know him, and Cochepaille, who
was intimidated, gave a military salute. M. Madeleine
turned to the jury and the court, and said in a gentle voice:

"Gentlemen of the jury, acquit the prisoner. Monsieur
le President, have me arrested. The man you are seeking
is not he, for—I am Jean Valjean."

Not a breath stirred. The first commotion of astonishment had been succeeded by a sepulchral silence; all felt
that species of religious terror which seizes on a crowd when
something grand is being accomplished. The President's
face, however, displayed sympathy and sorrow; he exchanged a rapid look with the public prosecutor, and a few

words in a low voice with the assessors. He then turned to the spectators, and asked with an accent which all understood :

" Is there a physician here ? "

The public prosecutor then said :

"Gentlemen of the jury, the strange and unexpected incident which has disturbed the trial inspires us, as it does yourselves, with a feeling which we need not express. You all know, at least by reputation, the worthy M. Madeleine, Mayor of M——. If there be a medical man here, we join with the President in begging him to attend to M. Madeleine and conduct him to his house."

M. Madeleine did not allow the public prosecutor to conclude, but interrupted him with an accent full of gentleness and authority. These are the words he spoke ; we produce them literally as they were written down by one of the witnesses of this scene, and as they still live in the ears of those who heard them now nearly forty years ago :

" I thank you, sir, but I am not mad, as you will soon see. You were on the point of committing a great error ; set that man at liberty : I am accomplishing a duty, for I am the hapless convict. I am the only man who sees clearly here, and I am telling you the truth. What I am doing at this moment God above is looking at, and that is sufficient for me. You can seize me, for here I am ; and yet I did my best. I hid myself under a name, I became rich, I became Mayor, and I wished to get back among honest men, but it seems that this is impossible. There are many things I cannot tell you, as I am not going to describe my life to you, for one day it will be known. It is true that I robbed the Bishop ; also true that I robbed Little Gervais, and they were right in telling you that Jean Valjean was a dangerous villain—though, perhaps, all the fault did not lie with him. Listen, gentlemen of the court. A man so debased as myself cannot remonstrate with Providence, or give advice to society ; but I will say that the infamy from which I sought to emerge is an injurious thing, and the galleys make the convict. Be good enough to bear that fact in mind. Before I went to Toulon I was a poor peasant, with but little intelligence ; but the galleys changed me. I was stupid, and I became wicked ; I was a log, and I became a brand. At a later date indulgence and goodness saved me, in the same way as severity had destroyed me. But, forgive me, you cannot understand what I am

saying. At my house the two-franc piece I stole seven
years ago from Little Gervais will be found among the
ashes in the fireplace. I have nothing more to add, so
seize me. Good Heavens! the public prosecutor shakes
his head. You say: 'M. Madeleine has gone mad;' you
do not believe me. This is afflicting; at least do not condemn
this man. What! these three do not recognise me! Oh,
I wish that Javert were here, for he would recognise me!"

Nothing could express the kindly yet terrible melancholy
of the accent which accompanied these words. He then
turned to the three convicts:

"Well, I recognise you. Brevet, do you not remember
me?" He broke off, hesitated for a moment, and said:

"Can you call to mind the chequered braces you used to
wear at the galleys?"

Brevet gave a start of surprise and looked at him from
head to foot in terror. He continued:

"Chenildieu, you have a deep burn in your right shoulder,
because you placed it one day in a pan of charcoal in order
to efface the three letters, T. F. P., which, however, are
still visible. Answer me—is it so?"

"It is true," said Chenildieu.

"Cochepaille, you have near the hollow of your left arm
a date made in blue letters with burnt gunpowder; the
date is that of the Emperor's landing at Cannes, March 1,
1815. Turn up your sleeve."

Cochepaille did so, and every eye was turned to his bare
arm; a gendarme brought up a lamp, and the date was
there. The unhappy man turned to the audience and the
judges, with a smile which to this day affects those who
saw it. It was the smile of triumph, but it was also the
smile of despair.

"You see plainly," he said, "that I am Jean Valjean."

In the hall there were now neither judges, accusers, nor
gendarmes; there were only fixed eyes and heaving hearts.
No one thought of the part he might be called on to perform
—the public prosecutor that he was there to prove a charge,
the President to pass sentence, and the prisoner's counsel to
defend. It was a striking thing that no question was asked,
no authority interfered. It is the property of sublime
spectacles to seize on all minds and make spectators of all
the witnesses. No one perhaps accounted for his feelings,
no one said to himself that he saw a great light shining,
but all felt dazzled in their hearts. It was evident that

they had Jean Valjean before them. The appearance of this man had been sufficient to throw a bright light on an affair which was so obscure a moment previously : without needing any explanation, the entire crowd understood, as if through a sort of electric revelation, at once and at a glance the simple and magnificent story of a man who denounced himself in order that another man might not be condemned in his place. Details, hesitation, any possible resistance, were lost in this vast luminous fact. It was an impression which quickly passed away, but at the moment was irresistible.

" I will not occupy the time of the court longer," Jean Valjean continued ; " I shall go away, as I am not arrested, for I have several things to do. The public prosecutor knows who I am, he knows where I am going, and he will order me to be arrested when he thinks proper."

He walked towards the door, and not a voice was raised, not an arm stretched forth to prevent him. All fell back, for there was something divine in this incident, which causes the multitude to recoil and make way for a single man. He slowly walked on ; it was never known who opened the door, but it is certain that he found it open when he reached it. When there, he turned and said :

" I am at your orders, sir."

Then he addressed the audience.

" I presume that all of you consider me worthy of pity ? Great God, when I think of what I was on the point of doing, I consider myself worthy of envy. Still I should have preferred that all this had not taken place."

He went out, and the door was closed as it had been opened, for men who do certain superior deeds are always sure of being served by some one in the crowd. Less than an hour after, the verdict of the jury acquitted Champmathieu, and Champmathieu, who was at once set at liberty, went away in stupefaction, believing all the men mad, and understanding nothing of this vision.

CHAPTER XXXVI.

DAY began to dawn. Fantine had passed a sleepless and feverish night, though full of bright visions, and towards morning fell asleep. Sister Simplice, who was watching, took advantage of this slumber to go and prepare a fresh dose of quinine. The worthy Sister had been for some time in the surgery, stooping over her drugs and bottles, and looking carefully at them on account of the mist which dawn spreads over objects. All at once she turned her head and gave a slight shriek. M. Madeleine had entered silently, and was standing before her.

" Is it you, sir ? " she exclaimed.

He answered in a low voice :

" How is the poor creature ? "

" Not so bad just at present, but she has frightened us terribly."

She explained to him what had occurred, how Fantine had been very ill the previous day, but was now better, because she believed that he had gone to Montfermeil to bring her child. The Sister did not dare question him, but she could see from his looks that he had not been there.

" All that is well," he said. " You did right in not un-deceiving her."

" Yes," the Sister continued, " but now that she is going to see you, sir, and does not see her child, what are we to tell her ? "

He remained thoughtful for a moment.

" God will inspire us," he said.

" Still, it is impossible to tell a falsehood," the Sister murmured in a low voice.

It was now bright day in the room, and it lit up M. Madeleine's face. The sister raised her eyes by chance.

" Good gracious, sir," she exclaimed, " what can have happened to you ? Your hair is quite white."

" What ! " he said.

Sister Simplice had no mirror, but she took from a drawer a small looking-glass which the infirmary doctor employed to make sure that a patient was dead. M. Madeleine took this glass, looked at his hair, and said, " So it is." He said it carelessly and as if thinking of something else, and the Sister felt chilled by some unknown terror of which she caught a glimpse in all this. He asked :

" Can I see her ? "

" Will you not procure her child for her, sir ? " the Sister said, hardly daring to ask the question.

" Of course ; but it will take at least two or three days."

" If she were not to see you till then, sir," the Sister con-tinued timidly, " she would not know that you had re-turned ; it would be easy to keep her quiet, and when her child arrived, she would naturally think that you had returned with it. That would not be telling a falsehood."

M. Madeleine appeared to reflect for a few moments, and then said with his calm gravity :

"No, Sister, I must see her, for I am possibly pressed for time."

The nun did not seem to notice the word "possibly," which gave an obscure and singular meaning to the Mayor's remark. She answered in a low voice :

"In that case you can go in, sir, though she is asleep."

He made a few remarks about a door that closed badly and whose creaking might awake the patient, then entered Fantine's room, went up to the bed, and opened the curtains. She was asleep ; her breath issued from her chest with that tragic sound peculiar to these diseases, which crushes poor mothers who sit up at nights by the side of their sleeping child for whom there is no hope. But this painful breathing scarce disturbed an ineffable serenity spread over her face, which transfigured her in her sleep. Her pallor had become whiteness ; her cheeks were carnations. Her long, fair eyelashes, the sole beauty that remained of her virginity and youth, quivered, though remaining closed. Her whole person trembled as if she had wings which were on the point of expanding and bearing her away. To see her thus, no one could have believed that she was in an almost hopeless state, for she resembled rather a woman who is about to fly away than one who is going to die. The branch, when the hand approaches to pluck the flowers, quivers and seems at once to retire and advance. The human body undergoes something like this quiver when the moment arrives for the mysterious fingers of death to pluck the soul.

M. Madeleine remained for some time motionless near this bed, looking first at the patient and then at the crucifix, as he had done two months previously, on the day when he came for the first time to see her in this asylum. They were both in the same attitude,—she sleeping, he praying ; but in those two months her hair had turned gray, and his white. The Sister had not come in with him : he was standing by the bedside, finger on lip, as if there were some one in the room whom he was bidding to be silent. She opened her eyes, saw him, and said calmly and with a smile :

"And Cosette ? "

She gave no start of surprise, no start of joy, for she was

joy itself. The simple question—"And Cosette?" was asked in such profound faith, with so much certainty, with such an utter absence of anxiety and doubt, that he could not find a word to say. She continued:

"I knew you were there, for though I was asleep, I saw. I have seen you for a long time, and have been looking after you all night; you were in a glory, and had around you all sorts of heavenly faces."

She looked up to the crucifix.

"But," she continued, "tell me, where is Cosette? why was she not laid in my bed so that I could see her the instant I woke?"

He answered something mechanically which he could never remember. Luckily the physician, who had been sent for, came to M. Madeleine's assistance.

"My dear girl," said the physician, "calm yourself, your child is here."

Fantine's eyes sparkled, and covered her whole face with brightness; she clasped her hands with an expression which contained all the violence and all the gentleness a prayer can have simultaneously.

"Oh," she exclaimed, "bring her to me!"

Touching maternal illusion! Cosette was still to her the little child who must be carried.

"Not yet," the physician continued, "not at this moment; you have a little fever hanging about you; the sight of your own child would agitate you and do you harm. You must get well first."

She impetuously interrupted him:

"But I am well! I tell you I am well. What a donkey this doctor is. I insist on seeing my child."

"There, you see," the physician said, "how violent you are! So long as you are like that, I will prevent your having your child. It is not enough to see her, but you must live for her. When you grow reasonable, I will bring her myself."

The poor mother hung her head.

"Doctor, I ask your pardon, I sincerely ask your pardon. In former times I should not have spoken as I did just now, but I have gone through so much unhappiness that I do not know at times what I am saying. I understand; you are afraid of the excitement; I will wait as long as you like, but I swear to you that it would not do me any harm to see my child. Is it not very natural that I should want to see

my child, who has been fetched from Montfermeil expressly
for me? I am not angry, for I know very well that I am
going to be happy. The whole night I have seen white
things and smiling faces. The doctor will bring me Cosette
when he likes; I have no fever now, because I am cured;
I feel that there is nothing the matter with me, but I will
behave as if I were ill, and not stir, so as to please these
ladies. When you see that I am quite calm, you will say,
We must give her her child."

M. Madeleine had seated himself in a chair by the bedside; she turned to him, visibly making an effort to appear
calm and "very good," as she said in that weakness of illness which resembles childhood, in order that, on seeing
her so peaceful, there might be no difficulty in bringing
Cosette to her. Still, while checking herself, she could not
refrain from asking M. Madeleine a thousand questions.

"Have you had a pleasant journey, sir? Oh, how kind
it was of you to go and fetch her for me! Only tell me
how she is. Did she stand the journey well? Alas! she
will not recognise, she will have forgotten me in all this
time, poor darling. Children have no memory. They are
like the birds, to-day they see one thing and another to-
morrow, and do not think about anything. Had she got
clean underclothing? did those Thénardiers keep her clean?
What food did they give her? Oh, if you only knew how I
suffered when I asked myself all these questions during the
period of my wretchedness! but now it is all passed away
and I am happy. Oh! how I should like to see her! Did
you not find her very pretty, sir? You must have been very
cold in the stage-coach? Can she not be brought here if
only for a moment? she could be taken away again directly
afterwards. You could do it if you liked, as you are the
Mayor."

He took her hand and said: "Cosette is lovely, she is
well, you will see her soon, but calm yourself. You speak
too eagerly and put your arms out of bed, which will make
you cough."

In fact, a fit of coughing interrupted Fantine at nearly
every word. She did not object, she feared lest she had injured the confidence she had wished to inspire, by some too
impassioned entreaties, and she began talking of indifferent
matters.

"Montfermeil is a rather pretty place, is it not? In
summer pleasure parties go there. Have those Thénardiers

a good trade? Not many people pass through the village, and theirs is a sort of pot-house."

M. Madeleine still held her hand, and was looking at her anxiously; it was evident that he had come to tell her something at which he now hesitated. The physician had left, and Sister Simplice alone remained near them. "I can hear her, I can hear her!" She held out her arms to command silence, held her breath, and began listening with ravishment. A child was playing in the yard, and probably belonged to one of the workmen. It was one of those accidents which constantly occur, and seem to form part of the mysterious *mise-en-scène* of mournful events. The child, a little girl, was running about to warm herself, laughing and singing loudly. Alas! what is there in which children's games are not mingled?

"Oh!" Fantine continued, "'tis my Cosette! I recognise her voice."

The child went away again. Her voice died away. Fantine listened for some time, and then her face was clouded, and M. Madeleine could hear her murmuring, "How unkind that doctor is not to let me see my child! That man has a bad face."

Still, her merry ideas returned to her, and she continued to talk to herself, with her head on the pillow. "How happy we are going to be! We will have a small garden, for M. Madeleine has promised me that. My child will play in the garden. She must know her alphabet by this time, and I will teach her to spell. She will chase butterflies, and I shall look at her. Then, she will take her first communion; let me see when that will be."

She began counting on her fingers:

"One, two, three, four—she is now seven years old; in five years, then, she will wear a white open-work veil, and look like a little lady. Oh, my good Sister, you cannot think how foolish I am, for I am thinking of my daughter's first communion."

And she began to laugh. He had let go Fantine's hand, and listened to these words, as one listens to the soughing breeze, with his eyes fixed on the ground, and his mind plunged into unfathomable reflections. All at once she ceased speaking, and this made him raise his head mechanically. Fantine had become frightful to look at. She no longer spoke, she no longer breathed; she was half sitting up, and her thin shoulder projected from her nightgown; her face, radiant a moment previously, was hard, and she seemed to be fixing her eyes, dilated by terror, upon something formidable that stood at the other end of the room.

"Good God!" he exclaimed, "what is the matter with you, Fantine?"

She did not answer; she did not take her eyes from the object, whatever it might be, which she fancied she saw; but she touched his arm with one hand, and with the other made him a sign to look behind him. He turned, and saw Javert.

Let us see what had happened. Half-past twelve was striking when M. Madeleine left the assize court of Arras; and he returned to the hotel just in time to start by the mail cart in which he had booked his place. A little before six in the morning he reached M——, and his first care was to post the letter for M. Laffitte, and then proceed to the infirmary and see Fantine. Still, he had scarce quitted the court ere the public prosecutor, recovering from his stupor, rose on his legs, deplored the act of mania on the part of the honourable Mayor of M——, declared that his convictions were in no way modified by this strange incident, which would be cleared up at a later date, and demanded, in the interim, the conviction of this Champmathieu, evidently the true Jean Valjean. The persistency of the public prosecutor was visibly in contradiction with the feelings of all,—the public, the court, and the jury. The counsel for the defence had little difficulty in refuting his arguments, and establishing that through the revelations of M. Madeleine, that is to say, the real Jean Valjean, circumstances were entirely altered, and the jury had an innocent man before them. The barrister deduced a few unluckily rather stale arguments, about judicial errors, etc., the President in his summing-up supported the defence, and the jury in a few moments acquitted Champmathieu. Still, the public prosecutor wanted a Jean Valjean; and, as he no longer had Champmathieu, he took Madeleine. Immediately after Champmathieu was acquitted, he had a conference with the President as to the necessity of seizing the person of the Mayor of M——, and after the first emotion had passed, the President raised but few objections. Justice must take its course; and then, to tell the whole truth, although the President was a kind and rather sensible man. he was at the same time a very ardent royalist, and had been offended by the way in which the Mayor of M——, in alluding to the landing at Cannes, employed the words " the Emperor " and not " Bonaparte." The order of arrest was consequently made out, and the prosecutor at once sent it off by express to M——, addressed to Inspector Javert, who, as we know, returned home immediately after giving his testimony.

Javert was just rising at the moment when the messenger handed him the order of arrest and the warrant. This messenger was himself a very skilful policeman, who informed Javert in two words of what had occurred at Arras. The order of arrest, signed by the public prosecutor, was thus conceived : " Inspector Javert will apprehend Monsieur Madeleine, Mayor of M——, who in this day's session was recognised as the liberated convict, Jean Valjean." Any one who did not know Javert and had seen him at the moment when he entered the infirmary anteroom, could not have guessed what was taking place, but would have considered him to be as usual. He was cold, calm, serious, his gray hair was smoothed down on his temples, and he went up the stairs with his usual slowness. But any one who was well acquainted with him, and examined him closely, would have shuddered ; the buckle of his leathern stock, instead of sitting in the nape of his neck, was under his left ear. This revealed an extraordinary agitation. Javert was a complete character, without a crease in his duty or in his uniform : methodical with criminals, and rigid with his coat buttons. For him to have his stock out of order, it was necessary for him to be suffering from one of those emotions which might be called internal earthquakes. He had merely fetched a corporal and four men from the guardhouse close by, left them in the yard, and had Fantine's room pointed out to him by the unsuspecting porteress, who was used to policemen asking for the Mayor.

On reaching Fantine's door, Javert turned the key, pushed the door with the gentleness either of a sick nurse or a spy, and entered. Correctly speaking, he did not enter : he stood in the half-opened door with his hat on his head, and his left hand thrust into the breast of his greatcoat, which was buttoned to the chin. Under his elbow could be seen the leaden knob of his enormous cane, which was concealed behind his back. He remained thus for many a minute, no one perceiving his presence. All at once Fantine raised her eyes, saw him, and made M. Madeleine turn. At the moment when Madeleine's glance met Javert's, the latter, without stirring or drawing near, became fearful. No human feeling can succeed in being so horrible as joy. It was the face of a fiend who has just found a condemned soul again. The certainty of at length holding Jean Valjean caused all he had in his soul to appear on his countenance, and the stirred-up sediment rose to the surface. The humiliation of having lost the trail for a while and having been mistaken with regard to Champmathieu was effaced by his pride at having guessed so correctly at the beginning, and having a right instinct for such a length of time. Javert's satisfaction was displayed in his sovereign attitude, and the deformity of triumph was spread over his narrow forehead. It was the fullest development of horror that a gratified face can show.

Javert at this moment was in heaven. Without distinctly comprehending the fact, but still with a confused intuition of his necessity and his success, he, Javert, personified justice, light, and truth in their celestial function of crushing evil. He had behind him, around him, at an infinite depth, authority, reason, the legal conscience, the public vindication, all the stars : he protected order, he drew the lightning from the law, he avenged society, he rendered assistance to the absolute. There was in his victory a remnant of defiance and contest : upright, haughty, and dazzling, he displayed the superhuman bestiality of a ferocious archangel in the bright azure of heaven. The formidable shadow of the deed he was doing rendered visible to his clutching fist the flashing social sword. Happy and indignant, he held beneath his heel, crime, vice, perdition, rebellion, and hell : he was radiant, he exterminated, he smiled, and there was an incontestable grandeur in this monstrous St. Michael. Javert, though terrifying, was not ignoble. Probity, sincerity, candour, conviction, and the idea of duty, are things which, by deceiving themselves, may become hideous, but which, even if hideous, remain grand ; their majesty, peculiar to the human conscience, persists in horror ; they are virtues which have but one vice, error. The pitiless honest joy of a fanatic, in the midst of his atrocity, retains a mournfully venerable radiance. Without suspecting it, Javert, in his formidable happiness, was worthy of pity,

like every ignorant man who triumphs. Nothing could be
more painful and terrible than this face, which revealed
what we may call all the evil of good.

Fantine had not seen Javert since the day the Mayor had
wrested her from him. Her sickly brain could form no
other thought but that he had come to fetch her. She
could not endure his frightful face : she felt herself dying.
She buried her face in her hands, and cried with agony :

" Monsieur Madeleine, save me ! "

Jean Valjean—we will not call him otherwise in future
—had risen, and said to Fantine in his gentlest, calmest
voice :

" Do not be alarmed : he has not come for you."

Then he turned to Javert and said :

" I know what you want."

And Javert answered :

" Come, make haste——"

There was something savage and frenzied in the accent
that accompanied these words : no orthographer could
write it down, for it was no longer human speech, but a
roar. He did not behave as usual, he did not enter into
the matter or display his warrant. To him Jean Valjean
was a sort of mysterious combatant, a dark wrestler with
whom he had been struggling for five years, without being
able to throw him. This arrest was not a beginning
but an end, and he confined himself to saying, " Come,
make haste." While speaking thus, he did not advance :
he merely darted at Jean Valjean the look which he threw
out as a grapple, and with which he violently drew
wretches to him. It was this look which Fantine had
felt pierce to her marrow two months before. On hearing
Javert's roar, Fantine opened her eyes again ; but the
Mayor was present, so what had she to fear ? Javert
walked into the middle of the room and cried :

" Well, are you coming ? "

The unhappy girl looked around her. No one was
present but the nun and the Mayor ; to whom, then, could
this humiliating remark be addressed ? only to herself.
She shuddered. Then she saw an extraordinary thing, so
extraordinary that nothing like it had ever appeared in the
darkest delirium of fever. She saw the policeman Javert
seize the Mayor by the collar, and she saw the Mayor bow
his head. It seemed to her as if the end of the world had
arrived.

"Monsieur le Maire!" Fantine screamed.

Javert burst into a laugh—that frightful laugh which showed all his teeth.

"There is no Monsieur le Maire here."

Jean Valjean did not attempt to remove the hand that grasped his collar; he said:

"Javert——"

Javert interrupted him: "Call me Monsieur the Inspector."

"I should like to say a word to you in private, sir," Jean Valjean continued.

"Speak up," Javert answered, "people talk aloud to me."

Jean Valjean went on in a low voice:

"It is a request I have to make of you."

"I tell you to speak up."

"But it must only be heard by yourself——"

"What do I care for that? I am not listening!"

Jean Valjean turned to him and said rapidly, and in a very low voice:

"Grant me three days! three days to go and fetch this unhappy woman's child! I will pay whatever you ask, and you can accompany me if you like."

"You must be joking," Javert cried. "Why, I did not think you such a fool! You ask three days of me that you may bolt! You say that it is to fetch this girl's brat! ah, ah, that is rich, very rich."

Fantine had a tremor.

"My child," she exclaimed, "to go and fetch my child? Then she is not here! Sister, answer me,—where is Cosette? I want my child! Monsieur Madeleine, M. le Maire!"

Javert stamped his foot.

"There's the other beginning now; will you be quiet, wench? A devil's own country, where galley-slaves are magistrates, and street-walkers are nursed like countesses. Well, well, it will be altered now, and it's time for it."

He looked fixedly at Fantine, and added, as he took a fresh hold of Jean Valjean's cravat, shirt, and coat collar:

"I tell you there is no M. Madeleine and no Monsieur le Maire, but there is a robber, a brigand, a convict of the name of Jean Valjean, and I've got him,—that's what there is."

Fantine rose, supporting herself on her stiffened arms and hands: she looked at Jean Valjean; she looked at

Javert; she looked at the nun; she opened her mouth as
if to speak, but there was a rattle in her throat, her teeth
chattered, she stretched out her arms, convulsively opening
her hands, clutching like a drowning man, and then
suddenly fell back on the pillow. Her head struck against
the bed head, and fell back on her breast with gaping
mouth and open eyes;—she was dead. Jean Valjean laid
his hand on that one of Javert's which held him, opened it
as if it had been a child's hand, and then said to Javert:

"You have killed this woman."

"Enough of this," Javert shouted furiously. "I am not
here to listen to abuse, so you can save your breath. There
is a guard down below, so come quickly, or I shall handcuff you."

There was in the corner of the room an old iron bedstead
in a bad condition, which the Sisters used as a sofa when
they were sitting up at night. Jean Valjean went to this
bed, tore off in a twinkling the head piece, an easy thing for
muscles like his, seized the supporting bar, and looked at
Javert. Javert recoiled to the door. Jean Valjean, with the
iron bar in his hand, walked slowly up to Fantine's bed;
when he reached it, he turned and said to Javert in a scarcely
audible voice:

"I would advise you not to disturb me just at present."

One thing is certain,—Javert trembled. He thought of
going to fetch the guard, but Jean Valjean might take
advantage of the moment to escape. He therefore remained, clutched his stick by the small end, and leaned
against the door-post, without taking his eyes off Jean
Valjean. The latter rested his elbow on the bedstead, and
his forehead on his hand, and began contemplating Fantine,
who lay motionless before him. He remained thus, absorbed and silent, and evidently not thinking of anything
else in the world. On his face and in his attitude there was
only an indescribable pity. After a few minutes passed in
this reverie, he stooped over Fantine and spoke to her in a
low voice. What did he say to her? what could this out-
cast man say to this dead woman? No one on earth heard
the words, but did that dead woman hear them? There
are touching illusions, which are perhaps sublime realities.
One thing is indubitable, that Sister Simplice, the sole
witness of what took place, has frequently declared that at
the moment when Jean Valjean whispered in Fantine's ear,
she distinctly saw an ineffable smile playing round her pale

lips and in her vague eyeballs, which were full of the amazement of the tomb. Jean Valjean took Fantine's head in his
hands, and laid it on the pillow, as a mother might have
done to her child. Then he tied the strings of her nightgown,
and thrust her hair under her cap. When this was done,
he closed her eyes. Fantine's face at this moment seemed
strangely illumined, for death is the entrance into brilliant
light. Fantine's hand was hanging out of bed; Jean
Valjean knelt down by this hand, gently raised and kissed
it. Then he rose and turned to Javert :

" Now I am at your disposal."

CHAPTER XXXVII.

JAVERT put Jean Valjean in the town gaol. The arrest of
M. Madeleine produced an extraordinary commotion in
M——, but it is sad to have to say that nearly everybody
abandoned him on hearing that he was a galley-slave. In
less than two hours all the good he had done was forgotten,
and he was only a galley-slave. It is but fair to say,
though, that they did not yet know the details of the affair
at Arras.

Only three or four persons in the whole town remained
faithful to his memory, and his old servant was one of them.
On the evening of the same day this worthy old woman was
sitting in her lodge, still greatly startled and indulging in
sad thoughts. The factory had been closed all day, the
gates were bolted, and the street was deserted. There was
no one in the house but the two nuns, who were watching
by Fantine's body. Toward the hour when M. Medeleine
was wont to come in, the worthy porteress rose mechanically, took the key of M. Madeleine's bedroom from a drawer,
and the candlestick which he used at night to go upstairs ;
then she hung the key on the nail from which he usually
took it, and placed the candlestick by its side, as if she
expected him. Then she sat down again and began thinking. The poor old woman had done all this unconsciously.
She did not break off her reverie for two or three hours, and
then exclaimed : " Only think of that ! I have hung his key
on the nail ! "

At this moment the window of the lodge was opened, a
hand was passed through the opening, which seized the key
and lit the candle by hers. The porteress raised her eyes,

and stood with gaping mouth, but she repressed the cry which was in her throat; for she recognised this hand, this arm, this coat sleeve, as belonging to M. Madeleine. It was some minutes ere she could speak, for she "was struck," as she said afterwards when describing the adventure.

"Good gracious, M. le Maire," she at length exclaimed, "I fancied——"

She stopped, for the end of the sentence would have been disrespectful to the first part. Jean Valjean was still Monsieur le Maire with her. He completed her thought.

"That I was in prison?" he said. "I was so, but I pulled out a bar, leapt out, and here I am. I am going up to my room; go and fetch Sister Simplice, who doubtless is by the side of that poor woman."

The old servant hastened to obey; he said nothing further to her, for he was quite sure that she would guard him better than he could himself. It was never known how he managed to get into the yard without having the gate opened. He always carried about him a master-key, which opened a little side door, but he must have been searched and this key taken from him. This point was not cleared up. He went up the stairs that led to his room, and on reaching the landing, left the candle on the top stair, closed his window and shutters, and then entered the room with the candle. This precaution was useful, for it will be remembered that his window could be noticed from the street. He took a glance around him, at his table, his chair, his bed, which had not been slept in for three nights. No trace of that night's disorder remained, for the porteress "had done his room"; but she had picked out of the ashes and laid neatly on the table the two iron ends of the stick and the forty-sous piece, which was blackened by the fire. He took a sheet of paper, on which he wrote, "This is the two-franc piece stolen from Little Gervais to which I alluded in court," and he laid the coin on the paper, so that it should be the first thing seen on entering the room. He took from a drawer an old shirt which he tore up, and wrapped the two candlesticks in the rags. Still, he displayed no haste or agitation, and while wrapping up the candlesticks he ate a piece of black bread—probably the prison bread which he took with him on his escape. This fact was proved by the crumbs found on the boards when the authorities made an investigation at a later date.

There were two gentle taps at the door.

"Come in," he said.

It was Sister Simplice ; she was pale, her eyes were red, and the candle she held shook in her hand. Violent events of destiny have this peculiarity, that however perfect or cold we may be, they draw human nature out of our entrails and compel it to reappear on the surface. In the emotions of this day the nun had become a woman again ; she had wept and was trembling. Jean Valjean had just finished writing some lines on a piece of paper, which he handed to the Sister, with the remark, "Sister, you will deliver this to the Curé?"

As the paper was open, she turned her eyes on it. "You may read it," he said.

She read : "I request the Curé to take charge of all that I leave here. He will be good enough to defray out of it the costs of my trial and the interment of the woman who died this morning. The rest will be for the poor."

The Sister attempted to speak, but could only produce a few inarticulate sounds : at length she managed to say :

"Do you not wish to see the poor unhappy girl for the last time, sir?"

"No," he said, "I am pursued, and if I were to be arrested in her room it would disturb her."

He had scarce said this, ere a great noise broke out on the staircase : they heard a tumult of ascending steps, and the old servant cry in her loudest and most piercing voice :

"My good sir, I can take my oath that no one has come in here all day or all the evening, and I have not left my lodge once."

A man answered :

"But there is a light in that room."

They recognised Javert's voice. The room was so built that the door, on being thrown open, concealed a nook in the right-hand wall : Jean Valjean blew out the light and crept into the nook. Sister Simplice fell on her knees by the table, as the door opened and Javert entered. The voices of several men and the protestations of the old porteress could be heard. The nun did not raise her eyes : she was praying. Her candle was on the chimney and gave but little light, and on noticing the nun, Javert halted in great confusion. It will be remembered that the very basis of Javert, his element, the air he breathed, was reverence for all authority : he was all of one piece, and allowed no objection or limitation. With him, of course, ecclesiastical authority was the highest of all : he was religious, superficial, and correct on this point as on all. In his eyes, a priest was a spirit that does not deceive, a nun a creature who does not sin. Theirs were souls walled up against the world with only one door, which never opened except to let truth pass out. On noticing the Sister, his first movement was to withdraw, but he had another duty too, which imperiously urged him in an opposite direction. His second impulse was to remain, and at least venture one question. This was the Sister Simplice who had never told a falsehood in her life : Javert was aware of this, and especially revered her for it.

"Sister," he asked, "are you alone in the room ? "

There was a terrible moment, during which the old servant felt as if she were going to faint : the Sister raised her eyes and said, "Yes."

"In that case," Javert continued, "I beg your pardon for pressing you, but it is my duty,—you have not seen this evening a person, a man who has escaped and whom we are seeking—that fellow of the name of Jean Valjean. Have you seen him ? "

The Sister answered, "No."

She had told two falsehoods one upon the other, without hesitation, rapidly, as if devoting herself.

"I beg your pardon," said Javert ; and he withdrew with a deep bow.

O holy woman, it is many years since you were on this earth ; you have rejoined in the light your sisters the virgins and your brothers the angels ; may this falsehood be placed to your credit in Paradise !

The Sister's assertion was so decisive for Javert, that he did not notice the singular fact of the candle just blown out and which was still smoking on the table. An hour later a man, making his way through the fog, was hurrying away from M——, in the direction of Paris. This man was Jean Valjean ; and it was proved, by the testimony of two or three carriers who met him, that he was carrying a bundle and was dressed in a blouse. Where did he procure this blouse from ? It was never known ; but a few days before, an old workman had died in the infirmary of the sailors, only leaving a blouse. This might have been the one.

A last word in regard to Fantine. We have all one mother, the earth, and Fantine was given back to that mother. The Curé thought he was doing his duty, and perhaps did it, by keeping for the poor as much money as he possibly could out of what Jean Valjean left him. After all, who were the people interested ?—a convict and a street-walker : hence he simplified Fantine's interment, and reduced it to what is called the "public grave." Fantine was therefore interred in the gratis corner of the cemetery, which belongs to everybody and to nobody, and where the poor are lost. Fortunately God knows where to look for a soul. Fantine was laid in the darkness among a pile of promiscuous bones in the public grave. Her tomb was like her bed.

CHAPTER XXXVIII.

On a beautiful May morning last year (1861) a traveller, he who tells this story, was coming from Nivelles, and was proceeding toward La Hulpe. He was on foot, and following, between two rows of trees, a wide, paved road which undulates over a constant succession of hills, that raise the road and let it fall again, and form, as it were, enormous waves. He had passed Lillois and Bois-Seigneur Isaac, and noticed in the west the slate-covered steeple of Braine l'Alleud, which looks like an overturned vase. He had just left behind him a wood upon a hill, and at the angle of a cross road, by the side of a sort of worm-eaten gallows which bore the inscription, "Old barrier, No. 4," a wine-shop, having on its front the following notice : "The Four Winds, Echabeau, Private coffee-house."

About half a mile beyond this pothouse, he reached a small valley, in which there is a stream that runs through an arch formed in the causeway. The clump of trees, widespread but very green, which fills the valley on one side of the road, is scattered on the other over the fields, and runs gracefully and capriciously toward Braine l'Alleud. On the right, and skirting the road, was an inn, with a four-wheeled cart in front of the door, a large bundle of hop poles, a plough, a pile of dry shrubs near a quick-set hedge, lime smoking in a square hole, and a ladder lying along an old shed with straw partitions. A girl was hoeing in a field, where a large yellow bill—probably of a show at some Kermesse—was flying in the wind. At the corner of the inn, a badly-paved path ran into the bushes by the side of a pond, on which a flotilla of ducks was navigating. The traveller took this path.

After proceeding about one hundred yards, along a wall

of the fifteenth century, surmounted by a coping of crossed bricks, he found himself in front of a large arched stone gate, with a rectangular moulding, in the stern style of Louis XIV., supported by two flat medallions. A severe façade was over this gate; a wall perpendicular to the façade almost joined the gate and flanked it at a right angle. On the grass-plat in front of the gate lay three harrows, through which the May flowers were growing pell-mell. The gate was closed by means of two decrepit folding-doors, ornamented by an old rusty hammer.

The sun was delightful, and the branches made that gentle May rustling, which seems to come from nests even more than from the wind. A little bird, probably in love, was singing with all its might. The wayfarer stooped and looked at a rather large circular excavation in the stone to the right of the gate, which resembled a sphere. At this moment the gates opened and a peasant woman came out. She saw the wayfarer, and noticed what he was looking at.

" It was a French cannon-ball that made it," she said, and then added " What you see higher up there, on the gate near a nail, is the hole of a heavy shell, which did not penetrate the wood."

" What is the name of this place ? " the traveller asked.

" Hougomont," said the woman.

The traveller raised his head. He walked a few steps, and then looked over the hedge. He could see on the horizon through the trees a sort of hillock, and on this mound something which, at a distance, resembled a lion. He stood on the battlefield of Waterloo.

Hougomont ! This was the fatal spot, the beginning of the resistance, the first check which that great woodman of Europe, called Napoleon, encountered at Waterloo ; the first knot under the axe-blade. It was a château, and is now but a farm. For the antiquarian Hougomont is Hugomons : it was built by Hugo, Sire de Sommeril, the same who endowed the sixth chapelry of the Abbey of Villers. The wayfarer pushed open the door, elbowed an old carriage under a porch, and entered the yard. The first thing that he noticed in this enclosure was a gate of the sixteenth century, which now resembles an arcade, as all has fallen around it. A monumental aspect frequently springs up from ruins. Near the arcade there is another gateway in the wall, with key-stones in the style of Henri IV., through which can be seen the trees of an orchard. By the side of this gateway a dunghill, mattocks, and shovels, a few carts, an old well with its stone slab and iron windlass, a frisking colt, a turkey displaying its tail, a chapel surmounted by a little belfry, and a blossoming pear-tree growing in espalier along the chapel wall,—such is this yard, the conquest of which was a dream of Napoleon's. This nook of earth, had he been able to take it, would probably have given him the world. Chickens are scattering the dust there with their beaks, and you hear a growl,—it is a large dog, which shows its teeth and fills the place of the English. The English were admirable here ; Cooke's four companies of Guards resisted at this spot for seven hours the obstinate attack of an army.

Hougomont, seen on the map, comprising buildings and enclosures, presents an irregular quadrangle, of which one angle has been broken off. In this angle is the southern gate within point-blank range of this wall. Hougomont has two gates, the southern one, which belongs to the château, and the northern, which belongs to the farm. Napoleon sent against Hougomont his brother Jérôme ; Guilleminot's, Foy's, and Bachelie's divisions were hurled at it ; nearly the whole of Reille's corps was employed there and failed ; and Kellermann's cannon-balls rebounded from this heroic wall. Bauduin's brigade was not strong enough to force Hougomont on the north, and Soye's brigade could only attack it on the south without carrying it.

The farm-buildings are on the southern side of the court, and a piece of the northern gate, broken by the French, hangs from the wall. It consists of four planks nailed on two cross beams, and the scars of the attack may still be distinguished upon it. The northern gate, which was forced by the French, and in which a piece has been let in to replace the panel hanging to the wall, stands, half open, at the extremity of the yard ; it is cut square in a wall which is stone at the bottom, brick at the top, and which closes the yard on the north side. It is a simple gate, such as may be seen in all farm-yards, with two large folding doors made of rustic planks ; beyond it are fields. The dispute for this entrance was furious ; for a long time all sorts of marks of bloody hands could be seen on the side-post of the gate, and it was here that Bauduin fell. The storm of the fight still lurks in the courtyard : horror is visible there ; the incidents of the fearful struggle are petrified in it ; people are living and dying in it,—it was only yesterday. The walls are in the pangs of death, the stones fall, the breaches cry out, the holes are wounds, and the bent and quivering trees seem as if making an effort to fly.

This yard was in better condition in 1815 than it is to-day. Structures which have since been removed, formed in it redans and angles. The English barricaded themselves in it ; the French penetrated but could not hold their ground there. By the side of the chapel stands a wing of the château, the sole relic left of the Manor of Hougomont, in ruins, one might almost say gutted. The château was employed as a keep, the chapel served as a block-house. Men exterminated each other there. The French, fired upon from all sides, from behind walls, from granaries, from cellars, from every window, from every air-hole, from every crack in the stone, brought up fascines, and set fire to the walls and men ; the musketry fire was replied to by a tempest of flame.

In the ruined wing you can look through windows defended by iron bars, into the dismantled rooms of a brick building ; the English Guards were ambuscaded in these rooms, and the spiral staircase, hollowed out from ground-floor to roof, appears like the interior of a broken shell. The staircase has two landings ; the English, besieged on this landing and massed on the upper stairs, broke away the lowest. These are large slabs of blue stone which form a pile among the nettles. A dozen steps still hold to the wall ; on the first the image of a trident is carved, and these inaccessible steps are solidly set in their bed. All the rest resemble a toothless jaw. There are two trees here, one of them dead, and the other, which was wounded on the foot, grows green again in April. Since 1815 it has taken to growing through the staircase.

In the chapel, men massacred each other, and the interior, which is grown quiet again, is strange. Mass has not been said in it since the carnage, but the altar has been left—an altar of coarse wood supported by a foundation of rough stone. Four whitewashed walls, a door opposite the altar, two small arched windows, a large wooden crucifix over the door, above the crucifix a square air-hole stopped up with hay ; in a corner, on the ground, an old window-sash, with the panes all broken,—such is the chapel. Near the altar is a wooden statue of St. Anne, belonging to the fifteenth century ; the head of the infant Saviour has been carried away by a shot. The French, masters for a moment of the chapel and then dislodged, set fire to it. The flames filled the building, and it became a furnace ; the door was burnt, the flooring was burnt, but the wooden Christ was not burnt ; the fire nibbled away the feet, of which only the blackened stumps can now be seen, and then stopped. It was a miracle, say the country people. It was at the door of this chapel that a body was picked up, holding an axe in its hand ; it was the body of Sub-lieutenant Legros.

On coming out of the chapel you see a well on your left hand. As there are two wells in this yard, you ask yourself why this one has no bucket and windlass ? Because water is no longer drawn from it. Why is it not drawn? Because it is full of skeletons. The last man who drew water from this well was a man called Willem van Kylsom : he was a peasant who lived at Hougomont, and was gardener there. On June 18th, 1815, his family took to flight and concealed themselves in the woods. The forest round the Abbey of Villiers sheltered for several days and nights the dispersed luckless country people. Even at the present day certain vestiges, such as old burnt trunks of trees, mark the spot of these poor encampments among the thickets. Willem van Kylsom remained at Hougomont "to take care of the château," and concealed himself in a cellar. The English discovered him there ; he was dragged from his lurking-place, and the frightened man was forced by blows with the flat of a sabre to wait on the combatants. They were thirsty, and this Willem brought them drink, and it was from this well he drew the water. Many drank there for the last time, and this well, from which so many dead men drank, was destined to die too. After the action, the corpses were hastily interred ; death has a way of its own of harassing victory, and it causes pestilence to follow glory. Typhus is an annexe of triumph. This well was deep and was converted into a tomb. Three hundred dead were thrown into it, perhaps with too much haste. Were they all dead ? The legend says no.

One house in this ruin, the farm-house, is still inhabited, and the poor of this house opens on the yard. By the side of a pretty Gothic lock on this gate there is an iron handle. At the moment when the Hanoverian lieutenant, Wilda, seized this handle in order to take shelter in the farm, a French sapper cut off his hand with a blow of his axe. The old gardener, Van Klysom, who has long been dead, was grandfather of the family which now occupies the house. A door on the left hand of the yard, as we said, leads into the orchard, which is terrible. It is in three

parts, one might almost say in three acts. The first part
is a garden, the second the orchard, the third a wood.
These three parts have one common enclosure ; near the
entrance, the buildings of the château and the farm, on the
left a hedge, on the right a wall, and at the end a wall.
The right-hand wall is of brick, the bottom one of stone.
You enter the garden first ; it slopes, is planted with gooseberry bushes, is covered with wild vegetation, and is closed
by a monumental terrace of cut stones with balustrades.
It was a seigneurial garden in the French style, that
preceded Le Notre : now it is ruins and briers. The
pilasters are surmounted by globes that resemble stone
cannon-balls. Forty-three balustrades are still erect ; the
others are lying in the grass, and nearly all have marks of
musket-balls. One fractured balustrade remains upright
like a broken leg.

It was in this garden, which is lower than the orchard,
that six voltigeurs of the 1st Light Regiment, having got in
and unable to get out, and caught like bears in a trap,
accepted combat with two Hanoverian companies, one of
which was armed with rifles. The Hanoverians lined the
balustrade and fired down : the voltigeurs, firing up, six
intrepid men against two hundred, and having no shelter
but the gooseberry bushes, took a quarter of an hour in
dying. You climb up a few steps and reach the orchard,
properly so called. Here, on these few square yards,
fifteen hundred men fell in less than an hour. The wall
seems ready to recommence the fight, for the thirty-eight
loopholes pierced by the English at irregular heights may
still be seen. In front of the wall are two English tombs
made of granite. There are only loopholes in the south
wall, for the principal attack was on that side. This wall
is concealed on the outside by a quickset hedge. The
French came up under the impression that they had only to
carry this hedge, and found the wall an obstacle and an
ambuscade ; the English Guards, behind the thirty-eight
loopholes, firing at once a storm of canister and bullets ;
and Soye's brigade was dashed to pieces against it.
Waterloo commenced thus.

The orchard, however, was taken. The French had no
ladders, but they climbed up with their nails. A hand-
to-hand fight took place under the trees, and all the grass
was soaked with blood, and a battalion of Nassau, seven
hundred strong, was cut to pieces here. On the outside, the

wall against which Kellermann's two batteries were pointed, is pock-marked with cannon-balls. This orchard is sensitive like any other to the month of May ; it has its buttercups and its daisies, the grass is tall in it, the plough-horses browse in it, hair ropes on which linen is hung to dry occupy the space between the trees, and make the visitor bow his head, and as you walk along your foot sinks in mole holes. In the middle of the grass you notice an uprooted, outstretched, but still flourishing tree. Major Blackman leant against it to die. Under another large tree close by fell the German General Duplat, a French refugee belonging to a family that fled upon the revocation of the edict of Nantes. Close at hand an old sickly apple-tree, poulticed with a bandage of straw and clay, hangs its head. Nearly all the apple-trees are dying of old age, and there is not one without its cannon-ball or bullet-shot. Skeletons of dead trees abound in this orchard, ravens fly about in the branches, and at the end is a wood full of violets.

CHAPTER XXXIX.

LET us go back, for such is the story-teller's privilege, and place ourselves once again in the year 1815, a little prior to the period when the matters related in the first part of this book begin. If it had not rained on the night between the 17th and 18th June, 1815, the future of Europe would have been changed ; a few drops of rain more or less made Napoleon oscillate. In order to make Waterloo the end of Austerlitz, Providence only required a little rain, and a cloud crossing the sky at a season when rain was not expected was sufficient to overthrow an empire. The battle of Waterloo could not begin till half-past eleven, and that gave Blücher time to come up. Why? Because the ground was moist and it was necessary for it to become firmer, that the artillery might manœuvre. Napoleon was an artillery officer, and always showed himself one ; all his battle plans were made for projectiles. Making artillery converge on a given point was his key to victory. He treated the strategy of the opposing general as a citadel, and breached it ; he crushed the weak point under grape-shot, and he began and ended his battles with artillery. On the 18th of June, 1815, he counted the more on his artillery, because he held the numerical superiority.

Wellington had only one hundred and fifty-nine guns; Napoleon had two hundred and forty. Had the earth been dry and the artillery able to move, the action would have begun at 6 a.m. It would have been won and over by 2 p.m., three hours before the Prussian interlude. How much blame was there on Napoleon's side for the loss of this battle ? is the shipwreck imputable to the pilot ? was the evident physical decline of Napoleon at that period complicated by a certain internal diminution ? had twenty years of war worn out the blade as well as the scabbard, the soul as well as the body ? was the veteran being awkwardly displayed in the captain ? In a word, was the genius, as many historians of reputation have believed, eclipsed ? In that class of great material men who may be called the giants of action, is there an age when genius becomes short-sighted ? Old age has no power over ideal genius; with the Dantes and the Michael Angelos old age is growth, but is it declension for the Hannibals and the Buonapartes? had Napoleon lost the direct sense of victory ? had the man who formerly knew all the roads to victory and pointed to them with a sovereign finger, from his flashing car, now a mania for leading his tumultuous team of legions to the precipices ? was he attacked at the age of forty-six by a supreme madness? was the Titanic charioteer of destiny now only a Phaëton ?

We think not. His plan of action, all confess, was a masterpiece. Go straight at the centre of the allied line, make a hole through the enemy, cut him in two, drive the British half over Halle, and the Prussians over Tingres, carry Mont. St. Jean, seize Brussels, drive the German into the Rhine and the Englishman into the sea. All this, for Napoleon, was in this battle; afterwards he would see.

We need hardly say that we do not pretend to tell the story of Waterloo here ; one of the generating scenes of the drama we are recounting is attaching to this battle, but the story of Waterloo has been already told, and magisterially discussed, from one point of view by Napoleon, from another by Charras. We leave the historians to contend.

Those who would get a clear idea of the battle of Waterloo need only imagine a capital A laid on the ground. The left leg of the A is the Nivelles road, the right one the Genappe road, while the string of the A is the broken way running from Ohain to Braine l'Alleud. The top of the A is Mont St. Jean, where Wellington is, the left lower point is Hougomont, where Reille is with Jérôme Bonaparte; the right lower point is La Belle Alliance, where Napoleon is. A little below the point where the string of the A meets and cuts the right leg is La Haye Sainte; and in the centre of this string is the exact spot where the battle was concluded. It is here that the lion is placed, the involuntary symbol of the supreme heroism of the old Guard.

The triangle contained at the top of the A between the two legs and the string is the plateau of Mont St. Jean; the dispute for this plateau was the whole battle. The wings of the two armies extend to the right and left of the Genappe and Nivelles roads, d'Erlon facing Picton, Reille facing Hill. Behind the point of the A, behind the plateau of Mont St. Jean, is the forest of Soignies. As for the plain itself, imagine a vast undulating ground; each ascent commands the next ascent, and all the undulations ascend to Mont St. Jean, where they are bounded by the forest.

Two hostile armies on a battlefield are two wrestlers,—one tries to throw the other; they cling to everything; a thicket is a basis; for want of a village to support it, a regiment gives way; a fall in the plain, a transverse hedge in a good position, a wood, a ravine, may arrest the heel of that column which is called an army, and prevent it slipping. The one who leaves the field is beaten; and hence the necessity for the responsible chief to examine the smallest clump of trees, and investigate the slightest rise in the ground. The two generals had attentively studied the plain of Mont St. Jean, which is called at the present day the field of Waterloo. In the previous year, Wellington, with prescient sagacity, had examined it as suitable for a great battle. On this ground and for this duel of June 18, Wellington had the good side and Napoleon the bad; for the English army was above, the French army below.

Everybody knows the first phase of this battle; the troubled, uncertain, hesitating opening, dangerous for both armies, but more so for the English than the French. It had rained all night; the ground was saturated; the rain had collected in hollows of the plain as in tubs; at certain points the ammunition wagons had sunk in up to the axle-trees and the girths of the horses; if the wheat and barley laid low by this mass of   ing vehicles had not filled the ruts, and made a litter under the wheels, any movement, especially in the valleys, in the direction of Papelotte, would have been impossible. The battle began

late, for Napoleon, as we have explained, was accustomed
to hold all his artillery in hand like a pistol, aiming first
at one point, then at another of the battle, and he resolved
to wait until the field batteries could gallop freely, and for
this purpose it was necessary that the sun should appear
and dry the ground. But the sun did not come out; it
was no longer the field of Austerlitz. When the first
cannon shot was fired, the English General Colville drew
out his watch, and saw that it was twenty-five minutes to
twelve.

The battle was commenced furiously, more furiously
perhaps than the Emperor desired, by the French left wing
on Hougomont. At the same time Napoleon attacked the
centre by hurling Quiot's brigade on La Haye Sainte, and
Ney pushed the French right wing against the English
left, which was leaning upon Papelotte. The attack on
Hougomont was, to a certain extent, a feint, for the plan
was to attract Wellington there, and make him strengthen
his left. This plan would have succeeded had not the four
companies of Guards and Perponcher's Belgian division
firmly held the position, and Wellington, instead of massing
his troops, found it only necessary to send as a reinforcement four more companies of Guards and a battalion of
Brunswickers. The attack of the French right on
Papelotte was serious; to destroy the English left, cut
the Brussels road, bar the passage for any possible
Prussians, force Mont St. Jean, drive back Wellington on
Hougomont, then on Braine l'Alleud, and then on Halle,—
nothing was more distinct. Had not a few incidents supervened, this attack would have succeeded. Papelotte was
taken; La Haye Sainte carried.

There is a circumstance to note here. In the English
Infantry, especially in Kempt's brigade, there were many
recruits, and these young soldiers valiantly withstood our
formidable foot, and they behaved excellently as sharp-
shooters. The soldier when thrown out as a skirmisher,
being left to some extent to his own resources, becomes, as
it were, his own general; and these recruits displayed
something of the French invention and fury. These
novices showed enthusiasm, and it displeased Wellington.

After the capture of La Haye Sainte, the battle vacillated.
There is an obscure interval in this day, between twelve
and four; the middle of this battle is almost indistinct, and
participates in the gloom of the conflict.

CHAPTER XL.

TOWARDS four o'clock in the afternoon, the situation of the English army was serious. The Prince of Orange commanded the centre, Hill the right, and Picton the left. The Prince of Orange, wild and intrepid, shouted to the Dutch Belgians: "Nassau Brunswick, never yield an inch." Hill, fearfully weakened, had just fallen back on Wellington, while Picton was dead. At the very moment when the English took from the French the flag of the 105th line regiment, the French killed General Picton with a bullet through his head. The battle had two bases for Wellington, Hougomont and La Haye Sainte. Hougomont still held out, though on fire, while La Haye Sainte was lost. Of the German battalion that defended it, forty-two men only survived; all the officers but five were killed or taken prisoners. Three thousand combatants had been massacred in that focus; a sergeant of the English Guards, the first boxer of England and reputed invulnerable by his comrades, had been killed there by a little French drummer. Barny was dislodged, and Alten was sabred; several flags had been lost, one belonging to Alten's division and one to the Luxembourg battalion, which was borne by a Prince of the Deux-ponts family. The Scots Greys no longer existed; Ponsonby's heavy dragoons were cut to pieces,—this brave cavalry had given way before the lancers of Bex and the cuirassiers of Traver. Of twelve hundred sabres only six hundred remained; of three lieutenant-colonels, two were kissing the ground, Hamilton wounded, and Mather killed. Ponsonby had fallen, pierced by seven lance wounds; Gordon was dead, March was dead, and two divisions, the fifth and sixth, were destroyed. Hougomont attacked, La Haye Sainte taken; there was only one knot left, the centre, which still held out. Wellington reinforced it; he called in Hill from Merbe-Braine and Chassé, who was at Braine l'Alleud.

The centre of the English army, slightly concave, very dense and compact, was strongly situated; it occupied the plateau of Mont St. Jean, having the village behind it, and before it the slope, which at that time was rather steep. It was supported by that strong stone house, which at that period was a domainial property of Nivelles, standing at the cross-road, and an edifice dating from the sixteenth century, so robust that the cannon-balls rebounded without doing it any injury. All round the plateau the English had cut through the hedges at certain spots, formed embrasures in the hawthorns, thrust guns between branches and loopholed the shrubs,—their artillery was ambuscaded under the brambles. This Punic task, incontestably authorised by the rules of war which permit snares, had been so well effected that Haxo, who had been sent by the Emperor at eight o'clock to reconnoitre the enemy's batteries, returned to tell Napoleon that there was no obstacle, with the exception of the barricades blocking the Nivelles and Genappe roads. It was the season when the wheat is still standing, and along the edge of the plateau a battalion of Kempt's brigade, the 95th, was lying in the tall corn. Thus supported and protected, the centre of the Anglo-Dutch army was well situated.

The danger of this position was the forest of Soignies, at that time contiguous to the battlefield and intersected by the ponds of Groenendael and Boitsford. An army could not have fallen back into it without being dissolved, regiments would have been broken up at once, and the artillery lost in the marshes. The retreat, according to the opinion of several professional men, contradicted, it is true, by others, would have been a flight. Wellington added to this centre a brigade of Chassé's removed from the right wing, one of Wicke's from the left wing, and Clinton's division. He gave his English — Halkett's regiments, Mitchell's brigade, and Maitland's guards — as epaulements and counterforts, the Brunswick infantry, the Nassau contingent, Kielmansegge's Hanoverians, and Ompteda's Germans. He had thus twenty-six battalions under his hand ; as Charras says, " the right wing deployed behind the centre." An enormous battery was masked by earth bags, at the very spot where what is called "the Museum of Waterloo" now stands, and Wellington also had in a little hollow Somerset's Dragoon Guards, counting one thousand four hundred sabres. They were the other moiety of the so justly celebrated English cavalry ; though Ponsonby was destroyed, Somerset remained. The battery which, had it been completed, would have been almost a redoubt, was arranged behind a very low wall, hastily lined with sand bags and a wide slope of earth. This work was not finished ; there was not time to stockade it.

Wellington, anxious but impassive, was on horseback,

and remained for the whole day in the same attitude, a little in front of the old mill of Mont St. Jean, which still exists, and under an elm tree, which an Englishman, an enthusiastical Vandal, afterwards bought for two hundred francs, cut down and carried away. Wellington was coldly heroic; there was a shower of cannon-balls, and his aide-de-camp Gordon was killed by his side. Lord Hill, pointing to a bursting shell, said to him, "My Lord, what are your instructions, and what orders do you leave us, if you are killed?"—"Do as I am doing," Wellington answered. To Clinton he said laconically, "Hold out here to the last man." The day was evidently turning badly, and Wellington cried to his old comrades of Vittoria, Talavera, and Salamanca, "Boys, can you think of giving way? What would they say of us in old England?"

About four o'clock, the English line fell back all at once; nothing was visible on the crest of the plateau but artillery and sharp-shooters, the rest had disappeared. The regiments, driven by the French shell and cannon-balls, fell back into the hollow, which at the present day is intersected by the lane that runs to the farm of Mont St. Jean. A retrograde movement began, the English front withdrew. Wellington was recoiling. "It is the beginning of the retreat," Napoleon cried.

Though sick and suffering on horseback from a local injury, the emperor had never been so good-tempered as on this day. From the morning his impenetrability had been smiling, and on June 18th, 1815, this profound soul, coated with granite, was radiant. The man who had been sombre at Austerlitz was gay at Waterloo. The greatest predestined men offer these contradictions, for our joys are a shadow and the supreme smile belongs to God. *Ridet Cæsar, Pompeius flebit*, the legionaries of the Fulminatrix legion used to say. On this occasion Pompey was not destined to weep, but it is certain that Cæsar laughed. At one o'clock in the morning, amid the rain and storm, he had explored with Bertrand the hills near Rossomme, and was pleased to see the long lines of English fires illumining the horizon from Frischemont to Braine l'Alleud. It seemed to him as if destiny had made an appointment with him on a fixed day and was punctual. He stopped his horse, and remained for some time motionless, looking at the lightning and listening to the thunder. The fatalist was heard to cast into the night the mysterious words,—"We are agreed." Napoleon was deceived. They were no longer in accord.

He had not taken a moment's sleep ; every instant of the past night had been marked with joy for him. He rode through the entire line of main guards, stopping every now and then to speak to the videttes. At half-past two he heard the sound of a marching column near Hougomont, and believed for a moment in a retreat on the side of Wellington. He said to Bertrand,—"The English rear-guard is preparing to decamp. I shall take prisoners the six thousand English who have just landed at Ostende." He talked cheerfully, and had regained the spirits he had displayed during the landing of March 1st, when he showed the Grand Marshal the enthusiastic peasant of the Juan Gulf and said,—"Well, Bertrand, here is a reinforcement already." On the night between June 17 and 18 he made fun of Wellington : "This little Englisman requires a lesson," said Napoleon. The rain became twice as violent, and it thundered while the Emperor was speaking. At 3.30 a.m. he lost one illusion ; officers sent to reconnoitre informed him that the enemy was making no movement. Nothing was stirring, not a single bivouac fire was extinguished, and the English army was sleeping. The silence was profound on earth, and there was only noise in the heavens. At four o'clock a peasant was brought to him by the scouts : this peasant had served as guide to a brigade of English cavalry, probably Vivian's, which had taken up a position on the extreme left in the village of Ohain. At five o'clock two Belgian deserters informed him that they had just left their regiments, and the English army meant fighting. "So much the better," cried Napoleon, "I would sooner crush them than drive them back."

At daybreak he dismounted on the slope which forms the angle of the Plancenoit road, had a kitchen table and a peasant chair brought from the farm of Rossomme, sat down with a truss of straw for a carpet, and laid on the table the map of the battlefield, saying to Soult,—"It is a pretty chess-board." Owing to the night rain, the commissariat wagons, which stuck in the muddy roads, did not arrive by daybreak. The troops had not slept, were wet through and fasting, but this did not prevent Napoleon from exclaiming cheerfully to Soult,—"We have ninety chances out of a hundred in our favour." At eight o'clock the Emperor's breakfast was brought, and he invited several generals to share it with him. While breakfasting somebody said that Wellington had been the last evening but one at a ball in Brussels, and Soult, the rough soldier with his archbishop's face, remarked, "The ball will be to-day." The Emperor teased Ney for saying,—"Wellington will not be so simple as to wait for your Majesty." This was his usual manner. After breakfast he reflected for a quarter of an hour ; then two generals sat down on the truss of straw with a pen in their hand, and a sheet of paper on their knee, and the Emperor dictated to them the order of the battle.

At nine o'clock, at the instant when the French army, echeloned and moving in five columns, began to deploy, the divisions in two lines, the artillery between, the bands in front, drums rattling and bugles braying—a powerful, mighty, joyous army, a sea of bayonets and helmets on the horizon, the Emperor, much affected, twice exclaimed,— "Magnificent ! magnificent !"

Between nine o'clock and half-past ten, incredible though it seems, the whole army took up position, and was drawn up in six lines, forming, to repeat the Emperor's expression, "the figure of six V's." A few minutes after the formation of the line, and in the midst of that profound silence which precedes the storm of a battle, the Emperor, seeing three 12-pounder batteries defile, which had been detached by his orders from d'Erlon, Reille, and Lobau's brigades, and which were intended to begin the action at the spot where the Nivelles and Genappe roads crossed, tapped Haxo on the shoulder, and said, "There are twenty-four pretty girls, General." Sure of the result, he encouraged with a smile the company of sappers of the first corps as it passed him, which he had selected to barricade itself in Mont St. Jean, so soon as the village was carried. All this security was only crossed by one word of human pity : on seeing at his left at the spot where there is now a large tomb, the admirable Scots Greys massed with their superb horses, he said, "It is a pity." Then he mounted his horse, rode toward Rossomme, and selected as his observatory a narrow strip of grass on the right of the road running from Genappe to Brussels, and this was his second station. The third station, the one he took at seven in the evening, is formidable,—it is a rather lofty mound which still exists, and behind which the guard was massed in a hollow. Around this mound the balls ricochetted on the pavement of the road and reached Napoleon. As at Brienne, he had round his head the whistle of bullets and canister. Almost at the spot where his horse's hoofs stood, cannon-balls, old sabre-blades, and shapeless rust-eaten projectiles, have been picked up ; a few years ago, a live shell was dug up, the fusee of which had broken off. It was at this station that the Emperor said to his guide, Lacoste, a hostile timid peasant, who was fastened to a hussar's saddle, and tried at each volley of canister to hide himself behind Napoleon, " You dolt, it is shameful ; you will be killed in the back."

The undulations of the plains on which the encounter between Napoleon and Wellington took place, are, as every-body knows, no longer as they were on June 18th, 1815. On taking from this mournful plain the material to make a monument, it was deprived of its real relics, and history, disconcerted, no longer recognises itself ; in order to glorify, they disfigured. Wellington, on seeing Waterloo two years after, exclaimed, "My battlefield has been altered." Where the huge pyramid of earth surmounted by a lion now stands, there was a crest which on the side of the Nivelles road had a practicable ascent, but which on the side of the Genappe road was almost an escarpment. The elevation of this escarpment may still be imagined by the height of the two great tombs which skirt the road from Genappe to Brussels : the English tomb on the left, the German tomb on the right. There is no French tomb,—for France the whole plain is a sepulchre. Through the thousands of cart-loads of earth employed in erecting the mound, which is one hundred and fifty feet high and half a mile in circum-ference, the plateau of Mont St. Jean is now accessible by a gentle incline, but on the day of the battle, and especially on the side of La Haye Sainte, it was steep and abrupt. The incline was so sharp that the English gunners could not see beneath them the farm situated in the bottom of the valley, which was the centre of the fight. On June 18, 1815, the rain had rendered the steep road more difficult, and the troops not only had to climb up but slipped in the mud. Along the centre of the crest of the plateau ran a species of ditch, which it was impossible for a distant observer to guess. We will state what this ditch was. Braine l'Alleud is a Belgian village and Ohain is another ; these villages, both concealed in hollows, are connected by a road about a league and a half in length, which traverses an undulating plain, and frequently buries itself between

hills, so as to become at certain spots a ravine. In 1815, as
to-day, this road crossed the crest of the plateau of Mont
St. Jean ; but at the present day it is level with the ground,
while at that time it was a hollow way. The two slopes
have been carried away to form the monumental mound.
This road was, and still is, a trench for the greater part of
the distance ; a hollow trench, in some places twelve feet
deep, whose scarped sides were washed down here and
there by the winter rains. On the day of the battle, this
hollow way, whose existence nothing revealed, a trench on
the top of the escarpment, a trench concealed in the earth,
was invisible, that is to say, terrible.

On the morning of Waterloo, then, Napoleon was satisfied. He had reason to be so,—for the plan he had drawn
up was admirable. Once the battle had begun, its various
incidents :—the resistance of Hougomont ; the tenacity of
La Haye Sainte ; Bauduin killed, and Foy placed *hors de
combat* ; the unexpected wall against which Soye's brigade
was broken ; the fatal rashness of Guilleminot, who had no
petards or powder-bags to destroy the farm gates ; the
sticking of the artillery in the mud ; the fifteen guns without
escort captured by Uxbridge in a hollow way ; the slight
effect of the shells falling in the English lines, which buried
themselves in the moistened ground, and only produced a
volcano of mud, so that the troops were merely plastered
with mud ; the inutility of Piret's demonstration on Braine
l'Alleud, and the whole of his cavalry, fifteen squadrons,
almost annihilated ; the English right slightly disquieted
and the left poorly attacked ; Ney's strange mistake in
massing instead of echeloning the four divisions of the
first corps ; a depth of twenty-seven ranks and a line of two
hundred men given up in this way to the canister ; the
frightful gaps made by the cannon-balls in these masses ;
the attacking columns disunited ; the oblique battery
suddenly unmasked on their flank ; Bourgeois, Donzelot,
and Durutte in danger ; Quiot repulsed ; Lieutenant Viot,
that Hercules who came from the Polytechnic School,
wounded at the moment when he was beating in with an
axe the gates of La Haye Sainte, under the plunging fire of
the English barricade on the Genappe road ; Marcognet's
division caught between infantry and cavalry, shot down
from the wheat by Best and Pack, and sabred by Ponsonby ;
its battery of seven guns spiked ; the Prince of Saxe Weimar
holding and keeping in defiance of Count d'Erlon, Frische-

mont and Smohain ; the flags of the 105th and 45th regiments which he had captured ; the Prussian black Hussar stopped by the scouts of the flying column of three hundred chasseurs, who were beating the country between Wavre and Plancenoit ; the alarming things which this man said ; Grouchy's delay; the fifteen hundred men killed in less than an hour in the orchard of Hougomont ; the eighteen hundred laid low even in a shorter space of time round La Haye Sainte ;—all these stormy incidents, passing like battle-clouds, before Napoleon, had scarce disturbed his glance or cast a gloom over his imperial face.

At the moment when Wellington drew back, Napoleon started up. He suddenly saw the plateau of Mont St. Jean deserted, and the front of the English army disappear. The Emperor half-raised himself in his stirrups, and the flash of victory passed into his eyes. If Wellington were driven back into the forest of Soignies, and destroyed, it would be the definitive overthrow of England by France ; it would be Cressy, Poictiers, Malplaquet, and Ramilies avenged, the man of Marengo would erase Agincourt. The Emperor, while meditating on this tremendous result, turned his telescope to all parts of the battlefield. His Guards, standing at ease behind him, gazed at him with a sort of religious awe. He was reflecting, he examined the slopes, noted the inclines, scrutinised the clumps of trees, the patches of barley, and the paths ; he seemed to be counting every tuft of gorse. He looked with some fixity at the English barricades, two large masses of felled trees, the one on the Genappe road defended by two guns, the only ones of all the English artillery which commanded the battlefield, and the one on the Nivelles road, behind which flashed the Dutch bayonets of Chassé's brigade. He noticed near this barricade the old chapel of St. Nicholas, which is at the corner of the cross-road leading to Braine l'Alleud. He bent down and spoke in a low voice to the guide Lacoste. The guide shook his head with a probably treacherous negative.

The Emperor drew himself up and reflected ; Wellington was retiring, and all that was needed now was to complete this retreat by an overthrow. Napoleon hurriedly turned and sent off a messenger at full speed to Paris to announce that the battle was gained Napoleon was one of those geniuses from whom thunder issues, and he had just found his thunder-stroke ; he ordered Milhaud's cuirassiers to carry the plateau of Mont St. Jean.

They were three thousand five hundred. They formed a front a quarter of a league in length. They were gigantic men mounted on colossal horses. They formed twenty-six squadrons, and had behind them, as a support, Lefebvre Desnouette's division, composed of the one hundred and six gendarmes, the Chasseurs of the Guard, eleven hundred and ninety-seven sabres, and the Lancers of the Guard, eight hundred and eighty lances. They wore helmets without plumes, and cuirasses of wrought steel, and were armed with pistols and straight sabres. In the morning the whole army had admired them when they came up, at nine o'clock, with bugles sounding, in close column, with one battery on their flank, the other in their centre, and deployed in two ranks, and took their place in that powerful second line, so skilfully formed by Napoleon, which, having at its extreme left Kellermann's cuirassiers, and on its extreme right Milhaud's cuirassiers, seemed to be endowed with two wings of iron.

Aide-de-camp Bernard brought them the Emperor's order : Ney drew his sabre and placed himself at their head, and the mighty squadrons started. Then a formidable spectacle was seen ; the whole of this cavalry, with raised sabres, with standards flying, and formed in columns of division, descended, with one movement and as one man, with the precision of a bronze battering-ram opening a breach, the hill of La Belle Alliance. They entered the formidable valley in which so many men had already fallen, disappeared in the smoke, and then, emerging from the gloom, re-appeared on the other side of the valley, still in a close compact column, mounting at a trot, under a tremendous canister fire, the frightful muddy incline of the plateau of Mont St. Jean. They ascended it, stern, threatening, and imperturbable ; between the breaks in the artillery and musketry fire, the colossal tramp could be heard. As they formed two divisions, they were in two columns ; Wathier's division was on the right, Delord's on the left. At a distance it appeared as if two immense steel lizards were crawling toward the crest of the plateau ; they traversed the battlefield like a flash.

Nothing like it had been seen since the taking of the great redoubt of the Moskova by the heavy cavalry : Murat was missing, but Ney was there. It seemed as if this mass had become a monster, and had but one soul ; each squadron undulated, and swelled like the rings of a polype. This could be seen through a vast smoke which was rent asunder at intervals ; it was one pell-mell of helmets, shouts, and sabres, a stormy bounding of horses among cannon, and a disciplined and terrible array ; while above it all flashed the cuirasses like the scales of the dragon. Such narratives seem to belong to another age; something like this vision was doubtless traceable in the old Orphean epics describing the men-horses, the ancient hippanthropists, those Titans with human faces and equestrian chests, whose gallop escaladed Olympus,—horrible, sublime, invulnerable beings, gods and brutes.   It was a curious numerical coincidence that twenty-six battalions were preparing to receive the charge of these twenty-six squadrons.   Behind the crest of the plateau, in the shadow of the masked battery, thirteen English squares, each of two battalions and formed two deep, with seven men in the first line and six in the second, were waiting, calm, dumb, and motionless, with their muskets, for what was coming.   They did not see the cuirassiers, and the cuirassiers did not see them ; they merely heard this tide of men ascending.   They heard the swelling sound of three thousand horses, the alternating and symmetrical sound of the hoofs, the clang of the cuirasses, the clash of the sabres, and a species of great and formidable breathing.   There was a long and terrible silence, and then a long file of raised arms, brandishing sabres, and helmets, and bugles and standards, and three thousand heads with great moustaches, shouting " Vive l'Empereur ! " appeared above the crest.   The whole of this cavalry debouched on the plateau, and it was like the beginning of an earthquake.

All at once, tragic to relate, the head of the column of cuirassiers facing the English left reared with a fearful clamour.   On reaching the culminating point of the crest, furious and eager to make their exterminating dash on the English squares and guns, the cuirassiers noticed between them and the English a trench, a grave.   It was the hollow road of Ohain.   It was a frightful moment,—the ravine was there, unexpected, yawning, almost precipitous, beneath the horses' feet, and with a depth of twelve feet between its two sides.   The second rank thrust the first into the abyss ; the horses reared, fell back, struggled with all four feet in the air, crushing and throwing their riders.   There was no means of escaping ; the entire column was one huge projectile. The force acquired to crush the English crushed the French, and the inexorable ravine would not yield till it was filled up. Men and horses rolled into it pell-mell, crushing each other, and making one large charnel-house of the gulf, and when this grave was full of living men the rest passed over them. Nearly one-third of Dubois' brigade rolled into this abyss. This commenced the loss of the battle. A local tradition, which evidently exaggerates, says that two thousand horses and fifteen hundred men were buried in the hollow way of Ohain. These figures probably comprise the other corpses cast into the ravine on the day after the battle. Napoleon, before ordering this charge, had surveyed the ground, but had been unable to see this hollow way, which did not form even a ripple on the crest of the plateau. Warned, however, by the little white chapel which marks its juncture with the Nivelles road, he had asked Lacoste a question, probably as to whether there was any obstacle. The guide answered no, and we might almost say that from a peasant's shake of the head came the catastrophe of Napoleon.

CHAPTER XLI.

THE ravine and the artillery were unmasked simultaneously, —sixty guns and the thirteen squares thundered at the cuirassiers at point-blank range. The intrepid General Delord gave a military salute to the English battery. The whole of the English field artillery had entered the squares at a gallop; the cuirassiers had not even a moment for reflection. The disaster of the hollow way had decimated but not discouraged them, they were of that nature of men whose hearts grow large when their number is diminished. Wathier's column alone suffered in the disaster: but Delord's column, which he had ordered to wheel to the left, as if he suspected the trap, arrived entire. The cuirassiers rushed at the English squares at full gallop, with hanging bridles, sabres in their mouths, and pistols in their hands. There are moments in a battle when the soul hardens a man, so that it changes the soldier into a statue, and all flesh becomes granite. The English battalions, though fiercely assailed, did not move. Then there was a frightful scene. All the faces of the English squares were attacked simultaneously, and a frenzied whirl surrounded them. But the cold infantry remained impassive; the front rank kneeling received the cuirassiers on their bayonets, while the second fired at them · behind the second rank the artillerymen loaded their guns, the front of the square opened to let an eruption of canister pass, and then closed again. The cuirassiers responded by attempts to crush their foe; their great horses reared, leapt over the bayonets, and landed in the centre of the four living walls. The cannon-balls made gaps in the cuirassiers, and the cuirassiers made breaches in the squares. Files of men disappeared, trampled down by the horses, and bayonets were buried in the entrails of these centaurs. Hence arose horrible wounds, such as were probably never seen elsewhere. The squares, where broken by the impetuous cavalry, contracted without yielding an inch of ground; inexhaustible in canister they produced an explosion in the midst of the assailants. The aspect of this combat was monstrous: these squares were no longer battalions, but craters; these cuirassiers were no longer cavalry, but a tempest,—each square was a volcano attacked by a storm; the lava fought with the lightning.

The square on the extreme right, the most exposed of all, being in the open field, was nearly annihilated in the first attack. It was formed of the 75th Highlanders. The piper in the centre, while his comrades were being exterminated around him, was seated on a drum, with his pibroch under his arm, playing mountain airs. These Scotchmen died, thinking of Ben Lomond, as the Greeks did, remembering Argos. A cuirassier's sabre stopped the tune by killing the player.

The cuirassiers, relatively few in number, and reduced by the catastrophe of the ravine, had against them nearly the whole English army; but they multiplied themselves, and each man was worth ten. Some Hanoverian battalions, however, gave way: Wellington saw it and thought of his cavalry. Had Napoleon at this moment thought of his infantry, the battle would have been won. This forgetfulness was his great and fatal blunder. All at once the assailants found themselves assailed; the English cavalry were on their backs, before them the squares, behind them Somerset with the one thousand four hundred Dragoon Guards. Somerset had on his right Dornberg with the German chevau-legers, and on his left Trip with the Belgian carbineers; the cuirassiers, attacked on the flank and in front, before and behind, by infantry and cavalry, were compelled to make a front on all sides. But what did they care? they were a whirlwind, their bravery became indescribable.

Besides, they had behind them the still thundering battery, and it was only in such a way that these men could be wounded in the back. One of these cuirasses, with a hole through the left scapula, is in the Waterloo Museum. For such Frenchmen, nothing less than such Englishmen was required. It was no longer a mêlée, it was a headlong fury, a hurricane of flashing swords. In an instant the one thousand four hundred Dragoons were only eight hundred; and Fuller, their Lieutenant-colonel, was dead. Ney dashed up with Lefebvre Desnouette's lancers and chasseurs; the plateau of Mont St. Jean was taken and retaken, and taken again. The cuirassiers left the cavalry to attack the infantry, or, to speak more correctly, all these men collared each other and did not loose their hold. The squares still held out after twelve assaults. Ney had four horses killed under him, and one half of the cuirassiers remained on the plateau. This struggle lasted two hours. The English army was profoundly shaken; and there is no doubt that, had not the cuirassiers been weakened in their attack by the disaster of the hollow way, they would have broken through the centre and decided the victory. This extraordinary cavalry petrified Clinton, who had seen Talavera and Badajoz. Wellington, three parts vanquished, admired heroically; he said in a low voice, "Splendid!" The cuirassiers annihilated seven squares out of thirteen, captured or spiked sixty guns, and took six English regimental flags, which three cuirassiers and three chasseurs of the Guard carried to the Emperor before the farm of La Belle Alliance.

The situation of Wellington was growing worse. This strange battle resembled a fight between two savage wounded men, who constantly lose their blood while continuing the struggle. Which would be the first to fall? The combat for the plateau continued. How far did the cuirassiers get? no one could say; but it is certain that on the day after the battle, a cuirassier and his horse were found dead on the weighing machine of Mont St. Jean, at the very spot where the Nivelles, Genappe, La Hulpe, and Brussels roads intersect each other. This horseman had pierced the English lines. One of the men who picked up this corpse still lives at Mont St. Jean; his name is Dehaye, and he was eighteen years of age at the

time. Wellington felt himself giving way, and the crisis
was close at hand. The cuirassiers had not succeeded, in
the sense that the English centre had not been broken.
Everybody held the plateau, and nobody held it ; but, in
the end, the greater portion remained in the hands of the
English. Wellington had the village and the plain ; Ney,
only the crest and the slope. Both sides seemed to have
taken root in this mournful soil. But the weakness of
the English seemed irremediable, for the hæmorrhage of
this army was horrible. Kempt on the left wing asked
for reinforcements.   "There are none," Wellington replied.
Almost at the same moment, by a strange coincidence
which depicts the exhaustion of both armies, Ney asked
Napoleon for infantry, and Napoleon answered, "Infantry?
where does he expect me to get them ?   Does he expect me
to make them ? "

But the English army was the worse of the two ; the
furious attacks of these great squadrons with their iron
cuirasses and steel chests had crushed their infantry. A
few men round the colours marked the place of a regiment,
and some battalions were only commanded by a captain or
a lieutenant. Alten's division, already so maltreated at
La Haye Sainte, was nearly destroyed ; the intrepid
Belgians of Van Kluze's brigade lay among the wheat
along the Nivelles road : hardly any were left of those
Dutch Grenadiers who, in 1811, fought Wellington in
Spain, on the French side, and who, in 1815, joined the
English and fought Napoleon. The loss in officers was
considerable ; Lord Uxbridge, who had his leg interred the
next day, had a fractured knee. If on the side of the
French in this contest of the cuirassiers, Delord, l'Heretier,
Colbert, Duof, Travers, and Blancard were *hors de combat*,
on the side of the English, Alten was wounded, Barnes
was wounded, Delancy killed, Van Meeren killed, Ompteda
killed, Wellington's staff decimated,—and England had
the heaviest scale in this balance of blood. The 2nd
regiment of foot-guards had lost five lieutenant-colonels,
four captains, and three ensigns ; the first battalion of the
30th had lost twenty-four officers, and one hundred and
twelve men ; the 79th Highlanders had twenty-four officers
wounded, and eighteen officers and four hundred and fifty
men killed. Cumberland's Hanoverian Hussars, an entire
regiment, having Colonel Hacke at their head, who at
a later date was tried and cashiered, turned bridle during

the flight and fled into the forest of Soignies, spreading the rout as far as Brussels. The wagons, ammunition trains, baggage trains, and ambulance carts full of wounded, on seeing the French, gave ground, and approaching the forest, rushed into it; the Dutch, sabred by the French cavalry, broke in confusion. From Vert Coucou to Groenendael, a distance of two leagues on the Brussels roads, there was, according to the testimony of living witnesses, a dense crowd of fugitives, and the panic was so great that it assailed the Prince de Condé at Mechlin and Louis XVIII. at Ghent. With the exception of the weak reserve échelonned behind the field hospital established at the farm of Mont St. Jean, and Vivian's and Vandeleur's brigades, which flanked the left wing, Wellington had no cavalry left, and many of the guns lay dismounted. These facts are confessed by Siborne, and Pringle, exaggerating the danger, goes so far as to state that the Anglo-Dutch army was reduced to thirty-four thousand men. The Iron Duke remained firm, but his lips blanched. The Austrian commissioner Vincent, and the Spanish commissioner Alava, who were present at the battle, thought the Duke lost; at five o'clock Wellington looked at his watch, and could be heard to mutter these ominous words, "Blücher or night."

It was about this time that a distant line of bayonets glistened on the heights on the side of Frischemont. This was the turning-point of the colossal drama.

CHAPTER XLII.

Napoleon's awful mistake is known to all; Grouchy expected, Blücher coming up, death instead of life. Destiny has such turnings as this: men anticipate the throne of the world, and St. Helena becomes visible. If the little shepherd who served as guide to Bülow, Blücher's lieutenant, had advised him to debouche from the forest above Frischemont, instead of below Plancenoit, the form of the nineteenth century would have been different, for Napoleon would have won the battle of Waterloo. By any other road than that below Plancenoit the Prussian army would have come upon a ravine impassable by artillery, and Bülow would not have arrived. Now one hour's delay—the Prussian general Muffling declares it—and Blücher would not have found Wellington erect,—"the battle was lost." It was high time, as we see, for Bülow to arrive, and as it was he had been greatly delayed. He had bivouacked at Dieu-le-Mont and started at daybreak, but the roads were impracticable, and his divisions stuck in the mud. The ruts came up to the axle-tree of the guns ; moreover, he was compelled to cross the Dyle by the narrow bridge of Wavre : the street leading to the bridge had been burned by the French, and artillery train and limbers, which could not pass between two rows of blazing houses, were compelled to wait till the fire was extinguished. It was noon before Bülow's vanguard had reached Chapelle Saint Lambert.

Had the action commenced two hours earlier, it would have been over at four o'clock, and Blücher would have fallen upon the battle gained by Napoleon. At midday, the Emperor had been the first to notice through his telescope on the extreme horizon, something which fixed his attention, and he said, "I see over there a cloud which appears to me to be troops." Then he asked the Duke of Dalmatia, "Soult, what do you see in the direction of Chapelle Saint Lambert?" The Marshal, after looking through his telescope, replied, "Four or five thousand men, sire." It was evidently Grouchy, still they remained motionless in the mist. All the staff examined the cloud pointed out by the Emperor, and some said, "They are columns halting," but the majority were of opinion that they were trees. The truth is that the cloud did not move, and the Emperor detached Doncoul's division of light cavalry to reconnoitre in the direction of this obscure point.

Bülow, in fact, had not moved, for his vanguard was very weak and could effect nothing. He was obliged to wait for the main body of the army, and had orders to concentrate his troops before forming line ; but at five o'clock, Blücher, seeing Wellington's danger, ordered Bülow to attack, and employed the remarkable phrase, "We must let the English army breathe." A short time after, Losthin's, Hiller's, Hacke's, and Ryssel's brigades deployed in front of Lobau's corps, the cavalry of Prince William of Prussia debouched from the Bois de Paris, Plancenoit was in flames, and the Prussian cannon-balls began pouring even upon the ranks of the guard in reserve behind the Emperor.

The rest is known,—the irruption of a third army ; the battle dislocated ; eighty-six pieces of artillery thundering simultaneously ; Pirch I. coming up with Bülow ; Ziethen's cavalry led by Blücher in person ; the French driven back ;

Marcognet swept from the plateau of Ohain ; Durutte dislodged from Papelotte ; Donzelot and Quiot falling back Lobau attacked on the flank ; a new battle rushing at nightfall on the weakened French regiments ; the whole English line assuming the offensive, and pushed forward ; the gigantic gap made in the French army by the combined English and Prussian batteries ; the extermination, the disaster in front, the disaster on the flank, and the guard forming line amid this fearful convulsion. As they felt they were going to death, they shouted, "Long live the Emperor !" History has nothing more striking than this death-rattle breaking out into acclamations. The sky had been covered the whole day, but at this very moment, eight o'clock in the evening, the clouds parted in the horizon, and the sinister red glow of the setting sun was visible through the elms on the Nivelles road. The rising sun had shone on Austerlitz.

Each battalion of the Guard, for this final effort, was commanded by a general ; Friant, Michel, Roguet, Harlot, Mallet, and Pont de Morvan, were there. When the tall bearskins of the Grenadiers of the Guard with the large eagle device appeared, symmetrical in line, and calm, in the twilight of this fight, the enemy felt a respect for France ; they fancied they saw twenty victories entering the battlefield with outstretched wings, and the men who were victors, esteeming themselves vanquished, fell back ; but Wellington shouted, "Up, Guards, and take steady aim." The red regiment of English Guards, which had been lying down behind the hedges, rose ; a storm of canister rent the tricolour flag waving above the heads of the French ; all rushed forward, and the supreme carnage commenced. The Imperial Guard felt in the darkness the army giving way around them, and the vast staggering of the rout ; they heard the cry of "Sauve qui peut !" substituted for the "Vive l'Empereur !" and with flight behind them they continued to advance, hundreds falling at every step they took. None hesitated or evinced timidity ; the privates were as heroic as the generals. Not a man flinched from the suicide.

Ney, desperate and grand in the consciousness of accepted death, offered himself to every blow in this combat. He had his fifth horse killed under him here. Bathed in perspiration, with a flame in his eye, and foam on his lips, his uniform unbuttoned, one of his epaulettes half-cut through by the sabre-cut of a horse-guard, and his decoration of the

great eagle dinted by a bullet,—bleeding, muddy, magnificent, and holding a broken sword in his hand, he shouted,
" Come and see how a Marshal of France dies on the battlefield ! " But it was in vain; he did not die. He was haggard
and indignant, and hurled at Drouet d'Erlon the question,
"Are you not going to get yourself killed ? " He yelled
amid the roar of all this artillery, crushing a handful of
men, " Oh ! there is nothing for me ! I should like all these
English cannon-balls to enter my chest ! " You were reserved for French bullets, unhappy man.

The rout in the rear of the Guard was dismal ; the army
suddenly gave way on all sides simultaneously, at Hougomont, La Haye Sainte, Papelotte, and Plancenoit. The
cry of "treachery" was followed by that of " Sauve qui
peut ! " An army which disbands is like a thaw,—all gives
way, cracks, floats, rolls, falls, comes into collision, and
dashes forward. Ney borrows a horse, leaps on it, and
without hat, stock, or sword, dashes across the Brussels
road, stopping at once English and French. He tries to
hold back the army, he recalls it, he insults it, he clings
wildly to the rout to hold it back. The soldiers fly from
him, shouting, "Long live Marshal Ney ! " Two regiments
of Durotte's move backward and forward in terror, and as
it were tossed between the sabres of the Hussars and the
musketry fire of Kempt's, Best's, and Pack's brigades. A
rout is the highest of all confusions, for friends kill each
other in order to escape, and squadrons and battalions dash
against and destroy each other. Lobau at one extremity
and Reille at the other are carried away by the torrent.
In vain does Napoleon build a wall of what is left of the
Guard ; in vain does he expend his own special squadrons
in a final effort. Quiot retires before Vivian, Kellermann
before Vandeleur, Lobau before Bülow, Moraud before
Pirch, and Domor and Subervie before Prince William of
Prussia. Guyot, who led the Emperor's squadrons to the
charge, falls beneath the horses of English Dragoons.
Napoleon gallops along the line of fugitives, harangues,
urges, threatens, and implores them ; all the mouths that
shouted "Long live the Emperor" in the morning remain wide open ; they hardly knew him. The Prussian
cavalry, who had come up fresh, dash forward, cut down,
kill, and exterminate. The artillery horses dash forward
with the guns ; the train soldiers unharness the horses from
the caissons and escape on them ; wagons overthrown and

with their four wheels in the air, block up the road and
supply opportunities for massacre. Men crush each other
and trample over the dead and over the living. A multitude
wild with terror fill the roads, the paths, the bridges, the
plains, the hills, the valleys, and the woods, which are
thronged by this flight of forty thousand men. Cries,
desperation ; knapsacks and muskets cast into the wheat ;
passages cut with the edge of the sabres ; no comrades, no
officers, no generals recognised—an indescribable terror.
Ziethen sabring France at his ease. The lions become
kids. Such was this flight.

At Genappes, an effort was made to turn and rally ; Lobau
collected three hundred men ; the entrance of the village was
barricaded, but at the first round of Prussian canister all began
flying again, and Lobau was made prisoner. The marks of
this shot may still be seen, buried in the gable of an old
brick house on the right of the road, just before you reach
Genappes. The Prussians dashed into Genappes, doubtless
furious at being such small victors, and the pursuit was
monstrous, for Blücher commanded extermination. Roguet
had given the mournful example of threatening with death
any French Grenadier who brought in a Prussian prisoner,
and Blücher surpassed Roguet. Duchesme, general of the
Young Guard, who was pursued into the doorway of an inn
in Genappes, surrendered his sword to a Hussar of Death,
who took the sword and killed the prisoner. The victory
was completed by the assassination of the vanquished. Let
us punish as we are writing history,—old Blücher dis-
honoured himself. This ferocity set the seal on the disaster ;
the desperate rout passed through Genappes, passed through
Quatre Bras, passed through Sombreffe, passed through
Frasnes, passed through Thuin, passed through Charleroi,
and only stopped at the frontier. Alas ! and who was it
flying in this way ? It was the Grand Army.

Did this madness, this terror, this overthrow of the
greatest bravery that ever astonished history, take place
without a cause ? No. The shadow of a mighty right
hand is cast over Waterloo ; it is the day of destiny, and
the force which is above man produced that day. Hence
the terror, hence all those great souls laying down their
swords. Those who had conquered Europe fell crushed,
having nothing more to say or do, and feeling a terrible
presence in the shadow. On that day, the perspective of
the human race was changed, and Waterloo is the hinge

of the nineteenth century. The disappearance of the great man was necessary for the advent of the great age, and He to whom there is no reply undertook the task.

In the gathering night, Bernard and Bertrand seized by the skirt of his coat, in a field near Genappes, a haggard, thoughtful, gloomy man, who, carried so far by the current of the rout, had just dismounted, passed the bridle over his arm, and was now, with wandering eye, returning alone to Waterloo. It was Napoleon, the mighty somnambulist of the shattered dream, still striving to advance.

CHAPTER XLIII.

The battle of Waterloo is an enigma as obscure for those who gained it as for him who lost it. To Napoleon it is a panic ; Blücher sees nothing in it but fire ; Wellington does not understand it at all. Look at the reports : the bulletins are confused ; the commentaries are entangled ; the latter stammer, the former stutter. Jomini divides the battle of Waterloo into four moments ; Muffling cuts it into three acts ; Charras, although we do not entirely agree with him in all his appreciations, has alone caught with his haughty eye the characteristic lineaments of this catastrophe of human genius contending with divine chance. All the other historians suffer from a certain bedazzlement in which they grope about. It was a flashing day, in truth the overthrow of the military monarchy which, to the great stupor of the kings, has dragged down all kingdoms, the downfall of strength and the rout of war.

In this event, which bears the stamp of superhuman necessity, men play but a small part ; but, if we take Waterloo from Wellington and Blücher, does that deprive England and Germany of anything ? No. Neither illustrious England nor august Germany is in question in the problem of Waterloo, for, thank Heaven, nations are great without the mournful achievements of the sword. Neither Germany, nor England, nor France is held in a scabbard ; at this day when Waterloo is only a clash of sabres, Germany has Goethe above Blücher, and England Byron above Wellington. A mighty dawn of ideas is peculiar to our age, and in this dawn England and Germany have their own magnificent flash. They are majestic because they think ; the high level they bring to civilisation

is intrinsic to them ; it comes from themselves and not from
an accident. Any aggrandisement the nineteenth century
may have cannot boast of Waterloo as its fountain-head ;
for only barbarous nations grow suddenly after a victory—
it is the transient vanity of torrents swollen by a storm.
Civilised nations, especially at the present day, are not
elevated or debased by the good or evil fortune of a captain,
and their specific weight in the human family results from
something more than a battle. Their honour, dignity,
enlightenment, and genius, are not numbers which those
gamblers, heroes and conquerors, can stake in the lottery
of battles. Very often a battle lost is progress gained, and
less of glory, more of liberty. The drummer is silent and
reason speaks ; it is the game of who loses, wins. Let us,
then, speak of Waterloo coldly from both sides, and render
to chance the things that belong to chance, and to God
what is God's. What is Waterloo,—a victory? No ; a
prize in the lottery, won by Europe and paid by France ;
it was hardly worth while erecting a lion for it.

Waterloo, by the way, is the strangest encounter recorded
in history ; Napoleon and Wellington are not enemies, but
contraries. Never did God, who delights in antitheses,
produce a more striking contrast or a more extraordinary
confrontation. On one side precision, foresight, geometry,
prudence, a retreat assured, reserves prepared, an obstinate
coolness, an imperturbable method, strategy profiting by
the ground, tactics balancing battalions, carnage measured
by a plumb-line, war regulated watch in hand, nothing left
voluntarily to accident, old classic courage and absolute
correctness. On the other side we have intuition, divination, military strangeness, superhuman instinct, a flashing
glance ; something that gazes like the eagle and strikes like
lightning, all the mysteries of a profound mind, association
with destiny ; the river, the plain, the forest, and the hill
summoned, and to some extent compelled to obey, the
despot going so far as even to tyrannise over the battlefield ;
faith in a star blended with strategetic science, heightening,
but troubling it. Wellington was the Bareme of war,
Napoleon was its Michael Angelo, and this true genius was
conquered by calculation. On both sides somebody was
expected ; and it was the exact calculator who succeeded.
Napoleon waited for Grouchy, who did not come ; Wellington
waited for Blücher, and he came.

Wellington is the classical war taking its revenge ;

Bonaparte, in his dawn, had met it in Italy and superbly defeated it. The old owl fled before the young vulture. The old tactics had been not only overthrown, but scandalised. Who was this Corsican of six-and-twenty years of age? what meant this splendid ignoramus who, having everything against him, nothing for him, without provisions, ammunition, guns, shoes, almost without an army, with a handful of men against masses, dashed at allied Europe, and absurdly gained impossible victories? Who was this new-comer of war who possessed the effrontery of a planet? The academic military school excommunicated him, while bolting, and hence arose an implacable rancour of the old Cæsarism against the new, of the old sabre against the flashing sword, and of the chess-board against genius. On June 18th, 1815, this rancour got the best; and beneath Lodi, Montebello, Montenotte, Mantua, Marengo, and Arcola, it wrote,—Waterloo. It was a triumph of mediocrity, sweet to majorities, and destiny consented to this irony. In his decline, Napoleon found a young Suvarov before him,—in fact, it is only necessary to blanch Wellington's hair in order to have a Suvarov. Waterloo is a battle of the first class, gained by a captain of the second.

What must be admired in the battle of Waterloo is England, the English firmness, the English resolution, the English blood, and what England had really superb in it, is (without offence) herself; it is not her captain, but her army. Wellington, strangely ungrateful, declares in his despatch to Lord Bathurst, that his army, the one which fought on June 18th, 1815, was a "detestable army." What does the gloomy pile of bones buried in the trenches of Waterloo think of this? England has been too modest to herself in her treatment of Wellington, for making him so great is making herself small. Wellington is merely a hero like any other man. The Scots Greys, the Life Guards, Maitland and Mitchell's regiments, Pack and Kempt's infantry, Ponsonby and Somerset's cavalry, the Highlanders playing the bagpipes under the shower of canister, Ryland's battalions, the fresh recruits who could hardly manage a musket, and yet held their ground against the old bands of Essling and Rivoli—all this is grand. Wellington was tenacious, that was his merit, and we do not deny it to him, but the lowest of his privates and his troopers was quite as solid as he, and the iron soldier is as good as the iron duke. For our part, all our glorification is offered to the English soldier, the English army, the English nation; and if there must be a trophy, it is to England that this trophy is owing. The Waterloo column would be more just, if, instead of the figure of a man, it raised to the clouds the statue of a people.

With the fall of the Dictatorship, an entire European system crumbled into dust, and the Empire sank into a darkness resembling that of the expiring Roman world. Louis XVIII. returned to Paris, and the dancing of July 8th effaced the enthusiasm of the 20th of March.

CHAPTER XLIV.

WE must return, for the story requires it, to the fatal field of battle. On the 18th of June, 1815, the moon was full. Its light favoured Blücher's ferocious pursuit, denounced the trail of the fugitives, surrendered this disastrous crowd to the Prussian cavalry, and assisted the massacre. Such tragical complacency of the night is witnessed at times in catastrophes. After the last cannon was fired the plain of Mont St. Jean remained deserted. The English occupied the French encampment, for the usual confirmation of victory is to sleep in the beds of the conquered. They established their bivouac a little beyond Rossomme, and while the Prussians followed up the fugitives, Wellington proceeded to the village of Waterloo to draw up his report for Lord Bathurst. If ever the *sic vos non vobis* were applicable, it is most certainly to this village of Waterloo, which did nothing, and was half a league away from the action. Mont St. Jean was cannonaded, Hougomont burned, Papelotte burned, Plancenoit burned, La Haye Sainte carried by storm, and La Belle Alliance witnessed the embrace of the two victors; but these names are scarce known, and Waterloo, which had nothing to do with the battle, has all the honour of it.

We are not of those who glorify war, and when the opportunity offers, we tell it the truth. War has frightful beauties which we have not concealed; but it has also, we must allow, some ugly features. One of the most surprising is the rapid stripping of the dead after victory; the dawn that follows a battle always rises on naked corpses. Who does this? Who sullies the triumph in this way? Whose is the hideous, furtive hand which slips into the pocket of victory?

Who are the villains dealing their stroke behind the glory ? Some philosophers, Voltaire among them, assert that they are the very men who have made the glory ; they say that those who keep their feet plunder those lying on the ground, and the hero of the day is the vampire of the night. After all, a man has the right to strip a corpse of which he is the author. We do not believe it, however ; reaping a crop of laurels and stealing the shoes of a dead man do not seem to us possible from the same hand. One thing is certain, that, after the conquerors, come the robbers.

Every army has a train, and there the accusation should lie. Batlike beings, half servants, half brigands, all the species of night-bird which the twilight called war engenders, wearers of uniform who do not fight, malingerers, formidable invalids, interloping sutlers, trotting with their wives in small carts, and stealing things which they sell again, beggars offering themselves as guides to officers, villains, marauders,—all these, armies marching in former times (we are not alluding to the present day) had with them, so that, in the special language, they were called "the stragglers." No army and no nation were responsible for these beings,—they spoke Italian, and followed the Germans ; they spoke French, and followed the English. The detestable maxim, "Live on the enemy," produced this leprosy, which strict discipline could alone cure. A larger or smaller amount of marauders followed an army, according as the chief was more or less severe. Hoche and Morceau had no camp followers, and Wellington, we gladly do him the justice of stating, had but few.

However, during the night of June 18th, the dead were stripped. Wellington was strict ; he ordered that everybody caught in the act should be shot, but rapine is tenacious, and marauders plundered in one corner of the field while some were being shot in the other. About midnight a man was prowling, or rather crawling, about the hollow road of Ohain. He was, according to all appearance, one of those whom we have just described, neither English nor French, nor peasant nor soldier, less a man than a ghoul, attracted by the smell of the dead, whose victory was robbery, and who had come to plunder Waterloo. He was dressed in a blouse, which looked something like a gown, was anxious and daring, and looked behind while he went onwards. Who was this man ? Night knew probably more about him than did day. He had no bag, but evidently capacious pockets under his blouse. From time to time he stopped, examined the plain around him as if to see whether he was watched, bent down quickly, disturbed something lying silent and motionless on the ground, and then drew himself up again and skulked away.

Whoever had carefully examined, would have seen behind the house, which stands at the intersection of the Nivelles and Mont St. Jean roads, a sort of small vivandière's cart with a tilt of tarpaulin stretched over wickerwork, drawn by a hungry-looking, staggering horse, which was nibbling the nettles. In this cart, a woman was seated on chests and bundles, and there was probably some connection between this cart and the prowler. There was not a cloud in the sky, and though the ground may be blood red, the moon remains white ; that is the indifference of nature. In the fields, branches of trees broken by cannon-balls, but still holding on by the bark, waved softly in the night breeze. A breath shook the brambles, and there was a quiver in the grass that resembled the departure of souls. In the distance could be confusedly heard the march of the English patrols and rounds. Hougomont and La Haye Sainte continued to burn, making, one in the west, the other in the east, two large bodies of flames, to which were joined the English bivouac fires, stretching along the hills on the horizon, in an immense semicircle. The scene produced the effect of an unfastened ruby necklace, with a carbuncle at either end.

We have already described the catastrophe of the Ohain road. At the spot where this lamentable disaster occurred, all was now silence. The hollow way was filled with an inextricable pile of horses and their riders. There was no slope now, for the corpses levelled the road with the plain, and came up flush to the top, like a fairly measured bushel of barley. A pile of dead above, a stream of blood below,—such was the road on the night of June 18th, 1815. The blood ran as far as the Nivelles road, and extravasated there in a wide pool, in front of the barricade, at a spot which is still pointed out. It will be remembered that the destruction of the cuirassiers took place at the opposite point, near the Genappes road. The depth of the corpses was proportionate to that of the hollow way ; toward the middle, at the spot where Delord's division passed, the layer of dead was thinner.

The night prowler whom we have just introduced to the reader proceeded in that direction, searching this immense

tomb. He looked around and held a hideous review of the
dead ; he walked with his feet in the blood. All at once he
stopped. A few paces before him in the hollow way, at the
point where the pile of dead ended, an open hand, illumined
by the moon, emerged from the heap of men and horses.
This hand had on one finger something that glittered ; it
was a gold ring. The man bent down, and when he rose
again there was no longer a ring on this finger. He did
not exactly rise ; he remained in a savage and shy attitude,
turning his back to the pile of dead, investigating the horizon,
supporting himself on his two forefingers, and his head
spying over the edge of the hollow way. The four paws
of the jackals are suited for certain actions. Then, making
up his mind, he rose, but at the same moment he started,
for he felt that some one was holding him behind. He
turned and found that it was the open hand which had
closed and seized the skirt of his coat. An honest man
would have been frightened. This man began to laugh.

"Oh ! " he said, " it is only the dead man. I like a ghost
better than a gendarme."

The hand, however, soon relaxed its hold, for efforts are
quickly exhausted in the tomb.

" Can this dead man be alive ? " the marauder continued ;
" let me have a look."

He bent down again, removed all the obstacles, seized the
hand, liberated the head, pulled out the body, and a few
minutes later dragged an inanimate or at least fainting man
into the shadow of the hollow way. He was an officer of
cuirassiers of a certain rank, for a heavy gold epaulette
peeped out from under his cuirass. This officer had lost his
helmet, and a furious sabre cut crossed his face, which was
covered with blood. He did not appear, however, to have
any bones broken, and through some fortunate accident, if
such a word be possible here, the dead had formed an arch
over him so as to save him from being crushed. His eyes
were closed. He had on his cuirass the silver cross of the
Legion of Honour, and the prowler tore away this cross,
which disappeared in one of the gulfs he had under his
blouse. After this he felt the officer's fob, found a watch,
and took it ; then he felt in his vest and drew from it a
purse. When he was at this stage of the assistance he was
rendering the dying man, the officer opened his eyes.

" Thanks," he said feebly.

The roughness of the man's movements, the freshness of

the night, and the freely inhaled air had aroused him from his lethargy. The prowler did not answer, but raised his head. A sound of footsteps could be heard on the plain ; it was probably some patrol approaching. The officer murmured, for there was still the agony of death in his voice :

" Who won the battle ? "

" The English," the marauder answered.

The officer continued :

" Search my pockets. You will find a purse and a watch, which you can take."

Though this was already done, the prowler did what was requested, and said :

" There is nothing in them."

" I have been robbed," the officer continued ; " I am sorry. They would have been yours."

The footsteps of the patrol became more and more distinct.

" Some one is coming," the marauder said, preparing to go away.

The officer, raising his arm with difficulty, stopped him.

" You have saved my life ; who are you ? "

The prowler answered rapidly and in a low voice : " I belong, like yourself, to the French army, but I must leave you ; for if I were caught I should be shot,—I have saved your life, so now get out of the scrape as you can."

" What is your rank ? "

" Sergeant."

" Your name ? "

" Thénardier."

" I shall not forget that name," the officer said. " And you, remember mine. It is Pontmercy."

CHAPTER XLV.

JEAN VALJEAN had been retaken. As our readers will probably thank us for passing rapidly over painful details, we confine ourselves to the quotation of two paragraphs published by the newspapers of the day, a few months after the occurrence of the surprising events at M——. The first we take from the *Drapeau Blanc*, dated July 25th, 1823.

" A district of the Pas de Calais has just been the scene of an extraordinary occurrence. A man, who was a stranger to the department and called M. Madeleine, had some years previously revived by a new process an old local trade—the manufacture of jet and black beads. He made his own fortune, and, let us add, that of the district, and in acknowledgment of his services he was appointed Mayor. The police discovered that M. Madeleine was no other than an ex-convict, who had broken his ban, condemned in 1796 for robbery, of the name of Jean Valjean. He has been sent back to the galleys. It appears that prior to his arrest he succeeded in withdrawing from M. Laffitte's a sum of more than half a million, which he had banked there, and which it is said that he had honestly acquired by his trade. Since his return to Toulon, futile efforts have been made to discover where this amount is hidden."

The second article, which is rather more detailed, is extracted from the *Journal de Paris* of the same date.

"An ex-convict, named Jean Valjean, has just been tried at the Var assizes, under circumstances which attract attention. This villain had succeeded in deceiving the vigilance of the police, and had behaved so cleverly as to be made Mayor of one of our small towns in the north, where he established a rather considerable trade. He was at length unmasked, and arrested through the indefatigable zeal of the public authorities. He had, as his concubine, a girl of the town, who died of a fit at the moment of his arrest. This scoundrel, who is endowed with Herculean strength, managed to escape, but three or four days later the police again captured him in Paris, at the moment when he was entering one of those small coaches which run from the capital to the village of Montfermeil (Seine et Oise). It is said that he took advantage of these three or four days of liberty to withdraw from one of our chief bankers an amount estimated at six or seven hundred thousand francs. According to the indictment he buried it at some spot only known to himself, and it has not been found ; but, however this may be, this Jean Valjean had just been tried at Var assizes for a highway robbery, committed with violence some eight years ago upon one of those honest lads, who, as the patriarch of Ferney has said in immortal verse :

> " —De Savoie arrivent tous les ans
> Et dont la main légèrement essuie
> Ces longs canaux engorgés par la suie.

This bandit made no defence, but it was proved by the skilful and eloquent organ of public justice that Jean

Valjean was a member of a band of robbers in the south. Consequently Jean Valjean was found guilty and sentenced to death. The criminal refused to appeal to the Court of Cassation, but the King, in his inexhaustible mercy, deigned to commute his sentence into penal servitude for life. Jean Valjean was immediately sent on to the galleys at Toulon."

Jean Valjean changed his number at the galleys, and was known as 9430. Let us state here once and for all that with M. Madeleine the prosperity of M——'disappeared : all he had foreseen in his night of hesitation and fever was realised ; his absence was in truth the absence of the soul. After his fall there took place at M—— that selfish division of great fallen existences, that fatal break up of flourishing things, which is daily accomplished obscurely in the human community, and which history has only noticed once because it occurred after the death of Alexander. Lieutenants crown themselves kings ; overseers, in this case, suddenly became manufacturers, and envious rivalries sprang up. M. Madeleine's large workshops were shut up ; the buildings fell into a ruinous condition, and the artisans dispersed, some leaving the town, others the trade. All was henceforth done on a small scale instead of a large one, for lucre instead of the public welfare. There was no centre, but on all sides violent competition. M. Madeleine had commanded and directed everything. When he fell, a spirit of contest succeeded that of organisation, bitterness succeeded cordiality, and mutual hatred the goodwill of the common founder. The threads tied by M. Madeleine became knotted and broken ; the process was falsified, the articles became worse, and confidence was destroyed ; the outlets diminished, and there were fewer orders ; wages fell, there were stoppages, and lastly came bankruptcy.

CHAPTER XLVI.

BEFORE proceeding further, it will not be amiss to relate in some detail, a strange fact that occurred at about the same period at Montfermeil, and which may possibly possess some coincidence with certain police conjectures. There is at Montfermeil a very old superstition, which is the more curious and valuable because a popular superstition in the neighbourhood of Paris is like an aloe-tree in Siberia. We

are of those who respect everything which is in the condition of a rare plant. This, then, is the Montfermeil
superstition : it is believed that from time immemorial the
fiend has selected the forest as the spot where he buries his
treasure. Old women declare that it is not rare to meet at
nightfall, and in remote parts of the forest, a black man
resembling a wagoner or wood-cutter, dressed in wooden
shoes and canvas trousers and blouse, and recognisable
from the fact that he has on his head two enormous horns
in place of cap or hat. This man is usually engaged in
digging a hole, and there are three modes of action in the
event of meeting him. The first is to go up to the man and
address him ; in that case you perceive that he is simply a
peasant, that he appears black because it is twilight that
he is not digging a hole, but cutting grass for his kine, and
that what you had taken for horns is nothing but a dung-
fork he carries on his back, whose prongs seem to grow
out of his head. You go home and die within the week.
The second plan is to watch him, wait till he has dug his
hole and filled it up and gone away ; then you run up to
the hole and take out the treasure which the black man
had necessarily deposited in it. In this case you die
within the month. The last way is not to speak to the
black man at all, not to look at him, but run away as fast
as you can. You die within the year.

All three modes have their drawbacks, but the second,
which offers at any rate some advantages, among others
that of possessing a treasure, if only for a month, is the one
most generally adopted. Bold men whom chances tempt
have therefore, so it is declared, frequently reopened the
hole dug by the black man, and robbed the demon. It
seems, however, as if the profits are small : at any rate if
we may believe tradition, and particularly and especially
two enigmatical lines in dog Latin, which a wicked
Norman monk, a bit of a sorcerer, and of the name of
Tryphon, left on the subject. This Tryphon lies at St.
George's Abbey at Bocherville, near Rouen, and frogs are
born on his tomb. A man makes enormous exertions, then,
for the holes are generally very deep : he perspires, works
the whole night through (for the operation must be carried
out at night), gets a wet shirt, burns out his candle, breaks
his pick, and when he at last reaches the bottom of the hole
and lays his hand on the treasure, what does he find ?
what is the fiend's treasure ? a sou, at times a crown-piece,

a stone, a skeleton, a bleeding corpse, or a spectre folded up like a sheet of paper in a pocket-book, and sometimes nothing at all! This is what seems to be held forth to the indiscreet and prying by the lines of Tryphon :

Fodit et in fossâ thesauros condit opaca,
As, nummos, lapides, cadaver, simulacra, nirhilque.

It appears that in our time there are also found sometimes a gunpowder flask and balls, or an old pack of greasy, dirty cards which have evidently been used by the fiends. Tryphon does not record these two facts, because he lived in the twelfth century, and it does not appear that the fiend had the sense to invent gunpowder before Roger Bacon, or playing-cards before Charles VI. If you play with the cards you are safe to lose all you possess, while the gunpowder displays the peculiarity of bursting your gun in your face.

Now, very shortly after the time when it occurred to the police that Jean Valjean, during his four days of liberty, had been prowling round Montfermeil, it was noticed in the same village that a certain old road-mender of the name of Boulatruelle was " up to his tricks " in the forest. It was believed generally that this Boulatruelle had been to the galleys ; he was to some extent under police inspection, and as he could not find work anywhere, the administration employed him at a low wage as mender of the cross-road from Gagny to Lagny. This Boulatruelle was a man looked upon with suspicion by the villageois, as he was too respectful, too humble, ready to doff his cap to everybody, trembling and fawning before the gendarmes, and probably allied with the robbers, so it was said, and suspected of lurking about the roads after dark. He had nothing in his favour except that he was a drunkard.

What had been observed was this. For some time past Boulatruelle had left work at an early hour, and had gone into the forest with his pick-axe. He was met toward evening in the most desolate clearings, in the wildest thickets, apparently seeking something, and at times digging holes. The old women who passed at first took him for Beelzebub, and when they recognised Boulatruelle did not feel at all more easy in mind. Such meetings greatly annoyed Boulatruelle, and hence it was plain that he tried to hide himself, and that there was a mystery in what he was doing. It was said in the village, " It is clear that the fiend has made his appearance. Boulatruelle saw him, and is seeking for his treasure. The truth is he is just the fellow to rob the Evil One." The Voltairians added : "Will Boulatruelle cheat the demon or the demon cheat Boulatruelle ? " while the old women crossed themselves repeatedly. Boulatruelle, however, discontinued his forest rambles, and regularly resumed his work, whereupon something else was talked about. Some persons, however, remained curious, thinking that there was probably in the affair, not the fabulous treasure of the legend, but something more palpable and tangible than the fiend's banknotes, and that the road-mender had doubtless found out half the secret. The most puzzled were the schoolmaster and Thénardier the publican, who was everybody's friend, and had not disdained to strike up an intimacy even with Boulatruelle.

"He has been to the galleys," Thénardier would say. "Well, good Lord ! we do not know who is there, or who may go there."

One evening the schoolmaster remarked that in old times the authorities would have inquired what Boulatruelle was about in the wood, and that he would have been obliged to speak ; they would have employed torture if necessary, and Boulatruelle would not have resisted the ordeal of water, for instance. "Let us give him the ordeal of wine," said Thénardier. They set to work, and Boulatruelle drank enormously, but held his tongue. He combined, with admirable tact and in magisterial proportions, the thirst of a sponge with the discretion of a judge. Still, by returning to the charge, and by putting together the few obscure words that escaped him, Thénardier and the schoolmaster made out, as they thought, the following :

One morning, about daybreak, as he was going to his work, Boulatruelle was surprised at seeing under a bush a spade and a pick, which "looked as if they were hidden"; still he fancied that they belonged to Father Six-fours, the water-carrier, and did not think any more of the matter. On the evening of the same day, however, he saw, without being himself seen, as he was hidden behind a tree, "an individual who did not belong to these parts, and whom he, Boulatruelle, knew," proceeding toward the most retired part of the wood. This Thénardier translated as "a comrade at the galleys," but Boulatruelle obstinately refused to mention his name. This individual was carrying

a bundle, something square, like a box or small chest.
Boulatruelle was surprised, but it was not till some ten
minutes later that the idea of following the "individual"
occurred to him. But it was too late, the individual was
already among the trees, night had fallen, and Boulatruelle
was unable to catch him up. Then he resolved to watch
the outskirts of the wood, for the moon was shining.
Boulatruelle, some two or three hours after, saw this
individual come out of the wood, not carrying the box,
however, but a spade and pick. Boulatruelle allowed him
to pass, and did not address him, for he said to himself that
the other man was thrice as strong as he, and being armed
with a pick, would probably smash him on recognising him
and finding himself recognised; touching effusion on the
part of two old comrades who suddenly meet! But the
spade and pick were a ray of light for Boulatruelle; he
hurried to the bush at daybreak, and no longer found them
there. From this he concluded that this individual, on
entering the wood, had dug a hole with his pick, buried
his box in it, and then filled up the hole with his spade.
Now, as the box was too small to contain a corpse, it must
contain money, and hence his researches. Boulatruelle
explored the forest in all directions, and especially at spots
where the ground seemed to have been recently turned up.
But all in vain.

CHAPTER XLVII.

TOWARDS the end of October, in that same year, 1823, the
inhabitants of Toulon saw a vessel enter their port which
had sustained some damage in a heavy storm. It was the
Orion, which at a later date was employed at Brest as a
training ship, but now formed part of the Mediterranean
fleet. The presence of a man-of-war in a port has something about it which attracts and occupies the mob, and
every day, from morning till night, the quays and piers of
Toulon were covered with numbers of idlers, whose business
it was to look at the *Orion*. This vessel had long been in
a sickly state. During previous voyages barnacles had
collected on her hull to such an extent that she lost half
her speed; she had been taken into dry dock the year
previous to scrape off these barnacles, and then put to sea
again. But this scraping had injured the bolts, and when
off the Balearic Isles, she sprang a leak, and took in water,

as vessels were not coppered in those days. A violent
equinoctial gale supervened, which injured her larboard
bows and destroyed the fore chains. In consequence of
this damage the *Orion* put into Toulon, and was moored
near the arsenal for repairs.

One morning the crowd of idlers witnessed an accident.
The crew were engaged in furling the sails, and the top-
man, who had hold of the upper corner of the main-topsail,
lost his balance. He was seen to totter ; the crowd on the
arsenal quay uttered a cry, his head dragged him down-
wards, and he turned round the yard, with his hands
stretched down to the water, but he caught hold of the foot-
rope as he passed it, first with one hand then with the
other, and remained hanging from it. The sea was below
him at a dizzy depth, and the shock of his fall had given
the foot-rope a violent swinging movement. The man
swung at the end of the rope like a stone in a sling. To go
to his assistance would be running a frightful risk, and not
one of the sailors, all coast fishermen lately called in for
duty, dared to venture it. Still the unhappy top-man was
growing tired : his agony could not be seen in his face, but
his exhaustion could be distinguished in all his limbs, and
his arms were awfully dragged. Any effort he made to
raise himself only caused the foot-rope to oscillate the more,
and he did not cry out, for fear of exhausting his strength.
The minute was close at hand when he must leave go the
rope, and every now and then all heads were turned away
not to see it happen. There are moments in which a rope,
a pole, the branch of a tree, is life itself, and it is a fearful
thing to see a living being leave hold of it, and fall like ripe
fruit. All at once a man could be seen climbing up the
shrouds with the agility of a tiger-cat. As he was dressed
in red this man was a convict ; as he wore a green cap he
was a convict for life. On reaching the top a puff of wind
blew away his cap and revealed a white head, so that he
was not a young man.

In fact, a convict, employed on board in some prison task,
had at once run up to the officer of the watch, and in the
midst of the trouble and confusion, while all the sailors
trembled and recoiled, asked permission to risk his life in
saving the top-man. At a nod of assent from the officer he
broke with one blow of a hammer the chain riveted to his
ankle, took up a rope, and darted up the shrouds. No
one noticed at the moment with what ease this chain was

broken ; and the fact was not remembered till afterwards. In a second he was upon the yard, where he stood for a little while as if looking round him. These seconds, during which the wind swung the top-man at the end of a thread, seemed ages to the persons who were looking at him. At length the convict raised his eyes to heaven and advanced a step. The crowd breathed again, as they saw him run along the yard. On reaching the end he fastened to it the rope he had brought with him, let it hang down, and then began going down it hand over hand. This produced a feeling of indescribable agony, for, instead of one man hanging over the gulf, there were now two. He resembled a spider going to seize a fly ; but, in this case, the spider brought life and not death. Ten thousand eyes were fixed on the group : not a cry, not a word could be heard ; every mouth held its breath, as if afraid of increasing in the slightest degree the wind that shook the two wretched men. The convict, in the interim, had managed to get close to the sailor, and it was high time, for a minute later the man, exhausted and desperate, would have let himself drop into the sea. The convict fastened him securely with the rope to which he clung with one hand, while he worked with the other. At length he was seen to climb back to the yard and haul the sailor up : he supported him there for a moment to let him regain his strength, then took him in his arms and carried him along the yard to the cap, and thence to the top, where he left him with his comrades. The crowd applauded him, and several old sergeants of the chain-gang had tears in their eyes : women embraced each other on the quay, and every voice could be heard shouting with a species of frenzy,—" This man must be pardoned ! "

The convict, however, had made it a point of duty to descend again immediately, and go back to his work. In order to do so more rapidly he slid down a rope and ran along a lower yard. All eyes followed him, and at one moment the spectators felt afraid, for they fancied they could see him hesitate and totter, either through fatigue or dizziness ; all at once the crowd uttered a terrible cry,— the convict had fallen into the sea. The fall was a danger- ous one, for the *Algésiras* frigate was anchored near the *Orion*, and the poor galley slave had fallen between the two ships, and might be sucked under one of them. Four men hastily got into a boat, and the crowd encouraged them, for all felt anxious again. The man did not come to the surface again, and disappeared in the sea without making a ripple, just as if he had fallen into a barrel of oil. They dragged for him, but in vain ; they continued the search till nightfall, but his body was not even found. The next day the Toulon paper printed the following lines :—"Nov. 17, 1823.—Yesterday a convict, one of a gang on board the *Orion*, fell into the sea and was drowned, as he was returning from assisting a sailor. His body has not been found, and is supposed to be entangled among the piles at the arsenal point. The man was registered under the number 9430, and his name was Jean Valjean."

CHAPTER XLVIII.

MONTFERMEIL lies between Livry and Chelles, on the southern slope of the high plateau which separates the Ourcq from the Marne. At present, it is a rather large place, adorned with stucco villas all the year round, and with holiday-making citizens on Sunday. In 1823 there were neither so many white houses nor so many happy citizens as there are now, and it was merely a village in the woods. A visitor certainly came across here and there a few country houses of the last century, recognisable by their air of pretension, their balconies of twisted iron, and the tall windows, in which the little squares produce all sorts of green hues on the white of the closed shutters. But Montfermeil was not the less a village ; retired cloth-dealers and persons fond of country life had not yet discovered it. It was a quiet, pleasant spot, which was not on a road to anywhere. Persons lived there cheaply that peasant life which is so tranquil and abundant. The only thing was that water was scarce, owing to the elevation of the plateau, and it had to be fetched from some distance. That end of the village which was on the Gagny side obtained its water from the splendid ponds in the forest there ; but the other end, which surrounds the church and is on the Chelles side, could only obtain drinking water from a little spring about a quarter of an hour's walk from Montfermeil, near the road to Chelles ; laying in water was therefore a hard task for every family. The large houses and the aristocracy, among which Thénardier's pot-house may be reckoned, paid a liard a bucket to a man whose trade it was, and who earned by it about eight sous a day. But this man only worked till seven o'clock in summer, and till five in winter ; and once night had set in and the ground-floor shutters were closed, any person who had no water to drink must either go for it or go without it.

This was the terror of the poor being whom the reader has not perhaps forgotten—little Cosette. It will be remembered that Cosette was useful to the Thénardiers in two ways,—they made the mother pay and the child act as servant. Hence when the mother ceased payment, for the reason which we know, the Thénardiers kept Cosette, who took the place of a servant. In this quality she had to fetch water when it was wanted, and the child, terrified at the idea of going to the spring at night, was very careful that the house should never be without water. Christmas of 1823 was peculiarly brilliant at Montfermeil ; the beginning of the winter was mild, and there had been neither snow nor frost. Some mountebanks, who came from Paris, had obtained leave from the mayor to erect their booth in the village high street, and a party of travelling hawkers had put up their stalls in the church square, and even in the lane in which Thénardier's pot-house was situated. This filled the inns and pot-houses, and produced a noisy, joyous life in this quiet little place.

On that Christmas evening several men, carters and pedlars, were sitting drinking, round four or five candles, in Thénardier's tap-room. This room was like those usually found in pot-houses ; there were tables, pewter pots, bottles, drinkers, and smokers, but little light, and a good deal of uproar. The date of the year was, however, indicated by the two objects, fashionable at that time among tradespeople, which were on a table—a kaleidoscope and a lamp of clouded tin. Madame Thénardier was watching the supper, which was roasting before a bright clear fire, while her husband was drinking with his guests and talking politics.

Cosette was seated at her usual place, the cross-bar of the table, near the chimney ; she was in rags, her bare feet were thrust into wooden shoes, and she was knitting, by the firelight, stockings intended for the young Thénardiers. Two merry children could be heard laughing and prattling in an adjoining room ; they were Eponine and Azelma. A cat-o'-nine-tails hung from a nail by the side of the chimney. At times, the cry of a baby somewhere in the house was,

audible through the noise of the tap-room ; it was a little
boy Madame Thénardier had given birth to one winter,
"without knowing how," she used to say ; "it was the
effect of the cold," and who was a little over three years
of age. The mother suckled him, but did not love him ;
when his cries became too troublesome, Thénardier would
say,—"There's your brat squalling ; go and see what he
wants." "Bah !" the mother would answer, "I am sick
of him." And the poor deserted little fellow would continue
to cry in the darkness.

Up to the present, only a side view of the Thénardiers
has been offered the reader of this book ; the time has
now arrived to turn this couple round, and look at them
on all sides. Thénardier had passed his fiftieth year,
Madame Thénardier was just on her fortieth, which is
fifty in a woman ; and in this way there was a balance of
age between husband and wife. Our readers may probably
have retained from the first meeting some recollection of
this tall, light-haired, red, fat, square, enormous, and
active woman. She did everything in the house ; made
the beds, cleaned the rooms, was cook and laundress,
produced rain and fine weather, and played the devil. Her
only assistant was Cosette, a mouse in the service of an
elephant. All trembled at the sound of her voice—windows,
furniture, and people ; and her large face, dotted with
freckles, looked like a skimmer. She had a beard, and
was the ideal of a Billingsgate porter dressed in female
attire. She swore splendidly, and boasted of being able
to crack a walnut with a blow of her fist. Had it not
been for the romances she had read, and which at times
made the finikin woman appear under the ogress, no one
would ever have dreamed of thinking that she was feminine.
She seemed to be the product of a cross between a young
damsel and a fish fag. When people heard her speak,
they said,—"'Tis a gendarme ;" when they saw her
drink, they said,—"'Tis a carter ;" and when they saw
her treatment of Cosette, they said,—"'Tis the hangman."
When she was at rest, a tooth protruded from her mouth.

The other Thénardier was a short, thin, sallow, angular,
bony, weak man, who looked ill, and was perfectly well
—his knavery began there. He smiled habitually through
caution, and was polite to nearly everybody, even to the
beggar whom he refused a halfpenny. He had the eye
of a ferret and the face of a man of letters, and greatly

resembled the portraits of Abbé Delille. His coquetry consisted in drinking with carriers, and no one had ever been able to intoxicate him. He wore a blouse and under it an old black coat, and had pretensions to literature and materialism. There were some names he frequently uttered in order to support an argument, such as Voltaire, Raynal, Parny, and, strangely enough, St. Augustine. He declared that he had "a system." He was a thorough scamp, however. It will be remembered that he asserted he had been a soldier, and told people with some pomp how at Waterloo, where he was sergeant in the 6th or 9th Light something, he alone, against a squadron of Hussars of Death, had covered with his body and saved "a severely wounded general." Hence came his flaming sign, and the name by which his house was generally known, the Sergeant of Waterloo. He was liberal, classical, and a Bonapartist; he had subscribed to the Champ d'Asile, and it was said in the village that he had studied for the priesthood. We believe that he had simply studied in Holland to be an innkeeper. This scoundrel of a composite order was in all probability some Fleming of Lille, a Frenchman at Paris, a Belgian at Brussels, conveniently striding over two frontiers. We know his prowess at Waterloo, and, as we see, he exaggerated slightly. Ebb and flow and wandering adventures were the elements of his existence. A tattered conscience entails an irregular life, and probably at the stormy period of June 18th, 1815, Thénardier belonged to that variety of marauding sutlers to whom we have alluded, who go about the country selling to some and robbing others, and moving about in a halting cart after marching troops, with the instinct of always joining the victorious army. When the campaign was over, having, as he said, "some brads," he opened a pot-house at Montfermeil. These "brads," consisting of purses and watches, gold rings, and silver crosses, collected in ditches filled with corpses, did not make a heavy total, and had not lasted this sutler, now become innkeeper, very long.

Thénardier had something rectangular in his movements, which, with an oath, recalls the barrack,—with the sign of the cross, the seminary. He was a clever speaker, and liked to be thought educated, but the schoolmaster noticed that he made mistakes. He drew up a traveller's bill in a masterly way, but practised eyes sometimes found orthographical errors in it. Thénardier was cunning, greedy, indolent, and skilful ; he did not despise his servant girls, and for that reason his wife no longer kept any. This giantess was jealous, and fancied that this little yellow man must be an object of universal covetousness. Thénardier above all, as a crafty and well-balanced man, was a villain of the temperate genus, and this breed is the worst, as hypocrisy is mixed up in them. It was not that Thénardier was not at times capable of passion, at least quite as much as his wife, but it was very rare, and at such moments—as he owed a grudge to the whole human race, as he had within him a profound furnace of hatred, as he was one of those persons who avenge themselves perpetually, who accuse everybody who passes before them for what falls upon them, and who are ever ready to cast on the first comer, as a legitimate charge, the whole of the annoyances, bankruptcies, and deceptions of their life,—when all this leaven was working in him and boiling in his mouth and eyes, he was fearful. Woe to him who came under his fury then.

Besides all his other qualities, Thénardier was attentive and penetrating, silent or chattering, according to occasion, and always with great intelligence. He had the glance of sailors who are accustomed to wink when looking through a telescope. Thénardier was a statesman. Any new-comer, on entering the pot-house, said upon seeing the woman, " That is the master of the house ; " but it was an error,—she was not even the mistress, for her husband was both master and mistress. She did and he created, he directed everything by a species of invisible and continuous magnetic action ; a word, sometimes a sign, from him was sufficient, and the mastodon obeyed. The husband was to his wife, though she did not know it, a species of peculiar and sovereign being. However much she might dissent from " Monsieur Thénardier,"—an inadmissible hypothesis, —she would never have proved him publicly in the wrong for any consideration. She would never have committed " in the presence of strangers " that fault which wives so often commit, and which is called, in parliamentary language, " exposing the crown." Although their agreement only resulted in evil, there was contemplation in Madame Thénardier's submission to her husband. This mountain of noise and flesh moved under the little finger of this frail despot ; seen from its dwarfish and grotesque aspect, it was the great universal thing—adoration of matter by the mind. There was something strange in Thénardier, and hence came the absolute dominion of this man over this woman. At certain moments she saw him as a lighted candle, at others she felt him as a claw. This woman was a formidable creature, who only loved her children, and only feared her husband. She was a mother because she was mammiferous; her maternal feelings ceased, however, with her girls, and, as we shall see, did not extend to boys. He, the man, had but one thought—to get rich.

He did not succeed. A suitable stage was wanting for this great talent. Thénardier ruined himself at Montfermeil, if ruin is possible at zero; in Switzerland or the Pyrenees he would have become a millionaire. But where fate fastens a landlord he must browse. In this year, 1823, Thénardier was in debt to the amount of 1500 francs, which rendered him anxious. Whatever might be the obstinate injustice of destiny against him, Thénardier was one of those men who thoroughly understand, and in the most modern fashion, the theory which is a virtue in barbarous nations, and an article of sale among civilised nations—hospitality. He was also an admirable poacher, and renowned for the correctness of his aim. He had a certain cool and quiet laugh, which was peculiarly dangerous.

His theories of innkeeping burst forth from him at times in flashes, and he had professional aphorisms which he drove into his wife's mind. "The duty of a landlord," he said one day savagely, and in a low voice, "is to sell to the first comer, ragouts, rest, light, fire, dirty sheets, chamber maids, fleas, and smiles; to arrest passers-by, empty small purses, and honestly lighten heavy ones; to shelter respectfully travelling families, rasp the husband, peck the wife, and pluck the children; to set a price on the open window, the shut window, the chimney-corner, the easy-chair, the sofa, the stool, the feather-bed, the mattress, and the palliasse; to know how much the reflection wears off the looking-glass, and charge for it, and by the five hundred thousand devils to make the traveller pay for everything, even to the flies his dog eats!"

This man and this woman were cunning and rage married —a hideous and terrible pair. While the husband ruminated and combined, the she Thénardier did not think about absent creditors, had not thought of yesterday or to-morrow, and lived violently only for the moment. Such were these two beings, between whom Cosette stood, enduring their double pressure, like a creature who was being at once crushed my a millstone and torn with a pair of pincers. Man and wife had each a different way. Cosette was beaten, that came from the wife; she went about barefoot in winter, that came from her husband. Cosette went up and down stairs, washed, brushed, scrubbed, swept, ran about, panted for breath, moved heavy weights, and, little though she was, did all the hard work. She could expect no pity from a ferocious mistress and a venomous master, and the Sergeant of Waterloo was, as it were, a web in which Cosette was caught and trembled. The ideal of oppression was realised by this gloomy household, and it was something like a fly serving spiders. The poor child was passively silent. When they find themselves in such condition at the dawn of existence, so young, so feeble, among men, what goes on in these souls fresh from God!

CHAPTER XLIX.

FOUR new travellers arrived. Cosette was musing, sadly, for though only eight years of age she had already suffered so much that she thought with the mournful air of an old woman. Her eyelid was blackened by a blow which the woman had given her, which made madame say now and then, "How ugly she is with her black eye!" Cossette was thinking then that it was late, very late; that she had been suddenly obliged to fill the jugs and bottles in the rooms of the travellers who had just arrived, and that there was no water in the cistern. What reassured her most was the fact that but little water was drunk at the Sergeant of Waterloo. There was no lack of thirsty souls, but it was that sort of thirst which applies more readily to the wine-jar than to the water-bottle. Any one who asked for a glass of water among the glasses of wine would have appeared a savage to all these men. At one moment, however, the child trembled; her mistress raised the cover of a stew-pan, bubbling on a stove, then took a glass and hurried to the cistern. The child had turned, and was watching all her movements. A thin stream of water ran from the tap and filled the glass. "Hilloh," she said, "there is no water;" then she was silent for a moment, during which the child held her breath.

"Well," Madame Thénardier continued, as she examined the half-filled glass, "this will be enough."

Cosette resumed her work, but for more than a quarter of an hour she felt her heart beating in her chest. She counted the minutes that passed thus, and wished that it were next morning. From time to time one of the topers looked out into the street and said, "It's as black as pitch," or "A man would have to be a cat to go into the street at this hour without a lantern," and Cosette shivered. All at once, one of the pedlars lodging at the inn came in and said in a harsh voice :

"My horse has had no water."

"Oh yes, it has," said Madame Thénardier.

"I tell you it has not, mother," the pedlar went on.

Cosette had crept out from under the table.

"Oh yes, sir," she said, "your horse drank a bucketful, and I gave it the water and talked to it."

This was not true.

"There's a girl no bigger than one's fist who tells a lie as big as a house," the dealer exclaimed. "I tell you it has not had any water, you little devil ; it has a way of breathing which I know well when it has not drunk."

Cosette persisted, and added in a voice rendered hoarse by agony, and which was scarce audible :

"Oh, indeed, the horse drank a lot."

"Enough of this," the dealer said savagely, "give my horse water."

Cosette went back under the table.

"Well, that is but fair," said madame, "if the brute has not drunk it ought to drink." Then she looked around her. "Why, where is the little devil ?"

She stooped down, and discovered Cosette hidden at the other end of the table, almost under the feet of the topers.

"Come out of that," her mistress shouted.

Cosette came out of the hole in which she had hidden herself, and the landlady continued :

"Miss What's-your-name, give the horse water."

"There is no water, madame," Cosette said faintly.

The Thénardiers threw the street door wide open.

"Well, go after some."

Cosette hung her head, and went for an empty bucket standing in a corner near the chimney ; it was larger than herself, and she could have sat down in it comfortably. Madame Thénardier returned to her stove and tasted the contents of a stew-pan with a wooden spoon, while growling :

"There's plenty at the spring. I believe it would have been better to sift the onions."

Then she rummaged in a drawer which contained half-pence, pepper, and shallots.

"Here, Miss Toad," she added, "as you come back, you will bring a loaf from the baker's. Here's a fifteen-sous piece."

Cosette had a small pocket in her apron, in which she placed the coin; then she stood motionless, bucket in hand, and with the door open before her. She seemed to be waiting for some one to come to her help.

"Be off," her mistress shouted.

Cosette went out. The door closed.

The row of open-air booths, it will be remembered, extended along the street from the church as far as Thénardier's inn. These stalls, owing to the approaching and passing of persons going to midnight mass, were all lit up with candles in paper funnels, which, as the school-master, who was seated at this moment in Thénardier's taproom, declared, produced a "magical effect." To make up for this not a star glittered in the sky. The last of these shops, right facing Thénardier's door, was a child's toy establishment, all flashing with tinsel, glass beads, and magnificent things in block-tin. Right in front, the dealer had placed upon a white napkin an enormous doll, nearly two feet high, which was dressed in a pink crape gown, with golden wheat-ears in her hair, which was real hair, and had enamel eyes. The whole day had this marvel been displayed, to the amazement of all passers-by under ten years of age, but not a mother in Montfermeil had been rich enough or extravagant enough to give it to her child. Eponine and Azelma had spent hours in contemplating it, and Cosette herself, furtively, it is true, had dared to look at it.

At the moment when Cosette went out, bucket in hand, sad and desolate as she was, she could not refrain from raising her eyes to the prodigious doll, the "lady," as she called it. The poor child stopped petrified, for she had not seen this doll so close before. The whole stall seemed to her a palace, and this doll was not a doll, but a vision. Joy, splendour, wealth, and happiness appeared in a sort of chimerical radiance to the unhappy little creature who was deeply buried in mournful and cold wretchedness. Cosette measured with the simple and sad sagacity of

childhood the abyss which separated her from this doll.
She said to herself that a person must be a queen or
a princess to have a "thing" like that. She looked at the
fine dress, the long smooth hair, and thought, "How happy
that doll must be!" She could not take her eyes off this
fantastic shop, and the more she looked the more dazzled
she became, and she fancied she saw Paradise. There
were other dolls behind the large one, which appeared to
her fairies and genii. The tradesman, who walked about
at the back of the shop, seemed to her something more
than mortal. In this adoration she forgot everything, even
the task on which she was sent, but suddenly the rough
voice of her mistress recalled her to the reality. "What,
you little devil, you have not gone! just wait till I come to
you, you little toad." Madame Thénardier had taken a look
out into the street, and noticed Cosette in ecstasy. The
child fled with her bucket, running as fast as she could.

As Thénardier's inn was in that part of the village near
the church, Cosette had to fetch the water from the spring
in the forest on the Chelles side. She did not look at
another stall; so long as she was in the lane and the
vicinity of the church, the illuminated booths lit up the
road, but the last gleam of the last stall soon disappeared,
and the poor child found herself in darkness. She went
further into it, but, as she felt some emotion while walking,
she shook the handle of her bucket as much as she could,
which produced a noise that gave her company. The
further she went, the more dense the gloom became; there
was no one in the streets except a woman, who turned on
seeing her pass, and muttered between her teeth, "Wherever can the child be going? can she be a goblin?" Then
she recognised Cosette. "Why," she said, "it is the
Lark." Cosette in this way went through the labyrinth
of winding, deserted streets which end the village of
Montfermeil on the side of Chelles; and so long as she had
houses, or even walls, on both sides of the way, she walked
rather boldly. From time to time she saw a candle
glimmering through the crack of a shutter; it was light
and life, people were there, and this reassured her.
Still, in proportion as she advanced, her step became
slower, as if mechanically. and when she had passed the
corner of the last house, Cosette stopped. Going beyond
the last stall had been difficult, but going further than
the last house became an impossibility. She put her

bucket on the ground, plunged her hand into her hair, and began scratching her head slowly—a gesture peculiar to terrified and undecided children. It was no longer Mont-fermeil, but the fields, and black deserted space was before her. She looked despairingly at this space in which there was nobody, but where there were beasts, and there might be ghosts. She looked out, and heard the beasts walking in the grass, and distinctly saw the ghosts moving among the trees. Then she took her bucket again, and fear gave her boldness. "Well," she said, "I will tell her that there was no water;" and she boldly re-entered Montfermeil. She had scarce gone one hundred yards when she stopped, and began scratching her head again. Now it was her mistress who appeared to her—her hideous mistress with her hyena mouth, and her eyes flashing with passion. The child took a lamentable glance before and behind her. What should she do? What would become of her? Where should she go? It was from her mistress she recoiled; she turned back in the direction of the spring, and began running. She left the village running, she entered the wood running, looking at nothing, hearing nothing. She did not stop till breath failed her, but she still went on ahead, wildly. While running she felt inclined to cry, for the nocturnal rustling of the forest completely surrounded her. She did not think, she did not see; the immensity of night was opposed to this little creature; on one side was darkness, on the other an atom. It was only seven or eight minutes' walk from the skirt of the wood to the spring, and Cosette knew the road from having gone there several times by day. Strange to say, she did not lose her way, for a remnant of instinct vaguely guided her; still she did not look either to the right or left, for fear of seeing things in the branches and shrubs. In this way she reached the spring; it was a narrow natural basin hollowed by the water in the dry soil, about two feet in depth, surrounded by moss and that goffered grass which is called Henri IV.'s ruff, and paved with a few heavy stones. A brook escaped from it with a gentle, tranquil murmur.

Cosette did not take time to breathe. It was very dark, but she was accustomed to come to this fountain. She felt in the obscurity for a young oak that leant over the spring, and usually served her as a support, caught a branch, stooped down, and plunged the bucket into the water. She

was in such a violent state that her strength was tripled.
While thus bent, she did not notice that the pocket of her
apron emptied itself into the stream, and that the fifteen-
sous piece fell into the water.   Cosette neither saw nor
heard it fall ; she drew up the bucket nearly full, and placed
it on the grass.   This done, she felt that she was exhausted
with fatigue ; she would have liked to start again at once,
but the effort of filling the bucket had been so great that
she found it impossible to move a step.   She fell on to the
grass, and lay there utterly exhausted.   She shut her eyes,
then opened them again, not knowing why, but unable to
do otherwise.   By her side the water stirring in the bucket
made circles that resembled snakes of white fire.   Over her
head the sky was covered with large black clouds, which
seemed like smoke ; the tragic mask of the gloom seemed
to bend vaguely over this child.   Jupiter was setting in the
profundity ;   the child gazed with a wondering eye at
this large star, which she did not know, and which
terrified her.   The planet, in fact, was at this moment very
near the horizon, and was passing through a dense fog,
which gave it a horrible redness.   The fog, which was
of a gloomy purple hue, enlarged the planet and it looked
like a luminous wound.   A cold wind blew from the plain ;
the wood was dark, but there was no rustling of leaves,
and none of the vague and fresh gleams of summer.   Large
branches stood out frightfully, and shapeless, stunted
bushes soughed in the glades.   The tall grass twined under
the breeze like eels, and the brambles writhed like long
arms provided with claws seeking to clutch their prey.
A few withered patches of fern, impelled by the breeze,
passed rapidly, and seemed to be flying before something
that was following.   The prospect was dismal.   Darkness
makes the brain giddy.   This penetration of darkness
is indescribably dismal for a child.   Forests are apocalypses,
and the beating of the wings of a little soul produces an
agonising sound beneath their monstrous vault.

Without being conscious of what she experienced, Cosette
felt herself affected by this black enormity of nature : it was
no longer terror alone that overpowered her, but something
even more terrible than terror.   She shuddered, and words
fail us to describe the strange nature of this shudder which
chilled her to the heart.   Her eye had become wild, and
she felt as if she could not prevent herself from returning to
the same spot on the morrow.   Then, by a species of instinct,

and in order to emerge from this singular state which she did not understand, but which terrified her, she began counting aloud one, two, three, four, up to ten, and when she finished, she began again. This restored her a true perception of the things that surrounded her : she felt the coldness of her hands which she had wetted in drawing the water. She rose, for fear had seized upon her again, a natural and insurmountable fear. She had only one thought left, to fly, fly at full speed through the wood, and across the fields, as far as the houses, the windows, and the lighted candles. Her eye fell on the bucket before her ; and such was the terror with which her mistress inspired her that she did not dare fly without the bucket. She seized the handle with both hands and found it difficult to lift. She proceeded thus for about a dozen yards, but the bucket was full and heavy, and she was compelled to set it on the ground. She breathed for a moment, and then lifted the bucket and started again, this time going a little further. But she was still obliged to stop once more, and after a few moments' rest set out again. She walked with body bent forward and drooping head, like an old woman ; and the weight of the bucket stiffened her thin arms. The iron handle swelled and froze her small wet hands. From time to time she was forced to stop, and each time she did so, the cold water from the bucket splashed her bare legs. This occurred in the heart of a wood, at night in winter, far from any human eye. She was a child of eight years of age, and God alone at this moment saw this sorrowful sight. And doubtless her mother, alas ! For there are things which open the eyes of the dead in their graves.

She breathed with a kind of mournful rattle ; sobs contracted her throat, but she did not dare cry, for she was so afraid of her mistress, even at a distance. It was her habit always to imagine Madame Thénardier present. Still, she did not make much progress in this way, and she walked very slowly, although she strove to lessen the length of her halts and walk as long as she possibly could between them. She thought with agony that it would take her more than an hour to get back to Montfermeil in this way, and that her mistress would beat her. This agony was mingled with her terror at being alone in the wood at night ; she was worn out with fatigue, and had not yet left the forest. On reaching an old chestnut tree which she knew, she made a longer halt than the others to rest herself thoroughly ; then

she collected all her strength, took up the bucket again, and
began walking courageously. Still the poor little creature
in her despair could not refrain from exclaiming : "Oh,
my God! my God!" All at once she suddenly felt that the
bucket no longer weighed anything ; a hand, which seemed
to her enormous, had seized it, and was vigorously lifting
it. She raised her head, and saw a tall black form walking
by her side ; it was a man who had come up behind her,
and whom she had not heard. This man, without saying a
word, had seized the handle of the bucket which she was
carrying. There is an instinct in all the crises of life. The
child felt no fear.

CHAPTER L.

On the afternoon of this same Christmas Day, 1823, a man
walked for a long time about the most desolate part of the
Boulevard de l'Hôpital, at Paris. This man seemed like a
person looking for a lodging, and seemed to stop by choice
at the most shabby houses in this part of the Faubourg
St. Marceau. As we shall see presently, this man had
really hired a bedroom in this isolated district. Both in
dress and person, he realised the type of what might be
called the respectable mendicant, or extreme misery combined with extreme cleanliness. This is a very rare blending, which inspires intelligent minds with the twofold
respect which is felt for the very poor and the very worthy
man. He wore a very old and carefully brushed round hat,
a threadbare coat of coarse yellow ochre coloured cloth, a
colour which was not absolutely odd at that day, a long
waistcoat with enormous pockets, black breeches which
had turned gray at the knees, black worsted stockings, and
stout shoes with brass buckles. He looked like the ex-tutor
of a good family returned from emigration. From his
white hair, wrinkled forehead, livid lips, and his face in
which everything revealed weariness of life, he might have
been supposed much beyond sixty years of age ; but his
firm though slow step, and the singular vigour imprinted
on all his movements, made him look scarce fifty. The
wrinkles on his forehead were well placed, and would have
favourably disposed any one who observed him closely ; his
lip was contracted by a strange curve, which seemed stern
but was humble, and there was a lugubrious serenity in his
look. He carried in his left hand a small parcel tied up in

a handkerchief; and in his right he had a stick cut from a
hedge. This stick had been carved with some care, and
was not bad-looking; advantage had been taken of the
knots, and a coral knob had been formed with red wax; it
was a cudgel, and it seemed a cane.

There are few people on this Boulevard, especially in
winter. This man, however, seemed to avoid rather than
seek them, though without affectation. At this period Louis
XVIII. went almost daily to Choisy le Roi, which was one
of his favourite drives. At two o'clock the royal carriage
and escort could almost invariably be seen passing at full
gallop along the Boulevard de l'Hôpital. This did as well
as a clock or watch for the poor women of the district, who
said, "It is two o'clock, for he is returning to the Tuileries."
And some ran, and others fell into line, for a king who
passes always produces a tumult. Moreover, the appearance and disappearance of Louis XVIII. produced a certain
effect in the streets of Paris, for it was rapid but majestic.
This impotent king had a taste for galloping; unable to
walk, he wished to run; and this cripple would have liked
to be drawn by lightning. He passed, peaceful and stern,
amid drawn sabres; his heavy gilded berline, with large
branches of lilies painted on the panels, rolled noisily along.
There was scarce time to take a glance at him; you saw in
the right-hand corner a broad, firm, red face, a healthy
forehead powdered *à l'oiseau royal*, a proud, harsh, artful
eye, an intelligent smile, two heavy epaulettes with hanging
fringe upon a civilian coat; the golden fleece, the cross of
St. Louis, the cross of the Legion of Honour, the silver plate
of the Holy Ghost, a large stomach, and a wide blue ribbon,
—it was the king. When out of Paris he carried his white
feathered hat on his knees, up to which came tall English
gaiters; when he returned to the city he put his hat on
his head, and bowed rarely. He looked at the people coldly,
and they returned the compliment; when he appeared for
the first time in the Faubourg St. Marceau, his entire
success consisted in a remark made by a workman to his
chum,—"It is that fat fellow who is the government."

The regular passage of the king at the same hour was
therefore the daily event of the Boulevard de l'Hôpital. The
promenader in the yellow coat plainly did not belong to
that quarter, and probably not to Paris, for he was ignorant
of the fact. When at two o'clock the royal carriage, surrounded by Life Guards with their silver aiguillettes, turned

into the Boulevard, after coming round the Salpetrière, he seemed surprised and almost terrified. As he was alone in the walk, he quickly concealed himself behind an angle of the wall ; but this did not prevent the Duc d'Havre from noticing him. The Duc, as Captain of the Guards on duty that day, was seated in the carriage opposite to the king, and said to his Majesty : 'There is an ill-looking fellow." The policemen, who cleared the way for the king, also noticed him, and one of them received orders to follow him. But the man turned into the solitary streets of the Faubourg, and, as night was setting in, the agent lost his trail, as is proved by a report addressed the same evening to Count Anglès, Minister of State and Prefect of Police. When the man in the yellow coat had thrown the officer off his track, he doubled his pace, though not without looking back many times to make sure that he was not followed. At a quarter-past four, he entered the Pewter Platter, which was at that time the office of the Lagny coach, which started at half-past four. The horses were put in, and the passengers, summoned by the driver, were hastily clambering up the iron steps of the vehicle. The man asked :

" Have you a seat ? "

" Only one, by my side, on the box," the driver said.

" I will take it."

" Get up then," the driver said.

Before starting, however, he took a glance at the passenger's poor dress, and the smallness of his bundle, and asked for the fare.

" Are you going all the way to Lagny ? " he said.

" Yes," the man answered.

The traveller paid his fare to Lagny and the coach started. After passing the city gate, the driver tried to get up a conversation, but the traveller only answered in monosyllables, so the driver began whistling and swearing at his horses. As the night was cold, he wrapped himself in his cloak, but the passenger did not seem to notice it. At about six o'clock they reached Chelles, where the driver stopped for a moment to let his horses breathe, at an inn opened in the old buildings of the Royal Abbey.

" I shall get down here," the man said.

He took his bundle and stick and jumped off the coach. A moment after he had disappeared, but he did not enter the inn. When the coachman started again a few moments after, he did not meet him in the high street of Lagny, and he turned round to his inside passengers :

"That man," he said, "does not belong to these parts, for I do not know him. He looks as if he had not a penny, and yet he don't care for money, as he paid his fare to Lagny and only came as far as Chelles. It is night, all the houses are closed, he has not gone into the inn, and yet I can't see him, so he must have sunk into the ground."

The man had not sunk into the ground, but walked hastily along the main street of Chelles, in the darkness ; then he turned to his left before reaching the church, into a cross-road that runs to Montfermeil, like a man who knows the country and had been there before. He followed this road rapidly, and at the spot where it is intersected by the old road that runs from Lagny to Gagny, he heard wayfarers coming. He hurriedly concealed himself in a ditch, and waited till they had passed ; the precaution, however, was almost superfluous, for, as we have said, it was a very dark December night, and only two or three stars were visible in the sky. The man did not return to the Montfermeil road, but went to his right, across the fields, and hurried in the direction of the wood. When he was in it, he slackened his pace, and began looking carefully at all the trees, walking step by step, as if seeking and following a mysterious road known to himself alone. There was a moment at which he seemed to lose himself and appeared undecided, but at last, by repeated groping, he reached a glade in which there was a pile of large white stones. He walked hurriedly toward these stones and attentively examined them, as if passing them in review. A large tree, covered with those excrescences which are the warts of vegetation, was a few paces from the heap ; he went up to it and passed his hand over the bark as if trying to recognise and count all the warts. Opposite this tree, which was an ash, there was a sickly chestnut shedding its bark, upon which a ring of zinc had been placed as a poultice ; he stood on tiptoe and felt this ring, then he examined for some time the ground in the space contained between the tree and the stones, as if assuring himself that the ground had not been freshly turned up. This done, he looked about him, to see which way his road lay, and resumed his walk through the wood.

It was this man who came across Cosette. While

proceeding in the direction of Montfermeil, he perceived this little shadow depositing a load on the ground, then taking it up again, and continuing her journey. He went up and saw that it was a young child carrying an enormous bucket. Then he had gone to the child, and silently taken hold of the handle of the bucket.

CHAPTER LI.

COSETTE, as we said, was not afraid. The man spoke to her in a serious, almost low voice :

"My child, what you are carrying is very heavy."

Cosette raised her head and replied, "Yes, sir."

"Give it to me," the man continued ; "I will carry it."

Cosette let go the bucket, and the man walked on by her side.

"It is really very heavy," he muttered ; then added, "What is your age, little one ? "

"Eight years, sir."

"And have you come far with this ? "

"From the spring in the wood."

"And how far have you to go ? "

"About a quarter of an hour's walk."

The man stopped for a moment, and then suddenly said :

"Then you have not a mother ? "

"I do not know," the child answered.

Before the man had time to speak, she continued :

"I do not think so ; other girls have one, but I have not."

And after a silence, she added :

"I believe that I never had one."

The man stopped, put the bucket on the ground, and laid his two hands on her shoulders, making an effort to see her face in the darkness. Cosette's thin sallow countenance was vaguely designed in the vivid gleam of the sky.

"What is your name ? " the man asked her.

"Cosette."

The man seemed to have an electric shock ; he looked at her again, then removed his hands, took the bucket up again, and continued his walk. A moment after he asked :

"Where do you live, little one ? "

"At Montfermeil, if you know the place."

"Are we going there ? "

" Yes, sir."

There was another pause, and then he began again :

" Who was it that sent you to fetch water from the wood at this hour ? "

" Madame Thénardier."

The man continued with an accent which he strove to render careless, but in which there was, for all that, a singular tremor.

" What is this Madame Thénardier ? "

" She is my mistress," the child said, " and keeps the inn."

" The inn ? " remarked the man ; " well, I am going to lodge there to-night. Show me the way."

" We are going to it."

Though the man walked rather quickly, Cosette had no difficulty in keeping up with him ; she no longer felt fatigue, and from time to time raised her eyes to this man with a sort of indescribable calmness and confidence. She had never been taught to turn her eyes toward Providence, and yet she felt within her something that resembled hope and joy, and which rose to heaven. After the lapse of a few minutes the man continued :

" Does Madame Thénardier keep no servant ? "

" No, sir."

" Is there no one but you ? "

" No, sir."

There was another interruption, and then Cosette raised her voice :

" That is to say, there are two little girls."

" What little girls ? "

" Ponine and Zelma."

The child simplified in this way the romantic names dear to Madame Thénardier.

" Who are they ? "

" They are Madame Thénardier's young ladies, as you may say,—her daughters."

" And what do they do ? "

" Oh ! " said the child, " they have handsome dolls, and things all covered with gold. They play about and amuse themselves."

" All day ? "

" Yes, sir."

" And you ? "

" Oh, I work."

"All day?"

The child raised her large eyes, in which stood a tear, invisible in the darkness, and replied softly:

"Yes, sir." After a silence she continued. "Sometimes, when I have finished my work and they allow me, I amuse myself."

"In what way?"

"As I can; they let me be, but I have not many toys. Ponine and Zelma do not like me to play with their dolls, and I have only a little leaden sword, no longer than that."

The child held out her little finger.

"And which does not cut?"

"Oh yes, sir," said the child, "it cuts lettuce and chops flies' heads off."

They reached the village, and Cosette guided the stranger through the streets. When they passed the baker's, Cosette did not think of the loaf which she was to bring in. The man had ceased questioning her, and preserved a gloomy silence, but when they had left the church behind them, on seeing all the open-air shops, he asked Cosette:

"Is it the fair-time?"

"No, sir, it is Christmas."

When they approached the inn, Cosette touched his arm timidly.

"Sir."

"What is it, my child?"

"We are close to the house."

"Well?"

"Will you let me carry my bucket now?"

"Why?"

"Because madame will be at me if she sees that it has been carried for me."

The man gave her the bucket. A moment later they were at the door of the pot-house.

Cosette could not help casting a side glance at the large doll which was still displayed at the toy-shop, and then tapped at the door; it opened, and Madame Thénardier appeared, candle in hand.

"Oh, it's you, you little devil: well, I'll be hanged if you have not taken time enough: you've been playing, I expect."

"Madame," said Cosette, with a violent tremor, "this gentleman wants a bedroom."

Madame Thénardier exchanged her coarse look for an

amiable grimace, a change peculiar to landladies, and greedily turned her eyes on the new-comer.

" Is this the gentleman ? " she said.

" Yes, madame," the man answered, touching his hat.

Rich travellers are not so polite. This gesture and the inspection of the stranger's clothes and luggage, which the landlady took in at a glance, caused the amiable grimace to disappear and the rough look to return. She continued dryly:

" Come in, my good man."

The "good man" entered ; the landlady gave him a second look, carefully examined his threadbare coat and broken-brimmed hat, and consulted her husband, who was still drinking with the carter, by a toss of the head, a curl of her nose, and a wink. The husband answered with that imperceptible movement of the forefinger which, laid on the puffed-out lips, signifies : Complete Destitution. Upon this the landlady exclaimed :

" My good man, I am very sorry, but I haven't a bed-room disengaged."

" Put me where you like," the man said, "in the loft or the stable. I will pay as if it were a bedroom."

" Forty sous."

" Be it so."

" Forty sous ! " a carrier whispered to the landlady ; " why, it is only twenty sous."

" It's forty for a man like him," Madame Thénardier replied in the same tone ; " I do not lodge poor people under."

" That is true," the husband added gently ; " it injures a house to have customers of that sort."

Meanwhile the man, after leaving his bundle and stick on a form, sat down at a table on which Cosette had hastened to place a bottle of wine and a glass. The pedlar who had asked for the bucket of water himself carried it to his horse, while Cosette returned to her place under the kitchen table and her knitting. The man, who had scarce moistened his lips with the glass of wine he poured out, gazed at the child with strange attention. Cosette was ugly, but had she been happy she might possibly have been pretty. We have already sketched her little overclouded face : Cosette was thin and sickly, and, though eight years of age, looked hardly six. Her large eyes, buried in a species of shadow, were almost extinguished by constant crying, while the corners of her mouth had the curve of habitual agony,

which may be observed in condemned prisoners and in
patients who are given over. Her hands were, as her
mother had guessed, "ruined with chilblains." The fire-
light, which shone upon her at this moment, brought out
the angles of her bones and rendered her thinness frightfully
visible ; as she constantly shivered, she had grown into the
habit of always keeping her knees pressed against each other.
Her entire clothing was one rag, which would have aroused
pity in summer, and caused horror in winter. She had only
torn calico upon her person, and not a rag of woollen
stuff ; her skin was here and there visible, and everywhere
could be distinguished blue or black marks, indicating the
spots where her mistress had beaten her. Her bare legs
were red and rough, and the hollow between her shoulder-
blades would have moved you to tears. The whole person
of this child, her attitude, the sound of her voice, the interval
between one word and the next, her look, her silence, her
slightest movement, expressed and translated but one idea
—fear. Fear was spread over her ; she was, so to speak,
clothed in it ; fear drew up her elbows against her hips,
withdrew her heels under her petticoats, made her occupy
as little room as possible, breathe when only absolutely
necessary, and had become what might be called the habit
of her body, without any possible variation save that of increasing. There was a corner in her eye in which terror
lurked. This fear was so great that Cosette on returning
wet through did not dare go to the fire, but silently began
her work again. The expression of this child's countenance
was habitually so gloomy and at times so tragical, that it
seemed at certain moments as if she were on the point of
becoming either an idiot or a demon. Never, as we said,
had she known what prayer was ; never had she set foot
in a church. "Can I spare the time for it ?" Madame
Thénardier used to say. The man in the yellow coat did
not take his eyes off Cosette. Suddenly her mistress cried :
"By the way, where's that loaf?"

Cosette, according to her custom whenever Madame
Thénardier raised her voice, quickly came from under the
table. She had completely forgotten the loaf, and had
recourse to the expedient of terrified children,—she lied.

"Madame, the baker's was shut."

"You ought to have knocked."

"I did knock, but he would not open."

"I shall know to-morrow whether that is the truth," said

her mistress, "and if it is not, you shall dance finely. Meanwhile, give me back my fifteen-sous piece."

Cosette plunged her hand into the pocket of her apron and turned white. The coin was no longer in it.

"Well," her mistress said, "did you not hear me?"

Cosette turned her pocket out, but there was nothing in it. What could have become of the money? The wretched little creature could not find a word to say. She was petrified.

"Have you lost it?" her mistress asked, "or are you trying to rob me?"

At the same time she stretched out her hand to the cat-o'-nine-tails; this formidable gesture restored Cosette the strength to cry:

"Mercy, madame; I will never do it again."

The man in the yellow coat had been feeling in his waist-coat pocket, though no one noticed it. Moreover, the other guests were drinking or card-playing, and paid no attention to him. Cosette had retreated in agony to the chimney-corner, shivering to make herself as little as she could, and protect her poor half-naked limbs. Her mistress raised her arm.

"I beg your pardon, madame," said the man, "but just now I saw something fall out of the little girl's pocket and roll away. It may be that."

At the same time he stooped and appeared to be searching for a moment.

"Yes, here it is," he continued, as he rose and held out a coin to the landlady.

"Yes, that's it," she said.

It was not the real coin, it was a twenty-sous piece, but madame made a profit by the transaction. She put it in her pocket, and confined herself to giving the child a stern glance, saying: "That had better not happen again."

Cosette returned to what her mistress called her niche, and her large eyes, fixed on the strange traveller, began to assume an expression they had never had before. It was no longer a simple astonishment, but a sort of stupefied confidence was mingled with it.

"Do you want any supper?" the landlady asked the traveller.

He did not reply, but seemed to be lost in thought. "What can this man be?" she muttered to herself; "he is some wretched beggar who has not a penny to pay for his supper. Will he be able to pay for his bedroom? It is lucky, after all, that he did not think of stealing the silver coin that was on the ground."

At this moment a door opened, and Eponine and Azelma came in. They were really two pretty little girls, rather tradesmen's daughters than peasants, and very charming, one with her auburn, well-smoothed tresses, the other with long black plaits hanging down her back; both were quick, clean, plump, fresh, and pleasant to look on through their beaming health. They were warmly clothed, but with such maternal art that the thickness of the stuff did not remove anything of the coquetry of the style; winter was foreseen, but spring was not effaced. In their dress, their gaiety, and the noise which they made, there was a certain queenliness. When they came in, their mother said to them in a scolding voice, which was full of adoration, "There you are, then."

Then, drawing them on to her knees in turn, smoothing their hair, retying their ribbons, and letting them go with that gentle shake which is peculiar to mothers, she exclaimed, "How smart they are!" They sat down by the fireside, with a doll which they turned over on their knees with all sorts of joyous prattle. At times Cosette raised her eyes from her knitting and mournfully watched their playing. Eponine and Azelma did not look at Cosette, for to them she was like the dog. These three little girls did not count four-and-twenty years among them, and already represented human society,—on one side envy, on the other, disdain. The doll was very old and broken, but it did not appear the less wonderful to Cosette, who never in her life possessed a doll, a "real doll," to employ an expression which all children will understand. All at once the landlady, who was going about the room, noticed that Cosette was idling, and watching the little girls instead of working.

"Ah, I have caught you," she exclaimed; "that's the way you work, is it? I'll make you work with the cat-o'-nine-tails."

The stranger, without leaving his chair, turned to Madame Thénardier.

"Oh, madame," he said, with an almost timid smile, "let her play."

Such a wish would have been a command from any traveller who had ordered a good supper and drunk a couple of bottles of wine, and who did not look like a beggar. But the landlady did not tolerate a man who had such a hat, having a desire! and one who wore such a coat daring to have a will of his own! Hence she answered sharply :

" She must work, since she eats ; I do not keep her to do nothing."

" What is she doing, pray ? " the stranger continued, in that gentle voice which formed such a strange contrast with his beggar clothes and porter shoulders.

The landlady deigned to reply :

" She is knitting stockings, if you please, for my little girls, who have none, so to speak, and are forced to go about barefooted."

The man looked at Cosette's poor red feet, and said :

" When will she have finished that pair of stockings ? "

" She has three or four good days' work, the idle slut."

" And how much may such a pair be worth when finished ? "

The landlady gave a contemptuous glance.

" At least thirty sous."

" Will you sell them to me for five francs ? " the man continued.

M. Thénardier thought it his duty to speak.

" Yes, sir, if such be your fancy, you can have the pair of stockings for five francs ; we cannot refuse travellers anything."

" Cash payment," the landlady said in her peremptory voice.

" I buy the pair of stockings," the man said, and added, as he drew a five-franc piece from his pocket and laid it on the table, " I pay for them."

Then he turned to Cosette :

" Your labour is now mine, so play, my child."

Thénardier came up and silently put the coin in his pocket. The landlady could make no answer, but she bit her lips, and her face assumed an expression of hatred. Cosette was trembling, but still ventured to ask :

" Is it true, madame ? May I play ? "

" Play," her mistress said, in a terrible voice.

And while her lips thanked the landlady, all her little soul thanked the traveller. Thénardier had returned to his glass, and his wife whispered in his ear :

" What can this yellow man be ? "

" I have seen," Thénardier replied, with a sovereign air, " millionaires who wore a coat like his."

Cosette had laid down her needle, but did not dare leave her place, for, as a rule, she moved as little as possible. She took from a box behind her a few old rags and her little leaden sword. Eponine and Azelma paid no attention to what was going on, for they were carrying out a very important operation. They had seized the cat, thrown the doll on the ground, and Éponine, who was the elder, was wrapping up the kitten, in spite of its writhings, in a quantity of red and blue rags. While performing this serious and difficult task, she was saying to her sister in the sweet and adorable language of children, the grace of which, like the glistening of butterflies' wings, disappears when you try to preserve it:

"Look, sister, this doll is more amusing than the other, you see, for it moves, it cries, and is warm; so we will play with it. It is my little daughter, and I am a lady; you will call upon me and look at it. By degrees you will see its whiskers, and that will surprise you, and then you will see its ears and its tail, and that will surprise you too, and you will say to me, 'Oh my goodness!' and I shall answer, 'Yes, madame, it is a little child I have like that; little children are like that just now.'" Azelma listened to Eponine with wonder. In the same way as birds make a nest of anything, children make a doll of no matter what. While Eponine and Azelma were wrapping up the kitten, Cosette on her side was performing the same operation on her sword. This done, she laid it on her arm, and sang softly to lull it to sleep. A doll is one of the most imperious wants, and at the same time one of the most delicious instincts, of feminine childhood. To clean, clothe, adorn, dress, undress, dress again, teach, scold a little, nurse, lull, send to sleep, and imagine that something is somebody— the whole future of a woman is contained in this. While dreaming and prattling, making little trousseaux and cradles, while sewing little frocks and aprons, the child becomes a girl, the girl becomes a maiden, and the maiden a woman. The first child is a continuation of the last doll. A little girl without a doll is nearly as unhappy and quite as impossible as a wife without children; Cosette, therefore, made a doll of her sword. The landlady, in the meanwhile, walked up to the "yellow man." "My husband is right," she thought; "it is perhaps M. Laffitte. Some rich men are so whimsical." She leant her elbow on the table and said, "Sir——"

At the word "Sir" the man turned round, for the female Thénardier had up to the present only addressed him as "My good man."

"You see, sir," she continued, assuming her gentle air, which was still more dreadful to see than her fierce look, "I am glad to see the child play, and do not oppose it, and it is all right for once, as you are generous. But, you see, she has nothing, and must work."

"Then she is not a child of yours?" the man asked.

"Oh! Lord, no, sir; she is a poor little girl we took in out of charity. She is a sort of imbecile, and I think has water on the brain, for she has a big head. We do all we can for her, but we are not rich, and though we write to her people, we have not had an answer for six months. It looks as if the mother were dead."

"Ah!" said the man, and fell back into his reverie.

"The mother couldn't have been much," the landlady added, "for she deserted her child."

During the whole of this conversation Cosette, as if an instinct warned her that she was being talked about, did not take her eyes off her mistress. She listened and heard two or three indistinct words here and there. Cosette, under her table, looked at the fire which was reflected in her fixed eyes; she had begun rocking her doll again, and while lulling it to sleep, sang in a low voice: "My mother is dead, my mother is dead, my mother is dead." On being pressed again by the landlady, the yellow man, the "millionaire," consented to take some supper.

"What will you have, sir?"

"Bread and cheese."

"He is certainly a beggar," the landlady thought. Cosette, under the table, still sang her song. All at once she broke off. She turned, and perceived the doll lying on the ground a few paces from the kitchen table, which the children had thrown down on taking up the kitten. She let the wrapped-up sword, which only half satisfied her, fall, and then slowly looked round the room. The landlady was whispering to her husband and reckoning some change. Eponine and Azelma were playing with the kitten, the guests were eating, drinking, or singing, and no one noticed her. She had not a moment to lose, so she crept on her hands and knees from under the table, assured herself once again that she was not watched, and seized the doll. A moment after she was back in her seat, and turned so that the doll which she held in her arms should be in the shadow. The happiness of playing with this doll was almost too much for her. No one had seen her, excepting the traveller, who was slowly eating his poor supper. This joy lasted nearly a quarter of an hour, but in spite of the caution which Cosette took, she did not notice that one of the doll's feet was peeping out, and that the fire lit it up very distinctly. This pink luminous foot emerging from the glow suddenly caught the eye of Azelma, who said to Eponine, "Look there, sister."

The two little girls were stupefied : Cosette had dared to take their doll ! Eponine rose, and without letting the cat go, ran to her mother and plucked her skirt.

"Let me be," said the mother ; " what do you want now ? "

" Mother," said the girl, "just look ! "

And she pointed to Cosette, who, yielding entirely to the ecstasy of possession, saw and heard nothing more. The landlady's face assumed that peculiar expression, which is composed of the terrible blended with the commonplace, and which has caused such women to be christened Megæras. This time wounded pride exasperated her wrath : Cosette had leapt over all bounds, and had made an assault on the young ladies' doll. A czarina who had seen a moujik trying on her Imperial son's blue ribbon, would not have had a different face. She cried in a voice which indignation rendered hoarse : " Cosette ! "

Cosette started as if the earth had trembled beneath her, and turned round.

" Cosette ! " her mistress repeated.

Cosette gently laid the doll on the ground with a species of veneration mingled with despair. Then, without taking her eyes off it, she clasped her hands, and, frightful to tell of a child of her age, wrung them ; then what none of the emotions of the day had wrung from her,—neither the walk in the wood, the weight of the bucket, the loss of the coin, the sight of the lash, nor the harsh words of her mistress— she burst into tears. She sobbed. The traveller had risen from his chair. " What is the matter ? " he asked the landlady.

" Don't you see ? " she replied, pointing to the evidence of the crime which lay at Cosette's feet.

" Well, what ? " the man continued.

" That lazy beggar," the landlady answered, " has had the audacity to touch my children's doll."

"So much noise about that!" the man said; "well, suppose that she did play with the doll!"

"She has touched it with her dirty hands," the landlady continued, "her frightful hands."

Here Cosette redoubled her sobs.

"Will you be quiet?" her mistress yelled.

The man went straight to the street door, opened it, and walked out : the landlady took advantage of his absence to give Cosette a kick under the table, which made her scream. The door opened again, and the man reappeared, carrying in his hands the fabulous doll to which we have alluded, and which all the village children had been contemplating since the morning He placed it upright in front of Cosette, saying :

"Here, this is for you."

It is probable that, during the hour he had been sitting in a reverie, he had confusedly noticed the toyman's shop, which was so brilliantly illumined with lamps and candles, that it could be seen through the taproom window like an aurora borealis. Cosette raised her eyes : she had looked at the man coming toward her with the doll as if he were the sun ; she heard the extraordinary words : "It is for you ;" she looked at him, looked at the doll, then drew back slowly, and concealed herself entirely in a corner under the table. She did not cry, she did not speak, but looked as if she dared hardly breathe. The landlady, Eponine, and Azelma were so many statues : the topers themselves had stopped drinking, and there was a solemn silence in the taproom. The mother, petrified and dumb, began her conjectures again. "Who is this man? is he poor or a millionaire? He is, perhaps, both, that is to say, a thief." The husband's face offered that expressive wrinkle which marks the human countenance each time that the ruling instinct appears on it with all its bestial power. The landlord looked in turn at the doll and the traveller : he seemed to be sniffing round the man, as he would have done round a money-bag. This only lasted for a second. Then he went up to his wife and whispered :

"That thing cost at least thirty francs. No nonsense. Down in the dust to the man."

Coarse natures have this in common with simple natures, that they have no transitions.

"Well, Cosette," the landlady said, in a voice which strove to be gentle, and which was composed of the bitter honey of wicked women, "why don't you take your doll?"

Cosette ventured to crawl out of her hole.

"My little Cosette," her mistress continued fawningly, "this gentleman gives you the doll. Take it. It is yours."

Cosette looked upon the wonderful doll with a sort of terror. Her face was still bathed in tears, but her eyes were beginning to fill, like the sky at dawn, with strange rays of joy. What she felt at this moment was something like what she would have felt had some one suddenly said to her, "Little girl, you are Queen of France."

It seemed to her that if she touched the doll, thunder would issue from it; and this was true to some extent, for she said to herself that her mistress would scold and beat her. Still, the attraction gained the victory. She at length crawled up to the doll and murmured timidly as she turned to the landlady :

"May I, madame?"

No expression could describe her look, which was at once despairing, terrified, and ravished.

"Of course," said her mistress, "since this gentleman gives it to you."

"Is it true, sir?" Cosette continued. "Is the lady really mine?"

The stranger's eyes were full of tears, and he seemed to have reached that point of emotion when a man does not speak in order that he may not weep. He nodded to Cosette, and placed the "lady's" little hand in hers. Cosette quickly drew back her hand as if the lady's burned her, and looked down at the brick floor. We are compelled to add that at this moment she put her tongue out to an enormous length ; all at once she turned and passionately seized the doll.

"I will call her Catherine," she said.

It was a strange sight when Cosette's rags met and held the doll's ribbons and fresh muslins.

"May I put her in a chair, madame?" she continued.

"Yes, my child," her mistress answered.

It was now the turn of Eponine and Azelma to look enviously at Cosette. She placed Catherine in a chair, and then sat down on the ground before her, motionless, without saying a word, and in a contemplative attitude.

"Why don't you play, Cosette?" the stranger said.

"Oh! I am playing," the child answered.

This unknown man, this stranger, who seemed like a visitor sent by Providence to Cosette, was at that moment the person whom Madame Thénardier hated most in the world; still, she must put a constraint on herself. This emotion was more than she could endure, accustomed to dissimulation though she was by the copy which she had to take of her husband in all his actions. She hastened to send her children to bed, and then asked the yellow man's leave to send off Cosette, "who had been very tired during the day," she added with a maternal air. Cosette went off to bed carrying Catherine in her arms. The landlady went from time to time to the other end of the room, where her husband was, in order to relieve her mind. She exchanged with him a few sentences, which were the more furious that she dared not speak them aloud.

"Old idiot! what has he got in his noddle to come and disturb us in this way! to wish that little monster to play! to give her dolls! dolls worth forty francs, to a wretch whom I would gladly sell for forty sous! a little more, and he would call her Your Majesty like the Duchesse de Berry. Can he be in his senses? The mysterious old fellow must be cracked."

"Why so? it is very simple," Thénardier replied. "Suppose it amuses him? It amuses you that the little one should work—it amuses him to see her play. He has a right, for a traveller can do as he likes so long as he pays. If this old man is a philanthropist, how does it concern you? If he is an ass, it is no business of yours. What do you interfere for, so long as he has money?"

This was the language of a master and the reasoning of a landlord, neither of which admitted a reply.

The man was resting his elbow on the table, and had resumed his thoughtful attitude; the other travellers, pedlars and carriers, had gone away. They regarded him from a distance with a sort of respectful fear; this poorly clad individual, who lavished gigantic dolls on ragged girls, was assuredly a magnificent and formidable man. Several hours passed, midnight mass was finished, the matin bell had been rung, the pot-house was closed, the fire was out in the taproom, but the stranger still remained at the same spot and in the same posture. From time to time he changed the elbow on which he was leaning, that was all; but he had not uttered a syllable since Cosette went off to bed. The Thénardiers alone, through politeness and curiosity, remained in the room.

"Is he going to spend the night like that?" grumbled the landlady. When it struck two, she declared herself conquered, and said to her husband, "I am off to bed; you can do as you like." The husband sat down at a table in a corner, lit a candle, and began reading the *Courier Français.* A good hour passed, during which the worthy host read the paper through thrice from the date of the number to the imprint, but the stranger did not stir. Thénardier moved, coughed, spat, and made his chair creak, but the man made no movement. "Can he be asleep?" Thénardier thought. The man was not asleep, but no movement aroused him. At length the landlord doffed his cap, walked up gently, and ventured to say:

"Do you not wish for repose, sir?"

"Yes, you are right," said the stranger; "where is your stable?"

"I will show you the way, sir," Thénardier replied, with a smile.

He took the candle. The man fetched his stick and bundle, and Thénardier led him to a room on the first floor, which was most luxurious, with its mahogany furniture, and the bed with its red calico curtains.

"What is this?" the traveller asked.

"Our own wedding bedroom," the landlord replied; "my wife and I occupy another, and this room is only entered three or four times a year."

"I should have preferred the stable," the man said roughly. Thénardier pretended not to hear this disagreeable reflection, but lit two new wax candles standing on the mantelpiece. A rather large fire was flashing in the grate. Upon the mantelpiece was also a woman's head-dress, made of silver tissue and orange flowers, under a glass shade.

"And what is this?" the stranger continued.

"That, sir," Thénardier said, "is my wife's wedding bonnet."

The traveller looked at the object in a way that seemed to say,—"Then there was a time when this monster was a virgin."

This was a falsehood of Thénardier's; when he hired the house to convert it into a pot-house, he found this room thus furnished, and bought the lot, thinking that it would cast a graceful shadow over his "spouse," and that his house would derive from it what the English call respectability. When the traveller turned round, Thénardier had disappeared, without saying good-evening, as he did not wish to treat with disrespectful cordiality a man whom he intended to flay royally the next morning. The landlord went to his room, where his wife was in bed, but not asleep. As soon as she heard her husband's footstep, she said to him :

"You know that I am going to kick Cosette out of doors to-morrow ? "

Thénardier coldly answered :

" Are you ? "

They exchanged no further words, and a few minutes after the candle was extinguished. For his part, the stranger had placed his stick and bundle in a corner. When the landlord had withdrawn, he sat down in an easy-chair and remained pensive for a time ; then he took off his shoes, seized one of the candlesticks, and left the room, looking about him as if in search of something. He went along a passage and reached the staircase ; here he heard a very gentle sound, like the breathing of a child. He followed this sound, and reached a triangular closet under the stairs, or, to speak more correctly, formed by the stairs themselves. Here, among old hampers and potsherds, in dust and cobwebs, there was a bed, if we may apply the term to a palliasse so rotten as to show the straw, and a blanket so torn as to show the mattress. There were no sheets, and all this lay on the ground ; in this bed Cosette was sleeping. The man walked up and gazed at her ; Cosette was fast asleep and full dressed ; in winter she did not take off her clothes, that she might be a little warmer. She was holding to her bosom the doll, whose large open eyes glistened in the darkness ; from time to time she gave a heavy sigh, as if about to awake, and pressed the doll almost convulsively in her arms. There was nothing by her bedside but one of her wooden shoes. Through an open door close by a large dark room could be seen, and the stranger entered. At the end, two little white beds were visible through a glass door. They belonged to Eponine and Azelma. Behind this a wicker, curtainless cradle was half hidden, in which the little boy who had cried all the evening was sleeping.

The stranger conjectured that this room communicated with that of the Thénardiers. He was about to return, when his eye fell on the chimney, one of those vast inn chimneys in which there is always so little fire when there is a frost, and which are so cold to look at. In this chimney

there was no fire, not even ashes; but wnat there was in
it attracted the traveller's attention. He saw two little
children's shoes of coquettish shape and unequal size; and
the traveller recollected the graceful and immemorial custom
of children who place their shoe in the chimney on Christmas
night, in order to obtain some glittering present from their
good fairy in the darkness. Eponine and Azelma had not
failed in this observance. The traveller bent down; the
fairy, that is, the mother, had already paid her visit, and in
each shoe a handsome ten-sous piece could be seen shining.
The man rose and was going away, when he observed
another object in the darkest corner of the hearth; he looked
at it, and recognised a hideous wooden shoe, half broken
and covered with ashes and dried mud. It was Cosette's;
with the touching confidence of children who may be dis-
appointed, but are never discouraged, she had also placed
her shoe in the chimney. Hope in a child who has never
known aught but despair is a sublime and affecting thing.
There was nothing in this shoe; but the stranger felt in
his pocket and laid a louis d'or in it. Then he went back
to his room with stealthy step.

CHAPTER LII.

THE following morning, nearly two hours before daybreak,
Thénardier was seated, pen in hand, at a table in the tap-
room, and making out the bill of the yellow-coated traveller.
His wife, standing behind him, was watching him; they
did not exchange a syllable; on one side there was a profound meditation, on the other that profound admiration
with which people watch a marvel of the human mind expanding. A noise could be heard in the house; it was the
Lark sweeping the stairs. At the end of a quarter of an hour
and some erasures, Thénardier produced this masterpiece:

" *Bill of Monsieur in No.* 1.

Supper	3	francs
Room	10	,,
Candles	5	,,
Fire	4	,,
Attendance	1	,,

Total 23 francs."

"Twenty-three francs!" the wife exclaimed, with an admiration mingled with some hesitation.

Like all great artists, Thénardier was not satisfied, and said, "Pooh!"

"Monsieur Thénardier, you are right; he certainly owes it," the wife muttered, thinking of the doll given to Cosette in the presence of her children: "it is fair, but it is too much; he will not pay it."

Thénardier gave his cold laugh, and said, "He will pay it."

This laugh was the supreme signification of certainty and authority; what was said in this way must be. The wife made no objection, but began arranging the tables, while her husband walked up and down the room; a moment after he added:

"Why, I owe fifteen hundred francs."

He sat down in the ingle-nook, meditating with his feet in the warm ashes.

"By the bye," the wife continued, "you don't forget that I mean to kick Cosette out to-day? The monster! she eats my heart with her doll; I would sooner marry Louis XVIII. than keep her a day longer in the house."

Thénardier lit his pipe, and said between two puffs,— "You will hand the man the bill."

Then he went out, and had scarce left the room ere the traveller entered; Thénardier at once appeared behind and stood in the half-open door, only visible to his wife. The yellow man carried his stick and bundle in his hand.

"Up so soon?" the landlady said; "are you going to leave us already, sir?"

While speaking, she turned the bill in her hands with an embarrassed air and made creases in it with her nails; her harsh face had an unusual look of timidity and scruple. It seemed to her difficult to present such a bill to a man who looked so thoroughly poor. The traveller seemed absent and preoccupied, as he replied:

"Yes, madame, I am going away."

"Then you had no business to transact at Montfermeil, sir?" she continued.

"No, I am merely passing through, that is all. What do I owe, madame?"

The landlady, without replying, handed him the folded paper; he opened and looked at it, but his attention was visibly elsewhere.

"Do you do a good business here?" he asked.

"So-so, sir," the landlady answered, stupefied at not see-ing any other explosion; then she went on with an elegiac and lamentable accent:

"Oh, sir, times are very bad! and then there are so few respectable people in these parts. It is lucky we have now and then generous and rich travellers like yourself, sir, for the expenses are so high. Why, that little girl eats us out of house and home."

"What little girl?"

"Why, you know, Cosette, the Lark, as they call her hereabout."

"Oh!" said the man.

She continued:

"What dolts these peasants are with their nicknames! She looks more like a bat than a lark. You see, sir, we don't ask for charity, but we can't give it. Our earnings are small and our expenses great. The licence, the door and window tax, and so on! You know, sir, that the Government claims a terrible deal of money. And then I have my own daughters, and have nothing to spend on other people's children."

The man replied, in a voice which he strove to render careless, and in which there was a tremor:

"And suppose you were freed of her?"

"Of whom?—of Cosette?"

The landlady's red and violent face was illumined by a hideous grin.

"Ah, sir, my good sir; take her, keep her, carry her off, sugar her, stuff her with truffles, eat her, drink her, and may all the saints in Paradise bless you."

"It is settled."

"You really will take her away at once?"

"At once; call her."

"Cosette," the landlady shouted.

"In the meanwhile," the man continued, "I will pay my score; how much is it?"

He took a glance at the bill, and could not restrain a start of surprise. He looked at the landlady and said slowly, "Twenty-three francs?" There was in his pro-nunciation of the two words the accent which separates the point of exclamation from the point of interrogation. Madame Thénardier had had time to prepare for the collision, and hence answered with assurance:

" Yes, sir, twenty-three francs."

The stranger laid five five-franc pieces on the table.

"Go and fetch the girl," he said.

At this moment Thénardier walked into the middle of the room, and said:

" The gentleman owes twenty-six sous."

" Twenty-six sous ! " the wife exclaimed.

"Twenty sous for the bedroom," Thénardier continued coldly, "and six for the supper. As for the girl, I must talk a little with the gentleman first. Leave us, wife."

The landlady was dazzled by one of those unforeseen flashes which emanate from talent. She felt that the great actor had come on the stage, made no answer, and went out. As soon as they were alone, Thénardier offered the traveller a chair ; he sat down, but Thénardier remained standing, and his face assumed a singular expression of kindliness and simplicity.

" I must tell you, sir," he said, " that I adore the child."

The stranger looked at him fixedly.

"What child ? "

Thénardier continued :

"How strange it is, but you grow attached to them. What is the meaning of all that money ? put it back in your pocket ; I adore the child."

" What child ? " the stranger asked.

"Why, our little Cosette ! don't you wish to take her from us ? Well, I speak frankly, and as true as you are an honest man, I cannot consent. I should miss the child, for I have known her since she was a baby ; it is true that she costs us money, that she has her faults, that we are not rich, and that I paid more than upwards of four hundred francs for medicines alone in one of her illnesses. She has neither father nor mother, and I brought her up ; and I have bread both for her and for me. Look you, I am fond of the child ; affection grows on you ; I am a good foolish fellow, and don't reason ; I love the girl, and though my wife is quick, she loves her too. She is like our own child, and I want to hear her prattle in the house."

The stranger still looked at him steadily, as he continued :

" Excuse me, sir, but a child can't be given like that to the first passer-by. You will allow that I am right ? I don't say that you are not rich and look like a very worthy man, and that it may be for her welfare ? but I am bound to know. You understand ? Supposing that I let her go and sacrificed myself, I should like to know where she is going, and not let her out of sight ; I should wish to know where she is, and go and see her now and then, to convince the child that her foster-father is watching over her. In short, there are some things which are not possible ; I don't even know your name. I must at least see some scrap of paper, a bit of a passport—something."

The stranger, without ceasing to fix on him that look which pierces to the bottom of the conscience, said in a grave, firm voice :

" Monsieur Thénardier, people do not take a passport to go four leagues from Paris. If I take Cosette away, I take her away, that is all. You will not know my name, my residence, or where she is, and it is my intention that she shall never see you again. I break the string which she has round her foot, and away she flies. Do you agree to that ? Yes or no ? "

As demons and genii recognise by certain signs the presence of a superior deity, so Thénardier understood that he had to deal with a very strong man. It was a sort of intuition, and he comprehended it with his distinct and sagacious promptitude. On the previous evening, while drinking, smoking, and singing, he had constantly looked at the stranger, watching him like a cat, and studying him like a mathematician. He had both watched him on his own account, through pleasure and instinct, and played the spy on him as if paid to do so. Not a gesture or movement of the yellow-coated man escaped him, and even before the stranger so clearly manifested his interest in Cosette, Thénardier divined it. He surprised the profound glances of this old man which constantly reverted to the child. Why this interest ? who was this man ? why was his attire so wretched when his purse was so full ? These questions he asked himself and could not answer them, and they irritated him ; he reflected on them the whole night. He could not be Cosette's father ; was he her grandfather ? then, why did he not make himself known at once ? When a man has a claim, he proves it, and this man evidently had no claim on Cosette. In that case, what was it ? Thénardier lost himself in suppositions ; he caught a gleam of everything and saw nothing. However this might be, on beginning the conversation, feeling sure that there was a secret in all this, and that the man was interested in remaining in the shadow, he felt himself strong ; but on hearing

the stranger's firm and distinct answer, when he saw that
this mysterious person was simply mysterious, he felt himself weak. He had not expected anything of this sort, and
it routed his conjectures. He rallied his ideas, and weighed
all this in a second. Thénardier was one of those men who
judge of a situation at a glance, and he considered that this was
the moment to advance straight and rapidly. He behaved
like great captains at that decisive instant which they alone
can recognise. He unmasked his battery at once.

" Sir," he said, " I must have one thousand five hundred
francs."

The stranger took from his side-pocket an old black
leathern portfolio, and drew from it three bank-notes which
he laid on the table. Then he placed his large thumb on
the notes, and said to the landlord :

" Bring Cosette."

While this was going on, what was Cosette about ? On
waking, she ran to her sabot and found the gold coin in it ;
it was not a napoleon, but one of those new twenty-franc
pieces of the Restoration, on which the Prussian queue was
substituted for the crown of laurels. Cosette was dazzled,
and her destiny was beginning to intoxicate her ; she knew
not what a gold piece was, she had never seen one, and she
hurriedly hid it in her pocket, as if she had stolen it. She
felt it was really hers, she guessed whence the gift came,
but she experienced a feeling of joy full of fear. She was
happy, but she was more stupefied ; these magnificent
things did not seem to her real,—the doll frightened her,
the gold coin frightened her, and she trembled vaguely at
this magnificence. The stranger alone did not frighten
her ; on the contrary, he reassured her since the previous
evening. Through her amazement and her sleep, she
thought in her little childish mind of this man, who looked
so old, and poor, and sad ; and who was so rich and good.
Ever since she met him in the wood, all had changed for
her, as it were. Cosette, less happy than the meanest
swallow, had never yet known what it is to take refuge in
the shadow and beneath the wing of her mother ; for five
years, that is to say, so far back as her thoughts went, the
poor child had trembled and shuddered. She had ever been
exposed in her nudity to the bleak blast of misfortune, and
she now felt as if she were clothed ; formerly her soul was
cold, now it was warm. Cosette no longer felt afraid of her
mistress, for she was no longer alone ; she had some one

by her side.   She had set about her daily work very quickly, and the louis, which she had placed in the same pocket from which the fifteen-sous piece had fallen on the previous night, caused her thoughts to stray.   She did not dare touch it, but she looked at it for five minutes at a time.   While sweeping the stairs, she stood motionless, forgetting her broom and the whole world, engaged in watching this star sparkle in her pocket.   It was during one of these contemplations that her mistress came to her ; by her husband's order she had come to fetch the child, and, extraordinary to say, did not slap her, or even call her a hard name.

" Cosette," she said, almost gently, "come directly."

A moment after, Cosette entered the taproom.   The stranger took his bundle and untied it.   It contained a complete mourning dress for a child of seven years of age.

" My child," the man said, "take these and go and dress yourself quickly."

The day was breaking, when those inhabitants of Montfermeil who were beginning to open their doors saw a poorly clad man and a girl, holding a large doll, going along the Paris road toward Livry.   No one knew the man, and few recognised Cosette in her new dress. Cosette was going away.   With whom ? she was ignorant. Where to? she did not know.   All she understood was that she was leaving Thénardier's pot-house behind her ; no one thought of saying good-bye to her, or she to any one. She left the house, hated and hating.   Poor gentle being, whose heart up to this hour had only been crushed !

Cosette walked gravely, opening her large eyes and look- ing at the sky.   She had placed her louis in the pocket of her new apron, and from time to time stooped down and looked at it, and then at her companion.   She felt somehow as if she were near God.

Madame Thénardier, according to her custom, had left her husband to act, and anticipated grand results.   When the man and Cosette had left, Thénardier let a good quarter of an hour elapse, then took her on one side, and showed her the fifteen hundred francs.

" No more than that ? " she said.

It was the first time since her marriage that she had ventured to criticise an act of her master, and the blow went home.

" You are right," he said, "and I am a fool.   Give me my hat."   He thrust the three notes into his pocket and went out, but he made a mistake and first turned to the right. Some neighbours of whom he inquired put him on the right track, and he walked along at a great rate, talking to himself.

"This man is evidently a millionaire dressed in yellow, and as for me, I am an animal. He gave first twenty sous, then five francs, then fifty francs, then fifteen hundred francs, and all with the same facility. He would have given fifteen thousand francs! but I shall catch him up." And, then, the bundle of clothes prepared beforehand was singular, and there was a mystery behind it. Now mysteries must not be let go when you hold them, for the secrets of the rich are sponges full of gold, if you know how to squeeze them. All these thoughts whirled about his brain. "I am an animal," he said. On leaving Montfermeil and reaching the angle formed by the Lagny road, you can see it running for a long distance before you upon the plateau. On getting to this point he calculated that he should see the man and child, and looked as far as he could, but saw nothing. He inquired again, and passers-by told him that the people he was looking for had gone in the direction of Gagny wood. He followed them, for, though they had the start of him, a child walks slowly. He went fast, and then, again, the country was familiar to him. All at once he stopped and smote his forehead, like a man who has forgotten the main thing, and thinks of retracing his steps.

"I ought to have taken my gun," he said to himself. Thénardier was one of those double natures that pass at times among us without our knowledge, and disappear unknown, because destiny has only shown us one side of them : it is the fate of many men to live thus half submerged. In an ordinary situation Thénardier had everything that was necessary to make him—we do not say to be—what is conventionally termed an honest tradesman, or a worthy citizen. At the same time, certain circumstances being given, certain shocks stirring up his nature from the bottom, he had everything that was required to make him a villain. He was a shopkeeper in whom there was a monster. Satan must at times crouch in a corner of the lair in which Thénardier lived, and dream before this hideous masterpiece. After hesitating an instant, he thought :

"Bah! they would have time to escape."

And he continued on his way, going rapidly ahead and almost with an air of certainty, displaying the sagacity of a fox that scents a flock of partridges. In fact, when he had passed the ponds and cut across the wide turfed glade which covers the old waterway of the Abbey de Chelles, he noticed under a shrub a hat, on which he built up many conjectures. The shrub was low, and Thénardier saw that the man and Cosette were sitting under it. The child could not be seen, but the doll's head was visible. Thénardier was not mistaken; the man had sat down there to let the child rest a little, and the tavern-keeper dodged round the shrub and suddenly appeared before those whom he sought.

"Pardon me, sir," he said, panting, "but here are your fifteen hundred francs."

The man raised his eyes.

"What is the meaning of this?"

Thénardier answered respectfully:

"It means, sir, that I take Cosette back."

The child shuddered, and clung to the man. The latter answered, looking fixedly at Thénardier and leaving a space between each word:

"You—take—Cosette—back?"

"Yes, sir, I do. I must tell you that I have reflected. The truth is, that I have no right to give her to you. Look you, I am an honest man: the little one does not belong to me, but to her mother, who intrusted her to me, and I can only give her back to her mother. You will say to me, 'Her mother is dead.' Good. In that case, I can only surrender Cosette to a person who brings me a written authority from her mother. That is surely quite clear."

The man, without answering, felt in his pocket, and Thénardier saw the portfolio with the bank-notes reappear. He gave a start of joy.

"Good," he thought, "I have him; he is going to bribe me."

Before opening the portfolio the traveller looked around him. The place was utterly deserted, and there was not a soul in the wood or the valley. The man opened the pocket-book and took out, not the handful of bank-notes which Thénardier anticipated, but a simple sheet of paper, which he opened and handed to the landlord, saying: "You are right: read."

Thénardier took the paper and read.

"M—— SUR M——, *March 25, 1823.*

"MONSIEUR THÉNARDIER,—You will deliver Cosette to the bearer, who will pay up all little matters.—Yours,

"FANTINE."

"Do you know that signature?" the man continued.

It was indeed Fantine's, and Thénardier recognised it, and had nothing to say. He felt a double annoyance, first at having to renounce the bribery which he expected, and, secondly, that of being beaten. The man added :

"You can keep that paper as your discharge."

Thénardier folded it up neatly, and growled : "The signature is tolerably well imitated. Well, be it so."

Then he attempted a desperate effort.

"So far so good, sir, since you are the bearer; but the expenses must be paid, and there is a heavy sum owing me."

The man rose, and said as he dusted his threadbare cuff : "Monsieur Thénardier, in January the mother calculated that she owed you 120 francs ; in February you sent in an account of 500 francs ; you received 300 at the end of that month, and 300 more early in March. Since then nine months have elapsed at the agreed on price of 15 francs, which makes 135 francs. You had received 100 francs too much, so this leaves 35 francs owing you, and I have just given you 1500."

Thénardier felt just like the wolf when it is caught by the leg in a steel trap.

"Who in the fiend's name is this man?" he thought.

He behaved like the wolf : he shook himself : impudence had carried him through before now.

"Monsieur, I don't know your name," he said boldly, and putting off his respectful manner, "if you do not give me 3000 francs I shall take Cosette back."

The stranger said quietly, "Come, Cosette." He took the child with his left hand, and with the right picked up his stick. Thénardier noticed the enormity of the stick and the solitude of the spot. The man buried himself in the wood, leaving the landlord motionless and confounded. As he walked away, Thénardier regarded his broad shoulders and enormous fists, then his eye fell on his own thin arms. "I must have been a fool," he said, "not to bring my gun, as I was going to hunt."

Still the tavern-keeper did not abandon the pursuit. "I

will know where he goes," he said, and began following them at a distance. Two things remained in his hands, irony in the shape of the scrap of paper signed "Fantine," and a consolation in the 1500 francs. The man led Cosette in the direction of Bondy : he walked slowly, with drooping head and in a pensive attitude. Winter had rendered the wood transparent, and hence Thénardier did not lose sight of them, while keeping some distance off. From time to time the man turned round and looked to see whether he were followed, and suddenly perceived Thénardier. He drew Cosette into a clump of trees, in which they both disappeared. "Confusion!" said Thénardier, as he doubled his pace. The closeness of the trees compelled him to draw nearer to them, and when the man was at the thickest part he turned round and saw Thénardier, although the latter tried to conceal himself behind a stem. The man gave him a restless glance, then tossed his head and continued his walk. Thénardier followed him, but, after going some two hundred yards, the man turned and looked at him so menacingly that the landlord thought it "useless" to go any further. He turned back.

On the evening of the day on which Jean Valjean drew Cosette from the claws of the Thénardiers he re-entered Paris. At nightfall he passed through the Barrière de Monceaux with the child, and got into a cabriolet which conveyed him to the Esplanade of the Observatory. Here he got down, and the pair proceeded in the darkness toward the Boulevard de l'Hôpital. The day had been strange and full of emotions for Cosette : they had eaten behind hedges bread and cheese bought at isolated wine-shops ; they had often changed vehicles, and gone a distance on foot. She did not complain, but she felt tired, and Jean Valjean perceived it by her hand, which dragged more and more. He took her on his back, and Cosette, without letting go of Catherine, laid her head on his shoulder and fell asleep.

CHAPTER LIII.

FORTY years ago the solitary walker who ventured into the lost districts of the Salpetrière, and went up the Boulevard as far as the Barrière d'Italie, reached a quarter where it might be said that Paris disappeared. It was not solitude, for there were passers-by; it was not the country, for there were houses and streets ; it was not a town, for the streets had ruts as large as those in the high-roads, and grass grew in them ; and it was not a village, for the houses were too lofty. What was it then? It was an inhabited place where there was nobody, a deserted spot where there was somebody. It was the old quarter of the Marché-aux-Chevaux. The rambler, if he risked himself beyond the tottering walls of the market, if he even consented to pass the Rue du Petit-banquier, reached the corner of the Rue des Vignes St. Marcel, a but little known latitude, after leaving on his right a garden protected by high walls, next a field in which stood tan mills, resembling gigantic beaver dams, next an enclosure encumbered with planks, tree-stumps, sawdust, and chips, on the top of which a large dog barked ; then a long low wall, all in ruins, with a small, decrepit back gate, covered with moss, which burst into flower in spring, and lastly, in the most desolate spot, a hideous and decrepit building, on which could be read in large letters STICK NO BILLS. Here, close to a foundry, and between two garden walls, could be seen, at the time of which we write, a poor house, which, at the first glance, seemed small as a cottage, but was in reality large as a cathedral. It turned its gable end to the public thoroughfare, and hence came its apparent smallness ; nearly the whole house was concealed.

This house was only one storey high. On examining it, the first fact that struck you was that the door could never have been other than that of a low lodging-house, while the window, had it been carved in stone instead of made of stucco, might have belonged to a mansion. The door was nothing but a collection of worm-eaten planks, clumsily held together by roughly planed cross beams. It opened immediately on a steep staircase, muddy, dirty, and dusty, of the same width as itself, which could be seen from the street mounting steep as a ladder, and disappearing in the gloom between two walls. The top of the clumsy opening in which the door stood was masked by a thin deal plank, in which a triangular hole had been cut. On the inside of the door a brush dipped in ink had clumsily traced No. 52, while over the skylight the same brush had painted No. 50, so people hesitated. Dust-coloured rags hung like a drapery over the triangular skylight. The window was wide, tolerably lofty, filled with large panes of glass, and protected by Venetian shutters ; but these panes had various wounds, at once concealed and betrayed by an ingenious bandage of paper, and the Venetian shutters, broken and hanging from their hinges, threatened passers-by more than they protected the inhabitants. The horizontal screen-boards were wanting here and there, and these places had been filled up with boards nailed on perpendicularly ; so that the affair began by being a Venetian screen, and ended by being a shutter. This door, which had an unclean look, and this window, which looked honest, though fallen in the world, produced the effect of two beggars walking side by side with two different faces under the same rags, the one having always been a mendicant, while the other had once been a gentleman. The staircase led to a very large building, which resembled a shed which had been converted into a house. This building had, as its intestinal tube, a long passage, upon which opened, right and left, compartments of various dimensions, habitable at a pinch, and more like booths than cells. These rooms looked out on the dreary landscape around ; all was dark, wearisome, dull, melancholy, and sepulchral, and traversed, according as the cracks were in the roof or the door, by cold sunbeams or sharp draughts. An interesting and picturesque peculiarity of houses of this description is the enormous size of the cobwebs. To the left of the door, on the boulevard, and at about six feet from the ground, a bricked-up window formed a square hole, which was filled with stones that passing urchins had thrown into it. A portion of this building has been recently demolished, but what still remains will allow an idea to be formed of what it was. The whole affair is not more than a century old ; one hundred years are the youth of a church and the old age of a human abode. It seems as if the house of man shares his brief tenure, and the House of God His eternity. The postman called this house No. 50-52, but it was known in the quarter by the name of Maison Gorbeau.

Jean Valjean stopped before No. 50-52. Like the dull bird, he had selected this deserted spot in which to build his nest. He felt in his pocket, took out a latchkey, opened and carefully shut the door again, and went upstairs, still carrying Cosette on his back. When he reached the landing he took from his pocket a key, with which he opened another door. The room he entered was a sort of spacious garret, furnished with a mattress laid on the ground, a table, and a few chairs. There was a burning stove in the corner, and the boulevard lamp faintly illumined this poor interior. At the end of the room was a closet with a poor bedstead, to which Jean Valjean carried the child and laid her on it, without waking her. He struck a light and lit a candle,—all this had been prepared on the previous day,—and he then began gazing at Cosette with a look full of ecstasy, in which the expression of kindness and tenderness almost attained delirium. The little girl, with that calm confidence which only appertains to extreme strength and extreme weakness, had fallen asleep without knowing with whom she was, and continued to sleep without knowing where she was. Jean Valjean bent down and kissed the child's hand. Nine months previously he had kissed her mother's hand, who had also just fallen asleep, and the same painful, religious, poignant feeling filled his heart. He knelt down by the side of Cosette's bed.

Long after daybreak the child was still asleep. A pale beam of the December sun filtered through the window and made large strips of light and shadow on the ceiling. Suddenly a heavily laden wagon, passing along the boulevard, shook the house like a blast of wind, and made it tremble from top to bottom.

"Yes, madame," Cosette cried, waking with a start, " I am coming directly."

And she jumped out of bed, her eyelids still half closed by the weight of sleep, and stretched out her arms to a corner of the wall.

"Oh, goodness, my broom !" she said.

She opened her eyes thoroughly, and saw Jean Valjean's smiling face.

"Ah, it is true," the child said. "Good-morning, sir."

Children accept at once and familiarly joy and happiness, for they are themselves by nature happiness and joy. Cosette saw Catherine at the foot of her bed, caught her up, and while playing, asked Jean Valjean a hundred questions :—"Where was she ? was Paris large ? was Madame Thénardier a long way off ? and would she never return ? " etc. etc. etc. All at once she exclaimed, " How pretty it is here !"

It was a frightful hole, but she felt herself free.

" Must I sweep ? " she at length continued.

" Play," said Jean Valjean.

The day passed in this way, and Cosette, not feeling any anxiety at understanding nothing, was inexpressibly happy with her doll and this good man.

The next morning at daybreak Jean Valjean was again standing by Cosette's bedside ; he was motionless and waiting for her to awake : something new was entering his soul. Jean Valjean had never loved anything. For twenty-five years he had been alone in the world, and had never been father, lover, husband, or friend. At the galleys he was wicked, gloomy, chaste, ignorant, and ferocious—the heart of the old convict was full of virginities. His sister and his sister's children had only left in him a vague and distant reminiscence, which in the end entirely faded away : he had made every effort to find them again, and, not being able to do so, forgot them,—human nature is thus constituted. The other tender emotions of his youth, if he had any, had fallen into an abyss. When he saw Cosette, when he carried her off, he felt his entrails stirred up : all the passion and affection there was in him was aroused and rushed toward this child. He went up to the bed on which she slept, and he trembled with joy : he felt pangs like a mother, and knew not what it was, for the great and strange emotion of a heart which is preparing to love is a very obscure and sweet thing. Still, as he was fifty-five years of age, and Cosette eight, all the love he might have felt during life was melted into a species of ineffable glow. This was the second white apparition he had seen. The Bishop had caused the dawn of virtue to rise on his horizon. Cosette now evoked the dawn of love.

The first days passed in this bewilderment. On her side Cosette became unconsciously different, poor little creature ! She was so little when her mother left her that she did not remember ; and like all children, who resemble the young vine-twigs that cling to everything, she tried to love, and had not succeeded. All had repulsed her, the Thénardiers, their children, and other children ; she had loved the dog which died, and after that nothing and nobody would have anything to do with her. It is a sad thing to say, but at the age of eight she had a cold heart ; it was not her fault, it was not that she lacked the faculty of loving, but it was, alas ! the possibility. Hence, from the first day, all that

felt and thought within her began to love the good man ;
and she experienced what she had never known before, a
feeling of expansion. The man no longer even produced
the effect upon her of being old or poor ; she found Jean
Valjean handsome, in the same way as she found the garret
pretty. Such are the effects of dawn, childhood, youth, and
joy. The novelty of earth and life has something to do in
it, and nothing is so charming as the colouring reflection
of happiness upon an attic ; in this way we have all a blue
garret in our past. Nature had placed a profound interval,
of fifty years, between Jean Valjean and Cosette ; but destiny
filled up this separation. Destiny suddenly united, and
affianced with its irresistible power, these two uprooted
existences so different in age, so similar in sorrow, and the
one, in fact, was the complement of the other. Cosette's
instinct sought a father, in the same way as Jean Valjean's
sought a child, and to meet was to find each other. At the
mysterious moment when their two hands clasped they were
welded together, and when their two souls saw each other
they recognised that each was necessary to the other, and
joined in a close embrace. Taking the words in their most
comprehensive and absolute meaning, we may say that,
separated from everything by the walls of the tombs, Jean
Valjean was the Widower as Cosette was the Orphan, and
this situation caused Jean Valjean to become in a celestial
manner Cosette's father. And, in truth, the mysterious
impression produced upon Cosette in the Chelles wood by
Jean Valjean's hand grasping hers in the darkness was not
an illusion but a reality. The coming of this man, in its
influence on the destiny of this child, had been as the
advent of God.

Moreover, Jean Valjean had selected his asylum well.
He seemed to be almost perfectly secure. The room he
occupied with Cosette was the one whose window looked
out on the boulevard, and as it was the only one of the sort
in the house, he had not to fear the curiosity of neighbours,
either in front or on his side. The ground floor of 50-52,
a sort of rickety penthouse, was employed as a tool-house
by nursery-gardeners and had no communication with the
first floor. The latter, as we have said, contained several
rooms, and a few garrets, one of which alone was occupied
by the old woman who looked after Jean Valjean. It was
this old woman who was known as the chief lodger, but
who in reality performed the duties of porter, that let him the

room on Christmas Day. He had represented himself as an annuitant ruined by the Spanish bonds, who meant to live there with his little daughter. He paid six months' rent in advance, and requested the old woman to furnish the room in the way we have seen, and it was this woman who lit the stove and prepared everything on the evening of their arrival. Weeks passed away, and these two beings led a happy life in this wretched garret. With the dawn Cosette began laughing, chattering, and singing, for children, like birds, have their matin song. At times it happened that Jean Valjean took her little red chilblained hand and kissed it; the poor child, accustomed to be beaten, did not know what this meant, and went away quite ashamed. At one moment she became serious, and looked at her little black frock. Cosette was no longer dressed in rags, but in mourning; she had left wretchedness, and was entering life. Jean Valjean set to work teaching her to read. At times he thought that it was with the idea of doing evil that he learned to read at the galleys, and this idea had turned to teaching a child to read. Then the old galley-slave smiled the pensive smile of the angels. He felt in it a premeditation of heaven, and he lost himself in a reverie, for good thoughts as well as wicked have their depths. Teaching Cosette to read, and letting her play, almost constituted Jean Valjean's entire life; and then, he spoke to her about her mother, and made her play. She called him "father," and knew him by no other name. He spent hours in watching her dress and undress her doll, and listening to her prattle. From this moment life appeared to him full of interest; men seemed to him good and just; he no longer reproached any one in his thoughts, and perceived no reason why he should not live to a great age, now that this child loved him. He saw a future illumined by Cosette, as by a delicious light; and as the best men are not exempt from a selfish thought, he said to himself at times joyfully that she would be by no means handsome.

It is only a personal opinion, yet we fancy that at the point which Jean Valjean had reached when he began to love Cosette, he required this fresh impulse to continue in the right path. He had just seen, under new aspects, the wickedness of men and the wretchedness of society, but the aspects were incomplete, and only fatally showed him one side of the truth,—the fate of woman comprised in Fantine, and public authority personified in Javert; he had returned

to the galleys, but this time for acting justly ; he had drunk
the new cup of bitterness to the dregs ; disgust and weariness seized upon him ; the very recollection of the Bishop
was approaching an eclipse, and though it would have
perhaps reappeared afterwards luminous and triumphant,
still this holy recollection was beginning to fade. Who
knows whether Jean Valjean was not on the eve of growing
discouraged and relapsing ? but he loved and became strong
again. Alas ! he was no less tottering than Cosette ; he
protected her and she strengthened him ; through him, she
was able to advance in her life ; through her, he could
continue in the path of virtue. O unfathomable and divine
mystery of the compensations of destiny !

Jean Valjean was prudent enough never to go out in the
daytime. Every evening he walked out for an hour or
two, sometimes alone, but generally with Cosette, in the
most retired streets, and entering the churches at nightfall.
When he did not take Cosette with him, she remained with
the old woman, but it was her delight to go out with him.
She preferred an hour with him to the ravishing *tête-à-*
têtes with Catherine. He walked along holding her by the
hand, and talking pleasantly with her, for Cosette's temper
turned to be very playful.

The old woman cleaned, cooked, and bought food for
them. They lived quietly, always having a little fire, but
as if they were very poor. Jean Valjean had made no
change in the furniture since the first day, except that he
had a wooden door put up in place of the glass door in
Cosette's sleeping-closet. He still wore his yellow coat,
black breeches, and old hat, and in the streets he was
taken for a poor man. It happened at times that charitable
women turned and gave him a sou, which Jean Valjean
accepted with a deep bow. It happened at times also that
he met some wretch asking for charity ; in such a case
he looked behind him to see that no one was watching,
furtively approached the beggar, gave him money, now
and then silver, and hurried away. This entailed incon-
veniences, for people began to know him in the district
under the name of the alms-giving beggar. The old chief
lodger, a spiteful creature, full of envy and uncharitableness
toward her neighbours, watched him closely, though he did
not suspect it. She was rather deaf, which rendered her
prone to gossip, and there remained to her from the past
two teeth, one atop and one at bottom, which she constantly

rattled against each other. She questioned Cosette, who, knowing nothing, could say nothing except that she came from Montfermeil. One day this spy saw Jean Valjean go into one of the uninhabited rooms in a way that seemed to her peculiar. She followed him with the stealthy step of an old cat, and was able to watch him, herself unseen, through the crack of the door, to which Jean Valjean turned his back, doubtless as a greater precaution. She saw him take out of his pocket a pair of scissors, needle, and thread, and then begin ripping up the lining of his coat, and pull out a piece of yellow paper, which he unfolded. The old woman recognised with horror that it was a thousand-franc note, the second or third she had seen in her life, and she fled in terror. A moment after Jean Valjean addressed her, and requested her to change the note for him, adding that it was his half-year's dividend, which he had received on the previous day. "When?" the old woman thought; "he did not go out till six in the evening, and the bank is certainly not open at that hour." The old woman went to change the note and made her conjectures; the amount of money being considerably multiplied gave rise to a host of breathless conferences among the gossips of the Rue des Vignes St. Marcel.

Some days afterwards, it happened that Jean Valjean, in his shirt sleeves, was chopping wood in the passage, and the old woman was in his room cleaning up. She was alone, for Cosette was admiring the wood-chopping. She saw the coat hanging on a nail, and investigated it. The lining had been sewn up again, but the good woman felt it carefully, and fancied she could notice folds of paper between the cloth and the lining. More bank-notes, of course! She also noticed that there were all sorts of things in the pockets; not only the needles, scissors, and thread she had seen, but a large portfolio, a big clasp-knife, and, most suspicious fact of all, several different coloured wigs. Each pocket of this coat seemed to be a species of safeguard against unexpected events.

Thus, the occupants of the old building reached the last days of winter.

CHAPTER LIV.

There was, in the neighbourhood of St. Medard's church, a poor man who usually sat on the edge of a condemned well, to whom Jean Valjean liked to give alms. He never passed him without giving him a trifle, and at times spoke to him. The persons who envied this beggar said that he belonged to the police, and he was an ex-beadle seventy-five years of age, who was constantly telling his beads. One evening when Jean Valjean passed alone, he perceived the beggar at his usual place under the lamp which had just been lit. The man, according to his habit, seemed to be praying and was bent over. Jean Valjean went up to him and placed his usual charity in his hand, and the beggar suddenly raised his eyes, looked fixedly at Jean Valjean, and then let his head hang again. This movement was like a flash, but Jean Valjean gave a start; he fancied that he had seen by the flickering light of the lamp, not the placid and devout face of the old beadle, but a terrifying and familiar face. He had such a feeling as he would have had had he suddenly found himself face to face with a tiger in the darkness. He recoiled, terrified and petrified, not daring to breathe, remain, or fly, staring at the beggar, who had let his head fall, and did not appear to know that he was there. At this strange moment, an instinct, perhaps that of self-preservation, urged Jean Valjean not to utter a syllable. The beggar was of the same height, wore the same rags, and looked as he did every day. "Stuff," said Jean Valjean, "I am mad, dreaming; it is impossible!" And he went home sorely troubled in mind. He hardly dared confess to himself that the face which he fancied he had seen was Javert's. At night, on reflecting, he regretted that he had not spoken to the man, and made him raise his head a second time. The next evening he returned and found the beggar at his seat. "Good-day, my man," Jean Valjean said resolutely, as he gave him a sou. The beggar raised his head and replied in a complaining voice, "Thank you, my good gentleman." It was certainly the old beadle. Jean Valjean felt fully reassured, and began laughing. "How on earth could I have thought that it was Javert? Is my sight growing poor already?" And he thought no more of it.

Some days after, it might be about eight in the evening,

he was giving Cosette a spelling lesson, when he heard the
house door open and then close again. This appeared to
him singular, for the old woman, who alone lived in the
house besides himself, always went to bed at nightfall to
save candle. Jean Valjean made Cosette a sign to be
silent, for he heard some one coming upstairs. After all
it might be the old woman, who felt unwell, and had been
to the chemist's. Jean Valjean listened; the footstep was
heavy and sounded like a man's, but the old woman wore
thick shoes, and nothing so closely resembles a man's footstep as an old woman's. For all that, though, Jean Valjean
blew out his candle. He had sent Cosette to bed, saying
in a whisper, "Make no noise," and while he was kissing
her forehead the footsteps stopped. Jean Valjean remained
silently in his chair, with his back turned to the door,
and holding his breath in the darkness. After a long
interval, hearing nothing more, he turned noiselessly, and,
on looking at his door, saw a light through the keyhole,
which formed a sort of sinister star in the blackness of the
door and the wall. There was evidently some one there
holding a candle in his hand and listening. A few minutes
passed, and then the light went away : still he did not hear
the sound of footsteps, which seemed to indicate that the
man who came to listen had taken off his shoes. Jean
Valjean threw himself full-dressed on his bed, and could not
close his eyes all night. At daybreak, when he was just
yielding to fatigue, he was aroused by the creaking of a
door which opened into a room at the end of the passage,
and then heard the same footstep which had ascended the
stairs the previous evening drawing nearer. He put his
eye to the keyhole, which was rather large, in the hope of
seeing the man who had listened at his door overnight. It
was really a man, who this time passed Jean Valjean's door
without stopping. The passage was still too dark for him
to distinguish his face ; but when the man reached the
staircase a ray of light from outside fell upon him, and Jean
Valjean saw his back perfectly. He was a tall man, dressed
in a long coat, with a cudgel under his arm, and he was
very like Javert. Jean Valjean might have tried to see him
on the boulevard through his window, but for that purpose
he must have opened it, and that he dared not do. It was
plain that this man came in with a key and was quite at
home. Who gave him this key ? what did it mean ? At
seven o'clock, when the old woman came to clean up, Jean

Valjean gave her a piercing glance, but did not question her. The good woman was as calm as usual, and while sweeping she said to him :

" I suppose you heard some one come in last night, sir ? "

At her age, and on that boulevard, eight in the evening is the blackest night.

"Yes, I remember," he said, with the most natural accent : " who was it ? "

" A new lodger in the house."

" What is his name ? "

" I forget : Dumont or Daumont, something like that."

" And what may he be ? "

The old woman looked at him with her little ferret eyes, and answered :

" He lives on his property, like yourself."

Perhaps she meant nothing, but Jean Valjean fancied that he could detect a meaning. When the old woman had gone off he made a rouleau of some hundred francs which he had in a chest of drawers and put it in his pocket. Whatever precautions he took to keep the money from rattling, a five-franc piece fell from his hand and rolled noisily on the floor. At nightfall he went down and looked attentively all along the boulevard : he saw nobody, and it seemed utterly deserted. It is true that some one might have been concealed behind the trees. He went up again, and said to Cosette, " Come ! " He took her by the hand, and both went out.

Jean Valjean at once left the boulevard and began threading the streets, making as many turnings as he could, and at times retracing his steps to make sure that he was not followed. The moon was at its full, and Jean Valjean was not sorry for that, for as the luminary was still close to the horizon it formed large patches of light and shade in the streets. Jean Valjean was able to slip along the houses and walls on the dark side and watch the bright side ; perhaps he did not reflect sufficiently that the dark side escaped his notice. Still, in all the deserted lanes which border the Rue de Poliveau he felt certain that no one was following him.

Cosette walked on without asking any questions. The sufferings of the first six years of her life had introduced something passive into her nature. Moreover—and this is a remark to which we shall have to revert more than once —she was accustomed to the singularities of her companion, and the strange mutations of fate. And then she felt in safety as she was with him. Jean Valjean did not know any more than Cosette whither he was going ; he trusted to God, as she trusted to him. He fancied that he also held some one greater than himself by the hand, and felt an invisible being guiding him. However, he had no settled idea, plan, or scheme ; he was not absolutely certain that it was Javert ; and then again it might be Javert ignorant that he was Jean Valjean. Was he not disguised ? Was he not supposed to be dead ? Still, during the last few days several things had occurred which were becoming singular, and he wanted nothing more. He was resolved not to return to No. 50-52, and, like the animal driven from its lair, he sought a hole in which to hide himself until he could find a lodging. Jean Valjean described several labyrinths in the Quartier Mouffetard, which was as fast asleep as if it were still under mediæval discipline and the yoke of the Curfew, and combined several streets into a clever strategic system. There were lodging-houses where he now was, but he did not enter them, as he did not find anything to suit him, and he did not suppose for a moment that if persons were on his trail they had lost it again.

As eleven o'clock struck in the tower of St. Étienne du Mont he passed the police-office at No. 14, in the Rue de Pointoise. A few minutes after, the instinct to which we have referred made him look round, and he distinctly saw, by the office lamp which betrayed them, three men who were following him rather closely, pass in turn under this lamp on the dark side of the street. One of these men turned into the office, and another, who was in front, appeared to him decidedly suspicious.

" Come, child," he said to Cosette, and he hastened out of the Rue de Pontoise. He made a circuit, skirted the Passage des Patriarches, which was closed at that hour, and eventually turned into the Rue des Postes. There is an open space here, where the Rollin College now stands, and into which the Rue Neuve St. Geneviève runs.

The moon lighted up this open space brightly, and Jean Valjean hid himself in a doorway, calculating that if the men were still following him he could not fail to have a good look at them as they crossed the open space. In fact, three minutes had not elapsed when the men appeared. There were now four of them, all tall, dressed in long brown coats and round hats, and holding large sticks in their hands. They were no less alarming through their stature and huge fists, than through their sinister movements in the darkness; they looked like four spectres disguised as citizens. They stopped in the centre of the square, and formed a group as if consulting, and apparently undecided. The leader turned and pointed with his right hand in the direction Jean Valjean had taken, while another seemed to be pointing with some degree of obstinacy in the opposite direction. At the moment when the first man turned the moon shone full in his face. Jean Valjean recognised Javert perfectly.

Uncertainty was at an end for Jean Valjean; but fortunately it still lasted with the men. He took advantage of their hesitation, for it was time lost by them and gained by him. He left the gateway in which he was concealed, and pushed on along the Rue des Postes toward the region of the Jardin des Plantes. As Cosette was beginning to feel tired, he took her in his arms and carried her. No one was passing, and the lamps had not been lit on account of the moon. He doubled his pace.

He left behind him the Rue de la Clef, skirted the Jardin des Plantes, and reached the quay. Here he turned; the quay was deserted, the streets were deserted. There was no one behind him, and he breathed again. He reached the Austerlitz bridge, where a toll still existed at the time, and he handed the tollman a sou.

"It is two sous," said the man; "you are carrying a child who can walk. Pay for two."

He paid, though greatly vexed that his passing had given rise to any remark. A heavy cart was passing the river at the same time as himself, and also proceeding to the right bank. This was useful for him, as he could cross the whole of the bridge in its shadow. On reaching the arches of the bridge, Cosette, whose feet were numbed, asked to be put down; he did so, and took her by the hand again. After crossing the bridge, he saw a little to his right building-yards, towards which he proceeded. In order to reach them he must cross an open, brilliantly lighted space, but he did not hesitate. His pursuers were evidently thrown out, and Jean Valjean believed himself out of danger; he might be looked for, but he was not followed. A little street, the Rue du Chemin Vert Saint Antoine, ran between two timber-yards; it was narrow, dark, and seemed expressly made for him, but before entering it he looked back. From the spot where he was he

could see the whole length of the bridge of Austerlitz ; four
shadows had just come upon it, and were walking toward
the right bank. Jean Valjean gave a start like a recaptured
animal ; one hope was left him ; it was that the four men
had not been upon the bridge at the moment when he
crossed the large illumined space with Cosette. In that
case, by entering the little street before him, he might
escape, if he could reach the timber-yards, kitchen-gardens,
fields, and land not yet built on. It seemed to him that he
might trust to this little silent street. He entered it.

Some three hundred yards further on, he came to a spot
where the road formed two forks, and Jean Valjean had
before him, as it were, the two branches of a Y. Which
should he choose ? He did not hesitate, but took the right
one, because the other ran towards the faubourg, that is to
say, inhabited parts, while the right branch went in the
direction of the country, or deserted parts. Still they did
not walk very rapidly, for Cosette checked Jean Valjean's
pace, and hence he began carrying her again, and Cosette
laid her head on his shoulder and did not say a word. At
times he looked back, while careful to keep on the dark
side of the street. The first two or three times that he
turned he saw nothing, the silence was profound, and he
continued his walk with a little more confidence. All at
once, on turning suddenly, he fancied that he saw something
moving on the dark part of the street which he had just
passed. He rushed forward rather than walked, hoping to
find some side lane by which he could escape, and once
again break his trail. He reached a wall, which, however,
did not render further progress impossible, for it was a wall
skirting a cross lane, into which the street Jean Valjean
had entered ran. Here he must make his mind up again
whether to turn to the right or left. He looked to the
right ; the lane ran for some distance between buildings,
which were barns or sheds, and then stopped. The end of
the blind alley, a tall white wall, was distinctly visible. He
looked to the left ; on this side the lane was open, and at a
distance of about two hundred yards fell into a street, of
which it was an affluent. On that side safety lay. At the
moment when Jean Valjean turned to his left in order to
reach this street he saw at the angle formed by the street
and the lane a species of black and motionless statue. It
was evidently a man posted there to prevent him passing.
Jean Valjean was startled.

This part of Paris where Jean Valjean now was, situated
between the Faubourg St. Antoine and la Rapée, was one
of those which have been utterly transformed by those
recent works, which some call disfiguring, others
beautifying. The fields, the timber-yards, and old buildings have been removed, and there are now brand-new wide
streets, arenas, circuses, hippodromes, railway stations,
and a prison, Mazas,—progress as we see with its cor-
rective. Half a century back, in that popular language all
made up of traditions which insists on calling l'Institut
"les Quatre Nations," and l'Opera Comique "Feydeau,"
the precise spot where Jean Valjean now stood was called
"le Petit Picpus." Little Picpus, which by the way scarce
existed and was never more than the outline of a quarter,
had almost the monastic look of a Spanish town. The
streets were scarce paved, and hardly any houses lined
them ; excepting two or three streets, to which we are about
to refer, all was wall and solitude. There was not a shop
or a vehicle, scarce a candle lighted in the windows, and
every light was put out by ten o'clock. The quarter consisted of gardens, convents, timber-yards, and kitchen-
grounds, and there were a few low houses with walls as
lofty as themselves. Such was the quarter in the last
century ; the Revolution fiercely assailed it, and the Republican board of works demolished and made gaps in it :
rubbish was allowed to be shot there. Thirty years ago
this quarter was disappearing under the erasure of new
buildings, and now it is completely blotted out.

Little Picpus, of which no modern map retains a trace, is
very clearly indicated in the plan of 1727, published at Paris
by Denis Thirery. Little Picpus had what we have just
called a Y of streets formed by the Rue du Chemin Vert St.
Antoine dividing into two branches, the left-hand one taking
the name of the Petite Rue Picpus, and the right-hand that
of Rue Polonceau. The two branches of the Y were joined
at their summit by a sort of cross-bar called Rue Droit-Mur.
Any one who, coming from the Seine, reached the end of
Rue Polonceau, had on his left Rue Droit-Mur, turning
sharply at a right angle, in front of him the wall of that
street, and on his right a truncated prolongation of the Rue
Droit-mur called the Cul de sac Genrot.

Jean Valjean was at this place. As we said, on perceiving
the black shadow standing on watch at the corner of the
Rue Droit-Mur and the Petite Rue Picpus, he was startled,

for he was doubtless watched by this phantom. What was to be done ? he had no time to retrograde, for what he had seen moving in the shadow a few moments previously in his rear was of course Javert and his squad. Javert was probably already at the beginning of the street at the end of which Jean Valjean was. Javert, according to appearances, was acquainted with this labyrinth, and had taken his precautions by sending one of his men to guard the outlet. These conjectures, which so closely resembled certainty, whirled suddenly in Jean Valjean's troubled brain like a handful of dust raised by an unexpected puff of wind. He examined the blind alley, that was barred ; he examined the Rue Picpus, a sentry was there, and he saw his black shadow distinctly thrown on the white moonlit pavement. To advance was to fall into this man's clutches ; to fall back was throwing himself into Javert's arms.

In order to understand what follows, the reader must form an exact idea of the Rue Droit-Mur, and in particular of the angle which the visitor left on his left when he turned out of the Rue Polonceau into this lane. The lane was almost entirely bordered on the right by poor-looking houses, on the left by a single building of severe outline, composed of several structures which rose gradually from one floor to two as they approached Petite Rue Picpus, so that this mansion, which was very lofty on that side, was very low on the side of Rue Polonceau, where, at the corner to which we have alluded, it sank so low as to be only a wall. This wall did not run parallel with the lane, but formed a very deep cant, concealed by its corners from any observers in Rue Polonceau and Rue Droit-Mur. From this cant the wall extended along Rue Polonceau up to a house bearing the number 49, and in Rue Droit-Mur, where it was much shorter, up to the frowning building to which we have referred, whose gable it intersected, thus forming a new re-entering angle in the street. This gable had a gloomy appearance, for only one window was visible, or, to speak more correctly, two shutters covered with sheet zinc and always closed. The description of the locality which we are now giving is strictly correct, and will doubtless arouse a very precise souvenir in the mind of the old inhabitants of the locality.

The cant in the wall was entirely filled up by a thing that resembled a colossal and wretched gateway ; it was a vast collection of perpendicular planks, the top ones wider than those below, and fastened together by long cross strips of iron. By the side of this gate was a *porte-cochère* of ordinary dimensions, which had apparently been made in the wall about fifty years previously. A lime tree displayed its branches above the cant, and the wall was covered with ivy towards the Rue Polonceau.

In Jean Valjean's desperate situation this gloomy building had an uninhabited and solitary look about it which tempted him. He hurriedly examined it, and said to himself that if he could only enter it he might perhaps be saved. In the centre of the frontage of this building, turned to the Rue Droit-Mur, there were old leaden drain-pipes at all the windows of the different floors. The various branches which led to a central pipe formed a species of tree on the façade; these ramifications with their hundred elbows imitated those old vine branches which cling to the front of old farm-houses. This and a large espalier of lead and iron branches was the first thing that caught Jean Valjean's attention. He put Cosette down with her back against a post, bidding her be silent, and hurried to the spot where the main pipe reached the ground. Perhaps there might be a way to scale it and enter the house, but the pipe was worn out, and scarce held in its cramps; besides, all the windows of this silent house were defended by thick iron bars, even the garrets. And then the moon shone full on this front, and the man watching at the end of the street would see Jean Valjean climb up; and then what was he to do with Cosette? how was he to hoist her up a three-storeyed house? He gave up all idea of climbing by the pipe, and crawled along the wall to re-enter Rue Polonceau. When he reached the cant where he had left Cosette he noticed that no one could see him there. As we stated, he was safe from all eyes, no matter on what side; moreover, he was in the shadow; and then, lastly, there were two gates, which might perhaps be forced. The wall, over which he saw the lime tree and the ivy, evidently belonged to a garden in which he could at least conceal himself, though there was no foliage on the trees, and pass the rest of the night. Time was slipping away, and he must set to work at once. He felt the *porte-cochère*, and at once perceived that it was fastened up inside and out; and then went to the other great gate with more hope. It was frightfully decrepit, its very size rendered it less solid. the planks were rotten, and the iron bands, of which there were only three, were rusty. It seemed possible to break through this affair. On examining this gate, however, he saw that it was not a gate ; it had no hinges, lock, or partition in the centre ; the iron bands crossed it from side to side without any solution of continuity. Through the cracks of the planks he caught a glimpse of coarsely mortared rag stone, which passers-by might have seen ten years back. He was forced to confess to himself with consternation that this fancied gate was simply a make-believe. It was easy to pull down a board, but he would find himself face to face with a wall.

At this moment a muffled, regular sound began to grow audible a short distance off, and Jean Valjean ventured to take a peep round the corner of the street. Seven or eight soldiers were entering the street. He could see their bayonets gleaming, and they were coming towards him. These soldiers, at the head of whom he distinguished Javert's tall form, advanced slowly and cautiously, and frequently halted ; it was plain that they were exploring all the corners and all the doors and lanes. It was —and here conjecture could not be wrong—some patrol which Javert had met and requested to assist him. Judging from the pace at which they marched, and the halts they made, they would require about a quarter of an hour to reach the spot where Jean Valjean was. It was a frightful thought ; a few moments separated Jean Valjean from the awful precipice which yawned before him for the third time. And the galleys were now not merely the galleys, but Cosette lot for ever, that is to say, a life in death.

There was now only one thing possible. Jean Valjean had one peculiarity—that he might be said to carry two wallets ; in one he had the thoughts of a saint, in the other the formidable talents of a convict, and he felt in one or the other as opportunity offered. Among other resources, owing to his numerous escapes from the Toulon galleys, he had become a perfect master in the incredible art of raising himself without ladder, cramping irons, and by his mere muscular strength, and holding on by his shoulders and knees, in the right angle of a wall, to the sixth floor if necessary ; an art which rendered so terrible and so celebrated that corner of the yard in the Paris Conciergerie by which the condemned convict Battemolle escaped twenty years ago. Jean Valjean measured the height of the wall above which he saw the lime tree, and found that it was about eighteen feet. The lower part of the angle which it made with the gable end of the large building was filled up with a triangular mass of masonry, very common in Parisian corners. This mass was about five feet high, and the space to be cleared from the top of it was not more than fourteen ; but the difficulty was Cosette, for she could not climb a wall. Abandon her? Jean Valjean did not think of it, but carrying her was impossible ; a man requires his whole strength to carry out such an ascent, and the slightest burden would displace his centre of gravity and hurl him down. He required a rope, but he had none. Where was he to find a rope at midnight in the Rue Polonceau? Assuredly at this moment if Jean Valjean had possessed a kingdom he would have given it for a rope. All extreme situations have their flashes, which at one moment blind, at another illumine us. Jean Valjean's desperate glance fell on the lamp-post in the blind alley. In those days there were no gaslights in the streets of Paris ; at nightfall lamps were lit at regular distances, which were pulled up and down by a rope that crossed the street, and fitted into a groove in a post. The end of the rope was kept in an iron box under the lantern, of which the lamplighter had the key, and the rope itself was protected by a metal case. Jean Valjean leaped across the street, burst the lock of the box with the point of his knife, and a moment later was again by Cosette's side holding a rope. Such gloomy finders of expedients, when struggling with fatality, set rapidly to work. We have mentioned that the lamps were not lit on this night ; the one in the blind alley therefore was naturally extinguished, and any one might have passed close without noticing that it was no longer in its place.

Meanwhile the hour, the place, the darkness, Jean Valjean's preoccupation, his singular gestures, his coming and going, were all beginning to alarm Cosette. Any other child would have begun crying loudly long before, but she confined herself to pulling the skirt of his coat. The noise of the approaching patrol constantly became more distinct.

" Father," she whispered, " I am afraid. Who is coming?"

" Hush ! " the unhappy man replied, " it is Madame Thénardier."

The child trembled, and he added :

" Do not say a word, but leave me to act ; if you cry out or sob she will catch you and take you back again."

Then, without haste, but without doing anything twice over, with a firm and sharp precision, which was the more remarkable at such a moment, when the patrol and Javert might be instantly expected, he undid his cravat, fastened it under Cosette's armpits, while careful not to hurt her, fastened the rope to the cravat, took the other end in his teeth, took off his shoes and stockings, which he threw over the wall, and began raising himself in the corner of the wall with as much certainty as if he had cramping irons under his heels and elbows. Half a minute had not elapsed ere he was astride the coping. Cosette looked at him in stupor, without saying a word; for Jean Valjean's mention of the landlady's name had frozen her. All at once she heard Jean Valjean say to her, in a very low voice:

"Lean against the wall."

She obeyed.

"You must not say a word, or feel frightened," he continued.

And she felt herself lifted from the ground. Before she had time to look round she found herself on the top of the wall. Jean Valjean placed her on his back, took her two little hands in his left hand, and crawled along the wall till he reached the cant. As he had suspected, there was a building here, whose roof began at the top of the bastard gate and descended in a gentle slope nearly to the ground, grazing the lime tree. This was a fortunate circumstance, for the wall was much higher on this side than on that of the street, and Jean Valjean could scarce see the ground, so far was it beneath him. He had just reached the sloping roof, and had not yet loosed his hold of the coping, when a violent uproar announced the arrival of the patrol, and he heard Javert's thundering voice:

"Search the blind alley; all the streets are guarded, and I will wager that he is in it."

The soldiers rushed forward. Jean Valjean slipped down the roof, still supporting Cosette, reached the lime tree, and leapt to the ground. Either through terror or courage the child had not uttered a whisper. Her hands were only a little scraped.

CHAPTER LV.

JEAN VALJEAN found himself in a sort of garden, very large and of a most singular appearance, one of those gloomy gardens that appear made to be looked at in winter and by night. This garden was of an oblong shape, with a walk of tall poplars at the end, tall shrubs in the corner, and an unshadowed space, in the centre of which an isolated tree could be distinguished. There were also a few stunted fruit-trees bristling like brambles, vegetable plots, a melon bed whose frames glistened in the moonlight, and an old well. Here and there were stone benches that seemed black with moss; the walks were bordered with small, gloomy-looking, and upright shrubs; grass covered one half of the walks, and a green moss the other half.

Jean Valjean had by his side the building, by help of whose roof he had descended, a pile of faggots, and behind the latter, close to the wall, a stone statue, whose mutilated face was merely a shapeless mask, appearing indistinctly in the darkness. The building was a species of ruin, contain- ing several dismantled rooms, of which one was apparently employed as a shed. The large edifice of the Rue Droit-mur had two façades looking into this garden at right angles, and these façades were even more melancholy than those outside. All the windows were barred, and not a single light could be seen, while at the upper window there were scuttles as in prisons. One of these frontages threw its shadow upon the other, which fell back on the garden like an immense black cloth. No other house could be noticed, and the end of the garden was lost in mist and night. Still, walls could be indistinctly noticed intersecting each other, as if there were other gardens beyond, and the low roofs in the Rue Polonceau. Nothing more stern and solitary than this garden could well be imagined; there was no one in it, as was natural at such an hour, but it did not look as if the spot were made for any one to walk in, even in broad daylight.

Jean Valjean's first care was to find his shoes and stock- ings again and put them on; then he entered the shed with Cosette. A man who is escaping never considers himself sufficiently concealed, and the child, who was still thinking of Madame Thénardier, shared his instinct for concealment. Cosette trembled and clung close to him : for she could hear the tumultuous noise of the patrol searching the street and

lane, the blows of musket-butts against the stones, Javert's
appeals to the men whom he had posted, and his oaths,
mingled with words which could not be distinguished. At
the expiration of a quarter of an hour this species of stormy
grumbling appeared to be retiring, and Jean Valjean could
scarce breathe. He had gently laid his hand on Cosette's
mouth. The solitude in which he found himself was so
strangely calm, however, that the furious uproar so close at
hand did not even cast the shadow of a trouble over it. All
at once, in the midst of this profound calm, a new sound
burst forth ; a heavenly, divine, ineffable sound, as ravishing as the other had been horrible. It was a hymn that
issued from the darkness, a dazzling blending of prayer and
harmony in the dark and fearful silence of the night : female
voices, but composed at once of the pure accent of virgins
and the simple voices of children, such voices as do not
belong to earth, and resemble those which the new-born
still hear, and the dying begin to hear. This chant came
from the gloomy building that commanded the garden, and
at the moment when the noise of the demons was retiring,
it seemed like a choir of angels approaching in the dark.
Cosette and Jean Valjean fell on their knees ; they knew
not what it was, they knew not where they were, but both
man and child, the penitent and the innocent, felt that they
must fall on their knees. The voices had this strangeness
about them, that they did not prevent the edifice from
appearing deserted ; it seemed like a supernatural chant in
an uninhabited house. While the voices sang Jean Valjean
thought of nothing else ; he no longer saw the night, but
an azure sky. He fancied that the wings which we all of
us have within us were expanding in him. The singing
ceased ; it had probably lasted some time, but Jean Valjean
could not have said how long, for hours of ecstasy never
occupy more than a minute. All had become silent again :
there was no sound in the garden, no sound in the street ;
all that which threatened, all that which reassured, had
faded away. The wind shook on the coping of the wall
some dry grass, which produced a soft and mournful sound.

The night wind had risen, which proved that it must be
between one and two in the morning. Cosette said nothing,
and as she was leaning her head against him, Jean Valjean
fancied that she was asleep. He bent down and looked at
her : her eyes were wide open, and she had a pensive look
which hurt Jean Valjean. She was still trembling.

"Are you sleepy?" he asked her.

"I am very cold," she answered; a moment after she continued :

"Is she still there?"

"Who?" Jean Valjean asked.

"Madame Thénardier."

Jean Valjean had forgotten the means he had employed to keep Cosette silent.

"Ah," he said, "she is gone, and you have nothing to fear."

The child sighed, as if a weight had been taken off her chest.

The ground was damp, the shed open on all sides, and the wind grew more cutting every moment. He took off his coat and wrapped Cosette up in it.

"Are you less cold now?" he said.

"Oh! yes, father."

"Well, wait for me a minute."

He went out of the ruin, and began walking along the large building in search of some better shelter. He came to doors, but they were closed, and there were bars on all the ground-floor windows. After passing the inner angle of the edifice he noticed that he had come to some arched windows, and perceived a faint light. He raised himself on tiptoe and looked through one of the windows; they all belonged to a large hall, paved with stones, in which nothing could be distinguished but a little light and great shadows. The light came from a night-lamp burning in the corner. This hall was deserted and nothing was stirring in it, and yet, after a long look, he fancied that he could see on the ground, something that seemed to be covered with a pall and resembled a human form. It was stretched out flat, with its face against the stones, its arms forming a cross, and motionless as death. From a species of snake which dragged along the pavement, it looked as if this sinister form had a rope round its neck. The whole hall was bathed in that mist of badly-lighted places, which intensifies the horror. He had the courage to place his face to the pane, and watch whether the figure would stir; but though he remained for a time, which appeared to him very long, the outstretched form made no movement. All at once he felt himself assailed by an indescribable horror, and he ran off toward the shed without daring to look back; he fancied that if he turned his head he should see the figure walking after him and waving its arms. When he reached the ruin he was panting, his knees gave way, and the perspiration was running down his back. Where was he? Who could have imagined anything like this species of sepulchre in the heart of Paris? What was this strange house? An edifice full of nocturnal mystery, calling souls in the darkness with the voice of angels, and when they arrive, suddenly offering them this frightful vision ; promising to open the bright gate of heaven, and, instead, opening the horrible gate of the tomb! Cold, anxiety, apprehension, and the emotion of the night, brought on him a real fever, and all his ideas were confused in his brain. He went up to Cosette ; she was asleep, with her head upon a stone. He sat down by her side, and began gazing at her ; gradually, as he looked, he grew calm and regained possession of his clearness of mind.

He plainly perceived this truth, the basis of his life henceforth, that, so long as she was there, so long as he had her by his side, he would require nothing except for her, nor fear anything save on her account. He did not even feel the cold particularly, for, though he had taken off his coat, it was to cover her. Still, through the reverie into which he had fallen, he had heard for some time past a singular noise, like a bell being rung, and it was in the garden. It could be heard distinctly, though faintly, and resembled those cattle bells which produce a gentle melody at night in the grazing fields. This noise made Jean Valjean turn, and he saw that there was some one in the garden. A being looking like a man was walking among the melon frames, rising, stooping, and stopping with regular movements, as if he was dragging or stretching out something on the ground. This man was apparently lame. Jean Valjean gave the continual, trembling start of the unhappy ; everything is hostile and suspicious to them ; they distrust the day because it allows them to be seen, and night because it helps in surprising them. Just now he shuddered because the garden was deserted, and now he shuddered because there was some one in it. He fell back from chimerical into real terror. He said to himself that Javert and the police had probably not gone away, that they had, in any case, left watchmen in the street ; and that if this man discovered him he would give an alarm and hand him over to the police. He gently raised the still sleeping Cosette in his arms, and carried her behind a mass of old furniture in the most remote part of the shed. Cosette did not stir. From this spot he observed the movements of the being in the melon bed; the strange thing was that the noise of the bell followed this man's every movement. When he approached, the sound approached; when he went away, the sound went away. If he made a sudden movement a little peal followed the movement, and when he stopped, the noise ceased. It appeared evident that the bell was fastened to this man; but in that case what could be the meaning of it? What was this man to whom a bell was fastened, as if he were a ram or an ox? While asking himself these questions he touched Cosette's hands. They were icy.

"O God!" he said.

Then he said in a whisper,—"Cosette!"

She did not open her eyes. He shook her sharply, but she did not awake.

"Can she be dead?" he said to himself, and he rose shivering from head to foot.

The most frightful thoughts crossed his mind pell-mell. There are moments when hideous suppositions assail us like a band of furies, and violently force the bolts of our brain. When it is a question about people whom we love, our prudence invents all sorts of follies. He remembered that sleep in the open air on a cold night might be mortal. Cosette was lying stretched out motionless at his feet. He listened for her breath; she was breathing, but so faintly that it seemed as if the respiration would cease at any moment. How was he to warm her? how was he to wake her? All that did not refer to this slipped from his mind, and he rushed wildly from the shed. It was absolutely necessary that within a quarter of an hour Cosette should be in bed before a fire.

Jean Valjean walked straight up to the man whom he saw in the garden. He took from his pocket the rouleau of silver. This man was looking down, and did not see him coming, and in a few strides Jean Valjean was by his side, and addressed him with the cry, "One hundred francs."

The man started and raised his eyes.

"One hundred francs to be gained," Jean Valjean continued, "if you will find me a shelter for this night."

The moon fully lit up Jean Valjean's bewildered face.

"Why, it is you, Father Madeleine!" the man said.

This name uttered thus in the darkness at this strange spot, by this strange man, made Jean Valjean recoil, for he expected everything save that. The man who addressed him was a stooping, lame old man, dressed nearly like a peasant, and wearing on his left leg a leathern knee-cap, from which hung a rather large bell. It was impossible to distinguish his face, which was in the shadow; still the man had doffed his bonnet, and said all in a tremor:

"Oh, Lord, how did you get here, Father Madeleine? which way did you come in? Why, you must have fallen from heaven. Well, if ever you do fall, it will be from there. And then, what a state you are in! you have no cravat, no hat, and no coat! do you know that you would have frightened anybody who did not know you? No coat! Oh, my goodness, are the saints going mad at present? But how *did* you get in here?"

One word did not wait for the next. The old man spoke with a rustic volubility in which there was nothing alarming; and it was all said with a mixture of stupefaction and simple kindness.

"Who are you? and what is this house?" Jean Valjean asked.

"Oh, Lord, that is too strong," the old man exclaimed; "why, did you not get me the situation, and in this house too? What, don't you recognise me?"

"No," said Jean Valjean, "and how is it that you know me?"

"You saved my life," the man said.

He turned, a moonbeam played on his face, and Jean Valjean recognised old Fauchelevent.

"Ah!" he said, "it is you; oh, now I recognise you."

"That is lucky," the old man said reproachfully.

"And what are you doing here?" Jean Valjean asked.

"Why! I am covering my melons."

Old Fauchelevent really held in his hand at the moment when Jean Valjean accosted him a piece of matting, which he was engaged in spreading over the melon frame. He had laid a good many pieces during the hour he had been in the garden, and it was this operation that produced the peculiar movements which Jean Valjean had noticed from the shed. He continued:

"I said to myself, there is a bright moon and it is going to freeze, so I had better put these greatcoats on my melons. And," he added, as he looked at Jean Valjean with a grin, "you should have done the same. But how have you got here?"

Jean Valjean, feeling himself known by this man, at least under the name of Madeleine, only advanced cautiously. He multiplied his questions, and, curiously enough, they changed parts,—he, the intruder, became the questioner.

"And what is that bell you have on your knee?"

"That?" Fauchelevent said; "that is so that they may avoid me."

"What on earth do you mean?"

Old Fauchelevent gave an inimitable wink.

"Oh, Lord, there are only women in this house, and lots of girls. It seems that I should be dangerous to meet, and so the bell warns them; when I come, they go."

"What is this house?"

"Oh, nonsense, you know."

"Indeed I do not."

"Why, you got me the gardener's place here."

"Answer me as if I knew nothing."

"Well, it is the convent of the Little Picpus, then."

Jean Valjean's recollections returned to him. Chance, that is to say, Providence, had brought him to the very convent in the Quartier St. Antoine, where Fauchelevent after his accident had been engaged on his recommendation two years back. He repeated, as if speaking to himself:

"Little Picpus!"

"But come, tell me," Fauchelevent continued, "how the deuce did you get in here, Father Madeleine? for though you are a saint, you are a man, and no men are admitted here."

"Why, you are."

"Well, only I."

"And yet," Jean Valjean continued, "I must remain."

"O Lord!" Fauchelevent exclaimed.

Jean Valjean walked up to the gardener and said in a grave voice:

"Fauchelevent, I saved your life."

"I was the first to remember it," Fauchelevent answered.

"Well, you can do for me to-day what I did for you formerly."

Fauchelevent took Jean Valjean's muscular hands in his old, wrinkled, and trembling hands, and for some seconds seemed as if unable to speak. At length he exclaimed:

" Oh ! it would be a blessing from heaven, if I could repay you a slight portion ! Save your life ! M. Madeleine, you can dispose of the old man as you please."

An admirable joy had transfigured the aged gardener, and his face seemed radiant.

" What do you wish me to do ? " he continued.

" I will explain. Have you a room ? "

" I have a cottage, behind the ruins of the old convent, in a corner which no one visits, with three rooms."

" Good," said Jean Valjean ; " now I will ask two things of you."

" What are they, M. Le Maire ? "

" First, that you will tell nobody what you know about me. Second, that you will not try to learn anything further."

" As you please. I know that you can do nothing but what is honest, and that you have ever been a man after God's heart. And then, again, it was you who got me this situation, and I am at your service."

" Enough ; now come with me, and we will go and fetch the child."

" Ah," said Fauchelevent, " there is a child."

He did not add a word, but followed Jean Valjean as a dog follows his master. In less than half an hour, Cosette, who had become rosy again by the heat of a good fire, was asleep in the old gardener's bed. Jean Valjean had put on his cravat and coat again ; his hat, which he had thrown over the wall, had been found and picked up ; and Fauchelevent took off his knee-cap and bell, which now adorned the wall by the side of a door. The two men were seated near the fire at a table on which Fauchelevent had placed a lump of cheese, biscuits, a bottle of wine and two glasses, and the old man said to Jean Valjean as he laid his hand on his knee :

" Ah, Father Madeleine ! you did not know me at first. You save people's lives and forget them afterwards ! Oh ! that is wrong ; for they remember you. You are ungrateful."

CHAPTER LVI.

THE events, the reverse of which, so to speak, we have just seen, had occurred under the simplest conditions. When Jean Valjean, on the night of the day on which Javert arrested him by Fantine's death-bed, broke out of M—— jail, the police supposed that the escaped convict would proceed to Paris. Paris is a maelstrom in which everything is lost and disappears in the whirlpool of the streets : no forest can conceal a man so well as that crowd, and fugitives of every description are aware of the fact. They go to Paris to be swallowed up, for that is at times a mode of safety. The police are aware of this too, and it is at Paris they seek what they have lost elsewhere. They sought there the ex-mayor of M——, and Javert was summoned to assist in the search, and in truth powerfully assisted in recapturing Jean Valjean. The zeal and intelligence he displayed in this office were noticed by M. Chabouillet, Secretary to the Prefecture under Count Anglès, and this gentleman, who had before been a friend to Javert, had the police-inspector of M—— appointed to the Paris district. Here Javert proved himself variously, and—let us say it, though the word seems inappropriate when applied to such services—honourably useful.

He thought no more of Jean Valjean—with these hounds ever on the hunt the wolf of to-day causes the wolf of yesterday to be forgotten,—until in December, 1823, he, who never read newspapers, read one. But Javert, who was a legitimist, was anxious to learn the details of the triumphal entry of the " Prince Generalissimo " into Bayonne. When he had finished the article that interested him, a name—the name of Jean Valjean—at the foot of a column, attracted his attention. The newspaper announced that the convict Jean Valjean was dead, and published the fact in such formal terms that Javert did not doubt it. He musing said, " That is the best bolt," then threw away the paper, and thought no more of the subject. Some time after, it happened that a report was sent by the Prefecture of the Seine et Oise to that of Paris about the abduction of a child, which took place, it was said, under peculiar circumstances, in the parish of Montfermeil. A little girl of seven or eight years of age, who had been entrusted by her mother to a publican in the town, had been stolen by a stranger. The child answered to the name of

Cosette, and her mother was a certain Fantine, who had died in an hospital, it was not known when or where. This report passed under Javert's eyes, and rendered him thoughtful. The name of Fantine was familiar to him : he remembered that Jean Valjean had made him laugh by asking him for a respite of three days to go and fetch this creature's child. He remembered that Jean Valjean was arrested at Paris at the very moment when he was getting into the Montfermeil coach, and some facts had led to the supposition at the time that he had taken a trip to the vicinity of the village on the previous day, for he had not been seen in the village itself. What was his business at Montfermeil ? no one was able to guess ; but Javert now understood it—Fantine's daughter was there, and Jean Valjean had gone to fetch her. Now this child had just been stolen by a stranger ; who could the stranger be ? could it be Jean Valjean ?—but he was dead. Javert, without saying a word to anybody, took the coach at the " Pewter Platter," and took a trip to Montfermeil.

He expected to find a great clearing up there, but only found a great obscurity. At the beginning, the Thénardiers, in their vexation, had chattered, and the disappearance of the Lark produced a sensation in the village. There were at once several versions of the story, which finally settled down into an abduction, and hence the police report. Still, after he had got over his first outburst of temper, Thénardier, with his admirable instinct, very speedily comprehended that it is never useful to set the authorities at work, and that his complaint about the abduction of Cosette would have the primary result of fixing the flashing gaze of justice upon himself, and many dark matters he was mixed up in. The thing that owls least like is to have a candle brought to them. And then, again, how would he get out of the fifteen hundred francs which he had received ? He stopped short, put a gag in his wife's mouth, and affected amazement when people spoke about " the stolen child." He did not at all understand ; he had certainly complained at the first moment about his little darling being taken from him so suddenly ; he should have liked to keep her for two or three days longer through affection ; but it was her grandfather who had come to fetch her in the most natural way in the world. He added the " grandfather," which produced a good effect, and it was on this story that Javert fell upon reaching Montfermeil : the grandfather caused Jean Valjean to fade out of

memory. Javert, however, drove a few questions like probes
into Thénardier's story : " Who was this grandfather, and
what was his name ? " Thénardier answered simply, " He
is a rich farmer ; 1 saw his passport, and I fancy his name
was M. Guillaume Lambert." Lambert is a respectable and
most reassuring name, and so Javert returned to Paris.
"Jean Valjean is really dead," he said to himself, " and I
am a fool."

He was beginning to forget the whole affair again, when
in the course of March, 1824, he heard talk of an odd
character who lived in the parish of St. Medard, and was
surnamed the "beggar who gives alms." This man was
said to be an annuitant, whose name no one exactly knew,
and who lived alone with a little girl eight years old, who
knew nothing about herself, except that she came from
Montfermeil. Montfermeil ! that name constantly returned,
and made Javert prick up his ears. An old begging spy,
an ex-beadle, to whom this person was very charitable,
added a few more details. "He was a very unsociable
person ; he never went out till night ; he spoke to nobody,
except to the poor now and then, and let no one approach
him. He wore a horrible old yellow coat, which was worth
several millions, as it was lined all through with bank-
notes." This decidedly piqued Javert's curiosity. In order
to see this annuitant closer without startling him, he one
day borrowed the beadle's rags and the place where the old
spy crouched every evening, snuffling his orisons through
his nose, and spying between his prayers. "The suspicious
individual" really came up to Javert, thus travestied, and
gave him alms. At this moment Javert raised his head,
and the shock which Jean Valjean received on fancying that
he recognised Javert, Javert received on fancying that he
recognised Jean Valjean. Still, the darkness might have
deceived him ; and Jean Valjean's death was official.
Javert felt serious doubts, and when in doubt, Javert, a
scrupulous man, never collared anybody. He followed his
man to No. 50-52, and made the old woman talk, which
was no difficult task. She confirmed the fact of the greatcoat lined with millions, and told the story about the
thousand-franc note ; she had seen it ! she had felt it ! Javert
hired a room, and took possession of it that same night.
He listened at the door of the mysterious lodger, in the hope
of hearing his voice, but Jean Valjean saw his candle
through the keyhole, and baulked the spy by keeping silence.

On the following day, Jean Valjean decamped, but the
noise of the five-franc piece which he let drop was noticed
by the old woman, who supposed that he was about to
leave, and hastened to forewarn Javert. Hence, when Jean
Valjean left the house at night, Javert was waiting for him
behind the trees with two men. Javert had requested
assistance at the Prefecture, but had not mentioned the
name of the individual whom he hoped to seize. That was
his secret, and he kept it for three reasons : first, because
the slightest indiscretion might give Jean Valjean the
alarm ; next, because laying hands on an old escaped
convict, supposed to be dead, a condemned man whom
justice had already classified for ever among "the malefactors of the most dangerous class," was a magnificent
success, which the older policemen of Paris would certainly
not leave to a new-comer like Javert—and he was afraid lest
he might be robbed of his galley-slave ; lastly, because
Javert, having artistic tastes, was fond of anything unexpected. He hated those successes which are deflowered
by being talked of a long time beforehand ; and he liked to
elaborate his masterpieces in the darkness, and suddenly
unveil them. Javert followed Jean Valjean from tree to
tree, and then from street corner to street corner, and had
not once taken his eye off him ; even at the moment when
Jean Valjean fancied himself the safest, Javert's eye was
upon him. Why did Javert not arrest him, though ?
Because he was still in doubt. It must be borne in mind
that, at this period, the police were not exactly at their ease,
and the free press annoyed them. A few arbitrary arrests,
denounced by the newspapers, had found an echo in the
Chambers, and rendered the Prefecture timid. Attacking
individual liberty was a serious matter; the agents were
afraid of being deceived, for the Prefect made them answer-
able, and a mistake was dismissal. Just imagine the effect
which would have been produced in Paris by the following
short paragraph reproduced by twenty papers: "Yesterday,
an old, white-haired grandfather, a respectable fund-holder,
who was taking a walk with his granddaughter, eight
years of age, was arrested and taken to the House of
Detention, as an escaped convict." Let us repeat also that
Javert had scruples of his own ; the warnings of his
conscience were added to those of the Prefect, and he really
doubted. Jean Valjean had his back turned to him, and
was walking in the dark ; sorrow, anxiety, despondency,

the fresh misfortune of being compelled to fly by night and seek a chance refuge for Cosette and himself in Paris, the necessity of regulating his pace by that of a child—all this had unconsciously changed Jean Valjean's demeanour, and imparted to him such a senility, that the very police, incarnated in Javert, might be deceived, and were deceived. The impossibility of approaching close, his attire as an old emigré tutor, Thénardier's statement which made him out a grandpapa, and, lastly, the belief in his death at the galleys, added to the uncertainty that clouded Javert's mind. For a moment he had the idea of suddenly asking for his papers; but, if the man was not Jean Valjean, and if he were not a respectable fund-holder, he was, in all probability, some fellow deeply entangled in the meshes of Parisian crime; some leader of a band who gave alms to hide his other talents, and who had his "pals," his accomplices, and his lurking-places, where he could conceal himself. All the turnings this man made in the streets seemed to indicate that all was not quite right with him, and arresting him too quickly would be "killing the goose with the golden eggs." Where was the harm of waiting? Javert felt quite certain that he could not escape. He walked along, therefore, in great perplexity, asking himself a hundred questions about this enigmatical personage. It was not till some time after that he decidedly recognised Jean Valjean in the Rue Pontoise, by the bright light that streamed from a wine shop.

There are in the world only two beings that quiver profoundly,—the mother who recovers her child, and the tiger who finds his prey again. Javert suffered the same quiver. So soon as he had positively recognised Jean Valjean, the formidable convict, he noticed that he had only two companions, and asked for support at the police office in the Rue Pontoise. Before catching hold of a thorn bush, people put on gloves. This delay and the halt at the Rollin Square to arrange with his agents, all but made him lose the trail, but he quickly guessed that Jean Valjean wished to place the river between himself and his hunters. He hung his head and reflected, like a bloodhound putting its nose to the ground to lift the scent, and then, with the powerful correctness of his instinct, walked to the Austerlitz bridge. One remark of the toll-collector's put him on his track. "Have you seen a man with a little girl?" "I made him pay two sous," the collector answered. Javert

reached the bridge just in time to see Jean Valjean leading
Cosette across the moonlit square; he saw him enter the
Rue du Chemin Vert St. Antoine; he thought of the blind
alley arranged there like a trap, and the sole issue from it
by the little Rue Picpus; and in order to stop the earth, as
sportsmen say, he sent off a policeman by a detour to guard
the issue. A patrol, which was returning to the arsenal,
happening to pass, he requested its assistance, for in such
games as this soldiers are trumps, and, moreover, it is a
principle that, in forcing a boar from its lair, the hunter
must be scientific, and there must be a strong pack of
hounds. These arrangements made, Javert, feeling that
Jean Valjean was caught between the blind alley on the
right, his own agent on the left, and himself behind, took
a pinch of snuff. Then he began playing and enjoying a
delicious and infernal moment; he let his man go before him,
knowing that he had him, but desiring to defer as long as
possible the moment of arresting him; delighted at feeling
him caught, and at seeing him free, and watching him with
the pleasure of the spider that lets the fly flutter for a
while, and the cat that lets the mouse run. The paw and
the talon have a monstrous sensuality in the fluttering
movements of the animal imprisoned in their grasp; what
a delight such a strangling must be! Javert was playing;
the meshes of his net were so solidly made, he was certain
of success, and now he only needed to close his hand.
Accompanied as he was, the very idea of resistance was impossible, however energetic, vigorous, and desperate Jean
Valjean might be.

Javert advanced slowly, examining and searching every
corner of the street, as he would the pockets of a thief; but
when he reached the centre of the web he did not find his
fly. One can imagine his exasperation. He questioned
his watchmen, but they quietly declared that they had not
seen the man pass.

Even at the moment, however, when Javert perceived
that Jean Valjean had slipped from his clutches he did not
lose his head. Certain that the convict could not be very
far off, he established watches, organised mousetraps and
ambuscades, and beat up the quarter the whole night
through. The first thing he saw was the cut cord of the
lanthorn. This was a valuable sign, which, however, led
him astray so far that it made him turn all his attention to
the Genrot blind alley. There are in this alley low walls,

surrounding gardens which skirt open fields, and Jean Valjean had evidently fled in that direction. The truth is, that if he had gone a little further down the blind alley he would, in all probability, have done so and been a lost man. Javert explored the gardens and fields as if looking for a needle, and at daybreak he left two intelligent men on duty, and returned to the Prefecture of the Police, crestfallen as a spy who has been caught by a thief.

CHAPTER LVII.

HALF a century ago nothing more resembled the most ordinary *porte-cochère* than that of No. 62 Petite Rue Picpus. This door, generally half open in the most inviting manner, allowed you to see two things which are not of a very mournful nature—a courtyard with walls covered with vines, and the face of a lounging porter. Above the bottom wall tall trees could be seen, and, when a sunbeam enlivened the yard, and a glass of wine had enlivened the porter, it was difficult to pass before No. 62 and not carry away a pleasant thought. And yet, you had had a glimpse of a very gloomy place. The threshold smiled, but the house prayed and wept. It was the convent of the Perpetual Adoration.

This convent, which had existed for many years prior to 1824 in the Rue Picpus, was a community of Bernardines belonging to the Obedience of Martin Verga. These Bernardines, consequently, were not attached to Clairvaux, like other Bernardines, but to Citeaux, like the Benedictines. In other words, they were subjects, not of St. Bernard, but of St. Benedict.

Next to the rules of the Carmelites, who walk barefoot, wear a piece of wicker-work on their throat, and never sit down, the hardest rules are those of the Bernardo-Benedictines of Martin Verga. They are dressed in black with a wimple, which, by the express order of St. Benedict, comes up to the chin; a serge gown with wide sleeves, a large woollen veil, the wimple cut square on the chest, and the coif, which comes down to their eyes—such is their dress. All is black, excepting the coif, which is white. Novices wear the same garb, but all white, while the professed nuns also wear a rosary by their side.

The Bernardo-Benedictines of this Obedience abstain from

meat the whole year ; fast all Lent, and on many other days, special to themselves ; get up in their first sleep, from one to three o'clock in the morning in order to read their breviary and chant matins ; sleep in serge sheets at all seasons, and on straw ; never bathe or light fires ; chastise themselves every Friday ; observe the rule of silence ; only speak during recreation, which is very short, and wear coarse flannel chemises for six months, from 14th September, which is the Exaltation of the Holy Cross, up to Easter. These six months are a moderation—the rule says all the year, but the flannel chemise, insupportable in the heat of summer, produced fevers and nervous spasms. Even with this relief, when the nuns put on the flannel chemise on 14th September, they suffer from fever for three or four days. Obedience, poverty, chastity, perseverance—such are their vows, which are greatly aggravated by the rule. The prioress is elected for three years by mothers, called " Mères Vocales," because they have a voice in the Chapter. She can be only re-elected twice, which fixes the longest possible reign of a prioress at nine years. They never see the officiating priest, who is hidden from them by a green baize curtain nine feet high. At the sermon, when the preacher is in the chapel, they draw their veil over their face ; they must always speak low, and walk with their eyes fixed on the ground. Only one man is allowed to enter the convent, and he is the Diocesan Archbishop. There is certainly another, who is the gardener ; but he is always an aged man, and in order that he may be constantly alone in the garden, and that the nuns may avoid him, a bell is fastened to his knee. The nuns must display absolute and passive submission to the prioress, and it is canonical subjection in all its self-denial. Each of them performs in turn what they call the " reparation." This reparation is a prayer for all the sins, faults, irregularities, violations, iniquities, and crimes performed upon earth. For twelve consecutive hours, from four in the evening till four the next morning, the sister who performs the reparation remains on her knees, on the stone before the Holy Sacrament, with her hands clasped, and a rope round her neck. When the fatigue becomes insupportable she prostrates herself with her face on the ground, and her arms forming a cross,—that is her sole relief. In this attitude she prays for all the guilty in the world ; it is a grand, almost a sublime idea. As this act is accomplished in front of a stake on the top of which a wax candle is burning, it is called either "making reparation," or "being at the stake." The nuns through humility, indeed, prefer the latter expression, which contains an idea of punishment and abasement. Making reparation is a function in which the whole soul is absorbed; the sister at the stake would not turn round were a thunderbolt to fall behind her. Moreover, there is always a nun on her knees before the Holy Sacrament; this station lasts an hour, and they relieve each other like sentries. That is the Perpetual Adoration.

The prioress and mothers nearly all have names imprinted with peculiar gravity, recalling, not saints and martyrs, but the incidents in the life of the Saviour—such as Mother Nativity, Mother Conception, Mother Presentation, and Mother Passion; still the names of saints are not interdicted. When you see them, you never see more of them than their mouth; and they all have yellow teeth, for a tooth-brush never entered the convent. Cleaning the teeth is the first rung of the ladder, at the foot of which is "losing the soul." They do not call anything "mine"; they have nothing of their own, and must not be attached to anything. They say "our" of everything, thus: our veil, our beads. No one must lock herself in under any pretence, or have a room of her own, and they live with open doors. When they pass each other, one says, "The most Holy Sacrament of the Altar be blessed and adored," and the other answers, "For ever." There is the same ceremony when one sister raps at another sister's door; the door has scarce been touched, ere a gentle voice was heard saying hurriedly from within, "For ever." Like all practices, this one becomes mechanical through habit; and a sister will sometimes say "For ever," before the other has had time to utter the long sentence, "The most holy Sacrament of the Altar be blessed and adored!" Among the Visitandines, the one who enters says "Ave Maria," to which the other replies, "Gratiâ plena"; this is their greeting, which is truly full of grace. At each hour of the day, three supplementary strokes are struck on the chapel bell, and at this signal, prioress, vocal mothers, professed nuns, lay sisters, novices, and postulants, break off what they are saying, doing, or thinking, and all repeat together—if it be five o'clock, for instance—"At five o'clock, and at every hour, may the most Holy Sacrament of the Altar be blessed and adored," and so on according to the hour. This custom, which is intended to break off thoughts and ever lead them back to God, exists in many communities, the form alone varying. Thus, at the Infant Jesus, they say, "At the present hour, and at every hour, may the love of Jesus inflame my heart!"

The Bernardo-Benedictines of Martin Verga sing the offices to a grave, full chant, and always in a loud voice, during the whole of the service. Whenever there is an asterisk in the missal, they pause, and say in a low voice, "Jesus, Marie, Joseph." In the service for the dead they employ such a deep note, that female voices can scarce descend to it, and there results from it a striking and tragical effect. The sisters of Little Picpus had a vault under their high altar for the burial of their community, but the Government, as they call it, would not allow coffins to be placed in this vault, and they therefore left the convent when they were dead; this afflicted and consternated them like an infraction. They had obtained the slight consolation of being buried at a special hour and in a special corner of the old Vaugirard Cemetery, which was established in a field that had once belonged to the community.

When a nun is summoned to the parlour, even if she be the prioress, she pulls down her veil in such a way as only to show her mouth. The prioress alone can communicate with strangers: the others can only see their nearest relations, and that very rarely. If by chance a person from the outer world requests to see a nun whom she had formerly known or loved, a lengthened negotiation is required. If it be a woman, the permission may possibly be granted. The nun comes and is spoken to through the shutters, which are only opened for a mother or a sister. We need hardly say that permission is never granted to men.

Such is the rule of St. Benedict, aggravated by Martin Verga. These nuns are not gay, rosy, and fresh, as we find sometimes in other orders: they are pale and serious. Between 1825 and 1830 three of them went mad.

At the period when this story is laid, there was a boarding-school attached to the convent, the pupils being young ladies of noble birth, and generally rich. Among them could be noticed Mlles de Ste Aulaire and de Bélisseu, and an English girl, bearing the illustrious Catholic name of Talbot. These young ladies, educated by the nuns between four walls, grew up with a horror of the world and of the century. One of them said to us one day, "Seeing the street pavement made me shudder from head to foot."

They were dressed in blue with a white cap, and a Holy Ghost, in silver or copper gilt, on the chest. On certain high festivals, especially Saint Martha's day, they were allowed, as a high favour and supreme happiness, to dress themselves like nuns, and perform the offices and practices of St. Benedict for the whole day. At first the nuns lent them their black robes, but this was deemed a profanity, and the prioress forbade it, so the novices alone were permitted to make such loans. It is remarkable that these representations, doubtless tolerated in the convent through a secret spirit of proselytism, and in order to give their children some foretaste of the sacred dress, were a real happiness and true recreation for the boarders. They were amused by them, for "it was a novelty and changed them," —candid reasons of children, which do not succeed, however, in making us worldly-minded people understand the felicity of holding a holy-water brush in one's hand, and standing for hours before a lectern and singing quartettes. The pupils conformed to all the practices of the convent, though not to all the austerities.

For all this, though, the young ladies filled this grave house with delightful reminiscences. At certain hours childhood sparkled in this cloister. The bell for recreation was rung, the gate creaked on its hinges, and the birds whispered to each other, "Here are the children." An irruption of youth inundated this garden, which with its cross walks resembled a pall. Radiant faces, white foreheads, ingenuous eyes, full of gay light—all sorts of dawn —spread through the gloom. After the psalm-singing, the bell-ringing, and the services, the noise of girls, softer than the buzzing of bees, suddenly burst out. The hive of joy opened, and each brought her honey ; they played, they called each other, they formed groups, and ran about ; pretty little white teeth chattered at corners ; in the distance veils watched the laughter, shadows guarded the beams— but what matter ! they were radiant, and laughed. These four mournful walls had their moment of radiance ; vaguely whitened by the reflection of so much joy, they watched this gentle buzzing of the swarm. It was like a shower of roses falling on this mourning. The girls sported beneath the eye of the nuns, for the glance of impeccability does not disturb innocence ; and, thanks to these children, there was a simple hour among so many austere hours. The little girls jumped about and the elder danced, and nothing could be so ravishing and august as all the fresh, innocent expansion of these childish souls.

The refectory, a large, rectangular room, which only received light through an arched window, looking on the garden, was gloomy and damp, and its only door opened on the garden. Two narrow tables, with wooden benches on each side, formed two long parallel lines from one end to the other of the refectory. The walls were white, the tables black; for these two mourning colours are the sole variations in convents. The meals were poor, and the food of even the children scanty. A single plate of meat and vegetables or salt-fish was the height of luxury. This ordinary, reserved for the boarders alone, was, however, an exception. The children ate and held their tongues under the guardianship of the mother of the week, who, from time to time, if a fly dared to move or buzz contrary to regulation, noisily opened and closed a wooden book. This silence was seasoned with the *Lives of the Saints*, read aloud from a little desk standing at the foot of the crucifix, the reader being a grown-up pupil, appointed for the week. At regular distances on the bare table there were earthenware bowls, in which the pupils themselves washed their cups and forks and spoons, and sometimes threw in a piece of hard meat or spoiled fish, but this was severely punished. Any child who broke the silence made a cross with her tongue. Where? On the ground. She licked the stones. Dust, that finale of all joys, was ordered to chastise these poor little rosebuds that were guilty of prattling.

They played in a garden walk, bordered by a few stunted fruit trees. In spite of the extreme watch and the severity of the punishment, when the wind shook the trees they at times succeeded in picking up furtively a green apple, or a spoiled apricot, or a wasp-inhabited pear. I will here let a letter speak which I have before me, a letter written by an ex-boarder five-and-twenty years ago, who is now the Duchesse de ——, and one of the most elegant women in Paris. I quote exactly. "We hide our pear or our apple, as we can. When we go up to lay our veil on the bed before supper we thrust it under a pillow, and eat it at night in bed, and when that is not possible we eat it in the ——." This was one of their liveliest pleasures. On one occasion, at a period when the archbishop was paying a visit at the convent, one of the young ladies, Mademoiselle

Bouchard, who was related to the Montmorencys, laid a wager that she would ask him for a holiday, an enormity in such an austere community. The wager was taken, but not one of those who took it believed in it. When the moment arrived for the archbishop to pass before the boarders, Mlle Bouchard, to the indescribable horror of her companions, stepped out of the ranks and said, "Monseigneur, a holiday." Mademoiselle Bouchard was fresh and tall, and had the prettiest pink-and-white face in the world. M. de Quélen smiled, and said, "What, my dear child, a day's holiday! three, if you like. I grant three days." The prioress could do nothing, as the archbishop had said it. It was a scandal for the convent, but a joyful thing for the school. Just imagine the effect.

There were within the walls of Little Picpus three perfectly distinct buildings—the great convent, inhabited by the nuns, the schoolhouse, in which the boarders were lodged, and, lastly, what was called the little convent. The latter was a house with a garden, in which all sorts of old nuns of various orders, the remains of convents broken up in the Revolution, dwelt in common; a reunion of all the black, white, and gray. The church, so built as to separate the great convent from the school, was, of course, common to the school, the great and little convents. The public were even admitted by a sort of quarantine entrance from the street : but everything was so arranged that not one of the inhabitants of the convent could see a single face from the outer world. Imagine a church whose choir was seized by a gigantic hand, and crushed so as no longer to form, as in ordinary chapels, a prolongation behind the altar, but a sort of obscure cavern on the side of the officiating priest ; imagine this hall closed by the green baize curtain to which we have referred ; pile up in the shade of this curtain upon wooden seats the nuns on the left, the boarders on the right, and the lay sisters and novices at the end, and you will have some idea of the Little Picpus nuns attending divine service. This cavern, which was called the choir, communicated with the convent by a covered way, and the church obtained its light from the garden. When the nuns were present at those services at which their rule commanded silence, the public were only warned of their presence by the sound of the seats being noisily raised and dropped.

During the six years between 1819 and 1825 the prioress of Little Picpus was Mademoiselle de Blémeur, called in religion Mother Innocent. She belonged to the family of that Marguerite de Blémeur, who was authoress of the *Lives of the Saints of the Order of St. Benedict.* She was a lady of about sixty years, short, stout, and with a voice "like a cracked pot," says the letter from which we have already quoted ; but she was an excellent creature, the only merry soul in the convent, and on that account adored. She followed in the footsteps of her ancestress Marguerite, the Dacier of the Order ; she was lettered, learned, competent, versed in the curiosities of history, stuffed with Latin, Greek, and Hebrew, and more a monk than a nun. The sub-prioress was an old Spanish nun, almost blind, Mother Cineres.

The nuns were kind to the children, and only stern to themselves ; there were no fires lit except in the school-house, and the food there was luxurious when compared with that of the convent. The only thing was that when a child passed a nun and spoke to her, the latter did not answer. This rule of silence produced the result, that in the whole convent language was withdrawn from human creatures and given to inanimate objects. At one moment it was the church bell that spoke, at another the gardener's ; and a very sonorous gong, placed by the side of the sister porter, and which could be heard all through the house, indicated by various raps, which were a sort of acoustic telegraphy, all the actions of natural life which had to be accomplished, and summoned a nun, if required, to the parlour. Each person and each thing had its raps : the prioress had one and one ; the sub-prioress one and two ; six-five announced school hour, so that the pupils talked of going to six-five. Nineteen strokes announced a great event—it was the opening of the cloister door, a terrible iron plate all bristling with bolts, which only turned on its hinges before the archbishop. With the exception of that dignitary and the gardener, no other man entered the convent, but the boarders saw two others—one was the chaplain, Abbé Banès, an ugly old man, whom they were allowed to contemplate through a grating ; while the other was M. Ansiaux, the drawing-master, whom the letter, which we have already quoted, calls "M. Anciot," and describes as an odious old hunchback. So we see that all the men were picked.

Such was this curious house.

After sketching its moral features, it may not be

time lost to indicate in a few words its material configuration, of which the reader already possesses some idea.

The convent of the Little Picpus occupied a large trapeze, formed by the four streets to which we have so frequently alluded, and which surrounded it like a moat. The convent was composed of several buildings and a garden. The main building, regarded in its entirety, was a juxtaposition of hybrid constructions, which, looked at from a balloon, would very exactly form a gallows laid on the ground. The long arm of the gallows occupied the whole of the Rue Droit-Mur, comprised between the Little Rue Picpus and the Rue Polonceau, while the shorter arm was a tall, gray, stern, grated façade, looking on the Little Rue Picpus, of which the *porte-cochère*, No. 62, was the extremity. Toward the centre of this façade dust and ashes whitened an old low-arched gate, where the spiders made their webs, and which was only opened for an hour or two on Sundays, and on the rare occasions when the coffin of a nun left the convent; this was the public entrance to the church. The elbow of the gallows was a square room, used as an office, and which the nuns called the "buttery." In the long arm were the cells of the mothers, sisters, and novices; in the short one the kitchens, the refectory, along which a cloister ran, and the church. Between No. 62 and the corner of Aumarais lane was the school, which could not be seen from the exterior. The rest of the trapeze formed the garden, which was much lower than the level of the Rue Polonceau, and this caused the walls to be much loftier inside than out. The garden, which was slightly arched, had at its centre and on the top of a mound a fine-pointed and conical fir-tree, from which ran, as from the boss of a shield, four large walks, with eight smaller ones arranged two and two, so that, had the enclosure been circular, the geometrical plan of the walks would have resembled a cross laid upon a wheel. The walks, which all ran to the extremely irregular walls of the garden, were of unequal length, and were bordered by gooseberry bushes. At the end a poplar walk ran from the ruins of the old convent, which was at the angle of the Rue Droit-Mur, to the little convent, which was at the corner of the Aumarais lane. In front of the little convent was what was called the small garden. If we add to this *ensemble* a courtyard, all sorts of varying angles formed by the inside buildings, prison walls,

and the long black line of roofs that ran along the other
side of the Rue Polonceau, as the sole prospect, we can
form an exact idea of what the house of the Bernardines of
Little Picpus was five-and-forty years ago.

CHAPTER LVIII.

It was into this house that Jean Valjean had as Fauchelevent said, "fallen from heaven." He had climbed the
garden wall which formed the angle of the Rue Polonceau.
The hymn of angels which he heard in the middle of the
night was the nuns chanting matins; the hall of which
he had caught a glimpse in the darkness was the
chapel; the phantom he had seen stretched out on the
ground was the sister making reparation; and the bell
which had so strangely surprised him was the gardener's
bell fastened to Fauchelevent's knee. So soon as Cosette
was in bed, Jean Valjean and Fauchelevent supped on a
glass of wine and a lump of cheese before a good blazing
log; then, as the only bed in the cottage was occupied by
Cosette, each threw himself on a truss of straw. Before
closing his eyes Jean Valjean said, "I must stop here
henceforth," and this remark trotted about Fauchelevent's
head all night. In fact, neither of them slept; Jean
Valjean, feeling himself discovered and Javert on his
track, understood that he and Cosette were lost if they
entered Paris. Since the new blast of wind had blown him
into this convent, Jean Valjean had but one thought—that
of remaining in it. Now, for a wretch in his position, this
convent was at once the most dangerous and the safest
place;—the most dangerous, because as no man was
allowed to enter it, if he were discovered it would be a
crime, and Jean Valjean would only take one step from the
convent to the prison; the safest, because if he succeeded
in remaining in it, who would come to seek him there?
Inhabiting an impossible spot was salvation.

For his part, Fauchelevent racked his brains. He began
by declaring to himself that he understood nothing. How
did M. Madeleine come there, with such walls?—and
convent walls cannot be passed at a stride. How was he
here with a child? People do not scale a perpendicular
wall with a child in their arms. Who was this child?
Where did they both come from? Since Fauchelevent had

been in the convent he had received no news from M——
sur M——, and did not know what had occurred there.
Father Madeleine had that look which discourages
questioning, and moreover, Fauchelevent said to himself:
"A saint is not to be cross-questioned." It was only from
a few words which escaped Jean Valjean, that the gardener
fancied he could come to the conclusion that M. Madeleine
had probably been made bankrupt by the hard times, and
was pursued by his creditors; or else, he was compromised
in a political affair and was in hiding, which idea did not
displease Fauchelevent, because, like most of the peasants
in the north of France, he was a staunch Bonapartist.
M. Madeleine had chosen the convent as his asylum, and
it was simple that he should wish to remain there. But
the inexplicable thing, to which Fauchelevent constantly
recurred and which addled his brains, was that M.
Madeleine was here, and here with this child. Fauchelevent saw them, touched them, spoke to them, and did
not believe it. The gardener was stumbling among conjectures and saw nothing clear but this, " M. Madeleine
saved my life." This sole certainty was sufficient, and
decided him; he said to himself, " It is my turn now."
He added in his conscience, " M. Madeleine did not
deliberate long when he had to get under the cart to save
me," and he decided upon saving M. Madeleine. He,
however, asked himself several questions, to which he
gave divers answers. "After what he did for me, should
I save him, if he were a robber? just the same. If he
were an assassin, would I save him? just the same. Since
he is a saint, shall I save him? just the same."

What a problem it was, though, to enable him to remain
in the convent! Still, Fauchelevent did not recoil before
this almost chimerical attempt; this poor Picard peasant,
who had no other ladder but his devotion, his goodwill,
and a small stock of old rustic craft, this time turned to a
generous purpose, undertook to scale the impossibilities of
the convent, and the rough escarpments of the rule of
St. Benedict. Fauchelevent was an old man, who had
been selfish throughout his life, and who, at the end of his
days, limping, infirm, and taking no interest in the world,
found it pleasant to be grateful, and seeing a virtuous
action to be done, he flung himself upon it like a man
who, on the point of death, lays his hand on a glass of
good wine which he had never tasted, and eagerly drinks

it off. We may add, that the air which he had been
breathing for some years in this convent, had destroyed his
personality, and had eventually rendered some good deed
a necessity for him. He, therefore, formed the resolution
of devoting himself for M. Madeleine. We have just
called him a "poor Picard peasant"; the qualification is
correct but incomplete. At the present stage of our story
a little physiological examination of Father Fauchelevent
becomes useful. He was a peasant, but he had been a
notary, which added chicanery to his cunning, and penetration to his simplicity. Having, through various reasons,
failed in his business, he descended from a notary to be a
carter and day-labourer; but in spite of the oaths and
lashes necessary for horses, as it seems, something of the
notary had clung to him. Fauchelevent, in fact, belonged
to that species which the impertinent and light vocabulary
of the last century qualified as "a bit of a rustic and a bit
of a townsman; pepper and salt." Fauchelevent, though
sorely tried, and much worn by fate, a sort of poor old
threadbare soul, was still a man to act on the first impulse,
and spontaneously; a precious quality which prevents a
man from ever being wicked. His defects and vices, for
he had such, were on the surface, and altogether his
physiognomy was one of those which please the observer.
His old face had none of those ugly wrinkles on the top of
the forehead which signify wickedness or stupidity. At
daybreak, after thinking enormously, Father Fauchelevent
opened his eyes and saw M. Madeleine sitting on his truss
of straw, and looking at the sleeping Cosette; Fauchelevent sat up too, and said:

"Now that you are here, how will you manage to get
in?" This remark summed up the situation, and aroused
Jean Valjean from his reverie. The two men held counsel.

"In the first place," said Fauchelevent, "you must
begin by not setting foot outside this cottage, neither you
nor the little one. One step in the garden and we are done."

"That is true."

"Monsieur Madeleine," Fauchelevent continued, "you
have arrived at a very lucky moment; I ought to say, a
very unhappy one; there is one of our ladies dangerously
ill. In consequence of this folk will not look much this
way. It seems that she is dying, and the forty-hour
prayers are being said. The whole community is aroused,
and that occupies them. The person who is on the point

of going off is a saint. In fact, though, we are all saints here; the only difference between them and me is that they say 'our cell,' and I say 'my cottage.' There will be a service for the dying, and then the service for the dead. For to-day we shall be all quiet here; but I do not answer for to-morrow."

"Still," Jean Valjean observed, "this cottage is retired; it is hidden by a sort of ruin; there are trees, and it cannot be seen from the convent."

"And I may add that the nuns never approach it."

"Well?" Jean Valjean asked.

The interrogation that marked this "well" signified, "I fancy that we can remain concealed here," and it was to this interrogation that Fauchelevent replied.

"There are the little ones."

"What little ones?" Jean Valjean asked.

As Fauchelevent opened his mouth to answer, a stroke rang out from a bell.

"The nun is dead," he said; "there is the knell."

And he made Jean Valjean a sign to listen. A second stroke rang out.

"It is the passing bell, Monsieur Madeleine. The bell will go on so minute after minute for twenty-four hours, till the body leaves the church. You see they play about; at recreations they need only lose a ball, and, in spite of the prohibition, they will come and look for it here and ransack everything. Those cherubs are little devils."

"Who?" Jean Valjean asked.

"The little ones; I can tell you that you would soon be discovered. They would cry out, 'Why, it's a man!' But there is no danger to-day, for there will be no re-creation. The day will be spent in prayer. You hear the bell, as I told you, one stroke a minute—it is the knell."

"I understand, Father Fauchelevent; they are boarders."

And Jean Valjean thought to himself:

"It is a chance for educating Cosette."

Fauchelevent exclaimed:

"By Job, I should think they are boarders! they would sniff round you, and then run away. To be a man here is to have the plague, as you can see; a bell is fastened to my paw as if I were a wild beast."

Jean Valjean reflected more and more deeply. "This convent would save us," he muttered, and then added aloud:

"Yes, the difficulty is to remain."

" No," said Fauchelevent, " it is to go out."

Jean Valjean felt the blood rush back to his heart.

" Go out ? "

" Yes, M. Madeleine, in order to come in, you must go out."

And, after waiting till a knell had died out in air, Fauchelevent continued :

" You must not be found here like that. Where do you come from ? for me, you fall from heaven, because I know you, but the nuns require that people should come in by the front door."

All at once a complicated ringing of another bell could be heard.

" Ah ! " said Fauchelevent, " the vocal mothers are being summoned to a Chapter—a Chapter is always held when any one dies. She died at daybreak, and they generally die at daybreak. But can't you go out by the way that you came in ? Come, I don't want to ask you a question —but where did you come in ? "

Jean Valjean turned pale : the mere idea of going back to that formidable street made him tremble.

" Impossible ! " he said. " Suppose, Father Fauchelevent, that I really fell from above."

" Why, I believe so," Fauchelevent continued ; " you need not tell me so. Well, there is another peal ; it is to tell the porter to go and warn the municipal authorities that they should send and inform the physician of the dead, so that he may come and see there is a dead woman here. All that is the ceremony of dying. The good ladies are not very fond of such visits, for a doctor believes in nothing ; he raises the veil, and sometimes raises something else. What a hurry they have been in to warn the doctor this time ! What is up, I wonder ? Your little girl is still asleep ; what is her name ? "

" Cosette."

" Is she your daughter ? I mean, are you her grandfather ? "

" Yes."

" To get her out will be easy. I have my special door, which opens into the yard ; I knock, the porter opens. I have my dorser on my back, with the little girl in it, and go out. You will tell her to be very quiet, and she will be under the hood. I will leave her for the necessary time with an old friend of mine, a fruiteress in the Rue du

Chemin Vert, who is deaf, and where there is a little bed.
I will shout in her ear that it is my niece, and bid her
keep her for me till to-morrow; then the little one will
come in with you, for I mean to bring you in again. But
how will you manage to get out?"

Jean Valjean shook his head.

"The great point is that no one sees me, Father Fauchelevent. Find means to get me out in the same way as Cosette."

Fauchelevent scratched the tip of his ear with the middle
finger of his left hand, which was a sign of serious embarrassment. A third peal caused a diversion.

"That is the doctor going away," said Fauchelevent.
"He has had a look and said, 'She is dead, all right.'
When the doctor has countersigned the passport for
Paradise, the undertakers send a coffin. If it is a mother,
the mothers put her in it; if a sister, the sisters; and after
that I nail up. That is part of my gardening, for a
gardener is a bit of a gravedigger. A box is brought,
in which there is nothing, and it is carried off with something in it; and that's what a burial is. *De Profundis.*"

A horizontal sunbeam illumined the face of the sleeping
Cosette, who opened her lips and looked like an angel
imbibing light. Jean Valjean was gazing at her again,
and no longer listened to Fauchelevent. Not to be heard
is no reason why a man should hold his tongue, so the
worthy old gardener quickly continued his chatter:

"The grave is dug in the Vaugirard Cemetery. I have
a friend there, Father Mestrenne, the gravedigger. The
nuns of this house possess the privilege of being carried
to that cemetery at nightfall: they have a decree of the
prefecture expressly for them. But what events since
yesterday! Mother Crucifixion is dead, and Father
Madeleine——"

"Is buried," Jean Valjean said, with a sad smile.

Fauchelevent marked the word.

"Well, if you were here altogether it would be a real
burial."

A fourth peal rang out. Fauchelevent quickly took
down his knee-cap and put it on.

"This time it is for me. The Mother Prioress wants me.
There, I have pricked myself with the tongue of my buckle.
M. Madeleine, don't stir, but wait for me. There is something up; if you are hungry, there is bread, wine, and
cheese."

And he left the cottage, saying, " Coming, coming."

Jean Valjean watched him hurrying across the garden as rapidly as his leg would allow, while taking a side glance at his melon frames. Less than ten minutes after, Father Fauchelevent, whose bell routed all the nuns as he passed, tapped gently at a door, and a soft voice answered, " For ever, for ever," that is to say, " Come in." It was the door of the parlour reserved expressly for the gardener, and adjoining the chapter room. The prioress, seated on the only chair in the room, was waiting for Fauchelevent.

To have an agitated and serious air is peculiar, on critical occasions, to certain characters and professions, and notably to priests and monks. At the moment when Fauchelevent entered, this double form of preoccupation was imprinted on the face of the Prioress, who was that charming and learned Mlle du Blémeur, or Mother Innocent, who was usually so cheerful. The gardener gave a timid bow, and remained in the doorway of the cell ; the prioress, who was telling her beads, raised her eyes, and said :

" Oh, it is you, Father Fauvent ? "

This abbreviation had been adopted in the convent. Fauchelevent again began to bow.

" Father Fauvent, I summoned you."

" Here I am, Reverend Mother."

" I wish to speak with you."

" And I, on my side," said Fauchelevent, with a boldness which made him tremble inwards, " have something to say to the most Reverend Mother."

" Well, speak."

Fauchelevent, the ex-notary, belonged to that class of peasants who possess coolness. During the two years Fauchelevent had lived in the convent, he had achieved a success in the community. Remote as he was from all these veiled women, he saw nothing before him but an agitation of shadows, but, by constant attention and penetration, he had succeeded in putting flesh on these phantoms, and these dead lived for him. He had turned his mind to discover the meaning of the various peals, and had succeeded, so that this enigmatical and mysterious convent had nothing hidden from him ; and this sphynx whispered all its secrets in his ear. Fauchelevent, while knowing everything, concealed everything, and that was his art; the whole convent believed him to be stupid, and that is a great merit in religion. The vocal mothers set value on Fauchelevent, for he was a curious dumb man and inspired confidence. Moreover, he was regular, and only went out when absolutely compelled by the claims of his orchard or kitchen garden, and this discretion was placed to his credit. But, for all that, he had made two men talk,—the porter of the convent, and he thus knew all the peculiarities of the parlour; and the gravedigger at the cemetery, and he knew the regularities of the burial; so that he possessed a double light about these nuns—the light of life and the light of death. But he made no abuse of his knowledge, and the congregation were attached to him. Old, lame, seeing nothing, and probably rather deaf; what qualifications! It would be difficult to fill up his place. The good man, with the assurance of a servant who knows his value, began a rustic address to the prioress, which was rather diffuse and very artful. He talked a good deal about his age, his infirmities, years henceforward, reckoning double for him, the growing demands of his work, nights to pass, as, for instance, the last, in which he was obliged to draw matting over the melon frames owing to the moon; and he ended with this, that he had a brother (the prioress gave a start)— a brother who was not young (a second start, but not so alarmed)—that if leave were granted, this brother would come and live with him and help him; that he was an excellent gardener, and would be of more use to the community than himself and that, on the other hand, if his brother's services were not accepted, as he, the elder, felt worn out and unequal to his work, he would be compelled, to his great regret, to give up his situation; and that his brother had a little girl whom he would bring with him, and who would be brought up in the house, and might, who knew? become a nun some day. When he had finished speaking, the prioress broke off her occupation of letting the beads of her rosary slip through her fingers, and said:

"Could you procure a strong iron bar between this and to-night?"

"What to do?"

"To act as a lever."

" Yes, Reverend Mother," Father Fauchelevent replied.

The prioress, without adding a syllable, rose and walked into the adjoining room, where the Chapter was assembled. Fauchelevent was left alone.

CHAPTER LIX.

ABOUT a quarter of an hour passed ere the prioress came in again and sat down on her chair. The two speakers appeared preoccupied.

" Father Fauvent, do you know the chapel? "

" I have a little cage in it where I hear mass and the offices. "

" A stone will have to be lifted. "

" What stone? "

" The one at the side of the altar. "

" The stone that closes the vault? That is a job where two men would be useful. "

" Mother Ascension, who is as strong as a man, will help you. "

" A woman is never a man. "

" We have only a woman to help you, but she will do her best. The merit is to work according to your strength. A convent is not a work-yard. "

" And a woman is not a man. My brother is a strong fellow! "

" The four chanting mothers will help you. "

" All right, Reverend Mother, I will open the vault; and when it is open? "

" You must shut it again. "

" Is that all? "

" No. "

" Give me your orders, most Reverend Mother. "

" Fauvent, we place confidence in you. "

" I am here to do everything. "

" And to hold your tongue about everything. "

" Yes, Reverend Mother. "

" When the vault is opened—— "

" I will shut it again. "

" But, first—— "

" What, Reverend Mother? "

" You must let down something into it. "

There was a silence, and the prioress, after a pout of the lower lip, which looked like hesitation, continued :

" Father Fauvent, you are aware that a mother died this morning."

" No."

" Did you not hear the bell ? "

" Nothing can be heard at the end of the garden."

" She died at daybreak."

" And besides, this morning, the wind did not blow in my direction."

" It is Mother Crucifixion, a blessed saint."

The prioress was silent, moved her lips for a moment, as if in mental prayer, and went on :

" Three years ago, through merely seeing Mother Crucifixion pray, a Jansenist, Madame de Béthune, became orthodox."

" Oh, yes, I hear the passing bell now, Reverend Mother."

" The mothers have carried her into the dead-room adjoining the church."

" I know."

" No other man but you can or ought to enter that room, so keep careful watch. It would be a fine thing to see another man enter the charnel-house ! In her lifetime Mother Crucifixion performed conversions, after her death she will perform miracles."

" She will do them," Fauchelevent added.

" Father Fauvent, the community was blessed in Mother Crucifixion. Of course it is not granted to every one to die, like Cardinal de Bérulle, while reading the Holy Mass, and exhale his soul to God while uttering the words, *Hanc igitur oblationem*. But though she did not attain such happiness, Mother Crucifixion had a very blessed death. She retained her senses up to the last moment ; she spoke to us, and then conversed with the angels. She gave us her last commands ; if you had more faith, and if you had been in her cell, she would have crude your leg by touching it. She smiled, and we all felt that she was living again in God—there was Paradise in such a death."

Fauchelevent fancied that it was the end of a prayer ; " Amen," he said.

" Father Fauvent, what the dead wish must be carried out."

The prioress told a few beads.   Fauchelevent held his
tongue ; then the lady continued :

"Father Fauvent, Mother Crucifixion will be buried in
the coffin in which she has slept for twenty years."

" That is but fair."

" It is a continuation of sleep."

" Then I shall have to nail her up in that coffin ? "

" Yes."

" And we shall not employ the undertaker's coffin ? "

" Exactly."

" I am at the orders of the most Reverend Community."

" The four singing mothers will help you."

" To nail up the coffin?   I do not want them."

" No, to let it down."

" Where ? "

" Into the vault."

" What vault ? "

" Under the altar."

Fauchelevent started.

" The vault under the altar ? "

" We must obey the dead.   It was the last wish of
Mother Crucifixion to be buried in the vault under the
chapel altar, not to be placed in profane soil, and to remain
when dead at the place where she had prayed when alive.
She asked this of us, indeed ordered it."

" But it is forbidden."

" Forbidden by man, ordered by God."

" If it should come to be known ? "

" We have confidence in you."

" Oh ! I am a stone of your wall."

" The Chapter is assembled ; the vocal mothers whom I
have just consulted once again, and who are deliberating,
have decided that Mother Crucifixion should be interred
according to her wish, under our altar.   Only think,
Father Fauvent, if miracles were to take place here ! what
a glory in God for the community ! miracles issue from
tombs."

" But, Reverend Mother, supposing the Sanitary Commissioner——"

" St. Benedict II., in a matter of burial, resisted Con-
stantine Pogonatus."

" Still the Inspector——"

" Chonodemairus, one of the seven German kings who
entered Gaul during the empire of Constantius, expressly

recognised the right of monks to be buried in religion, that is to say, beneath the altar."

"But the Inspector of the Prefecture——"

"The world is as nothing in presence of the cross. What do we know about the State, the regulations, the administration, and the public undertaker? Any witnesses would be indignant at the way in which we are treated; we have not even the right to give our dust to Christ! your salubrity is a revolutionary invention. God subordinate to a Police Inspector, such is the age!"

The prioress breathed, and then turned to Fauchelevent.

"Father Fauvent, is it settled?"

"It is, Reverend Mother."

"Can we reckon on you?"

"I will obey."

"You will close the coffin, and the sisters will carry it into the chapel. The office for the dead will be read, and then we shall return to the cloisters. Between eleven and twelve you will come with your iron bar, and everything will be performed with the utmost secrecy: there will be no one in the chapel but the four singing mothers, Mother Ascension, and yourself."

"And the sister at the stake?"

"She will not turn round."

"But she will hear."

"She will not listen. Moreover, what the convent knows the world is ignorant of."

There was another pause, after which the prioress continued:

"You will remove your bell, for it is unnecessary for the sister at the stake to notice your presence."

"Reverend Mother?"

"What is it, Father Fauvent?"

"Has the physician of the dead paid his visit?"

"He will do so at four o'clock to-day: the bell has been rung to give him notice. But do you not hear any ringing?"

"I only pay attention to my own summons."

"Very good, Father Fauvent. About three-quarters of an hour before midnight, do not forget."

"Reverend Mother?"

"What is it?"

"If you have other jobs like this, my brother is a strong fellow for you, a Turk."

"You will be as quick as possible."

"I cannot do things quickly, for I am infirm, and for that reason require an assistant. I halt."

"Halting is not a crime, and may be a blessing. The Emperor Henry II., who combated the Antipope Gregory and re-established Benedict VIII., has two surnames—the saint and the cripple. Father Fauvent, now I think of it, take a whole hour, for it will not be too much. Be at the High Altar with your crowbar at eleven o'clock, for the service begins at midnight and all must be finished a good quarter of an hour previously."

"I will do everything to prove my zeal to the community. I will nail up the coffin, and be in the chapel at eleven o'clock precisely; the singing mothers and Mother Ascension will be there. Two men would be better, but no matter, I shall have my crowbar, we will open the vault, let down the coffin, and close it again. After that there will not be a trace, and the government will have no suspicion. Reverend Mother, is all arranged thus?"

"No."

"What is there still?"

"There is the empty coffin."

This was a difficulty; Fauchelevent thought of it, and so did the prioress.

"Father Fauvent, what must be done with the other coffin?"

"It must be buried."

"Yes, but the bearers, while placing it in the hearse, and lowering it into the grave, will soon perceive that there is nothing in it."

"Oh, the de——!" Fauchelevent exclaimed. The prioress began a cross, and looked intently at the gardener; the *vil* stuck in his throat, and he hastily improvised an expedient to cause the oath to be forgotten.

"Reverend Mother, I will put earth in the coffin, which will produce the effect of a body."

"You are right, for earth is the same as a human being. So you will manage the empty coffin?"

"I take it on myself."

The face of the prioress, which had hitherto been troubled and clouded, now grew serene. She made the sign of a superior dismissing an inferior, and Fauchelevent walked toward the door. As he was going out the prioress gently raised her voice.

"Father Fauvent, I am satisfied with you ; to-morrow, after the interment, bring me your brother, and tell him to bring me his daughter."

CHAPTER LX.

THE strides of halting men are like the glances of squinters, they do not reach their point very rapidly. Monsieur Fauchelevent was perplexed, and he spent upwards of a quarter of an hour in returning to the cottage in the garden. Cosette was awake, and Jean Valjean had seated her by the fireside. At the moment when Fauchelevent entered Jean Valjean was pointing to the gardener's *hotte* leaning in a corner, and saying to her :

"Listen to me carefully, little Cosette. We are obliged to leave this house, but shall return to it, and be very happy. The good man will carry you out in that thing upon his back, and you will wait for me with a lady till I come to fetch you. If you do not wish Madame Thénardier to catch you again, obey and say not a word."

Cosette nodded her head gravely. At the sound Fauchelevent made in opening the door Valjean turned round.

"Well ? "

"All is arranged, and nothing is so," said Fauchelevent. "I have leave to bring you in, but to bring you in you must go out. That is the difficulty ; it is easy enough with the little one."

"You will carry her out ? "

"Will she be quiet ? "

"I answer for that."

"But you, Father Madeleine ? "

And after an anxious silence Fauchelevent cried :

"Why, go out in the same way as you came in."

Jean Valjean, as on the first occasion, confined himself to saying "Impossible ! "

Fauchelevent, speaking to himself rather than to Jean Valjean, growled :

"There is another thing that troubles me. I said that I would put earth in it, but now I come to think of it, earth instead of a body will not do, for it will move about and the men will notice it. You understand, Father Madeleine, the government will perceive the trick ? "

Jean Valjean looked at him, and fancied that he must be raving ; Fauchelevent continued :

"How the deuce are you going to get out? for everything must be settled to-morrow, as the prioress expects you then."

Then he explained to Valjean that it was a reward for a service which he, Fauchelevent, was rendering the community. It was part of his duty to attend to the funerals, nail up the coffin, and assist the gravedigger at the cemetery. The nun who had died that morning requested to be buried in the coffin which served her as bed in the vault under the altar of the chapel. This was forbidden by the police regulations, but she was one of those women to whom nothing could be refused. The prioress and the vocal mothers intended to carry out the wishes of the deceased, and so, all the worse for the government. He, Fauchelevent, would nail up the coffin in the cell, lift the stone in the chapel, and let down the body into the vault. As a reward for this the prioress would admit into the house his brother as gardener, and his niece as boarder. The prioress had told him to bring his brother the next day after the pretended funeral, but he could not bring M. Madeleine in from outside if he were not there. There was his first embarrassment, and then he had a second in the empty coffin.

"What do you mean by the empty coffin?" Valjean asked.

"Why, the government coffin."

"I do not understand you."

"A nun dies, and the physician of the municipality comes and says, 'There is a nun dead.' Government sends a coffin, the next day it sends a hearse and undertaker's men to fetch the coffin and carry it to the cemetery. They will come and lift the coffin, and there's nothing in it."

"Put something in it."

"A dead person? I haven't such a thing."

"Well, then, a living one."

"Who?"

"Myself," said Jean Valjean.

Fauchelevent, who was seated, sprang up as if a shell had exploded under his chair.

"You?"

"Why not?"

Jean Valjean had one of those rare smiles which resembled a sunbeam in a wintry sky.

"You know that you said, Fauchelevent, Mother Cruci-fixion is dead, and I added, 'And Father Madeleine is buried.' It will be so."

"Oh, you are joking, not speaking seriously."

"Most seriously. Must I not get out of here?"

"Of course."

"Well, the point is to get out of here unseen, and that is a way. But just tell me, how does it all take place? where is the coffin?"

"In what is called the dead-house. It is upon two trestles, and covered with the pall."

"What is the length of the coffin?"

"Six feet."

"What is this dead-house?"

"A ground-floor room with a grated window looking on the garden, and two doors, one leading to the church, the other to the convent."

"What church?"

"The street church, the one open to everybody."

"Have you the keys of these doors?"

"No, I have the key of the one communicating with the convent, but the porter has the other."

"When does he open it?"

"Only to let the men pass who come to fetch the body. When the coffin has gone out the door is locked again."

"Who nails up the coffin?"

"I do."

"Who places the pall over it?"

"I do."

"Are you alone?"

"No other man, excepting the doctor, is allowed to enter the dead-house. It is written on the wall."

"Could you hide me in that house to-night, when all are asleep in the convent?"

"No, but I can hide you in a dark hole opening out of the dead-house, in which I put the burial tools, of which I have the key."

"At what hour to-morrow will the hearse come to fetch the body?"

"At three in the afternoon. The interment takes place at the Vaugirard Cemetery a little before nightfall, for the ground is not very near here."

"I will remain concealed in your tool-house during the

night and morning. How about food? for I shall be hungry."

"I will bring you some."

"You can nail me up in the coffin at two o'clock." Fauchelevent recoiled and cracked his finger-bones.

"Oh, it is impossible!"

"Nonsense! to take a hammer and drive nails into a board?"

What seemed to Fauchelevent extraordinary was quite simple to Jean Valjean, for he had gone through worse straits, and any man who has been a prisoner knows how to reduce himself to the diameter of the mode of escape. A prisoner is affected by flight, just as a sick man is by the crisis which saves or destroys him, and an escape is a cure. What will not a man undergo for the sake of being cured? To be nailed up and carried in a box, to live for a long time in a packing-case, to find air where there is none, to economise one's breath for hours, to manage to choke without dying, was one of Jean Valjean's melancholy talents.

Besides, a coffin in which there is a living body, this convict's expedient, is also an imperial expedient. If we may believe the monk Austin Castillejo, it was the way employed by Charles V., who, wishing to see La Plombes for the last time after his abdication, contrived to get her in and out of the monastery of Saint Yuste. Fauchelevent, when he had slightly recovered, exclaimed:

"But how will you manage to breathe?"

"I will manage it."

"In that box? why, the mere idea of it chokes me."

"You have a gimlet. You will make a few holes round the mouth, and nail down the lid, without closing it tightly."

"Good! and suppose you cough or sneeze?"

"A man who is escaping does not do such a thing."

And Jean Valjean added:

"Father Fauchelevent, we must make up our mind: I must either be captured here or go out in the hearse."

"After all, there is no other way," said Fauchelevent.

"The only thing I am anxious about is what will take place at the cemetery."

"There is the very thing I am not anxious about," said Fauchelevent; "if you feel sure of getting out of the coffin I feel sure of getting you out of the grave. The gravedigger is a friend of mine and a drunkard of the name of Fathe

Mestienne; he puts the dead in the grave, and I put the gravedigger in my pocket. I will tell you what will occur; we shall arrive a little before twilight, three-quarters of an hour before the cemetery gates are closed. The hearse will drive up to the grave, and I shall follow, for that is my business. I shall have a hammer, a chisel, and pincers in my pocket. The hearse stops, the undertaker knots a cord round your coffin and lets you down; the priest says the prayers, makes the sign of the cross, sprinkles the holy water, and bolts. I remain alone with Father Mestienne, and he is a friend of mine, I tell you. One of two things is certain; he will either be drunk or not be drunk. If he is not drunk, I shall say to him, 'Come and have a dram before the Good Quince closes.' I take him away, make him drunk, which does not take long, as he has always made a beginning; I lay him under the table, take his card, and return to the cemetery without him. You will have only to deal with me. If he is drunk I shall say to him, 'Be off, I will do your work for you.' He will go, and I get you out of the hole."

Jean Valjean held out his hand, which Father Fauchelevent seized with a touching peasant devotion.

"It is settled, Father Fauchelevent. All will go well."

"Providing that nothing is deranged," Fauchelevent thought; "suppose the affair were to have a terrible ending!"

The next day, as the sun was setting, the few passers-by on the Boulevard du Maine took off their hats to an old-fashioned hearse, ornamented with death's-head, thigh-bones, and tears. In this hearse was a coffin covered with a white pall, on which lay an enormous black cross, like a tall dead woman with hanging arms. A draped carriage, in which could be noticed a priest in his surplice, and a chorister in his red skull cap, followed. Two mutes in a gray uniform with black facings walked on the right and left of the hearse, while behind them came an old man in workman's garb, who halted. The procession proceeded toward the Vaugirard Cemetery. This cemetery formed an exception to the others in Paris. It had its peculiar usages, just as it had a large gate and a side gate, which old people in the quarters, tenacious to old names, called the horseman's gate and the footman's gate. The Bernardo-Benedictines of the Little Picpus had obtained, as we have stated, permission to be buried there in a separate corner, and by night, because the cemetery had formerly belonged to their community. The gravediggers, having thus an evening duty in summer and a night duty in winter, were subjected to special rules. The gates of Parisian cemeteries were closed at that period at sunset, and as this was a police measure the Vaugirard Cemetery was subjected to it like the rest. The two gates adjoined a pavilion, built by the architect Perronet, in which the porter lived, and they were inexorably closed at the moment when the sun disappeared behind the dome of the Invalides. If any gravedigger were detained at that moment in the cemetery, he had only one way to get out, his card, with which the undertaker's department supplied him. There was a species of letter-box in the shutter of the porter's window; the gravedigger threw his card into this box, the porter heard it fall, pulled the string, and the small gate opened. If the gravedigger had not his card he gave his name; the porter got up, recognised him, and opened the gate with his key; but in that case the gravedigger paid a fine of fifteen francs.

The sun had not yet set when the hearse with the white pall and black cross entered the avenue of this cemetery, and the halting man who followed it was no other than Fauchelevent. The interment of Mother Crucifixion in the vault under the altar, getting Cosette out, and introducing Jean Valjean into the dead-house, had been effected without the slightest hitch.

Fauchelevent limped after the hearse with great satisfaction; his twin plots, the one with the nuns, the other with M. Madeleine, one for, the other against, the convent, were getting on famously. The calmness of Jean Valjean was one of those powerful tranquillities which are contagious, and Fauchelevent no longer doubted of success. What he still had to do was nothing; during the last two years he had made the gravedigger drunk a dozen times, and he played with him. He could do what he liked with Father Mestienne, and his head exactly fitted Fauchelevent's cap. The gardener's security was complete.

At the moment when the procession entered the avenue leading to the cemetery, Fauchelevent looked at the hearse with delight, and rubbed his huge hands as he said in a low voice, " What a lark ! "

All at once the hearse stopped ; it had reached the gates, and the permission for burying must be shown. The undertaker conversed with the porter, and during this colloquy, which occupied two or three minutes, a stranger stationed himself behind the hearse by Fauchelevent's side. He was a sort of workman, wearing a jacket with wide pockets, and holding a spade under his arm. Fauchelevent looked at the stranger, and asked him :

" Who are you ? "

The man replied, " The gravedigger."

If any man could survive a cannon-ball right in the middle of his chest, he would cut such a face as Fauchelevent did.

" Why, Father Mestienne is the gravedigger."

" Was."

" How, was ? "

" He is dead."

Fauchelevent was prepared for anything except this, that a gravedigger could die ; and, yet, it is true that grave-diggers themselves die ; while digging holes for others, they prepare one for themselves. Fauchelevent stood with widely opened mouth, and had scarce strength to stammer :

" Why, it is impossible."

" After Napoleon, Louis XVIII. After Mestienne, Gribier. Rustic, my name is Gribier."

Fauchelevent, who was very pale, stared at Gribier ; he was a tall, thin, livid, thoroughly funereal man. He looked like a broken-down doctor who had turned gravedigger. Fauchelevent burst into a laugh.

" Ah, what funny things do happen ! Father Mestienne is dead ; little Father Mestienne is dead, but long live little Father Lenoir ! Do you know who he is ? a bottle of Surêne, morbigou ! real Paris Surêne. And so Father Mestienne is dead ; I feel sorry for him, as he was a jolly fellow. But you are a jolly fellow too, are you not, comrade ? We will drink a glass together, eh ? "

The man answered, " I have studied, and I never drink."

The hearse had set out again, and was now going along the main avenue. Fauchelevent had decreased his pace, and limped more through anxiety than infirmity. The gravedigger walked in front of him, and Fauchelevent once again surveyed this unknown Gribier. He was one of those men who, when young, look old, and who, though thin, are very strong.

" Comrade ! " Fauchelevent cried.

The man turned round.

" I am the convent gravedigger."

" My colleague," the man said.

Fauchelevent, uneducated though very sharp, understood that he had to deal with a formidable species, a fine speaker ; he growled :

"So, then, Father Mestienne is dead."

The man answered, "Completely. The good God consulted his bill-book. Father Mestienne was due, and so Father Mestienne is dead."

"Are we not going to form an acquaintance ? " Fauchelevent stammered.

"It is formed. You are a rustic, I am a Parisian."

"People never know one another thoroughly till they have drunk together, for when a man empties his glass he empties his heart. You will come and drink with me, such an offer cannot be refused."

"Work first."

Fauchelevent thought, "It's all over with me."

They had only a few more yards to go before reaching the nuns' corner. The gravedigger added :

"Peasant, I have seven children to feed. Their hunger is the enemy of my thirst."

The hearse left the main avenue, and turned down a smaller one, which indicated the immediate proximity of the grave. Fauchelevent reduced his pace, but could not reduce that of the hearse. Fortunately, the ground was saturated with winter rains, and rendered their progress slower. He drew closer to the gravedigger.

"There is such a capital Argenteuil wine," he muttered.

Here a remark is necessary. Fauchelevent, however great his agony might be, proposed drinking, but did not explain himself on one point. Who was to pay ? As a general rule, Fauchelevent proposed and Father Mestienne paid. A proposal to drink evidently resulted from the new situation created by the new gravedigger, and that proposal the gardener must make, but he left, not undesignedly, the proverbial quarter of an hour called Rabelais in obscurity. However affected Fauchelevent might be, he did not feel anxious to pay.

The hearse went on, and Fauchelevent looked all about him with the greatest anxiety ; heavy drops of perspiration fell from his forehead. The hearse stopped ; the chorister got out of the coach, and then the priest : one of the small front wheels of the hearse was slightly raised by a heap of earth, beyond which an open grave was visible.

"Here's another lark!" Fauchelevent said in consternation.

CHAPTER LXI.

WHO was in the coffin? It was, as we know, Jean Valjean, who had so contrived as to be able to live in it, and could almost breathe. It is a strange thing to what an extent security of conscience produces other security; the whole combination premeditated by Valjean had been going on since the previous evening, and was still going on excellently. He calculated, like Fauchelevent, upon Father Mestienne, and did not suspect the end. Never was a situation more critical or a calamity more perfect.

The four planks of a coffin exhale a species of terrible peace, and it seemed as if some of the repose of the dead were blended with Valjean's tranquillity. From the bottom of this coffin he had been able to follow and did follow all the phases of the formidable drama which he performed with death. A short while after Fauchelevent had finished nailing down the coffin lid, Valjean felt himself raised and then carried along. Through the cessation of the jolting he felt that they had passed from the pavement to the stamped earth, that is to say, the hearse had left the streets, and had turned into the boulevards. From the hollow sound he guessed that he was crossing the bridge of Austerlitz; at the first halt, he understood that he was entering the cemetery, and at the sound he said to himself, "Here is the grave."

He suddenly felt hands seize the coffin, and then heard a harsh scraping on the planks: he guessed that a rope was being fastened round the coffin in order to let it down into the grave. After this, he felt dizzy for a while; in all probability the men had made the coffin oscillate and let the head down before the feet. He perfectly recovered when he found himself horizontal and motionless. He felt a certain amount of cold, as a chill and solemn voice was raised above him, and he heard the Latin words, which he did not understand, pass away so slowly that he could distinguish each in turn. Then he, listening attentively, heard something like the sound of retreating footsteps.

"They are going away," he thought. "I am alone."

All at once he heard over his head a noise which appeared to him like a thunder-clap; it was a spadeful of earth falling on the coffin,—a second spadeful fell, and one of the holes by which he breathed was stopped,—a third spadeful fell and then a fourth. There are some things stronger than the strongest man. Jean Valjean lost consciousness.

This is what took place above the coffin which contained Jean Valjean. When the hearse had gone away, when the priest and the chorister had driven off in the coach, Fauchelevent, who did not once take his eyes off the gravedigger, saw him stoop down and seize his spade, which was standing upright in the heap of earth. Fauchelevent formed a supreme resolution : he placed himself between the grave and the digger, folded his arms, and said :

" I'll pay."

The gravedigger looked at him in amazement, and replied :

" What, peasant ? "

Fauchelevent repeated, " I'll pay for the wine."

" Go to the deuce," said the gravedigger.

And he threw a spadeful of earth on the coffin, which produced a hollow sound. Fauchelevent tottered, and was himself ready to fall into the grave. He cried, in a voice with which a death-rattle was beginning to be mingled :

" Come along, mate, before the Good Quince closes."

The gravedigger filled his spade again. and Fauchelevent continued, " I'll pay."

And he seized the gravedigger's arm.

" Listen to me, mate ; I am the convent gravedigger, and have come to help you. It is a job which can be done by night, so let us begin by going to have a dram."

And while speaking, while clinging to this desperate pressing, he made the melancholy reflection, " And suppose he does drink, will he get drunk ? "

" Provincial," said the gravedigger, " since you are so pressing, I consent. We will drink, but after work, not before."

And he raised his spade, but Fauchelevent restrained him.

" It is Argenteuil wine."

" Why," said the gravedigger, " you must be a bell-ringer ; ding-dong, ding-dong. You can only say that. Go and have yourself pulled."

And he threw the second spadeful.

Fauchelevent had reached that moment when a man is no longer aware of what he says.

"But come and drink," he cried, "since I offer to pay."

"When we have put the child to bed," said Gribier.

He threw the third spadeful and then added, as he dug the spade into the ground :

"It will be very cold to-night! and the dead woman would hallo after us if we were to leave her here without a blanket."

At this moment the gravedigger stooped to fill his spade and his jacket pocket gaped. Fauchelevent's wandering glance fell mechanically into his pocket and remained there. The sun was not yet hidden by the horizon, and there was still sufficient light to distinguish something white at the bottom of this gaping pocket.

All the brightness of which a Picard peasant's eye is capable glistened in Fauchelevent's,—an idea had struck him. Unnoticed by the gravedigger, he thrust his hand into his pocket from behind, and drew out the white thing at the bottom. The gravedigger threw the fourth spadeful into the grave, and as he hurried to raise a fifth, Fauchelevent looked at him with profound calmness, and said :

"By the way, my novice, have you your card ? "

"What card ? "

"The sun is just going to set."

"Very good, it can put on its nightcap."

"The cemetery gates will be shut."

"Well, and what then ? "

"Have you your card ? "

"Ah, my card!" the gravedigger said ; and he felt in one pocket and then in another, he passed to his fobs and turned them inside out.

"No," he said, "I have not got my card, I must have forgotten it."

"Fifteen francs fine," said Fauchelevent.

The gravedigger turned green, for the pallor of livid men is green.

"O Lord, have mercy upon me," he exclaimed ; "fifteen francs fine ! "

The gravedigger let his spade fall.

Fauchelevent's turn had arrived.

"Come, conscript," said the old gardener, "no despair ; you need not take advantage of the grave to commit suicide. Fifteen francs are fifteen francs, and, besides, you can avoid paying them. I am old and you a new-comer, and

I am up to all the tricks and dodges. I will give you a piece of friendly advice. One thing is clear, the sun is setting, it is touching the dome, and the cemetery will shut in five minutes."

" That is true."

" Five minutes will not be enough for you to fill up this grave, which is deuced deep, and reach the gates in time to get out before they close."

" Perfectly correct."

" In that case, fifteen francs fine. But you have time, —where do you live ? "

"Hardly a quarter of an hour's walk from here, at No. 87 Rue de Vaugirard."

" You have just time enough to get out, if you look sharp."

"So I have."

" Once outside the gates, you will gallop home and fetch your card, and when you return the porter will open the gate for you gratis. And you will bury your dead woman, whom I will stop from running away during your absence."

" I owe you my life, peasant."

" Be off at once," said Fauchelevent.

The gravedigger, who was beside himself with gratitude, shook his hand and ran off.

When he had disappeared behind a clump of trees, Fauchelevent listened till his footsteps died away, then bent over the grave, and said in a low voice, " Father Madeleine ! "

There was no reply. Fauchelevent trembled : he tumbled all of a heap into the grave, threw himself on the coffin lid, and cried :

" Are you there ? "

There was silence in the coffin, and Fauchelevent, who could not breathe for trembling, took out his cold chisel and hammer and prized off the coffin lid. He could see Jean Valjean's face in the gloom, pale, and with the eyes closed. The gardener's hair stood on an end ; he got up, and then fell against the side of the grave. He gazed at Jean Valjean, who lay livid and motionless. Fauchelevent murmured in a voice faint as a breath, " He is dead ! "

And drawing himself up, he folded his arms so violently that his clenched fists struck his shoulders, and cried, " That is the way in which I save him ! "

Then the poor old man began sobbing and soliloquising, for it is a mistake to suppose that there is no soliloquy in nature. Powerful agitations often talk aloud.

And he tore his hair. A shrill grating sound was audible at a distance through the trees : it was the closing of the cemetery gate. Fauchelevent bent over Jean Valjean, and all at once bounded back to the further end of the grave —Jean Valjean's eyes were open and staring at him.

If seeing a death is fearful, seeing a resurrection is nearly as frightful. Fauchelevent became like stone. He was pale, haggard, confounded by such excessive emotion, not knowing if he had to do with a dead man or a living man, and looking at Jean Valjean, who looked at him.

" I was falling asleep," said Valjean.

And he sat up. Fauchelevent fell on his knees.

" Holy Virgin ! how you frightened me ! "

Then he rose and cried, " Thank you, Father Madeleine ! "

Jean Valjean had only fainted, and the fresh air aroused him again. Joy is the reflux of terror, and Fauchelevent had almost as much difficulty in recovering himself as had Jean Valjean.

" Then you are not dead ! oh, what a clever fellow you are ! I called to you so repeatedly that you came back. When I saw your eyes closed, I said, ' There, he is suffocated ! ' I should have gone stark mad, fit for a strait waistcoat, and they would have put me in Bicêtre. What would you have me do if you were dead ? And your little girl ! the greengrocer's wife would not have understood it at all. A child is left upon her hands, and the grandfather is dead ! What a story ! oh, my good saints in Paradise, what a story ! Well, you are alive, that's the great thing."

" I am cold," said Valjean.

This remark completely recalled Fauchelevent to the reality, which was urgent. These two men, who had scarce recovered, had a troubled mind, they knew not why, which emanated from the gloomy place where they were.

" Let us get out of this at once," said Fauchelevent.

He felt in his pocket and produced a flask.

" But a dram first," he said.

The flask completed what the fresh air had began. Valjean drank a mouthful of spirits and regained perfect possession of himself. He got out of the coffin, and helped Fauchelevent to nail on the lid again : three minutes later they were out of the grave.

Fauchelevent was calm, and took his time. The cemetery was closed, and there was no fear of Gribier returning. That "conscript" was at home, busily seeking his card, and prevented from finding it because it was in Fauchelevent's pocket. Without it he could not return to the cemetery. Fauchelevent took the spade, and Valjean the pick, and they together buried the empty coffin. When the grave was filled up, Fauchelevent said :

"Come along : you carry the pick and I will carry the spade."

Jean Valjean felt some difficulty in moving and walking, for in the coffin he had grown stiff, and become to some extent a corpse. The rigidity of death had seized upon him between these four planks, and he must, so to speak, become thawed.

"You are stiff," said Fauchelevent, "it is a pity that I am a cripple, or we would have a run."

"Nonsense," said Valjean, "half a dozen strides will make my legs all right again."

They went along the avenues by which the hearse had passed, and, on reaching the gate, Fauchelevent threw the gravedigger's card into the box ; the porter pulled the string, and they went out.

"How famously it has all gone," said Fauchelevent ; "it was an excellent idea you had, Father Madeleine ! "

They passed through the Vaugirard barrier in the simplest way in the world, for, in the vicinity of a cemetery, a spade and a pick are two passports. The Rue de Vaugirard was deserted.

"Father Madeleine," Fauchelevent said, as they walked along, "you have better eyes than I have, so show me No 87."

"Here it is," said Valjean.

"There is no one in the street," Fauchelevent continued, "give me the pick, and wait for me a couple of minutes."

Fauchelevent entered No. 87, went right to the top, guided by that instinct which ever leads the poor man to the garret, and rapped at a door in the darkness. A voice replied, "Come in." It was Gribier's voice.

Fauchelevent pushed the door. The gravedigger's room was like all these wretched abodes, an impoverished and crowded garret. A packing-case—possibly a coffin—occupied the place of a chest of drawers, a butter-jar was the water-cistern, a palliasse represented the bed, while the floor filled the place of chairs and table. In one corner, on an old ragged piece of carpet, were a thin woman and a heap of children. The whole of this poor interior displayed signs of a convulsion, and it seemed as if an earthquake "for one" had taken place there. The blankets were torn away, the rags scattered about, the jug was broken, the mother had been crying, and the children probably beaten,—there were evident signs of an obstinate and savage search. It was plain that the gravedigger had been wildly looking for his card, and made everything in the garret responsible for it, from his jug to his wife. He looked desperate, but Fauchelevent was too eager to notice this sad side of his success : he went in, and said, " I have brought you your spade and pick."

Gribier looked at him in stupefaction.

"Is it you, peasant ? "

"And to-morrow morning you will find your card with the porter of the cemetery."

And he placed the spade and pick on the floor.

"What does this mean ? " Gribier asked.

" It means that you let your card fall out of your pocket, that I found it on the ground when you had left, that I have buried the dead woman, filled up the grave, done your work, the porter will give you your card, and you will not pay fifteen francs. That's what it is, conscript ! "

" Thanks, villager," said Gribier, quite bewildered. " The next time I will treat."

An hour later, in the depth of night, two men and a child presented themselves at No. 62 Little Rue Picpus. The elder of the two men raised the knocker and rapped. It was Fauchelevent, Jean Valjean, and Cosette. The two men had fetched Cosette from the greengrocer's, where Fauchelevent had left her on the previous evening. Cosette had spent the four-and-twenty hours in understanding nothing, and silently trembling ; she trembled so greatly that she had not cried, nor had she eaten or slept. The worthy greengrocer had asked her a hundred questions, but had only obtained as answer a gloomy look, ever the same. Cosette did not breathe a syllable of what she had seen or heard during the last two days, for she guessed that she was passing through a crisis, and felt deeply that she must be "good." Who has not experienced the sovereign power of the words, "say nothing," uttered with a certain accent in the ear of a little startled being ?

Fear is dumb ; besides, no one can keep a secret like a
child.

The only thing was that when she saw Jean Valjean
again after these mournful four-and-twenty hours, she
uttered such a cry of joy that any thoughtful person who
had heard it would have divined in this cry an escape from
a gulf.

Fauchelevent belonged to the convent, and knew all the
passwords ; hence doors readily opened to him, and thus
was solved the double and startling problem, "how to get
in, and how to get out."

The prioress, rosary in hand, was waiting for them, and
a vocal mother, with her veil down, was standing near her.
A discreet candle lit up, or, to speak more correctly, pretended to light up, the parlour. The prioress bent a
searching glance on Jean Valjean, and then proceeded to
interrogate him. Fauchelevent took upon himself the task
of answering her questions. He informed her that the
name of his supposed brother was Ultime ; his age, fifty ; his
trade, a gardener ; and that Cosette was his grandchild.

Jean Valjean had not said a word. The prioress looked
attentively at Cosette, and whispered to the vocal mother,
"She will be ugly."

The two mothers consulted for a few minutes in a very
low voice in a corner of the parlour, and then the prioress
turned and said :

"Father Fauvent, you will get another knee-cap and
bell, for we shall require two in future."

On the morrow two bells were really heard in the garden,
and the nuns could not resist the temptation of raising a
corner of their veils. They could see under the shade of
the trees two men digging side by side, Fauvent and another.
It was an enormous event, and silence was so far broken
that they whispered, "It is an assistant gardener," while
the vocal mothers added, "It is a brother of Father
Fauvent's."

Jean Valjean was in fact permanently installed. He had
the leathern knee-cap and bell, and was henceforth official.
He called himself Ultime Fauchelevent. The most powerful determining cause of his admission was the remark of
the prioress with reference to Cosette : "She will be ugly."
The prioress, once she had prognosticated this, felt an
affection for Cosette, and gave her a place in the boarding-
school. This is very logical after all ; for, although there

may be no looking-glasses in a convent, women are conscious of their face. Now, girls who feel themselves pretty have a disinclination to take the veil, and as profession is generally in an inverse ratio to the beauty, more is hoped from ugly than from pretty girls.

CHAPTER LXII.

IN the convent, Cosette continued to be silent. She very naturally thought herself Valjean's daughter, but as she knew nothing, she could say nothing, and in any case would have said nothing, as we have remarked ; for nothing trains children to silence like misfortune. Cosette had suffered so greatly that she feared everything, even to speak, even to breathe, for a word had so often brought down an avalanche upon her! She had scarce begun to grow reassured since she had belonged to Jean Valjean, but she grew very soon accustomed to the convent. The only thing she regretted was Catherine, but she did not dare say so ; one day, however, she remarked to Valjean, "If I had known, I would have brought her with me."

Cosette, on becoming a pupil at the convent, was obliged to assume the garb of the pupils of the house. Jean Valjean begged, and obtained the old clothes she left off—the same mourning clothes he made her put on when he removed her from the Thénardiers', and they were not much worn. Jean Valjean placed these clothes and her shoes and stockings, with a quantity of camphor and other odorous drugs with which convents abound, in a small valise which he managed to procure. He placed this valise on a chair by his bedside, and always had the key about him.

"Father," Cosette asked him one day, "what is that box which smells so nice?"

Father Fauchelevent was rewarded for his good deed ; for, in the first place, he was happy, and, in the second place, he had much less to do, owing to the division of labour. Lastly, as he was very fond of snuff, he had from M. Madeleine's presence the advantage that he took thrice as much as before, and in a far more voluptuous manner, because M. Madeleine paid for it.

The nuns did not adopt the name of Ultime ; they called Jean Valjean "the other Fauvent." Had these holy women had any of Javert's temper about them, they must have noticed that when anything had to be procured from outside for the garden it was always the elder Fauvent, the cripple, who went out, and never the other ; but either because eyes constantly fixed on God know not how to spy, or because they preferred to watch one another, they paid no attention to the fact. However, Jean Valjean did quite right in keeping shy and not stirring, for Javert watched the quarter for a whole month.

This convent was to Jean Valjean like an island surrounded by gulfs, and these four walls were henceforth the world for him ; he saw enough of the sky there to be secure, and enough of Cosette to be happy. He lived with old Fauchelevent in the hovel at the end of the garden. This lath and plaster tenement, which still existed in 1825, was composed of three rooms which had only the bare walls. The largest room was surrendered by force, for Jean Valjean resisted in vain, by Father Fauchelevent to M. Madeleine. The wall of this room had for ornament, in addition to the two nails for hanging up the knee-cap and the *hotte*, a Royalist note for ten livres, date '93, fastened above the mantelpiece. This Vendean assignat had been nailed to the wall by the previous gardener, an ex-chouan, who died in the convent, and was succeeded by Fauchelevent.

Jean Valjean worked every day in the garden, and was very useful. As he had once been a pruner he was glad to become a gardener. It will be remembered that he had a great number of receipts and secrets which he turned to a profit ; nearly all the trees in the orchard were wild stocks, but he grafted them, and made them produce excellent fruit.

Cosette had permission to spend an hour daily with him, and as the sisters were sad and he was kind, the child compared him with them and adored him. At the fixed hour she ran to the cottage, and when she entered it filled it with paradise. Jean Valjean expanded, and felt his own happiness grow with the happiness which he caused Cosette. The joy which we inspire has this charming thing about it, that far from being weakened, like ordinary reflections, it returns to us more radiant than before. In her hours of recreation Jean Valjean watched her from a distance, playing and running, and distinguished her laugh from that of the others, for Cosette now laughed. Her face had also changed to a certain extent, for laughter is the sun which drives winter from the human face. When Cosette returned to her studies Jean Valjean watched the windows of her schoolroom, and at night would rise to gaze at the windows of her dormitory.

God has His inscrutable designs, and the convent contributed, like Cosette, to maintain and complete the Bishop's work in Jean Valjean. It is certain that one of the sides of virtue leads to pride, and there is a bridge built there by the demon. Jean Valjean was perhaps unconsciously very near this bridge when Providence threw him into the convent of the Little Picpus. So long as he had only compared himself with the Bishop, he had found himself unworthy, and had been humble, but for some time past he had been beginning to compare himself with men, and pride was growing up. Who knows whether he might not have ended by gently returning to hatred?

The convent checked him on this slope; it was the second place of captivity which he had seen. In his youth, in what had been to him the commencement of life, and again very recently, he had seen another, a frightful spot, a terrible spot, whose severities had ever appeared to him to be the iniquity of justice and the crime of the law. At the present day after the hulks he saw the convent, and reflecting that he had been a member of the galleys and was now, so to speak, a spectator of the convent, he anxiously confronted them in his thoughts.

At times he leant on his spade, and fell into a profound reverie. He recalled his old comrades; how wretched they were! They rose at dawn and worked till night; they were scarce granted time to sleep; they lay down on camp-beds and were only allowed mattresses two inches thick; their rooms were only warmed in the severest months of the year; they were dressed in hideous red jackets; they were allowed, as an indulgence, canvas trousers in the great heat, and woollen bandages on their backs in the severe cold; they only ate meat and drank wine when they worked on fatigue parties; they lived without names, solely designated by numbers, lowering their eyes, lowering their voices, with shorn hair, under the stick, and in disgrace.

Then his thoughts turned to the beings whom he had before him. These beings also lived with cropped hair, downcast eyes, and low voices, not in disgrace, but amid the mockery of the world, and if their backs were not bruised by a stick, their shoulders were lacerated by the discipline. Their names had vanished too among human beings, and they only existed under severe appellations. They never ate meat nor drank wine; they often remained without food till night; they were dressed, not in red jackets, but in black woollen palls, heavy in summer and light in winter, and were unable to reduce it or add to it at all, and they wore for six months in the year serge chemises, which caused them a fever. They slept not in rooms warmed merely in the severe cold, but in cells in which fires were never kindled; they slept not on mattresses two inches thick, but on straw; lastly, they were not even allowed to sleep; every night, after a day of labour, they were compelled to get up, dress themselves, and go and pray in a freezing dark chapel, with their knees upon the stones. On certain days, moreover, each of these beings was obliged, in turn, to remain for twelve hours prostrate on the ground, with her arms extended like a cross.

The former were men; the latter were women. What had the men done? they had robbed, violated, plundered, killed, assassinated. They were bandits, forgers, poisoners, incendiaries, murderers, and parricides. What had these women done? nothing. On one side, brigandage and fraud, cozening, violence, lubricity, homicide, every sort of sacrilege, every variety of crime; on the other, only one thing,—innocence, perfect innocence, which was still attached to the earth by virtue, and already attached to heaven by holiness. On one side, confessions of crimes made in a whisper; on the other, confessions of faults made aloud. And what crimes, and what faults! On one side miasma, on the other an ineffable perfume; on one side a moral pestilence, closely guarded, held down by cannon, and slowly devouring its plague-sufferers; on the other, a chaste kindling of all the souls on the same hearth. There darkness, here shadow, but a shadow full of light, and light full of radiance.

Jean Valjean perfectly understood the expiation of the former, as personal, but he did not understand the expiation of the others, of these creatures who were without reproach or stain, and he asked himself with trembling: expiation for what? A voice answered in his conscience; the most divine proof of human generosity, Expiation for others.

Here we lay aside any and every personal theory; we are only the narrator, we are standing in Jean Valjean's place, and transferring his impressions. He had before his eyes the sublime summit of abnegation, the highest pinnacle of possible virtue, that innocence which forgives men their faults, and expiates them in their place; servitude endured, torture accepted, punishment demanded by souls which have not sinned, that they may absolve souls which have erred; the love of humanity swallowed up in the love of God, but remaining distinct and suppliant in it; gentle, feeble beings who have the wretchedness of those who are punished and the smile of those who are rewarded.

And he remembered that he had dared to complain. He often rose in the middle of the night to listen to the grateful song of these innocent creatures, weighed down by severity, and his blood ran cold when he thought that men who were justly chastised only raised their voices to Heaven to blaspheme, and that he, wretch as he was, had threatened God. It was a striking thing, which made him reflect deeply, and imagine it a warning of Providence, that all the things he had done to escape from the other place of expiation, such as climbing walls, difficulties, dangerous adventures, and risks of death, he had gone through again, in entering the present place. Was it a symbol of his destiny?

This house was a prison too, and bore a mournful likeness to the other abode from which he had fled, and yet he had never had such an idea here. He saw again the gratings, bolts, and iron bars, to guard whom? angels. The lofty walls which he had seen around tigers he saw again around lambs.

It was a place of expiation, and not of punishment, and yet it was even more austere, gloomy, and pitiless than the other. These virgins were more harshly bowed than the galley-slaves: a rough, cold wind, the wind which had chilled his youth, blew through the barred and padlocked cage of the vultures; but a sharper and more painful wind passed through the cotes of these doves.

Why was this?

When he thought of these things, all within him bowed down before this mystery of sublimity. In these meditations pride vanished: he felt himself insignificant, and wept many times: all that had entered his life during the past six months, led him back to the Bishop's holy injunctions,— Cosette by love, the convent by humility.

At times in those hours of the night when the garden was deserted, he might have been seen kneeling in front of that window through which he had gazed on the night of his arrival, turned towards the spot where he knew that the sister who was making reparation was prostrated in prayer. He prayed thus kneeling before this sister—it seemed as if he dared not kneel directly to God.

All that surrounded him, this peaceful garden, these fragrant flowers, these children uttering merry cries, these grave and simple women, these silent cloisters, slowly penetrated him, and gradually his soul was composed of silence like this cloister, of perfume like these flowers, of peace like this garden, of simplicity like these women, and of joy like these children. And then he thought how two houses of God had in turn received him at the two critical moments of his life, the first when all doors were closed and human society repulsed him, the second at the moment when human society was beginning to hunt him down again, and the hulks were yawning for him ; and that, had it not been for the former, he would have fallen back into crime, and but for the latter, into punishment. All his heart melted into gratitude, and he loved more and more.

Several years passed thus, and Cosette grew.

CHAPTER LXIII.

EIGHT or nine years after the events last recorded, there might be noticed on the Boulevard du Temple and in the regions of the Château d'Eau, a boy of about eleven or twelve years of age, who would have tolerably well realised the ideal of a Parisian gamin. This child was dressed in a man's trousers, but he had not got them from his father, and a woman's jacket, which did not come from his mother. Some persons had clothed him in rags out of charity. Yet he had a father and a mother, but his father did not think of him, and his mother did not love him. He was one of those children worthy of pity before all, who have father and mother and are orphans.

This child was never so comfortable anywhere as in the street, for the paving-stones were less hard to him than his mother's heart. His parents had kicked him out into life, and he had simply tried his wings. He was a noisy, pale, active, sharp, impudent lad, with a cunning and sickly

look. He came and went, sang, played at hop-scotch,
searched the gutters, pilfered a little, but gaily, like cats
and sparrows, laughed when he was called a scamp, and
felt angry when called a thief. He had no bed, no bread,
no fire, no love : but he was happy because he was free.
When these poor beings are men, the mill of social order
nearly always crushes them, but so long as they are
children they escape because they are small. The slightest
hole saves them.

Still, so abandoned as this child was, it happened every
two or three months that he said, "Well, I'll go and see
mamma." Then he quitted the Boulevard, the Circus, the
Porte St. Martin, went along the quay, crossed the bridge,
reached Salpetrière, and arrived where ? Exactly at
that double number, 50-52, which the reader knows, the
Maison Gorbeau. At this period No. 50-52, which
was habitually deserted and eternally decorated with a
bill of "Lodgings to Let," was, strange to say, inhabited
by several persons, who had no acquaintance with each
other, as is always the case in Paris. All belonged to that
indigent class, which begins with the last small tradesman in difficulties, and is prolonged from wretchedness to
wretchedness to those two beings to whom all the material
things of civilisation descend, the scavenger and the rag-
picker.

The chief lodger of Jean Valjean's day was dead, and her
place had been taken by another exactly like her. I forget
now what philosopher said, "There is never any want of
old women." This new old woman was called Madame
Burgon, and had nothing remarkable in her life save a
dynasty of three parrots, which had successively reigned
over her soul. The most wretched of all the persons inhabiting the house were a family of four persons, father,
mother, and two nearly grown-up daughters, all four
living in the same attic, one of the cells to which we
have alluded.

This family offered at the first glance nothing very
peculiar beyond its denudation ; and the father, on hiring
the room, stated that his name was Jondrette. A short
time after he moved in, which had borne a striking resemblance—to employ the memorable remark of the chief
lodger—to the coming in of nothing at all, this Jondrette
had said to the woman, who, like her predecessor, was also
porteress and swept the stairs, " Mother So-and-so, if any

one were to ask by chance for a Pole, or an Italian, or perhaps a Spaniard, I am the party."

This was the family of the merry little vagabond. He joined it, and found distress, and, what is sadder still, not a smile ; a cold hearth and cold heart. When he entered, they asked him, "Where do you come from ?" and he answered, "From the street :" when he went away, "Where are you going ?" and he answered, "To the street." His mother would say to him, "What do you want here ?" The boy lived in this absence of affection like the pale grass which grows in cellars. He was not hurt by it being so, and was not angry with any one : he did not know exactly how a father and mother ought to be. Moreover, his mother loved his sisters.

We have forgotten to mention that on the boulevard the lad was called little Gavroche. Why was he called Gavroche? probably, because his father's name was Jondrette. Breaking the thread seems the instinct of some wretched families. The room which the Jondrettes occupied at the Maison Gorbeau was the last in the passage, and the cell next to it was occupied by a very poor young man of the name of Monsieur Marius. Let us see who and what Monsieur Marius was.

CHAPTER LXIV.

In the Rue Boucherat, Rue de Normandie, and Rue de Saintonge, there are still a few persons remaining, who can remember a gentleman of the name of M. Gillenormand, and speak kindly about him. This man was old when they were young, and this profile has not entirely disappeared, with those who look sadly at the vague congregation of shadows called the past, from the labyrinth of streets near the Temple, which in the reign of Louis XIV. received the names of all the provinces of France, exactly in the same way as in our time the names of all the capitals of Europe have been given to the streets in the new Tivoli quarter ; a progression, by the bye, in which progress is visible.

M. Gillenormand, who was most lively in 1831, was one of those men who have become curious to look on, solely because they have lived a long time, and are strange, because they once resembled everybody and now no longer resemble any one. He was a peculiar old man, and most certainly the man of another age, the complete and rather haughty bourgeois of the eighteenth century, who carried his honest old bourgeoisie with the same air as Marquises did their marquisate. He had passed his ninetieth year, walked upright, talked loudly, saw clearly, drank heartily, and ate, slept, and snored. He still had his two-and-thirty teeth, and only wore spectacles to read with. He was of an amorous temper, but said that for the last ten years he had decidedly and entirely given up the sex. "He could not please," he said: and he did not add "I am too old," but "I am too poor. If I were not ruined—he, he, he !" In fact, all that was left him was an income of about fifteen thousand francs. His dream was to make a large inheritance, and have one hundred thousand francs a year, in order to keep mistresses. He was superficial, rapidly and easily angered, and he would storm at the slightest thing, most usually an absurd trifle. When he was contradicted, he raised his cane, and thrashed his people, as folk used to do in the great age. He had a daughter, upwards of fifty years of age and unmarried, whom he gave a hearty thrashing to when he was in a passion, and whom he would have liked to whip, for he fancied her eight years of age. He boxed his servant's ears energetically, and would say, "Ah, carrion !" M. Gillenormand admired his own discernment in everything, and declared himself extremely sagacious.

He lived in the Marais, at No. 6 Rue des Filles des Calvaire. The house was his own. He occupied an old and vast suite of rooms on the first floor, furnished up to the ceiling with large Gobelins and Beauvais tapestry, representing shepherd scenes ; the subjects of the ceiling and panels were repeated in miniature upon the chairs. He surrounded his bed with an immense screen of Coromandel lacquer work ; long curtains hung from the windows, and made very splendid, large, broken folds. The garden immediately under the windows was reached by a flight of twelve or fifteen steps running from one of them, which the old gentleman went up and down very nimbly. In addition to a library adjoining his bed-room, he had a boudoir, which he was very fond of ; a gay retreat, hung with a magnificent fleur-de-lysed tapestry. M. Gillenormand inherited this from a stern maternal great-aunt, who died at the age of one hundred. He had had

two wives. His manners were midway between those
of the courtier, which he had never been, and of the
barrister, which he might have been. He was gay and
pleasing when he liked; in his youth he had been one
of those men who are always deceived by their wives
and never by their mistresses, because they are at once
the most disagreeable husbands and the most charming
lovers imaginable. He was a connoisseur of pictures,
and had in his bedroom a marvellous portrait of somebody unknown, painted by Jordaens in a bold style, and
with an infinitude of details. M. Gillenormand's coat
was not in the style of Louis XV. or even Louis XVI.,
but it was in the style of the Incredibles of the Directory.
He had believed himself quite a youth at that time, and
followed the fashions. His coat was of light cloth with
large cuffs, he wore a long swallow tail, and large steel
buttons. Add to these, short breeches and shoe buckles.
He always had his hands in his pockets, and said authoritatively, "The French Revolution is a collection of
ragamuffins."

In Gillenormand sorrow was translated into passion; he
was furious at being in despair. He had every prejudice
and took every licence. One of the things of which he
composed his external relief and internal satisfaction was,
as we have indicated, having remained a gay fellow, and
passing energetically for such. He gave alms readily and
handsomely, he was benevolent, brusque, and charitable,
and had he been rich his downfall would have been magnificent. He liked everything that concerned him to be
done grandly. He had married twice, as we said; by his
first wife he had a girl, who did not marry, and by the
second another girl, who died at the age of thirty, and who
married through love, or chance, or otherwise, a soldier of
fortune who had served in the armies of the Republic and
the Empire, won the cross at Austerlitz, and his colonel's
commission at Waterloo. "He is the disgrace of my
family," the old gentleman used to say. He took a great
deal of snuff, and had a peculiarly graceful way of shaking
his shirt-frill with the back of his hand. He believed very
little in God.

As for M. Gillenormand's two daughters, they were born
at an interval of ten years. In their youth they had been
very little alike, and both in character and face were as
little like sisters as was possible. The younger was a

charming creature, who turned to the light, loved flowers, poetry, and music, was enthusiastic, ethereal, and mentally betrothed from her youth up to some heroic figure. The elder had her chimera too; she saw in the azure a contractor, some fat and very rich man, a splendidly stupid husband, a million converted into a man, or else a prefect, the reception at the prefecture, an usher in the anteroom with a chain round his neck, the official balls, the addresses at the mansion-house to be "Madame la Prefête"—all this buzzed in her imagination. The two sisters wandered each in her own reverie, at the period when they were girls, and both had wings, the one those of an angel, the other those of a goose.

No ambition is fully realised, at least not in this nether world, and no paradise becomes earthly in our age. The younger married the man of her dreams, but she was dead, while the elder did not marry. At the period when she enters into our narrative, she was an old virtue, an incombustible pride, with one of the most acute noses and most obtuse intellects imaginable. It is a characteristic fact that, beyond her family, no one had ever known her family name; she was called Mademoiselle Gillenormand the elder. In the matter of cant, Mademoiselle Gillenormand could have given points to a Miss, and she was modestly carried to the verge of blackness. She had one frightful reminiscence in her life—one day a man saw her garter.

Age had only heightened this pitiless modesty. Her chemisette was never sufficiently opaque, and never was high enough. She multiplied brooches and pins in places where no one dreamed of looking. The peculiarity of prudery is to station the more sentries the less the fortress is menaced. Still, let who will explain these old mysteries of innocence, she allowed herself to be kissed without displeasure by an officer in the Lancers, who was her grand-nephew, and Théodule by name. In spite of this favoured Lancer, however, the ticket of "Prude" which we have set upon her, suited her exactly. Mademoiselle Gillenormand's was a species of twilight soul, and prudery is a semi-virtue, and a semi-vice. She added to prudery the congenial lining of bigotry; she belonged to the Sisterhood of the Virgin, wore a white veil on certain saints' days, muttered special orisons, revered "the holy blood," venerated "the sacred heart," remained for hours in contemplation before an old-fashioned Jesuit altar in a closed chapel, and allowed her soul to soar among the little marble clouds and through the large beams of gilt wood. She kept house for her father; such families, consisting of an old man and an old maid, are not rare, and have the ever-touching appearance of two weaknesses supporting each other.

There was also in this house a child, a little boy, who was always trembling and dumb in the old gentleman's presence. M. Gillenormand never spoke to this boy except with a stern voice, and at times with upraised cane. "Come here, sir,—scamp, scoundrel, come here! Answer me, fellow! Let me see you, vagabond!" etc. etc. He adored him; it was his grandson, and we shall meet him again.

M. Gillenormand in former times had frequented several very good and highly noble salons. Although a bourgeois, M. Gillenormand was welcome in them, and as he had a twofold stock of wit, namely, that which he had, and that attributed to him, he was sought after and made much of. There are some people who desire influence and to be talked about, no matter what price they pay; and when they cannot be oracles, they make themselves buffoons. M. Gillenormand was not of that nature; and his domination in the Royalist drawing-rooms which he frequented did not cost him any of his self-respect. He was an oracle everywhere, and at times he held his own against M. de Bonald, and even M. Bengy-Puy-Vallée.

He was generally accompanied by his daughter, a tall young lady, who at that time was forty and looked fifty; and by a pretty boy of nine years of age, red and white, fresh, with happy, confident eyes, who never appeared in this drawing-room without hearing all the voices buzz around him: "How pretty he is! What a pity! poor boy!" This lad was the one to whom we referred just now, and he was called "poor boy" because he had for father "a brigand of the Loire." This brigand was that son-in-law of M. Gillenormand, who has already been mentioned, and whom the old gentleman called the "disgrace of his family."

CHAPTER LXV.

HAD any one at that period passed through the little town of Vernon, and walked on the handsome stone bridge, which, let us hope, will soon be succeeded by some hideous wire bridge, he would have noticed, on looking over the parapet, a man of about fifty, wearing a leathern cap, and trousers and jacket of coarse gray cloth, to which something yellow, which had been a red ribbon, was sewn, with a face tanned by the sun, and almost black, and hair almost white, with a large scar on his forehead and running down his cheek, bowed and prematurely aged, walking almost every day, spade and pick in hand, in one of the walled enclosures near the bridge, which border, like a belt of terraces, the left bank of the Seine. These are delicious enclosures full of flowers, of which you might say, were they much larger, "they are gardens," and if they were a little smaller, "they are bouquets." All these enclosures join the river at one end and a house at the other. The man in the jacket and wooden shoes, to whom we have alluded, occupied in 1817 the narrowest of these enclosures and the smallest of these houses. He lived there alone and solitary, silently and poorly, with a woman who was neither young nor old, neither pretty nor ugly, neither peasant nor bourgeoise, who waited on him. The square of land which he called his garden was celebrated in the town for the beauty of the flowers he cultivated, and they were his occupation.

Through his toil, perseverance, attention, and watering-pot, he had succeeded in creating after the Creator; and he had invented sundry tulips and dahlias which seemed to have been forgotten by nature. He was ingenious, and preceded Soulange Bodin in the formation of small patches of peat-soil for the growth of the rare and precious shrubs of America and China. From daybreak in summer he was in his walks, pricking out, clipping, hoeing, watering, or moving among his flowers, with an air of kindness, sorrow, and gentleness. At times he would stand thoughtful and motionless for hours, listening to the song of a bird in a tree, the prattle of a child in a house, or else gazing at a drop of dew on a blade of grass, which the sun converted into a carbuncle. He lived very poorly, and drank more milk than wine : a child made him give way, and his servant scolded him. He was timid to such an extent that he seemed stern, went out rarely, and saw no one but the poor, who tapped at his window, and his curé, Abbé Mabœuf, a good old man, Still, if the inhabitants of the town or strangers, curious to see his roses or tulips, came and tapped at his little door, he opened it with a smile. He was the brigand of the Loire.

Any one who, at the same time, read military Memoirs and Biographies, the *Moniteur*, and the bulletins of the Grand Army, might have been struck by a name which pretty often turns up, that of George Pontmercy. When quite a lad this Pontmercy was a private in the Saintonge regiment, and when the Revolution broke out, this regiment formed part of the army of the Rhine, for the regiments of the Monarchy kept their provincial names even after the fall of the Monarchy, and were not brigaded till 1794. Pontmercy fought at Spires, Worms, Neustadt, Turkheim, Alzey, and at Mayence, where he was one of the two hundred who formed Houchard's rear-guard. He, with eleven others, held out against the corps of the Prince of Hesse behind the old rampart of Andernach, and did not fall back on the main body until the enemy's guns had opened a breach from the parapet to the talus. He was under Kleber at Marchiennes, and at the fight of Mont Palissel, where his arm was broken by a rifle-ball; then he went to the frontier of Italy, and was one of the thirty who defended the Col de Tenda with Joubert. Joubert was appointed adjutant-general, and Pontmercy sub-lieutenant; he was by Berthier's side in the middle of the canister on that day of Lodi which made Bonaparte say, "Berthier was gunner, trooper, and grenadier." He saw his old general Joubert fall at Novi at the moment when he was shouting, with uplifted sabre, "Forward!" Having embarked with his company on board a cutter, which sailed from Genoa to some little port of the coast, he fell into a wasps' nest of seven or eight English sail. The Genoese commandant wished to throw his guns into the sea, hide the soldiers in the hold, and pass like a merchant vessel, but Pontmercy had the tricolour flag hoisted at the peak, and proudly passed under the guns of the British frigates. Twenty leagues further on, his audacity increasing, he attacked and captured a large English transport conveying troops to Sicily, and so laden with men and horses that the vessel's deck was almost flush with the sea. In 1805 he belonged to Malher's division, which took Gunzbourg from the Arch-duke Ferdinand, and at Wettingen he caught in his arms, amid a shower of bullets, Colonel Maupilet, who was mortally wounded at the head of the 9th Dragoons. He distinguished himself at Austerlitz in that admirable march in columns of companies performed under the enemy's fire; and when the Russian Imperial Horse Guards destroyed one of the battalions of the 4th Line Infantry, Pontmercy was among those who took their revenge, and drew back these Guards. For this the Emperor gave him the Cross. Pontmercy saw in turn Wurmser made prisoner at Mantua, Mélas at Alessandria, and Mack at Ulm, and he belonged to the eighth corps of the grand army which Mortier commanded, and which took Hamburg. Then he joined the 55th regiment of the Line, which was the old regiment of Flanders; at Eylau, he was in the cemetery where the heroic Captain Louis Hugo, uncle of the author of this book, withstood, with his company of eighty-three men, for two hours, the whole effort of the enemy's army. Pontmercy was one of the three who left this cemetery alive. He was at Friedland; then he saw Moscow, the Beresina, Lutzen, Bautzen, Dresden, Wacha, Leipsic, and the defiles of Gelnhausen; then at Montmereil, Château-Thierry, Craon, the banks of the Marne, the banks of the Aisne, and the formidable position of Laon. At Arnay le Duc, as captain, he sabred ten Cossacks, and saved not his general, but his corporal; he was cut to pieces on this occasion, and seven-and-twenty splinters were taken out of his left arm alone. Eight days before the capitulation of Paris he exchanged with a comrade and entered the cavalry; for he had what was called under the old régime a "double hand," that is to say, an equal aptitude in handling, as private, a sabre or musket, as officer, a squadron or a company. From this aptitude, improved by military education, special arms sprang, for instance, the dragoons, who are at once cavalry and infantry. He accompanied Napoleon to Elba, and at Waterloo was a major of cuirassiers in Dubois' brigade. It was he who took the colours of the Limburg battalion, and himself threw them at the Emperor's feet. He was covered with blood, for, on seizing the colours, he received a sabre cut across the face. The Emperor, who was pleased, cried out to him, "You are a Colonel, a Baron, and officer of the Legion of Honour!" Pontmercy answered, "Sire, I thank you on behalf of my widow." An hour later he fell into the ravine of Ohain. And now who was this George Pontmercy? He was the same brigand of the Loire.

We have already seen some portion of his history. After Waterloo, Pontmercy, drawn as we remember out of the hollow way of Ohain, succeeded in rejoining the army, and dragged himself from ambulance to ambulance as far as the cantonments of the Loire. The Restoration put him on half-pay, and then sent him to Vernon, under honourable surveillance. King Louis XVIII., regarding all that was done in the Hundred Days as if it had not happened, recognised neither his quality as officer of the Legion of Honour, nor his commission as Colonel, nor his title as Baron. He for his part neglected no opportunity to sign himself, "Colonel Baron de Pontmercy." He had only one old blue coat, and never went out without attaching to it the rosette of the Legion of Honour.

He had nothing but his scanty half-pay as Major, and he had taken the smallest house in Vernon, where he lived alone, in what way we have just seen. Under the Empire and between two wars he found time to marry Mademoiselle Gillenormand. The old bourgeois, who was indignant in his heart, concluded with a sigh and saying, "The greatest families are forced into it." In 1815, Madame Pontmercy, a most admirable woman in every respect, and worthy of her husband, died, leaving a child. This child would have been the Colonel's delight in his solitude, but the grandfather imperiously claimed him, declaring that if he were not given up to him he would disinherit him. The father yielded for the sake of the little one, and, unable to love his son, he took to loving flowers.

He had, however, given up everything, and did not join the opposition or conspire. He shared his thoughts between the innocent things he did and the great things he had done, and he spent his time in hoping for a carnation or calling to mind Austerlitz. M. Gillenormand kept up no relations with his son-in-law; the Colonel was to him a "bandit," and he was for the Colonel an "ass." M. Gillenormand never spoke about the Colonel, except at times to make mocking allusions to "his barony." It was expressly stipulated that Pontmercy should never attempt to see his son or speak to him, under penalty of having him thrown on his hands disinherited. To the Gillenormands, Pontmercy was a plague patient, and they intended to bring up the child after their fashion. The Colonel perhaps did wrong in accepting these terms, but he endured them in the belief that he was acting rightly, and only sacrificing himself.

The inheritance of the grandfather was a small matter, but that of Mlle Gillenormand the elder was considerable, for this aunt was very rich on her mother's side, and her sister's son was her natural heir. The boy who was called Marius, knew that he had a father, but nothing more, and no one opened his lips to him on the subject. Still, in the society to which his grandfather took him, the whisperings and winks eventually produced light in the boy's mind ; he understood something at last, and, as he naturally accepted, by a species of infiltration and slow penetration, the ideas and opinions which were, so to speak, his breathing medium, he gradually came to think of his father only with shame.

While he was thus growing up in this way, the Colonel every two or three months came furtively to Paris, like a convict who is breaking his ban, and posted himself at St. Sulpice, at the hour when Aunt Gillenormand took Marius to Mass. Trembling lest the aunt should turn round, concealed behind a pillar, motionless, and scarce daring to breathe, he looked at this boy—the scarred warrior was frightened at this old maid.

From this very circumstance emanated his friendship with the curé of Vernon, Abbé Mabœuf. This worthy priest had a brother, churchwarden of St. Sulpice, who had several times noticed this man contemplating his child, and the scar on his cheek, and the heavy tear in his eye. This man, who looked so thoroughly a man, and who wept like a child, struck the churchwarden, and this face adhered to his memory. One day when he went to Vernon to see his brother he met on the bridge Colonel Pontmercy, and recognised his man of St. Sulpice. The churchwarden told the affair to the curé, and both made some excuse to pay a visit to the Colonel. This visit led to others, and the Colonel, though at first very close, eventually opened his heart, and the curé and the churchwarden learnt the whole story, and how Pontmercy sacrificed his own happiness to the future of his child. The result was that the curé felt a veneration and tenderness for him, and the Colonel, on his side, took the curé into his affection. Twice a year, on January 1st and St. George's Day, Marius wrote his father letters dictated by his aunt. This was all M. Gillenormand allowed. The father sent very tender replies, which the grandfather thrust into his pocket without reading.

The salon frequented by his grandfather was all that Marius Pontmercy knew of the world. It was the sole opening by which he could look out into life. This opening was gloomy, and more cold than heat, more night than day, reached him through this trap. This boy, who was all joy and light on entering the strange world, became thus, in a short time, sad, and what is more contrary still to his age, serious.

Marius Pontmercy, like most children, received some sort of education. When he left the hands of Aunt Gillenormand, his grandfather intrusted him to a worthy professor of the finest classical innocence. This young mind, just expanding, passed from a prude to a pedant. Marius spent some years at college, and then joined the law-school; he was royalist, fanatic, and austere. He loved but little his grandfather, whose gaiety and cynicism ruffled him, and he was gloomy as regarded his father. In other respects, he was an ardent yet cold, noble, generous, proud, religious, and exalted youth; worthy almost to harshness, and fierce almost to savageness.

CHAPTER LXVI.

THE completion of Marius' classical studies was coincident with M. Gillenormand's retirement from society; the old gentleman bade farewell to the Faubourg St. Germain and Madame de T.'s drawing-room, and withdrew to his house in the Marais. His servants were, in addition to the porter, that Nicolette who succeeded Magnon, and that wheezing, short-winded Basque, to whom we have already alluded. In 1827 Marius attained his seventeenth year; on coming home one evening he saw his grandfather holding a letter in his hand.

"Marius," said M. Gillenormand, "you will start to-morrow for Vernon."

"What for?" Marius asked.

"To see your father."

Marius trembled, for he had thought of everything excepting this, that he might one day be obliged to see his father. Nothing could be more unexpected, more surprising, and, let us add, more disagreeable for him. Marius, in addition to his motives of political antipathy, was convinced that his father, the trooper, as M. Gillenormand called him in his good-tempered days, did not love him; that was evident, as he had abandoned him thus and left him to others. He was so stupefied that he did not question his grandfather, but M. Gillenormand continued:

" It seems that he is ill, and asks for you."

And after a silence he added :

" Start to-morrow morning. I believe there is a coach which leaves at six o'clock and gets to Vernon at nightfall. Go by it, for he says that the matter presses."

He then crumpled up the letter, and put it in his pocket. Marius could have started the same night, and have been with his father the next morning ; a diligence at that time used to run at night to Rouen, passing through Vernon. But neither M. Gillenormand nor Marius dreamed of inquiring. On the evening of the following day Marius arrived at Vernon, and asked the first passer-by for the " house of Monsieur Pontmercy." For in his mind he was of the same opinion as the Restoration, and did not recognise either his father's barony or colonelcy. The house was shown him ; he rang, and a woman holding a small hand-lamp opened the door for him.

" Monsieur Pontmercy ? " Marius asked.

The woman stood motionless.

" Is this his house ? " Marius continued.

The woman shook her head in the affirmative.

" Can I speak to him ? "

The woman made a negative sign.

" Why, I am his son," Marius added ; " and he expects me."

" He no longer expects you," the woman said.

Then he noticed that she was in tears. She pointed to the door of a parlour, and he went in. In this room, which was lighted by a tallow candle placed on the mantelpiece, there were three men, one standing, one on his knees, and one lying full length upon the floor in his shirt. The one on the floor was the Colonel ; the other two were a physician and a priest praying. The Colonel had been attacked by a brain fever three days before, and having a foreboding of evil, he wrote to M. Gillenormand, asking for his son. The illness grew worse, and on the evening of Marius' arrival at Vernon, the Colonel had an attack of delirium. He leaped out of bed, in spite of the maid-servant, crying, " My son does not arrive, I will go to meet him." Then he left his bedroom, and fell on the floor of the anteroom ;—he had just expired. The physician and the curé were sent for, but both arrived too late ; the son too had also arrived too late. By the twilight gleam of the candle, a heavy tear, which had fallen from the Colonel's dead eye, could be noticed on his pallid cheek. The eye was lustreless, but the tear had not dried up. This tear was his son's delay.

Marius gazed upon this man whom he saw for the first time and the last, upon this venerable and manly face, these open eyes which no longer saw, this white hair, and the robust limbs upon which could be distinguished here and there brown lines, which were sabre cuts, and red stars, which were bullet holes. He gazed at the gigantic scar which imprinted heroism on this face, upon which God had imprinted gentleness. He thought that this man was his father, and that this man was dead, and he remained cold. The sorrow he felt was such as he would have felt in the presence of any other man whom he might have seen lying dead before him.

Mourning and lamentation were in this room. The maid-servant was weeping in a corner, the priest was praying, and could be heard sobbing, the physician wiped his eyes, and the corpse itself wept. The physician, priest, and woman looked at Marius through their affliction without saying a word, for he was the stranger. Marius, who was so little affected, felt ashamed and embarrassed at his attitude, and he let the hat which he held in his hand fall on the ground, in order to induce a belief that sorrow deprived him of the strength to hold it. At the same time he felt a species of remorse, and despised himself for acting thus. But was it his fault? he had no cause to love his father.

The Colonel left nothing, and the sale of the furniture scarce covered the funeral expenses. The maid-servant found a scrap of paper, which she handed to Marius. On it were the following lines, written by the Colonel :—

"For my Son.—The Emperor made me a Baron on the field of Waterloo, and as the Restoration contests this title, which I purchased with my blood, my son will assume it and wear it. Of course he will be worthy of it." On the back the Colonel had added, "At this same battle of Waterloo a sergeant saved my life. This man's name is Thénardier. Not long ago, I believe he kept a small inn in a village near Paris, either Chelles or Montfermeil. If my son meet this Thénardier, he will do all he can for him."

Not through any affection for his father, but owing to that vague respect for death which is ever so imperious in the heart of man, Marius took this paper and put it away. Nothing was left of the Colonel. M. Gillenormand had his sword and uniform sold to the Jews; the neighbours plundered the garden, and carried off the rare flowers, while the others became brambles and died. Marius only remained forty-eight hours in Vernon. After the funeral he returned to Paris and his legal studies, thinking no more of his father than if he had never existed. In two days the Colonel was buried, and in three forgotten.

Marius wore crape on his hat. That was all.

Marius had maintained the religious habits of his child-hood. One Sunday, when he went to hear Mass at St. Sulpice, in the same Lady's Chapel to which his aunt took him when a boy, being on that day more than usually absent and thoughtful, he placed himself behind a pillar, and knelt, without paying attention to the fact, upon a Utrecht velvet chair, on the back of which was written, "Monsieur Mabeuf, Churchwarden." The Mass had scarce begun when an old gentleman presented himself, and said to Marius:

"This is my place, sir."

Marius at once stepped aside, and the old gentleman took his seat. When Mass was ended Marius stood pensively for a few moments, till the old gentleman came up to him and said:

"I ask your pardon, sir, for having disturbed you just now, and for troubling you afresh at this moment, but you must have considered me ill-bred, and so I wish to explain the matter to you."

"It is unnecessary, sir," said Marius.

"No, it is not," the old man continued, "for I do not wish you to have a bad opinion of me. I am attached to this seat, and it seems to me that the Mass is better here, and I will tell you my reason. To this spot I saw during ten years, at regular intervals of two or three months, a poor worthy father come, who had no other opportunity or way of seeing his son, because they were separated through family arrangements. He came at the hour when he knew that his son would be brought to Mass. The boy did not suspect that his father was here—perhaps did not know, the innocent, that he had a father. The latter kept behind a pillar so that he might not be seen, looked at his child and wept; for the poor man adored him, as I could see. This spot has become, so to speak, sanctified for me, and I have fallen into the habit of hearing Mass here. I prefer it to the bench to which I should have a right as churchwarden.

I even knew the unfortunate gentleman slightly. He had a father-in-law, a rich aunt, and other relatives, who threatened to disinherit the boy if the father ever saw him, and he sacrificed himself that his son might one day be rich and happy. They were separated through political opinions, and though I certainly approve of such opinions, there are persons who do not know where to stop. Good gracious! because a man was at Waterloo he is not a monster; a father should not be separated from his child on that account. He was one of Bonaparte's colonels, and is dead, I believe. He lived at Vernon, where I have a brother who is curé, and his name was something like Pontmarie, or Montpercy. He had, on my word, a handsome sabre cut."

"Pontmercy," Marius said, turning pale.

"Precisely, Pontmercy; did you know him?"

"He was my father, sir."

The old churchwarden clasped his hands and exclaimed:

"Ah! you are the boy! Yes, yes, he would be a man now. Well, poor boy, you may say that you had a father who loved you dearly."

Marius offered his arm to the old gentleman, and conducted him to his house. The next day he said to M. Gillenormand:

"Some friends of mine have arranged a shooting party; will you permit me to go away for three days?"

"Four," the grandfather answered, "go and amuse yourself;" and he whispered to his daughter with a wink, "Some love affair!"

We shall learn presently where Marius went. He was away three days, then returned to Paris, went straight to the library of the law-school, and asked for a file of the *Moniteur*. He read it; he read all the histories of the Republic and the Empire; the *Mémorial de St. Hélène*; all the memoirs, journals, bulletins, and proclamations; he devoured all. The first time he came across his father's name in a bulletin of the grand army he had a fever for a whole week. He called upon the generals under whom George Pontmercy had served; among others, Count H——. The churchwarden, whom he saw again, told him of the life at Vernon, the colonel's retirement, his flowers, and his solitude. Marius had at last a perfect knowledge of this rare, sublime, and gentle man, this species of lion-lamb—who had been his father.

While occupied with this study, which filled all his moments as well as all his thoughts, he scarce ever saw the Gillenormands. He appeared at meals, but when sought for by them he could not be found. His aunt sulked, but old Gillenormand smiled. "Stuff, stuff, it is the right age;" at times the old man would add, "Confound it, I thought that it was an affair of gallantry, but it seems that it is a passion." It was a passion in truth, for Marius was beginning to adore his father.

At the same time an extraordinary change took place in his ideas, and the phases of this change were numerous and successive. As this is the history of many minds in our day, we deem it useful to follow these phases step by step, and indicate them all. The history he had just read startled him, and the first effect was bewilderment. The Republic, the Empire, had hitherto been to him but monstrous words,—the Republic a guillotine in the twilight; the Empire a sabre in the night. He had looked into it, and where he had only expected to find a chaos of darkness he had seen, with a species of extraordinary surprise, mingled with fear and delight, stars flashing,—Mirabeau, Vergniaud, Saint Just, Robespierre, Camille Desmoulins, and Danton,—and a sun rise, Napoleon. He knew not where he was, and he recoiled, blinded by the brilliancy. Gradually, when the first surprise had worn off, he accustomed himself to this radiance. He regarded the deed without dizziness, and examined persons without terror. The Revolution and the Empire stood out in luminous perspective before his visionary eyeballs. He saw each of these two groups of events and facts contained in two enormous facts; the Revolution in the sovereignty of civic right restored to the masses, the Empire in the sovereignty of the French idea imposed on Europe. He saw the great figure of the people emerge from the Revolution, the great figure of France from the Empire, and he declared to himself on his conscience that all this was good.

What his bewilderment neglected in this first appreciation, which was far too synthetical, we do not think it necessary to indicate here. We are describing the state of a mind advancing, and all progress is not made in one march. This said, once for all, as to what precedes and what is to follow, we will continue.

He then perceived, that up to this moment he had no more understood his country than he did his father. He

had known neither the one nor the other, and he had
spread a species of voluntary night over his eyes. He
now saw, and on one side he admired, on the other he
adored. He was full of regret and remorse, and he thought
with despair that he could only tell to a tomb all that he
had in his mind. Oh, if his father were alive, if he had
him still, if God in His compassion and His goodness
had allowed this father to be still alive, how he would
have flown, how he would have cried to his father :
"Father, here I am, it is I! I have the same heart as
you! I am your son!" How he would have kissed his
white head, bathed his hair with his tears, gazed at his
scar, pressed his hand, adored his clothes, and embraced
his feet! Oh, why did this father die so soon, before justice
had been done him, before he had known his son's love ?
At the same time he became more truly serious, more truly
grave, more sure of his faith and his thoughts. At each
instant beams of light arrived to complete his reason, and
a species of internal growth went on within him. He felt a
natural aggrandisement produced by the two things so new
to him—his father and his country.

As a door can be easily opened when we hold the key, he
explained to himself what he had hated, and understood
what he had abhorred. Henceforth he saw clearly the
providential, divine, and human meaning, the great things
which he had been taught to detest, and the great men
whom he had been instructed to curse. When he thought
of his previous opinions, which were but of yesterday, and
which yet seemed to him so old, he felt indignant and
smiled. From the rehabilitation of his father he had
naturally passed to that of Napoleon. It must be said,
however, that the latter was not effected without labour.
From childhood he had been imbued with the judgments of
the party of 1814 about Bonaparte. Now all the prejudices
of the Restoration, all its interests, and all its instincts,
tended to disfigure Napoleon, and it execrated him even
more than Robespierre. It had worked rather cleverly
upon the weariness of the nation, and the hatred of mothers.
Bonaparte had become a species of almost fabulous monster,
and in order to depict him to the imagination of the people,
which, as we said just now, resembles that of children, the
party of 1814 brought forward in turn all the frightful
masques, from that which is terrible while remaining grand,
down to that which is terrible while becoming grotesque,

from Tiberius down to old Boguey. Marius had never had on the subject of—that man, as he was called—any other ideas but these in his mind, and they were combined with his natural tenacity. He was a headstrong little man, who hated Napoleon.

On reading history, especially on studying documents and records, the veil which hid Napoleon from Marius' sight was gradually rent asunder, he caught a glimpse of something immense, and suspected that up to this moment he had been mistaken about Bonaparte, as about all the rest; each day he saw more clearly, and he began climbing slowly, step by step, at the beginning almost reluctantly, but then with intoxication, and as if attracted by an irresistible fascination, first, the gloomy steps, then the dimly lighted steps, and at last the luminous and splendid steps of enthusiasm.

One night he was alone in his little garret, his candle was lighted, and he was reading at a table by the open window. All sorts of reveries reached him from the space, and were mingled with his thoughts. He was reading the bulletins of the grand army, those Homeric strophes written on the battlefield; he saw in them at intervals the image of his father, and ever that of the Emperor; the whole of the great Empire was before him; he felt, as it were, a tide within him swelling and mounting; it seemed at moments as if his father passed close to him like a breath, and whispered in his ear; he gradually became strange, he fancied he could hear drums, cannon, and bugles, the measured tread of the battalions, and the hollow, distant gallop of the cavalry; from time to time his eyes were raised and surveyed the colossal constellations flashing in the profundities, and then they fell again upon the book, and he saw in that other colossal things stirring confusedly. His heart was contracted, he was transported, trembling and gasping; and all alone, without knowing what was within him or what he obeyed, he rose, stretched his arms out of the window, looked fixedly at the shadow, the silence, the dark infinitude, the eternal immensity, and shouted, " Long live the Emperor ! "

From this moment it was all over. The ogre of Corsica, the usurper, the tyrant, the monster, who was the lover of his own sisters, the actor who took lessons of Talma, the prisoner of Jaffa, the tiger, Buonaparté,—all this faded away, and made room in his mind for a radiance in which the pale marble phantom of Cæsar stood out serenely at an inaccessible height. The Emperor had never been to his father more than the beloved captain, whom a man admires and for whom he devotes himself, but to Marius he was far more. He was the predestined constructor of the French group which succeeded the Roman group in the dominion of the universe, he was the prodigious architect of an earthquake, the successor of Charlemagne, Louis XI., Henri IV., Richelieu, Louis XIV., and the Committee of Public Safety; he had doubtless his spots, his faults, and even his crimes, that is to say, he was a man, but he was august in his faults, brilliant in his spots, and powerful in his crime. He was the predestined man who compelled all nations to say: The great nation. He was even more, he was the very incarnation of France, conquering Europe by the sword he held, and the world by the lustre which he emitted. Marius saw in Bonaparte the dazzling spectre which will ever stand on the frontier and guard the future. He was a despot, but a dictator—a despot resulting from a republic, and completing a revolution. Napoleon became for him the man-people, as the Saviour is the man-God.

As we see, after the fashion of all new converts to a religion, his conversion intoxicated him, and he dashed into faith and went too far. The points of his moral compass were changed, and what had once been sunset was now sunrise; and all these revolutions took place in turns, without his family suspecting it. When, in this mysterious labour, he had entirely lost his old Bourbonic and Ultra skin, when he had pulled off the aristocrat, the Jacobite, and the Royalist, when he was a perfect Revolutionist, profoundly democratic, and almost republican, he went to an engraver's and ordered one hundred cards, with the address "Baron Marius Pontmercy." This was but the logical consequence of the change which had taken place in him, a change in which everything gravitated round his father. Still, as he knew nobody and could not show his cards at any porter's lodge, he put them in his pocket.

By another natural consequence, in proportion as he drew nearer to his father, his memory, and the things for which the Colonel had fought during five-and-twenty years, he drew away from his grandfather. As we said, M. Gillenormand's humour had not suited him for a long time past, and there already existed between them all the dissonances produced by the contact of a grave young man with a frivolous old man. Marius met his grandfather upon them as on a bridge, but when the bridge fell there was a great gulf between them ; and then, before all else, Marius had indescribable attacks of revolt when he reflected that it was M. Gillenormand who, through stupid motives, pitilessly tore him from the Colonel, thus depriving father of son and son of father. Through his reverence for his father, Marius had almost grown into an aversion from his grandfather.

Nothing of this, however, was revealed in his demeanour ; he merely became colder than before, laconic at meals, and rarely at home. When his aunt scolded him for it he was very gentle, and alleged as excuse his studies, examinations, conferences, etc. The grandfather, however, still adhered to his infallible diagnostic : " He is in love ; I know the symptoms." Marius was absent every now and then.

" Where can he go ? " the aunt asked.

In one of his trips, which were always very short, he went to Montfermeil in order to obey his father's intimation, and sought for the former sergeant of Waterloo, Thénardier, the landlord. Thénardier had failed, the public-house was shut up, and no one knew what had become of him. In making this search Marius remained away for four days.

" He is decidedly getting out of order," said the grandfather.

They also fancied they could notice that he wore under his shirt something hung round his neck by a black ribbon.

CHAPTER LXVII.

WE have made reference to a Lancer : he was a greatgrand-nephew of M. Gillenormand's, on the father's side, who led a garrison life, far away from the domestic hearth. Lieutenant Théodule Gillenormand fulfilled all the conditions required for a man to be a pretty officer : he had a young lady's waist, a victorious way of clanking his sabre, and turned-up moustache. He came very rarely to Paris, so rarely that Marius had never seen him, and the two cousins only knew each other by name. Théodule was, we think we said, the favourite of Aunt Gillenormand, who preferred him because she never saw him ; for not seeing people allows of every possible perfection being attributed to them.

One morning Mlle Gillenormand the elder returned to her apartments, as much affected as her general placidity would allow. Marius had again asked his grandfather's permission to make a short trip, adding that he wished to start that same evening. "Go," the grandfather answered; and he added to himself, as he pursed up his eye, "Another relapse of sleeping from home." Mlle Gillenormand went up to her room greatly puzzled, and cast to the staircase this exclamation, "It's too much!" and this question, "But where is it that he goes?" She caught a glimpse of some more or less illicit love adventure, of a woman in the shadow, a meeting, a mystery, and would not have felt vexed to have a closer peep at it through her spectacles. Scenting a mystery is like the first bite at a piece of scandal, and holy souls do not detest it. In the secret compartments of bigotry there is some curiosity for scandal.

She was, therefore, suffering from a vague appetite to learn a story. In order to distract this curiosity, which agitated her a little beyond her wont, she took refuge in her talents, and began festooning with cotton upon cotton one of those embroideries of the Empire and the Restoration, in which there are a great many cabriolet wheels. It was a clumsy job, and the workwoman was awkward. She had been sitting over it for some hours when the door opened. Mlle Gillenormand raised her nose, and saw Lieutenant Théodule before her, making his regulation salute. She uttered a cry of delight; for a woman may be old, a prude, devout, and an aunt, but she is always glad to see a Lancer enter her room.

"You here, Théodule!" she exclaimed. "Are you travelling on horseback, with your regiment?"

"No, my aunt. We are changing garrison, and I have come to see you by special permission. My servant is leading my horse, and I shall travel by the diligence. By the way, there is one thing I want to ask you."

"What is it?"

"It appears that my cousin Marius Pontmercy is going on a journey too?"

"How do you know that?" the aunt said, her curiosity being greatly tickled.

"On reaching Paris I went to the coach-office to take my place in the coupé."

"Well?"

"A traveller had already taken a seat in the Impériale, and I saw his name in the way-bill: it was Marius Pont-mercy."

"Oh, the scamp," the aunt exclaimed. "Ah! your cousin is not a steady lad like you. To think that he is going to pass the night in a diligence!"

"Like myself."

"You do it through duty, but he does it through dissipation."

"The deuce!" said Théodule.

Here an event occurred to Mademoiselle Gillenormand the elder: she had an idea. If she had been a man she would have struck her forehead. She addressed Théodule.

"You are aware that your cousin does not know you?"

"I have seen him, but he never deigned to notice me."

"Where is the diligence going to?"

"To Andelys."

"Is Marius going there?"

"Unless he stops on the road, like myself. I get out at Vernon, to take the Gaillon coach. I know nothing about Marius' route."

"Marius! what an odious name! what an idea it was to call him that! well, your name, at least, is Théodule."

"I would rather it was Alfred," the officer said.

"Listen, Théodule; Marius absents himself from the house; he goes about the country; he sleeps out. We should like to know the meaning of all this."

Théodule replied, with the calmness of a bronze man, "Some petticoat!"

"That is evident!" the aunt exclaimed, and then continued, "Do us a pleasure by following Marius a little. As he does not know you, that will be an easy matter. Since there is a girl in the case, try to get a look at her, and write and tell us all about it, for it will amuse your grandfather."

Théodule had no excessive inclination for this sort of watching, but he accepted the commission, and said, "As you please, aunt," and added in an aside, "I am a Duenna now!"

Marius, on the evening that followed this dialogue, got into the diligence, not suspecting that he was watched. As for the watcher, the first thing he did was to fall asleep, and his sleep was complete and conscientious. Argus snored the whole night. At daybreak the guard shouted, "Vernon; passengers for Vernon, get out here!" and Lieutenant Théodule got out.

"All right," he growled, still half asleep, "I get out here."

Then his memory growing gradually clearer, he thought of his aunt, the ten louis, and the account he had promised to render of Marius' sayings and doings. This made him laugh.

"He is probably no longer in the coach," he thought, while buttoning up his jacket. "He may have stopped at Poissy, he may have stopped at Triel, if he did not get out at Meulan, he may have done so at Mantes, unless he stopped at Rolleboise, or only went as far as Passy, with the choice of turning on his left to Estreux, or on his right to La Rocheguyon. Run after him, aunty. What the deuce shall I write to the old lady?"

At this moment the leg of a black trouser appeared against the window-pane of the coupé.

"Can it be Marius?" the lieutenant said.

It was Marius. A little peasant girl was offering flowers to the passengers, and crying "Bouquets for your ladies." Marius went up to her, and bought the finest flowers in her basket.

"By Jove," said Théodule, as he leaped out of the coupé, "the affair is growing piquant. Who the deuce is he going to carry those flowers to? she must be a deucedly pretty woman to deserve so handsome a bouquet. I must have a look at her."

And then he began following Marius, no longer by order, but through personal curiosity, like those dogs which hunt on their own account. Marius paid no attention to Théodule. Some elegant women were getting out of the diligence, but he did not look at them; he seemed to see nothing around him.

"He must be preciously in love," Théodule thought. Marius proceeded toward the church.

"That's glorious!" Théodule said to himself, "the church, that's the thing. Rendezvous spiced with a small amount of mass are the best. Nothing is so exquisite as an ogle exchanged in the presence of the Virgin."

On reaching the church, Marius did not go in, but disappeared behind one of the buttresses of the apse.

"The meeting outside," Théodule said; "now for a look at the girl."

And he walked on tiptoe up to the corner which Marius had gone round, and on reaching it stopped in stupefaction. Marius, with his forehead in both his hands, was kneeling in the grass upon a tomb, and had spread his flowers out over it. At the head of the grave was a cross of black wood, with this name in white letters : COLONEL BARON PONT-MERCY. He heard Marius sobbing.

The girl was a tomb.

It is here that Marius had come the first time that he absented himself from Paris ; it was to this spot he retired each time that M. Gillenormand said, "He sleeps out." Lieutenant Théodule was absolutely discountenanced by this unexpected elbowing of a tomb, and felt a disagreeable and singular sensation, which he was incapable of analysing, and which was composed of respect for a tomb, mingled with respect for a colonel. He fell back, leaving Marius alone in the cemetery, and there was discipline in this retreat ; death appeared to him wearing heavy epaulettes, and he almost gave it the military salute. Not knowing what to write to his aunt, he resolved not to write at all ; and there would probably have been no result from Théodule's discovery of Marius' armour had not, by one of those mysterious arrangements so frequent in accident, the scene at Vernon had almost immediately a sort of counterpart in Paris.

Marius returned from Vernon very early on the morning of the third day, and wearied by two nights spent in a diligence, and feeling the necessity of repairing his want of sleep by an hour at the swimming-school, he hurried up to his room, only took the time to take off his travelling coat and the black ribbon which he had round his neck, and went to the bath. M. Gillenormand, who rose at an early hour like all old men who are in good health, heard him come in, and hastened as quick as his old legs would carry him up the stairs leading to Marius' garret, in order to welcome him back, and try and discover his movements. But the young man had taken less time in descending than the octogenarian in ascending, and when Father Gillenormand entered the garret Marius was no longer there. The bed had been unoccupied, and on it lay the coat and black ribbon unsuspectingly.

"I prefer that," said M. Gillenormand, and a moment later he entered the drawing-room, while Mlle Gillenormand the elder was already seated embroidering her cabriolet wheels. The entrance was triumphant, M. Gillenormand held in one hand the coat, in the other the neck-ribbon, and shouted :

"Victory ! we are going to penetrate the mystery, we are going to know the cream of the joke, we are going to lay our hands on the libertinage of our cunning gentleman. Here is the romance itself, for I have the portrait."

In fact, a box of shagreen leather, much like a miniature, was suspended from the ribbon. The old man took hold of this box, and looked at it for some time without opening, with the air of pleasure, eagerness, and anger of a poor starving fellow, who sees a splendid dinner, of which he will have no share, carried past under his nose.

"It is evidently a portrait, and I am up to that sort of thing. It is worn tenderly on the heart,—what asses they are ! 'some .abominable gorgon, who will probably make me shudder, for young men have such bad tastes nowadays."

"Let us look, father," the old maid said.

The box opened by pressing a spring, but they only found in it a carefully folded-up paper.

"From the same to the same," said M. Gillenormand, bursting into a laugh. "I know what it is, a love-letter!"

"Indeed ! let us read it," said the aunt ; and she put on her spectacles. They unfolded the paper and read as follows :—

"For my Son.—The Emperor made me a Baron on the field of Waterloo, and as the Restoration contests this title which I purchased with my blood, my son will assume it and wear it ; of course he will be worthy of it."

What the father and daughter felt, it is not possible to describe ; but they were chilled as if by the breath of a death's head. They did not exchange a syllable. M. Gillenormand merely said in a low voice, and as if speaking to himself, "It is that trooper's handwriting." The hand examined the slip of paper, turned it about in all directions, and then placed it again in the box.

At the same instant, a small square packet, wrapped up in blue paper, fell from a pocket of the coat. Mlle Gillenormand picked it up and opened the blue paper. It contained Marius' one hundred cards, and she passed one to M. Gillenormand, who read, "Baron Marius Pontmercy." The old man rang, and Nicolette came in. M. Gillenormand took the ribbon, the box, and the coat, threw them on the ground in the middle of the room, and said :

"Remove that rubbish."

A long hour passed in the deepest silence; the old man and the old maid were sitting back to back and thinking, probably both of the same things. At the end of this hour, Mlle Gillenormand said, "Very pretty!" A few minutes after, Marius came in; even before he crossed the threshold he perceived his grandfather holding one of his cards in his hand. On seeing Marius he exclaimed, with his air of bourgeois and grimacing superiority, which had something crushing about it :

"Stay! stay! stay! stay! stay! You are a baron at present; I must congratulate you. What does this mean?"

Marius blushed slightly, and answered :

"It means that I am my father's son."

M. Gillenormand left off laughing, and said harshly, "I am your father."

"My father," Marius continued with downcast eyes and a stern air, "was a humble and heroic man, who gloriously served the Republic of France, who was great in the greatest history which men have ever made, who lived for a quarter of a century in a bivouac, by day under a shower of grape-shot and bullets, and at night in snow, mud, wind, and rain. He was a man who took two flags, received twenty wounds, died in forgetfulness and abandonment, and who had never committed but one fault, that of loving too dearly two ungrateful beings—his country and myself."

This was more than M. Gillenormand could bear; at the word Republic he had risen, or, more correctly, sprung up. Each of the words that Marius had just uttered had produced on the old gentleman's face the same effect as the blast of a forge-bellows upon a burning log. From gloomy he became red, from red, purple, and from purple, flaming.

"Marius," he shouted, "you abominable boy! I know not who your father was, and do not wish to know. I know nothing about it, but what I do know is, that there never were any but scoundrels among all those people; they were all rogues, assassins, red-caps, robbers! I say all, I say all! I know nobody! I saw all; do you understand me, Marius? You must know that you are as much a baron as my slipper is! They were all bandits who served

Robespierre! they were all brigands who served B-u-o-naparte! all traitors who betrayed, betrayed, betrayed their legitimate king! all cowards who ran away from the Prussians and the English at Waterloo. That is what I know. If your father was among them, I am ignorant of the fact, and am sorry for it. I am your humble servant!"

In his turn, Marius became the brand, and M. Gillenormand the bellows. Marius trembled all over, he knew not what to do, and his head was aglow. He was the priest who sees his consecrated wafers cast to the wind, the fakir who notices a passer-by spit on his idol. It was impossible that such things could be said with impunity in his presence, but what was he to do? His father had just been trampled under foot, and insulted in his presence, but by whom? by his grandfather. How was he to avenge the one without outraging the other? It was impossible for him to insult his grandfather, and equally impossible for him not to avenge his father. On one side was a sacred tomb, on the other was white hair. He tottered for a few moments like a drunken man, then raised his eyes, looked fixedly at his grandfather, and shouted in a thundering voice:

"Down with the Bourbons, and that great pig of a Louis XVIII.!"

Louis XVIII. had been dead four years, but that made no difference to him. The old man, who had been scarlet, suddenly became whiter than his hair. He turned to a bust of the Duc de Berry which was on the mantelpiece, and bowed to it profoundly with a sort of singular majesty. Then he walked twice, slowly and silently, from the mantelpiece to the window, and from the window to the mantelpiece, crossing the whole room, and making the boards creak as if he were a walking marble statue. The second time he leant over his daughter, who was looking at the disturbance with the stupor of an old sheep, and said to her with a smile which was almost calm:

"A baron like this gentleman, and a bourgeois like myself, can no longer remain beneath the same roof."

And suddenly drawing himself up, livid, trembling, and terrible, with his forehead dilated by the fearful radiance of passion, he stretched out his arm toward Marius, and shouted "Begone!"

Marius left the house, and on the morrow M. Gillenormand said to his daughter:

"You will send every six months sixty pistoles to that blood-drinker, and never mention his name to me."

Having an immense amount of fury to expend, and not knowing what to do with it, he continued to address his daughter as "you" instead of "thou" for upwards of three months.

Marius, on his side, left the house indignant, and a circumstance aggravated his exasperation. There are always small fatalities of this nature to complicate domestic dramas : the anger is augmented although the wrongs are not in reality increased. In hurriedly conveying, by the grandfather's order, Marius' rubbish to his bedroom, Nicolette, without noticing the fact, let fall, probably on the attic stairs, which were dark, the black shagreen case in which was the paper written by the Colonel. As neither could be found, Marius felt convinced that "Monsieur Gillenormand"—he never called him otherwise from that date—had thrown "his father's will" into the fire. He knew by heart the few lines written by the Colonel, and consequently nothing was lost ; but the paper, the writing, that sacred relic,—all that was his heart itself. What had been done with it?

Marius went away without saying where he was going and without knowing, with thirty francs, his watch, and some clothes in a carpet-bag. He jumped into a cabriolet, engaged it by the hour, and drove at random to the Latin Quarter. What would Marius do?

CHAPTER LXVIII.

AT this period, which was apparently careless, a certain revolutionary quivering was vaguely felt. There were breezes in the air which returned from the depths of '89 and '92 ; and the young men, if we may be forgiven the expression, were in the moulting stage. Men became transformed, almost without suspecting it, by the mere movement of time, for the hand which moves round the clock-face also moves in the mind. Each took the forward step he had to take; the royalists became liberals, and the liberals, democrats. It was like a rising tide complicated by a thousand ebbs, and it is the peculiarity of ebbs to cause things to mingle. Hence came very singular combinations of ideas, and men adored liberty and Napoleon at the same time. We are writing history here, and such were the mirages of that period. Opinions pass through phases, and Voltairian royalism, a strange variety, had a no less strange companion in Bonapartist liberalism.

Other groups of minds were more serious. At one spot principles were sounded, and at another men clung to their rights. They became impassioned for the absolute, and obtained glimpses of infinite realisations. There is nothing like the dogma to originate a dream, and nothing like a dream to engender the future ; the Utopia of to-day is flesh and bone to-morrow. Advanced opinions had a false bottom, and a commencement of mystery threatened "Established order," which was suspicious and cunning. This is a most revolutionary sign. There were not as yet in France any of those vast subjacent organisations, like the Tugenbund of Germany or the Carbonari of Italy ; but here and there were dark subterranean passages with extensive ramifications. The Cougourde was started at Aix ; and there was at Paris, among other affiliations of this nature, the Society of the Friends of the A B C.

Who were the Friends of the A B C ? A society, whose ostensible object was the education of children, but the real one the elevation of men. They called themselves Friends of the A B C, and the people were the *abaissés* whom they wished to raise. The Friends of the A B C were few in number ; it was a secret society, in a state of embryo, and we might almost call it a coterie, if coteries produced heroes. They assembled at two places in Paris ; at a cabaret called Corinthe, near the Halles, to which we shall revert hereafter, and near the Pantheon, in a small café on the Place St. Michel, known as the Café Musain, and now demolished : the first of these meeting-places was contiguous to the workmen, and the second to the students. The ordinary discussions of the Friends of the A B C were held in a back room of the Café Musain. This room, some distance from the coffee-room, with which it communicated by a very long passage, had two windows and an issue by a secret staircase into the little Rue des Grès. They smoked, drank, played, and laughed there ; they spoke very loudly about everything, and in a whisper about the other thing. On the wall hung—which would have been a sufficient hint for a police-agent—an old map of France under the Republic.

Most of the Friends of the A B C were students, who maintained a thorough understanding with a few workmen.

Here are the names of the principal members, which belong in a certain measure to history : Enjolras, Combeferre, Jean Prouvaire, Feuilly, Courfeyrac, Bahorel, Lesgle or Laigle, Joly, and Grantaire. These young men formed a species of family through their friendship, and all came from the South, excepting Laigle. This group is remarkable, although it has vanished in the invisible depths which are behind us. At the point of this drama which we have now attained, it will not be labour lost, perhaps, to throw a ray of light upon these heads, before the reader watches them enter the shadow of a tragical fate.

Enjolras, whom we named first, it will be seen afterwards why, was an only son, and rich. He was a charming young man, capable of becoming terrible ; he was angelically beautiful, and looked like a stern Antinous. On noticing the pensive depth of his glance you might have fancied that he had gone through the revolutionary apocalypse in some preceding existence. He knew the traditions of it like an eye-witness, and was acquainted with all the minor details of the great thing. His was a pontifical and warlike nature, strange in a young man ; he was a churchman and a militant ; from the immediate point of view a soldier of democracy, but, above the contemporary movement, a priest of the ideal. He had a slightly red eyelid, a thick and easily disdainful lower lip, and a lofty forehead ; a good deal of forehead on a face is like a good deal of sky in a horizon. Like certain young men of the beginning of the present century and the end of the last, who became illustrious at an early age, he looked excessively young, and was as fresh as a schoolgirl, though he had his hours of pallor. Although a man, he seemed still a boy, and his two-and-twenty years looked like only seventeen. He was serious, and did not appear to know that there was on the earth a being called woman. He had only one passion, justice, and only one thought, overthrowing the obstacle. On the Mons Aventinus, he would have been Gracchus ; in the Convention, he would have been St. Just. He scarcely noticed roses, was ignorant of spring, and did not hear the birds sing ; the bare throat of Evadne would have affected him as little as it did Aristogiton ; to him, as to Harmodius, flowers were only good to conceal the sword. He was stern in his joy, and before all that was not the Republic, he chastely lowered his eyes — he was the marble lover of liberty. His language had a sharp inspiration and a species of rhythmic strain. Woe to the girl who ventured to ensnare him ! If any grisette of the Place Cambray, or the Rue St. Jean de Beauvais, seeing this face so like that of a page, his long light lashes, his blue eyes, his hair floating wildly in the breeze, his pink cheeks, cherry lips, and exquisite teeth, had felt a longing for all this dawn, and tried the effect of her charms upon Enjolras, a formidable look of surprise would have suddenly shown her the abyss, and taught her not to confound the avenging cherub of Ezekiel with the gallant cherub of Beaumarchais.

By the side of Enjolras, who represented the logic of the revolution, Combeferre represented its philosophy. Between the logic and the philosophy of revolutions, there is this difference, that the logic may conclude in war, while its philosophy can only lead to peace. Combeferre completed and rectified Enjolras ; he was not so tall, but broader. He wished that the extended principles of general ideas should be poured over minds, and said, " Revolution, but civilisation ! " and he opened the vast blue horizon around the peaked mountain. Hence there was something accessible and practicable in all Combeferre's views ; and the revolution with him was more respectable than with Enjolras. Enjolras expressed its divine right and Combeferre its natural right, and while the former clung to Robespierre, the latter bordered upon Condorcet. Combeferre loved more than Enjolras the ordinary life of mankind ; and if these two young men had gained a place in history, the one would have been the just man, the other the sage. Enjolras was more manly, Combeferre more humane. Combeferre was gentle as Enjolras was stern, through natural purity ; he loved the word citizen, but preferred man. He read everything, went to the theatres, attended the public lectures, learned from Arago the polarisation of light, and grew quite excited about a lecture in which Geoffrey Saint Hilaire explained the double functions of the external and internal carotid arteries, the one which makes the face, and the other which produces the brain ; he was conversant with, and followed, science step by step, confronted St. Simon with Fourier, deciphered hieroglyphics, broke pebbles which he found, drew from memory a bombyx butterfly, pointed out the errors in French in the Dictionary of the Academy, studied Puységur and Deleuze, affirmed nothing, not even miracles, denied nothing, not even ghosts, turned over the file of the *Moniteur*, and reflected. He declared that the future was in the hands of the schoolmaster, and busied himself with educational questions. He wished that society should labour without relaxation at the elevation of the intellectual and moral standard, at coining science, bringing ideas into circulation, and making the minds of youth grow; and he feared that the present poverty of methods, the wretchedness from the literary point of view of confining studies to two or three centuries called classical, the tyrannical dogmatism of official pedants, scholastic prejudices, and routine, would in the end convert our colleges into artificial oyster-beds. He was learned, a purist, polite, and Polytechnic, a delver, and at the same time pensive, "even to a chimera," as his friends said. He believed in all dreams, railways, the suppression of suffering in surgical operations, fixing the image of the camera obscura, electric telegraphy, and the steering of balloons. He was but slightly terrified by the citadels built on all sides against the human race by superstitions, despotisms, and prejudices, for he was one of those men who think that science will in the end turn the position. Enjolras was a chief, and Combeferre a guide; you would have liked to fight under one and march with the other. Not that Combeferre was incapable of fighting. He did not refuse to seize obstacles round the waist and attack them by main force; but it pleased him better to bring the human race into harmony with its destiny, gradually, by the instruction of axioms and the promulgation of positive laws; and with a choice between two lights, his inclination was for illumination rather than fire. A fire may certainly produce a dawn, but why not wait for daybreak? A volcano illumines, but the sun does so far better. Combeferre perhaps preferred the whiteness of the beautiful to the flashing of the sublime, and a brightness clouded by smoke, a progress purchased by violence, only half satisfied his tender and serious mind. A headlong hurling of a people into the truth, a '93, startled him; still stagnation was more repulsive to him, for he smelt in it putrefaction and death. In a word, he desired neither halt nor haste, and while his tumultuous friends who were chivalrously attracted by the absolute, adored and summoned the splendid revolutionary adventurer, Combeferre inclined to leave progress, right progress, to act—it might be cold but it was pure, methodical but irreproachable, and phlegmatic but imperturbable. Combeferre would have knelt down and prayed that this future might arrive with all its candour, and that nothing might disturb the immense virtuous evolution of the people. "The good must be innocent," he repeated incessantly.

Jean Prouvaire was of an even more gentle nature than Combeferre. He was called Jehan, through that little momentary fantasy which was blended with the powerful and profound movement, from which issued the most necessary study of the Middle Ages. Jean Prouvaire was addicted to love, cultivated a pot of flowers, played the flute, wrote verses, loved the people, pitied women, wept over children, confounded in the same confidence the future and God, and blamed the Revolution for having caused a royal head to fall, that of André Chénier. He had a voice which was habitually delicate, and suddenly became masculine ; he was erudite, and almost an Orientalist. He was good before all, and through a motive which those will easily understand who know how closely goodness borders on grandeur, he loved immensity in poetry. He knew Italian, Latin, Greek, and Hebrew, and he employed his knowledge to read only four poets—Dante, Juvenal, Æschylus, and Isaiah. In French he preferred Corneille to Racine, and Agrippa d'Aubigné to Corneille. He was fond of strolling about the fields of wild oats and cornflowers, and occupied himself with clouds almost as much as with events. His mind had two attitudes—one turned to man, the other to God ; he either studied or contemplated. The whole day long he studied social questions—wages, capital, credit, marriage, religion, liberty of thought, liberty of love, education, the penal code, wretchedness, partnership, property, production, and division, that enigma of the lower world which casts a shadow over the human ant-heap, and at night he looked at the stars, those enormous beings. Like Enjolras, he was rich, and an only son ; he talked softly, hung his head, looked down, smiled with an embarrassed air, dressed badly, had an awkward gait, blushed at nothing, and was very timid ; for all that he was intrepid.

Feuilly was a fan-maker, doubly an orphan, who with difficulty earned three francs a day, and had only one idea —to deliver the world. He had another preoccupation as well, instructing himself, which he called self-deliverance. He had taught himself to read and write ; and all that he knew he had learned alone. Feuilly had a generous heart, and hugged the world. This orphan had adopted the people, and as he had no mother, he meditated on his country. He had wished that there should not be in the world a man who had no country, and he brooded over what we now call the "idea of nationalities" with the profound divination of the man of the people. He had studied history expressly that he might be indignant with a knowledge of the fact, and in this youthful assembly of Utopians who were specially interested about France, he represented the foreign element. His speciality was Greece, Poland, Roumania, Hungary, and Italy; he pronounced these names incessantly, in season and out of season, with the tenacity of right. The violations committed by Turkey on Greece and Thessaly, of Russia on Warsaw, and Austria on Venice, exasperated him, and above all the great highway robbery of 1772 aroused him. There can be no more sovereign eloquence than truth in indignation, and he was eloquent with that eloquence. He never left off talking about the infamous date 1772, the noble and valiant people suppressed by treachery, this crime committed by three accomplices, and the monstrous ambush, which is the prototype and pattern of all those frightful suppressions of states, which have since struck several nations, and have, so to speak, erased their name from the baptismal register. All the social assaults of the present day emanate from the division of Poland, and it is a theorem, to which all our political crimes are corollaries. There is not a despot or a traitor who for a century past has not revised, confirmed, countersigned, and margined with the words *ne varietur*, the division of Poland. Such was Feuilly's usual text. This poor workman had made himself the guardian of justice, and she rewarded him by making him grand.

Courfeyrac had a father whose name was M. de Courfeyrac. One of the incorrect ideas of the bourgeoisie of the Restoration in the matter of the aristocracy and the nobility was a belief in the particle. The particle, as we know, has no meaning, but the bourgeois of the time of *La Minerve* esteemed this poor *de* so highly that persons thought themselves obliged to abdicate it. M. de Chauvelin called himself M. Chauvelin, M. de Caumartin, M. Caumartin, M. de Constant de Rebecque, Benjamin Constant, and M. de Lafayette, M. Lafayette. Courfeyrac was unwilling to remain behindhand, and called himself Courfeyrac quite short. As concerns this gentleman, we might almost stop here and content ourselves with saying as to the rest, *for* Courfeyrac *read* Tholomyès; Courfeyrac, in fact, had those sallies of youth which might be called a mental *beauté du diable*. At a later date this expires like the prettiness of the kitten; and all this grace produces, upon two feet the bourgeois, and on four paws the tomcat. The only thing was that Courfeyrac was an honest fellow, and beneath an apparent external similitude, the difference between Tholomyès and himself was great, and the latent man who existed within them was very different in the former from what it was in the latter. In Tholomyès there was an attorney, and in Courfeyrac a Paladin; Enjolras was the chief, Combeferre the guide, and Courfeyrac the centre. The others gave more light, but he produced more heat; and he had in truth all the qualities of a centre, in the shape of roundness and radiation.

Bahorel had been mixed up in the sanguinary tumult of June, 1822, on the occasion of the burial of young Lallemand. Bahorel was a being of good temper and bad company, an honest fellow and a spendthrift, prodigal and meeting with generosity, chattering and meeting with eloquence, bold and meeting with effrontery; and the very best clay for the devil's moulding imaginable. He displayed daring waist-coats and scarlet opinions; he was a turbulent on a grand scale, that is to say, that he liked nothing so much as a quarrel unless it were a riot, and nothing so much as a riot except a revolution. He was ever ready to break a pane of glass, tear up the paving-stones, and demolish a government, in order to see the effect—he was a student in his eleventh year. He sniffed at the law, but did not practise it, and he had taken as his motto "never a lawyer," and as his coat of arms a night-table surmounted by a square cap. Whenever he passed in front of the law-school, which rarely happened to him, he buttoned up his overcoat and took hygienic precautions. He said of the school gate, "What a fierce old man!" and of the Dean M. Devincourt, "What a monument!" He found in his lectures a subject for coarse songs, and in his professors an occasion for laughter. He spent in doing nothing a very considerable allowance, something like three thousand francs, and his parents were peasants in whom he had inculcated a respect for their son. He used to say of them, "They are peasants, and not townspeople, that is why they are so intelligent." Bahorel, as a capricious man, visited several cafés; and while the others had habits he had none. He strolled about: if *errare* is human, strolling is Parisian. Altogether, he had a penetrating mind, and thought more than people fancied. He served as the connecting link between the Friends of the A B C and other groups which were still unformed, but which were to take form afterwards.

In this assembly of young men, there was a bald-headed member. The Marquis d'Avaray, whom Louis XVIII. made a duke because he helped him to get into a hired cab on the day when he emigrated, used to tell how, when the King landed in 1814 at Calais upon his return to France, a man handed him a petition.

"What do you want?" the King said.

"A postmastership, sire."

"What is your name?"

"L'Aigle."

The King frowned, but looked at the signature of the petition, and read the name thus written, LESGLE. This, anything but Bonapartist orthography, touched the King, and he began smiling. "Sire," the man with the petition went on, "my ancestor was a whipper-in of the name of Lesgueules, and my name came from that. I called myself Lesgueules, by contraction Lesgle, and by corruption L'Aigle." This remark caused the King to smile still more, and at a later date he gave the man the post-office at Meaux, purposely or through a mistake. The bald Mentor of the group was son of this Lesgle or Legle, and signed himself Legle (of Meaux). His comrades, to shorten this, called him Bossuet, who, as everybody knows, was christened the Eagle of Meaux.

Bossuet was a merry fellow, who was unlucky, and his speciality was to succeed in nothing. On the other hand, he laughed at everything. At the age of five-and-twenty he was bald; his father left him a house and a field, but the son knew nothing so pressing as to lose them both in a swindling speculation, and nothing was left him. He had learning and sense, but he failed in everything, and everything cozened him; whatever he built up broke down under him. If he chopped wood, he cut his fingers; and if he had a mistress, he speedily discovered that she had also a friend. At every moment some misfortune happened to him, and hence came his joviality; and he used to say, "I live under the roof of falling tiles." Feeling but slight astonishment, for every accident was foreseen by him, he accepted ill-luck serenely, and smiled at the pin-pricks of destiny like a man who is listening to a good joke. He was poor, but his

wallet of good-humour was inexhaustible ; he speedily
reached his last halfpenny, but never his last laugh.
When adversity entered his room he bowed to his old
acquaintance cordially ; he tickled catastrophes in the ribs,
and was so familiar with fatality as to call it by a nickname.

These persecutions of fate had rendered him inventive,
and he was full of resources. He had no money, but
contrived to make a "frenzied outlay" whenever he
thought proper. One night he went so far as to devour
a hundred francs in a supper with a girl, which inspired
him in the middle of the orgie with the memorable remark,
"Fille de cinq Louis (Saint Louis) ; pull off my boots."
Bossuet was advancing slowly to the legal profession, and
studied law much after the fashion of Bahorel. Bossuet
had but little domicile, at times none at all, and he lived
first with one and then with the other, but most frequently
with Joly.

Joly was a student of medicine, of two years' younger
standing than Bossuet, and was the young imaginary sick
man. What he had gained by his medical studies was to
be more a patient than a doctor, for at the age of twenty-
three he fancied himself a valetudinarian, and spent his life
in looking at his tongue in a mirror. He declared that a
man becomes magnetised like a needle, and in his room he
placed his bed with the head to the south and the feet to the
north, so that at night the circulation of his blood might not
be impeded by the great magnetic current of the globe. In
storms he felt his pulse, but for all that was the gayest of
all. All these incoherences, youth, mania, dyspepsia, and
fun, lived comfortably together, and the result was an
eccentric and agreeable being, whom his comrades, lavish
of liquid consonants, called Jollly. Joly was accustomed to
touch his nose with the end of his cane, which is the sign of
a sagacious mind.

All these young men, who differed so greatly, and of
whom, after all, we must speak seriously, had the same
religion—Progress. They were all the direct sons of the
French Revolution, and the lightest among them became
serious when pronouncing the date of '69. Their fathers
in the flesh were, or had been, feuilletants, royalists, or
doctrinaires, but that was of little consequence ; this pell-
mell, anterior to themselves, who were young, did not
concern them, and the pure blood of principles flowed
in their veins ; they attached themselves, without any

intermediate tinge, to incorruptible right and absolute duty.

Amid all these impassioned hearts and convinced minds there was a sceptic ; how did he get there ? through juxtaposition. The name of this sceptic was Grantaire, and he usually wrote it after the manner of this rebus ; R [*grand R*—great R]. Grantaire was a man who carefully avoided believing in anything ; he was, however, one of these students who had learned the most during a Parisian residence. He knew that the best coffee was at Lemblier's, and the best billiard-table at the Café Voltaire ; that excellent cakes and agreeable girls could be found at the Hermitage on the Boulevard du Maine, broiled chickens at Mother Saquet's, excellent matelottes at the Barrière de la Cunette, and a peculiar white wine at the Barrière du Combat. Besides all this, he was a mighty drinker. He was abominably ugly, and Irma Boissy, the prettiest bootbinder of that day, in her indignation at his ugliness, passed the verdict : " Grantaire is impossible." But Grantaire's fatuity was not disconcerted by this. He looked tenderly and fixedly at every woman, and assumed an expression of " If I only liked ! " and he tried to make his companions believe that he was in general demand with the sex.

All such words as rights of the people, rights of man, the social contract, the French Revolution, republic, democracy, humanity, civilisation, progress, had as good as no meaning with Grantaire, and he smiled at them. Scepticism, that curse of the intellect, had not left one whole idea in his mind. He lived in irony, and his axiom was, " There is only one thing certain, my full glass." He ridiculed every act of devotion in every party, in the brother as much as the father, young Robespierre as heartily as Loizerolles. " They made great progress by dying," he would exclaim ; and would say of the crucifix, " There is a gallows which was successful." Idler, gambler, libertine, and often intoxicated, he annoyed these young democrats by incessantly singing, " I love the girls and I love good wine," to the tune of " Long live Henry IV."

However, this sceptic had a fanaticism. It was neither an idea, a dogma, an act, nor a sense ; it was a man,— Enjolras. Grantaire admired, loved, and revered Enjolras. Whom did this anarchical doubter cling to in this phalanx of absolute minds ? to the most absolute. In what way did Enjolras subjugate him ? by ideas ? No, but by character.

This is a frequently-observed phenomenon, and a sceptic who clings to a believer is as simple as the law of complementary colours. What we do not possess attracts us ; no one loves daylight like the blind man ; the dwarf adores the drum-major, and the frog has its eyes constantly fixed on heaven to see the bird fly. Grantaire, in whom doubt grovelled, liked to see faith soaring in Enjolras, and he felt the want of him, without clearly understanding it, or even dreaming of explaining the fact to himself. This chaste, healthy, firm, upright, harsh, and candid nature charmed him, and he instinctively admired his contrary. His soft, yielding, dislocated, sickly, and shapeless ideas attached themselves to Enjolras as to a vertebra, and his moral rickets supported themselves by this firmness. Grantaire, by the side of Enjolras, became somebody again ; and he was, moreover, himself composed of two apparently irreconcilable elements,—he was ironical and cordial. His mind dispensed with belief, but his heart could not dispense with friendship.

Grantaire, a true satellite of Enjolras, dwelt in this circle of young men : he lived there, he solely enjoyed himself there, and he followed them everywhere. His delight was to see their shadows coming and going through the fumes of wine, and he was tolerated for his good-humour. Enjolras, as a believer, disdained this sceptic, and as a sober man scorned this drunkard, but he granted him a little haughty pity.

CHAPTER LXIX.

On a certain afternoon, which had, as we shall see, some coincidence with events before related, Laigle de Meaux was sensually leaning against the door-post of the Café Musain. He looked like a caryatid out for a holiday, and having nothing to carry but his reverie. Leaning on one's shoulder is a mode of lying down upright which is not disliked by dreamers. Laigle de Meaux was thinking, without melancholy, of a slight misadventure which had occurred to him on the previous day but one at the law-school, and modified his personal plans for the future, which, as it was, were somewhat indefinite.

Reverie does not prevent a cabriolet from going by, or a dreamer from noticing the cabriolet. Laigle, whose eyes were absently wandering, saw through this somnambulism a two-wheeled vehicle moving across the Place St. Michel at a foot-pace and apparently undecided. What did this cab want? why was it going so slowly? Laigle looked at it, and saw inside a young man seated by the side of the driver and in front of the young man a carpet-bag. The bag displayed to passers-by this name, written in large black letters on the card sewn to the cloth: MARIUS PONT-MERCY. This name made Laigle change his attitude: he drew himself up, and shouted to the young man in the cab, "M. Marius Pontmercy."

The cab stopped, on being thus hailed, and the young man, who also appeared to be thinking deeply, raised his eyes.

"Well?" he said.

"Are you M. Pontmercy?"

"Yes."

"I was looking for you," Laigle de Meaux continued.

"How so?" asked Marius, for it was really he, who had just left his grandfather's, and had before him a face which he saw for the first time. "I do not know you."

"And I don't know you either."

Marius fancied that he had to do with a practical joker, and, as he was not in the best of tempers at the moment, frowned. Laigle imperturbably continued:

"You were not at lecture the day before yesterday!"

"Very possibly."

"It is certain."

"Are you a student?" Marius asked.

"Yes, sir, like yourself. The day before yesterday I entered the law-school by chance; as you know, a man has an idea like that sometimes. The Professor was engaged in calling over, and you are aware how ridiculously strict they are in the school at the present moment. Upon the third call remaining unanswered, your name is erased from the list, and sixty francs are gone."

Marius began to listen, and Laigle continued:

"It was Blondeau who was calling over. You know Blondeau has a pointed and most malicious nose, and scents the absent with delight. He craftily began with the letter P, and I did not listen, because I was not compromised by that letter. The roll-call went on capitally, there was no erasure. and the universe was present. Blondeau was sad, and I said to myself aside, 'Blondeau, my

love, you will not perform the slightest execution to-day.'
All at once Blondeau calls out, 'Marius Pontmercy.' No
one answered, and so Blondeau, full of hope, repeats in a
louder voice, 'Marius Pontmercy,' and takes up his pen.
I have bowels, sir, and I said to myself hurriedly, 'The name
of a good fellow is going to be erased. Attention! he is
not a proper student, a student who studies, a reading man,
a pedantic sap, strong in science, literature, theology, and
philosophy. No, he is an honourable idler, who lounges
about, enjoys the country, cultivates the grisette, pays his
court to the ladies, and is perhaps with my mistress at this
moment. I must save him : death to Blondeau!' At this
moment Blondeau dipped his pen, black with erasures, into
the ink, looked round his audience, and repeated for the third
time, 'Marius Pontmercy!' I answered, 'Here!' and so
your name was not erased."

"Sir!" Marius exclaimed.

"And mine was," Laigle de Meaux added.

"I do not understand you," said Marius.

Laigle continued :

"And yet it was very simple. I was near the desk to
answer, and near the door to bolt. The Professor looked
at me with a certain fixedness, and suddenly Blondeau, who
must be the crafty nose to which Boileau refers, leaps to the
letter L, which is my letter, for I come from Meaux, and my
name is L'Esgle."

"L'Aigle!" Marius interrupted, "what a glorious name."

"Blondeau arrives, sir, at that glorious name, and
exclaims 'L'Aigle!' I answer, 'Here!' Then Blondeau
looks at me with the gentleness of a tiger, smiles, and
says : 'If you are Pontmercy, you are not L'Aigle,' a phrase
which appears offensive to you, but which was only lugubrious for me. After saying this, he erased me."

Marius exclaimed :

"I am really mortified, sir——"

"Before all," L'Aigle interrupted, "I ask leave to embalm
Blondeau in a few phrases of heartfelt praise. I will
suppose him dead, and there will not be much to alter in his
thinness, paleness, coldness, stiffness, and smell, and I say,
Erudimini qui judicatis terram. Here lies Blondeau the Nosy,
Blondeau Nasica, the ox of discipline, *bos disciplinæ,* the
mastiff of duty, the angel of the roll-call, who was straight,
square, exact, rigid, honest, and hideous. God erased him
as he erased me."

Marius continued, " I am most grieved——"

" Young man," said Laigle, " let this serve you as a lesson ; in future be punctual."

" I offer you a thousand apologies."

" And do not run the risk of getting your neighbour erased."

" I am in despair——"

Laigle burst into a laugh.

" And I am enchanted. I was on the downward road to become a lawyer, and this erasure saves me. I renounce the triumphs of the bar. I will not defend the orphan or attack the widow. I have obtained my expulsion, and I am indebted to you for it, M. Pontmercy. I intend to pay you a solemn visit of thanks,—where do you live ? "

" In this cab," said Marius.

"A sign of opulence," Laigle remarked calmly ; " I congratulate you, for you have apartments at nine thousand francs a year."

At this moment Courfeyrac came out of the café. Marius smiled sadly.

" I have been in this lodging for two hours, and am eager to leave it, but I do not know where to go."

" Come home with me," Courfeyrac said to him.

" I ought to have the priority," Laigle observed, " but then I have no home."

" Hold your tongue, Bossuet," Courfeyrac remarked.

" Bossuet," said Marius, " why, you told me your name was Laigle."

"Of Meaux," Laigle answered, "metaphorically, Bossuet."

Courfeyrac got into the cab.

" Hotel de la Porte St. Jacques, driver," he said.

The same evening, Marius was installed in a room in the Hotel de la Porte St. Jacques, next door to Courfeyrac.

CHAPTER LXX

In a few days Marius was a friend of Courfeyrac. Marius by the side of Courfeyrac breathed freely, a great novelty for him. Courfeyrac asked him no questions, and did not even think of doing so, for at that age faces tell everything at once, and words are unnecessary. One morning, however, Courfeyrac suddenly asked him the question :

" By the way, have you any political opinions ? "

" What do you mean ? " said Marius.

" What are you ? "

" Bonapartist—democrat."

" The gray colour of the reassured mouse," Courfeyrac remarked.

On the next day he led Marius to the Café Musain, and whispered in his ear with a smile, " I must introduce you to the Revolution," and he led him to the room of the Friends of the A B C. He introduced him to his companions, saying in a low voice, " a pupil," which Marius did not at all comprehend. Marius had fallen into a mental wasp's nest, but though he was silent and grave, he was not the less winged and armed.

Marius hitherto solitary, and inclining to soliloquies and asides through habit and taste, was somewhat startled by the swarm of young men around him. The tumultuous movement of all these minds at liberty and at work made his ideas whirl. He heard philosophy, literature, art, history, and religion spoken of in an unexpected way ; he caught a glimpse of strange aspects, and as he did not place them in perspective, he was not sure that he was not gazing at chaos. On giving up his grandfather's opinions for those of his father, he believed himself settled ; but he now suspected, anxiously, and not daring to confess it to himself, that it was not so. It seemed as if there was no "sacred thing" for these young men, and Marius heard singular remarks about all sorts of matters which were offensive to his still timid mind. For instance, it happened accidentally that Marius passed along the Rue Jean Jacques Rousseau between Enjolras and Courfeyrac and the latter seized his, arm.

" Pay attention ! this is the Rue Plutriere, now called

Rue Jean Jacques Rousseau, on account of a singular family that lived here sixty years back, and they were Jean Jacques and Thérèse. From time to time little creatures were born; Thérèse fondled them, and Jean Jacques took them to the Foundling."

And Enjolras reproved Courfeyrac.

"Silence before Jean Jacques! for I admire that man. I grant that he abandoned his children, but he adopted the people."

Not one of these young men ever uttered the words: the Emperor. Jean Prouvaire alone sometimes said Napoleon; all the rest spoke of Bonaparte. Enjolras pronounced it Buonaparte. Marius was confusedly astonished. *Initium sapientiæ.*

One of the conversations among the young men at which Marius was present, and in which he mingled now and then, was a thorough shock for his mind. It came off in the back room of the Café Musain, and nearly all the Friends of the A B C were collected on that occasion, and the chandelier was solemnly lighted. They talked about one thing and another, without passion and with noise. With the exception of Enjolras and Marius, who were silent, each harangued somewhat haphazard. Conversations among chums at times display these peaceful tumults. It was a game and a pell-mell as much as a conversation; words were thrown and caught up, and students were talking in all the four corners.

No female was admitted into this back room, excepting Louison, the washer-up of cups, who crossed it from time to time to go from the wash-house to the "laboratory."

The collision of young minds has this admirable thing about it, that the spark can never be foreseen or the lightning divined. What will shoot forth presently? no one knows. The burst of laughter is heard, and at the next moment seriousness makes its entrance. A stern thought, which strangely issued from a clash of words, suddenly flashed through the medley in which Grantaire, Bahorel, Prouvaire, Bossuet, Combeferre, and Courfeyrac were blindly slashing and pointing. How is it that a phrase suddenly springs up in conversation, and under-lines itself at once in the attention of those who trace it? as we have just said, no one knows. In the midst of the general confusion Bossuet concluded some remark he made to Combeferre with the date: "June 18, 1815, Waterloo."

At this name of Waterloo, Marius, who had been leaning over a glass of water, removed his hand from under his chin, and began looking intently at the company.

"Pardieu !" Courfeyrac exclaimed (*Parbleu* at this period was beginning to grow out of fashion). "That number eighteen is strange, and strikes me, for it is Bonaparte's fatal number. Place Louis before and Brumaire behind, and you have the man's whole destiny, with this expressive peculiarity, that the beginning has its heel gyved by the end."

Enjolras, who had hitherto been dumb, now broke the silence, and said :

"Courfeyrac, you mean that the crime is urged by the expiation."

This word *crime* exceeded the measure which Marius, who was already greatly affected by this sudden reference to Waterloo, could accept. He rose, walked slowly to the map of France hanging on the wall, on the bottom of which could be seen an island in a separate compartment ; he placed his finger on this and said :

"Corsica, a small island, which made France very great."

This was the breath of frozen air ; all broke off, for they felt that something was about to begin. Bahorel, who was assuming a victorious attitude in answering Bossuet, gave it up in order to listen ; and Enjolras, whose blue eye was fixed on no one and seemed to be examining space, answered without looking at Marius :

"France requires no Corsica to be great. France is great because she is France. *Quia nominor leo.*"

Marius felt no desire to give way ; he turned to Enjolras, and his voice had a strange vibration, produced by his internal emotion.

"Heaven forbid that I should diminish France ; but it is not diminishing her to amalgamate Napoleon with her. Come, let us talk. I am a new-comer among you, but I confess that you astonish me. Where are we ? who are we ? who are you ? who am I ? Let us come to an understanding about the Emperor. I hear you call him Buonaparte, laying a stress on the *u*, like the Royalists, but I must tell you that my grandfather does better still, for he says, 'Buonaparté.' I fancied you young men, but where do you keep your enthusiasm, and what do you do with it ? whom do you admire, if it is not the Emperor.

and what more do you want? if you will not have that great man, what great man would you have? He had everything, he was complete, and in his brain was the cube of human faculties. He made codes like Justinian, and dictated like Cæsar; his conversation blended the lightning of Pascal with the thunder of Tacitus; he made history and wrote it, and his bulletins are Iliads; he combined the figures of Newton with the metaphor of Mahomet. He left behind him in the East words great as the Pyramids, at Tilsit he taught majesty to Emperors, at the Academy of Sciences he answered Laplace, at the Council of State he held his own against Merlin, he gave a soul to the geometry of some and to the sophistry of others, for he was a legist with the lawyers, a sidereal with the astronomers. Like Cromwell, blowing out one of two candles, he went to the Temple to bargain for a curtain tassel; he saw everything, knew everything, but that did not prevent him from laughing heartily by the cradle of his new-born son. And, all at once, startled Europe listened, armies set out, parks of artillery rolled along, bridges of boats were thrown over rivers, clouds of cavalry galloped in the hurricane, and shouts, bugles, and the crashing of thrones could be heard all around. The frontiers of kingdoms oscillated on the map, the sound of a superhuman sword being drawn from its scabbard could be heard, and he was seen, standing erect on the horizon, with a gleam in his hand, and a splendour in his eyes, opening in the thunder his two wings, the Grand Army and the Old Guard. He was the archangel of war."

All were silent, and Enjolras hung his head. Silence always produces to some extent the effect of acquiescence, or a species of setting the back against the wall. Marius, almost without drawing breath, continued with increased enthusiasm:

"Let us be just, my friends! What a splendid destiny it is for a people to be the empire of such an Emperor, when that people is France and adds its genius to the genius of that man! To appear and reign; to march and triumph; to have as bivouacs every capital; to select grenadiers and make kings of them; to decree the downfall of dynasties; to transfigure Europe at double-quick step; to feel when you threaten that you lay your hand on the sword-hilt of God; to follow, in one man, Hannibal, Cæsar, and Charlemagne; to be the people of a ruler who accompanies your every daybreak with the brilliant announcement of a battle gained ; to be aroused in the morning by the guns of the Invalides ; to cast into the abysses of light prodigious words which are eternally luminous — Marengo, Arcola, Austerlitz, Jena, and Wagram ! — to produce at each moment on the zenith of centuries constellations of victories ; to make the French Emperor a pendant of the Roman Empire ; to be the great nation, and give birth to the great army ; to send legions all over the world, as the mountain sends its eagles in all directions to conquer, rule, and crush ; to be in Europe a people gilt by glory ; to sound a Titanic flourish of trumpets through history ; to conquer the world twice, by conquest and by amazement—all this is sublime, and what is there greater ? "

" To be free," said Combeferre.

Marius in his turn hung his head. This simple and cold remark had traversed his epical effusion like a steel blade, and he felt it fainting away within him. When he raised his eyes, Combeferre was no longer present ; probably satisfied with his reply to the apotheosis, he had left the room, and all, excepting Enjolras, had followed him. Enjolras, alone with Marius, was looking at him gravely. Marius, however, having slightly collected his ideas, did not confess himself defeated, and he was in all probability about to begin afresh upon Enjolras, when he suddenly heard some one singing on the staircase. It was Combeferre, and this is what he sung.

> " Si César m'avait donné
> La gloire et la guerre,
> Et qu'il me fallût quitter
> L'amour de ma mère,
> Je dirais au grand César :
> Reprends ton sceptre et ton char,
> J'aime mieux ma mère, ô gué !
> J'aime mieux ma mère ! "

The tender and solemn accent with which Combeferre sang this couplet imparted to it a species of strange grandeur. Marius, with his eye pensively fixed on the ceiling, repeated almost mechanically " my mother ? "

At this moment he felt Enjolras' hand on his shoulder.

" Citizen," said Enjolras to him, " my mother is the Republic."

CHAPTER LXXI.

THAT evening left Marius in a profound agitation, with a sorrowful darkness in his soul. He felt what the earth probably feels when it is opened by the ploughshare that the grain may be deposited; it only feels the wound, and the joy of giving birth does not come until later.

Marius was gloomy. He had only just made himself a faith, and must he reject it again? He declared to himself that he would not: he resolved not to doubt, and began doubting involuntarily. To stand between two religions, one of which you have not yet lost, and the other which you have not yet entered, is unendurable, and twilight only pleases batlike souls. Marius had an open eye-ball and wanted true light; and the semi-lustre of doubt hurt him. Whatever might be his desire to remain where he was and cling to it, he was invincibly constrained to continue, to advance, to think, to go further. Whither would this lead him? He feared lest, after taking so many steps which had drawn him near his father, he was now going to take steps which would carry him away from him. His discomfort increased with all the reflections that occurred to him, and an escarpment became formed around him. He agreed neither with his grandfather nor his friends; he was daring for the one and behind-hand for the others; and he found himself doubly isolated, on the side of old age and on the side of youth. He left off going to the Café Musain.

In the troubled state of his conscience he did not think at all of certain serious sides of existence, but the realities of life will not allow themselves to be forgotten, and so they suddenly came to jog his memory. One morning the landlord came into Marius' room, and said to him:

" Monsieur Courfeyrac is responsible for you? "

" Yes."

" But I am in need of money."

"Ask Courfeyrac to come and speak with me," said Marius.

When Courfeyrac arrived the landlord left them, and Marius told his friend what he had not dreamed of telling him yet,—that he was, so to speak, alone in the world, and had no relations.

" What will become of you? " said Courfeyrac.

" I do not know," Marius answered.

" What do you intend doing ? "

" I do not know."

" Have you any money ? "

" Fifteen francs."

" Are you willing to borrow from me ? "

" Never."

" Have you clothes ? "

" There they are."

" Any jewellery ? "

" A gold watch."

" I know a dealer in clothes who will take your overcoat and a pair of trousers."

" Very good."

" You will only have a pair of trousers, a waistcoat, a hat, and coat left."

" And my boots."

" What ? you will not go barefoot ? what opulence ! "

" That will be enough."

" I know a jeweller who will buy your watch."

" All right."

" No, it is not all right ; what will you do after ? "

" Anything I can that is honest."

" Do you know English ? "

" No."

" Or German ? "

" No."

" All the worse."

" Why so ? "

" Because a friend of mine, a publisher, is preparing a sort of encyclopædia, for which you could have translated English or German articles. The pay is bad, but it is possible to live on it."

" I will learn English and German."

" And in the meanwhile ? "

" I will eat my clothes and my watch.

The clothes-dealer was sent for, and gave twenty francs for the coat and trousers ; next they went to the jeweller's, who bought the watch for forty-five francs.

"That's not so bad," said Marius to Courfeyrac, on returning to the hotel ; " with my fifteen francs that makes eighty."

" And your bill here ? " Courfeyrac observed.

" Oh, I forgot that," said Marius.

The landlord presented his bill, which Marius was bound to pay at once; it amounted to seventy francs.

"I have ten francs left," said Marius.

"The deuce," Courfeyrac replied; "you will spend five francs while learning English, and five while learning German. That will be swallowing a language very quickly, or a five-franc piece very slowly."

Aunt Gillenormand, who was not a bad-hearted woman in sad circumstances, discovered her nephew's abode; and one morning, when Marius returned from college, he found a letter from his aunt and the "sixty pistoles," that is to say, six hundred francs in gold, in a sealed-up box. Marius sent the thirty louis back to his aunt with a respectful note, in which he stated that he would be able in future to take care of himself—at that moment he had just three francs left. The aunt did not tell grandpapa of this refusal, through fear of raising his exasperation to the highest pitch; besides, had he not said, "Never mention that blood-drinker's name in my presence." Marius quitted the Hotel of the Porte St. Jacques, as he was unwilling to contract debt.

Life became stern to Marius. Eating his clothes and his watch was nothing, but he also went through that indescribable course which is called "champing the bit." This is a horrible thing, which contains days without bread, nights without sleep, evenings without candle, a house without fire, weeks without work, a future without hope, a threadbare coat, an old hat at which the girls laugh, the door which you find locked at night because you have not paid your rent, the insolence of the porter and the eating-house keeper, the grins of neighbours, humiliations, dignity trampled under foot, disgust, bitterness, and desperation. Marius learnt how all this is devoured, and how it is often the only thing which a man has to eat. At that moment of life when a man requires pride because he requires love, he felt himself derided because he was meanly dressed, and ridiculous because he was poor. At the age when youth swells the heart with an imperial pride, he looked down more than once at his worn-out boots, and knew the unjust shame and burning blushes of wretchedness. It is an admirable and terrible trial, from which the weak come forth infamous and the strong sublime. It is the crucible into which destiny throws a man whenever it wishes to have a scoundrel or a demigod. For there are many great deeds done in the small struggles of life.

There was a time in Marius' life when he swept his own landing, when he bought a halfpennyworth of Brie cheese of the fruiterer, when he waited till nightfall to go into the baker's and buy a loaf, which he carried stealthily to his garret as if he had stolen it. At times there might have been seen slipping into the butcher's shop at the corner among the gossiping cooks who elbowed him, a young awkward man with books under his arm, who had a timid and frightened air, who, on entering, removed his hat from his dripping forehead, made a deep bow to the astonished butcher's wife, another to the foreman, asked for a mutton-chop, paid three or four pence, wrapped the chop in paper, placed it under his arm between two books, and went away. It was Marius, and on this chop, which he cooked himself, he lived for three days. On the first day he ate the lean, on the second he ate the fat, and on the third he gnawed the bone. Several times did Aunt Gillenormand make overtures and send him the sixty pistoles, but Marius always returned them, saying that he wanted for nothing.

He was still in mourning for his father when the revolution we have described took place within him, and since then he had not left off black clothes ; but the clothes left him. A day arrived when he had no coat, though his trousers would still pass muster. What was he to do ? Courfeyrac, to whom he on his side had rendered several services, gave him an old coat. For thirty sous Marius had it turned by some porter, and it became a new coat. But it was green, and Marius henceforth did not go out till nightfall, which caused his coat to appear black. As he still wished to be in mourning, he wrapped himself in night.

Through all this he contrived to pass his examination. He was supposed to inhabit Courfeyrac's rooms, which were decent, and where a certain number of legal tomes, supported by broken-backed volumes of novels, represented the library prescribed by the regulations. He had his letters addressed to Courfeyrac's lodgings. When Marius was called to the bar he informed his grandfather of the fact in a cold letter, which, however, was full of submission and respect. M. Gillenormand took the letter with a trembling hand, read it, tore it in four parts, and threw them into the basket. Two or three days later, Mlle Gillenormand heard her father, who was alone in his room, talking aloud, which always happened when he was agitated. She listened and heard the old gentleman say, " If you were not an ass,

you would know that you cannot be a baron and a lawyer
at the same time."

It is with misery as with everything else, it gradually
becomes endurable. A man vegetates, that is to say, is
developed in a certain poor way, which is, however,
sufficient for life. This is the sort of existence which
Marius Pontmercy had secured.

He had got out of the narrowest part, and the defile had
grown slightly wider before him. By labour, courage,
perseverance, and will, he contrived to earn about seven
hundred francs a year by his work. He had taught himself
English and German, and, thanks to Courfeyrac, who introduced him to his friend the publisher, he filled the modest
post of hack in his office. He wrote prospectuses, translated
newspapers, annotated editions, compiled biographies, and
one year with the other, his net receipts were seven hundred
francs. He lived upon them—how ? not badly as we shall
show.

Marius occupied at No. 50-52, for the annual rent of
thirty francs, a garret without a fireplace, which was called
a "cabinet," and only contained the indispensable articles
of furniture, and this furniture was his own. He paid three
francs a month to the old principal lodger for sweeping out
his room, and bringing him every morning a little hot water,
a new-laid egg, and a halfpenny roll. On this roll and
egg he breakfasted, and the outlay varied from two to four
sous according as eggs were dear or cheap. At six in the
evening he went to the Rue St. Jacques, to dine at Rousseau's,
exactly opposite Basset's, the print-shop, at the corner of
the Rue des Mathurins. He did not take soup, but he ordered
a plate of meat for six sous, half a plate of vegetables
for three sous, and dessert three sous. For three sous he
had as much bread as he liked, and for wine, he drank
water. On paying at the bar, where Madame Rousseau, at
that period a fat and good-looking dame, was majestically
enthroned, he gave a sou for the waiter, and Madame
Rousseau gave him a smile. Then he went away ; for sixteen sous he had a smile and a dinner.

Thus, with breakfast four sous, dinner sixteen, his food
cost him three hundred and sixty-five francs a year. Add
thirty francs for rent, and the thirty-six francs for the old
woman, and a few minor expenses, and for four hundred
and fifty francs Marius was fed, lodged, and served.
His clothes cost him a hundred francs, his linen fifty, his

washing fifty; the whole did not exceed six hundred and fifty francs. He had fifty left, and was rich : at times he would lend ten francs to a friend, and Courfeyrac once actually borrowed sixty francs of him. As for firing, as Marius had no chimney, he "simplified "it. Marius always had two complete suits ; one old, for everyday wear, and the other new, for special occasions, and both were black. He had but three shirts, one on, one in the drawer, and one at the wash, and he renewed them as they became worn out. As they were usually torn, he had a fashion of buttoning up his coat to the chin.

It had taken Marius years to reach this flourishing condition, rude and difficult years, in which he underwent great struggles, but he had not given up for a single day. As regarded want, he had suffered everything and he had done everything except run into debt. He gave himself the credit of never having owed a farthing to any one, for to him debt was the beginning of slavery. He said to himself that a creditor is worse than a master ; for a master only holds your person, while a creditor holds your dignity and may insult it. Sooner than borrow, he did not eat, and he had known many days of fasting. Knowing that unless a man is careful, reduction of fortune may lead to baseness of soul, he jealously watched over his pride. Many a remark or action which, under other circumstances, he would have regarded as deference, now seemed to him platitudes, and he refrained from them. He ventured nothing, as he did not wish to fall back ; he had on his face a stern blush, and he was timid almost to rudeness. In all his trials he felt encouraged, and to some extent supported, by a secret force within him ; for the soul helps the body and at times raises it, and is the only bird that upholds its cage.

By the side of his father's name, another name was engraved on Marius' heart, that of Thénardier. Marius, in his grave and enthusiastic nature, enveloped in a species of glory the man to whom he owed his father's life, that intrepid sergeant who saved his colonel among the balls and bullets of Waterloo. He never separated the memory of this man from that of his father, and he associated them in his veneration : it was a species of shrine with two steps, the high altar for the Colonel, the low one for Thénardier. What doubled the tenderness of his gratitude was the thought of the misfortune into which he knew that Thénardier had fallen, and was swallowed up. Marius had learnt at Montfermeil the ruin and bankruptcy of the unfortunate landlord, and since then he had made extraordinary efforts to find his trail, and try to reach him in the frightful abyss of misery through which Thénardier had disappeared. Marius went everywhere : he visited Chelles, Bondy, Gournay, Nogent, and Lagny ; and obstinately continued his search for three years, spending in these explorations the little money he saved. No one was able to give him the slightest information of Thénardier, and it was supposed he had gone to a foreign country. His creditors had sought him too, with less love, but with quite as much perseverance as Marius, and had been unable to lay hands on him. Marius accused and felt angry with himself for not succeeding in his search ; it was the only debt the Colonel had left him, and he felt bound in honour to pay it. "What," he thought, "when my father lay dying on the battlefield, Thénardier contrived to find him in the midst of the smoke and grape-shot, and carry him off on his shoulders, although he owed him nothing, while I, who owe so much to Thénardier, am unable to come up with him in the shadow where he is dying of want, and in my turn bring him back from death to life. Oh, I will find him ! " In fact, Marius would have given one of his arms to find Thénardier, and his last drop of blood to save him from want. To see Thénardier, do him some service, and say to him, "You do not know me, but I know you : I am here, dispose of me as you please," was his sweetest and most magnificent dream.

At this period Marius was twenty years of age. It was three years since he had left his grandfather's house. They remained on the same terms, without attempting a reconciliation or trying to meet. What good would it have been to meet ?—to come into collision again ? Which of them would have got the better ? Marius was the bronze vessel, but Father Gillenormand was the iron pot.

We are bound to say that Marius was mistaken as to his grandfather's heart. He imagined that M. Gillenormand had never loved him, and that this sharp, harsh, laughing old gentleman, who cursed, shouted, stormed, and raised his cane, only felt for him at the most that slight and severe affection of the Gerontes in the play. Marius was mistaken ; there are fathers who do not love their children ; but there is not a grandfather who does not adore his grandson. In his heart, as we said, M. Gillenormand idolised Marius.

He idolised him, it is true, after his fashion, with an accompaniment of abuse and even of blows, but when the lad had disappeared he felt a black gap in his heart. He insisted upon his name not being mentioned, but regretted that he was so strictly obeyed. At the outset he hoped that this Bonapartist, this Jacobin, this terrorist would return ; but weeks passed, months passed, years passed, and, to the great despair of M. Gillenormand, the drinker of blood did not reappear. "I could not do otherwise, though, than turn him out," the grandfather said ; and asked himself, "If it were to be done again, would I do it ?" His pride at once answered Yes, but his old head, which he silently shook, sorrowfully answered, No. He had his hours of depression, for he missed Marius, and old men require affection as much as they do the sun to warm them. However strong he might naturally be, the absence of Marius had changed something in him ; for no consideration in the world would he have taken a step towards the "little scamp"; but he suffered. He lived in greater retirement than ever at the Marais ; he was still gay and violent as of yore, but his gaiety had a convulsive harshness, as if it contained grief and passion, and his violence generally terminated with a sort of gentle and sombre depression. He would say to himself at times, "Oh, if he were to come back, what a hearty box of the ears I would give him !"

As for the aunt, she thought too little to love much ; to her Marius was only a black and vague profile, and in the end she paid much less attention to him than to the cat or the parrot which she probably had. What added to Father Gillenormand's secret suffering was that he shut it up within himself, and did not allow it to be divined. His chagrin was like one of those newly invented furnaces which consume their own smoke. At times it happened that officious friends would speak to him about Marius, and ask, "How is your grandson, and what is he doing ?" The old bourgeois would answer, with a sigh if he were sad, or with a flip to his frill if he wished to appear gay, "Baron Pontmercy is shabbily pleading in some county court."

While the old gentleman regretted, Marius applauded himself. As is the case with all good hearts, misfortune had freed him from bitterness ; he thought of M. Gillenormand gently, but he was resolved never to accept anything from a man *who had been unjust to his father.* This was the mitigated translation of his first indignation. Moreover, he was glad that he had suffered, and was still suffering, for he did so for his father.

Marius lived in solitude ; through the inclination he had to remain outside everything, and also through the commotion he had undergone, he held aloof from the society presided over by Enjolras. They remained excellent friends, and were ready to help each other when the opportunity offered, but nothing more. Marius had two friends, one, young Courfeyrac, the other, old M. Mabœuf, and he inclined to the latter. In the first place, he owed to him the revolution which had taken place in him, and his knowledge and love of his father : " He operated on me for the cataract," he would say. Certainly, this churchwarden had been decisive ; but for all that, M. Mabœuf had only been in this affair the calm and impassive agent of Providence. He had enlightened Marius accidentally and unconsciously, just as a candle does which some one brings into a room, but he had been the candle, and not the some one. As for the internal political revolution which had taken place in Marius, M. Mabœuf was entirely incapable of understanding, wishing, or directing it. As we shall meet M. Mabœuf again, hereafter, a few remarks about him will not be useless.

CHAPTER LXXII.

WHEN M. Mabœuf said to Marius, " I certainly approve of political opinions." he expressed the real state of his mind. All political opinions were a matter of indifference to him, and he approved of them all without distinction, that they might leave him at peace. M. Mabœuf's political opinion was to love plants passionately, and books even more. He possessed, like everybody else, his termination in *ist*, without which no one could have lived at that day, but he was neither Royalist, Bonapartist, Chartist, Orleanist, nor Anarchist. He was a botanist.

He did not understand how men could come to hate each other for trifles like the Charter, democracy, legitimacy, monarchy, the republic, etc., when there were in the world all sorts of mosses, grasses, and plants which they could look at. He was very careful not to be useless : his having books did not prevent him reading them, and being a

botanist did not prevent him being a gardener. When
he knew Colonel Pontmercy, there was this sympathy
between them, that the Colonel did for flowers what he
did for fruits. M. Mabœuf had succeeded in producing
pears as sweet as those of St. Germain; it is one of those
combinations from which sprang, as it seems, the autumn
Mirabelle plum, which is still celebrated, and no less
perfumed than the summer one. He attended mass more
through gentleness than devotion, and because, while he
loved men's faces but hated their noise, he found them at
church congregated and silent. Feeling that he must hold
some position in the State, he selected that of churchwarden.
He had never succeeded in loving any woman so much as a
tulip bulb, or any man so much as an Elzevir. He had long
passed his sixtieth year, when some one asked him one day,
"How is it that you never married?" "I forgot it," he
said. When he happened to say—and to whom does it not
happen?—"Oh, if I were rich!" it was not when ogling a
pretty girl, like Father Gillenormand, but when contemplating a quarto. He lived alone with an old housekeeper; he
was rather gouty, and when he slept, his old chalk-stoned
fingers formed an arch in the folds of the sheets. He had
written and published a *Flora of the Environs of Cauteretz*,
with coloured plates, a work of some merit, the plates of
which he possessed and which he sold himself. People
rang at his door in the Rue Mézières two or three times a
day to buy a copy; he made a profit of about two thousand
francs a year by the book, and that was nearly his whole
fortune. Although poor, he had contrived by patience and
privations, and with time, to form a valuable collection of
all sorts of rare examples. He never went out without a
book under his arm, and frequently returned with two.
The sole ornaments of his four rooms on the ground-floor,
which, with a small garden, formed his lodging, were
herbals and engravings by old masters. The sight of a
musket or a sabre froze him, and in his life he had never
walked up to a cannon, not even at the Invalides. He had
a tolerable stomach, a brother a curé, very white hair, no
teeth left in his mouth or in his mind, a tremor all over him,
a Picard accent, a childish laugh, and the air of an old sheep.
With all that, he had no other friend among the living than
an old bookseller at the Porte St. Jacques of the name of
Royol; and the dream of his life was to naturalise indigo
in France.

His maid-servant was also a variety of innocence. The good woman was an old maid, and Sultan, her tom-cat, filled her heart, and sufficed for the amount of passion within her. Not one of her dreams had ever gone so far as a man. She had never got beyond her cat—like him she had moustaches. She knew how to read, and M. Mabœuf had christened her Mother Plutarch.

M. Mabœuf had taken a fancy to Marius, because the young man, being young and gentle, warmed his old age without startling his timidity. Youth, combined with gentleness, produces on aged people the effect of sun without wind. When Marius was saturated with military glory, gun-powder, marches, and counter-marches, and all the prodigious battles in which his father gave and received such mighty sabre cuts, he went to see M. Mabœuf, who talked to him about the hero in his connection with flowers.

About the year 1830 his brother the curé died, and almost immediately after, as when night arrives, the entire horizon became dark for M. Mabœuf. The bankruptcy of a notary despoiled him of ten thousand francs—all he possessed of his brother's capital and his own—while the revolution of July produced a crisis in the book trade. In times of pressure the first thing which does not sell is a *Flora*, and that of the Environs of Cauteretz stopped dead. Weeks passed without a purchaser. At times M. Mabœuf started at the sound of the house bell, but Mother Plutarch would say to him sadly, "It is the water-carrier, sir." In a word, M. Mabœuf left the Rue Mézières one day, abdicated his office as church-warden, gave up St. Sulpice, sold a portion, not of his books, but of his engravings, for which he cared least, and installed himself in a small house on the Boulevard Mont Parnasse, where, however, he only remained three months, for two reasons—in the first place, the ground-floor and garden cost three hundred francs, and he did not dare set aside more than two hundred francs for rent; and secondly, as he was close to the Fatou shooting gallery, he heard pistol-shots, which he could not endure. He carried off his *Flora*, his copper-plates, his herbals, portfolios, and books, and settled down near the Salpetrière, in a sort of hut, in the village of Austerlitz, where he rented for fifty crowns a year three rooms, a garden enclosed by a hedge, and a well. He took advantage of this removal to sell nearly all his furniture. On the day when he entered his new house he was in very good spirits, and drove in with his own hands the nails on which to hang the engravings ; he dug in his garden for the rest of the day, and at night, seeing that Mother Plutarch had an anxious look and was thoughtful, he tapped her on the shoulder and said with a smile, "We have the indigo." Only two visitors, the publisher and Marius, were allowed admission to this hut.

Marius felt a liking for this candid old man, who saw himself slowly assailed by poverty and yet was not depressed by it. Marius met Courfeyrac and sought M. Mabœuf— very rarely, however—once or twice a month at the most. Marius' delight was to take long walks alone, either on the external boulevards at the Champ de Mars, or in the least frequented walks of the Luxembourg. He often spent half a day in looking at a kitchen garden, the patches of lettuce, the fowls on the dungheap, and the horse turning the mill-wheel. Passers-by looked at him with surprise, and some thought his dress suspicious and his face dangerous, while it was only a poor young man thinking without an object. It was in one of these walks that he discovered the Maison Gorbeau, and the isolation and the cheapness tempting him, he took a room there. He was only known by the name of M. Marius.

Some of his father's old generals and old comrades invited him to come and see them, when they knew him, and Marius did not refuse, for they were opportunities to speak about his father. He called thus from time to time upon Count Pajol, General Bellavesne, and General Frérion at the Invalides. There was generally music and dancing, and on such evenings Marius put on his best suit; but he never went to such parties except on days when it was freezing tremendously hard, for he could not pay for a vehicle, and he would not go unless his boots were like looking-glasses. He would say at times, though not at all bitterly, "Men are so constituted that in a drawing-room you may have mud everywhere except on your boots. In order to give you a proper reception only one irreproach-able thing is expected from you—is it your conscience ? no, your boots."

About the middle of the year 1831 the old woman who waited on Marius told him that his neighbours, the wretched Jondrette family, were going to be turned out. Marius, who spent nearly his whole time out of doors, scarce knew that he had neighbours.

"Why are they turned out?" he asked.

"Because they do not pay their rent, and owe two quarters."

"How much is it?"

"Twenty francs," said the old woman.

Marius had thirty francs in reserve in a drawer.

"Here are twenty-five francs," he said to the woman; "pay the rent of the poor people, give them five francs, and do not tell them that the money comes from me."

CHAPTER LXXIII.

MARIUS was now a fine-looking young man or medium height, with heavy jet-black hair, a lofty and intelligent forehead, open and impassioned nostrils, a sincere and calm air, and something haughty, pensive, and innocent was spread over his whole face. His profile, in which all the lines were rounded without ceasing to be firm, had that Germanic gentleness which entered France through Alsace and Lorraine, and that absence of angles which renders it so easy to recognise the Sicambri among the Romans, and which distinguishes the leonine from the aquiline race. He had reached the season of life when the mind of men is composed of depth and simplicity in nearly equal proportions. A serious situation being given, he had all that was necessary to be stupid, but, with one more turn of the screw, he could be sublime. His manner was reserved, cold, polite, and unexpansive; but, as his mouth was beautiful, his lips bright vermilion, and his teeth the whitest in the world, his smile corrected any severity in his countenance. At certain moments, this chaste forehead and voluptuous smile offered a strange contrast.

In the period of his greatest need he remarked that people turned to look at him when he passed, and he hurried away or hid himself, with death in his soul. He thought that they were looking at his shabby clothes and laughing at them; but the fact is, they were looking at his face, and thinking about it. This silent misunderstanding between himself and pretty passers-by had rendered him savage, and he did not select one from the simple reason that he fled from all. He lived thus indefinitely—stupidly, said Courfeyrac, who also added,—"Do not aspire to be venerable, and take one bit of advice,

my dear fellow. Do not read so many books, and look at
the wenches a little more, for they have some good about
them. Oh, Marius ! you will grow brutalised if you go
on shunning women and blushing."

On other occasions, Courfeyrac, when he met him, would
say, " Good-morning, Abbé." When Courfeyrac had made
any remark of this nature, Marius for a whole week would
shun women, young and old, more than ever, and Courfeyrac into the bargain. There were, however, in the
whole immense creation, two women whom Marius did
not shun, or to whom he paid no attention. To tell the
truth, he would have been greatly surprised had any one
told him that they were women. One was the hairy-faced
old woman who swept his room, and induced Courfeyrac to
remark,—" Seeing that his servant wears her beard, Marius
does not wear his ; " the other was a young girl whom he
saw very frequently and did not look at. For more than a year
Marius had noticed in a deserted walk of the Luxembourg,
the one which is bordered by the Parapet de la Pepinière,
a man and a very young lady nearly always seated side
by side at the most solitary end of the walk, near the
Rue de l'Ouest. Whenever that accident, which mingles
with the promenades of people whose eye is turned inwards,
led Marius to this walk, and that was nearly daily, he met
this couple there. The man seemed to be about sixty years
of age ; he appeared sad and serious, and the whole of his
person presented the robust but fatigued appearance of
military men who have retired from service. If he had
worn a decoration, Marius would have said, " He is an old
officer." He looked kind but unapproachable, and never
fixed his eye on that of another person. He wore blue
trousers, a coat of the same colour, and a broad-brimmed
hat, all of which were constantly new ; a black cravat, and
a quaker's, that is to say, dazzlingly white, but very coarse
shirt. A grisette who passed him one day said, " What
a clean old widower." His hair was perfectly white.

The first time that the young girl who accompanied him
sat down with him upon the bench, which they seemed to
have adopted, she was about thirteen or fourteen, so thin
as to be almost ugly, awkward, insignificant, and promising
to have perhaps very fine eyes some day ; but they were
always raised to the old gentleman with a species of displeasing assurance. She wore the garb, at once old and
childish, of boarders at a convent,—a badly-cut dress of

coarse black merino. They looked like father and daughter. Marius examined for two or three days this old man, who was not yet aged, and this little girl, who was not yet a maiden, and then paid no further attention to them. They, on their side, seemed not even to see him, and talked together with a peaceful and careless air. The girl talked incessantly and gaily, the old man spoke but little, and at times he fixed upon her eyes filled with ineffable paternity. Marius had formed the mechanical habit of walking in this alley, and invariably found them there. This is how matters went on :—

Marius generally arrived by the end of the walk furthest from the bench ; he walked the whole length, passed them, then turned back to the end by which he had arrived, and began again. He took this walk five or six times nearly every day in the week, but these persons and himself never even exchanged a bow. The man and the girl, though they appeared, and perhaps because they appeared, to shun observation, had naturally aroused to some little extent the attention of some students, who walked from time to time along La Pepinière ; the studious after lectures, the others after their game of billiards. Courfeyrac, who belonged to the latter, had watched them for some time, but finding the girl ugly, he got away from them very rapidly, firing at them like Parthian a sobriquet. Being solely struck by the dress of the girl and the old man's hair, he christened the former Mlle Lanoire, and the father Monsieur Leblanc, so that, as no one knew them otherwise, this name adhered to them in the absence of a better one. The students said, "Ah, M. Leblanc is at his bench," and Marius, like the rest, found it convenient to call this strange gentleman M. Leblanc. We will follow their example. Marius saw them nearly daily, at the same hour, during a year. He considered the man agreeable, but the girl rather dull.

In the second year, just at the point of our story which the reader has now reached, it happened that Marius broke off his daily walk in the Luxembourg, without exactly knowing why, and was nearly six months without setting foot in the garden. One day, however, he returned to it ; it was a beauteous summer day, and Marius was joyous as men are when the weather is fine. He felt as if he had in his heart all the birds' songs that he heard, and all the patches of blue sky, of which he caught a glimpse between the leaves. He went straight to "his" walk, and when he reached the end he noticed the well known couple seated on the same bench, but when he drew near he found that, while it was the same man, it did not seem to be the same girl. The person he now saw was a tall and lovely creature, possessing the charming outlines of the woman, at the precise moment when they are still combined with the most simple graces of the child—a fugitive and pure moment which can alone be rendered by the two words "fifteen years." He saw admirable auburn hair, tinted with gilt veins, a forehead that seemed made of marble, cheeks that seemed made of a rose-leaf, and of a pale carnation hue, an exquisite mouth, from which a smile issued like a flash, and words like music, and a head which Raphael would have given to a Virgin, set upon a neck which Goujon would have given to a Venus. And, that nothing might be wanting in this ravishing face, the nose was not beautiful, but pretty, neither straight nor bent, neither Italian nor Greek, it was the Parisian nose, that is to say, something witty, fine, irregular, and pure, which is the despair of painters and the charm of poets.

When Marius passed her he could not see her eyes, which she constantly cast down; he only saw her long lashes, which revealed modesty. This did not prevent the lovely girl from smiling while she listened to the white-haired man who was speaking to her, and nothing could be so ravishing as this fresh smile with the downcast eyes. At the first moment Marius thought that it was another daughter of the old gentleman's, a sister of the former. But when the invariable habit of his walk brought him again to the bench, and he examined her attentively, he perceived that it was the same girl. In six months the girl had become a maiden, that was all, and nothing is more frequent than this phenomenon. There is a moment in which girls become roses instantly,—yesterday you left them children, to-day you find them objects of anxiety. This girl had not only grown; she had become idealised. As three days in April suffice to cover some trees with flowers, six months had sufficed to clothe her with beauty—her April had arrived. We sometimes see poor and insignificant persons suddenly wake up, pass from indigence to opulence, lay out money in all sorts of extravagance, and become brilliant, prodigal, and magnificent. The reason is that they have just received their dividends; and the girl had been paid six months' income.

And then she was no longer the boarding-school miss, with her plush bonnet, merino dress, thick shoes, and red hands; taste had come to her with beauty, and she was well dressed, with a species of simple, rich, and unaffected elegance. She wore a black brocade dress, a cloak of the same material, and a white crape bonnet; her white gloves displayed the elegance of her hand, which was playing with the ivory handle of a parasol, and her satin boot revealed the smallness of her foot; when you passed her, her whole toilette exhaled a youthful and penetrating perfume. As for the man, he was still the same. The second time that Marius passed, the girl raised her eyelids, and he could see that her eyes were of a deep cerulean blue, but in this veiled azure there was only the glance of a child. She looked at Marius carelessly, as she would have looked at the child playing under the sycamores, or the marble vase that threw a shadow over the bench; and Marius continued his walk, thinking of something else. He passed the bench four or five times, but did not once turn his eyes toward the young lady. On the following days he returned as usual to the Luxembourg; as usual he found the "father and daughter" there, but he paid no further attention to them. He thought no more of the girl now that she was lovely than he had done when she was ugly. He always passed very close to the bench on which she was sitting, but that was simply the result of habit.

One day the air was mild, the Luxembourg was flooded with light and shade, the sky was as pure as if the angels had washed it that morning, the sparrows were twittering shrilly in the foliage of the chestnut trees, and Marius opened his whole soul to nature. He was thinking of nothing, he loved and breathed, he passed by the bench, the young lady raised her eyes to him, and their two glances met. What was there this time in her look? Marius could not have said,—there was nothing and there was everything, it was a strange flash. She let her eyes fall, and he continued his walk. What he had just seen was not the simple and ingenuous eye of a child, but a mysterious gulf, the mouth of which had had opened and then suddenly closed again. There is a day on which every maiden looks in this way, and woe to the man on whom her glance falls!

This first glance of a soul which does not yet know itself is like dawn in the heavens; it is the awakening of something radiant and unknown. Nothing could render the mysterious charm of this unexpected flash which suddenly illumines the adorable darkness, and is composed of all the innocence of the present and all the passion of the future. It is a sort of undecided tenderness, which reveals itself accidentally and waits ; it is a snare which innocence sets unconsciously, and in which it captures hearts without wishing or knowing it. It is a virgin who looks at you like a woman. It is rare for a profound reverie not to spring up wherever this flame falls ; all purity and all candour are blended in this heavenly and fatal beam, which possesses, more than the best-managed ogles of coquettes, the magic power of suddenly causing that dangerous flower, full of perfume and poison, called love, suddenly to expand in the soul.

On returning to his garret in the evening, Marius took a glance at his clothes, and perceived for the first time that he had been guilty of the extraordinary impropriety and stupidity of walking in the Luxembourg in his "everyday dress," that is to say, with a broken-brimmed hat, clumsy boots, black trousers, white at the knees, and a black coat pale at the elbows. The next day, at the accustomed hour, Marius took out of the drawers his new coat, his new trousers, his new hat, and his new boots ; he dressed himself in this complete panoply, put on gloves, an extraordinary luxury, and went off to the Luxembourg. On the road he met Courfeyrac, and pretended not to see him. Courfeyrac, on reaching home, said to his friends :

"1 have just met Marius' new hat and new coat, and Marius inside them. He was going, 1 fancy, to pass some examination, for he looked so stupid."

On reaching the Luxembourg Marius walked round the basin and gazed at the swans ; then he proceeded toward "his" walk slowly, and as if with regret. He seemed to be at once forced and prevented from going, but he did not explain this to himself, and he fancied he was behaving as he did every day. On turning into the walk he saw M. Leblanc and the young lady at the other end, seated on "their" bench. He buttoned up his coat to the top, pulled it down so that it should make no creases, examined with some complacency the lustre of his trousers, and marched upon the bench. There was attack in this march, and assuredly a desire for conquest, and hence I say that he marched upon this bench, as I would say, Hannibal marched on Rome.

Still, all his movements were mechanical, and he had not in any way altered the habitual preoccupation of his mind and labours. He was thinking at this moment that the *Manuel des Baccalaureat* was a stupid book, and that it must have been edited by wondrous ignoramuses, who analysed as masterpieces of the human mind three tragedies of Racine and only one comedy of Molière. He had a shrill whistling in his ear, and while approaching the bench, he pulled down his coat, and his eyes were fixed on the maiden. He fancied that she filled the whole end of the walk with a vague blue light. As he drew nearer his pace gradually decreased. On coming within a certain distance of the bench, though still some distance from the end of the walk, he stopped, and did not know how it was that he turned back. The young lady was scarce able to notice him, and see how well he looked in his new suit. Still he held himself very erect, for fear any one behind might be looking at him.

He reached the opposite end, then returned, and this time approached a little nearer to the bench. He even got within the distance of three trees, but then he felt an impossibility of going further, and hesitated. He fancied he could see the young lady's face turned toward him ; however, he made a great and manly effort, subdued his hesitation, and continued to advance. A few moments after he passed in front of the bench, upright and firm, but red up to the ears, and not daring to cast a glance either to the right or left, and with his hand thrust into his coat like a statesman. At the moment when he passed under the guns of the fort he felt his heart beat violently. She was dressed as on the previous day, and he heard an ineffable voice which must be "her" voice. She was talking quietly, and she was very beautiful ; he felt it, though he did not attempt to look at her.

He passed the bench, went to the end of the walk which was close by, then turned and again passed the young lady. This time he was very pale, and his feelings were most disagreeable. He went away from the bench and the maiden, and while turning his back, he fancied that she was looking at him, and this made him totter. He did not again attempt to pass the bench ; he stopped at about the middle of the walk and then sat down, a most unusual thing for him, taking side-glances, and thinking in the innermost depths of his mind that after all it was difficult for a person whose white bonnet and black dress he admired to be absolutely insensible to his showy trousers and new coat. At the end of a quarter of an hour he rose, as if about to walk toward this bench which was surrounded by a halo, but he remained motionless. For the first time in fifteen months he said to himself that the gentleman who sat there daily with his daughter must have noticed him, and probably considered his assiduity strange. For the first time, too, he felt it was rather irreverent to designate this stranger, even in his own thoughts, by the nickname of M. Leblanc.

He remained thus for some minutes with hanging head, making sketches in the sand with the stick he held in his hand. Then he suddenly turned in the direction opposite the bench, and went home. That day he forgot to go to dinner ; he noticed the fact at eight in the evening, and, as it was too late to go to the Rue St. Jacques, he ate a lump of bread. He did not retire till he had carefully brushed and folded up his coat.

Next day, Ma'am Bougon—so Courfeyrac called the old porteress, principal lodger, and charwoman of No. 50-52, though her real name was Madame Bourgon, as we have stated, but that scamp of a Courfeyrac respected nothing— Ma'am Bougon, to her stupefaction, noticed that Marius again went out in his best coat. He returned to the Luxembourg, but did not go beyond his half-way bench ; he sat down there, as on the previous day, regarding from a distance, and seeing distinctly, the white bonnet, the black dress, and, above all, the blue radiance. He did not move or return home till the gates of the Luxembourg were closed. He did not see M. Leblanc and his daughter go away, and hence concluded that they left the garden by the gate in the Rue de l'Ouest. Some weeks after, when reflecting on the subject, he could never remember where he dined that day. On the next day, the third, Ma'am Bougon received another thunder-stroke ; Marius went out in his new coat. " Three days running ! " she exclaimed. She tried to follow him, but Marius walked quickly, and with immense strides : it was a hippopotamus attempting to catch up a chamois.

Marius had gone to the Luxembourg, where M. Leblanc and the young lady were already. Marius approached as near to them as he could, while pretending to read his book, though still a long distance off, and then sat down on his bench, where he spent four hours in watching the sparrows, which he fancied were ridiculing him, hopping about in the walk. A fortnight passed in this way; Marius no longer went to the Luxembourg to walk, but always to sit down in the same spot, without knowing why. Every morning he put on his new coat, not to be conspicuous, and he began again on the morrow. She was, decidedly, marvellously beautiful; the sole remark resembling a criticism that could be made was, that the contradiction between her glance, which was sad, and her smile, which was joyous, gave her face a slightly startled look, which at times caused this gentle face to become strange without ceasing to be charming.

On one of the last days of the second week Marius was as usual seated on his bench, holding in his hand an open book of which he had not turned a page for several months, when he suddenly started—an event was occurring at the end of the walk. M. Leblanc and his daughter had left their bench, the girl had taken her father's arm, and both were proceeding slowly toward the middle of the walk where Marius was. He shut his book, then opened it again and tried to read, but he trembled, and the halo came straight toward him. "Oh, heaven!" he thought, "I shall not have time to throw myself into an attitude." The white-haired man and the girl, however, advanced; it seemed to him as if this endured a century, and was only a second. "What do they want here?" he asked himself. "What! she is going to pass here; her feet will tread this sand, this walk, two paces from me?" He heard the soft measured sound of their footsteps approaching him, and he imagined that M. Leblanc was taking a wry glance at him. "Is this gentleman going to speak to me?" he thought. He hung his head, and when he raised it again they were close to him. The girl passed, and in passing looked at him,—looked at him intently, with a thoughtful gentleness which made Marius tremble from head to foot. It seemed to him as if she reproached him for keeping away from her so long, and was saying, "I have come instead." Marius was dazzled by these eyeballs full of beams and abysses. He felt that his brain was on fire. She had come toward him, what joy! and then, how she had looked at him! She appeared to him lovelier than she had ever been, lovely with a beauty at once feminine and angelic, a perfect beauty, which would have made Petrarch sing and Dante kneel. He felt as if he were floating in the blue sky, but, at

the same time, he was horribly annoyed because he had
dust on his boots, and he felt sure that she had looked at
his boots too.

He looked after her till she disappeared, and then he
walked about the garden like a maniac. Marius had
reached that startling and charming hour which commences
great passions. A look had affected all this. When the
mine is loaded, when the fire is ready, nothing is more
simple, and a glance is a spark. It was all over; Marius
loved a woman, and his destiny was entering upon the
unknown.

Isolation, pride, separation from all things, a taste for
nature, the absence of daily and material labour, the soul-
struggles of chastity, and his benevolent ecstasy in the
presence of creation, had prepared Marius for that possession
which is called passion. His reverence for his father had
gradually become a religion, and, like all religions, withdrew into the depths of the soul : something was wanting
for the foreground, and love came. A whole month passed,
during which Marius went daily to the Luxembourg : when
the hour arrived nothing could stop him. "He is on duty,"
Courfeyrac said. Marius lived in ravishment, and it is
certain that the young lady looked at him. In the end he
had grown bolder, and went nearer the bench ; still he did
not pass in front of it, obeying at once the timid instincts
and prudent instincts of lovers. He thought it advisable
not to attract the father's attention, and hence arranged his
stations behind trees and the pedestals of statues, with
profound Machiavellism, so as to be seen as much as
possible by the young lady and as little as possible by the
old gentleman. At times he would be standing for half
an hour motionless in the shadow of some Leonidas or
Spartacus, holding in one hand a book, over which his eyes,
gently raised, sought the lovely girl, and she, for her part,
turned her charming profile toward him with a vague smile.
While talking most naturally and quietly with the white-
haired man, she fixed upon Marius all the reveries of
a virginal and impassioned glance. It is an old and
immemorial trick which Eve knew from the first day of the
world, and which every woman knows from the first day of
her life. Her mouth replied to the one and her eyes
answered the other.

It must be supposed, however, that M. Leblanc eventually
noticed something, for frequently when Marius arrived he

got up and began walking. He left their accustomed seat, and adopted the bench at the other end of the walk, close to the Gladiator, as if to see whether Marius would follow them. Marius did not understand it, and committed this blunder. The "father" began to become unpunctual, and no longer brought his "daughter" every day. At times he came alone, and then Marius did not stop, and this was another blunder. Marius paid no attention to these symptoms : from the timid phase he had passed by a natural and fatal progress into a blind phase. His love was growing, and he dreamed of it every night, and then an unexpected happiness occurred to him, like oil on fire, and redoubled the darkness over his eyes. One evening at twilight he found on the bench which "M. Leblanc and his daughter" had just quitted, a simple, unembroidered handkerchief, which, however, was white and pure, and seemed to him to exhale ineffable odours. He seized it with transport, and noticed that it was marked with the letters U. F. Marius knew nothing about the lovely girl, neither her family, her name, nor her abode ; these two letters were the first thing of hers which he seized, adorable initials, upon which he at once begun to erect his scaffolding. U. was evidently the Christian name : "Ursule!" he thought, "what a delicious name!" He kissed the handkerchief, smelt it, placed it on his heart during the day, and at night upon his lips to go to sleep.

"I can see her whole soul !" he exclaimed.

This handkerchief belonged to the old gentleman, who had simply let it fall from his pocket. On the following days, when Marius went to the Luxembourg, he kissed the handkerchief, and pressed it to his heart. The lovely girl did not understand what this meant, and expressed her surprise by imperceptible signs.

"O modesty !" said Marius.

Since we have uttered the word *modesty*, and as we conceal nothing, we are bound to say that on one occasion, however, through all his ecstasy "his Ursule" caused him serious vexation. It was on one of the days when she induced M. Leblanc to leave the bench and walk about. There was a sharp spring breeze which shook the tops of the plane trees ; and father and daughter, arm in arm, had just passed in front of Marius, who rose and watched them, as was fitting for a man in his condition. All at once a puff of wind, more merry than the rest, and probably ordered to

do the business of spring, dashed along the walk, enveloped
the maiden in a delicious rustling worthy of the nymphs of
Virgil and the fauns of Theocritus, and raised her dress,
that dress more sacred than that of Isis, almost as high
as her garter. A leg of exquisite shape became visible.
Marius saw it, and he was exasperated and furious. The
maiden rapidly put down her dress, with a divinely startled
movement, but he was not the less indignant. There was
no one in the walk, it was true, but there might have been
somebody ; and if that somebody had been there ? Is such
a thing conceivable ? what she had just done was horrible !
Alas ! the poor girl had done nothing, and there was only
one culprit, the wind, but Marius was determined to be
dissatisfied, and was jealous of his shadow.

When "his Ursule," after reaching the end of the walk,
turned back with M. Leblanc, and passed in front of the
bench on which Marius was sitting, he gave her a stern,
savage glance. The girl drew herself slightly up, and
raised her eyelids, which means, "Well, what is the matter
now ?" This was their first quarrel.

With the help of time every point grows blunted, and
Marius' anger with "Ursule," though so just and legitimate, passed away. He ended by pardoning her, but it
was a mighty effort, and he sulked with her for three days.
Still, through all this, and owing to all this, his passion
increased, and became insane.

We have seen how Marius discovered, or fancied he had discovered, that her name was Ursule. Appetite comes while
loving, and to know that her name was Ursule was a great
deal already, but it was little. In three or four weeks Marius
had devoured this happiness and craved another ; he wished
to know where she lived. He had made the first fault in
falling into the trap of the Gladiator's bench ; he had
committed a second by not remaining at the Luxembourg
when M. Leblanc went there alone ; and he now committed
a third, an immense one—he followed "Ursule." She
lived in the Rue de l'Ouest, in the most isolated part, in
a new three-storeyed house of modest appearance. From
this moment Marius added to his happiness of seeing her at
the Luxembourg the happiness of following her home. His
hunger increased ; he knew what her name was, her
Christian name at least, the charming, the real name of
a woman ; he knew where she lived, and he now wanted to
know who she was. One evening, after following them

home and watching them disappear in the gateway, he went in after them, and valiantly addressed the porter.

"Is that the gentleman of the first floor who has just come in?"

"No," the porter answered, "it is the gentleman of the third floor."

Another step made! This success emboldened Marius.

"Front?" he asked.

"Our rooms all look on the street," said the porter.

"And what is the gentleman's position?" Marius continued.

"He lives on his property. He is a very good man, who does a deal of good to the wretched, though he is not rich."

"What is his name?" Marius added.

The porter raised his head and said:

"Do you happen to be a police spy, sir?"

Marius went off much abashed, but highly delighted, for he was progressing.

"Good," he thought, "I know that her name is Ursule, that she is the daughter of a retired gentleman, and that she lives there, on a third floor in the Rue de l'Ouest."

On the morrow M. Leblanc and his daughter made but a short appearance at the Luxembourg, and went away in broad daylight. Marius followed them to the Rue de l'Ouest, as was his habit, and on reaching the gateway M. Leblanc made his daughter go in first, then stopped, turned, and looked intently at Marius. The next day they did not come to the Luxembourg, and Marius waited in vain the whole day. At nightfall he went to the Rue de l'Ouest, and noticed a light in the third-floor windows, and he walked about beneath these windows till the light was extinguished. The next day there was no one at the Luxembourg. Marius waited all day, and then went to keep his night-watch under the windows. This took him till ten o'clock, and his dinner took care of itself, for fever nourishes the sick man, and love the lover. Eight days passed in this way, and M. Leblanc and his daughter did not again appear at the Luxembourg. Marius made sorrowful conjectures, for he did not dare watch the gateway by day; he contented himself with going at night to contemplate the reddish brightness of the window-panes. He saw shadows pass now and then, and his heart beat.

On the eighth day, when he arrived beneath the windows, there was no light. "What," he said to himself, "the lamp is not lighted, can they have gone out?" He waited till ten o'clock, till midnight, till one o'clock, but no light was kindled at the third-floor windows, and nobody entered the house. He went away with very gloomy thoughts. On the morrow—for he only lived from morrow to morrow, and he had no to-day, so to speak—he saw nobody at the Luxembourg, as he expected, and at nightfall he went to the house. There was no light at the windows, the shutters were closed, and the third floor was all darkness. Marius rapped, walked in, and said to the porter:

"The gentleman on the third floor?"

"Gone away," the porter answered.

Marius tottered, and asked feebly:

"Since when?"

"Yesterday."

"Where is he living now?"

"I do not know."

"Then he did not leave his new address?"

"No."

And the porter, raising his eyes, recognised Marius.

"What? it's you, is it?" he said; "why, you really do keep a bright look-out."

CHAPTER LXXIV.

A QUARTETTE of bandits, Babet, Gueulemer, Claquesous, and Montparnasse, governed, from 1830-1835, the lowest depths of Paris. Gueulemer was a Hercules out of place, and his den was the Arche-Marion sewer. He was six feet high, had lungs of marble, muscles of bronze, the respiration of a cavern, the bust of a colossus, and a bird's skull. You fancied you saw the Farnèse Hercules attired in ticking trousers and a cotton velvet jacket. Gueulemer built in this mould might have subdued monsters, but he had found it shorter to become one. A low forehead, wide temples, under forty years of age, rough short hair, and a bushy beard; from this you can see the man. His muscles demanded work, and his stupidity would not accept it: he was a great slothful strength, and an assassin through nonchalance. People believed him to be a Creole, and he had probably laid his hands upon Marshal Brune when massacred, as he was a porter at Avignon in 1815. From that stage he had become a bandit.

Babet's transparency contrasted with the meat of Gueulemer; he was thin and learned,—transparent but impenetrable : you might see the light through his bones, but not through his eyes. He called hmself a chemist, and had played in the vaudeville at St. Mihiel. His trade was to sell in the open air plaster busts and portraits of the "chief of the State," and, in addition, he pulled teeth out. He had shown phenomena at fairs, and possessed a booth with a trumpet and the following show-board—"Babet, dentist, and member of the academies, performs physical experiments on metals and metalloids, extirpates teeth, and undertakes stumps given up by the profession. Terms—one tooth, one franc fifty centimes ; two teeth, two francs ; three teeth, two francs fifty centimes. Take advantage of the opportunity." (The last sentence meant, Have as many teeth pulled out as possible.) He was married and had children, but did not know what had become of wife or children : he had lost them, just as another man loses his handkerchief.

What was Claquesous ? He was night ; and never showed himself till the sky was bedaubed with blackness. In the evening he emerged from a hole, to which he returned before daybreak. Where was this hole ? no one knew. In the greatest darkness, and when alone with his accomplices, he turned his back when he spoke to them. Was his name Claquesous ? no : he said, "My name is Not-at-all." If a candle were brought in he put on a mask, and he was a ventriloquist in the bargain, and Babet used to say, "Claquesous is a night-bird with two voices." Claquesous was vague, wandering, and terrible : no one was sure that he had a name, for Claquesous was a nickname : no one was sure that he had a voice, for his stomach spoke more frequently than his mouth ; and no one was sure that he had a face, as nothing had ever been seen but his mask. He disappeared like a ghost, and when he appeared he seemed to issue from the ground.

Montparnasse was a mournful being. He was a lad not yet twenty, with a pretty face, lips that resembled cherries, beautiful black hair, and the brightness of spring in his eyes. He had every vice, and aspired to every crime, and the digestion of evil gave him an appetite for worse. He was the gamin turned pickpocket, and the pickpocket had become a garrotter. He was genteel, effeminate, graceful, robust, active, and ferocious. The left-hand brim of his hat was turned up to make room for the tuft of hair, in the style of 1829. He lived by robbery committed with violence, and his coat was cut in the latest fashion, though worn at the seams. Montparnasse was an engraving of the fashions, in a state of want, and committing murders. The cause of all the attacks made by this young man was a longing to be well dressed : the first grisette who said to him, "You are handsome," put the black spot in his heart, and made a Cain of this Abel. Finding himself good-looking, he wished to be elegant, and the first stage of elegance is idleness : but the idleness of the poor man is crime. Few garrotters were so grand as Montparnasse, and at the age of eighteen he had several corpses behind him. More than one wayfarer lay in the shadow of this villain with outstretched arms, and with his face in a pool of blood. Curled, pomaded, with his waist pinched in, the hips of a woman, the bust of a Prussian officer, the buzz of admiration of the girls of the boulevard around him, a carefully-tied cravat, a life-preserver in his pocket, and a flower in his buttonhole—such was this dandy of the tomb.

These four bandits formed a species of Proteus, winding through the police ranks and striving to escape the indiscreet glances of Vidocq "under various faces, trees, flame, and fountain," borrowing each other's names and tricks, asylums for one another, laying aside their personality as a man removes a false nose at a masquerade ; at times simplifying themselves so as to be only one man, at others multiplying themselves to such an extent that Coco-Latour himself took them for a mob. These four men were not four men ; they were a species of four-headed robber working Paris on a grand scale ; the monstrous polyp of evil inhabiting the crypt of society. Owing to their ramifications and the subjacent network of their relations, Babet, Gueulemer, Claquesous, and Montparnasse had the general direction of all the villainies in the department of the Seine, and carried out upon the passers-by the low class of coups d'état. The finders of ideas in this style, the men with nocturnal imaginations, applied to them to execute them ; the four villains were supplied with the canvas, and they produced the scenery. They were always in a position to supply a proportionate and proper staff for every robbery which was sufficiently lucrative and required a stout arm. If a crime were in want of persons to carry it out, they sublet the accomplices, and they always had a band of actors at the service of all the tragedies of the caverns.

They generally met at nightfall, the hour when they awoke, on the steppes that border the Salpêtrière. There they conferred, and, as they had the twelve dark hours before them, they settled their employment. "Patron Minette" was the name given in the subterranean lurking-places to the association of these four men. In the old and fantastic popular language, which is daily dying out, Patron Minette signifies the morning, just as "between dog and wolf" signifies night. This appellation was probably derived from the hour when their work finished, for dawn is the moment for spectres to fade away and for bandits to part. These four men were known by this title. When the President of the Assizes visited Lacenaire in prison, he questioned him about a crime which the murderer denied. "Who committed it?" the President asked, and Lacenaire gave this answer, which was enigmatical for the magistrate, but clear for the police, "It is, perhaps, Patron Minette."

The plot of a play may be at times divined from the list of names, and a party of bandits may, perhaps, be appreciated in the same way. Here are the names to which the principal members of Patron Minette answered, exactly as they survive in special memoirs.

Panchaud, *alias* Printanier, *alias* Bigrenaille; Brujon (there was a dynasty of Brujons, about whom we may still say a word); Boulatruelle, the roadmender, already introduced; Laveuve; Finistère; Homer-Hogu, a negro; Mardisoir; Dépêche; Fauntleroy, *alias* Bouquetière; Glorieux, a liberated convict; Barrecarrosse; *alias* Monsieur Dupont; L'esplanade-du-Sud; Poussàgrive, Carmagnolet; Kruideniers, *alias* Bizarro; Mangedentelle; Les-pieds-en-l'air; Demi-leard, *alias* Deux-milliards; etc. etc.

These names have faces, and express not merely beings, but species. Each of these names responds to a variety of the poisonous fungi which grow beneath human civilisation. These beings, very careful about showing their faces, were not of those whom we may see passing by day, for at that period, weary of their night wanderings, they went to sleep in the lime-kilns, the deserted quarries of Montmarte or Montrouge, or even in the snow. They ran to earth.

CHAPTER LXXV.

SUMMER passed away, then autumn : winter arrived. Neither M. Leblanc nor the young girl had set foot again in the Luxembourg, while Marius had but one thought, that of seeing again this sweet and adorable face. He sought it ever, he sought it everywhere, but found nothing. He was no longer Marius, the enthusiastic dreamer, the resolute, ardent, and firm man, the bold challenger of destiny, the brain that built up future upon future, the young mind encumbered with plans, projects, pride, ideas, and resolves,—he was a lost dog.

Once he had a meeting which produced a strange effect upon him. In the little streets adjoining the Boulevard des Invalides he passed a man dressed like a workman, and wearing a deep-peaked cap, under which white locks peered out. Marius was struck by the beauty of this white hair, and looked at the man, who was walking slowly, and as if absorbed in painful meditation. Strange to say, he fancied that he could recognise M. Leblanc,—it was the same hair, the same profile, as far as the peak allowed him to see, and the same gait, though somewhat more melancholy. But why this workman's clothing ? What was the meaning of this disguise ? Marius was greatly surprised, and when he came to himself again his first impulse was to follow this man, for he might, perhaps, hold the clue which he had so long been seeking ; at any rate, he must have a close look at the man, and clear up the enigma ; but he hit on this idea too late, for the man was no longer there. He had turned into some side street, and Marius was unable to find him again. This meeting troubled him for some days, and then faded away. "After all," he said to himself, "it is probably only a resemblance."

Marius still lived in the Gorbeau tenement. He paid no attention to anybody there. At this period, in truth, there were no other tenants in the house but himself and those Jondrettes whose rent he had once paid, without ever having spoken, however, to father, mother, or daughters. The other lodgers had removed, were dead, or turned out for not paying their rent. On one day of this winter the sun had shown itself a little during the afternoon—it was the second of February, old Candlemas day—and Marius had just left his room, for night was falling. It was the hour to go and

dine, for he had been obliged to revert to that practice, such
is the infirmity of ideal passions.

Marius slowly walked along the boulevard, in the direction
of the Rue St. Jacques. He walked thoughtfully, with
hanging head. All at once he felt himself elbowed in the
fog. He turned and saw two girls in rags, one tall and thin,
the other not quite so tall, who passed hurriedly, panting,
frightened, and as if running away ; they were coming
toward him, and ran against him as they passed. Marius
noticed in the twilight their livid faces, uncovered heads,
dishevelled hair, ragged petticoats, and bare feet. While
running they talked together, and the elder said :

" The slops came, and nearly caught me."

And the other answered, " I saw them, and so I bolted."

Marius understood that the police had nearly caught the
two girls, and that they had managed to escape. They
buried themselves beneath the trees behind him, and for
a few minutes produced a sort of vague whiteness in the
obscurity. Marius had stopped for a moment, and was just
going on, when he noticed a small gray packet lying at his
feet. He stooped down and picked it up ; it was a sort of
envelope, apparently containing papers.

" Why," he said, " these poor girls must have let it fall."

He turned back and called to them, but could not find
them. He thought they must be some distance off, so he
thrust the parcel into his pocket and went to dinner.

At night, as he undressed to go to bed, his hand felt in
his coat pocket the parcel which he had picked up in the
boulevard. He thought that it would be as well to open it,
as the packet might contain the girls' address, if it belonged
to them, or in any case the necessary information to restore
it to the person to whom it belonged. He opened the
envelope, which was unsealed, and which contained four
letters, also unsealed. The addresses were on all four,
and they exhaled a frightful perfume of tobacco. The first
letter was addressed to *Madame, Madame la Marquise de
Grucheray, on the Square opposite the Chamber of Deputies.*
Marius said to himself that he would probably find the information he wanted, and as the letter was not sealed he could
read it without impropriety. It was drawn up as follows :—

" MADAME LA MARQUISE,
        "The virtue of kindness and piety is that which
binds sosiety most closely. Call up your Christian feelings,

and dain a glance of compasion at this unfortunate Spaniard
and victim to his loyalty and atachment to the sacred cause
of legitimacy, who shed his blood, devoted the whole of
his fortune to defend this cause, and is now in the greatest
missery. He does not doubt that you, honnored lady, will
grant some asistence to preserve an existence entirely painful for a soldier of honour and edducation, who is covered
with wounds, and he reckons beforehand on the humanity
which annimates you, and the interest which your ladyship
takes in so unhapy a nacion. His prayer will not be in
vain, and His gratitude will retain her charming memory.

" With the most respectful feelings, I have the honour to
be, madame,

" DON ALVARES, Spanish captain of cavvalry,
a Royalist refugee in France, who is travelling for
his country, and who wants the means to continue
his jurney."

No address was attached to the signature, but Marius
hoped to find it in the second letter, of which the superscrip-
tion was : *To Madame, Madame la Comtesse de Montvernet,
No. 9 Rue Cassette.* This is what Marius read :

" MY LADY COMTESS,
" It is a unhapy mother of a familly of six children,
of which the yungest is only eight months old ; I ill since
my last confinement, deserted by my husband, and havving
no ressourse in the world, living in the most frightful
indijance.
"Trusting in your ladyship, she has the honour to be,
madame, with profound respect,
" ANTOINETTE BALIZARD."

Marius passed to the third letter, which was, like the
preceding, a petition, and he read in it :

" Monsieur Pabourgeot, Elector, wholesale dealer in caps,
Rue St. Denis, at the corner of the Rue Aux-Fers.

" I venture to adress this letter to you, to ask you
to grant me the pretious favour of your sympathies, and to
interest you in a litterary man, who has just sent a drama to
the Théâtre Français. The subject is historical, and the
scene takes place in Auvergne in the time of the Empire ;
the style, I believe, is natural, laconic, and may posess

some merit. There are couplets for singing at four places. The comic, the serious, and the unexpected elements are blended in it with a variety of characters, and a tinge of romance is lightly spread through the whole plot, which moves misteriously, and the finale takes place amid several brilliant tableaux. My principal desire is to sattisfy the desire which progressively animates sosiety, that is to say, fashion, that capritious and vague whirligig which changes with nearly every wind.

"In spite of these quallities, I have reason to fear that jealousy and the selfishness of privileged authors may obtain my exclusion from the stage, for I am not unaware of the vexation which is caused to new-comers.

"Monsieur Pabourgeot, your just reputation as the en-lightened protector of litterary men, emboldens me to send to you my daughter, who will explain to you our indijant situation, wanting for bread and fire in this winter season. To tell you that I wish you to accept the homage which I desire to make to you of my drama, and all those that may succeed it, is to prove to you how much I desire the honour of sheltering myself under your ægis, and adorning my writings with your name. If you dain to honour me with the most modest offering, I will at once set to work writing a coppy of verses, by which to pay you my debt of grattitude. These verses, which I will try to render as perfect as possible, will be sent to you before they are insirted in the beginning of the drama, and produced on the stage.

"My most respectful homage to Monsieur and Madame Pabourgeot,   GENFLOT, man of letters.

"P.S.—If it was only forty sous. I appologise for sending my daughter, and not paying my respects personaly, but sad reasons of dress do not allow me, alas ! to go out."

Marius then opened the last letter, which was addressed to—*The Benevolent gentleman of the church of St. Jacques du Haut-pas,* and it contained the following few lines :—

"BENEVOLENT MAN,
     "If you will dain to accompany my 'daughter you will witness a misserable calamity, and I will show you my certificates.

"At the sight of these dokuments your generous soul will be moved by a feeling of sensitive benevolence, for true philosophers always experience lively emotions.

"Allow, compasionate man, that a man must experience the most cruel want, and that it is very painful to obtain any relief, by having it attested by the authorities, as if a man were not at liberty to suffer and die of inanicion, while waiting till our missery is releaved. Fate is too cruel to some and too lavish or protecting for others. I await your presence or your offering, if you dain to make one, and I beg you to believe in the grateful feelings with which I have the honour of being, really magnamious sir,

"Your very humble and most obedient servant,
"P. FABANTOU, dramatic artist."

After reading these four letters Marius did not find himself much advanced. In the first place not one of the writers gave his address; and next, they appeared to come from four different individuals, Don Alvarez, Madame Balizard, Genflot the poet, and Fabantou the dramatic artist; but these letters offered this peculiarity, that they were all in the same handwriting. What could be concluded from this, save that they came from the same person? Moreover—and this rendered the conjecture even more probable—the paper, which was coarse and yellow, was the same for all four, the tobacco smell was the same, and though an attempt had evidently been made to vary the handwriting, the same orthographical mistakes were reproduced with the most profound tranquillity, and Genflot, the literary man, was no more exempt from them than the Spanish captain. To strive to divine this mystery was time thrown away, and if he had not picked it up it would have looked like a mystification; Marius was too sad to take kindly even a jest of accident, and lend himself to a game which the street pavement appeared desirous to play with him. He felt as if he were playing at blind-man's buff among these four letters and they were mocking him. Nothing, besides, indicated that these letters belonged to the girls whom Marius had met in the boulevard. After all they were papers evidently of no value. Marius returned them to the envelope, threw the lot into a corner, and went to bed.

At about seven in the morning he had got up and break-fasted, and was trying to set to work, when there came a gentle tap at the door. As he possessed nothing he never locked his door, except very rarely, when he had a pressing job to finish. As a rule, even when out, he left the key in the lock. There was a second knock, quite as gentle as the first.

"Come in," said Marius.

The door opened.

"What is the matter, Ma'am Bougon?" Marius continued, without taking his eyes off the books and MSS. on his table.

A voice, which was not Ma'am Bougon's, replied: "I beg your pardon, sir."

It was a hollow, cracked, choking voice, the voice of an old man, rendered hoarse by dram-drinking and exposure to the cold.

A girl who was quite young was standing in the half-open door. The skylight, through which light entered, was exactly opposite the door, and threw upon this form a sallow gleam. She was a wretched, exhausted, fleshless creature, and had only a chemise and a petticoat upon her shivering and frozen nudity. For waistbelt she had a piece of string, for head-dress another,—pointed shoulders emerged from her chemise; she was of an earthy pallor, her hands were red, her mouth degraded, and she had lost teeth; her eye was sunken and hollow, and she had the outline of an abortive girl and the look of a corrupted old woman, or fifty years blended with fifteen. She was one of those beings who are at once weak and horrible, and who make those shudder whom they do not cause to weep.

Marius had risen, and was gazing with a species of stupor at this being, who almost resembled the shadows that traverse dreams. What was most crushing of all was, that this girl had not come into the world to be ugly, and in her childhood she must even have been pretty. The grace of youth was still struggling with the hideous and premature senility of debauchery and poverty. A remnant of beauty was expiring on this countenance of sixteen, like the pallid sun which dies out under the frightful clouds on the dawn of a winter's day. This face was not absolutely strange to Marius, and he fancied that he had already seen it somewhere.

"What do you want, miss?" he asked.

The girl replied, with her drunken galley-slave's voice.

"It is a letter for you, Monsieur Marius."

She addressed him by name, and hence he could not doubt but that she had to do with him; but who was this girl, and how did she know his name? Without waiting for any authority, she walked in. She walked in boldly, looking at the whole room and the unmade bed with a sort of assurance that contracted the heart. Her feet were bare, and large holes in her petticoat displayed her long legs and thin knees. She was shivering, and held in her hand a letter, which she offered to Marius. On opening the letter, he noticed that the large, clumsy wafer was still damp, which proved that the missive had not come a long distance, and he read :

" My amicable neighbour and young sir !
" I have herd of your kindness to me, and that you paid my half-year's rent six months ago. I bless you for it, young sir. My eldest daughter will tell you that we have been without a morsel of bread for two days,—four persons, and my wife ill. If I am not deseived in my opinion, I dare to hope that your generous heart will be affected by this statment, and will arouse in you a desire to be propicious to me, by daining to lavish on me a trifling charity.
" I am, with the distinguished consideration which is due to the benefactors of humanity,   JONDRETTE.

" P.S.—My daughter will wait for your orders, my dear Monsieur Marius."

This letter, in the midst of the obscure adventure which had been troubling Marius since the previous evening, was like a candle in a cellar ; all was suddenly lit up. This letter came from where the other letters came. It was the same handwriting, the same style, the same orthography, the same paper, and the same tobacco smell. There were five letters, five stories, five names, five signatures, and only one writer. The Spanish captain Don Alvarez, the unhappy mother Balizard, the dramatic author Genflot, and the old comedian Fabantou, were all four Jondrette, if, indeed, Jondrette's name were really Jondrette.

During the lengthy period that Marius had lived in the tenement, he had had, as we stated, but very few opportunities to see, or even catch a glance of, his very low neighbours. His mind was elsewhere, and where the mind is, there is the eye. He must have passed the Jondrettes more than once in the passage and on the stairs, but they were to him merely shadows. He had paid

so little attention to them, that on the previous evening
he had run against the Jondrette girls on the boulevard
without recognising them; for it was evidently they;
and it was with great difficulty that this girl, who had
just entered the room, aroused in him, through disgust
and pity, a vague fancy that he had met her somewhere
before.

Now he saw everything clearly. He understood that
his neighbour Jondrette in his distress had hit upon the
trade of working upon the charity of benevolent persons;
that he procured addresses and wrote under supposititious
names, to people whom he supposed to be rich and charitable, letters which his children delivered at their risk and
peril, for this father had attained such a stage that he
hazarded his daughters; he was gambling with destiny
and staked them. Marius comprehended that, in all
probability, judging from their flight of the previous
evening, their panting, their terror, and the slang words
he overheard, these unfortunates carried on some other
dark trades, and the result of all this was, in the heart
of human society such as it is constituted, two wretched
beings, who were neither children, nor girls, nor women,
but a species of impure and innocent monsters, which were
the produce of wretchedness.

While Marius was bending on the young girl an astonished
and painful glance, she was walking about the garret with
the boldness of a spectre, and without troubling herself in
the slightest about her state of nudity. At some moments
her unfastened and torn chemise fell almost to her waist.
She moved the chairs about, disturbed the toilette articles
on the chest of drawers, felt Marius' clothes, and rummaged
in every corner.

"Why," she said, "you have a looking-glass!"

And she hummed, as if she had been alone, bits of
vaudeville songs and wild choruses, which her guttural
and hoarse voice rendered mournful. But beneath this
boldness there was something constrained, alarmed, and
humiliated, for effrontery is a disgrace. Nothing could
well be more sad than to see her fluttering about the
room with the movement of a broken-winged bird startled
by a dog. It was palpable that with other conditions of
education and destiny, the gay and free demeanour of
this girl might have been something gentle and charming.
Among animals, the creature born to be a dove is never

changed into an osprey; that is only possible with men. Marius was thinking, and left her alone, and she walked up to the table.

"Ah!" she said, "books."

A gleam darted from her glassy eye : she continued, and her accent expressed the attitude of being able to boast of something to which no human creature is insensible :

"I know how to read."

She quickly seized the book lying on the table, and read rather fluently :

"General Bauduin received orders to carry with the five battalions of his brigade the Château of Hougomont, which is in the centre of the plain of Waterloo——"

She broke off.

"Ah, Waterloo, I know all about that. It was a battle in which my father was engaged, for he served in the army. We are thorough Bonapartists, we are. Waterloo was fought against the English."

She laid down the book, took up a pen, and exclaimed, "And I can write, too."

She dipped the pen in the ink, and turned to Marius, saying :

"Would you like a proof? stay, I will write a line to show you."

And ere he had time to answer she wrote on a sheet of white paper in the middle of the table, "Here are the slops." Then, throwing down the pen, she added :

"There are no errors in spelling, as you can see, for my sister and I were well educated. We have not always been what we are now. We were not made——"

Here she stopped, fixed her glassy eye on Marius, and burst into a laugh, as she said, with an intonation which contained every possible agony, blended with every possible cynicism :

"Bosh!"

"Do you ever go to the play, Monsieur Marius?" she continued. "I do so. I have a brother who is a friend of the actors, and who gives me tickets every now and then. I don't care for the gallery much, though, for you are so squeezed up; at times too there are noisy people there, and others who smell bad."

Then she stared at Marius, gave him a strange look, and said to him :

"Do you know, M. Marius, that you are a very good-looking fellow!"

And at the same moment the same thought occurred to both, which made her smile and him blush. She walked up to him, and laid a hand upon his shoulder: "You don't pay any attention to me, but I know you, M. Marius. I meet you here on the staircase, and then I see you go in to a swell of the name of M. Mabœuf, who lives over at Austerlitz, when I am out that way. Your curly hair becomes you very well."

Her voice tried to be very soft, and only succeeded in being very low; a part of her words was lost in the passage from the larynx to the lips, as on a pianoforte some keys of which are broken. Marius had gently recoiled.

"I have a packet," he said, with his cold gravity, "which, I believe, belongs to you. Allow me to deliver it to you."

And he handed her the envelope which contained the four letters; she clapped her hands and said:

"We looked for it everywhere."

Then she quickly seized the parcel, and undid the envelope, while saying:

"Lord of Lords! how my sister and I *did* look for it! And so you found it? on the boulevard, did you not? it must have been there. You see, it was dropped while we were running, and it was my brat of a sister who made the stupid blunder. When we got home we could not find it, and, as we did not wish to be beaten, which is unnecessary, which is entirely unnecessary, which is absolutely unnecessary, we said at home that we had delivered the letters, and that the answer was Nix! and here are the poor letters! Well, and how did you know that they were mine? Oh, yes, by the writing. So, then, it was you that we ran against last night? We could not see anything, and I said to my sister, 'Is it a gentleman?' and she answered, 'Yes, I think it is a gentleman.'"

While saying this she had unfolded the petition addressed to the "benevolent gentleman of the church of St. Jacques du Haut-pas."

"Hilloh!" she said, "this is the one for the old swell who goes to Mass. Why, 'tis just the hour, and I will carry it to him. He will perhaps give us something for breakfast."

Then she burst into a laugh, and added :

" Do you know what it will be if we breakfast to-day ? We shall have our breakfast of the day before yesterday, our dinner of the day before yesterday, our breakfast of yesterday, our dinner of yesterday, all at once this morning. Well, hang it all ! if you are not satisfied, rot, dogs ! "

And she gazed at him with haggard eyes.

After feeling in the depths of all his pockets, Marius succeeded in getting together five francs and sixteen sous ; it was at this moment all that he possessed in the world. " Here is my to-day's dinner," he thought, " and to-morrow will take care of itself." He kept the sixteen sous, and gave the girl the five-franc piece, which she eagerly clutched.

She pulled her chemise up over her ˙shoulders, gave Marius a deep curtsey, and a familiar wave of the hand, and walked towards the door, saying :

" Good-day, sir, but no matter, I'll go and find my old swell."

As she passed she noticed on the bureau an old crust of dry bread, mouldering in the dust ; she caught it up, and bit into it savagely, grumbling :

" It is good, it is hard ; it breaks my teeth ! "

Then she went out.

CHAPTER LXXVI.

FOR five years Marius had lived in poverty, want, and even distress, but he now saw that he had never known what real misery was. Now he had seen it—it was the phantom which had just passed before him. For, in truth, he who has only seen man's misery has seen nothing, he must see woman's misery ; while he who has seen woman's misery has seen nothing, for he must see the misery of the child. When man has reached the last extremity he has also reached the limit of his resources ; and, then, woe to the defenceless beings that surround him ! Work, wages, bread, fire, courage, and food, will all fail him at once ; the light of day seems extinguished outside, the moral light is extinguished within him. In these shadows man comes

across the weakness of the wife and the child, and violently
bends them to ignominy.

This girl was to Marius a sort of emissary from the
darkness, and she revealed to him a hideous side of night.
Marius almost reproached himself for the preoccupations of
reverie and passion which, up to this day, had prevented
him from taking a glance at his neighbours. They doubtless seemed very depraved, very corrupt, very vile, and
indeed very odious; but persons who fall without being
degraded are rare. Besides, there is a stage where the
unfortunate and the infamous are mingled and confounded
in one word, a fatal word, *Les Misérables*, and with whom
lies the fault? And then again, should not the charity be
the greater the deeper the fall is?

While reading himself this lecture, for there were
occasions on which Marius was his own pedagogue, and
reproached himself more than he deserved, he looked at the
wall which separated him from the Jondrettes, as if his
pitying glance could pass through the partition, and warm
the unhappy beings. The wall was a thin coating of
plaster, supported by laths and beams, and which, as we
have stated, allowed the murmurs of words and voices to be
distinctly heard. A man must be a dreamer like Marius
not to have noticed the fact before. No paper was hung on
either side of the wall, and its clumsy construction was
plainly visible. Almost unconsciously Marius examined this
partition; for at times reverie examines, scrutinises, and
observes much as thought does. All at once he rose, for he
had just noticed near the ceiling a triangular hole produced
by the gap between three laths. The plaster which once
covered this hole had fallen off, and by getting on his
bureau he could see through this aperture into the room
of the Jondrettes. Commiseration has, and should have,
its curiosity, and it is permissible to regard misfortune
traitorously when we wish to relieve it. "Let me see,"
thought Marius, "what these people are like, and what
state they are in." He got upon the bureau, put his eye to
the aperture, and looked.

Cities, like forests, have their dens, in which all that is
most vile and terrible hides itself. The only difference is,
that what hides itself thus in cities is ferocious, unclean,
and little, that is to say, ugly; what conceals itself in the
forests is ferocious, savage, and grand, that is to say,
beautiful. Den for den, those of the beasts are preferable to

those of men; and caverns are better than hiding-places.
Marius was poor, and his room was indigent; but, in the
same way as his poverty was noble, his room was clean.
The garret into which he was now looking was abject,
dirty, fetid, infectious, dark, and sordid. The furniture only
consisted of a straw-bottomed chair, a rickety table, a few
old earthenware articles, and in the corners two indescribable beds. The only light came through a skylight with
four panes of glass festooned with spider-webs. Through
this came just sufficient light for the face of a man to seem
the face of a spectre. The walls had a leprous look, and
were covered with gashes and scars, like a face disfigured
by some horrible disease, and a putrid damp oozed from
them. Obscene designs, clumsily drawn in charcoal, could
be distinguished on them.

The room which Marius occupied had a broken brick
flooring, but in this one the people walked on the old
plaster, which had grown black under the feet. Upon this
uneven flooring, where the dust was, so to speak, encrusted,
and which had but one virginity, that of the broom, were
capriciously grouped constellations of old shoes, boots, and
frightful rags; this room, however, had a chimney, and for
this reason was let at forty francs a year. There was
something of everything in this fireplace,—a chafing-dish,
a pot, some broken planks, rags hanging from nails, a
bird-cage, ashes, and even a little fire, for two logs were
smoking there sadly. A thing which augmented the horror
of this garret was the fact of its being large; it had angles,
nooks, black holes under the roof, bays, and promontories.
Hence came frightful, inscrutable corners, in which it
seemed as if spiders large as one's fist, wood-lice as
large as one's foot, and possibly some human monsters,
must lurk.

One of the beds was near the door, the other near the
window, but the ends of both ran down to the mantelpiece, and faced Marius. In a corner near the hole
through which Marius was peeping, a coloured engraving
in a black frame, under which was written in large letters,
THE DREAM, leant against the wall. It represented a
sleeping woman and a sleeping child, the child lying
on the woman's knees, an eagle in the clouds with a
crown in its beak, and the woman removing the crown
from the child's head, without awaking it, however;
in the background Napoleon, surrounded by a halo, was

leaning against a dark blue column, with a yellow capital, that bore the following inscription :—

MARINGO
AUSTERLITS
IENA
WAGRAMME
ELOT

Below this frame a sort of wooden panel, longer than it was wide, was standing on the ground and leaning against the wall. It looked like a picture turned from the spectator, or some signboard detached from a wall and forgotten while waiting to be hung again. At the table, on which Marius noticed pen, ink, and paper, a man was seated of about sixty years of age, short, thin, livid, haggard, with a sharp, cruel, and listless look— a hideous scamp. If Lavater had examined this face he would have found in it the vulture blended with the attorney's clerk ; the bird of prey and the man of trickery rendering each other more ugly and more perfect—the man of trickery rendering the bird of prey ignoble, and the bird of prey rendering the man of trickery horrible. This man had a long gray beard, and wore a woman's chemise, which allowed his hairy chest, and naked arms, bristling with gray hairs, to be seen. Under this chemise might be noticed muddy trousers, and boots out of which his toes stuck. He had a pipe in his mouth, and was smoking ; there was no bread in the garret, but there was still tobacco. He was writing, probably some letter like those which Marius had read. On one corner of the table could be seen an old broken-backed volume, the form of which, the old 12mo of circulating libraries, indicated that it was a romance ; on the cover figured the following title, printed in large capitals,—GOD, THE KING, HONOUR, AND THE LADIES : BY DUCRAY DUMINIL, 1814. While writing, the man was talking aloud, and Marius heard his words :

"Only to think that there is no equality, even when a man is dead ! Just look at Père La Chaïse ! The great ones, those who are rich, are up above, in the Acacia Avenue which is paved, and reach it in a coach. The little folk, the poor people, the wretched—they are put down at the bottom where there is mud up to the knees, in holes, and in the damp, and they are placed there that they may rot all the sooner. You can't go to see them without sinking into the ground."

Here he stopped, smote the table with his fist, and added, while he gnashed his teeth :

"Oh! I could eat the world !"

A big woman, who might have been forty or one hundred, was crouched up near the chimney-piece on her naked feet. She too was only dressed in a chemise, a cotton petticoat, pieced with patches of old cloth, and an apron of coarse canvas concealing one half of the petticoat. Though this woman was sitting all of a heap, you could see that she was very tall, and a species of giantess by her husband's side. She had frightful hair, of a reddish auburn, beginning to turn gray, which she thrust back every now and then with her enormous strong hands, which had flat nails. By her side, on the ground, was lying an open volume, of the same form as the other, probably part of the same romance. On one of the beds Marius caught a glimpse of a slender little wan girl, sitting up almost naked, and with hanging feet, who did not seem to hear, see, or live; she was, doubtless, the younger sister of the one who had come to his room. She appeared to be eleven or twelve years of age, but on examining her attentively it could be seen that she was at least fourteen. It was the girl who said on the boulevard the previous night, "I bolted." She was of that backward class who keep down for a long time and then shoot up quickly and suddenly. It is indigence which produces these human plants, and these creatures have neither infancy nor adolescence. At fifteen they seem twelve, and at sixteen they appear twenty; to-day it is a little girl, to-morrow a woman; we might almost say that they stride through life in order to reach the end more rapidly. At this moment, however, she had the look of a child.

In this lodging there was not the slightest sign of work ; not a loom, a spinning-wheel, or a single tool, but in one corner were some iron implements of dubious appearance. It was that dull indolence which follows despair and precedes death. Marius gazed for some time at this mournful interior, which was more terrifying than the interior of a tomb, for here were felt the movements of a human soul, and the palpitation of life.

Marius, with a heavy heart, was just going to descend from the species of observatory which he had improvised, when a noise attracted his attention, and made him remain at his post. The door of the garret was suddenly opened, and the elder daughter appeared on the threshold. She had on her feet clumsy men's shoes covered with mud, which had even plashed her red ankles, and she was covered with an old ragged cloak, which Marius had not noticed an hour previously, and which she had probably left at his door, in order to inspire greater sympathy, and put on again when she went out. She came in, shut the door after her, stopped to take breath, for she was panting, and then cried, with an expression of triumph and joy, " He is coming ! "

The father turned his eyes, the mother turned her head, and the little girl did not move.

" Who? the philanthropist ? " the father asked.

" Yes."

" Of the church of St. Jacques ? "

" Yes. He is following me."

" Are you sure ? "

" He is coming in a hackney coach, I tell you."

" How are you sure ? if he is coming in a coach, how is it that you got here before him ? did you give him the address, and are you certain you told him the last door on the right in the passage ? I only hope he will not make a mistake. Did you find him at church ? did he read my letter, and what did he say to you ? "

" Ta, ta, ta," said the girl, " how you gallop, my good man. I went into the church, he was at his usual place, I made a curtsey and handed him the letter, he read it, and said to me, ' Where do you live, my child ? ' I said, ' I will show you the way, sir ; ' he said, ' No, give me your address, for my daughter has some purchases to make. I will take a hackney coach, and be at your abode as soon as you.' I gave him the address, and when I mentioned the house he seemed surprised, and hesitated for a moment, but then said, ' No matter, I will go.' When mass was over I saw him leave the church and get into a coach with his daughter. And I carefully told him the last door on the right at the end of the passage."

" And what tells you that he will come ? "

" I have just seen the coach turn into the Rue du Petit Banquier, and that is why I ran."

" How do you know it is the same coach ? "

" Because I noticed the number, of course."

" What was it ? "

" Four hundred and forty."

" Good, you are a clever girl. And so you are sure that he will come ? "

" He is at my heels," she replied.

The man drew himself up, and there was a species of illumination on his face.

" Wife," he cried, " you hear ! Here is the philanthropist ; put out the fire."

The stupefied mother did not stir, but the father, with the agility of a mountebank, seized the cracked pot, which stood on the chimney-piece, and threw water on the logs. Then he said to his elder daughter :

" Pull the straw out of the chair."

As his daughter did not understand him, he seized the chair and kicked the seat out ; his leg passed through it, and while drawing it out, he asked the girl :

" Is it cold ? "

" Very cold, it is snowing."

The father turned to the younger girl, who was on the bed, near the window, and shouted in a thundering voice :

" Come off the bed directly, idler ; you never will do anything ; break a pane of glass ! "

The little girl jumped off the bed, shivering.

" Break a pane ! " he continued.

The girl was quite stunned, and did not move.

" Do you hear me ? " the father repeated ; " I tell you to break a pane."

The child, with a sort of terrified obedience, stood on tiptoe, and broke a pane with her fist ; the glass fell with a great clash.

" All right ! " said the father.

He was serious and active, and his eye rapidly surveyed every corner of the garret ; he was like a general who makes his final preparations at the moment when an action is about to begin. The mother, who had not yet said a word, rose and asked in a slow, dull voice, the words seeming to issue as it frozen :

" Darling, what do you intend to do ? "

" Go to bed," the man replied.

The tone admitted of no deliberation ; the mother obeyed, and threw herself heavily on one of the beds. A sobbing was now audible in a corner.

" What is that ? " the father cried.

The younger girl, without leaving the gloom in which she was crouching, showed her bleeding hand. In breaking the glass she had cut herself; she had crawled close to her mother's bed, and was now crying silently. It was the mother's turn to draw herself up and cry.

"You see what nonsensical acts you commit! she has cut herself in breaking the window."

"All the better," said the man, "I expected it."

"How all the better?" the woman continued.

"Silence!" the father replied, "I suppress the liberty of the press."

Then, tearing the chemise which he wore, he made a bandage, with which he quickly wrapped up the girl's bleeding hand; this done, his eye settled on the torn shirt with satisfaction.

"And the shirt too!" he said; "all this looks well."

An icy blast blew through the pane and entered the room. The external fog penetrated it, and dilated like a white wadding pulled open by invisible fingers. The snow could be seen falling through the broken pane, and the cold promised by the Candlemas sun had really arrived. The father took a look around him, as if to make sure that he had forgotten nothing, then he fetched an old spade and strewed the ashes over the wet logs so as to conceal them entirely. Then getting up and leaning against the chimney-piece, he said:

"Now we can receive the philanthropist."

The elder girl walked up to her father, and laid her hand in his.

"Feel how cold I am!" she said.

"Pshaw!" the father answered, "I am much colder than that."

The mother cried impetuously:

"You always have everything better than the others, the evil even."

"To kennel!" the man said.

The mother, looked at by him in a certain way, held her tongue, and there was a momentary silence in the den. The elder girl was carelessly removing the mud from the edge of her cloak, and her younger sister continued to sob. The mother had taken her head between her hands, and covered it with kisses, while whispering:

"Pray do not go on so, my treasure; it will be nothing, so don't cry, or you will vex your father."

"No," the father cried, "on the contrary, sob away, for that does good."

Then he turned to the elder girl :

" Why, he is not coming ! suppose he were not to come !
I should have broken my pane, put out my fire, unseated
my chair, and torn my shirt all for nothing."

" And hurt the little one," the mother murmured.

" Do you know," the father continued, " that it is infer-
nally cold in this devil's own garret ? Suppose the man did
not come ! but no, he is keeping us waiting, and says to
himself, ' Well, they will wait my pleasure, they are sent
into the world for that ! ' Oh ! how I hate the rich, and
with what joy, jubilation, enthusiasm, and satisfaction,
would I strangle them all ! I will bet that that old
brute——"

At this moment there was a gentle tap at the door ; the
man rushed forward and opened it, while exclaiming with
deep bows and smiles of adoration :

" Come in, sir, deign to enter, my respected benefactor,
as well as your charming daughter."

A man of middle age and a young lady stood in the doorway ; Marius had not left his post, and what he felt at this
moment is beyond the human tongue.

It was She ; and any one who has loved knows the radiant
meaning conveyed in the three letters that form the word
She. It was certainly she, though Marius could hardly
distinguish her through the luminous vapour which had
suddenly spread over his eyes. It was the gentle creature
he had lost, the star which had gleamed on him for six
months, it was the forehead, the mouth, the lovely mouth
which had produced night by departing. The eclipse was
over, and she now reappeared—reappeared in this darkness,
in this attic, in this filthy den, in this horror. Marius
trembled. What ! it was she ! the palpitation of his heart
affected his sight, and he felt ready to burst into tears.
What ! he saw her again after seeking her so long ! it
seemed to him as if he had lost his soul and had just found
it again. She was still the same, though, perhaps, a little
paler ; her delicate face was framed in a violet velvet bonnet,
her waist was hidden by a black satin pelisse, and a glimpse
of her little foot in a silk boot could be caught under her
long dress. She was accompanied by M. Leblanc, and she
walked into the room and placed a rather large parcel on
the table. The elder girl had withdrawn behind the door
and looked with a jealous eye at the velvet bonnet, the satin
pelisse, and the charming, happy face.

The garret was so dark that persons who came into it felt much as if they were going into a cellar. The two new-comers, therefore, advanced with some degree of hesitation, scarce distinguishing the vague forms around them, while they were perfectly seen and examined by the eyes of the denizens in the attic, who were accustomed to this gloom. M. Leblanc walked up to Father Jondrette, with his sad and gentle smile, and said :

"You will find in this parcel, sir, new apparel, woollen stockings, and blankets."

"Our angelic benefactor overwhelms us," Jondrette said, bowing to the ground ; then, bending down to the ear of his elder daughter, he added in a hurried whisper, while the two visitors were examining this lamentable interior :

"Did I not say so ? clothes but no money. They are all alike. By the way, how was the letter to the old ass signed ? "

"Fabantou."

"The actor ; all right."

It was lucky that Jondrette asked this, for at the same moment M. Leblanc turned to him, and said, with the air of a person who is trying to remember the name :

"I see that you are much to be pitied, Monsieur——"

"Fabantou," Jondrette quickly added.

"Monsieur Fabantou, yes, that is it, I remember."

"An actor, sir, who has been successful in his time."

Here Jondrette evidently believed the moment arrived to trap his philanthropist, and he shouted in a voice which had some of the bombast of the country showman, and the humility of the professional beggar,—"A pupil of Talma, sir ! I am a pupil of Talma ! Fortune smiled upon me formerly, but now, alas ! the turn of misfortune has arrived. You see, my benefactor, we have no bread, no fire. My poor babies have no fire. My sole chair without a seat ! a pane of glass broken ! in such weather as this ! my wife in bed, ill ! "

"Poor woman !" said M. Leblanc.

"My child hurt," Jondrette added.

The child, distracted by the arrival of the strangers, was staring at the "young lady," and ceased sobbing.

"Cry, I tell you—roar !" Jondrette whispered to her. At the same time he squeezed her bad hand. All this was done with the talent of a conjurer. The little one uttered piercing cries, and the adorable girl whom Marius called in his heart, " his Ursule," eagerly went up to her.

" Poor dear child ! " she said.

" You see, respected young lady," Jondrette continued, " her hand is bleeding. It is the result of an accident which happened to her while working at a factory to earn six sous a day. It is possible that her arm will have to be cut off."

" Really ? " the old gentleman said in alarm.

The little girl, taking this remark seriously, began sobbing again her loudest.

" Alas, yes, my benefactor ! " the father answered.

For some minutes past Jondrette had been looking at the " philanthropist " in a peculiar way, and while speaking seemed to be scrutinising him attentively, as if trying to recall his recollections. All at once, profiting by a moment during which the new-comers were questioning the little girl about her injured hand, he passed close to his wife, who was lying in her bed with a surprised and stupid air, and said to her in a hurried whisper :

" Look at that man ! "

Then he turned to M. Leblanc, and continued his lamentations.

" Look, sir ! my sole clothing consists of a chemise of my wife's, all torn, in the heart of winter. I cannot go out for want of a coat, and if I had the smallest bit of a coat I would go and call on Mademoiselle Mars, who knows me, and is much attached to me ; does she still live in the Rue de la Tour des Dames? Do you know, sir, that we played together in the provinces, and that I shared her laurels? Célimène would come to my help, sir, and Elmire give alms to Belisarius. But no, nothing ! and not a halfpenny piece in the house ! my wife ill, not a sou ! my daughter dangerously injured, not a sou ! my wife suffers from shortness of breath—it comes from her age, and then the nervous system is mixed up in it. She requires assistance, and so does my daughter. But the physician and the apothecary, how are they to be paid, if I have not a farthing ? I would kneel down before a decime, sir. You see to what the arts are reduced ! And do you know, my charming young lady, and you, my generous protector, who exhale virtue and goodness, and who perfume the church where my poor child sees you daily when she goes to say her prayers ! for I am bringing up my daughters in religion, sir, and did not wish them to turn to the stage. I do not jest, sir ; I read them lectures of honour, morality, and virtue. Just ask them ! They must go straight ; for they have a father. They are not wretched girls who begin by having no family, and finish by marrying the public. Such a girl is Miss Nobody, and becomes Madame All the World. There must be nothing of that sort in the Fabantou family ! I intend to educate them virtuously, and they must be respectable, and honest, and believe in God's holy name. Well, sir, worthy sir, do you know what will happen to-morrow ? To-morrow is the fatal 4th of February, the last respite my landlord has granted me, and if I do not pay my rent by to-night, my eldest daughter, myself, my wife with her fever, my child with her wound, will be all four of us turned out of here into the street, shelterless in the rain and snow. That is the state of the case, sir ! I owe four quarters, a year's rent, that is to say, sixty francs."

Jondrette lied, for four quarters would only have been forty francs, and he could not owe four, as it was not six months since Marius had paid two for him. M. Leblanc took a five-franc piece from his pocket and threw it on the table. Jondrette had time to growl in his grown-up daughter's ear :

"The scamp ! what does he expect me to do with his five francs ? They will not pay for the chair and pane of glass. There's the result of making an outlay."

In the meanwhile, M. Leblanc had taken off a heavy brown coat, which he wore over his blue one, and thrown it on the back of a chair.

"Monsieur Fabantou," he said, "I have only these five francs about me, but I will take my daughter home and return to-night. Is it not to-night that you have to pay ? "

Jondrette's face was lit up with a strange expression, and he hurriedly answered :

"Yes, respected sir, I must be with my landlord by eight o'clock."

"I will be here by six, and bring you the sixty francs."

"My benefactor ! " Jondrette exclaimed wildly ; and he added in a whisper :

"Look at him carefully, wife."

M. Leblanc had given his arm to the lovely young lady, and was turning to the door.

"Till this evening, my friends," he said.

"At six o'clock ? " Jondrette asked.

" At six o'clock precisely."

At this moment the overcoat left on the back of the chair caught the eye of the elder girl.

"Sir," she said, "you are forgetting your greatcoat."

Jondrette gave his daughter a crushing glance, accompanied by a formidable shrug of the shoulders, but M. Leblanc turned and replied smilingly :

"I do not forget it, I leave it."

"Oh, my protector," said Jondrette, "my august benefactor, I am melting into tears ! permit me to conduct you to your vehicle."

"If you go out," M. Leblanc remarked, "put on that overcoat, for it is really very cold."

Jondrette did not let this be said twice, but eagerly put on the brown coat. And they went out, all three, Jondrette preceding the two strangers.

Marius had lost nothing of all this scene, and yet in reality he had seen nothing of it. His eyes had remained fixed on the young girl ; his heart had, so to speak, seized and entirely enfolded her from her first step into the garret. During the whole time she had been there he had lived that life of ecstasy which suspends material perceptions, and concentrates the whole mind upon one point. He contemplated not the girl, but the radiance which was dressed in a satin pelisse and a velvet bonnet. Had the planet Sirius entered the room he would not have been more dazzled. While she was opening the parcel, and unfolding the clothes and blankets, questioning the sick mother kindly, and the little wounded girl tenderly, he watched her every movement, and tried to hear her words. Though he knew her eyes, her forehead, her beauty, her waist, and her walk, he did not know the sound of her voice. He fancied that he had caught a few words once at the Luxembourg, but he was not absolutely sure. He would have given ten years of his life to hear her, and to carry off in his soul a little of this music, but all was lost in the lamentable braying of Jondrette's trumpet. This mingled a real anger with Marius' ravishment, and he devoured her with his eyes, for he could not imagine that it was really this divine creature whom he perceived among these unclean beings in this monstrous den ; he fancied that he saw a humming-bird among frogs.

When she left the room he had but one thought,—to follow her, to attach himself to her trail, not to leave her till he knew where she lived, or at least not to lose her again after having so miraculously found her. He leapt off the bureau, and seized his hat, but just as he laid his hand on the latch and was going out a reflection arrested him; the passage was long, the staircase steep, Jondrette chattering, and M. Leblanc had doubtless not yet got into his coach again. If, turning in the passage, or on the stairs, he were to perceive him, Marius, in this house, he would assuredly be alarmed, and find means to escape him again, and so all would be over for the second time. What was to be done? wait awhile? but during this delay the vehicle might start off. Marius was perplexed, but at length risked it, and left the room. There was no one in the passage, and he ran to the stairs, and as there was no one upon them, he hurried down and reached the boulevard just in time to see a hackney-coach turning the corner of the Rue du Petit Banquier, on its road to Paris.

Marius rushed in that direction, and, on reaching the corner of the boulevard, saw the hackney-coach again rapidly rolling along the Rue Mouffetard; it was already some distance off, and he had no means of catching it up. Running after it was an impossibility; and, besides, a man running at full speed after the vehicle would be seen from it, and the father would recognise him. At this moment, by an extraordinary and marvellous accident, Marius perceived a cab passing along the boulevard, empty. There was only one thing to be done, get into this cab and follow the hackney-coach; that was sure, efficacious, and without danger. Marius made the driver a sign to stop, and shouted to him, "By the hour!" Marius had no cravat on, he wore his old working coat, from which buttons were missing, and one of the plaits of his shirt was torn. The driver stopped, winked, and held out to Marius his left hand, as he gently rubbed his forefinger with his thumb.

"What do you mean?" Marius asked.

"Payment in advance," said the coachman.

Marius remembered that he had only sixteen sous in his pocket.

"How much is it?"

"Forty sous."

"I will pay on returning."

The driver, in reply, whistled the air of La Palisse, and lashed his horse. Marius watched the cab go off with a haggard look; for the want of twenty-four sous, he lost his

joy, his happiness, his love ! he fell back into night ! he had
seen, and was becoming blind again.   He thought bitterly,
and, we must add, with deep regret, of the five francs which
he had given that very morning to the wretched girl.   If he
had still had them, he would have been saved, would have
emerged from limbo and darkness, and have been drawn
from isolation, spleen, and bereavement ; he would have
reattached the black thread of his destiny to the beauteous
golden thread which had just floated before his eyes, only
to be broken again !   He returned to his garret in despair.
He might have said to himself that M. Leblanc had promised
to return that evening, and that then he must contrive to
follow him better ; but in his contemplation he had scarce
heard him.

Just as he was going up the stairs h noticed on the other
side of the wall, and against the deserted wall of the Rue de
la Barrière des Gobelins, Jondrette, wrapped up in the
"philanthropist's" overcoat, and conversing with one ot
those ill-looking men who are usually called prowlers at the
barrière; men with equivocal faces and suspicious soliloquies,
who look as if they entertain evil thoughts, and most usually
sleep by day, which leads to the supposition that they work
at night.   These two men, standing to talk in the snow,
which was falling heavily, formed a group which a policeman would certainly have observed, but which Marius
scarce noticed.   Still, though his preoccupation was so
painful, he could not help saying to himself that the man
to whom Jondrette was talking was like a certain Panchaud,
alias Printanier, *alias* Bigrenaille, whom Courfeyrac had
once pointed out to him, and who was regarded in the
quarter as a very dangerous night-bird.

CHAPTER LXXVII.

MARIUS mounted the stairs slowly, and at the moment when
he was going to enter his cell he perceived behind him, in
the passage, the elder of Jondrette's girls following him.
This girl was odious in his sight, for it was she who had his
five francs, but it was too late to ask them back from her,
for both the hackney-coach and the cab were now far away.
Besides, she would not return them to him.   As for questioning her about the abode of the persons who had been here
just now, that was useless, and it was plain that she did not

know, for the letter signed Fabantou was addressed to the
"benevolent gentleman of the church of St. Jacques du
Haut-pas." Marius went into his room and threw the door
to after him, but it did not close ; he turned and saw a hand
in the aperture.

"Who's that ? " he asked.

It was the girl.

"Oh ! it's you ! " Marius continued almost harshly,
" always you ! What do you want of me ? "

She seemed thoughtful, and made no answer, and she no
longer had her boldness of the morning ; she did not come
in, but stood in the dark passage, where Marius perceived
her through the half-open door.

" Well, answer," said Marius, " what do you want
of me ? "

She raised her dull eye, in which a sort of lustre seemed
to be vaguely illumined, and said :

" Monsieur Marius, you look sad ; what is the matter
with you ? "

" Nothing."

" Yes, there is ! "

" Leave me alone ! "

Marius pushed the door again, but she still held it.

" Stay," she said, " you are wrong. Though you are not
rich, you were kind this morning ; be so again now. You
gave me food, and now tell me what is the matter with you.
It is easy to see that you are in sorrow, and I do not wish
you to be so. What can I do to prevent it, and can I be of
any service to you ? Employ me ; I do not ask for your
secrets, and you need not tell them to me, but I may be of
use to you. Surely I can help you, as I help my father.
When there are any letters to deliver, or any address to be
found by following people, or asking from door to door, I
am employed. Well, you can tell me what is the matter
with you, and I will go and speak to persons. Now and
then it is sufficient for some one to speak to persons in order
to find out things, and all is arranged. Employ me."

An idea crossed Marius' mind, for no branch is despised
when we feel ourselves falling. He walked up to the girl.

" Listen to me," he said ; " you brought an old gentleman
and his daughter here."

" Yes."

" Do you know their address ? "

" No."

" Find it for me."

The girl's eye, which was dull, had become joyous, but now it became gloomy.

" Is that what you want ? " she asked.

" Yes."

" Do you know them ? "

" No."

" That is to say," she added quickly, " you don't know her, but you would like to know her."

This " them," which became " her," had something most significant and bitter about it.

" Well, can you do it ? " Marius said.

" You shall have the ' lovely young lady's ' address."

In these words there was again a meaning which annoyed Marius, so he went on :

" Well, no matter ! the father and daughter's address, their address, I say."

She looked at him fixedly.

" What will you give me for it ? "

" Whatever you like."

" Whatever I like ? You shall have the address."

She hung her head, and then closed the door with a hurried gesture ; Marius was alone again. He fell into a chair, with his head and elbows on his bed, sunk in thoughts which he could not grasp, and suffering from a dizziness. All that had happened since the morning, the apparition of the angel, her disappearance, and what this creature had just said to him, a gleam of hope floating in an immense despair—this is what confusedly filled his brain. All at once he was violently dragged out of his reverie, for he heard Jondrette's loud, hard voice uttering words full of the strangest interest for him.

" I tell you that I am sure, and that I recognised him."

Of whom was Jondrette talking, and whom had he recognised ? M. Leblanc, the father of " his Ursule." What ! did Jondrette know him ? Was Marius going to obtain, in this sudden and unexpected fashion, all the information without which his life was obscure for himself ? was he at last going to know who she was whom he loved, and who her father was ? Was the thick cloud that covered them on the point of clearing off ? would the veil be rent asunder ? Oh, heavens ! He bounded rather than ascended upon the bureau and resumed his place at the aperture in the partition : once more he saw the interior of Jondrette's den. There was no change in the appearance of the family, save that the mother and daughters had put on stockings and flannel waistcoats taken out of the parcel, and two new blankets were thrown on the beds. The man had evidently just returned, for he was out of breath; his daughters were seated near the fireplace on the ground, the elder tying up the younger's hand. The mother was crouching on the bed near the fireplace, with an astonished face, while Jondrette was walking up and down the room with long strides. His eyes had an extraordinary look. The woman, who seemed frightened and struck with stupor before him, ventured to say:

"What, really, are you sure?"

"Sure! it is eight years ago, but I can recognise him! I recognised him at once. What! did it not strike you?"

"No."

"And yet I said to you, 'Pay attention!' Why, it is his figure, his face, very little older—for there are some people who never age, though I do not know how they manage it—and the sound of his voice. He is better dressed, that's all! Ah! you mysterious old villain, I hold you!"

He stopped and said to his daughters:

"Be off, you two!—It is funny that it did not strike you."

They rose to obey, and the mother stammered:

"With her bad hand?"

"The air will do it good," said Jondrette. "Off with you."

It was evident that this man was one of those who are not answered. The girls went out, but just as they passed the door the father clutched the elder by the arm, and said, with a peculiar accent:

"You will be here at five o'clock precisely, both of you, for I shall want you."

Marius redoubled his attention. When left alone with his wife, Jondrette began walking up and down the room again, and took two or three turns in silence. All at once he turned to his wife, folded his arms, and exclaimed:

"And shall I tell you something? the young lady——"

"Well, what?" the wife retorted.

Marius could not doubt, they were really talking about her. He listened with ardent anxiety, and all his life was in his ears. But Jondrette had stooped down, and was whispering to his wife. Then he rose, and ended aloud:

" It is she."

"That one ? " the wife asked.

"That one ! " said the husband.

No expression could render all there was in the mother's *that one*; it was surprise, rage, hatred, and passion mingled and combined in a monstrous intonation. A few words, doubtless a name which her husband whispered in her ear, were sufficient to arouse this huge, crushed woman, and to make her more than repulsive and frightful.

"It is not possible," she exclaimed; "when I think that my daughters go about barefooted, and have not a gown to put on! What! a satin pelisse, a velvet bonnet, clothes worth more than two hundred francs, so that you might take her for a lady ! no ! you are mistaken ! and, then, the other was hideous, while this one is not ugly, indeed, rather good-looking : oh, it cannot be ! "

"And I tell you that it is. Shall I tell you something else ? "

" What ? " she asked.

He replied in a low, guttural voice, "That my fortune is made."

The wife looked at him in the way which means, "Can the man who is talking to me have suddenly gone mad ? " He continued :

"Thunder ! I have been a long time a parishioner of the parish of die-of-hunger-if-you-have-any-fire, and die-of-cold-if-you-have-any-bread ! I have had enough of that misery! I am not jesting, for I no longer consider this comical. I have had enough jokes, good God ! and want no more farces, by the Eternal Father ! I wish to eat when I am hungry, and drink when I am thirsty : to gorge, sleep, and do nothing. I want to have my turn now, and mean to be a bit of a millionaire before I rot ! " He walked up and down the room and added, " Like the rest ! "

" What do you mean ? " his wife asked.

" Listen carefully. The Crœsus is trapped, or as good as trapped. It is done, arranged, and I have seen the people. He will come at six this evening to bring the sixty francs, the vagabond ! Did you notice how I plummed him about my landlord on February 4th ? Why, it is not a quarter-day, the ass. Well, he will come at six o'clock, and at that hour the neighbour has gone to dinner, and Mother Bougon is washing up dishes in town, so there will be no one in the house. The neighbour never comes in before eleven o'clock. The little ones will be on the watch, you will help us, and he will execute himself."

"And suppose he does not ? " the wife asked.

Jondrette made a sinister gesture, and said, " We will do it for him."

And he burst into a laugh : it was the first time that Marius saw him laugh, and this laugh was cold and gentle, and produced a shudder. Jondrette opened a cupboard near the fireplace, and took out an old cap, which he put on his head after brushing it with his cuff.

" Now," he said, " I am going out, for I have some more people to see, good men. I shall be away as short a time as possible, for it is a famous affair ; and do you keep house."

He went out, but had only gone a short distance when the door opened again, and his sharp, intelligent face reappeared in the aperture.

"I forgot," he said, "you will get a chafing-dish of charcoal ready."

And he threw into his wife's apron the five-franc piece which the " philanthropist " left him.

Jondrette closed the door again, and then Marius heard his steps as he went along the passage and down the stairs. It struck one at this moment from St. Medard's.

Dreamer as he was, Marius possessed, as we have said, a firm and energetic nature. His habits of solitary contemplation, by developing compassion and sympathy within him, had perhaps diminished the power of being irritated, but left intact the power of becoming indignant : he had the benevolence of a brahmin and the sternness of a judge, and while he pitied a toad he crushed a viper. At present he had a nest of vipers before him, and he said, " I must set my foot upon these villains." Not one of the enigmas which he hoped to see cleared up was solved ; on the contrary, they had become rather denser, and he had learned no more about the pretty girl of the Luxembourg and the man whom he called M. Leblanc, save that Jondrette knew them. Through the dark words which had been uttered he only saw one thing distinctly, that a snare was preparing, an obscure but terrible snare ; that they both ran an imminent danger, she probably, and the father certainly, and that he must save them, and foil the hideous combinations of the Jondrettes by destroying their spider's web.

He watched the woman for a moment ; she had taken an old iron furnace from the corner, and was rummaging among the tools. He got off the bureau as gently as he could, taking care not to make any noise. In his terror at what was preparing, and the horror with which the Jondrettes filled him, he felt a species of joy at the idea that it might perhaps be in his power to render such a service to her whom he loved. But what was he to do? should he warn the menaced persons? where was he to find them? for he did not know their address. They had reappeared to him momentarily, and then plunged again into the immense profundities of Paris. Should he wait for M. Leblanc at the gate at the moment when he arrived that evening and warn him of the snare? But Jondrette and his comrades would see him on the watch. The place was deserted, they would be stronger than he, they would find means to get him out of the way, and the man whom Marius wished to save would be lost. It had just struck one, and as the snare was laid for six o'clock, Marius had five hours before him. There was only one thing to be done; he put on his best coat, tied a handkerchief round his neck, took his hat, and went out, making no more noise than if he were walking barefoot on moss; besides, the woman was still rummaging among the old iron.

Once outside the house, he turned into the Rue du Petit Banquier. About the middle of the street he found himself near a very low wall, which it was possible to bestride in some places, and which surrounded unoccupied ground. He was walking slowly, deep in thought as he was, and the snow deadened his footsteps, when all at once he heard voices talking close to him. He turned his head, but the street was deserted; it was open day, and yet he distinctly heard the voices. He thought of looking over the wall, and really saw two men seated in the snow, and conversing in a low voice. They were strangers to him: one was a bearded man in a blouse, and the other a hairy man in rags. The bearded man wore a Greek cap, while the other was bareheaded, and had snow in his hair. By thrusting out his head over them Marius could hear the hairy man say to the other, with a nudge:

"With Patron Minette it cannot fail."

"Do you think so?" asked the bearded man, and the hairy man added:

"It will be five hundred balls for each, and the worst that can happen is five years, six years, or ten at the most."

The other replied with some hesitation, and shuddering under his Greek cap:

"That is a reality; and people must not go to meet things of that sort."

"I tell you that the affair cannot fail," the hairy man continued. "Father What's-his-name's trap will be all ready."

Then they began talking of a melodrama which they had seen on the previous evening at the Gaîté.

Marius walked on; but it seemed to him that the obscure remarks of these men, so strangely concealed behind this wall, and crouching in the snow, must have some connection with Jondrette's abominable scheme; that must be the *affair*. He went toward the Faubourg St. Marceau, and asked at the first shop he came to where he could find a police commissary. He was told at No. 14 Rue de Pontoise, and he proceeded there. As he passed a baker's he bought a two-sous roll and ate it, as he foresaw that he should not dine. On the way he rendered justice to Providence. He thought that if he had not given the five francs in the morning to the girl he should have followed M. Leblanc's hackney-coach, and consequently known nothing. There would, in that case, have been no obstacle to Jondrette's ambuscade, and M. Leblanc would have been lost, and doubtless his daughter with him.

On reaching No. 14 Rue de Pontoise, he went up to the first floor and asked for the commissary.

"He is not in at present," said a clerk, "but there is an inspector to represent him. Will you speak to him? is your business pressing?"

"Yes," said Marius.

The clerk led him to the commissary's office. A very tall man was leaning here against the fender of a stove, and holding up with both hands the skirts of a mighty coat with three capes. He had a square face, thin and firm lips, thick grayish whiskers, and a look which seemed as if it was searching your pockets. Of this look you might have said, not that it pierced, but that it felt. This man did not appear much less ferocious or formidable than Jondrette; for sometimes it is just as dangerous to meet the dog as the wolf.

"What do you want?" he asked Marius, without adding sir.

"The police commissary."

" He is absent, but I represent him."

" It is a very secret affair."

" Then speak."

" And very urgent."

" In that case speak quick."

This man, who was calm and quick, was at once terrifying and reassuring. He inspired both fear and confidence. Marius told him of his adventure—that a person whom he only knew by sight was to be drawn that very evening into a trap—that he, Marius Pontmercy, barrister, residing in the next room to the den, had heard the whole plot through the partition—that the scoundrel's name who invented the snare was Jondrette—that he would have accomplices, probably prowlers at the barrières, among others one Panchaud, *alias* Printanier, *alias* Bigrenaille—that Jondrette's daughters would be on the watch—that there were no means of warning the threatened man, as not even his name was known—and that, lastly, all this would come off at six in the evening, at the most deserted spot on the Boulevard de l'Hôpital, in the house No. 50-52.

At this number the Inspector raised his head, and said coldly :

" It must be in the room at the end of the passage."

" Exactly," Marius replied, and added, " Do you know the house ? "

The Inspector remained silent for a moment, and then answered, while warming his boot-heel at the door of the stove :

" Apparently so."

He went on between his teeth, talking less to Marius than to his cravat.

" Patron Minette must be mixed up in this."

This remark struck Marius.

" Patron Minette ! " he said, " yes, I heard that name mentioned."

And he told the Inspector of the dialogue between the hairy man and the bearded man in the snow behind the wall in the Rue du Petit Banquier. The Inspector growled :

" The hairy man must be Burgon, and the bearded man Demi-liard, *alias* Deux-milliards."

He was again looking down and meditating. As for Father What's-his-name, I guess who he is. There, I have burnt my greatcoat, they always make too large a fire in these cursed stoves. No. 50-52, formerly the property of one Gorbeau."

Then he looked at Marius.

" You only saw the hairy man and the bearded man ? "

" And Panchaud."

" You did not see a small dandy prowling about there ? "

" No."

" Nor a heavy lump of a fellow, resembling the elephant in the Jardin des Plantes ? "

" No."

" Nor a scamp who looks like an old red-tail ? "

" No."

" As for the fourth, no one sees him, not even his pals and assistants. It is not surprising, therefore, that you did not perceive him."

" No. Who are all these men ? " Marius asked.

The Inspector continued, " Besides, it is not their hour." He fell into silence, and presently added :

" 50-52. I know the tenement. It is impossible for us to hide ourselves in the interior without the actors perceiving us, and then they would escape by putting off the farce. They are so modest, and frightened at an audience. That won't do, for I want to hear them sing and make them dance."

This soliloquy ended, he turned to Marius, and asked, as he looked at him searchingly :

" Would you be afraid ? "

" Of what ? " Marius asked.

" Of these men."

" No more than I am of you," Marius answered roughly, for he was beginning to notice that this policeman had not yet said " Sir."

The Inspector looked at Marius more intently still, and continued, with a sort of sententious solemnity :

" You speak like a brave man and like an honest man. Courage does not fear crime, nor honesty the authorities."

Marius interrupted him :

" That is all very well, but what do you intend doing ?

The Inspector restricted himself to saying :

" The lodgers in that house have latchkeys to let themselves in at night. You have one ? "

" Yes," said Marius.

" Have you it about you ? "

" Yes."

"Give it to me," the Inspector said.

Marius took the key out of his waistcoat pocket, handed it to the Inspector, and added :

"If you take my advice you will bring a strong force."

The Inspector gave Marius such a glance as Voltaire would have given a Provincial Academician who proposed a rhyme to him ; then he thrust both hands into his immense coat-pockets and produced two small steel pistols, of the sort called "knock-me-downs." He handed them to Marius, saying sharply and quickly :

"Take these. Go home. Conceal yourself in your room, and let them suppose you out. They are loaded ; both with two bullets. You will watch, as you tell me there is a hole in the wall. People will arrive ; let them go on a little. When you fancy the matter ripe, and you think it time to stop it, you will fire a pistol, but not too soon. The rest concerns me. A shot in the air, in the ceiling, I don't care where,—but, mind, not too soon. Wait till they begin to put the screw on. You are a lawyer, and know what that means."

Marius took the pistols, and placed them in a side pocket of his coat.

"They bulge like that, and attract attention," said the Inspector ; "put them in your trousers' pockets."

Marius did so.

"And now," the Inspector continued, "there is not a moment for any one to lose. What o'clock is it? Half-past two. You said seven ? "

"Six o'clock," Marius corrected.

"I have time," the Inspector added ; "but only just time. Do not forget anything I have said to you. A pistol-shot."

"All right," Marius replied.

And as he put his hand on the latch to leave the room the Inspector shouted to him :

"By the way, if you should want me between this and then, come or send here. You will ask for Inspector Javert."

About three o'clock, Marius actually came across Jondrette in the Rue Mouffetard, and followed him. Jondrette was walking along, not at all suspecting that an eye was already fixed upon him. He left the Rue Mouffetard, and Marius saw him enter one of the most hideous lodging-houses in the Rue Gracieuse, where he remained for about a

quarter of an hour, and then returned to the Rue Mouffetard.
He stopped at an ironmonger's shop, which was at that
period at the corner of the Rue Pierre-Lombard : and a few
minutes after Marius saw him come out of the shop, holding a large cold chisel set in a wooden handle, which he
hid under his greatcoat. He then turned to his left and
hurried toward the Rue du Petit Banquier. Day was
drawing in, the snow, which had ceased for a moment,
had begun again, and Marius concealed himself at the
corner of the Rue du Petit Banquier, which was deserted
as usual, and did not follow Jondrette. It was lucky that
he acted thus, for Jondrette, on reaching the spot where
Marius had listened to the conversation of the hairy man
and the bearded man, looked round, made sure that he
was not followed, clambered over the wall, and disappeared.
The unused ground which this wall enclosed communicated
with the back-yard of a livery stable keeper of bad repute,
who had been a bankrupt, and still had a few vehicles
standing under sheds.

Marius thought it would be as well to take advantage of
Jondrette's absence and return home. Besides, time was
slipping away, and every evening Ma'am Bougon, when
she went to wash up dishes in town, was accustomed to
close the gate, and, as Marius had given his latchkey
to the Inspector, it was important that he should be in time.
Night had nearly set in along the whole horizon, and in
the whole immensity there was only one point still illumined
by the sun, and that was the moon, which was rising
red behind the low dome of the Salpetrière. Marius hurried
to No. 50-52, and the gate was still open when he arrived.
He went up the stairs on tiptoe, and glided along the
passage-wall to his room. This passage, it will be remembered, was bordered on either side by rooms which
were now to let, and Ma'am Bougon, as a general rule, left
the doors open. While passing one of these doors, Marius
fancied that he could see in the uninhabited room four
men's heads vaguely lit up by a remnant of daylight, which
fell through a window. Marius did not attempt to see,
as he did not wish to be seen himself; and he managed
to re-enter his room noiselessly and unseen. It was high
time, for, a moment after, he heard Ma'am Bougon going
out, and the house-gate shutting.

Marius sat down on his bed : it might be about half-
past five, and only half an hour separated him from

what was about to happen. He heard his arteries beat
as you hear the ticking of a clock in the darkness, and
he thought of the double march which was taking place
at this moment in the shadows,—crime advancing on one
side, and justice coming up on the other. It no longer
snowed; the moon, now very bright, dissipated the mist,
and its rays, mingled with the white reflection from the
fallen snow, imparted a twilight appearance to the room.
There was a light in Jondrette's room, and Marius could see
the hole in the partition glowing with a ruddy brilliancy
that appeared to him the colour of blood. It was evident
that this light could not be produced by a candle. There
was no movement in the den, no one stirred there, no one
spoke, there was not a breath, the silence was chilling and
profound, and had it not been for the light, Marius might
have fancied himself close to a grave. He gently took off
his boots, and thrust them under the bed. Several minutes
elapsed, and then Marius heard the house-gate creaking on
its hinges, a heavy quick step ran up the stairs, and along
the passage, the hasp of the door was noisily raised,—
it was Jondrette returned home. All at once several voices
were raised, and it was plain that the whole family were at
home. They were merely silent in the master's absence,
like the whelps in the absence of the wolves.

Marius heard him lay something heavy on the table,
probably the chisel which he had bought.

"The mousetrap is open, and the cats are here," said he,
and then lowering his voice, he added, "put this in the
fire."

Marius heard some charcoal bars stirred with a pair
of iron pincers, or some steel instrument, and Jondrette
asked:

"Have you tallowed the hinges of the door, so that they
may make no noise?"

"Yes," the mother answered.

"What o'clock is it?"

"Close on six. It has struck the half-hour at St·
Medard."

"Hang it!" said Jondrette, "the girls must go on the
watch. Come here and listen to me."

There was a whispering, and then Jondrette's voice was
again uplifted.

"Has Ma'am Bougon gone?"

"Yes," the mother answered.

"Are you sure there is nobody in the neighbour's room ? "

"He has not come in all day, and you know that this is his dinner-hour."

"Are you sure ? "

"Quite."

"No matter," Jondrette added, "there is no harm in going to see whether he is in. Daughter, take the candle and go."

Marius fell on his hands and knees, and silently crawled under the bed; he had scarce done so ere he saw light through the cracks of his door.

"Papa," a voice exclaimed, "he is out."

He recognised the elder girl's voice.

" Have you been in his room ? " the father asked.

"No," the girl replied, "but as his key is in his door he has gone out."

The father shouted :

"Go in all the same."

The door opened, and Marius saw the girl come in, candle in hand. She was the same as in the morning, save that she was even more fearful in this light. She walked straight up to the bed, and Marius suffered a moment of intense anxiety, but there was a looking-glass hanging from a nail by the bedside, and it was to that she proceeded. She stood on tiptoe and looked at herself; a noise of iron being moved could be heard in the other room. She smoothed her hair with her hand, and smiled in the glass, and sang, in her cracked and sepulchral voice. Still Marius trembled, for he thought that she could not but hear his breathing. She walked to the window and looked out, while saying aloud with the half-insane look she had :

" How ugly Paris is when it has put on a white sheet ! "

She returned to the glass and began taking a fresh look at herself, first full face and then three-quarters.

"Well," asked the father, "what are you doing there ? "

"I am looking under the bed and the furniture," she said, as she continued to smooth her hair ; "but there is nobody."

"You she-devil," the father yelled. "Come here directly, and lose no time."

"Coming, coming," she said, "there's no time to do anything here."

She took a parting glance at the glass and went off,

closing the door after her. A moment later Marius heard
the sound of the girls' naked feet pattering along the
passage, and Jondrette's voice shouting to them :

" Pay attention ! one at the barrière and the other at the
corner of the Rue du Petit Banquier. Do not lose the
gate of this house out of sight, and if you see anything
come back at once—at once—you have a key to let yourselves in."

The elder daughter grumbled :

" To stand sentry barefooted in the snow, what a treat ! "

" To-morrow you shall have beetle-coloured silk boots,"
the father said.

They went down the stairs, and a few seconds later the
sound of the gate closing below announced that they had
reached the street. The only persons in the house now
were Marius, the Jondrettes, and probably, too, the
mysterious beings of whom Marius had caught a glimpse
in the twilight behind the door of the untenanted garret.

CHAPTER LXXVIII.

MARIUS judged that the time had come for him to resume
his place at his observatory. In a second, and with the
agility of his age, he was at the hole in the partition,
and peeped through. The interior of Jondrette's lodging
offered a strange appearance, and Marius was able to
account for the peculiar light he had noticed. A candle
was burning in a verdigrised candlestick, but it was not
this which really illumined the room ; the whole den was
lit up with the ruddy glow of a brasier standing in the
fireplace, and filled with incandescent charcoal—it was the
chafing-dish which the wife had prepared in the morning.
The burner was red, a bluish flame played round it, and
rendered it easy to recognise the shape of the chisel
purchased by Jondrette, which was heating in the charcoal.
In a corner, near the door, could be seen two heaps, one
apparently of old iron, the other of ropes, arranged for some
anticipated purpose.

The heat of the chafing-pan was so great that the candle
on the table was melting and guttering on the side turned
toward it. An old copper dark lantern, worthy of a
Diogenes who had turned Cartouche, was standing on the
mantelpiece. The chafing-dish, which stood in the fire-

place, close to the decaying logs, sent its smoke up the
chimney, and thus produced no smell. Jondrette's den, if
our readers remember what we have said about the house,
was admirably selected to serve as the scene of a violent
and dark deed, and as a covert for crime. It was the
furthest room in the most isolated house on the most
deserted Parisian boulevard; and if a snare were not there
already it would have been invented there. The whole
length of a house and a number of uninhabited rooms
separated this lair from the boulevard, and the only window
in it looked out on fields enclosed by walls and boardings.
Jondrette had lit his pipe, was seated on the bottomless
chair and smoking, and his wife was speaking to him in
a low voice.

If Marius had been Courfeyrac, that is to say, one of
those men who laugh at every opportunity, he would have
burst into a roar when his eye fell on Mother Jondrette.
She had on a bonnet with black feathers, like the hats
worn by the heralds at the coronation of Charles X., an
immense tartan shawl over her cotton skirt, and the man's
shoes, which her daughter had disdained in the morning.

"By the way," said Jondrette, "in such weather as this
he will come in a hackney-coach. Light your lamp and
go down, and keep behind the front gate; when you hear
the vehicle stop you will open the gate at once, light him
upstairs, and along the passage, and when he has come
in here you will go down as quickly as you can, pay the
coachman, and discharge him."

"Where's the money to come from?" the woman asked.

Jondrette felt in his pocket, and gave her five francs.

"What is this?" she exclaimed.

"The monarch which our neighbour gave us this morning," and he added, "We shall want two chairs, though."

"What for?"

"Why, to sit down."

Marius shuddered on hearing the woman make the quiet
answer:

"Well, I will go and fetch our neighbour's."

And with a rapid movement she opened the door, and
stepped into the passage. Marius had not really the time
to get off the bureau and hide under his bed.

"Take the candle," Jondrette shouted.

"No," she said, "it would bother me, for I have two
chairs to carry. Besides, the moon is shining."

Marius heard the heavy hand of Mother Jondrette fumbling for his key in the darkness. The door opened, and he remained nailed to his post by alarm and stupor. The woman came in; the skylight sent a moonbeam between two large patches of shade, and one of these patches entirely covered the wall against which Marius was standing, so that he disappeared. Mother Jondrette did not see Marius, took the two chairs, the only two that Marius possessed, and went off, noisily slamming the door after her. She re-entered the den.

" Here are the two chairs."

"And here is the lantern," the husband said. "Make haste down."

He placed the chairs on either side of the table, turned the chisel in the chafing-dish, placed in front of the fire-place an old screen, which concealed the charcoal-pan, and then went to the corner where the heap of rope lay, and stooped down as if examining something. Marius then perceived that what he had taken for a shapeless heap was a rope ladder, very well made with wooden rungs, and two hooks to hang it by. This ladder and a few large tools, perfect crowbars, which were mingled with the heap of old iron in the corner, had not been there in the morning, and had evidently been brought in the afternoon, during the absence of Marius.

The table and the two chairs were exactly opposite Marius, and, as the charcoal-pan was concealed, the room was only illumined by the candle, and the smallest article on the table or the chimney-piece cast a long shadow; a cracked water-jug hid half a wall. There was in this room a hideous and menacing calm, and an expectation of something awful could be felt. Jondrette had let his pipe go out, a sign of deep thought, and had just sat down again. The candle caused the stern and fierce angles of his face to stand out; he was frowning, and suddenly thrust out his right hand now and then, as if answering the final counsels of a dark internal soliloquy. In one of the obscure replies he made to himself he opened the table drawer, took out a long carving-knife hidden in it, and felt its edge on his thumb nail. This done, he put the knife in the drawer, which he closed again. Marius, on his side, drew the pistol from his pocket, and cocked it, which produced a sharp, clicking sound. Jondrette started, and half rose from his chair.

"Who's that?" he shouted.

Marius held his breath. Jondrette listened for a moment, and then said laughingly :

"What an ass I am! it is the partition creaking."

Marius held the pistol in his hand.

At this moment the distant and melancholy vibration of a bell shook the windows; six o'clock was striking at St. Medard's. Jondrette marked each stroke by a shake of the head, and when he had counted the last he snuffed the candle with his fingers. Then he began walking up and down the room, listened at the door, began walking again, and then listened once more. "I only hope he'll come," he growled, and then returned to his chair. He was hardly seated ere the door opened. Mother Jondrette had opened it, and remained in the passage making a horrible grimace, which one of the holes in the dark lantern lit up from below.

"Step in, sir," she said.

"Enter, my benefactor!" Jondrette repeated, as he hurriedly rose.

M. Leblanc appeared with that air of serenity which rendered him singularly venerable, and laid four louis on the table.

"Monsieur Fabantou, here is the money for your rent, and something more to put you a little straight. After that we will see."

"May Heaven repay you, my generous benefactor!" said Jondrette, and then rapidly approached his wife.

"Dismiss the hackney-coach."

She slipped away, while her husband made an infinitude of bows, and offered a chair to M. Leblanc. A moment after she returned, and whispered in his ear, "All right!"

The snow, which had not ceased to fall since morning, was now so thick that neither the arrival nor the departure of the coach had been heard. M. Leblanc had seated himself, and Jondrette now took possession of the chair opposite to him.

No sooner was M. Leblanc seated than he turned his eyes to the beds, which were empty.

"How is the poor little wounded girl?" he asked.

"Very bad," Jondrette replied with a heart-broken and grateful smile. "Very bad, my good sir. Her elder sister has taken her to La Bourbe to have her hand dressed. But you will see them, as they will return almost immediately."

"Madame Fabantou seems to me better?" M. Leblanc continued, taking a glance at the strange garb of Mother Jondrette, who, standing between him and the door, as if already guarding the outlet, was looking at him in a menacing and almost combative posture.

"She is dying," Jondrette said, "but what would you have, sir? that female has so much courage. She is not a female but an ox."

Mother Jondrette, affected by the compliment, protested with the affectation of a flattered monster :

"You are always too kind to me, Monsieur Jondrette."

"Jondrette?" said M. Leblanc, "why, I thought your name was Fabantou."

"Fabantou, *alias* Jondrette," the husband quickly replied, "a professional name."

And, giving his wife a shrug, which M. Leblanc did not see, he continued with an emphatic and caressing inflection of voice :

"Ah! that poor dear and I have ever lived happily together, for what would be left us if we had not that! we are so wretched, respectable sir. I have arms but no labour, a heart but no work. I do not know how the Government manage it, but, on my word of honour, sir, I am no Jacobin, I wish them no harm, but if I were the ministers, on my most sacred word, things would go differently. For instance, I wished my daughters to learn the trade of making paper boxes. You will say to me, 'What! a trade?' Yes, a trade, a simple trade, a bread-winner. What a fall, my benefactor! what degradation, after persons have been in such circumstances as we were, but, alas! nothing is left us from our prosperous days. Nothing but one article—a picture, to which I cling, but which I am ready to part with, as we must live."

While Jondrette was saying this with a kind of apparent disorder, which did not in any way alter the thoughtful and sagacious expression of his face, Marius raised his eyes and saw some one at the back of the room, whom he had not seen before. A man had just entered, but so softly that the hinges had not been heard to creak. This man had on an old worn-out, torn knitted jacket of violet colour, wide cotton velvet trousers, thick socks on his feet, and no shirt ; his neck was bare, his arms were naked and tattooed, and his face was daubed with black. He seated himself silently, and with folded arms, on the nearest bed, and, as he was behind Mother Jondrette, he could be but dimly distinguished. That sort of magnetic instinct which warns the eye caused M. Leblanc to turn almost at the same moment as Marius. He could not suppress a start of surprise, which Jondrette noticed.

"Ah, I see," Jondrette exclaimed, as he buttoned his coat complacently, "you are looking at your surtout? it fits me, really fits me capitally."

"Who is that man?" M. Leblanc asked.

"That?" said Jondrette, "oh, a neighbour; pay no attention to him."

The neighbour looked singular, but chemical factories abound in the Faubourg St. Marceau, and a workman may easily have a black face. M. Leblanc's whole person displayed a confident and intrepid candour, as he continued:

"I beg your pardon, but what were you saying, M. Fabantou?"

"I was saying, sir, and dear protector," Jondrette replied, as he placed his elbows on the table and gazed at M. Leblanc with fixed and tender eyes, very like those of a boa-constrictor, "I was saying that I had a picture to sell."

There was a slight noise at the door; a second man came in and seated himself on the bed behind Mother Jondrette. Like the first, he had bare arms and a mask, either of ink or soot. Though this man literally glided into the room he could not prevent M. Leblanc noticing him.

"Take no heed," said Jondrette, "they are men living in the house. I was saying that I had a valuable picture left; look here, sir."

He rose, walked to the wall, against which the panel to which we have already referred was leaning, and turned it round, while still letting it rest on the wall. It was something, in fact, that resembled a picture, and which the candle almost illumined. Marius could distinguish nothing, as Jondrette was standing between him and the picture, but he fancied he could catch a glimpse of a coarse daub, and a sort of principal character standing out of the canvas, with the bold crudity of a showman's pictures.

"What is that?" M. Leblanc asked.

Jondrette exclaimed:

"A masterpiece, a most valuable picture, my benefactor! I am as much attached to it as I am to my daughters, for it recalls dear memories; but, as I told you, and I will not go back from my word, I am willing to dispose of it, as we are in such poverty."

Either by accident, or some vague feeling of anxiety, M. Leblanc's eye, while examining the picture, returned to the end of the room. There were now four men there, three seated on the bed and one leaning against the door-post, but all four bare-armed, motionless, and with blackened faces. One of those on the bed was leaning against the wall with closed eyes, apparently asleep; this one was old, and the white hair on the blackened face was horrible. The other two were young, one was hairy, the other bearded. Not a single one had shoes, and those who did not wear socks were barefooted. Jondrette remarked that M. Leblanc's eyes rested on these men.

"They are friends, neighbours," he said, "their faces are black because they are chimney-sweeps. Do not trouble yourself about them, sir, but buy my picture. Have pity on my misery. I will not ask much for it; what value do you set upon it?"

"Well," M. Leblanc said, looking Jondrette full in the face, like a man setting himself on guard, "it is some pot-house sign, and worth about three francs."

Jondrette replied gently:

"Have you your pocket-book about you? I shall be satisfied with a thousand crowns."

M. Leblanc rose, set his back against the wall, and took a hurried glance round the room. He had Jondrette on his left by the window, and on his right the woman and the four men by the door. The four men did not stir, and did not even appear to see him. Jondrette had begun talking again with a plaintive accent, and with such a wandering eye that M. Leblanc might fairly believe that he simply had before him a man driven mad by misery.

"If you do not buy my picture, dear benefactor," Jondrette said, "I have no resource remaining, and nothing is left me but to throw myself into the river. When I think that I wished my two daughters to learn how to make paper boxes for new-year's gifts. Well, for that you require a table with a backboard to prevent the glasses falling on the ground, a stove made expressly, a pot with three compartments for the three different degrees of strength which the glue must have, according as it is used for wood, paper, and cloth; a board to cut pasteboard on, a hammer, a pair of pincers, and the deuce knows what, and all that to gain four sous a day! and you must work fourteen hours! and each box passes thirteen times through the hands of the workgirl! and moistening the paper! and not spoiling anything! and keeping the glue hot! the devil! I tell you, four sous a day! How do you expect them to live?"

While speaking, Jondrette did not look at M. Leblanc, who was watching him. M. Leblanc's eye was fixed on Jondrette, and Jondrette's on the door, while Marius' gasping attention went from one to the other. M. Leblanc seemed to be asking himself, Is he a lunatic? and Jondrette repeated twice or thrice with all sorts of varied inflections in the suppliant style, "All that is left me is to throw myself into the river! the other day I went for that purpose down three steps by the side of the bridge of Austerlitz." All at once his eyes glistened with a hideous radiance, the little man drew himself up and became frightful, he walked a step toward M. Leblanc, and shouted, in a thundering voice:

"But all that is not the question! Do you know me?"

CHAPTER LXXIX.

THE door of the garret had been suddenly flung open, disclosing three men in blue cloth blouses and wearing masks of black paper. The first was thin, and carried an iron-shod cudgel; the second, who was a species of Colossus, held a pole-axe by the middle; while the third, a broad-shouldered fellow, not so thin as the first, but not so stout as the second, was armed with an enormous key stolen from some prison-gate. It seemed as if Jondrette had been awaiting the arrival of these men, and a hurried conversation took place between him and the man with the cudgel.

"Is all ready?" asked Jondrette.

"Yes," the thin man replied.

"Where is Montparnasse?"

"He's stopped to talk to your eldest daughter."

"Is the trap ready?"

"Yes."

"With two good horses?"

"Excellent."

"Is it waiting where I ordered?"

"Yes."

"All right," said Jondrette,

M. Leblanc was very pale. He looked all round the room like a man who understands into what a snare he has fallen, and his head, turned toward all the heads that surrounded him, moved on his neck with an attentive and surprised slowness, but there was nothing in his appearance that resembled fear. He had formed an improvised bulwark of the table, and this man, who a moment before merely looked like an old man, had suddenly become an athlete, and laid his robust fist on the back of his chair with a formidable and surprising gesture. This old man, so firm and brave in the presence of such a danger, seemed to possess one of those natures which are courageous in the same way as they are good—easily and simply. The father of a woman we love is never a stranger to us, and Marius felt proud of this unknown man.

Three of the men whom Jondrette called chimney-sweeps had taken from the mass of iron, one a large chisel, another a pair of heavy pincers, and the third a hammer, and posted themselves in front of the door, without saying a word. The old man remained on the bed, merely opening his eyes, and Mother Jondrette was sitting by his side. Marius thought that the moment for interference was at hand, and raised his right hand to the ceiling in the direction of the passage, ready to fire his pistol. Jondrette, after finishing his colloquy with the three men, turned again to M. Leblanc, and repeated the question, with that low, restrained, and terrible laugh of his:

"Do you not recognise me?"

M. Leblanc looked him in the face and answered, "No!"

Jondrette then went up to the table, he bent over the candle with folded arms, and placed his angular and ferocious face as close as he could to M. Leblanc's placid face, and in this posture of a wild beast which is going to bite, he exclaimed:

"My name is not Fabantou or Jondrette, but my name is Thénardier, the landlord of the inn at Montfermeil! Do you hear me? Thénardier! Now do you recognise me?"

An almost imperceptible flush shot athwart M. Leblanc's forehead, and he answered, with his ordinary placidity, and without the slightest tremor in his voice:

"No more than before."

Marius did not hear this answer, and any one who had seen him at this moment in the darkness would have found him haggard, stunned, and crushed. At the moment when Jondrette said, " My name is Thénardier," Marius trembled in all his limbs, and he leant against the wall, as if he felt a cold sword-blade thrust through his heart. Then his right hand, raised in readiness to fire, slowly dropped, and at the moment when Jondrette repeated, " Do you hear me, Thénardier ? " Marius' relaxing fingers almost let the pistol fall. Jondrette, by revealing who he was, did not affect M. Leblanc, but he stunned Marius, for he knew this name of Thénardier, which was apparently unknown to M. Leblanc. Only remember what that name was for him ! He had carried it in his heart, recorded in his father's will ! he bore it in the deepest shrine of his memory in the sacred recommendation " A man of the name of Thénardier saved my life ; if my son meet this man he will do all he can for him." This name, it will be remembered, was one of the pieties of his soul, and he blended it with his father's name in his worship. What ! This man was Thénardier, the landlord of Montfermeil, whom he had so long and so vainly sought ! He found him now, and in what a state ! His father's saviour was a bandit ! this man, to whom Marius burned to devote himself, was a monster ! the liberator of Colonel Pontmercy was on the point of committing a crime, whose outline Marius could not yet see very distinctly, but which resembled an assassination ! And on whom ? Great Heaven, what a fatality, what a bitter mockery of fate ! His father commanded him from his tomb to do all in his power for Thénardier. During four years Marius had had no other idea but to pay this debt of his father's, and at the very moment when he was about to deliver over to justice a brigand, in the act of crime, destiny cried to him, " It is Thénardier ! " and he was at length about to requite this man, for saving his father's life amid a hail-storm of grape-shot on the heroic field of Waterloo, by sending him to the scaffold ! But, on the other hand, how could he witness a murder, and not prevent it ? What, should he condemn the victim and spare the assassin ? could he be bound by any ties of gratitude to such a villain ? All the ideas which Marius had entertained for four years were, as it were, run through the body by this unexpected stroke. He trembled, all depended on him, and he held in his hands the unconscious beings who were moving before his eyes.

If he fired the pistol, M. Leblanc was saved and Thénardier lost ; if he did not fire, M. Leblanc was sacrificed and Thénardier might, perhaps, escape. Must he hunt down the one, or let the other fall ? there was remorse on either side. What should he do ? which should he choose ? He felt as if he were going mad. His knees gave way under him, and he had not even time to deliberate, as the scene he had before him was being performed with such furious precipitation. It was a tornado of which he had fancied himself the master, but which was carrying him away : he was on the verge of fainting.

In the meanwhile Thénardier (we will not call him otherwise in future) was walking up and down before the table, with a sort of wild and frenzied triumph. He seized the candlestick and placed it on the chimney-piece with such a violent blow that the candle nearly went out, and the tallow spattered the wall. Then he turned round furiously to M. Leblanc and spat forth these words.

"Ah ! I have found you again, my excellent philanthropist ! my millionaire with the threadbare coat ! the giver of dolls ! the old niggard ! Ah, you do not recognise me. I suppose it wasn't you who came to my inn at Montfermeil just eight years ago, on the Christmas night of 1823 ! it wasn't you who carried off Fantine's child, the Lark ! it wasn't you who wore a yellow watchman's coat, and had a parcel of clothes in your hand, just as you had this morning. Tell me, wife ! It is his mania, it appears, to carry to houses bundles of woollen stockings, the old charitable humbug ! Are you a cap-maker, my Lord millionaire ? you give your profits to the poor, what a holy man ! what a mountebank ! Ah, you do not recognise me ! well, I recognise you, and did so directly you thrust your muzzle in here. Ah, you will be taught that it is not a rosy game to go like that to people's houses, under the excuse that they are inns, with such a wretched coat and poverty-stricken look that they feel inclined to give you a sou, and then, to play the generous, rob them of their bread-winner, and threaten them in the woods. I'll teach you that you won't get off, by bringing people when they are ruined a coat that is too large and two paltry hospital blankets, you old scamp, you child-stealer ! "

He stopped, and for a moment seemed to be speaking to himself. It appeared as if his fury fell into some hole, like the Rhone : then, as if finishing aloud the things he had

just been saying to himself, he struck the table with his
fist, and cried :

"With his simple look !"

Then he apostrophised M. Leblanc.

"By heaven ! you made a fool of me formerly, and are
the cause of all my misfortunes. You got for fifteen
hundred francs a girl who certainly belonged to rich
parents, who had already brought me in a deal of money,
and from whom I should have got an annuity ! That girl
would have made up to me all I lost in that wretched pot-
house, where I threw away like an ass all my blessed
savings ! Oh, I wish that what was drunk at my house
were poison to those who drank it ! However, no matter !
Tell me, I suppose you thought me a precious fool when
you went off with the Lark. You had your cudgel in the
forest, and were the stronger. To-day I shall have my
revenge, for I hold all the trumps ; you are done, my good
fellow. Oh ! how I laugh when I think that he fell into
the trap !"

Thénardier stopped out of breath ; his little narrow chest
panted like a forge-bellows. His eye was full of the ignoble
happiness of a weak, cruel, and cowardly creature who is at
length able to trample on the man he feared, and insult him
whom he flattered ; it is the joy of a dwarf putting his heel
on the head of Goliath, the joy of a jackal beginning to
rend a sick bull, which is unable to defend itself, but still
has sufficient vitality to suffer. M. Leblanc did not interrupt
him, but said, when he ceased speaking :

"I do not know what you mean, and you are mistaken.
I am a very poor man, and anything but a millionaire. I
do not know you, and you take me for somebody else."

"Ah !" Thénardier said hoarsely, "a fine dodge ! So
you adhere to that joke, eh, old fellow ? Ah, you do not
remember, you do not see who I am !"

"Pardon me, sir," M. Leblanc replied, with a polite
accent, which had something strange and grand about it
at such a moment, " I see that you are a bandit."

"Bandit ! yes, I know that you rich swells call us so. It
is true that I have been bankrupt. I am in hiding, I have
no bread, I have not a farthing, and I am a bandit ! For
three days I have eaten nothing, and I am a bandit ! ah, you
fellows warm your toes, you wear pumps made by Sakoski,
you have wadded coats like archbishops, you live on the
first floors of houses where a porter is kept, you eat truffles,

asparagus at forty francs the bundle in January, and green
peas. You stuff yourselves, and when you want to know
whether it is cold you look in the newspaper to see what
Chevalier's thermometer marks ; but we are the thermo-
meters. But we will eat you, we will devour you, poor
little chap ! Monsieur le millionnaire, learn this : I was
an established man, I held a licence, I was an elector, and
am still a citizen, while you, perhaps, are not one ! "

Here Thénardier advanced a step toward the men near
the door, and added with a quiver :

" When I think that he dares to come and address me
like a cobbler."

Then he turned upon M. Leblanc with a fresh outburst
of frenzy :

" And know this, too, my worthy philanthropist, I am
not a doubtful man, or one whose name is unknown, and
who carries off children from houses ! I am an ex-French
soldier, and ought to have the cross ! I was at Waterloo, and
in the battle I saved the life of a General called the Comte
de Pontmercy ! The picture you see here, and which was
painted by David at Bruqueselles—do you know whom it
represents ? it represents me, for David wished to im-
mortalise the exploit. I have the General on my back,
and I am carrying him through the grape-shot. That is
the story ! the General never did anything for me, and he
is no better than the rest, but, for all that, I saved his life
at the peril of my own, and I have my pockets filled with
certificates of the fact. I am a soldier of Waterloo. And
now that I have had the goodness to tell you all this, let
us come to a finish ; I want money, I want a deal of money,
an enormous amount of money, or I shall exterminate you,
by the thunder of heaven."

Marius had gained a little mastery over his agony, and
was listening. The last possibility of doubt had vanished ;
it was really the Thénardier of the will. Marius shuddered
at the charge of ingratitude cast at his father, and which
he was on the point of justifying so fatally, and his perplexities were redoubled.

The masterpiece, the picture by David, which he offered
M. Leblanc, was, as the reader will have perceived, nought
else than his public-house sign, painted by himself, and
the sole relic he had preserved from his shipwreck at
Montfermeil. As he had stepped aside Marius was now
enabled to look at this thing, and in the daub he really

recognised a battle, a background of smoke, and one man carrying another. It was the group of Thénardier and Pontmercy; the saviour sergeant and the saved colonel. Marius felt as if intoxicated, for this picture represented to some extent his loving father; it was no longer an inn sign-board but a resurrection; in it a tomb opened, from it a phantom rose. Marius heard his heart beating at his temples; he had the guns of Waterloo in his ears; his bleeding father vaguely painted on this ill-omened board startled him, and he fancied that the shapeless figure was gazing fixedly at him. When Thénardier regained breath he fastened his bloodshot eyes on M. Leblanc, and said to him in a low, sharp voice:

"What have you to say before we put the handcuffs on you?"

M. Leblanc was silent. In the midst of this silence a ropy voice uttered this mournful sarcasm in the passage:

"If there's any wood to be chopped, I'm your man."

It was the fellow with the pole-axe amusing himself. At the same time an immense, hairy, earth-coloured face appeared in the door with a frightful grin, which displayed not teeth but tusks. It was the face of the man with the pole-axe.

"Why have you taken off your mask?" Thénardier asked him furiously.

"To laugh," the man answered.

For some minutes past M. Leblanc had seemed to be watching and following every movement of Thénardier, who, blinded and dazzled by his own rage, was walking up and down the room, in the confidence of knowing the door guarded, of holding an unarmed man, and of being nine against one, even supposing that his wife only counted for one man. In his speech to the man with the pole-axe he turned his back to M. Leblanc; the latter took advantage of the opportunity, upset the chair with his foot, the table with his fist, and with one bound, ere Thénardier was able to turn, he was at the window. To open it and bestride the sill only took a second, and he was half out when six powerful hands seized him and energetically dragged him back into the room. The three "chimney-sweeps" had rushed upon him, and at the same time Mother Thénardier seized him by the hair. At the noise which ensued the other bandits ran in from the passage, and the old man on the bed, who seemed the worse for liquor, came up tottering with a roadmender's hammer in his hand. One of the sweeps, whose blackened face the candle lit up, and in whom Marius recognised, in spite of the blackening, Panchaud, *alias* Printanier, *alias* Bigrenaille, raised above M. Leblanc's head a species of life-preserver, made of two lumps of lead at the ends of an iron bar. Marius could not resist this sight. "My father," he thought, "forgive me!" and his finger sought the trigger. He was on the point of firing, when Thénardier cried :

"Do not hurt him."

This desperate attempt of the victim, far from exasperating Thénardier, had calmed him. There were two men in him, the ferocious man and the skilful man. Up to this moment, in the exuberance of triumph, and while standing before his motionless victim, the ferocious man had prevailed, but when the victim made an effort and appeared inclined to struggle, the skilful man reappeared and took the mastery.

"Do him no harm!" he repeated, and his first service was, though he little suspected it, that he stopped the discharge of the pistol, and paralysed Marius, to whom the affair did not appear so urgent, and who in the presence of this new phase saw no harm in waiting a little longer. Who knew whether some accident might not occur, which would deliver him from the frightful alternative of letting Ursule's father perish, or destroying the Colonel's saviour? A herculean struggle had commenced. With one blow of his fist in the chest M. Leblanc sent the old man rolling in the middle of the room, and then with two back-handers knocked down two other assailants, and held one under each of his knees. The villains groaned under this pressure as under a granite millstone, but the four others had seized the formidable old man by the arms and neck, and were holding him down upon the two "sweeps." Thus, master of two, and mastered by the others, crushing those beneath him, and crushed by those above him, M. Leblanc disappeared beneath this horrible group of bandits, like a boar attacked by a howling pack of dogs. They succeeded in throwing him on to the bed nearest the window, and held him down. Mother Thénardier did not once let go his hair.

"Don't you interfere," Thénardier said to her, "you will tear your shawl."

The woman obeyed, as the she-wolf obeys the wolf, with a snarl.

" You fellows," Thénardier continued, " can search him."

M. Leblanc appeared to have given up all thought of resistance, and they searched him. He had nothing about him but a leathern purse containing six francs and his handkerchief. Thénardier put the latter in his own pocket.

" What! no pocket-book ? " he asked.

" No, and no watch," one of the sweeps replied.

" No matter," the masked man who held the large key muttered in the voice of a ventriloquist, " he is a tough old bird."

Thénardier went to the corner near the door, and took up some ropes, which he threw to them.

" Fasten him to the foot of the bed," he said, and noticing the old man whom M. Leblanc had knocked down still motionless on the floor, he asked :

" Is Boulatruelle dead ? "

" No," Bigrenaille answered, " he's drunk."

" Sweep him into a corner," Thénardier said.

Two of the sweeps thrust the drunkard with their feet to the side of the old iron.

" Babet, why did you bring so many ? " Thénardier said in a whisper to the man with the cudgel, " it was unnecessary."

" They all wanted to be in it," the man answered, " for the season is bad, and there's nothing doing."

The bed upon which M. Leblanc had been thrown was a sort of hospital bed, on four clumsy wooden legs. The bandits tied him firmly in an upright posture to the end of the bed, farthest from the window and nearest the chimney-piece. When the last knot was tied Thénardier took a chair and sat down almost facing the prisoner. He was no longer the same man ; in a few minutes his countenance had passed from frenzied violence to tranquil and cunning gentleness. Marius had a difficulty in recognising in this polite smile of an official the almost bestial mouth which had been foaming a moment previously ; he regarded this fantastic and alarming metamorphosis with stupor, and he felt as a man would feel who saw a tiger changed into an attorney.

" Sir," said Thénardier, making a sign to the bandits who still held M. Leblanc to fall back ; " leave me to talk with the gentleman," he said. All withdrew to the door, and he resumed :

" You did wrong to try and jump out of the window, for

you might have broken a leg. Now, with your permission, we will talk quietly ; and, in the first place, I will communicate to you a thing I have noticed, that you have not yet uttered the slightest cry."

Thénardier was right, the fact was so, although it had escaped Marius in his trouble. M. Leblanc had merely said a few words without raising his voice, and even in his struggle near the window with the six bandits he had preserved the profoundest and most singular silence. Thénardier went on :

"Good heavens ! you might have tried to call for help, and I should not have thought it improper. Such a thing as 'Murder !' is shouted on such occasions ; I should not have taken it in ill part. It is very simple that a man should make a bit of a row when he finds himself with persons who do not inspire him with sufficient confidence. If you had done so we should not have interfered with you or thought of gagging you, and I will tell you the reason why. This room is very deaf ; it has only that in its favour, but it has that. You might explode a bombshell here and it would not produce the effect of a drunkard's snore at the nearest post. It is a convenient lodging. But still you did not cry out. All the better, and I compliment you on it, and will tell you what conclusion I draw from the fact. My dear sir, when a man cries for help, who come ? the police ; and after the police ? justice. Well, you did not cry out, and so you are no more desirous than we are for the arrival of the police. The fact is—and I have suspected it for some time—that you have some interest in hiding something ; for our part, we have the same interest, and so we may be able to come to an understanding."

While saying this Thénardier was trying to drive the sharp points that issued from his eyes into his prisoner's conscience. Besides, his language, marked with a sort of moderate and cunning insolence, was reserved and almost chosen, and in this villain who was just before only a bandit could now be seen "the man who had studied for the priesthood." The silence which the prisoner had maintained, this precaution which went so far as the very forgetfulness of care for his life, this resistance so opposed to the first movement of nature, which is to utter a cry, troubled and painfully amazed Marius, so soon as his attention was drawn to it.

Thénardier's well-founded remark but rendered denser
the mysterious gloom behind which was concealed the
grave and peculiar face, to which Courfeyrac had thrown
the sobriquet of M. Leblanc. But whoever this man
might be, though bound with cords, surrounded by
bandits, and half buried, so to speak, in a grave where
the earth fell upon him at every step—whether in the
presence of Thénardier furious or of Thénardier gentle
—he remained impassive, and Marius could not refrain
from admiring this face so superbly melancholy at such
a moment. His was evidently a soul inaccessible to
terror, and ignorant of what it is to be alarmed. He
was one of those men who overcome the amazement
produced by desperate situations. However extreme the
crisis might be, however inevitable the catastrophe, he
had none of the agony of the drowning man, who opens
horrible eyes under water. Thénardier rose without any
affectation, removed the screen from before the fireplace,
and thus unmasked the chafing-pan full of burning charcoal, in which the prisoner could perfectly see the chisel
at a white heat, and studded here and there with small red
stars. Then he came back and sat down near M. Leblanc.

"I will continue," he said; "we can come to an understanding, so let us settle this amicably. I did wrong to
let my temper carry me away just now. For instance,
because you are a millionaire, I told you that I insisted
on money, a great deal of money, an immense sum of
money, and that was not reasonable. Good heavens!
you may be rich, but you have burdens; for who is
there that has not? I do not wish to ruin you, for I am
not a bailiff after all. I am not one of those men who,
because they have advantage of position, employ it to
be ridiculous. Come, I will make a sacrifice on my side,
and be satisfied with two hundred thousand francs."

M. Leblanc did not utter a syllable, and so Thénardier
continued:

"You see that I put plenty of water in my wine. I
do not know the amount of your fortune, but I am aware
that you do not care for money, and a benevolent man
like you can easily give two hundred thousand francs
to an unfortunate parent. Of course, you are reasonable
too; you cannot have supposed that I would take all
that trouble this morning, and organise this affair to-
night, which is a well-done job, in the opinion of these

gentlemen, merely to ask you for enough money to go and drink fifteen-sous wine and eat veal at Desnoyer's. But two hundred thousand francs, that's worth the trouble; once that trifle has come out of your pocket I will guarantee that you have nothing more to apprehend. You will say, 'But I have not two hundred thousand francs about me.' Oh, I am not exorbitant, and I do not insist on that. I only ask one thing of you : be good enough to write what I shall dictate."

Here Thénardier stopped, but added, laying a stress on the words and casting a smile on the chafing-dish :

"I warn you that I shall not accept the excuse that you cannot write."

A grand inquisitor might have envied that smile.

Thénardier pushed the table close up to M. Leblanc, and took pen, ink, and paper out of the drawer, which he left half open, and in which the long knife-blade flashed. He laid the sheet of paper before M. Leblanc.

"Write !" he said.

The prisoner at last spoke.

"How can you expect me to write ? my arms are tied."

"That is true, I beg your pardon," said Thénardier; "you are quite right." And turning to Bigrenaille, he added, " Unfasten the gentleman's right arm."

Panchaud, *alias* Printanier, *alias* Bigrenaille, obeyed Thénardier's orders, and when the prisoner's hand was free, Thénardier dipped the pen in the ink and handed it to him.

"Make up your mind, sir, that you are in our absolute power ; no human interference can liberate you, and we should really be sorry to be forced to proceed to disagreeable extremities. I know neither your name nor your address, but I warn you that you will remain tied up here until the person commissioned to deliver the letter you are going to write has returned. Now be good enough to write."

"What ?" the prisoner asked.

Thénardier began dictating : " My dear daughter."

The prisoner started, and raised his eyes to Thénardlier, who went on :

"Come to me at once, for I want you particularly. The person who delivers this letter to you has instructions to bring you to me. I am waiting. Come in perfect confidence."

M. Leblanc wrote this down, and Thénardier resumed :

"By the way, efface that 'Come in perfect confidence,' for it might lead to a supposition that the affair is not perfectly simple, and create distrust."

M. Leblanc erased the words.

"Now," Thénardier added, "sign it. What is your name?"

The prisoner laid down the pen, and asked :

"For whom is this letter?"

"You know very well," Thénardier answered; "for the little one, I have just told you."

It was evident that Thénardier avoided mentioning the name of the girl in question : he called her "the Lark," he called her "the little one," but he did not pronounce her name. It was the precaution of a clever man who keeps his secret from his accomplices, and mentioning the name would have told them the whole affair, and taught them more than there was any occasion for them to know. So he repeated :

"Sign it. What is your name?"

"Urbain Fabre," said the prisoner.

Thénardier, with the movement of a cat, thrust his hand into his pocket and drew out the handkerchief found on M. Leblanc. He sought for the mark, and held it to the candle.

"U. F., all right, Urbain Fabre. Well, sign it U. F."

The prisoner did so.

"As two hands are needed to fold a letter, give it to me and I will do so."

This done, Thénardier added :

"Write the address, to 'Mademoiselle Fabre,' at your house. I know that you live somewhere near here in the neighbourhood of St. Jacques du Haut-pas, as you attend Mass there every day, but I do not know in what street. I see that you understand your situation, and as you have not told a falsehood about your name you will not do so about your address. Write it yourself."

The prisoner remained pensive for a moment, and then took up the pen and wrote :

"Mademoiselle Fabre, at M. Urbain Fabre's, No. 17 Rue St. Dominique d'Enfer."

Thénardier seized the letter with a sort of feverish convulsion.

"Wife," he shouted, and the woman came up. "Here

is the letter, and you know what you have to do. There is a hackney-coach down below, so be off at once." Then he turned to the man with the pole-axe, and said, "As you have taken off your false nose you can accompany her. Get up behind the coach. You know where you left it?"

"Yes," said the man, and depositing the axe in a corner, he followed the woman. As they were going away, Thénardier thrust his head out of the door and shouted down the passage.

"Mind and do not lose the letter! Remember you have two hundred thousand francs about you."

A minute had not elapsed when the crack of a whip could be heard rapidly retiring.

"All right," Thénardier growled, "they are going at a good pace; with a gallop like that she will be back in three quarters of an hour."

He drew up a chair to the fireside, and sat down with folded arms, holding his muddy boots to the chafing-dish.

"My feet are cold," he said.

Only five bandits remained in the den with Thénardier and the prisoner. It was plain that these men performed a crime like a job, tranquilly, without passion or pity, and with a sort of fatigue. They were heaped up in a corner like brutes, and were silent. Thénardier was warming his feet, and the prisoner had fallen back into his taciturnity. A sinister calmness had succeeded the formidable noise which had filled the garret a few moments previously. The candle, on which a large mushroom had formed, scarce lit up the immense room; the chafing-dish had grown black, and all these monstrous heads cast misshapen shadows upon the walls and the ceiling. No other sound was audible save the regular breathing of the old drunkard, who was asleep. Marius was waiting in a state of anxiety, which everything tended to augment. The enigma was more impenetrable than ever; who was this "little one," whom Thénardier had also called "the Lark,"—was she "his Ursule?" The prisoner had not seemed affected by this name of the Lark, and had answered with the most natural air in the world, "I do not know what you mean." On the other hand, the two letters U. F. were explained, they were Urbain Fabre, and Ursule's name was no longer Ursule. This is what Marius saw most clearly. A sort of frightful fascination kept him nailed to the spot, whence he surveyed and commanded the whole scene. He stood there almost incapable of reflection and movement, as if annihilated by the frightful things which he saw close to him ; and he waited, hoping for some incident, no matter its nature, unable to collect his thoughts, and not knowing what to do.

"In any case," he said, "if she is the Lark, I shall see her, for Mother Thénardier will bring her here. In that case I will give my life and blood, should it be necessary, to save her, and nothing shall stop me.".

Nearly half an hour passed in this way ; Thénardier seemed absorbed in dark thoughts, and the prisoner did not stir. Still Marius fancied that he could hear at intervals a low, dull sound in the direction of the prisoner. All at once Thénardier addressed his victim.

"By the way, M. Fabre," he said, "I may as well tell you something at once."

As these few words seemed the commencement of an explanation, Marius listened carefully. Thénardier continued :

"My wife will be back soon, so do not be impatient. I believe that the Lark is really your daughter, and think it very simple that you should keep her, but listen to me for a moment. My wife will go to her with your letter, and I told Madame Thénardier to dress herself in the way you saw, that your young lady might make no difficulty about following her. They will both get into the hackney-coach with my comrade behind ; near a certain barrier there is a trap drawn by two excellent horses ; your young lady will be driven up to it in the hackney-coach, and get into the trap with my pal, while my wife returns here to report progress. As for your young lady, no harm will be done her ; she will be taken to a place where she will be all safe, and so soon as you have handed me the trifle of two hundred thousand francs she will be restored to you. If you have me arrested, my pal will settle the Lark, that's all."

The prisoner did not utter a word, and after a pause Thénardier continued :

"It is simple enough, as you see, and there will be no harm, unless you like to make harm. I have told you all about it, and warned you, that you might know."

He stopped, but the prisoner did not interrupt the silence, and Thénardier added :

"So soon as my wife has returned and said to me, 'The Lark is on her way,' we will release you, and you can sleep at home if you like. You see that we have no ill intentions."

Frightful images passed across the mind of Marius.
What! they were not going to bring the girl here! One
of the monsters was going to carry her off in the darkness!
where? Oh, if it were she! and it was plain that it was so.
Marius felt the beating of his heart stop; what should he
do? fire the pistol and deliver all these villains into the
hands of justice? But the hideous man with the pole-axe
could not be the less out of reach with the girl, and Marius
thought of Thénardier's words, whose sanguinary meaning
he could read,—"If you have me arrested, my pal will settle
the Lark." Now he felt himself checked, not only by the
Colonel's will, but by his love, and the peril of her whom he
loved. The frightful situation, which had already lasted
above an hour, changed its aspect at every moment, and
Marius had the strength to review in turn all the most
frightful conjectures, while seeking a hope and finding
none. The tumult of his thoughts contrasted with the
lugubrious silence of the den. In the midst of this silence,
the sound of the staircase door being opened and
shut became audible. The prisoner gave a start in his
bonds.

"Here's my wife," said Thénardier.

He had scarce finished speaking when Mother Thénardier
rushed into the room, red, out of breath, and with flashing
eyes, and shouted as she struck her thighs with her two
big hands:

"A false address."

The brigand, who had accompanied her, appeared behind,
and took up his pole-axe again.

"A false address?" Thénardier repeated, and she went
on:

"No Monsieur Urbain Fabre known at No. 17 Rue St.
Dominique. They never heard of him."

She stopped to snort, and then continued:

"Monsieur Thénardier, that old villain has made a fool
of you; for you are too good-hearted, I keep on telling you.
I would have cut his throat to begin with! and if he had
sulked I would have boiled him alive! that would have
made him speak and tell us where his daughter is, and
where he keeps his money. That is how I should have
managed the affair. People are right when they say that
men are more stupid than women. Nobody at No. 17, it is
a large gateway. No Monsieur Fabre at No. 17, and we
went at a gallop, with a fee for the driver and all! I spoke

to the porter and his wife, who is a fine, tall woman, and they did not know anybody of the name."

Marius breathed again, for She, Ursule, or the Lark—he no longer knew her name—was saved. While the exasperated woman was vociferating, Thénardier sat down at the table ; he remained for some minutes without saying a word, balancing his right leg and looking at the chafing-dish with an air of savage reverie. At last he said to the prisoner slowly, and with a peculiarly ferocious accent :

"A false address? why, what did you hope for by that?"

"To gain time !" the prisoner thundered.

And at the same moment he shook off his bonds, which were cut through : the prisoner was only fastened to the bed by one leg. Ere the seven men had time to look about them and rush forward, he had stretched out his hand toward the fireplace, and the Thénardiers and the brigands, driven back by surprise to the end of the room, saw him almost free, and in a formidable attitude, waving round his head the red-hot chisel, from which a sinister glare shot.

In the judicial inquiry that followed this affair it was stated that a large sou, cut and worked in a peculiar manner, was found in the garret, when the police made their descent upon it. It was one of those marvels of industry which the patience of the galleys engenders in the darkness and for the darkness—marvels which are nought but instruments of escape. These hideous and yet delicate products of a prodigious art are in the jewellery trade what slang metaphors are in poetry ; for there are Benvenuto Cellinis at the galleys, in the same way as there are Villons in language. The wretch who aspires to deliverance, finds means, without tools, or, at the most, with an old knife, to saw a sou in two, hollow out the two parts without injuring the dies, and form a thread in the edge of the sou, so that the sou may be reproduced. It screws and unscrews at pleasure, and is a box ; and in this box a watch-spring saw is concealed, which, if well managed, will cut through fetters and iron bars. It is believed that the unhappy convict possesses only a sou ; but, not at all, he possesses liberty. It was a sou of this nature which was found by the police under the bed near the window, and a small saw of blue steel, which could be easily concealed in the sou, was also discovered. It is probable that at the moment when the bandits searched the prisoner he had the double sou about him, and hid it in his palm ; and his right hand being at liberty afterwards, he unscrewed it, and employed the saw to cut the ropes. This would explain the slight noise and the almost imperceptible movements which Marius had noticed. As, however, he was unable to stoop down for fear of betraying himself, he had not cut the cord on his left leg. The bandits gradually recovered from their surprise.

"Be easy," said Bigrenaille to Thénardier, "he is still held by one leg, and will not fly away. I put the pack-thread round that paw."

Here the prisoner raised his voice:

"You are villains, but my life is not worth so much trouble to defend. As for imagining that you could make me speak, make me write what I do not wish to write, or make me say what I do not intend to say——"

He pulled up the sleeve of his left arm, and added:

"Look here!"

At the same time he stretched out his arm, and placed on the naked flesh the red-hot chisel, which he held in his right hand by the wooden handle. Then could be heard the frizzling of the burnt flesh, and the smell peculiar to torture-rooms spread through the garret. Marius tottered in horror, and the brigands themselves shuddered—but the face of the strange old man was scarce contracted, and while the red-hot steel was burying itself in the smoking wound, he—impassive and almost august—fixed on Thénardier his beautiful glance, in which there was no hatred, and in which suffering disappeared in a serene majesty. For in great and lofty natures the revolt of the flesh and of the senses when suffering from physical pain make the soul appear on the brow, in the same way as the mutiny of troops compels the captain to show himself.

"Villains," he said, "be no more frightened of me than I am of you."

And, tearing the chisel out of the wound, he hurled it through the window, which had been left open. The horrible red-hot tool whirled through the night, and fell some distance off in the snow, which hissed at the contact. The prisoner continued:

"Do to me what you like."

He was defenceless.

"Seize him," said Thénardier.

Two of the brigands laid their hands on his shoulders, and the masked man with the ventriloquist voice stood in front of him, ready to dash out his brains with a blow of the key at the slightest movement on his part. At the same time Marius heard below him, but so close that he could not see the speakers, the following remarks exchanged in a low voice :

"There is only one thing to be done."

"Cut his throat !"

"Exactly."

It was the husband and wife holding counsel, and then Thénardier walked slowly to the table, opened the drawer, and took out the knife. Marius clutched the handle of the pistol in a state of extraordinary perplexity. For above an hour he had heard two voices in his conscience, one telling him to respect his father's will, while the other cried to him to succour the prisoner. These two voices continued their struggle uninterruptedly, and caused him an agony. He had vaguely hoped up to this moment to find some mode of reconciling these two duties, but nothing possible had occurred to him. Still the peril pressed ; the last moment of delay was passed, for Thénardier, knife in hand, was reflecting a few paces from the prisoner. Marius looked wildly around him, which is the last mechanical resource of despair. All at once he started ; at his feet on his table a bright moonbeam lit up and seemed to point out to him a sheet of paper. On this sheet he read this line, written in large letters that very morning by the elder of Thénardier's daughters :

"HERE ARE THE SLOPS."

An idea, a flash, crossed Marius' mind ; this was the solution of the frightful problem that tortured him, sparing the assassin and saving the victim. He knelt down on the bureau, stretched forth his arm, seized the paper, softly detached a lump of plaster from the partition, wrapped it up in the paper, and threw it through the hole into the middle of the den. It was high time, for Thénardier had overcome his last fears, or his last scruples, and was going toward the prisoner.

"There's something falling," his wife cried.

"What is it ? " her husband asked.

The woman had bounded forward, and picked up the lump of plaster wrapped in paper, which she handed to her husband.

"How did it get here ? " Thénardier asked.

"Why, hang it," his wife asked, "how do you expect that it did? through the window, of course."

"I saw it pass," said Bigrenaille.

Thénardier rapidly unfolded the paper, and held it close to the candle.

"Eponine's handwriting,—the devil!"

He made a signal to his wife, who hurried up to him, and showed her the line written on the paper, then added in a hollow voice:

"Quick, the ladder! we must leave the bacon in the trap."

"Without cutting the man's throat?" the Megæra asked.

"We haven't the time."

"Which way?" Bigrenaille remarked.

"By the window," Thénardier replied; "as Ponine threw the stone through the window, that's a proof that the house is not beset on that side."

The mask with the ventriloquist voice laid his key on the ground, raised his arms in the air, and opened and shut his hands thrice rapidly, without saying a word. This was like the signal for clearing for action aboard ship; the brigands who held the prisoner let him go, and in a twinkling the rope-ladder was dropped out of window, and securely fastened to the sill by the two iron hooks. The prisoner paid no attention to what was going on around him, he seemed to be thinking or praying. So soon as the ladder was fixed, Thénardier cried:

"The lady first."

And he dashed at the window, but as he was stepping out, Bigrenaille roughly seized him by the collar.

"No, no, my old joker, after us!" he said.

"After us!" the bandits yelled.

"You are children," said Thénardier, "we are losing time, and the police are at our heels."

"Very well then," said one of the bandits, "let us draw lots as to who shall go first."

Thénardier exclaimed:

"Are you mad? are you drunk? Why, what a set of humbugs; lose time, I suppose, draw lots, eh? with a wet finger? a short straw? write our names and put them in a cap?"

"May I offer my hat?" a voice said at the door.

All turned; it was Javert, who held his hat in his hand and offered it smilingly.

Javert had posted his men at nightfall, and ambushed himself behind the trees of the Rue de la Barrière des Gobelins, which joins No. 50-52 on the other side of the boulevard. He began by opening his " pocket," in order to thrust into it the two girls ordered to watch the approaches to the den, but he had only " nailed " Azelma ; {as for Eponine, she was not at her post, she had disappeared, and he had not been able to seize her. Then Javert took up his post, and listened for the appointed signal. The departure and return of the hackney-coach greatly perplexed him ; at length he grew impatient, and feeling sure · that there " was a nest there," and of being in " luck's way," and having recognised several of the bandits who went in, he resolved to enter without waiting for the pistol-shot. It will be remembered that he had Marius' latchkey, and he arrived just in time.

The startled bandits dashed at the weapons, which they had thrown into corners at the moment of their attempted escape ; and in less than a second, these seven men, formidable to look at, were grouped in a posture of defence, one with his pole-axe, another with his key, a third with his life-preserver, the others with chisel, pincers, and hammer, and Thénardier with his knife in his fist. The woman picked up an enormous paving-stone which lay in the angle of the room, and which served her daughter as a footstool. Javert restored his hat to his head, and walked into the room, with folded arms, his cane hanging from his wrist, and his sword in his scabbard.

" Halt ! " he shouted, " you will not leave by the window, but by the door, which is not so unhealthy. You are seven and we are fifteen, so do not let us quarrel like water-carriers, but behave as gentlemen."

Bigrenaille drew a pistol from under his blouse, and placed it in Thénardier's hand, as he whispered : .

" It is Javert, and I dare not fire at that man. Dare you ? "

" I should think so," Thénardier answered.

" Well, fire."

Thénardier took the pistol and aimed at Javert ; the Inspector who was only three paces from him, looked at him fixedly, and contented himself with saying :

" Don't fire, for the pistol won't go off."

Thénardier pulled the trigger ; there was a flash in the pan.

" Did I not tell you so ? " Javert remarked.

Bigrenaille threw his life-preserver at Javert's feet.

" You are the Emperor of the devils, and I surrender."

" And you ? " Javert asked the other bandits.

They answered, " We too."

Javert remarked calmly :

"That is all right, I begged you to behave like gentlemen."

" I only ask one thing," Bigrenaille remarked, " that my 'baccy mayn't be stopped whiie I'm in solitary confinement."

" Granted," said Javert.

Then he turned and shouted, " You can come in now."

A squad of police, sword in hand, and agents armed with bludgeons and sticks, rushed in at Javert's summons, and bound the robbers. This crowd of men, scarce illumined by the candle, filled the den with shadows.

" Handcuff them all," Javert cried.

" Just come this way," a voice shouted, which was not that of a man, but of which no one could have said, " It is a woman's voice." Mother Thénardier had entrenched herself in one of the angles of the window, and it was she from whom this roar had come. The police and the agents fell back ; she had thrown off her shawl and kept her bonnet on ; her husband, crouching behind her, almost disappeared under the fallen shawl, and she covered him with her body, while raising the paving-stone above her head with both hands, like a giantess about to heave a rock.

" Heads below ! " she screeched.

All fell back upon the passage, and there was a large open space in the centre of the garret. The hag took a glance at the bandits, who had suffered themselves to be bound, and muttered, in a hoarse and guttural voice,— " The cowards ! "

Javert smiled, and walked into the open space which the woman guarded with her eyes.

" Don't come nearer," she shrieked, "or I'll smash you. Be off ! "

" What a grenadier ! " said Javert, " the mother ! you have a beard like a man, but I have claws like a woman."

And he continued to advance. Mother Thénardier, with flying hair and terrible looks, straddled her legs, bent back, and wildly hurled the paving-stone at Javert. He stooped, the stone passed over him, struck the wall, from which it dislodged a mass of plaster, and then ricochetted from angle to angle till it fell exhausted at Javert's feet. At the same moment Javert reached the Thénardiers; one of his large hands settled on the wife's shoulder, the other on the husband's head.

"Handcuffs here!" he shouted.

The policemen flocked in, and in a few seconds Javert's orders were carried out. The woman, quite crushed, looked at her own and her husband's manacled hands, fell on the ground, and, bursting into tears, cried:

"My daughters."

"Oh, they are all right," said Javert.

By this time the police had noticed the drunken man sleeping behind the door, and shook him; he woke up, and stammered:

"Is it all over, Jondrette?"

"Yes," Javert answered.

The six bound bandits were standing together, with their spectral faces, three daubed with black, and three masked.

"Keep on your masks," said Javert.

And, passing them in review, like a Frederick II. at a Potsdam parade, he said to the three "sweeps":

"Good-day, Bigrenaille." "Good-day, Brujon." "Good-day, Deux-milliards."

Then turning to the three masks, he said to the man with the pole-axe, "Good-day, Gueulemer," and to the man with the cudgel, "Good-day, Babet," and to the ventriloquist, "Here's luck, Claquesous."

At this moment he noticed the prisoner, who had not said a word since the arrival of the police, and held his head down.

"Untie the gentleman," said Javert, "and let no one leave the room."

After saying this he sat down in a lordly way at the table, on which the candle and the inkstand were still standing, took a stamped paper from his pocket, and began writing his report. When he had written a few lines, which are always the same formula, he raised his eyes.

"Bring the gentleman here whom these gentlemen had tied up."

The agents looked round.

"Well," Javert asked, "where is he?"

The prisoner of the bandits, M. Leblanc, M. Urbain Fabre, the father of Ursule or the Lark, had disappeared. The door was guarded, but the window was not. So soon as he found himself released, and while Javert was writing, he took advantage of the trouble, the tumult, the crowd, the darkness, and the moment when attention was not fixed upon him, to rush to the window. An agent ran up and looked out ; he could see nobody, but the rope-ladder was still trembling.

"The devil!" said Javert between his teeth, "he must have been the best of the lot."

On the day after that in which these events occurred in the house on the Boulevard de l'Hôpital, a lad, who apparently came from the bridge of Austerlitz, was trudging along the right-hand walk in the direction of the Barrière de Fontaine-bleau, at about nightfall. This boy was pale, thin, dressed in rags, wearing canvas trousers in the month of February, and singing at the top of his lungs. He reached No. 50-52 Gorbeau, and, finding the gate closed, began giving it re-echoing and heroic kicks. The old porteress made her appearance.

"Hilloh! it's the old woman," said the boy. "Good-evening, my dear Bougonmuche, I have come to see my ancestors."

The old woman answered with a composite grimace, an admirable instance of hatred taking advantage of old age and ugliness, which was unfortunately lost in the darkness,—
"There's nobody here, scamp."

"Nonsense," the boy said, "where's father?"

"At La Force."

"Hilloh! and mother?"

"At Saint Lazare."

"Very fine! and my sist ers?"

"At Les Madelonnettes."

The lad scratched the back of his ear, looked at Ma'am Bougon, and said, "Ah!"

Then he turned on his heels, and a moment later the old woman, who was standing in the gateway, heard him singing in his clear young voice, as he went off under the elms which were quivering in the winter breeze.

CHAPTER LXXX.

1831 and 1832, the two years immediately attached to the Revolution of July, contain the most peculiar and striking moments of history, and these two years, amid those that precede and follow them, stand out like mountains. They possess the true revolutionary grandeur, and precipices may be traced in them. The social masses, the foundations of civilisation, the solid group of superimposed and adherent interests, and the secular profiles of the ancient Gaelic formations, appear and disappear every moment through the stormy clouds of systems, passions, and theories. These apparitions and disappearances were called resistance and movement, but, at intervals, truth, the daylight of the human soul, flashes through all.

Revolutions have a terrible arm and a lucky hand; they hit hard and choose well. Even when incomplete, bastardised, and reduced to the state of a younger revolution, like that of 1830, they nearly always retain sufficient providential light not to fall badly, and their eclipse is never an abdication. Still we must not boast too loudly, for revolutions themselves are mistaken, and grave errors have been witnessed ere now. Let us return to 1830, which was fortunate in its deviation. In the establishment which was called order after the Revolution was cut short, the king was worth more than the Royalty. Louis Philippe was a rare man.

Son of a father to whom history will certainly grant extenuating circumstances, but as worthy of esteem as his father was of blame; possessing all the private virtues and several of the public virtues, careful of his health, his fortune, his person, and his business affairs; knowing the value of a minute, but not always the value of a year; sober, serious, peaceful, and patient; a good man and a good prince; sleeping with his wife, and having in his palace lackeys whose business it was to show the conjugal couch to the citizens—a regular ostentation which had grown useful after the old illegitimate displays of the elder branch; acquainted with all the languages of Europe, and, what is rarer still, with all the languages of all the interests, and speaking them; an admirable representative of the "middle classes," but surpassing them, and in every way greater; possessing the excellent sense, while appreciating the blood from which he sprang, of claiming merit for his personal value, and very particular on the question of his race by declaring himself an Orleans and not a Bourbon; a thorough first prince of the blood, so long as he had only been Most Serene Highness, but a frank bourgeois on the day when he became His Majesty; diffuse in public, and concise in private life; branded as a miser, but not proved to be one; in reality, one of those saving men who are easily prodigal to satisfy their caprices or their duty; well read, and caring but little for literature; a gentleman, but not a cavalier; simple, calm, and strong; adored by his family and his household; a seductive speaker, a disabused and cold-hearted statesman, swayed by the immediate interest, governing from hand to mouth; incapable of rancour and of gratitude; pitilessly employing superiorities upon mediocrities, and clever in confounding by parliamentary majorities those mysterious unanimities which growl hoarsely beneath thrones; expansive, at times imprudent in his expansiveness, but displaying marvellous skill in his imprudence; fertile in expedients, faces, and masks; terrifying France by Europe, and Europe by France; loving his country undeniably, but preferring his family; valuing domination more than authority, and authority more than dignity; a temperament which has this mournful feature about it, that, by turning everything to success, it admits of craft and does not absolutely repudiate baseness, but at the same time has this advantage, that it preserves politics from violent shocks, the state from fractures, and society from catastrophes; minute, correct, vigilant, attentive, sagacious, and indefatigable; contradicting himself at times, and belying himself; bold against Austria at Ancona, obstinate against England in Spain, bombarding Antwerp and paying Pritchard; singing the Marseillaise with conviction; inaccessible to despondency, to fatigue, to a taste for the beautiful and ideal, to rash generosity, to Utopias, chimeras, anger, vanity, and fear; possessing every form of personal bravery; a general at Valmy, a private at Jemappes; eight times attacked by regicides, and constantly smiling; brave as a grenadier, and courageous as a thinker; merely anxious about the chances of a European convulsion, and unfitted for great political adventures; ever ready to risk his life, but not his work; disguising his will under influence for the sake of being obeyed rather as an intellect than as king; gifted with observation and not with divination; paying but slight attention to minds, but a connoisseur in men, that is to say, requiring to see ere he could judge; endowed with prompt and penetrating sense, fluent tongue, and a prodigious memory, and incessantly drawing on that memory, his sole similitude with Cæsar, Alexander, and Napoleon; knowing facts, details, dates, and proper names, but ignorant of the various passions and tendencies of the crowd, the internal aspirations and concealed agitation of minds—in one word, of all that may be called the invisible currents of consciences; accepted by the surface, but agreeing little with the lower strata of French society; getting out of scrapes by skill; governing too much and not reigning sufficiently; his own Prime Minister; excellent in the art of setting up the littleness of realities as an obstacle to the immensity of ideas; mingling with a true creative faculty of civilisation, order, and organisation, I do not know what pettifogging temper and chicanery; the founder of a family and at the same time its man-of-law; having something of Charlemagne and something of an attorney in him; but, on the whole, as a lofty and original figure, as a prince who managed to acquire power in spite of the anxiety of France, and influence in spite of the jealousy of Europe,—Louis Philippe would be ranked among the eminent men of his age, and among the most illustrious governors known in history, if he had loved glory a little, and had a feeling for what is grand to the same extent as he had a feeling for what is useful.

Louis Philippe had been handsome, and when aged, remained graceful: though not always admired by the nation, he was always so by the mob, for he had the art of pleasing and the gift of charm. He was deficient in majesty, and neither wore a crown though king, nor displayed white hair though an old man. His manners belonged to the ancient régime, and his habits to the new, a mixture of the noble and the citizen which suited 1830. Louis Philippe was transition on a throne. He went but rarely to Mass, not at all to the chase, and never to the opera: he was incorruptible by priests, whippers-in, and ballet girls, and this formed part of his citizen popularity. He had no Court, and went out with an umbrella under his arm, and this umbrella for a long time formed part of his glory. He was a bit of a mason, a bit of a gardener, and a bit of a surgeon: he bled a postilion who had fallen from his horse, and no more thought of going out without his lancet than Henry III. would without his dagger. The Royalists ridiculed this absurd king, the first who shed blood in order to cure.

At the moment, when the drama we are recounting is about to enter one of those tragic clouds which cover the beginning of the reign of Louis Philippe, it was quite necessary that this book should give an explanation about that king. Louis Philippe had entered upon the royal authority without violence or direct action on his part, through a revolutionary change of wind, which was evidently very distinct from the real object of the Revolution, but in which he, the Duc d'Orleans, had no personal initiative. He was born a prince, and believed himself elected king; he had not given himself these functions, nor had he taken them; they were offered to him and he accepted, convinced, wrongly as we think, but still convinced, that the office was in accordance, and acceptance in harmony, with duty. Hence came an honest possession, and we say in all conscience that, as Louis Philippe was honest in the possession, and democracy honest in its attack, the amount of terror disengaged from social struggles can not be laid either on the king or the democracy.

Toward the end of April matters became aggravated, and the fermentation assumed the proportions of an ebullition. Since 1830 there had been small partial revolts, quickly suppressed, but breaking out again, which were the sign of a vast subjacent conflagration, and of something terrible smouldering. A glimpse could be caught of the lineaments of a possible revolution, though it was still indistinct and badly lighted. France was looking at Paris, and Paris at the Faubourg St. Antoine. The wine-shops in the Rue de Charonne were grave and stormy, though the conjunction of these two epithets applied to wine-shops appears singular. The Government was purely and simply put upon its trial on this, and men publicly discussed whether "they should fight or remain quiet." There were back rooms in which workmen swore to go into the streets at the first cry of alarm, "and fight without counting their enemies." Once they had taken the pledge, a man seated in a corner of the wine-shop shouted in a sonorous voice, "You hear! You have sworn!" Sometimes they went up to a private room on the first floor, where scenes almost resembling masonic ceremonies took place, and the novice took oaths, "in order to render a service to himself as well as to the fathers of families,"—such was the formula. In the taprooms, "subversive" pamphlets were read, and, as a secret report of the day says, "they spurned the Government."

Remarks like the following could be heard,—"I do not know the names of the chiefs; we shall not know the day till two hours beforehand." A workman said, "We are three hundred, let us each subscribe ten sous, and we shall have one hundred and fifty francs, with which to manufacture bullets and gunpowder." Another said, "I do not ask for six months, I do not ask for two. Within a fortnight we shall be face to face with the Government, for it is possible to do so with twenty-five thousand men." Another said, "I do not go to bed at nights now, for I am making cartridges." From time to time well-dressed men came, who pretended to be embarrassed, shook hands with the more important, and then went away, never staying longer than ten minutes, and significant remarks were exchanged in whispers, "The plot is ripe, the thing is ready;" to borrow the remark of one of the audience, "This was buzzed by all present." The excitement was so great, that one day a workman said openly in a wine-shop, "But we have no weapons;" to which a comrade replied, "The soldiers have them," unconsciously parodying Bonaparte's proclamation to the army of Italy. "When they had any very great secret," a report adds, "they did not communicate it," though we do not understand what they could conceal after what they had said. The meetings were sometimes periodical; at certain ones there were never more than eight or ten members present, and they were always the same, but at others any one who liked went in, and the room was so crowded that they were obliged to stand; some went there through enthusiasm and passion, others "because it was on the road to their work." In the same way as during the Revolution, there were female patriots in these wine-shops, who kissed the new-comers.

All this fermentation was public, we might almost say calm, and the impending insurrection prepared its storm quietly in the face of the Government. No singularity was lacking in this crisis, which was still subterranean, but already perceptible. The citizens spoke peacefully to the workmen of what was preparing. They said, "How is the revolt going on?" in the same tone as they would have said, "How is your wife?" A furniture broker in the Rue Moreau asked, "Well, when do you attack?" and another shopkeeper said, "They will attack soon, I know it. A month ago there were fifteen thousand of you, and now there are twenty-five thousand." He offered his gun, and a neighbour offered a pocket pistol which was marked for sale at seven francs. The revolutionary fever spread, and no point of Paris or of France escaped it. The artery throbbed everywhere, and the network of secret societies began spreading over the country like the membranes which spring up from certain inflammations, and are formed in the human body. From the "Association of the Friends of the People," which was at the same time public and secret, sprang the "Society of the Rights of Man," which thus dated one of its orders of the day, *Pluviôse, year* 40 *of the Republican Era*; a society which was destined even to survive the decrees that suppressed it, and which did not hesitate to give to its sections significant titles like the following :

"*Pikes. The Tocsin. The Alarm Gun. The Phrygian Cap. January* 21. *The Beggars. The Mendicants. March Forward. Robespierre. The Level. Ça ira.*"

The Society of the Rights of Man engendered the Society of Action, composed of impatient men who detached themselves and hurried forward. Other associations tried to recruit themselves in the great mother societies : and the Sectionists complained of being tormented. Such were the "Gaulish Society," and the "Organising Committee of the Municipalities " ; such the associations for the "Liberty of the Press," for "Individual Liberty," for the "Instruction of the People," and against "Indirect Taxes." Next we have the "Society of Equalitarian Workmen " divided into three fractions—the Equalitarians, the Communists, and the Reformers. Then, again, the "Army of the Bastilles," a cohort possessing military organisation, four men being commanded by a corporal, ten by a sergeant, twenty by a sublieutenant, and forty by a lieutenant ; there were never more than five men who knew each other. This is a creation which is boldly combined, and seems to be marked with the genius of Venice. The central committee which formed the head had two arms—the Society of Action and the Army of the Bastilles. A legitimist association, the "Knights of Fidelity," agitated among these republican affiliations, but was denounced and repudiated. The Parisian societies ramified through the principal cities ; Lyons, Nantes, Lille had their Society of the Rights of Man, The Charbonnière, and the Free Men. Aix had a revolutionary society called the Cougourde. We have already mentioned that name.

At Paris the Faubourg St. Marceau buzzed no less than the

Faubourg St. Antoine, and the schools were quite as excited as the faubourgs. A coffee-shop in the Rue Saint Hyacinthe, and the Estaminet des Sept Billiards in the Rue des Mathurins St. Jacques, served as the gathering-place for the students. The Society of the Friends of the A B C affiliated with the Mutualists of Angers, and the Cougourde of Aix assembled, as we have seen, at the Café Musain. The same young men met, as we have also said, at a wine-shop and eating-house near the Rue Mondetour, called Corinthe. These meetings were secret, but others were as public as possible, and we may judge of their boldness by this fragment from an examination that was held in one of the ulterior trials. " Where was the meeting held ? " " In the Rue de la Paix." " At whose house ? " " In the street." " What sections were there ? " " Only one." " Which one ? " " The Manuel section." " Who was the chief ? " " Myself." " You are too young to have yourself formed this serious resolve of attacking the Government. Whence came your instructions ? " " From the central committee." The army was undermined at the same time as the population, as was proved at a later date by the movements of Béfort, Luneville, and Epinal. Hopes were built on the 52nd, 5th, 8th, and 37th Regiments, and on the 20th Light Infantry. In Burgundy and the southern towns the tree of liberty was planted, that is to say, a mast surmounted by a red cap. Such was the situation. It was rendered more sensible and marked by the Faubourg St. Antoine than by any other group of the population. This old faubourg, peopled like an ant-heap, laborious, courageous, and passionate as a hive of bees, quivered in expectation and the desire of a commotion. All was agitation there, but labour was not suspended on that account.

CHAPTER LXXXI.

MARIUS witnessed the unexpected denouement of the snare upon the track of which he had placed Javert, but the Inspector had scarce left the house, taking his prisoners with him in three hackney-coaches, ere Marius stepped out of the house in his turn. It was only nine in the evening, and Marius went to call on Courfeyrac, who was no longer the imperturbable inhabitant of the Pays Latin. He had gone to live in the Rue de la Verrière, " for political reasons," and this district was one of those in which insurrectionists of the day were fond of installing themselves. Marius said to Courfeyrac, "I am going to sleep here," and Courfeyrac pulled off one of his two mattresses, laid it on the ground, and said, "There you are!" At seven o'clock the next morning Marius returned to No. 50-52, paid his quarter's rent, and what he owed to Ma'am Bougon, had his books, bed, table, bureau, and two chairs, placed on a truck, and went away, without leaving his address. When Javert returned in the morning to question Marius about the events of the previous evening, he only found Ma'am Bougon, who said to him,—"Gone away." Ma'am Bougon was convinced that Marius was in some way an accomplice of the robbers arrested the previous evening. "Who would have thought it!" she exclaimed to the porteresses of the quarter, "a young man whom you might have taken for a girl!"

Marius had two reasons for moving so promptly, the first was that he now felt a horror of this house, in which he had seen so closely, and in all its most repulsive and ferocious development, a social ugliness more frightful still, perhaps, than the wicked rich man—the wicked poor man. The second was that he did not wish to figure at the trial, which would in all probability ensue, and be obliged to give evidence against Thénardier. Javert believed that the young man, whose name he forgot, had been frightened and had run away, or else had not even returned home; he made some efforts, however, to find him, which were unsuccessful. A month elapsed, then another. Marius was still living with Courfeyrac, and had learned from a young barrister, an habitual walker of the Salle des pas Perdus, that Thénardier was in solitary confinement, and every Monday he left a five-franc piece for him at the wicket of La Force. Marius, having no money left, borrowed the five francs of Courfeyrac; it was the first time in his life that he borrowed money. These periodical five francs were a double enigma for Courfeyrac who gave them, and for Thénardier who received them. "Where can they go to?" Courfeyrac thought. "Where can they come from?" Thénardier asked himself.

Marius, however, was heart-broken, for everything had disappeared again under a trap-door. He saw nothing ahead of him, and his life was once more plunged into the mystery in which he had been groping. He had seen again momentarily and very closely the girl whom he loved, the old man who appeared her father, the strange beings who were his only interest and sole hope in this world, and at the moment when he fancied that he should grasp them, a breath had carried off all these shadows. Not a spark of certainty and truth had flashed even from that most terrific collision, and no conjecture was possible. He no longer knew the name of which he had felt so certain, and it certainly was not Ursule, and the Lark was a nickname. And then, what must he think of the old man? Did he really hide himself from the police? The white-haired workman whom Marius had met in the vicinity of the Invalides reverted to his mind, and it now became probable that this workman and M. Leblanc were one and the same. He disguised himself then, and this man had his heroic side and his equivocal side. Why did he not call for help? why did he fly? was he, yes or no, the father of the girl? and, lastly, was he really the man whom Thénardier fancied he recognised? Thénardier might have been mistaken. These were all so many insoluble problems. All this, it is true, in no way lessened the angelic charm of the maiden of the Luxembourg, and hence arose the poignant distress. Marius had a passion in his heart, and night over his eyes. He was impelled, he was attracted, and he could not stir ; all had vanished, except love, and he had lost the sudden instincts and illuminations of even that love. All his life was now summed up in two words—absolute uncertainty, in an impenetrable fog,—and though he still longed to see her, he no longer hoped it. As a climax, want returned, and he felt its icy breath close to him and behind him. In all these torments, and for a long time, he had discontinued his work, and nothing is more dangerous than discontinued work, for it is a habit which a man loses—a habit easy to give up, but difficult to reacquire.

A certain amount of reverie is good, like a narcotic taken in discreet doses. It lulls to sleep the at times harsh fevers of the working brain, and produces in the mind a soft and fresh vapour which corrects the too sharp outlines of pure thought, fills up gaps and spaces here and there, and rounds the angles of ideas. But excess of reverie submerges and drowns, and woe to the mental workman who allows himself to fall entirely from thinking into reverie! he believes that he can easily rise again, and says that, after all, it is the same thing, but it is an error! Through going out to dream, a day arrives when a man goes out to throw himself into the water. Marius went down this incline slowly, with his eyes fixed upon her whom he no longer saw. She was Marius' entire thought, he dreamed of nothing else. He felt confusedly that his old coat was becoming an impossible coat, and that his new coat was growing an old coat, that his boots were wearing out, that his hat was wearing out, that his shirts were wearing out, that is to say, that his life was wearing out; and he said to himself, Could I but see her again before I die!

One sole sweet idea was left him, and it was that she had loved him, that her glance had told him so, and that she did not know his name, but that she knew his soul, and that however mysterious the spot might be where she now was, she loved him still. Might she not be dreaming of him as he was dreaming of her? At times in those inexplicable hours which every loving heart knows, as he had only reason to be sad, and yet felt within him a certain quivering of joy, he said to himself, "Her thoughts are visiting me," and then added, "Perhaps my thoughts also go to her." This illusion, at which he shook his head a moment after, sometimes, however, contrived to cast rays which resembled hope into his soul at intervals. Now and then, especially at that evening hour which most saddens dreamers, he poured out upon virgin paper the pure, impersonal, and ideal reveries with which love filled his brain. He called this "writing to her." We must not suppose, however, that his reason was in disorder, quite the contrary. He had lost the faculty of working and going firmly toward a determined object, but he retained clear-sightedness and rectitude more fully than ever. Marius saw by a calm and real, though singular, light, all that was taking place before him, even the most indifferent men and facts, and spoke correctly of everything with a sort of honest weariness and candid disinterestedness. Happy, even in agony, is the man to whom God has granted a soul worthy of love and misfortune! He who has not seen the things of this world and the heart of man in this double light, has seen nothing of the truth, and knows nothing, for the soul that loves and suffers is in a sublime state. Days succeeded each other, and nothing new occurred; it really seemed to him that the gloomy space which he still had to traverse was becoming daily reduced. He fancied that he could already see distinctly the brink of the bottomless abyss.

"What!" he repeated to himself, "shall I not see her again before that takes place?"

After going up the Rue St. Jacques, leaving the barrière on one side, and following for some distance the old inner boulevard, you reach the Rue de la Santé, then the Glacière, and just before coming to the small stream of the Gobelins, you notice a sort of field, the only spot on the long and monotonous belt of Parisian boulevards, where Ruysdael would be tempted to sit down. As the place is worth seeing, no one goes to it : scarce a cart or a wagon passes in a quarter of an hour. It once happened that Marius' solitary rambles led him to this field, and on that day there was a rarity on the boulevard, a passer-by. Marius, really struck by the almost savage grace of the field, asked him,—"What is the name of this spot?"

The passer-by answered, "It is the Lark's field;" and added, "It was here that Ulback killed the shepherdess of Ivry."

But, after the words "the Lark," Marius heard no more, for a word at times suffices to produce a congelation in a man's dreamy condition : the whole thought is condensed round an idea, and is no longer capable of any other perception. The Lark, that was the appellation which had taken the place of Ursule in the depths of Marius' melancholy. "Stay," he said, with that sort of unreasoning stupor peculiar to such mysterious asides, "this is her field, I shall learn here where she lives." This was absurd but irresistible, and he came daily to this Lark's field.

CHAPTER LXXXII.

JAVERT'S triumph at the Maison Gorbeau had seemed complete, but was not so. In the first place, and that was his chief anxiety, Javert had not been able to make a prisoner of the prisoner : the victim who escapes is more suspicious than the assassin, and it was probable that this man who escaped, though a precious capture for the bandits, might be equally so for the authorities. Next, Montparnasse slipped out of Javert's clutches, and he must wait for another opportunity to lay hands on that "cursed little fop." Montparnasse, in fact, having met Eponine on the boulevard, keeping watch, went off with her; and it was lucky for him that he did so, as he was now free. As for Eponine, Javert "nailed" her, but it was a poor consolation, and sent her to join Azelma at Les Madelonnettes. Lastly, in the drive from No. 50-52 to La Force, one of the chief men arrested, Claquesous, had disappeared. No one knew how he did it, and the sergeants and agents did not at all understand it: he had turned into vapour, slipped through the handcuffs, and passed through a crack in the coach; but no one could say anything except that on reaching the prison there was no Claquesous. There was in this either enchantment or a police trick. Had Claquesous melted away in the darkness like a snow-flake in the water? was there an unavowed connivance on the part of the agents? did this man belong to the double enigma of disorder and order? Javert did not accept these combinations, and struggled against such compromises; but his squad contained other inspectors besides himself, more thoroughly initiated, perhaps, though his subordinates in the secrets of the Prefecture; and Claquesous was such a villain that he might be a very excellent agent. To be on such intimate relations with the night is capital for brigands and admirable for the police, and there are double-edged rogues of this sort. However this might be, Claquesous was lost and could not be found, and Javert seemed more irritated than surprised. As for Marius, "that scrub of a barrister who was probably frightened," and whose name he had forgotten, Javert did not trouble himself much about him, and, besides, a barrister can always be found. But, was he only a barrister?

The examination began, and the magistrate thought it advisable not to put one of the members of the Patron Minette in solitary confinement, as it was hoped he might chatter. This was Brujon, the hairy man of the Rue du Petit Banquier; he was turned into the Charlemagne Court, and the eyes of the spies were kept upon him. This name of Brujon is one of the recollections of La Force. In the hideous yard called the New Building—which the governor named the Court of St. Bernard, and the robbers christened the Lion's den, and on the wall covered with scars and leprosy, that rose on the left to the height of the roof and close to a rusty old iron gate which led to the old chapel of the Hôtel de la Force, converted into a dormitory for prisoners—there might have been seen, twelve years ago, a species of Bastille, clumsily engraved with a nail in the stone, and beneath it this signature—

BRUJON, 1811.

The Brujon of 1811 was the father of the Brujon of 1832. The latter, of whom we could only catch a glimpse in the garret, was a very crafty and artful young fellow, with a downcast and plaintive air. It was in consequence of this air that the magistrate turned him loose, believing him more useful in the Charlemagne yard than in a secret cell. Robbers do not interrupt their labours because they are in the hands of justice, and do not trouble themselves about such a trifle. Being in prison for one crime does not prevent another being commenced. There are artists who have a picture in the Exhibition, but for all that work at a new one in their studio. Brujon seemed stupefied by prison; he might be seen standing for hours in the yard near the canteen man's stall, gazing like an idiot at the duty list of prices, which began with *garlic, fifty-two centimes*, and ended with *cigar, five centimes*. Or else he passed his time in trembling, shaking his teeth, declaring he had the fever, and inquiring whether one of the twenty-six beds in the Infirmary were vacant.

All at once, toward the second half of February, 1832, it was discovered that Brujon, the sleepy-looking man, had had three messages delivered, not in his own name, but in those of his comrades, by the prison porters. These messages had cost him fifty sous altogether, an exorbitant sum, which attracted the corporal's attention. After making inquiries and consulting the tariff of messages hung up in the prisoners' visiting-room, this authority found out that the fifty sous were thus divided,—one message to the Pantheon, ten sous; one to Val de Grâce, fifteen sous; and one to the Barrière de Grenelle, twenty-five sous, the latter being the dearest in the whole list. Now at these very places resided these very dangerous prowlers at the barrière, Kruideniers, *alias* Bizarro, Glorieux an ex-convict, and Barrecarrosse, and the attention of the police was directed to these through this incident. It was assumed that these men belonged to the Patron Minette, of which band two chiefs, Babet and Gueulemer, were locked up. It was supposed that Brujon's messages, which were not delivered at the houses, but to persons waiting in the street, contained information about some meditated crime. The three ruffians were arrested, and the police believed they had scented some machination of Brujon's.

A week after these measures had been taken, a night watchman, who was inspecting the ground-floor sleeping-ward of the New Building, saw through the trap Brujon sitting up in bed and writing something. The turnkey went in, Brujon was placed in solitary confinement for a month, but what he had written could not be found. Hence the police were just as wise as before. One thing is certain, that on the next day a "Postilion" was thrown from Charlemagne into the Lion's den over the five-storeyed building that separated the two yards. Prisoners give the name of "Postilion" to a ball of artistically moulded bread, which is sent to "Ireland," that is to say, thrown from one yard into another. This ball falls into the yard, the man who picks it up opens it and finds in it a note addressed to some prisoner in the yard. If it be a prisoner who finds the note he delivers it to the right address ; if it be a turnkey, or one of those secretly-bought prisoners, called "sheep" in prisons, and "foxes" at the galleys, the note is carried to the wicket and delivered to the police. This time the postilion reached its address, although the man for whom it was intended was at the time in a separate cell. This person was no other than Babet, one of the four heads of Patron Minette. It contained a rolled-up paper, on which only two lines were written.

"Babet, there's a job to be done in the Rue Plumet, a gate opening on the garden."

It was what Brujon had written during the night. In spite of male and female searchers, Babet contrived to send the note from La Force to the Salpetrière to a "lady friend" of his locked up there. She in her turn handed the note to a girl she knew of the name of Magnon, whom the police were actively seeking, but had not yet arrested. This Magnon was closely connected with the Thénardiers, and, by going to see Eponine, was able to serve as a bridge between the Salpetrière and the Madelonnettes. At this very period Eponine and Azelma were discharged for want of evidence, and when Eponine went out, Magnon, who was watching for her at the gate of the Madelonnettes, handed her the note from Brujon to Babet, with instructions to look into the affair. Eponine went to the Rue Plumet, recognised the grating and the garden, observed the house, watched for some days, and then carried to Magnon a biscuit, which the latter sent to Babet's mistress at the Salpetrière. A biscuit, in the dark language of prisons, means, "Nothing to be done."

In less than a week from this Babet and Brujon happened to meet, as one was going before the magistrate, the other returning. "Well," Brujon asked, "the Rue P.?" "Biscuit," Babet answered. Thus the fœtus of crime engendered by Brujon at La Force became abortive; but this abortion had consequences, for all that, perfectly foreign to Brujon's plans, as will be seen. In fancying we are tying one thread we often tie another.

CHAPTER LXXXIII.

MARIUS no longer called on any one, but at times he came across Father Mabœuf. While Marius was slowly descending the mournful steps which might be called the cellar stairs, and lead to places without light, on which you hear the footsteps of the prosperous above your head, M. Mabœuf was also descending. The *Flora of Cauterets* did not sell at all now, and the indigo experiments had not been successful in the little garden of Austerlitz, which looked in a bad direction. M. Mabœuf could only cultivate in it a few rare plants which are fond of moisture and shade. For all that, though, he was not discouraged : he had obtained a strip of ground at the Jardin des Plantes, on which to carry on his experiments "at his own charge." To do this he pledged the plates of his *Flora*, and he reduced his breakfast to two eggs, of which he left one for his old servant, whose wages he had not paid for fifteen months past. And very frequently his breakfast was his sole meal. He no longer laughed with his childish laugh, he had grown morose, and declined to receive visitors, and Marius did well not to call on him. At times, at the hour when M. Mabœuf proceeded to the Jardin des Plantes, the old man and the young man passed each other on the Boulevard de l'Hôpital ; they did not speak, and merely shook their heads sorrowfully. It is a sad thing that the moment arrives when misery parts friends !

Royol the publisher was dead, and now M. Mabœuf knew nothing but his books, his garden, and his indigo ; these were the three shapes which happiness, pleasure, and hope had assumed for him. This fed his life ; and he would say

to himself, "When I have made my blue balls, I shall be
rich; I will redeem my plates from the Mont de Piété,
bring my *Flora* into fashion again with charlatanism, the
big drum, and advertisements in the papers, and buy, I
know where, a copy of Pierre de Medine's *Art of Navigation*,
with woodcuts, edition 1539." In the meanwhile, he toiled
all day at his indigo patch, and at night went home to water
his garden and read his books. M. Mabœuf at this period
was close on eighty years of age.

One evening he had a strange apparition. He had returned home while it was still daylight, and found that Mother
Plutarch, whose health was not so good as it might be, had
gone to bed. He had dined upon a bone on which a little
meat remained, and a lump of bread which he had found on
the kitchen table, and had seated himself on a stone post
which served for a bench in his garden. Near this bench
there was, after the fashion of old kitchen gardens, a sort of
tall building of planks in a very rickety condition, a hutch
on the ground-floor, and a storeroom on the first floor.
There were no rabbits in the hutch, but there were a few
apples, the remnant of the winter stock, in the storeroom.
M. Mabœuf was reading two books in which he took great
interest. The first of these books was the celebrated treatise
of President Delanere, *On the Inconstancy of Delusions*, and
the other was the quarto work of Mutor de la Rubandière,
On the Demons of Vauvert and the goblins of la Bièvre.
The latter book interested him the more, because his garden
had been in olden times one of the places haunted by the
goblins. Twilight was beginning to whiten what is above and
blacken what is below. While reading, M. Mabœuf looked
over the book which he held in his hand at his plants, and
among others at a magnificent rhododendron, which was one
of his consolations. Four days of wind and sun had passed
without a drop of rain, the stems were bending, the buds
drooping, the leaves falling, and they all required watering;
this rhododendron especially looked in a very sad way. M.
Mabœuf was one of those men for whom plants have souls;
he had been at work all day in his indigo patch, and was
worn out with fatigue, but for all that he rose, laid his books
on the bench, and walked in a bent posture, and with tottering steps, up to the well. But when he seized the chain he
had not sufficient strength to unhook it; he then turned and
took a glance of agony at the sky, which was glittering with
stars. The evening had that serenity which crushes human

sorrow under a lugubrious and eternal joy. The night promised to be as dry as the day had been.

"Stars everywhere!" the old man thought, "not the smallest cloud! not a drop of water!"

And his head, which had been raised a moment before, fell again on his chest, then he looked once more at the sky, murmuring:

"A little dew! a little pity!"

He tried once again to unhook the well-chain, but could not succeed; at this moment he heard a voice saying:

"Father Mabœuf, shall I water the garden for you?" At the same time a sound like that of a wild beast breaking through was heard in the hedge, and he saw a tall thin girl emerge, who stood before him looking at him boldly. She looked less like a human being than some form engendered of the darkness. Ere Father Mabœuf, whom, as we said, was easily terrified, found time to answer a syllable, this creature, whose movements had in the gloom a sort of strange suddenness, had unhooked the chain, let down and drawn up the bucket, and filled the watering-pot; and the old gentleman saw this apparition, which was barefooted and wore a ragged skirt, running along the flower-beds and distributing life around her. The sound of the water pattering on the leaves filled M. Mabœuf's soul with ravishment, and the rhododendron now seemed to him to be happy. The first bucket emptied, the girl drew a second, then a third, and watered the whole garden. To see her moving thus along the walks in which her outline appeared quite black, and waving on her long thin arms her ragged shawl, she bore a striking resemblance to a bat. When she had finished, Father Mabœuf went up to her with tears in his eyes, and laid his hand on her forehead.

"God will bless you," he said, "you are an angel, since you care for flowers."

"No," she replied, "I am the devil, but I don't care."

The old man continued, without waiting for or hearing the reply:

"What a pity that I am so unhappy and so poor, and can do nothing for you!"

"You can do something," she said.

"What is it?"

"Tell me where M. Marius lives."

The old man did not understand.

"What Monsieur Marius?"

He raised his glassy eyes and seemed seeking something which had vanished.

"A young man who used to come here."

"Ah, yes," he exclaimed, "I know whom you mean. Wait a minute! Monsieur Marius, Baron Marius Pontmercy, pardïeu! lives, or rather he does not live——well, I do not know."

While speaking, he had stooped to straighten a rhododendron branch, and continued :

"Ay! yes, I remember now. He passes very frequently along the boulevard, and goes in the direction of the Lark's field in the Rue Croule Barbe. Look for him there, he will not be difficult to find."

When M. Mabœuf raised his head again, he was alone, and the girl had disappeared. He was decidedly a little frightened.

"Really," he thought, "if my garden were not watered, I should fancy that it was a ghost."

A few days after this visit of a ghost to Father Mabœuf— it was on a Monday, the day of the five-franc piece, which Marius borrowed of Courfeyrac for Thénardier, Marius placed the coin in his pocket, and before carrying it to the prison, resolved to "take a little walk," hoping that on his return this would make him work. It was, however, everlastingly so. As soon as he rose, he sat down before a book and paper to set about some translation, and his job at this time was the translation into French of a celebrated German quarrel, the controversy between Gans and Savigny. He took up Gans, he took up Savigny, read four pages, tried to write one but could not, saw a star between his paper and himself, and got up from his chair, saying, "I will go out, that will put me in the humour," and he proceeded to the Lark's field, where he saw the star more than ever, and Gans and Savigny less. He went home, tried to resume his task, and did not succeed ; he could not join a single one of the threads broken in his brain, and so said to himself, "I will not go out to-morrow, for it prevents me from working." But he went out every day.

He lived in the Lark's field more than at Courfeyrac's lodging, and his right address was Boulevard de la Santé, at the seventh tree past the Rue Croule Barbe. On this morning he had left the seventh tree and was seated on the parapet of the bridge over the little stream. The merry sunbeams were flashing through the expanded and luminous leaves. He thought of "Her," and his reverie, becoming a reproach, fell back on himself; he thought bitterly of the indolence and mental paralysis which were gaining on him, and of the night which constantly grew denser before him, so that he could no longer even see the sun. Still, through this painful evolution of indistinct ideas which was not even a soliloquy, as action was so weak in him, and he had no longer the strength to try and feel sad; through this melancholy absorption, we say, sensations from without reached him. He heard behind, below, and on both sides of him, the washerwomen of the Gobelins beating their linen, and above him the birds twittering and singing in the elms. On one side the sound of liberty, happy care-lessness, and winged leisure, on the other the sound of labour. These two joyous sounds made him think deeply and almost reflect. All at once he heard amid his poignant ecstasy a familiar voice saying :

"Ah ! here he is ! "

He raised his eyes and recognised the unhappy girl who had come to him one morning, Eponine, the elder of Thénardier's daughters ; he now knew what her name was. Strange to say, she had grown poorer and more beautiful, two things which he had not thought possible. She had accomplished a double progress toward light and toward distress. Her feet were bare and her clothes torn, as on the day when she so boldly entered his room, but the rags were two months older and the holes larger. She had the same hoarse voice, the same forehead wrinkled and bronzed by exposure, the same free, absent, and wandering look, but she had, in addition, on her countenance, some-thing startled and lamentable, which passing through prisons adds to misery. She had pieces of straw and hay in her hair, not that, like Ophelia, she had gone mad through contagion with Hamlet's lunacy, but because she had slept in some stable-loft ; and with all this, she was beautiful. O youth, what a star art thou ! She had stooped in front of Marius with a little joy on her livid face, and something like a smile, and it was some minutes ere she could speak.

"I have found you ! " she said at last. "Father Mabœuf was right, it was in this boulevard ! How I have sought

you, if you only knew! Do you know that I have been
in quod for a fortnight! They let me go as there was no
charge against me, and besides I had not attained years
of discretion by two months. Oh, how I have looked for
you the last six weeks! So you no longer live down
there?"

"No," said Marius.

"Ah, I understand, on account of that thing; well, such
disturbances are unpleasant, and you moved. Hilloh, why
do you wear an old hat like that? a young man like you
ought to be handsomely dressed. Do you know, Monsieur
Marius, that M. Mabœuf calls you Baron Marius—I forget
what; but you are not a baron, are you? Barons are old
swells, who walk in front of the Luxembourg Palace, where
there is the most sun, and read the *Quotidienne* for a sou.
I went once with a letter for a baron who was like that;
he was more than a hundred years of age. Tell me, where
do you live now?"

Marius did not answer.

"Ah," she added, "you have a hole in your shirt-front;
I must mend it for you."

Then she continued with an expression which gradually
grew gloomier:

"You do not seem pleased to see me?"

Marius held his tongue. She was also silent for a
moment, and then exclaimed:

"If I liked, I could compel you to look pleased."

"What do you mean?" Marius asked.

She bit her lip, and apparently hesitated, as if suffering
from some internal struggle. At length she seemed to
make up her mind.

"All the worse; but no matter, you look sad and I wish
you to be pleased. Only promise me, though, that you will
laugh, for I want to see you laugh and hear you say,
'Ah! that is famous!' Poor M. Marius! you know you
promised you would give me all I wanted."

"Yes, but speak, can't you?"

She looked at M. Marius intently and said, "I have the
address."

Marius turned pale, and all his blood flowed to his heart.

"What address?"

"The address which you asked me for;" and she added,
as if with a great effort, "the address—you know?"

"Yes," Marius stammered.

"The young lady's."

These words uttered, she heaved a deep sigh. Marius leapt from the parapet on which he was sitting, and wildly seized her hand.

"Oh! lead me to it! tell me! ask of me what you please! where is it?"

"Come with me," she answered; "I don't exactly know the street or the number, and it is quite on the other side of town, but I know the house well, and will take you to it."

She withdrew her hand, and continued in a tone which would have made an observer's heart bleed, but did not at all affect the intoxicated and transported lover:

"Oh, how pleased you are!"

A cloud passed over Marius' forehead, and he clutched Eponine's arm.

"Swear one thing."

"Swear?" she said, "what do you mean by that? what would you have me swear?"

And she burst into a laugh.

"Your father! promise me, Eponine, swear to me that you will never tell your father that address."

She turned to him with an air of stupefaction. "Eponine! how do you know that is my name."

"Promise me what I ask you."

But she did not seem to hear him.

"That is nice! you call me Eponine!"

Marius seized both her arms.

"Answer me in Heaven's name! pay attention to what I am saying,—swear to me that you will not tell your father the address which you know."

"My father?" she remarked. "Oh, yes, my father. He's all right in a secret cell. Besides, what do I care for my father!"

"But you have not promised!" Marius exclaimed.

"Let me go!" she said, as she burst into a laugh, "how you are shaking me! Yes, yes, I promise it, I swear it! how does it concern me? I will not tell my father the address. There, does that suit you, is that it?"

"And no one else?" said Marius.

"And no one else."

"Now," Marius continued, "lead me there."

"At once?"

"Yes."

"Come on! Oh, how glad he is!" she said.

A few yards farther on she stopped.

"You are following me too closely, M. Marius; let me go on in front and do you follow me, as if you were not doing so. A respectable young man like you must not be seen with such a woman as I am."

No language could render all that was contained in the word "woman" thus pronounced by this child. She went a dozen paces and stopped again. Marius rejoined her, and she said to him aside without turning to him:

"By the bye, you know that you promised me something?"

Marius felt in his pocket; he had nothing in the world but the five-franc piece destined for father Thénardier, but he laid the coin in Eponine's hand. She let it slip through her fingers to the ground, and looking at him frowningly said:

"I do not want your money."

CHAPTER LXXXIV.

Towards the middle of the last century a President of the Parliament of Paris who kept a mistress under the rose, for at that day the nobility displayed their mistresses and the bourgeois concealed theirs, had "a small house," built in the Faubourg St. Germain, in the deserted Rue de Blomet, which is now called Rue Plumet. This house consisted of a pavilion two storeys in height: two sitting-rooms on the ground-floor, two bedrooms on the first, a kitchen below, a boudoir above, an attic beneath the roof, and the whole was surrounded by a large garden with railings looking out on the street. This was all that passers-by could see. But behind the pavilion was a narrow yard, with an outhouse containing two rooms, where a nurse and a child could be concealed if necessary. In the back of this outhouse was a secret door leading into a long, paved winding passage, open to the sky, and bordered by two lofty walls. This passage, concealed with prodigious art, and, as it were, lost between the garden walls, whose every turn and winding it followed, led to another secret door, which opened about a quarter of a mile off almost in another quarter, at the solitary end of the Rue de Babylone. The President went in by this door, so that even those who might have watched him, and observed that he mysteriously went somewhere

every day, could not have suspected that going to the Rue
de Babylone was going to the Rue Blomet. By clever
purchases of ground, the ingenious magistrate had been
enabled to make this hidden road upon his own land, and
consequently without supervision. At a later date he sold
the land bordering the passage in small lots for gardens,
and the owners of these gardens on either side believed that
they had a parting-wall before them, and did not even
suspect the existence of this long strip of pavement winding
between two walls among their flower-beds and orchards.
The birds alone saw this curiosity, and it is probable that
the linnets and tom-tits of the last century gossiped a good
deal about the President.

The pavilion, built of stone, in the Mansard taste, and
panelled and furnished in the Watteau style, rock-work
outside, periwig within, and begirt by a triple hedge of
flowers, had something discreet, coquettish, and solemn
about it, befitting the caprices of love and a magistrate.
This house and this passage, which have now disappeared,
still existed fifteen years ago. In '93 a brazier bought the
house for the purpose of demolishing it, but as he could not
pay, the nation made him bankrupt, and thus it was the
house that demolished the brazier. Since then the house
had remained uninhabited, and fell slowly into ruin, like
every residence to which the presence of man no longer
communicates life. The old furniture was left in it, and
the ten or twelve persons who pass along the Rue Plumet
were informed that it was for sale or lease by a yellow and
illegible placard which had been fastened to the garden
gate since 1810. Toward the end of the Restoration the
same passers-by might have noticed that the bill had
disappeared, and even that the first-floor shutters were
open. The house was really occupied, and there were
short curtains at the windows, a sign that there was a
lady in the house. In October, 1809, a middle-aged man
presented himself and took the house as it stood, including
of course the outhouse and the passage leading to the Rue de
Babylone, and he had the two secret doors of this passage
put in repair. The house was still furnished much as the
President had left it, so the new tenant merely ordered a
few necessary articles, had the paving of the yard put to
rights, new stairs put in, and the windows mended, and
eventually installed himself there with a young girl and an
old woman, without any disturbance, and rather like a man

slipping in than one entering his own house. The neighbours, however, did not chatter, for the simple reason that there were none.

The tenant was in reality Jean Valjean, and the girl was Cosette. The domestic was a female of the name of Toussaint, whom Jean Valjean had saved from the hospital and wretchedness, and who was old, rustic, and stammered, three [qualities which determined Jean Valjean on taking her with him. He hired the house in the name of M. Fauchelevent, annuitant. In all we have recently recorded the reader will have doubtless recognised Valjean even sooner than Thénardier did. Why had he left the convent of the Little Picpus, and what had occurred there? Nothing had occurred. It will be borne in mind that Jean Valjean was happy in the convent, so happy that his conscience at last became disturbed by it. He saw Cosette daily, he felt paternity springing up and being developed in him more and more; he set his whole soul on the girl; he said to himself that she was his, that no power on earth could rob him of her, that it would be so indefinitely, that she would certainly become a nun, as she was daily gently urged to it, that henceforth the convent was the world for him as for her, that he would grow old in it and she grow up, that she would grow old and he die there; and that, finally, no separation was possible. While reflecting on this, he began falling into perplexities : he asked himself if all this happiness were really his, if it were not composed of the happiness of this child, which he confiscated and deprived her of, and whether this were not a robbery? He said to himself that this child had the right to know life before renouncing it, that depriving her beforehand, and without consulting her, of all joys under the pretext of saving her from all trials, and profiting by her ignorance and isolation to make an artificial vocation spring up in her, was denaturalising a human creature and being false to God. And who knew whether Cosette, some day meditating on this, and feeling herself a reluctant nun, might not grow to hate him? It was a last thought, almost selfish and less heroic than the others, but it was insupportable to him. He resolved to leave the convent.

He resolved, and recognised with a breaking heart that he must do so. As for objections, there were none, for six years of residence between these walls, and of disappearance, had necessarily destroyed or dispersed the element of fear.

He could return to human society at his ease, for he had grown old and all had changed. Who would recognise him now? And then, looking at the worst, there was only danger for himself, and he had not the right to condemn Cosette to a cloister, for the reason that he had been condemned to the galleys; besides, what is danger in the presence of duty? Lastly, nothing prevented him from being prudent and taking precautions; and as for Cosette's education, it was almost completed and terminated. Once the resolution was formed, he awaited the opportunity, which soon offered: old Fauchelevent died. Jean Valjean requested an audience of the reverend Prioress, and told her that as he had inherited a small property by his brother's death, which would enable him to live without working, he was going to leave the convent, and take his daughter with him; but as it was not fair that Cosette, who was not going to profess, should have been educated gratuitously, he implored the reverend Prioress to allow him to offer the community, for the five years which Cosette had passed among them, the sum of five thousand francs. It was thus that Jean Valjean quitted the convent of the Perpetual Adoration.

On leaving it he carried with his own hands, and would not entrust to any porter, the small valise, of which he always had the key about him. This valise perplexed Cosette, owing to the aromatic smell which issued from it. Let us say at once that this trunk never quitted him again, he always had it in his bedroom, and it was the first, and at times the only thing which he carried away in his removals. Cosette laughed, called this valise the inseparable, and said, "I am jealous of it." Jean Valjean, however, felt a profound anxiety when he returned to the outer air. He discovered the house in the Rue Plumet, and hid himself in it, henceforth remaining in possession of the name of Ultime Fauchelevent. At the same time he hired two other lodgings in Paris, so that he might attract less attention than if he had always remained in the same quarter; that he might, if necessary, absent himself for a while if anything alarmed him; and, lastly, that he might not be taken unawares, as on the night when he so miraculously escaped from Javert. These two lodgings were of a very mean appearance, and in two quarters very distant from each other, one being in the Rue de l'Ouest, the other in the Rue de l'Homme-armé. He spent a few weeks now and then at one or the other of these lodgings, taking Cosette with him and leaving Toussaint behind. He was waited on by the porters, and represented himself as a person living in the country, who had a lodging in town. This lofty virtue had three domiciles in Paris in order to escape the police.

Properly speaking, however, Jean Valjean's house was at the Rue Plumet, and he had arranged his existence there in the following fashion :—Cosette and the servant occupied the pavilion : she had the best bedroom, with the painted press, the boudoir with the gilt beading, the President's drawing-room with its hangings and vast easy-chairs, and the garden. Jean Valjean placed in Cosette's room a bed with a canopy of old damask in three colours, and an old and handsome Persian carpet, purchased at Mother Gauchér's in the Rue Figuier Saint Paul, while, to correct the sternness of these old splendours, he added all the light gay furniture of girls, an étagère, bookshelves with gilt books, a desk and blotting-case, a work-table inlaid with mother-of-pearl, a silver dressing-case, and toilette articles of Japanese china. Long damask curtains of three colours, like those on the bed, festooned the first-floor windows, while on the ground-floor they were of tapestry. All through the winter Cosette's small house was warmed from top to bottom. While Valjean himself lived in the sort of porter's lodge at the end of the back-yard, which was furnished with a mattress and common bedstead, a deal table, two straw-bottomed chairs, an earthenware water-jug, a few books on a plank, and his dear valise in a corner, but he never had any fire. He dined with Cosette, and black bread was put on the table for him ; and he had said to Toussaint, when she came, "This young lady is mistress of the house." " And you, sir ? " Toussaint replied, quite stupefied. " Oh ! I am much better than the master,—I am the father."

Cosette had been taught housekeeping in the convent, and checked the expenses, which were very small. Daily Jean Valjean took Cosette for a walk, leading to the most sequestered allée of the Luxembourg, and every Sunday they attended mass at the Church of St. Jacques du Haut-pas, because it was a long distance off. As it is a very poor district, he gave away a considerable amount of alms, and the wretched flocked around him in the church, which caused Thénardier to head his letter to him in the way we have seen. He was fond of taking Cosette to visit the indigent and the sick, but no stranger ever entered the house in the Rue Plumet. Toussaint bought the provisions, and

Jean Valjean himself fetched the water from a fountain close by, on the boulevard. The wood and wine were kept in a semi-subterranean building covered with rock-work, near the door in the Rue Babylone, and which had formerly served the President as a grotto, for in the age of the Follies and small houses, love was not possible without a grotto. In the door opening on the Rue Babylone there was a letter-box, but, as the inhabitants of the house in the Rue Plumet received no letters, this box, once on a time the go-between in amourettes, and the confidant of a love-sick lawyer, was now only of service to receive the tax-papers and the guard-summonses. For M. Fauchelevent, annuitant, belonged to the National Guard, and had been unable to escape the close meshes of the census of 1831. The municipal inquiries made at that period extended even to the convent of the Little Picpus, whence Jean Valjean emerged venerable in the sight of the Major, and consequently worthy of mounting guard. Three or four times a year Jean Valjean donned his uniform and went on duty, and did so readily enough, for it was a disguise which enabled him to mix with everybody, while himself remaining solitary. Jean Valjean had attained his sixtieth year, or the age of legal exemption ; but he did not look more than fifty ; besides, he had no wish to escape his Sergeant-major and cheat Count Lobau. He had no civil status, hid his name, his identity, his age, everything, and, as we just said, he was a willing National Guard ; all his ambition was to resemble the first-comer who pays taxes. The ideal of this man was internally an angel, externally a bourgeois.

Let us mention one fact, by the way. When Jean Valjean went out with Cosette he dressed himself in the way we have seen, and looked like a retired officer, but when he went out alone, and he did so usually at night, he was attired in a workman's jacket and trousers, and a cap whose peak was pulled deep over his eyes. Was this precaution or humility ? Both at once. Cosette was accustomed to the enigmatical side of her destiny, and hardly noticed her father's singularities ; as for Toussaint, she revered Jean Valjean, and considered everything he did right. One day her butcher, who got a glimpse of her master, said, " He's a queer-looking stick," and she replied, " He's a—a—a—saint." All three never left the house except by the gate in the Rue de Babylone ; and unless they were noticed through the garden gate it would be difficult to guess that they lived in the Rue Plumet. This gate was always locked, and Jean Valjean left the garden untended that it might not be noticed. In this, perhaps, he deceived himself.

This garden, left to itself for more than half a century, had become extraordinary and charming : passers-by forty years ago stopped in the street to gaze at it, without suspecting the secrets which it hid behind its fresh green screen. More than one dreamer at that day allowed his eyes and thoughts indiscreetly to penetrate the bars of the old locked, twisted, shaky gate, which hung from two mould-covered pillars and was surmounted by a pediment covered with undecipherable arabesques. There was a stone bank in a corner, there were one or two mouldering statues, and some trellis-work, unnailed by time, was rotting against the walls ; there was no turf or walk left, but there was dog's-grass everywhere. The artificiality of gardening had departed, and nature had returned ; weeds were abundant, and the festival of the gilly-flowers was splendid there. Nothing in this garden impeded the sacred efforts of things toward life, and growth was at home there, and held high holiday. The trees had bent down to the briars, the briars had mounted towards the trees ; the plants had clambered up, the branches had bent down. What crawls on the ground had gone to meet what expands in the air, and what floats in the wind stooped down to what drags along the moss ; brambles, branches, leaves, fibres, tufts, twigs, tendrils, and thorns were mixed together, wedded and confounded ; vegetation had celebrated and accomplished here, in a close and profound embrace, and beneath the satisfied eye of the Creator, the holy mystery of its fraternity, which is a symbol of human paternity.

Although the pavement of Paris was all around, the classical and splendid mansions of the Rue de Varennes two yards off, the dome of the Invalides close by, and the Chamber of Deputies no great distance ; although the carriages from the Rues de Bourgogne and St. Dominique rolled along luxuriously in the vicinity, and yellow, brown, and white, and red omnibuses crossed the adjoining square, the Rue Plumet was a desert ; and the death of the old proprietors, a revolution which had passed, the overthrow of old fortunes, absence, forgetfulness, and forty years of desertion and widowhood, had sufficed to bring back to this privileged spot ferns, torch-weeds, hemlock, ragwort, tall grass, dock-leaves, lizards, beetles, and restless and rapid insects.

It seemed as if this garden, created in former times to conceal libertine mysteries, had been transformed and become fitting to shelter chaste mysteries. There were no longer any cradles, bowling-greens, covered walks, or grottos; but there was a magnificent tangled obscurity which fell all around, and Paphos was changed into Eden. A penitent feeling had refreshed this retreat, and the coquettish garden, once on a time so compromised, had returned to virginity and modesty. A president assisted by a gardener, a good fellow who believed himself the successor of Lamoignon, and another good fellow who fancied himself the successor of Lenôtre, had turned it about, clipped it, and prepared it for purposes of gallantry; but nature had seized it again, filled it with shadow, and prepared it for love. There was too in this solitude a heart which was quite ready, and love had only to show itself; for there were here a temple composed of verdure, grass, moss, the sighs of birds, gentle shadows, waving branches, and a soul formed of gentleness, faith, candour, hope, aspirations, and illusions.

Cosette left the convent while still almost a child. She was but little more than fourteen, and at the "ungrateful age," as we have said. With the exception of her eyes, she seemed rather ugly than pretty; still she had no ungraceful feature, but she was awkward, thin, timid and bold at the same time, in short, a grown-up little girl. Her education was finished, that is to say, she had been taught religion, and more especially devotion, also "history," that is to say, the thing so called in a convent; geography, grammar, the participles, the kings of France, and a little music, drawing, etc.; but in other respects she was ignorant of everything, which is at once a charm and a peril. The mind of a young girl ought not to be left in darkness, for at a later date too sudden and quick looming as produced in it as in a *camera obscura*. She should be gently and discreetly enlightened, rather by the reflection of realities than by their direct and harsh light; for this is a useful and gracefully obscure semi-light which dissipates childish fears and prevents falls. There is only the maternal instinct, that admirable intuition into which the recollections of the virgin and the experience of the wife enter, that knows how or of what this semi-light should be composed. Nothing can take the place of this instinct, and in forming a girl's mind, all the nuns in the world are not equal to one mother. Cosette had had no mother, she had only had a great many mothers : as for Jean Valjean, he had within him every possible tenderness and every possible anxiety ; but he was only an old man who knew nothing at all. Now, in this work of education, in this serious matter of preparing a woman for life, what knowledge is needed to contend against the other great ignorance which is called innocence ! Nothing prepares a girl for passions like the convent, for it directs her thoughts to the unknown. The heart is driven back on itself, and hence come visions, suppositions, conjectures, romances sketched, adventures longed for, fantastic constructions, and edifices built entirely on the inner darkness of the mind, gloomy and secret dwellings in which the passions alone find a lodging so soon as passing through the convent gate allows it. The convent is a compression which must last the whole life, if it is to triumph over the human heart. On leaving the convent, Cosette could not have found anything sweeter or more dangerous than the house in the Rue Plumet. It was the commencement of solitude with the commencement of liberty, a closed garden, but a rich, sharp, voluptuous, and flagrant soul ; there were the same dreams as in the convent, but glimpses could be caught of young men,—it was a grating, but it looked on the street. Still, we repeat, when Cosette first came here, she was but a child. Jean Valjean gave over to her this uncultivated garden, and said to her, " Do what you like with it." This amused Cosette, she moved all the tufts and all the stones in search of " beasts " ; she played about while waiting till the time came to think, and she loved this garden for the sake of the insects which she found in the grass under her feet, while waiting till she should love it for the sake of the stars she could see through the branches above her head.

And then, too, she loved her father, that is to say, Jean Valjean, with all her soul, with a simple filial passion, which rendered the worthy man a desired and delightful companion to her. Our readers will remember that M. Madeleine was fond of reading, and Jean Valjean continued in the same track ; he had learned to speak well, and he possessed the secret wealth and the eloquence of a humble, true, and self-cultivated intellect. He had retained just

sufficient roughness to season his kindness, and he had a
rough mind and a soft heart.   During their *tête-à-têtes* in
the Luxembourg garden he gave her long explanations
about all sorts of things, deriving his information from
what he had read, and also from what he had suffered.
While Cosette was listening to him her eyes vaguely
wandered around.   This simple man was sufficient for
Cosette's thoughts, in the same way as the wild garden
was for her eyes.   When she had chased the butterflies for
a while she would run up to him panting, and say, "Oh !
how tired I am !" and he would kiss her forehead.
Cosette adored this good man, and she was ever at his
heels, for wherever Jean Valjean was, happiness was.   As
he did not live either in the pavilion or the garden, she
was more attached to the paved back-yard than to the
flower-laden garden, and preferred the little outhouse with
the straw chairs to the large drawing-room hung with
tapestry, along which silk-covered chairs were arranged.
Jean Valjean at times said to her with a smile of a man
who is delighted to be annoyed,—"Come, go to your own
rooms ! leave me at peace for a little while."
She scolded him in that charming tender way which is
so graceful when addressed by a daughter to a parent.
"Father, I feel very cold in your room ; why don't you
have a carpet and a stove !"
"My dear child, there are so many persons more de-
serving than myself who have not even a roof to cover them."
"Then, why is there fire in my room and everything that
I want ?"
"Because you are a woman and a child."
"Nonsense ! then men must be cold and hungry ?"
"Some men."
"Very good ! I'll come here so often that you will be
obliged to have a fire."
Or else it was :
"Father, why do you eat such wretched bread as that ?"
"Because I do, my daughter."
"Well, if you eat it I shall eat it too."
And so to prevent Cosette from eating black bread Jean
Valjean ate white. Cosette remembered her childhood but
confusedly, and she prayed night and morning for the
mother whom she had never known. The Thénardiers
were like two hideous beings seen in a dream, and she
merely remembered that she had gone "one day at night"

to fetch water in a wood—she thought that it was a long
distance from Paris. It seemed to her as if she had
commenced life in an abyss, and that Jean Valjean had
drawn her out of it, and her childhood produced on her
the effect of a time when she had had nought but centi-
pedes, spiders, and snakes around her. When she thought
at night before she fell asleep, as she had no very clear
idea of being Jean Valjean's daughter, she imagined that
her mother's soul had passed into this good man, and had
come to dwell near her. When he was sitting down she
rested her cheek on his white hair, and silently dropped a
tear, while saying to herself, "Perhaps this man is my
mother!" Cosette, strange though it is to say, in her
profound ignorance, as a girl educated in a convent, and
as, too, maternity is absolutely unintelligible to virginity,
eventually imagined that she had had as little of a mother
as was possible. This mother's name she did not know,
and whenever it happened that she spoke to Jean Valjean
on the subject he held his tongue. If she repeated her
question he answered by a smile, and once, when she
pressed him, the smile terminated in a tear. This silence
on his part cast a night over Fantine: was it through
prudence? was it through respect? or was it through a
fear of entrusting this name to the chances of another
memory besides his own?

So long as Cosette was young, Jean Valjean readily talked
to her about her mother, but when she grew up it was impossible for him to do so—he felt as if he dared not do it.
Was it on account of Cosette or of Fantine? He felt a
species of religious horror at making this shadow enter
Cosette's thoughts, and rendering a dead woman a third
person in their society. The more sacred this shade was to
him, the more formidable was it. He thought of Fantine,
and felt himself overwhelmed by the silence. He saw
vaguely in the darkness something that resembled a finger
laid on a lip. Had all the modesty which was in Fantine,
and which, during her existence, came out of her violently,
returned after her death, to watch indignantly over the dead
woman's peace, and sternly guard her in the tomb? was
Jean Valjean himself unconsciously oppressed by it? We
who believe in death are not prepared to reject this
mysterious explanation, and hence arose the impossibility
of pronouncing, even to Cosette, the name of Fantine. One
day Cosette said to him :

"Father, I saw my mother last night in a dream. She had two large wings, and in life she must have been a sainted woman."

"Through martyrdom," Jean Valjean replied. Altogether, though, he was happy; when Cosette went out with him she leant on his arm, proudly and happily, in the fulness of her heart. Jean Valjean felt his thoughts melt into delight at all these marks of such exclusive tenderness, so satisfied with himself alone. The poor wretch inundated with an angelic joy, trembled; he assured himself with transports that this would last his whole life; he said to himself that he had not really suffered enough to deserve such radiant happiness, and he thanked God, in the depths of his soul, for having allowed him, villain as he was, to be thus loved by an innocent being.

CHAPTER LXXXV.

ONE day Cosette happened to look at herself in the glass, and said, "Good gracious!" She fancied that she was almost pretty, and this threw her into a singular trouble. Up to this moment she had not thought of her face, and though she saw herself in the mirror she did not look at herself. And, then, she had often been told that she was ugly; Jean Valjean alone would say gently, "Oh no, oh no!" However this might be, Cosette had always believed herself ugly, and had grown up in this idea with the facile resignation of childhood. And now all at once her looking-glass said to her, as Jean Valjean had done, "Oh no!" She did not sleep that night. "Suppose I were pretty," she thought, "how droll it would be if I were pretty!" and she remembered those of her companions whose beauty produced an effect in the convent, and said to herself, "What! I might be like Mademoiselle So-and-so!"

On the next day she looked at herself, but not accidentally, and doubted. "Where was my sense?" she said, "no, I am ugly." She had simply slept badly, her eyes were heavy and her cheeks pale. She had not felt very joyous on the previous day when she fancied herself pretty, but was sad at no longer believing it. She did not look at herself again, and for upwards of a fortnight tried to dress her hair with her back to the glass. In the evening, after dinner, she usually worked at her embroidery in the drawing-room, while Jean Valjean read by her side. Once she raised her eyes from her work, and was greatly surprised by the anxious way in which her father was gazing at her. Another time she was walking along the street, and fancied she heard some one behind her, whom she did not see, say, "A pretty woman, but badly dressed." "Nonsense," she thought, "it is not I, for I am well dressed and ugly." At that time she wore her plush bonnet and merino dress. One day, at last, she was in the garden, and heard poor old Toussaint saying, "Master, do you notice how pretty our young lady is growing?" Cosette did not hear her father's answer, for Toussaint's words produced a sort of commotion in her. She ran out of the garden up to her room, looked in the glass, which she had not done for three months, and uttered a cry—she had dazzled herself.

She was beautiful and pretty, and could not refrain from being of the same opinion as Toussaint and her glass. Her waist was formed, her skin had grown white, her hair was glossy, and an unknown splendour was lit up in her blue eyes. The consciousness of her beauty came to her fully in a minute, like the sudden dawn of day; others, besides, noticed her, Toussaint said so; it was evidently to herself that the passer-by alluded, and no doubt was possible. She returned to the garden, believing herself a queen, hearing the birds sing, though it was winter, seeing the golden sky, the sun amid the trees, flowers on the shrubs; she was wild, distraught, and in a state of ineffable ravishment. On his side, Jean Valjean experienced a profound and inexplicable contraction of the heart; for some time past, in truth, he had contemplated with terror the beauty which daily appeared more radiant in Cosette's sweet face. It was a laughing dawn for all, but most mournful for him.

Cosette had been for a long time beautiful ere she perceived the fact, but, from the first day, this unexpected light which slowly rose and gradually enveloped the girl's entire person hurt Jean Valjean's sombre eyes. He felt that it was a change in a happy life, so happy that he did not dare stir in it, for fear of deranging it somewhere. This man, who had passed through every possible distress, who was still bleeding from the wounds dealt him by his destiny, who had been almost wicked, and had become almost a saint, who, after dragging the galley chain, was now dragging the invisible but weighty chain of indefinite infamy; this man whom the law had not liberated, and who might at any moment be recaptured and taken from the obscurity of virtue to the broad daylight of further opprobrium—this man accepted everything, excused everything, pardoned everything, blessed everything, wished everything well, and only asked one thing of Providence, of men, of the laws, of society, of nature, of the world—that Cosette should love him, that Cosette might continue to love him! that God would not prevent the heart of this child turning to him and remaining with him! Loved by Cosette, he felt cured, at rest, appeased, overwhelmed, rewarded, and crowned. With Cosette's love all was well, and he asked no more. Had any one said to him, "Would you like to be better off?" he would have answered, "No." Had God said to him, "Do you wish for heaven?" he would have answered, "I should lose by it." All that could affect this situation, even on the surface, appeared to him the beginning of something else. He had never known thoroughly what a woman's beauty was, but he understood instinctively that it was terrible. This beauty, which continually expanded more triumphantly and superbly by his side, upon the ingenuous and formidable brow of the child, from the depths of his ugliness, old age, misery, reprobation, and despondency, terrified him, and he said to himself, "How beautiful she is! what will become of me?" Here lay the difference between his tenderness and that of a mother; what he saw with agony a mother would have seen with joy.

The first symptoms speedily manifested themselves. From the day when Cosette said to herself, "I am decidedly good-looking," she paid attention to her toilet. She remembered the remark of the passer-by—pretty, but badly dressed—a blast of the oracle which passed by her and died out, after depositing in her heart one of those two germs which are destined at a later period to occupy a woman's entire life—coquettishness. The other is love. With faith in her beauty, all her feminine soul was expanded within her; she had a horror of merinos, and felt ashamed of plush. Her father never refused her anything, and she knew at once the whole science of the hat, the dress, the mantle, the slipper, and the sleeve of the fabric that suits, and the colour that is becoming, the science which makes the Parisian woman something so charming, profound, and dangerous. The expression *femme capiteuse* was invented for the Parisian. In less than a month little Cosette was in this Thebaïs of the Rue de Babylone, not only one of the prettiest women, which is something, but one of the best dressed in Paris, which is a great deal more. She would have liked to meet her "passer-by," to see what he would say, and teach him a lesson. The fact is, that she was in every respect ravishing, and could admirably distinguish a bonnet of Gerard's from one of Herbautt's. Jean Valjean regarded these ravages with anxiety, and while feeling that he could never do more than crawl or walk at the most, he could see Cosette's wings growing. However, by the simple inspection of Cosette's toilet, a woman would have seen that she had no mother. Certain small proprieties and social conventionalisms were not observed by Cosette ; a mother, for instance, would have told her that an unmarried girl does not wear brocade.

The first day that Cosette went out in her dress and cloak of black brocade, and her white crape bonnet, she took Jean Valjean's arm, gay, radiant, blushing, proud, and striking. "Father," she said, "how do you think I look?" Jean Valjean replied, in a voice which resembled the bitter voice of an envier, "Charming." During the walk he was as usual, but when he returned home he asked Cosette :

"Will you not put on that dress and bonnet, you know which, again?"

This took place in Cosette's room ; she returned to the wardrobe in which her boarding-school dress was hanging.

"That disguise?" she said, "how can you expect it, father? oh, no, indeed, I shall never put on those horrors again : with that thing on my head I look a regular dowdy."

Jean Valjean heaved a deep sigh.

From that moment he noticed that Cosette, who hitherto had wished to stay at home, saying, "Father, I amuse myself much better here with you," now constantly asked to go out. In truth, what good is it for a girl to have a pretty face and a delicious toilet if she does not show them? He also noticed that Cosette no longer had the same liking for the back-yard, and at present preferred remaining in the garden, where she walked, without displeasure, near the railings. Jean Valjean never set foot in the garden, but remained in the back-yard, like the dog. Cosette, knowing herself to be beautiful, lost the grace of being ignorant of the fact, an exquisite grace, for beauty heightened by simplicity is ineffable, and nothing is so adorable as a beauteous innocent maiden, who walks along unconsciously, holding in her hand a key of a paradise. But what she lost in ingenuous grace she regained in a pensive and serious charm. Her whole person, impregnated with the joys of youth, innocence, and beauty, exhaled a splendid melancholy. It was at this period that Marius saw her again at the Luxembourg, after an interval of six months.

Cosette was in her shadow, as Marius was in his, ready prepared to be kindled. Destiny, with its mysterious and fatal patience, brought slowly together these two beings, all charged with, and pining in, the stormy electricity of passion, these two souls which bore love, as the clouds bore thunder, and were destined to come together and be blended in a glance like the clouds in a storm. At the hour when Cosette unconsciously gave that glance which troubled Marius, Marius did not suspect that he too gave a glance which troubled Cosette. For a long time she had seen and examined him in the way girls see and examine, while looking elsewhere. Marius was still thinking Cosette ugly, when Cosette had already considered Marius handsome, but as the young man paid no attention to her he was an object of indifference. Still she could not refrain from saying to herself that he had silky hair, fine eyes, regular teeth, an agreeable voice, when she heard him talking with his companions, that he perhaps walked badly, but with a grace of his own, that he did not appear at all silly, that his whole person was noble, gentle, simple, and proud, and, lastly, that though he seemed poor he had the bearing of a gentleman.

On the day when their eyes met, and at length suddenly said to each other the first obscure and ineffable things which the eye stammers, Cosette did not understand it at first. She returned pensively to the house in the Rue de l'Ouest, where Jean Valjean was spending six weeks, according to his wont. When she awoke the next morning she thought of the young stranger, so long indifferent and cold, who now seemed to pay attention to her, and this attention did not appear at all agreeable to her; on the contrary, she felt a little angry with the handsome, disdainful man. A warlike feeling was aroused, and she felt a very childish joy at the thought that she was at length about to be avenged; knowing herself to be lovely, she felt, though in an indistinct way, that she had a weapon. Women play with their beauty as lads do with their knives, and cut themselves with it. Our readers will remember

Marius' hesitations, palpitations, and terrors; he remained
on his bench, and did not approach, and this vexed Cosette.
One day she said to Jean Valjean, "Father, suppose we
take a walk in that direction?" Seeing that Marius did
not come to her, she went to him, for, in such cases, every
woman resembles Mahomet. And then, strange it is, the
first sympton of true love in a young man is timidity; in a
girl it is boldness. This will surprise, and yet nothing is
more simple; the two sexes have a tendency to approach,
and each assumes the qualities of the other. On this day
Cosette's glance drove Marius mad, while his glance made
Cosette tremble. Marius went away confiding, and Cosette
restless. Now they adored each other. The first thing
that Cosette experienced was a confused and deep sorrow:
it seemed to her that her soul had become black in one day,
and she no longer recognised herself. The whiteness of
the soul of maidens, which is composed of coldness and
gaiety, resembles snow; it melts before love, which is its
sun.

Cosette knew not what love was, and she had never heard
the word uttered in its earthly sense, and hence did not
know what name to give to that which now troubled her.
But are we the less ill through being ignorant of the name
of our disease? She loved with the more passion, because
she loved in ignorance; she did not know whether it is
good or bad, useful or dangerous, necessary or mortal,
eternal or transient, permitted or prohibited,—she loved.
She would have been greatly surprised had any one said to
her, "You do not sleep? that is forbidden. You do not
eat? that is very wrong. You have an oppression and
beating of the heart? that cannot be tolerated. You blush
and turn pale when a certain person dressed in black appears
at the end of a certain green walk? why, that is abominable!" She would not have understood, and would have
replied, "How can I be to blame in a matter in which I can
do nothing, and of which I know nothing?"

It happened that the love which presented itself was the
one most in harmony with the state of her soul; it was a
sort of distant adoration, a dumb contemplation, the deifica-
tion of an unknown man. It was the apparition of youth
to youth, the dream of nights become a romance, and
remaining a dream, the wished-for phantom at length
realised and incarnated, but as yet having no name, or
wrong, or flaw, or claim, or defect; in a way, the distant

lover who remained idealised, a chimera which assumed a shape. Any more palpable and nearer meeting would at this first stage have startled Cosette, who was still half plunged in the magnifying fog of the cloister. It was not a lover she wanted, not even an admirer, but a vision, and she began adoring Marius as something charming, luminous, and impossible.

As extreme simplicity trenches on extreme coquetry, she smiled upon him most frankly. She daily awaited impatiently the hour for the walk; she saw Marius, she felt indescribably happy, and sincerely believed that she was expressing her entire thoughts when she said to Jean Valjean, "What a delicious garden the Luxembourg is!" Marius and Cosette were in the dark in regard to each other: they did not speak, they did not bow, they did not know each other, but they met: and like the stars in the heavens, which are millions of leagues separate, they lived by looking at each other. It is thus that Cosette gradually became a woman, and was developed into a beautiful and loving woman, conscious of her beauty and ignorant of her love. She was a coquette into the bargain, through her innocence.

All situations have their instincts, and old and eternal mother Nature warned Jean Valjean darkly of the presence of Marius. Jean Valjean trembled in the depth of his mind: he saw nothing, knew nothing, and yet regarded with obstinate attention the darkness in which he was, as if he felt on one side something being built up, on the other something crumbling away. Marius, who was also warned by the same mother Nature, did all in his power to conceal himself from the father, but, for all that, Jean Valjean sometimes perceived him. Marius' manner was no longer wise; he displayed clumsy prudence and awkward temerity. He no longer came quite close to them, as he had formerly done, he sat down at a distance, and remained in an ecstasy: he had a book, and pretended to read it; why did he pretend? Formerly he came in an old coat, and now he came every day in his new one. Jean Valjean was not quite sure whether he did not have his hair dressed: he had a strange way of rolling his eyes, and wore gloves: in short, Jean Valjean cordially detested the young man. Cosette did not allow anything to be guessed. Without knowing exactly what was the matter with her, she had a feeling that it was something which must be hidden. There

was a parallelism which annoyed Jean Valjean between the
taste for dress which had come to Cosette, and the habit
of wearing new clothes displayed by this stranger. It was
an accident, perhaps—of course it was—but a menacing
accident.

He never opened his mouth to Cosette about this stranger.
One day, however, he could not refrain, and said, with that
vague despair, which suddenly thrusts the probe into its
own misfortune, "That young man looks like a pedant."
Cosette, a year previously, when still a careless little girl,
would have answered, "Oh no, he is very good-looking."
Ten years later, with the love of Marius in her heart, she
would have replied, "An insufferable pedant, you are quite
right." At the present moment of her life and heart, she
restricted herself to saying, with supreme calmness, "That
young man!" as if she looked at him for the first time in
her life. "How stupid I am," Jean Valjean thought, "she
had not even noticed him, and now I have pointed him out
to her." Oh, simplicity of old people! oh, depth of children!
It is another law of these first years of suffering and care,
of these sharp struggles of first love with first obstacles,
that the maiden cannot be caught in any snare, while the
young man falls into all. Jean Valjean had begun a secret
war against Marius, which Marius, in the sublime stupidity
of his passion and his age, did not guess. Jean Valjean
laid all sorts of snares for him. He changed his hours, he
changed his bench, he forgot his handkerchief, and went
alone to the Luxembourg, and Marius went headlong into
the trap, and to all these notes of interrogation which Jean
Valjean planted in the road, he ingenuously answered,
"Yes." Cosette, however, remained immured in her
apparent carelessness and imperturbable tranquillity, so that
Jean Valjean arrived at this conclusion, "That humbug is
madly in love with Cosette, but Cosette does not even know
that he exists."

For all that, though, he had a painful tremor in his heart,
for the minute when Cosette would love might arrive at any
instant. Does not all this commence with indifference?
Only once did Cosette commit a fault and startle him; he
arose from his bench to go home after three hours' sitting,
and she said, "What, already?" Jean Valjean did not give
up his walks at the Luxembourg, as he did not wish to do
anything singular, or arouse Cosette's attention, but during
the hours so sweet for the two lovers, while Cosette was

sending her smile to the intoxicated Marius, who only perceived this, and now saw nothing more in the world than a radiant adored face, Jean Valjean fixed on Marius flashing and terrible eyes. He who had ended by no longer believing himself capable of a malevolent feeling, had moments when he felt, if Marius were present, as if he were growing savage and ferocious, and those old depths of his soul which had formerly contained so much anger opened again against this young man. It seemed to him as if unknown craters were again being formed within him. Jean Valjean said to himself, " What does he come to seek ? an adventure. What does he want ? a love-affair. A love-affair ! and I ! What ? I was first the most wretched of men, and then the most unhappy. I have spent sixty years on my knees, I have suffered all that a man can suffer, I have grown old without ever having been young ; I have lived without family, parents, friends, children, or wife ; I have left some of my blood on every stone, on every bramble, on every wall ; I have been gentle, though men were harsh to me, and good though they were wicked. I have become an honest man again, in spite of everything ; I have repented of the evil I did, and pardoned the evil done to me, and at the moment when I am rewarded, when all is finished when I touched my object, when I have what I wish, and it is but fair as I have paid for it and earned it—all this is to fade away, and I am to lose Cosette, my love, my joy, my soul, because it has pleased a long-legged ass to saunter about the Luxembourg garden ! "

Then his eyeballs were filled with extraordinary brilliancy. Marius continued to act madly, and one day followed Cosette to the Rue de l'Quest. Another day he spoke to the porter, and the porter spoke in his turn, and said to Jean Valjean, " Do you happen to know, sir, a curious young man, who has been making inquiries about you ? " The next day Jean Valjean gave Marius that look which Marius at length noticed, and a week later Jean Valjean went away. He made a vow that he would never again set foot in the Rue de l'Ouest or the Luxembourg, and returned to the Rue Plumet. Cosette did not complain, she said nothing, she asked no questions, she did not attempt to discover any motive, for she had reached that stage when a girl fears

that her thoughts may be perused, or she may betray herself.
Jean Valjean had no experience of these miseries, the
only ones which are charming, and the only ones he did
not know, and on this account he did not comprehend the
grave significance of Cosette's silence. Still he noticed
that she became sad, and he became gloomy. Inexperience
was contending on both sides. Once he made an essay,
by asking Cosette, "Will you go to the Luxembourg?"
A beam illuminated Cosette's pale face; "Yes," she said.
They went there, but three months had elapsed, and Marius
no longer went there—there was no Marius present. The
next day Jean Valjean again asked Cosette, "Will you go
to the Luxembourg?" She answered sadly and gently,
"No." Jean Valjean was hurt by the sadness, and heart-
broken by the gentleness.

What was taking place in this young and already so
impenetrable mind? what was going to be accomplished?
what was happening to Cosette's soul? Sometimes, instead
of going to bed, Jean Valjean would remain seated by his
bedside with his head between his hands, and spent whole
nights in asking himself, "What has Cosette on her
mind?" and in thinking of the things of which she might
be thinking. Oh! How he lamented his self-denial and
his madness in bringing Cosette back to the world. He
was the poor hero of the sacrifice, seized and hurled down
by his own devotion! How he said to himself, "What have
I done?" However, nothing of this was visible to Cosette—
neither temper, nor roughness—it was ever the same serene,
kind face. Jean Valjean's manner was even more tender
and paternal than before; and if anything could have
evidenced his joy it was more gentleness.

On her side, Cosette was pining; she suffered from
Marius' absence, as she had revelled in his presence,
singularly, and not exactly knowing why. When Jean
Valjean ceased taking her for her usual walk, a feminine
instinct had whispered to her heart that she must not appear
to be attached to the Luxembourg, and that if she displayed
indifference in the matter her father would take her back
to it. But days, weeks, and months, succeeded each other,
for Jean Valjean had tacitly accepted Cosette's tacit consent.
She regretted it, but it was too late, and on the day when
they returned to the Luxembourg, Marius was no longer
there. He had disappeared then, it was all over : what
could she do? would she ever see him again? She felt

a contraction of the heart which nothing dilated and which daily increased : she remained crushed, absorbed, attentive to one thought alone, with a vague and fixed eye, like a person gazing through the darkness at the deep black spot where a phantom has just vanished. Still she did not allow Jean Valjean to see anything but her pallor, and her face was ever gentle to him. This pallor, though, was more than sufficient to render Jean Valjean anxious, and at times he would ask her :

" What is the matter with you ? "

And she answered :

" Nothing."

After a silence, she would add, as if guessing that he was sad too :

" And, father, is there anything the matter with you ? "

" With me ? oh nothing," he would reply.

These two beings, who had loved each other so exclusively, and one of them with such a touching love, and had lived for a long time one through the other, were now suffering side by side, one on account of the other, without confessing it, without anger, and with a smile.

The more unhappy of the two was Jean Valjean, for youth, even in its sorrow, has always a brilliancy of its own. He felt irresistibly that Cosette was slipping from him. In the isolated life they led, and since they had gone to reside in the Rue Plumet, they had one habit. They sometimes had the pleasure of going to see the sun rise, a species of sweet joy, which is agreeable to those who are entering life and those who are leaving it. To walk about at daybreak is equivalent, to the man who loves solitude, to walking about at night with the gaiety of nature added. The streets are deserted and the birds sing. Cosette, herself a bird, generally woke at an early hour. These morning excursions were arranged on the previous evening ; he proposed, and she accepted. This was arranged like a plot ; they went out before day, and it was a delight for Cosette, as these innocent eccentricities please youth. Jean Valjean had, as we know, a liking to go to but little-frequented places, to solitary nooks, and forgotten spots. There were at that time, in the vicinity of the gates of Paris, poor fields, almost forming part of the city, where sickly wheat grew in summer, and which in autumn, after the harvest was got in, did not look as if they had been reaped, but skinned. Jean Valjean had a predilection

for these fields, and Cosette did not feel wearied there ;
it was solitude for him and liberty for her. There she
became a little girl again ; she ran about and almost played,
she took off her bonnet, laid it on Jean Valjean's knees,
and plucked flowers. She watched the butterflies, but did
not catch them, for humanity and tenderness spring up
with love, and the maiden who has in her heart a trembling
and fragile ideal feels pity for a butterfly's wing. She
twined poppies into wreaths, which she placed on her head,
and when the sun poured its beams on them and rendered
them almost purple, they formed a fiery crown for her fresh
pink face. Even after their life had grown saddened they
kept up their habit of early walks.

CHAPTER LXXXVI.

THEIR life thus gradually became overcast ; only one amusement was left them which had formerly been a happiness,
and that was to carry bread to those who were starving,
and clothes to those who were cold. In these visits to the
poor, in which Cosette frequently accompanied Jean Valjean,
they found again some portion of their old expansiveness,
and, at times, when the day had been good, when a good deal
of distress had been relieved, and many children warmed
and reanimated, Cosette displayed a little gaiety at night.
It was at this period that they paid the visit to Jondrette's
den. The day after that visit Jean Valjean appeared at
an early hour in the pavilion, calm as usual, but with a large
wound in his left arm, which was very inflamed and
venomous, that resembled a burn, and which he accounted
for in some way or other. This wound kept him at home
for a whole month, for he would not see any medical man,
and when Cosette pressed him, he said, "Call in the dog-
doctor." Cosette dressed his wound morning and night
with an air of such divine and angelic happiness at being
useful to him, that Jean Valjean felt all his old joy
return, his fears and anxieties dissipated, and he gazed
at Cosette, saying, "Oh, the excellent wound ! the good
evil ! "

Cosette, seeing her father ill, had deserted the pavilion,
and regained her taste for the little outhouse and the back
court. She spent nearly the whole day by the side of Jean
Valjean, and read to him any books he chose, which were

generally travels. Jean Valjean was regenerated : his happiness returned with ineffable radiance ; the Luxembourg, the young unknown prowler, Cosette's coldness, all these soul-clouds disappeared, and he found himself saying, " I once imagined all that ; I am an old madman ! " His happiness was such that the frightful discovery of the Thénardiers in the Jondrettes, which was so unexpected, had to some extent glided over him. He had succeeded in escaping, his trail was lost, and what did he care for the rest ! he only thought of it to pity those wretches. They were in prison, and henceforth incapable of mischief, he thought, but what a lamentable family in distress ! In the convent Sister Ste Mechthilde had taught Cosette music ; she had a voice such as a linnet would have if it possessed a soul, and at times she sang melancholy songs in the wounded man's obscure room, which Jean Valjean was delighted with. Spring arrived, and the garden was so delicious at that season of the year, that Jean Valjean said to Cosette, " You never go out, and I wish you to take a stroll." "As you please, father," said Cosette. And, to obey her father, she resumed her walks in the garden, generally alone, for, as we have mentioned, Jean Valjean, who was probably afraid of being seen from the gate, hardly ever entered it.

Jean Valjean's wound had been a diversion ; when Cosette saw that her father suffered less, and was recovering and seemed happy, she felt a satisfaction which she did not even notice, for it came so softly and naturally. Then, too, it was the month of March, the days were drawing out, winter was departing, and it always takes with it some portion of our sorrow ; then came April, that daybreak of summer, fresh as every dawn, and gay like all childhoods, and somewhat tearful at times like the new-born babe that it is. Nature in that month has charming beams which pass from the sky, the clouds, the trees, the fields, and the flowers, into the human heart. Cosette was still too young for this April joy, which resembled her, not to penetrate her ; insensibly, and without suspecting it, the dark cloud departed from her mind. In spring there is light in sad souls, as there is at midday in cellars. Cosette was no longer so very sad ; it was so, but she did not attempt to account for it. In the morning, after breakfast, when she succeeded in drawing her father into the garden for a quarter of an hour, and walked him up and down, while supporting his bad arm, she did not notice that she laughed every moment and was happy. Jean Valjean was delighted to see her become ruddy-cheeked and fresh once more.

"Oh! the famous wound!" he repeated to himself in a low voice. And he was grateful to the Thénardiers.

Cosette's sorrow, so poignant and so sharp four or five months previously, had, without her knowledge, attained the convalescent stage. Nature, spring, youth, love for her father, the gaiety of the flowers and birds, filtered gradually day by day, and drop by drop, something that almost resembled oblivion into her virginal and young soul. Was the fire entirely extinguished? or were layers of ashes merely formed? The fact is, that she hardly felt at all the painful and burning point, and on the day when she suddenly thought of Marius, "Why," she said, "I had almost forgotten him." This same week she noticed, while passing the garden gate, a very handsome officer in the lancers, with a wasp-like waist, a delightful uniform, the cheeks of a girl, a sabre under his arm, waxed moustaches, and lacquered schapska. In other respects, he had light hair, blue eyes flush with his head, a round, vain, insolent, and pretty face; he was exactly the contrary of Marius. He had a cigar in his mouth, and Cosette supposed that he belonged to the regiment quartered in the barracks of the Rue de Babylone. The next day she saw him pass again, and remarked the hour. From this moment—was it an accident?—she saw him pass nearly every day. The officer's comrades perceived that there was in this badly-kept garden, and behind this poor, old-fashioned railing, a very pretty creature, who was nearly always there when the handsome lieutenant passed, who is no stranger to the reader, as his name was Théodule Gillenormand.

"Hilloh!" they said to him, "there's a little girl making eyes at you, just look at her."

"Have I the time," the lancer replied, "to look at all the girls who look at me?"

It was at this identical time that Marius was slowly descending to the abyss, and said, "If I could only see her again before I die!" If his wish had been realised, if he had at that moment seen Cosette looking at a lancer, he would have been unable to utter a word, but expired of grief. Whose fault would it have been? nobody's. Marius possessed one of those temperaments which bury themselves in chagrin and abide in it : Cosette was one of those who plunge into it and again emerge. Cosette, however, was passing through that dangerous moment, the fatal phase of feminine reverie left to itself, in which the heart of an isolated maiden resembles those vine tendrils which cling, according to chance, to the capital of a marble column or to the sign-post of an inn. It is a rapid and decisive moment, critical for every orphan, whether she be poor or rich. What was there in Cosette's soul ? passion calmed or lulled to sleep, love in a floating state : something which was limpid and brilliant, perturbed at a certain depth, and sombre lower still. The image of the handsome officer was reflected on the surface, but was there any reminiscence at the bottom, quite at the bottom ? perhaps so, but Cosette did not know.

A singular incident occurred.

In the first fortnight of April Jean Valjean went on a journey ; this, as we know, occurred from time to time at very lengthened intervals, and he remained away one or two days at the most. Where did he go ? no one knew, not even Cosette : once only she had accompanied him in a hackney coach, upon the occasion of one of these absences, to the corner of a little lane, which was called, "L'Impasse de la blanchette." He got out there, and the coach carried Cosette back to the Rue de Babylone. It was generally when money ran short in the house that Jean Valjean took these trips. Jean Valjean, then, was absent, and he had said, "I shall be back in three days." At night Cosette was alone in the drawing-room, and in order to wile away the time, she opened her piano and began singing to her own accompaniment the song of Euryanthe, "Hunters wandering in the wood," which is probably the finest thing we possess in the shape of music. When she had finished she remained passive, till she suddenly fancied she heard some one walking in the garden. It could not be her father, for he was away, and it could not be Toussaint, as she was in bed, for it was ten o'clock at night. Cosette went to the drawing-room shutters, which were closed, and put her ear to them ; and it seemed to her that it was the footfall of a man who was walking very gently. She hurried up to her room on the first-floor, opened a Venetian frame in her shutter, and looked out into the garden. The moon was shining bright as day, and there was nobody in it. She opened her window : the garden was perfectly calm, **and all** that could be seen of the street was as deserted as usual.

Cosette thought that she had been mistaken. She had supposed that she heard the noise; it was an hallucination produced by Weber's gloomy and prodigious chorus, which opens before the mind prodigious depths, which trembles before the eye like a dizzy forest, in which we hear the cracking of the dead branches under the restless feet of the hunters, of whom we catch a glimpse in the obscurity. She thought no more of it. Moreover, Cosette was not naturally very timid: she had in her veins some of the blood of the gipsy, and the adventurer who goes about barefooted. As we may remember, she was rather a lark than a dove, and she had a stern and brave temper.

The next evening, at nightfall, she was walking about the garden. In the midst of the confused thoughts which occupied her mind, she fancied she could distinguish now and then a noise like that of the previous night, as if some one were walking in the gloom under the trees not far from her, but she said to herself that nothing so resembles the sound of a footfall on grass as the grating of two branches together, and she took no heed of it—besides, she saw nothing. She left the " thicket," and had a small grass-plat to cross ere she reached the house. The moon, which had just risen behind her, projected Cosette's shadow, as she left the clump of bushes, upon the grass in front of her, and she stopped in terror. By the side of her shadow the moon distinctly traced on the grass another singularly startling and terrible shadow—a shadow with a hat on its head. It was like the shadow of a man standing at the edge of the clump a few paces behind Cosette. For a moment she was unable to speak or cry, or call out, or stir, or turn her head, but at last she collected all her courage and boldly turned round. There was nobody; she looked on the ground and the shadow had disappeared. She went back into the shrubs, bravely searched in every corner, went as far as the railings, and discovered nothing. She felt really chilled: was it again an hallucination? what! two days in succession? one hallucination might pass, but two! The alarming point was, that the shadow was most certainly not a ghost, for ghosts never wear round hats.

The next day Jean Valjean returned, and Cosette told him what she fancied she had seen and heard. She expected to be reassured, and that her father would shrug his shoulders and say, "You are a little goose,"—but Jean Valjean became anxious.

"Perhaps it is nothing," he said to her. He left her with some excuse, and went into the garden, where she saw him examine the railings with considerable attention. In the night she woke up ; this time she was certain, and she distinctly heard some one walking just under her windows. She walked to her shutter and opened it. There was in the garden really a man holding a large stick in his hand. At the moment when she was going to cry out the moon lit up the man's face—it was her father. She went to bed again, saying, "He seems really very anxious!" Jean Valjean passed that and the two following nights in the garden, and Cosette saw him through the hole in her shutter. On the third night the moon was beginning to rise later, and it might be about one in the morning when she heard a hearty burst of laughter, and her father's voice calling her :

"Cosette!"

She leapt out of bed, put on her dressing-gown, and opened her window ; her father was standing on the grass-plat below.

"I have woke you up to reassure you," he said ; "look at this,—here's your shadow in the round hat."

And he showed her on the grass a shadow, which the moon designed, and which really looked rather like the spectre of a man wearing a round hat. It was an outline produced by a zinc chimney-pot with a cowl, which rose above an adjoining roof. Cosette also began laughing, all her mournful suppositions fell away, and the next morning at breakfast she jested at the ill-omened garden, haunted by the ghost of chimney-pots. Jean Valjean quite regained his ease ; as for Cosette, she did not notice particularly whether the chimney-pot were really in the direction of the shadow which he had seen or fancied she saw, and whether the moon were in the same part of the heavens. She did not cross-question herself as to the singularity of a chimney-pot which is afraid of being caught in the act, and retires when its shadow is looked at, for the shadow did retire when Cosette turned round, and she fancied herself quite certain of that fact. Cosette became quite reassured, for the demonstration seemed to her perfect, and the thought left her brain that there could have been any one walking about the garden by night. A few days afterwards, however, a new incident occurred.

CHAPTER LXXXVII.

IN the garden, near the railings looking out on the street, there was a stone bench, protected from the gaze of the curious by a hedge, but which could have been easily reached by thrusting an arm through the railings and the hedge. One evening in this same month of April, Jean Valjean had gone out, and Cosette, after sunset, was seated on this bench. The wind was freshening in the trees, and Cosette was reflecting. An objectless sorrow was gradually gaining on her, the invincible sorrow which night produces, and which comes perhaps—for who knows?—from the mystery of the tomb which is yawning at the moment. Possibly Fantine was in that shadow.

Cosette rose, and slowly went round the garden, walking on the dew-laden grass, and saying to herself through the sort of melancholy somnambulism in which she was plunged, "I ought to have wooden shoes to walk in the garden at this hour; I shall catch cold." She returned to the bench, but at the moment when she was going to sit down she noticed at the place she had left a rather large stone, which had evidently not been there a moment before. Cosette looked at the stone, asking herself what it meant; all at once the idea that the stone had not reached the bench of itself, that some one had placed it there, and that an arm had been passed through the grating, occurred to her and frightened her. This time it was a real fear, for there was the stone. No doubt was possible; she did not touch it, but fled without daring to look behind her, sought refuge in the house, and at once shuttered, barred, and bolted the French window opening on the steps. Then she asked Toussaint:

"Has my father come in?"

"No, miss."

(We have indicated once for all Toussaint's stammering, and we ask leave no longer to accentuate it, as we feel a musical notation of an infirmity to be repulsive.)

Jean Valjean, a thoughtful man, and stroller by night, often did not return till a late hour.

"Toussaint," Cosette continued, "be careful to put up the bars to the shutters looking on the garden, and to place the little iron things in the rings that close them."

"Oh, I am sure I will, miss."

Toussaint did not fail, and Cosette was well aware of the fact, but she could not refrain from adding :

"For it is so desolate here."

"Well, that's true," said Toussaint ; "we might be murdered before we had the time to say Ouf! and then, too, master does not sleep in the house. But don't be frightened, miss. I fasten up the windows like Bastilles. Lone women ! I should think that is enough to make a body shudder. Only think ! to see men coming into your bedroom and hear them say, 'Hold your tongue !' and then they begin to cut your throat. It is not so much the dying, for everybody dies, and we know that we must do so, but it is the abomination of feeling those fellows touch you ; and then their knives are not sharp, perhaps ; oh, Lord !"

"Hold your tongue," said Cosette, "and fasten up everything securely."

Cosette, terrified by the drama improvised by Toussaint, and perhaps too by the apparitions of the last week, which returned to her mind, did not even dare to say to her, "Just go and look at the stone laid on the bench," for fear of having to open the garden gate again, and the men might walk in. She had all the doors and windows carefully closed, made Toussaint examine the whole house from cellar to attic, locked herself in her bedroom, looked under the bed, and slept badly. The whole night through she saw the stone as large as a mountain and full of caverns. At sunrise—the peculiarity of sunrise is to make us laugh at all our terrors of the night, and our laughter is always proportioned to the fear we have felt—at sunrise, Cosette, on waking, saw her terror like a nightmare, and said to herself, "What could I be thinking about ! it was like the steps which I fancied I heard last week in the garden at night ! It is like the shadow of the chimney-pot, am I going to turn coward now ?" The sun which poured through the crevices of her shutters and made the damask curtains one mass of purple, reassured her so fully that all faded away in her mind, even to the stone.

"There was no more a stone on the bench than there was a man in a round hat in the garden. I dreamt of the stone like the rest."

She dressed herself, went down into the garden, and felt a cold perspiration all over her—the stone was there. But this only lasted for a moment, for what is terror by night is curiosity by day.

" Nonsense ! " she said, " I'll see."

She raised the stone, which was of some size, and there was something under it that resembled a letter ; it was an envelope of white paper. Cosette seized it ; there was no address on it, and it was not sealed up. Still, the envelope, though open, was not empty, for papers could be seen inside. Cosette no longer suffered from terror, nor was it curiosity ; it was a commencement of anxiety. Cosette took out a small quire of paper, each page of which was numbered, and bore several lines written in a very nice and delicate hand, so Cosette thought. She looked for a name, but there was none ; for a signature, but there was none either. For whom was the packet intended ? probably for herself, as a hand had laid it on the bench. From whom did it come ? An irresistible fascination seized upon her ; she tried to turn her eyes away from these pages, which trembled in her hand. She looked at the sky, the street, the acacias all bathed in light, the pigeons circling round an adjoining roof, and then her eye settled on the manuscript, and she said to herself that she must know what was inside it. This is what she read :

The reduction of the Universe to a single being, the expansion of a single being as far as God, such is love.

Love is the salutation of the angel to the stars.

———

How sad is the soul when it is sad from love !

———

What a void is the absence of the being who alone fills the world ! Oh ! how true it is that the beloved being becomes God ! One would conceive that God would be jealous if the Father of all had not evidently made creation for the soul, and the soul for love !

———

A glimpse of a smile under a white crape hat with a lilac coronet is enough for the soul to enter into the palace of dreams.

———

God is behind all things, but all things hide God. Things are black, creatures are opaque. To love a being is to render her transparent.

———

Certain thoughts are prayers. There are moments when,

whatever be the attitude of the body, the soul is on its knees.

_____

Separated lovers deceive absence by a thousand chimerical things which still have their reality. They are prevented from seeing each other, they cannot write to each other; they find a multitude of mysterious means of correspondence. They commission the song of the birds, the perfume of flowers, the laughter of children, the light of the sun, the sighs of the wind, the beams of the stars, the whole creation. And why not? All the works of God were made to serve love. Love is powerful enough to charge all nature with its messages.

O Spring! thou art a letter which I write to her.

_____

The future belongs still more to the heart than to the mind. To love is the only thing which can occupy and fill up eternity. The infinite requires the inexhaustible.

_____

Love partakes of the soul itself. It is of the same nature. Like it, it is a divine spark; like it, it is incorruptible, indivisible, imperishable. It is a point of fire which is within us, which is immortal and infinite; which nothing can limit and which nothing can extinguish. We feel it burn even in the marrow of our bones, and we see it radiate even to the depths of the sky.

_____

God can add nothing to the happiness of those who love one another but to give them unending duration. After a life of love, an eternity of love is an augmentation indeed; but to increase in its intensity the ineffable felicity which love gives to the soul in this world is impossible, even with God. God is the plenitude of heaven; love is the plenitude of man.

_____

When love has melted and mingled two beings into an angelic and sacred unity, the secret of life is found for them; they are then but the two terms of a single destiny; they are then but the two wings of a single spirit. Love, soar!

_____

The day that a woman who is passing before you sheds a light upon you as she goes, you are lost, you love. You have then but one thing to do: to think of her so earnestly that she will be compelled to think of you.

What love begins can be finished only by God.

True love is in despair and in raptures over a glove lost or a handkerchief found, and it requires eternity for its devotion and its hopes.   It is composed at the same time of the infinitely great and the infinitely small.

If you are stone, be lodestone; if you are plant, be sensitive; if you are man, be love.

Nothing suffices love.   We have happiness, we wish for paradise; we have paradise, we wish for Heaven.

O ye who love each other, all this is in love.   Be wise enough to find it.   Love has, as much as Heaven, contemplation, and more than Heaven, passionate delight.

"Does she still come to the Luxembourg?" "No, Monsieur."   "She hears Mass in this church, does she not?"   "She comes here no more."   "Does she still live in this house?"   "She has moved away!"   "Whither has she gone to live?"   "She did not say."
What a gloomy thing not to know the address of one's soul?

Love has its childlikenesses, the other passions have their littlenesses.   Shame on the passions which render man little!   Honour to that which makes him a child!

There is a strange thing, do you know it?   I am in the night.   There is a being who has gone away and carried the heavens with her.

You who suffer because you love, love still more.   To die of love is to live by it.

O joy of the birds!   It is because they have their nest that they have their song.

Love is a celestial respiration of the air of paradise.

Deep hearts, wise minds take life as God has made it; it is a long trial, an unintelligible preparation for the unknown destiny.   This destiny, the true one, begins for man at the first step in the interior of the tomb. Then something appears to him and he begins to discern the definite. The definite! Think of this word. The living see the infinite; the definite reveals itself only to the dead. Meantime, love and suffer, hope and contemplate. Woe, alas! to him who shall have loved bodies, forms, appearances only. Death will take all from him. Try to love souls, you shall find them again.

————

I met in the street a very poor young man who was in love. His hat was old, his coat was threadbare—there were holes at his elbows; the water passed through his shoes and the stars through his soul.

————

What a grand thing to be loved! What a grander thing still to love! The heart becomes heroic through passion. It is no longer composed of anything but what is pure; it no longer rests upon anything but what is elevated and great. An unworthy thought can no more spring up in it than a nettle upon a glacier. The soul lofty and serene, inaccessible to common passions and common emotions, rising above the clouds and the shadows of this world, its follies, its falsehoods, its hates, its vanities, its miseries, inhabits the blue of the skies, and only feels more the deep and subterranean commotions of destiny, as the summit of the mountains feels the quaking of the earth.

————

Were there not some one who loved, the sun would be extinguished.

————

While reading these lines Cosette gradually fell into a reverie, and at the moment when she raised her eyes from the last page the pretty officer passed triumphantly in front of the gate, for it was his hour. Cosette found him hideous. She began gazing at the roll of paper again; it was in an exquisite handwriting, Cosette thought, all written by the same hand, but with different inks, some very black, others pale, as when ink is put in the stand, and consequently on different days. It was, therefore, a thought expanded on the paper, sigh by sigh, irregularly, without order, without choice, without purpose, accidentally. Cosette had never read anything like it; this manuscript, in which she saw more light than obscurity, produced on her the effect of the door of a shrine left ajar. Each of these mysterious lines flashed in her eyes, and inundated her heart with a strange light. The education which she had received had always spoken to her of the soul, and not of love, much as if a person were to speak of the burning log and say nothing about the flame. This manuscript of fifteen pages suddenly and gently revealed to her the whole of love, sorrow, destiny, life, eternity, the beginning and the end. It was like a hand which opened and threw upon her a galaxy of beams. She felt in these few lines an impassioned, ardent, generous, and honest nature, a sacred will, an immense grief, and an immense hope ; a contracted heart, and an expanded ecstasy. What was the manuscript? a letter. A letter without address, name, or signature, pressing, and disinterested, an enigma composed of truths, a love-message fit to be borne by an angel and read by a virgin ; a rendezvous appointed off the world, a sweet love-letter written by a phantom to a shadow. It was a tranquil and crushed absent man, who seemed ready to seek a refuge in death, and who sent to his absent love the secret of destiny, the key of life. It had been written with the foot in the grave and the hand in heaven, and these lines, which had fallen one by one on the paper, were what might be called drops of the soul.

And now, from whom could these pages come? Who could have written them? Cosette did not hesitate for a moment,—only from one man, from *him*! Daylight had returned to her mind and everything reappeared. She experienced an extraordinary joy and a profound agony. It was he ! he who wrote to her ! he had been there ! his arm had been passed through the railings ! while she was forgetting him he had found her again ! But had she forgotten him ? no, never ! she was mad to have thought so for a moment, for she had ever loved, ever adored him. The fire was covered, and had smouldered for a while, but, as she now plainly saw, it had spread its ravages, and again burst into a flame which entirely kindled her. This letter was like a spark that had fallen from the other soul into hers ; she felt the fire begin again, and she was penetrated by every word of the manuscript. "Oh yes," she said to herself, "how well I recognise all this ! I had read it all already in his eyes."

As she finished reading it for the third time Lieutenant Théodule returned past the railings, and clanked his spurs on the pavement. Cosette was obliged to raise her eyes, and she found him insipid, silly, stupid, useless, fatuous, displeasing, impertinent, and very ugly. The officer thought himself bound to smile, and she turned away ashamed and indignant; she would have gladly thrown something at his head. She ran away, re-entered the house, and locked herself in her bedroom, to re-read the letter, learn it by heart, and dream. When she had read it thoroughly she kissed it and hid it in her bosom. It was all over. Cosette had fallen back into the profound seraphic love, the Paradisaic abyss had opened again. The whole day through Cosette was in a state of bewilderment; she hardly thought, and her ideas were confused in her brain; she could not succeed in forming any conjectures, and she hoped through a tremor, what? vague things. She did not dare promise herself anything, and she would not refuse herself anything. A pallor passed over her face, and a quiver over her limbs, and she fancied at moments that it was all a chimera, and said to herself, "Is it real?" then she felt the well-beloved paper under her dress, pressed it to her heart, felt the corners against her flesh, and if Jean Valjean had seen her at that moment he would have shuddered at the luminous and strange joy which overflowed from her eyelids. "Oh yes," she thought, "it is certainly his! this comes from him for me!" And she said to herself that an intervention of the angels, a celestial accident, had restored him to her. O transfiguration of love! O dreams! this celestial accident, this intervention of angels, was the ball of bread cast by one robber to another from the Charlemagne yard to the lions' den, over the buildings of La Force.

When night came Jean Valjean went out, and Cosette dressed herself. She arranged her hair in the way that best became her, and put on a dress whose body, being cut a little too low, displayed the whole of the neck, and was therefore, as girls say, "rather indecent." It was not the least in the world indecent, but it was prettier than the former fashion. She dressed herself in this way without knowing why. Was she going out? No. Did she expect a visitor? No. She went down into the garden as it grew dark; Toussaint was engaged in her kitchen, which looked out on the back-yard. Cosette began walking under the branches, removing them from time to time with her hand, as some were very low, and thus reached the bench. The stone was still there, and she sat down and laid her beautiful white hand on the stone, as if to caress and thank it. All at once she had that indescribable feeling which people

experience even without seeing, when some one is standing
behind them. She turned her head and rose—it was he.
He was bareheaded, and seemed pale and thin, and his
black clothes could be scarce distinguished. The twilight
rendered his glorious forehead livid, and covered his eyes
with darkness, and he had, beneath a veil of incomparable
gentleness, something belonging to death and night. His
face was lit up by the flush of departing day, and by the
thoughts of an expiring soul. He seemed as if he were
not yet a spectre, but was no longer a man. His hat was
thrown among the shrubs a few paces from him. Cosette,
though ready to faint, did not utter a cry; she slowly
recoiled, as she felt herself attracted, but he did not stir.
Through the ineffable sadness that enveloped him she felt
the glance of the eyes which she could not see. Cosette,
in recoiling, came to a tree, and leaned against it; had it
not been for this tree she would have fallen. Then she
heard his voice, that voice which she had really never heard
before, scarce louder than the rustling of the foliage, as he
murmured :

"Pardon me for being here ; my heart is swollen, I could
not live as I was, and I have come. Have you read what
I placed on that bench? do you recognise me at all ? do
not be frightened at me. Do you remember that day when
you looked at me, now so long ago ? It was in the Luxembourg garden, near the Gladiator, and the days on which
you passed before me were June 16 and July 2 : it is nearly
a year ago. I have not seen you for a very long time
now. I inquired of the woman who lets out chairs, and
she said that you no longer came there. You lived in the
Rue de l'Ouest, on the third-floor front of a new house.
You see that I know. I followed you, what else could I
do ? and then you disappeared. I fancied that I saw you
pass once as I was reading the papers under the Odéon
Arcade, and ran after you, but no, it was a person wearing
a bonnet like yours. At night I come here—fear nothing,
no one sees me—and I walk very softly that you may
not hear me, for you might be alarmed. The other
evening I was behind you, you turned round, and I fled.
Once I heard you sing, and I was happy ; does it harm
you that I should listen to you through the shutters while
singing ? no, it cannot harm you. You see you are my
angel, so let me come now and then, and I believe that I
am going to die. If you only knew how I adore you ! But

forgive me, I am speaking to you, I know not what I am
saying, perhaps I offend you—do I offend you?"

"Oh, my mother!" she said.

And she sank down as if she were dying. He seized her
in his arms, and pressed her to his heart, not knowing
what he did. He supported her while himself tottering.
He felt as if his head were full of smoke; flashes passed
between his eyelashes; his ideas left him, and it seemed to
him as if he were accomplishing a religious act, and yet
committing a profanation. However, he had not the least
desire for this ravishing creature, whose form he felt against
his chest; he was distractedly in love. She took his hand,
and laid it on her heart; he felt the paper there, and
stammered:

"You love me then?"

She answered in so low a voice, that it was almost an
inaudible breath:

"Silence! you know I do."

And she hid her blushing face in the chest of the proud
and intoxicated young man. He fell on to the bench, and
she by his side. They no longer found words, and the
stars were beginning to twinkle. How came it that their
lips met? how comes it that the bird sings, the snow melts,
the rose opens, May bursts into life, and the dawn grows
white behind the black trees on the rustling tops of the
hills? One kiss, and that was all; both trembled and
gazed at each other in the darkness with flashing eyes.
They neither felt the fresh night nor the cold stone, nor
the damp grass, nor the moist soil,—they looked at each
other, and their hearts were full of thoughts. Their hands
were clasped without their cognisance. She did not ask
him, did not even think of it, how he had managed to enter
the garden, for it seemed to her so simple that he should be
there. From time to time Marius' knee touched Cosette's
knee, and both quivered. At intervals Cosette stammered
a word; her soul trembled on her lips like the dewdrop on
a flower.

Gradually they conversed, and expansiveness succeeded
the silence which is plenitude. The night was serene and
splendid above their heads, and these two beings, pure as
spirits, told each other everything,—their dreams, their intoxication, their ecstasy, their chimeras, their depressions,
how they had adored and longed for each other at a
distance, and their mutual despair when they ceased to

meet. They confided to each other in an ideal intimacy which nothing henceforth could increase, all their most hidden and mysterious thoughts. They told each other, with a candid faith in their illusions, all that love, youth, and the remnant of childhood which they still had, brought to their minds; their two hearts were poured into each other, so that at the end of an hour the young man had the maiden's soul and the maiden his. They were mutually penetrated, enchanted, and dazzled. When they had finished, when they had told each other everything, she laid her head on his shoulder and asked him:

"What is your name?"

"Marius," he said; "and yours?"

"Mine is Cosette."

CHAPTER LXXXVIII.

AT La Force, about this time, the following had occurred. An escape had been concerted between Babet, Brujon, Gueulemer, and Thénardier, although Thénardier was in secret confinement. Babet had managed the affair on his own account during the day, and Montparnasse was to help them outside. Brujon, while spending a month in a punishment room, had time, first, to make a rope, and, secondly, to ripen a plan. Formerly, these severe places, in which prison discipline leaves the prisoner to himself, were composed of four stone walls, a stone ceiling, a brick pavement, a camp-bed, a grated skylight, and a gate lined with iron, and were called dungeons; but the dungeon was considered too horrible, so now it is composed of an iron gate, a grated skylight, a camp-bed, a brick pavement, a stone ceiling, four stone walls, and it is called a "punishment room." A little daylight is visible about midday. The inconvenience of these rooms, which, as we see, are not dungeons, is to leave beings to think who ought to be set to work. Brujon, therefore, reflected, and he left the punishment room with a cord. As he was considered very dangerous in the Charlemagne yard, he was placed in the New Building, and the first thing he found there was Gueulemer, the second a nail; Gueulemer, that is to say, crime, and a nail, that is to say, liberty.

Brujon, of whom it is time to form a complete idea, was,

with the appearance of a delicate complexion and a deeply premeditated languor, a polished, intelligent robber, who possessed a caressing look and an atrocious smile. His look was the result of his will, and his smile the result of his nature. His first studies in his art were directed to roofs, and he had given a great impulse to the trade of lead-stealers, who strip roofs and carry away gutters by the process called *au gras double.* What finally rendered the moment favourable for an attempted escape was that workmen were at this very moment engaged in relaying and retipping the prison slates. The St. Bernard was not absolutely isolated from the Charlemagne and St. Louis yards, for there were on the roof scaffolding and ladders, in other words, bridges and staircases, on the side of deliverance. The New Building, which was the most cracked and decrepit affair possible to imagine, was the weak point of the building. Saltpetre had so gnawed the walls that it had been found necessary to prop up and shore the ceilings of the dormitories, because stones became detached and fell on the prisoners' beds. In spite of this antiquity, the error was committed of confining in the New Building the most dangerous prisoners, and placing in it the "heavy cases," as is said in the prison jargon. The New Building contained four sleeping-wards, one above the other, and a garret-floor called the "Fine Air." A large stove pipe, probably belonging to some old kitchen of the Ducs de la Force, started from the ground-floor, passed through the four storeys, cut in two the sleeping-wards, in which it figured as a sort of flattened pillar, and issued through a hole in the roof. Gueulemer and Brujon were in the same ward, and had been placed through precaution on the ground-floor. Accident willed it that the head of their beds rested against the stove pipe. Thénardier was exactly above their heads in the attic called Fine Air.

The passer-by, who stops in the Rue Culture Sainte Catherine, after passing the firemen's barracks, and in front of the bath-house gateway, sees a courtyard full of flowers and shrubs in boxes, at the end of which is a small white rotunda with two wings, enlivened by green shutters, the bucolic dream of Jean Jacques. Not ten years ago there rose above this rotunda a black, enormous, frightful, naked wall, which was the outer wall of La Force. This wall behind this rotunda was like a glimpse of Milton caught behind Berquin. High though it was, this wall was surmounted by an even blacker roof, which could be seen beyond,—it was the roof of the New Building.

Four dormer-windows protected by bars could be seen in it, and they were the windows of Fine Air, and a chimney passed through the roof, which was the chimney of the sleeping-wards. Fine Air, the attic-floor of the New Building, was a species of large hall, closed with triple gratings and iron-lined doors, starred with enormous nails. When you entered by the north end, you had on your left the four dormers, and on your right facing these, four square and spacious cages, separated by narrow passages, built up to breast-height of masonry, and the rest to the roof of iron bars. Thénardier had been confined in solitary punishment since the night of Febuary 3. It was never discovered how, or by what connivance, he succeeded in procuring and concealing a bottle of that prepared wine, invented, so 'tis said, by Desrues, in which a narcotic is mixed, and which the band of the Endormeurs rendered celebrated. There are in many prisons treacherous turnkeys, half gaolers, half robbers, who assist in escapes, and sell to the police a faithless domesticity.

On this very night, then, when little Gavroche picked up the two straying children, Brujon and Gueulemer, who knew that Babet, who had escaped that same morning, was waiting for them in the street with Montparnasse, gently rose, and began breaking open with a nail, which Brujon had found, the stove pipe against which their beds were. The rubbish fell on Brujon's bed, so that it was not heard, and the gusts of wind mingled with the thunder shook the doors on their hinges, and produced a frightful and hideous row in the prison. Those prisoners who awoke pretended to fall asleep again, and left Brujon and Gueulemer to do as they pleased ; and Brujon was skilful, and Gueulemer was vigorous. Before any sound had reached the watchman sleeping in the grated cell which looked into the ward, the wall was broken through, the chimney escaladed, the iron trellis which closed the upper opening of the chimney forced, and the two formidable bandits were on the roof. The rain and the wind were tremendous, and the roof was slippery.

"What a fine night for an escape!" said Brujon.

An abyss of six feet in width and eighty feet deep separated them from the surrounding wall, and at the bottom of this abyss they could see a sentry's musket gleaming in the darkness. They fastened to the ends of the chimney bars which they had just broken the rope which Brujon had woven in the cell, threw the other end over the outer wall, crossed the abyss at a bound, clung to the coping of the wall, bestraddled it, glided in turn along the rope to a little roof which joins the bath-house, pulled their rope to them, jumped into the yard of the bath-house, pulled the porter's string, opened the gateway, and found themselves in the street. Not three-quarters of an hour had elapsed since they were standing on the bed, nail in hand, and with their plan in their heads ; a few minutes after, they had rejoined Babet and Montparnasse, who were prowling in the neighbourhood. On drawing the cord to them they broke it, and a piece had remained fastened to the chimney on the roof, but they had met with no other accident beyond almost entirely skinning their fingers. On this night Thénardier was warned, though it was impossible to discover how, and did not go to sleep. At about one in the morning, when the night was very black, he saw two shadows passing, in the rain and gusts, the window opposite his cage. One stopped just long enough to give a look ; it was Brujon. Thénardier saw him, and understood—that was enough for him. Thénardier, reported to be a burglar, and detained on the charge of attempting to obtain money at night by violence, was kept under constant watch, and a sentry, relieved every two hours, walked in front of his cage with a loaded musket. The Fine Air was lighted by a skylight, and the prisoner had on his feet a pair of fetters weighing fifty pounds. Every day at four in the afternoon, a turnkey, escorted by two mastiffs—such things still happened at that day—entered his cage, placed near his bed a black loaf of two pounds' weight, a water-jug, and a bowl of very weak broth in which a few beans floated, inspected his fetters, and tapped the bars. This man with his dogs returned twice during the night.

Thénardier had obtained permission to keep a sort of iron pin which he used to nail his bread to the wall, in order, as he said, "to preserve it from the rats." As Thénardier was under a constant watch, this pin did not seem dangerous ; still it was remembered at a later day that a turnkey had said, "It would be better only to leave him a wooden skewer." At two in the morning the sentry, who was an old soldier, was changed, and a recruit substituted for him. A few minutes after, the

man with the dogs paid his visit, and went away without
having noticed anything, except the youth and peasant
look of the "Tourlourou." Two hours after, when they
came to relieve this conscript, they found him asleep, and
lying like a log by the side of Thénardier's cage. As
for the prisoner, he was no longer there ; his severed fetters
lay on the ground, and there was a hole in the ceiling
of his cage, and another above it in the roof. A plank
of his bed had been torn out and carried off, for it could
not be found. In the cell was also found the half-empty
bottle, containing the rest of the drugged wine with which
the young soldier had been sent to sleep. The soldier's
bayonet had disappeared. At the moment when all this
was discovered, Thénardier was supposed to be out of
reach ; the truth was, that he was no longer in the New
Building, but was still in great danger. Thénardier, on
reaching the roof of the New Building, found the remainder
of Brujon's rope hanging from the chimney bars, but as
the broken cord was much too short, he was unable to
cross the outer wall as Brujon and Gueulemer had done.

When you turn out of the Rue des Ballets into the
Rue du Roi de Sicile, you notice almost directly on your
right a dirty hole. In the last century a house stood here,
of which only the back wall exists, a perfect ruin of
a wall which rises to the height of a third storey between
the adjacent buildings. This ruin can be recognised by
two large square windows, still visible ; the centre one,
the one nearest the right-hand gable, is barred by a shored-
up beam, and through these windows could be seen,
formerly, a lofty lugubrious wall, which was a portion of
the outer wall of La Force. The gap which the demolished
house has left in the street is half filled up with a hoarding
of rotten planks, supported by five stone pillars, and inside
is a small hut built against the still standing ruin. The
boarding has a door in it which, a few years ago, was
merely closed with a hasp. It was the top of this ruin
which Thénardier had attained a little after three in the
morning. How did he get there? This was never explained or understood. The lightning flashes must at once
have impeded and helped him. Did he employ the ladders
and scaffolding of the slaters to pass from roof to roof, over
the buildings of the Charlemagne yard, those of the St.
Louis yard, the outer, and thence reach the ruined wall in
the Rue du Roi de Sicile? But there were gaps in this

route which seemed to render it impossible. Had he laid
the plank from his bed as a bridge from the roof of Fine
Air to the outer wall, and crawled on his stomach along
the coping, all round the prison till he reached the ruin?
But the outer wall of La Force was very irregular, it rose
and sank; and then, too, the sentries must have seen
the fugitive's dark outline,—and thus the road taken by
Thénardier remains almost inexplicable. Had he, illumined
by that frightful thirst for liberty which changes precipices
into moats, iron bars into reeds, a cripple into an athlete,
a gouty patient into a bird, stupidity into instinct, instinct
into intellect, and intellect into genius, invented and improvised a third mode of escape? However this may
be, Thénardier, dripping with perspiration, wet through
with rain, with his clothes in rags, his hands scarified,
his elbows bleeding, and his knees lacerated, reached
the ruin-wall, lay down full length on it, and then his
strength failed him. A perpendicular wall as high as a
three-storeyed house separated him from the street, and
the rope he had was too short. He waited there, pale,
exhausted, despairing, though just now so hopeful, still
covered by night, but saying to himself that day would
soon come; horrified at the thought that he should shortly
hear it strike four from the neighbouring clock of St. Paul,
the hour when the sentry would be changed and be found
asleep under the hole in the roof. Thénardier regarded
with stupor at such a depth below, and in the light of the
lamps, the wet black pavement—that desired and terrific
pavement which was death and which was liberty. He
asked himself whether his three accomplices had succeeded
in escaping, whether they were waiting for him, and if they
would come to his help? He listened: excepting a patrol,
no one had passed through the street since he had been
lying there. Nearly all the market carts from Montreuil,
Charonne, Vincennes, and Bercy came into town by the
Rue St. Antoine.

Four o'clock struck, and Thénardier trembled. A few
minutes after, the startled and confused noise which follows
the discovery of an escape broke out in the prison. The
sound of doors being opened and shut, the creaking of gates
on their hinges, the tumult at the guardroom, and the clang
of musket butts on the pavement of the yards, reached his
ears; lights flashed past the grated windows of the sleeping-
wards, a torch ran along the roof of the New Building, and

the sappers were called out. Three caps which the torch lit up in the rain, came and went along the roofs, and at the same time Thénardier saw, in the direction of the Bastille, a livid gleam mournfully whitening the sky. He was on the top of a wall ten inches wide, lying in the pitiless rain, with a gulf on his right hand and on his left, unable to stir, suffering from the dizziness of a possible fall and the horror of a certain arrest, and his mind, like the clapper of a bell, went from one of these ideas to the other : " Dead if I fall, caught if I remain. " In this state of agony he suddenly saw in the still perfectly dark street, a man, who glided along the walls and came from the Rue Pavée, stop in the gap over which Thénardier was, as it were, suspended. This man was joined by a second, who walked with similar caution, then by a third, and then by a fourth. When these men were together, one of them raised the hasp of the hoarding gate, and all four entered the enclosure where the hut is, and stood exactly under Thénardier. These men had evidently selected this place to consult in, in order not to be seen by passers-by, or the sentry guarding the wicket of La Force a few paces distant. We must say, too, that the rain kept this sentry confined to his box. Thénardier, unable to distinguish their faces, listened to their remarks with the desperate attention of a wretch who feels himself lost. He felt something like hope pass before his eyes, when he heard these men talking slang. The first said, in a low voice but distinctly, something which we had better translate.

" Let us be off. What are we doing here ? "

The second replied :

" It is raining hard enough to put out the fire of hell. And then the police will pass soon ; besides, there is a sentry on. We shall get ourselves arrested here. "

Two words employed, *icigo* and *icicaille*, which both mean here, and which belong, the first to the flash language of the barrières, and the second to that of the Temple, were rays of light for Thénardier. By *icigo* he recognised Brujon, who was a prowler at the barrières, and by *icicaille* Babet, who, among all his other trades, had been a second-hand clothes-dealer at the Temple. The antique slang of the great century is only talked now at the Temple, and Babet was the only man who spoke it in its purity. Had it not been for *icicaille*, Thénardier could not have recognised him, for he had completely altered his voice. In the meanwhile the third man had interfered.

"There is nothing to hurry us, so let us wait a little. What is there to tell us that he does not want us?"

Through this, which was only French, Thénardier recognised Montparnasse, whose pride it was to understand all the slang dialects and not speak one of them. As for the fourth man, he held his tongue, but his wide shoulders denounced him, and Thénardier did not hesitate; it was Gueulemer. Brujon replied almost impetuously, but still in a low voice:

"What is that you are saying? The landlord has not been able to escape. A man must be a clever hand to tear up his shirt and cut his sheets in slips to make a rope; to make holes in doors; manufacture false papers; make false keys; file his fetters through; hang his rope out of the window; hide and disguise himself. The old chap cannot have done this, for he does not know how to work."

Babet added, still in the correct classic slang which Poiailler and Cartouche spoke, and which is to the new, bold, and coloured slang which Brujon employed what the language of Racine is to that of André Chénier.

"Your landlord has been caught in the act, for he is only an apprentice. He has let himself be duped by a spy, perhaps by a sheep, who played the pal. Listen, Montparnasse; do you hear those shouts in the prison? You saw all those candles; he is caught again, and will get off with twenty years. I am not frightened, I am no coward, as is well known, but there is nothing to be done, and we shall be trapped. Do not feel offended, but come with us, and let us drink a bottle of old wine together."

"Friends must not be left in a difficulty," Montparnasse growled.

"I tell you he is caught again," Brujon resumed, "and at this moment the landlord is not worth a halfpenny. We can do nothing for him, so let us be off. I feel at every moment as if a policeman were holding me in his hand."

Montparnasse resisted but feebly; the truth is, that these four men, with the fidelity which bandits have of never deserting each other, had prowled the whole night round La Force, in spite of the peril they incurred, in the hope of seeing Thénardier appear on the top of some wall. But the night which became really too favourable, for the rain rendered all the streets deserted, the cold which attacked them, their dripping clothes, their worn-out shoes, the alarming noises which had broken out in the prison, the hours which had elapsed, the patrols they had met, the hope which departed and the fear that returned,—all this urged them to retreat. Montparnasse himself, who was perhaps Thénardier's son-in-law in a certain sense, yielded, and in a moment they would be gone. Thénardier gasped on his wall like the shipwrecked crew of the *Méduse* did on their raft, when they watched the ship which they had sighted, fade away on the horizon. He did not dare call to them, for a cry overheard might ruin everything, but he had an idea, a last idea, an inspiration,—he took from his pocket the end of Brujon's rope which he had detached from the chimney of the New Building, and threw it at their feet.

"A cord!" said Babet.

"My cord!" said Brujon.

"The landlord is there," said Montparnasse. They raised their eyes, and Thénardier thrust out his head a little.

"Quiet," said Montparnasse; "have you the other end of the rope, Brujon?"

"Yes."

"Fasten the two ends together, we will throw the rope to him, he will attach it to the wall, and it will be long enough for him to come down."

Thénardier ventured to raise his voice:

"I am wet through."

"We'll warm you."

"I cannot stir."

"You will slip down, and we will catch you."

"My hands are swollen."

"Only just fasten the rope to the wall."

"I can't."

"One of us must go up," said Montparnasse.

"Three storeys!" Brujon ejaculated.

An old plaster conduit pipe, which had served as a chimney for a stove, formerly lit in the hut, ran along the wall almost to the spot where Thénardier was lying. This pipe, which at that day was full of cracks and holes, has since fallen down, but its traces may be seen. It was very narrow.

"It would be possible to mount by that," said Montparnasse.

"By that pipe?" Babet exclaimed; "a man? oh no, a boy is required."

"Yes, a boy," Brujon said in affirmative.

" Where can we find one ? " Gueulemer said.

" Wait a minute," Montparnasse said, " I have it."

He gently opened the hoarding door, assured himself that there was no passer-by in the street, went out, shut the gate cautiously after him, and ran off in the direction of the Bastille. He knew that in that vicinity he could find Gavroche. Seven or eight minutes elapsed, eight thousand centuries for Thénardier; Babet, Brujon, and Gueulemer did not open their lips : the door opened again, and Montparnasse came in, panting and leading Gavroche. The rain continued to make the street completely deserted. Little Gavroche stepped into the enclosure and looked calmly at the faces of the bandits. The rain was dripping from his hair, and Gueulemer said to him :

" Brat, are you a man ? "

Gavroche shrugged his shoulders, and replied :

" A child like me is a man, and men like you are children."

" What a well-hung tongue the brat has ! " Babet exclaimed.

" The boy of Paris is not made of wet paste," Brujon added.

" What do you want of me ? " said Gavroche.

Montparnasse answered :

" Climb up that pipe."

" With this rope," Babet remarked.

" And fasten it," Brujon continued.

" At the top of the wall," Babet added.

" To the cross-bar of the window," Brujon said finally.

" What next ? " asked Gavroche.

" Here it is," said Gueulemer.

The gamin examined the rope, the chimney, the wall, and the window, and gave that indescribable and disdainful smack of the lips which signifies, " What is it ? "

" There is a man up there whom you will save," Montparnasse replied.

" Are you willing ? " Brujon asked.

" Ass ! " the lad replied, as if the question seemed to him extraordinary ; and he took off his shoes.

Gueulemer seized Gavroche by one arm, placed him on the roof of the penthouses, where mouldering planks bent under the boy's weight, and handed him the rope which Brujon had joined again during the absence of Montparnasse. The gamin turned to the chimney, which it

was an easy task to enter, thanks to a large crevice close
to the roof. At the moment when he was going to ascend,
Thénardier, who saw safety and life approaching, leant
over the edge of the wall; the first gleam of day whitened
his dark forehead, his livid cheek-bones, his sharp savage
nose, his bristling gray beard, and Gavroche recognised
him.

"Hilloh!" he said, "it's my father; well, that won't
stop me."

And, taking the rope between his teeth, he resolutely
commenced his ascent. He reached the top of the wall,
straddled across it like a horse, and securely fastened the
rope to the topmost cross-bar of the window. A moment
after, Thénardier was in the street; so soon as he touched
the pavement, so soon as he felt himself out of danger, he
was no longer wearied, chilled, or trembling; the terrible
things he had passed through were dissipated like smoke,
and all his strange and ferocious intellect was re-aroused,
and found itself erect and free, ready to march onward.
The first remark this man made was :

"Well, whom are we going to eat?"

It is unnecessary to explain the meaning of this frightfully
transparent sentence, which signifies at once killing, as-
sassinating, and robbing. The real meaning of "to eat" is
"to devour."

"We must get into hiding," said Brujon. "We will
understand each other in three words, and then separate at
once. There was an affair that seemed good in the Rue
Plumet, a deserted street, an isolated house, old rust-eaten
railings looking on a garden, and lone women."

"Well, why not try it?" Thénardier asked.

"Your daughter Éponine went to look at the thing,"
Babet answered.

"And gave Magnon a biscuit," Brujon added; "there's
nothing to be done there."

"The girl's no fool," said Thénardier, "still, we must
see."

"Yes, yes," Brujon remarked, "we must see."

Not one of the men seemed to notice Gavroche, who,
during this colloquy, was sitting on one of the posts; he
waited some minutes, perhaps in the hope that his father
would turn to him, and then put on his shoes again,
saying :

"Is it all over? you men don't want me any more, I

suppose, as I've got you out of the scrape? I'm off, for I must go and wake my brats."

And he went off. The five men left the enclosure in turn. When Gavroche had disappeared round the corner of the Rue des Ballets, Babet took Thénardier on one side.

"Did you notice that brat?" he asked him.

"What brat?"

"The one who climbed up the wall and handed you the rope."

"Not particularly."

"Well, I don't know, but I fancy it's your son."

"Nonsense," said Thénardier; "do you think so?"

CHAPTER LXXXIX.

THE reader will have understood that Eponine, on recognising through the railings the inhabitant of the house in the Rue Plumet, to which Magnon sent her, began by keeping the bandits aloof from the house, then led Marius to it, and that after several days of ecstasy before the railings, Marius, drawn by that force which attracts iron to the magnet, and the lover toward the stones of the house in which she whom he loves resides, had eventually entered Cosette's garden, as Romeo did Juliet's. It had even been an easier task for him than for Romeo; for Romeo was obliged to scale a wall, while Marius had only to move one of the bars of the decrepit railing loose in its rusty setting, like the teeth of old people. As Marius was thin, he easily passed through. As there never was anybody in the street, and as Marius never entered the garden save at night, he ran no risk of being seen. From that blessed and holy hour when a kiss affianced these two souls, Marius went to the garden every night. If, at this moment of her life, Cosette had fallen in love with an unscrupulous libertine, she would have been lost, for there are generous natures that surrender themselves, and Cosette was one of them. One of the magnanimities of a woman is to yield, and love, at that elevation where it is absolute, is complicated by a certain celestial blindness of modesty. But what dangers you incur, ye noble souls! you often give the heart and we take the body : your heart is left you, and you look at it in the darkness with a shudder. Love has no middle term : it

either saves or destroys, and this dilemma is the whole of
human destiny. No fatality offers this dilemma of ruin or
salvation more inexorably than does love, for love is life, if
it be not death : it is a cradle, but also a coffin. God willed
it that the love which Cosette came across was one of those
loves which save. So long as the month of May of that
year, 1832, lasted, there were every night in this poor
untrimmed garden, and under this thicket, which daily
became more fragrant and more thick, two beings composed of all the chastities and all the innocences, overflowing
with all the felicities of heaven, nearer to the archangels
than to man, pure, honest, intoxicated, and radiant, and
who shone for each other in the darkness. It seemed to
Cosette as if Marius had a crown, and to Marius as if
Cosette had a halo. They touched each other, they looked
at each other, they took each other by the hand, they drew
close to each other ; but there was a distance which they
never crossed. Not that they respected it, but they were
ignorant of it. Marius felt a barrier in Cosette's purity,
and Cosette felt a support in the loyalty of Marius. The
first kiss had also been the last : since then Marius had
never gone beyond touching Cosette's hand or neck-hand-
kerchief or a curl with his lips. Cosette was to him a
perfume, and not a woman, and he inhaled her. She
refused nothing, and he asked for nothing : Cosette was
happy and Marius satisfied. They lived in that ravishing
state which might be called the bewilderment of a soul by a
soul ; it was the ineffable first embrace of two virginities in
the ideal, two swans meeting on the Jungfrau. At this
hour of love, the hour when voluptuousness is absolutely
silenced by the omnipotence of ecstasy, Marius, the pure
and seraphic Marius, would have sooner been able to go
home with a street-walker than raise Cosette's gown as
high as her ankle. Once, in the moonlight, Cosette
stooped to pick up something on the ground, and her dress
opened and displayed her neck. Marius turned his eyes
away.

What passed between these two lovers ? Nothing. They
adored each other. Said Cosette to Marius :

" Do you know that my name is Euphrasie ? "

" Euphrasie ? no, it is Cosette."

"Oh ! Cosette is an ugly name, which was given me
when I was little, but my real name is Euphrasie. Don't
you like that name ? "

"Yes, but Cosette is not ugly."

"Do you like it better than Euphrasie?"

"Well—yes."

"In that case, I like it better too. That is true, Cosette is pretty. Call me Cosette."

Another time she looked at him intently, and exclaimed :

"You are handsome, sir, you are good-looking, you have wit, you are not at all stupid, you are much more learned than I, but I challenge you with, 'I love you.'"

And Marius fancied that he heard a strophe sung by a star. Or else she gave him a little tap, when he coughed, and said :

"Do not cough, sir, I do not allow anybody to cough in my house without permission. It is very wrong to cough and frighten me. I wish you to be in good health, because if you were not I should be very unhappy. What will you have me do for you?"

And this was simply divine.

Once Marius said to Cosette :

"Just fancy, I supposed for a while that your name was Ursula."

This made them laugh the whole evening. In the middle of another conversation he happened to exclaim :

"Oh! one day at the Luxembourg I felt disposed to settle an invalid!"

But he stopped short, and did not complete the sentence, for he would have been obliged to allude to Cosette's garter, and that was impossible. There was a strange feeling connected with the flesh, before which this immense innocent love recoiled with a sort of holy terror. Marius imagined life with Cosette like this, without anything else ; to come every evening to the Rue Plumet, remove the old complacent bar of the President's railings, sit down elbow to elbow on this bench, look through the trees at the scintillation of the commencing night, bring the fold in his trouser-knee into cohabitation with Cosette's ample skirts, to caress her thumb-nail, and to inhale the same flower in turn for ever and indefinitely. During this time the clouds passed over their heads. Each time the wind blows it carries off more of a man's thoughts than of clouds from the sky. We cannot affirm that this chaste, almost stern love was absolutely without gallantry. "Paying compliments" to her whom we love is the first way of giving caresses and an attempted semi-boldness. A compliment is something

like a kiss through a veil, and pleasure puts its sweet point
upon it, while concealing itself.

"Oh !" Marius muttered, "how lovely you are ! I dare
not look at you ; that is why I stare at you. You are
a grace. I know not what is the matter with me. The
hem of your dress, where the end of your slipper passes
through, upsets me. And then, what an enchanting light
when your thoughts become visible, for your reason astonishes
me, and you appear to me at times to be a dream. Speak,
I am listening to you, and admiring you. Oh, Cosette,
how strange and charming it is ! I am really mad. You
are adorable, mademoiselle. I study your feet with the
microscope and your soul with the telescope."

And Cosette made answer :

" And I love you a little more through all the time which
has passed since this morning."

They idolised each other. The permanent and the im-
mutable exist ; a couple love, they laugh, they make little
pouts with their lips, they intertwine their fingers, and that
does not prevent eternity. Two lovers conceal themselves
in a garden in the twilight, in the invisible, with the birds
and the roses, they fascinate each other in the darkness
with their souls which they place in their eyes, they mutter,
they whisper, and during this period immense constellations
of planets fill infinity. Cosette and Marius lived vaguely in
the intoxication of their madness, and they did not notice
the cholera which was decimating Paris in that very month.
They had made as many confessions to each other as they
could, but they had not extended very far beyond their names.
Marius had told Cosette that he was an orphan, Pontmercy
by name, a barrister by profession, and gaining a livelihood
by writing things for publishers ; that his father was a
colonel, a hero, and he, Marius, had quarrelled with his
grandfather who was very rich. He also incidentally remarked that he was a baron, but this did not produce much
effect on Cosette. Marius a baron ? she did not understand
it, and did not know what the word meant ; Marius was
Marius to her. For her part, she confided to him that she had
been educated at the convent of the Little Picpus, that her
mother was dead, like his, that her father's name was
Fauchelevent, that he was very good and gave a great
deal to the poor, but was himself poor, and deprived
himself of everything, while depriving her of nothing.
Strange to say, in the species of symphony which Marius

had lived in since he found Cosette again, the past, even
the most recent, had become so confused and distant to
him that what Cosette told him completely satisfied him.
He did not even dream of talking to her about the nocturnal
adventure in the garret, the Thénardiers, the burning, and
the strange attitude and singular flight of her father.
Marius momentarily forgot all this ; he did not know at
night what he had done in the morning, where he had
breakfasted or who had spoken to him ; he had a song in his
ears which rendered him deaf to every other thought, and
he only existed during the hours when he saw Cosette. As
he was in heaven at that time, it was perfectly simple that
he should forget the earth. Both of them bore languidly
the undefinable weight of immaterial joys ; that is the way
in which those somnambulists, called lovers, live.

Jean Valjean suspected nothing ; for Cosette, a little less
dreamy than Marius, was gay, and that sufficed to render
Jean Valjean happy. Cosette's thoughts, her· tender preoccupations, and the image of Marius which filled her soul,
removed none of the incomparable purity of her splendid,
chaste, and smiling forehead. She was at the age when
the virgin wears her love as the angel wears its lily. Jean
Valjean was, therefore, happy ; and, besides, when two
lovers understand each other, things always go well, and
any third party who might trouble their love is kept in
a perfect state of blindness by a small number of precautions, which are always the same with all lovers. Hence
Cosette never made any objections ; if he wished to take a
walk, very good, my little papa, and if he stayed at home,
very good, and if he wished to spend the evening with
Cosette, she was enchanted. As he always went to his
outhouse at ten o'clock at night, on those occasions Marius
did not reach the garden till after that hour, when he heard
from the street Cosette opening the door. We need hardly
say that Marius was never visible by day, and Jean Valjean
did not even remember that Marius existed. One morning,
however, he happened to say to Cosette, "Why, the back
of your dress is all white!" On the previous evening
Marius, in a transport, had pressed Cosette against the wall.
Old Toussaint, who went to bed at an early hour, only
thought of sleeping so soon as her work was finished, and
was ignorant of everything, like Jean Valjean.

Marius never set foot in the house when he was with
Cosette ; they concealed themselves in a niche near the

steps, so as not to be seen or heard from the street, and sat there, often contenting themselves with the sole conversation of pressing hands twenty times a minute, and gazing at the branches of the trees. At such moments, had a thunderbolt fallen within thirty feet of them, they would not have noticed it, so profoundly was the reverie of the one absorbed and plunged in the reverie of the other. It was a limpid purity, and the houses were all white, and nearly all alike. This genus of love is a collection of lily leaves and doves' feathers. The whole garden was between them and the street, and each time that Marius came in and out he carefully restored the bar of the railings, so that no disarrangement was visible. He went away generally at midnight, and returned to Courfeyrac's lodgings. Courfeyrac used to rally him on the growing irregularity of his habits.

Various complications, however, were approaching. One evening Marius was going to the rendezvous along the Boulevard des Invalides ; he was walking as usual with his head down, and as he was turning the corner of the Rue Plumet, he heard some one say close to him :

"Good-evening, Monsieur Marius."

He raised his head, and recognised Eponine. This produced a singular effect : he had not once thought of this girl since the day when she led him to the Rue Plumet ; he had not seen her again, and she had entirely left his mind. He had only motives to be grateful to her, he owed to her his present happiness, and yet it annoyed him to meet her. It is an error to believe that passion, when it is happy and pure, leads a man to a state of perfection ; it leads him simply, as we have shown, to a state of forgetfulness. In this situation, man forgets to be wicked, but he also forgets to be good, and gratitude, duty, and essential and material recollections, fade away. At any other time Marius would have felt very differently toward Eponine, but, absorbed by Cosette, he had not very clearly comprehended that this Eponine was Eponine Thénardier, and that she bore a name written in his father's will—that name to which he would have so ardently devoted himself a few months previously. We show Marius as he was. His father himself disappeared somewhat from his mind beneath the splendour of his love. Hence he replied with some embarrassment :

"Ah, is it you, Eponine ?"

"Why do you treat me so coldly ? Have I done you any injury ?"

"No," he answered.

Certainly he had no fault to find with her; far from it. Still, he felt that he could not but say "you" to Eponine, now that he said "thou" to Cosette. As he remained silent, she exclaimed:

"Tell me——"

Then she stopped, and it seemed as if words failed this creature, who was formerly so impudent and bold. She tried to smile and could not, so continued:

"Well——"

Then she was silent again, and looked down on the ground.

"Good-evening, Monsieur Marius," she abruptly said, and went away.

CHAPTER XC.

THE next day—it was June 3rd, 1832, a date to which we draw attention owing to the grave events which were at that moment hanging over the horizon of Paris in the state of lightning-charged clouds—Marius at nightfall was following the same road as on the previous evening, with the same ravishing thoughts in his heart, when he saw between the boulevard trees Eponine coming toward him. Two days running,—that was too much; so he sharply turned back, changed his course, and went to the Rue Plumet by the Rue Monsieur. This caused Eponine to follow him as far as the Rue Plumet, a thing she had never done before: hitherto she had contented herself with watching him as he passed along the boulevard, without attempting to meet him: last evening was the first time that she ventured to address him. Eponine followed him, then, without his suspecting it: she saw him move the railing-bar aside and step into the garden.

"Hilloh!" she said, "he enters the house."

She went up to the railing, felt the bars in turn, and easily distinguished the one which Marius had removed. She sat down on the stone work of the railing, close to the bar, as if she were guarding it. It was exactly at the spot where the railings joined the next wall, and there was there a dark corner, in which Eponine entirely disappeared. She remained thus for more than an hour without stirring or breathing, absorbed in thought. About ten o'clock at night, one of the two or three passers along the Rue

Plumet, an old belated citizen, who was hurrying along the deserted and ill-famed street, while passing the railing, heard a dull menacing voice saying :

" I am not surprised now that he comes every evening."

The passer-by looked around him, saw nobody, did not dare to peer into this dark corner, and felt horribly alarmed. He redoubled his speed, and was quite right in doing so, for in a few minutes six men, who were walking separately, and at some distance from each other, under the walls, and who might have been taken for a drunken patrol, entered the Rue Plumet : the first who reached the railings stopped and waited for the rest, and a second after, all six were together, and began talking in whispered slang :

" It's here," said one of them.

" Is there a dog in the garden ? " another asked.

" I don't know. In any case I have brought a ball which we will make it swallow."

" Have you got some mastic to break a pane ? "

" Yes."

" The railings are old," remarked the fifth man, who seemed to have the voice of a ventriloquist.

" All the better," said the second speaker, " it will make no noise when sawn, and won't be so hard to cut through."

The sixth, who had not yet opened his mouth, began examining the railings as Eponine had done an hour ago, and thus reached the bar which Marius had unfastened. Just as he was about to seize this bar, a hand suddenly emerging from the darkness, clutched his arm ; he felt himself roughly thrust back, and a hoarse voice whispered to him, " There's a cab (a dog)." At the same time he saw a pale girl standing in front of him. The man had that emotion which is always produced by things unexpected ; his hair stood hideously on end. Nothing is more formidable to look at than startled wild beasts. He fell back and stammered :

" Who is this she-devil ? "

" Your daughter."

It was, in truth, Eponine speaking to Thénardier. On the appearance of Eponine, the other five men, that is to say, Claquesous, Gueulemer, Babet, Montparnasse, and Brujon, approached noiselessly, without hurry or saying a word, but with the sinister slowness peculiar to these men of the night. Some hideous tools could be distinguished in their hands.

" Well, what are you doing here ? what do you want ? are you mad ? " Thénardier exclaimed. as far as is possible to exclaim in a whisper. "Have you come to prevent us from working ?"

Eponine burst into a laugh and leapt on his neck. "I am here, my dear little pappy, because I am here ; are not people allowed to sit down in copings at present ? it is you who oughtn't to be here ; and what have you come to do, since it is a biscuit ? I told Magnon so ; there is nothing to be done here. But embrace me, my dear pappy, it is such a time since I saw you. You are out, then ! "

Thénardier tried to free himself from Eponine's arms, and growled :

"There, there, you have embraced me. Yes, I am out, and not in. Now, be off."

But Eponine did not lose her hold, and redoubled her caresses.

"My dear pappy, how ever did you manage ? You must have been very clever to get out of that scrape, so tell me all about it. And where is mamma ? give me some news of her."

Thénardier answered :

"She's all right. I don't know ; leave me and be off, I tell you."

"I do not exactly want to go off," Eponine said with the pout of a spoiled child ; "you send me away, though I haven't seen you now for four months, and I have scarce had time to embrace you."

And she caught her father again round the neck.

"Oh, come, this is a bore," said Babet.

"Make haste," said Gueulemer, "the police may pass."

Eponine turned to the five bandits :

"Why, that's Monsieur Brujon. Good-evening, Monsieur Babet ; good-evening, Monsieur Claquesous. What, don't you know me, Monsieur Gueulemer ? How are you, Montparnasse ? "

"Yes, they know you," said Thénardier ; "but now good-night, and be off ; leave us alone."

"It is the hour of the foxes, and not of the chickens," said Montparnasse.

"Don't you see that we have work here ? " Babet added.

Eponine took Montparnasse by the hand. "Mind," he said, "you will cut yourself, for I have an open knife."

"My dear Montparnasse," Eponine replied very gently, "confidence ought to be placed in people, and I am my father's daughter, perhaps. Monsieur Babet, Monsieur Gueulemer, I was ordered to examine into this affair."

It is remarkable that Eponine did not speak slang; ever since she had known Marius that frightful language had become impossible to her. She pressed Gueulemer's great coarse fingers in her little bony hand, which was as weak as that of a skeleton, and continued: "You know very well that I am no fool, and people generally believe me. I have done you a service now and then; well, I have made inquiries, and you would run a needless risk. I swear to you that there is nothing to be done in this house."

"There are lone women," said Gueulemer.

"No, they have moved away."

"Well, the candles haven't," Babet remarked, and he pointed over the trees to a light which was moving about the garret; it was Toussaint who was up late in order to hang up some linen to dry. Eponine made a final effort.

"Well," she said, "they are very poor people, and there isn't a penny-piece in the house."

"Go to the devil," cried Thénardier; "when we have turned the house topsy-turvy, and placed the cellar at top and the attics at the bottom, we will tell you what there is inside, and whether they are francs, sous, or liards."

And he thrust her away that he might pass.

"You shall not enter. You are six, but what do I care for that? You are men and I am a woman. You won't frighten me, I can tell you, and you shall not enter this house, because it does not please me. If you come nearer I bark; I told you there was a dog, and I am it. I do not care a farthing for you, so go your way, for you annoy me! Go where you like, but don't come here, for I forbid it. Come on as you like, you have your knives, and I have my feet."

She advanced a step toward the bandits and said, with the same frightful laugh:

"Confound it! I'm not frightened. This summer I shall be hungry, and this winter I shall be cold. What asses these men must be to think they can frighten a girl! Afraid of what? You have got dolls of mistresses who crawl under the bed when you talk big, but I am afraid of nothing!"

She fixed her eye on Thénardier, and said,—"Not even of you, father."

Then she continued, as she turned her spectral, bloodshot eyeballs on each of the bandits in turn:

"What do I care whether I am picked up to-morrow on

the pavement of the Rue Plumet stabbed by my father, or am found within a year in the nets of St. Cloud or on Swan's Island, among old rotting corks and drowned dogs ! "

She was compelled to break off, for she was attacked by a dry cough, and her breath came from her weak, narrow chest like the death-rattle.

She continued :

" I have only to cry out and people will come, patatras. You are six, but I am all Paris."

Thénardier moved a step toward her.

" Don't come near me," she cried.

He stopped, and said gently :

"Well, no, I will not approach you, but do not talk so loud. Do you wish to prevent us from working, my daughter ? And yet we must earn a livelihood. Do you no longer feel any affection for your father ? "

" You bore me," said Eponine.

" Still we must live, we must eat——"

" Rot of hunger."

This said, she sat down on the coping of the railings, singing to herself.

She had her elbow on her knee, and her chin in her hand, and she balanced her foot with a careless air. Her ragged gown displayed her thin shoulder-blades, and the neighbouring lamp lit up her profile and attitude. Nothing more resolute or more surprising could well be imagined. The six burglars, amazed and savage at being held in check by a girl, went under the shadow of the lamp and held counsel, with humiliated and furious shrugs of their shoulders. She, however, looked at them with a peaceful yet stern air.

" There's something the matter with her," said Babet, " some reason for it. Can she be in love with the dog ? and, yet, it's a pity to miss the affair. There are two women who live alone, an old cove who lives in a yard, and very decent curtains at the windows. The old swell must be a Jew, and I consider the affair a good one."

" Well, do you fellows go in," Montparnasse exclaimed, " and do the trick. I will remain here with the girl, and if she stirs——"

He let the knife which he held in his hand glisten in the lamplight. Thénardier did not say a word, and seemed ready for anything they pleased. Brujon, who was a bit of

an oracle, and who, as we know, "put up the job," had
not yet spoken, and seemed thoughtful. He was supposed
to recoil at nothing, and it was notorious that he had
plundered a police-office through sheer bravado. Moreover,
he wrote verses and songs, which gave him a great
authority. Babet questioned him.

"Have you nothing to say, Brujon?"

Brujon remained silent for a moment, then tossed his
head in several different ways, and at length decided on
speaking.

"Look here. I saw this morning two sparrows fighting,
and to-night I stumble over a quarrelsome woman : all that
is bad, so let us be off."

They went away. Eponine, who did not take her eyes off
them, saw them return by the road along which they had
come. She rose and crawled after them, along the walls
and the houses. She followed them thus along the boulevard ; there they separated, and she saw the six men bury
themselves in the darkness, where they seemed to fade away.

While all this was going on, Marius was by Cosette's
side. The sky had never been more star-spangled and
more charming, the trees more rustling, or the smell of
the grass more penetrating ; never had the birds fallen
asleep beneath the frondage with a softer noise ; never had
the universal harmonies of serenity responded better to the
internal music of the soul ; never had Marius been more
enamoured, happier, or in greater ecstasy. But he had
found Cosette sad, she had been crying, and her eyes were
red. It was the first cloud in this admirable dream.
Marius' first remark was :

"What is the matter with you?"

And she replied :

"I will tell you."

Then she sat down on the bench near the house, and
while he took his seat, all trembling, by her side, she
continued :

"My father told me this morning to hold myself in readiness, for he had business to attend to, and we were probably
going away."

Marius shuddered from head to foot. When we reach
the end of life, death signifies a departure, but at the
beginning, departure means death. For six weeks past
Marius had slowly and gradually taken possession of
Cosette ; it was a perfectly ideal, but profound possession.

Marius possessed Cosette in the way that minds possess ; but he enveloped her with his entire soul, and jealously seized her with an incredible conviction. He possessed her touch, her breath, her perfume, the deep flash of her blue eyes, the softness of her skin when he touched her hand, the charming mark which she had on her neck, and all her thoughts. They had agreed never to sleep without dreaming of each other, and had kept their word. He, therefore, possessed all Cosette's dreams. Marius felt Cosette live in him ; to have Cosette, to possess Cosette, was to him not very different from breathing. It was in the midst of this faith, this intoxication, this virgin, extraordinary, and absolute possession that the words "We are going away" suddenly fell on him, and the stern voice of reality shouted to him, "Cosette is not thine." Marius awoke. For six weeks, as we said, he had been living out of life, and the word "depart" made him roughly re-enter it. He could not find a word to say, and Cosette merely noticed that his hand was very cold. She said to him in her turn :

" What is the matter with you ? "

He answered, in so low a voice that Cosette could scarce hear him :

" I do not understand what you said."

She continued :

" This morning my father told me to prepare my clothes and hold myself ready, that he would give me his linen to put in a portmanteau, that he was obliged to make a journey, that we were going away, that we must have a large trunk for myself and a small one for him, to get all this ready within a week, and that we should probably go to England."

"Why, it is monstrous ! " Marius exclaimed.

It is certain that, at this moment, in Marius' mind, no abuse of power, no violence, no abomination of the most prodigious tyrants, no deed of Busiris, Tiberius, or Henry VIII., equalled in ferocity this one,—M. Fauchelevent taking his daughter to England because he had business to attend to. He asked, in a faint voice :

" And when will you start ? "

" He did not say when."

" And when will you return ? "

" He did not tell me."

And Marius rose and said coldly :

" Will you go, Cosette ? "

Cosette turned to him, her beautiful eyes full of agony, and answered, with a species of wildness :

" Where ? "

" To England ; will you go ? "

" What can I do ? " she said, clasping her hands

" Then you will go ? "

" If my father goes."

" So you are determined to go ? "

Cosette seized Marius' hand, and pressed it as sole reply.

" Very well," said Marius, " in that case I shall go elsewhere."

Cosette felt the meaning of this remark even more than she comprehended it ; she turned so pale that her face became white in the darkness, and stammered :

" What do you mean ? "

Marius looked at her, then slowly raised his eyes to heaven, and replied :

" Nothing."

When he looked down again he saw Cosette smiling at him ; the smile of the woman whom we love has a brilliancy which is visible at night.

" How foolish we are ! Marius, I have an idea."

" What is it ? "

" Follow us if we go away ! I will tell you whither ! and you can join me where I am."

Marius was now a thoroughly wide-awake man, and had fallen back into reality ; hence he cried to Cosette :

" Go with you ! are you mad ? why, it would require money, and I have none ! Go to England ! why, I already owe more than ten louis to Courfeyrac, one of my friends, whom you do not know ! I have an old hat, which is not worth three francs, a coat with buttons missing in front, my shirt is all torn, my boots let in water, I am out at elbows, but I have not thought of it for six weeks, and did not tell you. Cosette, I am a wretch ; you only see me at night and give me your love : were you to see me by day you would give me a halfpenny. Go to England ! Why I have not enough to pay for the passport ! "

He threw himself against a tree, with his arms over his head, and his forehead pressed to the bark, neither feeling the wood that grazed his skin nor the fever which spotted his temples, motionless and ready to fall, like the statue of despair. He remained for a long time in this state—people would remain for an eternity in such abysses. At length he turned and heard behind a little stifled, soft, and sad sound ; it was Cosette sobbing ; she had been crying for more than two hours by the side of Marius, who was reflecting. He went up to her, fell on his knees, seized her foot, which peeped out from under her skirt, and kissed it. She let him do so in silence, for there are moments when a woman accepts, like a sombre and resigned duty, the worship of love.

"Do not weep," he said.

She continued :

"But I am, perhaps, going away, and you are not able to come with me."

He said, "Do you love me?"

She replied by sobbing that Paradisaic word, which is never more charming than through tears, "I adore you."

He pursued, with an accent which was an inexpressible caress :

"Do not weep. Will you do so much for me as to check your tears?"

"Do you love me?" she said.

He took her hand.

"Cosette, I have never pledged my word of honour to any one, because it frightens me, and I feel that my father is by the side of it. Well, I pledge you my most sacred word of honour that if you go away I shall die."

There was in the accent with which he uttered these words such a solemn and calm melancholy that Cosette trembled, and she felt that chill which is produced by the passing of a sombre and true thing. In her terror she ceased to weep.

"Now listen to me," he said ; "do not expect me to-morrow."

"Why not?"

"Do not expect me till the day after."

"Oh, why?"

"You will see."

"A day without your coming !—oh, it is impossible."

"Let us sacrifice one day to have, perhaps, a whole life."

And Marius added in a low voice and aside : "He is a man who makes no change in his habits, and he never received anybody before the evening."

"What man are you talking about?" Cosette asked.

"I? I did not say anything."

"What do you hope for, then?"

" Wait till the day after to-morrow."

" Do you desire it ? "

"Yes, Cosette."

He took her head between his two hands, as she stood on tiptoe to reach him, and tried to see his hopes in his eyes. Marius added :

" By the bye, you must know my address, for something might happen ; I live with my friend Courfeyrac, at No. 16 Rue de la Verrerie."

He felt in his pockets, took out a knife, and scratched the address on the plaster of the wall. In the meanwhile, Cosette had begun looking in his eyes again.

"Tell me your thought, Marius, for you have one. Tell it to me. Oh, tell it to me, so that I may pass a good night."

" My thought is this ; it is impossible that God can wish to separate us. Expect me the day after to-morrow."

"What shall I do till then ? " Cosette said. " You are in the world, and come and go : how happy men are ! but I shall remain all alone. Oh, I shall be so sad ! what will you do to -morrow night, tell me ? "

" I shall try something."

"In that case I shall pray to Heaven, and think of you, so that you may succeed. I will not question you any more, as you do not wish it, and you are my master. I will spend my evening in singing the song from *Euryanthe*, of which you are so fond, and which you heard one night under my shutters. But you will come early the next evening, and I shall expect you at nine o'clock exactly. I warn you. Oh, good heavens ! how sad it is that the days are so long ! You hear ; I shall be in the garden as it is striking nine."

" And I too."

And without saying a word, moved by the same thought, carried away by those electric currents which place two lovers in continual communication, both intoxicated with voluptuousness, even in their grief, fell into each other's arms without noticing that their lips were joined together, while their upraised eyes, overflowing with ecstasy and full of tears, contemplated the stars. When Marius left, the street was deserted, for it was the moment when Eponine followed the bandits into the boulevard. While Marius dreamed with his head leaning against a tree an idea had crossed his mind, an idea, alas ! which he himself considered mad and impossible. He had formed a desperate resolution.

CHAPTER XCI.

FATHER GILLENORMAND at this period had just passed his
ninety-first birthday, and still lived with his daughter at
No. 6 Rue des Filles de Calvaire, in the old house, which
was his own property.   He was, it will be remembered, one
of those antique old men whom age falls on without bending them, and whom even sorrow cannot bow.   Still, for
some time past, his daughter had said, "My father is
breaking."   He no longer boxed the ears of the maid-
servants, or banged so violently the staircase railing when
Basque kept him waiting.   The Revolution of July had not
exasperated him for more than six months, and he had seen
almost with tranquillity in the *Moniteur* this association of
words, M. Humblot-Conté, Peer of France.   The truth is,
that the old man was filled with grief ; he did not bend, he
did not surrender, for that was not possible, either with his
moral or physical nature ; but he felt himself failing in-
wardly.   For four years he had been awaiting Marius, with
the conviction that the cursed young scamp would ring his
bell some day, and now he had begun to say to himself that
Marius might remain away a little too long.   It was not
death that was insupportable to him, but the idea that
perhaps he might not see Marius again.   This idea had
never occurred to him until this day, and at present it rose
before him constantly, and chilled him to death.   Absence,
as ever happens in natural and true feelings, had only
heightened the grandfather's love for the ungrateful boy
who had gone away.   M. Gillenormand was, or fancied
himself, utterly incapable of taking a step toward his grandson : "I would rot first," he said to himself.   He did not
think himself at all in the wrong, but he thought of Marius
only with profound tenderness, and the dumb despair of an
old man who is going down into the valley of the shadows.
He was beginning to lose his teeth, which added to his
sorrow.   M. Gillenormand, without confessing it to himself, however, for he would have been furious and ashamed
of it, had never loved a mistress as he loved Marius.   He
had hung up in his room, as the first thing he might see
on awaking, an old portrait of his other daughter, the
one who was dead, Madame de Pontmercy, taken when she
was eighteen.   He incessantly regarded this portrait, and
happened to say one day, while gazing at it :

" I can notice a likeness."

" To my sister ? " Mlle Gillenormand remarked ; " oh, certainly."

The old man added, " And to him too."

When he was once sitting, with his knees against each other and his eyes almost closed, in a melancholy posture, his daughter ventured to say to him :

" Father, are you still so furious against——? " She stopped, not daring to go further.

" Against whom ? " he asked.

" That poor Marius."

He raised his old head, laid his thin wrinkled fist on the table, and cried, in his loudest and most irritated accent :

" Poor Marius, you say ! that gentleman is a scoundrel, a scamp, a little vain ingrate, without heart or soul, a proud and wicked man ! "

And he turned away, so that his daughter might not see a tear which he had in his eyes. Three days later he interrupted a silence which had lasted four hours to say to his daughter gruffly :

" I have had the honour of begging Mademoiselle Gillenormand never to mention his name to me."

Aunt Gillenormand gave up all attempts, and formed this profound diagnostic : " My father was never very fond of my sister after her folly. It is clear that he detests Marius."

On the evening of June 4th, which did not prevent Father Gillenormand from having an excellent fire in his chimney, he had dismissed his daughter, who was sewing in the adjoining room. He was alone in his apartment with the pastoral hangings, with his feet on the andirons, half enveloped in his nine-leaved Coromandel screen, sitting at a table on which two candles burned under a green shade, swallowed up in his needleworked easy-chair, and holding a book in his hand, which he was not reading. Father Gillenormand was thinking of Marius bitterly and lovingly, and, as usual, bitterness gained the upper hand. His savage tenderness always ended by boiling over and turn- ing into indignation, and he was at the stage when a man seeks to make up his mind and accept that which is to be. He was explaining to himself that there was no longer any reason for Marius' return, that if he had meant to come home he would have done so long before, and all idea of it must be given up. He tried to form the idea that it was all

over, and that he should die without seeing that "gentleman" again. But his whole nature revolted, and his old
paternity could not consent. "What," he said, and it was
his mournful burthen, "he will not come back!" and his
old bald head fell on his chest, and he vaguely fixed a
lamentable and irritated glance upon the ashes on his
hearth. In the depth of this reverie his old servant Basque
came in and asked:

"Can you receive M. Marius, sir?"

The old man sat up, livid, and like a corpse which is
roused by a galvanic shock. All his blood flowed to his
heart, and he stammered:

"M. Marius! who?"

"I do not know," Basque replied, intimidated and disconcerted by his master's air, "for I did not see him. It
was Nicolette who said to me just now, 'There is a young
man here, say it is M. Marius.'"

Father Gillenormand stammered in a low voice, "Show
him in."

And he remained in the same attitude with hanging head
and eye fixed on the door. It opened, and a young man
appeared—it was Marius, who stopped in the doorway as if
waiting to be asked in. His almost wretched clothes could
not be seen in the obscurity produced by the shade, and
only his calm, grave, but strangely sorrowful face could
be distinguished. Father Gillenormand, as if stunned by
stupor and joy, remained for a few minutes, seeing nothing
but a brilliancy, as when an apparition rises before us. He
was ready to faint; he perceived Marius through a mist.
It was really he, it was really Marius! At length, after
four years! He took him in entirely, so to speak, at a
glance, and found him handsome, noble, distinguished,
grown, a thorough man, with a proper attitude and a
charming air. He felt inclined to open his arms and call
the boy to him, his entrails were swelled with ravishment,
affectionate words welled up and overflowed his bosom. At
length all this tenderness burst forth and reached his lips,
and through the contrast which formed the basis of his
character a harshness issued from it. He said roughly:

"What do you want here?"

Marius replied with an embarrassed air:

"Sir——"

Monsieur Gillenormand would have liked for Marius to
throw himself into his arms, and he was dissatisfied both

with Marius and himself.   He felt that he was rough and Marius cold, and it was an insupportable and irritating anxiety to the old gentleman to feel himself so tender and imploring within, and unable to be otherwise than harsh externally.   His bitterness returned, and he abruptly interrupted Marius.

"In that case why do you come?"

The "in that case" meant "if you have not come to embrace me."   Marius gazed at his ancestor's marble face.

"Sir——"

The old gentleman resumed in a stern voice:

"Have you come to ask my pardon? have you recognised your error?"

He believed that he was putting Marius on the right track, and that "the boy" was going to give way.   Marius trembled, for it was a disavowal of his father that was asked of him, and he lowered his eyes and replied, "No, sir."

"Well, in that case," the old man exclaimed impetuously, and with a sharp sorrow full of anger, "what is it you want of me?"

Marius clasped his hands, advanced a step, and said, in a weak, trembling voice:

"Take pity on me, sir."

This word moved M. Gillenormand; had it come sooner it would have softened him, but it came too late.   The old gentleman rose, and rested both hands on his cane; his lips were white, his forehead vacillated, but his lofty stature towered over the stooping Marius.

"Pity on you, sir! the young man asks pity of the old man of ninety-one!   You are entering life, and I am leaving it; you go to the play, to balls, to the coffee-house, the billiard-table; you are witty, you please women, you are a pretty fellow, while I spit on my logs in the middle of summer; you are rich with the only wealth there is, while I have all the poverty of old age, infirmity, and isolation. You have your two-and-thirty teeth, a good stomach, a quick eye, strength, appetite, health, gaiety, a forest of black hair, while I have not even my white hair left.   I have lost my teeth, I am losing my legs, I am losing my memory.   Such is my state; you have a whole future before you, full of sunshine, while I am beginning to see nothing, as I have advanced so far into night.   You are in love, that is a matter of course, while I am not beloved by a soul in the world, and yet you ask me for pity ! By Jove, Molière forgot that. If that is the way in which you barristers jest at the palace of justice, I compliment you most sincerely upon it, for you are droll fellows."

And the octogenarian added, in a serious and wrathful voice :

"Well, what is it you want of me ? "

"I am aware, sir," said Marius, "that my presence here displeases you, but I have only come to ask one thing of you, and then I shall go away at once."

"You are a fool," the old man said; "who told you to go away ? "

This was the translation of the tender words which he had at the bottom of his heart. "Ask my pardon, why don't you? and throw your arms round my neck." M. Gillenormand felt that Marius was going to leave him in a few moments, that his bad reception offended him, and that his harshness expelled him ; he said all this to himself, and his grief was augmented by it ; as his grief immediately turned into passion and his harshness grew the greater. He had wished that Marius should understand, and Marius did not understand, which rendered the old gentleman furious. He continued :

"What ! you insulted me, your grandfather ; you left my house to go the Lord knows whither ; you broke your aunt's heart ; you went away to lead a bachelor's life, of course that's more convenient, to play the fop, come home at all hours, and amuse yourself ; you have given me no sign of life, you have incurred debts without even asking me to pay them, and at the end of four years you return to my house and have nothing more to say to me than that ! "

This violent way of forcing the grandson into tenderness only produced silence on the part of Marius. M. Gillenormand folded his arms, a gesture which with him was peculiarly imperious, and bitterly addressed Marius :

" Let us come to an end. You have come to ask something of me, you say ! well, what is it ? speak."

"Sir," said Marius, with the look of a man who feels that he is going to fall over a precipice, "I have come to ask your permission to marry."

M. Gillenormand rang the bell, and Basque poked his head into the door.

"Send my daughter here.

A second later, the door opened again, and Mlle Gillenormand did not enter, but showed herself. Marius was standing silently, with drooping arms and the face of a criminal, while M. Gillenormand walked up and down the room. He turned to his daughter and said to her :

"It is nothing. This is M. Marius, wish him good-evening. This gentleman desires to marry ; that will do. Be off."

The sound of the old man's sharp, hoarse voice announced a mighty fury raging within him. The aunt looked at Marius in terror, seemed scarce to recognise him, did not utter a syllable, and disappeared before her father's breath, like a straw before a hurricane. In the meanwhile M. Gillenormand had turned back, and was now leaning against the mantelpiece.

"You marry ! at the age of one-and-twenty ! you have settled all that, and have only a permission to ask, a mere formality ! Sit down, sir. Well, you have had a revolution since I had the honour of seeing you last ; the Jacobins had the best of it, and you are of course pleased ; are you not a republican since you became a baron ? those two things go famously together, and the republic is a sauce for the barony. Are you one of the decorated of July ? did you give your small aid to take the Louvre, sir ? Close by, in the Rue St. Antoine, opposite the Rue des Nonaindières, there is a cannon-ball imbedded in the wall of a house three storeys up, with the inscription, July 28, 1830. Go and look at it, for it produces a famous effect. Ah ! your friends do very pretty things ! By the way, are they not erecting a fountain on the site of the Duc de Berry's monument ? So you wish to marry ? May I ask, without any indiscretion, who the lady is ? "

He stopped, and before Marius had time to answer, he added violently :

"Ah ! have you a profession, a fortune ? how much do you earn by your trade as a lawyer ? "

"Nothing," said Marius, with a sort of fierceness and almost stern resolution.

"Nothing ? then you have only the twelve hundred livres which I allow you to live on ? "

Marius made no reply, and M. Gillenormand continued :

"In that case, I presume that the young lady is wealthy ? "

"Like myself."

"What ? no dowry ? "

" No."

" Any expectations ? "

" I do not think so."

" Quite naked ! and what is the father ? "

" I do not know."

" And what is her name ? "

" Mademoiselle Fauchelevent."

" Mademoiselle Fauchewhat ? "

" Fauchelevent."

" Ptt ! " said the old gentleman.

" Sir ! " Marius exclaimed.

M. Gillenormand interrupted him, with the air of a man who is talking to himself :

" That is it, one-and-twenty, no profession, twelve hundred livres a year, and the Baroness Pontmercy will go and buy two sous' worth of parsley at the greengrocer's."

" Sir," Marius replied in the wildness of the last vanishing hope, " I implore you, I conjure you in Heaven's name, with clasped hands I throw myself at your feet,—sir, permit me to marry her ! "

The old man burst into a sharp, melancholy laugh, through which he coughed and spoke :

" Ah, ah, ah ! you said to yourself, ' I'll go and see that old periwig, that absurd ass ! What a pity that I am not five-and-twenty yet, how I would send him a respectful summons ! Old fool, you are too glad to see me, I feel inclined to marry Mademoiselle Lord-knows-who, the daughter of M. Lord-knows-what. She has no shoes, and I have no shirt, that matches ; I am inclined to throw into the river my career, my youth, my future, my life, and take a plunge into wretchedness with a wife round my neck— that is my idea, and you must consent : ' and the old fossil will consent. Go in, my lad, fasten your paving-stone round your neck, marry your Pousselevent, your Coupelevent,— never, sir, never ! "

" Father—— "

" Never ! "

Marius lost all hope through the accent with which this " never " was pronounced. He crossed the room slowly, with hanging head, tottering, and more like a man that is dying than one who is going away. M. Gillenormand looked after him, and at the moment when the door opened and Marius was about to leave the room he took four strides with the senile vivacity of an impetuous and self-willed old man, seized Marius by the collar, pulled him back energetically into the room, threw him into an easy-chair, and said :

" Tell me all about it."

The word " father " which had escaped from Marius' lips produced this revolution. Marius looked at M. Gillenormand haggardly, but his inflexible face expressed nought now but a rough and ineffable goodness. The ancestor had made way for the grandfather.

" Well, speak ; tell me of your love episodes, tell me all. Sapristi ! how stupid young men are ! "

" My father ! " Marius resumed.

The old gentleman's entire face was lit up with an indescribable radiance.

" Yes, that is it, call me father, and you'll see."

There was now something so gentle, so good, so open, and so paternal in this sharpness, that Marius, in this sudden passage from discouragement to hope, was, as it were, stunned and intoxicated. As he was seated near the table the light of the candles fell on his seedy attire, which Father Gillenormand studied with amazement.

" Well, father," said Marius.

" What," M. Gillenormand interrupted him, " have you really no money ?   You are dressed like a thief."

He felt in a drawer and pulled out a purse, which he laid on the table.

" Here are one hundred louis to buy a hat with."

" My father," Marius continued, " my kind father. If you only knew how I love her !   You cannot imagine it. The first time I saw her was at the Luxembourg, where she came to walk.   At the beginning I paid no great attention to her, and then I know not how it happened, but I fell in love with her.   Oh ! how wretched it made me.   I see her now every day at her own house, and her father knows nothing about it : just fancy, they are going away, we see each other at night in the garden, her father means to take her to England, and then I said to myself, ' I will go and see my grandfather and tell him about it.'   I should go mad first, I should die, I should have a brain fever, I should throw myself into the water.   I must marry her, or else I shall go mad.   That is the whole truth, and I do not believe that I have forgotten anything.   She lives in a garden with a railing to it, in the Rue Plumet : it is on the side of the Invalides."

Father Gillenormand was sitting, radiant with joy, by Marius' side : while listening and enjoying the sound of his voice he enjoyed at the same time a lengthened pinch of snuff. At the words Rue Plumet he broke off his sniffing, and allowed the rest of the snuff to fall on his knees.

"Rue Plumet! did you say Rue Plumet? only think! Is there not a barrack down there? oh yes, of course there is. Marius! I think it very proper that a young man like you should be in love, for it becomes your age, and I would sooner have you in love than a Jacobin. I would rather know you caught by a petticoat, ay, by twenty petticoats, than by Monsieur de Robespierre. For my part, I do myself the justice of saying that, as regards sans-culottes, I never loved any but women. Pretty girls are pretty girls, hang it all! and there is no harm in that. And so she receives you behind her father's back, does she? that's all right, and I had affairs of the same sort, more than one. Do you know what a man does in such cases? he does not regard the matter ferociously, he does not hurl himself into matrimony, or conclude with marriage and M. le Maire in his scarf. No, he is a sharp fellow, and a man of common sense. Glide, mortals, but do not marry. Such a young man goes to his grandfather, who is well inclined after all, and who has always a few rolls of louis in an old drawer, and he says to him, 'Grandpapa, that's how matters stand,' and grandpapa says, 'It is very simple, youth must enjoy itself, and old age be smashed up. I have been young and you will be old. All right, my lad, you will requite it to your grandson. Here are two hundred pistoles, go and amuse yourself, confound you!' that is the way in which the matter should be arranged; a man does not marry, but that is no obstacle : do you understand?"

Marius, petrified and incapable of uttering a word, shook his head in the negative. The old gentleman burst into a laugh, winked his aged eyelid, tapped him on the knee, looked at him between the eyes with a mysterious and radiant air, and said with the tenderest shrug of the shoulders possible :

"You goose! make her your mistress!"

Marius turned pale ; he had understood nothing of what his grandfather had been saying. Nothing of all this could affect Cosette who was a lily, and the old gentleman was wandering. But this derogation had resulted in a sentence which Marius understood, and which was a mortal insult to Cosette, and the words, "Make her your mistress," passed through the stern young man's heart like a sword-blade. He rose, picked up his hat which was on the ground, and walked to the door with a firm, assured step. Then he turned, gave his grandfather a low bow, drew himself up again, and said :

"Five years ago you outraged my father ; to-day you have outraged my wife. I have nothing more to ask of you, sir ; farewell ! "

Father Gillenormand, who was stupefied, opened his mouth, stretched out his arms, strove to rise, but ere he was able to utter a word, the door had closed again, and Marius had disappeared. The old gentleman remained for a few minutes motionless, and as if thunder-struck, unable to speak or breathe, as though a garrotter's hand were compressing his throat. At length he tore himself out of his easy-chair, ran to the door as fast as a man can run at ninety-one, opened it, and cried :

"Help ! help !".

His daughter appeared, and then his servants ; he went on with a lamentable rattle in his throat :

"Run after him ! catch him up ! how did I offend him ? he is mad and going away ! O Lord, O Lord ! this time he will not return."

He went to the window which looked on the street, opened it with his old trembling hands, bent half his body out of it, while Basque and Nicolette held his skirts, and cried :

"Marius ! Marius ! Marius ! Marius ! "

But Marius could not hear him, for at this very moment he was turning the corner of the Rue St. Louis. The octogenarian raised his hands twice or thrice to his temples with an expression of agony, tottered back, and sank into an easy-chair, pulseless, voiceless, and tearless, shaking his head and moving his lips with a stupid air, and having nothing left in his eyes or heart but something deep and mournful, which resembled night.

That very day, about four in the afternoon, Jean Valjean was seated on one of the most solitary slopes of the Champ de Mars. Either through prudence, a desire to reflect, or simply in consequence of one of those insensible changes of habits which gradually introduce themselves into all existences, he now went out very rarely with Cosette. He had on his workman's jacket and gray canvas trousers, and his long peaked cap concealed his face. He was at present calm and happy by Cosette's side ; what had startled and troubled him for a while was dissipated ; but, during the last week or fortnight, anxieties of a fresh nature had sprung up. One day, while walking along the boulevard, he noticed Thénardier ; thanks to his disguise, Thénardier did not recognise him, but after that Jean Valjean saw him several times again, and now felt certain that Thénardier was prowling about the quarter. This was sufficient to make him form a grand resolution, for Thénardier present was every peril at once ; moreover, Paris was not quiet, and political troubles offered this inconvenience to any man who had something in his life to hide, that the police had become very restless and suspicious and, when trying to find a man like Pepin or Morey, might very easily discover a man like Jean Valjean. He, therefore, resolved to leave Paris, even France, and go to England ; he had warned Cosette, and hoped to be off within a week. He was sitting on the slope, revolving in his mind all sorts of thoughts,— Thénardier, the police, the journey, and the difficulty of obtaining a passport. From all these points of view he was anxious ; and lastly, an inexplicable fact, which had just struck him, and from which he was still hot, added to his alarm. On the morning of that very day he, the only person up in the house, and walking in the garden before Cosette's shutters were opened, suddenly perceived this line on the wall, probably scratched with a nail :

16 *Rue de la Verrerie.*

It was quite recent, the lines were white on the old black mortar, and a bed of nettles at the foot of the wall was powdered with fine fresh plaster. This had probably been inscribed during the night. What was it ? an address ? a signal for others, or a warning for himself ? In any case, it was evident that the secrecy of the garden was violated, and that strangers entered it. He remembered the strange incidents which had already alarmed the house, and his mind was at work on this subject ; but he was careful not to say a word to Cosette about the line written on the wall, for fear of alarming her. In the midst of his troubled thoughts he perceived, from a shadow which the sun threw, that some one was standing on the crest of the slope immediately behind him. He was just going to turn, when a folded paper fell on his knees, as if a hand had thrown it over his head; he opened the paper, and read this word, written in large characters, and in pencil,— "REMOVE."

Jean Valjean rose smartly, but there was no longer any one on the slope; he looked round him, and perceived a person, taller than a child and shorter than a man, dressed in a gray blouse and dust-coloured cotton-velvet trousers, bestriding the parapet, and slipping down into the moat of the Champ de Mars. Jean Valjean at once went home, full of thought.

Marius had left M. Gillenormand's house in a wretched state; he had gone in with very small hopes, and came out with an immense despair. He began walking about the streets, the resource of those who suffer, and he thought of nothing which he might have remembered. At two in the morning he went to Courfeyrac's lodging, and threw himself on his mattress full dressed: it was bright sunshine when he fell asleep, with that frightful oppressive sleep which allows ideas to come and go in the brain. When he awoke he saw Courfeyrac, Enjolras, Feuilly, and Combeferre, all ready to go out, and extremely busy. Courfeyrac said to him:

"Are you coming to General Lamarque's funeral?"

It seemed to him as if Courfeyrac were talking Chinese. He went out shortly after them, and put in his pockets the pistols which Javert had entrusted to him at the affair of February 3, and which still remained in his possession. They were still loaded, and it would be difficult to say what obscure notion he had in his brain when he took them up. The whole day he wandered about, without knowing where; it rained at times, but he did not perceive it; he bought for his dinner a halfpenny roll, put it in his pocket, and forgot it. It appears that he took a bath in the Seine without being conscious of it, for there are moments when a man has a furnace under his skull, and Marius had reached one of those moments. He hoped for nothing, feared nothing now; he had reached this condition since the previous day. He awaited the evening with a feverish impatience, for he had but one clear idea left, that at nine o'clock he should see Cosette. This last happiness was now his sole future; after that came the shadow. At times, while walking along the most deserted boulevards, he imagined that he could hear strange noises in Paris; then he thrust his head out of his reverie, and said,—" Can they be fighting ?" At nightfall, at nine o'clock precisely, he was at the Rue Plumet, as he had promised Cosette. He had not seen her for eight-and-forty hours, he was about to see her again. Every other thought was effaced, and he only felt an extraordinary and profound joy. Those minutes in which men live ages have this sovereign and admirable thing about them, that, at the moment when they pass, they entirely occupy the heart.

Marius removed the railing and rushed into the garden. Cosette was not at the place where she usually waited for him, and he crossed the garden, and went to the niche near the terrace. " She is waiting for me there," he said, but Cosette was not there. He raised his eyes and saw that the shutters of the house were closed ; he walked round the garden, but the garden was deserted. Then he returned to the house, and, mad with love, terrified, exasperated with grief and anxiety, he rapped at the shutters, like a master who returns home at a late hour. He rapped, he rapped again, at the risk of seeing the window open and the father's frowning face appear, and ask him,—" What do you want ?" This was nothing to what he caught a glimpse of. When he had rapped, he raised his voice, and called Cosette. " Cosette !" he cried ; " Cosette !" he repeated imperiously. There was no answer, and it was all over ; there was no one in the garden, no one in the house. Marius fixed his desperate eyes on this mournful house, which was as black, as silent, and more empty than a tomb. He gazed at the stone bench on which he had spent so many adorable hours by Cosette's side ; then he sat down on the garden steps, with his heart full of gentleness and resolution ; he blessed his love in his heart, and said to himself that since Cosette was gone there was nothing left him but to die. All at once he heard a voice which seemed to come from the street, crying through the trees :

" Monsieur Marius !"

He drew himself up.

" Hilloh ?" he said.

"Are you there, M. Marius ?"

" Yes."

" Monsieur Marius," the voice resumed, "your friends are waiting for you at the barricade in the Rue de la Chanvrerie."

This voice was not entirely strange to him, and resembled

Eponine's rough, hoarse accents. Marius ran to the railings, pulled aside the shifting bar, passed his head through, and saw some one, who seemed to be a young man, rapidly disappearing in the twilight.

CHAPTER XCII.

M. MABŒUF had continued to descend. The indigo experiments had succeeded no better at the Jardin des Plantes than in his garden of Austerlitz. The previous year he owed his housekeeper her wages, and now, as we have seen, he owed his landlord his rent. The Government pawnbrokers' office sold the copper-plates of his *Flora*, at the expiration of thirteen months, and some brazier had made stew-pans of them. When his plates had disappeared, as he could no longer complete the unbound copies of his *Flora*, which he still possessed, he sold off plates and text to a second-hand bookseller, as defective. Nothing was then left him of the labour of his whole life, and he began eating the money produced by the copies. When he saw that this poor resource was growing exhausted he gave up his garden, and did not attend to it; before, and long before, he had given up the two eggs and the slice of beef which he ate from time to time, and now dined on bread and potatoes. He had sold his last articles of furniture, then everything he had in duplicate, in linen, clothes, and coverlids, and then his herbals and plates; but he still had his most precious books, among them being several of great rarity. M. Mabœuf never lit a fire in his room, and went to bed with the sun, in order not to burn a candle; it seemed as if he no longer had neighbours, for they shunned him when he went out, and he noticed it. The wretchedness of a child interests a mother, the wretchedness of a youth interests an old man, but the wretchedness of an old man interests nobody, and it is the coldest of all distresses. Still M. Mabœuf had not entirely lost his childlike serenity; his eye acquired some vivacity when it settled on his books, and he smiled when he regarded a rare edition of *Diogenes Laertius* which he had, and which was a unique copy. His glass case was the only furniture which he had retained beyond what was indispensable. One day Mother Plutarch said to him:

"I have no money to buy dinner with."

What she called dinner consisted of a loaf and four or five potatoes.

"Can't you get it on credit?" said M. Mabœuf.

"You know very well that it is refused me."

M. Mabœuf opened his bookcase, looked for a long time at all his books in turn like a father, obliged to decimate his children, would look at them before selecting, then took one up quickly, put it under his arm, and went out. He returned two hours after with nothing under his arm, laid thirty sous on the table, and said:

"You will get some dinner."

From this moment Mother Plutarch saw a dark veil, which was not raised again, settle upon the old gentleman's candid face. The next day, the next after that, and every day, M. Mabœuf had to begin again; he went out with a book and returned with a piece of silver. As the second-hand booksellers saw that he was compelled to sell they bought for twenty sous books for which he had paid twenty francs, and frequently to the same dealers. Volume by volume his whole library passed away, and he said at times, "And yet I am eighty years of age," as if he had some lurking hope that he should reach the end of his days ere he reached the end of his books. His sorrow grew, but once he had a joy: he went out with a Robert Estienne, which he sold for thirty-five sous on the Quai Malaquais, and came home with an Aldus which he had bought for forty sous in the Rue de Grès. "I owe five sous," he said quite radiantly to Mother Plutarch, but that day he did not dine. He belonged to the Horticultural Society, and his poverty was known. The President of the Society called on him, promised to speak about him to the Minister of Commerce and Agriculture, and did so. "What do you say?" the minister exclaimed, "I should think so! an old savant! a botanist! an inoffensive man! we must do something for him." The next day M. Mabœuf received an invitation to dine with the minister, and, trembling with joy, showed the letter to Mother Plutarch. "We are saved!" he said. On the appointed day he went to the minister's, and noticed that his ragged cravat, his long, square-cut coat, and shoes varnished with white of egg, astounded the footman. No one spoke to him, not even the minister, and at about ten in the evening, while still waiting for a word, he heard the minister's wife, a handsome lady in a low-necked dress, whom he had not dared to approach, ask, "Who can that old gentleman be?" He went home on foot at midnight through the pouring rain; he had sold an Elzevir to pay his hackney-coach in going.

Every evening, before going to bed, he had fallen into the habit of reading a few pages of his *Diogenes Laertius*; for he knew enough of Greek to enjoy the peculiarities of the text which he possessed, and had no other joy now left him. A few weeks passed away, and all at once Mother Plutarch fell ill. There is one thing even more sad than having no money to buy bread at a baker's, and that is, not to have money to buy medicine at the chemist's. One night the doctor had ordered a most expensive potion, and then the disease grew worse, and a nurse was necessary. M. Mabœuf opened his bookcase, but there was nothing left in it; the last volume had departed, and the only thing left him was the *Diogenes Laertius*. He placed the unique copy under his arm and went out—it was June 4, 1832; he proceeded to Royol's successor at the Porte St. Jacques, and returned with one hundred francs. He placed the pile of five-franc pieces on the old servant's table, and entered his bedroom without uttering a syllable. At dawn of the next day he seated himself on the overturned post in his garden, and over the hedge he might have been seen the whole morning, motionless, with drooping head, and eyes vaguely fixed on the faded flower-beds. It rained every now and then, but the old man did not seem to notice it: but in the afternoon extraordinary noises broke out in Paris, resembling musket-shots, and the clamour of a multitude. Father Mabœuf raised his head, noticed a gardener passing, and asked:

"What is the matter?"

The gardener replied, with the spade on his back, and with the most peaceful accent:

"It's the rebels."

"What! rebels?"

"Yes, they are fighting."

"Why are they fighting?"

"The Lord alone knows," said the gardener.

"In what direction?"

"Over by the arsenal."

Father Mabœuf went into his house, took his hat, mechanically sought for a book to place under his arm, found none, said, "Ah, it is true!" and went out with a wandering look.

CHAPTER XCIII.

In the spring of 1832, although for three months cholera
had chilled minds and cast over their agitation a species of
dull calm, Paris had been for a long time ready for a commotion. As we have said, the great city resembles a piece
of artillery when it is loaded,—a spark need only fall and
the gun goes off. In June, 1832, the spark was the death
of General Lamarque. Lamarque was a man of renown
and of action, and had displayed in succession, under the
Empire and the Restoration, the two braveries necessary
for the two epochs, the bravery of the battlefield and the
bravery of the oratorical tribune. He was eloquent as he
had been valiant, and a sword was felt in his words; like
Foy, his predecessor, after holding the command erect, he
held liberty erect; he sat between the left and the extreme
left, beloved by the people because he accepted the chances
of the future, and beloved by the mob because he had served
the Emperor well. He was, with Gérard and Drouet, one
of Napoleon's marshals *in petto*, and the hiatus of 1815
affected him like a personal insult. He hated Wellington
with a direct hatred, which pleased the multitude, and for
the last seventeen years, scarcely paying attention to intermediate events, he had majestically nursed his grief for
Waterloo. In his dying hour he pressed to his heart a
sword which the officers of the Hundred Days had given
him, and while Napoleon died uttering the word *army*,
Lamarque died pronouncing the word *country*. His death,
which was expected, was feared by the people as a loss, and
by the Government as an opportunity. This death was a
mourning, and, like everything which is bitter, mourning
may turn into revolt. This really happened on the previous
evening, and on the morning of June 5th, the day fixed for
the interment of Lamarque, the Faubourg St. Antoine, close
to which the procession would pass, assumed a formidable
aspect. This tumultuous network of streets was filled with
rumours, and people armed themselves as they could.
Carpenters carried off the bolts of their shop "to break
in doors with"; one of them made a dagger of a stocking-
weaver's hook, by breaking off the hook and sharpening the
stump. Another in his fever "to attack" slept for three
nights in his clothes.

On June 5, then, a day of sunshine and shower, the

funeral procession of General Lamarque passed through
Paris with the official military pomp, somewhat increased
by precautions. Two battalions with covered drums and
trailing muskets, ten thousand of the National Guard with
their sabres at their side, and the batteries of the artillery of
the National Guard escorted the coffin, and the hearse was
drawn by young men. The officers of the Invalides followed
immediately after, bearing laurel branches, and then came
a countless, agitated, and strange multitude, the sectionists
of the friends of the people, the school of law, the school of
medicine, refugees of all nations, Spanish, Italian, German,
Polish flags, horizontal tri-colour flags, every banner possible, children waving green branches, stone-cutters and
carpenters out of work at this very time, and printers easy
to recognise by their paper caps, marching two and two,
three and three, uttering cries, nearly all shaking sticks,
and some sabres, without order, but with one soul, at one
moment a mob, at another a column. Squads selected their
chiefs, and a man armed with a brace of pistols, which were
perfectly visible, seemed to pass others in review, whose files
made way for him. On the side-walks of the boulevards,
on the branches of the trees, in the balconies, at the
windows and on the roofs, there was a dense throng of
men, women, and children, whose eyes were full of anxiety.
An armed crowd passed, and a startled crowd looked at it;
on its side Government was observing, with its hand on the
sword-hilt. Four squadrons of carbineers, mounted, and
with their trumpeters at the head, with their cartouche
boxes full, and their musquetoons loaded, might be seen on
the Place Louis XV., in the Pays Latin, and at the Jardin
des Plantes; the Municipal Guard were echelonned from
street to street; at the Halle-aux-Vins was a squadron of
dragoons, at the Grève one half of the 12th Light Infantry,
while the other half was at the Bastille; the 6th Dragoons
were at the Celestins, and the court of the Louvre was
crammed with artillery; all the rest of the troops were
confined to barracks, without counting the regiments in
the environs of Paris. The alarmed authorities held suspended over the threatening multitude twenty-four thousand
soldiers in the city, and thirty thousand in the suburbs.

Various rumours circulated in the procession, legitimist
intrigues were talked about, and they spoke about the Duke
of Reichstadt, whom God was marking for death at the very
moment when the crowd designated him for Emperor. A

person who was never discovered announced that at appointed hours two overseers, gained over, would open to the people the gates of a small arm-factory. An enthusiasm blended with despondency was visible in the uncovered heads of most of the persons present, and here and there too in this multitude, suffering from so many violent but noble emotions, might be seen criminal faces and ignoble lips, that muttered, "Let us plunder."

The hearse passed the Bastille, followed the canal, crossed the small bridge, and reached the esplanade of the bridge of Austerlitz, where it halted. A circle was formed round the hearse, and the vast crowd was hushed. Lafayette spoke, and bade farewell to Lamarque : it was a touching and august moment,—all heads were uncovered, and all hearts beat. All at once a man on horseback, dressed in black, appeared in the middle of the group with a red flag, though others say with a pike surmounted by a red cap. Lafayette turned his head away, and Excelmans left the procession. This red flag aroused a storm and disappeared in it : from the Boulevard Bourdon to the bridge of Austerlitz one of those clamours which resemble billows stirred up the multitude, and two prodigious cries were raised, "Lamarque at the Pantheon!" "Lafayette at the Hôtel ¸de Ville!" Young men, amid the acclamations of the crowd, began dragging Lamarque in the hearse over the bridge of Austerlitz, and Lafayette in a hackney-coach along the Quai Morland. In the crowd that surrounded and applauded Lafayette people noticed and pointed out to each other a German of the name of Ludwig Snyder, who has since died a centenarian, who also went through the campaign of 1776, and had fought at Trenton under Washington, and under Lafayette at Brandywine.

The municipal cavalry galloped along the left bank to stop the passage of the bridge, while on the right the dragoons came out of the Celestins and deployed along the Quai Morland. The people who were drawing Lafayette suddenly perceived them at a turning of the quay, and cried, "The dragoons!" The troops advanced at a walk, silently, with their pistols in their holsters, sabres undrawn, and musquetoons slung with an air of gloomy expectation. Two hundred yards from the little bridge they halted, the coach in which Lafayette was went up to them, they opened their ranks to let it pass, and then closed up again. At this moment the dragoons and the crowd came in contact, and the women fled in terror. What took place in this fatal minute? no one could say, for it is the dark moment when two clouds clash together. Some state that a bugle-call sounding the charge was heard on the side of the Arsenal, others that a dragoon was stabbed with a knife by a lad. The truth is, that three shots were suddenly fired, one killing Major Cholut, the second an old deaf woman who was closing her window in the Rue Contrescarpe, while the third grazed an officer's shoulder. A woman cried, "They have begun too soon!" and all at once a squadron of dragoons was seen galloping up on the opposite side with drawn sabres, and sweeping everything before it.

At such a moment the last word is said, the tempest is unchained, stones shower, the fusilade bursts forth: many rush to the water's edge and cross the small arm of the Seine, which is now filled up: the timber-yards on Ile Louviers, that ready-made citadel, bristle with combatants, stakes are pulled up, pistols are fired, a barricade is commenced, the young men driven back, pass over the bridge of Austerlitz with the hearse at the double, and charge the Municipal Guard: the carbineers gallop up, the dragoons sabre; the crowd disperses in all directions, a rumour of war flies to the four corners of Paris: men cry "To arms" and run, overthrow, fly, and resist. Passion spreads the riot as the wind does fire.

Nothing is more extraordinary than the commencement of a riot, for everything breaks out everywhere at once. Before a quarter of an hour had elapsed, fighting was going on simultaneously at twenty different points of Paris. Two intrepid men, tried by the great wars, Marshal de Lobau and General Bugeaud, commanded the troops—Bugeaud under Lobau.

At the Tuileries there was not an additional sentry posted, and Louis Philippe was full of serenity.

CHAPTER XCIV.

AT the moment when the insurrection, ʰreaking out through the collision between the people and the troops in front of the Arsenal, produced a retrograde movement in the multitude that followed the hearse, and which pressed with the whole length of the boulevards upon the head of the procession, there was a frightful reflux. The ranks were broken, and all ran or escaped, some with cries of attack, others with the pallor of flight. The great stream which covered the boulevards divided in a second, overflowed on the right and left, and spread in torrents over two hundred streets at once, as if a dyke had burst. At this moment a ragged lad who was coming down the Rue Menilmontant, holding in his hand a branch of flowering laburnum which he had picked on the heights of Belleville, noticed in the shop of a seller of curiosities an old holster pistol. He threw his branch on the pavement, and cried:

"Mother What's-your-name, I'll borrow your machine."

And he ran off with the pistol. Two minutes after, a crowd of frightened citizens flying through the Rue Basse met the lad, who was brandishing his pistol and singing loudly. It was little Gavroche going to the wars. On the boulevard he noticed that his pistol had no hammer. Gavroche was acquainted with all the popular tunes in circulation, and mingled with them his own chirping, and, as a young vagabond, he made a *pot-pourri* of the voices of nature and the voices of Paris.

He reached the Rue du Pont aux Choux, and noticed that there was only one shop still open in that street, and it was worthy of reflection that it was a confectioner's. It was a providential opportunity to eat one more apple-puff before entering the unknown. Gavroche stopped, felt in his pockets, turned them inside out, found nothing, not even a sou, and began shouting, "Help!" It is hard to go without the last cake, but for all that Gavroche went on his way. Two minutes after he was in the Rue St. Louis, and on crossing the Rue du Parc Royal he felt the necessity of compensating himself for the impossible apple-puff, and gave himself the immense treat of tearing down in open daylight the playbills. A little further on, seeing a party of stout gentry, who appeared to him to be retired from business, he shrugged his shoulders and spat out this mouthful of philosophic bile:

"How fat annuitants are! they wallow in good dinners. Ask them what th y do with their money, and they don't know. They eat it, eat their bellyful."

Holding a pistol without a cock in the streets is such a public function, that Gavroche felt his humour increase at every step. He cried between the scraps of the Marseillaise which he sang:

"All goes well. I suffer considerably in my left paw. I

have broken my rheumatism, but I am happy, citizens. The bourgeois have only to hold firm, and I am going to sing them some subversive couplets. I have just come from the boulevard, my friends, where it's getting warm, and the soup is simmering ; it is time to skim the pot. Forward, my men, and let their impure blood inundate the furrows ! I give my days for my country. I shall not see my concubine again, it's all over. Well, no matter ! long live joy ! let us fight, egad, for I have had enough of despotism ! "

At this moment the horse of a lancer, in the National Guard, who was passing, fell. Gavroche laid his pistol on the pavement, helped the man up, and then helped to raise the horse, after which he picked up his pistol and went his way again.

Gavroche at length reached the Marché St. Jean, and there he joined himself to a band led by Enjolras, Courfeyrac, Combeferre, and Feuilly. They were all more or less armed, and Bahorel and Prouvaire had joined them, and swelled the group. Enjolras had a double-barrelled fowling-piece, Combeferre a National Guard's musket bearing the number of a legion, and in his waist-belt two pistols, which his unbuttoned coat allowed to be seen, Jean Prouvaire an old cavalry musquetoon, and Bahorel a carbine ; Courfeyrac brandished a sword drawn from a cane, while Feuilly with a naked sabre in his hand walked along shouting, " Long live Poland ! " They reached the Quai Morland without neckcloths or hats, panting for breath, drenched with rain, but with lightning in their eyes. Gavroche calmly approached them :

" Where are we going ? "

" Come on," said Courfeyrac.

Behind Feuilly marched, or rather bounded, Bahorel, a fish in the water of revolt. He had a crimson waistcoat, and uttered words which smash everything. His waistcoat upset a passer-by, who cried wildly, " Here are the reds ! "

" The reds, the reds," Bahorel answered, " that's a funny fear, citizen. For my part, I do not tremble at a poppy, and the little red cap does not inspire me with any terror. Citizen, believe me, let us leave a fear of the red to horned cattle."

He noticed a corner wall, on which was placarded the most peaceful piece of paper in the world, a permission to eat eggs, a Lent mandamus addressed by the Archbishop of Paris to his " flock." Bahorel exclaimed :

"A flock! a polite way of saying geese." And he tore the paper down. This conquered Gavroche, and from this moment he began studying Bahorel.

"Bahorel," Enjolras observed, "you are wrong, you should have left that order alone, for we have nothing to do with it, and you needlessly exposed your passion. Keep your stock by you; a man does not fire out of the ranks any more with his mind than with his gun."

"Every man has his own way, Enjolras," Bahorel replied; "the bishop's prose offends me, and I insist on eating eggs without receiving permission to do so. Yours is the cold burning style, while I amuse myself; moreover, I am not expending myself, but getting the steam up, and if I tore that order down, Hercle! it is to give me an appetite."

A tumultuous crowd accompanied them—students, artists, young men affiliated to the Cougourde of Aix, artisans, and lightermen, armed with sticks and bayonets, and some, like Combeferre, with pistols passed through their trouser-belts. An old man, who appeared very aged, marched in this band; he had no weapon, and hurried on, that he might not be left behind, though he looked thoughtful. It was M. Mabœuf. We will tell what had occurred. Enjolras and his friends were on the Bourdon Boulevard near the granaries, at the moment when the dragoons charged, and Enjolras, Courfeyrac, and Combeferre were among those who turned into the Rue Bassompierre shouting "To the barricades!" In the Rue Lesdiguières they met an old man walking along, and what attracted their attention was that he was moving very irregularly, as if intoxicated. Moreover, he had his hat in his hand, although it had rained the whole morning, and was raining rather hard at that very moment. Courfeyrac recognised Father Mabœuf, whom he knew through having accompanied Marius sometimes as far as his door. Knowing the peaceful and more than timid habits of the churchwarden and bibliomaniac, and stupefied at seeing him in the midst of the tumult, within two yards of cavalry charges, almost in the midst of the musketry fire, bareheaded in the rain, and walking about among bullets, he accosted him, and the rebel of five-and-twenty and the octogenarian exchanged this dialogue.

"Monsieur Mabœuf, you had better go home."

"Why?"

"There is going to be a row."

"Very well."

"Sabre-cuts and shots, M. Mabœuf."

"Very well."

"Cannon-shots."

"Very well. Where are you gentlemen going?"

"To upset the Government."

"Very well."

And he began following them, but since that moment had not said a word. His step had become suddenly firm, and when workmen offered him an arm, he declined it with a shake of the head. He walked almost at the head of the column, having at once the command of a man who is marching and the face of a man who is asleep.

"What a determined old fellow!" the students muttered, and the rumour ran along the party that he was an ex-conventionalist, an old regicide. The band turned into the Rue de la Verrerie, and little Gavroche marched at the head, singing at the top of his voice, which made him resemble a bugler.

They were going to St. Merry. The band swelled every moment, and near the Rue des Billettes, a tall, grayish-haired man, whose rough bold face Courfeyrac, Enjolras, and Combeferre noticed, though not one of them knew him, joined them. Gavroche, busy singing, whistling, shouting, and rapping on the window-shutters with his pistol-butt, paid no attention to this man. As they went through the Rue de la Verrerie they happened to pass Courfeyrac's door.

"That's lucky," said Courfeyrac, "for I have forgotten my purse and lost my hat."

He left the band and bounded upstairs, where he put on an old hat and put his purse in his pocket. He also took up a large square box of the size of a portmanteau, which was concealed among his dirty linen. As he was running downstairs again his porteress hailed him.

"Monsieur de Courfeyrac!"

"Porteress, what is your name?" Courfeyrac retorted.

She stood in stupefaction.

"Why, you know very well, sir, that my name is Mother Veuvain."

"Well then, if ever you call me M. de Courfeyrac again, I shall call you Mother de Veuvain; now speak, what is it?"

"Some one wishes to speak to you."

"Who is it?"

"I don't know."

"Where is he?"

"In my lodge."

"The devil!" said Courfeyrac.

"But he has been waiting for more than an hour for you to come in."

At the same time a species of young workman, thin, livid, small, marked with freckles, dressed in an old blouse and a pair of patched cotton-velvet trousers, who looked more like a girl attired as a boy than a man, stepped out of the lodge and said to Courfeyrac in a voice which was not the least in the world a feminine voice:

"Monsieur Marius, if you please?"

"He is not in."

"Will he come in to-night?"

"I don't know anything about it."

And Courfeyrac added, "I shall not be in to-night."

The young man looked at him intently, and asked.

"Why so?"

"Because I shall not."

"Where are you going, then?"

"How does that concern you?"

"Shall I carry your chest for you?"

"I am going to the barricades."

"May I go with you?"

"If you like," Courfeyrac replied; "the street is free, and the pavement belongs to everybody."

And he ran off to rejoin his friends; when he had done so, he gave one of them the box to carry; and it was not till a quarter of an hour after that he noticed that the young man was really following them.

A band does not go exactly where it wishes, and we have explained that a puff of wind directs it. They passed St. Merry, and found themselves, without knowing exactly how, in the Rue St. Denis.

CHAPTER XCV.

THE Parisians, who, at the present time, on entering the Rue Rambuteau from the side of the markets, notice on their right, opposite the Rue Mondétour, a basket-maker's shop having for sign a basket in the shape of Napoleon the Great, do not suspect the terrible scenes which this very site saw hardly thirty years ago. Here were the Rue de la

Chanvrerie, which old title-deeds write Chanverrerie, and the celebrated wine-shop called Corinth.

For the clearness of our narrative, we may be permitted to have recourse to the simple mode which we employed for Waterloo. Those persons who wish to represent to themselves in a tolerably exact manner the mass of houses which at that day stood at the north-east corner of the markets, at the spot where the opening of the Rue Rambuteau now is, need only imagine an N whose two vertical strokes are the Rue de la Grande Truanderie, and the Rue de la Chanvrerie, and of which the Rue de la Petite Truanderie would be the cross-stroke. The old Rue Mondétour intersected the three strokes with the most tortuous angles, so that the Dædalian entanglement of these four streets was sufficient to make, upon a space of one hundred square yards, between the markets and the Rue St. Denis on one side, between the Rue du Cygne and the Rue des Precheurs, on the other side, seven islets of houses, strangely cut, of different heights, standing sideways, and as if accidentally, and scarce separated by narrow cracks, like the blocks of stone in a dock. We say narrow cracks, and cannot give a fairer idea of these obscure, narrow, angular lanes, bordered by tenements eight storeys in height. These houses were so decrepit that in the Rues de la Chanvrerie and La Petite Truanderie, the frontages were supported by beams running across from one house to the other. The street was narrow and the gutter wide; the passer-by walked on a constantly damp pavement, passing shops like cellars, heavy posts shod with iron, enormous piles of filth, and gates armed with extraordinarily old palings. The Rue Rambuteau has devastated all this. The name of Mondétour exactly describes the windings of all this laystall. A little farther on it was found even better expressed by the Rue Pirouette, which threw itself into the Rue Mondétour. The wayfarer who turned out of the Rue St. Denis into the Rue de la Chanvrerie saw it gradually contract before him, as if he had entered an elongated funnel. At the end of the street, which was very short, he found the passage barred on the side of the markets by a tall row of houses, and he might have fancied himself in a blind alley had he not perceived on his right and left two black cuts through which he could escape. It was the Rue Mondétour, which joined on one side the Rue des Precheurs, on the other the Rue du Cynge. At the end of this sort of

blind alley, at the corner of the right-hand cutting, a house
lower than the rest, forming a species of cape in the street,
might be noticed. It is in this house, only two storeys
high, that an illustrious cabaret had been installed for more
than three hundred years.

The spot was good, and the landlords succeeded each
other from father to son. In the time of Mathurin Régnier
this inn was called the "Rose-pot," and as rebuses were
fashionable, it had as sign a post painted pink, which represented a "Poteau rose," hence the Pot-aux-roses. In
the last century worthy Natoire, one of the fantastic masters
disdained at the present day by the stiff school, having got
tipsy several times in this inn at the same table where
Régnier had got drunk, painted out of gratitude a bunch
of currants on the pink post. The landlord, in his delight,
changed his sign, and had the words gilt under the bunch,
"au Raisin de Corinthe," hence the name of Corinth.
Nothing is more natural to drunkards than ellipses, for
they are the zig-zags of language. Corinth had gradually
dethroned the rose-pot, and the last landlord of the dynasty,
Father Hucheloup, not being acquainted with the tradition,
had the post painted blue.

A ground-floor room in which was the bar, a first-floor
room in which was a billiard-table, a spiral wooden staircase piercing the ceiling, wine on the tables, smoke on the
walls, and candles by daylight—such was the inn. A staircase with a trap in the ground-floor room led to the cellar,
and the apartments of the Hucheloups were on the second
floor, reaching by a staircase more like a ladder, and through
a door hidden in the wall of the large first-floor room.
Under the roof were two garrets, the nests of the maid-
servants, and the kitchen shared the ground-floor with the
bar. Father Hucheloup might have been born a chemist,
but was really a cook, and customers not only drank but
ate in his wine-shop. Hucheloup had invented an excellent
dish, which could be only eaten at his establishment; it was
stuffed carp, which he called *carpes au gras*. The Rue de
la Chanvrerie and Corinth have disappeared under the
pavement of the Rue Rambuteau. As we have said, Corinth
was a meeting-place, if not a gathering-place, of Courfeyrac
and his friends, and it was Grantaire who discovered it.
People drank there, ate there, and made a row there: they paid
little, paid badly or paid not at all, but were always welcome.
Father Hucheloup was a worthy fellow. Hucheloup, whom

we have just called a worthy fellow, was an eating-house keeper with a moustache, an amusing variety. He always looked ill-tempered, appeared wishful to intimidate his customers, growled at persons who came in, and seemed more disposed to quarrel with them than serve them. And yet we maintain people were always welcome. This peculiarity filled his bar, and brought to him young men who said, " Let us go and have a look at Father Hucheloup." He had been a fencing-master, and would suddenly break out into a laugh ; he had a rough voice, but was a merry fellow. His was a comical foundation with a tragical look ; and he asked for nothing better than to frighten you, something like the snuff-boxes which had the shape of a pistol— the detonation produces a sneeze. He had for wife Mother Hucheloup, a bearded and very ugly being. About 1830 Father Hucheloup died, and with him disappeared the secret of the *carpes au gras*. His widow, who was almost inconsolable, carried on the business, but the cooking degenerated, and became execrable, and the wine, which had always been bad, was frightful. Courfeyrac and his friends, however, continued to go to Corinth—through pity, said Bossuet.

Widow Hucheloup was short of breath and shapeless, and had rustic recollections. The first-floor room, where the restaurant was, was a large, long apartment, crowded with stools, chairs, benches, and tables, and an old rickety billiard-table. It was reached by the spiral staircase which led to a square hole in the corner of the room, like a ship's hatchway. This apartment, lighted by only one narrow window and a constantly-burning lamp, had a garret-look about it, and all the four-legged articles of furniture behaved as if they had only three.

Two servant-girls, called Matelotte and Gibelotte, and who were never known by any other names, helped Ma'am Hucheloup in placing on the tables bottles of blue wine, and the various messes served to the hungry guests in earthenware bowls. Matelotte, stout, round, red-haired, and noisy, an ex-favourite sultana of the defunct Hucheloup, was uglier than the ugliest mythological monster ; and yet, as it is always proper that the servant should be a little behind the mistress, she was not so ugly as Ma'am Hucheloup. Gibelotte, tall, delicate, white with a lymphatic whiteness, with blue circles round her eyes, and drooping lids, ever exhausted and oppressed, and suffering from what

may be called chronic lassitude, the first to rise, the last to
go to bed, waited on everybody, even the other servant,
silently and gently, and smiling a sort of vague, sleepy
smile through her weariness.

Laigle of Meaux, as we know, liked better to live with
Joly than any one else, and he had a lodging much as the
bird has a branch. The two friends lived together, ate
together, slept together, and had everything in common,
Musichetta perhaps included. They were, to use the expression of the schools, *bini*, or twins. On the morning of
June 5 they went to breakfast at Corinth. Joly had a cold
in his head, and Laigle's coat was threadbare, while Joly
was well dressed. It was about nine in the morning when
they pushed open the door of Corinth, and went up to the
first-floor room, where they were received by Matelotte and
Gibelotte.

" Oysters, cheese, and ham," said Laigle.

They sat down at a table ; the room was empty, there was
no one in it but themselves. Gibelotte, recognising Joly
and Laigle, placed a bottle of wine on the table, and they
attacked the first dozen of oysters. A head appeared in the
hatchway, and a voice said :

" As I was passing, I smelt a delicious perfume of Brie
cheese ; so I stepped in."

It was Grantaire ; he took a stool and sat down at the
table. Gibelotte, on seeing Grantaire, placed two bottles of
wine on the table, which made three.

"Are you going to drink these two bottles ? " Laigle
asked Grantaire ; who replied :

" All men are ingenious, but you alone are ingenuous.
Two bottles never yet astonished a man."

The others began with eating, but Grantaire began with
drinking ; a pint was soon swallowed.

" Why, you must have a hole in your stomach," said
Laigle.

" Well, you have one in your elbow," Grantaire retorted,
and after emptying his glass, he added :

" Oh yes, Laigle of the funeral orations, your coat is
old."

"I should hope so," Laigle replied, " for my coat and
I live comfortably together. It has assumed all my wrinkles,
does not hurt me anywhere, has moulded itself on my
deformities, and is complacent to all my movements, and
I only feel its presence because it keeps me warm."

"Grantaire," Joly asked, "have you come from the boulevard ? "

" No."

" Laigle and I have just seen the head of the procession pass. It is a marvellous sight."

"How quiet this street is !" Laigle exclaimed. "Who could suspect that Paris is turned topsy-turvy ? How easy it is to see that formerly there were monasteries all round here ! There was all around where we are now sitting a busy swarm of monks, shod and barefooted, tonsured and bearded, gray, black, white, Franciscans, Minimi, Capuchins, Carmelites, little Augustines, great Augustines, old Augustines——"

" Don't talk about monks," Grantaire interrupted, " for it makes me feel that I want to scratch myself." Then he exclaimed :

" Bouh ! I have just swallowed a bad oyster, and that has brought back my hypochondria. Oysters are spoiled, servant-girls are ugly, and I hate the human race. I passed just now before the great public library in the Rue Richelieu, and that pile of oyster-shells, which is called a library, disgusts me with thinking. What paper ! what ink ! what pothooks and hangers ! all that has been written ! what ass was it who said man was a featherless biped ? And then, too, I met a pretty girl I know, lovely as spring, and worthy to be called Floreal, who was ravished, transported, happy in Paradise, the wretch, because yesterday a hideous banker, spotted with small-pox, deigned to throw his handkerchief to her ! Alas ! woman looks out for a keeper quite as much as a lover ; cats catch mice as well as birds. This girl, not two months ago, was living respectably in a garret, and fitted little copper circles into the eyelet-holes of stays, what do you call it ? She sewed, she had a flock bed, she lived by the side of a pot of flowers, and was happy. Now she is a bankeress, and the transformation took place last night. I met the victim this morning perfectly happy, and the hideous thing was that the wretched creature was quite as pretty this morning as she was yesterday, and there was no sign of the financier on her face. Roses have this more or less than women, that the traces which the caterpillars leave on them are visible. Ah ! there is no morality left in the world, and I call as witnesses the myrtle, symbol of love, the laurel, symbol of war, the olive, that absurd symbol of peace, the apple-tree, which nearly choked Adam with its pips, and the fig-tree, the grandfather of petticoats. As for justice, do you know what justice is? The Gauls cover Clusium, Rome protects Clusium and asks what wrong Clusium has done them. Brennus answers, "The wrong which Alba did to you, the wrong that Fidène did to you, the wrong that the Equi, Volscians, and Sabines did to you. They were your neighbours, and the Clusians are ours. We understand neighbourhood in the same way as you do. You stole Alba, and we take Clusium." Rome says, "You shall not take Clusium." Brennus took Rome, and then cried *Væ victis*! That is what justice is! Oh, what birds of prey there are in the world! What eagles, what eagles! the thought makes my flesh creep."

And after this burst of eloquence Grantaire had a burst of coughing, which was well deserved.

"Talking of a revolution," said Joly, "it seebs that Barius is decidedly in love."

"Do you know who with?" Laigle asked.

"Do."

"No?"

"Do, I tell you."

"The loves of Marius!" Grantaire exclaimed, "I can see them from here. Marius is a fog and will have found a vapour. Marius belongs to the poetic race, and poet and madman are convertible terms. *Thymbræus Apollo*. Marius and his Marie, or his Maria, or his Mariette, or his Marion, must be a funny brace of lovers. I can fancy what it is: ecstasies in which kissing is forgotten. Chaste on earth but connected in the infinitude. They are souls that have feelings, and they sleep together in the stars."

Grantaire was attacking his second bottle, and perhaps his second harangue, when a new head emerged from the staircase hatchway. It was a boy under ten years of age, ragged, very short and yellow, with a bull-dog face, a quick eye, and an enormous head of hair: he was dripping with wet, but seemed happy. The lad choosing without hesitation among the three, though he knew none of them, addressed Laigle of Meaux.

"Are you M. Bossuet?" he asked.

"I am called so," Laigle replied; "what do you want?"

"A tall, light-haired gent said to me on the boulevard, 'Do you know Mother Hucheloup's?' I said, 'Yes, in the Rue Chanvrerie, the old one's widow.' Says he to me,

'Go there, you will find Monsieur Bossuet there, and say to
him from me, A—B—C.' I suppose it's a trick played you,
eh? he gave me ten sous."

"Joly, lend me ten sous," said Laigle; and turning to
Grantaire, "Grantaire, lend me ten sous."

This made twenty sous, which Laigle gave the lad.
"Thank you, sir," he said.

"What is your name?" Laigle asked.

"Navet, Gavroche's friend."

"Stay with us," Laigle said.

"Breakfast with us," Grantaire added.

The lad replied, "I can't, for I belong to the procession,
and have to cry, 'Down with Polignac.'"

And, drawing his foot slowly behind him, which is the
most respectful of bows possible, he went away. When
he was gone, Laigle said in a low voice:

"A—B—C, that is to say, funeral of General Lamarque."

"The tall, fair man," Grantaire observed, "is Enjolras,
who has sent to warn you."

"Shall we go?" asked Bossuet.

"It's raididg," said Joly; "I have sword to go through
fire, but dot through water, and I do dot wish to bake
by cold worse."

"I shall stay here," Grantaire remarked; "I prefer a
breakfast to a hearse."

"Conclusion, we remain," Laigle continued; "in that
case, let us drink. Besides, we may miss the funeral without missing the row."

"Ah, the row!" cried Joly, "I'b id that."

Laigle rubbed his hands.

"So the Revolution of 1830 is going to begin over again."

"I do not care a rap for your revolution," Grantaire
remarked, "and I do not execrate the present Government,
for it is the crown tempered by the cotton night-cap, a
sceptre terminating in an umbrella. In such weather
as this Louis Philippe might use his royalty for two objects,
stretch out the sceptre-end against the people, and open
the umbrella-end against the sky."

The room was dark, and heavy clouds completely veiled
the daylight. There was no one in the wine-shop or in the
streets, for everybody had gone "to see the events."

"Is it midday or midnight?" Bossuet asked. "I can
see nothing; bring a candle, Gibelotte."

Grantaire was drinking sorrowfully.

" Enjolras disdains me," he muttered. " Enjolras said to himself, ' Joly is ill and Grantaire is drunk,' and so he sent Navet to Bossuet. And yet, if he had fetched me, I would have followed him. All the worse for Enjolras ! I will not go to his funeral."

This resolution formed, Bossuet, Grantaire, and Joly did not stir from the wine-shop, and at about 2 P.M. the table at which they sat was covered with empty bottles. Two candles burnt on it, one in a perfectly green copper candlestick, the other in the neck of a cracked water-bottle. Grantaire had led Joly and Bossuet to wine, and Bossuet and Joly had brought Grantaire back to joy. As for Grantaire, he gave up wine at midday, as a poor inspirer of dreams. Wine is not particularly valued by serious sots, for inebriety there is black magic and white magic, and wine is only the white magic. Grantaire was attracted rather than arrested by the blackness of a formidable intoxication yawning before him, and he had given up bottles and taken to the dram glass, which is an abyss. Not having at hand either opium or hashish, and wishing to fill his brain with darkness, he turned to that frightful mixture of brandy, stout, and absinthe, which produces such terrible lethargies. Of these three vapours, beer, brandy, and absinthe, the lead of the soul is made : they are three darknesses in which the celestial butterfly is drowned ; and three dumb furies, night-mare, night, and death, which hover over the sleeping Psyche, are produced, in a membranous smoke vaguely condensed into a bat's wing. Grantaire had not yet reached that phase, far from it : he was prodigiously gay, and Bossuet and Joly kept even with him. Grantaire added to the eccentric accentuation of words and ideas the incoherency of gestures ; he laid his left hand on his knee with a dignified air, and with his neckcloth unloosed, straddling his stool, and with his full glass in his right hand, he threw these solemn words at the stout servant-girl, Matelotte.

" Open the gates of the palace ! Let every man belong to the French Academy, and have the right of embracing Madame Hucheloup ! Let us drink."

And turning to the landlady, he added :

" Antique female, consecrated by custom, approach, that I may contemplate thee."

And Joly exclaimed :

" Batelotte and Gibelotte, don't give Grantaire ady bore drink. He is spending a frightful sum, and odly since this borning has devoured in shabeful prodigality two francs, dwenty-five centibes."

And Grantaire went on :

" Who has unhooked the stars without my leave, in order to place them on the table in lieu of candles ? "

Bossuet, who was very drunk, had retained his calmness, and was sitting on the sill of the open window, letting the rain drench his back, while he gazed at his two friends. All at once he heard behind him a tumult, hurried footsteps, and shouts of " To arms ! " He turned, and noticed in the Rue St. Denis at the end of the Rue Chanvrerie, Enjolras passing, carbine in hand, Gavroche with his pistol, Feuilly with his sabre, Courfeyrac with his sword, Jean Prouvaire with his musquetoon, Combeferre with his fowling-piece, Bahorel with his musket, and the whole armed and stormy band that followed them. The Rue de la Chanvrerie was not a pistol-shot in length, so Bossuet improvised a speaking-trumpet with his two hands round his mouth, and shouted :

" Courfeyrac ! Courfeyrac ! hilloh ! "

Courfeyrac heard the summons, perceived Bossuet, and walked a few steps down the Rue de la Chanvrerie, exclaiming, " What do you want ? " which was crossed by a " Where are you going ? "

"To make a barricade," Courfeyrac answered.

" Well, why not make it here ? the spot is good.'

" That is true, Eagle," said Courfeyrac.

And at a sign from Courfeyrac the band rushed into the Rue de la Chanvrerie.

The ground was, in fact, admirably suited ; the entrance of the street was wide, the end narrowed, and, like a blind alley, Corinth formed a contraction in it ; the Rue Mondétour could be easily barred right and left, and no attack was possible save by the Rue St. Denis, that is to say, from the front, and in the open. Bossuet, drunk, had had the inspiration of Hannibal fasting. At the sound of the band rushing on, terror seized on the whole street, and not a passer-by but disappeared. More quickly than a flash of lightning, shops, stalls, gates, doors, Venetian blinds, and shutters of every size, were shut from the ground-floor to the roofs, at the end, on the right, and on the left. An old terrified woman fixed up a mattress before her window with clothes-props, in order to deaden the musketry ; the public-house alone remained open—and for an excellent reason, because the insurgents had rushed into it.

"O Lord, Lord !" Ma'am Hucheloup sighed.

Bossuet ran down to meet Courfeyrac, and Joly, who had gone to the window, shouted :

"Courfeyrac, you ought to have brought an umbrella. You will catch cold."

In a few minutes twenty iron bars were pulled down from the railings in front of the inn, and ten yards of pavement dug up. Gavroche and Bahorel seized, as it passed, the truck of a lime-dealer, of the name of Anceau, and found in it three barrels of lime, which they placed under the piles of paving-stones ; Enjolras had raised the cellar-flap, and all Ma'am Hucheloup's empty casks went to join the barrels of lime ; Feuilly, with his fingers accustomed to illumine the delicate sticks of fans, reinforced the barrels and the trucks with two massive piles of stones. The supporting shores were pulled away from the frontage of an adjoining house, and laid on the casks. When Courfeyrac and Bossuet turned round, one half the street was already barred by a rampart, taller than a man, for there is nothing like the hand of the people to build up anything that is built by demolishing. Matelotte and Gibelotte were mixed up with the workmen, and the latter went backwards and forwards, loaded with rubbish, and her lassitude helped at the barricade. She served paving-stones as she would have served wine, with a sleepy look. An omnibus drawn by two white horses passed the end of the street : Bossuet jumped over the stones, ran up, stopped the driver, ordered the passengers to get out, offered his hand to "the ladies," dismissed the conductor, and returned, pulling the horses on by the bridle.

"Omnibuses," he said, "must not pass before Corinth. *Non licet omnibus adire Corinthum.*"

A moment after the unharnessed horses were struggling down the Rue Mondétour, and the omnibus lying on its side completed the barricade. Ma'am Hucheloup, quite upset, had sought refuge on the first-floor ; her eyes were wandering and looked without seeing, and her cries of alarm dared not issue from her throat.

"It is the end of the world," she muttered.

Joly deposited a kiss on Ma'am Hucheloup's fat, red, wrinkled neck, and said to Grantaire, "My dear fellow, I have always considered a woman's neck an infinitely delicate thing." But Grantaire had reached the highest regions of dithyramb. When Matelotte came up to the first-floor he seized her round the waist, and burst into loud peals of laughter at the window.

Enjolras, who was standing on the top of the barricade, gun in hand, raised his handsome, stern face. Enjolras, as we know, blended the Spartan with the Puritan ; he would have died at Thermopylæ with Leonidas, and burnt Drogheda with Cromwell.

"Grantaire," he cried, "go and sleep off your wine elsewhere ; this is the place for intoxication, and not for drunkenness. Do not dishonour the barricade."

These angry words produced on Grantaire a singular effect, and it seemed as if he had received a glass of cold water in his face. He appeared suddenly sobered, sat down near the window, gazed at Enjolras with inexpressible tenderness, and said to him :

"Let me sleep here."

"Go and sleep elsewhere," Enjolras cried.

But Grantaire, still fixing on him his tender and misty eyes, answered :

"Let me sleep here till I die here."

Enjolras looked at him disdainfully.

"Grantaire, you are incapable of believing, thinking, wishing, living, and dying."

Grantaire replied in a grave voice :

"You will see."

He stammered a few more unintelligible words, then his head fell noisily on the table, and, as is the usual effect of the second period of ebriety into which Enjolras had roughly and suddenly thrust him, a moment later he was asleep.

CHAPTER XCVI.

BAHOREL, delighted with the barricade, exclaimed : "How well the street looks when dressed for a ball ! "

Courfeyrac, while gradually demolishing the public-house, tried to console the widowed landlady.

"Mother Hucheloup, were you not complaining the other day that you had been summoned by the police, because Gibelotte shook a counterpane out of the window ? "

"Yes, my good Monsieur Courfeyrac. Ah ! good gracious ! are you going to put that table too in your horror ? Yes, and the Government also condemned me to a fine of one hundred francs on account of a flower-pot that fell out of the garret into the street. Is that not abominable ? "

" Well, Mother Hucheloup, we are going to avenge you."

Mother Hucheloup did not exactly see the advantage accruing to her from the reparation made her. The rain had ceased, and recruits began to arrive. Artisans brought under their blouses a barrel of gunpowder, a hamper containing carboys of vitriol, two or three carnival torches, and a basket full of lamps, "remaining from the king's birthday," which was quite recent, as it was celebrated on May 1. It was said that this ammunition was sent by a grocer in the Faubourg St. Antoine of the name of Pepin. The only lantern in the Rue de la Chanvrerie, and all those in the surrounding streets, were broken. Enjolras, Combeferre, and Courfeyrac directed everything, and now two barricades were erected simultaneously, both of which were supported by Corinth and formed a square ; the larger one closed the Rue de la Chanvrerie, and the smaller the Rue Mondétour on the side of the Rue du Cygne. This latter barricade, which was very narrow, was merely made of barrels and paving-stones. There were about fifty workmen there, of whom thirty were armed with guns, for on the road they had borrowed a gunsmith's entire stock.

Nothing could be stranger or more motley than this group ; one had a sleeved waistcoat, a cavalry sabre, and a pair of holster pistols, another was in shirt sleeves, with a round hat, and a powder-flask hung at his side, while a third was cuirassed with nine sheets of gray paper, and was armed with a saddler's awl. There was one who shouted, " Let us exterminate to the last, and die on the point of our bayonet ! " This man had no bayonet. Another displayed over his coat the belts and pouch of a National Guard, with these words sewn in red worsted on the cover—" public order." There were many muskets, bearing the number of legions, few hats, no neckties, a great many bare arms, and a few pikes ; add to this all ages, all faces, short pale youths, and bronzed labourers at the docks. All were in a hurry, and while assisting each other, talked about the possible chances—that they were sure of one regiment, and Paris would rise. These were terrible remarks, with which a sort of cordial joviality was mingled ; they might have been taken for brothers, though they did not know each other's names. Great dangers have this beauty about them, that they throw light on the fraternity of strangers.

A fire was lighted in the kitchen, and men were melting in a bullet-mould, bowls, spoons, forks, and all the pewter articles of the public-house. They drank while doing this, and caps and slugs lay pell-mell on the table with glasses of wine. In the billiard-room Ma'am Hucheloup, Matelotte, and Gibelotte, variously affected by terror,—as one was brutalised by it, another had her breath stopped, while the third was awakened—were tearing up old sheets and making lint. Three insurgents helped them, three hairy, bearded, and moustached fellows, who pulled the linen asunder with the fingers of a sempstress, and who made them tremble. The tall man, whom Courfeyrac, Combeferre, and Enjolras had noticed, as he joined the band at the corner of the Rue des Billettes, was working at the small barricade, and making himself useful. Gavroche was working at the large one, and as for the young man who had waited for Courfeyrac at his lodgings and asked after M. Marius, he disappeared just about the time when the omnibus was overthrown.

Gavroche, who was perfectly radiant, had taken the arrangements on himself; he came, went, ascended, descended, went up again, rustled and sparkled. He seemed to be there for the encouragement of all; had he a spur? certainly in his misery : had he wings? certainly in his joy. Gavroche was a whirlwind, he was seen incessantly and heard constantly, and he filled the air, being everywhere at once. He was a sort of almost irritating ubiquity, and it was impossible to stop with him. The enormous barricade felt him on its crupper; he annoyed the idlers, excited the slothful, reanimated the fatigued, vexed the thoughtful, rendered some gay, and gave others time to breathe, set some in a passion, and all in motion ; he piqued a student and stung a workman, he halted, then started again, flew over the turmoil and the efforts, leapt from one to the other, murmured, buzzed, and harassed the whole team ; he was the fly of the immense revolutionary coach. Perpetual movement was in his little arms, and perpetual clamour in his little lungs.

"Push ahead ; more paving-stones, more barrels, more vehicles ! where are there any? We want a hod-load of plaster to stop up this hole. Your barricade is very small, and must mount. Put everything into it, smash up the house ; a barricade is Mother Gibou's tea. Hilloh ! there's a glass door."

This made the workmen exclaim :

"A glass door ! what would you have us do with that ? "

"A glass door in a barricade is excellent," said Gavroche, "for, though it does not prevent the attack, it bothers them in taking it. Have you never boned apples over a wall on which there was broken glass ? A glass door will cut the corns of the National Guards when they try to climb up the barricade. By Job ! glass is treacherous. Well, you fellows have no very bright imagination."

He was furious with his useless pistol, and went from one to the other, saying, "A gun ! I want a gun ! Why don't you give me a gun ? "

"A gun for you ? " said Combeferre.

"Well, why not ? " Gavroche answered ; "I had one in 1830, when we quarrelled with Charles X."

Enjolras shrugged his shoulders.

"When all the men have guns we will give them to boys."

Gavroche turned fiercely, and answered him :

"If you are killed before me I will take yours."

"Gamin ! " said Enjolras.

"Puppy ! " said Gavroche.

The journals of the day which stated that the barricade in the Rue de la Chanvrerie, that "almost impregnable fortress," as they called it, reached the level of a first-floor, are mistaken, for the truth is, that it did not exceed an average height of six or seven feet. It was so built that the combatants could, at will, either disappear behind it or ascend to its crest, by means of a quadruple row of paving-stones arranged like steps inside. Externally the front of the barricade, composed of piles of paving-stones and barrels, held together by joists and planks, passed through the wheels of the truck and the omnibus, had a bristling and inextricable appearance. A gap, sufficiently wide for one man to pass, was left between the house wall and the end of the barricade farthest from the wine-shop, so that a sortie was possible. The pole of the omnibus was held upright by ropes, and a red flag fixed to this pole floated over the barricade. The small Mondétour barricade, concealed behind the wine-shop, could not be seen, but the two barricades combined formed a real redoubt. Enjolras and Courfeyrac had not thought it advisable to barricade the other portion of the Rue Mondétour, which opens on to the markets, as they doubtless wished to maintain a possible communication with the outside, and had but little fear of being attacked by the difficult and dangerous Rue des Prêcheurs. With the exception of this issue left free, which constituted what Folard would have called in a strategic style, a zigzac, and of the narrow passage in the Rue de la Chanvrerie, the interior of the barricade, in which the wine-shop formed a salient angle, presented an irregular quadrilateral, enclosed on all sides. There was a space of twenty yards between the great barricade and the tall houses which formed the end of the street, so that it might be said that the barricade leant against these houses, which were all inhabited, but closed from top to bottom.

All this labour was completed without any obstacle, in less than an hour, during which this handful of men had not seen a single bearskin-cap or bayonet. The few citizens who still ventured at this moment of riot into the Rue St. Denis took a glance into the Rue de la Chanvrerie, perceived the barricade, and doubled their pace. When the two barricades were completed and the flag was hoisted, a table was pulled from the wine-shop into the street, and Courfeyrac got upon it. Enjolras brought up the square chest, which Courfeyrac opened, and it proved to be full of cartridges. When they saw these cartridges the bravest trembled, and there was a moment's silence. Courfeyrac distributed the cartridges smilingly, and each received thirty : many had powder, and began making others with the bullets which had been cast ; as for the powder barrel, it was on a separate table, near the door, and was held in reserve. The assembly, which was traversing the whole of Paris, did not cease, but in the end it had become a monotonous sound, to which they no longer paid any attention. This noise at one moment retired, at another came nearer, with lugubrious undulations. The guns and carbines were loaded altogether, without precipitation and with a solemn gravity. Enjolras then stationed three sentries outside the barricades, one in the Rue de la Chanvrerie, the second in the Rue des Prêcheurs, the third at the corner of the Petite Truanderie. Then, when the barricades were built, the posts assigned, the guns loaded, the sentries set, the insurgents alone in these formidable streets, through which no one now passed, surrounded by dumb and, as it were, dead houses, in which no human movement palpitated, enveloped in the menacing darkness, in the midst of that

silence and obscurity in which they felt something advancing,
and which had something tragical and terrifying about it,
isolated, armed, determined, and tranquil, they waited.

During the hours of waiting, what did they do? we are
bound to tell it, because this is historical. While the men
were making cartridges and the women lint, while a large
stewpan full of melted tin and lead, intended for the bullet-
mould, was smoking on a red-hot chafing-dish, while the
vedettes were watching with shouldered guns on the
barricade, while Enjolras, whom it was impossible to
distract, watched the vedettes, Combeferre, Courfeyrac,
Jean Prouvaire, Feuilly, Bossuet, Joly, Bahorel, and a
few others, assembled, as in the most peaceful days of their
student conversations, and in one corner of the wine-shop
converted into a casemate, two paces from the barricade which
they had raised, and with their loaded and primed muskets
leaning against the back of their chairs, these fine young
men, so near their last hour, wrote love verses. The hour,
the spot, the recollections of youth recalled, a few stars
which were beginning to glisten in the sky, the funereal
repose of these deserted streets, the imminence of the inexorable adventure which was preparing, gave a pathetic
charm to the verses murmured in a low voice in the twilight
by Jean Prouvaire, who, as we said, was a gentle poet.

In the meanwhile a lamp had been lit on the small
barricade, and on the large one, one of those wax torches
such as may be seen on Shrove Tuesday in front of the
vehicles crowded with masks that are proceeding to the
Courtille. These torches, we know, came from the
Faubourg St. Antoine. The torch was placed in a species
of lantern of paving-stones closed on three sides to protect
it from the wind, and arranged so that the entire light
should fall on the flag. The street and the barricade
remained plunged in darkness, and nothing was visible
save the red flag formidably illumined, as if by an enormous
dark lantern. This light added a strange and terrible purple
to the scarlet of the flag.

Night had quite set in, and nothing occurred, only confused rumours and fusillades now and then could be heard,
but they were rare, badly maintained, and distant. This
respite, which was prolonged, was a sign that the Government was taking its time and collecting its strength. These
fifty men were waiting for the coming of sixty thousand.
Enjolras was attacked by that impatience which seizes on

powerful minds when they stand on the threshold of formidable events. He looked up Gavroche, who was busy manufacturing cartridges in the ground-floor room, by the dubious
light of two candles placed on the bar for precaution, on
account of the gunpowder sprinkled over the tables. These
two candles threw no rays outside, and the insurgents
allowed no light in the upper floors. Gavroche was at this
moment greatly occupied, though not precisely with his
cartridge.

The recruit from the Rue des Billettes had come into the
room and seated himself at the least-lighted table. A Brown
Bess of the large model had fallen to his share, and he held
it between his legs. Gavroche up to this moment, distracted
by a hundred "amusing" things, had not even seen this man.
When he entered, Gavroche looked after him, mechanically
admiring his musket, but when the man was seated, the
gamin suddenly rose. Those who might have watched this
man would have noticed him observe everything in the
barricade, and the band of insurgents, with singular attention, but when he entered the room he fell into a state of
contemplation, and seemed to see nothing of what was
going on. The gamin approached this pensive man, and
began walking round him on tiptoe, in the same way as
people move round a man whom they are afraid of awaking.
At the same time all the grimaces of an old man passed over
his childish face, at once so impudent and so serious, so
giddy and so profound, so gay and so affecting, and these
grimaces signified, "Oh, stuff! it is not possible, I must
see double—I am dreaming—can it be?—no, it is not—yes,
it is—no, it is not." Gavroche balanced himself on his heels,
clenched his fists in his pockets, moved his neck like a bird,
and expended on an enormously outstretched lip all the
sagacity of a lower lip. He was stupefied, uncertain,
convinced, and dazzled. All about him was at work, the
instinct that scents and the intellect that combines ; it was
plain that an event was happening to Gavroche. It was
when he was deepest in thought that Enjolras accosted him.

"You are little," he said, "and will not be seen. Go
out of the barricades, slip along the houses, pass through
as many streets as you can, and come back to tell me what
is going on."

Gavroche drew himself up.

"So little ones are good for something! that's lucky!
I'm off. In the meanwhile trust the little and distrust

the big," and Gavroche, raising his head and dropping his voice, added, as he pointed to the man of the Rue des Billettes :

" You see that tall fellow ? "

" Well ? "

" He's a spy."

" Are you sure ? "

" Not a fortnight back he pulled me down by the ear from the cornice of the Pont Royal where I was taking the air."

Enjolras hurriedly left the gamin and whispered a few words to a labourer from the wine-docks who was present. The labourer went out and returned almost immediately, followed by three others. The four men, four broad-shouldered porters, stationed themselves silently behind the table at which the man was seated, in evident readiness to fall upon him, and then Enjolras walked up to the man and asked him :

" Who are you ? "

At this sudden question the man started, he looked into the depths of Enjolras's candid eyeballs, and seemed to read his thoughts. He gave a smile, which was at once the most disdainful, energetic, and resolute possible, and answered, with a haughty gravity :

" I see what you mean,—well, yes ! "

" Are you a spy ? "

" I am an agent of the authority ! "

" And your name is——? "

" Javert."

Enjolras gave the four men a sign, and in a twinkling, before Javert had time to turn round, he was collared, thrown down, bound, and searched. They found on him a small round card fixed between two pieces of glass, and bearing on one side the arms of France, with the motto, " Surveillance and vigilance," and on the other this notice, " Javert, police Inspector, fifty-two years of age," and the signature of the Prefect of Police of that day, M. Gisquet. He had also a watch and a purse containing some pieces of gold, and both were left him. Behind his watch at the bottom of his fob a paper was found, which Enjolras un-folded, and on which he read these lines, written by the Prefect of Police himself :

" So soon as his political mission is concluded, Javert will assure himself by a special watch whether it is true that criminals assemble on the slope of the right bank of the Seine, near the bridge of Jena."

When the search was ended Javert was raised from the ground, his arms were tied behind his back, and he was fastened in the middle of the room to the celebrated post, which in olden times gave its name to the wine-shop. Gavroche, who had watched the whole scene and approved of everything with a silent shake of the head, went up to Javert, and said :

"The mouse has trapped the cat."

All this took place so quickly that it was completed before those outside the wine-shop were aware of it. Javert had not uttered a cry, but, on seeing him fastened to the post, Courfeyrac, Bossuet, Combeferre, Joly, and the men scattered over the two barricades, flocked in. Javert, who was surrounded with cords so that he could not stir, raised his head with the intrepid serenity of a man who has never told a falsehood.

"It is a spy," said Enjolras, and turning to Javert, "You will be shot two minutes before the barricade is taken."

Javert replied, with his most imperious accent :

"Why not at once?"

"We are saving of powder."

"Then settle the affair with a knife."

"Spy," said the beautiful Enjolras, "we are judges, and not assassins."

Then he called Gavroche.

"You be off now and do what I told you."

"I am off," Gavroche cried, but stopped just as he reached the door.

"By the way, you will give me his gun. I leave you the musician but I want his clarionette."

The gamin gave a military salute, and gaily slipped round the large barricade.

The tragical picture we have undertaken would not be complete, the reader would not see in their exact and real relief those great moments of social lying-in and revolutionary giving birth, in which there is convulsion blended with effort, if we were to omit in our sketch an incident full of an epic and savage horror which occurred almost immediately after Gavroche's departure.

Bands of rioters, it is well known, resemble snowballs, and, as they roll along, agglomerate many tumultuous men, who do not ask each other whence they come.

Among the passers-by who joined the band led by Enjolras, Combeferre, and Courfeyrac, there was a man wearing a porter's jacket, much worn at the shoulders, who gesticulated and vociferated, and had the appearance of a drunken savage. This man, whose name or nickname was Le Cabuc, and entirely unknown to those who pretended to know him, was seated, in a state of real or feigned intoxication, with four others, round a table which they had dragged out of the wine-shop. This Cabuc, while making the others drink, seemed to be gazing thoughtfully at the large house behind the barricade, whose five storeys commanded the whole street, and faced the Rue St. Denis. All at once he exclaimed :

"Do you know what, comrades? we must fire from that house. When we are at the windows, hang me if any one can come up the street."

"Yes, but the house is closed," said one of the drinkers.

"We'll knock."

"They won't open."

"Then we'll break in the door."

Le Cabuc ran up to the door, which had a very massive knocker, and rapped ; as the door was not opened he rapped again, and no one answering, he gave a third rap, but the silence continued.

"Is there any one in here?" Le Cabuc shouted. But nothing stirred, and so he seized a musket and began hammering the door with the butt end. It was an old, low, narrow, solid door, made of oak, lined with sheet-iron inside and heavy bars, and a thorough postern gate. The blows made the whole house tremble, but did not shake the door. The inhabitants, however, were probably alarmed, for a little square trap-window was at length lit up and opened on the third storey, and a candle and the gray-haired head of a terrified old man, who was the porter, appeared in the orifice. The man who was knocking left off.

"What do you want, gentlemen?" the porter asked.

"Open the door!" said Le Cabuc.

"I cannot, gentlemen."

"Open, I tell you!"

"It is impossible, gentlemen."

Le Cabuc raised his musket and took aim at the porter, but as he was below and it was very dark, the porter did not notice the fact.

"Will you open? yes or no."

"No, gentlemen."

"You really mean it?"

"I say no, my kind——"

The porter did not finish the sentence, for the musket was fired; the bullet entered under his chin and came out of his neck, after passing through the jugular vein. The old man fell in a heap, without heaving a sigh, the candle went out, and nothing was visible save a motionless head lying on the sill of the window, and a small wreath of smoke ascending to the roof.

"There," said Le Cabuc, as he let the butt of his musket fall on the pavement again.

He had scarce uttered the word ere he felt a hand laid on his shoulder with the tenacity of an eagle's talon, and he heard a voice saying to him:

"On your knees!"

The murderer turned, and saw before him Enjolras's white, cold face. Enjolras held a pistol in his hand. He had hurried up on hearing the shot fired, and clutched with his left hand Le Cabuc's blouse, shirt, and braces.

"On your knees!" he repeated.

And with a sovereign movement the frail young man of twenty bent, like a reed, the muscular and robust porter, and forced him to kneel in the mud. La Cabuc tried to resist, but he seemed to have been seized by a superhuman hand. Enjolras, pale, barenecked, with his dishevelled hair and feminine face, had at that moment an inexpressible something of the ancient Themis. His dilated nostrils, his downcast eyes, gave to his implacable Greek profile that expression of wrath and that expression of chastity which, in the opinion of the old world, are becoming to justice. All the insurgents ran up, and then ranged themselves in a circle at a distance, feeling that it was impossible for them to utter a word in the presence of what they were going to see. Le Cabuc, conquered, no longer attempted to struggle, and trembled all over: Enjolras loosed his grasp, and took out his watch.

"Pray or think!" he said, "you have one minute to do so."

"Mercy!" the murderer stammered, then hung his head and muttered a few inarticulate execrations.

Enjolras did not take his eyes off his watch; he let the minute pass, and then put the watch again in his fob. This done, he seized Le Cabuc by the hair, who clung to his knees with a yell, and placed the muzzle of the pistol to his ear. Many of these intrepid men, who had so tranquilly entered upon the most frightful of adventures, turned away their heads. The explosion was heard, the assassin fell on his head on the pavement, and Enjolras drew himself up, and looked round him with a stern air of conviction. Then he kicked the corpse and said :

" Throw this outside."

Three men raised the body of the wretch, which was still writhing in the last mechanical convulsions of expiring life, and threw it over the small barricade into the Mondétour lane. Enjolras stood pensive ; some grand darkness was slowly spreading over his formidable serenity. Presently he raised his voice, and all were silent.

"Citizens," said Enjolras, " what that man did is frightful, and what I have done is horrible ; he killed, and that is why I killed, and I was obliged to do so, as insurrection must have its discipline. Assassination is even more of a crime here than elsewhere, for we stand under the eye of the Revolution, we are the priests of the Republic, we are the sacred victims to duty, and we must not do aught that would calumniate our combat. I, therefore, tried and condemned this man to death ; for my part, constrained to do what I have done, but abhorring it, I have also tried myself, and you will shortly see what sentence I have passed."

All who listened trembled.

" We will share your fate," Combeferre exclaimed.

" Be it so ! " Enjolras continued. " One word more. In executing that man I obeyed Necessity ; but Necessity is a monster of the old world, and its true name is Fatality. Now it is the law of progress that monsters should disappear before angels, and Fatality vanish before Fraternity. It is a bad moment to utter the word love, but no matter, I utter it, and I glorify it. Love, thou hast a future ; Death I make use of thee, but I abhor thee. Citizens, in the future there will be no darkness, no thunder-claps ; neither ferocious ignorance, nor bloodthirsty retaliation ; and as there will be no Satan left, there will be no St. Michael. In the future no man will kill another man, the earth will be radiant, and the human race will love. The day will come, citizens, when all will be concord, harmony, light, joy, and life, and we are going to die in order that it may come."

Enjolras was silent, his virgin lips closed, and he stood for some time at the spot where he had shed blood, in the motionlessness of a marble statue. His fixed eyes caused people to talk in whispers around him. Jean Prouvaire and Combeferre shook their heads silently, and leaning against each other in an angle of the barricade, gazed, with an admiration in which there was compassion, at this grave young man, who was an executioner and priest, and had at the same time the light and the hardness of crystal. Let us say at once, that after the action, when the corpses were conveyed to the Morgue and searched, a police-agent's card was found on Le Cabuc; the author of this work had in his hands in 1848 the special report on this subject made to the Prefect of Police in 1832. Let us add that, if we may believe a strange but probably well-founded police tradition, Le Cabuc was Claquesous. It is certainly true that after the death of Cabuc Claquesous was never heard of again, and left no trace of his disappearance. He seemed to have become amalgamated with the invisible; his life had been gloom, and his end was night. The whole insurgent band were still suffering from the emotion of this tragical trial, so quickly begun and so quickly ended, when Courfeyrac saw again at the barricade the small young man who had come to his lodgings to ask for Marius. This lad, who had a bold and reckless look, had come at night to rejoin the insurgents.

CHAPTER XCVII.

THE voice which summoned Marius through the twilight to the barricade in the Rue de la Chanvrerie had produced on him the effect of the voice of destiny. He wished to die, and the opportunity offered; he rapped at the door of the tomb, and a hand held out the key to him from the shadows. Such gloomy openings in the darkness just in front of despair are tempting; Marius removed the bar which had so often allowed him to pass, left the garden, and said, " I will go." Mad with grief, feeling nothing fixed and solid in his brain, incapable of accepting anything henceforth of destiny, after the two months spent in the intoxication of youth and love, and crushed by all the reveries of despair at once, he had only one wish left—to finish with it all at once. He began walking rapidly, and he happened to be armed, as he had Javert's pistols in his pocket. The young man whom he fancied that he had seen had got out of his sight in the streets.

Marius, who left the Rue Plumet by the boulevard, crossed the esplanade and bridge of the Invalides, the Champs Elysées, the square of Louis XV., and reached the Rue de Rivoli. The shops were open there, the gas blazed under the arcades, ladies were making purchases, and people were eating ices at the Café Laiter, and cakes at the English pastrycook's. A few post-chaises, however, were leaving at a gallop the Hôtel des Princes and Meurice's. Marius entered the Rue St. Honoré by the passage Delorme. The shops were closed there, the trades-men were conversing before their open doors, people walked along, the lamps were lighted, and from the first-floor upwards the houses were illumined as usual. Cavalry were stationed on the square of the Palais Royal. Marius followed the Rue St. Honoré, and the farther he got from the Palais Royal the fewer windows were lit up; the shops were entirely closed, nobody was conversing on the thresholds, the street grew darker, and at the same time the crowd denser, for the passers-by had now become a crowd. No one could be heard speaking in the crowd, and yet a hollow, deep buzzing issued from it. Near the Arbre sec Fountain there were mobs motionless, and sombre groups standing among the comers and goers like stones in the middle of a running stream. At the entrance of the Rue des Pouvaires, the crowd no longer moved, it was a resisting, solid, compact, almost impenetrable mob of persons packed together and conversing in a low voice. There were hardly any black coats or round hats present, only fustian jackets, blouses, caps, and bristling beards. This multitude undulated confusedly in the night mist, and its whispering had the hoarse accent of a rustling, and though no one moved, a tramping in the mud could be heard. Beyond this dense crowd there was not a window lit up in the surrounding streets, and the solitary and de-creasing rows of lanterns could only be seen in them. The street-lanterns of that day resembled large red stars suspended from ropes, and cast on to the pavement a shadow which had the shape of a large spider. These streets, however, were not deserted, and piled muskets, moving bayonets, and troops bivouacking could be dis-tinguished in them. No curious person went beyond this limit, and circulation ceased there; there the mob ended and the army began.

Marius willed with the will of a man who no longer hopes;

he had been summoned and was bound to go. He found means to traverse the crowd and bivouacking troops ; he hid himself from the patrols and avoided the sentries. He made a circuit, came to the Rue de Béthisy, and proceeded in the direction of the markets ; at the corner of the Rue des Bourdonnais the lanterns ceased. After crossing the zone of the mob he passed the border of troops, and now found himself in something frightful. There was not a wayfarer, nor a soldier, nor a light, nothing but solitude, silence, and night, and a strangely-piercing cold ; entering a street was like entering a cellar. Still he continued to advance ; some one ran close past him ; was it a man? a woman? were there more than one ? He could not have said, for it had passed and vanished. By constant circuits he reached a lane, which he judged to be the Rue de la Poterie, and toward the middle of that lane he came across an obstacle. He stretched out his hands and found that it was an overturned cart, and his feet recognised pools of water, holes, scattered and piled-up paving-stones—it was a barricade which had been begun and then abandoned. He clambered over the stones and soon found himself on the other side of the obstacle ; he walked very close to the posts, and felt his way along the house walls. A little beyond the barricade he fancied that he could see something white before him, and on drawing nearer it assumed a form. It was a pair of white horses, the omnibus horses un-harnessed by Bossuet in the morning, which had wandered, haphazard, from street to street all day, and at last stopped here, with the stolid patience of animals which no more comprehend the actions of man than man comprehends the actions of Providence. Marius left the horses behind him, and as he entered a street which seemed to be the Rue du Contrat-social, a musket-shot, which came, no one could say whence, and traversed the darkness at hazard, whizzed close past him, and pierced above his head a copper shaving-dish, hanging from a hairdresser's shop. In 1846, this dish with the hole in it was still visible at the corner of the pillars of the markets. This shot was still life, but from this moment nothing further occurred ; the whole itineracy resembled a descent down black steps, but for all that Marius did not the less advance.

Any being hovering over Paris at this moment, with the wings of a bat or an owl, would have had a gloomy spectacle under his eyes. The entire old district of the markets, which is like a city within a city, which is traversed by the Rues St. Denis and St. Martin, and by a thousand lanes which the insurgents had converted into their redoubt and arsenal, would have appeared like an enormous black hole dug in the centre of Paris. Here the eye settled on an abyss, and, owing to the broken lamps and the closed shutters, all brilliancy, life, noise, and movement had ceased in it. The invisible police of the revolt were watching everywhere and maintaining order, that is to say, night. To hide the small number in a vast obscurity, and to multiply each combatant by the possibilities which this obscurity contains, is the necessary tactics of the insurrection, and at nightfall every window in which a candle gleamed received a bullet; the light was extinguished, and sometimes the occupant killed. Hence, nothing stirred; there was nought but terror, mourning, and stupor in the houses, and in the streets a sort of sacred horror.

As often happens, nature seemed to have come to an understanding with what men were going to do, and nothing deranged the mournful harmonies of the whole scene. The stars had disappeared, and heavy clouds filled the entire horizon with their melancholy masses. There was a black sky over these dead streets, as if an intense pall were cast over the immense tomb. While a thoroughly political battle was preparing on the same site which had already witnessed so many revolutionary events,—while the youth, the secret associations, and the schools, in the name of principles, and the middle classes in the name of interests, were coming together to try a final fall,—while everybody was hurrying up and appealing to the last and decisive hour of the crisis, in the distance and beyond that fatal district, at the lowest depths of the unfathomable cavities of that old wretched Paris, which is disappearing under the splendour of happy and opulent Paris, the gloomy voice of the people could be heard hoarsely growling.

Marius had reached the markets; there all was calmer, darker, and even more motionless than in the neighbouring streets. It seemed as if the frozen peace of the tomb had issued from the ground and spread over the sky. A ruddy tinge, however, brought out from the black background the tall roofs of the houses which barred the Rue de la Chanvrerie on the side of St. Eustache. It was the reflection of the torch burning on the Corinth barricade, and Marius walked toward that ruddy hue; it led him to the Marché-aux-

Poirées, and. he caught a glimpse of the Rue des Prêcheurs, into which he turned. The sentry of the insurgents watching at the other end did not notice him; he felt himself quite close to what he was seeking, and he walked on tiptoe. He thus reached the corner of that short piece of the Mondétour lane which was, as will be remembered, the sole communication which Enjolras had maintained with the outer world. At the corner of the last house on his left, he stopped and peeped into the lane. A little beyond the dark corner formed by the lane and the Rue de la Chanvrerie, which formed a large patch of shadow, in which he was himself buried, he noticed a little light on the pavement, a portion of a wine-shop, a lamp flickering in a sort of shapeless niche, and men crouching down with guns on their knees,—all this was scarce ten yards from him, and was the interior of the barricade. The houses that lined the right-hand side of the lane hid from him the rest of the wine-shop, the large barricade, and the flag. Marius had but one step to take, and then the unhappy young man sat down on a post, folded his arms, and thought of his father.

He thought of that heroic Colonel Pontmercy, who had been such a proud soldier, who had defended under the Republic the frontier of France, and reached under the Emperor the frontier of Asia; who had seen Genoa, Alessandria, Milan, Turin, Madrid, Vienna, Dresden, Berlin, and Moscow; who had left on all the victorious battlefields of Europe drops of the same blood which Marius had in his veins; who had grown gray before his time in discipline and command; who had lived with his waistbelt buckled, his epaulettes falling on his chest, his cockade blackened by smoke, his brow wrinkled by his helmet, in barracks, in camp, in bivouacs, and in hospitals, and who, at the expiration of twenty years, had returned from the great wars with his scarred cheek and smiling face, simple, tranquil, admirable, pure as an infant, having done everything for France, and nothing against her. He said to himself that his own day had now arrived, that his hour had at length struck, that after his father, he too was going to be brave, intrepid, and bold, to rush to meet bullets, offer his chest to the bayonets, shed his blood, seek the enemy, seek death; that he, in his turn, was about to wage war and go into the battlefield, and that the battle he would enter was the street, and the war he was about to wage civil war! He saw civil war opening like a gulf before him, and that he was going to fall into it ; then he shuddered.

He thought of his father's sword, which his grandfather had sold to the old clothes-dealer, and which he had so painfully regretted. He said to himself that this valiant and chaste sword had done well to escape from him, and disappear angrily in the darkness ; that it fled away thus because it was intelligent, and foresaw the future,—the riots, the war of gutters, the war of paving-stones, fusillades from cellar-traps, and blows dealt and received from behind ; that, coming from Marengo and Austerlitz, it was unwilling to go to the Rue de la Chanvrerie, and after what it had done with the father refused to do that with the son ! He said to himself that if that sword had been here, if, after receiving it at his dead father's bedside, he had dared to take it, and carry it into this nocturnal combat between Frenchmen in the streets, it would assuredly have burned his hands, and have flashed before him like the sword of the archangel ! He said to himself that it was fortunate it was not there, and that it had disappeared,—that this was well, this was just, that his grandfather had been the true guardian of his father's glory, and that it was better for the Colonel's sword to have been put up for auction, sold to the second-hand dealer, or broken up as old iron, than come to-day to make the flank of the country bleed. And then he began weeping bitterly. It was horrible, but what was he to do? he could not live without Cosette, and since she had departed all that was left him was to die. ·Had he not pledged her his word of honour that he would die? She had gone away knowing this, and it was plain that she was pleased with Marius' dying ; and then it was clear that she no longer loved him, since she had gone away thus without warning him, without a word, without a letter, and yet she knew his address ! Of what use was it to live? and why should he live now? And then, to have come so far and then recoil! to have approached the danger and run away! to have come to look at the barricade and then slip off! to slip off, trembling and saying, "After all, I have had enough of that. I have seen it ; that is sufficient. It is civil war; and I will be off!" To abandon his friends who expected him, who perhaps had need of him, who were a handful against an army ! To be false to everything at once,—to love, to friendship, to his word ! to give his poltroonery the pretext of patriotism! Oh, that was impossible; and if his father's phantom were there in the shadows, and saw him recoil, it would lash him with the flat of its sabre, and cry to him, " Forward, coward !"

A prey to this oscillation of his thoughts, he hung his head, but suddenly raised it again, for a species of splendid rectification had just taken place in his mind. There is a dilatation of thought peculiar to the vicinity of the tomb; and to be near death makes a man see correctly. The vision of the action upon which he saw himself perhaps on the point of entering, no longer appeared to him lamentable, but superb; the street was transfigured by some internal labour of the soul, before his mental eye. All the tumultuous notes of interrogation of reverie crowded back upon him, but without troubling him; and he did not leave a single one unanswered. Why would his father be indignant? are there not cases in which insurrection attains to the dignity of duty? what was there degrading for the son of Colonel Pontmercy in the combat which was about to commence? It is no longer Montmirail or Champaubert, it is something else; it is no longer a question of a sacred territory, but of a holy idea.

No one but will have noticed in himself that the mind— and this is the marvel of its unity complicated with ubiquity —has the strange aptitude of reasoning almost coldly in the most violent extremities, and it often happens that weird passions and deep despair, in the very agony of their blackest soliloquies, handle subjects and discuss theses. Logic is mingled with the convulsion, and the thread of syllogism runs without breaking through the storm of the thoughts :—such was Marius' state of mind. While thinking thus, crushed, but resolute, and yet hesitating and shuddering at what he was going to do, his eyes wandered about the interior of the barricade. The insurgents were conversing in whispers, without moving, and that almost silence which marks the last phase of expectation was perceptible. Above them at a third-floor window, Marius distinguished a species of spectator or witness, who seemed singularly attentive,—it was the porter killed by Le Cabuc. From below, this head could be vaguely perceived in the reflection of the torch burning on the barricade, and nothing was stranger in this dense and vacillating light than this motionless, livid, and amazed face, with its bristling hair, open and fixed eyes, and gaping mouth, bending over the street in an attitude of curiosity. One would have said that he who was dead was contemplating those who were going to die. A long stream of blood which had flowed from his head, descended from the window to the first floor, where it stopped.

CHAPTER XCVIII.

NOTHING came yet : it had struck ten by St. Merry's, and Enjolras and Combeferre were sitting, musket in hand, near the sally port of the great barricade. They did not speak, but were listening, trying to catch the dullest and most remote sound of marching. Suddenly, in the midst of this lugubrious calm, a clear, young, gay voice, which seemed to come from the Rue St. Denis, burst forth, and began singing distinctly, to the old popular tune of *Au clair de la lune*, these lines, terminating with a cry that resembled a cock-crow.

> Mon nez est en larmes,
> Mon ami Bugeaud,
> Prêt-moi tes gendarmes
> Pour leur dire un mot.
> En capote bleue,
> La poule au shako,
> Voici la banlieue !
> Co-cocorico !

They grasped each other by the hand.
" It is Gavroche," said Enjolras.
" He is warning us," said Combeferre.
Hurried footsteps troubled the deserted streets, and a being more active than a clown was seen climbing over the omnibus, and Gavroche leaped into the square, out of breath, and saying :
" My gun ! here they are."
An electric thrill ran along the whole barricade, and the movement of hands seeking guns was heard.
" Will you have my carbine ? " Enjolras asked the gamin.
" I want the big gun," Gavroche answered ; and he took Javert's musket.
Two sentries had fallen back and come in almost simultaneously with Gavroche ; they were those from the end of the street and the Petite Truanderie. The vedette in the lane des Prêcheurs remained at his post, which indicated

that nothing was coming from the direction of the bridges and the markets. The Rue de la Chanvrerie, in which a few paving-stones were scarce visible in the reflection of the light cast on the flag, offered to the insurgents the aspect of a large black gate vaguely opening into a cloud of smoke. Every man proceeded to his post : forty-three insurgents, among whom were Enjolras, Combeferre, Courfeyrac, Bossuet, Joly, Bahorel, and Gavroche, knelt behind the great barricade, with the muzzles of their guns and carbines thrust out between the paving-stones as through loopholes, attentive, silent, and ready to fire. Six, commanded by Feuilly, installed themselves at the upper windows of Corinth. Some minutes more elapsed, and then a measured, heavy tramp of many feet was distinctly heard from the direction of St. Leu. This noise, at first faint, then precise, and then heavy and re-echoing, approached slowly, without halt or interruption, and with a tranquil and terrible continuity. Nothing was audible but this. It was at once the silence and noise of the statue of the commendatore. But the stormy footfall had something enormous and multiple about it, which aroused the idea of a multitude at the same time as that of a spectre ; you might have fancied that you heard the fearful statue Legion on the march. The tramp came nearer, nearer still, and then ceased ; and the breathing of many men seemed to be audible at the end of the street. Nothing, however, was visible ; though quite at the end in the thick gloom could be distinguished a multitude of metallic threads, fine as needles and almost imperceptible, which moved about like that indescribable phosphoric network which we perceive under our closed eyelids just at the moment when we are falling asleep. These were bayonets and musket barrels on which the reflection of the torch confusedly fell. There was another pause, as if both sides were waiting. All at once a voice, which was the more sinister because no one could be seen, and because it seemed as if the darkness itself was speaking, shouted :

"Who goes there ? "

At the same time the click of muskets being cocked could be heard. Enjolras replied with a sonorous and haughty accent :

"The French Revolution ! "

" Fire ! " the voice commanded.

A flash lit up all the frontages in the street, as if the door of a furnace had been suddenly opened, then shut. A frightful shower of bullets hurled against the barricade, and the flag fell. The discharge had been so violent and dense that it had cut the staff asunder, that is to say, the extreme point of the omnibus pole. Bullets ricochetting from the corners of the houses, penetrated the barricade, and wounded several men. The impression produced by this first discharge was chilling. The attack was rude, and of a nature to make the boldest think. It was plain that they had to do with a whole regiment at least.

"Comrades," Courfeyrac cried, "let us not waste our powder, but wait till they have entered the street before returning their fire."

"And before all," Enjolras said, "let us hoist the flag again!"

He picked up the flag, which had fallen at his feet. They heard from without the ring of ramrods in barrels: the troops were reloading. Enjolras continued:

"Who has a brave heart among us? who will plant the flag on the barricade again?"

Not one replied, for to mount the barricade at this moment, when all the guns were doubtless again aimed at it, was simply death, and the bravest man hesitates to condemn himself. Enjolras even shuddered as he repeated:

"Will no one offer?"

Since they had arrived at Corinth and had commenced building the barricade, no one had paid any further attention to Father Mabœuf. M. Mabœuf, however, had not quitted the insurgents. He had gone into the ground-floor room of the wine-shop and seated himself behind the bar, where he was, so to speak, annihilated in himself. He seemed no longer to see or think. Courfeyrac and others had twice or thrice accosted him, warning him of the peril, and begging him to withdraw, but he had not appeared to hear them. When no one was speaking to him his lips moved as if he were answering some one, and so soon as people addressed him, his lips left off moving, and his eyes no longer seemed alive. A few hours before the barricade was attacked he had assumed a posture which he had not quitted since, with his two hands on his knees, and his head bent forward, as if he were looking into a precipice. Nothing could have drawn him out of this attitude, and it did not appear as if his mind were in the barricade. When every one else went to his post the only persons left in the room were Javert tied to the post, an insurgent with drawn sabre watching over

Javert, and Mabœuf. At the moment of the attack, at the detonation, the physical shock affected, and, as it were, awoke him : he suddenly rose, crossed the room, and at the moment when Enjolras repeated his appeal, "Does no one offer ? " the old man was seen on the threshold of the wineshop. His presence produced a species of commotion in the groups, and the cry was raised :

"It is the voter, the conventionalist, the representative of the people ! "

He probably did not hear it : he walked straight up to Enjolras, the insurgents making way for him with a religious fear, tore the flag from Enjolras, who recoiled with petrifaction, and then, no one daring to arrest or help him, this old man of eighty, with shaking head, but firm step, slowly began ascending the staircase of paving-stones formed inside the barricade. This was so gloomy and so grand that all around him cried, "Hats off !" With each step he ascended, the scene became more frightful, his white hair, his decrepit face, his tall, bald, and wrinkled forehead, his hollow eyes, his amazed and open mouth, and his old arm raising the red banner, stood out from the darkness and were magnified in the sanguinary brightness of the torch, and the spectators fancied they saw the spectre of '93 issuing from the ground, holding the flag of terror in its hand. When he was on the last step, when this trembling and terrible phantom, standing on the pile of ruins, in the presence of twelve hundred invisible gun-barrels, stood facing death, and as if stronger than it, the whole barricade assumed a supernatural and colossal aspect in the darkness. There was one of those silences which only occur at the sight of prodigies, and in the midst of this silence the old man brandished the red flag and cried :

"Long live the revolution ! long live the republic ! fraternity ! equality ! and death ! "

A low and quick talking, like the murmur of a hurried priest galloping through a mass, was heard,—it was probably the police commissary making the legal summons at the other end of the street ; then the same loud voice which had shouted " Who goes there " cried :

" Withdraw ! "

M. Mabœuf, livid, haggard, with his eyeballs illumined by the mournful flames of mania, raised the flag about his head and repeated :

" Long live the republic ! "

"Fire!" the voice commanded.

A second discharge, resembling a round of grapeshot, burst against the barricade; the old man sank on his knees, then rose again, let the flag slip from his hand, and fell back on the pavement like a log, with his arms stretched out like a cross. Streams of blood flowed under him, and his old, pale, melancholy face seemed to be gazing at heaven. One of those emotions stronger than man, which makes him forget self-defence, seized on the insurgents, and they approached the corpse with respectful horror.

"What men these regicides are!" said Enjolras.

Courfeyrac whispered in Enjolras's ear:

"This is only between ourselves, as I do not wish to diminish the enthusiasm, but this man was anything but a regicide. I knew him, and his name was Mabœuf. I do not know what was the matter with him to-day, but he was a brave idiot. Look at his head."

"The head of an idiot and the heart of Brutus!" Enjolras replied, then he raised his voice.

"Citizens! such is the example which the old give to the young. We hesitated and he came; we recoiled and he advanced. This is what those who tremble with old age teach those who tremble with fear! This aged man is august before his country; he has had a long life and a magnificent death! Now let us place his corpse under cover, let each of us defend this dead old man as he would defend his living father, and let his presence in the midst of us render the barricade impregnable!"

A murmur of gloomy and energetic adhesion followed these words. Enjolras bent down, raised the old man's head, and sternly kissed him on the forehead; then, stretching out his arms and handling the dead man with tender caution, as if afraid of hurting him, he took off his coat, pointed to the bloodstained holes, and said:

"This is our flag now!"

A long black shawl of Widow Hucheloup's was thrown over Father Mabœuf: six men made a litter of their muskets, the corpse was laid on them, and they carried it with bare heads and solemn slowness to a large table in the ground-floor room. These men, entirely engaged with the grave and sacred thing they were doing, did not think of the perilous situation in which they were, and when the corpse was carried past the stoical Javert, Enjolras said to the spy.

"Your turn will come soon."

During this period little Gavroche, who alone had not left his post, and had remained on the watch, fancied he could see men creeping up to the barricade : all at once he cried, "Look out !" Courfeyrac, Enjolras, Jean Prouvaire, Combeferre, Joly, Bahorel, and Bossuet, all hurried tumultuously out of the wine-shop, but it was almost too late ; for they saw a flashing line of bayonets undulating on the crest of the barricade. Municipal Guards of tall stature penetrated, some by striding over the omnibus, others through the sally port, driving before them the gamin, who fell back, but did not fly. The moment was critical ; it was that first formidable minute of inundation when the river rises to the level of the dam and the water begins to filter through the fissures of the dyke. One second more and the barricade had been captured. Bahorel dashed at the first Municipal Guard who entered, and killed him with a shot from his carbine ; the second killed Bahorel with a bayonet-thrust. Another had already levelled Courfeyrac, who was shouting "Help !" while the tallest of all of them, a species of Colossus, was marching upon Gavroche, with his bayonet at the charge. The gamin raised in his little arms Javert's enormous musket, resolutely aimed it at the giant, and pulled the trigger. But the gun did not go off, as Javert had not loaded it : the Municipal Guard burst into a laugh, and advanced upon the lad. Before the bayonet had reached Gavroche, however, the musket fell from the soldier's hands, for a bullet struck him in the middle of the forehead, and he fell on his back. A second bullet struck the other Guard, who had attacked Courfeyrac, in the middle of the chest, and laid him low.

The shots were fired by Marius who had just entered the barricade.

Marius, still concealed at the corner of the Rue Mondétour, had watched the first phase of the combat with shuddering irresolution. Still he was unable to resist for any length of time that mysterious and sovereign dizziness which might be called the appeal from the abyss : and at the sight of the imminence of the peril, of M. Mabœuf's death, that mournful enigma, Bahorel killed, Courfeyrac shouting for help, this child menaced, and his friends to succour or revenge, all hesitation vanished, and he rushed into the medley, pistols in hand. With the first shot he saved Gavroche, and with the second delivered Courfeyrac. On hearing the shots and the cries of the Guards, the assailants swarmed up the entrenchment, over the crest of which could now be seen more than half the bodies of Municipal Guards, troops of the line, and National Guards from the suburbs, musket in hand. They already covered more than two-thirds of the barricade, but no longer leapt down into the enclosure, and hesitated, as if they feared some snare. They looked down into the gloomy space as they would have peered into a lion's den; and the light of the torch only illumined bayonets, bearskin shakos, and anxious and irritated faces.

Marius had no longer a weapon, as he had thrown away his discharged pistols, but he had noticed the barrel of gunpowder near the door of the ground-floor room. As he half turned to look in that direction a soldier levelled his musket at him, and at the moment when the soldier was taking steady aim at Marius, a hand was laid on the muzzle of his musket and stopped it up; the young workman in the velvet trousers had rushed forward. The shot was fired, the bullet passed through the hand, and probably through the workman, for he fell, but it did not hit Marius. Marius, who was entering the wine-shop, hardly noticed this; still he had confusedly seen the gun pointed at him, and the hand laid on the muzzle, and had heard the explosion. But in minutes like this things that men see vacillate, and they do not dwell on anything, for they feel themselves obscurely impelled toward deeper shadows still, and all is mist. The insurgents, surprised but not terrified, had rallied, and Enjolras cried, " Wait, do not throw away your shots ! " and, in truth, in the first moment of confusion they might wound each other. The majority had gone up to the first-floor and attic windows, whence they commanded the assailants, but the more determined, with Enjolras, Courfeyrac, Jean Prouvaire, and Combeferre, were haughtily standing against the houses at the end, unprotected, and facing the lines of soldiers and guards who crowned the barricade. All this was done without precipitation, and with that strange and menacing gravity which precedes a combat ; on both sides men were aiming at each other within point-blank range, and they were so near that they could converse. When they were at the point where the spark was about to shoot forth, an officer wearing a gorget and heavy epaulettes stretched out his sword and said :

"Throw down your arms!"

"Fire!" Enjolras commanded.

The two detonations took place at the same moment, and everything disappeared in smoke, a sharp and stifling smoke, in which the dying and the wounded writhed, with faint and hollow groans. When the smoke dispersed, the two lines of combatants could be seen, thinned out, but still in the same spot, and silently reloading their guns. All at once a thundering voice was heard shouting:

"Begone, or I will blow up the barricade!"

All turned to the quarter whence the voice came.

Marius had entered the wine-shop, fetched the barrel of gunpowder, and then, taking advantage of the smoke and obscure mist which filled the entrenched space, glided along the barricade up to the cage of paving-stones in which the torch was fixed. To tear out the torch, place in its stead the barrel of powder, throw down the pile of paving-stones on the barrel, which was at once unheaded with a sort of terrible obedience, had only occupied so much time as stooping and rising again; and now all, National Guards and Municipal Guards, officers and privates, collected at the other end of the barricade, gazed at him in stupor, as he stood with one foot on the paving-stones, the torch in his hand, his haughty face illumined by a fatal resolution, approaching the flame of the torch to the formidable heap, in which the broken powder-barrel could be distinguished, and uttering the terrifying cry:

"Begone, or I will blow up the barricade!"

Marius, on this barricade after the octogenarian, was the vision of the young revolution after the apparition of the old one.

"Blow up the barricade!" a sergeant said, "and yourself too!"

Marius answered, "And myself too!"

And he lowered the torch toward the barrel of gunpowder; but there was no one left on the barricade; the assailants, leaving their dead and their wounded, fell back pell-mell and in disorder to the end of the street, and disappeared again in the night. It was a *sauve qui peut*, and the barricade was saved. All surrounded Marius, and Courfeyrac fell on his neck.

"Here you are!"

"What happiness!" said Combeferre.

"You arrived just in time," said Bossuet.

"Were it not for you I should be dead!" Courfeyrac remarked.

"Without you I should have been goosed," Gavroche added.

Marius added :

"Who is the leader ? "

"Yourself," Enjolras replied.

Marius the whole day through had had a furnace in his brain, but now it was a tornado, and this tornado which was in him produced on him the effect of being outside him and carrying him away. It seemed to him as if he were already an immense distance from life, and his two luminous months of joy and love suddenly terminated at this frightful precipice. Cosette lost to him, this barricade, M. Mabœuf letting himself be killed for the Republic, himself chief of the insurgents—all these things seemed to him a monstrous nightmare, and he was obliged to make a mental effort in order to remind himself that all which surrounded him was real. Marius had not lived long enough yet to know that nothing is so imminent as the impossible, and that what must be always foreseen is the unforeseen. He witnessed the performance of his own drama, as if it were a piece of which he understood nothing. In his mental fog he did not recognise Javert, who, fastened to his post, had not made a movement of his head during the attack on the barricade, and saw the revolt buzzing round him with the resignation of a martyr and the majesty of a judge. In the meanwhile, the assailants no longer stirred ; they could be heard marching and moving at the end of the street, but did not venture into it, either because they were waiting for orders, or else required reinforcements, before rushing again upon this impregnable redoubt. The insurgents had posted sentries, and some who were medical students had begun dressing wounds. All the tables had been dragged out of the wine-shop, with the exception of the two reserved for the lint and the cartridges, and the one on which Father Mabœuf lay ; they had been added to the barricade, and the mattresses off the beds of Widow Hucheloup and the girls had been put in their place. On these mattresses the wounded were laid ; as for the three poor creatures who inhabited Corinth, no one knew what had become of them, but they were at length found hidden in the cellar,—"Like lawyers," Bossuet said ; and added, "Women, fie ! "

A poignant emotion darkened the joy of the liberated

barricade ; the roll-call was made, and one of the insurgents was missing. Who was he? one of the dearest and most valiant, Jean Prouvaire. He was sought for among the dead, but was not there ; he was sought for among the wounded, and was not there ; he was evidently a prisoner. Combeferre said to Enjolras :

"They have our friend, but we have their agent ; do you insist on the death of this spy ? "

"Yes," Enjolras replied, " but less than the life of Jean Prouvaire."

This was said in the bar-room close to Javert's post.

"Well," Combeferre continued, " I will fasten a handkerchief to my cane, and go as a flag of truce to offer to give them their man for our man."

"Listen," said Enjolras, as he laid his hand on Combeferre's arm.

There was a meaning click of guns at the end of the street, and a manly voice could be heard crying :

" Long live France ! long live the future ! "

They recognised Prouvaire's voice ; a flash passed, and a detonation burst forth ; then the silence returned.

" They have killed him," Combeferre exclaimed.

Enjolras looked at Javert and said to him :

" Your friends have just shot you."

It is a peculiarity of this sort of war, that the attack on barricades is almost always made in the front, and that the assailants generally refrain from turning positions, either because they suspect ambuscades, or are afraid to enter winding streets. The whole attention of the insurgents was, consequently, directed to the great barricade, which was evidently the constantly threatened point, and where the contest must infallibly recommence. Marius, however, thought of the little barricade, and went to it ; it was deserted, and only guarded by the lamp which flickered among the paving-stones. However, the Mondétour lane and the branches of the little Truanderie were perfectly calm. As Marius, after making his inspection, was going back, he heard his name faintly uttered in the darkness :

" Monsieur Marius ! "

He started, for he recognised the voice which had summoned him two hours back through the garden railings in the Rue Plumet, but this voice now only seemed to be a gasp ; he looked around him and saw nobody. Marius fancied that he was mistaken, and that it was an illusion added by his mind to the extraordinary realities which were pressing round him. He took a step to leave the remote angle in which the barricade stood.

"Monsieur Marius!" the voice repeated; this time he could not doubt, for he had heard distinctly; he looked around but saw nothing.

"At your feet," the voice said.

He stooped down, and saw in the shadow a form crawling toward him on the pavement. It was the speaker. The lamp enabled him to distinguish a blouse, torn cotton-velvet trousers, bare feet, and something that resembled a pool of blood; Marius also caught a glimpse of a pale face raised to him, and saying :

"Do you not recognise me?"

"No."

"Eponine."

Marius eagerly stooped down; it was really that hapless girl, dressed in male clothes.

"What brought you here? what are you doing?"

"Dying," she said to him.

There are words and incidents that wake up crushed beings; Marius cried with a start :

"You are wounded! wait, I will carry you into the wine-shop! your wound will be dressed! is it serious? how shall I catch hold of you so as not to hurt you? where is it you suffer? Help, good God! but what did you come here for?"

And he tried to pass his hand under her to lift her, and as he did so he touched her hand—she uttered a faint cry.

"Have I hurt you?" Marius asked.

"A little."

"But I only touched your hand."

She raised her hand to Marius' eyes, and he could see a hole right through it.

"What is the matter with your hand?" he said.

"It is pierced."

"Pierced?"

"Yes."

"What with?"

"A bullet."

"How?"

"Did you see a musket aimed at you?"

"Yes, and a hand laid on the muzzle."

"It was mine."

Marius shuddered.

"What madness ! Poor child ! But all the better, if that is your wound ; it is nothing, so let me carry you to a bed. Your wound will be dressed, people do not die of a bullet through the hand."

She murmured :

" The bullet passed through my hand but came out of my back, so it is useless to move me from here. I will tell you how you can do me more good than a surgeon ; sit down by my side on that stone."

He obeyed ; she laid her head on his knees, and without looking at him, said :

"Oh, how good that is, how comforting ! There ! I do not suffer now."

She remained silent for a moment, then turned her head with an effort, and gazed at Marius.

"Do you know what, M. Marius ? it annoyed me that you entered that garden, though it was very foolish of me, as I showed you the house, and then, too, I ought to have remembered that a young gentleman like you——"

She broke off, and leaping over the gloomy transitions which her mind doubtless contained, she added with a heartrending smile :•

"You thought me ugly, did you not ? "

Then she continued :

"You are lost, and no one will leave the barricade now. I brought you here, you know, and you are going to die, I feel sure of it. And yet, when I saw the soldier aiming at you, I laid my hand on the muzzle of his gun. How droll it is, but the reason was that I wished to die with you. When I received that bullet I dragged myself here, and as no one saw me I was not picked up. I waited for you, and said, 'Will he not come ? ' Oh, if you only knew how I bit my blouse, for I was suffering so terribly ; but now I feel all right. Do you remember the day when I came into your room and looked at myself in your glass, and the day when I met you on the boulevard near the washer-women ? How the birds sang, and it is not so very long ago. You gave me five francs, and I said to you, 'I do not want your money.' I hope you picked up your coin, for you are not rich, and I did not think of telling you to pick it up. The sun was shining, and it was not at all cold. Do you remember, M. Marius ! Oh, I am so happy, for everybody is going to die."

She had a wild, grave, and heartrending look, and her ragged blouse displayed her naked throat. While speaking, she laid her wounded hand on her chest, in which there was another hole, and whence every moment a stream of blood spirted like a jet of wine from an open bung. Marius gazed at this unfortunate creature with profound compassion.

"Oh!" she suddenly continued, "it is coming back: I choke!"

She raised her blouse and bit it, and her limbs stiffened on the pavement. At this moment Gavroche's crowing voice could be heard from the barricade: the lad had got on to a table to load his musket, and was gaily singing the song so popular at that day:

> En voyant Lafayette,
> Le gendarme répète :
> Sauvons-nous ! sauvons-nous ! sauvons-nous !

Eponine raised herself and listened, then she muttered : "It is he."

And, turning to Marius, added :

"My brother is here, but he must not see me, or he would scold me."

"Your brother?" Marius asked, as he thought most bitterly and sadly of the duties toward the Thénardiers which his father had left him; "which is your brother?"

"That little fellow."

"The one who is singing?"

"Yes."

Marius made a move.

"Oh, do not go away," she said, "it will not be long now."

She was almost sitting up, but her voice was very low, and every now and then interrupted by the death-rattle. She put her face as close as she could to that of Marius, and added with a strange expression :

"Come, I will not play you a trick. I have had a letter addressed to you in my pocket since yesterday. I was told to put it in the post; but kept it, as I did not wish it to reach you. But perhaps you will not be angry with me when we meet again ere long; for we shall meet again, shall we not? Take your letter."

She convulsively seized Marius' hand with her wounded

hand, but seemed no longer to feel the suffering. She placed Marius' hand in her blouse pocket, and he really felt a paper.

"Take it," she said.

Marius took the letter, and she gave a nod of satisfaction and consolation.

" Now, for my trouble ; promise me ——"

And she stopped.

"What ? " Marius asked.

" Promise me ! "

" I do promise ! "

" Promise to kiss me on the forehead when I am dead— I shall feel it."

She let her head fall again on Marius' knees and her eyes closed — he fancied the poor soul had departed. Eponine remained motionless, but all at once, at the moment when Marius believed her eternally asleep, she slowly opened her eyes, on which the gloomy profundity of death was visible, and said to him with an accent whose gentleness seemed already to come from another world :

" And then, Monsieur Marius, I think that I was a little bit in love with you."

She tried to smile once more, and expired.

CHAPTER XCIX.

MARIUS kept his promise. He kissed that livid forehead, upon which an icy perspiration beaded. It was not an infidelity to Cosette, but a pensive and sweet farewell to an unhappy soul. He had not taken without a quiver the letter which Eponine gave him ; for he at once suspected an event in it, and was impatient to read it. The heart of man is so constituted,—and the unfortunate child had scarce closed her eyes ere Marius thought of unfolding the paper. He gently laid her on the ground and went off, for something told him that he could not read this letter in the presence of a corpse. He walked up to a candle on the ground-floor room ; it was a little note, folded and sealed with the elegant care peculiar to women. The address was in a feminine handwriting, and ran :

"To Monsieur, Monsieur Marius Pontmercy, at M. Courfeyrac's, No. 16 Rue de la Verrerie."

He broke the seal and read :

"My well-beloved,—Alas, my father insists on our going away at once. We shall be this evening at No. 7 Rue de l'Homme Armé, and within a week in London.— COSETTE. June 4."

Such was the innocence of their love, that Marius did not even know Cosette's handwriting.

What had happened may be told in a few words. Eponine had done it all. After the night of June 3 she had had a double thought,—to foil the plans of her father and the bandits upon the house in the Rue Plumet, and separate Marius and Cosette. She had changed rags with the first scamp she met, who thought it amusing to dress up as a woman, while Eponine disguised herself as a man. It was she who gave Jean Valjean the expressive warning, and he had gone straight home and said to Cosette, "We shall start this evening, and go to the Rue de l'Homme Armé with Toussaint. Next week we shall be in London." Cosette, startled by this unexpected blow, had hastily written two lines to Marius, but how was she to put the letter in the post ? She never went out alone, and Toussaint, surprised by such an errand, would certainly show the letter to M. Fauchelevent. In this state of anxiety, Cosette noticed through the railings Eponine in male clothes, who now incessantly prowled round the garden. Cosette had summoned "this young workman," and gave him the letter and a five-franc piece, saying, "Carry this letter at once to its address," and Eponine put the letter in her pocket. The next day she went to Courfeyrac's and asked for Marius, not to hand him the letter, but "to see," a thing which every jealous, loving soul will understand. There she waited for Marius, or at any rate Courfeyrac—always to see. When Courfeyrac said to her, "We are going to the barricades," an idea crossed her mind—to throw herself into this death as she would have done into any other, and thrust Marius into it. She followed Courfeyrac, assured herself of the spot where the barricade was being built ; and, feeling certain, since Marius had not received the letter, that he would go at nightfall to the usual meeting-place, she went to the Rue Plumet, waited for Marius there, and gave him that summons in the name of his friends, which, as she thought, must lead him to the barricade. She reckoned on Marius' despair when he did not find

Cosette, and she was not mistaken, and then she returned to the Rue de la Chanvrerie. We have just seen what she did there; she died with that tragic joy of jealous hearts, which drags the beloved being down to death with them, saying, "No one shall have him!"

Marius covered Cosette's letter with kisses. She loved him then! and for a moment he had an idea that he ought not to die; but then he said to himself, "Her father is taking her to England, and my grandfather will not give his consent to the marriage; no change has taken place in fatality." Dreamers like Marius undergo such supreme despondencies, and desperate resolves issue from them; the fatigue of living is insupportable, and death is sooner over. Then he thought that two duties were left him to accomplish; to inform Cosette of his death and send her his last farewell, and to save from the imminent catastrophe which was approaching that poor boy, Eponine's brother and Thénardier's son. He had a pocket-book about him, the same which had contained the paper on which he had written so many love-thoughts for Cosette; he tore out a leaf, and wrote in pencil these few lines:

"Our marriage was impossible; I asked my grandfather's consent, and he refused to give it; I have no fortune, nor have you. I ran to your house, and did not find you there; you remember the pledge I made to you; I keep it. I die. I love you, and when you read this, my soul will be near you, and will smile upon you."

Having nothing with which to seal this letter, he merely folded it, and wrote on it the address.

"To Mademoiselle Cosette Fauchelevent, at M. Fauchelevent's, No. 7 Rue de l'Homme Armé."

The letter folded, he stood for a moment in thought, then opened his pocket-book again, and wrote with the same pencil these lines on the first page:

"My name is Marius Pontmercy. Carry my body to my grandfather, M. Gillenormand, No. 6 Rue des Filles du Calvaire, in the Marais."

He returned the book to his coat pocket, and then summoned Gavroche. The lad, on hearing Marius' voice, ran up with his joyous and devoted face.

"Will you do something for me?"

"Everything," said Gavroche. "God of Gods! my goose would have been cooked without you."

"You see this letter?"

"Yes."

"Take it. Leave the barricade at once" (Gavroche began scratching his ear anxiously). "and to-morrow morning you will deliver it at its address, No. 7 Rue de l'Homme Armé."

The heroic lad replied:

"Well, but during that time the barricade will be attacked, and I shall not be here."

"The barricade will not be attacked again till daybreak, according to all appearances, and will not be taken till to-morrow afternoon."

The new respite which the assailants granted to the barricade was really prolonged; it was one of those intermittences frequent in night fights, which are always followed by redoubled obstinacy.

"Well," said Gavroche, "suppose I were to deliver your letter to-morrow morning?"

"It will be too late; for the barricade will probably be blockaded, all the issues guarded, and you will be unable to get out. Be off at once."

Gavroche could not find any reply, so he stood there undecided, and scratching his head sorrowfully. All at once he seized the letter with one of those birdlike movements of his.

"All right," he said.

And he ran off toward the Mondétour lane. Gavroche had an idea which decided him, but which he did not mention; it was the following:

"It is scarce midnight, the Rue de l'Homme Armé is no great distance off. I will deliver the letter at once, and be back in time."

What are the convulsions of a city compared with the convulsions of a soul? man is even a greater profundity than the people. Jean Valjean at this very moment was suffering from a frightful internal earthquake, and all the gulfs were reopened within him. He too was quivering like Paris, on the threshold of a formidable and obscure revolution. A few hours had sufficed to cover his destiny and his conscience with shadows, and of him, as of Paris, it might be said, "The two principles are face to face." The white angel and the black angel are about to wrestle with each other on the brink of the abyss; which will hurl the other down?

On the evening of that same day, Jean Valjean, accompanied by Cosette and Toussaint, proceeded to the Rue de l'Homme Armé, where a tremendous incident was fated to take place. Cosette had not left the Rue Plumet without an attempt at resistance, and for the first time since they had lived together, the will of Cosette and the will of Jean Valjean had shown themselves distinct, and had contradicted each other, though they did not come into collision. There was objection on one side and inflexibility on the other : for the abrupt advice to move, thrown to Jean Valjean by a stranger, had alarmed him to such a point as to render him absolute. He fancied himself tracked and pursued, and Cosette was compelled to yield. The pair reached the Rue de l'Homme Armé without exchanging a syllable, for each was deep in personal thought ; Jean Valjean so anxious that he did not notice Cosette's sadness, and Cosette so sad that she did not notice Jean Valjean's anxiety. Jean Valjean had brought Toussaint with him, which he had never done in his previous absences, but he foresaw that he might possibly never return to the Rue Plumet, and he could neither leave Toussaint behind him nor tell her his secret. Moreover, he felt her to be devoted and sure ; the treachery of a servant to a master begins with curiosity, and Toussaint, as if predestined to be Jean Valjean's servant, was not curious. In his departure from the Rue Plumet, which was almost a flight, Jean Valjean took away with him nothing but the fragrant little portmanteau, christened by Cosette the *inseparable*. Packed trunks would have required porters, and porters are witnesses ; a hackney-coach had been called to the gate in the Rue de Babylone and they went away in it. It was with great difficulty that Toussaint obtained permission to pack up a little stock of linen and clothes, and a few toilet articles ; Cosette, herself, only took her desk and blotting-book. Jean Valjean, in order to heighten the solitude and mystery of this disappearance, had so arranged as to leave the Rue Plumet at nightfall, which had given Cosette the time to write her note to Marius. They reached the Rue de l'Homme Armé when it was quite dark, and went to bed in perfect silence.

The apartments in this street were situated on a second floor in a back yard, and consisted of two bedrooms, a dining-room, and a kitchen adjoining, with a closet in which was a flock-bed, which fell to the lot of Toussaint.

The dining-room was at the same time the anteroom, and separated the two bedrooms; the apartments were provided with the necessary articles of furniture. Human nature is so constituted that men become reassured almost as absurdly as they are alarmed; hence Jean Valjean had scarce reached the Rue de l'Homme Armé ere his anxiety cleared away and was gradually dissipated. There are calming places which act to some extent mechanically on the mind, and when a street is obscure the inhabitants are peaceful. Jean Valjean felt a contagious tranquillity in this lane of old Paris, which is so narrow that it is barred against vehicles by a cross-beam, which is dumb and deaf amid the noisy town, full of twilight in broad daylight, and, so to speak, incapable of feeling emotions between its two rows of aged houses, which are silent, as old people generally are. There is in this street a stagnant oblivion, and Jean Valjean breathed again in it, for how was it possible that he could be found there? His first care was to place the *inseparable* by his side; he slept soundly, and night counsels, we might add, night appeases. The next morning he woke up almost gay. He considered the dining-room charming, though it was hideous, for it was furnished with an old round table, a low sideboard surmounted by a mirror, a rickety easy-chair, and a few chairs encumbered with Toussaint's parcels. In one of these parcels Jean Valjean's National Guard uniform could be seen through an opening.

As for Cosette, she ordered Toussaint to bring a basin of broth to her bedroom, and did not make her appearance till evening. At about five o'clock, Toussaint, who went about very busy with this small moving, placed a cold fowl on the dinner-table, which Cosette consented to look at, through deference for her father. This done, Cosette, protesting a persistent headache, said good-night to Jean Valjean, and shut herself up in her bedroom. Jean Valjean ate a wing of the fowl with appetite, and with his elbows on the table, and, gradually growing reassured, regained possession of his serenity. While he was eating his modest dinner, he vaguely heard twice or thrice stammering Toussaint say to him, "There is a disturbance, sir, and people are fighting in Paris." But, absorbed in a multitude of internal combinations, he had paid no attention to her; truth to tell, he had not heard her. He rose and began walking from the door to the window, and from the window to the door with calmness. Cosette, his sole preoccupation, reverted to his

mind, not that he was alarmed by this headache, a slight
nervous attack, a girl's pouting, a momentary cloud, which
would disappear in a day or two, but he thought of the
future, and, as usual, thought of it gently. After all, he
saw no obstacle to his happy life resuming its course : at
certain hours everything seems possible, at others everything
appears easy, and Jean Valjean was in one of those good
hours. They usually arrive after bad hours, as day does
after night, through that law of succession and contrast
which is the basis of our nature, and which superficial minds
call antithesis. In this peaceful street where he had sought
shelter, Jean Valjean freed himself from all that had troubled
him for some time past, and, from the very fact that he had
seen so much darkness, he was beginning to perceive a little
azure. To have left the Rue Plumet without any complication or accident was a good step gained, and perhaps it
would be wise to leave the country, were it only for a few
months, and go to London. Well, they would go ; what
did he care whether he were in England or France, provided
that he had Cosette by his side ? He arranged in his mind,
and with all possible facility, the departure for England with
Cosette, and he saw his felicity reconstructed, no matter
where, in the perspectives of his reverie.

While slowly walking up and down, his eye suddenly
fell on something strange. He noticed, facing him in the
inclined mirror over the sideboard, and read distinctly :

" My well-beloved,—Alas, my father insists on our going
away at once. We shall be this evening at No. 7 Rue de
l'Homme Armé, and within a week in London.— COSETTE.
June 4."

Jean Valjean stopped with haggard gaze. Cosette, on
arriving, had laid her blotting-book on the sideboard facing
the mirror, and, immersed in her painful thoughts, had
forgotten it there, without even noticing that she had left it
open at the very page on which she had dried the few lines
she had written and entrusted to the young workman passing along the Rue Plumet. The writing was imprinted on
the blotting-paper and the mirror reflected the writing.
The result was what is called in geometry a symmetrical
image, so that the writing reversed on the blotting-paper
was placed straight in the mirror, and offered its natural
direction, and Jean Valjean had before his eyes the letter
written on the previous evening by Cosette to Marius. It

was simple and crushing. Jean Valjean walked up to the mirror and read the lines again, but did not believe in them. They produced on him the effect of an apparition in a flash of lightning : it was an hallucination—it was impossible— it was not. Gradually his perception became more precise, he looked at Cosette's blotting-book, and the consciousness of the real fact returned to him. He took up the blotting- book and said, "It comes from that." He feverishly examined the lines imprinted on the blotting-paper, but as they ran backward he could see no meaning in the strange scrawl. Then he said to himself, "Why, it means nothing ; there is nothing written there." And he drew a long breath with inexpressible relief. Who has not felt such wild delight in horrible moments ? the soul does not surrender to despair till it has exhausted every illusion.

He held the book in his hand and gazed at it, stupidly happy, almost ready to laugh at the hallucination of which he had been the dupe. All at once his eyes fell again on the mirror, and he saw the vision again ; the lines stood on it with inexorable clearness. This time it was no mirage, it was palpable, it was the writing turned straight in the mirror, and he comprehended the fact. Jean Valjean tottered, let the blotting-book slip from his grasp, and fell into the old easy-chair by the side of the sideboard with hanging head and glassy, wandering eye. He said to him- self that it was evident that the light of this world was eclipsed, and that Cosette had written that to somebody. Then he heard his soul, which had become terrible again, utter a hoarse roar in the darkness. Just attempt to take from the lion the dog he has in his cage ! Strange, and sad to say, at that moment Marius had not yet received Cosette's letter ; accident had treacherously carried it to Jean Valjean before delivering it to Marius. Jean Valjean up to that day had never been conquered by a trial. He had been subjected to frightful assaults. Not a blow of evil fortune had been spared to him, and the ferocity of fate, armed with all social revenge and contempt, had taken him for its victim and ferociously attacked him. He had accepted, when it was necessary, every extremity ; he had surrendered his reacquired inviolability as man, given up his liberty, risked his head, lost everything and suffered everything, and he had remained disinterested and stoical, to such an extent that at times he seemed to be oblivious of self, like a martyr. His conscience, hardened to all possible

assaults of adversity, might seem quite impregnable, but
any one who had now gazed into his heart would have been
compelled to allow that it was growing weak. In truth, of
all the tortures he had undergone in this long trial to which
fate had subjected him, this was the most formidable, and
never had such a vice held him before. Alas ! the supreme
trial, we may say the sole trial, is the loss of the being
whom we love.

Poor old Jean Valjean did not, assuredly, love Cosette
otherwise than as a father ; but, as we have already remarked, the very bereavement of his life had introduced all
the forms of love into this paternity. He loved Cosette as
his daughter, loved her as his mother, and loved her as his
sister, and, as he had never had a mistress or a wife, that
feeling too, the most clinging of all, was mingled with the
others, vague, ignorant, pure with the purity of blindness,
unconscious, heavenly, angelic, and divine, less as a feeling
than as an instinct, less as an instinct than as an attraction,
imperceptible, invisible, but real ; and love, properly so
called, was in his enormous tenderness for Cosette as the
vein of gold is in the mountain, dark and virginal. Our
readers must study for a moment this state of the heart ; no
marriage was possible between them, not even that of souls,
and yet it is certain that their destinies were wedded. Excepting Cosette, that is to say, excepting a childhood, Jean
Valjean, during the whole of his life, had known nothing
about things that may be loved. Those passions and loves
which succeed each other had not produced in him those
successive stages of green, light green, or dark green, which
may be noticed on leaves that survive the winter, and in
men who pass their fiftieth year. In fine, as we have more
than once urged, all this internal fusion, all this whole,
whose resultant was a lofty virtue, ended by making Jean
Valjean a father to Cosette. A strange father, forged out
of the grandsire, the son, the brother, and the husband,
which were in Jean Valjean ; a father in whom there was
even a mother ; a father who loved Cosette and adored her,
and who had this child for his light, his abode, his family,
his country, and his paradise. Hence, when he saw that it
was decidedly ended, that she was escaping from him,
slipping through his fingers, concealing herself, that she
was a cloud, that she was water, when he had before his
eyes this crushing evidence ; another is the object of her
heart, another is the wish of her life, she has a lover, I am

only the father, I no longer exist,—when he could no longer doubt, when he said to himself, "She is leaving me," the sorrow he experienced went beyond the limits of the possible. Then, as we have just stated, he had a quivering of revolt from head to foot ; he felt even in the roots of his hair the immense reawaking of selfishness, and the " I " yelled in the depths of this man's soul.

There are such things as internal earthquakes ; the penetration of a desperate certainty into a man is not effected without removing and breaking certain profound elements which are at times the man himself. Grief, when it attains that pitch, is a frantic flight of all the forces of the conscience, and such crises are fatal. Few among us emerge from them without change, and firm in our duty, for when the limit of suffering is exceeded the most imperturbable virtue is disconcerted. Jean Valjean took up the blotting-book and convinced himself afresh ; he bent down as if petrified, and with fixed eye, over the undeniable lines, and such a cloud collected within him that it might be believed that the whole interior of his soul was in a state of collapse. He examined this revelation through the exaggerations of reverie with an apparent and startling calmness, for it is a formidable thing when a man's calmness attains the coldness of a statue. He measured the frightful step which his destiny had taken without any suspicion on his part. He recalled his fears of the past summer, so madly dissipated. He recognised the precipice : it was still the same, but Jean Valjean was no longer at the top but at the bottom. It was an extraordinary and crushing fact that he had fallen without perceiving it ; the whole light of his life had fled while he still fancied he could see the sun. His instinct did not hesitate ; he brought together certain circumstances, certain dates, certain blushes, and certain palenesses of Cosette, and said to himself, " It is he ! " The divination of despair is a species of mysterious bow which never misses its mark, and with its first shaft it hit Marius. He did not know the name, but at once found the man ; he perceived distinctly at the bottom of the implacable evocation of memory the unknown prowler of the Luxembourg, that villainous seeker of amourettes, that romantic idler, that imbecile, that coward, for it is cowardice to exchange loving glances with girls who have by their side a father who loves them. After feeling quite certain that this young man was at the bottom of the situation, and that all this came from him, Jean

Valjean, the regenerated man, the man who had toiled so heavily in his soul, the man who had made so many efforts to resolve his whole life, his whole misery, and his whole misfortune into love, looked into himself, and saw there a spectre—hatred.

While Jean Valjean was thinking, Toussaint came in : he rose and asked her :

" Do you know where about it is ? "

Toussaint, in her stupefaction, could only answer

" I beg your pardon, sir."

Jean Valjean continued :

" Did you not say just now that they were fighting ? "

" Oh yes, sir," Toussaint replied ; " over at St. Merry."

There are some mechanical movements which come to us, without our cognisance, from our deepest thoughts. It was doubtless under the impulse of a movement of this nature, of which he was scarce conscious, that Jean Valjean found himself five minutes later in the street. He was bareheaded, and sat down on the bench before his house, seemingly listening.

The night had come.

How much time did he pass thus ? what was the ebb and flow of this tragical meditation ? did he draw himself up ? did he remain bowed down ? had he been bent till he was broken ? could he recover himself and stand again upon something solid in his conscience ? Probably he could not have said himself. The street was deserted ; and a few anxious citizens who hurriedly returned home scarce noticed him, for each for himself is the rule in times of peril. The lamplighter came as usual to light the lamp, which was exactly opposite the door of No. 7, and went away. Jean Valjean would not have appeared to be a living man to any one who might have examined him in this gloom, for he sat on his bench motionless, like a statue of ice. His despair was got beyond congelation. The tocsin and vague stormy rumours could be heard, and in the midst of all these convulsions of the bell blended with the riot, the clock of St. Paul struck the eleventh hour, solemnly and without hurrying, for the tocsin is man, the hour is God. The passing of the hour produced no effect on Jean Valjean, and he did not stir. Almost immediately after, however, a sudden detonation broke out in the direction of the markets, followed by a second even more violent,—it was probably that attack on the barricade

of the Rue de la Chanvrerie which we have just seen repulsed by Marius. At this double discharge, whose fury
seemed increased by the stupor of the night, Jean Valjean
started ; he turned in the direction whence the sound came,
but then fell back on his bench, crossed his arms, and his
head slowly bent down again on his chest. He resumed
his dark dialogue with himself.

All at once he raised his eyes, for there was some one
in the street ; he heard footsteps close to him, and by the
light of the lamp he perceived a vivid, young, and radiant
face, in the direction of the street which runs past the
Archives. It was Gavroche, who had just arrived from
the Rue de la Chanvrerie. Gavroche was looking up in
the air, and appeared to be seeking. He saw Jean Valjean
distinctly, but paid no attention to him. Gavroche, after
looking up in the air, looked down on the ground ; he
stood on tiptoe, and felt the doors and ground-floor windows
—they were all shut, bolted, and barred. After examining
the fronts of several houses barricaded in this way the
gamin shrugged his shoulders, and then resumed his self-
colloquy with himself, thus, " By Jove ! " Then he looked
up in the air again. Jean Valjean, who, in a moment
previously, in the state of mind in which he was, would
neither have spoken to nor answered any one, felt an
irresistible impulse to address this lad.

" My little boy," he said, " what is the matter with you ?"

" Why, I'm hungry," Gavroche answered bluntly. And
he added, " Little yourself."

Jean Valjean felt in his pocket and pulled out a five-
franc piece. But Gavroche, who was a species of wag-
tail, and rapidly passed from one gesture to another, had
just picked up a stone. He had noticed the lamp.

" Hilloh ! " he said, " you have still got lights here.
You are not acting rightly, my friends, that is disorderly
conduct. Break it for me."

And he threw the stone at the lamp, whose glass fell
with such a noise that the citizens concealed behind their
curtains in the opposite house cried, " There is '93 ! " The
lamp oscillated violently and went out ; the street suddenly
became dark.

" That's it, old street," said Gavroche, " put on your
nightcap." Then, turning to Jean Valjean, he said :

" What do you call that gigantic monument which you
have there at the end of the street ? it's the Archives, isn't

it? let's pull down some of those great brutes of columns and make a tidy barricade."

Jean Valjean walked up to Gavroche.

"Poor creature," he said in a low voice, and as if speaking to himself, "he is hungry."

And he placed the five-franc piece in his hand. Gavroche raised his nose, amazed at the size of this double sou; he looked at it in the darkness, and the whiteness of the double sou dazzled him. He was acquainted with five-franc pieces by hearsay, and their reputation was agreeable to him; he was delighted to see one so closely, and said, "Let us contemplate the tiger." He looked at it for some moments in ecstasy; then, turning to Jean Valjean, he held out the coin to him, and said majestically :

"Citizen, I prefer breaking the lamps. Take back your ferocious animal, for I am not to be corrupted. It has five claws, but it can't scratch me."

"Have you a mother?" Jean Valjean asked.

Gavroche replied :

"Perhaps more than you."

"Well," Jean Valjean continued, "keep that money for your mother."

Gavroche was affected. Moreover, he had noticed that the man who was addressing him had no hat on, and this inspired him with confidence.

"Really, then," he said, "it is not to prevent me ¹ the lamps?"

"Break as many as you like."

"You are a worthy man," said Gavroche.

And he put the five-franc piece in one of his pockets. Then, with increasing confidence, he added :

"Do you belong to this street?"

"Yes, why?"

"Can you point me out No. 7?"

"What do you want at No. 7?"

Here the lad stopped, for he feared lest he had said too much. He energetically plunged his nails into his hair, and confined himself to answering :

"Ah, there it is."

An idea flashed across Jean Valjean's mind, for agony has lucidities of that nature. He said to the boy :

"Have you brought me the letter which I am expecting?"

"You?" said Gavroche, "you ain't a woman."

"The letter is for Mademoiselle Cosette, is it not?"

"Cosette?" Gavroche grumbled; "yes, I think it is that absurd name."

"Well," Jean Valjean continued, "I am to deliver the letter to her, so give it to me."

"In that case, you must be aware that I am sent from the barricade?"

"Of course," said Jean Valjean.

Gavroche thrust his hand into another of his pockets, and produced a square folded letter; then he gave the military salute.

"Respect for the despatch," he said; "it comes from the Provisional Government."

"Give it to me," said Jean Valjean.

Gavroche held the paper above his head.

"You must not imagine that it is a love-letter, though it is for a woman; it is for the people; we are fighting, and we respect the sex; we are not like people in the world of fashion, where there are lions that send poulets to camels."

"Give it to me."

"After all," Gavroche continued, "you look like an honest man."

"Make haste."

"Here it is."

And he handed the paper to Jean Valjean.

"And make haste, Monsieur Chose, since Mamselle Chosette is waiting."

Gavroche felt pleased at having made this pun. Jean Valjean added:

"Must the answer be taken to St. Merry?"

"You would make in that way," Gavroche exclaimed, "one of those cakes vulgarly called blunders. That letter comes from the barricade in the Rue de la Chanvrerie, and I am going back to it. Good-night, citizen."

This said, Gavroche went away, or, to speak more correctly, resumed his birdlike flight to the spot whence he had escaped. He plunged again into the darkness, as if there were a hole there, with the rigid rapidity of a projectile: the lane of l'Homme Armé became once again silent and solitary. In a twinkling, this strange lad, who had shadow and dream within him, buried himself in the gloom of these rows of black houses, and was lost in it like smoke in darkness, and it might have been fancied that he was dispersed and had vanished, had not, a few minutes after his disappearance, a noisy breakage of glass, and the splendid echo of a lamp falling on the pavement, suddenly reawakened the indignant citizens. It was Gavroche passing along the Rue de Chaume.

Jean Valjean re-entered with Marius's letter : he groped his way upstairs, pleased with the darkness like an owl that holds its prey, gently opened and closed the door, listened whether he could hear any sound, convinced himself that Cosette and Toussaint were, according to all appearances, asleep, and plunged into the Fumade lighting bottle three or four matches before he could procure a spark, for his hand trembled so, as though what he had just done was a robbery. At last his candle was lit, he sat down at the table, opened the letter, and read. In such violent emotions men do not read, they hurl down, so to speak, the paper they hold, clutch it like a victim, crumple it, bury in it the nails of their fury or delight, they run to the end, they dash at the beginning : the attention is feverish, it understands the essential facts, it seizes on one point, and all the rest disappears. In the note from Marius to Cosette Jean Valjean only saw these words :

"—I die : when you read this my soul will be near you."

In the presence of this line he felt a horrible bewilderment ; he remained for a moment as if crushed by the change of emotion which took place in him. He gazed at Marius' letter with a species of drunken amazement ; he had before his eyes this splendour, the death of the hated being. He uttered a frightful cry of internal joy. So all was over, and the dénouement arrived more quickly than he could have dared to hope. The being that encumbered his destiny was disappearing ; he went away of his own accord, freely and willingly, without his doing anything in the matter, without any fault on the part of him, Jean Valjean; "that man" was going to die, perhaps was already dead. Here his fever made its calculations,—"No, he is not yet dead. The letter was evidently written to be read by Cosette on the next morning : since the two volleys he had heard between eleven o'clock and midnight nothing had occurred : the barricade would not be seriously attacked till daybreak, but no matter, from the moment when 'that man' is mixed up in this war, he was lost ; he is caught in the cogwheels. Jean Valjean felt himself delivered ; he was going to find himself once more alone with Cosette, the rivalry ceased, and the future began again. He need only keep the note in his pocket, and Cosette would never know what had become of 'that man'; I have only to let things take their course. That man cannot escape, and if he is not dead yet, it is certain that he is going to die. What happiness!" All this said internally, he became gloomy: he went down and aroused the porter. About an hour later Jean Valjean left the house in the uniform of a National Guard, and armed. The porter had easily obtained for him in the neighbourhood the articles to complete his equipment: he had a loaded musket and a full cartouche-box. He proceeded in the direction of the markets.

CHAPTER C.

THE insurgents, under the eye of Enjolras, had turned the night to good account: the barricade had not only been repaired, but increased. It had been raised two feet, and iron bars planted in the paving-stones resembled couched lances. All sorts of rubbish, added and brought from all sides, complicated the external confusion, and the redoubt had been cleverly converted into a wall inside and a thicket outside. The staircase of paving-stones, which allowed the top of the barricade to be reached, was restored, the ground floor of the room of the inn was cleared out, the kitchen converted into an infirmary, the wounds were dressed, the powder, scattered about the tables and floor, was collected, bullets were cast, cartridges manufactured, lint plucked, the fallen arms distributed; the dead were carried off and laid in a heap, in the Mondétour lane, of which they were still masters. The pavement remained for a long time red at that spot. Among the dead were four suburban National Guards, and Enjolras ordered their uniforms to be laid on one side. Enjolras had advised two hours' sleep, and his advice was an order; still, only three or four took advantage of it, and Feuilly employed the two hours in engraving this inscription on the wall, facing the wine-shop—

"VIVENT LES PEUPLES."

These three words, carved in the stone with a nail, could still be read on this wall in 1848. The three women took advantage of the respite to disappear entirely, which allowed the insurgents to breathe more at their ease; and they contrived to find refuge in some neighbouring house. Most of the wounded could and would still fight. There were, on a pile of mattresses and trusses of straw laid in the kitchen converted into an infirmary, five men seriously wounded, of whom two were Municipal Guards ; the wounds of the latter were dressed first. No one remained in the ground-floor room save Mabœuf, under his black cerecloth, and Javert, fastened to the post.

In the interior of this room, which was scarce lighted by a solitary candle, the mortuary table at the end being behind the post like a horizontal bar, a sort of large vague cross resulted from Javert standing and Mabœuf lying down. Although the pole of the omnibus was mutilated by the bullets, sufficient remained for a flag to be attached to it. Enjolras, who possessed that quality of a chief of always doing what he said, fastened to it the bullet-pierced and bloodstained coat of the killed old man. No meal was possible, for there was neither bread nor meat. The fifty men during the sixteen hours they had stood at the barricade speedily exhausted the scanty provisions of the inn. At a given moment every barricade that holds out becomes the raft of the *Méduse*, and the combatants must resign themselves to hunger. They had reached the early hours of that Spartan day, June 6, when at the barricade of St. Merry, Jeanne, surrounded by insurgents who cried for bread, answered, " What for ? it is three o'clock ; at four we shall be dead." As they could no longer eat, Enjolras prohibited drinking ; he put the wine under an interdict, and served out the spirits. Some fifteen full bottles, hermetically sealed, were found in the cellar, which Enjolras and Combeferre examined. Enjolras, in spite of the murmurs, put his veto on the fifteen bottles, and in order that no one might touch them, and that they should be to some extent sacred, he had placed them under the table on which Father Mabœuf lay.

At about two in the morning they counted their strength ; there were still thirty-seven. Day was beginning to appear, and the torch, which had been returned to its stone lantern, was extinguished. The interior of the barricade, that species of small yard taken from the street, was bathed in darkness, and resembled, through the vague twilight horror, the deck of a dismasted ship. The combatants moved about like black forms. Above this frightful nest of gloom the storeys of the silent houses stood out lividly, and above them again the chimney-pots were assuming a roseate hue.

The sky had that charming tint which may be white and may be blue, and the birds flew about in it with twitterings of joy. The tall house which formed the background of the barricade looked to the east, and had a pink reflection on its roof. At the third-floor window the morning breeze blew about the gray hair on the head of the dead man.

Enjolras had gone out to reconnoitre, and had left by the Mondétour lane, keeping in the shadow of the houses. The insurgents, we must state, were full of hope : the way in which they had repulsed the night attack almost made them disdain beforehand the attack at daybreak. They waited for it and smiled at it, and no more doubted of their success than of their cause ; moreover, help was evidently going to reach them, and they reckoned on it. With that facility of triumphant prophecy which is a part of the strength of the combating Frenchman, they divided into three certain phases the opening day,—at six in the morning a regiment, which had been worked upon, would turn ; at midday, insurrection all over Paris ; at sunset, the revolution. The tocsin of St. Merry, which had not ceased once since the previous evening, could be heard, and this was a proof that the other barricade, the great one, Jeanne's, still held out. All these hopes were interchanged by the groups with a species of gay and formidable buzzing, which resemble the war-hum of a swarm of bees. Enjolras reappeared returning from his gloomy walk in the external darkness. He listened for a moment to all this joy with his arms folded, and then said, fresh and rosy in the growing light of dawn,—

"The whole army of Paris is out, and one-third of that army is preparing to attack the barricade behind which you now are. There is, too, the National Guard. I distinguished the shakos of the fifth line regiment, and the colours of the sixth legion. You will be attacked in an hour ; as for the people, they were in a state of ferment yesterday, but this morning they do not stir. There is nothing to wait for, nothing to hope ; no more from a faubourg than from a regiment. You are abandoned."

These words fell on the buzzing groups, and produced the same effect as the first drops of a storm do on a swarm. All remained dumb, and there was a moment of inexpressible silence, in which death might have been heard flying past. This moment was short, and a voice shouted to Enjolras from the thickest of the crowd :

"Be it so. Let us raise the barricade to a height of

twenty feet, and all fall upon it. Citizens, let us offer the
protest of corpses, and show that if the people abandon the
republicans, the republicans do not abandon the people."

These words disengaged the thoughts of all from the
painful cloud of individual anxieties, and an enthusiastic
shout greeted them. The name of the man who spoke thus
was never known ; he was some unknown blouse-wearer,
an unknown man, a forgotten man, a passing hero, that
great anonymous always mixed up in human crises and
in social births, who at the given moment utters the decisive
word in a supreme fashion, and who fades away into darkness, after having represented for a minute, in the light
of a flash, the people and God. This inexorable resolution
was so strongly in the air of June 6, 1832, that almost at
the same hour the insurgents of the St. Merry barricade
uttered this cry which became historical,—"Whether they
come to our help or whether they do not, what matter !
Let us all fall here, to the last man." As we see, the two
barricades, though essentially isolated, communicated.

After the unknown man, who decreed the "protest of
corpses," had spoken, and given the formula of the common
soul, a strangely satisfied and terrible cry issued from every
mouth, funereal in its meaning, and triumphal in its accent.

"Long live death ! Let us all stay."

"Why all ? " Enjolras asked.

"All, all ! "

Enjolras continued :

"The position is good and the barricade fine. Thirty
men are sufficient, then why sacrifice forty ? "

They replied:

"Because not one of us will go away."

"Citizens," Enjolras cried, and there was in his voice an
almost irritated vibration, "the republic is not rich enough
in men to make an unnecessary outlay. If it be the duty
of some to go away, that duty must be performed like any
other."

Enjolras, the man of principle, had that species of omnipotence, which is evolved from the absolute, over his
co-religionists. Still, however great that omnipotence might
be, they murmured. A chief to the tips of his fingers,
Enjolras, on seeing that they murmured, insisted. He
continued haughtily :

"Let those who are afraid to be only thirty say so."

The murmurs were redoubled.

"Besides," a voice in the throng remarked, "to go away is easily said ; but the barricade is surrounded."

" Not on the side of the markets," said Enjolras.   "The Rue Mondétour is free, and the Marché des Innocents can be reached by the Rue des Prêcheurs."

"And then," another voice in the group remarked, "we should be caught by falling in with some grand rounds of the line or the National Guard.   They will see a man passing in blouse and cap ; 'Where do you come from ? don't you belong to the barricade ?' and they will look at your hands, you smell of powder, and will be shot."

Enjolras, without answering, touched Combeferre's shoulder, and both entered the ground-floor room. They came out again a moment after, Enjolras holding in his outstretched hands the four uniforms which he had laid on one side, and Combeferre followed him carrying the cross-belts and shakos.

" In this uniform," Enjolras said, " it is easy to enter the ranks and escape.   Here are four at any rate."

And he threw the four uniforms on the unpaved ground ; but as no one moved in the stoical audience Combeferre resolved to make an appeal.

"Come," he said, "you must show a little pity.   Do you know what the question is here ? it is about women.   Look you, are there wives, yes or no ? are there children, yes or no ? are these nothing, who rock a cradle with their foot, and have a heap of children around them ? let him among you who has never seen a nursing-woman's breast hold up his hand.   Ah, you wish to be killed.   I wish it too, I who am addressing you, but I do not wish to feel the ghosts of women twining their arms around me.   Die,— very good, but do not cause people to die.   Suicides like those which are about to take place here are sublime, but suicide is restricted and does not allow of extension, and so soon as it affects your relations, suicide is called murder.   Think of the little fair heads, and think too of the white hair.   Listen to me,—Enjolras tells me that just now he saw at the corner of the Rue du Cygne a candle at a poor window on the fifth floor, and on the panes the shaking shadow of an old woman who appeared to have spent the night in watching at the window ; she is perhaps the mother of one of you.   Well, let that man go, and hasten to say to his mother,—'Mother, here I am !'   Let him be easy in his mind, for the work will

be done here all the same. When a man supports his
relatives by his toil, he has no longer any right to sacrifice
himself, for that is deserting his family. And then, too,
those who have daughters, and those who have sisters!
only think of them. You let yourselves be killed, you are
dead, very good; and to-morrow? it is terrible when girls
have no bread, for a man begs, but a woman sells. Oh,
those charming, graceful, and gentle creatures with flowers
in their bonnets, who fill the house with chastity, who sing,
who prattle, who are like a living perfume, who prove the
existence of angels in heaven by the purity of virgins on
earth, that Jeanne, that Lise, that Mimi, those adorable
and honest creatures, who are your blessing and your pride,
—ah, my God! they will starve. What would you have
me say to you? There is a human flesh-market, and you
will not prevent them entering it with your shadowy hands
trembling around them. Think of the street, think of the
pavement covered with strollers, think of the shops before
which women in low-necked dresses come and go in the
mud. Those women, too, were pure.

"Come, those who have families must be good fellows and
give us a shake of the hand and go away, leaving us to do
the job here all alone. I am well aware that courage
is needed to go away, and that it is difficult, but the more
difficult the more meritorious it is. You say, 'I have
a gun and am at the barricade; all the worse, I remain.'
All the worse is easily said. My friends, there is a morrow,
and that morrow you will not see, but your families will
see it. And what sufferings! Stay, do you know what
becomes of a healthy child with cheeks like an apple, who
chatters, prattles, laughs, and smiles as fresh as a kiss,
when he is abandoned? I saw one, quite little, about so
high; his father was dead and poor people had taken
him in through charity, but they had not bread for themselves. The child was always hungry; it was winter-time,
but though he was always hungry he did not cry. He was
seen to go close to the stove, whose pipe was covered with
yellow earth. The boy detached with his fingers a piece of
this earth and ate it,—his breathing was hoarse, his face
livid, his legs soft, and his stomach swollen. He said
nothing, and when spoken to made no answer. He is
dead. He was brought to the Necker Hospital to die, where
I saw him; for I was a student there. Now, if there be
any fathers among you, fathers whose delight it is to take

a walk on Sunday, holding in their powerful hand a child's
small fingers, let each of these fathers fancy this lad his
own. That poor brat I can remember perfectly; I fancy
I see him now; and, when he lay on the dissecting table, his
bones stood out under his skin like the tombs under the
grass of a cemetery. We found a sort of mud in his
stomach, and he had ashes between his teeth. Come, let
us examine our conscience and take the advice of our heart;
statistics prove that the mortality among deserted children
is fifty-five per cent. I repeat, it is a question of wives, of
mothers, of daughters, and babes. Am I saying anything
about you? I know very well what you are. I know that
you are all brave. I know that you have all in your hearts
the joy and glory of laying down your lives for the great
cause. I know very well that you feel yourselves chosen to
die usefully and magnificently, and that each of you clings
to his share of the triumph. Very good. But you are
not alone in this world, and there are other beings of whom
you must think; you should not be selfish."

All hung their heads with a gloomy air, strange contradictions of the human heart in the sublimest moments!
Combeferre, who spoke thus, was not an orphan, he
remembered the mothers of others and forgot his own, he
was going to let himself be killed, and was "selfish."
Marius had but one idea, to die, and he did not wish to
avert his attention from it, but he thought in his gloomy
somnambulism that in destroying himself he was not
prohibited from saving somebody. He raised his voice:
"Enjolras and Combeferre are right," he said, "let us
have no useless sacrifice. I join them, and we must make
haste. Combeferre has told you decisive things: there are
men among you who have families, mothers, sisters, wives,
and children. Such must leave the ranks."

Not a soul stirred.

"Married men and supporters of families will leave the
ranks," Marius repeated.

His authority was great, for, though Enjolras was really
the chief of the barricade, Marius was its saviour.

"I order it," Enjolras cried.

"I implore it," Marius said.

Then these heroic men, stirred up by Combeferre's speech,
shaken by Enjolras' order, and moved by Marius' entreaty,
began denouncing one another. "It is true," a young man
said to a middle-aged man, "you are a father of a family—

begone !" "No! you ought to do so rather," the man replied, "for you have two sisters to support;" and an extraordinary contest broke out, in which each struggled not to be thrust out of the tomb.

"Make haste," said Combeferre, "in a quarter of an hour there will no longer be time."

"Citizens," Enjolras added, "we have a republic here, and universal suffrage reigns. Point out yourselves the men who are to leave us."

They obeyed, and at the end of a few minutes five were unanimously pointed out and left the ranks.

"There are five of them !" Marius exclaimed.

There were only four uniforms.

"Well," the five replied, "one will have to remain behind."

And it was who should remain, and who should find reasons for others not to remain. The generous quarrel recommenced.

"You have a wife who loves you." "You have your old mother." "You have neither father nor mother; so what will become of your three little brothers?" "You are the father of five children." "You have a right to live, for you are only seventeen, and it is too early to die."

These great revolutionary barricades were meeting-places of heroisms. The improbable was simple there, and these men did not astonish one another.

"Make haste," Courfeyrac repeated.

Somebody cried out from the group, to Marius.

"You must point out the one who is to remain."

"Yes !" the five said, "do you choose, and we will obey you."

Marius did not believe himself capable of any emotion; still at this idea of choosing a man for death all the blood flowed back to his heart, and he would have turned pale could he have grown paler. He walked up to the five, who smiled upon him, and each, with his eye full of that great flame which gleams through history on Thermopylæ, cried to him :

"Me ! me ! me !"

And Marius stupidly counted them. There were still five ! then his eyes settled on the four uniforms. All at once a fifth uniform fell, as if from heaven, on the other four ; the fifth man was saved. Marius raised his eyes, and recognised M. Fauchelevent. Jean Valjean had just entered the barricade· e.ther through information he had obtained, through instinct, or through accident, he arrived by the Mondétour lane, and, thanks to his National Guard uniform, passed without difficulty. The vedette stationed by the insurgents in the Rue Mondétour had no cause to give the alarm signal for a single National Guard, and had let him enter the street, saying to himself, "He is probably a reinforcement, or at the worst a prisoner." The moment was too serious for a sentry to turn away from his duty or his post of observation. At the moment when Jean Valjean entered the redoubt, no one noticed him, for all eyes were fixed on the five chosen men and the four uniforms. Jean Valjean, however, had seen and heard, and silently took off his coat and threw it on the pile formed by the other coats. The emotion was indescribable.

" Who is this man ? " Bossuet asked.

" He is a man," Combeferre replied, " who saves his fellow-man."

Marius added in a grave voice :

" I know him."

This bail was sufficient for all, and Enjolras turned to Jean Valjean.

" Citizen, you are welcome."

And he added :

" You are aware that you will die."

Jean Valjean, without answering, helped the insurgent whom he had saved to put on his uniform.

CHAPTER CI.

THE situation of all, in this fatal hour, and at this inexorable spot, had as resultant and apex the supreme melancholy of Enjolras. Enjolras had within him the plenitude of the revolution ; he was imperfect, however, so far as the absolute can be so ; he had too much of St. Just and not enough of Anacharsis Clootz : still his mind, in the society of the Friends of the A B C, had eventually received a certain magnetism of Combeferre's ideas. For some time past he had been gradually emerging from the narrow form of dogmatism and yielding to the expansion of progress, and in the end he had accepted, as the definitive and magnificent evolution, the transformation of the great French republic into the immense human republic. As for the immediate means, in a violent situation, he wished them to be violent ;

in that he did not vary ; and he still belonged to that epic and formidable school which is resumed in the words " '93." Enjolras was standing on the paving-stone steps, with one of his elbows on the muzzle of his gun. He was thinking ; he trembled, as men do when a blast passes ; for spots where death lurks produce this tripodal effect. A sort of stifled fire came from his eye. All at once he raised his head, his light hair fell back like that of the angel on the dark quadriga composed of stars, and he cried :

" Citizens, do you picture to yourselves the future ? The streets of towns inundated with light, green branches on the thresholds, the nation's sisters, men just, old men blessing children, the past loving the present, men thinking at perfect liberty, believers enjoying perfect equality, for religion, heaven, God, the direct priest, the human conscience converted into an altar, no more hatred, the fraternity of the workshop and the school, notoriety the sole punishment and reward, work for all, right for all, peace for all, no more bloodshed, no more wars, and happy mothers ! To subdue matter is the first step, to realise the ideal is the second. Reflect on what progress has already done ; formerly the first human races saw the terror the hydra that breathed upon the waters, the dragon that vomited fire, the griffin which was the monster of the air, and which flew with the wings of an eagle and the claws of a tiger, pass before their eyes, frightful beasts which were below man. Man, however, set his snares, the sacred snares of intellect, and ended by catching the monsters in them. We have subdued the hydra, and it is called the steamer ; we have tamed the dragon, and it is called the locomotive ; we are on the point of taming the griffin, we hold it already, and it is called the balloon. The day on which that Promethean task is terminated and man has defini- tively attached to his will the triple antique chimera, the dragon, the hydra, and the griffin, he will be master of water, fire, and air, and he will be to the rest of animated creation what the ancient gods were formerly to him. Courage, and forward ! Citizens, whither are we going ? to science made the government, to the strength of things converted into the sole public strength, to the natural law having its sanction, and penalty in itself and promulgating itself by evidence, and to a sunrise of truth corresponding with the dawn of day. We are proceeding to a union of the peoples ; we are proceeding to a unity of man.

No more fictions, no more parasites. The real governed by the true, is our object. Civilisation will hold its assize on the summit of Europe, and eventually in the centre of the continent, in a great parliament of intellect. Something like this has been seen already ; the Amphictyons held two sessions a year—one at Delphi, the place of the gods, the other at Thermopylæ, the place of souls. Europe will have her Amphictyons, the globe will have its Amphictyons, France bears the sublime future within her, and this is the gestation of the nineteenth century. What Greece sketched out is worthy of being finished by France. Listen to me. Feuilly, valiant workman, man of the people, man of the peoples, I venerate thee ; yes, thou seest clearly future times, yes, thou art right. Thou hast neither father nor mother, Feuilly, and thou hast adopted humanity as thy mother, and right as thy father. Thou art about to die here, that is to say, to triumph. Citizens, whatever may happen to-day, we are about to make a revolution, by our defeat as well as by our victory. In the same way as conflagrations light up a whole city, revolutions light up the whole human race. And what a revolution shall we make ? I have just told you, the revolution of the True. From the political point of view, there is but one principle, the sovereignty of man over himself. This sovereignty of myself over myself is called liberty, and where two or three of these liberties are associated the State begins. But in this association there is no abdication, and each sovereignty concedes a certain amount of itself to form the common right. This quality is the same for all, and this identity of concession which each makes to all, is called Equality. The common right is nought but the protection of all radiating over the right of each. This protection of all over each is called Fraternity. The point of intersection of all these aggregated sovereignties is called Society, and this intersection being a junction, the point is a knot. Hence comes what is called the social tie. Some say the social contract, which is the same thing, as the word contract is etymologically formed with the idea of a tie. Let us come to an understanding about equality, for if liberty be the summit, equality is the base. Equality, citizens, is not the whole of society on a level, a society of tall blades of grass and small oaks, or a number of entangled jealousies ; it is, civilly, every aptitude having the same opening ;

politically, all votes having the same weight, and religiously, all consciences having the same right. Equality has an organ in gratuitous and compulsory education, and it should begin with the right to the alphabet. The primary school imposed on all, the secondary school offered to all, such is the law, and from the identical school issues equal instruction. Yes, instruction! Light! light! everything comes from light and everything returns to it. Citizens, the nineteenth century is great, but the twentieth century will be happy. Then there will be nothing left resembling ancient history. Men will no longer have to fear, as at the present day, a conquest, an invasion, usurpation, an armed rivalry of nations, an interruption of civilisation depending on a marriage of kings, a birth in hereditary tyrannies, a division of peoples by Congress, a dismemberment by the collapse of dynasties, a combat of two religions, clashing like two goats of the darkness, on the bridge of infinity; there will be no cause longer to fear famine, exhaustion, prostitution through distress, misery through want of work, and the scaffold, and the sword, and battles, and all the brigandages of chance in the forest of events. We might almost say there will be no more events, we shall be happy. The human race will accomplish its law as the terrestrial globe fulfils its law; harmony will be restored between the soul and the planet, and the soul will gravitate round the truth as the planet does round light. Friends, the hour we are now standing in is a gloomy hour, but there are such terrible purchases of the future. Oh! the human race will be delivered, relieved, and consoled! We affirm it on this barricade, and where should the cry of love be raised if not on the summit of the sacrifice? Oh, my brothers, this is the point of junction between those who think and those who suffer, this barricade is not made of paving-stones, beams, and iron bars, it is made of two aggregations, one of ideas and one of sufferings. Misery here encounters the ideal; day embraces the night there, and says to it, I am about to die with thee, and thou wilt be born again with me. Faith springs from the embrace of all the desolations; suffering bring hither their agony and ideas their immortality. This agony and this immortality are about to be mingled and compose one death. Brothers, the man who dies here dies in the radiance of the future, and we shall enter a tomb all filled with dawn."

Enjolras broke off rather than ceased; his lips moved silently as if he were talking to himself, which attracted attention, and in order still to try to hear him they held their tongues. There was no applause, but they whispered together for a long time. Language being breath, the rustling of intellects resembles the rustling of leaves.

Let us tell what was going on in Marius' thoughts. Our readers will remember his state of mind, for everything was only a vision to him. His understanding was troubled, for he was (we urge the fact), beneath the shadow of the great gloomy wings opened above the dying. He felt that he had entered the tomb, he fancied that he was already on the other side of the wall, and he only saw the faces of the living with the eyes of a dead man. How was M. Fauchelevent present? why was he here, and what did he come to do? Marius did not ask himself all these questions. Moreover, as our despair has this peculiarity about it that it envelopes others as it does ourselves, it appeared to him logical that everybody should die. Still he thought of Cosette with a contraction of the heart. However, M. Fauchelevent did not speak to him, did not look at him, and did not even seem to hear Marius when he raised his voice, saying, "I know him." As for Marius, this attitude of M. Fauchelevent relieved him, and if such a word were permissible for such impressions, we might say that it pleased him. He had ever felt an absolute impossibility in addressing this enigmatical man, who was at once equivocal and imposing to him. It was a very long time too since he had seen him; and this augmented the impossibility for a timid reserved nature like Marius'.

The five men selected left the barricade by the Mondétour lane, perfectly resembling National Guards. One of them wept as he went away, and before doing so they embraced those who remained. When the five men sent back to life had left Enjolras thought of the one condemned to death. He went to the ground-floor room, where Javert, tied to the post, was reflecting.

"Do you want anything?" Enjolras asked him.

Javert answered:

"When will you kill me?"

"Wait. We require all our cartridges at this moment."

"In that case, give me some drink," Javert said.

Enjolras himself held out to him a glass of water, and, as Javert was bound, helped him to drink.

" Is that all ? " Enjolras resumed.

" I feel uncomfortable at this post," Javert replied ; " you did not act kindly in leaving me fastened to it the whole night. Bind me as you please, but you might surely lay me on a table, like the other man."

And with a nod of the head he pointed to M. Mabœuf's corpse. It will be remembered that there was at the end of the room a long wide table on which bullets had been run and cartridges made. All the cartridges being made, and all the powder expended, this table was free. By Enjolras' order four insurgents unfastened Javert from the post, and while they did so a fifth held a bayonet to his chest. His hand remained fastened behind his back, a thin strong cord was attached to his feet, which enabled him to walk fifteen inches, like those who are going to ascend the scaffold, and he was forced to walk to the table at the end of the room, on which they laid him, securely fastened round the waist. For greater security, a system of knotting was employed by means of a cord fastened to the neck, which rendered any escape impossible ; it was the sort of fastening called in prisons a martingale, which starts from the nape of the neck, is crossed on the stomach, and is turned round the hands after passing between the legs. While Javert was being bound a man standing in the doorway regarded him with singular attention, and the shadow this man cast caused Javert to turn his head. He raised his eyes and recognised Jean Valjean, but he did not even start, he merely looked down haughtily, and restricted himself to saying, " It is very natural."

It was growing light rapidly, but not a window opened, not a door was ajar ; it was the dawn, not the awakening. The end of the Rue de la Chanvrerie opposite the barricade had been evacuated by the troops, as we stated ; it appeared to be free and open for passers-by with a tranquillity that was ominous. The Rue St. Denis was as silent as the Avenue of the Sphynxes at Thebes ; there was not a living being on the square, which a sunbeam whitened. Nothing is so melancholy as this brightness of deserted streets. Nothing could be seen, but something could be heard, and there was a mysterious movement at a certain distance off. It was evident that the critical moment was arriving, and, as on the previous evening, the vedettes fell back, but this time all of them did so. The barricade was stronger than at the prior attack, for since the departure of the five it had been heightened. By the advice of the vedette who had been watching the region of the markets, Enjolras, through fear of a surprise in the rear, formed a serious resolution. He barricaded the small passage of the Mondétour lane, which had hitherto remained free, and for this purpose a further portion of the street was unpaved. In this way the barricade, walled in on three sides—in front by the Rue de la Chanvrerie, on the left by the Rue du Cygne, and on the right by the Rue Mondétour—was truly almost impregnable, but it is true that they were fatally enclosed within it. It had three fronts but no issue; it was a fortress but a mousetrap, as Courfeyrac said with a smile. Enjolras had some thirty paving-stones piled up by the door of the inn, which, as Bossuet said, had been "removed over and above." The silence was now so profound in the direction whence the attack must come, that Enjolras ordered all his men to return to their fighting-posts, and a ration of brandy was distributed to each man.

They had not long to wait. A rattling of chains, the alarming rolling of a heavy weight, a clang of bronze leaping on the pavement, and a species of solemn noise, announced that a sinister engine was approaching. There was a tremor in the entrails of these old peaceful streets, pierced and built for the fruitful circulation of interests and ideas, and which are not made for the monstrous rolling of the wheels of war. The fixity of the eyes turned toward the end of the street became stern, as a cannon appeared. The gunners pushed the gun on; the limber was detached, and two men supported the carriage, while four were at the wheels, others followed with the tumbril, and the lighted match could be seen smoking.

"Fire!" shouted Enjolras.

The whole barricade burst into a flame, and the detonation was frightful; an avalanche of smoke covered and concealed the gun and the men. A few seconds after the cloud was dispersed, and the gun and the men reappeared; the gunners were bringing it up to the front of the barricade, slowly, correctly, and without hurry, not one had been wounded. Then the captain of the gun, hanging with his whole weight on the breech to elevate the muzzle, began pointing the gun, with the gravity of an astronomer setting a telescope.

"Bravo for the gunners!" cried Bossuet.

And all the men at the barricade clapped their hands. A moment after the gun, standing in the very centre of the street across the gutter, was in position, and a formidable mouth yawned at the barricade.

"Come, we are going to be gay," said Courfeyrac, "here is the brute; after the fillip, the blow with the fist. The army is extending its heavy paw toward us, and the barricade is going to be seriously shaken. The musketry fire feels, and the cannon takes."

"Reload your guns," said Enjolras.

In what manner would the facing of the barricade behave against a cannon-ball? would a breach be formed? that was the question. While the insurgents were reloading their guns the artillerymen loaded the cannon. The anxiety within the redoubt was profound; the shot was fired, and the detonation burst forth.

"Present!" a joyous voice cried.

And at the same time as the cannon-ball struck the barricade, Gavroche bounded inside it. He came from the direction of the Rue du Cygne, and actively clambered over the accessory barricade which fronted the labyrinth of the little Truanderie. Gavroche produced a greater effect at the barricade than the cannon-ball did; for the latter was lost in the heap of rubbish. It had broken a wheel of the omnibus, and finished the old truck; on seeing which the insurgents bursts into a laugh.

"Pray go on," Bossuet cried to the gunners.

Gavroche was surrounded, but he had no time to report anything, as Marius, shuddering, drew him on one side.

"What have you come to do here?"

"What a question?" the boy said, "and you, pray?"

And he gazed fixedly at Marius with his epic effrontery: his eyes were dilated by the proud brightness which they contained. It was with a stern accent that Marius continued:

"Who told you to return? I only trust that you have delivered my letter at its address."

Gavroche felt some degree of remorse in the matter of the letter; for, in his hurry to return to the barricade, he had got rid of it rather than delivered it. He was forced to confess to himself that he had confided somewhat too lightly in this stranger, whose face he had not even been able to distinguish. It is true that this man was bareheaded, but that was not enough. In short, he reproached himself quietly for his conduct, and feared Marius' reproaches. He took the simplest process to get out of the scrape—he told an abominable falsehood.

"Citizen, I delivered the letter to the porter. The lady was asleep, and she will have the letter when she wakes."

Marius had two objects in sending the letter,—to bid Cosette farewell and save Gavroche. He was obliged to satisfy himself with one half of what he wanted. The connection between the sending of the letter and M. Fauchelevent's presence at the barricade occurred to his mind, and he pointed him out to Gavroche.

"Do you know that man?"

"No," said Gavroche.

Gavroche, in truth, as we know, had only seen Jean Valjean by night. The troubled and sickly conjectures formed in Marius' mind were dissipated; did he know M. Fauchelevent's opinions? perhaps he was a republican. Hence his presence in the action would be perfectly simple. In the meanwhile, Gavroche had run to the other end of the barricade, crying, "My gun!" and Courfeyrac ordered it to be given to him. Gavroche warned "his comrades," as he called them, that the barricade was surrounded; and that he had found great difficulty in reaching it. A battalion of the line, with their arms piled in the little Truanderie, was observing on the side of the Rue du Petit Cygne, on the opposite side the Municipal Guard occupied the Rue des Prêcheurs, while in front of them they had the main body of the army. This information given, Gavroche added:

"I authorise you to give them a famous pill."

Enjolras was in the meanwhile watching at his loophole with open ears; for the assailants, doubtless little satisfied with the gunshot, had not repeated it. A company of line infantry had come up to occupy the extremity of the street behind the gun. The soldiers unpaved the street, and erected with the stones a small low wall, a species of breastwork, only eighteen inches high, and facing the barricade. At the left-hand angle of this work could be seen the head of a suburban column, massed in the Rue St. Denis. Enjolras, from his post, fancied he could hear the peculiar sound produced by canister when taken out of its box, and he saw the captain of the gun change his aim and turn the gun's muzzle slightly to the left. Then the gunners began loading, and the captain of the gun himself took the portfire and walked up to the vent.

"Fall on your knees all along the barricade," Enjolras shouted.

The insurgents, who were scattered in front of the wine-shop, and who had left their posts on Gavroche's arrival, rushed pell-mell toward the barricade ; but ere Enjolras' order was executed, the discharge took place with the frightful rattle of a round of grapeshot ; it was one, in fact. The shot was aimed at the opening in the redoubt, and ricochetted against the wall, killing two men and wounding three. If this continued the barricade would be no longer tenable, for the grapeshot entered it. There was a murmur of consternation.

"Let us stop a second round," Enjolras said : and, levelling his gun, he aimed at the firer, who was leaning over the breech and rectifying the aim. The firer was a handsome young sergeant of artillery, fair, gentle-faced, and having the intelligent look peculiar to that predestined and formidable arm which, owing to its constant improvement, must end by killing war. Combeferre, who was standing by Enjolras' side, gazed at this young man.

"What a pity," said Combeferre, "what a hideous thing such butchery is ! Well, when there are no kings left, there will be no war. Enjolras, you aim at that sergeant, but do not notice him. Just reflect that he is a handsome young man ; he is intrepid. You can see that he is a thinker, and these young artillerymen are well educated ; he has a father, mother, and family ; he is probably in love, he is but twenty-five years of age at the most, and might be your brother."

"He is so;" said Enjolras.

"Yes," Combeferre added, "and mine too. Do not kill him."

"Let me alone. It must be."

And a tear slowly coursed down Enjolras' marble cheek. At the same time he pulled the trigger and the fire flashed forth. The artilleryman turned twice on his heel, with his arms stretched out before him, and his head raised as if to breathe the air, and then fell across the cannon motionless. His back could be seen, from the middle of which a jet of blood gushed forth ; the bullet had gone right through his chest, and he was dead. It was necessary to bear him away and fill up his place, and thus a few minutes were gained. Opinions varied in the barricade, for the firing of the piece was going to begin again, and the barricade could not hold out for a quarter of an hour under the grapeshot ; it was absolutely necessary to deaden the rounds. Enjolras gave the command.

"We must have a mattress, then."

"We have none," said Combeferre, "the wounded are lying on them."

Jean Valjean, seated apart on a bench, near the corner of the wine-shop, with his gun between his legs, had not up to the present taken any part in what was going on. He did not seem to hear the combatants saying around him, "There is a gun that does nothing." On hearing the order given by Enjolras, he rose. It will be remembered that on the arrival of the insurgents in the Rue de la Chanvrerie, an old woman, in her terror of the bullets, placed her mattress in front of her window. This window, a garret window, was on the roof of a six-storeyed house, a little beyond the barricade. The mattress, placed crosswise, leaned at the bottom upon two clothes-props, and was held above by two ropes, which, at a distance, seemed like packthread, and which were fastened to nails driven into the mantelpiece. These cords could be distinctly seen against the sky, like hairs.

"Can any one lend me a double-barrelled carbine?" Jean Valjean asked.

Enjolras, who had just reloaded his, handed it to him. Jean Valjean aimed at the garret-window and fired; one of the two cords of the mattress was cut asunder, and it only hung by one thread. Jean Valjean fired the second shot, and the second cord lashed the garret-window; the mattress glided between the two poles and fell into the street. The insurgents applauded, and every voice cried :

"There is a mattress."

"Yes," said Combeferre, "but who will go and fetch it?"

The mattress, in truth, had fallen outside the barricade, between the besiegers and besieged. Now, as the death of the sergeant of artillery had exasperated the troops, for some time past they had been lying flat behind the pile of paving-stones which they had raised; and in order to make up for the enforced silence of the gun, they had opened fire on the barricade. The insurgents, wishing to save their ammunition, did not return this musketry : the fusillade broke against the barricade, but the street which it filled with bullets was terrible. Jean Valjean stepped out of the gap, entered the street, passed through the hail of bullets, went to the mattress, picked it up, placed it on his back, and, re-entering the barricade, he himself placed the mattress in the gap, and fixed it against the wall, so that the gunners should not see it. This done, they waited for the next round, which was soon fired. The gun belched forth its canister with a hoarse roar, but there was no ricochet, and the grapeshot was checked by the mattress. The expected result was obtained, and the barricade saved.

"Citizen,' Enjolras said to Jean Valjean, "the republic thanks you."

Bossuet admired, and laughingly said :

"It is immoral for a mattress to have so much power : it is the triumph of that which yields over that which thunders. But no matter, glory to the mattress that annuls a cannon !"

CHAPTER CII.

AT that moment Cosette awoke. Her bedroom was narrow, clean, discreet, with a long window on the east side looking out into the courtyard of the house. Cosette knew nothing of what was going on in Paris, for she had returned to her bedroom at the time when Toussaint said, "There is a row." Cosette had slept but a few hours, though well. She had had sweet dreams, which resulted perhaps from the fact that her small bed was very white. Somebody, who was Marius, appeared to her in light ; and she rose with the sun in her eyes, which at first produced the effect of a continuation of her dream upon her. Her first thought on coming out of the dream was of a smiling nature, and she felt quite reassured. Like Jean Valjean a few hours before, she was passing through that reaction of the soul which absolutely desires no misfortune. She began hoping with all her strength, without knowing why, and then suffered from a contraction of the heart. She had not seen Marius for three days, but she said to herself that he must have received her letter, that he knew where she was, and that he was so clever, and would find means to get to her,—and most certainly to-day, and perhaps that very morning. It was bright day, but the sunbeam was nearly horizontal, and so she thought that it must be early, but that she ought to rise in order to receive Marius. She felt that she could not live without Marius, and that consequently was sufficient, and Marius would come. No objection was admissible, all this was certain. It was monstrous enough to have suffered for three days : Marius absent for three days, that was horrible on the part of the good God. Now this cruel suspense sent from on high was a trial passed through ; Marius was about to come and bring good news. Thus is youth constituted : it wipes away its tears quickly, and finding sorrow useless, does not accept it. Youth is the smile of the future of an unknown thing, which is itself : it is natural for it to be happy, and it seems as if its breath were made of hope.

However, Cosette could not succeed in recalling to mind what Marius had said to her on the subject of this absence, which was only to last one day, and what explanation he had given her about it. Every one will have noticed with what skill a coin let fall on the ground runs to hide itself, and what art it has in rendering itself invisible. There are thoughts which play us the same trick ; they conceal themselves in a corner of our brain : it is all over, they are lost, and it is impossible to recall them to memory. Cosette felt somewhat vexed at the little useless effort her memory made, and said to herself that it was very wrong and culpable of her to forget words pronounced by Marius. She left her bed, and performed the two ablutions of the soul and the body, her prayers and her toilette.

Everybody was still asleep in the house. No shutter was opened, and the porter's lodge was still closed. Toussaint was not up, and Cosette naturally thought that her father was asleep. She must have suffered greatly, and must still be suffering, for she said to herself that her father had been unkind, but she reckoned on Marius. The eclipse of such a light was decidedly impossible. At moments she heard some distance off a sort of heavy shock, and thought how singular it was that gates were opened and shut at so early an hour ; it was the sound of the cannon-balls battering the barricade. There was a martin's nest a few feet below Cosette's window in the old smoke-blackened cornice, and the mouth of the nest projected a little beyond the cornice, so that the interior of this little Paradise could be seen from above. The mother was there expanding her wings like a fan over her brood ; the male bird fluttered round, went away, and then returned, bringing in his bill food and kisses. The rising day gilded this happy thing, the great law, increase and multiply, was there smiling and august, and the sweet mystery was unfolded in the glory of the morn. Cosette, with her hair in the sunshine, her soul in flames, enlightened by love within and the dawn without, bent forward as if mechanically, and, almost without daring to confess to herself that she was thinking at the same time of Marius, she began looking at these birds, this family, this male and female, this mother and her little ones, with all the profound restlessness which the sight of a nest gives to a maiden.

CHAPTER CIII.

THE fire of the assailants continued. The musketry and grapeshot alternated, though without producing much mischief. The upper part of Corinth alone suffered, and the first-floor and garret-windows, pierced by slugs and bullets, gradually lost their shape. The combatants posted there were compelled to withdraw, but, in fact, such are the tactics of an attack on a barricade, to skirmish for a long time and exhaust the ammunition of the insurgents, if they commit the error of returning the fire. When it is discovered by the slackening of their fire that they have no powder or ball left, the assault is made. Enjolras had not fallen into this trap, and the barricade did not reply. At each platoon fire, Gavroche thrust his tongue into his cheek, a sign of supreme disdain.

"That's good," he said, "tear up the linen, for we require lint."

Courfeyrac addressed the grapeshot on its want of effect, and said to the cannon :

"You are becoming diffuse, my good fellow."

In a battle, intrigues take place as at a ball ; and it is probable that the silence of the redoubt was beginning to render the assailants anxious, and make them fear lest some unexpected incident had occurred. They felt a need of seeing clearly through this pile of paving-stones, and what was going on behind this impassive wall, which received shots without answering them. The insurgents suddenly perceived a helmet glistening in the sun upon an adjoining roof ; a sapper was leaning against a tall chimney-pot and apparently a sentry there. He looked down into the barricade.

"That's a troublesome spy," said Enjolras.

Jean had returned Enjolras his fowling-piece, but still had his own musket. Without saying a word he aimed at the sapper, and a second later the helmet, struck by a bullet,

fell noisily into the street. The soldier disappeared with
all possible haste. A second watchman took his place, and
it was an officer. Jean Valjean, who had reloaded his
musket, aimed at the new-comer, and sent the officer's
helmet to join the private's. The officer was not obstinate,
but withdrew very quickly. This time the hint was understood, and no one again appeared on the roof.

"Why did you not kill the man?" Bossuet asked Jean
Valjean, who, however, made no reply.

Bossuet muttered in Combeferre's ear :

"He has not answered my question."

"He is a man who does kind actions with musket-shots,"
said Combeferre.

Those who have any recollection of this now distant
epoch know that the suburban National Guards were valiant
against the insurrection, and they were peculiarly brave and
obstinate in the days of June, 1832.

Zeal sometimes went as far as extermination ; a platoon
of National Guards constituted themselves of their own
authority a council of war, and tried and executed in five
minutes an insurgent prisoner. It was an improvisation of
this nature which killed Jean Prouvaire. On June 6, 1832,
a company of suburban National Guards, commanded by
Captain Fannicot, to whom we have already referred,
decimated the Rue de la Chanvrerie for his own good
pleasure, and on his own authority. This fact, singular
though it is, was proved by the judicial report drawn up in
consequence of the insurrection of 1832. Captain Fannicot,
an impatient and bold bourgeois, a species of condottiere
of order, and a fanatical and insubmissive governmentalist,
could not resist the attraction of firing prematurely, and
taking the barricade all by himself, that is to say, with his
company. Exasperated at the successive apparition of the
red flag and the old coat, which he took for the black flag,
he loudly blamed the generals and commanders of corps,
who were holding counsel, as they did not think the decisive
moment for assault had arrived, but were "letting the insurrection stew in its own gravy," according to a celebrated
expression of one of them. As for him, he thought the
barricade ripe, and as everything that is ripe is bound to
fall he made the attempt.

He commanded men as resolute as himself. "Madmen,"
a witness called them. His company, the same which had
shot Jean Prouvaire, was the first of the battalion posted at

the street corner. At the moment when it was least expected the captain dashed his men at the barricade, but this movement, executed with more goodwill than strategy, cost Fannicot's company dearly. Before it had covered two-thirds of the street a general discharge from the barricade greeted it ; four, the boldest men of all, running at the head, were shot down in point-blank range at the very foot of the barricade, and this courageous mob of National Guards, very brave men, but not possessing the military tenacity, was compelled to fall back after a few moments, leaving fifteen corpses in the street. The momentary hesitation gave the insurgents time to reload, and a second and most deadly discharge assailed the company before the men were able to regain their shelter at the corner of the street. In a moment they were caught between two fires, and received the volley from the cannon, which, having no orders to the contrary, did not cease firing. The intrepid and imprudent Fannicot was one of those killed by this round of grapeshot : he was laid low by the cannon. This attack, which was more furious than serious, irritated Enjolras.

"The asses !" he said, "they have their men killed and expend our ammunition for nothing."

Enjolras spoke like the true general of the riot that he was : insurrection and repression do not fight with equal arms ; for the insurrection, which can be soon exhausted, has only a certain number of rounds to fire and of combatants to expend. An expended cartouche-box and a killed man cannot have their place filled up. Repression, on the other hand, having the army, does not count men, and bare Vincennes does not count rounds. Repression has as many regiments as the barricade has men, and as many arsenals as the barricade has cartouche-boxes. Hence these are always contests of one man against a hundred, which ever end by the destruction of the barricade, unless revolution, suddenly dashing up, casts into the balance its flashing archangel's glaive.

Courfeyrac, seated on a stone beside Enjolras, continued to insult the cannon, and each time that the gloomy shower of projectiles which is called a grapeshot passed, with its monstrous noise, he greeted it with an ironical remark.

"You are wasting your breath, my poor old brute, and I feel sorry for you, as your row is thrown away. That is not thunder, but a cough."

And those around him laughed. Courfeyrac and Bossuet,

whose valiant good-humour increased with danger, made up
for the want of food, like Madame Scarron, by jests, and as
wine was short, poured out gaiety for all.

"I admire Enjolras," Bossuet said, "and his temerity
astonishes me. He lives alone, which, perhaps, renders him
a little sad; and Enjolras is to be pitied for his greatness,
which attaches him to widowhood. We fellows have all,
more or less, mistresses, who make us mad, that is to say
brave, and when a man is as full of love as a tiger, the least
he can do is to fight like a lion. That is a way of avenging
ourselves for the tricks which our grisettes play us. Roland
lets himself be killed to vex Angelique, and all our heroism
comes from our women. A man without a woman is like a
pistol without a hammer, and it is the woman who makes
the man go off. Well, Enjolras has no woman, he is not in
love, and finds means to be intrepid. It is extraordinary
that a man can be cold as ice and daring as fire."

Enjolras did not appear to listen; but any one who had
been near him might have heard him murmur in a low
voice, "*Patria*." Bossuet laughed again, when Courfeyrac
shouted:

"Here's something fresh."

And assuming the voice of a groom of the chambers, who
announces a visitor, he added:

"Mr. Eight-Pounder."

In fact, a new character had come on the stage; it was a
second piece of artillery. The gunners rapidly got it into
position by the side of the first one, and this was the beginning of the end. A few minutes later both guns, being
actively served, were at work against the barricade, and the
platoon fire of the line and the suburban National Guards
supported the artillery. Another cannonade was audible
some distance off. At the same time as the two guns were
furiously assaulting the redoubt in the Rue de la Chanvrerie,
two other pieces placed in position, one in the Rue St. Denis,
the other in the Rue Aubrey-le-Boucher, were pounding the
St. Merry barricade. The four guns formed a lugubrious
echo to each other. Of the two guns now opened on the
barricade of the Rue de la Chanvrerie, one fired shell, the
other solid shot. The gun which fired the latter was pointed
at a slight elevation, and the firing was so calculated that
the ball struck the extreme edge of the crest of the barricades, and hurled the broken paving-stones on the heads of
the insurgents. This mode of fire was intended to drive the

combatants from the top of the redoubt, and compel them to close up in the interior ; that is to say, it announced the assault. Once the combatants were driven from the top of the barricade by the cannon and from the windows of the public-house bv the canister, the columns of attack could venture into the street without being aimed at, perhaps without even being seen, suddenly escalade the barricade, as on the previous evening, and take it by surprise.

" The annoyance of these guns must be reduced," said Enjolras, and he shouted, " Fire at the artillerymen."

All were ready,—the barricade, which had so long been silent, was belted with flame ; seven or eight rounds succeeded each other with a sort of rage and joy ; the street was filled with a blinding smoke, and at the expiration of a few minutes there might be confusedly seen through the mist, all striped with flame, two-thirds of the artillerymen lying under the gun-wheels. Those who remained standing continued to serve the guns with a stern tranquillity, but the fire was reduced.

" Things are going well," said Bossuet to Enjolras, " that is a success."

Enjolras shook his head, and replied :

" Another quarter of an hour of that success, and there will not be a dozen cartridges left in the barricade."

It appears that Gavroche heard the remark, for Courfeyrac all at once perceived somebody in the street, at the foot of the barricade, amid the shower of bullets. Gavroche had fetched a hamper from the pot-house, passed through the gap, and was quickly engaged in emptying into it the full cartouche-boxes of the National Guards killed on the slope of the barricade.

" What are you doing there ? " Courfeyrac said.

Gavroche looked up.

" Citizen, I am filling my hamper."

" Do you not see the grapeshot ? "

Gavroche replied :

" Well, it is raining, what then ? "

Courfeyrac cried, " Come in."

" Directly," said Gavroche.

And with one bound he reached the street. It will be borne in mind that Fannicot's company, in retiring, left behind it a number of corpses ; some twenty dead lay here and there all along the pavement of the street. That made twenty cartouche-boxes for Gavroche, and a stock of cartridges for the barricade. The smoke lay in the street like a fog ; any one who has seen a cloud in a mountain gorge, between two precipitous escarpments, can form an idea of this smoke, contracted, and as it were rendered denser, by the two dark lines of tall houses. It rose slowly, and was incessantly renewed ; whence came a gradual obscurity, which dulled even the bright daylight. The combatants could scarce see each other from either end of the street, which was, however, very short. This darkness, probably desired and calculated on by the chiefs who were about to direct the assault on the barricade, was useful for Gavroche. Under the cloak of this smoke, and thanks to his shortness, he was enabled to advance a considerable distance along the street unnoticed, and he plundered the first seven or eight cartouche-boxes without any great danger. He crawled on his stomach, galloped on all-fours, took his hamper in his teeth, writhed, glided, undulated, wound from one corpse to another, and emptied the cartouche-box as a monkey opens a nut. They did not cry to him from the barricade, to which he was still rather close, to return, for fear of attracting attention to him. On one corpse, which was a corporal's, he found a powder-flask.

" For thirst," he said, as he put it in his pocket.

While moving forward he at length reached the point where the fog of the fire became transparent, so that the sharpshooters of the line drawn up behind their parapet of paving-stones, and the National Guard at the corner of the street, all at once pointed out to each other something stirring in the street. At the moment when Gavroche was taking the cartridges from a sergeant lying near a post a bullet struck the corpse.

"Oh! for shame," said Gavroche, "they are killing my dead for me."

A second bullet caused the stones to strike fire close to him, while a third upset his hamper. Gavroche looked and saw that it came from the National Guards. He stood upright, with his hair floating in the breeze, his hand on his hips, and his eyes fixed on the National Guards who were firing, and he sang :

> On est laid à Nanterre,
> C'est la faute à Voltaire,
> Et bête à Palaisseau,
> C'est la faute à Rousseau.

Then he picked up his hamper, put into it the cartridges scattered around without missing one, and walked toward the firing-party, to despoil another cartouche-box. Then a fourth bullet missed him. Gavroche sang :

> Je ne suis pas notaire,
> C'est la faute à Voltaire,
> Je suis petit oiseau,
> C'est la faute à Rousseau.

A fifth bullet only succeeded so far as to draw a third couplet from him :

> Joie est mon caractère,
> C'est la faute à Voltaire :
> Misère est mon trousseau,
> C'est la faute à Rousseau.

They went on for some time longer, and the sight was at once terrific and charming ; Gavroche, while fired at, ridiculed the firing, and appeared to be greatly amused. He was like a sparrow deriding the sportsmen, and answered each discharge by a couplet. The troops aimed at him incessantly, and constantly missed him, and the National Guards and the soldiers laughed, while covering him. He lay down, then rose again, hid himself in a doorway, then bounded, disappeared, reappeared, ran off, came back, replied to the grapeshot by taking a sight, and all the while plundered cartridges, emptied boxes, and filled his hamper. The insurgents watched him, as they panted with anxiety, but while the barricade trembled he sang. He was not a child, he was not a man, he was a strange goblin gamin, and he resembled the invulnerable dwarf of the combat. The bullets ran after him, but he was more active than they ; he played a frightful game of hide-and-seek with death : and each time that the snub-nosed face of the spectre approached the gamin gave it a fillip. One bullet, however, better aimed or more treacherous than the rest, at length struck the will-o'-the-wisp lad ; Gavroche was seen to totter and then sink. The whole barricade uttered a cry, but there was an Antæus in this pigmy : for a gamin to touch the pavement is like the giant touching the earth ; and Gavroche had only fallen to rise again. He remained in a sitting posture, a long jet of blood ran down his face, he raised both arms in the air, looked in the direction whence the shot had come, and began singing :

Je suis tombé par terre,
C'est la faute à Voltaire :
Le nez dans le ruisseau,
C'est la faute a——

He did not finish, for a second shot from the same marksman stopped him short. This time he lay with his face on the pavement, and did not stir again. This little great soul had taken flight.

CHAPTER CIV.

MARIUS had sprung out of the barricade. Combeferre had followed him. It was too late; Gavroche was dead. Combeferre brought in the hamper of cartridges, and Marius the boy. Alas! he thought he was requiting the son for what the father had done for his father; but Thénardier had brought in his father alive, while he brought in the lad dead. When Marius re-entered the barricade with Gavroche in his arms his face was inundated with blood, like the boy's; for, at the very instant when he stooped to pick up Gavroche, a bullet had grazed his skull, but he had not noticed it. Courfeyrac took off his neckcloth and bound Marius' forehead; Gavroche was deposited on the same table with Mabœuf, and the black shawl was spread over both bodies; it was large enough for the old man and the child. Combeferre distributed the cartridges which he had brought in, and they gave each man fifteen rounds to fire. Jean Valjean was still at the same spot, motionless on his bench. When Combeferre offered him his fifteen cartridges he shook his head.

"That is a strange eccentric," Combeferre said in a whisper to Enjolras. "He manages not to fight inside this barricade."

"Which does not prevent him from defending it," Enjolras answered.

"Heroism has its original characters," Combeferre resumed.

And Courfeyrac, who overheard him, said:

"He is a different sort from Father Mabœuf."

The redoubt in the Rue de la Chanvrerie, we repeat, appeared internally most calm; and all the incidents and phases were, or would shortly be, exhausted. The position had become from critical menacing, and from menacing was

probably about to become desperate. In proportion as the
situation grew darker an heroic gleam more and more
purpled the barricade. Suddenly, between two discharges,
the distant sound of a clock striking was heard.

" It is midday," said Combeferre.

The twelve strokes had not died out ere Enjolras drew
himself up to his full height, and hurled the loud cry from
the top of the barricade :

" Take up the paving-stones into the house, and line the
windows with them. One half of you to the stones, the
other half to the muskets. There is not a moment to lose."

A party of sappers, with their axes on their shoulders,
had just appeared in battle-array at the end of the street.
This could only be the head of a column : and of what
column ? evidently the column of attack ; for the sappers
ordered to demolish the barricade always precede the troops
told off to escalade it.

Enjolras' order was carried out with that correct speed
peculiar to ships and barricades, the only two battlefields
whence escape is impossible. In less than a minute two-
thirds of the paving-stones which Enjolras had ordered to
be piled up against the door of Corinth were carried to the
first floor and attic, and before a second minute had passed
these paving-stones, artistically laid on one another, walled
up one-half of the window. A few spaces carefully arranged
by Feuilly, the chief constructor, allowed the gun-barrels to
pass through. This armament of the windows was the
more easily effected because the grapeshot had ceased.
The two cannon were now firing solid shot at the centre
of the barricade, in order to make a hole, and if possible
a breach, for the assault. When the stones intended for
the final assault were in their places, Enjolras carried to
the first floor the bottles he had placed under the table on
which Mabœuf lay.

" Who will drink that ? " Bossuet asked him.

" They will," Enjolras answered.

Then the ground-floor window was also barricaded, and the
iron bars which closed the door at night were held in readiness. The fortress was complete, the barricade was the
rampart, and the wineshop the keep. With the paving-
stones left over the gap was stopped up. As the defenders
of a barricade are always obliged to save their ammunition,
and the besiegers are aware of the fact, the latter combine
their arrangements with a sort of irritating leisure, expose

themselves before the time to the fire, though more apparently than in reality, and take their ease. The preparations for the attack are always made with a certain methodical slowness, and after that comes the thunder. This slowness enabled Enjolras to revise and render everything perfect. He felt that since such men were about to die their death must be a masterpiece. He said to Marius:

"We are the two chiefs. I am going to give the final orders inside, while you remain outside and watch."

Marius posted himself in observation on the crest of the barricade, while Enjolras had the door of the kitchen, which it will be remembered served as the hospital, nailed up.

"No spattering on the wounded," he said.

He gave his final instructions in the ground-floor room in a sharp but wonderfully calm voice, and Feuilly listened and answered in the name of all.

"Have axes ready on the first floor to cut down the stairs. Have you them?"

"Yes," Feuilly answered.

"How many?"

"Two axes and a crowbar."

"Very good. In all twenty-six fighting-men left. How many guns are there?"

"Thirty-four."

"Eight too many. Keep those guns loaded like the others, and within reach. Place your sabres and pistols in your belts. Twenty men to the barricade. Six will ambush themselves in the garret and at the first-floor window, to fire on the assailants through the loopholes in the paving-stones. There must not be an idle workman here. Presently, when the drummer sounds the charge, the twenty men below will rush to the barricade, and the first to arrive will be the best placed."

These arrangements made, he turned to Javert, and said to him:

"I have not forgotten you."

And laying a pistol on the table, he added:

"The last man to leave here will blow out this spy's brains."

"Here?" a voice answered.

"No, let us not have this corpse near ours. It is easy to stride over the small barricade in Mondétour lane, as it is only four feet high. This man is securely bound, so lead him there and execute him."

Some one was at this moment even more stoical than Enjolras,—it was Javert. Here Jean Valjean appeared ; he was mixed up with the group of insurgents, but stepped forward and said to Enjolras :

"Are you the Commandant ? "

"Yes."

"You thanked mé just now."

"In the name of the Republic. The barricade has two saviours, Marius Pontmercy and yourself."

" Do you think that I deserve a reward ? "

"Certainly."

"Well, then, I ask one."

"What is it ? "

"To let me blow out that man's brains myself.

Javert raised his head, saw Jean Valjean, gave an imperceptible start, and said, "It is fair."

As for Enjolras, he was reloading his gun. He looked around him.

" Is there no objection ? "

And he turned to Jean Valjean.

"Take the spy."

Jean Valjean took possession of Javert by seating himself on the end of the table. He seized the pistol, and a faint clink showed that he had cocked it. Almost at the same moment the bugle-call was heard.

"Mind yourselves," Marius shouted from the top of the barricade.

Javert began laughing that noiseless laugh peculiar to him, and, looking intently at the insurgents, said to them :

"You are no healthier than I am."

"All outside," Enjolras cried.

The insurgents rushed tumultuously forth, and as they passed, Javert smote them on the back, so to speak, with the expression, "We shall meet again soon."

So soon as Jean Valjean was alone with Javert, he undid the rope which fastened the prisoner round the waist, the knot of which was under the table. After this, he made him a signal to rise. Javert obeyed with that indefinable smile, in which the supremacy of enchained authority is condensed. Jean Valjean seized Javert by the martingale, as he would have taken an ox by its halter, and dragging him after him, quitted the wine-shop slowly, for Javert, having his feet hobbled, could only take very short steps. Jean Valjean held the pistol in his hand, and they thus crossed the inner trapeze of the barricade ; the insurgents, prepared for the imminent attack, were looking the other way.

Marius alone, placed at the left extremity of the barricade, saw them pass. This group of the victim and his hangman was illumined by the sepulchral gleams which he had in his soul. Jean Valjean forced Javert to climb over the barricade with some difficulty, but did not loosen the cord. When they had crossed the bar, they found themselves alone in the lane, and no one could now see them. Among the dead could be distinguished a livid face, a pierced hand, and a half-naked female bosom ; it was Eponine. Javert looked askance at this dead girl, and said with profound calmness :

" I fancy I know that girl."

Then he turned to Jean Valjean, who placed the pistol under his arm, and fixed on Javert a glance which had no need of words to say, " Javert, it is I."

Javert answered, " Take your revenge."

Jean Valjean took a knife from his pocket and opened it.

" A clasp-knife," Javert exclaimed. " You are right, that suits you better."

Jean Valjean cut the martingale which Javert had round his neck, then he cut the ropes on his wrists, and stooping down, those on his feet ; then rising again, he said, " You are free."

It was not easy to astonish Javert, still, master though he was of himself, he could not suppress his emotion ; he stood gaping and motionless, while Jean Valjean continued:

" I do not believe that I shall leave this place. Still if by accident I do, I live under the name of Fauchelevent, at No. 7 Rue de l'Homme Armé."

Javert gave a tigerish frown, which opened a corner of his mouth, and muttered between his teeth :

" Take care."

" Begone," said Jean Valjean.

Javert added :

" You said Fauchelevent, Rue de l'Homme Armé ? "

" No. 7."

Javert repeated in a low voice,—" No. 7."

He buttoned his frock-coat, restored the military stiffness between his shoulders, made a half-turn, crossed his arms while supporting his chin with one of his hands, and walked off in the direction of the markets. Jean Valjean looked after him. After going a few yards, Javert turned and said :

"You annoy me. I would sooner be killed by you."

"Begone," said Jean Valjean.

Javert retired slowly, and a moment after turned the corner of the Rue des Prêcheurs. When Javert had disappeared, Jean Valjean discharged the pistol in the air, and then returned to the barricade, saying :

"It is all over."

This is what had taken place in the meanwhile. Marius, more occupied with the outside than the inside, had not hitherto attentively regarded the spy fastened up at the darkened end of the ground-floor room. When he saw him in the open daylight bestriding the barricade, he recognised him, and a sudden hope entered his mind. He remembered the inspector of the Rue de Pontoise, and the two pistols he had given him, which he, Marius, had employed at this very barricade, and he not only remembered his face, but recalled his name.

This recollection, however, was foggy and disturbed, like all his ideas. It was not an affirmation he made so much as a question which he asked himself. "Is that not the Police Inspector, who told me that his name was Javert?" Marius shouted to Enjolras, who had just stationed himself at the other end of the barricade :

"Enjolras !"

"What is it ? "

"What is that man's name ? "

"Which man ? "

"The police agent. Do you know his name ? "

"Of course I do, for he told it to us."

"What is it ? "

"Javert."

Marius started, but at this moment a pistol-shot was heard, and Jean Valjean reappeared, saying, "It is all over." A dreary chill passed through the heart of Marius.

The death-agony of the barricade was approaching. Everything added to the tragical majesty of this supreme moment. A thousand mysterious disturbances in the air, the breathing of armed masses set in motion in streets which could not be seen, the intermittent gallop of cavalry, the heavy concussion of artillery, the platoon firing and the cannonades crossing each other in the labyrinth of Paris ;

the smoke of the battle rising golden above the roofs'
distant and vaguely terrible cries, flashes of menace
everywhere, the tocsin of St. Merry, which now had the
sound of a sob, the mildness of the season, the splendour
of the sky, full of sunshine and clouds, the beauty
of the day, and the fearful silence of the houses. For,
since the previous evening, the two rows of houses in
the Rue de la Chanvrerie had become two walls, ferocious
walls with closed doors, closed windows, and closed shutters.

Suddenly the drum beat the charge, and the attack was
a hurricane. On the previous evening the barricade had
been silently approached in the darkness as by a boa, but,
at present, in broad daylight, within this gutted street,
surprise was impossible ; besides, the armed force was
unmasked, the cannon had begun the roar, and the
troops rushed upon the barricade. Fury was now skill.
A powerful column of line infantry, intersected at regular
intervals by National Guards and dismounted Municipal
Guards, and supported by heavy masses, that could be
heard if not seen, debouched into the street at the double,
with drums beating, bugles sounding, bayonets levelled,
and sappers in front, and, imperturbable under the shower
of projectiles, dashed straight at the barricade with all
the weight of a bronze battering-ram. But the wall held
out firmly, and the insurgents fired impetuously ; the
escaladed barricade displayed a flashing mane. The
attack was so violent that it was in a moment inundated
by assailants ; but it shook off the soldiers as the lion does
the dogs, and it was only covered with besiegers as the
cliff is with foam, to reappear a minute later, scarped,
black, and formidable.

The columns, compelled to fall back, remained massed
in the street, exposed but terrible, and answered the redoubt by a tremendous musketry-fire. Any one who
has seen fireworks will remember the piece composed of
a cross-fire of lightnings, which is called a bouquet.
Imagine this bouquet, no longer vertical but horizontal,
and bearing at the end of each jet a bullet, slugs, or
iron balls, and scattering death. The barricade was
beneath it. On either side was equal resolution : the
bravery was almost barbarous, and was complicated by
a species of heroic ferocity which began with self-sacrifice.
It was the epoch when a National Guard fought like a
Zouave. The troops desired to make an end of it, and

the insurrection wished to contend. The acceptance of death in the height of youth and health converts intrepidity into a frenzy, and each man in this action had the grandeur of the last hour. The street was covered with corpses. The barricade had Marius at one of its ends and Enjolras at the other. Enjolras, who carried the whole barricade in his head, reserved and concealed himself : three soldiers fell under his loophole without even seeing him, while Marius displayed himself openly, and made himself a mark. More than once half his body rose above the barricade. There is no more violent prodigal than a miser who takes the bit between his teeth, and no man more startling in action than a dreamer. Marius was formidable and pensive, and was in action as in a dream. He looked like a firing ghost. The cartridges of the besieged were becoming exhausted, but not so their sarcasms ; and they laughed in the tornado of the tomb in which they stood.

The interior of the barricade was so sown with torn cartridges that it seemed as if there had been a snowstorm. The assailants had the numbers, and the insurgents the position. They were behind a wall, and crushed at point-blank range the soldiers who were stumbling over the dead and wounded. This barricade, built as it was, and admirably strengthened, was really one of those situations in which a handful of men holds a legion in check. Still, constantly recruited and growing beneath the shower of bullets, the column of attack inexorably approached, and now, little by little, step by step, but certainly, contracted round the barricade.

The assaults succeeded each other, and the horror became constantly greater. Then there broke out on this pile of paving-stones, in this Rue de la Chanvrerie, a struggle worthy of the walls of Troy. These sallow, ragged, and exhausted men, who had not eaten for four-and-twenty hours, who had not slept, who had only a few rounds more to fire, who felt their empty pockets for cartridges—these men, nearly all wounded, with head or arm bound round with a bloodstained blackish rag, having holes in their coat from which the blood flowed, scarce armed with bad guns and old rusty sabres, became Titans. The barricade was ten times approached, assaulted, escaladed, and never captured. To form an idea of the struggle it would be necessary to imagine a mass of terrible valour set on fire, and that you are watching the flames. It was not a combat, but the interior of a furnace; mouths breathed flames there, and faces were extraordinary. The human form seemed impossible there, the combatants flashed flames, and it was a formidable sight to see these salamanders of the medley flitting about in this red smoke. The successive and simultaneous scenes of this butchery are beyond our power to depict, for epic alone has the right to fill ten thousand verses with a battle. They fought foot to foot, body to body, with pistol-shots, sabre-cuts, and fists, close by, at a distance, above, below, on all sides, from the roof of the house, from the wine-shop, and even from the traps of the cellars into which some had slipped. The odds were sixty to one, and the frontage of Corinth, half demolished, was hideous. The window, pock-marked with grapeshot, had lost glass and frame, and was only a shapeless hole, confusedly stopped up with paving-stones. Bossuet was killed, Feuilly was killed, Courfeyrac was killed, Joly was killed. Combeferre, pierced by three bayonet stabs in the breast at the moment when he was raising a wounded soldier, had only time to look up to heaven, and expired. Marius, still fighting, had received so many wounds, especially in the head, that his face disappeared in blood, and looked as if it were covered by a red handkerchief. Enjolras alone was not wounded; when he had no weapon he held out his arm to the right or left, and an insurgent placed some instrument in his hand. Of four swords, one more than Francis I. at Marignan, he now had but one stump remaining.

CHAPTER CV.

WHEN there were none of the chiefs alive save Enjolras and Marius, who were at the two ends of the barricade, the centre, which had so long been supported by Courfeyrac, Bossuet, Joly, Feuilly, and Combeferre, yielded. The cannon, without making a practicable breach, had severely injured the centre of the redoubt, then the crest of the wall had disappeared under the balls and fallen down, and the fragments which had collected both inside and out had in the end formed two slopes, the outer one of which offered an inclined plane by which to attack. A final assault was attempted thus, and this assault was successful;

the mass, bristling with bayonets and hurled forward at a
run, came up irresistibly, and the dense line of the attacking
column appeared in the smoke on the top of the scarp.
This time it was all over, and the band of insurgents
defending the centre recoiled pell-mell.

Then the gloomy love of life was rekindled in some;
covered by this forest of muskets, several did not wish to
die. This is the moment when the spirit of self-preservation
utters yells, and when the beast reappears in man. They
were drawn up against the six-storeyed house at the back
of the barricade, and this house might be their salvation.
This house was barricaded, and, as it were, walled up from
top to bottom, but before the troops reached the interior of
the redoubt, a door would have time to open and shut, and
it would be life for these desperate men, for at the back of
this house were streets, possible flight, and space. They
began kicking and knocking at the door, while calling,
crying, imploring, and clasping their hands. But no one
opened. The dead head looked down on them from the
third-floor window. But Marius and Enjolras, and seven
or eight men who had rallied round them, rushed forward
to protect them. Enjolras shouted to the soldiers, "Keep
back," and as an officer declined to obey he killed the
officer. He was in the inner yard of the redoubt, close to
Corinth, with his sword in one hand, and his carbine in
tho other, holding open the door of the wine-shop, which
he barred against the assailants. He shouted to the
desperate men, "There is only one door open, this one,"
and covering them with his person, and alone facing a
battalion, he made them pass in behind him. All rushed
in, and Enjolras, whirling his musket round his head,
drove back the bayonets and entered last of all, and tnere
was a frightful moment, during which the troops tried to
enter and the insurgents to bar the door. The latter was
closed with such violence that the five fingers of a soldier
who had caught hold of the door-post were cut off clean, and
remained in the crevice. Marius remained outside; a bullet
had broken his collar-bone, and he felt himself fainting and
falling. At this moment, when his eyes were already
closed, he felt the shock of a powerful hand seizing him,
and his fainting-fit scarce left him time for this thought,
mingled with the supreme recollection of Cosette, "I am
made prisoner. I shall be shot."

Enjolras, not seeing Marius among those who had sought

shelter in the house, had the same idea, but they had reached that moment when each could only think of his own death. Enjolras put the bar on the door, bolted and locked it, while the soldiers beat it with musket-butts, and the sappers attacked it with their axes outside. The assailants were grouped round this door, and the siege of the wine-shop now began. The soldiers, let us add, were full of fury; the death of the sergeant of artillery had irritated them, and then, more mournful still, during the few hours that preceded the attack a whisper ran along the ranks that the insurgents were mutilating their prisoners, and that there was the headless body of a soldier in the cellar. This species of fatal rumour is the general accompaniment of civil wars, and it was a false report of the same nature which at a later date produced the catastrophe of the Rue Transnonain. When the door was secured Enjolras said to the others :

"Let us sell our lives dearly."

Then he went up to the table on which Mabœuf and Gavroche were lying; under the black cloth two forms could be seen straight and rigid, one tall, the other short, and the two faces were vaguely outlined under the cold folds of the winding-sheet. A hand emerged from under it, and hung toward the ground ; it was the old man's. Enjolras bent down and kissed this venerable hand, in the same way as he had done the forehead on the previous evening. They were the only two kisses he had ever given in his life.

Let us be brief. The barricade had resisted like a gate of Thebes, and the wine-shop resisted like a house of Sara-gossa. Such resistances are violent, and there is no quarter, and a flag of truce is impossible ; people are willing to die provided that they can kill. When the assailants rushed into the wine-shop, their feet entangled in the panels of the broken door which lay on the ground, they did not find a single combatant. The winding staircase, cut away with axes, lay in the middle of the ground-floor room, a few wounded men were on the point of dying, all who were not killed were on the first floor, and a terrific fire was dis-charged thence through the hole in the ceiling which had been the entrance to the restaurant. These were the last cartridges, and when they were expended and nobody had any powder or balls left, each man took up two of the bottles reserved by Enjolras, and defended the stairs with these frightfully fragile weapons. They were bottles of aqua-fortis. We describe the gloomy things of carnage exactly as they are : the besieged makes a weapon of everything. The noise was indescribable, and a compressed burning smoke almost threw night over the combat. Words fail to describe horror when it has reached this stage. It was the heroism of monsters.

At last, by employing the skeleton of the staircase, by climbing up the walls, clinging to the ceiling and killing on the very edge of the trap the last who resisted, some twenty assailants, soldiers, National and Municipal Guards, mostly disfigured by wounds in the face received in this formidable ascent, blinded by blood, furious and savage, burst into the first-floor room. There was only one man standing there— Enjolras ; without catridges or sword, he only held in his hand the barrel of his carbine, whose butt he had broken on the heads of those who entered. He had placed the billiard-table between himself and his assailants, he had fallen back to the end of the room, and there, with flashing eye and head erect, holding the piece of a weapon in his hand, he was still sufficiently alarming for a space to be formed round him. A cry was raised :

" It is the chief ; it was he who killed the artilleryman ; as he has placed himself there, we will let him remain there. Shoot him on the spot."

" Shoot me," Enjolras said.

And, throwing away his weapon and folding his arms, he offered his chest. The boldness of dying bravely always moves men. So soon as Enjolras folded his arms, accepting the end, the din of the struggle ceased in the room, and the chaos was suddenly appeased in a species of sepulchral solemnity. It seemed as if the menacing majesty of Enjolras, disarmed and motionless, produced an effect on the tumult, and that merely by the authority of his tranquil glance, this young man, who alone was unwounded, superb, bloodstained, charming, and indifferent as if he were invulnerable, constrained this sinister mob to kill him respectfully. His beauty, heightened at this moment by his haughtiness, was dazzling, and as if he could be no more fatigued than wounded after the frightful four-and-twenty hours which had elapsed, he was fresh and rosy. It was to him that the witness referred when he said at a later date before the court-martial, "There was an insurgent whom I heard called Apollo." A National Guard who aimed at Enjolras lowered his musket, saying, " I feel as if I were going to

kill a flower." Twelve men formed into a platoon in the
corner opposite to the one in which Enjolras stood, and got
their muskets ready in silence. Then a sergeant shouted,
" Present."

An officer interposed :

" Wait a minute."

And, addressing Enjolras :

" Do you wish to have your eyes bandaged

" No."

" It was really you who killed the sergeant of artillery ? "

" Yes."

Grantaire had been awake for some minutes past.
Grantaire, it will be remembered, had been sleeping since
the past evening in the upper room, with his head lying on
a table. He realised, in all its energy, the old metaphor,
dead drunk. The hideous potion of absinthe, stout, and
alcohol, had thrown him into a lethargic state, and, as his
table was small, and of no use at the barricade, they had
left it to him. He was still in the same posture, with his
chest upon the table, his head reeling on his arms, and
surrounded by glasses and bottles. He was sleeping the
deadly sleep of the hybernating bear, or the filled leech.
Nothing had roused him, neither the platoon fire, nor the
cannon-balls, nor the canister which penetrated through the
window into the room where he was, nor the prodigious
noise of the assault. Still he at times responded to the
cannon by a snore. He seemed to be waiting for a bullet
to save him the trouble of waking ; several corpses lay
around him, and, at the first glance, nothing distinguished
him from these deep sleepers of death.

Noise does not waken a drunkard, but silence arouses
him, and this peculiarity has been more than once observed.
The fall of anything near him increased Grantaire's
lethargy ; noise lulled him. The species of halt which the
tumult made before Enjolras was a shock to this heavy
sleep. It is the effect of a galloping coach which stops
short. Grantaire started up, stretched out his arms, rubbed
his eyes, looked, yawned, and understood. Intoxication
wearing off resembles a curtain that is rent, and a man
sees at once, and at a single glance, all that it concealed.
Everything offers itself suddenly to the memory, and the
drunkard, who knows nothing of what has happened during
the last twenty-four hours, has scarce opened his eyes ere
he understands it all.

Concealed, as he was, in a corner, and sheltered, so to speak, by the billiard-table, the soldiers, who had their eyes fixed on Enjolras, had not even perceived Grantaire, and the sergeant was preparing to repeat the order to fire when all at once they heard a powerful voice crying at their side :

"Long live the Republic ! I belong to it."

Grantaire had risen ; and the immense gleam of all the combat which he had missed appeared in the flashing glance of the transfigured drunkard. He repeated, "Long live the Republic !" crossed the room with a firm step, and placed himself before the muskets by Enjolras' side.

"Kill us both at once," he said.

And turning gently to Enjolras, he asked him :

"Do you permit it ? "

Enjolras pressed his hand with a smile, and this smile had not passed away ere the detonation took place. Enjolras, pierced by eight bullets, remained leaning against the wall, as if nailed to it ; he merely hung his head ; Grantaire was lying stark dead at his feet. A few minutes later the soldiers dislodged the last insurgents who had taken refuge at the top of the house, and were firing through a partition in the garret. They fought desperately, and threw bodies out of windows, some still alive. Two voltigeurs, who were trying to raise the smashed omnibus, were killed by two shots from the attics ; a man in a blouse rushed out of them, with a bayonet thrust in his stomach, and lay on the ground expiring. A soldier and an insurgent slipped together down the tiles of the roof, and, as they would not loosen their hold, fell into the street, holding each other in a ferocious embrace. There was a similar struggle in the cellar ; cries, shots, and a fierce clashing ; then a silence. The barricade was captured. The soldiers commenced the search of the houses round about and the pursuit of the fugitives.

Marius was indeed a prisoner—prisoner to Jean Valjean. The hand which had clutched him behind at the moment when he was falling, and of which he felt the pressure as he lost his senses, was Jean Valjean's.

Jean Valjean had taken no other part in the struggle than that of exposing himself. Had it not been for h'm, in the supreme moment of agony no one would have thought of the wounded. Thanks to him, who was everywhere present in the carnage like a Providence, those who fell were picked

up, carried to the ground-floor room, and had their wounds
dressed, and in the intervals he repaired the barricade.   But
nothing that could resemble a blow, an attack, or even
personal defence, could be seen with him, and he kept quiet
and gave aid.   However, he had only a few scratches;
and the bullets had no billet for him.   If suicide formed
part of what he dreamed of when he came to this sepulchre,
he had not been successful, but we doubt whether he thought
of suicide, which is an irreligious act.   Jean Valjean did
not appear to see Marius in the thick of the combat, but in
truth he did not take his eyes off him.   When a bullet laid
Marius low Jean Valjean leaped upon him with the agility
of a tiger, dashed upon him as on a prey, and carried him off.

The whirlwind of the attack was at this moment so
violently concentrated on Enjolras and the door of the
wine-shop that no one saw Jean Vajean, supporting the
fainting Marius in his arms, cross the unpaved ground of
the barricade, and disappear round the corner of Corinth.
Our readers will remember this corner, which formed a
sort of cape in the street, and protected a few square feet of
ground from bullets and grapeshot, and from glances as
well.   There is thus at times in fires a room which does not
burn, and in the most raging seas, beyond a promontory, or
at the end of a reef, a little quiet nook.   It was in this
corner of the inner trapeze of the barricade that Eponine
drew her last breath.   Here Jean Valjean stopped, let
Marius slip to the ground, leant against a wall, and looked
around him.

The situation was frightful.   For the instant, for two or
three minutes perhaps, this piece of wall was a shelter, but
how to get out of this massacre ?   He recalled the agony he
had felt in the Rue Polonceau, eight years previously, and
in what way he had succeeded in escaping ; it was difficult
then, but now it was impossible.   He had in front of him
that implacable and silent six-storeyed house, which only
seemed inhabited by the dead man leaning out of his
window ; he had on his right the low barricade which
closed the Petite Truanderie ; to climb over this obstacle
appeared easy, but a row of bayonet-points could be seen
over the crest of the barricade ; they were line troops posted
beyond the barricade, and on the watch.   It was evident
that to cross the barricade was to meet the fire of a platoon,
and that any head which appeared above the wall of paving-
stones would serve as a mark for sixty muskets.   He had

on his left the battlefield, and death was behind the corner
of the wall.

What was he to do? a bird alone could have escaped
from this place. And he must decide at once, find an
expedient, and make up his mind. They were fighting
a few paces from him, but fortunately all were obstinately
engaged at one point, the wine-shop door; but if a single
soldier had the idea of turning the house or attacking it on
the flank all would be over. Jean Valjean looked at the
house opposite to him, he looked at the barricade by his
side, and then looked on the ground, with the violence of
supreme extremity, wildly, and as if he would have liked to
dig a hole with his eyes. By force of looking, something
vaguely discernible in such an agony was designed,
and assumed a shape at his feet, as if the eyes had the
power to produce the thing demanded. He perceived a few
paces from him, at the foot of the small barricade so
pitilessly guarded and watched from without, and beneath
a pile of paving-stones which almost concealed it, an iron
grating, laid flat and flush with the ground. This grating,
made of strong cross-bars, was about two feet square, and
the framework of paving-stones which supported it had
been torn out, and it was as it were unset. Through the
bars a glimpse could be caught of an obscure opening,
something like a chimney-pot or the cylinder of a cistern.
Jean Valjean dashed up, and his old skill in escapes rose to
his brain like a beam of light. To remove the paving-
stones, tear up the grating, take Marius, who was as inert as
a dead body, on his shoulders, descend with this burden on
his loins, helping himself with his elbows and knees, into
this sort of well, which was fortunately of no great depth,
to let the grating fall again over his head, to set foot on a
paved surface, about ten feet below the earth, all this was
executed like something done in delirium, with a giant's
strength and the rapidity of an eagle : this occupied but a
few minutes. Jean Valjean found himself with the still
fainting Marius in a sort of long subterranean corridor,
where there was profound peace, absolute silence, and
night. The impression which he had formerly felt in falling
out of the street into the convent recurred to him, still
what he now carried was not Cosette, but Marius.

He could now hardly hear above him, like a vague
murmur, the formidable tumult of the wine-shop being
taken by assault.

CHAPTER CVI.

JEAN VALJEAN found himself in the sewer of Paris—that wonderful underground city. It was an extraordinary transition, in the very heart of the city. Jean Valjean had left the city, and in a twinkling, the time required to lift a trap and let it fall again, he had passed from broad daylight to complete darkness, from midday to midnight, from noise to silence, from the uproar of thunder to the stagnation of the tomb, and, by an incident more prodigious even than that of the Rue Polonceau, from the extremest peril to the most absolute security. A sudden fall into a cellar, disappearance in the oubliette of Paris, leaving this street where death was all around for this species of sepulchre in which was life ; it was a strange moment. He stood for some minutes as if stunned, listening and amazed. The trap-door of safety had suddenly opened beneath him, and the heavenly kindness had to some extent snared him by treachery. Admirable ambuscades of Providence ! Still the wounded man did not stir, and Jean Valjean did not know whether what he was carrying in this fosse were alive or dead.

His first sensation was blindness, for all at once he could see nothing. He felt too that in a moment he had become deaf, for he could hear nothing more. The frenzied storm of murder maintained a few yards above him only reached him confusedly and indistinctly, and like a rumbling at a great depth. He felt that he had something solid under his feet, but that was all ; still it was sufficient. He stretched out one arm, then the other ; he touched the wall on both sides and understood that the passage was narrow ; his foot slipped, and he understood that the pavement was damp. He advanced one foot cautiously, fearing a hole, a cesspool, or some gulf, and satisfied himself that the pavement went onwards. A fetid gust warned him of the spot where he was. At the expiration of a few minutes he was no longer blind, a little light fell through the trap by which he descended, and his eye grew used to this cellar. He began to distinguish something. The passage in which he had run to earth—no other word expresses the situation better—was walled up behind him ; it was one of those blind alleys called in the special language branchments. Before him he had another wall, a wall of night. The light

of the trap expired ten or twelve feet from the spot where
Jean Valjean was, and scarce produced a livid whiteness on
a few yards of the damp wall of the sewer. Beyond that
the opaqueness was massive, to enter it seemed horrible,
and resembled being swallowed up by an earthquake. Yet
it was possible to bury oneself in this wall of fog, and it
must be done ; and must even be done quickly. Jean
Valjean thought that the grating which he had noticed in
the street might also be noticed by the troops, and that all
depended on chance. They might also come down into the
well and search, so he had not a minute to lose. He had
laid Marius on the ground, and now gathered him up—that
is again the right expression—took him on his shoulders,
and set out. He resolutely entered the obscurity.

The truth is, that they were not so safe as Jean Valjean
supposed. Perils of another nature, but equally great,
awaited them. After the flashing whirlwind of the combat
came the cavern of miasmas and snares, after the chaos,
the cloaca. Jean Valjean had passed from one circle of
the Inferno into another. When he had gone fifty yards
he was obliged to stop, for a question occurred to him ;
the passage ran into another, which it intersected, and two
roads offered themselves. Which should he take ? ought
he to turn to the left or right ? how was he to find his
way in this black labyrinth ? This labyrinth, we have said,
has a clue in its slope, and following the slope leads to the
river. Jean Valjean understood this immediately ; he said
to himself that he was probably in the sewer of the markets,
that, if he turned to the left and followed the incline, he
would arrive in a quarter of an hour at some opening on
the Seine between the Pont au Change and the Pont Neuf,
that is to say, appear in broad daylight in the busiest part of
Paris. Perhaps he might come out at some street opening,
and passers-by would be stupefied at seeing two bloodstained
men emerge from the ground at their feet. The police
would come up and they would be carried off to the nearest
guardroom ; they would be prisoners before they had come
out. It would be better, therefore, to bury himself in the
labyrinth, confine in the darkness, and leave the issue to
Providence.

He went up the incline, and turned to the right ; when
he had gone round the corner of the gallery the distant light
from the trap disappeared, the curtain of darkness fell
on him again, and he became blind once more. For all

that he advanced as rapidly as he could ; Marius' arms were passed round his neck, and his feet hung down behind. He held the two arms with one hand and felt the wall with the other. Marius' cheek touched his and was glued to it, as it was bloody, and he felt a warm stream which came from Marius drip on him and penetrate his clothing. Still, a warm breath in his ear, which touched the wounded man's mouth, indicated respiration, and consequently life. The passage in which Jean Valjean was now walking was not so narrow as the former, and he advanced with some difficulty. The rain of the previous night had not yet passed off, and formed a small torrent in the centre, and he was forced to hug the wall in order not to lave his feet in the water. He went on thus darkly, resembling beings of the night groping in the invisible, and subterraneously lost in the veins of gloom. Still, by degrees, either that a distant grating sent a little floating light into this opaque mist, or that his eyes grew accustomed to the obscurity, he regained some vague vision, and began to notice confusedly, at one moment the wall he was touching, at another the vault under which he was passing. The pupil is dilated at night, and eventually finds daylight in it, in the same way as the soul is dilated in misfortune and eventually finds God in it.

To direct himself was difficult, for the sewers represent, so to speak, the outline of the streets standing over them. There were in the Paris of that day two thousand two hundred streets, and imagine beneath them that forest of dark branches called the sewer. The system of drains existing at that day, if placed end on end, would have given a length of eleven leagues. Jean Valjean began by deceiving himself ; he fancied that he was under the Rue St. Denis, and it was unlucky that he was not so. There is under that street an old stone drain, dating from Louis XIII., which runs straight to the collecting sewer, called the Grand Sewer, with only one turn on the right, by the old Court of Miracles, and a single branch, the St. Martin sewer, whose four arms cut each other at right angles. But the gut of the little Truanderie, whose entrance was near the Corinth wine-shop, never communicated with the sewer of the Rue St. Denis ; it falls into the Montmartre drain, and that is where Jean Valjean now was.

He advanced anxiously, but calmly, seeing nothing, hearing nothing, plunged into chance, that is to say, swallowed up in Providence. By degrees, however, we are bound to state that a certain amount of horror beset him, and the shadow which enveloped him entered his mind. He was walking in an enigma. This aqueduct of the cloaca is formidable, for it intersects itself in a vertiginous manner, and it is a mournful thing to be caught in this Paris of darkness. Jean Valjean was obliged to find and almost invent his road without seeing it. In this unknown region each step that he ventured might be his last. How was he to get out of it? would he find an issue? would he find it in time? could he pierce and penetrate this colossal subterranean sponge with its passages of stone? would he meet there some unexpected knot of darkness? would he arrive at something inextricable and impassable? would Marius die of hæmorrhage, and himself of hunger? would they both end by being lost there, and form two skeletons in a corner of this night? He did not know; he asked himself all this and could not find an answer.

He suddenly had a surprise. At the most unexpected moment, and without ceasing to walk in a straight line, he perceived that he was no longer ascending; the water of the gutter plashed against his heels instead of coming to his toes. The sewer was now descending; why? was he about to reach the Seine suddenly? That danger was great, but the peril of turning back was greater still, and he continued to advance. He was not proceeding toward the Seine; the ridge which the soil of Paris makes on the right bank empties one of its water-sheds into the Seine, and the other into the Grand Sewer. The crest of this ridge, which determines the division of the waters, follows a most capricious line; the highest point is in the St. Avoye sewer, beyond the Rue Michel-le-comte, in the Louvre sewer, near the boulevards, and in the Montmartre drain. This highest point Jean Valjean had reached, and he was proceeding toward the belt sewer, or in the right direction, but he knew it not. Each time that he reached a branch he felt the corners, and if he found the opening narrower than the passage in which he was he did not enter, but continued his march, correctly judging that any narrower way must end in a blind alley, and could only take him from his object, that is to say, an outlet. He thus avoided the fourfold snare laid for him in the darkness by the four labyrinths which we have enumerated. At a certain moment he recognised that he was getting from under that part of

Paris petrified by the riot, where the barricades had suppressed circulation, and returning under living and normal Paris. He suddenly heard above his head a sound like thunder, distant but continuous; it was the rolling of vehicles.

He had been walking about half an hour, at least that was the calculation he made, and had not thought of resting; he had merely changed the hand which held Marius up. The darkness was more profound than ever, but this darkness reassured him. All at once he saw his shadow before him; it stood out upon a faint and almost indistinct redness, which vaguely empurpled the roadway at his feet and the vault above his head, and glided along the greasy walls of the passage. He turned his head in stupefaction, and saw behind him at a distance, which appeared immense, a sort of horrible star glistening, which seemed to be looking at him. It was the gloomy police star rising in the sewer. Behind this star there moved confusedly nine or ten black, upright, indistinct, and terrible forms.

The meaning was as follows: On the day of June 6 a *battue* of the sewers was ordered, for it was feared that the conquered should fly to them as a refuge, and Prefect Gisquet ordered occult Paris to be searched, while General Bugeaud swept public Paris; a double connected operation, which required a double strategy of the public force, represented above by the army and beneath by the police. Three squads of agents and sewermen explored the subway of Paris, the first the right bank, the second the left bank, and the third the City. The agents were armed with carbines, bludgeons, swords, and daggers, and what was at this moment pointed at Jean Valjean was the lantern of the patrol of the right bank. This patrol had just inspected the winding gallery and the three blind alleys which are under the Rue du Cadran. While the police were carrying their light about there, Jean Valjean in his progress came to the entrance of the gallery, found it narrower than the main gallery, and had not entered it. The police, on coming out of the Cadran gallery, fancied that they could hear the sound of footsteps in the direction of the outer drain, and they were really Jean Valjean's footsteps. The head sergeant of the patrol raised his lantern, and the squad began peering into the mist in the direction whence the noise had come.

It was an indescribable moment for Jean Valjean; luckily, if he saw the lantern well, the lantern saw him badly, for it was the light and he was the darkness. He was far off, and blended with the blackness of the spot, so he drew himself up against the wall and stopped. However, he did not explain to himself what was moving behind him; lack of sleep, want of food, emotions, had thrown him also into the visionary state. He saw a flash, and round this flash, sprites. What was it? he did not understand. When Jean Valjean stopped, the noise ceased; the police listened and heard nothing, they looked and saw nothing, and hence consulted together. There was at that period a sort of square at this point in the Montmartre drain, called *de service*, which has since been suppressed, owing to the small internal lake which the torrents of rain formed there, and the squad assembled on this square. Jean Valjean saw them make a sort of circle, and then bulldog heads came together and whispered. The result of this council held by the watch-dogs was that they were mistaken, that there had been no noise, that there was nobody there, that it was useless to enter the belt sewer, that it would be time wasted, but that they must hasten to the St. Merry drain, for if there were anything to be done and any "boussingot" to track, it would be there. The sergeant gave orders to left-wheel toward the watershed of the Seine. Had they thought of dividing into two squads and going in both directions, Jean Valjean would have been caught. It is probable that the instructions of the Prefecture, fearing the chance of a fight with a large body of insurgents, forbade the patrol from dividing. The squad set out again, leaving Jean Valjean behind; and in all this movement he perceived nothing except the eclipse of the lantern, which was suddenly turned away.

Before starting, the sergeant, to satisfy his police conscience, discharged his carbine in the direction where Jean Valjean was. The detonation rolled echoing along the crypt, like the rumbling of these Titanic bowels. A piece of plaster which fell into the gutter and plashed up the water a few yards from Jean Valjean warned him that the bullet had struck the vault above his head. Measured and slow steps echoed for some time along the wooden causeway, growing more and more deadened by the growing distance; the group of black forms disappeared; a light oscillated and floated, forming on the vault a ruddy circle, which decreased and disappeared;

the silence again became profound, the obscurity again
became complete, and blindness and deafness again took
possession of the gloom. Jean Valjean, not daring yet
to stir, remained leaning for a long time against the wall,
with outstretched ear and dilated eyeballs, watching the
vanishing of that phantom patrol.

CHAPTER CVII.

WE must do the police of that period the justice of saying
that even in the gravest public conjunctures, they imperturbably accomplished their duties as watchmen. A
riot was not in their eyes a pretext to leave the bridle to
malefactors and to neglect society for the reason that the
Government was in danger. The ordinary duties were
performed correctly in addition to the extraordinary duties,
and were in no way disturbed. In the midst of an in-
calculable political event, under the pressure of a possible
revolution, an agent, not allowing himself to be affected
by the insurrection and the barricade, would track a robber.
Something very like this occurred on the afternoon of
June 6, on the right bank of the Seine, a little beyond
the Pont des Invalides. There is no bank there at the
present day, and the appearance of the spot has been
altered. On this slope two men, a certain distance apart,
were observing each other; the one in front seemed to
be trying to get away, while the one behind wanted to
catch him up. It was like a game of chess played at a
distance and silently; neither of them seemed to be in a
hurry, and both walked slowly, as if they were afraid
that increased speed on the part of one would be imitated
by the other. It might have been called an appetite following a prey, without appearing to do so purposely; the prey
was crafty, and kept on guard.

The proportions required between the tracked ferret and
the tracking dog were observed. The one trying to escape
was thin and weak; the one trying to catch was a tall
fellow, and evidently a rough customer. The first, feeling
himself the weaker, avoided the second, but did so in a
deeply furious way; any one who could have observed
him would have seen in his eyes the gloomy hostility of
flight, and all the threat which there is in fear; the slope
was deserted, there were no passers-by, not even a boat-

man or raftsman in the boats moored here and there.
They could only be noticed easily from the opposite quay,
and any one who had watched them at that distance,
would have seen that the man in front appeared a bristling,
ragged, and shambling fellow, anxious and shivering
under a torn blouse, while the other was a classic and
official personage, wearing the frock-coat of authority
buttoned up to the chin. The reader would probably
recognise these two men, were he to see them more
closely. What was the object of the last one? probably
he wished to clothe the other man more warmly. When
a man dressed by the State pursues a man in rags, it is
in order to make of him also a man dressed by the State.
The difference of colour is the sole question,—to be dressed
in blue is glorious, to be dressed in red is disagreeable,
for there is a purple of the lower classes. It was probably
some disagreeable thing, and some purple of this sort,
which the first man desired to avoid.

If the other allowed him to go on ahead, and did not
yet arrest him, it was, in all appearance, in the hope of seeing
him arrive at some significative rendezvous and some group
worth capturing. This delicate operation is called tracking. What renders this conjecture highly probable, is the
fact that the buttoned-up man perceiving from the slope
an empty fiacre passing, made a sign to the driver; the
driver understood, evidently perceived with whom he had
to deal, turned round, and began following the two men
along the quay. This was not perceived by the ragged,
shambling fellow in front. The hackney-coach rolled along
under the trees of the Champs Elysées, and over the parapet
could be seen the bust of the driver, whip in hand. One
of the secret instructions of the police to the agents is
"always have a hackney-coach at hand in case of need."
While each of these men manœuvred with irreproachable
strategy, they approached an incline in the quay, which
allowed drivers coming from Passy to water their horses
in the river. This incline has since been suppressed for
the sake of symmetry,—horses die of thirst, but the eye
is flattered. It was probable that the man in the blouse
would ascend by this incline in order to try and escape
in the Champs Elysées, a place adorned with trees, but,
to make up for that, much frequented by police agents,
where the other could easily procure assistance. This
point of the quay is a very little distance from the house

brought from Moret to Paris in 1824, by Colonel Brack, and called the house of Francis I. A piquet is always stationed there. To the great surprise of his watcher, the tracked man did not turn up the road to the watering-place, but continued to advance along the bank parallel with the quay. His position was evidently becoming critical, for unless he threw himself into the Seine, what could he do ?

There were no means now left him of returning to the quay, no incline or no steps, and they were close to the spot marked by the turn in the Seine, near the Pont de Jena, where the bank, gradually contracting, ended in a narrow strip, and was lost in the water. There he must inevitably find himself blockaded between the tall wall on his right, the river on his left and facing him, and authority at his heels. It is true that this termination of the bank was masked from sight by a pile of rubbish seven feet high, the result of some demolition. But did this man hope to conceal himself profitably behind this heap ? the expedient would have been puerile. He evidently did not dream of that, for the innocence of robbers does not go so far. The pile of rubbish formed on the waterside a sort of eminence extending in a promontory to the quay wall ; the pursued man reached this small mound and went round it, so that he was no longer seen by the other. The latter, not seeing, was not seen, and he took advantage of this to give up all dissimulation and walk very fast. In a few minutes he reached the heap and turned it, but there stood stupefied. The man he was pursuing was not there, it was a total eclipse of the man in the blouse. The bank did not run more than thirty yards beyond the heap, and then plunged under the water which washed the quay wall. The fugitive could not have thrown himself into the Seine, or have climbed up the quay wall, without being seen by his pursuer. What had become of him?

The man in the buttoned-up coat walked to the end of the bank and stood there for a moment, thoughtfully, with clenched fists and scowling eye. All at once he smote his forehead ; he had just perceived, at the point where the ground ended and the water began, a wide, low, arched, iron grating, provided with a heavy lock, and three massive hinges. This grating, a sort of gate pierced at the bottom of the quay, opened on the river as much as on the bank and a black stream poured from under it into the Seine

Beyond the heavy rusty bars could be distinguished a sort of arched and dark passage. The man folded his arms and looked at the grating reproachfully, and this look not being sufficient, he tried to push it open, he shook it, but it offered a sturdy resistance. It was probable that it had just been opened, although no sound had been heard, a singular thing with so rusty a gate, but it was certain that it had been closed again. This indicated that the man who had opened the gate had not a pick-lock but a key. This evidence at once burst on the mind of the man who was trying to open the grating, and drew from him this indignant apostrophe :

" That is strong ! a government key ! "

This said, hoping we know not what, either to see the man come out or others enter, he posted himself on the watch behind the heap of rubbish, with the patient rage of a yard-mastiff.

CHAPTER CVIII.

JEAN VALJEAN had resumed his advance, and had not stopped again. This march grew more and more laborious ; for the level of these arches varies ; the average height is about five feet six inches, and was calculated for a man's stature. Jean Valjean was compelled to stoop so as not to dash Marius against the roof, and was forced at each moment to bend down, then draw himself up and incessantly feel the wall. The dampness of the stones and of the flooring rendered them bad supports either for the hand or the foot, and he tottered in the hideous dungheap of the city. The intermittent flashes of the street gratings only appeared at lengthened intervals, and were so faint that the bright sunshine seemed to be moonlight; all the rest was fog, miasma, opaqueness, and blackness. Jean Valjean was hungry and thirsty ; thirsty especially ; and this place, like the sea, is one full of water where you cannot drink. His strength, which, as we know, was prodigious, and but slightly diminished by age, owing to his chaste and sober life, was, however, beginning to give way ; fatigue assailed him, and his decreasing strength increased the weight of his burden. Marius, who was perhaps dead, was heavy, like all inert bodies, but Jean Valjean held him in such a way that his chest was not compressed, and his breathing could always be as free as possible. He felt between his legs the rapid gliding of rats, and one was so startled as to bite him. From time to time a gush of fresh air came through the gratings, and this revived him.

It might be about 3 p.m. when he reached the belt sewer, and was at first amazed by the sudden widening. He unexpectedly found himself in a gallery whose two walls his outstretched arms did not reach, and under an arch which his head did not touch. The Grand Sewer, in fact, is eight feet wide and seven high. At the point where the Montmartre drain joins the Grand Sewer, two other subterranean galleries, that of the Rue de Provence and that of the Abattoir, form cross-roads. Between these four ways a less sagacious man would have been undecided, but Jean Valjean selected the widest, that is to say, the belt sewer. But here the question came back again,—should he ascend or descend? He thought that the situation was pressing, and that he must at all risks now reach the Seine, in other words, descend, so he turned to the left. It was fortunate that he did so. If Jean Valjean had remounted the gallery he would have arrived, exhausted by fatigue and dying, at a wall. He would have been lost.

Strictly speaking, by going back a little way, entering the passage of the Filles du Calvaire, he might have reached the Amelot sewer, and then if he did not lose his way in the species of F which is under the Bastille, he would have reached the issue on the Seine near the Arsenal. But for that he must have thoroughly known, in all its ramifications and piercings, tho enormous madrepore of the sewer. Now we dwell on the fact that he knew nothing of this frightful labyrinth in which he was marching, and had he been asked where he was he would have replied,—In the night. His instinct served him well ; going down, in fact, was the only salvation possible. He left on his right the two passages which ramify in the shape of a claw under the Rues Lafitte and St. Georges, and the long forked corridor of the Chaussée d'Antin. A little beyond an affluent, which was probably the Madeleine branch, he stopped, for he was very weary. A large grating, probably the one in the Rue d'Anjou, produced an almost bright light. Jean Valjean, with the gentle movements which a brother would bestow on his wounded brother, laid Marius upon the side bank of the drain, and his white face gleamed under the white light of the trap as from the bottom of a tomb. His eyes were closed, his hair was attached to his forehead like pincers dried in blood, his hands were hanging and dead, his limbs cold, and blood was clotted at the corner of his lip. Co-agulated blood had collected in his cravat knot, his shirt entered the wounds, and the cloth of his coat rubbed the gaping edges of the quivering flesh. Jean Valjean, removing the clothes with the tips of his fingers, laid his hand on his chest,—the heart still beat. Jean Valjean tore up his shirt, bandaged the wounds as well as he could, and stopped the blood that was flowing; then, stooping down in this half daylight over Marius, who was still un-conscious and almost breathless, he looked at him with indescribable hatred. In moving Marius' clothes he had found in his pockets two things, the loaf, which he had forgotten the previous evening, and his pocket-book. He ate the bread and opened the pocket-book. On the first page he read the lines written by Marius, as will be remembered :

"My name is Marius Pontmercy, carry my body to my grandfather's, M. Gillenormand, No. 6 Rue des Filles du Calvaire, in the Marais."

Jean Valjean read by the light of the grating these lines, and remained for a time as it were absorbed in himself, and repeating in a low voice, M. Gillenormand, No. 6 Rue des Filles du Calvaire. He returned the portfolio to Marius' pocket; he had eaten, and his strength had come back to him. He raised Marius again, carefully laid his head on his right shoulder, and began descending the sewer. The Grand Sewer, running along the course of the valley of Menilmontant, is nearly two leagues in length, and is paved for a considerable portion of the distance. This nominal torch of the streets of Paris, with which we enlighten for the reader Jean Valjean's subter-ranean march, he did not possess. Nothing informed him what zone of the city he was traversing, nor what distance he had gone; still, the growing paleness of the flakes of light which he met from time to time indicated to him that the sun was retiring from the pavement, and that day would be soon ended, and the rolling of vehicles over his head, which had become intermittent instead of con-tinuous, then having almost ceased, proved to him that he was no longer under central Paris, and that he was approaching some solitary region, near the external boulevards or the most distant quays, where there are fewer houses and streets, and the drain has fewer gratings.

The obscurity thickened around Jean Valjean; still he continued to advance, groping his way in the obscurity.

This obscurity suddenly became terrible.

He felt that he was entering the water, and that he had under his feet, pavement no longer, but mud. It often happens on certain coasts of Brittany or Scotland that a man, whether traveller or fisherman, walking at low water on the sands some distance from the coast, suddenly perceives that during the last few minutes he has found some difficulty in walking. The shore beneath his feet is like pitch, his heels are attached to it, it is no longer sand, but bird-lime; the sand is perfectly dry, but at every step taken, so soon as the foot is raised the imprint it leaves fills with water. The eye, however, has perceived no change, the immense expanse is smooth and calm, all the sand seems alike, nothing distinguishes the soil which is solid from that which is no longer so, and the little merry swarm of water-fleas continue to leap tumultuously round the feet of the wayfarer. The man follows his road, turns toward the land, and tries to approach the coast, not that he is alarmed; alarmed at what? Still he feels as if the heaviness of his feet increased at every step that he takes; all at once he sinks in, sinks in two or three inches. He is decidedly not on the right road, and he stops to look about him. Suddenly he looks at his feet, but they have disappeared, the sand covers them. He draws his feet out of the sand and tries to turn back, but he sinks in deeper still. The sand comes up to his ankles, he pulls himself out and turns to his left, when the sand comes to his knees, he turns to the right, and the sand comes up to his thighs, then he recognises with indescribable terror that he is caught in a quicksand, and has under him the frightful medium in which a man can no more walk than a fish can swim. At times the rider is swallowed up with his horse, at times the carter with his cart; it is a shipwreck otherwhere than in the water, it is the land drowning man. The land penetrated by the ocean becomes a snare. It presents itself as a plain, and opens like a wave.

Such a mournful adventure, always possible on some sea-shore, was also possible some thirty years ago in the sewer of Paris. Before the important works began in 1833 the subway of Paris was subject to sudden breakings in. The water filtered through a subjacent and peculiarly friable soil ; and the roadway, if made of paving-stones, as in the old drains, or of concrete upon beton, as in the new galleries, having no support, bent. A bend in a planking of this nature is a crevice, and a crevice is a bursting in. The roadway broke away for a certain length, and such a gap, a gulf of mud, was called in the special language *fontis*. What is a fontis? it is the quicksand of the seashore suddenly met with underground ; it is the quicksand of St. Michel in a sewer. The moistened soil is in a state of fusion, all its particles are held in suspense in a shifting medium ; it is not land and it is not water. The depth is at times very great. Nothing can be more formidable than meeting with such a thing ; if water predominate death is quick, for a man is drowned ; if earth predominate, death is slow, for he is sucked down.

Can our readers imagine such a death ? if it be frightful to sink in a quicksand on the seashore, what is it in a cloaca ? instead of fresh air, daylight, a clear horizon, vast sounds, the free clouds from which life rains, the barque perceived in the distance, that hope under every form, of possible passers-by, of possible help up to the last minute,—instead of all this, deafness, blindness, a black archway, the interior of a tomb already made, death in the mud under a tombstone ! slow asphyxia by uncleanliness, a sarcophagus where asphyxia opens its claws in the filth, and clutches you by the throat ; fetidness mingled with the death-rattle, mud instead of the sand, sulphuretted hydrogen in lieu of the hurricane, ordure instead of the ocean ! and to call and gnash the teeth, and writhe, and struggle and expire, with this enormous city which knows nothing of it above one's head. Inexpressible the horror of dying thus !

The depth of the fontis varied, as did their length and density, according to the nature of the subsoil. At times a fontis was three or four feet deep, at times eight or ten, and sometimes it was bottomless. In one the mud was almost solid, in another nearly liquid. The mud bears more or less well according to its degree of density, and a lad escapes where a man is lost. The first law of safety is to throw away every sort of loading, and every sewer-man who felt the ground giving way under him began by getting rid of his basket of tools. The fontis had various causes, friability of soil, some convulsion beyond man's depth, violent summer showers, the incessant winter rain, and long fine rains.

Jean Valjean found himself in presence of a fontis.

A giving way of the pavement, which was badly supported by the subjacent sand, had produced a deposit
of rain water, and when the filtering had taken place,
the ground broke in, and the roadway, being dislocated,
fell into the mud. How far? it was impossible to say,
for the darkness was denser there than anywhere else;
it was a slough of mud in a cavern of night. Jean Valjean
felt the pavement depart from under him as he entered
the slough; there was water at top and mud underneath. He
must pass it, for it was impossible to turn back; Marius
was dying, and Jean Valjean worn out. Where else could
he go? Jean Valjean advanced; the slough appeared but
of slight depth at the first few steps, but as he advanced
his legs sank in. He soon had mud up to the middle
of his legs, and water above his knees. He walked along,
raising Marius with both arms as high as he could above
the surface of the water; the mud now came up to his
knees and the water to his waist. He could no longer
draw back, and he sank in deeper and deeper. This mud,
dense enough for the weight of one man, could not evidently
bear two; Marius and Jean Valjean might have had a chance
of getting out separately, but, for all that, Jean Valjean
continued to advance, bearing the dying man, who was
perhaps a corpse. The water came up to his armpits, and
he felt himself drowning; he could scarce move in the
depth of mud in which he was standing, for the density
which was the support was also the obstacle. He still kept
Marius up, and advanced with an extraordinary expenditure
of strength, but he was sinking. He had only his head
out of water and his two arms sustaining Marius. In the
old paintings of the Deluge there is a mother holding her
child in the same way. As he still sank he threw back his
face to escape the water and be able to breathe; any one
who saw him in this darkness would have fancied he saw
a mask floating on the gloomy waters; he vaguely perceived
above him Marius' hanging head and livid face; he made
a desperate effort, and advanced his foot, which struck
against something solid, a resting-place. It was high time.

He drew himself up, and writhed, and rooted himself with
a species of fury upon this support. It produced on him the
effect of the first step of a staircase reascending to life. This
support, met with in the mud, at the supreme moment, was
the beginning of the other side of the roadway, which had

fallen in without breaking, and had bent under the water like a plank, and in a single piece. A well-constructed pavement forms a curve, and possesses such firmness. This fragment of roadway, partly submerged, but solid, was a real incline, and once upon it they were saved. Jean Valjean ascended it, and attained the other side of the slough. On leaving the water his foot caught against a stone and he fell on his knees. He found that this was just, and remained on them for some time, with his soul absorbed in words addressed to God. He rose, shivering, chilled, bent beneath the dying man he carried, dripping with filth, but with his soul full of a strange light.

He resumed his route once more. However, if he had not left his life in the fontis, he seemed to have left his strength there. This supreme effort had exhausted him, and his fatigue was now so great that he was obliged to rest every three or four paces, to take breath, and lean against the wall. Once he was obliged to sit down on the curb in order to alter Marius' position, and believed that he should remain there. But if his vigour were dead his energy was not so, and he rose again. He walked desperately, almost quickly, went thus one hundred yards without raising his head, almost without breathing, and all at once ran against the wall. He had reached an elbow of the drain, and, on arriving head down at the turning, had come against the wall. He raised his eyes, and at the end of the passage down there, far, very far away, perceived a light. But this time it was no terrible light, but white, fair light. It was daylight. Jean Valjean saw the outlet. A condemned soul that suddenly saw from the middle of the furnace the issue from Gehenna would feel what Jean Valjean felt. It would fly wildly with the stumps of its burnt wings toward the radiant gate. Jean Valjean no longer felt fatigue, he no longer felt Marius' weight, he found again his muscles of steel, and ran rather than walked. As he drew nearer, the outlet became more distinctly designed; it was an arch, not so tall as the roof, which gradually contracted, and not so wide as the gallery, which grew narrower at the same time as the roof became lowered. The tunnel finished on the inside in the shape of a funnel, a faulty reduction, imitated from the wickets of houses of correction, logical in a prison, but illogical in a drain, and which has since been corrected.

Jean Valjean reached the issue and then stopped; it was

certainly the outlet, but they could not get out. The arch
was closed by a strong grating, and this grating, which
apparently rarely turned on its oxidised hinges, was fastened
to the stone wall by a heavy lock, which, red with rust,
seemed an enormous brick. The keyhole was visible, as
well as the bolt deeply plunged into its iron box. It was
one of these Bastille locks of which ancient Paris was so
prodigal. Beyond the grating were the open air, the river,
daylight, the bank, very narrow, but sufficient to depart,
the distant quays, Paris, that gulf in which a man hides
himself so easily, the wide horizon, and liberty. On the
right could be distinguished, down the river, the Pont de
Jena, and up it the Pont des Invalides ; the spot would have
been a favourable one to await night and escape. It was
one of the most solitary points in Paris, the bank facing the
Gros Caillou. The flies went in and out through the
grating bars. It might be about half-past eight in the
evening, and day was drawing in : Jean Valjean laid
Marius along the wall on the dry part of the way, then
walked up to the grating and seized the bars with both
hands ; the shock was frenzied, but the effect *nil*. The
grating did not stir. Jean Valjean seized the bars one after
the other, hoping he might be able to break out the least
substantial one, and employ it as a lever to lift the gate off
the hinges, or break the lock, but not a bar stirred. A
tiger's teeth are not more solidly set in their jaws. Without a lever it was impossible to open the grating, and the
obstacle was invincible.

Must he finish, then, there ? what should he do ? what
would become of him ? he had not the strength to turn back
and recommence the frightful journey which he had already
made. Moreover, how was he to cross again that slough
from which he had only escaped by a miracle ? And after
the slough, was there not the police squad, which he
assuredly would not escape twice ; and then where should
he go, and what direction take ? following the slope would
not lead to his object, for if he reached another outlet, he
would find it obstructed by an iron plate or a grating. All
the issues were indubitably closed in that way ; accident
had left the grating by which thay had entered open, but
it was plain that all the other mouths of the sewer were
closed. They had only succeeded in escaping into a prison.

It was all over, and all that Jean Valjean had done was
useless : God opposed it. They were both caught in the

dark and immense web of death, and Jean Valjean felt the fearful spider already running along the black threads in the darkness. He turned his back to the grating and fell on the pavement near Marius, who was still motionless, and whose head had fallen between his knees. There was no outlet, that was the last drop of agony. Of whom did he think in this profound despondency? Neither of himself nor of Marius! of Cosette. In the midst of his annihilation a hand was laid on his shoulder, and a low voice said:

"Half shares."

Some one in this shadow? As nothing so resembles a dream as despair, Jean Valjean fancied that he was dreaming. He had not heard a footstep. Was it possible? He raised his eyes; a man was standing before him. This man was dressed in a blouse, his feet were naked, and he held his shoes in his hand; he had evidently taken them off in order to be able to reach Jean Valjean without letting his footsteps be heard. Jean Valjean had not a moment's hesitation: however unexpected the meeting might be, the man was known to him: it was Thénardier. Although, so to speak, aroused with a start, Jean Valjean, accustomed to alarms and to unexpected blows, which it is necessary to parry quickly, at once regained possession of all his presence of mind. Besides, the situation could not be worse, a certain degree of distress is no longer capable of crescendo, and Thénardier himself could not add any blackness to this night. There was a moment's expectation. Thénardier, raising his right hand to the level of his forehead, made a screen of it; then he drew his eyebrows together with a wink, which, with a slight pinching of the lips, characterises the sagacious attention of a man who is striving to recognise another. He did not succeed. Jean Valjean, as we said, was turning his back to the light, and was besides so disfigured, so filthy, and so bloodstained, that he could not have been recognised in broad daylight. On the other hand, Thénardier, with his face lit up by the light from the grating, a cellar brightness, it is true, livid but precise in its lividness, struck Jean Valjean at once, to employ the energetic popular metaphor. This inequality of conditions sufficed to ensure some advantage to Jean Valjean in the mysterious duel which was about to begin between the two situations and the two men. The meeting took place between Jean Valjean masked and Thénardier unmasked. Jean Valjean at once perceived that Thénardier did not recognise him; and they looked at each

other silently in this gloom, as if taking each other's measure.
Thénardier was the first to break the silence.

"How do you mean to get out?"

Jean Valjean not replying, Thénardier continued :

"It is impossible to pick the lock : and yet you must get
out of here."

"That is true," said Jean Valjean.

"Well, then, half shares."

"What do you mean?"

"You have killed the man ; very good.   I have the key."

Thénardier pointed to Marius, and continued,—"I do not
know you, but you must be a friend, and I wish to help you."

Jean Valjean began to understand.   Thénardier took him
for an assassin.   The latter continued :

"Listen, mate, you did not kill this man without looking
to see what he had in his pockets.   Give me my half and I
open the gate."

And half drawing a heavy key from under his ragged
blouse, he added :

"Would you like to see how the key is made? look here."

Jean Valjean was so astounded that he doubted whether
what he saw was real.   It was Providence appearing in a
horrible form, and the good angel issuing from the ground
in the shape of Thénardier.   The latter thrust his hand into
a wide pocket hidden under his blouse, drew out a rope, and
handed it to Jean Valjean.

"There," he said, "I give you the rope into the bargain."

"What am I to do with the rope?"

"You also want a stone, but you will find that outside,
as there is a heap of them."

"What am I to do with a stone?"

"Why, you ass, as you are going to throw the cove into
the river you want a rope and a stone, or else the body will
float on the water."

Jean Valjean took the rope mechanically, and Thénardier
snapped his fingers as if a sudden idea had occurred to him.

"Hilloh, mate, how did you manage to get through that
slough?   I did not dare venture into it.   Peuh ! you do not
smell pleasant."

After a pause he added :

"I ask you questions, but you are right not to answer :
this is an apprenticeship for the magistrate's ugly quarter
of an hour.   And then, by not speaking at all a man runs
no risk of speaking too loud.   No matter, though I cannot

see your face and do not know your name, you would do wrong in supposing that I do not know who you are and what you want. I know all about it: you have smashed that swell a little, and now want to get rid of him somewhere. You prefer the river, that great nonsense-hider, and I will help you out of the hobble. It is my delight to aid a good fellow when in trouble."

While commending Jean Valjean for his silence it was plain that he was trying to make him speak. He pushed his shoulder, so as to be able to see his profile, and exclaimed, though without raising the pitch of his voice :

"Talking of the slough, you are a precious ass. Why did you not throw the man into it ? "

Jean Valjean preserved silence. Thénardier continued, raising his rag of a cravat to the Adam's apple, a gesture which completes the capable air of a serious man.

" Really, you may have acted sensibly, for the workmen, when they come to-morrow to stop up the hole, would certainly have found the swell, and your trail would be followed up. Some one has passed through the sewer ; who? how did he get out? was he seen to do so? The police are full of sense : the drain is a traitor, and denounces you. Such a find is a rarity, it attracts attention, for few people employ the sewer for their little business, while the river belongs to everybody, and is the real grave. At the end of a month your man is fished up at the nets of St. Cloud : well, who troubles himself about that? it's cold meat, that's all. Who killed the man? Paris, and justice makes no inquiries. You acted wisely."

The more loquacious Thénardier became, the more silent Jean Valjean was. Thénardier shook his shoulder again.

"And now let's settle our business. You have seen my key, so show me your money."

Thénardier was haggard, firm, slightly menacing, but remarkably friendly. There was one strange fact : Thénardier's manner was not simple ; he did not appear entirely at his ease : while not affecting any mysterious air, he spoke in a low voice. From time to time he laid his finger on his lip, and muttered " Chut ! " it was difficult to guess why, for there were only themselves present. Jean Valjean thought that other bandits were probably hidden in some corner no great distance off, and that Thénardier was not anxious to share with them. The latter continued :

" Now for a finish. How much had the swell about him?"

Jean Valjean felt in his pockets. It was, as will be remembered, always his rule to have money about him, for the gloomy life of expedients to which he was condemned rendered it a law for him. This time, however, he was unprovided. In putting on his National Guard uniform, he had forgotten upon the previous evening, mournfully absorbed as he was, to take out his pocket-book, and he had only some change in his waistcoat-pocket. He turned out his pocket, which was saturated with slime, and laid on the curb a louis d'or, two five-franc pieces, and five or six double sous. Thénardier thrust out his lower lip with a significant twist of the neck.

" You did not kill him for much," he said.

He began most familiarly feeling in Jean Valjean's and Marius' pockets, and Jean Valjean, who was most anxious to keep his back to the light, allowed him to do so. While feeling in Marius' coat, Thénardier, with the dexterity of a conjuror, managed to tear off, without Jean Valjean perceiving the fact, a strip, which he concealed under his blouse; probably thinking that this piece of cloth might help him to recognise hereafter the assassinated man and the assassin. However, he found no more than the thirty francs.

" It is true," he said; " both together, you have no more than that."

And forgetting his phrase half shares, he took all. He hesitated a little at the double sous, but on reflection he took them too, while grumbling, " I don't care, it is killing people too cheaply."

This done, he again took the key from under his blouse.

" Now, my friend, you must be off. It is here as at the fairs; you pay when you go out. You have paid, so you can go."

And he began laughing. We may be permitted to doubt whether he had the pure and disinterested intention of saving an assassin, when he gave a stranger the help of this key, and allowed any one but himself to pass through this gate. Thénardier helped Jean Valjean to replace Marius on his back, and then proceeded to the grating on the tips of his naked feet. After making Jean Valjean a sign to follow him, he placed his finger on his lip, and remained for some seconds as if in suspense; but when the inspection was over he put the key in the lock. The bolt slid, and the gate turned on its hinges without either grinding or creaking. It was plain that this grating and these hinges, carefully oiled, opened more frequently than might be supposed. This gentleness was ill-omened ; it spoke of furtive comings and goings, of the mysterious entrances and exits of the men of the night, and the crafty footfall of crime. The sewer was evidently an accomplice of some dark band, and this taciturn grating was a receiver. Thénardier held the door ajar, left just room for Jean Valjean to pass, relocked the gate, and plunged back into the darkness, making no more noise. than a breath ; he seemed to walk with the velvety pads of a tiger. A moment later this hideous providence had disappeared, and Jean Valjean was outside.

CHAPTER CIX.

HE let Marius slip down on to the bank. They were out-side ; the miasmas, the darkness, the horror, were behind him ; the healthy, pure, living, joyous, freely respirable air inundated him. All around him was silence, but it was the charming silence of the sun setting in the full azure. Jean Valjean could not refrain from contemplating the vast clear shadow which he had above him, and pensively took a bath of ecstasy and prayer in the majestic silence of the eternal heavens. Then, as if the feeling of duty returned to him, he eagerly bent down over Marius, and lifting some water in the hollow of his hand, softly threw a few drops into his face. Marius' eyelids did not move, but he still breathed through his parted lips. Jean Valjean was again about to plunge his hand into the river, when he suddenly felt some annoyance, as when we feel there is some one behind us though we cannot see him. He turned round, and there was really some one behind him, as there had been just before.

A man of tall stature, dressed in a long coat, with folded arms, and carrying in his right hand a cudgel, whose leaden knob could be seen, was standing a few paces behind Jean Valjean, who was leaning over Marius. It was with the help of the darkness a species of apparition ; a simple man would have been frightened at it owing to the twilight, and a thoughtful one on account of the bludgeon. Jean Valjean recognised Javert. The reader has doubtless guessed that the tracker of Thénardier was no other than Javert. Javert, after his unhoped-for escape from the barricade, went to the Prefecture of Police, made a verbal report to the prefect in person in a short audience, and then immediately returned to duty, which implied—the note found on him will be remembered—a certain surveillance of the right bank of the river at the Champs Elysées, which had for some time past attracted the attention of the police. There he perceived Thénardier and followed him. The rest is known.

It will be also understood that the grating so obligingly opened for Jean Valjean was a clever trick on the part of Thénardier. He felt that Javert was still there; the watched man has a scent which never deceives him; and it was necessary to throw a bone to this greyhound. An assassin, what a chance! he could not let it slip. Thénardier, on putting Jean Valjean outside in his place, offered a prey to the policeman, made him loose his hold, caused himself to be forgotten in a greater adventure, recompensed Javert for his loss of time, which always flatters a spy, gained thirty francs, and fully intended for his own part to escape by the help of this diversion.

Jean Valjean had passed from one rock to another; these two meetings one upon the other, falling from Thénardier upon Javert, were rude. Javert did not recognise Jean Valjean, who, as we have said, no longer resembled himself. He did not unfold his arms, but secured his grasp of his bludgeon by an imperceptible movement, and said, in a sharp, calm voice :

"Who are you?"

"Myself."

"What do you mean?"

"I am Jean Valjean."

Javert placed his cudgel between his teeth, bent his knees, bowed his back, laid his two powerful hands on Jean Valjean's shoulders, which they held as in two vices, examined, and recognised him. Their faces almost touched, and Javert's glance was terrific. Jean Valjean remained inert under Javert's grip, like a lion enduring the claw of a lynx.

"Inspector Javert," he said, "you have me. Besides, since this morning I have considered myself your prisoner. I did not give you my address in order to try and escape you. Take me. Only grant me one thing."

Javert did not seem to hear, but kept his eyeballs fixed on Jean Valjean. His wrinkled chin thrust up his lips toward his nose, a sign of stern reverie. At length he loosed his hold of Jean Valjean, drew himself up, clutched his cudgel, and, as if in a dream, muttered rather than asked this question :

" What are you doing here ? and who is that man ? "

Jean Valjean replied, and the sound of his voice seemed to awaken Javert :

" It is of him that I wished to speak. Do with me as you please, but help me first to carry him home. 1 only ask this of you."

Javert's face was contracted in the same way as it always was when any one believed him capable of a concession ; still he did not say no. He stopped again, took from his pocket a handkerchief, which he dipped in the water, and wiped Marius' bloodstained forehead.

" This man was at the barricade," he said in a low voice, and as if speaking to himself ; " he was the one whom they called Marius."

He was a first-class spy, who had observed everything, listened to everything, heard everything, and picked up everything when he believed himself a dead man ; who even spied in his death-agony, and, standing on the first step of the sepulchre, took notes. He seized Marius' hand, and felt his pulse.

" He is wounded," said Jean Valjean.

" He is a dead man," said Javert.

Jean Valjean replied :

" No ; not yet."

" Then you brought him from the barricade here ? " Javert observed.

His preoccupation must have been great for him not to dwell on this alarming escape through the sewers, and not even notice Jean Valjean's silence after his question. Jean Valjean, on his side, seemed to have a sole thought ; he continued :

" He lives in the Marais, in the Rue des Filles du Calvaire, with his grandfather. I forget the name."

Jean Valjean felt in Marius' pocket, took out the pocketbook, opened it at the page on which Marius had written in pencil, and offered it to Javert. There was still sufficient floating light in the air to be able to read, and Javert, besides, had in his eyes the feline phosphorescence of nightbirds. He deciphered the few lines written by Marius, and growled, " Gillenormand, No. 6 Rue des Filles du Calvaire." Then he cried, " Driver ! "

Our readers will remember the coachman waiting above in case of need. A moment after the hackney-coach, which came down the incline leading to the watering-place, was on the bank. Marius was deposited on the back seat, and Javert sat down by Jean Valjean's side on the front one. When the door was closed the fiacre started off rapidly along the quays in the direction of the Bastille. They quitted the quay and turned into the streets ; and the driver, a black outline on his seat, lashed his lean horses. There was an icy silence in the hackney-coach. Marius motionless, with his body reclining in one corner, his head on his chest, his arms pendent, and his legs stiff, appeared to be only waiting for a coffin ; Jean Valjean seemed made of gloom, and Javert of stone ; and in this fiacre full of night, whose interior, each time that it passed a lamp, seemed to be lividly lit up as if by an intermittent flash, accident united and appeared to confront the three tragic immobilities —the corpse, the spectre, and the statue.

At every jolt over the pavement a drop of blood fell from Marius' hair. It was quite night when the hackney-coach reached No. 6 Rue des Filles du Calvaire. Javert got out first, examined at a glance the number over the gateway, and raising the heavy knocker of hammered steel, stamped in the old style with a goat and a satyr contending, gave a violent knock. The folding-door opened slightly, and Javert pushed it open. The porter half showed himself, yawning, and scarce awake, candle in hand. All were asleep in the house, for people go to bed early in the Marais, especially on days of rioting. This good old district, terrified by the Revolution, takes refuge in sleep, like children who, when they hear Bugaboo coming, quickly hide there heads under the counterpane. In the meanwhile Jean Valjean and the driver removed Marius from the hackney-coach, Valjean holding him under the armpits and the coachman under the knees. While carrying Marius in this way Jean Valjean passed his hands under his clothes, which were terribly torn, felt his chest, and assured himself that his heart still beat. It even beat a little less feebly, as if the motion of the vehicle had produced a certain return of life. Javert addressed the porter in the tone which becomes the government in the presence of the porter of a factious man.

" Any one live here of the name of Gillenormand ? "

" It is here. What do you want with him ? "

" We have brought home his son. "

" His son ? " the porter asked in amazement.

" He is dead."

Jean Valjean, who came ragged and filthy behind Javert, and whom the porter regarded with some horror, made him a sign that it was not so. The porter seemed neither to understand Javert's remark nor Jean Valjean's nod. Javert continued :

" He has been to the barricade, and here he is."

" To the barricade ! " the porter exclaimed.

" He has been killed. Go and wake his father."

The porter did not stir.

" Be off ! " Javert continued, and added, " There will be a funeral here to-morrow."

The porter limited himself to awaking Basque. Basque awoke Nicolette ; Nicolette awoke Aunt Gillenormand. As for the grandfather he was left to sleep, as it was thought that he would know the affair quite soon enough as it was. Marius was carried to the first floor, no one being acquainted with the fact in the rest of the house, and he was laid on an old sofa in M. Gillenormand's anteroom, and, while Basque went to fetch a physician and Nicolette opened the linen-presses, Jean Valjean felt Javert touch his shoulder. He understood, and went down, Javert following close at his heels. The porter saw them depart, as he had seen them arrive, with a startled sleepiness. They got into the hackney-coach again, and the driver mounted upon his box.

" Inspector Javert," Jean Valjean said, " grant me one thing more."

" What is it ? " Javert answered roughly.

" Let me go home for a moment, and you can then do with me what you please."

Javert remained silent for a few moments with his chin thrust into the collar of his greatcoat, and then let down the front window.

" Driver," he said, " No. 7 Rue de l'Homme Armé."

They did not speak during the entire ride. What did Jean Valjean want ? to finish what he had begun ; to warn Cosette, tell her where Marius was, give her perhaps some other useful information, and make, if he could, certain final arrangements. For his own part, as regarded what concerned him personally, it was all over ; he had been arrested by Javert, and did not resist. Any other than he, in such a situation, would perhaps have vaguely thought of the rope which Thénardier had given him, and the bars of

the first cell he entered ; but since his meeting with the
Bishop, Jean Valjean had within him a profound religious
hesitation against every assault, even on himself.   Suicide,
that mysterious attack on the unknown, which may contain
to a certain extent the death of the soul, was impossible to
Jean Valjean.

On entering the Rue de l'Homme Armé the coach stopped,
as the street was too narrow for vehicles to pass along it.
Jean Valjean and Javert got out.   The driver humbly
represented to "Mr. Inspector" that the Utrecht velvet of
his coach was quite spoilt by the blood of the assassinated
man and the filth of the assassin—that is how he understood
the affair, and he added that an indemnity was due to him.
At the same time, taking his licence-book from his pocket,
he begged Mr. Inspector to have the kindness to write him
a little bit of a certificate.   Javert thrust back the book
which the driver offered him and said :

"How much do you want, including the time you waited
and the journey?"

"It's seven hours and a quarter," the driver answered,
"and my velvet was bran new.   Eighty francs, Mr.
Inspector."

Javert took from his pocket four napoleons, and dismissed the hackney-coach.   Jean Valjean thought that it
was Javert's intention to take him on foot to the Blancs
Manteaux post, or that of the Archives, which were close
by.   They entered the street, which was as usual deserted.
Javert followed Jean Valjean, and, on reaching No. 7, the
latter rapped, and the gate opened.

"Very good," said Javert, "go up."

He added, with a strange expression, and as if making an
effort to speak as he was doing :

"I will wait for you here."

Jean Valjean looked at Javert, for this style of conduct
was not at all a habit of Javert's.   Still it could not surprise
him greatly that Javert should now place in him a sort of
haughty confidence, the confidence of the cat which grants
the mouse liberty to the length of its claw.   He thrust open
the gate, entered the house, shouted to the porter, who was
in bed, and had pulled the string without getting up, "It is
I," and mounted the staircase.   On reaching the first storey
he paused, for every Via dolorosa has its stations.   The
window was open, and as is the case in many old houses,
the staircase obtained light from, and looked out on, the

street. The street lantern, situated precisely opposite, threw some little light on the stairs, which caused the saving of a lamp. Jean Valjean, either to breathe or mechanically, thrust his head out of this window and looked down into the street. It is short, and the lamp lit it from one end to the other. Jean Valjean was bewildered with amazement.

Javert was gone.

Basque and the porter had carried Marius, who was still lying motionless on the sofa on which he had been laid on arriving, into the drawing-room. The physician, who had been sent for, hurried in, and Aunt Gillenormand had risen. Aunt Gillenormand came and went, horrified, clasping her hands, and incapable of doing anything but saying, " Can it be possible ? " She added at intervals, " Everything will be stained with blood." When the first horror had passed away a certain philosophy of the situation appeared even in her mind, and was translated by the exclamation, " It must end in that way." She did not go so far, though, as " Did I not say so ? " which is usual on occasions of this nature.

By the surgeon's orders a tester-bed was put up near the sofa. He examined Marius, and after satisfying himself that the pulse still beat, that the patient had no penetrating wound in the chest, and that the blood at the corners of the lips came from the nostrils, he had him laid flat on the bed, without a pillow, the head level with the body, and even a little lower, and with naked bust, in order to facilitate breathing. Mademoiselle Gillenormand, seeing that Marius was being undressed, withdrew, and told her beads in her bedroom. The body had received no internal injury ; a ball, deadened by the pocket-book, had deviated, and passed round the ribs with a frightful gash, but as it was not deep it was, therefore, not dangerous. The long subterranean march had completed the dislocation of the collar-bone, and there were serious injuries there. The arms were covered with sabre-cuts : no scar disfigured the face, but the head was cut all over with gashes : what would be the state of these wounds on the head ? did they stop at the scalp or did they reach the brain ? it was impossible to say yet. It was a serious symptom that they had caused the faintness. And men do not always wake from such fainting-fits ; the hæmorrhage, moreover, had exhausted the wounded man. From the waist downward, the lower part of the body had been protected by the barricade.

Basque and Nicolette tore up linen and prepared bandages : Nicolette sewed them and Basque rolled them. As they had no lint, the physician had temporarily checked the effusion of blood with cakes of wadding. By the side of the bed three candles burned on the table on which the surgeon's pocket-book lay open. He washed Marius' face and hair with cold water, and a bucketful was red in an instant. The porter, candle in hand, lighted him. The surgeon seemed to be thinking sadly : from time to time, he gave a negative shake of the head, as if answering some question which he mentally addressed to himself. Such mysterious dialogues of the physician with himself are a bad sign for the patient. At the moment when the surgeon was wiping the face and gently touching with his finger the still closed eyelids, a door opened at the end of the room, and a tall, pale figure appeared,—it was the grandfather. The riot during the last two days had greatly agitated, offended, and occupied M. Gillenormand ; he had not been able to sleep on the previous night, and he had been feverish all day. At night he went to bed at a very early hour, bidding his people bar up the house, and had fallen asleep through weariness.

Old men have a fragile sleep. M. Gillenormand's bedroom joined the drawing-room, and whatever precautions had been taken, the noise awoke him. Surprised by the crack of light which he saw in his door, he had got out of bed, and groped his way to the door. He was standing on the threshold, with one hand on the handle, his head slightly bent forward and shaking, his body enfolded in a white dressing-gown, as straight and creaseless as a winding-sheet : he was surprised, and looked like a ghost peering into a tomb. He noticed the bed, and on the mattress this young bleeding man, of the whiteness of wax, with closed eyes, open mouth, livid cheeks, naked to the waist, marked all over with vermilion, wounded, motionless, and brightly lighted.

The grandfather had from head to foot that shudder which ossified limbs can have. His eyes, whose cornea was yellow owing to their great age, were veiled by a sort of glassy stare ; his entire face assumed in an instant the earthy angles of a skeleton's head ; his arms fell pendent as if a spring had been broken in them, and his stupor was displayed by the outspreading of all the fingers of his two old trembling hands. His knees formed a salient angle, displaying through the opening of his dressing-gown his poor naked legs bristling with white hairs, and he murmured :

" Marius ! "

" He has just been brought here, sir," said Basque ; " he went to the barricade, and——"

" He is dead," the old gentleman exclaimed, in a terrible voice. " Oh ! the brigand ! "

Then a sort of sepulchral transfiguration drew up this centenarian as straight as a young man.

" You are the surgeon, sir," he said ; " begin by telling me one thing. He is dead, is he not ? "

The surgeon, who was frightfully anxious, maintained silence, and M. Gillenormand writhed his hands with a burst of terrifying laughter.

" He is dead, he is dead ! he has let himself be killed at the barricade through hatred of me ; it was against me that he did it ! ah, the blood-drinker, that is the way in which he returns to me. Woe of my life, he is dead ! "

He went to a window, opened it quite wide, as if he were stifling, and standing there began speaking to the night in the street.

" Pierced, sabred, massacred, exterminated, slashed, cut to pieces ! Do you see that, the beggar ! he knew very well that I expected him, and that I had his room ready, and that I had placed at my bed-head his portrait when he was a child ! He knew very well that he need only return, and that for years I had been recalling him, and that I sat at night by my fireside with my hands on my knees, not knowing what to do, and that I was crazy about him ! You knew that very well, you had only to return and say, ' It is I,' and you would be the master of the house, and I would obey you, and you could do anything you liked with your old ass of a grandfather ! You knew it very well, and said : ' No, he is a Royalist, I will not go ! ' and you went to the barricades, and have let yourself be killed out of spite ! in order to revenge yourself for what I said on the subject of Monsieur le Duc de Berry ! Is not that infamous ! Go to bed and sleep quietly, for he is dead. This is my awaking."

He went up to Marius, who was still livid and motionless, and began wringing his arms again. The old gentleman's white lips moved as it were mechanically, and allowed indistinct sentences to pass, which were scarce audible.

"Ah, heartless! ah, clubbist! ah, scoundrel! ah, Septem-
brist!" reproaches uttered in a low voice by a dying man
to a corpse.

At this moment Marius slowly opened his eyes, and
his glance, still veiled by lethargic surprise, settled on
M. Gillenormand.

"Marius!" the old man cried, "Marius, my little Marius!
my child! my beloved son! you open your eyes! you look
at me! you are alive! thanks!"

And he fell fainting.

CHAPTER CX.

JAVERT made his way slowly from the Rue de l'Homme
Armé. He walked with drooping head for the first time
in his life, and equally for the first time in his life with
his hands behind his back. Up to that day Javert had
only assumed, of Napoleon's two attitudes, the one which
expresses resolution, the arms folded on the chest; the
one indicating uncertainty, the arms behind the back,
was unknown to him. Now a change had taken place,
and his whole person, slow and sombre, was stamped with
anxiety. He buried himself in the silent streets, but
followed a certain direction; he went by the shortest road
to the Seine, reached the Quai des Ormes, walked along
it, passed the Grève, and stopped, a little distance from the
Place du Châtelet, at the corner of the Pont Notre Dame.
The Seine makes there, between that bridge and the Pont
au Change on one side, and the Quai de la Megisserie and
the Quai aux Fleurs on the other, a species of square lake
crossed by a rapid. This point of the Seine is feared by
sailors; nothing can be more dangerous than this rapid,
which was contracted at that period and irritated by the
stakes of the mill bridge, since demolished. The two
bridges, so close to each other, heighten the danger, for
the water hurries formidably through the arches. Men
who fall in there do not reappear, and the best swimmers
are drowned.

Javert leant his elbows on the parapet, his chin on his
hand, and while his hands mechanically closed on his thick
whiskers, he reflected. A novelty, a revolution, a catastrophe
had just taken place within him, and he must examine into
it. Javert was suffering horribly, and for some hours past

Javert had ceased to be simple. He was troubled; this brain, so limpid in its blindness, had lost its transparency, and there was a cloud in this crystal. Javert felt in his conscience duty doubled, and he could not hide the fact from himself. When he met Jean Valjean so unexpectedly on the Seine bank, he had something within him of the wolf that recaptures its prey and the dog that finds its master again. He saw before him two roads, both equally straight, but he saw two of them, and this terrified him, as he had never known in his life but one straight line. And, poignant agony, these two roads were contrary, and one of these right lines excluded the other. Which of the two was the true one? His situation was indiscribable: to owe his life to a malefactor, to accept this debt and repay him; to be, in spite of himself, on the same footing with an escaped convict, and requite one service with another service; to let it be said to him, "Be off," and to say in his turn, "Be free;" to sacrifice to personal motives duty, that general obligation, and to feel in these personal motives something general too, and perhaps superior; to betray society in order to remain faithful to his conscience—that all these absurdities should be realised, and accumulated upon him, was what startled him. One thing had astonished him, that Jean Valjean had shown him mercy; and one thing had petrified him, that he, Javert, had shown mercy to Jean Valjean.

A sacred galley-slave! a convict impregnable by justice, and that through the deed of Javert! Was it not frightful that Javert and Jean Valjean, the man made to punish and the man made to endure, that these two men, who were both the property of the law, should have reached the point of placing themselves both above the law? What! such enormities could happen and no one be punished? Jean Valjean, stronger than the whole social order, would be free, and he, Javert, would continue to eat the bread of the Government! His reverie gradually became terrible: he might through this reverie have reproached himself slightly on the subject of the insurgent carried home to the Rue des Filles du Calvaire, but he did not think of it. The slighter fault was lost in the greater, and, besides, this insurgent was evidently a dead man, and, legally, death checks prosecution. Jean Valjean,—that was the weight which he had on his mind; and he disconcerted him. All the axioms which had been the support of his whole life crumbled away before this man, and the generosity of Jean Valjean to him, Javert, overwhelmed him. Other facts which he remembered, and which he had formerly treated as falsehoods and folly, now returned to his mind as realities. M. Madeleine reappeared behind Jean Valjean, and the two figures were blended into one, which was venerable. Javert felt that something horrible, admiration for a convict, was entering his soul. Respect for a galley-slave, is it possible? he shuddered at it, and could not escape from it, although he struggled! he was reduced to confess in his soul the sublimity of this villain, and this was odious. A benevolent malefactor, a compassionate, gentle, helping, and merciful convict, repaying good for evil, pardon for hatred, preferring pity to vengeance, ready to destroy himself sooner than his enemy, saving the man who had struck him, kneeling on the pinnacle of virtue, and nearer to the angels than to man. Javert was constrained to confess to himself that such a monster existed.

The world was dismantled from top to bottom, and he was absolutely disconcerted! in what could men trust, when what they felt convinced of was crumbling away! What! the flaw in the cuirass of society could be formed by a magnanimous scoundrel! What! an honest servant of the law could find himself caught between two crimes, the crime of letting a man escape and the crime of arresting him! all was not certain, then, in the orders given by the State to the official! there could be blind alleys in duty! What, then! all this was real! was it true that an ex-bandit, bowed under condemnations, could draw himself up and end by being in the right? was this credible? were there, then, cases in which the law must retire before transfigured crime and stammer its apologies! Yes, it was so! and Javert saw it! and Javert touched it! and not only could he not deny it but he had a share in it. These were realities, and it was abominable that real facts could attain such a deformity. If facts did their duty they would restrict themselves to being proofs of the law; for facts are sent by God. Was, then, anarchy about to descend from on high? Thus, both in the exaggeration of agony and the optical illusion of consternation, everything which might have restricted and corrected his impression faded away, and society, the human race, and the universe henceforth were contained for his eyes in a simple and hideous outline —punishment, the thing tried, the strength due to the legislature, the decrees of sovereign courts, the magistracy, the government, prevention, and repression, official wisdom, legal infallibility, the principle of authority, all the dogmas on which political and civil security, the sovereignty, justice, logic flowing from the code and public truth, were a heap of ruins, chaos; he himself, Javert, the watcher of order, incorruptibility in the service of the police, the providence-dog of society, conquered and hurled to the ground, and on the summit of all this ruin stood a man in a green cap, and with a halo round his brow; such was the state of over-throw he had reached, such the frightful vision which he had in his mind. Was this endurable? no, it was a violent state, were there ever one, and there were only two ways of escaping from it; one was to go resolutely to Jean Valjean and restore to the dungeon the man of the galleys; the other——

Javert left the parapet, and, with head erect this time, walked firmly toward the guardroom indicated by a lantern at one of the corners of the Place du Châtelet. On reaching it he saw through the window a policeman, and went in. The police recognise each other merely by the way in which they push open the door of a guardroom. Javert mentioned his name, showed his card to the sergeant, and sat down at the table on which a candle was burning. There were on the table a pen, a leaden inkstand, and paper for drawing up verbal processes, and the reports of the night patrols. This table, always completed by a straw chair, is an institu-tion; it exists in all police-offices, it is always adorned with a boxwood saucer full of sawdust, and a box of red wafers, and it is the lower stage of the official style. It is here that the State literature commences. Javert took the pen and a sheet of paper and began writing. This is what he wrote :—

"SOME OBSERVATIONS FOR THE BENEFIT OF THE SERVICE.

"First : I beg M. le Préfet to glance at this.

"Secondly : Prisoners when they return from examination at the magistrate's office take off their shoes and remain barefooted on the slabs while they are being searched. Many cough on returning to the prison. This entails infirmary expenses.

"Thirdly : Tracking is good, with relays of agents at regular distances; but on important occasions two agents at the least should not let each other out of sight, because, if for any reason one agent were to fail in his duty, the other would watch him and take his place.

"Fourthly : There is no explanation why the special rules of the prison of Les Madelonnettes prohibit a prisoner from having a chair, even if he pay for it.

"Fifthly: At Les Madelonnettes there are only two gratings to the canteen, which allows the canteen woman to let the prisoners touch her hand.

"Sixthly : The prisoners called barkers, who call the other prisoners to the visitor's room, demand two sous from each prisoner for crying his name distinctly. This is a robbery.

"Seventhly : For a dropped thread, they retain ten sous from the prisoner in the weaving shop ; this is an abuse on the part of the manager, as the cloth is not the less good."

Javert wrote these lines in his calmest and most correct handwriting, not omitting to cross a *t*, and making the paper squeak beneath his pen. Under the last line he signed,

"JAVERT,

"Inspector of the 1st class.

"At the post of the Place du Châtelet, June 7, 1832, about one in the morning."

Javert dried the ink on the paper, folded it like a letter, sealed it, wrote on the back, " Note for the Administration," left it on the table, and quitted the guardroom. The glass door fell back after him. He again diagonally crossed the Place du Châtelet, reached the quay again, and went back with automatic precision to the same spot which he had left a quarter of an hour previously ; he bent down and found himself again in the same attitude on the same parapet slab. It seemed as if he had not stirred. The darkness was complete, for it was the sepulchral moment which follows midnight ; a ceiling of clouds hid the stars. Rains had swelled the river. The spot where Javert was leaning was, it will be remembered, precisely above the rapids of the Seine, perpendicularly over that formidable whirlpool which knots and unknots itself like an endless screw. Javert stooped down and looked ; all was dark, and nothing could be distinguished. A sound of spray was audible, but the river was invisible. At moments in this dizzy depth a flash appeared and undulated, for water has the power, even on the darkest night, of obtaining light,

no one knows whence, and changing itself into a lizard.
The light faded away, and all became indistinct again.
Immensity seemed open there, and what was beneath was
not water, but the gulf. The quay-wall, abrupt, confused,
mingled with the vapour, produced the effect of a precipice
of infinitude.

Javert remained for some moments motionless, gazing at
this opening of the darkness; he considered the invisible
with a fixedness which resembled attention. All at once
he took off his hat and placed it on the brink of the quay.
A moment after a tall black figure, which any belated
passer-by might have taken at a distance for a ghost,
appeared standing on the parapet, stooped toward the Seine,
then drew itself up, and fell straight into the darkness.
There was a dull splash, and the shadows alone were in
the secret of this obscure form which had disappeared
beneath the waters.

CHAPTER CXI.

SOME time after the events which we have just related
the Sieur Boulatruelle had a lively emotion. The Sieur
Boulatrouelle is the road-mender of Montfermeil of whom
we have already caught a glimpse in the dark portions of
this book. Boulatruelle, it will possibly be remembered,
was a man occupied with troublous and various things.
He broke stones and plundered travellers on the highway.
Road-mender and robber, he had a dream : he believed in
the treasures buried in the forest of Montfermeil. He hoped
some day to find money in the ground at the foot of a tree,
and in the meanwhile readily sought in the pockets of
passers-by. Still, for the present, he was prudent, for
he had just had a narrow escape. He was, as we know,
picked up with the other ruffians in Jondrette's garret.
There is some usefulness in a vice, for his drunkenness
saved him, and it never could be cleared up whether he
were there as a robber or as a robbed man. He was set
at liberty on account of his proved intoxication on the night
of the attack, and he returned to the woods. He went back
to his road from Gagny to Lagny, to break stones for the
State, under surveillance, with hanging head, very thoughtful, slightly chilled by the robbery, which had almost ruined
him, but turning with all the more tenderness to the wine
which had saved him.

As for the lively emotion which he had a short time after his return beneath the turf-roof of his road-mender's cabin, it was this. One morning Boulatruelle, while going as usual to work and to his lurking-place, possibly a little before daybreak, perceived among the branches a man whose back he could alone see, but whose shape, so he fancied, through the mist and darkness, was not entirely unknown to him. Boulatruelle, though a drunkard, had a correct and lucid memory, an indispensable defensive weapon for any man who is at all on bad terms with legal order.

" Where the deuce have I seen some one like that man ? " he asked.

But he could give himself no reply, save that he resembled somebody of whom he had a confused recollection. Boulatruelle, however, made his calculations, though he was unable to settle the identity. This man did not belong to those parts, and had come there evidently on foot, as no public vehicle passed through Montfermeil at that hour. He must have been walking all night. Where did he come from ? no great distance, for he had neither haversack nor bundle. Doubtless from Paris. Why was he in this wood ? why was he there at such an hour ? What did he want here ? Boulatruelle thought of the treasure : by dint of racking his memory he vaguely remembered having had, several years previously, a similar alarm on the subject of a man, who might very well be this man. While meditating he had, under the very weight of his meditation, hung his head, which was natural but not very clever. When he raised it again the man had disappeared in the forest and the mist.

" The deuce," said Boulatruelle, " I will find him again, and discover to what parish that parishioner belongs. This walker of Patron-Minette has a motive, and I will know it. No one must have a secret in my forest without my being mixed up in it."

He took up his pick, which was very sharp. " Here's something," he growled, " to search the ground and a man."

And as one thread is attached to another thread, hobbling as fast as he could in the direction which the man must have followed, he began marching through the coppice. When he had gone about a hundred yards, day, which was beginning to break, aided him. Footsteps on the sand here and there, trampled grass, broken heather, young branches bent into the shrubs and rising with a graceful slowness, like the arms of a pretty woman who stretches herself on waking, gave him a species of trail. He followed it, then lost it, and time slipped away; he got deeper into the wood and reached a species of eminence. A matutinal sportsman passing at a distance along a path, and whistling the air of Guillery, gave him the idea of climbing up a tree, and though old, he was active. There was on the mound a very large beech, worthy of Tityrus and Boulatruelle, and he climbed up the tree as high as he could. The idea was a good one, for while exploring the solitude on the side where the wood is most entangled, Boulatruelle suddenly perceived the man, but had no sooner seen him than he lost sight of him again. The man entered, or rather glided, into a rather distant clearing, masked by large trees, but which Boulatruelle knew very well, because he had noticed near a large heap of stones a sick chestnut tree, bandaged with a zinc belt nailed upon it. This clearing is what was formerly called the Blaru-bottom, and the pile of stones, intended no one knows for what purpose, which could be seen there thirty years ago, is doubtless there still. Nothing equals the longevity of a heap of stones, except that of a plank hoarding. It is there temporarily. What a reason for lasting !

Boulatruelle, with the rapidity of joy, tumbled off the tree, rather than came down it. The lair was found, and now he had only to seize the animal. The famous treasure he had dreamed of was probably there. It was no small undertaking to reach the clearing. By beaten paths, which make a thousand annoying windings, it would take a good quarter of an hour ; in a straight line through the wood, which is at that spot singularly dense, very thorny, and most aggressive, it would take half an hour at least. This is what Boulatruelle was wrong in not understanding ; he believed in the straight line, a respectable optical illusion, which has ruined many men. The wood, bristling though it was, appeared to him the right road.

" Let us go by the Rue de Rivoli of the wolves," he said.

Boulatruelle, accustomed to crooked paths, this time committed the error of going straight, and resolutely cast himself among the shrubs. He had to contend with holly, nettles, hawthorns, eglantines, thistles, and most irascible roots, and was fearfully scratched. At the bottom of the

ravine he came to a stream, which he was obliged to cross,
and at last reached the Blaru clearing after forty minutes,
perspiring, wet through, blowing, and ferocious. There
was no one in the clearing. Boulatruelle hurried to the
heap of stones; it was still in its place, and had not been
carried off. As for the man, he had vanished in the forest.
He had escaped; where? in which direction? into which
clump of trees? it was impossible to guess. And, most
crushing thing of all, there was behind the heap of stones
and in front of the zinc-banded tree a pick, forgotten or
abandoned, and a hole; but the hole was empty.

"Robber!" Boulatruelle cried, shaking his fists at the
horizon.

CHAPTER CXII.

MARIUS was for a long time neither dead nor alive. He
had for several weeks a fever, accompanied by delirium,
and very serious brain symptoms caused by the concussion
produced by the wounds in the head rather than the wounds
themselves. He repeated Cosette's name for whole nights
with the lugubrious loquacity of fever and the gloomy
obstinacy of agony. The width of certain wounds was a
serious danger, the suppuration of wide wounds always
being liable to reabsorption, and consequently killing
the patient, under certain atmospheric influences; and at
each change in the weather, at the slightest storm, the
physician became anxious. "Mind that the patient suffers
from no excitement," he repeated. The dressings were
complicated and difficult, for the fixing of bandages and
lint by the sparadrap had not been invented at that period.
Nicolette expended in lint a sheet "as large as a ceiling,"
she said; and it was not without difficulty that the
chloruretted lotions and nitrate of silver reached the end
of the gangrene. So long as there was danger, M.
Gillenormand, broken-hearted by the bedside of his grandson, was like Marius, neither dead nor alive.

Every day, and sometimes twice a day, a white-haired
and well-dressed gentleman, such was the description given
by the porter, came to inquire after the wounded man, and
left a large parcel of lint for the dressings. At length, on
September 7th, four months, day by day, from the painful
night on which he had been brought home dying to his
grandfather, the physician declared that he could answer

for him, and that convalescence was setting in. Marius, however, would be obliged to lie for two months longer on a couch, owing to the accidents produced by the fracture of the collar-bone. There is always a last wound like that which will not close, and prolongs the dressings, to the great annoyance of the patient. This long illness and lengthened convalescence, however, saved him from prosecution : in France there is no anger, even public, which six months do not extinguish. Riots, in the present state of society, are so much everybody's fault, that they are followed by a certain necessity of closing the eyes. Hence Marius was left tranquil.

M. Gillenormand first passed through every form of agony, and then through every form of ecstasy. They had great difficulty in keeping him from passing the whole night by Marius' side ; he had his large easy-chair brought to the bed ; and he insisted on his daughter taking the finest linen in the house to make compresses and bandages. Mademoiselle Gillenormand, as a sensible and elderly lady, managed to save the fine linen, while making her father believe that he was obeyed. M. Gillenormand would not listen to any explanation, that for the purpose of making lint fine linen is not so good as coarse, or new so good as worn. He was present at all the dressings, from which Mademoiselle Gillenormand modestly absented herself. Nothing was so touching as to see him hand the wounded man a cup of broth with his gentle senile trembling. He overwhelmed the surgeon with questions, and did not perceive that he constantly repeated the same. On the day when the physician informed him that Marius was out of danger he was beside himself. He gave his porter three louis d'or, and at night, when he went to his bedroom, danced a gavotte, making castanets of his thumb and forefinger, and sang a song.

Then he knelt on a chair, and Basque, who was watching him through the crack of the door, felt certain that he was praying. Up to that day he had never believed in God. At each new phase in the improvement of the patient, which went on steadily, the grandfather was extravagant. He performed a multitude of mechanical actions full of delight : he went up and down stairs without knowing why. A neighbour's wife, who was very pretty, by the way, was stupefied at receiving one morning a large bouquet : it was M. Gillenormand who sent it to her, and her husband got up a jealous scene. He called Marius Monsieur le Baron, and shouted, "Long live the Republic!" Every moment he asked the medical man, "There is no danger now, is there?" He looked at Marius with a grandmother's eyes, and gloated over him when he slept. He no longer knew himself, no longer took himself into account. Marius was the master of the house, there was abdication in his joy, and he was the grandson of his grandson. In his present state of merriment he was the most venerable of children: through fear of wearying or annoying the convalescent, he would place himself behind him in order to smile upon him. He was satisfied, joyous, enraptured, charming, and young, and his white hair added a gentle majesty to the gay light which he had on his face. When grace is mingled with wrinkles it is adorable; and there is a peculiar dawn in expansive old age.

As for Marius, while letting himself be nursed and petted, he had one fixed idea, Cosette. Since the fever and delirium had left him he no longer pronounced this name, and it might be supposed that he had forgotten it, but he was silent precisely because his soul was in it. He knew not what had become of Cosette: the whole affair of the Rue de la Chanvrerie was like a cloud in his memory; almost indistinct shadows floated in his mind. Eponine, Gavroche, Mabœuf, the Thénardiers, and all his friends, mournfully mingled with the smoke of the barricade, the strange passage of M. Fauchelevent through that bloodstained adventure, produced upon him the effect of an enigma in a tempest: he understood nothing of his own life, he knew not how or by whom he had been saved, and no one about him knew it either: all they were able to tell him was that he had been brought there at night in a hackney-coach: past, present, future, all this was to him like the mist of a vague idea; but there was in this mist one immovable point, a clear and precise lineament, something made of granite, a resolution, a will—to find Cosette again. For him the idea of life was not distinct from the idea of Cosette: he had decreed in his heart that he would not receive one without the other, and he unalterably determined to demand of his grandfather, of destiny, of fate, of Hades itself, the restitution of his lost Eden.

He did not conceal the obstacles from himself. Here let us underline one fact: he was not won or greatly affected by all the anxiety and all the tenderness of his grandfather.

In the first place he was not in the secret of them all, and next, in his sick man's reveries, which were perhaps still feverish, he distrusted this gentleness as a strange and new thing intended to subdue him. He remained cold to it, and the poor grandfather lavished his smiles in pure loss. Marius said to himself that it was all very well so long as he did not speak and let matters rest, but when he came to Cosette, he should find another face, and his grandfather's real attitude would be unmasked. Then the affair would be rude ; a warming up of family questions, a confrontment of position, every possible sarcasm and objection at once. Fauchelevent, Coupelevent, fortune, poverty, wretchedness, the stone on the neck, and the future, a violent resistance, and the conclusion,—a refusal. Marius stiffened himself against it beforehand. And then, in proportion as he regained life, his old wrongs reappeared, the old ulcers of his memory reopened ; he thought again of the past. Colonel Pontmercy placed himself once more between M. Gillenormand and him, Marius, and he said to himself that he had no real kindness to hope for from a man who had been so unjust and harsh to his father. And with health came back a sort of bitterness against his grandfather, from which the old man gently suffered. M. Gillenormand, without letting it be seen, noticed that Marius, since he had been brought home and regained consciousness, had never once called him father. He did not say Sir, it is true, but he managed to say neither one nor the other, by a certain way of turning his sentences.

A crisis was evidently approaching, and, as nearly always happens in such cases, Marius, in order to try himself, skirmished before offering battle ; this is called feeling the ground. One morning it happened that M. Gillenormand, alluding to a newspaper which he had come across, spoke lightly of the Convention, and darted a Royalist epigram at Danton, St. Just, and Robespierre. "The men of '93 were giants," Marius said sternly ; the old man was silent, and did not utter another syllable all the day. Marius, who had the inflexible grandfather of his early years ever present to his mind, saw in this silence a profound concentration of anger, augured from it an obstinate struggle, and augmented his preparations for the contest in the back nooks of his mind. He determined that in case of refusal he would tear off his bandages, dislocate his collar-bone, expose all the wounds still unhealed, and refuse all food. His wounds were his ammunition; he must have Cosette or die. He awaited the favourable moment with the crafty patience of sick persons, and the moment arrived.

One day M. Gillenormand, while his daughter was arranging the phials and cups on the marble slab of the sideboard, leant over Marius, and said in his most tender accent :

"Look you, my little Marius, in your place I would rather eat meat than fish ; a fried sole is excellent at the beginning of a convalescence, but a good cutlet is necessary to put the patient on his legs."

Marius, whose strength had nearly quite returned, sat up, rested his two clenched fists on his sheet, looked his grandfather in the face, assumed a terrible air, and said :

"That induces me to say one thing to you."

"What is it ? "

"That I wish to marry."

"Foreseen," said the grandfather, bursting into a laugh.

"How foreseen ? "

"Yes, foreseen. You shall have your little maid."

Marius, stupefied and dazzled, trembled in all his limbs, and M. Gillenormand continued :

"Yes, you shall have the pretty little dear. She comes every day in the form of an old gentleman to ask after you. Ever since you have been wounded she has spent her time in crying and making lint. I made inquiries ; she lives at No. 7 Rue de l'Homme Armé. Ah! there we are ! Ah, you want her, do you ? well, you shall have her. There's a take-in for you ; you had made your little plot, and had said to yourself, 'I will tell it point-blank to that grandfather, that mummy of the Regency and the Directory, that old beau ; he has had his frolics too, and his amourettes, and his grisettes, and his Cosettes ; he has had his fling, he has had his wings, and he has eaten the bread of spring ; he must surely remember it, we shall see. Battle!' Ah, you take the cockchafer by the horns, very good. I offer you a cutlet, and you answer me, 'By the bye, I wish to marry.' By Jupiter Ammon, that is a transition ! Ah, you made up your mind for a quarrel, but you did not know that I was an old coward. What do you say to that ? You are done, you did not expect to find your grandfather more stupid than yourself. You have lost the speech you intended to make me, master lawyer, and that is annoying. Well, all the worse, rage away ; I do what you want, and that cuts the speech short, ass. Listen! I have made my inquiries, for I too am cunning; she is charming, she is virtuous, she has made heaps of lint, she is a jewel, she adores you; if you had died there would have been three of us, and her coffin would have accompanied mine. I had the idea, as soon as you were better, of planting her there by your bedside, but it is only in romances that girls are introduced to the beds of handsome young wounded men in whom they take an interest. That would not do, for what would your aunt say? You were quite naked three parts of the time, sir; ask Nicolette, who never left you for a moment, whether it were possible for a female to be here? And, then, what would the doctor have said? for a pretty girl does not cure a fever. Well, say no more about it, it is settled and done. Take her. Look you, I saw that you did not love me, and I said, 'What can I do to make that animal love me?' I said, 'Stay, I have my little Cosette ready to hand. I will give her to him, and then he must love me a little, or tell me the reason why.' Ah! you believed that the old man would storm, talk big, cry no, and lift his cane against all this dawn. Not at all. Cosette, very good; love, very good; I ask for nothing better. Take the trouble, sir, to marry, be happy, my beloved child."

After saying this the old man burst into sobs; he took Marius' head and pressed it to his old bosom, and both began weeping. That is one of the forms of supreme happiness.

"My father!" Marius exclaimed.

"Ah, you love me then!" the old man said.

There was an ineffable moment; they were choking and could not speak; at length the old man stammered:

"Come! the stopper is taken out of him; he called me 'father.'"

Marius disengaged his head from his grandfather's arms, and said gently:

"Now that I am better, father, I fancy I could see her."

"Foreseen, too, you will see her to-morrow."

"Why not to-day?"

"Well, to-day; done for to-day. You have called me father twice, and it's worth that. I will see about it, and she shall be brought here."

Cosette and Marius saw each other again. We will not attempt to describe the interview; for there are things which we must not attempt to paint: the sun is of the number. The whole family, Basque and Nicolette included, were assembled in Marius' chamber at the moment when Cosette entered. She appeared in the doorway, and seemed to be surrounded by a halo : precisely at the moment this grandfather was going to blow his nose, but he stopped short, holding his nose in his handkerchief and looking over it.

"Adorable ! " he cried.

And then he blew a sonorous blast. Cosette was intoxicated, enraptured, startled, in heaven. She was as timid as a person can be through happiness ; she stammered, turned pale, and then pink, and wished to throw herself into Marius' arms, but dared not. She was ashamed of loving before so many people ; for the world is merciless to happy lovers, and always remains at the very moment when they most long to be alone. And yet they do not want these people at all. With Cosette, but behind her, had entered a white-haired man, serious, but still smiling, though the smile was wandering and poignant. It was "Monsieur Fauchelevent,"—it was Jean Valjean. He was "well-dressed," as the porter had said, in a new black suit and a white cravat. The porter was a thousand leagues from recognising in this correct citizen, this probable notary, the frightful corpse-bearer who had risen at the gate on the night of June 7th, ragged, filthy, hideous, and haggard, with a mask of blood and mud on his face, supporting in his arms the unconscious Marius ; still his porter's instincts were aroused. When M. Fauchelevent arrived with Cosette, the porter could not refrain from confiding this aside to his wife, " I don't know why, but I fancy that I have seen that face before." M. Fauchelevent remained standing by the door of Marius' room, as if afraid ; he held under his arm a packet rather like an octavo volume wrapped in paper. The paper was green, apparently from mildew.

" Has this gentleman always got books under his arm like that ? " Mademoiselle Gillenormand, who was not fond of books, asked Nicolette in a whisper.

" Well," M. Gillenormand, who had heard her, answered in the same key, " he is a savant, is that his fault ? Monsieur Bcuiard, whom I knew, never went out without a book either, and had always one close to his heart."

Then bowing, he said, in a loud voice :

" Monsieur Tranchelevent."

Father Gillenormand did not do it purposely, but an inattention to proper names was an aristocratic way of his.

" Monsieur Tranchelevent, I have the honour of requesting this lady's hand for my grandson, M. le Baron Marius
Pontmercy ? "

Monsieur " Tranchelevent " bowed.

" All right," the grandfather said.

And turning to Marius and Cosette, with both arms
extended in benediction, he cried :

" You have leave to adore each other."

They did not let it be said twice, and the prattling began.
They talked in a whisper, Marius reclining on his couch
and Cosette standing by his side. " Oh, Heaven ! " Cosette
murmured, " I see you again : it is you. To go and fight
like that ! But why ? it is horrible. For four months I
have been dead. Oh, how wicked it was of you to have
been at that battle ! What had I done to you ? I forgive
you, but you will not do it again. Just now, when they
came to tell me to come to you, I thought again that I
was going to die, but it was of joy. I was so sad ! I
did not take time to dress myself, and I must look
frightful ; what will your relations say at seeing me in a
tumbled collar ? But speak ! you let me speak all alone.
We are still in the Rue de l'Homme Armé. It seems that
your shoulder was terrible, and I was told that I could put
my hand in it, and then it seems that your flesh was cut
with scissors. How frightful that is ! I wept so that I
have no eyes left. It is strange that a person can suffer
like that. Your grandfather has a very kind look. Do not
disturb yourself, do not get on your elbow like that, or you
will do yourself an injury. Oh, how happy I am ! So our
misfortunes are all ended ! I am quite foolish. There were
things I wanted to say to you which I have quite forgotten.
Do you love me still ? We live in the Rue de l'Homme Armé.
There is no garden there. I made lint the whole time ;
look here, sir, it is your fault, my fingers are quite rough."

" Angel ! " said Marius.

Angel is the only word in the language which cannot be
worn out ; no other word would resist the pitiless use which
lovers make of it. Then, as there was company present,
they broke off, and did not say a word more, contenting
themselves with softly clasping hands. M. Gillenormand
turned to all the rest in the room, and cried :

" Speak loudly, good people ; make a noise, will you.
Come, a little row, hang it all, so that these children may
prattle at their ease."

And going up to Marius and Cosette, he whispered to
them :

"Go on ; don't put yourselves out of the way."

Aunt Gillenormand witnessed with stupor this irruption
of light into her antiquated house. This stupor had nothing
aggressive about it ; it was not at all the scandalised and
envious glance cast by an owl at two ring-doves ; it was the
stupid eye of a poor innocent of the age of fifty-seven ; it
was a spoiled life looking at that triumph, love.

"Mademoiselle Gillenormand the elder," her father said
to her, "I told you that this would happen."

He remained silent for a moment, and added :

"Look at the happiness of others."

Then he turned to Cosette.

"How pretty she is ! how pretty she is ! she is a Greuze !
So you are going to have all that for yourself, scamp ? Ah,
my boy, you have had a lucky escape from me ; for if I were
not fifteen years too old we would fight with swords and
see who should have her. There, I am in love with you,
mademoiselle ; but it is very simple, it is your right. What
a famous, charming little wedding we will have ! Saint
Denis du Saint Sacrement is our parish ; but I will procure
a dispensation, so that you may be married at St. Paul's,
for the church is better. It was built for the Jesuits, and is
more coquettish. It is opposite Cardinal Birague's fountain."

The grandfather pirouetted on his nonagenarian heels,
and began speaking again, like a spring which has been
wound up. Then he sat down by their side, made Cosette
take a chair, and took their four hands in his old wrinkled
hands.

"This darling is exquisite. This Cosette is a masterpiece ! She is a very little girl and a very great lady. She
will be only a baroness, and that is a derogation, for she
was born to be a marchioness. What eyelashes she has !
My children, drive it into your noddles that you are on
the right road. Love one another ; be foolish over it, for
love is the stupidity of men and the cleverness of God.
So adore one another. Still," he added, suddenly growing
sad, "what a misfortune ! more than half I possess is
sunk in annuities ; so long as I live it will be all right,
but when I am dead, twenty years hence, ah ! my poor
children, you will not have a farthing. Your pretty white
hands, Madame la Baronne, will be wrinkled by work."

Here a serious and calm voice was heard saying :

" Mademoiselle Euphrasie Fauchelevent has six hundred thousand francs."

It was Jean Valjean's voice. He had not yet uttered a syllable; no one seemed to remember that he was present, and he stood motionless behind all these happy people.

"Who is the Mademoiselle Euphrasie in question?" the startled grandfather asked.

"Myself," said Cosette.

"Six hundred thousand francs!" M. Gillenormand repeated.

"Less fourteen or fifteen thousand, perhaps," Jean Valjean said.

And he laid on the table the parcel which Aunt Gillenormand had taken for a book. Jean Valjean himself opened the packet; it was a bundle of bank-notes. They were turned over and counted; there were five hundred bank-notes for a thousand francs, and one hundred and sixty-eight for five hundred, forming a total of five hundred and eighty-four thousand francs.

"That's a famous book," said M. Gillenormand.

"Five hundred and eighty-four thousand francs!" the aunt murmured.

"That arranges a good many things, does it not, Mademoiselle Gillenormand the elder?" the grandfather continued. "That devil of a Marius has found a millionaire grisette upon the tree of dreams! Now trust to the amourettes of young people! Students find studentesses with six hundred thousand francs. Cherubin works better than Rothschild."

"Five hundred and eighty-four thousand francs!" Mademoiselle Gillenormand repeated; "five hundred and eighty-four thousand francs! we may as well say six hundred thousand."

As for Marius and Cosette, they were looking at each other during this period, and hardly paid any attention to the circumstances.

Of course our readers have understood, and no lengthened explanation will be required, that Jean Valjean after the Champmathieu affair was enabled by his escape for a few days to come to Paris, and withdraw in time from Laffitte's the sum he had gained under the name of M. Madeleine at M—— sur M——; and that, afraid of being recaptured, which in fact happened to him shortly after, he buried this sum in the forest of Montfermeil, at the spot called the Blaru-bottom. The sum, six hundred and thirty thousand francs, all in bank-notes, occupied but little space, and was contained in a box; but in order to protect the box from damp he placed it in an oak coffer filled with chips of chestnut-wood. In the same coffer he placed his other treasure, the Bishop's candlesticks. It will be remembered that he carried off these candlesticks in his escape from M—— sur M——. The man seen on one previous evening by Boulatruelle was Jean Valjean, and afterwards, whenever Jean Valjean required money, he fetched it from the Blaru clearing, and hence his absences to which we have referred. He had a pick concealed somewhere in the shrubs, in a hiding-place known to himself alone. When he found Marius to be convalescent, feeling that the hour was at hand when this money might be useful, he went to fetch it; and it was again he whom Boulatruelle saw in the wood, but this time in the morning, and not at night. Boulatruelle inherited the pick.

The real sum was five hundred and eighty-four thousand five hundred francs, but Jean Valjean kept back the five hundred francs for himself. "We will see afterwards," he thought. The difference between this sum and the six hundred and thirty thousand francs withdrawn from Laffitte's represented the expenditure of ten years, from 1823 to 1833. The five years' residence in the convent had only cost five thousand francs. Jean Valjean placed the two silver candlesticks on the mantelpiece, where they glistened, to the great admiration of Toussaint. Moreover, Jean Valjean knew himself freed from Javert; it had been stated in his presence, and he verified the fact in the *Moniteur* which had published it, that an Inspector of Police of the name of Javert had been found drowned under a washerwoman's boat between the Pont au Change and the Pont Neuf, and that a letter left by this man, hitherto irreproachable and highly esteemed by his chiefs, led to the belief in an attack of dementia and suicide. "In truth," thought Jean Valjean, "since he let me go when he had hold of me he must have been mad at that time."

All the preparations for the marriage were made. The physician, on being consulted, declared that it might take place in February. It was now December, and a few ravishing weeks of perfect happiness slipped away. The least happy man was not the grandfather; he would sit for a whole quarter of an hour contemplating Cosette.

"The admirably pretty girl!" he would exclaim, "and she has so soft and kind an air! She is the most charming creature I have ever seen in my life. Presently she will have virtues with a violet scent. She is one of the Graces, on my faith! A man can only live nobly with such a creature. Marius, my lad, you are a baron, you are rich, so do not be a pettifogger, I implore you."

Cosette and Marius had suddenly passed from the sepulchre into paradise : the transition had not been prepared, and they would have been stunned if they had not been dazzled.

" Do you understand anything of all this ? " Marius said to Cosette.

"No," Cosette answered, "but it seems to me as if le bon Dieu were looking at us."

Jean Valjean did everything, smoothed everything, conciliated everything, and rendered everything easy. He hurried toward Cosette's happiness with as much eagerness and apparently with as much joy as Cosette herself. As he had been Mayor, he was called to solve a delicate problem, the secret of which he alone possessed,—the civil status of Cosette. To tell her origin openly might have prevented the marriage, but he got Cosette out of all the difficulties. He arranged for her a family of dead people, a sure method of not incurring any inquiry. Cosette was the only one left of an extinct family. Cosette was not his daughter but the daughter of another Fauchelevent. Two brothers Fauchelevent had been gardeners at the convent of the Little Picpus : they went to this convent ; the best testimonials and most satisfactory character were given ; for the good nuns, little suited, and but little inclined to solve questions of paternity, had never known exactly of which of the two Fauchelevents Cosette was the daughter. They said what was wanted, and said it zealously. An act of notoriety was drawn up, and Cosette became by law Mademoiselle Euphrasie Fauchelevent, and was declared an orphan both on the father's and mother's side. Jean Valjean managed so as to be designated, under the name of Fauchelevent, as guardian of Cosette, with M. Gillenormand as supervising guardian. As for the five hundred and eighty-four thousand francs, they were a legacy left to Cosette by a dead person who wished to remain unknown : the original legacy had been five hundred and ninety-four thousand francs, but ten thousand had been

spent in the education of Mademoiselle Euphrasie, five
thousand of which had been paid to the convent. This
legacy, deposited in the hands of a third party, was to be
handed over to Cosette upon her majority, or at the period
of her marriage. All this was highly acceptable, as we
see, especially when backed up by more than half a million
francs. There were certainly a few singular points here
and there, but they were not seen, for one of the persons
interested had his eyes bandaged by love, and the others
by the six hundred thousand francs.

Cosette learned that she was not the daughter of the
old man whom she had so long called father ; he was only
a relation, and another Fauchelevent was her real father.
At another moment this would have grieved her, but in
the ineffable hour she had now reached it was only a slight
shadow, a passing cloud ; and she had so much joy that
this cloud lasted but a short time. She had Marius : the
young man came, the old man disappeared ; life is so.
And then, Cosette had been accustomed for many long years
to see enigmas around her ; every being who has had a
mysterious childhood is ever ready for certain renunciations.
Still she continued to call Jean Valjean "father." Cosette,
who was among the angels, was enthusiastic about Father
Gillenormand ; it is true that he overwhelmed her with
madrigals and presents. While Jean Valjean was con-
structing for Cosette an unassailable position in society,
M. Gillenormand attended to the wedding trousseau.
Nothing amused him so much as to be magnificent ; and
he had given Cosette a gown of Binche guipure, which
he inherited from his own grandmother. "These fashions
spring up again," he said, "antiquities are the great demand,
and the young ladies of my old days dress themselves like
the old ladies of my youth." He plundered his respectable
round-bellied commodes of Coromandel lacquer, which had
not been opened for years. "Let us shrive these dowagers,"
he said, "and see what they have in their paunch." He
noisily violated drawers full of the dresses of all his wives,
all his mistresses, and all his female ancestry. He lavished
on Cosette, Chinese satins, damasks, lampas, painted
moires, gros de Naples dresses, Indian handkerchiefs embroidered with gold that can be washed, Genoa and Alençon
point lace, sets of old jewellery, ivory bonbon boxes adorned
with microscopic battles, laces, and ribbons. Cosette,
astounded, wild with love for Marius and with gratitude

to M. Gillenormand, dreamed of an unbounded happiness, dressed in satin and velvet. Her wedding-basket seemed to her supported by séraphim, and her soul floated in ether with wings of Mechlin lace. The intoxication of the lovers was only equalled, as we stated, by the ecstasy of the grandfather, and there was something like a flourish of trumpets in the Rue des Filles du Calvaire. Each morning there was a new offering of bric-à-brac from the grandfather to Cosette, and all sorts of ornaments were spread out splendidly around her.

It was arranged that the couple should reside at M. Gillenormand's, and the grandfather insisted on giving them his bedroom, the finest room in the house. "It will make me younger," he declared. "It is an old place. I always had the idea that the wedding should take place in my room." He furnished this room with a heap of old articles of gallantry ; he had it hung with an extraordinary fabric which he had in the piece, and believed to be Utrecht, a gold satin ground with velvet auriculas. "It was with that stuff," he said, "that the bed of the Duchess d'Anville à la Rocheguyon was hung." He placed on the mantelpiece a figure in Saxon porcelain carrying a muff on its naked stomach. M. Gillenormand's library became the office which Marius required, for an office, it will be borne in mind, is insisted upon by the council of the order.

CHAPTER CXIII.

THE lovers saw each other every day. Cosette came with M. Fauchelevent. "It is turning things topsy-turvy," said Mademoiselle Gillenormand, "that the lady should come to the gentleman's house to have court paid to her in that way." But Marius' convalescence had caused the adoption of the habit, and the easy-chairs of the Rue des Filles du Calvaire, more convenient for a *tête-à-tête* than the straw-bottomed chairs of the Rue de l'Homme Armé, had decided it. Marius and M. Fauchelevent saw each other, but did not speak, and this seemed to be agreed on. Every girl needs a chaperon, and Cosette could not have come without M. Fauchelevent ; and for Marius, M. Fauchelevent was the condition of Cosette, and he accepted him. In discussing vaguely, and without any precision, political matters as connected with the improvement of all, they managed to

say a little more than yes and no. Once, on the subject
of instruction, which Marius wished to be gratuitous and
obligatory, multiplied in every form, lavished upon all like
light and air, and, in a word, respirable by the entire
people, they were agreed, and almost talked. Marius remarked on this occasion that M. Fauchelevent spoke well,
and even with a certain elevation of language, though
something was wanting. M. Fauchelevent had something
less than a man of the world, and something more.
Marius, in his innermost thoughts, surrounded with all
sorts of questions this M. Fauchelevent, who was to him
simple, well-wishing, and cold. At times doubts occurred
to him as to his own recollections; he had a hole in his
memory, a black spot, an abyss dug by four months of
agony. Many things were lost in it, and he was beginning
to ask himself whether it was the fact that he had seen
M. Fauchelevent, a man so serious and so calm, at the
barricade.

This was, however, not the sole stupor, which the appearances and disappearances of the past had left in his mind.
We must not believe that he was delivered from all those
promptings of memory which compel us, even when happy
and satisfied, to take a melancholy backward glance. The
head which does not turn to effaced horizons contains
neither thought nor love. At moments Marius buried his
face in his hands, and the tumultuous and vague past
traversed the fog which he had in his brain. He saw
Mabœuf fall again, he heard Gavroche singing under the
grapeshot, and he felt on his lips the coldness of Eponine's
forehead; Enjolras, Courfeyrac, Jean Prouvaire, Combeferre, Bossuet, Grantaire, all his friends rose before him,
and then disappeared. Were all these dear, dolorous,
valiant, charming, and tragic beings dreams? had they
really existed? The riot had robed everything in its smoke,
and these great fevers have great dreams. He questioned
himself, he groped within himself, and had a dizziness from
all these vanished realities. Where were they all, then?
was it really true that everything was dead? a fall into the
darkness had carried away everything, except himself; all
this had disappeared as it were behind the curtain of a
theatre. There are such curtains which drop on life, and
God passes on to the next act. In himself was he really
the same man? He, poor, was rich; he, the abandoned
man, had a family; he, the desperate man, was going to

marry Cosette. It seemed to him that he had passed through a tomb, and that he had gone in black and come out white. And in this tomb the others had remained. At certain times all these beings of the past, returned and present, formed a circle round him, and rendered him gloomy. Then he thought of Cosette, and became serene again, but it required no less than this felicity to efface this catastrophe. M. Fauchelevent had almost a place among these vanished beings. Marius hesitated to believe that the Fauchelevent of the barricade was the same as that Fauchelevent in flesh and bone, so gravely seated by the side of Cosette. The first was probably one of those nightmares brought to him and carried away in his hours of delirium. However, as their two natures were scarped, it was impossible for Marius to ask any question of M. Fauchelevent. The idea had not even occurred to him. Two men who have a common secret, and who, by a sort of tacit agreement, do not exchange a syllable on the subject, are not so rare as may be supposed. Once, however, Marius made an effort ; he turned the conversation on the Rue de la Chanvrerie, and turning to M. Fauchelevent, he said to him :

" Do you know that street well ? "

" What street ? "

" The Rue de la Chanvrerie."

" I have never heard the name of that street," M. Fauchelevent said in the most natural tone in the world.

The answer, which related to the name of the street, and not to the street itself, seemed to Marius more conclusive than it really was.

" Decidedly," he thought, " I must have been dreaming. I had an hallucination. It was some one who resembled him, and M. Fauchelevent was not there."

The enchantment, great though it was, did not efface other thoughts from Marius' mind. While the marriage arrangements were being made, and the fixed period was waited for, he made some difficult and scrupulous retrospective researches. He owed gratitude in several quarters, he owed it for his father, and he owed it for himself. There was Thénardier, and there was the stranger who had brought him back to M. Gillenormand's. Marius was anxious to find these two men again, as he did not wish to marry, be happy, and forget them, and feared lest these unpaid debts of honour might cast a shadow over his life, which would henceforth be so luminous. It was impossible for him to leave all these arrears unsettled behind him, and he wished, ere he entered joyously into the future, to obtain a receipt from the past. That Thénardier was a villain took nothing from the fact that he had saved Colonel Pontmercy. Thénardier was a bandit for all the world excepting for Marius. And Marius, ignorant of the real scene on the battlefield of Waterloo, did not know this peculiarity, that his father stood to Thénardier in the strange situation of owing him life without owing him gratitude. Not one of the agents whom Marius employed could find Thénardier's trail, and the disappearance seemed complete on that side. Mother Thénardier had died in prison before trial, and Thénardier and his daughter Azelma, the only two left of this lamentable group, had plunged again into the shadow. The gulf of the social Unknown had silently closed again upon these beings.

Mother Thénardier being dead, Boulatruelle being out of the question, Claquesous having disappeared, and the principal accused having escaped from prison, the trial for the trap in the Gorbeau attic had pretty nearly failed. The affair had remained rather dark, and the assize court had been compelled to satisfy itself with two subalterns, Panchaud, *alias* Printanier, *alias* Bigrénaille, and Demi-Liard, *alias* Deux-milliards, who had been tried and condemned to the galleys for fourteen years. Penal servitude for life was passed against their accomplices who had escaped ; Thénardier, as chief and promoter, was condemned to death, also in default. This condemnation was the only thing that remained of Thénardier, casting on this buried name its sinister gleam, like a candle by the side of a coffin. However, this condemnation, by thrusting Thénardier back into the lowest depths through the fear of being recaptured, added to the dense gloom which covered this man.

As for the other, the unknown man who had saved Marius, the researches had at first some result, and then stopped short. They succeeded in finding again the hackney-coach which had brought Marius to the Rue des Filles du Calvaire on the night of June 6. The driver declared that on the 6th June, by the order of a police agent, he had stopped from 3 p.m. till nightfall on the quay of the Champs Elysées, above the opening of the Grand Sewer; that at about nine in the evening the gate of the sewer which looks upon the river-bank opened; that a man came out, bearing on his shoulders another man, who appeared to be dead; that the agent, who was watching at this point, had arrested the living man, and seized the dead man; that he, the coachman, had taken " all these people " into his hackney-coach; that they drove first to the Rue des Filles du Calvaire, and deposited the dead man there; that the dead man was M. Marius, and that he, the coachman, recognised him thoroughly, though he was alive this time; that afterwards they got into his coach again, and a few yards from the gate of the Archives he was ordered to stop; that he was paid in the street and discharged, and that the agent took away the other man; that he knew nothing more, and that the night was very dark. Marius, as we said, remembered nothing. He merely remembered that he had been seized from behind by a powerful hand at the moment when he fell backwards from the barricade, and then all was effaced for him. He had only regained his senses when he was at M. Gillenormand's.

He lost himself in conjectures; he could not doubt as to his own identity, but how was it that he, who had fallen in the Rue de la Chanvrerie, had been picked up by the police agent on the bank of the Seine, near the bridge of the Invalides? Some one had brought him from the quarter of the markets to the Champs Elysées, and how? by the sewer? Extraordinary devotion! Some one; who? It was this man whom Marius was seeking. Of this man, who was his saviour, he could find nothing, not a trace, not the slightest sign. Marius, though compelled on this side to exercise a great reserve, pushed on his inquiries as far as the Prefecture of Police, but there the information which he obtained led to no better result than elsewhere. The Prefecture knew less about the matter than the driver of the hackney-coach; they had no knowledge of any arrest having taken place at the outlet of the great drain on June 6; they had received no report from the agent about this fact which, at the Prefecture, was regarded as a fable. The invention of this fable was attributed to the driver; for a driver anxious for drink-money is capable of anything, even imagination. The fact, however, was certain, and Marius could not doubt it, unless he doubted his own identity, as we have just said. Everything in this strange enigma was inexplicable; this man, this mysterious man, whom the driver had seen come out of the grating of the great drain, bearing the fainting Marius on his back, and whom the police agent caught in the act of saving an insurgent,— what had become of him? what had become of the agent himself? why had this agent kept silence? had the man succeeded in escaping? had he corrupted the agent? why did this man give no sign of life to Marius, who owed everything to him? the disinterestedness was no less prodigious than the devotion. Why did this man not reappear? perhaps he was above reward, but no man is above gratitude. Was he dead? who was the man? what face had he? No one was able to say; the driver replied,—"The night was very dark." Basque and Nicolette in their amazement had only looked at their young master, who was all bloody. The porter, whose candle had lit up Marius' tragic arrival, had alone remarked the man in question, and this was the description he gave of him, "The man was horrible."

In the hope of deriving some advantage from them for his researches, Marius kept the bloodstained clothes which he wore when he was brought to his grandfather's. On examining the coat it was noticed that the skirt was strangely torn, and a piece was missing. One evening Marius was speaking in the presence of Cosette and Jean Valjean about all this singular adventure, the countless inquiries he had made, and the inutility of his efforts; Monsieur Fauchelevent's cold face offended him, and he exclaimed with a vivacity which had almost the vibration of anger:

"Yes, that man, whoever he may be, was sublime. Do you know what he did, sir? He intervened like an archangel. He was obliged to throw himself into the midst of the contest, carry me away, open the sewer, drag me off, and carry me. He must have gone more than a league and a half through frightful subterranean galleries, bent and bowed in the darkness, in the sewer, for more than half a league, sir, with a corpse on his back! And for what object? for the sole object of saving that corpse, and that corpse was myself. He said to himself,—'There is, perhaps, a gleam of life left here, and I will risk my existence for this wretched spark!' and he did not risk his existence once, but twenty times! and each step was a danger, and the proof is, that on leaving the sewer, he was arrested. Do

you know, sir, that this man did all that? and he had no
reward to expect. Who was I? An insurgent. Who was
I? A conquered man. Oh! if Cosette's six hundred
thousand francs were mine——"

"They are yours," Jean Valjean interrupted.

"Well, then," Marius continued, "I would give them to
find that man."

Jean Valjean kept silence.

CHAPTER CXIV.

THE night of the 16th of February, 1833, was a blessed
night, for it had above its shadow the open sky. It was
the wedding-night of Marius and Cosette. The day had
been adorable; it was not the adorable blue feast dreamed
of by the grandfather, a fairy scene, with a confusion of
cherubims and cupids above the head of the married couple,
a marriage worthy of being represented over a door; but
it had been sweet and smiling. The fashion of marrying
in 1833 was not at all as it is now. France had not yet
borrowed from England that supreme delicacy of carrying off
the wife, flying on leaving the church, hiding oneself as if
ashamed of one's happiness, and combining the manœuvres
of a bankrupt with the ravishment of the Song of Songs.

People still supposed at that epoch, whimsically enough,
that a marriage is a private and social festival, that a
patriarchal banquet does not spoil a domestic solemnity;
that gaiety, even if it be excessive, so long as it is decent,
does no harm to happiness; and, finally, that it is venerable
and good for the fusion of these two destinies from which
a family will issue, to begin in the house, and that the
household may have in future the nuptial chamber as a
witness. And people were so immodest as to marry at
home. The wedding took place, then, according to this
fashion which is now antiquated, at M. Gillenormand's;
and though this affair of marrying is so simple and natural,
the publication of the banns, the drawing up of the deeds, the
mayoralty, and the church, always cause some complication,
and they could not be ready before February 16th. Now—
we note this detail for the pure satisfaction of being exact—
it happened that the 16th was Shrove Tuesday. There were
hesitations and scruples, especially on the part of Aunt
Gillenormand.

"A Shrove Tuesday!" the grandfather exclaimed; "all the better. Done for the 16th. Do you wish to put it off, Marius?"

"Certainly not," said the amorous youth.

"We'll marry then," said the grandfather.

The marriage, therefore, took place on the 16th, in spite of the public gaiety. It rained on that day, but there is always in the sky a little blue patch at the service of happiness, which lovers see, even when the rest of creation are under their umbrellas. On the previous day, Jean Valjean had handed to Marius, in the presence of M. Gillenormand, the five hundred and eighty-four thousand francs. As the marriage took place in the ordinary way, the deeds were very simple. Toussaint was henceforth useless to Jean Valjean, so Cosette inherited her, and promoted her to the rank of lady's-maid. As for Jean Valjean, a nice room was furnished expressly for him at M. Gillenormand's, and Cosette had said to him so irresistibly,—"Father, I implore you," that she had almost made him promise that he would come and occupy it. A few days before that fixed for the marriage, an accident happened to Jean Valjean; he slightly injured the thumb of his right hand. It was not serious, and he had not allowed any one to poultice it, or even see it, not even Cosette. Still, it compelled him to wrap up his hand in a bandage and wear his arm in a sling, and this, of course, prevented him from signing anything. M. Gillenormand, as supervising guardian to Cosette, took his place. We will not take the reader either to the mayoralty or to church. Two lovers are not usually followed so far, and we are wont to turn our back on the drama, so soon as it puts a bridegroom's bouquet in its button-hole. We will restrict ourselves to noting an incident which, though unnoticed by the bridal party, marked the drive from the Rue des Filles du Calvaire to St. Paul's.

The Rue Saint Louis was being repaired at the time, and it was blocked from the Rue du Parc Royal, hence it was impossible for the carriage to go direct to St. Paul's. As they were obliged to change their course, the most simple plan was to turn into the boulevard. One of the guests drew attention to the fact that, as it was Shrove Tuesday, there would be a block of vehicles. "Why so?" M. Gillenormand asked. "On account of the masks." "Famous," said the grandfather; "we will go that way. These young

people are going to marry and see the serious side of life,
and seeing the masquerade will be a slight preparation for
it." They turned into the boulevard : the first of the
wedding carriages contained Cosette and Aunt Gillenormand, M. Gillenormand and Jean Valjean. Marius, still
separated from his bride, according to custom, was in the
second. The nuptial procession, on turning out of the Rue
des Filles du Calvaire, joined the long file of vehicles making
an endless chain from the Madeleine to the Bastille, and
from the Bastille to the Madeleine. Masks were abundant
on the boulevard : and though it rained every now and
then, Pantaloon and Harlequin were obstinate. In the
good humour of that winter of 1833 Paris had disguised
itself as Venice. We do not see such Shrove Tuesdays
nowadays, for as everything existing is a wide-spread
carnival, there is no carnival left. The side-walks were
thronged with pedestrians, and the windows with gazers ;
and the terraces crowning the peristyles of the theatres were
covered with spectators. In addition to the masks, they
beheld that file, peculiar to Shrove Tuesday as to Long-
champs, of vehicles of every description, hackney-coaches,
carts, curricles, and cabs, marching in order rigorously
riveted to each other by police regulations, and, as it were,
running on tramways. Any one who happens to be in one
of these vehicles is at once spectator and spectacle. Policemen standing by the side of the boulevard kept in place
these two interminable files moving in a contrary direction,
and watched that nothing should impede the double current
of these two streams, one running up, the other down,
one towards the Chaussée d'Antin, the other towards the
Faubourg St. Antoine. The escutcheoned carriages of the
Peers of France and Ambassadors held the crown of the
causeway, coming and going freely ; and certain magnificent
and gorgeous processions, notably the Bœuf gras, had the
same privilege.

In the double file, along which Municipal Guards galloped
like watch-dogs, honest family arks, crowded with great-
aunts and grandmothers, displayed at windows healthy
groups of disguised children, pierrots of seven, and pierrettes
of six, ravishing little creatures, feeling that they officially
formed part of the public merriment, penetrated with the
dignity of their harlequinade, and displaying the gravity
of functionaries. From time to time a block occurred somewhere in the procession of vehicles ; one or other of the two

side files stopped until the knot was untied, and one impeded vehicle stopped the entire line. Then they started
again. The wedding-carriages were in the file, going
toward the Bastille on the right-hand side of the boulevard.
Opposite the Rue du Pont aux Choux there was a stoppage,
and almost at the same moment the file on the other side
proceeding toward the Madeleine stopped too. At this
point of the procession there was a carriage of masks.
These carriages, or, to speak more correctly, these cart-
loads of masks, are well known to the Parisians.

The tradition of the coaches of masks dates back to the
oldest times of the monarchy. In our time, these noisy
piles of creatures generally ride in some old van of which
they encumber the roof, or cover with their tumultuous
group a landau of which the hood is thrown back. You
see them on the seat, on the front stool, on the springs of
the hood, and on the pole, and they even straddle across
the lamps. They are standing, lying down, or seated,
cross-legged, or with pendent legs. The women occupy
the knees of the men, and this wild pyramid is seen for a
long distance over the heads of the crowd. These vehicles
form mountains of merriment in the midst of the mob, and
Collé, Panard, and Piron flow from them enriched with
slang, and the fish-fag's catechism is expectorated from
above upon the people.

Accident willed it, as we have just said, that one of the
shapeless groups of masked men and women collected in a
vast barouche stopped on the left of the boulevard, while
the wedding-party stopped on the right. The carriage in
which the masks were, noticed opposite to it the carriage in
which was the bride.

"Hilloh!" said a mask, "a wedding."

"A false wedding," another retorted, "we are the true
one."

And, as they were too far off to address the wedding-
party, and as they also feared the interference of the police,
the two masks looked elsewhere. The whole vehicle-load
had plenty of work a moment after, for the mob began
hissing it, which is the caress given by the mob to mas-
querades, and the two masks who had just spoken were
obliged to face the crowd with their comrades, and found
the projectiles from the Arsenal of the markets scarce sufficient to reply to the enormous barks of the people. A
frightful exchange of metaphors took place between the

masks and the crowd. In the meanwhile, two other masks in the same carriage, a Spaniard with an exaggerated nose, an oldish look, and enormous black moustaches, and a thin and very youthful fish-girl, wearing a half mask, had noticed the wedding also, and while their companions and the spectators were insulting each other, held a conversation in a low voice. Their aside was covered by the tumult and was lost in it. The showers had drenched the open carriage; the February wind is not warm, and so the fish-girl, while answering the Spaniard, shivered, laughed, and coughed. This was the dialogue, which we translate from the original slang :

"Look here."

"What is it, pa?"

"Do you see that old man there, in the wedding-coach, with his arm in a sling?" ·

"Yes; what about him?"

"I feel sure that I know him."

"Ah!"

"May my neck be cut, if I do not know that Parisian. Can you see the bride by stooping?"

"No."

"And the bridegroom?"

"There is no bridegroom in that coach"

"Nonsense."

"Unless it be the other old man."

"Come, try and get a look at the bride by stooping."

"I can't."

"No matter, that old fellow who has something the matter with his paw, I feel certain I know him."

"And what good will it do you, your knowing him?"

"I don't know. Sometimes!"

"I don't care a curse for old fellows."

"I know him."

"Know him as much as you like."

"How the deuce is he at the wedding?"

"Why, we are there too."

"Where does the wedding come from?"

"How do I know?"

"Listen."

"Well, what is it?"

"You must do something."

"What is it?"

"Get out of our trap and follow that wedding.

" What to do ? "

" To know where it goes and what it is. Make haste and
get down ; run, my daughter, for you are young."

" I can't leave the carriage."

" Why not ? "

" I am hired."

" Oh, the devil ! "

" I owe the Prefecture my day's work."

" That's true."

" If I leave the carriage, the first inspector who sees me
will arrest me. You know that."

" Yes, I know it ; but that old fellow bothers me."

" All old men bother you, and yet you ain't a chicken
yourself."

" He is in the first carriage."

" Well, what then ? "

" In the bride's carriage."

" What next ? "

" So he is the father."

" How does that concern me ? "

" I tell you he is the father."

" You do nothing but talk about that father."

" Listen."

" Well, what ? "

" I can only go away masked, for I am hidden here, and
no one knows I am here. But to-morrow there will be no
masks, for it is Ash Wednesday, and I run a risk of being
nailed. I shall be obliged to go back to my hole, but you
are free."

" Not quite."

" Well, more so than I am."

" Well, what then ? "

" You must try and find out for me what that wedding is,
and where it comes from."

" Of course ! that would be funny. It's so mighty easy
to find out a week after where a wedding-party has gone to
that passed on Shrove Tuesday. A pin in a bundle of hay.
Is it possible ? "

" No matter, you must try. Do you hear, Azelma ? "

The two files recommenced their opposite movement on
the boulevard, and the carriage of masks lost out of sight
that which contained the bride.

To realise one's dream—to whom is this granted ? There
must be elections for this in heaven ; we are the unconscious

candidates, and the angels vote. Cosette and Marius had been elected. Cosette, both at the mayoralty and at church, was brilliant and touching. Toussaint, helped by Nicolette, had dressed her. Cosette wore over a skirt of white taffetas her dress of Binche lace, a veil of English point, a necklace of fine pearls, and a crown of orange flowers ; all this was white, and in this whiteness she was radiant. It was an exquisite candour expanding and becoming transfigured in light ; she looked like a virgin on the point of becoming a goddess. Marius' fine hair was shining and perfumed, and here and there a glimpse could be caught, under the thick curls, of pale lines, which were the scars of the barricade. The grandfather, superb, with head erect, amalgamating in his toilet and manners all the elegances of the time of Barras, gave his arm to Cosette. He took the place of Jean Valjean, who, owing to his wound, could not give his hand to the bride. Jean Valjean, dressed all in black, followed and smiled.

"Monsieur Fauchelevent," the grandfather said to him, "this is a glorious day, and I vote the end of afflictions and cares. Henceforth there must be no sorrow anywhere. By Heaven ! I decree joy ! misfortune has no right to exist, and it is a disgrace for the azure of heaven that there are unfortunate men. Evil does not come from man, who, at the bottom, is good ; but all human miseries have their capital and central government in hell, otherwise called the Tuileries of the devil. There, I am making demagogic remarks at present ! For my part I have no political opinions left ; and all I stick to is that all men should be rich, that is to say, joyous."

When, at the end of all the ceremonies,—after pronouncing before the mayor and before the priest every possible yes, after signing the register at the municipality and in the sacristy, after exchanging rings, after kneeling side by side under the canopy of white moire in the smoke of the censer, —they arrived holding each other by the hand, admired and envied by all. Marius in black, she in white, preceded by the beadle in colonel's epaulettes, striking the flagstones with his halberd, between two rows of dazzled spectators, at the church doors which were thrown wide open, ready to get into their carriage,—and then all was over. Cosette could not yet believe it. She looked at Marius, she looked at the crowd, she looked at heaven ; it seemed as if she were afraid of awaking. Her astonished and anxious air imparted something strangely enchanting to her. In

returning they both rode in the same carriage, Marius seated
by Cosette's side, and M. Gillenormand and Jean Valjean
forming their vis-à-vis. Aunt Gillenormand had fallen back
a step and was in the second carriage. "My children," the
grandfather said, "you are now M. le Baron ànd Madame
la Baronne, with thirty thousand francs a year." And
Cosette, leaning close up to Marius, caressed his ear with
the angelic whisper, "It is true, then, my name is Marius,
and I am Madame Thou." These two beings were re-
splendent, they had reached the irrevocable and irrecover-
able moment, the dazzling point of intersection of all youth
and all joy. They said to each other in a whisper, "We
will go and see again our little garden in the Rue Plumet."
They realised Jean Prouvaire's views ; together they did not
count forty years. It was marriage sublimated ; and these
two children were two lilies. They did not see each other,
but contemplated each other. Cosette perceived Marius in
a glory, and Marius perceived Cosette upon an altar. And
upon this altar, and in this glory, the two apotheoses blending, behind a cloud for Cosette, in flashing flame for Marius,
there was the ideal thing, the real thing, the meeting-place
of kisses and of sleep, the nuptial pillow.

The delight of these two hearts overflowed upon the
crowd, and imparted merriment to the passers-by. People
stopped in the Rue St. Antoine, in front of St. Paul's,
to look through the carriage-window—the orange flowers
trembling on Cosette's head. Then they returned to the
Rue des Filles du Calvaire—home. Marius, side by side
with Cosette, ascended, triumphantly and radiantly, that
staircase up which he had been dragged in a dying state.
The beggars, collected before the gate and dividing the
contents of their purses, blessed them. There were flowers
everywhere, and the house was no less fragrant than the
church : after the incense, the rose. They fancied they
could hear voices singing in infinitude ; they had God
in their hearts ; destiny appeared to them like a ceiling
of stars ; they saw above their heads the flashing of the
rising sun. Marius gazed at Cosette's charming bare arm
and the pink things which could be vaguely seen through
the lace of her stomacher, and Cosette, catching Marius'
glance, blushed to the tips of her ears. A good many old
friends of the Gillenormand family had been invited, and
they thronged round Cosette, outvying each other in calling
her Madame la Baronne.

Cosette had never been more affectionate to Jean Valjean, and she was in unison with Father Gillenormand; while he built up joy in aphorisms and maxims, she exhaled love and beauty like a perfume. Happiness wishes everybody to be happy. In talking to Jean Valjean she formed inflections of her voice of the time when she was a little girl, and caressed him with a smile. A banquet had been prepared in the dining-room; an illumination *à giorno* is the necessary seasoning of a great joy; mist and darkness are not accepted by the happy. They do not consent to be black; night, yes; darkness, no; and if there be no sun, one must be made. The dining-room was a furnace of gay things; in the centre, above the white glistening tables, hung a Venetian chandelier, with all sorts of coloured birds, blue, violet, red, and green, perched among the candles; round the chandelier were girandoles, and on the walls were mirrors with three and four branches; glasses, crystal, plate, china, crockery, gold, and silver, all flashed and rejoiced. The spaces between the candelabra were filled up with bouquets, so that where there was not a light there was a flower. In the anteroom three violins and a flute played some of Haydn's quartettes. Jean Valjean had seated himself on a chair in the drawing-room, behind the door, which, being thrown back, almost concealed him. A few minutes before they sat down to table Cosette gave him a deep curtsey, while spreading out her wedding-dress with both hands, and with a tenderly mocking look, asked him :

" Father, are you satisfied ? "

"Yes," said Jean Valjean, "I am satisfied."

" Well, then, laugh."

Jean Valjean began laughing. A few minutes later Basque came in to announce that dinner was on the table. The guests, preceded by M. Gillenormand, who gave his arm to Cosette, entered the dining-room, and collected round the table in the prescribed order. There was a large easy-chair on either side of the bride, one for M. Gillenormand, the other for Jean Valjean. M. Gillenormand seated himself, but the other chair remained empty. All looked round for " Monsieur Fauchelevent," but he was no longer there, and M. Gillenormand hailed Basque.

" Do you know where M. Fauchelevent is ? "

"Yes, sir, I do," Basque replied. " Monsieur Fauchelevent requested me to tell you, sir, that his hand pained him, and that he could not dine with M. le Baron and

Madame la Baronne. He therefore begged to be excused,
but would call to-morrow. He has just left."

This empty chair momentarily chilled the effusion of the
wedding feast ; but though M. Fauchelevent was absent
M. Gillenormand was there, and the grandfather shone for
two. He declared that M. Fauchelevent acted rightly in
going to bed early if he were in pain, but that it was only
a small hurt. This declaration was sufficient ; besides,
what is a dark corner in such a submersion of joy ? Cosette
and Marius were in one of those egotistic and blessed
moments when people possess no other faculty than that
of perceiving joy ; and then M. Gillenormand had an idea,
" By Jupiter, this chair is empty ; come hither, Marius ;
your aunt, though she has a right to it, will permit you ; this
chair is for you ; it is legal, and it is pretty—Fortunatus by
the side of Fortunata." The whole of the guests applauded.
Marius took Jean Valjean's place by Cosette's side, and
things were so arranged that Cosette, who had at first been
saddened by the absence of Jean Valjean, ended by being
pleased at it. From the moment when Marius was the
substitute Cosette would not have regretted God. She
placed her little white satin-slippered foot upon Marius'
foot. When the easy-chair was occupied M. Fauchelevent
was effaced, and nothing was wanting. And five minutes
later all the guests were laughing from one end of the table
to the other, with all the forgetfulness of humour. At dessert
M. Gillenormand rose, with a glass of champagne in his
hand, only half full, so that the trembling of ninety-two
years might not upset it, and proposed the health of the
new-married couple.

The evening was lively, gay, and pleasant ; the sovereign
good humour of the grandfather gave the tone to the whole
festivity, and each was regulated by this almost centenarian
cordiality. There was a little dancing, and a good deal of
laughter ; it was a merry wedding, to which that worthy
old fellow "Once on a time" might have been invited ;
however, he was present in the person of Father Gillenormand. There was a tumult, and then a silence ; the
married couple disappeared. A little after midnight the
Gillenormand mansion became a temple. Here we stop,
for an angel stands on the threshold of wedding-nights,
smiling, and with finger on lip ; the mind becomes contemplative before this sanctuary in which the celebration
of love is held. There must be rays of light above such

houses, and the joy which they contain must pass through the walls in brilliancy, and vaguely irradiate the darkness. It is impossible for this sacred and fatal festival not to send a celestial radiance to infinitude. Love is the sublime crucible in which the fusion of man and women takes place; the one being, the triple being, the final being, the human trinity issue from it. This birth of two souls in one must have emotion for the shadows. The lover is the priest, and the transported virgin feels an awe. A portion of this joy ascends to God. When there is really marriage, that is to say, when there is love, the ideal is mingled with it, and a nuptial couch forms in the darkness a corner of the dawn. If it was given to the mental eye to perceive the formidable and charming visions of higher life, it is probable that it would see the forms of night, the unknown winged beings, the blue wayfarers of the invisible, bending down round the luminous house, satisfied and blessing, pointing out to each other the virgin bride, who is gently startled, and having the reflection of human felicity on their divine countenances. If, at this supreme hour, the pair, dazzled with pleasure, and who believe themselves alone, were to listen, they would hear in their chamber a confused rustling of wings, for perfect, happiness implies the guarantee of angels. This little obscure alcove has an entire heaven for its ceiling. When two mouths, which have become sacred by love, approach each other in order to create, it is impossible but that there is a tremor in the immense mystery of the stars above this ineffable kiss. These felicities are the real ones, there is no joy beyond their joys, love is the sole ecstasy, and all the rest weeps. To love or to have loved is sufficient; ask nothing more after that. There is no other pearl to be found in the dark folds of life, for love is a consummation.

CHAPTER CXV.

WHAT had become of Jean Valjean? Directly after he had laughed, in accordance with Cosette's request, as no one was paying any attention to him, Jean Valjean rose, and, unnoticed, reached the anteroom. It was the same room which he had entered eight months previously, black with mud, blood, and gunpowder, bringing back the grandson to the grandfather. The old panelling was garlanded with flowers and leaves, the musicians were seated on the sofa upon which Marius had been deposited. Basque, in black coat, knee-breeches, white cravat, and white gloves, was placing wreaths of roses round each of the dishes which was going to be served up. Jean Valjean showed him his arm in the sling, requested him to explain his absence, and quitted the house. The windows of the dining-room looked out on the street, and Jean Valjean stood for some minutes motionless in the obscurity of those radiant windows. He listened, and the confused sound of the banquet reached his ears ; he heard the grandfather's loud and dictatorial voice, the violins, the rattling of plates and glasses, the bursts of laughter, and in all this gay uproar he distinguished Cosette's soft, happy voice. He left the Rue des Filles du Calvaire and returned to the Rue de l'Homme Armé. In going home he went along the Rue Saint Louis, the Rue Culture Sainte Catherine, and the Blancs Manteaux ; it was a little longer, but it was the road by which he had been accustomed to come with Cosette during the last three months, in order to avoid the crowd and mud of the Rue Vieille du Temple. This road, which Cosette had passed along, excluded the idea of any other itinerary for him. Jean Valjean returned home, lit his candle, and went upstairs. The apartments were empty, and not even Toussaint was in there now. Jean Valjean's footsteps made more noise in the rooms than usual. All the wardrobes were open ; he entered Cosette's room, and there were no sheets on the bed. The pillow, without a case or lace, was laid on the blankets folded at the foot of the bed, in which no one was going to sleep again. All the small feminine articles to which Cosette clung had been removed ; only the heavy furniture and the four walls remained. Toussaint's bed was also unmade ; and the only one made, which seemed to be expecting somebody, was Jean Valjean's. Jean Valjean looked at the walls, closed some of the wardrobe drawers, and walked in and out of the rooms. Then he returned to his own room and placed his candle on the table ; he had taken his arm out of the sling, and used it as if he were suffering no pain in it. He went up to his bed, and his eyes fell—was it by accident or was it purposely ?—on the "inseparable," of which Cosette had been jealous, the little valise which never left him. On June 4th, when he arrived at the Rue de l'Homme Armé, he had laid it on a table ; he now walked up to this table with some eagerness, took the key out of his pocket, and opened the portmanteau. He slowly drew out the clothes in which, ten years previously, Cosette had left Montfermeil; first the little black dress, then the black handkerchief, then the stout shoes, which Cosette could almost have worn still, so small was her foot; next the petticoat, then the apron, and, lastly, the woollen stockings. These stockings, in which the shape of a little leg was gracefully marked, were no longer than Jean Valjean's hand. All these articles were black, and it was he who took them for her to Montfermeil. He laid each article on the bed as he took it out, and he thought, and remembered. It was in winter, a very cold December, she was shivering under her rags, and her poor feet were quite red in her wooden shoes. He, Jean Valjean, had made her take off these rags, and put on this mourning garb; the mother must have been pleased in her tomb to see her daughter wearing mourning for her, and above all to see that she was well clothed and was warm. He thought of that forest of Montfermeil, he thought of the weather it was, of the trees without leaves, of the wood without birds, and the sky without sun; but no matter, it was charming. He arranged the little clothes on the bed, the handkerchief near the petticoat, the stockings along with the shoes, the apron by the side of the dress, and he looked at them one after the other. She was not much taller than that, she had her large doll in her arms, she had put her louis d'or in the pocket of this apron, she laughed, they walked along holding each other's hand, and she had no one but him in the world.

Then his venerable white head fell on the bed, his old stoical heart broke, his face was buried in Cosette's clothes, and had any one passed upstairs at that moment he would have heard frightful sobs. The old formidable struggle, of which we have already seen several phases, began again. Jacob only wrestled with the angel for one night. Alas! how many times have we seen Jean Valjean caught round the waist in the darkness by his conscience, and struggling frantically against it. An extraordinary struggle! at certain moments the foot slips, at others, the ground gives way. How many times had that conscience, clinging to the right, strangled and crushed him! how many times had inexorable truth set its foot on his chest! how many times had he, felled by the light, cried for mercy! how many times had that implacable light, illumined within and over him by the

Bishop, dazzled him when he wished to be blinded ! how
many times had he risen again in the contest, clung to the
rock, supported himself by sophistry, and been dragged
through the dust, at one moment throwing his conscience
under him, at another thrown by it ! how many times, after
an equivocation, after the treacherous and specious reasoning
of egotism, had he heard his irritated conscience cry in his
ears, "Tripper! scoundrel!" how many times had his
refractory thoughts groaned convulsively under the evidence
of duty ! what secret wounds he had, which he alone felt
bleeding ! what excoriations there were in his lamentable
existence ! how many times had he risen, bleeding, mutilated, crushed, enlightened, with despair in his heart and
serenity in his soul ! and though vanquished, he felt himself
the victor, and after having dislocated, tortured, and broken
him, his conscience, erect before him, luminous and tranquil,
would say to him,—"Now go in peace !" What a mournful peace, alas ! after issuing from such a contest.

This night, however, Jean Valjean felt that he was
fighting his last battle. A crushing question presented
itself ; predestinations are not all straight ; they do not
develop themselves in a rectilinear avenue before the predestined man ; they have blind alleys, zigzags, awkward
corners, and perplexing cross-roads. Jean Valjean was
halting at this moment at the most dangerous of these
cross-roads. He had reached the supreme crossing of
good and evil, and had that gloomy intersection before his
eyes. This time again, as had already happened in other
painful interludes, two roads presented themselves before
him, one tempting, the other terrifying ; which should he
take ? The one which frightened him was counselled by
the mysterious pointing hand, which we all perceive every
time that we fix our eyes upon the darkness. Jean Valjean
had once again a choice between the terrible haven and
the smiling snare. Is it true, then ? the soul may be cured,
but not destiny. What a frightful thing ! an incurable
destiny ! The question which presented itself was this,—
In what way was Jean Valjean going to behave in regard
to the happiness of Cosette and Marius ? That happiness
he had willed, he had made ; and at this hour, in gazing
upon it, he could have the species of satisfaction which a
cutler would have who recognised his trade-mark upon
a knife, when he drew it all reeking from his chest. Cosette
had Marius, Marius possessed Cosette ; they possessed

everything, even wealth, and it was his doing. But, now
that this happiness existed and was there, how was he,
Jean Valjean, to treat it? should he force himself upon it
and treat it as if belonging to himself? Doubtless, Cosette
was another man's; but should he, Jean Valjean, retain
of Cosette all that he could retain? Should he remain the
sort of father, scarce seen but respected, which he had
hitherto been? should he introduce himself quietly into
Cosette's house? should he carry his past to this future
without saying a word? should he present himself there
as one having a right, and should he sit down, veiled, at
this luminous hearth? Should he smilingly take the hands
of these two innocent creatures in his tragic hands? should
he place on the andirons of the Gillenormand drawing-room
his feet which dragged after them the degrading shadow
of the law? Should he render the obscurity on his brow
and the cloud on theirs denser? should he join his
catastrophe to their two felicities? should he continue to be
silent? in a word, should he be the sinister dumb man of
destiny by the side of these two happy beings? We must
be accustomed to fatality and to meeting it, to raise our
eyes when certain questions appear to us in their terrible
nudity. Good and evil are behind this stern note of interrogation. What are you going to do? the sphynx asks.
This habit of trial Jean Valjean had, and he looked at the
sphynx fixedly, and examined the pitiless problem from all
sides. Cosette, that charming existence, was the raft of
this shipwrecked man ; what should he do, cling to it, or
let it go? If he clung to it, he issued from disaster, he
remounted to the sunshine, he let the bitter water drip off
his clothes and hair, he was saved and lived. Suppose he
let it go? then there was an abyss. He thus dolorously
held counsel with his thoughts, or, to speak more correctly,
he combated ; he rushed furiously within himself, at one
moment against his will, at another against his convictions.
It was fortunate for Jean Valjean that he had been able to
weep, for that enlightened him, perhaps. Still, the beginning
was stern ; a tempest, more furious than that which had
formerly forced him to Arras, was let loose within him.
The past returned to him in the face of the present ; he
compared and he sobbed. Once the sluice of tears was
opened, the despairing man writhed. He felt himself
arrested, alas ! in the deadly fight between one egotism and
one duty. When we thus recoil inch by inch before our

ideal, wildly, obstinately, exasperated at yielding, disputing the ground, hoping for a possible flight, and seeking an issue, what a sudden and sinister resistance is the foot of a wall behind us! to feel the sacred shadow forming an obstacle!

Hence we.have never finished with our conscience. The first step is nothing, it is the last that is difficult. What was the Champmathieu affair by the side of Cosette's marriage? what did it bring with it? what is returning to the hulks by the side of entering nothingness? Oh, first step to descend, how gloomy thou art! oh, second step, how black thou art! How could he help turning his head away this time? Martyrdom is a sublimation, a corrosive sublimation. It is a torture which consecrates. A man may consent to it for the first hour; he sits on the throne of red-hot iron, the crown of red-hot iron is placed on his head, he accepts the red-hot globe, he takes the red-hot sceptre, but he still has to don the mantle of flame, and is there not a moment when the miserable flesh revolts and the punishment is fled from? At length Jean Valjean entered the calmness of prostration, he wished, thought over, and considered the alternatives of the mysterious balance of light and shadow. Should he force his galleys on these two dazzling children, or consummate his own irremediable destruction? On one side was the sacrifice of Cosette, on the other of himself.

His confusing reverie lasted all night; he remained till daybreak in the same position, leaning over the bed, prostrate beneath the enormity of fate, crushed perhaps, alas! with clenched fists, and arms extended at a right angle like an unnailed crucified man thrown with his face on the ground. He remained thus for twelve hours, the twelve hours of a long winter's night, frozen, without raising his head or uttering a syllable. He was motionless as a corpse, while his thoughts rolled on the ground or fled away. Sometimes like the hydra, sometimes like the eagle. To see him thus you would have thought him a dead man; but all at once he started convulsively, and his mouth pressed to Cosette's clothes, kissed them; then you could see that he was alive.

CHAPTER CXVI.

THE day after a wedding is solitary, for people respect the retirement of the happy, and to some extent their lengthened slumbers. The confusion of visits and congratulations does not begin again till a later date. On the morning of February 17 it was a little past midday when Basque, with napkin and feather-brush under his arm, was dusting the anteroom, when he heard a low tap at the door. There had not been a ring, which is discreet on such a day. Basque opened and saw M. Fauchelevent; he conducted him to the drawing-room, which was still in great confusion, and looked like the battlefield of the previous day's joys.

"Really, sir," observed Basque, "we woke late."

"Is your master up?" Jean Valjean asked.

"How is your hand, sir?" Basque replied.

"Better. Is your master up?"

"Which one? the old or the new?"

"Monsieur Pontmercy."

"Monsieur le Baron!" said Basque, drawing himself up.

A baron is above all a baron to his servants; a portion of it comes to them, and they have what a philosopher would call the splashing of the title, and that flatters them. Marius, we may mention in passing, a militant republican as he had proved, was now a baron, in spite of himself. A little revolution had taken place in the family with reference to this title; at present it was M. Gillenormand who was attached to it, and Marius who threw it off. But Colonel Pontmercy had written, "My son will bear my title," and Marius obeyed. And then Cosette, in whom the woman was beginning to germinate, was delighted at being a baroness.

"Monsieur le Baron?" repeated Basque, "I will go and see. I will tell him that Monsieur Fauchelevent is here."

"No, do not tell him it is I. Tell him that some one wishes to speak to him privately, and do not mention my name."

"Ah!" said Basque.

"I wish to surprise him."

"Ah!" Basque repeated, giving himself his second "Ah!" as an explanation of the first.

And he left the room. Jean Valjean remained alone. A

few moments passed, during which Jean Valjean remained motionless at the spot where Basque left him. His eyes were hollow, and so sunk in their sockets by sleeplessness that they almost disappeared. His black coat displayed the fatigued creases of a coat which has been up all night, and the elbows were white with that down which friction with linen leaves on cloth. There was a noise at the door, and he raised his eyes. Marius came in with head erect, laughing mouth, a peculiar light over his face, a smooth forehead, and a flashing eye. He also had not slept.

"It is you, father!" he exclaimed, on perceiving Jean Valjean; "why, that ass Basque affected the mysterious. But you have come too early. It is only half-past twelve, and Cosette is asleep."

That word, father, addressed to M. Fauchelevent by Marius, signified supreme felicity. There had always been, as we know, an escarpment, a coldness, and constraint between them; ice to melt or break. Marius was so intoxicated that the escarpment sank, the ice dissolved, and M. Fauchelevent was for him, as for Cosette, a father. He continued; the words overflowed with him, which is peculiar to these divine paroxysms of joy,—

"How delighted I am to see you! if you only knew how we missed you yesterday! Good-day, father; how is your hand? better, is it not?"

And, satisfied with the favourable answer which he gave himself, he went on:

"We both spoke about you, for Cosette loves you so dearly. You will not forget that you have a room here, for we will not hear a word about the Rue de l'Homme Armé. I do not know how you were able to live in that street, which is sick, and mean, and poor, which has a barrier at one end, where you feel cold, and which no one can enter! You will come and install yourself here, and from to-day, or else you will have to settle with Cosette. She intends to lead us both by the nose, I warn you. You have seen your room, it is close to ours, and looks out on the gardens : we have had the lock mended, the bed is made, it is all ready, and you have only to move in. Cosette has placed close to your bed a large old easy-chair of Utrecht velvet, to which she said, 'Hold out your arms to him!' Every spring a nightingale comes to the clump of acacias which faces your windows, and you will have it in two months. You will have its nest on your left and ours on your right; at night

it will sing, and by day Cosette will talk. **Your room** faces
due south ; Cosette will arrange **your books in it, and al¹**
your matters. There is, I believe, a valise to which you are
attached, and I have arranged a corner of honour for it
You have won my grandfather, for you suit him : we will
live together. Do you know whist? you will overwhelm
my grandfather if you are acquainted with whist. You will
take Cosette for a walk on the day when I go to the Courts ;
you will give her your arm, as you used to do, you remember, formerly at the Luxembourg. We are absolutely
determined to be very happy, and you will share in our
happiness, do you hear, papa? By the bye, you will breakfast with us this morning ? "

" I have one thing to remark to you, sir," said Jean
Valjean ; " I am an ex-convict."

The limit of the perceptible acute sounds may be as well
exceeded for the mind as for the ear. These words, " I am
an ex-convict," coming from M. Fauchelevent's mouth and
entering Marius' ear went beyond possibility. Marius did
not hear ; it seemed to him as if something had just been
said to him, but he knew not what. He stood with gaping
mouth. Jean Valjean unfastened the black handkerchief
that supported his right arm, undid the linen rolled round
his hand, bared his thumb, and showed it to Marius.

" I have nothing the matter with my hand," he said.

Marius looked at the thumb.

" There was never anything the matter with it," Jean
Valjean added.

There was, in fact, no sign of a wound. Jean Valjean
continued :

" It was proper that I should be absent from your
marriage, and I was so as far as I could. I feigned this
wound in order not to commit a forgery, and render the
marriage-deeds null and void."

Marius stammered :

" What does this mean ? "

" It means," Jean Valjean replied, " that I have been to
the galleys."

" You are driving me mad," said the horrified Marius.

" Monsieur Pontmercy," said Jean Valjean, " I was nineteen years at the galleys for robbery. Then I was sentenced
to them for life, for robbery, and a second offence. At the
present moment I am an escaped convict."

Although Marius recoiled before the reality, refused the

facts, and resisted the evidence, he was obliged to yield
to it. He was beginning to understand, and as always
happens in such a case, he understood too much. He had
the shudder of a hideous internal flash : and an idea that
made him shudder crossed his mind. He foresaw a frightful destiny for himself in the future.

"Say all, say all," he exclaimed, "you are Cosette's
father ! "

And he fell back two steps, with a movement of indescribable horror. Jean Valjean threw up his head with such
a majestic attitude that he seemed to rise to the ceiling.

"It is necessary that you should believe me here, sir,
although the oath of men like us is not taken in a court of
justice——"

Here there was a silence, and then, with a sort of
sovereign and sepulchral authority, he added, speaking
slowly and laying a stress on the syllables :

"You will believe me. I, Cosette's father ! Before
Heaven, no, Monsieur le Baron Pontmercy. I am a
peasant of Faverolles, and earned my livelihood by pruning
trees. My name is not Fauchelevent, but Jean Valjean.
I am nothing to Cosette, so reassure yourself."

Marius stammered :

"Who proves it to me ? "

"I do, since I say it."

Marius looked at this man : he was mournful and calm,
and no falsehood could issue from such calmness. What is
frozen is sincere, and the truth could be felt in this coldness
of the tomb.

"I do believe you," said Marius.

Jean Valjean bowed his head, as if to note the fact, and
continued :

"What am I to Cosette? a passer-by. Ten years ago
I did not know that she existed. I love her, it is true,
for men love a child whom they have seen little when old
themselves ; when a man is old he feels like a grandfather
to all little children. You can, I suppose, imagine that
I have something which resembles a heart. She was an
orphan, without father or mother, and needed me, and
that is why I came to love her. Children are so weak
that the first comer, even a man like myself, may be their
protector. I performed this duty to Cosette. I cannot
suppose that so small a thing can be called a good action :
but if it be one, well, assume that I had done it. Record

that extenuating fact. To-day Cosette leaves my life, and our two roads separate. Henceforth I can do no more for her; she is Madame Pontmercy; her providence has changed, and she has gained by the change, so all is well. As for the six hundred thousand francs, you say nothing of them, but I will meet your thought half-way : they are a deposit. How was it placed in my hands? no matter. I give up the deposit, and there is nothing more to ask of me. I complete the restitution by stating my real name, and this too concerns myself, for I am anxious that you should know who I am."

And Jean Valjean looked Marius in the face. All that Marius experienced was tumultuous and incoherent, for certain blasts of the wind of destiny produce such waves in our soul. We have all had such moments of trouble in which everything is dispersed within us : we say the first things that occur to us, which are not always precisely those which we ought to say. There are sudden revelations which we connot bear, and which intoxicate like a potent wine. Marius was stupefied by the new situation which appeared to him, and spoke to this man almost as if he were angry at the avowal.

"But why," he exclaimed, "do you tell me all this? who forces you to do so? you might have kept your secret to yourself. You are neither denounced, nor pursued, nor tracked. You have a motive for making the revelation so voluntarily. Continue; there is something else ; for what purpose do you make this confession? for what motive?"

"For what motive?" Jean Valjean answered in a voice so low and dull that it seemed as if he were speaking to himself rather than Marius. "For what motive? in truth, does this convict come here to say, I am a convict. Well, yes, the motive is a strange one : it is through honesty. The misfortune is that I have a thread in my heart which holds me fast, and it is especially when a man is old that these threads are most solid. The whole of life is undone around, but they resist. Had I been enabled to tear away that thread, break it, unfasten or cut the knot, and go a long way off, I would be saved and needed only to start. There are diligences in the Rue du Bouloy ; you are happy, and I am off. I tried to break that thread. I pulled at it, it held out, it did not break, and I pulled out my heart with it. Then I said, I cannot live anywhere else, and must remain.

Well, yes, but you are right. I am an ass ; why not simply remain ? You offer me a bedroom in the house. Madame Pontmercy loves me dearly ; your grandfather asks nothing better than to have me. I suit him, we will all live together, have our meals in common, I will give my arm to Cosette, to Madame Pontmercy, forgive me, but it is habit, we will have only one roof, one table, one fire, the same chimney-corner in winter, the same walk in summer : that is joy, that is happiness, that is everything. We will live in one family."

At this word, Jean Valjean became fierce. He folded his arms, looked at the board at his feet, as if he wished to dig a pit in it, and his voice suddenly became loud.

"In one family ? no. I belong to no family ; I do not belong to yours ; I do not even belong to the human family. In houses where people are together, I am in the way. There are families ; but none for me. I am the unhappy man ; I am outside. Had I a father and mother ? I almost doubt it. On the day when I gave you that child in marriage, it was all ended. I saw that she was happy, and that she was with the man she loved, that there is a kind old gentleman here, a household of two angels, and every joy in this house, and I said to myself, Do not enter. I could lie, it is true ; deceive you all, and remain Monsieur Fauchelevent. So long as it was for her, I was able to lie, but now that it would be but for myself I ought not to do so. I only required to be silent, it is true, and all would have gone on. You ask me what compels me to speak ? a strange sort of thing, my conscience. It would have been very easy, however, to hold my tongue ; I spent the night in trying to persuade myself into it. You are shriving me, and what I have just told you is so extraordinary that you have the right to do so. Well, yes, I spent the night in giving myself reasons. I gave myself excellent reasons ; I did what I could. But there are two things in which I could not succeed ; I could neither break the string which holds me by the heart, fixed, sealed, and riveted here, nor silence some one who speaks to me in a low voice when I am alone. That is why I have come to confess all to you this morning,—all, or nearly all, for it is useless to tell what only concerns myself, and that I keep to myself. You know the essential thing. I took my mystery, then, and brought it to you, and ripped it up before your eyes. It was not an easy resolution to form, and I debated the point the whole night. Ah! you may fancy that I did not say to myself that this was not the Champmathieu affair, that in hiding my name I did no one any harm, that the name of Fauchelevent was given me by Fauchelevent himself in gratitude for a service rendered, and that I might fairly keep it, and that I should be happy in this room which you offer me, that I should not be at all in the way, that I should be in my little corner, and that while you had Cosette I should have the idea of being in the same house with her ; each would have his proportioned happiness. Continuing to be Monsieur Fauchelevent arranged everything. Yes, except my soul ; there would be joy all over me, but the bottom of my soul would remain black. Thus I should have remained Monsieur Fauchelevent. I should have hidden my real face in the presence of your happiness, I should have borne an enigma ; and in the midst of your broad sunshine, I should have been darkness ; thus, without crying beware, I should have introduced the hulks to your hearth, I should have sat down at your table with the thought that, if you knew who I was, you would expel me ; and let myself be served by the servants, who, had they known, would have said, 'What a horror!' I should have touched you with my elbow, which you have a right to feel offended at, and swindled you out of shakes of the hand. There would have been in your house a divided respect between venerable gray hairs and branded gray hairs ; in your most intimate hours, when all hearts formed themselves to each other, when we were all four together, the grandfather, you two, and I, there would have been a stranger there. Hence I, a dead man, would have imposed myself on you who are living, and I should have sentenced her for life. You, Cosette, and I would have been three heads in the green cap ! Do you not shudder? I am only the most crushed of men ; I should have been the most monstrous. And this crime I should have committed daily ! and this falsehood I should have told daily ! and this face of night I should have worn daily! and I should have given to you a share in my stigma daily, to you, my beloved, to you, my children, to you, my innocents. Holding one's tongue is nothing? keeping silence is simple? no, it is not simple, for there is a silence which lies, and my falsehood, and my fraud, and my indignity, and my cowardice, and my treachery, and my crime, I should have drunk drop by drop ; I should have spat it out, and thus drunk it again ; I should have ended at midnight and begun again at midday, and my good-day would have lied, and my good-night would have lied, and I should have slept upon it, and eaten it with my bread; and I should have looked at Cosette, and responded to the smile of the angel with the smile of the condemned man, and I should have been an abominable scoundrel, and for what purpose? to be happy. I happy! have I the right to be happy? I am out of life, sir."

Jean Valjean stopped, and Marius listened, but such enchainments of ideas and agonies cannot be interrupted. Jean Valjean lowered his voice again, but it was no longer the dull voice, but the sinister voice.

"You ask why I speak? I am neither denounced, nor pursued, nor tracked, you say. Yes, I am denounced! Yes, I am pursued! Yes, I am tracked! By whom? by myself. It is I who bar my own passage, and I drag myself along, and I push myself, and I arrest myself, and execute myself, and when a man holds himself he is securely held."

And, seizing his own collar, and dragging it toward Marius, he continued :

"Look at this fist. Do you not think that it holds this collar so as not to let it go? Well, conscience is a very different hand! If you wish to be happy, sir, you must never understand duty; for so soon as you have understood it, it is implacable. People may say that it punishes you for understanding it; but no, it rewards you for it, for it places you in a hell where you feel God by your side. A man has no sooner torn his entrails than he is at peace with himself."

And, with an indescribable accent, he added :

"Monsieur Pontmercy, this is not common sense. I am an honest man. It is by degrading myself in your eyes that I raise myself in my own. This has happened to me once before, but it was less painful; it was nothing. Yes, an honest man. I should not be one if you had, through my fault, continued to esteem me ; but now that you despise me, I am so. I have this fatality upon me, that as I am never able to have any but stolen consideration, this consideration humiliates and crushes me internally, and in order that I may respect myself, people must despise me. Then I draw myself up. I am a galley-slave who obeys his conscience. I know very well that this is not likely, but what would

you have me do? it is so. I have made engagements with
myself, and keep them. There are meetings which bind
us. There are accidents which drag us into duty. Look
you, Monsieur Pontmercy, things have happened to me in
my life."

Jean Valjean made another pause, swallowing his saliva
with an effort, as if his words had a bitter after-taste, and
he continued :

"When a man has such a horror upon him, he has no
right to make others share it unconsciously; he has no
right to communicate his plague to them ; he has no right
to make them slip over his precipice without their perceiving
it ; he has no right to drag his red cap over them ; and he
has no right craftily to encumber the happiness of another
man with his misery. To approach those who are healthy,
and to touch them in the darkness with his invisible ulcer, is
hideous. Fauchelevent may have lent me his name, but
I have no right to use it : he may have given it to me, but I
was unable to take it. A name is a self. Look you, sir,
I have thought a little and read a little, though I am a
peasant ; and you see that I express myself properly. I
explain things to myself, and have carried out my own
education. Well, yes ; to abstract a name and place oneself under it is dishonest. The letters of the alphabet may
be filched like a purse or a watch. To be a false signature
in flesh and blood, to be a living false key, to enter among
honest folk by picking their lock, never to look, but always
to squint, to be internally infamous,—no ! no ! no ! no ! It is
better to suffer, bleed, weep, tear one's flesh with one's nails,
pass the nights writhing in agony, and gnaw one's stomach
and soul. That is why I have come to tell you all this,—
voluntarily, as you remarked."

He breathed painfully, and uttered this last remark :

"Formerly, I stole a loaf in order to live ; to-day, I will
not steal a name in order to live."

"To live!" Marius interrupted, "you do not require
that name to live."

"Ah! I understand myself," Jean Valjean replied, raising
and drooping his head several times in succession. There
was a silence ; both held their tongue, sunk as they were
in a gulf of thought. Marius was sitting near a table, and
supporting the corner of his mouth on one of his fingers.
Jean Valjean walked backwards and forwards ; he stopped
before a glass and remained motionless. Then, as if

answering some internal reasoning, he said, as he looked
in this glass, in which he did not see himself :

" While at present I am relieved."

He began walking again, and went to the other end of
the room. At the moment when he turned he perceived
that Marius was watching his walk, and he said to him,
with an indescribable accent :

" I drag my leg a little.   You understand why now."

Then he turned round full to Marius.

" And now, sir, imagine this.   I have said nothing.   I
have remained Monsieur Fauchelevent.   I have taken my
place in your house.   I am one of your family.   I am in
my room.   I come down to breakfast in my slippers ; at
night we go to the play, all three.   I accompany Madame
Pontmercy to the Tuileries and to the Place Royale ; we
are together, and you believe me your equal.   One fine
day I am here, you are there.   We are talking and laughing, and you hear a voice cry this name,—Jean Valjean !
and then that fearful hand, the police, issues from the
shadow, and suddenly tears off my mask ! "

He was silent again.   Marius had risen with a shudder,
and Jean Valjean continued :

" What do you say to that ? "

Marius' silence replied, and Jean Valjean continued :

" You see very well that I did right in not holding my
tongue.   Be happy, be in heaven, be the angel of an angel,
be in the sunshine and content yourself with it, and do
not trouble yourself as to the way in which a poor condemned
man opens his heart and does his duty ; you have a wretched
man before you, sir."

Marius slowly crossed the room, and when he was by Jean
Valjean's side, offered him his hand.   But Marius was
compelled to take this hand which did not offer itself.   Jean
Valjean let him do so, and it seemed to Marius that he
was pressing a hand of marble.

" My grandfather has friends," said Marius.   " I will
obtain your pardon."

" It is useless," Jean Valjean replied ; " I am supposed
to be dead, and that is sufficient.   The dead are not
subjected to surveillance, and are supposed to rot quietly.
Death is the same thing as pardon."

And liberating the hand which Marius held, he added
with a sort of inexorable dignity :

" Moreover, duty, my duty, is the friend to whom I

have recourse, and I only need one pardon, that of my conscience."

At this moment the door opened gently at the other end of the drawing-room, and Cosette's head appeared in the crevice. Only her sweet face was visible. Her hair was in admirable confusion, and her eyelids were still swollen with sleep. She made the movement of a bird thrusting its head out of the nest, looked first at her husband, then at Jean Valjean, and cried to them laughingly—it looked like a smile issuing from a rose :

" I'll wager that you are talking politics. How stupid that is, instead of being with me ! "

Jean Valjean started.

" Cosette——" Marius stammered, and he stopped. They looked like two culprits ; Cosette, radiant, continued to look at them both, and there were in her eyes gleams of Paradise.

"I have caught you in the act," Cosette said, " I just heard through this, Father Fauchelevent saying, 'Conscience, doing his duty.' That is politics, and I will have none of it. People must not talk politics on the very next day ; it is not right."

" You are mistaken, Cosette," Marius replied, " we are talking of business. We are talking about the best way of investing your six hundred thousand francs."

" I am coming," Cosette interrupted. " Do you want me here ? "

And resolutely passing through the door, she entered the drawing-room. She was dressed in a full morning gown, with a thousand folds and with large sleeves, which descended from her neck to her feet. There are in the golden skies of old Gothic paintings, these charming bags to place angels in. She contemplated herself from head to foot in a large mirror, and then exclaimed with an ineffable out-burst of ecstasy :

" There was once upon a time a king and queen. Oh ! how delighted I am ! "

This said, she curtsied to Marius and Jean Valjean.

" There," she said, " I am going to install myself near you in an easy-chair ; we shall breakfast in half an hour. You will say all you like, for I know very well that gentlemen must talk, and I will be very good."

Marius took her by the arm and said to her lovingly :

" We are talking about business."

" By the way," Cosette answered, " I have opened my

window, and a number of *pierrots* (*sparrows* or *masks*) have just entered the garden. Birds, not masks. To-day is Ash Wednesday, but not for the birds."

" I tell you that we are talking of business, so go, my little Cosette, leave us for a moment. We are talking figures, and they would only annoy you."

" You have put on a charming cravat this morning, Marius. You are very coquettish, monseigneur. No, they will not annoy me."

" I assure you that they will."

" No, since it is you, I shall not understand you, but I shall hear you. When a woman hears voices she loves, she does not require to understand the words they say. To be together is all I want, and I shall stay with you,— there !"

" You are my beloved Cosette ! impossible."

" Impossible ! "

" Yes."

" Very good," Cosette remarked, " I should have told you some news. I should have told you that grandpapa is still asleep, that your aunt is at Mass, that the chimney of my papa Fauchelevent's room smokes, that Nicolette has sent for the chimney-sweep, that Nicolette and Toussaint have already quarrelled, and that Nicolette ridicules Toussaint's stammering. Well, you shall know nothing. Ah, it is impossible? you shall see, sir, that in my turn I shall say, It is impossible. Who will be caught then? I implore you, my little Marius, to let me stay here with you two."

" I assure you that we must be alone."

" Well, am I anybody ? "

Jean Valjean did not utter a word, and Cosette turned to him.

" In the first place, father, I insist on your coming and kissing me. What do you mean by saying nothing, instead of taking my part? Did one ever see a father like that? That will show you how unhappy marriage is, for my husband beats me. Come and kiss me at once."

Jean Valjean approached her, and Cosette turned to Marius.

" I make a face at you."

Then she offered her forehead to Jean Valjean, who moved a step towards her. All at once Cosette recoiled.

" Father, you are pale, does your arm pain you ? "

"It is cured," said Jean Valjean.

"Have you slept badly?"

"No."

"Are you sad?"

"No."

"Kiss me. If you are well, if you sleep soundly, if you are happy, I will not scold you."

And she again offered him her forehead, and Jean Valjean set a kiss on this forehead, upon which there was a heavenly reflection.

"Smile."

Jean Valjean obeyed, but it was the smile of a ghost.

"Now, defend me against my husband."

"Cosette——" said Marius.

"Be angry, father, and tell him I am to remain. You can talk before me. You must think me very foolish. What you are saying is very astonishing then! business, placing money in a bank, that is a great thing. Men make mysteries of nothing. I mean to stay. I am very pretty this morning. Marius, look at me."

And with an adorable shrug of the shoulders and an exquisite pout, she looked at Marius. Something like a flash passed between these two beings, and they cared little about a third party being present.

"I love you," said Marius.

"I adore you," said Cosette.

And they irresistibly fell into each other's arms.

"And now," Cosette continued, as she smoothed a crease in her gown with a little triumphant pout, "I remain."

"No," Marius replied imploringly, "we have something to finish."

"Again, no?"

Marius assumed a serious tone.

"I assure you, Cosette, that it is impossible."

"Ah, you are putting on your man's voice, sir; very good, I will go. You did not support me, father; and so you, my hard husband, and you, my dear papa, are tyrants. I shall go and tell grandpapa. If you believe that I intend to return and talk platitudes to you, you are mistaken. I am proud, and I intend to wait for you at present. You will see how wearisome it will be without me. I am going, very good."

And she left the room, but two seconds after the door

opened again, her fresh, rosy face passed once again between the two folding doors, and she cried to them :

" I am very anrgy."

The door closed again, and darkness returned. It was like a straggling sunbeam, which, without suspecting it, had suddenly traversed the night. Marius assured himself that the door was really closed.

" Poor Cosette," he muttered, " when she learns——"

At these words Jean Valjean trembled all over, and he fixed his haggard eyes on Marius.

"Cosette! oh, yes, it is true. You will tell Cosette about it. It is fair. Stay, I did not think of that. A man has strength for one thing, but not for another. I implore you, sir, I conjure you, sir, give me your most sacred word, do not tell her. Is it not sufficient for you to know it ? I was able to tell it of my own accord, without being compelled. I would have told it to the universe, to the whole world, and I should not have cared ; but she, she does not know what it is, and it would horrify her. A convict, what ! you would be obliged to explain to her ; tell her, It is a man who has been to the galleys. She saw the chain-gang once ; oh, my God ! "

He sank into a chair and buried his face in his hands ; it could not be heard, but from the heaving of his shoulders it could be seen that he was weeping. They were silent tears, terrible tears. There is a choking in the sob ; a species of convulsion seized on him, he threw himself back in the chair, letting his arms hang, and displaying to Marius his face bathed in tears, and Marius heard him mutter so low that his voice seemed to come from a bottomless abyss. "Oh ! I would like to die ! "

" Be at your ease," Marius said, " I will keep your secret to myself."

And, less affected than perhaps he ought to have been, but compelled for more than an hour to listen to unexpected horrors, gradually seeing a convict taking M. Fauchelevent's place, gradually overcome by this mournful reality, and led by the natural state of the situation to notice the gap which had formed between himself and this man, Marius added :

" It is impossible for me not to say a word about the trust money which you have so faithfully and honestly given up. That is an act of probity, and it is but fair that a reward should be given you ; fix the sum yourself, and it shall be paid you. Do not fear to fix it very high."

"I thank you, sir," Jean Valjean replied gently.

He remained pensive for a moment, mechanically passing the end of his forefinger over his thumb-nail, and then raised his voice :

"All is nearly finished ; there is only one thing left me."

"What is it ? "

Jean Valjean had a species of supreme agitation, and voicelessly, almost breathlessly, he stammered, rather than said :

"Now that you know, do you, sir, who are the master, believe that I ought not to see Cosette again ? "

"I believe that it would be better," Marius replied coldly.

"I will not see her again," Jean Valjean murmured. And he walked toward the door ; he placed his hand upon the handle, the door opened, Jean Valjean was going to pass out, when he suddenly closed it, then opened the door again, and returned to Marius. He was no longer pale, but livid ; and in his eyes there was a sort of tragic flame, instead of tears. His voice had grown strangely calm again.

"Stay, sir," he said, "if you like, I will come to see her ; for I assure you that I desire it greatly. If I had not longed to see Cosette I should not have made you the confession I have done, but have gone away ; but wishing to remain at the spot where Cosette is, and continue to see her, I was obliged to tell you everything honestly. You follow my reasoning, do you not ? it is a thing easy to understand. Look you, I have had her with me for nine years : we lived at first in that hovel on the boulevard, then in the convent, and then near the Luxembourg. It was there that you saw her for the first time, and you remember her blue plush bonnet. Next we went to the district of the Invalides, where there were a railway and a garden, the Rue Plumet. I lived in a little back yard where I could hear her pianoforte. Such was my life, and we never separated. That lasted nine years and seven months ; I was like her father, and she was my child. I do not know whether you understand me, M. Pontmercy, but it would be difficult to go away now, see her no more, speak to her no more, and have nothing left. If you have no objection I will come and see Cosette every now and then, but not too often, and I will not remain long. You can tell them to show me into the little room on the ground-floor ; I would certainly come in by the back door, which is used by the servants, but that might cause surprise, so it is better, I

think, for me to come by the front door. Really, sir, I
should like to see Cosette a little, but as rarely as you
please. Put yourself in my place, I have only that left.
And then, again, we must be careful, and if I did not come
at all it would have a bad effect, and appear singular. For
instance, what I can do is to come in the evening, when it
is beginning to grow dark."

"You can come every evening," said Marius, "and
Cosette will expect you."

"You are kind, sir," said Jean Valjean.

Marius bowed to Jean Valjean, happiness accompanied
despair to the door, and these two men parted.

Marius was completely unnerved. The kind of estrangement which he had ever felt for the man with whom he saw
Cosette was henceforth explained. There was in this person
something enigmatic, against which his instinct warned
him. This enigma was the most hideous of shames, the
galleys. This M. Fauchelevent was Jean Valjean, the
convict. To find suddenly such a secret in the midst of his
happiness is like discovering a scorpion in a turtle-dove's
nest. Was the happiness of Marius and Cosette in future
condensed to this proximity? was it an accomplished fact?
did the acceptance of this man form part of the consummated
marriage? could nothing else be done? Had Marius also
married the convict? Although a man may be crowned
with light and joy, though he be enjoying the grand hour
of life's purple, happy love, such shocks would compel even
the archangel in his ecstasy, even the demi-god in his glory,
to shudder.

As always happens in changes of view of this nature,
Marius asked himself whether he ought not to reproach
himself? Had he failed in divination? had he been deficient
in prudence? Had he voluntarily been headstrong? slightly
so, perhaps. Had he entered, without taking sufficient
precaution to light up the vicinity, upon this love-adventure,
which resulted in his marriage with Cosette? He verified
the visionary and chimerical side of his nature, a sort of
internal cloud peculiar to many organisations, and which in
the paroxysms of passion and grief expands, as the tempera-
ture of the soul changes, and invades the entire man to
such an extent that he merely becomes a conscience enveloped in a fog. We have more than once indicated this
characteristic element in Marius' individuality. He remembered that during the intoxication of his love in the Rue

Plumet, during those six or seven ecstatic weeks, he had not even spoken to Cosette about the drama in the Gorbeau hovel, during which the victim was so strangely silent both in the struggle and eventual escape. How was it that he had not spoken to Cosette about it? and yet it was so close and so frightful? how was it that he had not even mentioned the Thénardiers, and especially on the day when he met Eponine? He found almost a difficulty in explaining to himself now his silence at that period, but he was able to account for it. He remembered his confusion, his intoxica-tion for Cosette, his love absorbing everything, the carrying off of one by the other into the ideal world, and perhaps, too, as the imperceptible amount of reason mingled with that violent and charming state of the mind, a vague and dull instinct to hide and efface in his memory that formidable adventure with which he feared contact, in which he wished to play no part, from which he stood aloof, and of which he could not be narrator or witness without being an accuser. Moreover, these few weeks had been a flash, and they had formed him for nothing, save loving. In short, when all was revolved, and everything examined, supposing that he had described the Gorbeau trap to Cosette, had mentioned the Thénardiers to her, what would have been the conse-quence, even if he had discovered than Jean Valjean was a convict; would that have changed him, Marius, or his Cosette? Would he have shrunk back? Would he have loved her less? Would he have refused to marry her? No. Would it have made any change in what had happened? No. There was nothing, therefore, to regret, nothing to reproach, and all was well. There is a God for those drunkards who are called lovers, and Marius had blindly followed the road which he had selected with his eyes open. Love had bandaged his eyes to lead him whither?—to paradise.

But this paradise was henceforth complicated by an infernal proximity, and the old estrangement of Marius for this man, for this Fauchelevent who had become Jean Valjean, was at present mingled with horror. Yet in this horror, let us say it, there was some pity, and even a certain degree of surprise. This robber, this relapsed robber, had restored a deposit, and what a deposit? six hundred thousand francs. He alone held the secret of that deposit, he could have kept it all, but he gave it all up. Moreover, he had revealed his situation of his own accord, nothing compelled him to do so, and if he, Marius, knew who he was it was through himself. There was in this confession more than the acceptance of humiliation, there was the acceptance of peril. For a condemned man a mask is not a mask, but a shelter, and he had renounced that shelter. A false name is a security, and he had thrown away that false name. He, the galley-slave, could conceal himself for ever in an honest family, and he had resisted that temptation, and for what motive? through scruples of conscience. He had explained himself with the irresistible accent of truth. In short, whoever this Jean Valjean might be, his was incontestably an awakened conscience. Such attacks of justice and honesty do not belong to vulgar natures, and an awakening of the conscience is greatness of soul. Jean Valjean was sincere, and this sincerity, visible, palpable, irrefragable, and evident in the grief which it caused him, rendered his statements valuable, and gave authority to all that this man said. Here, for Marius, was a strange inversion of situations. What issued from M. Fauchelevent? distrust: what was disengaged from Jean Valjean? confidence. In the mysterious balance-sheet of this Jean Valjean which Marius mentally drew up, he verified the credit, he verified the debit, and tried to arrive at a balance. But all this was as in a storm; Marius striving to form a distinct idea of this man, and pursuing Jean Valjean, so to speak, to the bottom of his thoughts, lost him, and found him again in a fatal mist.

The honest restoration of the trust-money and the probity of the confession were good, and formed as it were a break in the cloud; but then the cloud became black again. However confused Marius' reminiscences might be, some shadows still returned to him. What, after all, was that adventure in the Jondrette garret? why on the arrival of the police did that man, instead of complaining, escape? here Marius found the answer,—because this man was a convict who had broken his ban. Another question, Why did this man come to the barricade? for at present Marius distinctly saw again that recollection, which reappeared in his emotions like sympathetic ink before the fire. This man was at the barricade, and did not fight, what did he want there? Before this question a spectre rose, and gave the answer, Javert. Marius perfectly remembered now the mournful vision of Jean Valjean dragging the bound Javert out of the barricade, and heard again behind the angle of

the little Mondétour lane the frightful pistol-shot. There
was, probably, a hatred between this spy and this galley-
slave ; the one annoyed the other. Jean Valjean went to
the barricade to revenge himself ; he arrived late, and was
probably aware that Javert was a prisoner there. Corsican
vendetta has penetrated certain lower strata of society, and
is the law with them ; it is so simple that it does not
astonish minds which have half returned to virtue, and
their hearts are so constituted that a criminal, when on the
path of repentance, may be scrupulous as to a robbery, and
not so as to vengeance. Jean Valjean had killed Javert,
or, at least, that seemed evident. The last question of all
admitted of no reply, and this question Marius felt like a
pair of pincers. How was it that the existence of Jean
Valjean had so long elbowed that of Cosette ? What was
this gloomy sport of Providence which had brought this
man and this child in contact ? are there chains for two
forged in heaven, and does God take pleasure in coupling
the angel with the demon ? a crime and an innocence can,
then, be chamber companions in the mysterious hulks of
misery ? In that defile of condemned men which is called
human destiny, two foreheads may pass along side by side,
one simple, the other formidable—one all bathed in the
divine whiteness of dawn, the other eternally branded ?
Who could have attached the lamb to the wolf, and, even
more incomprehensible still, the wolf to the lamb ? for the
wolf loved the lamb, the ferocious being adored the weak
being, and for nine years the angel had leant on the
monster for support. The childhood and maidenhood of
Cosette, and her virgin growth toward life and light, had
been protected by this deformed devotion. What, was this
Valjean carrying on the education of Cosette ? what was
this figure of darkness, whose care it was to preserve from
every shadow and every cloud the rising of a star ?

That was Jean Valjean's secret ; that was also God's
secret, and Marius recoiled before this double secret. God
has His instruments, and employs whom He likes as tool,
and is not responsible to him. Do we know how God sets
to work ? Jean Valjean had laboured on Cosette. and had
to some extent formed her mind, that was incontestable.
Well, what then ? The workman was horrible, but the
work was admirable, and God produces His miracles as He
thinks proper. He had constructed this charming Cosette
and employed Jean Valjean on the job, and it had pleased

him to choose this strange assistant. What explanation
have we to ask of Him? is it the first time that manure has
helped spring to produce the rose? Marius gave himself
these answers, and declared to himself that they were good.
On all the points which we have indicated he had not dared
to press Jean Valjean, though he did not confess to himself
that he dared not. In whatever circle of ideas Marius
might turn, he always came back to a certain horror of
Jean Valjean ; a sacred horror, perhaps, for, as we have
stated, he felt a *quid divinum* in this man. But, though it
was so, and whatever extenuating circumstances he might
seek, he was always compelled to fall back on this : he was
a convict, that is to say, a being who has not even a place
on the social ladder, being beneath the lowest rung.
Marius, in penal matters, democrat though he was, still
adhered to the inexorable system, and he entertained all
the ideas of the law about those whom the law strikes. He
had not yet made every progress, we are forced to say ; he
had not yet learned to distinguish between what is written
by man and what is written by God, between the law and
the right. He had examined and weighed the claim which
man sets up to dispose of the irrevocable, the irreparable ;
and the word vengeance was not repulsive to him. He
considered it simple that certain breaches of the written law
should be followed by eternal penalties, and he accepted
social condemnation as a civilising process. He was still
at this point, though infallibly certain to advance at a later
date, for his nature was good, and entirely composed of
latent progress.

In this medium of ideas Jean Valjean appeared to him
deformed and repelling, for he was the punished man, the
convict. This word was to him like the sound of the trumpet
of the last judgment, and after regarding Jean Valjean for
a long time, his last gesture was to turn away his head—
vade retrò. Marius, we must recognise the fact and lay
stress on it, while questioning Jean Valjean to such an
extent that Jean Valjean himself said, " You are shriving
me," had not, however, asked him two or three important
questions. It was not that they had not presented themselves to his mind, but he had been afraid of them. The
Jondrette garret ? the barricade ? Javert ? Who knew where
the revelations might have stopped ? Jean Valjean did not
seem the man to recoil, and who knows whether Marius,
after urging him on, might not have wished to check him ?

In certain supreme conjunctures has it not happened to all
of us that after asking a question we have stopped our ears,
in order not to hear the answer? a man is specially guilty
of such an act of cowardice when he is in love. It is not
wise to drive sinister situations into a corner, especially when
the indissoluble side of our own life is fatally mixed up with
them. What a frightful light might issue from Jean
Valjean's desperate explanations, and who knows whether
that hideous brightness might not have been reflected on
Cosette? Whether rightly or wrongly, Marius was terrified,
for he already knew too much, and he had rather to blind
than to enlighten himself. He wildly bore off Cosette in
his arms, closing his eyes upon Jean Valjean. In this state
of mind it was a crushing perplexity for Márius to think
that henceforth this man would have any contact with
Cosette; and he now almost reproached himself for not
having asked these formidable questions before which he
had recoiled, and from which an implacable and definitive
decision might have issued. He considered himself too kind,
too gentle, and, let us say it, too weak; and the weakness
had led him to make a fatal concession. He had allowed
himself to be affected, and had done wrong; he ought
simply and purely to have rejected Jean Valjean. Jean
Valjean was an incendiary, and he ought to have freed his
house from the presence of this man. He was angry with
himself, he was angry with that whirlwind of emotions
which had deafened, blinded, and carried him away. He
was dissatisfied with himself.

What was he to do now? the visits of Jean Valjean were
most deeply repulsive to him. Of what use was it that this
man should come to his house? what did he want here?
Here he refused to investigate the matter, he refused to
study; and he was unwilling to probe his own heart. He
had promised, he had allowed himself to be drawn into
a promise: Jean Valjean held that promise, and he must
keep his word even with a convict,—above all with a convict.
Still his first duty was toward Cosette; and a word, a
repulsion, which overcame everything else, caused him
a loathing. Marius confusedly revolved all these ideas in
his mind, passing from one to the other, and shaken by all.
Hence arose a deep trouble, which it was not easy to conceal
from Cosette, but love is a talent, and Marius succeeded
in doing it. However, he asked, without any apparent
motive, some questions of Cosette, who was as candid

as a dove is white, and suspected nothing ; he spoke to her of her childhood and her youth, and he convinced himself more and more that this convict had been to Cosette as good, paternal, and respectful as a man can be. All that Marius had dimly seen and conjectured was real. This darkly, mysterious nettle had loved and protected this lily.

CHAPTER CXVII.

THE next day, at nightfall, Jean Valjean tapped at the gateway of the Gillenormand mansion, and it was Basque who received him. Basque was in the yard at the appointed time, as if he had had his orders. It sometimes happens that people say to a servant, "You will watch for Mr. So-and-So's arrival." Basque, without waiting for Jean Valjean to come up to him, said :

"Monsieur le Baron has instructed me to ask you, sir, whether you wish to go upstairs or stay down here ? "

"Stay down here," Jean Valjean replied.

Basque, who, however, was perfectly respectful in his manner, opened the door of the ground-floor room, and said, "I will go and inform her ladyship." The room which Jean Valjean entered was a damp, arched, basement room, employed as a cellar at times, looking out on the street, with a flooring of red tiles, and badly lighted by an iron-barred window. This room was not one of those which are harassed by the broom and mop, and the dust was quiet there. The room, which was small and low-ceilinged, was furnished with a pile of empty bottles collected in a corner. The wall, covered with a yellow ochre wash, crumbled off in large patches ; at the end was a mantelpiece of black wood, with a narrow shelf, and a fire was lighted in it, which indicated that Jean Valjean's reply "remain down here" had been calculated on. Two chairs were placed, one in each chimney-corner, and between the chairs was spread, in guise of carpet, an old bedroom rug, which displayed more cord than wool. The room was illumined by the flickering of the fire, and the twilight through the window. Jean Valjean was fatigued, for several days he had not eaten or slept, and he fell into one of the arm-chairs. Basque returned, placed a lighted candle on the mantelpiece, and withdrew. Jean Valjean, who was sitting with hanging head, did not notice either Basque or the candle, till all at once he started up, for Cosette was behind him: he had not seen her come in, but he felt that she was coming. He turned round and contemplated her; she was adorably lovely. But what he gazed at with this profound glance was not the beauty but the soul.

"Well, father," Cosette exclaimed, "I knew that you were singular, but I could never have expected this. What an idea! Marius told me that it was your wish to see me here."

"Yes, it is."

"I expected that answer, and I warn you that I am going to have a scene with you. Let us begin with the beginning: kiss me, father."

And she offered her cheek, but Jean Valjean remained motionless.

"You do not stir, I mark the fact! it is the attitude of a culprit. But I do not care, I forgive you. Christ said, 'Offer the other cheek'; here it is."

And she offered the other cheek, but Jean Valjean did not stir; it seemed as if his feet were riveted to the floor.

"Things are growing serious," said Cosette. "What have I done to you? I am offended, and you must make it up with me; you will dine with us?"

"I have dined."

"That is not true, and I will have you scolded by M. Gillenormand. Grandfathers are made to lay down the law to fathers. Come, go with me to the drawing-room. At once."

"Impossible."

Cosette here lost a little ground; she ceased to order and began questioning.

"But why? and you choose the ugliest room in the house to see me in. It is horrible here."

"You know, Cosette——" Jean Valjean broke off. "You know, madame, that I am peculiar, and have my fancies."

"Madame—*you* know—more novelties; what does this all mean?"

Jean Valjean gave her that heart-broken smile to which he sometimes had recourse.

"You wished to be a lady, and are one."

"Not for you, father."

"Do not call me father."

"What?"

"Call me Monsieur Jean, or Jean, if you like "

"You are no longer father? I am no longer Cosette?
Monsieur Jean? why, what does it mean? These are
revolutions. What has happened? Look me in the face,
if you can. And you will not live with us! and you will
not accept our bedroom! What have I done to offend you?
Oh, what have I done? there must be something."

"Nothing."

"In that case then?"

"All is as usual."

"Why do you change your name?'

"You have changed yours."

He smiled the same smile again, and added:

"Since you are Madame Pontmercy, I may fairly be
Monsieur Jean."

"I do not understand anything, and all this is idiotic.
I will ask my husband's leave for you to be Monsieur Jean,
and I hope that he will not consent. You cause me great
sorrow, and though you may have whims, you have no
right to make your little Cosette grieve. That is wrong,
and you have no right to be naughty, for you are so good."

As he made no reply, she seized both his hands eagerly,
and with an irresistible movement raising them to her face,
she pressed them against her neck under her chin, which
is a profound sign of affection.

"Oh," she said, "be kind to me." And she continued:

"This is what I call being kind; to behave yourself,
come and live here, for there are birds here as in the
Rue Plumet; to live with us, leave that hole in the Rue
de l'Homme Armé, give us no more riddles to guess; to be
like everybody else, dine with us, breakfast with us, and
be my father."

He removed her hands:

"You no longer want a father, as you have a husband."

Cosette broke out:

"I no longer want a father! things like that have no
common sense, and I really do not know what to say."

"If Toussaint were here," Jean Valjean continued, like
a man seeking authorities and who clings to every branch;
"she would be the first to allow that I have always had
strange ways of my own. There is nothing new in it, for
I always loved my dark corner."

"But it is cold here, and we cannot see distinctly, and it
is abominable to wish to be Monsieur Jean, and I shall not
allow you to call me madame."

"As I was coming along just now," Jean Valjean replied, "I saw a very pretty piece of furniture at a cabinet-maker's in the Rue St. Louis. If I were a pretty woman, I should treat myself to it. It is a very nice toilet-table in the present fashion, made of rosewood, I think you call it, and inlaid. There is a rather large glass with drawers, and it is very nice."

"Hou! the ugly bear!" Cosette replied. And clenching her teeth, and parting her lips in the most graceful way possible, she blew at Jean Valjean; it was a Grace copying a cat.

"I am furious," she went on, "and since yesterday you have all put me in a passion. I do not understand it at all; you do not defend me against Marius, Marius does not take my part against you, and I am all alone. I have a nice room prepared, and if I could have put le bon Dieu in it, I would have done so; but my room is left on my hands and my lodger deserts me. I order Nicolette to prepare a nice little dinner, and—they will not touch your dinner, madame. And my father Fauchelevent wishes me to call him Monsieur Jean, and that I should receive him in a frightful old, ugly, mildewed cellar, in which the walls wear a beard, and empty bottles represent the looking-glasses, and spiders' webs the curtains. I allow that you are a singular man, it is your way, but a truce is granted to a newly-married woman; and you ought not to have begun to be singular again so soon. You are going to be very satisfied, then, in your Rue de l'Homme Armé; well, I was very wretched there. What have I done to offend you? you cause me great sorrow. Fie!"

And, suddenly growing serious, she looked intently at Jean Valjean and added:

"You are angry with me for being happy, is that it?"

Simplicity sometimes penetrates unconsciously very deep, and this question, simple for Cosette, was profound for Jean Valjean. Cosette wished to scratch, but she tore. Jean Valjean turned pale, he remained for a moment without answering, and then murmured with an indescribable accent, and speaking to himself:

"Her happiness was the object of my life, and at present God may order my departure. Cosette, thou art happy, and my course is run."

"Ah! you said 'thou' to me," Cosette exclaimed, and leaped on his neck.

Jean Valjean wildly strained her to his heart, for he felt as if he were almost taking her back again.

"Thank you, father," Cosette said to him.

The excitement was getting too painful for Jean Valjean ; he gently withdrew himself from Cosette's arms, and took up his hat.

"Well?" said Cosette.

Jean Valjean replied :

"I am going to leave you, madame, as you will be missed."

And on the threshold he added :

"I said to you 'thou'; tell your husband that it shall not happen again. Forgive me."

Jean Valjean left Cosette stupefied by this enigmatical leave-taking.

The following day, at the same hour, Jean Valjean came. Cosette asked him no questions, was no longer astonished, no longer exclaimed that it was cold, no longer alluded to the drawing-room ; she avoided saying either father or Monsieur Jean. She allowed herself to be called madame ; there was only a diminution of her delight perceptible, and she would have been sad, had sorrow been possible. It is probable that she had held with Marius one of those conversations in which the beloved man says what he wishes, explains nothing, and satisfies the beloved woman ; for the curiosity of lovers does not extend far beyond their love. The basement room had been furbished up a little ; Basque had suppressed the bottles, and Nicolette the spiders. Every following day brought Jean Valjean back at the same hour ; he came daily, as he had not the strength to take Marius' permission otherwise than literally. Marius arranged so as to be absent at the hour when Jean Valjean came, and the house grew accustomed to M. Fauchelevent's new mode of behaving. Toussaint helped in it ; "My master was always so," she repeated. The grandfather issued this decree—"He is an original"; and everything was said. Moreover, at the age of ninety no connection is possible ; everything is juxtaposition, and a new-comer is in the way ; there is no place for him, for habits are unalterably formed. Nobody caught a glimpse of the nether gloom.

Several weeks passed thus. A new life gradually took possession of Cosette. The relations which marriage creates, visits, the management of the household, and pleasures, that great business. The pleasures of Cosette were not costly, they consisted in only one, being with Marius. To go out with him, remain at home with him, was the great occupation of her life. It was for them an ever novel joy to go out arm in arm, in the sunshine, in the open streets, without hiding themselves, in the face of everybody. Cosette had one vexation, Toussaint could not agree with Nicolette (for the welding of the two old maids was impossible), and left. The grandfather was quite well; Marius had a few briefs now and then; Aunt Gillenormand peacefully lived with the married pair that lateral life which sufficed her, and Jean Valjean came daily. The madame and the Monsieur Jean, however, made him different to Cosette, and the care he had himself taken to detach himself from her succeeded. She was more and more gay, and less and less affectionate, and yet she loved him dearly still, and he felt it. One day she suddenly said to him, "You were my father, you are no longer my father; you were my uncle, you are no longer my uncle; you were Monsieur Fauchelevent, and are now Jean. Who are you then? I do not like all this. If I did not know you to be so good, I should be afraid of you." He still lived in the Rue de l'Homme Armé, as he could not resolve to remove from the quarter in which Cosette lived. At first he only stayed a few minutes with Cosette, and then went away, but by degrees he grew into the habit of making his visits longer. It might be said that he took advantage of the lengthening days; he arrived sooner and went away later. One day, the word father slipped over Cosette's lips, and a gleam of joy lit up Jean Valjean's old solemn face, but he chided her: "Say Jean."

"Ah, that is true," she replied, with a burst of laughter, "Monsieur Jean."

"That is right," he said, and he turned away that she might not see him wipe a tear from his eyes.

This was the last occasion. After this last gleam complete extinction took place. There was no more familiarity, no more good-day with a kiss, and never again that so deeply tender word "father." He had been, at his own request and with his own complicity, expelled from all those joys in succession, and he underwent this misery, that, after losing Cosette entirely in one day, he was then obliged to lose her again bit by bit. The eye eventually grows accustomed to cellar light, and he found it enough to have an apparition of Cosette daily. His whole life was concentrated in that hour; he sat down by her side, looked at her in silence, or else talked to her about former years, her childhood, the convent, and her little friends of those days. One afternoon —it was an early day in April, already warm, but still fresh, the moment of the sun's great gaiety—Marius said to Cosette, "We said that we would go and see our garden in the Rue Plumet again. Come, we must not be ungrateful." And they flew off like two swallows toward the spring. This garden in the Rue Plumet produced on them the effect of a dawn, for they already had behind them in life something that resembled the spring-time of their love. The house in the Rue Plumet, being taken on lease, still belonged to Cosette; they went to this garden and house, found themselves again, and forgot themselves there. In the evening Jean Valjean went to the Rue des Filles du Calvaire at the usual hour. "My lady went out with the baron," said Basque, "and has not returned yet." He sat down silently and waited an hour, but Cosette did not come in; he hung his head and went away. Cosette was so intoxicated by the walk in "their garden," and so pleased at having "lived a whole day in her past," that she spoke of nothing else the next day. She did not remark that she had not seen Jean Valjean.

"How did you go there?" Jean Valjean asked her.

"On foot."

"And how did you return?"

"On foot too."

For some time Jean Valjean had noticed the close life which the young couple led, and was annoyed at it. Marius' economy was strict, and that word had its absolute meaning with Jean Valjean; he hazarded a question.

"Why do you not keep a carriage? A little coupé would not cost you more than five hundred francs a month, and you are rich."

"I do not know," Cosette answered.

"It is the same with Toussaint," Jean Valjean continued; "she has left, and you have engaged no one in her place. Why not?"

"Nicolette is sufficient."

"But you must want a lady's-maid?"

"Have I not Marius?"

"You ought to have a house of your own, servants of your own, a carriage, and a box at the opera. Nothing is too good for you. Then why not take advantage of the fact of your being rich? Wealth adds to happiness."

Cosette made no reply. Jean Valjean's visits did not grow shorter, on the contrary, for when it is the heart that is slipping, a man does not stop on the incline. When Jean Valjean wished to prolong his visit and make the hour be forgotten, he sung the praises of Marius, he found him handsome, noble, brave, witty, eloquent, and good. Cosette added to the praise, and Jean Valjean began again. It was an inexhaustible subject, and there were volumes in the six letters composing Marius' name. In this way Jean Valjean managed to stop for a long time, for it was so sweet to see Cosette, and forget by her side. It was a dressing for his wound. It frequently happened that Basque would come and say twice,—"M. Gillenormand has sent me to remind Madame la Baronne that dinner is waiting." On those days Jean Valjean would return home very thoughtful. Was there any truth in that comparison of the chrysalis which had occurred to Marius' mind? Was Jean Valjean really an obstinate chrysalis, constantly paying visits to his butterfly? One day he remained longer than usual ; the next day he noticed there was no fire in the grate. "Stay," he thought, "no fire?"—and he gave himself this explanation—"It is very simple ; we are in April, and the cold weather has passed."

"Good gracious ! how cold it is here !" Cosette exclaimed as she came in.

"Oh no," said Jean Valjean.

"Then it was you who told Basque not to light a fire?"

"Yes ; we shall have May here directly."

"But fires keep on till June ; in this cellàr there ought to be one all the year round."

"I thought it was unnecessary."

"That is just like one of your ideas," Cosette remarked.

The next day there was a fire, but the two chairs were placed at the other end of the room, near the door. "What is the meaning of that?" Jean Valjean thought ; he fetched the chairs and placed them in their usual place near the chimney. This rekindled fire, however, encouraged him, and he made the conversation last even longer than usual. As he rose to leave Cosette remarked to him :

'My husband said a funny thing to me yesterday."

"What was it?"

"He said to me, 'Cosette, we have thirty thousand

francs a year,—twenty-seven of yours, and three that my grandfather allows me.' I replied, 'That makes thirty;' and he continued, 'Would you have the courage to live on the three thousand?' I answered, 'Yes, on nothing, provided that it be with you;' and then I asked him, 'Why did you say that to me?' He replied, 'I merely wished to know.'"

Jean Valjean had not a word to say. Cosette probably expected some explanation from him, but he listened to her in a sullen silence. He went back to the Rue de l'Homme Armé, and was so profoundly abstracted that, instead of entering his own house, he went into the next one. It was not till he had gone up nearly two flights of stairs that he noticed his mistake, and came down again. His mind was crammed with conjectures; it was evident that Marius entertained doubts as to the origin of the six hundred thousand francs, that he feared some impure source; he might even, who knew? have discovered that this money came from him, Jean Valjean; that he hesitated to touch this suspicious fortune, and was repugnant to use it as his own, preferring that Cosette and he should remain poor than be rich with dubious wealth. Moreover, Jean Valjean was beginning to feel himself shown to the door. On the following day he had a species of shock on entering the basement room; the fauteuils had disappeared, and there was not even a seat of any sort.

"Dear me, no chairs," Cosette exclaimed on entering; "where are they?"

"They are no longer here," Jean Valjean replied.

"That is rather too much."

Jean Valjean stammered:

"I told Basque to remove them."

"For what reason?"

"I shall only remain a few minutes to-day."

"Few or many, that is no reason for standing."

"I believe that Basque required the chairs for the drawing-room."

"Why?"

"You have probably company this evening."

"Not a soul."

Jean Valjean had not another word to say, and Cosette shrugged her shoulders.

"Have the chairs removed! The other day you ordered the fire to be left off! How singular you are!"

"Good-bye," Jean Valjean murmured.

He did not say, "Good-bye, Cosette," but he had not the strength to say, "Good-bye, madame."

He went away, crushed, for this time he had comprehended. The next day he did not come, and Cosette did not remark this till the evening.

"Dear me," she said, "Monsieur Jean did not come to-day."

She felt a slight pang at the heart, but she scarce noticed it, as she was at once distracted by a kiss from Marius. The next day he did not come either. Cosette paid no attention to this, spent the evening, and slept at night as usual, and only thought of it when she woke; she was so happy! She very soon sent Nicolette to Monsieur Jean's to see whether he were ill, and why he had not come to see her on the previous day, and Nicolette brought back Monsieur Jean's answer. "He was not ill, but was busy, and would come soon, as soon as he could. But he was going to make a little journey, and madame would remember that he was accustomed to do so every now and then. She need not feel at all alarmed or trouble herself about him." Nicolette, on entering Monsieur Jean's room, had repeated to him her mistress' exact words,—"That madame sent to know 'why Monsieur Jean had not called on the previous day?'"

"I have not called for two days," Jean Valjean said quietly. The observation escaped the notice of Nicolette, who reported nothing of it to Cosette.

CHAPTER CXVIII.

DURING the last months of spring and the early months of summer, 1833, the scattered wayfarers in the Marais, the shopkeepers, and the idlers in the doorways, noticed an old gentleman, decently dressed in black, who every day, at nearly the same hour in the evening, left the Rue de l'Homme Armé, in the direction of the Rue Sainte Croix de la Bretonnerie, passed in front of the Blancs Manteaux, reached the Rue Culture Sainte Catharine, and on coming to the Rue de l'Echarpe, turned to his left and entered the Rue St. Louis. There he walked slowly, with head stretched forward, seeing nothing, hearing nothing, with his eye incessantly fixed on a spot which always seemed his

magnet, and which was nought else than the corner of the
Rue des Filles du Calvaire. The nearer he came to this
corner, the more brightly his eye flashed, a sort of joy
illumined his eyeballs, like an internal dawn ; he had a
fascinated and affectionate air, his lips made obscure movements as if speaking to some one whom he could not see,
he smiled vaguely, and he advanced as slowly as he could.
It seemed as if, while wishing to arrive, he was afraid of
the moment when he came quite close. When he had only
a few houses between himself and the street which appeared
to attract him, his step became so slow that at moments he
seemed not to be moving at all. The vacillation of his head
and the fixedness of his eye suggested the needle seeking
the pole. Whatever time he might make his arrival last,
he must arrive in the end ; when he reached the corner of
the Rue des Filles du Calvaire, he trembled, thrust his head
with a species of gloomy timidity beyond the corner of the
last house, and looked into this street, and there was in
this glance something that resembled the bewilderment of
the impossible and the reflection of a closed paradise. Then
a tear, which had been gradually collecting in the corner
of his eyelashes, having grown large enough to fall, glided
down his cheeks, and sometimes stopped at his mouth.
The old man tasted its bitter flavour. He stood thus for
some minutes as if he were of stone ; then returned by the
same road, at the same pace, and the farther he got away
the more lustreless his eye became.

By degrees this old man ceased going as far as the corner
of the Rue des Filles du Calvaire ; he stopped half-way in
the Rue St. Louis ; at times a little farther off, at times a
little nearer. One day he stopped at the corner of the Rue
Culture Sainte Catharine and gazed at the Rue des Filles
du Calvaire from a distance ; then he silently shook his
head from right to left, as if refusing himself something,
and turned back. Ere long he did not reach even the Rue
St. Louis ; he arrived at the Rue Pavie, shook his head,
and turned back ; then he did not go beyond the Rue des
Trois Pavillons ; and then he did not pass the Blancs
Manteaux. He seemed like a clock which was not wound
up, and whose oscillations grow shorter and shorter till they
stop. Every day he left his house at the same hour, undertook the same walk, but did not finish it, and incessantly
shortened it, though probably unconscious of the fact. His
whole countenance expressed this sole idea, Of what good

is it ? His eyes were lustreless, and there was no radiance
in them. The tears were also dried up ; they no longer
collected in the corner of his eyelashes, and this pensive eye
was dry. The old man's head was still thrust forward ; the
chin moved at times, and the creases in his thin neck were
painful to look on. At times, when the weather was bad,
he had an umbrella under his arm, which he never opened.
The good women of the district said, " He is an innocent,"
and the children followed him, laughing.

It is a terrible thing to be happy ! How pleased we are
with it ! how all-sufficient we find it ! how, when possessed
of the false object of life, happiness, we forget the true one,
duty ! We are bound to say, however, that it would be
unjust to accuse Marius. Marius, as we have explained,
before his marriage asked no questions of M. Fauchelevent,
and since had been afraid to ask any of Jean Valjean. He
had regretted the promise which he had allowed to be drawn
from him, and had repeatedly said to himself that he had
done wrong in making this concession to despair. He had
restricted himself to gradually turning Jean Valjean out of
his house, and effacing him as far as possible from Cosette's
mind. He had to some extent constantly stationed himself
between Cosette and Jean Valjean, feeling certain that in
this way she would not perceive it, or think of it. It was
more than an effacement, it was an eclipse. Marius did
what he considered necessary and just ; he believed that he
had serious reasons, some of which we have seen, and some
we have yet to see, for getting rid of Jean Valjean, without
harshness, but without weakness. Chance having made
him acquainted, in a trial in which he was retained, with
an ex-clerk of Laffitte's bank, he had obtained, without
seeking it, mysterious information, which, in truth, he had
not been able to examine, through respect for the secret he
had promised to keep, and through regard for Jean Valjean's
perilous situation. He believed, at this very moment, that
he had a serious duty to perform, the restitution of the six
hundred thousand francs to some one whom he was seeking
as discreetly as he could. In the meanwhile, he abstained
from touching that money.

As for Cosette, she was not acquainted with any of these
secrets ; but it would be harsh to condemn her also.
Between Marius and her there was an omnipotent
magnetism, which made her do instinctively, and almost
mechanically, whatever Marius wished. She felt a wish of

Marius in the matter of Monsieur Jean, and she conformed to it.   Her husband had said nothing to her, but she underwent the vague but clear presence of his tacit intentions, and blindly obeyed.   Her obedience in this case consisted in not remembering what Marius forgot; and she had no effort to make in doing so.   Without her knowing why, her mind had so thoroughly become that of her husband, that whatever covered itself with a shadow in Marius' thoughts was obscured in hers.   Let us not go too far, however; as regards Jean Valjean, this effacement and this forgetfulness were only superficial; and she was thoughtless rather than forgetful.   In her heart she truly loved the man whom she had so long called father, but she loved her husband more, and this had slightly falsified the balance of this heart, which weighed down on one side only.   It happened at times that Cosette would speak of Jean Valjean and express her surprise, and then Marius would calm her.   "He is away, I believe; did he not say that he was going on a journey?"—"That is true," Cosette thought, "he used to disappear like that, but not for so long a time."   Twice or thrice she sent Nicolette to inquire in the Rue de l'Homme Armé whether Monsieur Jean had returned from his tour, and Jean Valjean sent answer in the negative.   Cosette asked no more, as she had on earth but one want, Marius.   Let us also say that Marius and Cosette had been absent too.   They went to Vernon, and Marius took Cosette to his father's tomb.   Marius had gradually abstracted Cosette from Jean Valjean, and Cosette had allowed it.   However, what is called much too harshly in certain cases the ingratitude of children is not always so reprehensible a thing as may be believed.

One day Jean Valjean went downstairs, took three steps in the street, sat down upon a stone block, the same one on which Gavroche had found him sitting in thought on the night of June 5th; he stayed there a few minutes, and then went up again.   This was the last oscillation of the pendulum; the next day he did not leave his room; the next to that he did not leave his bed.   The porter's wife, who prepared his poor meals for him, some cabbage or a few potatoes and a little bacon, looked at the brown earthenware plate, and exclaimed:

"Why, poor dear man, you ate nothing yesterday."

"Yes, I did," Jean Valjean answered.

"The plate is quite full."

"Look at the water-jug : it is empty."

"That proves that you have drunk, but does not prove that you have eaten."

"Well," said Jean Valjean, "suppose that I only felt hungry for water?"

"That is called thirst, and if a man does not eat at the same time it is called fever."

"I will eat to-morrow."

"Or on Trinity Sunday. Why not to-day? Whoever thought of saying, I will eat to-morrow? To leave my plate without touching it ; my rashers were so good."

Jean Valjean took the old woman's hand.

"I promise you to eat them," he said in his gentle voice.

"I am not pleased with you," the woman replied.

Jean Valjean never saw any other human creature but this good woman : there are in Paris streets through which people never pass, and houses which people never enter, and he lived in one of those streets and one of those houses. During the time when he still went out he had bought at a brazier's for a few sous a small copper crucifix, which he suspended from a nail opposite his bed ; that gibbet is ever good to look on. A week passed thus, and Jean Valjean still remained in bed. The porter's wife said to her husband, "The old gentleman upstairs does not get up, he does not eat, and he will not last long. He has a sorrow, and no one will get it out of my head but that his daughter has made a bad match."

The porter replied, with the accent of marital sovereignty :

"If he is rich, he can have a doctor ; if he is not rich, he can't. If he has no doctor, he will die."

"And if he has one?"

"He will die," said the porter.

The porter's wife began digging up with an old knife the grass between what she called her pavement, and while doing so grumbled :

"It's a pity. An old man who is so clean. He is as white as a pullet."

She saw a doctor belonging to the quarter passing along the bottom of the street, and took upon herself to ask him to go up.

"It's on the second floor," she said ; "you will only have to go in, for, as the old gentleman no longer leaves his bed, the key is always in the door."

The physician saw Jean Valjean and spoke to him :

when he came down again the porter's wife was waiting
for him.

" Well, doctor ? "

" He is very ill."

"What is the matter with him ? "

" Everything and nothing. He is a man who, from all
appearances, has lost a beloved person. People die of
that."

" What did he say to you ? "

" He told me that he was quite well."

"Will you call again, doctor ? "

" Yes," the physician replied ; "but another than I must
come too."

One evening Jean Valjean had a difficulty in rising on
his elbow ; he took hold of his wrist and could not find his
pulse ; his breathing was short, and stopped every now and
then, and he perceived that he was weaker than he had ever
yet been. Then, doubtless under the pressure of some
supreme desire, he made an effort, sat up, and dressed
himself. He put on his old workman's clothes ; for, as he
no longer went out, he had returned to them and preferred
them. He was compelled to pause several times while
dressing himself ; and the perspiration poured off his forehead, merely through the effort of putting on his jacket.
Ever since he had been alone he had placed his bed in the
anteroom, so as to occupy as little as possible of the deserted
apartments. He opened the valise, and took out Cosette's
clothing, which he spread on his bed. The Bishop's candlesticks were at their place on the mantelpiece ; he took two
wax candles out of a drawer and put them up, and then,
though it was broad summer daylight, he lit them. We
sometimes see candles lighted thus in open day in rooms
where dead men are lying. Each step he took in going
from one article of furniture to another exhausted him, and
he was obliged to sit down. It was not ordinary fatigue,
which expends the strength in order to renew it ; it was the
remnant of possible motion ; it was exhausted life falling
drop by drop in crushing efforts which will not be made
again.

One of the chairs on which he sank was placed near the
mirror, so fatal for him, so providential for Marius, in which
he had read Cosette's reversed writing on the blotting-book.
He saw himself in this mirror, and could not recognise
himself. He was eighty years of age ; before Marius'

marriage he had looked scarce fifty, but the last year had reckoned as thirty. What he had on his forehead was no longer the wrinkle of age, but the mysterious mark of death, and the laceration of the pitiless nail could be traced on it. His cheeks were flaccid, the skin of his face had that colour which leads to the belief that there is already earth upon it ; the two corners of his mouth drooped as in that mask which the ancients sculptured on the tomb. He had reached that stage, the last phase of dejection, in which grief no longer flows ; it is, so to speak, coagulated, and there is on the soul something like a clot of despair. Night had set in, and he with difficulty dragged a table and the old easy-chair to the chimney, and laid on the table pen, ink, and paper. This done, he fainted away, and when he regained his senses he was thirsty ; as he could not lift the water-jar, he bent down with an effort and drank a mouthful. Then he turned to the bed, and, still seated, for he was unable to stand, he gazed at the little black dress, and all those dear objects. Such contemplations last for hours which appear minutes. All at once he shuddered, and felt that the cold had struck him. He leant his elbows on the table which the Bishop's candlesticks illumined, and took up the pen. As neither the pen nor the ink had been used for a long time the nibs of the pen were bent, the ink was dried up, and he was therefore obliged to put a few drops of water in the ink, which he could not do without stopping and sitting down twice or thrice ; and he was forced to write with the back of the pen. He wiped his forehead from time to time, and his hand trembled as he wrote the few following lines :—

" Cosette, I bless you. I am about to explain to you. Your husband did right in making me understand that I ought to go away ; still, he was slightly in error as to what he believed, but he acted rightly. He is a worthy man, and love him dearly when I am gone from you. Monsieur Pontmercy, always love my beloved child. Cosette, this paper will be found ; this is what I wish to say to you ; you shall see the figures if I have the strength to remember them ; but listen to me, the money is really yours. This is the whole affair ; white jet comes from Norway, black jet comes from England, and black glass imitation comes from Germany. Jet is lighter, more valuable, and dearer, but imitations can be made in France as well as in Germany. You must have a small anvil two inches square, and a

spirit-lamp to soften the wax. The wax used to be made
with resin and lamp-black, and costs four francs the pound,
but I hit on the idea of making it of shell-lac and turpentine.
It only costs thirty sous, and is much better. The rings are
made of violet glass fastened by means of the wax on a
small black iron wire. The glass must be violet for iron
ornaments, and black for gilt ornaments. Spain buys large
quantities, it is the country of jet——"

Here he stopped, the pen slipped from his fingers, he
burst into one of those despairing sobs which rose at times
from the depths of his being ; the poor man took his head
between his hands and thought.

"Oh !" he exclaimed internally (lamentable cries heard
by God alone), "it is all over. I shall never see her again ;
it is a smile which flashed across me, and I am going to
enter night without even seeing her ; oh ! for one moment,
for one instant to hear her voice, to touch her, to look at
her, and then die. Death is nothing, but the frightful
thing is to die without seeing her. She would smile on me,
say a word to me, and would that do any one harm ? No,
it is all over, for ever. I am all alone, my God ! my God !
I shall see her no more."

At this moment there was a knock at his door.

CHAPTER CXIX.

THAT same day, or to speak more correctly, that same
evening, as Marius was leaving the dinner-table to withdraw
to his study, having a brief to get up, Basque handed him
a letter, saying, "The person who wrote the letter is in the
anteroom." Cosette had taken her grandfather's arm, and
was taking a turn round the garden. A letter may have
an ugly appearance, like a man, and the mere sight of coarse
paper and clumsy folding is displeasing. The letter which
Basque brought was of that description. Marius took it, and
it smelt of tobacco. Nothing arouses a recollection so much
as a smell, and Marius recognised the tobacco. He looked
at the address, "To Monsieur le Baron Pommerci. At his
house." The recognised tobacco made him recognise the
handwriting. It might be said that astonishment has its
flashes of lightning, and Marius was, as it were, illumined
by one of these flashes. The odour, that mysterious aid
to memory, had recalled to him a world : it was really the

paper, the mode of folding, the pale ink, it was really the well-known handwriting, and, above all, it was the tobacco. The Jondrette garret rose again before him. Hence—strange blow of accident !—one of the two trails which he had so long sought, the one for which he had latterly made so many efforts and believed lost for ever, came to offer itself voluntarily to him. He eagerly opened the letter and read :

" MONSIEUR LE BARON,—
    " If the Supreme Being had endowed me with talents, I might have been Baron Thénard, member of the Institute (academy of cienses), but I am not so, I merely bear the same name with him, and shall be happy if this reminisence recommends me to the excellense of your kindness. The benefits with which you may honor me will be reciprocal, for I am in possession of a secret conserning an individual. This individual conserns you. I hold the secret at your disposal, as I desire to have the honor?of being yuseful to you. I will give you the simple means for expeling from your honorable family this individual who has no right in it, Madam la Barronne being of high birth. The sanctuary of virtue could no longer coabit with crime without abdicating.
    " I await in the anteroom the order of Monsieur le Baron.
                                            " Respectfully."

The letter was signed " THÉNARD." This signature was not false, but only slightly abridged. However, the bombast and the orthography completed the revelation, the certificate of origin was perfect, and no doubt was possible. Marius' emotion was profound ; and after the feeling of surprise, he had a feeling of happiness. Let him now find the other man he sought, the man who had saved him, Marius, and he would have nothing more to desire. He opened a drawer in his bureau, took out several bank-notes, which he put in his pocket, closed the bureau again, and rang. Basque opened the door partly.
" Show the man in," said Marius.
Basque announced :
" M. Thénard."
A man came in, and it was a fresh surprise for Marius, as the man he now saw was a perfect stranger to him. This man, who was old, by the way, had a large nose, his chin

in his cravat, green spectacles, with a double shade of green
silk over his eyes, and his hair smoothed down and flattened
on his forehead over his eyebrows, like the wigs of English
coachmen of high life. His hair was gray. He was dressed
in black from head to foot, a very seedy but clean black, and
a bunch of seals, emerging from his fob, led to the supposition that he had a watch. He held an old hat in his hand,
and walked bent, and the curve in his back augmented the
depth of his bow. The thing which struck most at the
first glance was that this person's coat, too large, though
carefully buttoned, had not been made for him.

Had Marius been familiar with the occult institutions of
Paris, he would have known of an old Jew, in the Rue
Beautreillis, whose trade it was to supply rogues who wished
to disguise themselves with the needful costume. In one of
these borrowed suits, consisting, according to the Jew's
catalogue of "a carefully-dressed peruke, green spectacles,
bunch of seals, and two little quills an inch in length,
wrapped in cotton," and intended to support the character
of an ex-Ambassador, the visitor whom Basque had just
shown was arrayed. Marius' disappointment, on seeing a
different man from the one whom he expected enter, turned
into dislike towards the new-comer. He examined him from
head to foot, while the personage was giving him an exaggerated bow, and asked him curtly, "What do you
want?"

The man replied with an amiable grin, of which the
caressing smile of a crocodile would supply some idea:

"It appears to me impossible that I have not already had
the honour of seeing Monsieur le Baron in society. I have
a peculiar impression of having met you, my lord, a few
years back, at the Princess Bagration's, and in the salons
of his Excellency Vicomte Dambray, Peer of France."

It is always good tactics in swindling to pretend to
recognise a person whom the swindler does not know.
Marius paid attention to the man's words, he watched the
action and movement, but his disappointment increased; it
was a nasal pronunciation, absolutely different from the
sharp dry voice he expected. He was utterly routed.

"I do not know," he said, "either Madame Bagration or
Monsieur Dambray. I never set foot in the house of either
of them."

The answer was rough, but the personage continued with
undiminished affability:

"Then it must have been at Chateaubriand's, my lord, that I saw you! I know Chateaubriand intimately, and he is a most affable man. He says to me sometimes, 'Thénard, my good friend, will you not drink a glass with me?'"

Marius' brow became sterner and sterner. "I never had the honour of being introduced to Monsieur de Chateaubriand. Come to the point, what do you want with me?"

The man bowed lower still before this harsh voice.

"Monsieur le Baron, deign to listen to me. There is in America, in a country near Panama, a village called La Joya, and this village is composed of a single house. A large square house three storeys high, built of bricks dried in the sun, each side of the square being five hundred feet long, and each storey retiring from the one under it for a distance of twelve feet, so as to leave in front of it a terrace which runs all round the house. In the centre is an inner court, in which provisions and ammunition are stored; there are no windows, only loopholes, no door, only ladders —ladders to mount from the ground to the first terrace, and from the first to the second, and from the second to the third, ladders to descend into the inner court; no doors to the rooms, only traps; no staircases to the apartments, only ladders. At night the trap-doors are closed, the ladders are drawn up, and blunderbusses and carbines are placed in the loopholes; there is no way of entering; it is a house by day, a citadel by night. Eight hundred inhabitants, such is this village. Why such precautions? Because the country is dangerous, and full of anthropophagi. Then why do people go there? Because it is a marvellous country, and gold is found there."

"What are you driving at?" Marius, who had passed from disappointment to impatience, interrupted.

"To this, Monsieur le Baron. I am a worn-out ex-diplomatist. I am sick of our old civilisation, and wish to try the savages."

"What next?"

"Monsieur le Baron, egotism is the law of the world. The proletarian peasant-wench who works by the day turns round when the diligence passes, but the peasant woman who is labouring on her own field does not turn. The poor man's dog barks after the rich, the rich man's dog barks after the poor; each for himself; and self-interest is the object of mankind. Gold is the magnet."

"What next? conclude."

"I should like to go and settle at La Joya. There are three of us. I have my wife and my daughter, a very beautiful girl. The voyage is long and expensive, and I am short of funds."

"How does that concern me?" Marius asked.

The stranger thrust his neck out of his cravat, with a gesture peculiar to the vulture, and said, with a more affable smile than before :

"Monsieur le Baron cannot have read my letter?"

That was almost true, and the fact is that the contents of the epistle had escaped Marius; he had seen the writing rather than read the letter, and he scarce remembered it. A new hint had just been given him, and he noticed the detail, "My wife and daughter." He fixed a penetrating glance on the stranger; a magistrate could not have done it better; but he confined himself to saying :

"Be more precise."

The stranger thrust his hands into his trousers' pockets, raised his head without straightening his 'back-bone, but in his turn scrutinising Marius through his green spectacles.

"Very good, Monsieur le Baron. I will be precise. I have a secret to sell you."

"Does it concern me?"

"Slightly."

"What is it?'

Marius more and more examined the man while listening.

"I will begin gratis," the stranger said; "you will soon see that it is interesting."

"Speak."

"Monsieur le Baron, you have in your house a robber and assassin."

Marius gave a start.

"In my house? no," he said.

The stranger imperturbably brushed his hat with his arm, and went on :

"An assassin and robber. Remark, Monsieur le Baron, that I am not speaking here of old, forgotten facts, which might be effaced by prescription before the law—by repentance before God. I am speaking of recent facts, present facts, of facts still unknown to justice. I continue. This man has crept into your confidence, and almost into your family, under a false name. I am going to tell you his real name, and tell it you for nothing."

"I am listening."

" His name is Jean Valjean."

" I know it."

" I will tell, equally for nothing, who he is."

" Speak."

" He is an ex-convict."

" I know it."

" You have known it since I had the honour of telling you."

" No, I was aware of it before."

Marius' cold tone, this double reply, " I know it," and his refractory disinclination to speak, aroused some latent anger in the stranger, and he gave Marius a furious side-glance, which was immediately extinguished. Rapid though it was, the glance was one of those which are recognised if they have once been seen, and it did not escape Marius. Certain flashes can only come from certain souls; the eyeball, that cellar-door of the soul, is lit up by them, and green spectacles conceal nothing; you might as well put up a glass window to hell. The stranger continued, smiling :

" I will not venture to contradict Monsieur le Baron, but in any case you will see that I am well informed. Now, what I have to tell you is known to myself alone, and it affects the fortune of Madame la Baronne. It is an extraordinary secret, and is for sale. I offer it you first. Cheap, twenty thousand francs."

" I know that secret as I know the other," said Marius.

The personage felt the necessity of lowering his price a little.

" Monsieur le Baron, let us say ten thousand francs, and I will speak."

" I repeat to you that you have nothing to tell me. I know what you want to say to me."

There was a fresh flash in the man's eye, as he continued :

" Still I must dine to-day. It is an extraordinary secret, I tell you. Monsieur, I am going to speak. I am speaking. Give me twenty francs."

Marius looked at him fixedly.

" I know your extraordinary secret, just as I knew Jean Valjean's name, and as I know yours."

" My name ? "

" Yes."

" That is not difficult, Monsieur le Baron, for I had the honour of writing it and mentioning it to you. Thénard—"

" —dier."

" What ? "

" Thénardier."

" What does this mean ? "

In danger the porcupine bristles, the beetle feigns death, the old guard forms a square : this man began laughing. Then he flipped a grain of dust off his coat sleeve. Marius continued :

" You are also the workman Jondrette, the actor Fabantou, the poet Genflot, the Spanish Don Alvares, and Madame Balizard."

" Madame who ? "

" And you once kept a pot-house at Montfermeil."

" A pot-house ! never."

" And I tell you that you are Thénardier."

" I deny it."

" And that you are a scoundrel. Take that."

And Marius, taking a bank-note from his pocket, threw it in his face.

" Five hundred francs ! Monsieur le Baron ! "

And the man, overwhelmed and bowing, clutched the note and examined it.

" Five hundred francs," he continued, quite dazzled.

And he stammered half aloud, " No counterfeit."

Then suddenly exclaimed :

" Well, be it so ; let us be at our ease."

And with monkey-like dexterity, throwing back his hair, tearing off his spectacles, and removing the two quills to which we alluded just now, and which we have seen before in another part of this book, he took off his face as you or I take off our hat. His eye grew bright, the forehead, hideously wrinkled at top, became smooth, the nose sharp as a beak, and the ferocious and sagacious profile of the man of prey reappeared.

" Monsieur le Baron is infallible," he said in a sharp voice, from which the nasal twang had entirely disappeared ; " I am Thénardier."

And he drew up his curved back.

Thénardier, for it was really he, was strangely surprised ; he would have been troubled could he have been so. He had come to bring astonishment, and it was he himself who underwent it. This humiliation was paid for with five hundred francs, and he accepted it ; but he was not the less stunned. He saw for the first time this Baron Pontmercy, and in spite of his disguise this Baron Pontmercy recognised

him, and recognised him thoroughly; and not alone was
this baron acquainted with Thénardier, but he also seemed
acquainted with Jean Valjean. Who was this almost beard-
less young man, so cold and so generous; who knew
people's names, knew all their names, and opened his purse
to them; who bullied rogues like a judge, and paid them
like a dupe? Thénardier, it will be remembered, though
he had been Marius' neighbour, had never seen him, which
is frequently the case in Paris; he had formerly vaguely
heard his daughter speak of a very poor young man of the
name of Marius, who lived in the house, and he had written
him, without knowing him, the letter we formerly read. No
approximation between this Marius and M. le Baron Pontmercy was possible in his mind.

· However, he had managed through his daughter Azelma,
whom he put on the track of the married couple on February
16th, and by his own researches, to learn a good many
things, and in his dark den had succeeded in seizing more
than one mysterious thread. He had by sheer industry
discovered, or at least by the inductive process had divined,
who the man was whom he had met on a certain day in
the Grand Sewer. From the man he had easily arrived at
the name, and he knew that Madame la Baronne Pontmercy
was Cosette. But on that point he intended to be discreet;
who Cosette was he did not know exactly himself. He
certainly got a glimpse of some bastardism, and Fantine's
story had always appeared to him doubtful. But what was
the good of speaking? to have his silence paid? He had,
or fancied he had, something better to sell than that, and
according to all expectation, to go and make to Baron
Pontmercy, without further proof, the revelation, "Your
wife is only a bastard," would only have succeeded in
attracting the husband's boot to the broadest part of his
person.

In Thénardier's thoughts the conversation with Marius
had not yet begun; he had been obliged to fall back, modify
his strategy, leave a position, and make a change of front;
but nothing essential was as yet compromised, and he had
five hundred francs in his pocket. Moreover, he had something decisive to tell, and he felt himself strong even against
this Baron Pontmercy, who was so well informed and so
well armed. For men of Thénardier's nature every dialogue
is a combat, and what was his situation in the one which
was about to begin? He did not know to whom he was

speaking, but he knew of what he was speaking. He
rapidly made this mental review of his forces, and after
saying, "I am Thénardier," waited. Marius was deep in
thought; he at length held Thénardier, and the man whom
he had so eagerly desired to find again was before him. He
would be able at last to honour Colonel Pontmercy's recommendation. It humiliated him that that hero owed anything
to this bandit, and that the bill of exchange drawn by his
father from the tomb upon him, Marius, had remained up
to this day protested. It seemed to him, too, in the complex
state of his mind as regarded Thénardier, that he was bound
to avenge the colonel for the misfortune of having been
saved by such a villain. But, however this might be, he
was satisfied; he was at length going to free the colonel's
shadow from this unworthy creditor, and he felt as if he
were releasing his father's memory from a debtor's prison.
By the side of this duty he had another, clearing up if possible
the source of Cosette's fortune. The opportunity appeared
to present itself, for Thénardier probably knew something,
and it might be useful to see to the bottom of this man; so
he began with that. .Thénardier put away the "no counterfeit" carefully in his pocket, and looked at Marius with
almost tender gentleness. Marius was the first to break
the silence.

"Thénardier, I have told you your name, and now do you
wish me to tell you the secret which you have come to impart
to me? I have my information also, and you shall see that
I know more than you do. Jean Valjean. as you said, is an
assassin and a robber. A robber, because he plundered a
rich manufacturer, M. Madeleine, whose ruin he caused : an
assassin, because he murdered Inspector Javert."

"I do not understand you, M. le Baron," said Thénardier.

"I will make you understand; listen. There was in a
bailiwick of the Pas de Calais, about the year 1822, a man
who had been in some trouble with the authorities, and who
had rehabilitated and restored himself under the name of
Monsieur Madeleine. This man had become, in the fullest
extent of the term, a just man, and he made the fortune of
an entire town by a trade, the manufacture of black beads.
As for his private fortune, he had made that too, but
secondarily, and to some extent as occasion offered. He
was the foster-father of the poor, he founded hospitals,
opened schools, visited the sick, dowered girls, supported
widows, adopted orphans, and was, as it were, guardian

of the town. He had refused the Cross, and was appointed mayor. A liberated convict knew the secret of a penalty formerly incurred by this man ; he denounced and had him arrested, and took advantage of the arrest to come to Paris and draw out of Laffitte's—I have the facts from the cashier himself—by means of a false signature, a sum of half a million and more, which belonged to M. Mad-leine. The convict who robbed M. Madeleine was Jean Valjean'; as for the other act, you can tell me no more than I know either. Jean Valjean killed Inspector Javert with a pistol-shot, and I, who am speaking to you, was present."

Thénardier gave Marius the sovereign glance of a beaten man who sets his hand again on the victory, and has regained in a minute all the ground he had lost. But the smile at once returned, for the inferior, when in the presence of his superior, must keep his triumph to himself, and Thénardier confined himself to saying to Marius :

" Monsieur le Baron, we are on the wrong track."

And he emphasised this sentence by giving his bunch of seals an expressive twirl.

" What ! " Marius replied, " do you dispute it ? They are facts."

" They are chimeras. The confidence with which Monsieur le Baron honours me makes it my duty to tell him so. Before all, truth and justice, and I do not like to see people accused wrongfully. Monsieur le Baron, Jean Valjean did not rob M. Madeleine, and Jean Valjean did not kill Javert."

" That is rather strong. How is that ? '

" For two reasons."

" What are they ? speak."

" The first is this : he did not rob M. Madeleine, because Jean Valjean himself is M. Madeleine."

" What nonsense are you talking ? "

" And this is the second : he did not assassinate Javert, because the man who killed Javert was Javert."

" What do you mean ? "

" That Javert committed suicide."

" Prove it, prove it," Marius cried wildly.

Thénardier repeated slowly, scanning his sentence after the fashion of an ancient Alexandrian :

" Police-Agent-Javert-was-found-drowned-un-der-a-boat-at-Pont-au-Change."

" But prove it, then."

Thénardier drew from his side-pocket a large gray paper parcel, which seemed to contain folded papers of various sizes.

" I have my proofs," he said calmly, and he added :

" Monsieur le Baron, I wished to know Jean Valjean thoroughly on your behalf. I say that Jean Valjean and Madeleine are the same, and I say that Javert had no other assassin but Javert, and when I say this, I have the proofs, not MS. proofs, for writing is suspicious and complaisant, but printed proofs."

While speaking, Thénardier extracted from the parcel two newspapers, yellow, faded, and tremendously saturated with tobacco. One of these two papers, broken in all the folds, and falling in square rags, seemed much older than the other.

" Two facts, two proofs," said Thénardier, as he handed Marius the two open newspapers.

These two papers the reader knows ; one, the older, a number of the *Drapeau Blanc*, for July 25th, 1823, of which the exact text was given at p. 275, established the identity of M. Madeleine and Jean Valjean. The other, a *Moniteur*, of June 15th, 1832, announced the suicide of Javert, adding that it was found from a verbal report made by Javert to the Prefect, that he had been made prisoner at the barricade of the Rue de la Chanvrerie, and owed his life to the magnanimity of an insurgent, who, when holding him under his pistol, instead of blowing out his brains, fired in the air. Marius read ; there was evidence, a certain date, irrefragable proof, for these two papers had not been printed expressly to support Thénardier's statement, and the note published in the *Moniteur* was officially communicated by the Prefecture of Police. Marius could no longer doubt ; the cashier's information was false, and he was himself mistaken. Jean Valjean suddenly growing taller, issued from the cloud, and Marius could not restrain a cry of joy.

" What, then, this fellow is an admirable man ! all this fortune is really his ! He is Madeleine, the providence of an entire town ! he is Jean Valjean, the saviour of Javert ! he is a hero ! he is a saint ! "

" He is not a saint, and he is not a hero," said Thénardier, " he is an assassin and a robber."

And he added with the accent of a man beginning to feel

himself possessed of some authority, "Let us calm ourselves."

Robber, assassin, those words which Marius believed
had disappeared, and which had returned, fell upon him
like an icy douche.

" Still——" he said.

"Still," said Thénardier, "Jean Valjean did not rob
M. Madeleine, but he is a robber ; he did not assassinate
Javert, but he is an assassin."

"Are you alluding," Marius continued, "to that wretched
theft committed forty years back, and expiated, as is proved
from those very papers, by a whole life of repentance, self-
denial, and virtue?"

"I say assassination and robbery, M. le Baron, and
repeat that I am alluding to recent facts. What I have
to reveal to you is perfectly unknown and unpublished,
and you may perhaps find in it the source of the fortune
cleverly offered by Jean Valjean to Madame la Baronne.
I say skilfully, for it would not be a stupid act, by a
donation of that nature, to step into an honourable house,
whose comforts he would share, and at the same time
hide his crime, enjoy his robbery, bury his name, and
create a family."

"I could interrupt you here," Marius observed, "but
go on."

"Monsieur le Baron, I will tell you all, leaving the reward
to your generosity, for the secret is worth its weight in
gold. You will say to me, 'Why not apply to Jean
Valjean?' For a very simple reason. I know that he has
given up all his property in your favour, and I consider the
combination ingenious ; but he has not a halfpenny left ; he
would show me his empty hands, and as I want money for
my voyage to La Joya, I prefer you, who have everything,
to him, who has nothing. As I am rather fatigued, permit
me to take a chair."

Marius sat down, and made him a sign to do the same.
Thénardier installed himself in an easy-chair, took up the
newspapers, put them back in the parcel, and muttered as
he dug his nail into the *Drapeau Blanc* : "It cost me a
deal of trouble to procure this." This done, he crossed
his legs, threw himself into the chair in the attitude of men
who are certain of what they are stating, and then began
his narrative gravely, and laying a stress on his words :

"Monsieur le Baron, on June 6th, 1832, about a year

ago, and on the day of the riots, a man was in the great
sewer of Paris, at the point where the sewer falls into
the Seine between the Pont des Invalides and the Pont
de Jena."

Marius hurriedly drew his chair closer to Thénardier's.
Thenardier noticed this movement, and continued with
the slowness of an orator who holds his hearer, and feels
his adversary quivering under his words :

" This man, forced to hide himself, for reasons, however,
unconnected with politics, had selected the sewer as his
domicile, and had the key of it. It was, I repeat, June 6th,
and at about eight in the evening the man heard a noise in
the sewer; feeling greatly surprised, he concealed himself
and watched. It was a sound of footsteps ; some one was
walking in the darkness, and coming in his direction ;
strange to say, there was another man beside himself in
the sewer. As the outlet of the sewer was no great
distance off, a little light which passed through enabled
him to see the new-comer, and that he was carrying something on his back. He walked in a stooping posture ;
he was an ex-convict, and what he had on his shoulders
was a corpse. A flagrant case of assassination, were
there ever one ; as for the robbery, that is a matter of
course, for no one kills a man gratis. This convict was
going to throw the body into the river, and a fact worth
notice is, that, before reaching the outlet, the convict,
who had come a long way through the sewer, was obliged
to pass a frightful hole, in which it seems as if he might
have left the corpse ; but the sewer-men who came to
effect the repairs next day would have found the murdered
man there, and that did not suit the assassin. Hence he
preferred carrying the corpse across the slough, and his
efforts must have been frightful ; it was impossible to put
one's life in greater peril, and I do not understand how
he got out of it alive."

Marius' chair came nearer, and Thénardier took
advantage of it to draw a long breath ; then he
contin ied :

" Monsieur le Baron, a sewer is not the Champs de
Mars ; everything is wanting there, even space, and when
two men are in it together they must meet. This happened,
and the domiciled man and the passer-by were compelled
to bid each other good-evening, to their mutual regret.
The passer-by said to the domiciled man, ' You see what

I have on my back. I must go out, you have the key, so give it to me.' This convict was a man of terrible strength, and there was no chance of refusing him; still the man who held the key parleyed, solely to gain time. He examined the dead man, but could see nothing, except that he was young, well dressed, had a rich look, and was quite disfigured with blood. While talking, he managed to tear off, without the murderer perceiving it, a piece of the skirt of the victim's coat, as a convincing proof, you understand, a means of getting on the track of the affair, and bringing the crime home to the criminal   He placed the piece of cloth in his pocket; after which he opened the grating, allowed the man with the load on his back to go out, locked the grating again, and ran away, not feeling at all desirous to be mixed up any further in the adventure, or to be present when the assassin threw the corpse into the river. You now understand; the man who carried the corpse was Jean Valjean, the one who had the key is speaking to you at this moment, and the piece of coat-skirt——"

Thénardier completed the sentence by drawing from his pocket and holding level with his eyes a ragged piece of black cloth, all covered with dark spots. Marius had risen, pale, scarce breathing. with his eye fixed on the black patch, and, without uttering a syllable, or without taking his eyes off the rag, he fell back, and, with his right hand extended behind him, felt for the key of a wall-cupboard near the mantelpiece. He found this key, opened the cupboard, and thrust his hand into it without looking or once taking his eyes off the rag which Thénardier displayed. In the meanwhile Thénardier continued :

"Monsieur le Baron, I have the strongest grounds for believing that the assassinated young man was a wealthy foreigner, drawn by Jean Valjean into a trap, and carrying an enormous sum about him."

"I was the young man, and here is the coat!" cried Marius, as he threw on the floor an old bloodstained surtout. Then, taking the patch from Thénardier's hands, he bent over the coat and put it in its place in the skirt; the rent fitted exactly, and the fragment completed the coat. Thénardier was petrified, and thought, "I'm sold." Marius drew himself up, shuddering, desperate, and flashing; he felt in his pocket, and walking

furiously towards Thénardier, thrust almost into his
face his hand full of five hundred and thousand franc
notes.

"You are an infamous wretch! you are a liar, a
calumniator, and a villain! You came to accuse that
man, and you have justified him; you came to ruin
him, and have only succeeded in glorifying him. And it
is you who are the robber! it is you who are an
assassin! I saw you, Thénardier Jondrette, at that
den on the Boulevard de l'Hôpital. I know enough
about you to send you to the galleys, and even further
if I liked. There are a thousand francs, ruffian that
you are!"

And he threw a thousand-franc note at Thénardier.

"Ah, Jondrette—Thénardier, vile scoundrel, let this serve
you as a lesson, you hawker of secrets, you dealer in
mysteries, you searcher in the darkness, you villain, take
these five hundred francs, and be off. Waterloo protects
you."

"Waterloo!" Thénardier growled, as he pocketed the
five hundred francs.

"Yes, assassin! you saved there the life of a
colonel."

"A general!" Thénardier said, raising his head.

"A colonel," Marius repeated furiously; "I would not
give a farthing for a general. And you come here to
commit an infamy! I tell you that you have committed
every crime! Begone! disappear! Be happy, that is all
I desire! Ah, monster! here are three thousand francs
more: take them. You will start to-morrow for America
with your daughter, for your wife is dead, you abominable
liar! I will watch over your departure, bandit, and at the
moment when you set sail, pay you twenty thousand francs.
Go and get hanged elsewhere."

"Monsieur le Baron," Thénardier answered, bowing to
the ground, "accept my eternal gratitude."

And Thénardier left the room, understanding nothing of
all this, but stupefied and transported by this sweet crushing under bags of gold, and this lightning flashing over his
head in the shape of bank-notes. Let us finish at once
with this man. Two days after the events we have just
recorded he started for America, under a false name, with
his daughter Azelma, and provided with an order on a
New York banker for twenty thousand francs. The

moral misery of Thénardier, the spoiled bourgeois, was irremediable, and he was in America what he had been in Europe. The contact with a wicked man is sometimes sufficient to rot a good action, and to make something bad issue from it: with Marius' money Thénardier turned slave-dealer.

So soon as Thénardier had departed, Marius ran into the garden where Cosette was still walking.

"Cosette, Cosette," he cried, "come, come quickly, let us be off. Basque, a hackney-coach. Cosette, come! Heavens! it was he who saved my life! Let us not lose a minute! Put on your shawl."

Cosette thought him mad, and obeyed. He could not breathe, and laid his hand on his heart to check its beating. He walked up and down with long strides, and embraced Cosette. "Oh, Cosette," he said, "I am a scoundrel." Marius was amazed, for he was beginning to catch a glimpse of some strange, lofty, and sombre figure in this Jean Valjean. An extraordinary virtue appeared to him, supreme and gentle, and humble in its immensity, and the convict was transfigured into Christ. Marius was dazzled by this prodigy, and though he knew not exactly what he saw, it was grand. In an instant the hackney-coach was at the gate. Marius helped Cosette in, and followed her.

"Driver," he cried, " No. 7 Rue de l'Homme Armé."

"Oh, how glad I am," said Cosette. " Rue de l'Homme Armé. I did not dare speak to you about Monsieur Jean, but we are going to see him."

"Your father, Cosette! your father more than ever. Cosette, I see it all. You told me that you never received the letter I sent you by Gavroche. It must have fallen into his hands, Cosette, and he came to the barricade to save me. As it is his sole duty to be an angel, in passing he saved others : he saved Javert. He drew me out of that gulf to give me to you ; he carried me on his back through that frightful sewer. Ah! I am a monstrous ingrate! Cosette, after having been your providence, he was mine. Just imagine that there was a horrible pit, in which a man could be drowned a hundred times, drowned in muc Cosette ; and he carried me through it. I had fainted ; I saw nothing, l heard nothing, I could not know anything about my own adventures. We are going to bring him back with us, and whether he is willing or not he shall never leave us again. I only hope he is at home! I only hope we shall find him! I will spend the rest of my life in revering him. Yes, it must have been so, Cosette, and Gavroche must have given him my letter. That explains everything. You understand."

Cosette did not understand a word.

" You are right," she said to him.

CHAPTER CXX.

At the knock he heard at his door Jean Valjean turned round.

" Come in," he said feebly.

The door opened, and Cosette and Marius appeared. Cosette rushed into the room. Marius remained on the threshold, leaning against the door-post.

"Cosette!" said Jean Valjean, and he sat up in his chair, with his arms outstretched and opened, haggard, livid, and sinister, but with an immense joy in his eyes. Cosette, suffocated with emotion, fell on Jean Valjean's breast.

" Father," she said.

Jean Valjean, utterly overcome, stammered, "Cosette! she—you—madame! it is you! oh, my God!"

And clasped in Cosette's arms, he exclaimed :

" It is you! you are here ; you forgive me, then !"

Marius, drooping his eyelids to keep his tears from flowing, advanced a step, and muttered between his lips, which were convulsively clenched to stop his sobs :

" Father !"

" And you, too, you forgive me," said Jean Valjean.

Marius could not find a word to say, and Jean Valjean added, "Thank you." Cosette took off her shawl, and threw her bonnet on the bed.

" It is in my way," she said.

And sitting down on the old man's knees, she parted his gray hair with an adorable movement, and kissed his forehead. Jean Valjean, who was wandering, let her do so. Cosette, who only comprehended very vaguely, redoubled her caresses, as if she wished to pay Marius' debt, and Jean Valjean stammered :

" How foolish a man can be! I fancied that I should not see her again. Just imagine, Monsieur Pontmercy, that at the very moment when you came in I was saying, ' It is all over.' There is her little dress. ' I am a wretched man, I shall not see Cosette again,' I was saying at the very moment when you were coming up the stairs. What an idiot I was ! a man can be as idiotic as that ! But people count without le bon Dieu, who says,—' Men imagine that they are going to be abandoned ; no ; things will not happen like that. Down below there is a poor old fellow who wants an angel.' And the angel comes, and he sees

Cosette again, and he sees his little Cosette again. Oh! I was very unhappy."

For a moment he was unable to speak, then he went on :

"I really wanted to see Cosette for a little while every now and then, for a heart requires a bone to gnaw. Still, I felt plainly that I was in the way. I said to myself, They do not want you, so stop in your corner ; a man has no right to pay everlasting visits. Ah ! blessed be God ! I see her again. Do you know, Cosette, that your husband is very handsome ? What a pretty embroidered collar you are wearing, I like that pattern ; your husband chose it, did he not ? And, then, you will need cashmere shawls. Monsieur Pontmercy, let me call her Cosette, it will not be for long."

And Cosette replied :

" How unkind to have left us like that ! where have you been to ? why were you away so long ? Formerly, your absences did not last ever three or four days. I sent Nicolette, and the answer always was, 'He has not returned.' When did you get back ? why did you not let us know ? are you aware that you are greatly changed ? Oh, naughty papa, he has been ill, and we did not know it. Here, Marius, feel how cold his hand is ! "

" So you are here ! so you forgive me, Monsieur Pontmercy ? " Jean Valjean repeated.

At this remark, all that was swelling in Marius' heart found a vent, and he burst forth :

"Do you hear, Cosette ? he asks my pardon. And do you know what he did for me, Cosette ? He saved my life, he did more, he gave you to me, and, after saving me, and after giving you to me, Cosette, what did he do for himself? He sacrificed himself ; that is the man. And to me, who am so ungrateful, so pitiless, so forgetful, and so guilty, he says, 'Thank you !' Cosette, my whole life spent at this man's feet would be too little. That barricade, that sewer, that furnace, that pit, he went through them all for me and for you, Cosette ! He carried me through every form of death, which he held at bay from me and accepted for himself. This man possesses every courage, every virtue, every heroism, and every holiness, and he is an angel, Cosette."

" Stop, stop ! " Jean Valjean said in a whisper ; " why talk in that way ? "

" But why did you not tell me of it ? " exclaimed Marius, with a passion in which was veneration ; " it is your fault also. You save people's lives, and conceal the fact from them! You do more; under the pretext of unmasking yourself, you calumniate yourself. It is frightful."

"I told the truth," Jean Valjean replied.

"No," Marius retorted, "the truth is the whole truth, and you did not tell ,that. You were Monsieur Madeleine, why not tell me so? You saved Javert, why not tell me so? I owed my life to you, why not tell me so?"

"Because I thought like you, and found that you were right. It was necessary that I should leave you. Had you known of the sewer you would have compelled me to remain with you, and hence I held my tongue. Had I spoken, I should have been in the way."

"Been in the way of whom? of what?" Marius broke out. "Do you fancy that you are going to remain here? We mean to take you back with us. Oh! good heavens! when I think that I only learnt all this by accident! We shall take you away with us, for you form a part of ourselves; you are her father and mine. You shall not spend another day in this frightful house, so do not fancy you will be here to-morrow."

"To-morrow," said Jean Valjean, "I shall be no longer here, but I shall not be at your house."

"What do you mean?" Marius asked. "Oh! no, we shall not let you travel any more; you shall not leave us again, for you belong to us, and we will not let you go."

"This time it is for good," Cosette added. "We have a carriage below, and I mean to carry you off; if necessary, I shall employ force."

And, laughing, she feigned to raise the old man in her arms.

"Your room is still all ready in our house," she went on. "If you only knew how pretty the garden is just at present! the azaleas are getting on splendidly; the walks are covered with river sand, and there are little violet shells. You shall eat my strawberries, for it is I who water them. And no more madame and no more Monsieur Jean, for we live in a Republic, do we not, Marius? The programme is changed. If you only knew, father, what a sorrow I had; a redbreast had made its nest in a hole in the wall, and a horrible cat killed it for me. My poor, pretty little redbreast, that used to thrust its head out of its window and look at me! I cried over it, and could have killed the cat! But now, nobody weeps, everybody laughs, everybody is happy. You will

come with us ; how pleased grandfather will be ! You will
have your bed in the garden, you will cultivate it, and
we will see whether your strawberries are as fine as mine.
And, then, I will do all you wish, and you will obey me."

Jean Valjean listened without hearing ; he heard the
music of her voice rather than the meaning of her words,
and one of those heavy tears, which are the black pearls
of the soul, slowly collected in his eye. He murmured :

"The proof that God is good is that she is here."

"My father !" said Cosette.

Jean Valjean continued :

"It is true it would be charming to live together. They
have their trees full of birds, and I should walk about with
Cosette. It is sweet to be with persons who live, who say to
each other good-morning, and call each other in the garden.
We should each cultivate a little bed, she would give me
her strawberries to eat, and I would let her pick my roses.
It would be delicious, but——"

He broke off, and said gently, "It is a pity."

The tear did not fall, it was recalled, and Jean Valjean
substituted a smile for it. Cosette took both the old man's
hands in hers.

"My God !" she said, "your hands have grown colder.
Can you be ill? are you suffering ?"

"I—no," Jean Valjean replied, "I am quite well. It is
only——" He stopped.

"Only what ? "

"I am going to die directly."

Marius and Cosette shuddered.

"Die !" Marius exclaimed.

"Yes, but that is nothing," said Jean Valjean.

He breathed, smiled, and added :

"Cosette, you were talking to me, go on, speak again,
your redbreast is dead, then ? speak, that I may hear your
voice."

Marius, who was petrified, looked at the old man, and
Cosette uttered a piercing shriek.

"Father, father, you will live ! you are going to live. I
insist on your living, do you hear ?"

Jean Valjean raised his head to her, with adoration.

"Oh yes, forbid me dying. Who knows ? Perhaps, I
shall obey. I was on the road to death when you arrived,
but that stopped me. I fancied I was recovering."

"You are full of strength and life," Marius exclaimed.

"Can you suppose that a man dies like that? You have
known grief, but you shall know no more. It is I who
ask pardon of you, and on my knees! You are going to
live, and live with us, and live a long time. We will take
you with us, and shall have henceforth but one thought,
your happiness!"

"You hear," said Cosette, who was weeping fearfully,
"Marius says that you will not die."

Jean Valjean continued to smile.

"Even if you were to take me home with you, Monsieur
Pontmercy, would that prevent me being what I am? No.
God has thought the same as you and I, and He does not
alter His opinion. It is better for me to be gone. Death
is an excellent arrangement, and God knows better than we
do what we want. I am certain that it is right, that you
should be happy, that Monsieur Pontmercy should have
Cosette, that youth should espouse the dawn, that there
should be around you, my children, lilacs and nightingales,
that your life should be a lawn bathed in sunlight, that all
the enchantments of heaven should fill your souls, and that
I who am good for nothing should now die. Come, be
reasonable; nothing is possible now, and I fully feel that all
is over. An hour ago I had a fainting-fit, and last night
I drank the whole of that jug of water. How kind your
husband is, Cosette! You are much better with him than
with me!"

There was a noise at the door; it was the physician come
to pay his visit.

"Good-day, and good-bye, doctor," said Jean Valjean.
"Here are my poor children."

Marius went up to the physician, and addressed but one
word to him, "Sir?"—but in the manner of pronouncing
it there was a whole question. The physician answered
the question by an expressive glance.

"Because things are unpleasant," said Jean Valjean,
"that is no reason to be unjust to God."

There was a silence, and every chest was oppressed. Jean
Valjean turned to Cosette, and began contemplating her,
as if he wished to take the glance with him into eternity.
In the deep shadow into which he had already sunk ecstasy
was still possible for him in regarding Cosette. The reflection of her sweet countenance illumined his pale face,
for the sepulchre may have its brilliancy. The physician
felt his pulse.

"Ah, it was you that he wanted," he said, looking at Marius and Cosette.

And bending down to Marius' ear, he whispered, "Too late."

Jean Valjean, almost without ceasing to regard Cosette, looked at Marius and the physician with serenity, and the scarcely articulated words could be heard pass his lips.

"It is nothing to die, but it is frightful not to live."

All at once he rose—such return of strength is at times a sequel of the death-agony. He walked with a firm step to the wall, thrust aside Marius and the doctor, who wished to help him, detached from the wall the small copper crucifix hanging on it, returned to his seat with all the vigour of full health, and said, as he laid the crucifix on the table:

"There is the great Martyr."

Then his chest sank in, his head vacillated, as if the intoxication of the tomb were seizing on him, and his hands, lying on his knees, began pulling at the cloth of his trousers. Cosette supported his shoulders and sobbed, and tried to speak to him, but was unable to do so. Through the words mingled with that lugubrious saliva which accompanies tears, such sentences as this could be distinguished: "Father, do not leave us. Is it possible that we have only found you again to lose you?" It might be said that the death-agony moves like a serpent; it comes, goes, advances toward the grave, and then turns back toward life; there is groping in the action of death. Jean Valjean, after this partial syncope, rallied, shook his forehead as if to make the darkness fall off it, and became again almost quite livid. He caught hold of Cosette's sleeve and kissed it.

"He is recovering, doctor, he is recovering," Marius cried.

"You are both good," said Jean Valjean, "and I am going to tell you what causes me sorrow. It causes me sorrow, Monsieur Pontmercy, that you have refused to touch that money, but it is really your wife's. I will explain to you, my children, and that is why I am so glad to see you. Black jet comes from England, and white jet from Norway; it is all in that paper there which you will read. I invented the substitution of rolled-up snaps for welded snaps in bracelets; they are prettier, better, and not so dear. You can understand what money can be earned by it; so Cosette's fortune is really hers. I give you these details that your mind may be at rest!"

The porter's wife had come up, and was peeping through
the open door; the physician sent her off, but could not
prevent the zealous old woman shouting to the dying man
before she went.

"Will you have a priest?"

"I have one," Jean Valjean answered.

And he seemed to point with his finger to a spot over his
head, where he might have been fancied to see some one;
it is probable, in truth, that the Bishop was present at this
death scene. Cosette gently placed a pillow behind Jean
Valjean's loins, and he continued:

"Monsieur Pontmercy, have no fears, I conjure you. The
six hundred thousand francs really belong to Cosette. My
whole life would have been wasted if you had not employed
them. We have made those beads beautifully even in competition with what is called Berlin jewellery. For instance, the
black beads of Germany are unequalled, for a gross, containing twelve hundred well-cut beads, costs only three francs."

When a being dear to us is at the point of death we look
at him with a glance that holds him and would retain him
with us. The two dumb with anguish, not knowing what
to say to death, trembling and in despair, stood before him
hand in hand. With each moment Jean Valjean declined
and approached nearer to the dark horizon. His face grew
livid, though he smiled. Life was no longer there, but there
was something else. His breath failed, but his glance
expanded. He was a corpse on whom the wings could be
seen.

He made a sign to Cosette to approach, and then to
Marius. Clearly it was the last minute of the last hour,
and he began to speak to them in a voice so feeble that it
seemed to come from a distance, and it seemed as if there
were a wall between them and him.

"Come near, come near, both of you. I love you dearly.
Oh, how good it is to die like this! You, too, love me, my
Cosette. I was always sure you had a fondness for the
poor old man. You will weep for me a little, won't you?
But not too much, for I do not wish you to feel real sorrow.
You must amuse yourselves greatly, my children. I forgot
to tell you that more profit was made on the buckles without
tongues than on all the rest. The gross, twelve dozen, cost ten
francs to produce, and sold for sixty. Truly it was good business. You must not be astonished at the six hundred thousand francs, Monsieur Pontmercy. It is honest money. You

can be rich without any fear. You must have a carriage, a box at the opera from time to time, fine ball dresses, my Cosette; give good dinners to your friends, and be very happy.

"I was writing just now to Cosette. She will find my letter. To her I leave the two candlesticks on the mantel-piece. They are silver, but to me they are made of gold, of diamonds. They change the candles placed in them into consecrated tapers. I do not know if the man who gave me them is satisfied with me from on high. I have done what I could. You will not forget, children, that I am a poor man, and you will bury me in some corner with a stone to mark the place. I wish it. But no name on the stone. If only Cosette will come now and again to the spot, I shall be happy.

"You, too, Monsieur Pontmercy. I must own that I did not always like you. I ask your pardon. Now, you and she are only one for me. I am very grateful to you, for I feel that you will make Cosette happy. If you only knew, Monsieur Pontmercy, how her rose-pink cheeks were all my joy, and how miserable I was if she were but a little pale. There is in the chest of drawers a five-hundred franc bank-note. I have not touched it. It is for the poor. Cosette, do you see your little dress there on the bed? Do you remember it? And yet it was only ten years ago. How time flies!

"We have been very happy. Now it is over. Do not weep, my children, I am not going very far, and I shall see you from there. You will only have to look when it is night, and you will see me smile. Cosette, do you remember Montfermeil? You were in the wood, and very frightened. Do you remember when I took the handle of the bucket? It was the first time I touched your poor little hand. How cold it was! Ah, you had red hands then, miss, but now they are white enough. And the big doll! you remember? You called it Catherine, and were sorry you had not taken it with you to the convent. How many times you have made me laugh, my sweet angel! When it had rained you used to set straws afloat in the gutter and watch them go. One day I gave you a wicker racket and a shuttlecock with yellow, blue, and green feathers. You have forgotten it! You were so jolly when you were a little girl. How you played! And how you would place cherries in your ears!

"But these things are all over. The forests through which I walked with my child, the trees under which we have passed, the convent where we hid, the games and the happy laughter of infancy, all are but shadows. I imagined that these belonged to me, and I was stupid to do so.

"The Thénardiers were very wicked, but we must forgive them. Cosette, the time has now come to tell you the name of your mother. She was called Fantine. Remember this name: Fantine. Fall on your knees every time you pronounce it. She suffered terribly, and she loved you dearly. She knew as much of sorrow as you of happiness. Such are the distributions of God. He is above, He sees us all, and knows what He does amid His great stars. I am going, my children. Love each other dearly and always. Love—there is hardly any other thing in the world but that. Think sometimes of the poor old man who died here. Ah, my Cosette, it is not my fault that I did not see you all that time, for it broke my heart. I went as far as the corner of the street, and must have produced a strange effect upon those who saw me pass, for I was as if mad, and once even went out without my hat. I can no longer see clearly, my children, and I had still several things to say to you. But 'tis all the same. Think of me a little. You are blessed beings. I do not know what is the matter with me, but I see light. Come closer. I die happy. Let me lay my hands on your dearly beloved heads."

Cosette and Marius fell upon their knees, broken-hearted and choked with sobs, each under one of Jean Valjean's hands. Those reverend hands did not move again.

He fell back, and the light from the two candles illumined him. His white face looked up to heaven, and he let Cosette and Marius cover his hands with kisses. He was dead.

The night was starless and intensely dark. Without doubt, in the darkness, some great angel with outspread wings stood waiting for his soul.

CHAPTER CXXI.

THERE is, in the cemetery of Père Lachaise, in the neigh-bourhood of the poor side, far from the fashionable quarter of this city of tombs, far from those fantastic sepulchres, which blazon in the presence of eternity the hideous fashions of death, in a deserted corner alongside an old wall, under a lofty yew upon which bindweed climbs, and amid couch-grass and moss, a tombstone. This stone is no more exempt than others from the ravages of time. Water turns it green, and the atmosphere blackens it. It is not near any path, and people do not care to visit that part because the grass is long and they get their feet wet. When there is a little sunshine, lizards disport themselves on it. All around there is the rustling of wild oats, and in the spring linnets sing on the trees.

The tombstone is quite bare. They did not dream of cutting more than was necessary for a tomb, and no further care was taken than to make the stone long enough and narrow enough to cover a man.

No name appears on it.

Only, many, many years ago a hand wrote upon it in pencil these four lines which through rain and dust became almost illegible, and which to-day are probably effaced :

> Here sleeps a man whose lot was passing strange
> The whiles he lived. His loved one gone, death came
> Ev'n as the darkness of approaching night
> Comes swift upon the waning of the day.